SCIENCE FICTION OF THE British Empire

A Victorian-Edwardian Anthology

Edited by C.W. Gross

Original content copyright © 2020 C.W. Gross.

All rights reserved.

This anthology reprints stories and illustrations that are in the public domain in the United Kingdom and United States of America.

ISBN: 9798684230356

DEDICATION

To my beloved Ashley.

CONTENTS

A Note from the Editor   i

Introduction by C.W. Gross   Pg 1

The Battle of Dorking: Reminiscences of a Volunteer by George Tomkyns Chesney (United Kingdom, 1871)   Pg 18

The Storm of '92: A Grandfather's Tale told in 1932 by W.H.C. Lawrence (Canada, 1889)   Pg 54

The Swoop! or How Clarence Saved England: A Tale of the Great Invasion by P. G. Wodehouse (United Kingdom, 1909)   Pg 86

The Germ Growers: An Australian Story of Adventure and Mystery by Robert Potter (Australia, 1892)   Pg 128

Short Stories of Rudyard Kipling: *With the Night Mail: A Story of 2000 A.D.* (United Kingdom, 1905); *As Easy as A.B.C: A Tale of 2150 A.D.* (United Kingdom, 1912)   Pg 241

Anno Domini 2000, or Woman's Destiny by Sir Julius Vogel (New Zealand, 1889)   Pg 280

Sultana's Dream by Begum Rokeya Sakhawat Hussain (Bangladesh, 1905)   Pg 379

The Republic of Orissá: Annals From The Pages Of The Twentieth Century by Shoshee Chunder Dutt (India, 1845)   Pg 389

The Man in Asbestos: An Allegory of the Future by Stephen Leacock (Canada, 1911)   Pg 396

The Log of the Flying Fish: A Story of Aerial and Submarine Peril and Adventure by Harry Collingwood (United Kingdom, 1886)   Pg 406

The Ball and the Cross by G.K. Chesterton (United Kingdom, 1909)   Pg 607

A NOTE FROM THE EDITOR

The works reprinted in this volume date from the British Empire before World War One, in the decades preceding and following Queen Victoria's Diamond Jubilee in 1897. As such, they reflect the prevalent ideas in late 19th and early 20th century British culture concerning issues of race, gender, sexuality, economics, and politics. Many of the works reprinted herein contain ideas that are racist, white supremacist, ethnically denigrating, sexist and misogynist, feminist, heteronormative, colonialist and imperialist, genocidal, patriotic, seditionist, capitalist and industrialist, socialist, ableist and eugenicist. They are presented here not as an endorsement of their ideas, but as an accounting of historic British literature and should be understood as historic artefacts.

Enjoying tea in the year 2000 in Rudyard Kipling's With the Night Mail. *Illustration by Frank Leyendecker.*

INTRODUCTION
BY C.W. GROSS

The British Empire was largely accidental. During the 17th and 18th centuries, a small island nation accrued a patchwork scattering of commercial monopolies, isolated ports, utopian experiments, and colonies surrendered from other, more ambitious European powers. By the time of Queen Victoria's Diamond Jubilee in 1897, the British Empire was the largest the world had ever seen. The longest reigning monarch in British history to that point held dominion over nearly 400 million people and a quarter of the globe in both area and population. From Canada to Antarctica's Graham Land, from the West Indies to New Zealand, Cypress to South Africa, the British flag flew on every continent and over every ocean.

The shape of the Empire was amorphous, its machinery unwieldy, its values contradictory, and its legacy ambivalent. "By the imperial noonday," wrote Jan Morris in *The Spectacle of Empire: Style, Effect and the Pax Britannica* (1982), "the spectacle of the empire was flamboyant indeed, coloured as much by oriental despotism and barbaric gesture as by feudal example from nearer home. If it was modernist in some ways, it was antique in others. It embodied the marvellous energy of steam as well as the immemorial pride of horseflesh. It was queenly, but it was savage. It was partly the consequence of dukes, but partly the beat of jungle drums, and imperial activists of every kind were recruited willy-nilly into its presentation..."

The British Empire engaged in the ruthless practices of imperialism and colonialism with its monstrous effects on indigenous populations the world over. The British Empire also maintained an age of global peace and stability unknown since the days of Rome. In its first two centuries the Empire profited from the Trans-Atlantic Slave Trade, and in its third it employed its unrivalled naval hegemony to abolish it. It was a force for both moral good and unimagined evil, wrapped alike in a dull tweed suit. Its legacy is both post-colonial chaos and some of the most successful multicultural democracies in the world. Even multiculturalism as we know it is a colonial project of the British Empire.

A map of the British Empire circa 1886, created by J.C.R. Colomb and published by MacClure & Co.

Consider the example of Canada: The lure of luxurious fur drove the French to establish a colony along the St. Lawrence River in the early 1600's. However, when a pair of roguish *coureur des bois* (independent traders) named Pierre-Esprit Radisson and Médard des Groseilliers ran afoul of the authorities of Québec, they took their knowledge of the rich trappings of the northwoods to the English. King Charles II, desperate for cash after the misfortunes of the English Civil War, chartered the Hudson's Bay Company on their advice. Founded in 1670, and named for a trading monopoly over all the rivers that drain into Hudson's Bay, it remains an institution of Canadian society and one of the world's oldest extant commercial enterprises. The Hudson's Bay Company's monopoly was only interrupted by the Seven Years War between England and France. Québec fell in 1759 at the Battle of the Plains of Abraham, where national heroes General James Wolfe and General Louis-Joseph de Montcalm battled each other to a mutual death. New France was formally ceded to the British in 1763 with the Treaty of

Paris.

Provisions in the Treaty of Paris secured French Roman Catholic language and religious rights, establishing the province of Lower Canada as an officially multicultural, multilingual society. Furthermore, the Royal Proclamation of 1763 recognized the indigenous peoples of the Americas as sovereign nations, denying right of conquest to British colonies. For colonies to expand, they required formal land surrenders through legally constituted treaties. The Thirteen Colonies rejected this principle, and the Royal Proclamation became a proximate cause of the American Revolution. The looming threat of the United States, in turn, prompted the separate colonies of Upper and Lower Canada (now Ontario and Québec respectively), Nova Scotia, and New Brunswick to join together into a single Dominion of Canada in 1867. The Hudson's Bay Company's holdings – amounting to almost the entirety of modern Western Canada – were purchased in 1870, and the colonies of British Columbia and Prince Edward Island joined the Dominion in 1871.

The globe-spanning reach of the British Empire was celebrated by, and necessitated the existence of, the Standard of Empire Annual, *which described its mission as "enlarging mutual British understanding and knowledge, where all parts of the empire are concerned..."*

Though linked from coast to coast to coast on paper, the sovereign rights of indigenous peoples were still guaranteed by the Royal Proclamation. Canada, on behalf of Queen Victoria, negotiated a series of treaties from 1871 to 1921. Though appearing progressive in their recognition of indigenous nationhood, the interpretation of these treaties by the government was malignant. The promise of land where the British would not settle became reservations which imprisoned indigenous peoples. The promise of education became residential schools, where indigenous children were forcibly taken from their families and prohibited from speaking their native languages or practicing their cultural traditions, as well as being nightmarish places of terrifying physical, emotional, and sexual abuse. The promise of agricultural means for indigenous communities to support themselves became a peasant farming policy designed to maintain indigenous poverty and disenfranchisement. Many reserves in Canada continue to subsist under third world conditions, being denied even such basic necessities as clean water.

With the legal (if not humanitarian) obligations of the Royal Proclamation met, Canada's mission turned to yielding the prairies into productive farmland by

Canada's Parliament, Ottawa. Illustration from a Canadian Pacific Railway summer tours brochure of 1895.

which to feed the Empire. The Canadian Pacific Railway was completed in 1885, an integral link in the "All Red Route" that allowed travellers to voyage completely around the world without leaving the British Empire. Doors were opened to millions of British, American, German, Scandinavian, Ukrainian, Italian, and Doukhobor immigrants, as well as Chinese and Indian immigrants who were less welcome and fought severe government restrictions. Even this was uneven: while Canada instituted a Chinese head tax in 1885, there was relatively little animosity towards Japanese Canadians until the Second World War, due in no small part to Japan's participation in World War One as an ally of Britain. Before the 1880's, less than 1000 people of European ethnicity resided on the Canadian Prairies. By 1901 they had exploded to nearly 212,000. Canada's multicultural diversity and ethos of tolerance is a deliberate product of British colonial policy. It has taken time to develop and remains imperfectly implemented, also as a result of colonial policy.

More venerable than the Hudson's Bay Company was the East India Company, chartered in 1600 to establish trade with the Indian subcontinent. The directly precipitating event was Sir Walter Raleigh's 1592 capture of the Portuguese ship *Madre de Deus*, heavy laden with jewels, pearls, gold, spices, textiles, and valuable information on Asian trade routes. With permission of the Mughal Empire, the East India Company set up posts in Surat in 1608, Machilipatnam in 1611, Bengal in 1612, Madras in 1639, Hugli-Chuchura in 1640, Mumbai in 1668, and Kolata in 1690.

As the Mughals declined in power during the 1700's, the East India Company ascended. Critical to the spread of the East India Company's influence was the political diversity of India. At the time, the subcontinent was not organized as a modern nation-state, united across the subcontinent in a single ethnic, linguistic, and political unit. The concept of "India" itself was a product of the British Empire. Prior to direct British rule, the Mughals maintained a diverse array of kingdoms and principalities reflecting Europe prior to the creation of the nation-state. The East India Company was able to play these separate fiefdoms against each other, and slowly accumulate them during the 1700's and into the 1800's.

Resentment in these provinces and among the sepoy (ethnically Indian) soldiers of the company – including the use of Enfield rifle cartridges greased with pig and cow fat to offend both Muslims and Hindus respectively – lead to the Indian Rebellion of 1857 and direct colonial control of India through the British Raj. In 1877, Queen Victoria was proclaimed the Empress of India.

Despite the establishment of railways, canals, universities, hospitals, English Common Law, and government infrastructure, the rule of the British in India was not beneficent. Debate persists as to whether the Great Famine of 1876-1878, with its death toll of 5 to 10 million people, was an incident of incompetent British cash crop economics or a deliberate act of genocide. Some of worst famines in recorded human history happened during this time, totalling 11 major famines and several minor ones with a combined death toll of 35 million. India became a venue of economic exploitation, wealth being pulled from the country in raw resources and cash crops, and Indian entrepreneurialism suppressed in favour of creating a market for British goods like Lancashire textiles. There were also incidents like the Jallianwala Bagh massacre, in which British troops fired into a crowd of unarmed civilians, killing 400 and injuring over 1,000. The brutality of

"The Imperial Assembly of India at Delhi: the Viceregal Procession passing the Clock Tower and Delhi Institute in the Chandnee Chowk" as depicted in the Illustrated London News, 1877.

colonialism is indisputable.

Yet the most confusing aspect was British liberality, after the Rebellion of 1857, towards Indian tradition. Queen Victoria's proclamation to "the Princes, Chiefs and Peoples of India" declared freedom of religion with provisions that none should be disqualified from office on the basis of race or creed. Furthermore, it read that "in framing and administering the Law, due regard be paid to the ancient Rights, Usages, and Customs of India." A large part of the success of the British in India is due to this liberality.

Rather than wholesale, overt transformation of Indian traditions, the British opted to insert themselves into these traditions at the head. Princes were allowed to maintain their lands and inheritances while swearing fealty to the Crown. 560 of these principalities were supported by the British to act as a bulwark against another mutiny. Indians serving in the Legislative Council were from the aristocracy loyal to Britain. The British ruling class remained largely aloof to, and segregated from, the Indian community around them. Though official policy allowed ethnic Indians to serve in the Indian Civil Service, in practice the conditions to apply tended to exclude many qualified, educated Indians who then turned their prowess towards Indian nationalism.

Ironically, this led to criticisms that the British left India unprepared for independence. After 1947, the new country found itself with essentially a pre-modern political structure and pre-industrial economy thrust into the geopolitics of the post-WWII world. Much debate over the legacy of the British in India takes the form of "what ifs" and "could haves": Could India have formed a modern nation-state without the British? Would that have even mattered? Could India have built up the infrastructure the British did without them? Did the British build that infrastructure merely to suit the colonialist enterprise? Does intention matter? What if someone worse colonized India instead of the British? Or if India was divided like Africa? The fact remains that regardless of what might have happened, what happened is what happened, both good and ill.

This pattern repeated over and over again across the planet, across the 19th and early 20th centuries. The British Empire brought a sophisticated technological and political infrastructure at tremendous cost to indigenous peoples, mobilizing mass migration and creating complex multicultural societies with mixed legacies. As evident from these examples, the British Empire was not as crudely a "white supremacist" exercise as modern peoples might imagine. It was, in effect, a sense of *noblesse oblige*. As the British Empire grew, it developed a sense in which it did not conquer the world because it had the right to, or the power to, or even the economic need to... It did so because it had the *duty* to. For Queen Victoria's Diamond Jubilee, Rudyard Kipling penned the poem *Recessional* which includes the lines:

> If, drunk with sight of power, we loose
> > Wild tongues that have not Thee in awe,
> Such boastings as the Gentiles use,
> > Or lesser breeds without the Law—

Kipling did not, as it may be supposed, refer here to indigenous peoples. The lawless, boasting lesser breeds to which he refers are the Germans, embarking on their own Teutonic imperial project. In this anthology's first story, *The Battle of Dorking: Reminiscences of a Volunteer* by Sir George Tomkyns Chesney (United Kingdom, 1871), the invader of Britain is Germanic. In *The Storm of '92: A Grandfather's Tale told in 1932* by W.H.C. Lawrence (Canada, 1889) and *Anno Domini 2000, or Woman's Destiny* by Sir Julius Vogel (New Zealand, 1889), it is the United States of America that emerges as the Empire's foe.

Kipling's poem is a warning against imperial hubris, and reminder of the awesome responsibility that Britain has taken upon itself. The British Empire, as Kipling conceived it, was not motivated by a belief in the superiority of broadly conceived racial categories, but by the responsibilities forced upon it by a specifically *British* superiority in industry, philosophy, arts, culture, government, and jurisprudence. The spread of British rule was the definition of social progress, and even social justice.

So alien is this way of looking at imperialism today that the British Empire is an enigma. "Seen in the clearer light of retrospect," writes Jan Morris again, "even its loftiest aspirations seem illusory and theatrical, and so hard is it to disentangle its good from its bad, its truth from its deceptions, that most of us remember it less vividly now as a political organism than as a sort of gigantic exhibition."

The aforementioned examples of invasion literature, *The Battle of Dorking* and *The Storm of '92*, show the precariousness of the British Empire's position. Though its reach was vast, its spread left each arm vulnerable to threats from without and within.

Industrialization brought with it the spectre of mass warfare on an unimaginable scale. The American Civil War of 1861-65, the Japanese Boshin War of 1868-69, and the Franco-Prussian War of

Cover to the original 1871 edition of The Battle of Dorking.

1870-71 raised the paranoia that England herself could easily fall to an industrialized enemy. In the immediate wake of Prussia's victory over France – a complete rout of the largest army in Europe in only two months – Corps of Royal Engineers captain Sir George Tomkyns Chesney penned *The Battle of Dorking* as a cautionary tale. Struck by the disarray of the British Armed Forces and the looming threat of a credible adversary, Chesney found that his public appeals were fruitless until he sensationalized his fears in a fictional futurist narrative.

In *The Storm of '92*, the narrator recounts a future American invasion of Canada in 1892. It was itself a response to an American novella called *The Battle of the Swash and the Capture of Canada* by Samuel Barton, published the year before. In that 1888 story, a fisheries dispute led to war between Great Britain and the United States. Barton depicts Britain's main goal as humbling the United States and demanding that it takes Canada off the Empire's hands. "Oh! Let the United States have Canada; and much good may she do them!" says Lord Churchill to the Parliament in *The Battle of the Swash*, "I can never see where she has done us much. What I would propose in brief, is a 'forced sale' of Canada to the United States..."

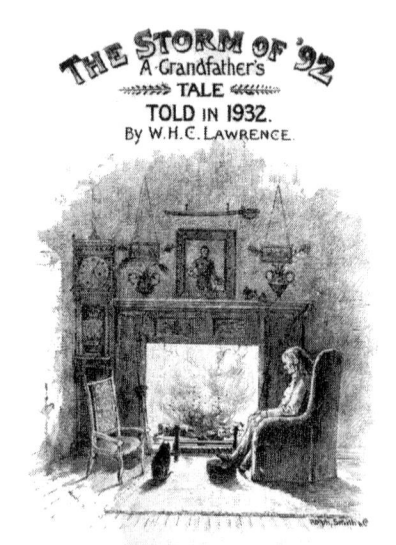

The Storm of '92 begins by disabusing the reader of any notions that Great Britain should want to rid itself of Canada or that Canada should want in any way to be part of the United States. Lawrence holds a still-current Canadian antipathy to identifying with the United States, seeing it then and now as an unruly free-for-all whose wars are instances of political and economic opportunism fermented by the media. The superiority of Canada's way of life, according to Lawrence, is its distinctively English and French cultural identity. Yet he is aware, as every Canadian must be, of the inherent threat posed by such a culturally, economically, and militarily dominating neighbour.

Some 400 invasion stories were published between *The Battle of Dorking* and World War One. These included such varied texts as the aggressively imperialistic *Kaitō Bōken Kidan: Kaitei Gunkan* (*The Submarine Battleship*) by Shunro Oshikawa (Japan, 1900) and its five sequels, the self-explanatory *Ikon Junen Nichiro Miraisen* (*The Bitter Future Ten-Year War between Japan and Russia*) by

Original cover image to The Storm of '92 *by Rolph, Smith & Co.*

8

Harada Masaemon (Japan, nd), a Japanese invasion of the United States in *In the Clutch of the War-God* by Milo Hastings (United States, 1911), a British invasion of the United States in *The Stricken Nation* by Henry Grattan Donnelly (United States, 1890), a German invasion of the United States in *Uncle Sam's Boys at The Invasion of the United States* by H. Irving Hancock (United States, 1916), *The Back Door* (Hong Kong, 1897) by an anonymous author warning of British Hong Kong's poor defenses, *The Yellow Wave: A Romance of the Asiatic Invasion of Australia* by Kenneth MacKay (Australia, 1895), and *The Great War in England in 1897* by William Le Queux (United Kingdom, 1894) in which a coalition of England and Germany emerge triumphant against France and Russia. The pre-WWI genre reached an early apotheosis with H.G. Wells' *The War of the Worlds* (United Kingdom, 1898): a Martian invasion of the UK describing a growing sense of imperial ennui. It was given a telling unofficial sequel that same year by Garret P. Serviss, titled *Edison's Conquest of Mars* (United States, 1898), in which the ascending world power revenges itself upon the red planet. *Edison's Conquest of Mars* has been republished in *Science Fiction of America's Gilded Age: An Anthology* edited by C.W. Gross.

In the midst of these was *The Swoop! or How Clarence Saved England: A Tale of the Great Invasion* (United Kingdom, 1909), a satirical novella by P.G. Wodehouse. Though predating his more famous creations, *The Swoop!* is still rooted in the farcical views of British high society Wodehouse would master with his Jeeves and Wooster series. The simultaneous invasion of Britain by the armies of Russia, Germany, Switzerland, Monaco, Morocco, China, the Ottomans, Somalia, and an African tribe in war canoes attracts little notice from the English distracted by the summer vacationing season. It is up to a Boy Scout, Clarence, to defend English country and English character.

The Germ Growers: An Australian Story of Adventure and Mystery by Robert Potter (Australia, 1892) imagines

Clarence triumphant on the cover of The Swoop! *Illustration by C. Harrison.*

invasion from a much different quarter: shapeshifting extraterrestrials developing virulent strains of plague in their secret facility in Australia. Predating H.G. Wells' *War of the Worlds* by six years, it is an imaginative inversion of its successor tale. This time it is the aliens, already among us, who employ biological warfare. The nature of these aliens as shapeshifters germinating disease is less suggestive of the kind of outright invasion feared by Chesney and Lawrence than as a kind of insidious rot from within... A rot that is essentially theological in nature. *The Germ Growers* is steeped in Christian imagery and allegories, framed as a rebellion of evil celestial beings against more beneficent ones, sowing disease (i.e.: sin) to weaken the human race.

Rudyard Kipling, the poet of the Empire, wrote only two proper science fiction tales during his illustrious career. *With the Night Mail: A Story of 2000 A.D.* (United Kingdom, 1905), set an amazing, futuristic, 100 years hence, describes an Aerial Board of Control that has been implemented to regulate air traffic, becoming a *de facto* world government. This particular short story follows Kipling's strength in writing about the regular, everyday functionaries of the imperial system. In this case, a mailman aboard an overnight London-to-Québec flight.

Though much out of favour for his jingoistic tenor today, this peek into the lives of imperial functionaries is the very fascination in Kipling's work. His is the unapologetic voice of the establishment, and not so much the elite of the establishment but the labourers, bureaucrats, and soldiers who carry out the work of the establishment. In 1942, long after Kipling had fallen out of favour, George Orwell wrote the following, not so much in defense of him ("Kipling *is* a jingo imperialist, he is morally insensitive and aesthetically disgusting. It is better to start by admitting that, and then to try to find out why it is that he survives...") as in explanation:

> But because he identifies himself with the official class, he does possess one thing which 'enlightened' people seldom or never possess, and that is a sense of responsibility... Although he had no direct connexion with any political party, Kipling was a Conservative, a thing that does not exist nowadays. Those who now call themselves Conservatives are either Liberals, Fascists or the accomplices of Fascists. He identified himself with the ruling power and not with the opposition. In a gifted writer this seems to us strange and even disgusting, but it did have the advantage of giving Kipling a certain grip on reality. The ruling power is always faced with the question, 'In such and such circumstances, what would you *do?*, whereas the opposition is not obliged to take responsibility or make any real decisions. Where it is a permanent and pensioned opposition, as in England, the quality of its thought deteriorates accordingly. Moreover, anyone who starts out with a pessimistic, reactionary view of life tends to be justified by events, for Utopia never arrives and 'the gods of the copybook headings', as Kipling himself put it, always return. Kipling sold out to the British governing class, not financially but emotionally. This warped his political judgement, for the British ruling class were not what

he imagined, and it led him into abysses of folly and snobbery, but he gained a corresponding advantage from having at least tried to imagine what action and responsibility are like.

Kipling revisits his futuristic world 150 years hence in *As Easy as A.B.C.: A Tale of 2150 AD* (United Kingdom, 1912). Absolute technocratic rule by the Aerial Board of Control has resulted in an atomistic society with a dwindling birthrate, a miserable society lacking social relationships or a thriving body politic. *With the Night Mail* and *As Easy as A.B.C.* are a fascinating exercise in an author revisiting a futurist story a further century off to see how it transforms, as well as for Kipling's prescience on the social effects of industry and globalization.

Sir Julius Vogel, Prime Minister of New Zealand from 1873 to 1875 and again in 1876, provides his own prognostications on life in the year 2000 in his country's first recorded science fiction novel. *Anno Domini 2000, or Woman's Destiny* (New Zealand, 1889) tells the story of Hilda Fitzherbert, the Imperial Prime Minister, and the unique challenges she faces as a woman in politics. Namely, the advances of the villainous Australian republican Sir Reginald Paramatta and her wooing by the monarch, Emperor Albert. Unfortunately, Albert's refusal of the hand of the daughter of the President of the United States precipitates a war between the Empire and its errant offshoot. As a rule, *Anno Domini 2000* reflects the progressive views towards women held in New Zealand: it was the first country in the world to enfranchise women, in 1893.

Illustration from With the Night Mail *by H.G. Seppings Wright.*

Even amidst the canon of Victorian-Edwardian feminist literature, *Sultana's Dream* by Begum Rokeya Sakhawat Hussain (Bangladesh, 1905) is unique.

Rokeya Khatun was both born and died in Bangladesh on a December 9th, the former in 1880 and the latter in 1932, which is recognized today as a national holiday in Bangladesh. Early on she adopted a love for her native language of Bengali against the common preference of educated Muslims to speak in Arabic and Persian. At the age of 18 she married deputy magistrate Khan Bahadur Sakhawat Hussain, who encouraged her studies in Bengali and English. It was through his endorsement that she wrote many stories and essays, including *Sultana's Dream*, in which she uses the medium of science fiction to postulate a reversal of fortune for women in her society, turning the tables on the men and hypothesizing a female-run utopia. After her husband passed away, Begum Rokeya used his estate to start the Sakhawat Memorial Girls' High School in 1909, which was moved to Calcutta in 1911 where it remains to this day. She also founded the Islamic Women's Association (Anjuman-e-Khawateen-e-Islam) dedicated to the education and improvement of Muslims, especially Muslim women, in British India.

In addition to being written by a Muslim female author in British India in the early 20th century, *Sultana's Dream* is unique for having been written in English. There was already a rich tradition of science fiction writing in Bengali, including such notable texts as *Aschary Vrittant* (*The Strange Tale*) by Ambika Dutt Vyas in 1884-88, *Shukra Bhraman* (*Transit to Venus*) by Jagadananda Roy in 1892, and *Niruddesher Kahini* (*The Story of the Missing One*) by Sir Jagadish Chandra Bose in 1896. The latter was especially provocative for its origins as an entry in a story contest for the hair oil Kuntalini. Entries had to feature the product in a prominent way, and *Niruddesher Kahini* prefigured chaos theory by using it to quell a cyclone. Despite this tradition, stories written in English were rare and *Sultana's Dream* is a significant example.

Another significant example of Indian science fiction in English is *The Republic of Orissá: Annals From The Pages Of The Twentieth Century* by Shoshee Chunder Dutt (India, 1845). Written before direct British rule in India, this short story still posits a future for the subcontinent that is free from British influence. Born in 1824, Chunder Dutt was a poet, historian, convert to Christianity, and wrote under two English pseudonyms, J.A.G. Barton and Horatio Bickerstaffe Rowney. His nephew, civil servant and writer Romesh Chunder Dutt, said of him that he used "the colonizer's values to eulogize freedom from subjugation." His argument for Indian liberation developed from the Christian and humanitarian values of the British themselves.

Just as Wodehouse satirized the genre of invasion literature, futurism was satirized by Stephen Leacock in *The Man in Asbestos: An Allegory of the Future* (Canada, 1911). Though largely forgotten today, Leacock was the most well-known Canadian writer prior to World War One and became the most popular English-language humourist in the world in the decade between 1915 and 1925. Robert Benchley, Groucho Marx, and Jack Benny all remarked on the debt they owed to Leacock. The effectiveness of his satire developed from his status as a political arch-conservative and patriot for the British Empire. Satire and cynicism are close cousins, as are conservatism and cynicism. Writers like Leacock and Alberta Robida, the French writer and artist of *The Twentieth Century* (France, 1883), need merely to take the ambitions of social reformers and filter them through the lens of human absurdity. The most accurate futurist is the one who can anticipate the stupidest possible use of a new technology, who can figure out the worst possible direction that progress can go in.

His early work *Nonsense Novels,* from which *The Man in Asbestos* is excerpted, is a fine example of this principle. A very short anthology of shorts, *Nonsense Novels* plays and prods the standard tropes of Victorian-Edwardian popular literature. Few genres are left untouched, be they the romances of the Scottish moors (*Hannah of the Highlands: or, The Laird of Loch Aucherlocherty*), robust tales of seafaring sailors (*Soaked in Seaweed: or, Upset in the Ocean (An Old-fashioned Sea Story.)*), spiritualist mysteries (*"Q." A Psychic Pstory of the Psupernatural*), detective whodunits (*Maddened by Mystery; or, The Defective Detective*) and science fiction. In *The Man in Asbestos*, a sleeper wakes sometime in the year 3000, but no one is quite sure because they stopped counting after death was eliminated. Machinery, chemical foods, a stabilized climate, and the revolt against fashion has eliminated work, change, and events. People could still die by accident, which is why most forms of sport and transportation have been banned, needless as they would have been anyways. Why travel when all is sameness? The sleeper, a social reformer, is appalled at the real meaning behind his efforts towards a total equality of outcome.

Back in England, Harry Collingwood rose to prominence in the latter part of the 19th century as a writer of boy's own stories. Born William Joseph Cosens Lancaster in 1843, this trained Royal Navy midshipman and civil engineer adopted the pen name "Harry Collingwood" from the protagonist of his first novel, *The Secret of the Sands* (United Kingdom, 1878). He went on to write over 40 novels, mainly of seafaring adventure, piracy, slavery, buried treasure, shipwrecks, and other disasters. A handful were historical novels of dubious accuracy. Three were straightforward science fiction.

The first of Collingwood's science fiction novels is presented in this volume: *The Log of the Flying Fish: A Story of Aerial and Submarine Peril and Adventure* (United Kingdom, 1886). In it, new discoveries in metallurgy and sources of energy allow for the creation of the Flying Fish, a craft that can act as both airship and submarine. This magnificent invention then

Harry Collingwood's intrepid explorers flee woolly mammoths in The Log of the Flying Fish. *Illustration by Gordon Browne.*

13

Routing African warriors in Harry Collingwood's The Log of the Flying Fish. *Illustration by Gordon Browne.*

takes a gang of British imperialists on a rapid excursion from sunken wrecks in the English Channel to the North Pole (where they find a lost world populated with woolly mammoths) to deepest Africa (where they discover real unicorns and run afoul of a local chieftain) to the top of Mount Everest.

One sees the typical preoccupations of British children's literature of the time in expeditions to uncharted lands. One also sees the typical insensitivity to indigenous cultures. Stories of this type, whether British, American, or Japanese, saw the world and the imperial exercise as backgrounds for pulse-pounding adventure in an age before Hollywood blockbusters. *The Log of the Flying Fish* is much like *The Huge Hunter; or, the Steam Man of the Prairies* by Edward S. Ellis (United States, 1868), also reprinted in *Science Fiction of America's Gilded Age*. In the latter, a boy inventor takes his eponymous steam-powered mechanical man on a jaunt through the American frontier to dig gold and fight Native Americans. The main difference is that, at the time, America's imperial ambitions were still continental in scale. Collingwood had the entire globe-spanning British Empire at his disposal.

The Flying Fish returned in Collingwood's two remaining science fiction novels, *With Airship and Submarine: A Tale of Adventure* (United Kingdom, 1908) and *The Cruise of the "Flying Fish": The Airship-Submarine* (United Kingdom, 1924). Another to try his hand with an airship, in his only science fictional novel, was G.K. Chesterton.

Though H.G. Wells is often drawn into comparison with Jules Verne, he was historically a more active participant in a protracted feud with three other

Edwardian men of letters: George Bernard Shaw, Hilaire Belloc, and G.K. Chesterton. On the side of the Fabian socialists were Wells and Shaw, who shared the kind of contempt for each other that can only be held by radicals who deem each other insufficiently radical. On the other side of the isle, Chesterton and Belloc enjoyed the camaraderie of a shared Roman Catholic faith. Together they posed such a rotund and unified front that Shaw gave them the shared epigram of "Chesterbelloc."

For his part, Chesterton was not above utilizing the same science fiction allegories as Wells. *The Ball and the Cross*, published in 1909, is a punchy story about a Jacobite Catholic named Maclan and a socialist atheist named Turnbull combing the world in search of a place to duel. After 20 years of publishing his secularist newsletter, Turnbull was homicidally gratified to have someone finally care enough about his opinion to disagree with it.

The Ball and the Cross is more akin to one of Chesterton's theological works but in a narrative form. Besides his famed *Father Brown* detective stories, about a sleuthing Catholic priest, Chesterton also published extensive works of Catholic apologetics and social commentary like *Orthodoxy* (United Kingdom, 1908) and *The Everlasting Man* (United Kingdom, 1925). In these works, Chesterton developed a distinctively disarming comedic voice. His theological points were made less with religious pieties or rational arguments than with comedic devices. This often left him open to accusations of flippancy. "I have occasionally in my life made jokes, and I have also occasionally been serious," he opined in a May 1910 letter to the *Illustrated London Times*. "And this, I had always understood, was the not unusual practice of my fellow-creatures. But I have discovered that this explanation is not considered sufficient in my case; I am always supposed to be engaged with some tortuous or topsy-turvy intention. When I state a dull truth about anything, it is said to be a showy paradox; when I lighten or brighten it with any common jest, it is supposed to be my solid and absurd opinion." And before this, in his book *All Things Considered* (United Kingdom, 1908):

> My fate in most controversies is rather pathetic. It is an almost invariable rule that the man with whom I don't agree thinks I am making a fool of myself, and the man with whom I do agree thinks I am making a fool of him. There seems to be some sort of idea that you are not treating a subject properly if you eulogise it with fantastic terms or defend it by grotesque examples. Yet a truth is equally solemn whatever figure or example its exponent adopts. It is an equally awful truth that four and four make eight, whether you reckon the thing out in eight onions or eight angels, or eight bricks or eight bishops, or eight minor poets or eight pigs. Similarly, if it be true that God made all things, that grave fact can be asserted by pointing at a star or by waving an umbrella. But the case is

stronger than this. There is a distinct philosophical advantage in using grotesque terms in a serious discussion.

 I think seriously, on the whole, that the more serious is the discussion the more grotesque should be the terms. For this, as I say, there is an evident reason. For a subject is really solemn and important in so far as it applies to the whole cosmos, or to some great spheres and cycles of experience at least. So far as a thing is universal it is serious. And so far as a thing is universal it is full of comic things. If you take a small thing, it may be entirely serious: Napoleon, for instance, was a small thing, and he was serious: the same applies to microbes. If you isolate a thing, you may get the pure essence of gravity. But if you take a large thing (such as the Solar System) it must be comic, at least in parts. The germs are serious, because they kill you. But the stars are funny, because they give birth to life, and life gives birth to fun. If you have, let us say, a theory about man, and if you can only prove it by talking about Plato and George Washington, your theory may be a quite frivolous thing. But if you can prove it by talking about the butler or the postman, then it is serious, because it is universal. So far from it being irreverent to use silly metaphors on serious questions, it is one's duty to use silly metaphors on serious questions. It is the test of one's seriousness. It is the test of a responsible religion or theory whether it can take examples from pots and pans and boots and butter-tubs. It is the test of a good philosophy whether you can defend it grotesquely. It is the test of a good religion whether you can joke about it.

 Thus, *The Ball and the Cross* begins with a farcical narrative about a Professor Lucifer who, from the security of his airship, taunts a monk named Michael about the irrationality of religious faith with a string of condescending invective that could have easily been pulled from the modern Internet. From there it launches into the even more farcical tale of Maclan and Turnbull, who constantly find their duelling over the most serious thing in the world frustrated by a world intent on stopping them. The airship does pop up periodically, however, and at the climax.

 Though Chesterton dealt with eternal things, the British Empire was already waning. The imperial project was already being questioned before Queen Victoria's death in 1901. The First World War was a tremendous blow not only the British Empire, but to the entirety of Western civilization. Optimistic faith in limitless moral and technological progress was shattered, and a new order emerged in which the British Empire waned as the United States and USSR began to rise. A kind of decadent nihilism took root in the Roaring Twenties, itself ended by the Great Depression and emergence of fascism. Though World War II was called

Britain's "finest hour" it also marked the definitive end of the Empire. An exhausted England was in no position to hold onto its vast domains in the face of accelerating sentiments of decolonization.

THE BATTLE OF DORKING: REMINISCENCES OF A VOLUNTEER BY GEORGE TOMKYNS CHESNEY (UNITED KINGDOM, 1871)

You ask me to tell you, my grandchildren, something about my own share in the great events that happened fifty years ago. 'Tis sad work turning back to that bitter page in our history, but you may perhaps take profit in your new homes from the lesson it teaches. For us in England it came too late. And yet we had plenty of warnings, if we had only made use of them. The danger did not come on us unawares. It burst on us suddenly, 'tis true; but its coming was foreshadowed plainly enough to open our eyes, if we had not been wilfully blind. We English have only ourselves to blame for the humiliation which has been brought on the land. Venerable old age! Dishonourable old age, I say, when it follows a manhood dishonoured as ours has been. I declare, even now, though fifty years have passed, I can hardly look a young man in the face when I think I am one of those in whose youth happened this degradation of Old England---one of those who betrayed the trust handed down to us unstained by our forefathers.

What a proud and happy country was this fifty years ago! Free-trade had been working for more than a quarter of a century, and there seemed to be no end to the riches it was bringing us. London was growing bigger and bigger; you could not build houses fast enough for the rich people who wanted to live in them, the merchants who made the money and came from all parts of the world to settle there, and the lawyers and doctors and engineers and other, and trades-people who got their share out of the profits. The streets reached down to Croydon and

Wimbledon, which my father could remember quite country places; and people used to say that Kingston and Reigate would soon be joined to London. We thought we could go on building and multiplying for ever. 'Tis true that even then there was no lack of poverty; the people who had no money went on increasing as fast as the rich, and pauperism was already beginning to be a difficulty; but if the rates were high, there was plenty of money to pay them with; and as for what were called the middle classes, there really seemed no limit to their increase and prosperity. People in those days thought it quite a matter of course to bring a dozen of children into the world--or, as it used to be said, Providence sent them that number of babies; and if they couldn't always marry off all the daughters, they used to manage to provide for the sons, for there were new openings to be found in all the professions, or in the Government offices, which went on steadily getting larger. Besides, in those days young men could be sent out to India, or into the army or navy; and even then emigration was not uncommon, although not the regular custom it is now. Schoolmasters, like all other professional classes, drove a capital trade. They did not teach very much, to be sure, but new schools with their four or five hundred boys were springing up all over the country.

Fools that we were! We thought that all this wealth and prosperity were sent us by Providence, and could not stop coming. In our blindness we did not see that we were merely a big workshop, making up the things which came from all parts of the world; and that if other nations stopped sending us raw goods to work up, we could not produce them ourselves. True, we had in those days an advantage in our cheap coal and iron; and had we taken care not to waste the fuel, it might have lasted us longer. But even then there were signs that coal and iron would soon become cheaper in foreign parts; while as to food and other things, England was not better off than it is now. We were so rich simply because other nations from all parts of the world were in the habit of sending their goods to us to be sold or manufactured; and we thought that this would last for ever. And so, perhaps, it might have lasted, if we had only taken proper means to keep it; but, in our folly, we were too careless even to insure our prosperity, and after the course of trade was turned away it would not come back again.

And yet, if ever a nation had a plain warning, we had. If we were the greatest trading country, our neighbours were the leading military power in Europe. They were driving a good trade, too, for this was before their foolish communism (about which you will hear when you are older) had ruined the rich without benefiting the poor, and they were in many respects the first nation in Europe; but it was on their army that they prided themselves most. And with reason. They had beaten the Russians and the Austrians, and the Prussians too, in bygone years, and they thought they were invincible. Well do I remember the great review held at Paris by the Emperor Napoleon during the great Exhibition, and how proud he looked showing off his splendid Guards to the assembled kings and princes. Yet, three years afterwards, the force so long deemed the first in Europe was ignominiously beaten, and the whole army taken prisoners. Such a defeat had never happened before in the world's history; and with this proof before us of the folly of disbelieving in the possibility of disaster merely because it had never fallen upon us, it might have been supposed that we should have the sense to take the lesson to heart. And the country was certainly roused for a time, and a cry was raised that the army ought to be reorganised, and our defences strengthened against the enormous power for sudden attacks which it was seen other nations were able to put forth. And a scheme of army reform was brought forward by the Government. It was a half-and-half affair at best; and, unfortunately, instead of being taken up in Parliament as a national scheme, it was made a party matter of, and so fell through. There was a Radical section of the House, too, whose votes had to be secured by conciliation, and which blindly demanded a reduction of armaments as the price of allegiance. This party always decried military establishments as part of a fixed policy for reducing the influence of the Crown and the aristocracy. They could not understand that the times had altogether changed, that the Crown had really no power, and that the Government merely existed at the pleasure of the House of Commons, and that even Parliament-rule was beginning to give way to mob-law. At any rate, the Ministry, baffled on all sides, gave up by degrees all the strong points of a scheme which they were not heartily in earnest about. It was not that there was any lack of money, if only it had been spent in the right way. The army cost enough, and more than enough, to give us a proper defence, and there were armed men of sorts in plenty and to spare, if only they had been decently organised. It was in organisation and forethought that we fell short, because our rulers did not heartily believe in the need for preparation. The fleet and the Channel, they said, were sufficient protection. So army reform was put off to some more convenient season, and the militia and volunteers were left untrained as before, because to call them out for drill would "interfere with the industry of the country." We could have given up some of the industry of those days, forsooth, and yet be busier than we are now. But why tell you a tale you have so often heard already? The nation, although uneasy, was misled by the false security its leaders professed to feel; the warning given by the disasters that overtook France was allowed to pass by unheeded. We would not even be at the trouble of putting our arsenals in a safe place, or of guarding the capital against a surprise, although the cost of doing so would not have been so much as missed from the national wealth. The French trusted in their army and its great reputation, we in our fleet; and in each case the result of this blind confidence was disaster, such as our forefathers in their hardest struggles could not have even imagined.

   I need hardly tell you how the crash came about. First, the rising in India drew away a part of our small army; then came the difficulty with America, which had been threatening for years, and we sent off ten thousand men to defend

Canada--a handful which did not go far to strengthen the real defences of that country, but formed an irresistible temptation to the Americans to try and take them prisoners, especially as the contingent included three battalions of the Guards. Thus the regular army at home was even smaller than usual, and nearly half of it was in Ireland to check the talked-of Fenian invasion fitting out in the West. Worse still--though I do not know it would really have mattered as things turned out--the fleet was scattered abroad: some ships to guard the West Indies, others to check privateering in the China seas, and a large part to try and protect our colonies on the Northern Pacific shore of America, where, with incredible folly, we continued to retain possessions which we could not possibly defend. America was not the great power forty years ago that it is now; but for us to try and hold territory on her shores which could only be reached by sailing round the Horn, was as absurd as if she had attempted to take the Isle of Man before the indepedence of Ireland. We see this plainly enough now, but we were all blind then.

It was while we were in this state, with our ships all over the world, and our little bit of an army cut up into detachments, that the Secret Treaty was published, and Holland and Denmark were annexed. People say now that we might have escaped the troubles which came on us if we had at any rate kept quiet till our other difficulties were settled; but the English were always an impulsive lot: the whole country was boiling over with indignation, and the Government, egged on by the press, and going with the stream, declared war. We had always got out of scrapes before, and we believed our old luck and pluck would somehow pull us through.

Then, of course, there was bustle and hurry all over the land. Not that the calling up of the army reserves caused much stir, for I think there were only about 5000 altogether, and a good many of these were not to be found when the time came; but recruiting was going on all over the country, with a tremendous high bounty, 50,000 more men having been voted for the army. Then there was a Ballot Bill passed for adding 55,500 men to the militia; why a round number was not fixed on I don't know, but the Prime Minister said that this was the exact quota wanted to put the defences of the country on a sound footing. Then the shipbuilding that began! Ironclads, despatch-boats, gunboats, monitors,---every building-yard in the country got its job, and they were offering ten shillings a-day wages for anybody who could drive a rivet. This didn't improve the recruiting, you may suppose. I remember, too, there was a squabble in the House of Commons about whether artisans should be drawn for the ballot, as they were so much wanted, and I think they got an exemption. This sent numbers to the yards; and if we had had a couple of years to prepare instead of a couple of weeks, I daresay we should have done very well.

It was on a Monday that the declaration of war was announced, and in a few hours we got our first inkling of the sort of preparation the enemy had made for the event which they had really brought about, although the actual declaration was made by us. A pious appeal to the God of battles, whom it was said we had aroused, was telegraphed back; and from that momnet all communication with the north of Europe was cut off. Our embassies and legations were packed off at an hour's notice, and it was as if we had suddenly come back to the middle ages. The dumb astonishment visible all over London the next morning, when the papers came out void of news, merely hinting at what had happened, was one of the most startling things in this war of surprises. But everything had been arranged beforehand; nor ought we to have been surprised, for we had seen the same Power, only a few months before, move down half a million of men on a few days' notice, to conquer the greatest military nation in Europe, with no more fuss than our War Office used to make over the transport of a brigade from Aldershot to Brighton,-- and this, too, without the allies it had now. What happened now was not a bit more wonderful in reality; but people of this country could not bring themselves to believe that what had never occurred before to England could ever possibly happen. Like our neighbours, we became wise when it was too late.

Of course the papers were not long in getting news—even the mighty organisation set at work could not shut out a special correspondent; and in a very few days, although the telegraphs and railways were intercepted right across Europe, the main facts oozed out. An embargo had been laid on all the shipping in every port from the Baltic to Ostend; the fleets of the two great Powers had moved out, and it was supposed were assembled in the great northern harbour, and troops were hurrying on board all the steamers detained in these places, most of which were British vessels. It was clear that invasion was intended. Even then we might have been saved, if the fleet had been ready. The forts which guarded the flotilla were perhaps too strong for shipping to attempt; but an ironclad or two, handled as British sailors knew how to use them, might have destroyed or damaged a part of the transports, and delayed the expedition, giving us what we wanted, time. But then the best part of the fleet had been decoyed down to the Dardanelles, and what remained of the Channel squadron was looking after Fenian filibusters off the west of Ireland; so it was ten days before the fleet was got together, and by that time it was plain the enemy's preparations were too far advanced to be stopped by a coup-de- main. Information, which came chiefly through Italy, came slowly, and was more or less vague and uncertain; but this much was known, that at least a couple of hundred thousand men were embarked or ready to be put on board ships, and that the flotilla was guarded by more ironclads than we could then muster. I suppose it was the uncertainty as to the point the enemy would aim at for landing, and the fear lest he should give us the go-by, that kept the fleet for several days in the Downs; but it was not until the Tuesday fortnight after the declaration of war that it weighed anchor and steamed away for the North Sea. Of course you have read about the Queen's visit to the fleet the day before, and how she sailed round the ships in her yacht, and went on board the flag-ship to take leave of the admiral; how, overcome with emotion, she told him that the safety of the country was committed to his keeping. You remember, too, the gallant old officer's reply, and how all the ships' yards were manned, and how lustily the tars cheered as her Majesty was rowed off. The account was of course telegraphed to London, and the high spirits of the fleet infected the whole town. I was outside the Charing Cross station when the Queen's special train from Dover arrived, and from the cheering and shouting which greeted her Majesty as she drove away, you might have supposed we had already won a great victory. The leading journal, which had gone in strongly for the army reduction carried out during the session, and had been nervous and desponding in tone during the past fortnight, suggesting all sorts of compromises as a way of getting out of the war, came out in a very jubilant form next morning. "Panic- stricken inquirers," it said, "ask now, where are the means of meeting the invasion? We reply that the invasion will never take place. A British fleet, manned by British sailors whose courage and enthusiasm are reflected in the people of this country, is already on the way to meet the presumptuous foe. The issue of a contest between British ships and those of any other country, under anything like equal odds, can never be doubtful. England awaits with calm confidence the issue of the impending action."

Such were the words of the leading article, and so we all felt. It was on Tuesday, the 10th of August, that the fleet sailed from the Downs. It took with it a submarine cable to lay down as it advanced, so that continuous communication was kept up, and the papers were publishing special editions every few minutes with the latest news. This was the first time such a thing had been done, and the feat was accepted as a good omen. Whether it is true that the Admiralty made use of the cable to keep on sending contradictory orders, which took the command out of the admiral's hands, I can't say; but all that the admiral sent in return was a few messages of the briefest kind, which neither the Admiralty nor any one else could have made any use of. Such a ship had gone off reconnoitring; such another had rejoined--fleet was in latitude so and so. This went on till the Thursday morning. I had just come up to town by train as usual, and was walking to my office, when the newsboys began to cry, "New edition--enemy's fleet in sight!" You may imagine the scene in London! Business still went on at the banks, for bills matured although the independence of the country was being fought out under our own eyes, so to say, and the speculators were active enough. But even with the people who were making and losing their fortunes, the interest in the fleet overcame everything else; men who went to pay in or draw out their money stopped to show the last bulletin to the cashier. As for the street, you could hardly get along for the crowd stopping to buy and read the papers; while at every house or office the members sat restlessly in the common room, as if to keep together for company, sending out some one of their number every few minutes to get the latest edition. At least this is what happened at our office; but to sit still was as impossible as to do anything, and most of us went out and wandered about among the crowd, under a sort of feeling that the news was got quicker at in this way. Bad as were the times coming, I think the sickening suspense of that day, and the shock which followed, was almost the worst that we underwent. It was about ten o'clock that the first telegram came; an hour later the wire announced that the admiral had signalled to form line of battle, and shortly afterwards that the order was given to bear down on the enemy and engage. At twelve came the announcement, "Fleet opened fire about three miles to leeward of us"--that is, the ship with the cable. So far all had been expectancy, then came the first token of calamity. "An ironclad has been blown up"--"the enemy's torpedoes are doing great damage"--"the flag-ship is laid abroad the enemy"--"the flag-ship appears to be sinking"--"the vice-admiral has signalled to"--there the cable became silent, and, as you know, we heard no more till, two days afterwards, the solitary ironclad which escaped the disaster steamed into Portsmouth.

    Then the whole story came out--how our sailors, gallant as ever, had tried to close with the enemy; how the latter evaded the conflict at close quarters, and, sheering off, left behind them the fatal engines which sent our ships, one after the other, to the bottom; how all this happened almost in a few minutes. The Government, it appears, had received warnings of this invention; but to the nation this stunning blow was utterly unexpected. That Thursday I had to go home early for regimental drill, but it was impossible to remain doing nothing, so when that was over I went up to town again, and after waiting in expectation of news which never came, and missing the midnight train, I walked home. It was a hot sultry night, and I did not arrive till near sunrise. The whole town was quite still--the lull before the storm; and as I let myself in with my latch-key, and went softly up-stairs to my room to avoid waking the sleeping household, I could not but contrast the peacefulness of the morning--no sound breaking the silence but the singing of the birds in the garden--with the passionate remorse and indignation that would break out with the day. Perhaps the inmates of the rooms were as wakeful as myself; but the house in its stillness was just as it used to be when I came home alone from balls or parties in the happy days gone by. Tired though I was, I could not sleep, so I went down to the river and had a swim; and on returning found the household was assembling for early breakfast. A sorrowful household it was, although the burden pressing on each was partly an unseen one. My father, doubting whether his firm could last through the day; my mother, her distress about my brother, now with his regiment on the coast, already exceeding that which she felt for the public misfortune, had come down, although hardly fit to leave her room. My sister Clara was worst of all, for she could not but try to disguise her special interest in the fleet; and though we had all guessed that her heart was given to the young lieutenant in the flag-ship--the first vessel to go down--a love unclaimed could not be told, nor could we express the sympathy we felt for the poor girl. That breakfast, the last meal we ever had together, was soon ended, and my father and I went up to town by an early train, and got there just as the fatal announcement of the loss of the fleet was telegraphed from Portsmouth.

The panic and excitement of that day--how the funds went down to 35; the run upon the bank and its stoppage; the fall of half the houses in the city; how the Government issued a notification suspending specie payment and the tendering of bills--this last precaution too late for most firms, Graham & Co. among the number, which stopped payment as soon as my father got to the office; the call to arms, and the unanimous response of the country--all this is history which I need not repeat. You wish to hear about my own share in the business of the time. Well, volunteering had increased immensely from the day war was proclaimed, and our regiment went up in a day or two from its usual strength of 600 to nearly 1000. But the stock of rifles was deficient. We were promised a further supply in a few days, which however, we never received; and while waiting for them the regiment had to be divided into two parts, the recruits drilling with the rifles in the morning, and we old hands in the evening. The failures and stoppage of work on this black Friday threw an immense number of young men out of employment, and we recruited up to 1400 strong by the next day; but what was the use of all these men without arms? On the Saturday it was announced that a lot of smooth-bore muskets in store at the Tower would be served out to regiments applying for them, and a regular scramble took place among the volunteers for them, and our people got hold of a couple of hundred. But you might almost as well have tried to learn rifle-drill with a broomstick as with old brown bess; besides, there was no smooth-bore ammunition in the country. A national subscription was opened for the manufacture of rifles at Birmingham, which ran up to a couple of millions in two days, but, like everything else, this came too late. To return to the volunteers: camps had been formed a fortnight before at Dover, Brighton, Harwich, and other places, of regulars and militia, and the headquarters of most of the volunteer regiments were attached to one or other of them, and the volunteers themselves used to go down for drill from day to day, as they could spare time, and on Friday an order went out that they should be permanently embodied; but the metropolitan volunteers were still kept about London as a sort of reserve, till it could be seen at what point the invasion would take place. We were all told off to brigades and divisions. Our brigade consisted of the 4th Royal Surrey Militia, the 1st Surrey Administrative Battalion, as it was called, at Clapham, the 7th Surrey Volunteers at Southwark, and ourselves; but only our battalion and the militia were quartered in the same place, and the whole brigade had merely two or three afternoons together at brigade exercise in Bushey Park before the march took place. Our brigadier belonged to a line regiment in Ireland, and did not join till the very morning the order came. Meanwhile, during the preliminary fortnight, the militia colonel commanded. But though we volunteers were busy with our drill and preparations, those of us who, like myself, belonged to Government offices, had more than enough of office work to do, as you may suppose. The volunteer clerks were allowed to leave office at four o'clock, but the rest were kept hard at the desk far into the night. Orders to the lord-lieutenants, to the magistrates, notifications, all the arrangements for cleaning out the workhouses for hospitals--these and a hundred other things had to be managed in our office, and there was as much bustle indoors as out. Fortunate we were to be so busy-- the people to be pitied were those who had nothing to do. And on Sunday (that was the 15th August) work went on just as usual. We had an early parade and drill, and I went up to town by the nine o'clock train in my uniform, taking my rifle with me in case of accidents, and luckily too, as it turned out, a mackintosh overcoat. When I got to Waterloo there were all sorts of rumours afloat. A fleet had been seen off the Downs, and some of the despatch-boats which were hovering about the coasts brought news that there was a large flotilla off Harwich, but nothing could be seen from the shore, as the weather was hazy. The enemy's light ships had taken and sunk all the fishing-boats they could catch, to prevent the news of their whereabouts reaching us; but a few escaped during the night and reported that the Inconstant frigate coming home from North America, without any knowledge of what had taken place, had sailed right into the enemy's fleet and been captured. In town the troops were all getting ready for a move; the Guards in the Wellington Barracks were under arms, and their baggage-waggons packed and drawn up in the Bird-cage Walk. The usual guard at the Horse Guards had been withdrawn, and orderlies and staff-officers were going to and fro. All this I saw on the way to my office, where I worked away till twelve o'clock, and then feeling hungry after my early breakfast, I went across Parliament Street to my club to get some luncheon. There were about half-a-dozen men in the coffee-room, none of whom I knew; but in a minute or two Danvers of the Treasury entered in a tremendous hurry. From him I got the first bit of authentic news I had had that day. The enemy had landed in force near Harwich, and the metropolitan regiments were ordered down there to reinforce the troops already collected in that neighbourhood; his regiment was to parade at one o'clock, and he had come to get something to eat before starting. We bolted a hurried lunch, and were just leaving the club when a messenger from the Treasury came running into the hall.

"Oh, Mr. Danvers," said he, "I've come to look for you, sir; the secretary says that all the gentlemen are wanted at the office, and that you must please not one of you go with the regiments."

"The devil!" cried Danvers.

"Do you know if that order extends to all the public offices?" I asked.

"I don't know," said the man, "but I believe it do. I know there's messengers gone round to all the clubs and luncheon-bars to look for the gentlemen; the secretary says it's quite impossible any one can be spared just now, there's so much work to do; there's orders just come to send off our records to Birmingham to-night."

I did not wait to condole with Danvers, but, just glancing up Whitehall to see if any of our messengers were in pursuit, I ran off as hard as I could for Westminster Bridge, and so to the Waterloo station.

The place had quite changed its aspect since the morning. The regular service of trains had ceased, and the station and approaches were full of troops, among them the Guards and artillery. Everything was very orderly: the men had piled arms, and were standing about in groups. There was no sign of high spirits or enthusiasm. Matters had become too serious. Every man's face reflected the general feeling that we had neglected the warnings given us, and that now the danger so long derided as impossible and absurd had really come and found us unprepared. But the soldiers, if grave, looked determined, like men who meant to do their duty whatever might happen. A train full of guardsmen was just starting for Guildford. I was told it would stop at Surbiton, and, with several other volunteers, hurrying like myself to join our regiment, got a place in it. We did not arrive a moment too soon, for the regiment was marching from Kingston down to the station. The destination of our brigade was the east coast. Empty carriages were drawn up in the siding, and our regiment was to go first. A large crowd was assembled to see it off, including the recruits who had joined during the last fortnight, and who formed by far the largest part of our strength. They were to stay behind, and were certainly very much in the way already; for as all the officers and sergeants belonged to the active part, there was no one to keep discipline among them, and they came crowding around us, breaking the ranks and making it difficult to get into the train. Here I saw our new brigadier for the first time. He was a soldier-like man, and no doubt knew his duty, but he appeared new to volunteers, and did not seem to know how to deal with gentlemen privates. I wanted very much to run home and get my greatcoat and knapsack, which I had bought a few days ago, but feared to be left behind; a good-natured recruit volunteered to fetch them for me, but he had not returned before we started, and I began the campaign with a kit consisting of a mackintosh and a small pouch of tobacco.

It was a tremendous squeeze in the train; for, besides the ten men sitting down, there were three or four standing up in every compartment, and the afternoon was close and sultry, and there were so many stoppages on the way that we took nearly an hour and a half crawling up to Waterloo. It was between five and six in the afternoon when we arrived there, and it was nearly seven before we marched up to the Shoreditch station. The whole place was filled up with stores and ammunition, to be sent off to the east, so we piled arms in the street and scattered about to get food and drink, of which most of us stood in need, especially the latter, for some were already feeling the worse for the heat and crush. I was just stepping into a public-house with Travers, when who should drive up but his pretty wife? Most of our friends had paid their adieus at the Surbiton station, but she had driven up by the road in his brougham, bringing their little boy to have a last look at papa. She had also brought his knapsack and greatcoat, and, what was still more acceptable, a basket containing fowls, tongue, bread-and-butter, and biscuits, and a couple of bottles of claret,---which priceless luxuries they insisted on my sharing.

 Meanwhile the hours went on. The 4th Surrey Militia, which had marched all the way from Kingston, had come up, as well as the other volunteer corps; the station had been partly cleared of the stores that encumbered it; some artillery, two militia regiments, and a battalion of the line, had been despatched, and our turn to start had come, and long lines of carriages were drawn up ready for us; but still we remained in the street. You may fancy the scene. There seemed to be as many people as ever in London, and we could hardly move for the crowds of spectators--fellows hawking fruits and volunteers' comforts, newsboys and so forth, to say nothing of the cabs and omnibuses; while orderlies and staff-officers were constantly riding up with messages. A good many of the militiamen, and some of our people too, had taken more than enough to drink; perhaps a hot sun had told on empty stomachs; anyhow, they became very noisy. The din, dirt, and heat were indescribable. So the evening wore on, and all the information our officers could get from the brigadier, who appeared to be acting under another general, was, that orders had come to stand fast for the present. Gradually the street became quieter and cooler. The brigadier, who, by way of setting an example, had remained for some hours without leaving his saddle, had got a chair out of a shop, and sat nodding in it; most of the men were lying down or sitting on the pavement--some sleeping, some smoking. In vain had Travers begged his wife to go home. She declared that, having come so far, she would stay and see the last of us. The brougham had been sent away to a by- street, as it blocked up the road; so he sat on a doorstep, she by him on the knapsack. Little Arthur, who had been delighted at the bustle and the uniforms, and in high spirits, became at last very cross, and eventually cried himself to sleep in his father's arms, his golden hair and one little dimpled arm hanging over his shoulder. Thus went on the weary hours, till suddenly the assembly sounded, and we all started up. We were to return to Waterloo. The landing on the east was only a feint--so ran the rumour--the real attack was on the south. Anything seemed better than indecision and delay, and, tired though we were, the march back was gladly hailed. Mrs Travers, who made us take the remains of the luncheon with us, we left to look for her carriage; little Arthur, who was awake again, but very good and quiet, in her arms.

 We did not reach Waterloo till nearly midnight, and there was some delay in starting again. Several volunteer and militia regiments had arrived from the north; the station and all its approaches were jammed up with men, and trains were being despatched away as fast as they could be made up. All this time no news had reached us since the first announcement; but the excitement then aroused had now passed away under the influence of fatigue and want of sleep, and most of us dozed off as soon as we got under way. I did, at any rate, and was awoke by the train stopping at Leatherhead. There was an up-train returning to town, and some persons in it were bringing up news from the coast. We could not, from our part of the train, hear what they said, but the rumour was passed up from one carriage to another. The enemy had landed in force at Worthing. Their position had been attacked by the troops from the camp near Brighton, and the action would be renewed in the morning. The volunteers had behaved very well. This was all the information we could get. So, then, the invasion had come at last. It was clear, at any rate, from what was said, that the enemy had not been driven back yet, and we should be in time most likely to take a share in the defence. It was sunrise when the train crawled into Dorking, for there had been numerous stoppages on the way; and here it was pulled up for a long time, and we were told to get out and stretch ourselves--an order gladly responded to, for we had been very closely packed all night. Most of us, too, took the opportunity to make an early breakfast off the food we had brought from Shoreditch. I had the remains of Mrs Travers's fowl and some bread wrapped up in my waterproof, which I shared with one or two less provident comrades. We could see from our halting-place that the line was blocked with trains beyond and behind. It must have been about eight o'clock when we got orders to take our seats again, and the train began to move slowly on towards Horsham. Horsham Junction was the point to be occupied--so the rumour went; but about ten o'clock, when halting at a small station a few miles short of it, the order came to leave the train, and our brigade formed in column on the highroad. Beyond us was some field-artillery; and further on, so we were told by a staff-officer, another brigade, which was to make up a division with ours. After more delays the line began to move, but not forwards; our route was towards the north-west, and a sort of suspicion of the state of affairs flashed across my mind. Horsham was already occupied by the enemy's advanced-guard, and we were to fall back on Leith Common, and take up a position threatening his flank, should he advance either to Guildford or Dorking. This was soon confirmed by what the colonel was told by the brigadier and passed down the ranks; and just now, for the first time, the boom of artillery came up on the light south breeze. In about an hour the firing ceased. What did it mean? We could not tell. Meanwhile our march continued. The day was very close and sultry, and the clouds of dust stirred up by our feet almost suffocated us. I had saved a soda-water-bottleful of yesterday's claret; but this went only a short way, for there were many mouths to share it with, and the thirst soon became as bad as ever. Several of the regiment fell out from faintness, and we made frequent halts to rest and let the stragglers come up. At last we reached the top of Leith Hill. It is a striking spot, being the highest point in the south of England. The view from it is splendid, and most lovely did the country look this summer day, although the grass was brown from the long drought. It was a great relief to get from the dusty road on to the common, and at the top of the hill there was a refreshing breeze. We could see now, for the first time, the whole of our division. Our own regiment did not muster more than 500, for it contained a large number of

Government office men who had been detained, like Danvers, for duty in town, and others were not much larger; but the militia regiment was very strong, and the whole division, I was told, mustered nearly 5000 rank and file. We could see other troops also in extension of our division, and could count a couple of field-batteries of Royal Artillery, besides some heavy guns, belonging to the volunteers apparently, drawn by carthorses. The cooler air, the sense of numbers, and the evident strength of the position we held, raised our spirits, which, I am not ashamed to say, had all the morning been depressed. It was not that we were not eager to close with the enemy, but that the counter-marching and halting ominously betokened a vacillation of purpose in those who had the guidance of affairs. Here in two days the invaders had got more than twenty miles inland, and nothing effectual had been done to stop them. And the ignorance in which we volunteers, from the colonel downwards, were kept of their movements, filled us with uneasiness. We could not but depict to ourselves the enemy as carrying out all the while firmly his well-considered scheme of attack, and contrasting it with our own uncertainty of purpose. The very silence with which his advance appeared to be conducted filled us with mysterious awe. Meanwhile the day wore on, and we became faint with hunger, for we had eaten nothing since daybreak. No provisions came up, and there were no signs of any commissariat officers. It seems that when we were at the Waterloo station a whole trainful of provisions was drawn up there, and our colonel proposed that one of the trucks should be taken off and attached to our train, so that we might have some food at hand; but the officer in charge, an assistant-controller I think they called him--this control department was a newfangled affair which did us almost as much harm as the enemy in the long-run--said his orders were to keep all the stores together, and that he couldn't issue any without authority from the head of his department. So we had to go without. Those who had tobacco smoked---indeed there is no solace like a pipe under such circumstances. The militia regiment, I heard afterwards, had two days' provisions in their haversacks; it was we volunteers who had no haversacks, and nothing to put in them. All this time, I should tell you, while we were lying on the grass with our arms piled, the General, with the brigadiers and staff, was riding about slowly from point to point of the edge of the common, looking out with his glass towards the south valley. Orderlies and staff- officers were constantly coming, and about three o'clock there arrived up a road that led towards Horsham a small body of lancers and a regiment of yeomanry, who had, it appears, been out in advance, and now drew up a short way in front of us in column facing to the south. Whether they could see anything in their front I could not tell, for we were behind the crest of the hill ourselves, and so could not look into the valley below; but shortly afterwards the assembly sounded. Commanding officers were called out by the General, and received some brief instructions; and the column began to march again towards London, the militia this time coming last in our brigade. A rumour regarding the object of this counter-march soon spread through the ranks. The enemy was not going to attack us here, but was trying to turn the position on both sides, one column pointing to Reigate, the other to Aldershot; and so we must fall back and take up a position at Dorking. The line of the great chalk-range was to be defended. A large force was concentrating at Guildford, another at Reigate, and we should find supports at Dorking. The enemy would be awaited in these positions. Such, so far as we privates could get at the facts, was to be the plan of operations. Down the hill, therefore, we marched. From one or two points we could catch a brief sight of the railway in the valley below running from Dorking to Horsham. Men in red were working upon it here and there. They were the Royal Engineers, some one said, breaking up the line. On we marched. The dust seemed worse than ever. In one village through which we passed--I forget the name now--there was a pump on the green. Here we stopped and had a good drink; and passing by a large farm, the farmer's wife and two or three of her maids stood at the gate and handed us hunches of bread and cheese out of some baskets. I got the share of a bit, but the bottom of the good woman's baskets must soon have been reached. Not a thing else was to be had till we got to Dorking about six o'clock; indeed most of the farm-houses appeared deserted already. On arriving there we were drawn up in the street, and just opposite was a baker's shop. Our fellows asked leave at first by twos and threes to go in and buy some loaves, but soon others began to break off and crowd into the shop, and at last a regular scramble took place. If there had been any order preserved, and a regular distribution arranged, they would no doubt have been steady enough, but hunger makes men selfish; each man felt that his stopping behind would do no good--he would simply lose his share; so it ended by almost the whole regiment joining in the scrimmage, and the shop was cleared out in a couple of minutes; while as for paying, you could not get your hand into your pocket for the crush. The colonel tried in vain to stop the row; some of the officers were as bad as the men. Just then a staff-officer rode by; he could scarcely make way for the crowd, and was pushed against rather rudely, and in a passion he called out to us to behave properly, like soldiers, and not like a parcel of roughs. "Oh, blow it, governor," said Dick Wake, "you aren't agoing to come between a poor cove and his grub." Wake was an articled attorney, and, as we used to say in those days, a cheeky young chap, although a good-natured fellow enough. At this speech, which was followed by some more remarks of the sort from those about him, the staff-officer became angrier still. "Orderly," cried he to the lancer riding behind him, "take that man to the provostmarshal. As for you, sir," he said, turning to our colonel, who sat on his horse silent with astonishment, "if you don't want some of your men shot before their time, you and your precious officers had better keep this rabble in a little better order;" and poor Dick, who looked crestfallen enough, would certainly have been led off at the tail of the sergeant's horse, if the brigadier had not come up and arranged matters, and marched us off to the hill beyond the town. This incident made us both angry and crestfallen. We were annoyed at being so roughly spoken to: at the same time we felt we had deserved it, and were ashamed of the misconduct. Then, too, we had lost confidence in our colonel, after the poor figure he cut in the affair. He was a good fellow, the colonel, and showed himself a brave one next day; but he aimed too much at being popular, and didn't understand a bit how to command.

To resume:--We had scarcely reached the hill above the town, which we were told was to be our bivouac for the night, when the welcome news came that a food-train had arrived at the station; but there were no carts to bring the things up, so a fatigue-party went down and carried back a supply to us in their arms,--loaves, a barrel of rum, packets of tea, and joints of meat--abundance for all; but there was not a kettle or a cooking-pot in the regiment, and we could not eat the meat raw. The colonel and officers were no better off. They had arranged to have a regular mess, with crockery, steward, and all complete, but the establishment never turned up, and what had become of it no one knew. Some of us were sent back into the town to see what we could procure in the way of cooking utensils. We found the street full of artillery, baggage-waggons, and mounted officers, and volunteers shopping like ourselves; and all the houses appeared to be occupied by troops. We succeeded in getting a few kettles and saucepans, and I obtained for myself a leather bag, with a strap to go over the shoulder, which proved very handy afterwards; and thus laden, we trudged back to our camp on the hill, filling the kettles with dirty water from a little stream which runs between the hill and the town, for there was none to be had above. It was nearly a couple of miles each way; and, exhausted as we were with marching and want of rest, we were almost too tired to eat. The cooking was of the roughest, as you may suppose; all we could do was to cut off slices of the meat and boil them in the saucepans, using our fingers for forks. The tea, however, was very refreshing; and, thirsty as we were, we drank it by the gallon. Just before it grew dark, the brigade-major came round, and, with the adjutant, showed our colonel how to set a picket in advance of our line a little way down the face of the hill. It was not necessary to place one, I suppose, because the town in our front was still occupied with troops; but no doubt the practice would be useful. We had also a quarter- guard, and a line of sentries in front and rear of our line, communicating with those of the regiments on our flanks. Firewood was plentiful, for the hill was covered with beautiful wood; but it took some time to collect it, for we had nothing but our pocket-knives to cut down the branches with.

So we lay down to sleep. My company had no duty, and we had the night undisturbed to ourselves; but, tired though I was, the excitement and the novelty of the situation made sleep difficult. And although the night was still and warm, and we were sheltered by the woods, I soon found it chilly with no better covering than my thin dust-coat, the more so as my clothes, saturated with perspiration during the day, had never dried; and before daylight I woke from a short nap, shivering with cold, and was glad to get warm with others by a fire. I then noticed that the opposite hills on the south were dotted with fires; and we thought at first they must belong to the enemy, but we were told that the ground up there was still held by a strong rearguard of regulars, and that there need be no fear of a surprise.

At the first sign of dawn the bugles of the regiments sounded the reveillé, and we were ordered to fall in, and the roll was called. About twenty men were absent, who had fallen out sick the day before; they had been sent up to London by train during the night, I believe. After standing in column for about half an hour, the brigademajor came down with orders to pile arms and stand easy; and perhaps half an hour afterwards we were told to get breakfast as quickly as possible, and to cook a day's food at the same time. This operation was managed pretty much in the same way as the evening before, except that we had our cooking pots and kettles ready. Meantime there was leisure to look around, and from where we stood there was a commanding view of one of the most beautiful scenes in England. Our regiment was drawn up on the extremity of the ridge which runs from Guildford to Dorking. This is indeed merely a part of the great chalk-range which extends from beyond Aldershot east to the Medway; but there is a gap in the ridge just here where the little stream that runs past Dorking turns suddenly to the north, to find its way to the Thames. We stood on the slope of the hill, as it trends down eastward towards this gap, and had passed our bivouac in what appeared to be a gentleman's park. A little way above us, and to our right, was a very fine country-seat to which the part was attached, now occupied by the headquarters of our division. From this house the hill sloped steeply down southward to the valley below, which runs nearly east and west parallel to the ridge, and carries the railway and the road from Guildford to Reigate; and in which valley, immediately in front of the chateau, and perhaps a mile and a half distant from it, was the little town of Dorking, nestled in the trees, and rising up the foot of the slopes on the other side of the valley which stretched away to Leith Common, the scene of yesterday's march. Thus the main part of the town of Dorking was on our right front, but the suburbs stretched away eastward nearly to our proper front, culminating in a small railway station, from which the grassy slopes of the park rose up dotted with shrubs and trees to where we were standing. Round this railway station was a cluster of villas and one or two mills, of whose gardens we thus had a bird's-eye view, their little ornamental ponds glistening like looking-glasses in the morning sun. Immediately on our left the park sloped steeply down to the gap before mentioned, through which ran the little stream, as well as the railway from Epsom to Brighton, nearly due north and south, meeting the Guildford and Reigate line at right angles. Close to the point of intersection and the little station already mentioned, was the station of the former line where we had stopped the day before. Beyond the gap on the east (our left), and in continuation of our ridge, rose the chalk-hill again. The shoulder of this ridge overlooking the gap is called Box Hill, from the shrubbery of boxwood with which it was covered. Its sides were very steep, and the top of the ridge was covered with troops. The natural strength of our position was manifested at a glance; a high grassy ridge steep to the south, with a stream in front, and but little cover up the sides. It seemed made for a battle-field. The weak point was the gap; the ground at the junction of the railways and the roads immediately at the entrance of the gap formed a little valley, dotted, as I have said, with buildings and gardens. This, in one sense, was the key of the position; for although it would not be tenable while we held the ridge commanding it, the enemy by carrying this point and advancing through the gap would cut our line in two. But you must not suppose I scanned the ground thus critically at the time. Anybody, indeed, might have been struck with the natural advantages of our position; but what, as I remember, most impressed me, was the peaceful beauty of the scene--the little town with the outline of the houses obscured by a blue mist, the massive crispness of the foliage, the outlines of the great trees, lighted up by the sun, and relieved by deep-blue shade. So thick was the timber here, rising up the southern slopes of the valley, that it looked almost as if it might have been a primeval forest. The quiet of the scene was the more impressive because contrasted in the mind with the scenes we expected to follow; and I can remember, as if it were yesterday, the sensation of bitter regret that it should now be too late to avert this coming desecration of our country, which might so easily have been prevented. A little firmness, a little prevision on the part of our rulers, even a little common- sense, and this great calamity would have been rendered utterly impossible. Too late, alas! We were like the foolish virgins in the parable.

  But you must not suppose the scene immediately around was gloomy: the camp was brisk and bustling enough. We had got over the stress of weariness; our stomachs were full; we felt a natural enthusiasm at the prospect of having so soon to take a part as the real defenders of the country, and we were inspirited at the sight of the large force that was now assembled. Along the slopes which trended off to the rear of our ridge, troops came marching up--volunteers, militia, cavalry, and guns; these, I heard, had come down from the north as far as Leatherhead the night before, and had marched over at daybreak. Long trains, too, began to arrive by the rail through the gap, one after the other, containing militia and volunteers, who moved up to the ridge to the right and left, and took up their position, massed for the most part on the slopes which ran up from, and in rear of, where we stood. We now formed part of an army corps, we were told, consisting of three divisions, but what regiments composed the other two divisions I never heard. All this movement we could distinctly see from our position, for we had hurried over our breakfast, expecting every minute that the battle would begin, and now stood or sat about on the ground near our piled arms. Early in the morning, too, we saw a very long train come along the valley from the direction of Guildford, full of redcoats. It halted at the little station at our feet, and the troops alighted. We could soon make out their bear-skins. They were the Guards, coming to reinforce this part of the line. Leaving a detachment of skirmishers to hold the line of the railway embankment, the main body marched up with a springy step and with the band playing, and drew up across the gap on our left, in prolongation of our line. There appeared to be three battalions of them, for they formed up in that number of columns at short intervals.

Shortly after this I was sent over to Box Hill with a message from our colonel to the colonel of a volunteer regiment stationed there, to know whether an ambulance-cart was obtainable, as it was reported this regiment was well supplied with carriage, whereas we were without any: my mission, however, was futile. Crossing the valley, I found a scene of great confusion at the railway station. Trains were still coming in with stores, ammunition, guns, and appliances of all sorts, which were being unloaded as fast as possible; but there were scarcely any means of getting the things off. There were plenty of waggons of all sorts, but hardly any horses to draw them, and the whole place was blocked up; while, to add to the confusion, a regular exodus had taken place of the people from the town, who had been warned that it was likely to be the scene of fighting. Ladies and women of all sorts and ages, and children, some with bundles, some empty-handed, were seeking places in the train, but there appeared no one on the spot authorised to grant them, and these poor creatures were pushing their way up and down, vainly asking for information and permission to get away. In the crowd I observed our surgeon, who likewise was in search of an ambulance of some sort: his whole professional apparatus, he said, consisted of a case of instruments. Also in the crowd I stumbled upon Wood, Travers's old coachman. He had been sent down by his mistress to Guildford, because it was supposed our regiment had gone there, riding the horse, and laden with a supply of things--food, blankets, and, of course, a letter. He had also brought my knapsack; but at Guildford the horse was pressed for artillery work, and a receipt for it given him in exchange, so he had been obliged to leave all the heavy packages there, including my knapsack; but the faithful old man had brought on as many things as he could carry, and hearing that we should be found in this part, had walked over thus laden from Guildford. He said that place was crowded with troops, and that the heights were lined with them the whole way between the two towns; also, that some trains with wounded had passed up from the coast in the night, through Guildford. I led him off to where our regiment was, relieving the old man from part of the load he was staggering under. The food sent was not now so much needed, but the plates, knives, and drinking-vessels, promised to be handy--and Travers, you may be sure, was delighted to get his letter; while a couple of newspapers the old man had brought were eagerly competed for by all, even at this critical moment, for we had heard no authentic news since we left London on Sunday. And even at this distance of time, although I only glanced down the paper, I can remember almost the very words I read there. They were both copies of the same paper: the first, published on Sunday evening, when the news had arrived of the successful landing at three points, was written in a tone of despair. The country must confess that it had been taken by surprise. The conqueror would be satisfied with the humiliation inflicted by a peace dictated on our own shores; it was the clear duty of the Government to accept the best terms obtainable, and to avoid further bloodshed and disaster, and avert the fall of our tottering mercantile credit. The next morning's issue was in quite a different tone. Apparently the enemy had received a check, for we were here exhorted to resistance. An impregnable position was to be taken up along the Downs, a force was concentrating there far outnumbering the rash invaders, who, with an invincible line before them, and the sea behind, had no choice between destruction or surrender. Let there be no pusillanimous talk of negotation, the fight must be fought out; and there could be but one issue. England, expectant but calm, awaited with confidence the result of the attack on its unconquerable volunteers. The writing appeared to me eloquent, but rather inconsistent. The same paper said the Government had sent off 500 workmen from Woolwich, to open a branch arsenal at Birmingham.

All this time we had nothing to do, except to change our position, which we did every few minutes, now moving up the hill farther to our right, now taking ground lower down to our left, as one order after another was brought down the line; but the staff-officers were galloping about perpetually with orders, while the rumble of the artillery as they moved about from one part of the field to another went on almost incessantly. At last the whole line stood to arms, the bands struck up, and the general commanding our army corps came riding down with his staff. We had seen him several times before, as we had been moving frequently about the position during the morning; but he now made a sort of formal inspection. He was a tall thin man, with long light hair, very well mounted, and as he sat his horse with an erect seat, and came prancing down the line, at a little distance he looked as if he might be five-and-twenty; but I believe he had served more than fifty years, and had been made a peer for services performed when quite an old man. I remember that he had more decorations than there was room for on the breast of his coat, and wore them suspended like a necklace round his neck. Like all the other generals, he was dressed in blue, with a cocked-hat and feathers--a bad plan, I thought, for it made them very conspicuous. The general halted before our battalion, and after looking at us a while, made a short address: We had a post of honour next her Majesty's Guards, and would show ourselves worthy of it, and of the name of Englishmen. It did not need, he said, to be a general to see the strength of our position; it was impregnable, if properly held. Let us wait till the enemy was well pounded, and then the word would be given to go at him. Above everything, we must be steady. He then shook hands with our colonel, we gave him a cheer, and he rode on to where the Guards were drawn up.

Now then, we thought, the battle will begin. But still there were no signs of the enemy; and the air, though hot and sultry, began to be very hazy, so that you could scarcely see the town below, and the hills opposite were merely a confused blur, in which no features could be distinctly made out. After a while, the tension of feeling which followed the general's address relaxed, and we began to feel less as if everything depended on keeping our rifles firmly grasped: we were told to pile arms again, and got leave to go down by tens and twenties to the stream below to drink. This stream, and all the hedges and banks on our side of it, were held by our skirmishers, but the town had been abandoned. The position appeared an excellent one, except that the enemy, when they came, would have almost better cover than our men. While I was down at the brook, a column emerged from the town, making for our position. We thought for a moment it was the enemy, and you could not make out the colour of the uniforms for the dust; but it turned out to be our rearguard, falling back from the opposite hills which they had occupied the previous night. One battalion, of rifles, halted for a few minutes at the stream to let the men drink, and I had a minute's talk with a couple of the officers. They had formed part of the force which had attacked the enemy on their first landing. They had it all their own way, they said, at first, and could have beaten the enemy back easily if they had been properly supported; but the whole thing was mismanaged. The volunteers came on very pluckily, they said, but they got into confusion, and so did the militia, and the attack failed with serious loss. It was the wounded of this force which had passed through Guildford in the night. The officers asked us eagerly about the arrangements for the battle, and when we said that the Guards were the only regular troops in this part of the field, shook their heads ominously.

While we were talking, a third officer came up; he was a dark man with a smooth face and a curious excited manner. "You are volunteers, I suppose," he said, quickly, his eye flashing the while. "Well, now, look here; mind I don't want to hurt your feelings, or to say anything unpleasant, but I'll tell you what; if all you gentlemen were just to go back, and leave us to fight it out alone, it would be a devilish good thing. We could do it a precious deal better without you, I assure you. We don't want your help, I can tell you. We would much rather be left alone, I assure you. Mind I don't want to say anything rude, but that's a fact." Having blurted out this passionately, he strode away before any one could reply, or the other officers could stop him. They apologised for his rudeness, saying that his brother, also in the regiment, had been killed on Sunday, and that this, and the sun, and marching, had affected his head. The officers told us that the enemy's advanced-guard was close behind, but that he had apparently been waiting for reinforcements, and would probably not attack in force until noon. It was, however, nearly three o'clock before the battle began. We had almost worn out the feeling of expectancy. For twelve hours had we been waiting for the coming struggle, till at last it seemed almost as if the invasion were but a bad dream, and the enemy, as yet unseen by us, had no real existence. So far things had not been very different, but for the numbers and for what we had been told, from a Volunteer review on Brighton Downs. I remember that these thoughts were passing through my mind as we lay down in groups on the grass, some smoking, some nibbling at their bread, some even asleep, when the listless state we had fallen into was suddenly disturbed by a gunshot fired from the top of the hill on our right, close by the big house. It was the first time I had ever heard a shotted gun fired, and although it is fifty years ago, the angry whistle of the shot as it left the gun is in my ears now. The sound was soon to become common enough. We all jumped up at the report, and fell in almost without the word being given, grasping our rifles tightly, and the leading files peering forward to look for the approaching enemy. This gun was apparently the signal to begin, for now our batteries opened fire all along the line. What they were firing at I could not see, and I am sure the gunners could not see much themselves. I have told you what a haze had come over the air since the morning, and now the smoke from the guns settled like a pall over the hill, and soon we could see little but the men in our ranks, and the outline of some gunners in the battery drawn up next us on the slope on our right. This firing went on, I should think, for nearly a couple of hours, and still there was no reply. We could see the gunners--it was a troop of horse-artillery--working away like fury, ramming, loading, and running up with cartridges, the officer in command riding slowly up and down just behind his guns, and peering out with his field-glass into the mist. Once or twice they ceased firing to let their smoke clear away, but this did not do much good. For nearly two hours did this go on, and not a shot came in reply. If a battle is like this, said Dick Wake, who was my next-hand file, it's mild work, to say the least. The words were hardly uttered when a rattle of musketry was heard in front; our skirmishers were at it, and very soon the bullets began to sing over our heads, and some struck the ground at our feet. Up to this time we had been in column; we were now deployed into line on the ground assigned to us. From the valley or gap on our left there ran a lane right up the hill almost due west, or along our front. This lane had a thick bank about four feet high, and the greater part of the regiment was drawn up behind it; but a little way up the hill the lane trended back out of the line, so the right of the regiment here left it and occupied the open grass-land of the park. The bank had been cut away at this point to admit of our going in and out. We had been told in the morning to cut down the bushes on the top of the bank, so as to make the space clear for firing over, but we had no tools to work with; however, a party of sappers had come down and finished the job. My company was on the right, and was thus beyond the shelter of the friendly bank. On our right again was the battery of artillery already mentioned; then came a battalion of the line, then more guns, then a great mass of militia and volunteers and a few line up to the big house. At least this was the order before the firing began; after that I do not know what changes took place.

  And now the enemy's artillery began to open; where their guns were posted we could not see, but we began to hear the rush of the shells over our heads, and the bang as they burst just beyond. And now what took place I can really hardly tell you. Sometimes when I try and recall the scene, it seems as if it lasted for only a few minutes; yet I know, as we lay on the ground, I thought the hours would never pass away, as we watched the gunners still plying their task, firing at the invisible enemy, never stopping for a moment except when now and again a dull blow would be heard and a man fall down, then three or four of his comrades would carry him to the rear. The captain no longer rode up and down; what had become of him I do not know. Two of the guns ceased firing for a time; they had got injured in some way, and up rode an artillery general. I think I see him now, a very handsome man, with straight features and a dark mustache, his breast covered with medals. He appeared in a great rage at the guns stopping fire.

"Who commands this battery?" he cried.

"I do, Sir Henry," said an officer, riding forward, whom I had not noticed before.

The group is before me at this moment, standing out clear against the background of smoke, Sir Henry erect on his splendid charger, his flashing eye, his left arm pointing towards the enemy to enforce something he was going to say, the young officer reining in his horse just beside him, and saluting with his right hand raised to his busby. This for a moment, then a dull thud, and both horses and riders are prostrate on the ground. A round-shot had struck all four at the saddle-line. Some of the gunners ran up to help, but neither officer could have lived many minutes. This was not the first I saw killed. Some time before this, almost immediately on the enemy's artillery opening, as we were lying, I heard something like the sound of metal striking metal, and at the same moment Dick Wake, who was next me in the ranks, leaning on his elbows, sank forward on his face. I looked round and saw what had happened; a shot fired at a high elevation, passing over his head, had struck the ground behind, nearly cutting his thigh off. It must have been the ball striking his sheathed bayonet which made the noise. Three of us carried the poor fellow to the rear, with difficulty for the shattered limb; but he was nearly dead from loss of blood when we got to the doctor, who was waiting in a sheltered hollow about two hundered yards in rear, with two other doctors in plain clothes, who had come up to help. We desposited our burden and returned to the front. Poor Wake was sensible when we left him, but apparently too shaken by the shock to be able to speak. Wood was there helping the doctors. I paid more visits to the rear of the same sort before the evening was over.

All this time we were lying there to be fired at without returning a shot, for our skirmishers were holding the line of walls and enclosures below. However, the bank protected most of us, and the brigadier now ordered our right company, which was in the open, to get behind it also; and there we lay about four deep, the shells crashing and bullets whistling over our heads, but hardly a man being touched. Our colonel was, indeed, the only one exposed, for he rode up and down the lane at a footpace as steady as a rock; but he made the major and adjutant dismount, and take shelter behind the hedge, holding their horses. We were all pleased to see him so cool, and it restored our confidence in him, which had been shaken yesterday.

The time seemed interminable while we lay thus inactive. We could not, of course, help peering over the bank to try and see what was going on; but there was nothing to be made out, for now a tremendous thunderstorm, which had been gathering all day, burst on us, and a torrent of almost blinding rain came down, which obscured the view even more than the smoke, while the crashing of the thunder and the glare of the lightning could be heard and seen even above the roar and flashing of the artillery. Once the mist lifted, and I saw for a minute an attack on Box Hill, on the other side of the gap on our left. It was like the scene at a theatre--a curtain of smoke all round and a clear gap in the centre, with a sudden gleam of evening sunshine lighting it up. The steep smooth slope of the hill was crowded with the dark-blue figures of the enemy, whom I now saw for the first time--an irregular outline in front, but very solid in rear: the whole body was moving forward by fits and starts, the men firing and advancing, the officers waving their swords, the columns closing up and gradually making way. Our people were almost concealed by the bushes at the top, whence the smoke and their fire could be seen proceeding: presently from these bushes on the crest came out a red line, and dashed down the brow of the hill, a flame of fire belching out from the front as it advanced. The enemy hesitated, gave way, and finally ran back in a confused crowd down the hill. Then the mist covered the scene, but the glimpse of this splendid charge was inspiring, and I hoped we should show the same coolness when it came to our turn. It was about this time that our skirmishers fell back, a good many wounded, some limping along by themselves, others helped. The main body retired in very fair order, halting to turn round and fire; we could see a mounted officer of the Guards riding up and down encouraging them to be steady. Now came our turn. For a few minutes we saw nothing, but a rattle of bullets came through the rain and mist, mostly, however, passing over the bank. We began to fire in reply, stepping up against the bank to fire, and stooping down to load; but our brigade-major rode up with an order, and the word was passed through the men to reserve our fire. In a very few moments it must have been that, when ordered to stand up, we could see the helmet- spikes and then the figures of the skirmishers as they came on: a lot of them there appeared to be, five or six deep I should say, but in loose order, each man stopping to aim and fire, and then coming forward a little. Just then the brigadier clattered on horseback up the lane. "Now, then, gentlemen, give it them hot!" he cried; and fire away we did, as fast as ever we were able. A perfect storm of bullets seemed to be flying about us too, and I thought each moment must be the last; escape seemed impossible, but I saw no one fall, for I was too busy, and so were we all, to look to the right or left, but loaded and fired as fast as we could. How long this went on I know not--it could not have been long; neither side could have lasted many minutes under such a fire, but it ended by the enemy gradually falling back, and as soon as we saw this we raised a tremendous shout, and some of us jumped up on the bank to give them our parting shots. Suddenly the order was passed down the line to cease firing, and we soon discovered the cause; a battalion of the Guards was charging obliquely across from our left across our front. It was, I expect, their flank attack as much as our fire which had turned back the enemy; and it was a splendid sight to see their steady line as they advanced slowly across the smooth lawn below us, firing as they went, but as steady as if on parade. We felt a great elation at this moment; it seemed as if the battle was won. Just then somebody called out to look to the wounded, and for the first time I turned to glance down the rank along the lane. Then I saw that we had not beaten back the attack without loss. Immediately before me lay Bob Lawford of my office, dead on his back from a bullet through his forehead, his hand still grasping his rifle. At every step was some friend or acquaintance killed or wounded, and a few paces down the lane I found Travers, sitting with his back against the bank. A ball had gone through his lungs, and blood was coming from his mouth. I was lifting him up, but the cry of agony he gave stopped me. I then saw that this was not his only wound; his thigh was smashed by a bullet (which must have hit him when standing on the bank), and the blood streaming down mixed in a muddy puddle with the rain-water under him. Still he could not be left here, so, lifting him up as well as I could, I carried him through the gate which led out of the lane at the back to where our camp hospital was in the rear. The movement must have caused him awful agony, for I could not support the broken thigh, and he could not restrain his groans, brave fellow though he was; but how I carried him at all I cannot make out, for he was a much bigger man than myself; but I had not gone far, one of a stream of our fellows, all on the same errand, when a bandsman and Wood met me, bringing a hurdle as a stretcher, and on this we placed him. Wood had just time to tell me that he had got a cart down in the hollow, and would endeavour to take off his master at once to Kingston, when a staff-officer rode up to call us to the ranks. "You really must not straggle in this way, gentlemen," he said; "pray keep your ranks." "But we can't leave our wounded to be trodden down and die," cried one of our fellows. "Beat off the enemy first, sir," he replied. "Gentlemen, do, pray, join your regiments, or we shall be a regular mob." And no doubt he did not speak too soon; for besides our fellows straggling to the rear, lots of volunteers from the regiments in reserve were running forward to help, till the whole ground was dotted with groups of men. I hastened back to my post, but I had just time to notice that all the ground in our rear was occupied by a thick mass of troops, much more numerous than in the morning, and a column was moving down to the left of our line, to the ground before held by the Guards. All this time, although the musketry had slackened, the artillery-fire seemed heavier than ever; the shells screamed overhead or burst around; and I confess to feeling quite a relief at getting back to the friendly shelter of the lane. Looking over the bank, I noticed for the first time the frightful execution our fire had created. The space in front was thickly strewed with dead and badly wounded, and beyond the bodies of the fallen enemy could just be seen--for it was now getting dusk--the bear-skins and red coats of our own gallant Guards scattered over the slope, and marking the line of their victorious advance. But hardly a minute could have passed in thus looking over the field, when our brigade-major came moving up the lane on foot (I suppose his horse had been shot), crying, "Stand to your arms, volunteers! they're coming on again;" and we found ourselves a second time engaged in a hot musketry-fire. How long it went on I cannot now remember, but we could distinguish clearly the thick line of skirmishers, about sixty paces off, and mounted officers among them; and we seemed to be keeping them well in check, for they were quite exposed to our fire, while we were protected nearly up to our shoulders, when--I know not how--I became sensible that something had gone wrong. "We are taken in flank!" called out some one; and looking along the left, sure enough there were dark figures jumping over the bank into the lane and firing up along our line. The volunteers in reserve, who had come down to take the place of the Guards, must have given way at this point; the enemy's skirmishers had got through our line, and turned our left flank. How the next move came about I cannot recollect, or whether it was without orders, but in a short time we found ourselves out of the lane, and drawn up in a straggling line about thirty yards in rear of it--at our end, that is, the other flank had fallen back a good deal more---and the enemy were lining the hedge, and numbers of them passing over and forming up on our side. Beyond our left a confused mass were retreating, firing as they went, followed by the advancing line of the enemy. We stood in this way for a short space, firing at random as fast as we could. Our colonel and major must have been shot, for there was no one to give an order, when somebody on horseback called out from behind--I think it must have been the brigadier--"Now, then, volunteers! give a British, cheer, and go at them--charge!" and, with a shout, we rushed at the enemy. Some of them ran, some stopped to meet us, and for a moment it was a real hand-to-hand fight. I felt a sharp sting in my leg, as I drove my bayonet right through the man in front of me. I confess I shut my eyes, for I just got a glimpse of the poor wretch as he fell back, his eyes starting out of his head, and, savage though we were, the sight was almost too horrible to look at. But the struggle was over in a second, and we had cleared the ground again right up to the rear hedge of the lane. Had we gone on, I believe we might have recovered the lane too, but we were now all out of order; there was no one to say what to do; the enemy began to line the hedge and open fire, and they were streaming past our left; and how it came about I know not, but we found ourselves falling back towards our right rear, scarce any semblance of a line remaining, and the volunteers who had given way on our left mixed up with us, and adding to the confusion. It was now nearly dark. On the slopes which we were retreating to was a large mass of reserves drawn up in columns. Some of the leading files of these, mistaking us for the enemy, began firing at us; our fellows, crying out to them to stop, ran towards their ranks, and in a few moments the whole slope of the hill became a scene of confusion that I cannot attempt to describe, regiments and detachments mixed up in hopeless disorder. Most of us, I believe, turned towards the enemy and fired away our few remaining cartridges; but it was too late to take aim, fortunately for us, or the guns which the enemy had brought up through the gap, and were firing point-blank, would have done more damage. As it was, we could see little more than the bright flashes of their fire. In our confusion we had jammed up a line regiment immediately behind us, which I suppose had just arrived on the field, and its colonel and some staff-officers were in vain trying to make a passage for it, and their shouts to us to march to the rear and clear a road could be heard above the roar of the guns and the confused babel of sound. At last a mounted officer pushed his way through, followed by a company in sections, the men brushing past with firm-set faces, as if on a desperate task; and the battalion, when it got clear, appeared to deploy and advance down the slope. I have also a dim recollection of seeing the Life Guards trot past the front, and push on towards the town--a last desperate attempt to save the day-- before we left the field. Our adjutant, who had got separated from our flank of the regiment in the confusion, now came up, and managed to lead us, or at any rate some of us, up to the crest of the hill in the rear, to re-form, as he said; but there we met a vast crowd of volunteers, miltia, and waggons, all hurrying rearward from the direction of the big house, and we were borne in the stream for a mile at least before it was possible to stop. At last the adjutant led us to an open space a little off the line of fugitives, and there we re- formed the remains of the companies. Telling us to halt, he rode off to try and obtain orders, and find out where the rest of our brigade was. From this point, a spur of high ground running off from the main plateau, we looked down through the dim twilight into the battle-field below. Artillery-fire was still going on. We could see the flashes from the guns on both sides, and now and then a stray shell came screaming up and burst near us, but we were beyond the sound of musketry. This halt first gave us time to think about what had happened. The long day of expectancy had been succeeded by the excitement of battle; and when each minute may be your last, you do not think much about other people, nor when you are facing another man with a rifle have you time to consider whether he or you are the invader, or that you are fighting for your home and hearths. All fighting is pretty much alike, I suspect, as to sentiment, when once it begins. But now we had time for reflection; and although we did not yet quite understand how far the day had gone against us, an uneasy feeling of self-condemnation must have come up in the minds of most of us; while, above all, we now began to realise what the loss of this battle meant to the country. Then, too, we knew not what had become of all our wounded comrades. Reaction, too, set in after the fatigue and excitement. For myself, I had found out for the first time that beside the bayonet-wound in my leg, a bullet had gone through my left arm, just below the shoulder, and outside the bone. I remember feeling something like a blow just when we lost the lane, but the wound passed unnoticed till now, when the bleeding had stopped and the shirt was sticking to the wound.

This half-hour seemed an age, and while we stood on this knoll the endless tramp of men and rumbling of carts along the downs besides us told their own tale. The whole army was falling back. At last we could discern the adjutant riding up to us out of the dark. The army was to retreat and take up a position on Epsom Downs, he said; we should join in the march, and try and find our brigade in the morning; and so we turned into the throng again, and made our way on as best we could. A few scraps of news he gave us as he rode alongside of our leading section; the army had held its position well for a time, but the enemy had at last broken through the line between us and Guildford, as well as in our front, and had poured his men through the point gained, throwing the line into confusion, and the first army corps near Guildford were also falling back to avoid being outflanked. The regular troops were holding the rear; we were to push on as fast as possible to get out of their way, and allow them to make an orderly retreat in the morning. The gallant old lord commanding our corps had been badly wounded early in the day, he heard, and carried off the field. The Guards had suffered dreadfully; the household cavalry had ridden down the cuirassiers, but had got into broken ground and been awfully cut up. Such were the scraps of news passed down our weary column. What had become of our wounded no one knew, and no one liked to ask. So we trudged on. It must have been midnight when we reached Leatherhead. Here we left the open ground and took to the road, and the block became greater. We pushed our way painfully along; several trains passed slowly ahead along the railway by the roadside, containing the wounded, we supposed--such of them, at least, as were lucky enough to be picked up. It was daylight when we got to Epsom. The night had been bright and clear after the storm, with a cool air, which, blowing through my soaking clothes, chilled me to the bone. My wounded leg was stiff and sore, and I was ready to drop with exhaustion and hunger. Nor were my comrades in much better case; we had eaten nothing since breakfast the day before, and the bread we had put by had been washed away by the storm: only a little pulp remained at the bottom of my bag. The tobacco was all too wet to smoke. In this plight we were creeping along, when the adjutant guided us into a field by the roadside to rest awhile, and we lay down exhausted on the sloppy grass. The roll was here taken, and only 180 answered out of nearly 500 present on the morning of the battle. How many of these were killed and wounded no one could tell; but it was certain many must have got separated in the confusion of the evening. While resting here, we saw pass by, in the crowd of vehicles and men, a cart laden with commissariat stores, driven by a man in uniform. "Food!" cried some one, and a dozen volunteers jumped up and surrounded the cart. The driver tried to whip them off; but he was pulled off his seat, and the contents of the cart thrown out in an instant. They were preserved meats in tins, which we tore open with our bayonets. The meat had been cooked before, I think; at any rate we devoured it. Shortly after this a general came by with three or four staff-officers. He stopped and spoke to our adjutant, and then rode into the field. "My lads," said he, "you shall join my division for the present: fall in, and follow the regiment that is now passing." We rose up, fell in by companies, each about twenty strong, and turned once more into the stream moving along the road;--regiments' detachments, single volunteers or militiamen, country people making off, some with bundles, some without, a few in carts, but most on foot; here and there waggons of stores, with men sitting wherever there was room, others crammed with wounded soldiers. Many blocks occurred from horses falling, or carts breaking down and filing up the road. In the town the confusion was even worse, for all the houses seemed full of volunteers and militiamen, wounded or resting, or trying to find food, and the streets were almost choked up. Some officers were in vain trying to restore order, but the task seemed a hopeless one. One or two volunteer regiments which had arrived from the north the previous night, and had been halted here for orders, were drawn up along the roadside steadily enough, and some of the retreating regiments, including ours, may have preserved the semblance of discipline, but for the most part the mass pushing to the rear was a mere mob. The regulars, or what remained of them, were now, I believe, all in the rear, to hold the advancing enemy in check. A few officers among such a crowd could do nothing. To add to the confusion, several houses were being emptied of the wounded brought here the night before, to prevent their falling into the hands of the enemy, some in carts, some being carried to the railway by men. The groans of these poor fellows as they were jostled through the street went to our hearts, selfish though fatigue and suffering had made us. At last, following the guidance of a staff-officer who was standing to show the way, we turned off from the main London road and took that towards Kingston. Here the crush was less, and we managed to move along pretty steadily. The air had been cooled by the storm, and there was no dust. We passed through a village where our new general had seized all the public-houses, and taken possession of the liquor; and each regiment as it came up was halted, and each man got a drink of beer, served out by companies. Whether the owner got paid, I know not, but it was like nectar. It must have been about one o'clock in the afternoon that we came in sight of Kingston. We had been on our legs sixteen hours, and had got over about twelve miles of ground. There is a hill a little south of the Surbiton station, covered then mostly with villas, but open at the western extremity, where there was a clump of trees on the summit. We had diverged from the road towards this, and here the general halted us and disposed the line of the division along his front, facing to the south-west, the right of the line reaching down to the water-works on the Thames, the left extending along the southern slope of the hill, in the direction of the Epsom road by which we had come. We were nearly in the centre, occupying the knoll just in front of the general, who dismounted on the top and tied his horse to a tree. It is not much of a hill, but commands an extensive view over the flat country around; and as we lay wearily on the ground we could see the Thames glistening like a silver field in the bright sunshine, the palace at Hampton Court, the bridge at Kingston, and the old church tower rising above the haze of the town, with the woods of Richmond Park behind it. To most of us the scene could not but call up the associations of happy days of peace--days now ended and peace destroyed through national infatuation. We did not say this to each other, but a deep depression had come upon us, partly due to weakness and fatigue, no doubt, but we saw that another stand was going to be made, and we had no longer any confidence in ourselves. If we could not hold our own when stationary in line, on a good position, but had been broken up into a rabble at the first shock, what chance had we now of manoeuvring against a victorious enemy in this open ground? A feeling of desperation came over us, a determination to struggle on against hope; but anxiety for the future of the country, and our friends, and all dear to us, filled our thoughts now that we had time for reflection. We had had no news of any kind since Wood joined us the day before---we knew not what was doing in London, or what the Government was about, or anything else; and exhausted though we were, we felt an intense craving to know what was happening in other parts of the country.

Our general had expected to find a supply of food and ammunition here, but nothing turned up. Most of us had hardly a cartridge left, so he ordered the regiment next to us, which came from the north and had not been engaged, to give us enough to make up twenty rounds a man, and he sent off a fatigue-party to Kingston to try and get provisions, while a detachment of our fellows was allowed to go foraging among the villas in our rear; and in about an hour they brought back some bread and meat, which gave us a slender meal all round. They said most of the houses were empty, and that many had been stripped of all eatables, and a good deal damaged already.

It must have been between three and four o'clock when the sound of cannonading began to be heard in the front, and we could see the smoke of the guns rising above the woods of Esher and Claremont, and soon afterwards some troops emerged from the fields below us. It was the rear-guard of regular troops. There were some guns also, which were driven up the slope and took up their position round the knoll. There were three batteries, but they only counted eight guns amongst them. Behind them was posted the line; it was a brigade apparently of four regiments, but the whole did not look to be more than eight or nine hundred men. Our regiment and another had been moved a little to the rear to make way for them, and presently we were ordered down to occupy the railway station on our right rear. My leg was now so stiff I could no longer march with the rest, and my left arm was very swollen and sore, and almost useless; but anything seemed better than being left behind, so I limped after the battalion as best I could down to the station. There was a goods shed a little in advance of it down the line, a strong brick building, and here my company was posted. The rest of our men lined the wall of the enclosure. A staff-officer came with us to arrange the distribution; we should be supported by line troops, he said; and in few minutes a train full of them came slowly up from Guildford way. It was the last; the men got out, the train passed on, and a party began to tear up the rails, while the rest were distributed among the houses on each side. A sergeant's party joined us in our shed, and an engineer officer with sappers came to knock holes in the walls for us to fire from; but there were only half-a-dozen of them, so progress was not rapid, and as we had no tools we could not help.

It was while we were watching this job that the adjutant, who was as active as ever, looked in, and told us to muster in the yard. The fatigue-party had come back from Kingston, and a small baker's hand-cart of food was made over to us as our share. It contained loaves, flour, and some joints of meat. The meat and the flour we had not time or means to cook. The loaves we devoured; and there was a tap of water in the yard, so we felt refreshed by the meal. I should have liked to wash my wounds, which were becoming very offensive, but I dared not take off my coat, feeling sure I should not be able to get it on again. It was while we were eating our bread that the rumour first reached us of another disaster, even greater than that we had witnessed ourselves. Whence it came I know not; but a whisper went down the ranks that Woolwich had been captured. We all knew that it was our only arsenal, and understood the significance of the blow. No hope, if this were true, of saving the country. Thinking over this, we went back to the shed.

Although this was only our second day of war, I think we were already old soldiers so far that we had come to be careless about fire, and the shot and shell that now began to open on us made no sensation. We felt, indeed, our need of discipline, and we saw plainly enough the slender chance of success coming out of troops so imperfectly trained as we were; but I think we were all determined to fight on as long as we could. Our gallant adjutant gave his spirit to everybody; and the staff-officer commanding was a very cheery fellow, and went about as if we were certain of victory. Just as the firing began he looked in to say that we were as safe as in a church, that we must be sure and pepper the enemy well, and that more cartridges would soon arrive. There were some steps and benches in the shed, and on these a part of our men were standing, to fire through the upper loop-holes, while the line soldiers and others stood on the ground, guarding the second row. I sat on the floor, for I could not now use my rifle, and besides, there were more men than loop-holes. The artillery fire which had opened now on our position was from a longish range; and occupation for the riflemen had hardly begun when there was a crash in the shed, and I was knocked down by a blow on the head. I was almost stunned for a time, and could not make out at first what had happened. A shot or shell had hit the shed without quite penetrating the wall, but the blow had upset the steps resting against it, and the men standing on them, bringing down a cloud of plaster and brickbats, one of which had struck me. I felt now past being of use. I could not use my rifle, and could barely stand; and after a time I thought I would make for my own house, on the chance of finding some one still there. I got up therefore, and staggered homewards. Musketry fire had now commenced, and our side were blazing away from the windows of the houses, and from behind walls, and from the shelter of some trucks still standing in the station. A couple of field-pieces in the yard were firing, and in the open space in rear of the station a reserve was drawn up. There, too, was the staff-officer on horseback, watching the fight through his field-glass. I remember having still enough sense to feel that the position was a hopeless one. That straggling line of houses and gardens would surely be broken through at some point, and then the line must give way like a rope of sand. It was about a mile to our house, and I was thinking how I could possibly drag myself so far when I suddenly recollected that I was passing Travers's house,--one of the first of a row of villas then leading from the Surbiton station to Kingston. Had he been brought home, I wonder, as his faithful old servant promised, and was his wife still here? I remember to this day the sensation of shame I felt, when I recollected that I had not once given him--my greatest friend---a thought since I carried him off the field the day before. But war and suffering make men selfish. I would go in now at any rate and rest awhile, and see if I could be of use. The little garden before the house was as trim as ever--I used to pass it every day on my way to the train, and knew every shrub in it--and ablaze with flowers, but the hall-door stood ajar. I stepped in and saw little Arthur standing in the hall. He had been dressed as neatly as ever that day, and as he stood there in his pretty blue frock and white trousers and socks showing his chubby little legs, with his golden locks, fair face, and large dark eyes, the picture of childish beauty, in the quiet hall, just as it used to look--the vases of flowers, the hat and coats hanging up, the familiar pictures on the walls-- this vision of peace in the midst of war made me wonder for a moment, faint and giddy as I was, if the pandemonium outside had any real existence, and was not merely a hideous dream. But the roar of the guns making the house shake, and the rushing of the shot, gave a ready answer. The little fellow appeared almost unconscious of the scene around him, and was walking up the stairs holding by the railing, one step at a time, as I had seen him do a hundred times before, but turned round as I came in. My appearance frightened him, and staggering as I did into the hall, my face and clothes covered with blood and dirt, I must have looked an awful object to the child, for he gave a cry and turned to run toward the basement stairs. But he stopped on hearing my voice calling him back to his god-papa, and after a while came timidly up to me. Papa had been to the battle, he said, and was very ill: mamma was with papa: Wood was out: Lucy was in the cellar, and had taken him there, but he wanted to go to mamma. Telling him to stay in the hall for a minute till I called him, I climbed up-stairs and opened the bedroom-door. My poor friend lay there, his body resting on the bed, his head supported on his wife's shoulder as she sat by the bedside. He breathed heavily, but the pallor of his face, the closed eyes, the prostrate arms, the clammy foam she was wiping from his mouth, all spoke of approaching death. The good old servant had done his duty, at least,—he had brought his master home to die in his wife's arms. The poor woman was too intent on her charge to notice the opening of the door, and as the child would be better away, I closed it gently and went down to the hall to take little Arthur to the shelter below, where the maid was hiding. Too late! He lay at the foot of the stairs on his face, his little arms stretched out, his hair dabbled in blood. I had not noticed the crash among the other noises, but a splinter of a shell must have come through the open doorway; it had carried away the back of his head. The poor child's death must have been instantaneous. I tried to lift up the little corpse with my one arm, but even this load was too much for me, and while stooping down I fainted away.

When I came to my senses again it was quite dark, and for some time I could not make out where I was; I lay indeed for some time like one half asleep, feeling no inclination to move. By degrees I became aware that I was on the carpeted floor of a room. All noise of battle had ceased, but there was a sound as of many people close by. At last I sat up and gradually got to my feet. The movement gave me intense pain, for my wounds were now highly inflamed, and my clothes sticking to them made them dreadfully sore. At last I got up and groped my way to the door, and opening it at once saw where I was, for the pain had brought back my senses. I had been lying in Travers's little writing-room at the end of the passage, into which I made my way. There was no gas, and the drawing-room door was closed; but from the open dining-room the glimmer of a candle feebly lighted up the hall, in which half-a-dozen sleeping figures could be discerned, while the room itself was crowded with men. The table was covered with plates, glasses, and bottles; but most of the men were asleep in the chairs or on the floor, a few were smoking cigars, and one or two with their helmets on were still engaged at supper, occasionally grunting out an observation between the mouthfuls.

"Sind wackere Soldaten, diese Englischen Freiwilligen," said a broad-shouldered brute, stuffing a great hunch of beef into his mouth with a silver fork, an implement I should think he must have been using for the first time in his life.

"Ja, ja," replied a comrade, who was lolling back in his chair with a pair of very dirty legs on the table, and one of poor Travers's best cigars in his mouth; "Sie so gat laufen können."

"Ja wohl," responded the first speaker; "aber sind nicht eben so schnell wie die Französischen Mobloten."

"Gewiss," grunted a hulking lout from the floor, leaning on his elbow, and sending out a cloud of smoke from his ugly jaws; "und da sind hier etwas gute Schützen."

"Hast recht, lange Peter," answered number one; "wenn die Schurken so gut exerciren wie schützen könnten, so waren wir heute nicht hier!"

"Recht! recht!" said the second; "das exerciren macht den guten Soldaten."

What more criticisms on the shortcomings of our unfortunate volunteers might have passed I did not stop to hear, being interrupted by a sound on the stairs. Mrs Travers was standing on the landing-place; I limped up the stairs to meet her. Among the many pictures of those fatal days engraven on my memory, I remember none more clearly than the mournful aspect of my poor friend, widowed and childless within a few moments, as she stood there in her white dress, coming forth like a ghost from the chamber of the dead, the candle she held lighting up her face, and contrasting its pallor with the dark hair that fell disordered round it, its beauty radiant even through features worn with fatigue and sorrow. She was calm and even tearless, though the trembling lip told of the effort to restrain the emotion she felt.

"Dear friend," she said, taking my hand, "I was coming to seek you; forgive my selfishness in neglecting you so long; but you will understand"-- glancing at the door above--"how occupied I have been."

"Where," I began, "is--" "My boy?" she answered, anticipating my question. "I have laid him by his father. But now your wounds must be cared for; how pale and faint you look!--rest here a moment,"--and, descending to the dining-room, she returned with some wine, which I gratefully drank, and then, making me sit down on the top step of the stairs, she brought water and linen, and cutting off the sleeve of my coat, bathed and bandaged my wounds.

'Twas I who felt selfish for thus adding to her troubles; but in truth I was too weak to have much will left, and stood in need of the help which she forced me to accept; and the dressing of my wounds afforded indescribable relief. While thus tending me, she explained in broken sentences how matters stood. Every room but her own, and the little parlour into which with Wood's help she had carried me, was full of soldiers. Wood had been taken away to work at repairing the railroad, and Lucy had run off from fright; but the cook had stopped at her post, and had served up supper and opened the cellar for the soldiers' use: she herself did not understand what they said, and they were rough and boorish, but not uncivil. I should now go, she said, when my wounds were dressed, to look after my own home, where I might be wanted; for herself, she wished only to be allowed to remain watching there--glancing at the room where lay the bodies of her husband and child--where she would not be molested. I felt that her advice was good. I could be of no use as protection, and I had an anxious longing to know what had become of my sick mother and sister; besides, some arrangement must be made for the burial. I therefore limped away. There was no need to express thanks on either side, and the grief was too deep to be reached by any outward show of sympathy.

Outside the house there was a good deal of movement and bustle; many carts going along, the waggoners, from Sussex and Surrey, evidently impressed and guarded by soldiers; and although no gas was burning, the road towards Kingston was well lighted by torches held by persons standing at short intervals in line, who had been seized for the duty, some of them the tenants of neighbouring villas. Almost the first of these torch-bearers I came to was an old gentleman whose face I was well acquainted with, from having frequently travelled up and down in the same train with him. He was a senior clerk in a Government office, I believe, and was a mildlooking old man with a prim face and a long neck, which he used to wrap in a white double neckcloth, a thing even in those days seldom seen. Even in that moment of bitterness I could not help being amused by the absurd figure this poor old fellow presented, with his solemn face and long cravat doing penance with a torch in front of his own gate, to light up the path of our conquerors. But a more serious object now presented itself, a corporal's guard passing by, with two English volunteers in charge, their hands tied behind their backs. They cast an imploring glance at me, and I stepped into the road to ask the corporal what was the matter, and even ventured, as he was passing on, to lay my hand on his sleeve.

"Auf dem Wege, Spitzbube!" cried the brute, lifting his rifle as if to knock me down. "Must one prisoners who fire at us let shoot," he went on to add; and shot the poor fellows would have been, I suppose, if I had not interceded with an officer, who happened to be riding by.

"Herr Hauptmann," I cried, as loud as I could, "is this your discipline, to let unarmed prisoners be shot without orders?"

The officer, thus appealed to, reined in his horse, and halted the guard till he heard what I had to say. My knowledge of other languages here stood me in good stead, for the prisoners, northcountry factory hands apparently, were of course utterly unable to make themselves understood, and did not even know in what they had offended. I therefore interpreted their explanation: they had been left behind while skirmishing near Ditton, in a barn, and coming out of their hiding-place in the midst of a party of the enemy, with their rifles in their hands, the latter thought they were going to fire at them from behind. It was a wonder they were not shot down on the spot. The captain heard the tale, and then told the guard to let them go, and they slunk off at once into a by-road. He was a fine soldier-like man, but nothing could exceed the insolence of his manner, which was perhaps all the greater because it seemed not intentional, but to arise from a sense of immeasurable superiority. Between the lame freiwilliger pleading for his comrades, and the captain of the conquering army, there was, in his view, an infinite gulf. Had the two men been dogs, their fate could not have been decided more contemptuously. They were let go simply because they were not worth keeping as prisoners, and perhaps to kill any living thing without cause went against the hauptmann's sense of justice. But why speak of this insult in particular? Had not every man who lived then his tale to tell of humiliation and degradation? For it was the same story everywhere. After the first stand in line, and when once they had got us on the march, the enemy laughed at us. Our handful of regular troops was sacrificed almost to a man in a vain conflict with numbers; our volunteers and militia, with officers who did not know their work, without ammunition or equipment, or staff to superintend, starving in the midst of plenty, we had soon become a helpless mob, fighting desperately here and there, but with whom, as a manoeuvring army, the disciplined invaders did just what they pleased. Happy those whose bones whitened the fields of Surrey; they at least were spared the disgrace we lived to endure. Even you, who have never known what it is to live otherwise than on sufferance, even your cheeks burn when we talk of these days; think, then, what those endured who, like your grandfather, had been citizens of the proudest nation on earth, which had never known disgrace or defeat, and whose boast it used to be that they bore a flag on which the sun never set! We had heard of generosity in war; we found none; the war was made by us, it was said, and we must take the consequences. London and our only arsenal captured, we were at the mercy of our captors, and right heavily did they tread on our necks. Need I tell you the rest?--of the ransom we had to pay, and the taxes raised to cover it, which keep us paupers to this day?--the brutal frankness that announced we must give place to a new naval Power, and be made harmless for revenge?--the victorious troops living at free quarters, the yoke they put on us made the more galling that their requisitions had a semblance of method and legality? Better have been robbed at first hand by the soldiery themselves, than through our own magistrates made the instruments for extortion. How we lived through the degradation we daily and hourly underwent, I hardly even now understand. And what was there left to us to live for? Stripped of our colonies; Canada and the West Indies gone to America; Australia forced to separate; India lost for ever, after the English there had all been destroyed, vainly trying to hold the country when cut off from aid by their countrymen; Gibraltar and Malta ceded to the new naval Power; Ireland independent and in perpetual anarchy and revolution. When I look at my country as it is now--its trade gone, its factories silent, its harbours empty, a prey to pauperism and decay--when I see all this, and think what Great Britain was in my youth, I ask myself whether I have really a heart or any sense of patriotism that I should have witnessed such degradation and still care to live! France was different. There, too, they had to eat the bread of tribulation under the yoke of the conqueror! their fall was hardly more sudden or violent than ours; but war could not take away their rich soil; they had no colonies to lose; their broad lands, which made their wealth, remained to them; and they rose again from the blow. But our people could not be got to see how artificial our prosperity was--that it all rested on foreign trade and financial credit; that the course of trade once turned away from us, even for a time, it might never return; and that our credit once shaken might never be restored. To hear men talk in those days, you would have thought that Providence had ordained that our Government should always borrow at three per cent, and that trade came to us because we lived in a foggy little island set in a boisterous sea. They could not be got to see that the wealth heaped up on every side was not created in the country, but in India and China, and other parts of the world; and that it would be quite possible for the people who made money by buying and selling the natural treasures of the earth, to go and live in other places, and take their profits with them. Nor would men believe that there could ever be an end to our coal and iron, or that they would get to be so much dearer than the coal and iron of America that it would no longer be worth while to work them, and that therefore we ought to insure against the loss of our artificial position as the great centre of trade, by making ourselves secure and strong and respected. We thought we were living in a commercial millennium, which must last for a thousand years at least. After all the bitterest part of our reflection is, that all this misery and decay might have been so easily prevented, and that we brought it about ourselves by our own shortsighted recklessness. There, across the narrow Straits, was the writing on the wall, but we would not choose to read it. The warnings of the few were drowned in the voice of the multitude. Power was then passing away from the class which had been used to rule, and to face political dangers, and which had brought the nation with honour unsullied through former struggles, into the hands of the lower classes, uneducated, untrained to the use of political rights, and swayed by demagogues; and the few who were wise in their generation were denounced as alarmists, or as aristocrats who sought their own aggrandisement by wasting public money on bloated armaments. The rich were idle and luxurious; the poor grudged the cost of defence. Politics had become a mere bidding for Radical votes, and those who should have led the nation stooped rather to pander to the selfishness of the day, and humoured the popular cry which denounced those who would secure the defence of the nation by enforced arming of its manhood, as interfering with the liberties of the people. Truly the nation was ripe for a fall; but when I reflect how a little firmness and self-denial, or political courage and foresight, might have averted the disaster, I feel that the judgment must have really been deserved. A nation too selfish to defend its liberty, could not have been fit to retain it. To you, my grandchildren, who are now going to seek a new home in a more prosperous land, let not this bitter lesson be lost upon you in the country of your adoption. For me, I am too old to begin life again in a strange country; and hard and evil as have been my days, it is not much to await in solitude the time which cannot now be far off, when my old bones will be laid to rest in the soil I have loved so well, and whose happiness and honour I have so long survived.

THE END

THE STORM OF '92:
A GRANDFATHER'S TALE TOLD IN 1932
BY W.H.C. LAWRENCE
(CANADA, 1889)

"Gentlemen of the four United Provinces — I transfer to your charge and keeping all those parts of North America which remained faithful to the King, my grandfather, after the secession of our other American possessions. I transfer to your charge and keeping a vast territory which the kings, my predecessors, have clung to with a determined resolution for three centuries, for the possession of which we seven times went to war with powerful rivals: which cost us to retain and defend may thousands of lives and many millions of treasure. This territory so eagerly explored, so ardently coveted, I now, in the name of my people and by the advice of my Imperial Parliament, transfer to you and to yours, to have and to hold, to make or to mar, to build up or break down." — *Thomas Darcy McGee.*

THE STORM OF '92.

I am an old man now — beyond my three-score and ten, — and soon to pass away, as most of those who were actors with me in the stirring events of my times have already passed; a few lingering upon the journey, but all soon to reach the inevitable goal at last. Here in the quiet evening of my days, in this great City of Toronto where I was born, and surrounded by my children and their children, I have thought it my duty, while memory and strength remain to me, to write my story of the events which made Canada what she is to-day.

I say duty. Perhaps a garrulous old man is fond of thinking that a duty which rather pleases his vanity and magnifies a little that personal importance which he cannot but feel is no longer conceded him by the busy world in which he is fast being forgotten. He lives in the past. Thrust aside in the hurry and bustle — his feeble steps too slow for the stalwart throng who jostle by him, he learns to love the quiet of the chimney corner, where he may dream undisturbed his day dreams of men and scenes long past. Here, too, among the little heads ranged around his armchair, he finds his indulgent listeners who never tire of his oft-told tales. How often is he asked to tell the story of the old sword rusting on the wall; of those strange grass-grown mounds and pits which still seam the quiet 'fields, and which the little feet meet in their summer-day rambles after butterfly and flower. Forty years have passed since these long lines of earthworks witnessed the struggle of contending armies. Forty years have crumbled them with the frost and washed them with the rain, smoothing down the old redoubt and filling up the rifle-pit. Some day they will be all levelled, and the plow-share will again pass smoothly over them. But the memories they recall can never be effaced while the life of this nation lasts.

These are the footprints of the war fought to preserve our nationality. Who but the old, who took part in the struggle, can reap and garner the lessons it taught; who but the young can profit by these lessons — the new generation whose life is before them, into whose hands, for good or ill, their country's fortunes must be committed. Upon this young generation will rest the burden of maintaining the honour and welfare of Canada; may strength be given them to fulfil this trust as honest, faithful, loyal men.

If, in this year of grace and peace, 1932, I start out to tell how we became a nation, I ought to begin at the Confederation formed sixty years ago, for this was the first step which we took towards national unity. Perhaps there were some who even then recognized and hailed it as such; yet Confederation was accepted by roost as at least a refuge from the political evils of those times. How great an advance it was, it is almost impossible for one not acquainted with the old Canadas of those days to conceive; nor is it easy to understand how, in the face of the race jealousies and religious and party quarrels which then existed among the Provinces, it was accomplished. Can our country ever be sufficiently grateful to those patient and far seeing statesmen whose labours accomplished it? Upon most questions opposed with all that bitterness of faction feeling which is engendered by the very pettiness of the affairs of insignificant communities — in the contemplation of this great subject they forgot party bickerings and thought only of their country.

Confederation enlarged the horizon of our people, and with it their political views and aspirations. It led up to the adoption of that wise policy which built up our North-west. Without this splendid country, of whose vast capabilities and subsequent achievements people sixty years ago did not even dream, we could never have become a nation. Once Canada comprised the region north of the Ohio and west of the Mississippi. This was the Canada of Vaudreuil: the Canada of De la Roche was of even greater extent. But when Canada was in the cradle and too weak to protest, her splendid heritage was despoiled. A few arpents of snow were nothing to the careless Louis; vast and uninhabited territories seemed of trifling value to Europeans of later years. Happy was it that the great North-west was then altogether unknown; that her fairy godmother had hidden this treasure for her where none could then find it, until she was grown wise enough herself to discover its value and strong enough to preserve it. Here was space for her to stretch her strong young limbs.

But in those days nobody knew much about the western territories. Travellers told us of their natural beauty and wonderful wealth, but not many of us went to see for ourselves. Our well-to-do classes were fond of spending their summers in Europe, according to the fashion of the times, and did not consider, as we do, an ignorance of the geography of their own country a disgrace. It was only when the great rush of European travel to those "Canadian Alps," the Selkirks, began to be remarked, that they commenced to visit them. How strange the ignorance of the former generation must seem to the present. We knew just as little of the James' Bay region, and believed it was frozen up eleven months in the year! The Kootenay Lakes, Fraser Canyon, Mount Sir Donald — those great summer resorts of this day — were all but unknown then.

Under Confederation we prospered. Our form of government was well planned, and its administration was honest and effective. Our population was of two pure races, British and French, and we had escaped contamination from that stream of pauper immigration, the scum of Europe, which swept, in ever increasing volume, towards shores to the south of us and was in time the cause of so much perplexity and disaster to our American neighbours. Our people were loyal to that just power whose yoke was no heavier than a garland of roses, whose gentle sway we were proud to own.

There was one cloud upon our horizon — American hatred of England. As to the Homeric Greeks the wrath of the son of Pelous was the source of woes unnumbered, so to us was this American hatred of Britain the cause of all the suffering entailed by war. Yet it was not shared by the educated classes through-out the United States; it is not too much to say that it was deplored by them. Had these classes possessed the political influence that rightfully was due their social position and wealth, this unworthy animosity, the outcome of ignorance, prejudice and misunderstanding, would never have been permitted to cost the lives of thousands of innocent men, to make little children fatherless, to widow contented wives. It was the feeling of ignorant and dangerous classes in the Republic, whose ranks had been swollen by the hordes brought in through twenty years of indiscriminate immigration, unfit for self-government, rebellious against all laws, with nothing to lose themselves, plotting always to possess others' property; without respect even for the flag which sheltered them, — in whose minds national honour was an incomprehensible idea. Among such it was the hatred of the parvenu against the man of acknowledged social position, the hatred of the self-conscious stronger, whose claims are not admitted, against the rival he believes weaker. It was a feeling fostered for his own purposes by that shameless thing — the professional politician; a creature as devoid of heart as of conscience; whom may God judge!

For a century before, the Americans had entertained the hope that our country would one day seek admission to the American Union; and in Jefferson's great Constitution provision was made for such expected application. Our continued existence as a colony of Great Britain was a standing negation of their old time political doctrine that no European power should be permitted to gain a foothold upon the continent of North America. But the Monroe doctrine, as devoid of practical wisdom as it was contrary to natural justice, no longer commended itself to the broader views of educated Americans of my day. Any desire which such men entertained to annex Canada to the United States was founded upon a misapprehension.

Somehow most of them could not understand that we were content with our political condition, and desired no change. We were something of a puzzle to them. In truth, we feared the result of democratic government where the reins of power had fallen from the hands of the educated, to be grasped by the ignorant, the worthless and the base. To our eyes, their future was beset with difficulties and perils, and we mistrusted their ability to avoid them. Expressions of hatred towards Britain pained and repelled us. Not a sneer or unkindly reference in the speeches of their public men, or in their press, to a government we knew to be steadfast of purpose, just and honourable in dealing, magnanimous and lofty in ideals of statesmanship, but what wounded us to the quick.

We knew Britain better than they did. A persistently untruthful press had for years, by the free use of contemptuous epithets, sought to make Americans believe that as a power she was selfish, calculating, and grasping. We knew that while possessing the power to tax her colonies, and sometimes provoked by their adoption of tariffs hostile to her interests, she never exacted a far-thing from them, left them free to govern them-selves in their own way, and was always ready to protect them with fleets and armies, to the support of which they contributed nothing. Was all this selfish, — was it, as they said, "mean" and "hoggish?" Was it not rather the dealing of a nation honorable and magnanimous to a degree the world has rarely witnessed? For a century or more there was not one representative from her hundred colonies and dependencies in Britain's parliament; yet was there an act of oppression or of wilful misgovernment on her part in relation to one? Truly, her children could rise up and call her blessed; there is no brighter jewel in her imperishable crown than their loyal affection.

True, the Americans were misled by a little clique of political busy-bodies among us, who sought to make it appear we were anxious for change. It was difficult to silence these pestilent little gnats, although we saw the misunderstanding they were likely to occasion. A curse on them, I say. I attribute to them in large part responsibility for our subsequent troubles. The noise they made was even louder by contrast with the peaceful stillness of our busy and happy country. Our neighbours were led to believe that a majority among us desired political union with them, and when this idea was dispelled, a feeling arose in their breasts akin to that of a disappointed and rejected suitor encouraged to the point of a declaration by a heartless jilt.

But there were classes and interests in the United States which possessed a direct financial interest in our annexation, forcible or otherwise, and it was not long before our material progress was such as to directly challenge their attention and excite their cupidity. We had built, at enormous cost to ourselves, a transcontinental railway, and although at first Americans smiled at the idea of constructing such a line across what they believed to be wastes of almost perpetual snow, its success turned their derision to envy. But a few years after its completion, it began to control the traffic between Europe and Asia. Untrammelled by the fetters which Congress had imposed upon the American Pacific lines, it was found that it could outstrip them in the competition. Such political influence as these roads possessed — and the railway interest was always one of the most powerful in American politics — was directed towards crushing this young rival. But this was only one of many interests. American manufacturers, anxious to secure our markets for themselves, were angered at customs walls which they could not surmount. The Whiskey Trust, the Oil Trust, and a dozen other Trusts, foreseeing the splendid markets promised in the rapid settlement of our territories, were eager to make us parcel of the dominions subject to their rapacious tyranny. All these interests boded trouble. "Canada must be annexed," said their trade newspapers, "peacefully if we can, forcefully if we must." And these organs were paid to stir up bad blood and excite international complications. Working steadily and quietly, and under the cloak of a spurious "patriotism," the power they exercised was very great. They were assisted by disloyal newspapers published in our own country, which, perhaps at a loss to discover any other motive, we believed to be subsidized also.

If every age has its predominant vice, I would unhesitatingly say that the vice of the decade which preceded our war was that of newspaper mendacity. It was, perhaps, not altogether an unnatural growth, — the outcome, to some extent, of the competition of newspapers to furnish information of a more startling, amusing or entertaining nature than that supplied by the commonplace events of everyday life. The entertaining raconteur must of necessity have less regard for truth than other men; and it may be said in behalf of the newspapers that the public taste encouraged it, and that in their view what the public taste demanded and was willing to pay for must needs be furnished. There existed throughout the United States, amongst classes under their system politically influential, a public appetite for all news derogatory of Great Britain, its rulers, or its people; and the United States press for years catered, more or less, to suit this taste. Most of the great city dailies commanded the services of able correspondents in England, whose duty it was to collect and cable news daily, and perhaps supply a weekly letter. All information from these sources was spiced to suit the anti-British palate.

The American Press Association despatches were invariably untrustworthy. The evanescent nature of public interest, which makes the news of yesterday stale to-morrow, rendered the fabrication of desirable items a matter of little risk, for long before European newspapers could correct the blunders of the cable-grams, the public had forgotten the matter. Correspondents were also employed by the American papers in our principal cities. One of them, from the exuberance of his malignant fancy was generally known among us as "the Ottawa Liar." The false news constantly sent to the American press by this miscreant, did incalculable harm; he could be counted on to misrepresent every fact he wrote of. Still, there seemed no way to suppress him. For the libel of an individual, the law provided a remedy; for the libel of a nation, none. I remember that, about this time, an able and patriotic member rose in his place in the House of Commons to draw the attention of honorable members to such facts, with a view of providing for the purchase and control of all telegraph lines throughout Canada by the Government; and he instanced numerous falsehoods with regard to public affairs then being circulated, and pointed out the danger to the whole country in permitting the great engine of the telegraph to remain under private and irresponsible control; but his views were ahead of the times, and were not then acted upon. With reference to newspapers published in Canada, we could not adopt a press censorship, and no other course appeared feasible.

But there were then, as I have said, even journals in Canada that acquired the habit of speaking insultingly of Britain and slightingly of Canada. If the reader should come across any old fyles of these journals at this day — one sometimes sees them pasted as lining for old trunks, for which they were really useful — he will, in the light of the truthful history of later days, see what I mean. There is the same sneering tone about them all; the same purpose to belittle the country, to discredit the government, to provoke the antagonism of sectionalism, to rekindle everywhere the embers of dying strifes and re-awaken provincial jealousies among our people. Is it not surprising that Canadians of that day should buy and read such discreditable sheets? How would they fare with us now? The historian who in the future will treat of Canada under Confederation, must learn the worthless nature of any material found in them; in our day, public confidence in their honesty of purpose or truthfulness of speech was never great.

But as Fishery troubles were at the root of our final misunderstanding with the United States, I ought, perhaps, to say a few words about this question, although every history published in later years has told all there is to say. Great Britain (for Canada in those days had no independent right to conclude treaties) had made several agreements with the United States upon this subject. The first was comprised in a few words, forming the Third Article of the Treaty of 1783. This was superseded by the Treaty of 1818. The Reciprocity Treaty of 1854 was satisfactory to all parties, but our neighbours, piqued at what they construed as the unfriendly attitude of Great Britain during their War of the Rebellion, gave notice that they would terminate it, and did so. Again the matter was brought up, and again settled by the Treaty of Washington in 1871; again also, in 1873, was this treaty abrogated by the United States, so far as its Fishery Clauses were concerned. Its abrogation left the old Treaty of 1818 the only one in force, and nothing remained for us but to fall back upon it. This was through no choice of ours. We recognized as well as they that, drawn up to provide for the circumstances of an earlier day, it was unsuited to our later times; and we prepared and settled with our neighbours a treaty conceding to them, in more generous measure, the fishing rights and facilities they desired. This was acceptable to the Democratic administration in power in 1888, but inasmuch as, by the American Constitution, the Senate alone possessed the power to ratify treaties, and as the Senate possessed a small Republican majority unwilling to concede to their political opponents the credit of negotiating a satisfactory treaty to settle forever this perplexing subject, it was rejected on a strict party vote. After all our trouble, after all the earnest and honorable desire our country had evinced to satisfy our American friends, we found ourselves again thrown back on the old troublesome Treaty of 1818, the terms of which we still sought to modify in their favor by concessions voluntarily granted their fishermen by our Government.

The American fishermen were an enterprising and hardy set of men, and their vessels were largely manned by natives of our Maritime Provinces. But there seemed something connected with the life they led which made them more impatient of control and less disposed to respect constituted authority than men in other walks of life. They were fond of complaining of ill-treatment upon the most frivolous grounds.

Our fisheries were immensely valuable to us; but, to preserve them at all, economy and care were necessary. For half a century our statute books had contained regulations restricting our own people from improper use of them, and it was only careful observance of such regulations that enabled us to keep them. Not unnaturally, the American fisherman did not enter warmly into our plans for conserving our fisheries. He wished to fish them for the purpose of making money, and with no other object in view. We knew that his reckless and wasteful methods of fishing, in season and out of season, with all kinds of purse seines and other destructive appliances, and his persistent raiding of the spawning beds, had destroyed his own fishing grounds. Time was when in the waters about Cape Cod and along the Maine coast were grounds richer than any we ever possessed; and we knew how and why they were ruined. We saw the same fate threatening our Fishing Banks, if we permitted the same methods to be followed. Was it unreasonable that we should exercise a somewhat strict control of what was our own? But our troublesome visitor, whose repeated declarations that the privilege we conceded him of fishing in our waters was worth nothing to him lost something of its force by his continual presence there, was frequently committing infractions of regulations, and sometimes losing his vessel and outfit by seizure. The actual merits of the complaints he so loudly made on these occasions never reached the ears of the American public. Irritated and angry at the loss he had sustained, his story of the matter was one not likely, upon ordinary principles of evidence, to be the most temperate or truthful account possible; yet it was just this account, and no other, which the American press received and published. It was just our angry friend's account, and no other, which was believed by all Americans who read of the seizure.

We managed somehow to avoid trouble with these turbulent fishermen, although several little difficulties had to be tided over. At last one arose destined to have no such fortunate ending. This was the affair of the *James G. Blaine*, which happened in the month of April, 1892. You all know how it came about. The *Blaine* was a fishing schooner hailing from Gloucester, Massachusetts, found by our government cruiser *Acadia* fishing off the coast of Nova Scotia, in breach of Treaty stipulations, and she resisted capture. What followed is soon told. The *Acadia's* boat approached to board, but was fired on, and one man killed. She then boarded, despite the cutlasses of the fishermen. A melee ensued, several shots were fired on both sides, and when the capture was complete it was found that two of the *Blaine's* men were shot. This was the *casus belli*.

Already somewhat heated over recent discussions of the fishery disputes in the Senate, and misled by the untruthful and highly coloured reports of the affair (or "outrage," as it was at once called) which were telegraphed all over the United States, the Americans were disposed to consider the affair of the *Blaine* not as the justifiable capture of a vessel committing a breach of fishery regulations, but rather a wanton and barbarous massacre of harmless fishermen. I forgot to say that the men killed were native born Nova Scotians, but that made no difference. Mass meetings were held in almost every town and village throughout the United States, and violent and inflammatory harangues delivered. Many were for immediately declaring war upon Canada and England, and both political parties, ever counter-bidding for the Irish vote, vied with each other in the sympathy they expressed and the sanguinary threats their leaders gave utterance to. Resolutions calling upon the President to declare war at once, were supported upon the floor of nearly every State legislature. Congress was not then in session, although when it met, the situation was not improved. That men of education, such as many of the political leaders were, would endorse the unjustifiable utterances of the demagogues was not generally credited in England. True it was that the better class of American citizens saw no cause for the unseemly passion into which the nation appeared to be lashing itself, but they constituted but a small number, of little or no influence among the great rabble of democracy. The question was a political one, and was used as those who understood American democracy (which the people of England never did) expected it would be. The then contending political parties were pretty evenly divided, and the possession of the Irish vote was admitted to be essential to the supremacy of either. The chief point, in the estimation of both, was to secure or retain office, and a presidential election was then just about convulsing the country — a most critical time. As regards war with Great Britain, which might, some doubted, in the then state of the country — without a navy, involve consequences of some moment, the people did not think with much seriousness. The masses at large in our democratic communities never do weigh such dangers. Still, if war was the outcome, the politicians in America did not much care; men in plenty could be hired to do the fighting and war meant immense appropriations from the still overflowing treasury to build ships, and forts, and manufacture all kinds of war material; and the prospect of lucrative contracts of various kinds reconciled the legislators with the dangers of bringing on war and with the possible spilling of blood — for it was probable that they and their friends would secure the contracts and other people spill the blood. So they took high ground, and were determined to "stand no more nonsense about the fisheries." Besides, what difference would it make? Each party believed that if it did not fan the flame, the political support it counted on would only be transferred to its opponents, and the outcome, whatever it was to be, would be the same. So even the better and more temperate class of newspapers feared at this crisis to counsel temperate measures, and were almost as inflammatory as the rest. To adopt any other tone would have been, in the excited state of public feeling too dangerous. No paper wished to see its circulation dwindle to nothing, still less to have its offices gutted and its editors treated to tar and feathers. All were cool enough to perceive that an excited democracy was a dangerous element to deal with.

But a pretext had to be found. After the first out-burst of fiery harangue and invective, the true and official reports of the case came in and were telegraphed over the country. But without troubling too much about the accuracy of any statements, or the international law in the matter, a special session of Congress was called for, which, when convened, promptly passed resolutions demanding an explanation of Great Britain, in terms not altogether couched in the language of European diplomacy in such cases.

The result could have been anticipated. The courteous and temperate reply of the Foreign Office indicated that Downing Street was apparently unruffled and firm. Upon the very day the despatch reached this side of the water and was reported in Congress, it was pronounced unsatisfactory immediate action was taken upon it and we in Canada awoke to find ourselves at **WAR**.

How well I remember the day when the news came. I was then living in Toronto, near what is now the corner of 25th Street and Second Avenue,[1] and it was a beautiful morning in early summer when I picked up the newspaper at the breakfast table, and read the short telegram from Washington (one of the last sent over the wires from the United States) announcing that the Declaration of War had received the President's signature. While the exciting events of the few weeks immediately preceding, eagerly watched by us in Canada, had filled us with forebodings of our danger, they had yet scarcely prepared us for the intense anxiety and apprehension which the news excited. For myself, I remember that the few short lines of newspaper print seemed to dance before my eyes; and so many thoughts crowded upon my startled brain that I became almost oblivious to surroundings until I found myself in my old easy-chair in the library looking out upon the fresh-

---

[1] Before the bombardment and fire, the city had no numbered streets or avenues, but in the re-building a more modern plan was adopted.

cut lawn, over which the great overhanging elm was throwing its dancing shadows. Through the opened window there breathed the fresh breath of summer, and upon it was borne the air of some old, half-forgotten waltz which some barrel-organ in the next square was playing. Mechanically I had taken up my pipe and filled it, and the snap of the parlour match startled a trespassing robin which was hopping near the tennis net, and which stood motionless to regard me sideways with a solemn and enquiring eye. But my thoughts were far from him. My little boy Jack, then a toddler of three, stole to my side, but I did not notice his presence, or heed his prattled "Mama says, come to b'etfast, papa," until I was aroused by the gaze of his eyes, looking up close into mine to learn what was wrong. I kissed the child and sent him back with a few words. The thought of what war might bring to my happy home, and many such a home as mine, filled me with most painful apprehensions. For I knew what war meant to us in Canada. Attack upon our peaceful homes was certain, and might be speedy. Could we repel it? How would we fare amid the clash of arms?

With some hasty excuse about an early appointment at the office, and that I would breakfast down town, I pocketed the newspaper and rushed out of the house. As I turned southward into what is now Sixth Avenue, then called Yonge Street, on my way towards the city, signs of unusual disturbance were visible everywhere. Even at that early hour, barely nine o'clock, the street was thronged and the tram-cars crowded to their very steps. Knots of men in uniform were gathered here and there. All were bound in the same direction. As I strode along, I caught up with my old friend Dick Waller, of the Citizen's Bank, who had been squeezed off a car, and was consoling himself with lighting a cigar at the curb-stone. I found I was smoking my pipe, though not before aware of it, for the news had made me forget all business rules.

"Lively news, my boy," said Waller, gravely, as he greeted me. "This is no little Fort Garry picnic, such as you and I had under Sir Garnet."

"A serious matter, indeed. How do you think we'll come out?"

"Hard to say. The war may not last long. Any- way, we have got to obey orders, and sit through the performance. They can't carry the land off."

We chatted on until we reached his bank. "I think," said Waller, with a smile, as he turned to ascend the steps, "I shall ask the cashier this morning for my month's holidays, and try the fishing in Hudson's Bay. You had best come along, and bring the family, too." Poor fellow, I knew he was not the sort to shrink from danger. Before the snow came he was filling a soldier's grave.

Down Yonge Street the crowds increased, and made passage along the thoroughfare difficult. In front of newspaper offices, where bulletins were displayed, the sidewalk was black with people. Everybody not talking seemed absorbed in reading newspapers, some standing in the streets, some sitting at shop-doors. It was amusing to note the change in tone of some of the papers. I have in my scrap-book two extracts from a journal well known at that day, though now no longer published.

I give them here, that they may be contrasted. The first was written March 14, 1892, the latter on the morning in question. The first is as follows: —

> We have consistently endeavoured to point out to our readers the absurdity of supposing for a moment that this little country, sparsely inhabited and overburdened with debt as she is, could talk of a war with the United States. It is best to be frank, and let them know we would not attempt it. When Col. Crockett pointed his gun at the treed 'coon, the sagacious animal, feeling the gravity of the situation, was moved to remark to the Colonel, "Don't shoot, Davy; I guess I'll come down." Belligerent Canadians should ponder this fable.

The other, thus: —

> War has been declared upon our peaceful people, and but one answer comes from united Canada. It rolls from the fog-encircled rocks of Newfoundland to the far off sunny slopes of Vancouver: form, riflemen, form; ready, aye, ready.

Above many buildings the red ensign had been run up, and flapped lazily in the morning breeze. It was impossible to get near the bulletin boards, as the crowd only opened unwillingly to let vehicles pass, though with more alacrity when several mounted officers with fresh scarlet uniforms and clanking scab- bards cantered by, — their impeded progress being greeted by the first burst of cheering I heard. The push of the crowd was towards the drill shed, where it was said there was to be a muster of the city volunteer regiments, whose ranks had been, in the past few days, largely increased by enlistments. Upon
Fifth Street (then called King) the jam soon became almost impassable. Eastward, down towards where the market square then stood, I could catch the clear and cheerful cadence of the bugles of some corps sounding the *Assembly*.

It was now nearly ten o'clock, and I picked my steps westward towards the Club, for I felt somewhat hungry. Here, too, was a crowd, and a perfect babel of talk and excitement. Enrolment lists lay upon the tables for the formation of Veteran corps and Home guards, and the more elderly men (some whose rotund appearance in regulation uniform made me smile to imagine), were solemnly signing them with an expression of features which would, at any other time, have seemed intensely ludicrous. Some jests were thrown about, but generally fell flat, to the dis- comfiture of the jesters. The general feeling was that it was no time for joking. I remember a militia colonel who had participated in our last little rebel- lion formed the centre of one animated group, and gave his views with the dignity which his experience entitled him to assume, and his words were eagerly listened and deferred to. Suddenly the strains of a military band were heard approaching, and out every- body rushed, pell-mell, to see the troops. It was a then crack city regiment, which was proceeding under orders to encamp at the Garrison Common. The men turned out well, stepping gaily to the quick march of "Annie Laurie," which the throbbing drums and bugles sent fairly rolling in a burst of echoing sound through the narrow and crowded street. On they came, their colonel, an old Imperial officer, whose breast bore the Crimean medal, riding ahead. With a steady impulse and in perfect time, they were up and past us before we found that we had lost our voices from cheering.

I could tell you a thousand incidents of that day and that week. In the excitement it seemed as though the ordinary life of weeks was crowded into days or even hours. The city and its suburbs became alive with troops passing through to the camp on the commons. The Government had assumed control of all the railways, and trains came in with military supplies, and troops from every direction. The streets were filled with men in uniform. Business soon became a thing of the past. Most of the warehouses and offices were shut up altogether, as in the disturbed state of affairs no business could be transacted, and many shops had to close for want of men to attend to them. All sorts of rumours were afloat, — that England was despatching one enormous force to Halifax, and another to invade the United States, that the fleet was making ready, and that some iron-clads had actually cleared from Portsmouth under sealed orders. Alarmists hinted that these preparations were too late — that already bodies of the enemy's troops had been seen and reported hovering about the borders, and that an immediate attack in several quarters must be expected. These rumours disturbed our citizens greatly; for what we feared most was an attack upon the city itself. Many had drawn out all deposits in coin before the banks suspended. But what to do with valuables was a question. Some buried them in their gardens. Old Bowser, of the Post Office, who lived next door to me, sent in word that he was having a deep safety cellar constructed behind his house, into which to place the women and children in case of a sudden bombardment, and that he wanted my advice about it; but I never found time to see him. From the back windows I remember I afterwards noticed a great hole in the old man's lawn, with heaps of dirt about it, and saw him once or twice crawling out of it on all fours very red in the face, pulling a mucky shovel after him. Apparently he could find no one but the women to help him in his humane design of protection, and whether his burrow proved of any avail when the city was afterwards attacked I never learned.

For the first three or four days the citizens of Toronto spent most of their days and a great part of their nights in the streets, and the constant extras issued by the city newspapers (which for a time drove a thriving trade) served to keep up the excitement.

Almost every night the cry of "extra" in the shrill tones of the newsboys would startle and awaken the citizens from their slumbers, and the sheets containing latest cablegrams from England were eagerly bought by the thousand. The cables to Newfoundland were fortunately in our hands, and, as the government had assumed entire control of them, we were kept advised of all preparations making in

England. But one day it was found that communication over one of them was cut off, and subsequently learnt that this cable had been picked up at sea and cut. This was the work of some privateer of the enemy. A more serious danger threatened when a similar fate befell the wires to the North-west. The discovery of this interruption of communication was well calculated to alarm us. Were we betrayed by traitors in our midst, or had our western territory been invaded? It took but little time to repair the damage, but the annoyance of broken wires occurred so frequently afterwards as to interfere seriously with communication west of Ontario. This did not tend to lessen our difficulties and anxieties. We attributed the annoyance to disloyal sympathisers in our country. By systematically suspending from a telegraph pole every man not an official found near it, we in time discouraged this form of treason.

In the camps, which were formed in each military district, drilling went on at a great rate, and although no bounties were offered, or impressment system adopted by Parliament, I believe almost every man of suitable age belonged to some corps or other. Rifles we had in plenty and our cartridge factory in
Quebec was worked night and day to supply ammunition. Uniforms were not as essential, and artillery of the best pattern was shipped us from Woolwich with promptness. While reports came constantly that an invasion was threatened at this and that point, still we were not attacked. Our best battalions had long since been sent to the frontier. In the camp on the garrison common, where twelve thousand men were being drilled, the summer days seemed to pass in peace, disturbed only by the firing of men practising at the butts; and as the sunset gun each evening told that another day was over, the silence seemed to typify the doubt and expectancy felt by all.

Meanwhile, what was the enemy doing? From letters and newspapers smuggled across the boundaries at various points, it appeared that our neighbors, though preparing for war, seemed in no hurry to begin hostilities. The better class of their journals now began to lean to the opinion that the action of Congress had been precipitate and was unjustified. The great farming class, to which the war closed the European markets for grain and other produce, complained loudly of an act which sacrificed their interests and threatened them with ruin. They perceived that the impetus sure to be given to East Indian and Egyptian grain and cotton cultivation meant to them the permanent loss of the British markets. To Wall street and the financial interest the heavy fall in all American securities, immediate upon the declaration of war, alone meant a loss involving more than millions. The seaboard cities cried out that they would bear the brunt of the loss, as the United States possessed practically no navy; and the vessel owners gave up to despair. A strong feeling of antagonism to the Irish was provoked, and the non-partisan journals announced that it was time for the American people to make these troublesome foreigners understand that they were no longer to be permitted to dictate the foreign policy of the nation. On the whole it appeared that there was, from one cause or another, something of a recoil from what was seen to be in reality a civil and fratricidal war. It was even proposed in some newspapers that Canada should not be attacked. But such a policy was seen to be impossible, and events changed this generous feeling; in the excitement of what followed it was forgotten.

For Great Britain had not been idle. Twenty-five days had scarcely passed since the declaration of war when the watchers at Fire Island reported iron clads approaching the coast, and two days after, New York, the metropolis of the eastern gate, received a summons to pay a ransom of ten million pounds or suffer bombardment. What followed is well known — how the Hotspur, Northumberland, Monarch, Cymbeline, Ajax and Wivern steamed slowly up, shelled and burnt the city, leaving its modern palaces a heap of smoking ruins, the grave of thousands of helpless people, and then sullenly drew off and proceeded southward. When this news came, no one in Canada but recognized the stern fact that there was no drawing back now — it was war beyond all mistake. On the very night this news reached us, the great troopships Burrampootra, Mirzapoor, and Scindiah, their white hulls swarming with troops, stole like ghosts into the harbour of Halifax, bearing the Rifle Brigade in four battalions and the 25th Regiment, besides some artillery and lancers, in all over five thousand men; and following them in less than a week came the Simoom, Etruria, City of London, Benares, and other ships, convoyed by the Hercules and Invincible, landing fifteen thousand more. The Pacific cable brought us information, also, that East Indian troops were already despatched from Calcutta to land upon our western coast and hold British Columbia. This new cable was just about completed, and the first message sent across it from Melbourne was, "Canada, stand firm; Australia sends twenty thousand men. Shoulder to shoulder," This news was received in camp with the most tumultuous cheering. The idea that we would fight side by side with the historic regiments of the Imperial army made the younger men almost exult that war had come. It was expected that some part of the Imperial force would at once proceed westward to our aid, but their progress, owing to one cause or another, proved slow.

Camp life on the commons was hard, but not unpleasant work. Among our mess was my old friend Waller, who had his company, and Stuart and Elliott, my lieutenants. The latter we called "the boy," from his youthful appearance — he was scarcely twenty — and he was the life of us all with his jovial pranks and kindly manners. His father, Col. Elliott, a retired officer of the Royal Engineers, was a guest with us in camp, and a most entertaining guest he was. An old wound received at Sabraon had partly crippled him, or he would, despite his seventy years, have offered for active service. On the death of his wife, many years before, the old gentleman had left England to end his days in a colony. He settled down, among other old army friends, near Woodstock, and there lived with his household, consisting of an only son and Corporal Brown, his old and attached body servant. Brown had fought under the Colonel, and for twenty-five years had gallantly served the guns against his country's enemies in India and China. And so when the Colonel's son, whose cradle he had rocked, had come to man's estate, and went to the wars, nothing would satisfy the faithful old retainer short of enlisting again, so as to be near the boy and see that he came to no harm.

I remember our last Sunday in camp. We had church parade at eleven, and an impressive address from the bishop. It was a bright September day, and in the afternoon the camp was thronged with visitors from town. My sister came down with a party, and with her was her daughter Mabel. Elliott and Mabel were engaged, and I saw the young man's eyes glisten when, after the party had inspected our tents, which Brown had in apple-pie order, an afternoon ramble was proposed. It was not long till he found her side, and handsome enough the pair looked, he in a fresh uniform, and she in some white muslin stuff with cherry ribbons. We went up through the old woods which then skirted the bank of the Humber. You would not know the spot now, for the last of the oaks has long since gone, and there is only a maze of waterside streets there — populous and dirty — near where the grimy bridges are thrown across the river. It was in that day a lovely sylvan resort. My sister and I strolled slowly along and let the young couple proceed ahead, for we did not care to disturb what might be their last meeting for a long time.

Upon our return home I learned the first news of a move. Our senior major told me of it. The Government had received word that an attack was to be apprehended in the Niagara peninsula, and two brigades would leave camp soon after daybreak to re-inforce those at the point threatened. That evening I set off for a last visit home, and at Elliott's request took him with me that he might say good-bye to Mabel, who was a visitor at my house. I was sorry afterwards that I did, for it had somehow become known in town that we were at last ordered to the front, and she had heard it. The parting between the lovers I forbear to describe. In the light of what afterwards took place, the scene never recurs to me without causing a pang.

Five weeks in camp had made us anxious for a move, and we were now to have it. Our battalions were to parade at six, and we were to see some service at last.

The next morning broke bright and lovely, with scarcely a ripple upon the lake, as the second and tenth battalions, the former in rifle-green and the latter in the scarlet of the line, filed into the steamers Oban, Miramichi and Strathclyde. Part of the force, in all some 3,000 men, were to proceed by rail by way of Hamilton and St. Catharines, and meet us at a spot near Dalhousie, whence we were to proceed forward. Of our march through the city to the wharf, and the uproar of enthusiasm it excited, I will say nothing. I can see now the tremendous sea of faces that lined the streets, and hear the sobs of the women whose husbands were with us.

Evans, one of ours, I met as we were getting aboard. He had been camping on Lake Superior, and prospecting for silver in the bush in Algoma.

"Heard of the rumpus by the merest chance, old man," he said, breathlessly, as he grasped my hand. "We had paddled down the Nipigon for a supply of necessaries, when we found a *World* a month old in a deserted camp, which told all about it."

After a run of some three hours we sighted the lighthouses at Dalhousie, and ran in between the piers. Two long trains filled with redcoats were just pulling in to the little station as we tied up along side of it. Our battalion formed in companies close to the shore, and marched up the bank, halting near where the balance of our force were awaiting us. We learned from some officers of the latter that it was reported to them by farmers upon their arrival, that the enemy had been seen upon the river road north of Queenston moving towards Niagara, where an attack was expected. A troop of cavalry had gone forward to ascertain what truth, if any, there was in these rumours, and the return of this body was shortly expected. Without waiting their return, however, or the reports from the cavalry outposts, which we felt sure would immediately reach us, we formed for the advance. First came a strong troop of our little cavalry force, upon the road, with our Toronto and other regiments, and after them the 19th Battalion; then the two field batteries sullenly trundled along, followed by a line of waggons with camp equipments find stores. The rest of our cavalry brought up the rear. About two hundred yards distant from each flank marched a line of skirmishers. The cavalry, guns and carts, threw up clouds of dust, but as the latter carried our knapsacks and relieved the men of the weight of them, we were not disposed to grumble. Thus we proceeded eastward.

Marching was hot and dusty work, and several halts called at places where a spring, or farmhouse well, was met. There was no wind, and the sun beat down upon our moving cloud of dust. Once or twice our route lay through a peach orchard, and the men could not be altogether restrained from plucking the fruit. I got one or two, I remember, and thought them most refreshing. The whole country population seemed out by the roadside to see us go by. At each farm house, as we proceeded, more rumours met us. Someone said, he heard from a man who had just driven up from Queenston way, that the enemy had entrenched himself near some woods there, and had been attacked by some Lincoln and Wentworth troops. The result was not yet known, and this was all we could learn.

Suddenly a halt was called, and word was passed down that the head of column had sighted a volunteer standing upon a knoll some thousand yards ahead signalling to indicate that the enemy was in sight. While our little cavalry force moved forward to learn how matters stood, we relieved the monotony of the march by extending part of our infantry into line through some stubble fields on our south, leaving a good support to follow if necessary.

Nothing was yet to be seen of the enemy, and Ned Stanley of my company suggested that the heat must have affected the signaller's head, and that probably the only enemy near him was what he secured from the canteen when he filled his water bottle there. But Stanley was cross because the halt had interrupted a narrative he was giving those of us marching near him of his exploits at Cut Knife, and broken the interest of his hearers before he reached the point. Though nothing might be seen, the mere suggestion that the enemy was now actually in sight was, I found, a startling and unpleasant one to a man who had never been under fire. I won't hesitate to confess that my heart was thumping against my cross-belt, and the general stopping of talk led me to think that the men, too, felt the moment of suspense trying. After an advance across the stubble field, a belt of woods was seen to the south, along the edge of which ran a tall snake fence, and behind it, we somehow felt, the enemy was to be met with. The uncertainty rendered us uneasy. Another halt was sounded on the bugle. What this was for we did not know. It was now near three in the afternoon, and the sunlight was as bright and the heat as great as ever, and as for the dust, I think the column on the road were all pretty much of one color, though the flanking skirmishers fared better. We were getting hungry, too, and those who had anything in their haversacks made a lunch themselves and handed out portions to their comrades. I had only a biscuit, a badly-bruised peach and a bottle of pop, of the first and last of which I got half, and warm as the liquid was, I thought it nectar. The peach I gave to Stanley, who declared that a lime-kiln was a running stream compared to his throat. During this repast we were sitting or lying in the stubble fields, most of the men smoking their pipes and watching the woods, which our skirmishers were exploring. A soft haze seemed to overspread them, rounding their foliage into soft green masses, above which the tufted tops of the darker pines stood out more sharply defined.

After some delay, it was determined to make a halt for the night at this spot, and we were informed that we were to bivouac there. This was a surprise to most of us, as we had expected to be pushed on to Niagara that evening, and we could easily have reached it. However, we were glad enough to get off our pouches and take a rest, as most of our men were city bred, and were pretty well fagged out by the heat, dust, excitement and marching of the day. Strong guards and pickets were posted and numerous patrols sent out; fires were built, and the pots soon boiling merrily above the crackling flames. Fatigue parties were told off to visit the wagons, which were found well stored with beef and bread and even canned vegetables. Everything seemed right with our commissariat, anyway, and, pipe in mouth, stretched beneath the trees, the men were disposed to vote our first day of actual campaigning, anyway, as good as a picnic. Soon the stars began to twinkle, and later the moon rose.

It was a lovely night. The bright moonlight, so frequent in the Canadian autumn as the earliest frost approaches, bathed the whole landscape, field and forest, far and wide, in its soft light. Above, the great expanse of the heavens was glittering with countless stars, some brilliant and palpitating, as though momentarily fanned by the passing breath of the night wind as it traversed the depths above us, some undistinguishable in the star drift. Settled in a cosy seat of dry leaves beside an old log, and comfortably wrapped in my cloak, I lighted a cigar and gave myself over to the tranquil beauty of the scene. To one new to campaigning, the surroundings possessed a charm of novelty and adventure, which the uncertainty of the morrow but enhanced. The tall pines stood above, faintly breathing their aromatic odours. Here and there a few camp fires still burned, and disposed about them were the dark forms of the men, some sleeping, some chatting or polishing accoutrements. Their stacked rifles were near at hand, and belts and pouches hung from the bushes. There was no sound, save sometimes the faint barking of dogs in some distant farm house, or nearer, the neigh of a tethered charger. The road wound across the landscape, wan and deserted, with here and there a poplar looking ghostlike under the glamour of the moonlight. On the northern horizon stretched the dark blue line of the lake, and the far-off plashing of its waves on the beach floated to our ears like the breathing of a sea shell. As I fell into reverie, my thoughts wandered widely: of our country and its future — of the fate of this little nation which had drawn the sword against the mighty power of its attacking enemy. What had the coming years in store? Were we, with all our pride in Canada, with all our affection for the land of our fathers and our wish to remain part of its Empire, to become another Poland — conquered, disgraced? Was it already Fate's decree that we should witness our flag torn down, beaten back and banished from this continent, that we should live to listen with burning cheeks to the scarce-concealed sneers of our conquerors? Or would the fire and endurance of a race enured to danger bring us in safety through this trial. How long would be the night of danger — what the harvest of this awful sowing?

A light crackling in the dry leaves aroused me, and a figure stole to my side. It was Waller.

"Dreaming, old boy, of wife and weans, I suppose," he said, as he laid a kindly hand on my shoulder, and took my cigar to light his, "Sweethearts and wives is the soldier's toast, and their dear presence never fails to visit and brighten his dreams. Heigh- ho! you and I are getting old for campaigning!"

"I am glad you came, Waller; I was not asleep, but a good deal perplexed about what will become of things generally. I was thinking this over when you surprised me."

"You know my views of many things, old friend, and have often told me some of them were peculiar, "said Waller, more seriously. "Grieving about the future brings one needless sorrow. The honorable man who fears God and does his duty, may well possess a tranquil mind. I have always believed in a Providence that foresees and directs what will hap- pen, and that everything which does happen is for the best. I know you do, too. I believe this war in the inscrutable providence of the Almighty is for the best, and though it may seem cruel that it will desolate many homes and put many a poor fellow under the sod, it is yet for the best, because it is permitted to be. Is mere life — even human life — of such paramount value, that there is nothing to be desired by men in comparison with it? All nature is prodigal and contemptuous of life. The war will build up Canada. There is no bond between human hearts like that brought about by a common danger and a common grief — and our Provinces, but lately such strangers to one another, now face the one, and will shortly, God help us, share the other. 80 with ourselves, England and the Empire. Australia is sending us twenty thousand men, and it stirs our hearts toward them to know that they feel for us." "But the result — can we defend this territory?" "We are at least following the plainest dictates of duty in trying it. We cannot but try. The conflict is not of our seeking. What else can we do? But I think we will succeed. Thirty years ago, before railways and steamships were what they are now, it might have been more a question. We are fighting for home and nationality; the Americans for nothing in particular, save to satisfy a foolish and unjustifiable grudge against Britain. We command the services of the most superb fleet in the world, of unlimited money, and unlimited men. A republic never fights as a monarchy does; it lacks the sentiment of loyalty to one idea. You will recollect that in the war of the American Rebellion, five million people, without money or resources, contended against the armies of the Republic for four long years, and almost succeeded. The foreign element among the American people amounts to nearly fifty per cent., and how far they are disposed to fight for anything or anybody save their own pockets was instanced in the terrible Draft Riots in New York in 1863. We did not invite this war; we did all that honorable men could do to avoid it. We cherished no ill-will against those of our race who are attacking us, we bear no malice now. The bitter cup is held to our lips, and we must drink it. Come weal or woe, we must do our duty, and leave the rest to God."

"Your words have the ring of truth, Waller, and I hardly how to controvert them, or why I should try. Yet I feel there is something wrong about the whole business. What have we done to have the terrible disaster and loss brought upon us which you appear to contemplate so calmly? Somehow you almost anger me. Have you ever realized the fearful havoc of modern war? Is it the act of Christian nations to murder each other, to burn, sink and destroy, without cause? Is Christianity a mockery?"

"If you ask me," replied Waller, "I say, yes; the applied Christianity of our day is, in regard to politics, a failure and mockery. This war is forced upon us because the politicians in America hope by it to strangle our nation now, because they wish to possess themselves of its property, and remove at once a commercial rival they begin to fear. It exemplifies the parable of those servants who killed their lord's messengers, and last of all his son, that they might divide the inheritance among them. A code of morality which would make a Buddhist or Confucian blush for shame of the human race brings no colour to their sickly Christian cheeks. Years ago watchers in Canada saw their purpose. It was then their mutterings began. They made no secret of what they would attempt. Why was England so blind? With enemies on every hand, with foreign nations gnarring at her heels, and closing their ports to her manufactures, could she not take counsel with her children who alone were her faithful and undoubted allies? Foreign markets were the life of her people, and she saw she was losing them one by one, and yet would not change her policy. Wedded to Free Trade as she was, why could she not decree Free Trade throughout all her vast dominions, and shut out by prohibitive tariffs every foreigner from them? Such a measure would have secured to her manufactures, home and colonial, absolute supremacy in her own markets, and what greater could they demand? Free Trade among sixty millions made the United States enormously wealthy; what would Free Trade among three hundred millions do? What need for her to fight for foreign markets when she possessed these? It would have strengthened her colonies, till, feeling the strong blood of a new commerce pulsing through their veins, their prosperity would have advanced like the tide in the Solway. With these young and lusty nations at her back she could have defied the world."

There was a silence. I felt he had spoken the truth.

We fell to talking of some news just brought in by scouts, which he had picked up in the headquarters tent, until it darkened towards the dawn and the moon sank. After a pause, he went on in a changed tone.

"Billy, some of us may be knocked over in the scrimmage to-morrow, and it troubles me to think of those I may leave. Promise me, if I don't get back, to look after things and put the boy to school. I want you to stand by: it may be the last thing I'll ask you."

A pressure of my hand told him I promised. He placed his face close to mine, and looked fixedly in my eyes. Then, silently rising, he strode away in the darkness and was gone.

The first grey streaks of day had just appeared in the East, and the rising sun had not yet begun to redden the tops of the pines, when the reveille sounded out cheerful and strong and our forces prepared to move. In a half hour we were again upon the road, still due eastward. Shortly we began to notice a few scattered houses, with a spire or two peeping above the trees, and knew we were approaching the old town of Niagara. From this point we crossed into the fields to our right, the country being level as a table and not heavily timbered. Towards the south-east lay Queenston, and there, like a slender needle in the bright air, rose Brock's monument. Further west, and mingling with the fleecy clouds, floated upward the steam of the mighty cataract, — the morning incense of the great Manitou.

During the night the scouts had not been idle, and all uncertainty which had attended our march of yesterday was dispelled. We learnt that a raid had been made upon the little village of Queenston by some fifteen hundred troops, mostly (as was judged from their peculiar uniform and regimental colors and guidons — a golden sunburst above a harp, on a field of green), guerrillas — Irish Invincibles, and a sharp skirmish had taken place between them and some Welland and Lincoln volunteers, who surprised and attacked them there. Almost upon the spot where the great Brock fell was the first blood of the campaign spilt. The report ran that over one hundred and fifty men had been killed on both sides, and nearly twice that number wounded. The attack had been planned from Lewiston, apparently to destroy the monument, which was, however, saved for the time at least. As evening approached, both sides drew off without any decisive result, our volunteers retiring towards Niagara, while the Americans carried off their dead and wounded across the river, which crossing they were permitted to make without molestation. It was unofficially rumored that this was a reverse to us, inasmuch as we neglected to occupy and hold the village. Our failure to do so had resulted in the Americans landing a considerable force in the night and occupying the place themselves. They had also brought over artillery, which they were without in yesterday's skirmish, and effected some entrenchments. Their crossing appeared to threaten an advance through the peninsula northward and westward. We also learned that the invasion had begun in other parts of our country. The wires announced that a considerable body of the enemy had crossed the border from Vermont, near Island Pond, and the railway, by some blunder, not having been destroyed in advance of them, they were already as far as St. Johns, on their way to Montreal. It was no doubt their purpose to capture the city before British reinforcements could come up from Halifax. Their strength was reported as 20,000 men, though the wildest rumors were flying about in Montreal, where a panic existed, and nothing very definite could be a present ascertained.

The Victoria Rifles, Fifth Royal Scots, md 86th Regiment had been despatched to intercept them and delay their approach, while the Second Battalion of the Rifle Brigade was on the way rip from Quebec in steamers, and also by rail. The Voltigeurs de Quebec, 64th Rifles, and other volunteers were retained to defend the city until arrival of the regulars, and hold themselves ready to advance in support, if called for. We learnt also that Essex was invaded and Sandwich and Windsor occupied without much show of defence beyond some desultory skirmishing, the local militia having fallen rapidly back eastward.

This discouraging news was a damper on our spirits, for we felt that it presaged, beyond other possible calamities, an attack upon Toronto. What delayed the Imperial troops?

For us, however, there was nothing to do, at present, but to fulfil the duty which lay nearest at hand, and trust in Providence for the safety of the rest of the country. Our hands were full. The enemy were only a few miles away, and expecting us.

The little town of Niagara seemed already occupied with four or five regiments of militia, of whom we caught fleeting glimpses through the avenues of maples which lined the streets, as we passed along the road which skirted the town to the southward. Soon we came to a street upon which a railway track was laid. Before us was a broad common which looked like a parade ground, crossed by one or two roads lined with young trees. On the nearer edge of it, in front of us, were three or four old unused bar- racks, relics of by-gone war times, and skirting the farther edge a thin belt of timber. Our leading companies halted at the track, and we saw for the first time the general officer who was to command our brigade, distinguishable by his cocked hat and feathers, in the midst of a little group of mounted officers. His appearance inspired confidence, as he sat on his dark clean-limbed hunter, watching our movements, and twirling with his finger the long ends of the white moustache which graced his bronzed face. He was an officer who had fought England's battles in three continents already, and now would fight in the fourth. He looked as jaunty and self- possessed as though passing down Whitehall.

Our men had expected to pile arms and rest after our march, but we had hardly halted when the command was called out, "The brigade will deploy into line from the centre," and out skipped our markers at a double, the men following almost as quickly. What was on foot? Had the enemy advanced north- ward, and were we to fight on this ground? Other regiments were quickly deployed on our right and left alignment. The rattle of chain harness soundly sharply behind us, and, turning, we saw a battery of six guns come leaping along, to take ground to our immediate right, the horses plunging and the guns bounding over obstacles in fine style. Our line now reached from the river, or near it, so far as we could see, along the whole northern edge of the common. How far it extended westward we could not discern, as trees cut off the view. After placing the ranks in review order, the general and staff rode slowly past, and the old soldier stopped and addressed a few words to the men. We would probably soon meet the enemy, and he expected all to do their duty; at any rate the men were to obey officers. There was no nonsense about his informal little speech, and nothing about glory, or "eyes of your country upon you," or anything of the sort. Perhaps it was to him simply a disagreeable piece of business, without any romantic features; and he spoke in this view of it to us who were to help him through. However, the men responded by cheers.

Scarcely had we returned to close order when, at the edge of the woods at the farther side of the plain, appeared an armed force in dark uniforms, marching in column towards us.

"By jove, there comes the enemy, boys"; "The Yankees are up to us at last," and other exclamations broke from the ranks, as all eyes were turned on the advancing force. But the alarm proved groundless. The new comers were some companies of one of our own regiments, the 20th Halton battalion. They drew up close to the edge of the woods. Some mounted officers who galloped across the plain to meet them, quickly returned, with news of the dis- position of the enemy's forces at Queenston.

This battalion had taken part in the skirmish of the preceding evening and had bivouacked in the woods north of the village, to watch the enemy. Being of insufficient strength to successfully engage him after his second crossing in force, they withdrew further awaiting reinforcements, sending back a covered wagon train of their wounded and dead, with a company or two as an escort. Silently, for a few moments, we watched the slow movement of this sad train as it wound its painful way along towards the town. Then "The brigade will advance in columns of battalions from the left "came the order, repeated down the line, and stepping out gaily to the strains of "Garryowen," a favourite marching tune, we pressed forward. I can remember how pretty a sight I thought it, and I could not repress a feeling of enthusiasm, as in steady order the long columns drew out upon the plain, with bands playing. For the first time in eighty years a Canadian army was crossing that old field in the footsteps of those led by the gallant Brock upon his last march, and towards the spot where he found his grave; and, while upon our left the ruined and grass- grown mounds, which marked the site of Fort George, in his day a powerful earthwork, bore testimony to the lapse of time, I do not believe that the sentiments of patriotism which inspired his men, burned less warmly in the breasts of this army of a later day.

Our advance guard of cavalry had now reached the woods, and not a whit too soon did we follow them, as the enemy occupying Fort Niagara across the river, hitherto silent, began to indicate their appreciation of what was going on by plumping shells after us. None did us any harm, as their range was defective, and some splashed into the river and others whistled high over our heads. The incident served to make us uneasy for the prospects of the town should a bombardment take place.

Our head of column now took the road along the brow of the bank of the broad river, following its windings. A thunder shower during the morning had laid the dust, but substituted mud, about as disagreeable for marching. To our right stretched peach orchards, row upon row of small low-branching trees, in almost continuous and interminable succession, which shut out from us all view of the other columns, and must have, taken with the stiff and annoying wire fences, rendered their progress more slow and difficult than ours. Once or twice a halt was called, as we imagined, to preserve the alignment. As the day wore on the heat began to be felt, but our march was not rapid. The good wives at the scattered farm houses we passed were always at their gates to see us go by, and milk, fruit, and pro- visions were handed out with unsparing hands by them, their maidens and men folk. The little homes looked peaceful and prosperous, and we could not help thinking of the injustice of a war which would shortly desolate them.

Soon the graceful column of the monument, till then hidden by intervening foliage, was sighted, and we could discern the outline of the majestic figure which surmounted it, standing with uplifted hand as if beckoning us on towards the hill which we knew to be now held by the enemy. No doubt from its top their glasses were already following our movements, for we were now within less than two miles of it. We strained our ears for the first round of firing, for the ball was shortly to open.

It did so from the westward. First a rifle shot or two, and then a dropping fire, again growing into a more continuous rattle. The scouts and skirmishers were at it, and I noticed an orderly come cantering towards our front across the orchards, taking one or two fences in his way in good style. He reined up sharply, saluted and handed some paper to our colonel, upon which we were forthwith deployed into line across the fields to our right to connect and form line of battle with the 31st and 47th battalions, which were next us. Immediately our cavalry moved off towards the center rear, their horses switching their tails and kicking up the mud skittishly with their heels as they were spurred briskly down a pretty green lane and disappeared, with rattling scabbards, under the trees. The guns followed them to take position to cover our advance, leaving only a couple of batteries in reserve upon the road in case of an advance upon our left wing.

My company formed part of the fighting line, and extended westward at a double, as rapidly as the abominable wire fences we everywhere met would enable us, in the direction towards where the firing proceeded. The foliage of the peach orchards and grape vineyards was so dense we could see but little of what might be going on, half the time losing sight of the line of skirmishers which pushed forward in in our immediate front. But now the sound of artillery again mingled with the rifle fire, and from the base of the monument itself shot out quick puffs of smoke, indicating that a battery of heavy guns had opened fire. The rush and scream of the shells was startling at first, but the fire from the rifle pits lower down at different parts of the height did, I think, more damage later on.

We had now got past the orchards, and before us was a broad stubble field with some woods opposite, perhaps four hundred yards away. At their edge appeared heavy bunches of skirmishers in blue — dark tunics and lighter trousers, who opened fire before we reached the clearing, the balls clipping the leaves above our heads. The bugles sounded a halt. Our skirmishers were already lying down at the edge of the wood and replied briskly. The force opposing us was not a strong one, but on the open to the west of them we now for the first time noticed several blue and gray columns marching up with considerable precision of movement. While I was watching them, I was startled by a swift movement and inarticulate cry at my left hand, and turning quickly, saw poor Playter, a rear rank man of my company, lying on his face quivering all over. Poor fellow, a glance showed me he was past help. A rifle ball had dropped from somewhere and, striking him in the right breast, had passed clean through him. Though I had expected to see such sights, I confess I was for a moment horror-stricken at the suddenness of this. I tried to lift him, but he only fell over limp on his back, staring around with a piteous look in his closing eyes, his lips moving as though he would speak, while blood oozed from between them. In a few seconds he was dead, and I ordered him carried some paces back, where he was laid beneath a great spreading maple, two comrades covering his face with leaves before they returned to their places. He was the first I saw killed. I would he had been the last.

But attention was quickly recalled from this incident. A couple of gatlings were brought into position bearing on the woods, and a few minutes firing disorganized the enemy, whom we now proceeded to dislodge by a rapid advance, firing, across the open. The distance was quickly covered, though three or four staggered and fell before we gained the woods. The enemy's skirmishers made off before we reached them, pursued by our fire. All this time heavy firing appeared to be going on towards our right and centre, but the ground was level, and we could not perceive the effect of it.

It is not my purpose to detail the incidents of the day, for fighting is inhuman work, and a recital of the events on a battlefield is not always pleasant reading. Besides, the excitement of an engagement, and the exertion, smoke and din, prevent any close observation by one taking actual part in it.

I remember our men advancing and firing rapidly through the smoke, which soon piled up in heavy banks before us. It was evident that the line was hotly engaged upon the centre and right, though we could see nothing of how matters fared there. After a time the gunners on the hill seemed to have got our range so exactly that every shell burst over our heads, and men were dropping on all sides, struck and mangled with these screaming missiles. It was a hot corner, and became hotter when, half blinded by a line of flashing fire point blank in our faces, at what seemed half pistol shot distance, we became aware that a strong force of the enemy was moving swiftly down upon us in echelon, apparently to turn the left wing of our position and outflank us near the road. So well planned and quickly executed was this movement, that our raw troops were unable to withstand it. Already the advance ranks of the Americans were engaged hand to hand with our men, and the latter, panic stricken at the suddenness of the attack, fell back rapidly in a moment their formation was completely broken. Seeing their advantage, the enemy pressed on, and an enfilading fire began to pour along our ranks. "We're outflanked," was the cry on every hand, and the disorder began to spread along the line.

"Steady — take ground to the right," roared our colonel, as he dashed bareheaded towards the wavering wing; but the confusion was now so great that it was impossible to reform, and all order seemed lost.

But just here a startling surprise was awaiting us. Advancing at a run and coolly opening ranks to permit our disorganized left to pass through them, up came a superb body of Highlanders, their tall bonnets and waving tartans lending to them the appearance of gigantic stature as they gallantly pushed forward.

"In God's name, Lawrence, what forces are these — where did they drop from?" shouted Aylmer, our junior major, his eyes bulging with surprise and excitement.

"They're the 42nd— the Black Watch, sir," said Sergeant M'Pherson, saluting from the ranks, and unable to suppress his pride at the splendid support his countrymen were giving at this juncture. "They reached St. Catharines at noon and have just marched on the field. See how beautifully they go in! "

"Forty-second fiends or devils," said Aylmer, wiping the thick beads of perspiration from his brow, "I thought we had none but volunteers with us. The kilties have saved us." "Well done, 42nd," echoed the colonel.

Meanwhile the Black Watch bounded forward to the charge, our bugler sounded the command, and with hoarse shouts and curses our line advanced at a run. Rage at the loss of comrades, friends and schoolfellows we had seen killed beside us made us madmen. With bayonets almost locked, fierce blows, stabs and thrusts were given. Elliott, who was near me, slipped and fell. With borrow I saw a tall militiaman in blue with bayonet in position to lunge through the prostrate lad. Before I could think to save him, old Brown leaped in front of me with a roar like that of a wild beast, and drove his bayonet through the militiaman's throat. Nothing withstood our charge now. In turn disorganized by our rush, the enemy broke and fled, and our cavalry rode down their flanks and cut off their retreat, the sabres dealing death right and left. Through the little village and out of it was the pursuit continued, and then, under cover of the fire of our batteries, the assault on the hill began. I have never found out from that day to this whether it was ordered or whether our fellows made it from sheer impulse. I saw a column of redcoats at a double take the road up the height to the left. A stockade had been built across it which they blew up and then pressed on. Our line made the direct ascent, climbing over felled timber and swarming through underbrush up the steep acclivity. Hardly had we cleared them when a cheer came from above, and I saw men of the 19th running along from the westward and leaping into the rifle pits, apparently on the very bayonets of the defenders. The last stand of the enemy was made in the plateau beneath the monument, and from the bodies we found piled about, sanguinary fighting must have occurred here. But before we reached the brow of the hill, all was over and the day was ours. Such of the enemy as were not taken prisoners had retreated westward in the direction of the quarries. The bones of the gallant Brock were once more guarded by friends.

The dusk of evening was falling as we formed for roll-call upon the height, and looked out over the familiar landscape, now so changed from what we had known it in former years. The fields were strewed with corpses of men and horses, and tracked with shattered gun carriages, caissons and wagons, the ruin and devastation of war. Peacefully the river rolled its smooth olive green current many hundred feet below us. Across it, upon the hills, we saw the white tents of the enemy, and in front of them a small battery was beginning to throw a shell or two towards our position. On the northern horizon the great lake gleamed in the waning light, and at the river mouth flashed the electric search lights of British gunboats feeling their way into the river. Off to the westward, a slackening fire still continued, for the tide of battle and pursuit had rolled thither. The roofs of one or two houses in the village at our feet were blazing, and the cool breeze of evening, blowing up from the gorge, was lifting the lazy smoke, fanning and drifting it back over the fields.

The day was ours, but at great cost. Of my company of ninety-eight men, but forty-three answered to their names. Stuart I had seen fall, shot through the body, at the foot of the hill. Elliot, too, was missing.

I remembered last seeing the boy with us in the fighting near some sheds as we were pushing through the village, and, as soon as possible, I obtained leave to take a couple of men and search for him. A heart-breaking business it was, following back the course our men had taken. Many a quiet form we turned over, to recognize beneath the lantern's light the face of a comrade we felt we were looking upon for the last time. Surgeons and fatigue parties of various regiments moved about the field with us, furnishing assistance, where it could be rendered, to friend and foe alike. To many, a cup of water was all that could be given: some feebly cried for it as we passed: most lay silent.

Attracted by a light in a small shed, or cow-stable, we threw back the shattered door and entered. The low structure was feebly illuminated by a tallow candle which someone had placed in the socket of a bayonet, the point of which was stuck in the floor. Some surgeon had probably been using the place as a field operating room. It seemed untenanted now, and I was pushing out again, when a figure slowly lifted a hand in military salute, from a heap of straw in the corner. It was Corporal Brown. The poor old man's uniform was torn, and soaked and stained in dark patches, and my first glance at his white and drawn features told me that he had fought his last battle. Perhaps guessing my errand, he feebly motioned towards a silent figure at his side, whose hand he held, stretched out with that strange and awesome contortion of limb which violent death upon the field so often produces. Before even the flickering light had caught the silver trappings of an officer's uniform, I knew it was poor Elliot. I put my hand over his heart. It was still. His body was not yet cold, but his hand and brow were icy. I drew from his tunic his watch, and the locket attached to it, which I knew contained Mabel's miniature. There was blood upon them. I thought of his lonely old father, even now waiting for news of battle in his far off home, and of another — . I turned to Brown: "Corporal, we must move him, and yourself, too. The enemy are beginning to shell this place, and we may have to evacuate it before sunrise. Can you move?"

He could not. I followed his eyes as they slowly sought his wounded arm, and his thigh, which, broken by some heavy shot, hung helplessly down. He shook his head, and as he looked at the dead boy beside him his cheeks glistened. "It's too late for me, sir," he said, brokenly. "Tell the poor Colonel I tried — I tried — ."

There was the harsh, hurtling scream of a shell which sounded at our very ears, a crash of splintering rafters over our heads, and I remember no more.

When I again opened my eyes, it was with a sense of pain at the light, and upon gradually gaining consciousness, I first discerned a window through which light was reflected upon them. They felt very weak and weary, but I was enabled to perceive, through the window, roofs and chimneys burdened with deep snow, shining out, a pure bank of white, against the blue sky. A Sabbath calm pervaded the place- There was sunlight outside and the snow reflected it upon my face. I was lying upon a hard and narrow pallet in a bare and somewhat darkened room with rough whitewashed walls. My thoughts seemed con- fused and sluggish, and perception returned slowly. I saw other beds, rows of them ranged along each side of the ward, with what appeared to be, from their wan faces and sunken eyes, sick and wounded men in each. One or two hospital nurses moved softly about, gentle-faced women, with quiet voices and soothing hands. Upon the arm of each was a white band marked with the red cross. At a table near sat an officer, writing, dressed in the uniform of the United States army.

I must have dozed then, for when I again became conscious, the lamps were lighted in the ward and an arm was lifting my head to administer some medicine. It was one of the nurses, and from her I learned that I was in St. Catharines, and had been brought into the hospital nearly a month before, wounded in the head and right arm.

Afterwards I learned what had happened during my long fever and delirium. Our first little skirmish had been but the prelude to some real fighting. Despite the destruction of all bridges over the Niagara River, the enemy had advanced in strong force, under cover of heavy artillery fire, at Fort Erie and Chippewa. After several ineffectual attempts to check them, our colonial forces were compelled to retire and leave the Niagara peninsula, for a time at least, in their hands.

But the great military power of Britain was not long in asserting itself. The swift and magnificent

Atlantic passenger liners, as well as dozens of other vessels of her merchant marine, had been hard at work transporting troops to Halifax and Quebec, and now fifty thousand Imperial soldiers were occupying the country. Under their protection all the gunboats of draught sufficiently light to pass up the St. Lawrence canals had gained the lakes. At the western gates, eighty thousand East Indians, Sikhs and Ghoorkas, had been landed, and one-half of them were already on their way eastward; and these, with an equal number of colonials under arms, and the reinforcements constantly pushing forward from east and west, established a force sufficient to withstand and hurl back the first onslaught of the invaders.

I learnt much of what went on from the United States army surgeon in charge of the ward, who called twice a day to dress my arm, and who supplied me with his New York and Boston newspapers. This surgeon was a chatty man named Lewis, a native of Vermont, and no enemy could be kinder than he was.

My old friend Armstrong, of the 19th, was also a prisoner in the ward with me, and many a pleasant hour we spent in the doctor's room, smoking (for our pipes were not refused us), discussing the telegraphic news and letters of special correspondents from the seat of war, and listening to our host's droll Yankee anecdotes. Of our friends at home, or of the movements of our regiments we could learn nothing, for no letters came through the picket lines, and, prisoners as we were, this suspense was hard to bear. So the days passed.

I had not been in hospital quite a month since my recovery from fever when Lewis approached me one morning, on his daily rounds, with the remark, "Well, Cap', I guess I'll have to leave you to better hands. They tell me us cusses'll hev to git," and he explained that the British Army of the Lakes was reported moving southward, and that orders had been received from American Headquarters to abandon St. Catharines. He seemed to have lost none of his cheerfulness at this apparent reverse. He exchanged pipes with me, bet Armstrong ten dollars that he would be back in a month, and then shook hands with us and his other patients as his orderly came up to report that his horse was at the door. Through the window we saw him mount his horse and ride away, laughingly shaking his fist at us in adieu. I never saw him after, but if these lines should meet the eye of this warm-hearted man, they will remind him of the gratitude of those enemies his kindness made friends.

He got off none too soon, for, sure enough, I heard an unusual stir a few hours after, and towards noon the sound of bugles. Looking out of the windows we saw a splendid troop of the 17th Lancers ride by. In all my life I never saw such excitement as that produced upon us by the sight of this fine cavalry regiment. Those of the sick men who could hobble to the windows raised them and tried to cheer, but they choked with emotion; while those poor fellows in the cots too feeble to raise their heads lay motionless, their wet cheeks alone betraying the joy they felt.

I did not set out to write a history of the war, nor is there need I should. You know it all. True, our country suffered; some of our cities were burnt and enormous amounts of property and material of every kind were wasted and destroyed, money spent and lives lost. The War Indemnity and Confiscation Acts passed by Congress swept away millions of British capital invested in the United States. Such is the result of all wars. For a year or more Ontario was a huge battlefield, and Manitoba was for a time pretty much in the hands of the enemy. But we were not the only ones who suffered, for the gunboats made short work of the unprotected lake cities of our enemies, and Chicago and Milwaukee, Cleveland and Buffalo, Rochester and Oswego, were all destroyed. The fleets of Britain held possession almost undisputed of the seas surrounding the enemy's coast, and blockaded every port. The United States navy fought with spirit and bravery, but it possessed no vessels strong enough to withstand the batteries of the Imperial warships, and as for the wooden frigates of the old type, it appeared like sheer murder of brave men to order them out against ironclads. The coasts of the Atlantic States were harried, and many sea-board cities followed the fate of New York. On the other hand, several British ironclads were sunk by torpedo vessels and dynamite balloons.

The end is matter of history. An influential peace party of both nations, moved by the terrible injuries the two branches of the English speaking race were inflicting on each other, were successful in bringing about a cessation of hostilities. Both nations were thoroughly tired of war, and willing enough to conclude peace. This was done by the Treaty of London, whereby some concessions were made on both sides, which, for our part, we had offered to make before the war began.

My story is done, and however much moralizing has been indulged in by the wiseacres of the press during the past forty years, I shall waste no time in adverting to vaporings and ideas which events have proved to be valueless. Time tries all. There are people in the world, and Canada has had her share of them, whose only mission is to find fault and predict misfortune. Some of these have told us that we Canadians lived for years in a fool's paradise, speculating weakly about our future, but taking no steps to control it; as though there ever was a people that studied more earnestly its political environment, that cherished more ardently one national purpose and aspiration. Others of our critics say that we lacked spirit in declining to ask, long before, for an independence of the mother country which was to be had for the asking, and to seek an annexation to our neighbours which, forestalling the danger of conquest, would have saved a bloody war. Independence! The independence of the lamb drinking at the stream beside the wolf! Annexation! – to a democracy ruled by the most corrupt and worthless classes of its citizens.

These same fault-finders – how well we know them – are the men who, with shallow flippancy, sneered at those steadfast hearts who in years gone by in Canada held before us the hope that, one day, there would exist a mighty and united Empire in which we should take our honoured and equal place; and, foreseeing the dangers which would beset the growing strength of our manhood, bid us cherish the ties which bound us to the great family of British nations — the lion's whelps even then waxing strong. Parrot tongues proclaimed the great Brotherhood longed for by these patient and loyal patriots, a dream. So of old did Joseph dream. So Columbus, Galileo, Clarkson, Wilberforce, and all the leaders in the advancement of mankind, back to the days of barbarism — undaunted spirits — dreamers all: dreamers of empire then unknown, of progress then unimagined, of thoughts then uncomprehended. Dreamers of a time to come when this strange dreamer we call man, taught through succeeding generations, in the slow march of the centuries, wandering for cycles of painful years in the wilderness of ignorance and waywardness and misdoing, should gain at last the shining tablelands where all is Light.

A dream. I was in London at that great review we held at the close of the war, when fifty thousand men, picked from the forces of the Empire, marched proudly past the carriage where sat the gentle lady whose locks time had silvered, whose features betrayed the emotion she felt, Queen and Empress, ruler of the hearts and destinies of three hundred million souls. It seemed to me a dream indeed, and in it the days of chivalry had returned. These were her stalwart and loyal knights whose lances had flashed beneath her guerdon: from the sunburnt plains of Hindostan, and from the snows of Canada, from Africa, from Australasia, and the islands of the Southern seas, brothers all, shoulder to shoulder, for the Power that gave the dream had fashioned their hearts alike. And afterwards at that service of Thanksgiving in the vast dark Abbey, where England guards the ashes of those noblest of our race — strong souls that fought and toiled and prayed for her through all the centuries of her glorious history, it seemed to me, in the hushed pulse of the living multitude, the great dead within the sculptured splendour of their tombs, were worshipping with us.

A dream. Go now and stand at night time upon that dark old bridge spanning the legendary river which flows beside the Abbey walls, and see, close by the noble tower of Westminster, that more stately and sumptuous pile. Mark well its blazing lights, it lights a world. This is the new Senate House of the Great Council of the Empire. Hither come the elders of the people, princes and satraps from a hundred states, to rule the common destinies of our race.

There is peace to-day in Canada, and happiness among her twenty millions of prosperous people, forming the new nation of the Western world. Knit together as one nation, old differences silenced and forgotten, we have become heirs to a goodly heritage. Canada, rich in all the wealth of forest and mine, of fishery and fruitful field, the home of a happy and contented people, has reached a future undreamt of fifty years ago. Could one of my generation at that day have been permitted, by some miracle of prophetic vision to pierce the obscurity which then surrounded us, could he have seen the vast unknown prairies of the Northwest filled with the teeming and energetic life of a prosperous and busy community; have seen its mighty rivers, then a name only to most of us, their primeval silence now broken by the whistle of the steamboat and the hum of the mill, and their courses now made the bustling highways of Commerce: could this seer have traced its network of railways, pushing far into the wilderness of forest, and have viewed its cities, adorned with the stateliest triumphs of architecture and replete with all that wealth can create, or refinement approve, — and pictured to us what would come to pass, who would have hearkened to him? Yet this is Canada to-day.

Yes, this is Canada. The old things have passed away, and all things are new. And as we turn our faces towards this still brightening orient of splendid promise, the shadows fall behind us.

I am writing these few last lines from the old field at Niagara, which I am revisiting again after many years. It seems asleep, as of old, in the sunshine; and as we walk across it towards the ruined bastions of Fort George, the summer wind wanders there with us, and seems to whisper of the old and later wars. Here, two centuries ago, France and England fought. But over the fading footprints of these forgotten struggles, the later war has left, sharp cut, the mark of its iron heel. See, to our right, the long earthworks, with the black muzzles of the guns peering behind them; see beyond, — Ah, how countless they seem! — the long lines of graves, row upon row, field upon field, each with its numbered head-stone, in this great national cemetery. A nation's dead sleep here.

Forty years have passed, yet how little has nature changed. There is the sun, a great red ball, about to plunge his face in the cool waters of the lake. Hark, from the rampart, the boom of the sunset gun peals over the quiet reaches of the river, which seem, in the evening hush, to listen for it. The gnats no longer dance in the level beams. The happy songs of the birds are hushed, and hushed too, the querulous rasp of the grasshoppers in the grass. From out the old church tower the sound of bells fills all the summer air, calling to prayer. With hearts humbled and softened by a thousand sad memories which their voices recall, and stilling within us every ungenerous and unworthy passion awakened once by the storm of long ago, let us, too, bow our heads to Him whose hand has led us through the valley of its awful shadow, whose purposes we cannot fathom. The echoes of a bygone conflict have long, since been silenced: its dead will some day be forgotten.

But not in vain. Not in vain, in the fresh morning of their young life did these first-born of our nation's heroes pass into darkness. Still over them, upon that tall staff, floats the flag for love of which they died. Here in this sacred spot, let us resolve that Canada, preserved by their sacrifice, shall be a nation great, just and renowned; great in the great hearts, the high aims, the noble courage of her people; progressing ever onward in all that is worthy, beneficent and good, until nation shall no longer rise against nation, and men shall learn war no more.

THE END

THE SWOOP! OR HOW CLARENCE SAVED ENGLAND: A TALE OF THE GREAT INVASION BY P. G. WODEHOUSE (GREAT BRITAIN, 1909)

PREFACE

It may be thought by some that in the pages which follow I have painted in too lurid colours the horrors of a foreign invasion of England. Realism in art, it may be argued, can be carried too far. I prefer to think that the majority of my readers will acquit me of a desire to be unduly sensational. It is necessary that England should be roused to a sense of her peril, and only by setting down without flinching the probable results of an invasion can this be done. This story, I may mention, has been written and published purely from a feeling of patriotism and duty. Mr. Alston Rivers' sensitive soul will be jarred to its foundations if it is a financial success. So will mine. But in a time of national danger we feel that the risk must be taken. After all, at the worst, it is a small sacrifice to make for our country.

P. G. WODEHOUSE.
The Bomb-Proof Shelter, London, W.

PART ONE

CHAPTER ONE
AN ENGLISH BOY'S HOME

August the First, 19—

Clarence Chugwater looked around him with a frown, and gritted his teeth.

"England—my England!" he moaned.

Clarence was a sturdy lad of some fourteen summers. He was neatly, but not gaudily, dressed in a flat-brimmed hat, a coloured handkerchief, a flannel shirt, a bunch of ribbons, a haversack, football shorts, brown boots, a whistle, and a hockey-stick. He was, in fact, one of General Baden-Powell's Boy Scouts.

Scan him closely. Do not dismiss him with a passing glance; for you are looking at the Boy of Destiny, at Clarence MacAndrew Chugwater, who saved England.

To-day those features are familiar to all. Everyone has seen the Chugwater Column in Aldwych, the equestrian statue in Chugwater Road (formerly Piccadilly), and the picture-postcards in the stationers' windows. That bulging forehead, distended with useful information; that massive chin; those eyes, gleaming behind their spectacles; that tout ensemble; that je ne sais quoi.

In a word, Clarence!

He could do everything that the Boy Scout must learn to do. He could low like a bull. He could gurgle like a wood-pigeon. He could imitate the cry of the turnip in order to deceive rabbits. He could smile and whistle simultaneously in accordance with Rule 8 (and only those who have tried this know how difficult it is). He could spoor, fell trees, tell the character from the boot-sole, and fling the squaler. He did all these things well, but what he was really best at was flinging the squaler.

Clarence, on this sultry August afternoon, was tensely occupied tracking the family cat across the dining-room carpet by its foot-prints. Glancing up for a moment, he caught sight of the other members of the family.

"England, my England!" he moaned.

It was indeed a sight to extract tears of blood from any Boy Scout. The table had been moved back against the wall, and in the cleared space Mr. Chugwater, whose duty it was to have set an example to his children, was playing diabolo. Beside him, engrossed in cup-and-ball, was his wife. Reggie Chugwater, the eldest son, the heir, the hope of the house, was reading the cricket news in an early edition of the evening paper. Horace, his brother, was playing pop-in-taw with his sister Grace and Grace's fiance, Ralph Peabody. Alice, the other Miss Chugwater, was mending a Badminton racquet.

Not a single member of that family was practising with the rifle, or drilling, or learning to make bandages.

Clarence groaned.

"If you can't play without snorting like that, my boy," said Mr. Chugwater, a little irritably, "you must find some other game. You made me jump just as I was going to beat my record."

"Talking of records," said Reggie, "Fry's on his way to his eighth successive century. If he goes on like this, Lancashire will win the championship."

"I thought he was playing for Somerset," said Horace.

"That was a fortnight ago. You ought to keep up to date in an important subject like cricket."

Once more Clarence snorted bitterly.

"I'm sure you ought not to be down on the floor, Clarence," said Mr. Chugwater anxiously. "It is so draughty, and you have evidently got a nasty cold. Must you lie on the floor?"

"I am spooring," said Clarence with simple dignity.

"But I'm sure you can spoor better sitting on a chair with a nice book."

"I think the kid's sickening for something," put in Horace critically. "He's deuced roopy. What's up, Clarry?"

"I was thinking," said Clarence, "of my country—of England."

"What's the matter with England?"

"She's all right," murmured Ralph Peabody.

"My fallen country!" sighed Clarence, a not unmanly tear bedewing the glasses of his spectacles. "My fallen, stricken country!"

"That kid," said Reggie, laying down his paper, "is talking right through his hat. My dear old son, are you aware that England has never been so strong all round as she is now? Do you ever read the papers? Don't you know that we've got the Ashes and the Golf Championship, and the Wibbley-wob Championship, and the Spiropole, Spillikins, Puff-Feather, and Animal Grab Championships? Has it come to your notice that our croquet pair beat America last Thursday by eight hoops? Did you happen to hear that we won the Hop-skip-and-jump at the last Olympic Games? You've been out in the woods, old sport."

Clarence's heart was too full for words. He rose in silence, and quitted the room.

"Got the pip or something!" said Reggie. "Rum kid! I say, Hirst's bowling well! Five for twenty-three so far!"

Clarence wandered moodily out of the house. The Chugwaters lived in a desirable villa residence, which Mr. Chugwater had built in Essex. It was a typical Englishman's Home. Its name was Nasturtium Villa.

As Clarence walked down the road, the excited voice of a newspaper-boy came to him. Presently the boy turned the corner, shouting, "Ker-lapse of Surrey! Sensational bowling at the Oval!"

He stopped on seeing Clarence.

"Paper, General?"

Clarence shook his head. Then he uttered a startled exclamation, for his eye had fallen on the poster.

It ran as follows:—

SURREY
DOING
BADLY
GERMAN ARMY LANDS IN ENGLAND

CHAPTER TWO
THE INVADERS

Clarence flung the boy a halfpenny, tore a paper from his grasp, and scanned it eagerly. There was nothing to interest him in the body of the journal, but he found what he was looking for in the stop-press space. "Stop press news," said the paper. "Fry not out, 104. Surrey 147 for 8. A German army landed in Essex this afternoon. Loamshire Handicap: Spring Chicken, 1; Salome, 2; Yip-i-addy, 3. Seven ran."

Essex! Then at any moment the foe might be at their doors; more, inside their doors. With a passionate cry, Clarence tore back to the house.

He entered the dining-room with the speed of a highly-trained Marathon winner, just in time once more to prevent Mr. Chugwater lowering his record.

"The Germans!" shouted Clarence. "We are invaded!"

This time Mr. Chugwater was really annoyed.

"If I have told you once about your detestable habit of shouting in the house, Clarence, I have told you a hundred times. If you cannot be a Boy Scout quietly, you must stop being one altogether. I had got up to six that time."

"But, father——"

"Silence! You will go to bed this minute; and I shall consider the question whether you are to have any supper. It will depend largely on your behaviour between now and then. Go!"

"But, father——"

Clarence dropped the paper, shaken with emotion. Mr. Chugwater's sternness deepened visibly.

"Clarence! Must I speak again?"

He stooped and removed his right slipper.

Clarence withdrew.

Reggie picked up the paper.

"That kid," he announced judicially, "is off his nut! Hullo! I told you so! Fry not out, 104. Good old Charles!"

"I say," exclaimed Horace, who sat nearest the window, "there are two rummy-looking chaps coming to the front door, wearing a sort of fancy dress!"

"It must be the Germans," said Reggie. "The paper says they landed here this afternoon. I expect——"

A thunderous knock rang through the house. The family looked at one another. Voices were heard in the hall, and next moment the door opened and the servant announced "Mr. Prinsotto and Mr. Aydycong."

"Or, rather," said the first of the two newcomers, a tall, bearded, soldierly man, in perfect English, "Prince Otto of Saxe-Pfennig and Captain the Graf von Poppenheim, his aide-de-camp."

"Just so—just so!" said Mr. Chugwater, affably. "Sit down, won't you?"

The visitors seated themselves. There was an awkward silence.

"Warm day!" said Mr. Chugwater.

"Very!" said the Prince, a little constrainedly.

"Perhaps a cup of tea? Have you come far?"

"Well—er—pretty far. That is to say, a certain distance. In fact, from Germany."

"I spent my summer holiday last year at Dresden. Capital place!"

"Just so. The fact is, Mr.—er—"

"Chugwater. By the way—my wife, Mrs. Chugwater."

The prince bowed. So did his aide-de-camp.

"The fact is, Mr. Jugwater," resumed the prince, "we are not here on a holiday."

"Quite so, quite so. Business before pleasure."

The prince pulled at his moustache. So did his aide-de-camp, who seemed to be a man of but little initiative and conversational resource.

"We are invaders."

"Not at all, not at all," protested Mr. Chugwater.

"I must warn you that you will resist at your peril. You wear no uniform—"

"Wouldn't dream of such a thing. Except at the lodge, of course."

"You will be sorely tempted, no doubt. Do not think that I do not appreciate your feelings. This is an Englishman's Home."

Mr. Chugwater tapped him confidentially on the knee.

"And an uncommonly snug little place, too," he said. "Now, if you will forgive me for talking business, you, I gather, propose making some stay in this country."

The prince laughed shortly. So did his aide-de-camp. "Exactly," continued Mr. Chugwater, "exactly. Then you will want some pied-a-terre, if you follow me. I shall be delighted to let you this house on remarkably easy terms for as long as you please. Just come along into my study for a moment. We can talk it over quietly there. You see, dealing direct with me, you would escape the middleman's charges, and—"

Gently but firmly he edged the prince out of the room and down the passage.

The aide-de-camp continued to sit staring woodenly at the carpet. Reggie closed quietly in on him.

"Excuse me," he said; "talking shop and all that. But I'm an agent for the Come One Come All Accident and Life Assurance Office. You have heard of it probably? We can offer you really exceptional terms. You must not miss a chance of this sort. Now here's a prospectus—"

Horace sidled forward.

"I don't know if you happen to be a cyclist, Captain—er—Graf; but if you'd like a practically new motorbike, only been used since last November, I can let you—"

There was a swish of skirts as Grace and Alice advanced on the visitor.

"I'm sure," said Grace winningly, "that you're fond of the theatre, Captain Poppenheim. We are getting up a performance of 'Ici on parle Francais,' in aid of the fund for Supplying Square Meals to Old-Age Pensioners. Such a deserving object, you know. Now, how many tickets will you take?"

"You can sell them to your friends, you know," added Mrs. Chugwater.

The aide-de-camp gulped convulsively.

Ten minutes later two penniless men groped their way, dazed, to the garden gate.

"At last," said Prince Otto brokenly, for it was he, "at last I begin to realise the horrors of an invasion—for the invaders."

And together the two men staggered on.

CHAPTER THREE
ENGLAND'S PERIL

When the papers arrived next morning, it was seen that the situation was even worse than had at first been suspected. Not only had the Germans effected a landing in Essex, but, in addition, no fewer than eight other hostile armies had, by some remarkable coincidence, hit on that identical moment for launching their long-prepared blow.

England was not merely beneath the heel of the invader. It was beneath the heels of nine invaders.

There was barely standing-room.

Full details were given in the Press. It seemed that while Germany was landing in Essex, a strong force of Russians, under the Grand Duke Vodkakoff, had occupied Yarmouth. Simultaneously the Mad Mullah had captured Portsmouth; while the Swiss navy had bombarded Lyme Regis, and landed troops immediately to westward of the bathing-machines. At precisely the same moment China, at last awakened, had swooped down upon that picturesque little Welsh watering-place, Lllgxtplll, and, despite desperate resistance on the part of an excursion of Evanses and Joneses from Cardiff, had obtained a secure foothold. While these things were happening in Wales, the army of Monaco had descended on Auchtermuchty, on the Firth of Clyde. Within two minutes of this disaster, by Greenwich time, a boisterous band of Young Turks had seized Scarborough. And, at Brighton and Margate respectively, small but determined armies, the one of Moroccan brigands, under Raisuli, the other of dark-skinned warriors from the distant isle of Bollygolla, had made good their footing.

This was a very serious state of things.

Correspondents of the Daily Mail at the various points of attack had wired such particulars as they were able. The preliminary parley at Lllgxtplll between Prince Ping Pong Pang, the Chinese general, and Llewellyn Evans, the leader of the Cardiff excursionists, seems to have been impressive to a degree. The former had spoken throughout in pure Chinese, the latter replying in rich Welsh, and the general effect, wired the correspondent, was almost painfully exhilarating.

So sudden had been the attacks that in very few instances was there any real resistance. The nearest approach to it appears to have been seen at Margate.

At the time of the arrival of the black warriors which, like the other onslaughts, took place between one and two o'clock on the afternoon of August Bank Holiday, the sands were covered with happy revellers. When the war canoes approached the beach, the excursionists seem to have mistaken their occupants at first for a troupe of nigger minstrels on an unusually magnificent scale; and it was freely noised abroad in the crowd that they were being presented by Charles Frohmann, who was endeavouring to revive the ancient glories of the Christy Minstrels. Too soon, however, it was perceived that these were no harmless Moore and Burgesses. Suspicion was aroused by the absence of banjoes and tambourines; and when the foremost of the negroes dexterously scalped a small boy, suspicion became certainty.

In this crisis the trippers of Margate behaved well. The Mounted Infantry, on donkeys, headed by Uncle Bones, did much execution. The Ladies' Tormentor Brigade harassed the enemy's flank, and a hastily-formed band of sharp-shooters, armed with three-shies-a-penny balls and milky cocos, undoubtedly troubled the advance guard considerably. But superior force told. After half an hour's fighting the excursionists fled, leaving the beach to the foe.

At Auchtermuchty and Portsmouth no obstacle, apparently, was offered to the invaders. At Brighton the enemy were permitted to land unharmed. Scarborough, taken utterly aback by the boyish vigour of the Young Turks, was an easy prey; and at Yarmouth, though the Grand Duke received a nasty slap in the face from a dexterously-thrown bloater, the resistance appears to have been equally futile.

By tea-time on August the First, nine strongly-equipped forces were firmly established on British soil.

CHAPTER FOUR
WHAT ENGLAND THOUGHT OF IT

Such a state of affairs, disturbing enough in itself, was rendered still more disquieting by the fact that, except for the Boy Scouts, England's military strength at this time was practically nil.

The abolition of the regular army had been the first step. Several causes had contributed to this. In the first place, the Socialists had condemned the army system as unsocial. Privates, they pointed out, were forbidden to hob-nob with colonels, though the difference in their positions was due to a mere accident of birth. They demanded that every man in the army should be a general. Comrade Quelch, in an eloquent speech at Newington Butts, had pointed, amidst enthusiasm, to the republics of South America, where the system worked admirably.

Scotland, too, disapproved of the army, because it was professional. Mr. Smith wrote several trenchant letters to Mr. C. J. B. Marriott on the subject.

So the army was abolished, and the land defence of the country entrusted entirely to the Territorials, the Legion of Frontiersmen, and the Boy Scouts.

But first the Territorials dropped out. The strain of being referred to on the music-hall stage as Teddy-boys was too much for them.

Then the Frontiersmen were disbanded. They had promised well at the start, but they had never been themselves since La Milo had been attacked by the Manchester Watch Committee. It had taken all the heart out of them.

So that in the end England's defenders were narrowed down to the Boy Scouts, of whom Clarence Chugwater was the pride, and a large civilian population, prepared, at any moment, to turn out for their country's sake and wave flags. A certain section of these, too, could sing patriotic songs.

It was inevitable, in the height of the Silly Season, that such a topic as the simultaneous invasion of Great Britain by nine foreign powers should be seized upon by the press. Countless letters poured into the offices of the London daily papers every morning. Space forbids more than the gist of a few of these.

Miss Charlesworth wrote:—"In this crisis I see no alternative. I shall disappear."

Mr. Horatio Bottomley, in John Bull, said that there was some very dirty and underhand work going on, and that the secret history of the invasion would be published shortly. He himself, however, preferred any invader, even the King of

Bollygolla, to some K.C.'s he could name, though he was fond of dear old Muir. He wanted to know why Inspector Drew had retired.

The Daily Express, in a thoughtful leader, said that Free Trade evidently meant invaders for all.

Mr. Herbert Gladstone, writing to the Times, pointed out that he had let so many undesirable aliens into the country that he did not see that a few more made much difference.

Mr. George R. Sims made eighteen puns on the names of the invading generals in the course of one number of "Mustard and Cress."

Mr. H. G. Pelissier urged the public to look on the bright side. There was a sun still shining in the sky. Besides, who knew that some foreign marksman might not pot the censor?

Mr. Robert FitzSimmons offered to take on any of the invading generals, or all of them, and if he didn't beat them it would only be because the referee had a wife and seven small children and had asked him as a personal favour to let himself be knocked out. He had lost several fights that way.

The directors of the Crystal Palace wrote a circular letter to the shareholders, pointing out that there was a good time coming. With this addition to the public, the Palace stood a sporting chance of once more finding itself full.

Judge Willis asked: "What is an invasion?"

Signor Scotti cabled anxiously from America (prepaid): "Stands Scotland where it did?"

Mr. Lewis Waller wrote heroically: "How many of them are there? I am usually good for about half a dozen. Are they assassins? I can tackle any number of assassins."

Mr. Seymour Hicks said he hoped they would not hurt George Edwardes.

Mr. George Edwardes said that if they injured Seymour Hicks in any way he would never smile again.

A writer in Answers pointed out that, if all the invaders in the country were piled in a heap, they would reach some of the way to the moon.

Far-seeing men took a gloomy view of the situation. They laid stress on the fact that this counter-attraction was bound to hit first-class cricket hard. For some years gates had shown a tendency to fall off, owing to the growing popularity of golf, tennis, and other games. The desire to see the invaders as they marched through the country must draw away thousands who otherwise would have paid their sixpences at the turnstiles. It was suggested that representations should be made to the invading generals with a view to inducing them to make a small charge to sightseers.

In sporting circles the chief interest centered on the race to London. The papers showed the positions of the various armies each morning in their Runners and Betting columns; six to four on the Germans was freely offered, but found no takers.

Considerable interest was displayed in the probable behaviour of the nine armies when they met. The situation was a curious outcome of the modern custom of striking a deadly blow before actually declaring war. Until the moment when the enemy were at her doors, England had imagined that she was on terms of the most satisfactory friendship with her neighbours. The foe had taken full advantage of this, and also of the fact that, owing to a fit of absent-mindedness on the part of the Government, England had no ships afloat which were not entirely obsolete. Interviewed on the subject by representatives of the daily papers, the Government handsomely admitted that it was perhaps in some ways a silly thing to have done; but, they urged, you could not think of everything. Besides, they were on the point of laying down a Dreadnought, which would be ready in a very few years. Meanwhile, the best thing the public could do was to sleep quietly in their beds. It was Fisher's tip; and Fisher was a smart man.

And all the while the Invaders' Marathon continued.

Who would be the first to reach London?

CHAPTER FIVE
THE GERMANS REACH LONDON

The Germans had got off smartly from the mark and were fully justifying the long odds laid upon them. That master-strategist, Prince Otto of Saxe-Pfennig, realising that if he wished to reach the Metropolis quickly he must not go by train, had resolved almost at once to walk. Though hampered considerably by crowds of rustics who gathered, gaping, at every point in the line of march, he had made good progress. The German troops had strict orders to reply to no questions, with the result that little time was lost in idle chatter, and in a couple of days it was seen that the army of the Fatherland was bound, barring accidents, to win comfortably.

The progress of the other forces was slower. The Chinese especially had undergone great privations, having lost their way near Llanfairpwlgwnngogogoch, and having been unable to understand the voluble directions given to them by the various shepherds they encountered. It was not for nearly a week that they contrived to reach Chester, where, catching a cheap excursion, they arrived in the metropolis, hungry and footsore, four days after the last of their rivals had taken up their station.

The German advance halted on the wooded heights of Tottenham. Here a camp was pitched and trenches dug.

The march had shown how terrible invasion must of necessity be. With no wish to be ruthless, the troops of Prince Otto had done grievous damage. Cricket-pitches had been trampled down, and in many cases even golf-greens dented by the iron heel of the invader, who rarely, if ever, replaced the divot.

Everywhere they had left ruin and misery in their train.

With the other armies it was the same story. Through carefully-preserved woods they had marched, frightening the birds and driving keepers into fits of nervous prostration. Fishing, owing to their tramping carelessly through the streams, was at a standstill. Croquet had been given up in despair.

Near Epping the Russians shot a fox....

The situation which faced Prince Otto was a delicate one. All his early training and education had implanted in him the fixed idea that, if he ever invaded England, he would do it either alone or with the sympathetic co-operation of allies. He had never faced the problem of what he should do if there were rivals in the field. Competition is wholesome, but only within bounds. He could not very well ask the other nations to withdraw. Nor did he feel inclined to withdraw himself.

"It all comes of this dashed Swoop of the Vulture business," he grumbled, as he paced before his tent, ever and anon pausing to sweep the city below him with his glasses. "I should like to find the fellow who started the idea! Making me look a fool! Still, it's just as bad for the others, thank goodness! Well, Poppenheim?"

Captain von Poppenheim approached and saluted.

"Please, sir, the men say, 'May they bombard London?'"

"Bombard London!"

"Yes, sir; it's always done."

Prince Otto pulled thoughtfully at his moustache.

"Bombard London! It seems—and yet—ah, well, they have few pleasures."

He stood awhile in meditation. So did Captain von Poppenheim. He kicked a pebble. So did Captain von Poppenheim—only a smaller pebble. Discipline is very strict in the German army.

"Poppenheim."

"Sir?"

"Any signs of our—er—competitors?"

"Yes, sir; the Russians are coming up on the left flank, sir. They'll be here in a few hours. Raisuli has been arrested at Purley for stealing chickens. The army of Bollygolla is about ten miles out. No news of the field yet, sir."

The Prince brooded. Then he spoke, unbosoming himself more freely than was his wont in conversation with his staff.

"Between you and me, Pop," he cried impulsively, "I'm dashed sorry we ever started this dashed silly invading business. We thought ourselves dashed smart, working in the dark, and giving no sign till the great pounce, and all that sort of dashed nonsense. Seems to me we've simply dashed well landed ourselves in the dashed soup."

Captain von Poppenheim saluted in sympathetic silence. He and the prince had been old chums at college. A life-long friendship existed between them. He would have liked to have expressed adhesion verbally to his superior officer's remarks. The words "I don't think" trembled on his tongue. But the iron discipline of the German Army gagged him. He saluted again and clicked his heels.

The Prince recovered himself with a strong effort.

"You say the Russians will be here shortly?" he said.

"In a few hours, sir."

"And the men really wish to bombard London?"

"It would be a treat to them, sir."

"Well, well, I suppose if we don't do it, somebody else will. And we got here first."

"Yes, sir."

"Then—"

An orderly hurried up and saluted.

"Telegram, sir."

Absently the Prince opened it. Then his eyes lit up.

"Gotterdammerung!" he said. "I never thought of that. 'Smash up London and provide work for unemployed mending it.—GRAYSON,'" he read. "Poppenheim."

"Sir?"

"Let the bombardment commence."

"Yes, sir."

"And let it continue till the Russians arrive. Then it must stop, or there will be complications."

Captain von Poppenheim saluted, and withdrew.

CHAPTER SIX
THE BOMBARDMENT OF LONDON

Thus was London bombarded. Fortunately it was August, and there was nobody in town.

Otherwise there might have been loss of life.

CHAPTER SEVEN
A CONFERENCE OF THE POWERS

The Russians, led by General Vodkakoff, arrived at Hampstead half an hour after the bombardment had ceased, and the rest of the invaders, including Raisuli, who had got off on an alibi, dropped in at intervals during the week. By the evening of Saturday, the sixth of August, even the Chinese had limped to the metropolis. And the question now was, What was going to happen? England displayed a polite indifference to the problem. We are essentially a nation of sightseers. To us the excitement of staring at the invaders was enough. Into the complex international problems to which the situation gave rise it did not occur to us to examine. When you consider that a crowd of five hundred Londoners will assemble in the space of two minutes, abandoning entirely all its other business, to watch a cab-horse that has fallen in the street, it is not surprising that the spectacle of nine separate and distinct armies in the metropolis left no room in the British mind for other reflections.

The attraction was beginning to draw people back to London now. They found that the German shells had had one excellent result, they had demolished nearly all the London statues. And what might have conceivably seemed a drawback, the fact that they had blown great holes in the wood-paving, passed unnoticed amidst the more extensive operations of the London County Council.

Taking it for all in all, the German gunners had simply been beautifying London. The Albert Hall, struck by a merciful shell, had come down with a run, and was now a heap of picturesque ruins; Whitefield's Tabernacle was a charred mass; and the burning of the Royal Academy proved a great comfort to all. At a mass meeting in Trafalgar Square a hearty vote of thanks was passed, with acclamation, to Prince Otto.

But if Londoners rejoiced, the invaders were very far from doing so. The complicated state of foreign politics made it imperative that there should be no friction between the Powers. Yet here a great number of them were in perhaps as embarrassing a position as ever diplomatists were called upon to unravel. When nine dogs are assembled round one bone, it is rarely on the bone alone that teeth-marks are found at the close of the proceedings.

Prince Otto of Saxe-Pfennig set himself resolutely to grapple with the problem. His chance of grappling successfully with it was not improved by the stream of telegrams which arrived daily from his Imperial Master, demanding to know whether he had yet subjugated the country, and if not, why not. He had replied guardedly, stating the difficulties which lay in his way, and had received the following: "At once mailed fist display. On Get or out Get.—WILHELM."

It was then that the distracted prince saw that steps must be taken at once.

Carefully-worded letters were despatched by District Messenger boys to the other generals. Towards nightfall the replies began to come in, and, having read them, the Prince saw that this business could never be settled without a personal interview. Many of the replies were absolutely incoherent.

Raisuli, apologising for delay on the ground that he had been away in the Isle of Dogs cracking a crib, wrote suggesting that the Germans and Moroccans should combine with a view to playing the Confidence Trick on the Swiss general, who seemed a simple sort of chap. "Reminds me of dear old Maclean," wrote Raisuli. "There is money in this. Will you come in? Wire in the morning."

The general of the Monaco forces thought the best way would be to settle the thing by means of a game of chance of the odd-man-out class. He knew a splendid game called Slippery Sam. He could teach them the rules in half a minute.

The reply of Prince Ping Pong Pang of China was probably brilliant and scholarly, but it was expressed in Chinese characters of the Ming period, which Prince Otto did not understand; and even if he had it would have done him no good, for he tried to read it from the top downwards instead of from the bottom up.

The Young Turks, as might have been expected, wrote in their customary flippant, cheeky style. They were full of mischief, as usual. The body of the letter, scrawled in a round, schoolboy hand, dealt principally with the details of the booby-trap which the general had successfully laid for his head of staff. "He was frightfully shirty," concluded the note jubilantly.

From the Bollygolla camp the messenger-boy returned without a scalp, and with a verbal message to the effect that the King could neither read nor write.

Grand Duke Vodkakoff, from the Russian lines, replied in his smooth, cynical, Russian way:—"You appear anxious, my dear prince, to scratch the other entrants. May I beg you to remember what happens when you scratch a Russian?"

As for the Mad Mullah's reply, it was simply pure delirium. The journey from Somaliland, and his meeting with his friend Mr. Dillon, appeared to have had the worse effects on his sanity. He opened with the statement that he was a tea-pot: and that was the only really coherent remark he made.

Prince Otto placed a hand wearily on his throbbing brow.

"We must have a conference," he said. "It is the only way."

Next day eight invitations to dinner went out from the German camp.

It would be idle to say that the dinner, as a dinner, was a complete success. Half-way through the Swiss general missed his diamond solitaire, and cold glances were cast at Raisuli, who sat on his immediate left. Then the King of Bollygolla's table-manners were frankly inelegant. When he wanted a thing, he grabbed for it. And he seemed to want nearly everything. Nor was the behaviour of the leader of the Young Turks all that could be desired. There had been some talk of only allowing him to come down to dessert; but he had squashed in, as he briefly put it, and it would be paltering with the truth to say that he had not had far more champagne than was good for him. Also, the general of Monaco had brought a pack of cards with him, and was spoiling the harmony by trying to induce Prince Ping Pong Pang to find the lady. And the brainless laugh of the Mad Mullah was very trying.

Altogether Prince Otto was glad when the cloth was removed, and the waiters left the company to smoke and talk business.

Anyone who has had anything to do with the higher diplomacy is aware that diplomatic language stands in a class by itself. It is a language specially designed to deceive the chance listener.

Thus when Prince Otto, turning to Grand Duke Vodkakoff, said quietly, "I hear the crops are coming on nicely down Kent way," the habitual frequenter of diplomatic circles would have understood, as did the Grand Duke, that what he really meant was, "Now about this business. What do you propose to do?"

The company, with the exception of the representative of the Young Turks, who was drinking creme de menthe out of a tumbler, the Mullah and the King of Bollygolla bent forward, deeply interested, to catch the Russian's reply. Much would depend on this.

Vodkakoff carelessly flicked the ash off his cigarette.

"So I hear," he said slowly. "But in Shropshire, they tell me, they are having trouble with the mangel-wurzels."

The prince frowned at this typical piece of shifty Russian diplomacy.

"How is your Highness getting on with your Highness's roller-skating?" he enquired guardedly.

The Russian smiled a subtle smile.

"Poorly," he said, "poorly. The last time I tried the outside edge I thought somebody had thrown the building at me."

Prince Otto flushed. He was a plain, blunt man, and he hated this beating about the bush.

"Why does a chicken cross the road?" he demanded, almost angrily.

The Russian raised his eyebrows, and smiled, but made no reply. The prince, resolved to give him no chance of wriggling away from the point, pressed him hotly.

"Think of a number," he cried. "Double it. Add ten. Take away the number you first thought of. Divide it by three, and what is the result?"

There was an awed silence. Surely the Russian, expert at evasion as he was, could not parry so direct a challenge as this.

He threw away his cigarette and lit a cigar.

"I understand," he said, with a tinkle of defiance in his voice, "that the Suffragettes, as a last resource, propose to capture Mr. Asquith and sing the Suffragette Anthem to him."

A startled gasp ran round the table.

"Because the higher he flies, the fewer?" asked Prince Otto, with sinister calm.

"Because the higher he flies, the fewer," said the Russian smoothly, but with the smoothness of a treacherous sea.

There was another gasp. The situation was becoming alarmingly tense.

"You are plain-spoken, your Highness," said Prince Otto slowly.

At this moment the tension was relieved by the Young Turk falling off his chair with a crash on to the floor. Everyone jumped up startled. Raisuli took advantage of the confusion to pocket a silver ash-tray.

The interruption had a good effect. Frowns relaxed. The wranglers began to see that they had allowed their feelings to run away with them. It was with a conciliatory smile that Prince Otto, filling the Grand Duke's glass, observed:

"Trumper is perhaps the prettier bat, but I confess I admire Fry's robust driving."

The Russian was won over. He extended his hand.

"Two down and three to play, and the red near the top corner pocket," he said with that half-Oriental charm which he knew so well how to exhibit on occasion.

The two shook hands warmly.

And so it was settled, the Russian having, as we have seen, waived his claim to bombard London in his turn, there was no obstacle to a peaceful settlement. It was obvious that the superior forces of the Germans and Russians gave them, if they did but combine, the key to the situation. The decision they arrived at was, as set forth above, as follows. After the fashion of the moment, the Russian and German generals decided to draw the Colour Line. That meant that the troops of China, Somaliland, Bollygolla, as well as Raisuli and the Young Turks, were ruled out. They would be given a week in which to leave the country. Resistance would be useless. The combined forces of the Germans, Russians, Swiss, and Monacoans were overwhelming, especially as the Chinese had not recovered from their wanderings in Wales and were far too footsore still to think of serious fighting.

When they had left, the remaining four Powers would continue the invasion jointly.

Prince Otto of Saxe-Pfennig went to bed that night, comfortably conscious of a good work well done. He saw his way now clear before him.

But he had made one miscalculation. He had not reckoned with Clarence Chugwater.

PART TWO

CHAPTER ONE
IN THE BOY SCOUTS' CAMP

Night!

Night in Aldwych!

In the centre of that vast tract of unreclaimed prairie known to Londoners as the Aldwych Site there shone feebly, seeming almost to emphasise the darkness and desolation of the scene, a single light.

It was the camp-fire of the Boy Scouts.

The night was raw and windy. A fine rain had been falling for some hours. The date of September the First. For just a month England had been in the grip of the invaders. The coloured section of the hostile force had either reached its home by now, or was well on its way. The public had seen it go with a certain regret. Not since the visit of the Shah had such an attractive topic of conversation been afforded them. Several comic journalists had built up a reputation and a large price per thousand words on the King of Bollygolla alone. Theatres had benefited by the index of a large, new, unsophisticated public. A piece at the Waldorf Theatre had run for a whole fortnight, and "The Merry Widow" had taken on a new lease of life. Selfridge's, abandoning its policy of caution, had advertised to the extent of a quarter of a column in two weekly papers.

Now the Young Turks were back at school in Constantinople, shuffling their feet and throwing ink pellets at one another; Raisuli, home again in the old mountains, was working up the kidnapping business, which had fallen off sadly in his absence under the charge of an incompetent locum tenens; and the Chinese, the Bollygollans, and the troops of the Mad Mullah were enduring the miseries of sea-sickness out in mid-ocean.

The Swiss army had also gone home, in order to be in time for the winter hotel season. There only remained the Germans, the Russians, and the troops of Monaco.

In the camp of the Boy Scouts a vast activity prevailed.

Few of London's millions realise how tremendous and far-reaching an association the Boy Scouts are. It will be news to the Man in the Street to learn that, with the possible exception of the Black Hand, the Scouts are perhaps the most carefully-organised secret society in the world.

Their ramifications extend through the length and breadth of England. The boys you see parading the streets with hockey-sticks are but a small section, the aristocrats of the Society. Every boy in England, and many a man, is in the pay of the association. Their funds are practically unlimited. By the oath of initiation which he takes on joining, every boy is compelled to pay into the common coffers a percentage of his pocket-money or his salary. When you drop his weekly three and sixpence into the hand of your office-boy on Saturday, possibly you fancy he takes it home to mother. He doesn't. He spend two-and-six on Woodbines. The other shilling goes into the treasury of the Boy Scouts. When you visit your nephew at Eton, and tip him five pounds or whatever it is, does he spend it at the sock-shop? Apparently, yes. In reality, a quarter reaches the common fund.

Take another case, to show the Boy Scouts' power. You are a City merchant, and, arriving at the office one morning in a bad temper, you proceed to cure yourself by taking it out of the office-boy. He says nothing, apparently does nothing. But that evening, as you are going home in the Tube, a burly working-man treads heavily on your gouty foot. In Ladbroke Grove a passing hansom splashes you with mud. Reaching home, you find that the cat has been at the cold chicken and the butler has given notice. You do not connect these things, but they are all alike the results of your unjust behaviour to your office-boy in the morning. Or, meeting a ragged little matchseller, you pat his head and give him six-pence. Next day an anonymous present of champagne arrives at your address.

Terrible in their wrath, the Boy Scouts never forget kindness.

The whistle of a Striped Iguanodon sounded softly in the darkness. The sentry, who was pacing to and fro before the camp-fire, halted, and peered into the night. As he peered, he uttered the plaintive note of a zebra calling to its mate.

A voice from the darkness said, "Een gonyama-gonyama."

"Invooboo," replied the sentry argumentatively "Yah bo! Yah bo! Invooboo."

An indistinct figure moved forward.

"Who goes there?"

"A friend."

"Advance, friend, and give the countersign."

"Remember Mafeking, and death to Injuns."

"Pass friend! All's well."

The figure walked on into the firelight. The sentry started; then saluted and stood to attention. On his face was a worshipping look of admiration and awe, such as some young soldier of the Grande Armee might have worn on seeing Napoleon; for the newcomer was Clarence Chugwater.

"Your name?" said Clarence, eyeing the sturdy young warrior.

"Private William Buggins, sir."

"You watch well, Private Buggins. England has need of such as you."

He pinched the young Scout's ear tolerantly. The sentry flushed with pleasure.

"My orders have been carried out?" said Clarence.

"Yes, sir. The patrols are all here."

"Enumerate them."

"The Chinchilla Kittens, the Bongos, the Zebras, the Iguanodons, the Welsh Rabbits, the Snapping Turtles, and a half-patrol of the 33rd London Gazekas, sir."

Clarence nodded.

"'Tis well," he said. "What are they doing?"

"Some of them are acting a Scout's play, sir; some are doing Cone Exercises; one or two are practising deep breathing; and the rest are dancing an Old English Morris Dance."

Clarence nodded.

"They could not be better employed. Inform them that I have arrived and would address them."

The sentry saluted.

Standing in an attitude of deep thought, with his feet apart, his hands clasped behind him, and his chin sunk upon his breast, Clarence made a singularly impressive picture. He had left his Essex home three weeks before, on the expiration of his ten days' holiday, to return to his post of junior sub-reporter on the staff of a leading London evening paper. It was really only at night now that he got any time to himself. During the day his time was his paper's, and he was compelled to spend the weary hours reading off results of races and other sporting items on the tape-machine. It was only at 6 p.m. that he could begin to devote himself to the service of his country.

The Scouts had assembled now, and were standing, keen and alert, ready to do Clarence's bidding.

Clarence returned their salute moodily.

"Scout-master Wagstaff," he said.

The Scout-master, the leader of the troop formed by the various patrols, stepped forward.

"Let the war-dance commence."

Clarence watched the evolutions absently. His heart was ill-attuned to dances. But the thing had to be done, so it was as well to get it over. When the last movement had been completed, he raised his hand.

"Men," he said, in his clear, penetrating alto, "although you have not the same facilities as myself for hearing the latest news, you are all, by this time, doubtless aware that this England of ours lies 'neath the proud foot of a conqueror. It is for us to save her. (Cheers, and a voice "Invooboo!") I would call on you here and now to seize your hockey-sticks and rush upon the invader, were it not, alas! that such an action would merely result in your destruction. At present the invader is too strong. We must wait; and something tells me that we shall not have to wait long. (Applause.) Jealousy is beginning to spring up between the Russians and the Germans. It will be our task to aggravate this feeling. With our perfect organisation this should be easy. Sooner or later this smouldering jealousy is going to burst into flame. Any day now," he proceeded, warming as he spoke, "there may be the dickens of a dust-up between these Johnnies, and then we've got 'em where the hair's short. See what I mean, you chaps? It's like this. Any moment they may start scrapping and chaw each other up, and then we'll simply sail in and knock what's left endways."

A shout of applause went up from the assembled scouts.

"What I am anxious to impress upon you men," concluded Clarence, in more measured tones, "is that our hour approaches. England looks to us, and it is for us to see that she does not look in vain. Sedulously feeding the growing flame of animosity between the component parts of the invading horde, we may contrive to bring about that actual disruption. Till that day, see to it that you prepare yourselves for war. Men, I have finished."

"What the Chief Scout means," said Scout-master Wagstaff, "is no rotting about and all that sort of rot. Jolly well keep yourselves fit, and then, when the time comes, we'll give these Russian and German blighters about the biggest hiding they've ever heard of. Follow the idea? Very well, then. Mind you don't go mucking the show up."

"Een gonyama-gonyama!" shouted the new thoroughly roused troops. "Invooboo! Yah bo! Yah bo! Invooboo!"

The voice of Young England—of Young England alert and at its post!

CHAPTER TWO
AN IMPORTANT ENGAGEMENT

Historians, when they come to deal with the opening years of the twentieth century, will probably call this the Music-Hall Age. At the time of the great invasion the music-halls dominated England. Every town and every suburb had its Hall, most of them more than one. The public appetite for sight-seeing had to be satisfied somehow, and the music-hall provided the easiest way of doing it. The Halls formed a common place on which the celebrity and the ordinary man could meet. If an impulsive gentleman slew his grandmother with a coal-hammer, only a small portion of the public could gaze upon his pleasing features at the Old Bailey. To enable the rest to enjoy the intellectual treat, it was necessary to engage him, at enormous expense, to appear at a music-hall. There, if he happened to be acquitted, he would come on the stage, preceded by an asthmatic introducer, and beam affably at the public for ten minutes, speaking at intervals in a totally inaudible voice, and then retire; to be followed by some enterprising lady who had endeavoured, unsuccessfully, to solve the problem of living at the rate of ten thousand a year on an income of nothing, or who had performed some other similarly brainy feat.

It was not till the middle of September that anyone conceived what one would have thought the obvious idea of offering music-hall engagements to the invading generals.

The first man to think of it was Solly Quhayne, the rising young agent. Solly was the son of Abraham Cohen, an eminent agent of the Victorian era. His brothers, Abe Kern, Benjamin Colquhoun, Jack Coyne, and Barney Cowan had gravitated to the City; but Solly had carried on the old business, and was making a big name for himself. It was Solly who had met Blinky Bill Mullins, the prominent sand-bagger, as he emerged from his twenty years' retirement at Dartmoor, and booked him solid for a thirty-six months' lecturing tour on the McGinnis circuit. It was to him, too, that Joe Brown, who could eat eight pounds of raw meat in seven and a quarter minutes, owed his first chance of displaying his gifts to the wider public of the vaudeville stage.

The idea of securing the services of the invading generals came to him in a flash.

"S'elp me!" he cried. "I believe they'd go big; put 'em on where you like."

Solly was a man of action. Within a minute he was talking to the managing director of the Mammoth Syndicate Halls on the telephone. In five minutes the managing director had agreed to pay Prince Otto of Saxe-Pfennig five hundred pounds a week, if he could be prevailed upon to appear. In ten minutes the Grand Duke Vodkakoff had been engaged, subject to his approval, at a weekly four hundred and fifty by the Stone-Rafferty circuit. And in a quarter of an hour Solly Quhayne, having pushed his way through a mixed crowd of Tricky Serios and Versatile Comedians and Patterers who had been waiting to see him for the last hour and a half, was bowling off in a taximeter-cab to the Russian lines at Hampstead.

General Vodkakoff received his visitor civilly, but at first without enthusiasm. There were, it seemed, objections to his becoming an artiste. Would he have to wear a properly bald head and sing songs about wanting people to see his girl? He didn't think he could. He had only sung once in his life, and that was twenty years ago at a bump-supper at Moscow University. And even then, he confided to Mr. Quhayne, it had taken a decanter and a-half of neat vodka to bring him up to the scratch.

The agent ridiculed the idea.

"Why, your Grand Grace," he cried, "there won't be anything of that sort. You ain't going to be starred as a comic. You're a Refined Lecturer and Society Monologue Artist. 'How I Invaded England,' with lights down and the cinematograph going. We can easily fake the pictures."

The Grand Duke made another objection.

"I understand," he said, "it is etiquette for music-hall artists in their spare time to eat—er—fried fish with their fingers. Must I do that? I doubt if I could manage it."

Mr Quhayne once more became the human semaphore.

"S'elp me! Of course you needn't! All the leading pros, eat it with a spoon. Bless you, you can be the refined gentleman on the Halls same as anywhere else. Come now, your Grand Grace, is it a deal? Four hundred and fifty chinking o'Goblins a week for one hall a night, and press-agented at eight hundred and seventy-five. S'elp me! Lauder doesn't get it, not in England."

The Grand Duke reflected. The invasion has proved more expensive than he had foreseen. The English are proverbially a nation of shopkeepers, and they had put up their prices in all the shops for his special benefit. And he was expected to do such a lot of tipping. Four hundred and fifty a week would come in uncommonly useful.

"Where do I sign?" he asked, extending his hand for the agreement.

Five minutes later Mr. Quhayne was urging his taxidriver to exceed the speed-limit in the direction of Tottenham.

CHAPTER THREE
A BIRD'S-EYE VIEW OF THE SITUATION

Clarence read the news of the two engagements on the tape at the office of his paper, but the first intimation the general public had of it was through the medium of headlines:—

MUSIC-HALL SENSATION
INVADING GENERALS' GIGANTIC SALARIES
RUMOURED RESENTMENT OF V.A.F.
WHAT WILL WATER-RATS DO?
INTERVIEW WITH MR. HARRY LAUDER

Clarence chuckled grimly as the tape clicked out the news. The end had begun. To sow jealousy between the rival generals would have been easy. To sow it between two rival music-hall artistes would be among the world's softest jobs.

Among the general public, of course, the announcement created a profound sensation. Nothing else was talked about in train and omnibus. The papers had leaders on the subject. At first the popular impression was that the generals were going to do a comedy duo act of the Who-Was-It-I-Seen-You-Coming-Down-the-Street-With? type, and there was disappointment when it was found that the engagements were for different halls. Rumours sprang up. It was said that the Grand Duke had for years been an enthusiastic amateur sword-swallower, and had, indeed, come to England mainly for the purpose of getting bookings; that the Prince had a secure reputation in Potsdam as a singer of songs in the George Robey style; that both were expert trick-cyclists.

Then the truth came out. Neither had any specialities; they would simply appear and deliver lectures.

The feeling in the music-hall world was strong. The Variety Artists' Federation debated the advisability of another strike. The Water Rats, meeting in mystic secrecy in a Maiden Lane public-house, passed fifteen resolutions in an hour and a quarter. Sir Harry Lauder, interviewed by the Era, gave it as his opinion that both the Grand Duke and the Prince were gowks, who would do well to haud their blether. He himself proposed to go straight to America, where genuine artists were cheered in the streets and entertained at haggis dinners, and not forced to compete with amateur sumphs and gonuphs from other countries.

Clarence, brooding over the situation like a Providence, was glad to see that already the new move had weakened the invaders' power. The day after the announcement in the press of the approaching debut of the other generals, the leader of the army of Monaco had hurried to the agents to secure an engagement for himself. He held out the special inducement of card-tricks, at which he was highly skilled. The agents had received him coldly. Brown and Day had asked him to call again. Foster had sent out a message regretting that he was too busy to see him. At de Freece's he had been kept waiting in the ante-room for two hours in the midst of a bevy of Sparkling Comediennes of pronounced peroxidity and blue-chinned men in dusty bowler-hats, who told each other how they had gone with a bang at Oakham and John o'Groats, and had then gone away in despair.

On the following day, deeply offended, he had withdrawn his troops from the country.

The strength of the invaders was melting away little by little.

"How long?" murmured Clarence Chugwater, as he worked at the tape-machine. "How long?"

CHAPTER FOUR
CLARENCE HEARS IMPORTANT NEWS

It was Clarence's custom to leave the office of his newspaper at one o'clock each day, and lunch at a neighbouring Aerated Bread shop. He did this on the day following the first appearance of the two generals at their respective halls. He had brought an early edition of the paper with him, and in the intervals of dealing with his glass of milk and scone and butter, he read the report of the performances.

Both, it seemed, had met with flattering receptions, though they had appeared nervous. The Russian general especially, whose style, said the critic, was somewhat reminiscent of Mr. T. E. Dunville, had made himself a great favourite with the gallery. The report concluded by calling attention once more to the fact that the salaries paid to the two—eight hundred and seventy-five pounds a week each—established a record in music-hall history on this side of the Atlantic.

Clarence had just finished this when there came to his ear the faint note of a tarantula singing to its young.

He looked up. Opposite him, at the next table, was seated a youth of fifteen, of a slightly grubby aspect. He was eyeing Clarence closely.

Clarence took off his spectacles, polished them, and replaced them on his nose. As he did so, the thin gruffle of the tarantula sounded once more. Without changing his expression, Clarence cautiously uttered the deep snarl of a sand-eel surprised while bathing.

It was sufficient. The other rose to his feet, holding his right hand on a line with his shoulder, palm to the front, thumb resting on the nail of the little finger, and the other three fingers upright.

Clarence seized his hat by the brim at the back, and moved it swiftly twice up and down.

The other, hesitating no longer, came over to his table.

"Pip-pip!" he said, in an undertone.

"Toodleoo and God save the King!" whispered Clarence.

The mystic ceremony which always takes place when two Boy Scouts meet in public was complete.

"Private Biggs of the Eighteenth Tarantulas, sir," said the boy respectfully, for he had recognised Clarence.

Clarence inclined his head.

"You may sit, Private Biggs," he said graciously. "You have news to impart?"

"News, sir, that may be of vital importance."

"Say on."

Private Biggs, who had brought his sparkling limado and a bath-bun with him from the other table, took a sip of the former, and embarked upon his narrative.

"I am employed, sir," he said, "as a sort of junior clerk and office-boy by Mr. Solly Quhayne, the music-hall agent."

Clarence tapped his brow thoughtfully; then his face cleared.

"I remember. It was he who secured the engagements of the generals."

"The same, sir."

"Proceed."

The other resumed his story.

"It is my duty to sit in a sort of rabbit-hutch in the outer office, take the callers' names, and especially to see that they don't get through to Mr. Quhayne till he wishes to receive them. That is the most exacting part of my day's work. You wouldn't believe how full of the purest swank some of these pros. are. Tell you they've got an appointment as soon as look at you. Artful beggars!"

Clarence nodded sympathetically.

"This morning an Acrobat and Society Contortionist made such a fuss that in the end I had to take his card in to the private office. Mr. Quhayne was there talking to a gentleman whom I recognised as his brother, Mr. Colquhoun. They were engrossed in their conversation, and did not notice me for a moment. With no wish to play the eavesdropper, I could not help but overhear. They were talking about the generals. 'Yes, I know they're press-agented at eight seventy-five, dear boy,' I heard Mr. Quhayne say, 'but between you and me and the door-knob that isn't what they're getting. The German feller's drawing five hundred of the best, but

I could only get four-fifty for the Russian. Can't say why. I should have thought, if anything, he'd be the bigger draw. Bit of a comic in his way!' And then he saw me. There was some slight unpleasantness. In fact, I've got the sack. After it was over I came away to try and find you. It seemed to me that the information might be of importance."

Clarence's eyes gleamed.

"You have done splendidly, Private—no, Corporal Biggs. Do not regret your lost position. The society shall find you work. This news you have brought is of the utmost—the most vital importance. Dash it!" he cried, unbending in his enthusiasm, "we've got 'em on the hop. If they aren't biting pieces out of each other in the next day or two, I'm jolly well mistaken."

He rose; then sat down again.

"Corporal—no, dash it, Sergeant Biggs—you must have something with me. This is an occasion. The news you have brought me may mean the salvation of England. What would you like?"

The other saluted joyfully.

"I think I'll have another sparkling limado, thanks, awfully," he said.

The beverage arrived. They raised their glasses.

"To England," said Clarence simply.

"To England," echoed his subordinate.

Clarence left the shop with swift strides, and hurried, deep in thought, to the offices of the Encore in Wellington Street.

"Yus?" said the office-boy interrogatively.

Clarence gave the Scout's Siquand, the pass-word. The boy's demeanour changed instantly. He saluted with the utmost respect.

"I wish to see the Editor," said Clarence.

A short speech, but one that meant salvation for the motherland.

CHAPTER FIVE
SEEDS OF DISCORD

The days following Clarence's visit to the offices of the Encore were marked by a growing feeling of unrest, alike among invaded and invaders. The first novelty and excitement of the foreign occupation of the country was beginning to wear off, and in its place the sturdy independence so typical of the British character was reasserting itself. Deep down in his heart the genuine Englishman has a rugged distaste for seeing his country invaded by a foreign army. People were asking themselves by what right these aliens had overrun British soil. An ever-growing feeling of annoyance had begun to lay hold of the nation.

It is probable that the departure of Sir Harry Lauder first brought home to England what this invasion might mean. The great comedian, in his manifesto in the Times, had not minced his words. Plainly and crisply he had stated that he was leaving the country because the music-hall stage was given over to alien gowks. He was sorry for England. He liked England. But now, all he could say was, "God bless you." England shuddered, remembering that last time he had said, "God bless you till I come back."

Ominous mutterings began to make themselves heard.

Other causes contributed to swell the discontent. A regiment of Russians, out route-marching, had walked across the bowling-screen at Kennington Oval during the Surrey v. Lancashire match, causing Hayward to be bowled for a duck's-egg. A band of German sappers had dug a trench right across the turf at Queen's Club.

The mutterings increased.

Nor were the invaders satisfied and happy. The late English summer had set in with all its usual severity, and the Cossacks, reared in the kindlier climate of Siberia, were feeling it terribly. Colds were the rule rather than the exception in the Russian lines. The coughing of the Germans at Tottenham could be heard in Oxford Street.

The attitude of the British public, too, was getting on their nerves. They had been prepared for fierce resistance. They had pictured the invasion as a series of brisk battles—painful perhaps, but exciting. They had anticipated that when they had conquered the country they might meet with the Glare of Hatred as they patrolled the streets. The Supercilious Stare unnerved them. There is nothing so terrible to the highly-strung foreigner as the cold, contemptuous, patronising gaze of the Englishman. It gave the invaders a perpetual feeling of doing the wrong thing. They felt like men who had been found travelling in a first-class carriage with a third-class ticket. They became conscious of the size of their hands and feet. As they marched through the Metropolis they felt their ears growing hot and red. Beneath the chilly stare of the populace they experienced all the sensations of a man who has come to a strange dinner-party in a tweed suit when everybody else has dressed. They felt warm and prickly.

It was dull for them, too. London is never at its best in early September, even for the habitue. There was nothing to do. Most of the theatres were shut. The streets were damp and dirty. It was all very well for the generals, appearing every night in the glare and glitter of the footlights; but for the rank and file the occupation of London spelt pure boredom.

London was, in fact, a human powder-magazine. And it was Clarence Chugwater who with a firm hand applied the match that was to set it in a blaze.

CHAPTER SIX
THE BOMB-SHELL

Clarence had called at the offices of the Encore on a Friday. The paper's publishing day is Thursday. The Encore is the Times of the music-hall world. It casts its curses here, bestows its benedictions (sparely) there. The Encore criticising the latest action of the Variety Artists' Federation is the nearest modern approach to Jove hurling the thunderbolt. Its motto is, "Cry havoc, and let loose the performing dogs of war."

It so happened that on the Thursday following his momentous visit to Wellington Street, there was need of someone on the staff of Clarence's evening paper to go and obtain an interview from the Russian general. Mr. Hubert Wales had just published a novel so fruity in theme and treatment that it had been publicly denounced from the pulpit by no less a person than the Rev. Canon Edgar Sheppard, D.D., Sub-Dean of His Majesty's Chapels Royal, Deputy Clerk of the Closet and Sub-Almoner to the King. A morning paper had started the question, "Should there be a Censor of Fiction?" and, in accordance with custom, editors were collecting the views of celebrities, preferably of those whose opinion on the subject was absolutely valueless.

All the other reporters being away on their duties, the editor was at a loss.

"Isn't there anybody else?" he demanded.

The chief sub-editor pondered.

"There is young blooming Chugwater," he said.

(It was thus that England's deliverer was habitually spoken of in the office.)

"Then send him," said the editor.

Grand Duke Vodkakoff's turn at the Magnum Palace of Varieties started every evening at ten sharp. He topped the bill. Clarence, having been detained by a review of the Scouts, did not reach the hall till five minutes to the hour. He got to the dressing-room as the general was going on to the stage.

The Grand Duke dressed in the large room with the other male turns. There were no private dressing-rooms at the Magnum. Clarence sat down on a basket-trunk belonging to the Premier Troupe of Bounding Zouaves of the Desert, and waited. The four athletic young gentlemen who composed the troupe were dressing after their turn. They took no notice of Clarence.

Presently one Zouave spoke.

"Bit off to-night, Bill. Cold house."

"Not 'arf," replied his colleague. "Gave me the shivers."

"Wonder how his nibs'll go."

Evidently he referred to the Grand Duke.

"Oh, 'e's all right. They eat his sort of swank. Seems to me the profession's going to the dogs, what with these bloomin' amytoors an' all. Got the 'airbrush,

'Arry?"

Harry, a tall, silent Zouave, handed over the hairbrush.

Bill continued.

"I'd like to see him go on of a Monday night at the old Mogul. They'd soon show him. It gives me the fair 'ump, it does, these toffs coming in and taking the bread out of our mouths. Why can't he give us chaps a chance? Fair makes me rasp, him and his bloomin' eight hundred and seventy-five o' goblins a week."

"Not so much of your eight hundred and seventy-five, young feller me lad," said the Zouave who had spoken first. "Ain't you seen the rag this week?"

"Naow. What's in it? How does our advert, look?"

"Ow, that's all right, never mind that. You look at 'What the Encore Would Like to Know.' That's what'll touch his nibs up."

He produced a copy of the paper from the pocket of his great-coat which hung from the door, and passed it to his bounding brother.

"Read it out, old sort," he said.

The other took it to the light and began to read slowly and cautiously, as one who is no expert at the art.

"'What the Encore would like to know:—Whether Prince Otto of Saxe-Pfennig didn't go particularly big at the Lobelia last week? And Whether his success hasn't compelled Agent Quhayne to purchase a larger-sized hat? And Whether it isn't a fact that, though they are press-agented at the same figure, Prince Otto is getting fifty a week more than Grand Duke Vodkakoff? And If it is not so, why a little bird has assured us that the Prince is being paid five hundred a week and the Grand Duke only four hundred and fifty? And, In any case, whether the Prince isn't worth fifty a week more than his Russian friend?' Lumme!"

An awed silence fell upon the group. To Clarence, who had dictated the matter (though the style was the editor's), the paragraph did not come as a surprise. His only feeling was one of relief that the editor had served up his material so well. He felt that he had been justified in leaving the more delicate literary work to that master-hand.

"That'll be one in the eye," said the Zouave Harry. "'Ere, I'll stick it up opposite of him when he comes back to dress. Got a pin and a pencil, some of you?"

He marked the quarter column heavily, and pinned it up beside the looking-glass. Then he turned to his companions.

"'Ow about not waiting, chaps?" he suggested. "I shouldn't 'arf wonder, from the look of him, if he wasn't the 'aughty kind of a feller who'd cleave you to the bazooka for tuppence with his bloomin' falchion. I'm goin' to 'urry through with my dressing and wait till to-morrow night to see how he looks. No risks for Willie!"

The suggestion seemed thoughtful and good. The Bounding Zouaves, with one accord, bounded into their clothes and disappeared through the door just as a long-drawn chord from the invisible orchestra announced the conclusion of the Grand Duke's turn.

General Vodkakoff strutted into the room, listening complacently to the applause which was still going on. He had gone well. He felt pleased with himself.

It was not for a moment that he noticed Clarence.

"Ah," he said, "the interviewer, eh? You wish to—"

Clarence began to explain his mission. While he was doing so the Grand Duke strolled to the basin and began to remove his make-up. He favoured, when on the stage, a touch of the Raven Gipsy No. 3 grease-paint. It added a picturesque swarthiness to his appearance, and made him look more like what he felt to be the popular ideal of a Russian general.

The looking-glass hung just over the basin.

Clarence, watching him in the glass, saw him start as he read the first paragraph. A dark flush, almost rivalling the Raven Gipsy No. 3, spread over his face. He trembled with rage.

"Who put that paper there?" he roared, turning.

"With reference, then, to Mr. Hubert Wales's novel," said Clarence.

The Grand Duke cursed Mr. Hubert Wales, his novel, and Clarence in one sentence.

"You may possibly," continued Clarence, sticking to his point like a good interviewer, "have read the trenchant, but some say justifiable remarks of the Rev. Canon Edgar Sheppard, D.D., Sub-Dean of His Majesty's Chapels Royal, Deputy Clerk of the Closet, and Sub-Almoner to the King."

The Grand Duke swiftly added that eminent cleric to the list.

"Did you put that paper on this looking-glass?" he shouted.

"I did not put that paper on that looking-glass," replied Clarence precisely.

"Ah," said the Grand Duke, "if you had, I'd have come and wrung your neck like a chicken, and scattered you to the four corners of this dressing-room."

"I'm glad I didn't," said Clarence.

"Have you read this paper on the looking-glass?"

"I have not read that paper on the looking-glass," replied Clarence, whose chief fault as a conversationalist was that he was perhaps a shade too Ollendorfian. "But I know its contents."

"It's a lie!" roared the Grand Duke. "An infamous lie! I've a good mind to have him up for libel. I know very well he got them to put those paragraphs in, if he didn't write them himself."

"Professional jealousy," said Clarence, with a sigh, "is a very sad thing."

"I'll professional jealousy him!"

"I hear," said Clarence casually, "that he has been going very well at the Lobelia. A friend of mine who was there last night told me he took eleven calls."

For a moment the Russian General's face swelled apoplectically. Then he recovered himself with a tremendous effort.

"Wait!" he said, with awful calm. "Wait till to-morrow night! I'll show him! Went very well, did he? Ha! Took eleven calls, did he? Oh, ha, ha! And he'll take them to-morrow night, too! Only"—and here his voice took on a note of fiendish purpose so terrible that, hardened scout as he was, Clarence felt his flesh creep—"only this time they'll be catcalls!"

And, with a shout of almost maniac laughter, the jealous artiste flung himself into a chair, and began to pull off his boots.

Clarence silently withdrew. The hour was very near.

CHAPTER SEVEN
THE BIRD

The Grand Duke Vodkakoff was not the man to let the grass grow under his feet. He was no lobster, no flat-fish. He did it now—swift, secret, deadly—a typical Muscovite. By midnight his staff had their orders.

Those orders were for the stalls at the Lobelia.

Price of entrance to the gallery and pit was served out at daybreak to the Eighth and Fifteenth Cossacks of the Don, those fierce, semi-civilised fighting-machines who know no fear.

Grand Duke Vodkakoff's preparations were ready.

Few more fortunate events have occurred in the history of English literature than the quite accidental visit of Mr. Bart Kennedy to the Lobelia on that historic night. He happened to turn in there casually after dinner, and was thus enabled to see the whole thing from start to finish. At a quarter to eleven a wild-eyed man charged in at the main entrance of Carmelite House, and, too impatient to use the lift, dashed up the stairs, shouting for pens, ink and paper.

Next morning the Daily Mail was one riot of headlines. The whole of page five was given up to the topic. The headlines were not elusive. They flung the facts at the reader:—

> SCENE AT THE LOBELIA
> PRINCE OTTO OF SAXE-PFENNIG
> GIVEN THE BIRD BY
> RUSSIAN SOLDIERS
> WHAT WILL BE THE OUTCOME?

There were about seventeen more, and then came Mr. Bart Kennedy's special report.

He wrote as follows:—

"A night to remember. A marvellous night. A night such as few will see again. A night of fear and wonder. The night of September the eleventh. Last night.

"Nine-thirty. I had dined. I had eaten my dinner. My dinner! So inextricably are the prose and romance of life blended. My dinner! I had eaten my dinner on this night. This wonderful night. This night of September the eleventh. Last night!

"I had dined at the club. A chop. A boiled potato. Mushrooms on toast. A touch of Stilton. Half-a-bottle of Beaune. I lay back in my chair. I debated within myself. A Hall? A theatre? A book in the library? That night, the night of September the eleventh, I as near as a toucher spent in the library of my club with a book. That night! The night of September the eleventh. Last night!

"Fate took me to the Lobelia. Fate! We are its toys. Its footballs. We are the footballs of Fate. Fate might have sent me to the Gaiety. Fate took me to the Lobelia. This Fate which rules us.

"I sent in my card to the manager. He let me through. Ever courteous. He let me through on my face. This manager. This genial and courteous manager.

"I was in the Lobelia. A dead-head. I was in the Lobelia as a dead-head!"

Here, in the original draft of the article, there are reflections, at some length, on the interior decorations of the Hall, and an excursus on music-hall performances in general. It is not till he comes to examine the audience that Mr. Kennedy returns to the main issue.

"And what manner of audience was it that had gathered together to view the entertainment provided by the genial and courteous manager of the Lobelia? The audience. Beyond whom there is no appeal. The Caesars of the music-hall. The audience."

At this point the author has a few extremely interesting and thoughtful remarks on the subject of audiences. These may be omitted. "In the stalls I noted a solid body of Russian officers. These soldiers from the Steppes. These bearded men. These Russians. They sat silent and watchful. They applauded little. The programme left them cold. The Trick Cyclist. The Dashing Soubrette and Idol of Belgravia. The Argumentative College Chums. The Swell Comedian. The Man with the Performing Canaries. None of these could rouse them. They were waiting. Waiting. Waiting tensely. Every muscle taut. Husbanding their strength. Waiting. For what?

"A man at my side told a friend that a fellow had told him that he had been told by a commissionaire that the pit and gallery were full of Russians. Russians. Russians everywhere. Why? Were they genuine patrons of the Halls? Or were they there from some ulterior motive? There was an air of suspense. We were all waiting. Waiting. For what?

"The atmosphere is summed up in a word. One word. Sinister. The atmosphere was sinister.

"AA! A stir in the crowded house. The ruffling of the face of the sea before a storm. The Sisters Sigsbee, Coon Delineators and Unrivalled Burlesque Artists, have finished their dance, smiled, blown kisses, skipped off, skipped on again, smiled, blown more kisses, and disappeared. A long chord from the orchestra. A chord that is almost a wail. A wail of regret for that which is past. Two liveried menials appear. They carry sheets of cardboard. These menials carry sheets of cardboard. But not blank sheets. On each sheet is a number.

"The number 15.

"Who is number 15?

"Prince Otto of Saxe-Pfennig. Prince Otto, General of the German Army. Prince Otto is Number 15.

"A burst of applause from the house. But not from the Russians. They are silent. They are waiting. For what?

"The orchestra plays a lively air. The massive curtains part. A tall, handsome military figure strides on to the stage. He bows. This tall, handsome, military man bows. He is Prince Otto of Saxe-Pfennig, General of the Army of Germany. One of our conquerors.

"He begins to speak. 'Ladies and gentlemen.' This man, this general, says, 'Ladies and gentlemen.'

"But no more. No more. No more. Nothing more. No more. He says, 'Ladies and Gentlemen,' but no more.

"And why does he say no more? Has he finished his turn? Is that all he does? Are his eight hundred and seventy-five pounds a week paid him for saying, 'Ladies and Gentlemen'?

"No!

"He would say more. He has more to say. This is only the beginning. This tall, handsome man has all his music still within him.

"Why, then, does he say no more? Why does he say 'Ladies and Gentlemen,' but no more? No more. Only that. No more. Nothing more. No more.

"Because from the stalls a solid, vast, crushing 'Boo!' is hurled at him. From the Russians in the stalls comes this vast, crushing 'Boo!' It is for this that they have been waiting. It is for this that they have been waiting so tensely. For this. They have been waiting for this colossal 'Boo!'

"The General retreats a step. He is amazed. Startled. Perhaps frightened. He waves his hands.

"From gallery and pit comes a hideous whistling and howling. The noise of wild beasts. The noise of exploding boilers. The noise of a music-hall audience giving a performer the bird.

"Everyone is standing on his feet. Some on mine. Everyone is shouting. This vast audience is shouting.

"Words begin to emerge from the babel.

"'Get offski! Rotten turnovitch!' These bearded Russians, these stern critics, shout, 'Rotten turnovitch!'

"Fire shoots from the eyes of the German. This strong man's eyes.

"'Get offski! Swankietoff! Rotten turnovitch!'

"The fury of this audience is terrible. This audience. This last court of appeal. This audience in its fury is terrible.

"What will happen? The German stands his ground. This man of blood and iron stands his ground. He means to go on. This strong man. He means to go on if it snows.

"The audience is pulling up the benches. A tomato shatters itself on the Prince's right eye. An over-ripe tomato.

"'Get offski!' Three eggs and a cat sail through the air. Falling short, they drop on to the orchestra. These eggs! This cat! They fall on the conductor and the second trombone. They fall like the gentle dew from Heaven upon the place beneath. That cat! Those eggs!

"AA! At last the stage-manager—keen, alert, resourceful—saves the situation. This man. This stage-manager. This man with the big brain. Slowly, inevitably, the fireproof curtain falls. It is half-way down. It is down. Before it, the audience. The audience. Behind it, the Prince. The Prince. That general. That man of iron. That performer who has just got the bird.

"The Russian National Anthem rings through the hall. Thunderous! Triumphant! The Russian National Anthem. A paean of joy.

"The menials reappear. Those calm, passionless menials. They remove the number fifteen. They insert the number sixteen. They are like Destiny—Pitiless, Unmoved, Purposeful, Silent. Those menials.

"A crash from the orchestra. Turn number sixteen has begun...."

CHAPTER EIGHT
THE MEETING AT THE SCOTCH STORES

Prince Otto of Saxe-Pfennig stood in the wings, shaking in every limb. German oaths of indescribable vigour poured from his lips. In a group some feet away stood six muscular, short-sleeved stage-hands. It was they who had flung themselves on the general at the fall of the iron curtain and prevented him dashing round to attack the stalls with his sabre. At a sign from the stage-manager they were ready to do it again.

The stage-manager was endeavouring to administer balm.

"Bless you, your Highness," he was saying, "it's nothing. It's what happens to everyone some time. Ask any of the top-notch pros. Ask 'em whether they never got the bird when they were starting. Why, even now some of the biggest stars can't go to some towns because they always cop it there. Bless you, it——"

A stage-hand came up with a piece of paper in his hand.

"Young feller in spectacles and a rum sort o' suit give me this for your 'Ighness."

The Prince snatched it from his hand.

The note was written in a round, boyish hand. It was signed, "A Friend." It ran:—"The men who booed you to-night were sent for that purpose by General Vodkakoff, who is jealous of you because of the paragraphs in the Encore this week."

Prince Otto became suddenly calm.

"Excuse me, your Highness," said the stage-manager anxiously, as he moved, "you can't go round to the front. Stand by, Bill."

"Right, sir!" said the stage-hands.

Prince Otto smiled pleasantly.

"There is no danger. I do not intend to go to the front. I am going to look in at the Scotch Stores for a moment."

"Oh, in that case, your Highness, good-night, your Highness! Better luck to-morrow, your Highness!"

It had been the custom of the two generals, since they had joined the music-hall profession, to go, after their turn, to the Scotch Stores, where they stood talking and blocking the gangway, as etiquette demands that a successful artiste shall.

The Prince had little doubt but that he would find Vodkakoff there to-night.

He was right. The Russian general was there, chatting affably across the counter about the weather.

He nodded at the Prince with a well-assumed carelessness.

"Go well to-night?" he inquired casually.

Prince Otto clenched his fists; but he had had a rigorously diplomatic up-bringing, and knew how to keep a hold on himself. When he spoke it was in the familiar language of diplomacy.

"The rain has stopped," he said, "but the pavements are still wet underfoot. Has your grace taken the precaution to come out in a good stout pair of boots?"

The shaft plainly went home, but the Grand Duke's manner, as he replied, was unruffled.

"Rain," he said, sipping his vermouth, "is always wet; but sometimes it is cold as well."

"But it never falls upwards," said the Prince, pointedly.

"Rarely, I understand. Your powers of observation are keen, my dear Prince."

There was a silence; then the Prince, momentarily baffled, returned to the attack.

"The quickest way to get from Charing Cross to Hammersmith Broadway," he said, "is to go by Underground."

"Men have died in Hammersmith Broadway," replied the Grand Duke suavely.

The Prince gritted his teeth. He was no match for his slippery adversary in a diplomatic dialogue, and he knew it.

"The sun rises in the East," he cried, half-choking, "but it sets—it sets!"

"So does a hen," was the cynical reply.

The last remnants of the Prince's self-control were slipping away. This elusive, diplomatic conversation is a terrible strain if one is not in the mood for it. Its proper setting is the gay, glittering ball-room at some frivolous court. To a man who has just got the bird at a music-hall, and who is trying to induce another man to confess that the thing was his doing, it is little short of maddening.

"Hen!" he echoed, clenching and unclenching his fists. "Have you studied the habits of hens?"

The truth seemed very near to him now, but the master-diplomat before him was used to extracting himself from awkward corners.

"Pullets with a southern exposure," he drawled, "have yellow legs and ripen quickest."

The Prince was nonplussed. He had no answer.

The girl behind the bar spoke.

"You do talk silly, you two!" she said.

It was enough. Trivial as the remark was, it was the last straw. The Prince brought his fist down with a crash on the counter.

"Yes," he shouted, "you are right. We do talk silly; but we shall do so no longer. I am tired of this verbal fencing. A plain answer to a plain question. Did you or did you not send your troops to give me the bird to-night?"

"My dear Prince!"

The Grand Duke raised his eyebrows.

"Did you or did you not?"

"The wise man," said the Russian, still determined on evasion, "never takes sides, unless they are sides of bacon."

The Prince smashed a glass.

"You did!" he roared. "I know you did! Listen to me! I'll give you one chance. I'll give you and your precious soldiers twenty-four hours from midnight to-night to leave this country. If you are still here then—"

He paused dramatically.

The Grand Duke slowly drained his vermouth.

"Have you seen my professional advertisement in the Era, my dear

Prince?" he asked.

"I have. What of it?"

"You noticed nothing about it?"

"I did not."

"Ah. If you had looked more closely, you would have seen the words, 'Permanent address, Hampstead.'"

"You mean——"

"I mean that I see no occasion to alter that advertisement in any way."

There was another tense silence. The two men looked hard at each other.

"That is your final decision?" said the German.

The Russian bowed.

"So be it," said the Prince, turning to the door. "I have the honour to wish you a very good night."

"The same to you," said the Grand Duke. "Mind the step."

CHAPTER NINE
THE GREAT BATTLE

The news that an open rupture had occurred between the Generals of the two invading armies was not slow in circulating. The early editions of the evening papers were full of it. A symposium of the opinions of Dr. Emil Reich, Dr. Saleeby, Sandow, Mr. Chiozza Money, and Lady Grove was hastily collected. Young men with knobbly and bulging foreheads were turned on by their editors to write character-sketches of the two generals. All was stir and activity.

Meanwhile, those who look after London's public amusements were busy with telephone and telegraph. The quarrel had taken place on Friday night. It was probable that, unless steps were taken, the battle would begin early on Saturday. Which, it did not require a man of unusual intelligence to see, would mean a heavy financial loss to those who supplied London with its Saturday afternoon amusements. The matinees would suffer. The battle might not affect the stalls and dress-circle, perhaps, but there could be no possible doubt that the pit and gallery receipts would fall off terribly. To the public which supports the pit and gallery of a theatre there is an irresistible attraction about a fight on anything like a large scale. When one considers that a quite ordinary street-fight will attract hundreds of spectators, it will be plainly seen that no theatrical entertainment could hope to compete against so strong a counter-attraction as a battle between the German and Russian armies.

The various football-grounds would be heavily hit, too. And there was to be a monster roller-skating carnival at Olympia. That also would be spoiled.

A deputation of amusement-caterers hurried to the two camps within an hour of the appearance of the first evening paper. They put their case plainly and well. The Generals were obviously impressed. Messages passed and repassed between the two armies, and in the end it was decided to put off the outbreak of hostilities till Monday morning.

Satisfactory as this undoubtedly was for the theatre-managers and directors of football clubs, it was in some ways a pity. From the standpoint of the historian it spoiled the whole affair. But for the postponement, readers of this history might—nay, would—have been able to absorb a vivid and masterly account of the great struggle, with a careful description of the tactics by which victory was achieved. They would have been told the disposition of the various regiments, the stratagems, the dashing advances, the skilful retreats, and the Lessons of the War.

As it is, owing to the mistaken good-nature of the rival generals, the date of the fixture was changed, and practically all that a historian can do is to record the result.

A slight mist had risen as early as four o'clock on Saturday. By night-fall the atmosphere was a little dense, but the lamp-posts were still clearly visible at a distance of some feet, and nobody, accustomed to living in London, would have noticed anything much out of the common. It was not till Sunday morning that the fog proper really began.

London awoke on Sunday to find the world blanketed in the densest, yellowest London particular that had been experienced for years. It was the sort of day when the City clerk has the exhilarating certainty that at last he has an excuse for lateness which cannot possibly be received with harsh disbelief. People spent the day indoors and hoped it would clear up by tomorrow.

"They can't possibly fight if it's like this," they told each other.

But on the Monday morning the fog was, if possible, denser. It wrapped London about as with a garment. People shook their heads.

"They'll have to put it off," they were saying, when of a sudden—Boom! And, again, Boom!

It was the sound of heavy guns.

The battle had begun!

One does not wish to grumble or make a fuss, but still it does seem a little hard that a battle of such importance, a battle so outstanding in the history of the world, should have been fought under such conditions. London at that moment was richer than ever before in descriptive reporters. It was the age of descriptive reporters, of vivid pen-pictures. In every newspaper office there were men who could have hauled up their slacks about that battle in a way that would have made a Y.M.C.A. lecturer want to get at somebody with a bayonet; men who could have handed out the adjectives and exclamation-marks till you almost heard the roar of the guns. And there they were—idle, supine—like careened battleships. They were helpless. Bart Kennedy did start an article which began, "Fog. Black fog. And the roar of guns. Two nations fighting in the fog," but it never came to anything. It was promising for a while, but it died of inanition in the middle of the second stick.

It was hard.

The lot of the actual war-correspondents was still worse. It was useless for them to explain that the fog was too thick to give them a chance. "If it's light enough for them to fight," said their editors remorselessly, "it's light enough for you to watch them." And out they had to go.

They had a perfectly miserable time. Edgar Wallace seems to have lost his way almost at once. He was found two days later in an almost starving condition at Steeple Bumpstead. How he got there nobody knows. He said he had set out to walk to where the noise of the guns seemed to be, and had gone on walking. Bennett Burleigh, that crafty old campaigner, had the sagacity to go by Tube. This brought him to Hampstead, the scene, it turned out later, of the fiercest operations, and with any luck he might have had a story to tell. But the lift stuck half-way up, owing to a German shell bursting in its neighbourhood, and it was not till the following evening that a search-party heard and rescued him.

The rest—A. G. Hales, Frederick Villiers, Charles Hands, and the others—met, on a smaller scale, the same fate as Edgar Wallace. Hales, starting for Tottenham, arrived in Croydon, very tired, with a nail in his boot. Villiers, equally unlucky, fetched up at Richmond. The most curious fate of all was reserved for Charles Hands. As far as can be gathered, he got on all right till he reached Leicester Square. There he lost his bearings, and seems to have walked round and round Shakespeare's statue, under the impression that he was going straight to Tottenham. After a day and a-half of this he sat down to rest, and was there found, when the fog had cleared, by a passing policeman.

And all the while the unseen guns boomed and thundered, and strange, thin shoutings came faintly through the darkness.

CHAPTER TEN
THE TRIUMPH OF ENGLAND

It was the afternoon of Wednesday, September the Sixteenth. The battle had been over for twenty-four hours. The fog had thinned to a light lemon colour. It was raining.

By now the country was in possession of the main facts. Full details were not to be expected, though it is to the credit of the newspapers that, with keen enterprise, they had at once set to work to invent them, and on the whole had not done badly.

Broadly, the facts were that the Russian army, outmanoeuvered, had been practically annihilated. Of the vast force which had entered England with the other invaders there remained but a handful. These, the Grand Duke Vodkakoff among them, were prisoners in the German lines at Tottenham.

The victory had not been gained bloodlessly. Not a fifth of the German army remained. It is estimated that quite two-thirds of each army must have perished in that last charge of the Germans up the Hampstead heights, which ended in the storming of Jack Straw's Castle and the capture of the Russian general.

Prince Otto of Saxe-Pfennig lay sleeping in his tent at Tottenham. He was worn out. In addition to the strain of the battle, there had been the heavy work of seeing the interviewers, signing autograph-books, sitting to photographers, writing testimonials for patent medicines, and the thousand and one other tasks, burdensome but unavoidable, of the man who is in the public eye. Also he had caught a bad cold during the battle. A bottle of ammoniated quinine lay on the table beside him now as he slept.

As he lay there the flap of the tent was pulled softly aside. Two figures entered. Each was dressed in a flat-brimmed hat, a coloured handkerchief, a flannel shirt, football shorts, stockings, brown boots, and a whistle. Each carried a hockey-stick. One, however, wore spectacles and a look of quiet command which showed that he was the leader.

They stood looking at the prostrate general for some moments. Then the spectacled leader spoke.

"Scout-Master Wagstaff."

The other saluted.

"Wake him!"

Scout-Master Wagstaff walked to the side of the bed, and shook the sleeper's shoulder. The Prince grunted, and rolled over on to his other side. The Scout-Master shook him again. He sat up, blinking.

As his eyes fell on the quiet, stern, spectacled figure, he leaped from the bed.

"What—what—what," he stammered. "What's the beadig of this?"

He sneezed as he spoke, and, turning to the table, poured out and drained a bumper of ammoniated quinine.

"I told the sedtry pardicularly not to let adybody id. Who are you?"

The intruder smiled quietly.

"My name is Clarence Chugwater," he said simply.

"Jugwater? Dod't doe you frob Adab. What do you want? If you're forb sub paper, I cad't see you now. Cub to-borrow bordig."

"I am from no paper."

"Thed you're wud of these photographers. I tell you, I cad't see you."

"I am no photographer."

"Thed what are you?"

The other drew himself up.

"I am England," he said with a sublime gesture.

"Igglud! How do you bead you're Igglud? Talk seds."

Clarence silenced him with a frown.

"I say I am England. I am the Chief Scout, and the Scouts are England. Prince Otto, you thought this England of ours lay prone and helpless. You were wrong. The Boy Scouts were watching and waiting. And now their time has come. Scout-Master Wagstaff, do your duty."

The Scout-Master moved forward. The Prince, bounding to the bed, thrust his hand under the pillow. Clarence's voice rang out like a trumpet.

"Cover that man!"

The Prince looked up. Two feet away Scout-Master Wagstaff was standing, catapult in hand, ready to shoot.

"He is never known to miss," said Clarence warningly.

The Prince wavered.

"He has broken more windows than any other boy of his age in South London."

The Prince sullenly withdrew his hand—empty.

"Well, whad do you wad?" he snarled.

"Resistance is useless," said Clarence. "The moment I have plotted and planned for has come. Your troops, worn out with fighting, mere shadows of themselves, have fallen an easy prey. An hour ago your camp was silently surrounded by patrols of Boy Scouts, armed with catapults and hockey-sticks. One rush and the battle was over. Your entire army, like yourself, are prisoners."

"The diggids they are!" said the Prince blankly.

"England, my England!" cried Clarence, his face shining with a holy patriotism. "England, thou art free! Thou hast risen from the ashes of the dead self. Let the nations learn from this that it is when apparently crushed that the Briton is to more than ever be feared."

"Thad's bad grabbar," said the Prince critically.

"It isn't," said Clarence with warmth.

"It is, I tell you. Id's a splid idfididive."

Clarence's eyes flashed fire.

"I don't want any of your beastly cheek," he said. "Scout-Master Wagstaff, remove your prisoner."

"All the sabe," said the Prince, "id is a splid idfididive."

Clarence pointed silently to the door.

"And you doe id is," persisted the Prince. "And id's spoiled your big sbeech. Id—"

"Come on, can't you," interrupted Scout-Master Wagstaff.

"I ab cubbing, aren't I? I was odly saying—"

"I'll give you such a whack over the shin with this hockey-stick in a minute!" said the Scout-Master warningly. "Come on!"

The Prince went.

CHAPTER ELEVEN
CLARENCE—THE LAST PHASE

The brilliantly-lighted auditorium of the Palace Theatre.

Everywhere a murmur and stir. The orchestra is playing a selection. In the stalls fair women and brave men converse in excited whispers. One catches sentences here and there.

"Quite a boy, I believe!"

"How perfectly sweet!"

"'Pon honour, Lady Gussie, I couldn't say. Bertie Bertison, of the Bachelors', says a feller told him it was a clear thousand."

"Do you hear that? Mr. Bertison says that this boy is getting a thousand a week."

"Why, that's more than either of those horrid generals got."

"It's a lot of money, isn't it?"

"Of course, he did save the country, didn't he?"

"You may depend they wouldn't give it him if he wasn't worth it."

"Met him last night at the Duchess's hop. Seems a decent little chap. No side and that, if you know what I mean. Hullo, there's his number!"

The orchestra stops. The number 7 is displayed. A burst of applause, swelling into a roar as the curtain rises.

A stout man in crinkled evening-dress walks on to the stage.

"Ladies and gentlemen," he says, "I 'ave the 'onour to-night to introduce to you one whose name is, as the saying goes, a nouse'old word. It is thanks to 'im, to this 'ero whom I 'ave the 'onour to introduce to you to-night, that our beloved England no longer writhes beneath the ruthless 'eel of the alien oppressor. It was this 'ero's genius—and, I may say—er—I may say genius—that, unaided, 'it upon the only way for removing the cruel conqueror from our beloved 'earths and 'omes. It was this 'ero who, 'aving first allowed the invaders to claw each other to 'ash (if I may be permitted the expression) after the well-known precedent of the Kilkenny cats, thereupon firmly and without flinching, stepped bravely in with his fellow-'eros—need I say I allude to our gallant Boy Scouts?—and dexterously gave what-for in no uncertain manner to the few survivors who remained."

Here the orator bowed, and took advantage of the applause to replenish his stock of breath. When his face had begun to lose the purple tinge, he raised his hand.

"I 'ave only to add," he resumed, "that this 'ero is engaged exclusively by the management of the Palace Theatre of Varieties, at a figure previously undreamed of in the annals of the music-hall stage. He is in receipt of the magnificent weekly salary of no less than one thousand one 'undred and fifty pounds a week."

Thunderous applause.

"I 'ave little more to add. This 'ero will first perform a few of those physical exercises which have made our Boy Scouts what they are, such as deep breathing, twisting the right leg firmly round the neck, and hopping on one foot across the stage. He will then give an exhibition of the various calls and cries of the Boy Scouts—all, as you doubtless know, skilful imitations of real living animals. In this connection I 'ave to assure you that he 'as nothing whatsoever in 'is mouth, as it 'as been sometimes suggested. In conclusion he will deliver a short address on the subject of 'is great exploits. Ladies and gentlemen, I have finished, and it only now remains for me to retire, 'aving duly announced to you England's Darling Son, the Country's 'Ero, the Nation's Proudest Possession—Clarence Chugwater."

A moment's breathless suspense, a crash from the orchestra, and the audience are standing on their seats, cheering, shouting, stamping.

A small sturdy, spectacled figure is on the stage.

It is Clarence, the Boy of Destiny.

THE END

THE GERM GROWERS: AN AUSTRALIAN STORY OF ADVENTURE AND MYSTERY BY ROBERT POTTER (AUSTRALIA, 1892)

PRELIMINARY

When I first heard the name of Kimberley[2] it did not remind me of the strange things which I have here to record, and which I had witnessed somewhere in its neighbourhood years before. But one day, in the end of last summer, I overheard a conversation about its geography which led me to recognise it as a place that I had formerly visited under very extraordinary circumstances. The recognition was in this wise. Jack Wilbraham and I were spending a little while at a hotel in Gippsland, partly on a tour of pleasure and partly, so at least we persuaded ourselves, on business. The fact was, however, that for some days past, the business had quite retreated into the background, or, to speak more correctly, we had left it behind at Bairnsdale, and had come in search of pleasure a little farther south.

It was delicious weather, warm enough for light silk coats in the daytime, and cold enough for two pairs of blankets at night. We had riding and sea-bathing to our hearts' content, and even a rough kind of yachting and fishing. The ocean was before us—we heard its thunder night and day; and the lakes were behind us, stretching away to the promontory which the Mitchell cuts in two, and thence to the mouth of the Latrobe, which is the highway to Sale. Three times a week a coach passed our door, bound for the Snowy River and the more savage regions beyond. Any day for a few shillings we could be driven to Lake Tyers, to spend a day amidst scenery almost comparable with the incomparable Hawkesbury. Last of all, if we

---

[2] In North-west Australia.

grew tired of the bell-birds and the gum-trees and the roar of the ocean, we were within a day's journey of Melbourne by lake and river and rail.

It was our custom to be out all day, but home early and early to bed. We used to take our meals in a low long room which was well aired but poorly lighted, whether by day or night. And here, when tea was over and the womenkind had retired, we smoked, whenever, as often happened, the evening was cold enough to make a shelter desirable; smoked and chatted. There was light enough to see the smoke of your pipe and the faces of those near you; but if you were listening to the chatter of a group in the other end of the room the faces of the speakers were so indistinct as often to give a startling challenge to your imagination if you had one, and if it was accustomed to take the bit in its teeth. I sometimes caught myself partly listening to a story-teller in the other end of the room and partly fashioning a face out of his dimly seen features, which quite belied the honest fellow's real countenance when the flash of a pipelight or a shifted lamp revealed it more fully.

Jack and I were more of listeners than talkers, and we were usually amongst the earliest who retired. But one evening there was a good deal of talk about the new gold-field in the north-west, and a keen-looking bushman who seemed to have just returned from the place began to describe its whereabouts. Then I listened attentively, and at one point in his talk, I started and looked over at Jack, and I saw that he was already looking at me. I got up and left the room without a sign to him, but I knew that he would follow me, and he did. It was bright moonlight, and when we met outside we strolled down to the beach together. It was a wide, long, and lonely beach, lonely to the very last degree, and it was divided from the house by a belt of scrub near a mile wide. We said not a word to one another till we got quite near the sea. Then I turned round and looked Jack in the face and said, "Why, man, it must have been quite near the place."

"No," said he, "it may have been fifty miles or more away, their knowledge is loose, and their description looser, but it must be somewhere in the neighbourhood, and I suppose they are sure to find it."

"I do not know," said I; and after a pause I added, "Jack, it seems to me they might pass all over the place and see nothing of what we saw."

"God knows," he muttered, and then he sat down on a hummock of sand and I beside him. Then he said, "Why have you never told the story, Bob?"

"Don't you know why, Jack?" I answered. "They would lock me up in a madhouse; there would be no one to corroborate me but you, and if you did so you would be locked up along with me."

"That might be," said he, "if they believed you; but they would not believe you, they would think you were simply romancing."

"What would be the good of speaking then?" said I.

"Don't speak," he repeated, "but write, *litera scripta manet*, you will be believed sometime. But meanwhile you can take as your motto that verse in Virgil about the gate of ivory, and that will save you from being thought mad. You have a knack of the pen, Bob, you ought to try it."

"Well," said I, "let it be a joint concern between you and me, and I'll do my best."

Then we lit our pipes and walked home, and settled the matter in a very few words on the way. I was to write, but all I should write was to be read over to Jack, who should correct and supplement it from his own memory. And no account of anything which was witnessed by both of us was to stand finally unless it was fully vouched for by the memory of both. Thus for any part of the narrative which would concern one of us only that one should be alone responsible, but for all of it in which we were both concerned there should be a joint responsibility.

Out of this agreement comes the following history, and thus it happens that it is told in the first person singular, although there are two names on the title-page.

CHAPTER ONE
DISAPPEARANCES

Before I begin my story I must give you some account of certain passages in my early life, which seem to have some connection with the extraordinary facts that I am about to put on record.

To speak more precisely, of the connection of one of them with those facts there can be no doubt at all, and of the connection of the other with them I at least have none.

When I was quite a boy, scarce yet fifteen years old, I happened to be living in a parish on the Welsh coast, which I will here call Penruddock. There were some bold hills inland and some very wild and rugged cliffs along the coast. But there was also a well-sheltered beach and a little pier where some small fishing vessels often lay. Penruddock was not yet reached by rail, but forty miles of a splendid road, through very fine scenery, took you to a railway station. And this journey was made by a well-appointed coach on five days of every week.

The people of Penruddock were very full of a queer kind of gossip, and were very superstitious. And I took the greatest interest in their stories. I cannot say that I really believed them, or that they affected me with any real fear. But I was not without that mingled thrill of doubt and wonder which helps one to enjoy such things. I had a double advantage in this way, for I could understand the Welsh language, although I spoke it but little and with difficulty, and I often found a startling family likeness between the stories which I heard in the cottages of the peasantry three or four miles out of town and those which circulated among the English-speaking people in whose village I lived.

There was one such story which was constantly reproduced under various forms. Sometimes it was said to have happened in the last generation; sometimes as far back as the civil wars, of which, strange to say, a lively traditional recollection still remained in the neighbourhood; and sometimes it seemed to have been handed down from prehistoric times, and was associated with tales of enchantment and fairyland. In such stories the central event was always the unaccountable disappearance of some person, and the character of the person disappearing always presented certain unvarying features. He was always bold and fascinating, and yet in some way or other very repulsive. And when you tried to find out why, some sort of inhumanity was always indicated, some unconscious lack of sympathy which was revolting in a high degree or even monstrous. The stories had one other feature in common, of which I will tell you presently.

I seldom had any companions of my own age, and I was in consequence more given to dreaming than was good for me. And I used to marshal the heroes of these queer stories in my day-dreams and trace their likeness one to another. They were often so very unlike in other points, and yet so strangely like in that one point. I remember very well the first day that I thought I detected in a living man a resemblance to those dreadful heroes of my Welsh friend's folk-lore. There was a young fellow whom I knew, about five or six years my senior, and so just growing into manhood. His name, let us say, was James Redpath. He was well built, of middle height, and, as I thought, at first at least, quite beautiful to look upon. And, indeed, why I did not continue to think so is more than I can exactly say. For he possessed very fine and striking features, and although not very tall his presence was imposing. But nobody liked him. The girls especially, although he was so good-looking, almost uniformly shrank from him. But I must confess that he did not seem to care much for their society.

I went about with him a good deal at one time on fishing and shooting excursions and made myself useful to him, and except that he was rather cruel to dogs and cats, and had a nasty habit of frightening children, I do not know that I noticed anything particular about him. Not, at least, until one day of which I am going to tell you. James Redpath and I were coming back together to Penruddock, and we called at a cottage about two miles from the village. Here we found a little boy of about four years old, who had been visiting at the cottage and whom they wanted to send home. They asked us to take charge of him and we did so. On the way home the little boy's shoe was found to have a nail or a peg in it that hurt his foot, and we were quite unable to get it out. It was nothing, however, to James Redpath to carry him, and so he took him in his arms. The little boy shrank and whimpered as he did so. James had under his arm some parts of a fishing-rod and one of these came in contact with the little boy's leg and scratched it rather severely so as to make him cry. I took it away and we went on. I was walking a little behind Redpath, and as I walked I saw him deliberately take another joint of the rod, put it in the same place and then watch the little boy's face as it came in contact with the wire, and as the child cried out I saw quite a malignant expression of pleasure pass over James's face. The thing was done in a moment and it was over in a moment; but I felt as if I should like to have killed him if I dared. I always dreaded and shunned him, more or less, afterwards, and I began from that date to associate him with the inhuman heroes of my Welsh stories.

I don't think that I should ever have got over the dislike of him which I then conceived, but I saw the last of him, at least Penruddock saw the last of him, about three months later. I had been sitting looking over the sea between the pier and the cliffs and trying to catch a glimpse of the Wicklow Mountains which were sometimes to be seen from that point. Just then James Redpath came up from the beach beyond the pier, and passing me with a brief "good morning," went away inland, leaving the cliffs behind him. I don't know how long I lay there, it might be two hours or more, and I think I slept a little. But I suddenly started up to find it high day and past noon, and I began to think of looking for some shelter. There was not a cloud visible, but nevertheless two shadows like, or something like, the shadows of clouds lay near me on the ground. What they were the shadows of I could not tell, and I was about to get up to see, for there was nothing to cast such a shadow within the range of my sight as I lay. Just then one of the shadows came down over me and seemed to stand for a moment between me and the sun. It had a well-defined shape, much too well defined for a cloud. I thought as I looked that it was just such a shadow as might be cast by a yawl-built boat lying on the body of a large wheelbarrow. Then the two shadows seemed to move together and to move very quickly. I had just noticed that they were exactly like one another when the next moment they passed out of my sight.

I started to my feet with a bound, my heart beating furiously. But there was nothing more to alarm the weakest. It was broad day. Houses and gardens were to be seen close at hand and in every direction but one, and in that direction there were three or four fishermen drawing their nets. But as I looked away to the part of the sky where the strange cloudlike shadows had just vanished, I remembered with a shudder that other feature in common of the strange stories of which I told you just now. It was a feature that forcibly reminded me of what I had just witnessed. Sometimes in the later stories you would be told of a cloud coming and going in an otherwise cloudless sky. And sometimes in the elder stories you would be told of an invisible car, invisible but not shadowless. I used always to identify the shadow of the invisible car in the elder stories with the cloud in the later stories, the cloud that unaccountably came and went.

As I thought it all over and tried to persuade myself that I had been dreaming I suddenly remembered that James Redpath had passed by a few hours before, and as suddenly I came to the conclusion that I should never see him again. And certainly he never was again seen, dead or alive, anywhere in Wales or England. His father, and his uncle, and their families, continued to live about Penruddock, but Penruddock never knew James Redpath any more. Whether I myself saw him again or not is more than I can say with absolute certainty. You shall know as much as I know about it if you hear my story to the end.

CHAPTER TWO
THE RED SICKNESS

Of course James Redpath's disappearance attracted much attention, and was the talk not only of the village, but of the whole country-side. It was the general opinion that he must have been drowned by falling over the cliffs, and that his body had been washed out to sea. I proved, however, to have been the very last person to see him, and my testimony, as far as it went, was against that opinion. For I certainly had seen him walking straight inland. Of course he might have returned to the coast afterwards, but at least nobody had seen him return. I gave a full account of place and time as far as I could fix them, and I mentioned the queer-looking clouds and even described their shape. This I remember, was considered to have some value as fixing my memory of the matter, but no further notice was taken of it. And I myself did not venture to suggest any connection between it and Redpath's disappearance, because I did not see how I could reasonably do so. I had, nevertheless, a firm conviction that there was such a connection, but I knew very well that to declare it would only bring a storm of ridicule upon me.

But a public calamity just then befell Penruddock which made men forget James Redpath's disappearance. A pestilence broke out in the place of which nobody knew either the nature or the source. It seemed to spring up in the place. At least, all efforts to trace it were unsuccessful. The first two or three cases were attributed to some inflammatory cold, but it soon became clear that there were specific features about it, that they were quite unfamiliar, that the disease was extremely dangerous to life and highly infectious.

Then a panic set in, and I believe that the disease would soon have been propagated all over England and farther, if it had not been for the zeal and ability of two young physicians who happened very fortunately to be living in the village just then. Their names were Leopold and Furniss. I forget if I ever knew their Christian names. We used to call them Doctor Leopold and Doctor Furniss. They had finished their studies for some little time, but they found it advisable on the score of health to take a longish holiday before commencing practice, and they were spending part of their holiday at Penruddock. They were just about to leave us when the disease I am telling you of broke out.

The first case occurred in a valley about two miles from the village. In this valley there were several cottages inhabited mostly by farm labourers and artisans. These cottages lay one after another in the direction of the rising ground which separated the valley from Penruddock. Then there were no houses for a considerable space. Then, just over the hill, there was another and yet another. The disease had made its way gradually up the hill from one cottage to another, day after day a fresh case appearing. Then there had been no new cases for four days, but on the fifth day a new case appeared in the cottage just over the brow of the hill. And when this became known, also that every case (there had now been eleven) had hitherto been fatal, serious alarm arose. Then, too, the disease became known as the "red sickness." This name was due to a discoloration which set in on the shoulders, neck, and forehead very shortly after seizure.

How the two doctors, as we called them, became armed with the needful powers I do not know. They certainly contrived to obtain some sort of legal authority, but I think that they acted in great measure on their own responsibility.

By the time they commenced operations there were three or four more cases in the valley, and one more in the second cottage on the Penruddock side. There was a large stone house, partly ruinous, in the valley, near the sea, and hither they brought every one of the sick. Plenty of help was given them in the way of beds, bedding, and all sorts of material, but such was the height which the panic had now attained that no one from the village would go near any of the sick folk, nor even enter the valley. The physicians themselves and their two men servants, who seemed to be as fearless and brave as they, did all the work. Fortunately, the two infected cottages on the Penruddock side were each tenanted only by the person who had fallen ill, and the tenant in each case was a labourer whose work lay in the valley. The physicians burnt down these cottages and everything that was in them. Then they established a strict quarantine between the village and the valley. There was a light fence running from the sea for about a mile inland, along the brow of the rising ground on the Penruddock side. This they never passed nor suffered any one to pass, during the prevalence of the sickness. Butchers and bakers and other tradesmen left their wares at a given point at a given time, and the people from the valley came and fetched them.

The excitement and terror in Penruddock were very great. All but the most necessary business was suspended, and of social intercourse during the panic there was next to none. Ten cases in all were treated by the physicians, and four of these recovered. The last two cases were three or four days apart, but they were no less malignant in character: the very last case was one of the fatal ones. I learned nothing of the treatment; but the means used to prevent the disease spreading, besides the strict quarantine, were chiefly fire and lime. Everything about the sick was passed through the fire, and of these everything that the fire would destroy was destroyed. Lime, which abounded in the valley, was largely used.

A month after the last case the two physicians declared the quarantine at an end, and a month later all fear of the disease had ceased. And then the people of the village began to think of consoling themselves for the dull and uncomfortable time they had had, and of doing some honour to the two visitors who had served the village so well. With this double purpose in view a picnic on a large scale was organized, and there was plenty of eating and drinking and speech-making and dancing, all of which I pass over. But at that picnic I heard a conversation which made a very powerful impression on me then, and which often has seemed to provide a bond which binds together all the strange things of which I had experience at the time and afterwards.

In the heat of the afternoon I had happened to be with Mr. Leopold and Mr. Furniss helping them in some arrangements which they were making for the amusement of the children who took part in the picnic. After these were finished they two strolled away together to the side of a brook which ran through the park where we were gathered. I followed them, attracted mainly by Mr. Furniss's dog, but encouraged also by an occasional word from the young men. At the brook Mr. Furniss sat upon a log, and leaned his back against a rustic fence. The dog sat by him; a very beautiful dog he was, black and white, with great intelligent eyes, and an uncommonly large and well-shaped head. He would sometimes stretch himself at length, and then again he would put his paw upon his master's shoulder and watch Mr. Leopold and me.

Mr. Leopold stood with his back to an oak-tree, and I leant against the fence beside him listening to him. He was a tall, dark man, with a keen, thoughtful, and benevolent expression. He was quite strong and healthy-looking, and there was a squareness about his features that I think one does not often see in dark people. Mr. Furniss was of lighter complexion and hardly as tall; there was quite as much intelligence and benevolence in his face, but not so much of what I have called thoughtfulness as distinguished from intelligence, and there was a humorous glint in his eye which the other lacked. They began to talk about the disease which had been so successfully dealt with, and this was what they said:—

Leopold. Well, Furniss, an enemy hath done this.

Furniss. Done what? The picnic or the red sickness?

Leopold. The red sickness, of course. Can't you see what I mean?

Furniss. No, I can't. You're too much of a mystic for me, Leopold; but I'll tell you what, England owes a debt to you and me, my boy, for it was near enough to being a new edition of the black death or the plague.

Leopold. Only the black death and the plague were imported, and this was indigenous. It sprung up under our noses in a healthy place. It came from nowhere, and, thank God, it is gone nowhither.

Furniss. But surely the black death and the plague must have begun somewhere, and they too seem to have gone nowhither.

Leopold. You're right this far that they *all* must have had the same sort of beginning. Only it is given to very few to see the beginning, as you and I have seen it, or so near the beginning.

Furniss. Now, Leopold, I hardly see what you are driving at. I am not much on religion, as they say in America, but I believe there is a Power above all. Call that power God, and let us say that God does as He pleases, and on the whole that it is best that He should. I don't see that you can get much further than that.

Leopold. I don't believe that God ever made the plague, or the black death, or the red sickness.

Furniss. Oh, don't you? Then you are, I suppose, what the churchmen call a Manichee—you believe in the two powers of light and darkness, good and evil. Well, it is not a bad solution of the question as far as it goes, but I can hardly accept it.

Leopold. No, I don't believe in any gods but the One. But let me explain. That is a nice dog of yours, Furniss. You told me one day something about his breeding, and you promised to tell me more.

Furniss. Yes, it is quite a problem in natural history. Do you know, Tommy's ancestors have been in our family for four or five generations of men, and, I suppose, that is twenty generations of dogs.

Leopold. You told me something of it. You improved the breed greatly, I believe?

Furniss. Yes; but I have some distant cousins, and they have the same breed and yet not the same, for they have cultivated it in quite another direction.

Leopold. What are the differences?

Furniss. Our dogs are all more or less like Tommy here, gentle and faithful, very intelligent, and by no means deficient in pluck. My cousin's dogs are fierce and quarrelsome, so much so that they have not been suffered for generations to associate with children. And so they have lost intelligence and are become ill-conditioned and low-lived brutes.

Leopold. But I think I understood you to say that the change in the breed did not come about in the ordinary course of nature.

Furniss. I believe not. I heard my grandfather say that his father had told him that when he was a young man he had set about improving the breed. He had marked out the most intelligent and best tempered pups, and he had bred from them only and had given away or destroyed the others.

Leopold. And about your cousin's dogs?

Furniss. Just let me finish. It seems that while one brother began to cultivate the breed upward, so to speak, another brother was living in a part of the country where thieves were numerous and daring, and there were smugglers and gipsies, and what not, about. And so he began to improve the breed in quite another direction. He selected the fierce and snappish pups and bred exclusively from them.

Leopold. And so from one ancestral pair of, say, a hundred or a hundred and fifty years ago, you have Tommy there, with his wonderful mixture of gentleness and pluck, and his intelligence all but human, and your cousin has a kennel of unintelligent and bloodthirsty brutes, that have to be caged and chained as if they were wild beasts.

Furniss. Just so, but I don't quite see what you are driving at.

Leopold. Wait a minute. Do you suppose the germs of cow-pox and small-pox to be of the same breed?

Furniss. Well, yes; you know that I hold them to be specifically identical. I see what you are at now.

Leopold. But one of them fulfils some obscure function in the physique of the cow, some function certainly harmless and probably beneficent, and the other is the malignant small-pox of the London hospitals.

Furniss. So you mean to infer that in the latter case the germ has been cultivated downwards by intelligent purpose.

Leopold. What if I do?

Furniss. You think, then, that there is a secret guild of malignant men of medicine sworn to wage war against their fellow-men, that they are spread over all the world and have existed since before the dawn of history. I don't believe that there are any men as bad as that, and if there were, I should call them devils and hunt them down like mad dogs.

Leopold. I don't wish to use misleading words, but I will say that I believe there are intelligences, not human, who have access to realms of nature that we are but just beginning to explore; and I believe that some of them are enemies to humanity, and that they use their knowledge to breed such things as malignant small-pox or the red sickness out of germs which were originally of a harmless or even of a beneficent nature.

Furniss. Just as my cousins have bred those wild beasts of theirs out of such harmless creatures as poor Tommy's ancestors.

Leopold. Just so.

Furniss. And you think that we can contend successfully against such enemies.

Leopold. Why not? They can only have nature to work upon. And very likely their only advantage over us is that they know more of nature than we do. They cannot go beyond the limits of nature to do less or more. As long as we sought after spells and enchantments and that sort of nonsense we were very much at their mercy. But we are now learning to fight them with their own weapons, which consist of the knowledge of nature. Witness vaccination, and witness also our little victory over the red sickness.

Furniss. You're a queer mixture, Leopold, but we must get back to the picnic people.

And so they got up and went back together to the dancers, nodding to me as they went. I sat there for awhile, going over and over the conversation in my mind and putting together my own thoughts and Mr. Leopold's.

Then I joined the company and was merry as the merriest for the remainder of the day. But that night I dreamt of strange-looking clouds and of the shadows of invisible cars, and of demons riding in the cars and sowing the seeds of pestilence on the earth and catching away such evil specimens of humanity as James Redpath to reinforce the ranks of their own malignant order.

CHAPTER THREE
AT SEA

It is my purpose to pass briefly over everything in my own history which does not concern the tale that I have to tell, and there is very little therefore for me to say about the seven or eight years which followed upon the events at Penruddock which I have just recorded.

I went in due course to Oxford, where I stayed the usual time. I did not make any great failures there, nor did I gain much distinction. I was a diligent reader, but much of my reading was outside the regulation lines. The literature of my own country, the poetry of mediæval Italy, and the philosophy of modern Germany, more than divided my attention with classics and mathematics. Novels, mostly of the sensational type, amused me in vacations and on holidays, but very seldom found their way into my working days.

I travelled over most of England, Scotland, and Ireland, and spent some time in some of the principal cities of the Continent. I became a fair linguist, speaking German, French, and Italian, with some fluency, although my accent always bewrayed me. I took a second class in classics, bade adieu to Oxford, and began to make up my mind as to what I should do with my life. I had thought of the various professions in turn, and had decided against them all; and, finally, as I had no taste for idleness, and as I had some money, I resolved to invest it in sheep or cattle farming in some of the new countries. I thought successively of New Zealand, the United States, Canada, and Australia, and I was determined in favour of Australia by falling in with Jack Wilbraham. He and I had gone into residence at Oxford about the same time, but not at the same college, and we took our degrees in the same year; but we hardly belonged to the same set. Jack was more of a sporting than a reading man, and I was not much of either, at least as either was understood at the University. So Jack and I, although we heard of one another occasionally, did not meet until a few months before we left Oxford.

Then we became fast friends, and, as he had already determined to go to Australia, I made up my mind to go with him. We took our passage of course in the same ship. It was not yet the day of the great steamers and the canal was not yet open. We sailed from Liverpool in a clipper ship and we went round the Cape. But

I think that we were quite as comfortable and as well taken care of as we should be now in the best of the Orient or Peninsular boats. Our voyage was altogether without disaster. Indeed it was like a picnic of ninety days' duration, and I do not know that I had ever enjoyed any three months of my life as much. But there were no details that I need mention except the fact that we formed an acquaintance (Jack and I) which determined our immediate course on our arrival in Australia, and so led us on to the mysterious experience of which I have to tell.

Not indeed that our new acquaintance was one who might fairly be expected to introduce us to anything mysterious. Mr. Fetherston, as I shall call him here, was a thoroughly good fellow, and proved himself to be a staunch friend, but he was utterly destitute of imagination, and he had the greatest contempt for what he used to call "queer stories"; he used queer in a special sense; he meant simply mysterious, or savouring of what is commonly called the supernatural.

One bright evening in the tropics some such stories were going round. The air was delicious, and the moon and stars were just beginning to shine. The first mate, myself, and Mr. Fetherston were the principal talkers, but we had a good many listeners. The first mate began the conversation by telling two or three stories of the type I have mentioned; one of them especially took my fancy. I cannot remember it in detail, but I know that it was provokingly mysterious, and seemed to admit of no solution but a supernatural one. The main incident was something like this. A farmer who lived about twelve miles from Bristol left home one evening with the intention of spending the night in that city in order to transact some business there at an early hour in the morning. He had to stop at a station about half-way to see some one who lived near there, and then to take another train in. He got out all right at the half-way station and walked towards the man's house whom he wanted to see. A stranger met him on the way and drew him into conversation. As they came to certain cross roads the stranger turned, looked him in the face and said very deliberately, "Go home by next train, you will be just in time." Then he walked away quickly down one of the cross roads. The farmer stood like one stunned for a minute or two, and then hurried after the stranger intending to stop him. But he could see him no more. There were several houses and gardens about and he might have passed into one of them, but anyhow he was lost to sight. The farmer did as he was told and hurried home. He arrived just in time to save his house from being burned to the ground, and more than that, for his wife and children and servants were in bed and asleep.

When the story was told, Mr. Fetherston gave his opinion of it very freely. I never saw contempt more effectually expressed. He spoke without the least atom of temper. Men who get angry and denounce that sort of thing are usually afraid of believing it, or at least of seeming to believe it. Nothing was further from Mr. Fetherston's thought. But you saw plainly that such stories were for him on a level with the most senseless of nursery rhymes and nothing better than mere idiot's chatter. He did not say so in as many words nor at all offensively, but he made it quite clear nevertheless that he felt himself to be looking down from the platform of a mysterious intelligence on some very contemptible folly.

I felt as if reproach were in the air, and I knew that if it were deserved I was one of those who deserved it. So, although it would have been pleasanter to be silent, I felt that I was bound to speak.

So I said, "Mr. Fetherston, isn't it all a matter of evidence?"

Fetherston. Evidence! And pray on what evidence would you believe such a story as that which we have just heard?

Easterley. Upon the statement on the honour of any sane man that I knew and trusted: how I might account for it is another matter.

Fetherston. If a man whom I knew and trusted told me such a story on his honour I should trust him no longer, and I should believe him to be either insane or dishonest.

Easterley. Suppose that ten men whom you knew and trusted agreed in telling you the same story?

Fetherston (with a slight laugh). Then I should begin to suspect that I had gone mad myself, but I should never believe it.

Easterly. Yet you believe a story which is nearly two thousand years old and which is full of mystery from beginning to end: the story of a man who was born mysteriously, who exercised mysterious powers during his life, and after death by violence lived again mysteriously, and at last left this world mysteriously. [Now you must know I spoke here knowing what I was about, for Fetherston was an enthusiastic churchman, and in company with a clergyman who was one of us he had organized a regular Sunday service, and, on the very last Sunday, was one of a small number to whom the clergyman had administered the sacrament.] It seems to me, Mr. Fetherston, I went on to say, that you, like some people I have met, can believe a thing with one side of your head and disbelieve it with the other.

Fetherston. You are certainly like some people I have met. You throw the Christian religion overboard and then you take to believing a lot of puerile absurdities.

Easterly. Softly now, you must not say that I throw the Christian religion overboard. It may be that I do not accept it in quite the same sense as you, still I accept it. And as for the supernatural, if I said that I believed in it or that I did not believe in it, I should most likely to some extent deceive you.

Fetherston. You mean that you could not answer with a plain "yes" or "no."

Easterly. Not quite that; but I could not answer as you do with "yes" and "no." I should have to distinguish.

Fetherston. Distinguish then, please.

Easterley. Well, when you say that you don't believe in the supernatural,

I reply that what I don't believe in is the natural.

Fetherston. I am afraid I must ask you to explain your explanation.

Easterley. What I mean is this. I believe that there is nothing at all, from a bucket of saltwater to the head on your shoulders, of which a full account can be given by any man. You go further and further back until you can get no further, but still you see that you are not at the end. Every natural thing implies a principle which is outside nature.

Fetherston. But you believe that there is a law for everything?

Easterly. I believe that order prevails everywhere, and that everything has its place in that order; you may if you like call that order nature. Then I say that if there be ghosts they are part of nature; they have their place in nature as well as we. And we as well as the ghosts, and the air and the water as well as we, imply something that is not nature. Everything is natural and everything is supernatural.

Fetherston. Easterly, I am afraid you are a philosopher. Come with me to Central Australia and we'll knock the philosophy out of you and make you a practical man.

Easterley. Are you going to Central Australia?

Fetherston. Yes; I am to have charge of a company of surveyors who are to be engaged about the laying of the overland line to Port Darwin.

Easterley. I'll think of it. I rather think I should like it. I suppose we shall see no ghosts there, Fetherston?

Fetherston. I don't know about that. I dare say we may, for we shall often have to live on salt junk and damper.

So there our talk ended. I had heard of Mr. Fetherston's business before, and even I believe of his destination; but I had forgotten the particulars, and certainly it never had struck me that I should care to go with him. But now I thought I should like to talk it over with Jack. So I went in search of him. I found him by himself at the farthest aft part of the ship, standing just above the companion with his back against a rail. He had been chatting with two or three of the ladies, and they had just gone below. He came at once to meet me, and we both went forward and lit our pipes and smoked some time in silence. Then Jack spoke. "I see that you have something to say, Bob; what is it?"

"Fetherston," said I, "is going with a survey party to assist in laying the overland wire to Port Darwin: he proposes that we should go with him; he was only in jest, but I think I should like it."

Jack thought it would be a very good beginning: we should see much of the country, we should get experience, and have something to talk about. Poor Jack! if he had only known! We have never ventured to talk much about that journey, not much to one another, and not at all to anyone else; but I must not anticipate. We both took a fancy to the scheme. There would be much of the interest of exploring without any of the special risks. We would, no doubt, have some hardships to put up with, but there would be depôts at intervals along the way, and our communication would be kept open all through. So I spoke to Fetherston a few days later. "Fetherston," I said, "will you take two volunteers with you on your survey party northward? We shall pay our own expenses, but we shall want your guidance and protection, and we shall have nothing to give you in return but our company."

Fetherston said that he thought it might on such terms be easily managed, and it was managed accordingly.

CHAPTER FOUR
OVERLAND

Jack and I had intended to go on to Melbourne and thence to Sydney, but upon our arrival at Adelaide we found that arrangements had been made which required that Mr. Fetherston should start northward as soon as possible. We had, therefore, little enough time to make preparation for the journey, and so we had to give up for the present all thought of making acquaintance with the great Australian cities. Mr. Fetherston, although he was but little over thirty years old, was a veteran Australian explorer; for about ten years before he had been with Stuart on his third and successful expedition in search of a practicable route from Adelaide to the Indian Ocean, and all the time since, except about a year and a half in England and on the way there and back, he had spent in pioneering work in Queensland and the north.

The undertaking in which he was now engaged was in rather a critical condition. The entire length of the route, from Adelaide to Port Darwin, would be about two thousand miles, and over the central section of eight hundred miles, passing through, as some would have thought, the most difficult part of the line, the wire had been already carried. And after some further delay this had been connected with Adelaide. But about six hundred miles at the northern extremity still remained unfinished. The first expedition for the purpose had absolutely failed, and one or two attempts made since had not been any more successful. The chief superintendent of the work was either about to start for Port Darwin by sea, or was already on his way. And Mr. Fetherston's expedition was to meet him in the north. They expected to hear of one another somewhere about the Daly Waters. So there would be no work but simply travelling until that point was reached; none, at least, for Mr. Fetherston's party.

Mr. Fetherston introduced us to his chief assistant, Mr. Berry, telling us that we could do no better than take his advice about our preparation for the journey. Mr. Berry was also a veteran bushman and an experienced surveyor. He had been to Cooper's Creek twice, and he knew the Darling from Bourke to

Wentworth as well as King William Street and the North Terrace. So Jack and I put ourselves into his hands. We purchased two strong saddle horses, each with colonial saddles of the sort used by stockmen, and everything to match. We hired a man, specially recommended as a good bushman by Mr. Berry. This man was to ride one horse and to lead another, so that we should have one spare horse in case of accident. Mr. Fetherston introduced us also to the department which had oversight of the work. And they allowed us to pay a bulk sum to cover our expenses on the journey. The sum seemed to me very moderate, but, as Berry explained, "it was only to cover tucker and tents;" and the former was to be of a very simple and primitive sort, consisting simply of tea and sugar, salt meat and flour, and lime-juice, and we were to manage our cooking the best way we could. The store waggons would carry tobacco and soap; but these were to be sold, and Mr. Berry advised us to take a private supply of the former. We also procured a revolver each, and as many cartridges as we could conveniently carry. We each provided ourselves with a pair of blankets, an opossum rug, a couple of changes of coarse outside clothing, and half-a-dozen flannel shirts. Our dressing gear was limited to a comb and a toothbrush each, with a few coarse towels. The towels and shirts we hoped to be able to wash from time to time on the way, and Mr. Berry told us that at depôts along the line there would sometimes be a supply of flannel shirts, and moleskin trousers, and cabbage-tree hats. The cabbage-tree hat was the head gear that we adopted by his advice.

    Before leaving Adelaide we put our money in the bank, arranging that it should bear interest at some low rate for six months, and then we made our wills, which we left in the safe belonging to the bank. By Mr. Fetherston's advice we took very little money with us. A few sovereigns and some silver, he said, would be more than enough. Whatever we might buy at the Government depôts would be paid for by cheque, and if we should have occasion and opportunity to purchase fresh horses our cheques, endorsed by Mr. Fetherston, would be readily accepted.

    Mr. Berry, with the horses and waggons, left Adelaide within a week of our arrival here. Mr. Fetherston, Jack, and I, remained a week or ten days longer. It was arranged that we should join them at Port Augusta, whence the real start would be made. Most of the time thus gained Jack and I spent in trying to make ourselves as well acquainted as possible with the route we were to travel by, and its position with reference to the other parts of Australia. In the Government office there were several charts and plans which we were permitted to study and to copy. The route was in the main identical with Stuart's track, but of much of the northern extremity it seemed to us doubtful if it had ever been surveyed at all. Of the other parts, however, a good deal was known, and the creeks and ranges were laid down with much apparent precision. Parts of the route might prove to be almost impracticable after a dry season, but as far as our information went, the worst country would be met with, not in the far interior but somewhere between Port

Augusta and a point a little north of Lake Eyre.

Mr. Fetherston, Jack, and I, left Port Adelaide for Port Augusta the first week in November in a slow little steamer that took near a week on the passage; and we had to stay nearly another week at Port Augusta before the overland party arrived. I remember nothing of Port Augusta except a very miserable public-house, at which we lodged, and the sand hills, long, low, and white.

On the 20th of November we were well on the road, and we hoped to reach Daly Waters in about three months, and Mr. Fetherston expected that the line would be open to Port Darwin in about three months more. I may as well say here that it was in fact opened in the month of August, just nine months after we left Port Augusta.

We travelled over a very miserable country for some weeks. Not a really green thing was to be seen, and water was very scarce and bad. And the heat was excessive, far worse than we found it on any other part of the route; far worse, indeed, than any heat that I have ever endured either in Australia or elsewhere.

But after we had passed Lake Eyre a little way the country and the climate began to improve. And we had pleasant enough travelling until we got far beyond Alice's Springs. We had reached or passed the seventeenth degree of latitude before the water began to get very scarce or the ground very difficult again. There was not much variety in the scenery. We passed through long tracts of wooded country, and again over nearly treeless plains, and again over a succession of low hills, some bald and some covered with forest. Though none of them attained any considerable height, they sometimes assumed very remarkable forms. We met several creeks whose course was in the main dry, with here and there, however, ponds or water holes from ten or twenty to several hundred feet long. At the larger ponds we often got a variety of water fowl, but in general along the route there was a great scarcity of game.

Mr. Berry had in his own special service a certain Australian black with whom Jack and I formed an intimate acquaintance—of which and of whom I must tell you something; for if it had not been for him Jack and I would never have left the beaten track, and so this book would never have been written.

His name was Gioro; that was the way we came to spell it, although J o r o would perhaps have been the better and simpler spelling, He was the most remarkable Australian black that I have ever met, and I have met a great many under a great variety of conditions and circumstances, and I find myself unable to differ seriously from the common estimate which places them near the very end of the scale. As a general rule (and I have only known the one exception), they have no really great qualities, none of those which are sometimes attributed to other barbarous races, as, for instance, to the American red man and even to the negro. But Gioro had qualities that would have done honour to the highest race on earth. He always spoke the truth, and he seemed to take it for granted that those to whom he spoke would also speak the truth. He had lived with white men in the North, and they must have been fine fellows, for he spoke of them always with respect, whereas he spoke with disgust and contempt of certain mean whites of Adelaide who had attempted to cheat him in some way. He never put himself forward, but if he were put forward by others who were in power he accepted the position as his right quite simply. He was as honest as the sun, and he was loyal through and through. He had even the manner of a gentleman. Mr. Fetherston's tent was notably the largest in our camp, and the union jack floated over it on Sundays. And every Sunday all the officers and volunteers, that is to say, Mr. Fetherston, Mr. Berry and his assistant, Jack and myself, dined there in a sort of state; and it was Mr. Fetherston's wont to have in one of the men to make the number even. And Gioro took his turn with us two or three times and was far the best conducted of those who were so invited. His ease of manner was perfect: he was as gentle and suave as an English nobleman; there was not a spark of self-assertion about him, and yet there was, or there seemed to be, a quiet consciousness of equality with his entertainers. He was also very courteous without being in the least bit cringing. He was glad always to teach us anything that we didn't know and that he knew, and he was grateful for being taught something in turn. Jack, for instance, took a great interest in the boomerang, and Gioro took much pains to teach him how to use it and how to make it. Jack had been distinguished at Oxford for his athletics. And these were a great bond between him and Gioro. He taught him several athletic feats, and Gioro's great suppleness of body enabled him to acquire them readily.

It was curious to notice the impression which his character made upon the men. His name suggested a very ready abbreviation, and indeed, he was often known in the camp as "Jo." But I never heard any one but Jack address him so. And Jack, as I have said, was more intimate with him than any of us. One day, quite near the beginning of the expedition, Fetherston called him "Sir Gioro." I don't quite know what he meant, probably nothing more than a humourous recognition of the black man's unassuming dignity. Anyhow, the title stuck, and one heard his name afterwards, quite as often with the addition as without it.

He had not been at all corrupted by his intercourse with white men. That intercourse had indeed been very limited. He had spent the greater part of two years with some settlers near the Gulf, and he learned there a sort of pigeon English which enabled him to converse with us. He had come to Adelaide with some of the party who had been engaged in one of the unsuccessful attempts to complete the northern extremity of the overland wire. His engagement with Mr. Berry was terminable at pleasure on either side. From the account which he gave of himself I should think that he was about twenty-five years old: he had visited his own people since the commencement of his sojourn with white men, and he intended to visit them again. I had learned all this from him before we were halfway to the Daly Waters.

One evening, after we had passed the tropic, we camped earlier than usual because we had come upon a creek where there were tracks of wallaby and other game, and Gioro was very busy setting snares for them and showing us how to make and set such snares. The occupation seemed to remind him of his sojourn with the white men near the Gulf. So when we sat down to smoke, Gioro, Jack and I, Gioro said, "Way there," pointing to the north-east after looking at the stars, "two three white men, sheep, two three, two three, two three, great many; one man not white man, not black man, pigtail man, and Gioro." "And what," said Jack, "were they doing there, and what were you doing there?" "Pigtailman cook, wash clothes, white man ride after sheep, dogs too, Gioro ride, speak English, snare wallaby."

"How long did he stay there?" One year six months.

"How long since he left?" One year.

I will not give you much of Gioro's dialect; it was many days before I could readily understand him, and it was not a sort of dialect which is worth studying for its own sake. I learned from him that he belonged to a strong and populous tribe which occupied part of the country to the west of the Daly Waters. They had a king or chief whom Gioro held in the highest regard. His name was Bomero: the accent on the first syllable and the final "o" short like the "o" in rock. This Bomero was a great warrior and a mighty strong man, and possessed of great personal influence. It was my fate, as you shall hear, to make his acquaintance, and I found him by no means the equal of Gioro in any of the greatest qualities of the man or the gentleman. Like some public leaders among more civilised people he owed his position partly to his fluent persuasiveness, partly to his violent self-assertiveness, and more than all to what I must call his roguery. Black men and white men are wonderfully like in some things.

Bomero seemed to have attained his power on the strength of these endowments alone. At least I could not learn anything decisive about his ancestry. Indeed, I could not gather that his people had any but the most elementary sense of the family relation, although tribal feeling, as distinct from family feeling, was very strong among them. Gioro had some recollection of "Old man Bomero," and his recollections would sometimes appear to indicate that Old man Bomero was a remarkable black fellow, but I could not discover that he ever attained to any position of special eminence among them. He certainly had not been their king as Bomero was.

I was at this time beginning to have some thought of a couple of days' expedition into the unexplored country to the west of the Daly Waters, and I had hinted as much to Jack. And I thought that the present was a good opportunity to find how far Gioro might be depended on as a guide. So I filled his pipe with my own tobacco (he was quite able to distinguish and prefer the flavour), and then I gave Jack a look to bespeak his attention, and began to put my questions.

"When would Sir Gioro see his own people again?"

Several slow puffs, a keen, eager, honest look, yet, withal, a cautious look, and then,

"May be one two months."

Then I said, "No water out west—die of thirst?"

"Now," said Gioro, nodding his head affirmatively, "but in one two months, no, no."

I saw that he meant either that after three months there would be wet weather, or that within three months we should have a better-watered country westward. So I said, pointing west, "What's out there?"

"No water, no grass, no duck, no black fellow."

"But," said I, looking northward, "we go on one two months, and then?" making a half-turn to face the west.

"Then," said he, "plenty grass, plenty fish, plenty duck, plenty black fellow."

"Everywhere?" said I, sweeping my arm all round the horizon.

"No, no, here, there, there. Gioro know the way, Bomero know the way, find Bomero, find water."

"What," said I, not understanding him, "Bomero make rain?"

But he replied with great contempt, "Bomero make rain! No, no. Bomero not witchfellow. No fear. Bomero make witchfellow make rain."

I think it was on this occasion that we ascertained that Gioro fully intended to go away westward in search of his tribe, who, as he expected, would be found in about three months at a point with which he was familiar at some uncertain distance from the Daly Waters.

They kept a great feast every year. It seemed to have some connection with the Pleiades and Aldebaran, for it was always celebrated when these stars were in conjunction with the sun. Several kindred tribes kept it, each in his own place westward, and every three years all the tribes who kept the feast celebrated it all together in a place farther west still. The triennial celebration was approaching, and Gioro intended to be there. He knew the way by which Bomero and his people would be travelling; he would cross their course, meet them, and go with them to the trysting-place.

Jack suggested that he and I and Gioro should all go together and visit his tribe.

Gioro hesitated for a little while, but after some apparently careful thought he said yes, he thought we could go.

After that we often talked it over with him, learning from him what we could about the disposition of his tribesmen towards white men, and about the distance of the triennial meeting-place of the tribes. It was quite impossible to say how far or how near this meeting-place might be; and on this depended in my judgment the practicability of the scheme. But at least, I thought, if the black fellows were friendly we might, under Gioro's guidance and protection, see a good deal of strange life and return home in a few days by the way we came. As far as I could gather, Gioro was the only one of his tribe that had ever seen a white man, although they had often heard of them, and curiosity rather than fear seemed to have been for some time the dominant feeling about them. But quite lately, for some reason or other, their fear began to exceed their curiosity.

The cause of this change was evidently something that had happened in the far west; some encounter with white men as Jack and I thought at first. But we had reason afterwards, as you will hear, to think that we were mistaken.

One evening I said to Gioro, "When did you see your people last?" He looked at the stars, and I knew he was going to be exact. Then he said, "One year."

"Did you tell Bomero then about the white men?"

"Yes, tell Bomero. Bomero never see white man."

"What did Bomero say?"

"Bomero say, white man all same dibble dibble."

"But Bomero never saw dibble dibble?"

"Yes, Bomero saw dibble dibble one, two, three, two two, two three, great many."

"Where?"

"Far away west."

"Where black fellows meet every three years?"

"More far."

"Bomero saw white men, not dibble dibble."

"No fear, Bomero saw dibble dibble and run away. Bomero run away from no man, black man, pigtail man, white man; but Bomero run from dibble dibble."

"Did any black fellow but Bomero see dibble dibble?"

"Yes, two three black fellow, more, all run away."

"And what like was dibble dibble?"

"White man all same dibble dibble."

That was all I could ever get out of him on the subject.

I spoke to Mr. Fetherston about our purpose of going westward with Gioro. He shook his head very gravely. "Well, Easterley," said he, "if you will be guided by me you will do nothing of the sort. You see we know next to nothing of those north-west blacks, and if you go it is even betting that you never come back. If you get, say, a hundred miles west of here you will be entirely dependent on the blacks. You will have to live among them, and to live as they live, if they let you live at all."

"But we have our compasses and the telegraph line."

"That would be all very well if it were a country through which you could make a 'bee line.' But you will want water and food, and you cannot get either without the help of the blacks."

"But," said I, "Gioro will come back with us."

"Gioro is a very good fellow, but if I were you I would not put myself altogether in his hands like that. He won't understand your anxiety to get away; he will think you are very well as you are. His interest in his own people will make him careless about you."

"But I know Gioro well, and I should trust him anywhere." So said I, and Jack eagerly agreed with me.

"But," said Mr. Fetherston, "Gioro may die or may be killed; they fight a great deal, and those who have been among white men are often subject to special enmity."

"I expect we shall have to chance that," said Jack. "Any of us may die or be killed."

"Well, gentlemen, wilful men you know— I don't pretend to any right to constrain you, only let it be fully understood that if you go, you go against my wish and in defiance of my advice."

We agreed that everyone should know that, and so the matter dropped.

The road was now growing very difficult, the water scarcer, and the timber very much denser. But we pushed on little by little from day to day. We were ascending slowly the watershed between the north and south, and we had left behind us the last point to which the wire had yet been carried, when one morning Mr. Fetherston, after a specially careful observation, announced that within three days we might expect to meet the superintendent's party from the north, if all had gone well with them. The same afternoon Gioro took me aside, and told me that he meant to start the day after the next in search of Bomero and his people. We had come, he said, to certain landmarks that he recognised. The tribe would be already on the march, and he was confident that he could pick them up by following the water until it crossed their track. Next day was not Sunday, but we made a Sunday of it. We camped early, the Union Jack was hoisted, and Mr. Fetherston, the officers and volunteers, with one guest selected from the men in charge of the teams, sat down to dinner together. The man selected was a bushman of great and well-known experience, and, like Mr. Fetherston, he had been with Stuart on one or more of his exploring expeditions. I guessed from his presence that Mr. Fetherston intended that I should before the evening was over state my intention of going westward. Accordingly, when dinner was over and as we were about to light our pipes, I said before them all,

"Well, Mr. Fetherston, my friend Wilbraham and I are going to leave you for a few days at least. We propose to go westward with Sir Gioro, in order to see something of the aborigines. We may be back within a week, but we may push on with the blacks into the interior, and perhaps we may make for the north-west or west coast."

Mr. Fetherston turned to the man of whom I spoke just now and said:

"Well, Tim, what do you say to that?"

The man turned to me and said: "I didn't quite catch all you said, governor. Would you mind saying it again?"

I repeated what I had said. "Well," he replied, "it has been a main wet season out north, that I can see, and if you don't go more than forty or fifty miles from the track you may get back within a week safe enough." He paused for a moment, and looked me steadily in the face, and went on—

"But, governor, if you go for the second part of the programme you'll never see a white man again."

"Why so?" said I.

"Well," said he, "you are depending on Gioro. Now Gioro is a good fellow, far the best black fellow I ever knew by a very long way. And my best hope for you is that Gioro will take you back once he has had a look at his people. He will, if he knows what will happen as well as I know it."

"And what will happen?" said I.

"Well, they'll kill Gioro before he has been very long among them. Sooner or later they always kill the blacks that have been among white men."

"And then," struck in Jack, "I suppose they will kill us."

"They may and they may not. You have ten times a better chance that Gioro. But if they don't you will be as good as their slaves for life. You won't be able to get back unless they take you back, and they will never take you back."

"Suppose we start to return on our own account?"

"Well," said the man, "if you are not more than forty or fifty miles to the west of the wire when you make the start eastward, and if you are able to make straight for the wire you may get back. But if you are much further away, or if you have to go a long way round you'll die of thirst or hunger in the bush." I noticed that he put thirst first.

"And, mind," he went on, "the chances are that you will be three times fifty miles to the west before you think of turning back."

"Why?"

"Because it's easy enough to travel with the blacks, easy enough for men of your sort, men that are hardy and are up to larks. The blacks know how to get food and water and fire, and you can live while in their company. It's only when you leave them that you will be done for."

Here Jack chimed in again. "Never mind," said he, "Mr. Easterly and I are going to try it, win or lose. Besides, after what you have told us, I wouldn't let poor 'Jo' go alone. We'll save him and he'll help us."

The answer came slowly. "Jo is your trump card, certainly . . . . and your only one."

Then Fetherston spoke. "Gentlemen, if I were your master I should absolutely forbid you to go, but I have not the right to interfere with your liberty. But

I am glad that you have had the benefit of Mr. Blundell's experience." (Mr. Blundell was Tim.) "His opinion and mine coincide exactly."

"Well," said I, "Mr. Fetherston, we will be careful and we will bear in mind your advice, and I think it is on the whole most probable that you will see us back within the week."

"Possible," said Jack.

They all looked very sober then, and nothing more was said on the subject, and indeed little on any subject until the company broke up.

CHAPTER FIVE
AMONG THE BLACKS

Our preparation for this madcap expedition was very soon made. We took our horses, for on foot we could not keep up with Gioro, and it was better to have the full benefit of his fleetness. We strapped our blankets to the pommels of our saddles. Jack carried a small fowling-piece, and I carried a pistol. We both had serviceable knives. A few small packages of tea and tobacco and what we thought a fair supply of ammunition completed *impedimenta.*

We left our spare horse in charge of our man, and entrusted Mr. Fetherston with a cheque sufficient to pay the man's wages and to give him a small gratuity on his return to Adelaide. Meantime he was to be in Mr. Fetherston's service until we should rejoin the expedition, and if we did not rejoin it before its return to Adelaide then Tim Blundell was to have the horse. Early in the forenoon Gioro showed me a hill which seemed to be about ten miles away (it proved to be much further). He told us that at the foot of that hill we should find a creek which we had crossed at an earlier part of its course the afternoon before, and that creek we must follow down. Mr. Fetherston had the same hill marked on his chart, and his instructions were that when he was abreast of it he was to turn to the right nearly at right angles. So that when he should make this turn that must be our signal for parting with him. As we did not get abreast of the hill until it was rather late in the afternoon, we camped a little earlier than usual, and Gioro, Jack, and I deferred our departure until the next day. Shortly after sunrise we bade adieu to our friends with those noisy demonstrations on both sides which often serve the Englishman as a decent veil for those deeper feelings which he nearly always hesitates to show. The landscape here consisted of grassy slopes and plains, alternating with belts of well-forested country. We were in the middle of a plain when we parted from our fellow-travellers, and our courses were not in quite opposite directions; ours was about north-west, and theirs east-north-east. So while we remained in the plain we could see our fellow-travellers by simply looking to the right, and they us by looking to the left. So for a while there was much waving of hats on both sides. But the first belt of timber that we entered hid them from our sight. And then I think for the first time I became fully aware of the meaning of what we were doing.

"Jack, my boy!" said I, giving my horse a slight cut, so that he bounded forward, "we're in for it now."

"You don't seem sorry for if, Bob," said he, urging his horse to join me.

Truly neither of us was sorry for it. A new spirit of independence and love of adventure sprang up within us. We were young and well and strong. The morning air was fresh; the unaccustomed aspect of the forest, the screams of a flock of savage birds of the cockatoo sort that seemed as if they were making for the same hill as ourselves, the aspect of our native guide, who trotted on with his body slightly bent forward, and with the confident air of one who had "been there before," all stirred us to a sense of strangeness and expectance which was quite a joy. Even the warnings of Mr. Fetherston and Tim Blundell seemed only to intensify the joy.

"For if a path be dangerous known,
The danger's self is lure alone."

All the way from Port Augusta, Gioro had been dressed like the rest of us; he had worn a pair of moleskin trousers, a flannel shirt, and a cabbage-tree hat. But now he had discarded all these, and he wore nothing but a kilt of matting and a head-dress which consisted of a string bound round his brows adorned with the tails of the small wild animals of the bush and one large opossum tail hanging down behind. He ran on steadily towards the hill, which we reached in three or four hours from the start. It was rather a remarkable hill, as we saw when we reached it. Sloping gradually from the side on which we approached, it was on the opposite side steep and even precipitous. The creek ran on the far side, and the shadow of the hill lay still across it. It was about half-past ten when we reached it, and we rested until about an hour after noon. We made a can of tea and drank it. We had neither milk nor sugar, but we had a few biscuits and some slices of meat. Jack and I wondered where our next meal was to come from, but Gioro did not seem at all anxious. We could not, however, get a word out of him about the matter except "plenty duck."

We made a start in the direction of west by north, or thereabouts, Gioro leading the way and we following blindly. He ran more carefully and rather more slowly, but there was still the same air of confidence about him. It was now very hot, but as we were well within the tropics, and the sun at noon was now as nearly as we could reckon vertical, the only wonder was that it was not much hotter. We must have been still high up on the watershed, although descending it on the northern slope. There was plenty of grass everywhere, and a good deal of timber, not so much, however, as to obstruct our passage or impede our view. The country was undulating, but there were no steep hills to be traversed. We passed a considerable herd of kangaroo and two or three dingoes, and there were many birds, chiefly crows, parrots, and cockatoos.

It was getting near sundown when we reached the summit of one of those low hills, and Gioro clapped his hands and shouted. We saw nothing but another hill, but it was clear that he recognised it, for he clapped his hands again and again, pointed towards it and said, "Plenty duck." He did not shape his course so as to cross the hill, but made for the point where it merged into the plain. And when we reached that point a sudden turn revealed a beautiful sheet of water, not very wide, but several hundred yards long, and consisting of two parts lying nearly at right angles to each other. This was the same creek which we had passed in the morning, but here it was much wider and deeper. Gioro stopped short and signed to us to stop. We did so at once, for we saw that the farther part of the water was alive with duck, and on the wider part nearer to us were several black swans. We turned immediately towards a grove of trees that lay between us and the water, and we dropped down. Gioro laid his hand on me, looked at Jack, pointed to the water and said, "Shoot." Jack stole to the water-side and shot a swan easily. It was not very near the others and none of the birds flew away. It was most likely the first time that firearms had been discharged there. Jack then shot several ducks and rejoined us. Gioro threw off his kilt and swam out for the birds. The moment his woolly head was seen over water all the birds flew away. We lit a fire at once, prepared and cooked our birds, and made a hearty meal. As we began to eat I remembered for the first time that we had no salt. I suppose I made a wry face, for Gioro grinned and pointed to a small bag which was fastened outside his kilt. This was full of salt, which he had thoughtfully provided for the dainty appetites of his white friends.

We slept sound and long that night, and in the morning Jack and I had a delicious bath, and washed our shirts and dried them in the sun. Going back to our camp we found a pleasant surprise awaiting us. Gioro had snared some wild creature—I think it was a bandicoot—and had baked it for breakfast. It was very nice, at least we thought so, and he was quite delighted when he saw that we enjoyed it. After breakfast we made an early start.

Two more days passed like this one. Each evening Gioro guided us to water and food, and all the time our course was in the main west by north or west-north-west. It was clear that we were following some river or creek downward, and so there were considerable occasional variations in the direction that we took, but we never headed south of west or east of north. On the morning of the third day Gioro speared a large fish. I think it was a variety of perch; it was very good eating.

This third morning we left the creek nearly at right angles and struck across the forest, and our guide was evidently more sharply on the watch than ever. He travelled very slowly now and he seemed to be looking everywhere for some local indications. After about two miles travelling we came again upon a creek, as far as I could judge a different one. It was very narrow and scarcely running. There was one very fair pond, however, but Gioro took scarce any notice of it, but ran on to the dry or nearly dry bed of the creek beyond. Here he set up a triumphant yell, and signed to us to come and see. I saw plainly enough what I thought at first to be a cattle track coming from the north-east and passing right across the bed of the creek. I looked at Gioro and said, "Sheep?" "No, no," he shouted, "no sheep; black fellow, black fellow," and stooping down he pointed at the track. I stooped also and examined it, and sure enough I could see plainly the mark of human feet. "When shall we catch them up, Sir Gioro?" said I. "Tonight," he shouted; "to-night, Corrobboree! Corrobboree!"

We followed the track without pause, and by-and-by more tracks joined it, all from the north or east or from some point between these. There could be no doubt at all that we were approaching some camping-place of the blacks. Our course was now almost directly westward, with a very slight trend to the north, and the country still continued much of the same sort, undulating perhaps a little more, well grassed and fairly but not very thickly timbered. Wild animals and birds were much more numerous.

It was after sunset, the moon which was now nearly half way between new and full was well up in the sky, there was a strange glimmer in the west that looked like an aurora, and Gioro was in a state of high excitement when the pathway bending round the foot of a somewhat steeper hill than we had seen during the day suddenly brought us within sight of a single fire. It was evidently just freshly kindled, but there was no one near it now. Gioro stopped, looked at us, and put his hand to his mouth. Then we made a half turn silently, still following the track, and all in a moment we came in view of the most striking sight that I had yet seen in Australia, or for the matter of that anywhere in the world.

We saw an irregular line of large fires burning before us, and immediately behind them stretched a sheet of water much wider and longer than any that we had yet seen in the country. The fires were vividly reflected in the water, and seemed at the first glance quite innumerable. After a time one saw that there were at least sixty or eighty of them. Near each fire was a group of black men, clad like Gioro, holding in their hands long staves or spears, and dancing furiously. They kept springing into the air with their feet quivering, and striking their spears, butt ends downwards, violently upon the ground. Presently they burst into a wild shout, or series of shouts. The shouts came in measured cadence, but were frightfully discordant. Their dance kept time to their music, and the whole effect was wildly barbarous. There were huts in great numbers built of branches, and covered with leaves and bark. As far as I could see there was a hut for each fire, and women and children of all ages were to be seen in front of the huts, some few of them apparently partaking of the excitement of the dancers, but far the greater number stolidly looking on. The dress of the women was nearly the same as that of the men. The kilt of matting was the same, but the head-dress showed more effort after ornament. It covered more of the head, and it was adorned with the feathers of cockatoos and parrots. The children who ran about were mostly naked. There were several dogs, not at all Australian dingoes, but miserable half-starved mongrels of European breed. Many of the women were engaged in cooking food, and some whiffs of smoke which reached us were by no means of unpleasant flavour.

All the while the song and dance lasted we lay quite still, hidden by the scrub which grew very thick here, and seemed to be a sort of stunted eucalyptus, and very like the mallee of Southern Australia. Our horses were hidden by the turn of a hill, and by a large tree near, and when the song and dance would pause for a moment, we could hear them munching the grass. I was at first greatly afraid that they would be startled by the noise and by the fires, but somehow they seemed to take no notice. They were accustomed to camp fires and singing, but not to such singing as that. When the song and the dance were ended, Gioro touched us, pointed and whispered, "Bomero, boss black fellow, see!" We looked in the direction of his finger, and could easily see a very tall and bulkily built black, with a very massive head, and dressed with some attempt at distinction. His kilt of matting was larger than any of those worn by others, and was rather elaborately ornamented with feathers. His head-dress was very much larger, and he wore besides a sort of little cloak of skins thrown over his shoulder, and fastened with some kind of thong. Gioro whispered again, "Stay! Gioro speak to Bomero, then come back." With this he stood erect, spear in hand, and advanced towards the fire where the tall black stood, dancing all the time rather gently, and singing rather softly, but exactly the same step and tune which we had just heard and seen. We followed him closely with our eyes, and we were in a state of great excitement and suspense.

He was noticed almost immediately, but there was hardly any sign of surprise, and none at all of hostility. I suppose that his dance and song secured him for the time from either. Bomero stepped out to meet him, followed by three or four other blacks. Gioro continued his dance and song till he came quite up to them, and then he went round them still dancing and singing. He stopped right in front of Bomero. And there seemed to follow a sort of obeisance and salutation, and then a palaver.

As the palaver proceeded the blacks became greatly excited, and more of them gathered round. No doubt he was telling them about us. I felt for my pistol, and looked towards the horses. I could still hear them munching the grass.

Presently Gioro came towards us, looking quite cheerful and confident. He told us that Bomero wished to see us and bid us welcome. We fetched our horses, and we led them with us, holding ourselves in readiness to mount at a moment's notice.

As we marched up to the camp great excitement prevailed, and we were presently surrounded by a vast concourse of men, women, and children. Some half dozen of the blacks around Bomero armed themselves with boughs of trees, and kept the crowd at a sufficient distance.

Bomero came towards us with spear in hand, and two men on each side of him also with spears. We made a sort of military salute, which he seemed to understand, and made an attempt to return. Then he began to talk. When he ceased, I turned to Gioro and said, "What says Bomero?"

Gioro looked first at Bomero, and then at me, then quite rapidly, "Bomero, say, know all about white fellow; white fellow ride on horse, keep cattle, keep sheep, carry fire spear. Bomero say white fellow hold fire spear in hand, throw away only point, but point kill. Sometime one point, sometime two, three points, two three. Bomero say, Good-morrow to white fellow. White fellow all same black fellow. Black fellow take white fellow to great Corrobboree far away west when the one[3] white, star rise, and red star and little stars go."

I replied with all the dignity that I could muster, "Right, all right; say to Bomero, 'thanks.' King Bob and king Jack all same king Bomero. King Bob and king Jack will go with king Bomero to great Corrobboree when the one white star rises, and the red star and the little stars go."

Then we were told that our miami must be built and that we must have meat and sleep, as we should have to start with the sun. They fell to work, Gioro and two or three others, and built a sort of hut in an incredibly short time, and then we supped on fish and wild duck and paste made with water of the seeds of some native grass. I think it was "nardoo." We had also a fruit which I have seen nowhere else, about the size of a loquat, of a pinkish colour and subacid in taste. After supper we had a palaver, Gioro being the interpreter, and then we went to bed. Jack and I slept well and rose before sunrise in order to get a bath before starting. Several of the blacks followed us to the water's edge and some of them plunged into the water after us. I didn't half like it as they swam round and round us; but they were more afraid of us than we of them.

Then we breakfasted and made a start. For twelve days we travelled on, still heading mainly westward, running down a watercourse, then crossing to

---

[3] The red star is certainly Aldebaran, and the little stars the Pleiades. I could not for a long time understand "the one white star." There is at present no large white star in opposition to Aldebaran. I first thought that Arcturus might be meant, and that the feast had perhaps come down from a period when Arcturus was a white star. But I now think that Spica Virginis is "the one white star." I think that by "rises," or more properly, "has risen," Gioro meant "has culminated;" for Gioro usually spoke of "rising" and "setting" as "coming" and "going;" so if he had meant to speak of stars in opposition he would have said, "when the white star comes and the red star goes." Spica culminates about the time that Aldebaran sets; also there are no large stars near Spica, this may be why it is called "the one white star." I think I have read that some people for the same reason call it "the lonely one." Gioro probably meant, "When the lone white star has culminated, and the red star and the little stars are set."—R. E.

another. Bomero was the leader always, and he seemed to know the way quite well. We always camped at water, and when we crossed from one creek to another the distance was usually no more than three or four miles. We passed a good many hills, but none of them I should say rising more than a thousand feet from the plain, and few of them so much as that. As far as I could reckon we must have travelled twenty-five to thirty miles a day, and the greater part of that was westing. I believe that on the evening of the twelfth day after we fell in with Bomero's people we must have been all of three hundred or three hundred and fifty miles to the west of the telegraph wire.

During those twelve days we did our best to study the people and the country so as to prepare ourselves for anything that might happen. Jack made a rough chart of each day's march, and we both made an attempt to keep a sort of dead reckoning. It was very hard, however, to make any available record of our observations. The curiosity and perhaps the suspicion of the blacks made it next to impossible to write or draw by daylight, and at night we had only the light of our fires and a sort of torch that we managed to make of bark and fat.

We were beginning to know something of the language. There was a palaver every night, or, to speak more exactly, there were several palavers, in one of which we always joined, with Gioro for interpreter. And on several occasions Bomero harangued the tribe. These harangues were very interesting, even before we could understand any part of them or before Gioro explained a word of them. The manner and mode of delivery were very remarkable. Bomero was highly demonstrative, but he was never carried away by his own eloquence. The spirit of the prophet was always subject to the prophet. He could pull himself together in a moment and be as cool as you please. The matter of his harangues was chiefly the greatness of his tribe, and above all of the king of the tribe, the king's ability to guide his people to food and water, to beat any two or three men of his own tribe, and as many as you like of any other tribe, the great Corroborree that they were going to keep out away west, and the greatness of the tribes who kept it, of which tribes they were the greatest, and Bomero was the greatest of them.

These harangues were his method, it seemed, of keeping up his influence over his people in time of peace. And one could not but liken him, as Carlyle says, to "certain completed professors of parliamentary eloquence" nearer home.

The Pleiades were now seen to be setting earlier and earlier every evening. They were for a few nights obscured by clouds, and the next time they appeared they were perceptibly nearer the sun. This fact was observed at once and they hailed it with what at first seemed to be a series of shouts, but which proved to be a sort of barbaric chant, each stave of which ended with this refrain:—

"Go, go,
Red star and little stars."

And this was a chant as Gioro told us (and Bomero confirmed him) which their fathers and their fathers' fathers had sung before them from time immemorial. I wish that some of our savants would investigate this matter, for I cannot but think that this festival and its obvious connection with the constellation Taurus would throw some important light on the origin of these people and their connection with the other races of mankind.

Jack and I for obvious reasons gave them some illustrations of the use of our "fire spears." Mine they said was a "fire spear" of one point, and Jack's of two three points, two three; that is to say I used a bullet and Jack used shot. We were beginning to be favourites, and even Bomero himself liked us, for although he showed at first some signs of being jealous, we treated him with such deference that he soon forgot his jealousy. Jack had a black leather belt for wearing round the waist, and we made Bomero a formal present of this. We explained its use to him and put it round his kilt. We could see that he was nearly overcome with childish delight, and yet the wily fellow was knowing enough to repress all show of this feeling and to receive the gift with stolid gravity. He gave us in turn an eagle's feather each, which he took off the kilt just where the belt would cover it, and these we received with becoming gratitude.

A serious misfortune befell us about the eighth day, which was the occasion of another compliment to Bomero. Jack's horse fell dead lame, and we were obliged to let him loose in the bush. We presented the saddle to our black prince, and made a throne of it for him, and one evening that we camped earlier than usual we persuaded him to hold a levee. Jack explained the matter to Gioro, and Gioro to Bomero. This was how Jack explained it.

Gioro. What's levee?

Jack. Boss white fellow stands on daïs. No, sits on throne, throne all same saddle and stirrups; other white fellows march up, march down again, come this way, go that way, all same little stars and red star. Bow to boss white fellow. Boss white fellow bows to them. Boss black fellow all same boss white fellow.

Bomero took readily to the proposal. We picked out a fallen tree high enough and wide enough. We fixed up the saddle upon it, the stirrups touching the ground. Bomero got astride of this with a spear in each hand. I passed before him bowing, and Jack followed me. All the others followed him. They took to it as if they had been born courtiers. They would not be satisfied until every adult man had made his bow, and we had something to do to keep them from beginning all over again. It was ludicrous to the last degree. The tall, bulky black fellow sat on the saddle with the tree under him like a hobby-horse, his head was all stuck over with feathers and the tails of opossums; his little cloak of skins and kilt of platted leaves were fastened with Jack's belt, and he held his two spears, one in each hand, and he looked as sober and solemn as a judge, and the other fellows as much in earnest as if they were freemasons in full regalia, or doctors of divinity in academic dress. I stole a look at Jack, and the villain replied with one of those winks which never fail to upset me. He let the lid of one eye fall completely, the other eye remaining wide open, and not a wrinkle in his face. A loud laugh would have spoiled the fun, and might even have been dangerous, but I saved myself with a fit of coughing. After the levee Bomero told off two men to have charge of the saddle. And for the next few days Jack and I walked, each of us, half the march, and rode the other. Once only during these twelve days did I see anything to give me any special uneasiness. One evening we camped a little earlier than usual and I noticed that Gioro was watched and dogged by two very ill-looking fellows whom I had noticed as being in some sort leaders. They stepped behind a clump of trees as he was passing, and as he returned they hid themselves again while he passed. I mentioned this to Gioro and he proved to be aware of their hostility. They were big men, he said, in the tribe, but Bomero was the biggest of all the men, and he was Gioro's friend.

About the morning of the twelfth day there was some trouble. We had come to a point where it was necessary to leave the course of one creek and to strike that of another. But a very destructive fire had passed over the place, followed, as it seemed, by heavy rains, and the track was quite obliterated. Certain trees also which would have served as guides had been entirely destroyed. And to increase the confusion the weather was foggy. Dense clouds rested on and hid some hills which might have served as landmarks.

Bomero went out to reconnoitre, and he took Gioro and another with him, and when they returned I could see that his mind was made up as to the course he would take, but that he was, nevertheless, as much perplexed as ever. He gave the word and we struck out a little north of west, and after travelling about three times as far as it had yet fallen us to get from water to water we struck another creek. We marched along the creek for another day, scarce ever losing sight of it, and then we camped by the water again. Next morning we left the women and children in camp, and about half the men, and Bomero with the ablest and quickest of the men marched away in search of another creek. Jack and I went with him, and as my horse was in good working condition we took him with us. We struck water somewhat sooner than before and camped for the night. I saw that Bomero was still perplexed, and I gathered from Gioro that his perplexity was caused by the conviction that he was now considerably out of his course, that he had gone too far north and had overshot the mark, and that we should have to go a day's march south and east before we could resume the straight course to the place of meeting. The horizon was still clouded, and there was no sign at present of the clouds lifting soon.

All this, however, was by no means enough to account for Bomero's evident perturbation of mind. He was undoubtedly a clever and cool fellow, and one of much resource; there was abundance of water and food, we could not be far out of the track, and we had plenty of time, for as far as I could judge by the astronomical indications, we were a great many days and even weeks too soon; and the weather, barring the clouds, was everything that could be wished.

Jack and I talked it over, and Jack reminded me of Gioro's tale of the "dibble dibble all same white man" that Bomero had seen in the far west. "Depend upon it," said Jack, "he thinks he is coming upon them again. The place, as Gioro said, was 'more far' than the place of meeting for the great Corrobboree, and he thinks that he is now getting 'more far' than there."

"And what of the dibble dibble that he saw there?" said I.

"Oh, that's the point," said Jack. "No doubt they were white men; some pioneers from the north coast, perhaps, or maybe the men on some outlying station of some western squatter's run, and if so we shall get back to civilisation sooner than we think."

"I don't see much in it, Jack," said I; "we're not far enough west for that; if we were on the head-waters of the western slope we might be on the look-out for white pioneers, but I am afraid we are near as far from there as from the telegraph wire. Bomero's 'dibble dibble' was either a pure invention or the suggestion of a dream, or if he did come across white men he must have been farther west than he is here."

On the morning of the fourteenth day Bomero harangued the men who were with him; he stood upon a veritable stump, a huge tree near the creek had been undermined by the flood waters and had fallen and lay along the ground roots and all. Bomero stood upon it and spoke, Jack and I stood by and listened, Gioro stood between us; he was in a state of great excitement, and he threw in every now and then a word of interpretation for our benefit, but indeed, by this time, we were able to follow the speaker fairly enough ourselves. It very soon became quite evident that Gioro's tale of "dibble dibble" was at the bottom of our trouble; it was quite evident also that the spirit of the prophet was no longer subject to the prophet. Bomero pointed westward, where the clouds were now slowly rising from some not very distant hills, and what he said was to this effect.

There was a hill away west where certain doleful creatures dwelt. He had once been very near there, and they had tried to take his life. They had tried to spear him through the air, and he who never feared men, feared them. He should know in a few minutes if that hill yonder was their hill; and if it was then he and his people must run and run till they got well out of sight of that hill. They had missed the way to the great Corroboree, but that was no matter; they would easily find it again, and there was plenty of time yet before the red star and the little stars would be gone. If they saw when the clouds rose (and they were now rising) that the hill was not their hill, then they would stay where they were to-day, and the witch fellows would dance the witch dance until all was clear, and on the next day they would go back to where the women were, and then they would strike the track, and be the first at the meeting-place. But if when the clouds rose, and they were now rising, they saw three peaks, a tall one in the middle, a crooked one on one side, and a straight one on the other, then Bomero and Bomero's men must run, run, run, and never stop, except to breathe, while any one of the three peaks was to be seen. Let the black man knock his brains out with his waddy, or let the white man spear him with his fire spear, but the devils that rode through the air on clouds, faster than eagles, were worse than any black men or white men."

Bomero was evidently no longer master of himself or of his men. Whatever the cause of it was, there was a dreadful panic imminent, and no one could tell what was going to happen.

Just then the clouds lifted quite away from the hill, and there, sure enough, were the three peaks, the tall one in the middle, and the crooked one and the straight one on either side.

A low murmur burst from the men, and Bomero uttered a frightful howl, and plunged away madly round a hill that rose gently from the creek, and right on into the forest. All the men ran after him, most of them howling and shrieking; and my horse, which hung by the bridle to a branch close by, started, and snorted, and broke his rein, and rushed away before them at full gallop.

The catastrophe was so sudden that our breath seemed to be taken away, and I don't know how many minutes passed before either spoke. I know that every man of the blacks had got clean out of sight, and my horse, too, and there was as dead a silence as before the world was made, and still there was not a word from either of us. Then Jack said in a hollow voice:

"Why wasn't the horse hobbled, Bob?"

"Why, Jack, I had just taken the hobbles off, and made him ready for the road."

"Never mind, old fellow, I hardly know what I said; Gioro will come back."

"Yes," I said, "Gioro will come back."

And then, as if our confidence in Gioro's fidelity cleared the air, we sat down and lit our pipes. I don't know how much time passed, it seemed to be hours, but it couldn't have been near an hour, and Jack and I never exchanged a word. Then, sure enough, we saw Gioro coming, and he was leading my horse. I saw him first, and I jumped up and shouted for joy. Then Jack jumped up, but the shout died on his lips, and he said only, "There is something the matter."

And so there was. Both Gioro and the horse were wounded, and the wounds were deadly, for the spears that inflicted them were poisoned. The horse died first. I took Gioro's head on my lap, and gave him a few drops of water. He told me that he had caught the horse by the bridle in passing, and that then he stopped and returned. He had not forgotten us, he said, not for a moment, nor would he have started at all if the horse had not started. The horse had stopped several times, and when he had come up with him had gone on again. But at last he had secured him and was returning. But several spears were flung at him, and many missed him, but the big men who had watched and dogged him took better aim, and struck both horse and man. At first he thought nothing of it, but presently he knew that the spears were poisoned, and now he must die.

"Take care," said the poor fellow, almost with his last breath, "keep away, kill you too, like Gioro; back, back to the big long wire."

He died quite easily, and I felt as he lay in my arms that it would be the best thing that could happen us if the poisoned arrows of the blacks had made an end of us as well as of him. The poor fellow's faithfulness would have helped us to face death without flinching.

We found a large hole in the earth where a tree had been uprooted by a storm, and there, with the help of his boomerang and our own knives, we managed to give him decent burial. We both fell on our knees for a few minutes, but no words passed our lips, although I am sure our hearts were full enough.

Then we stood up, and with one impulse held out a hand each to the other. The grip that followed was a silent English grip. But it meant that we knew that our case was desperate, and that we would stand by one another to the last.

CHAPTER SIX
LEFT ALONE

All the events described at the close of the last chapter succeeded one another very rapidly. I do not think that four hours in all could have passed from the beginning of Bomero's last harangue until Jack and I stood together over Gioro's grave. The sun had not reached the meridian; the atmosphere was perfectly clear; and the triple peak which had been the signal of so much disaster stood out clear and well-defined in the west.

What were we to do now? Were we to stay here and die like starved bandicoots when the first drought should come on? That was the question in both our minds, and that was the form in which Jack expressed it. "Let us get some food first," said I, "and then we shall see. Thank God it is easy enough still to get food." We soon lit a fire and shot some duck, and with the help of some of the wild fruit already mentioned and the water of the creek we did well enough. Then we talked over the situation, and it soon became clear that only two courses were open to us if we were to return to civilisation, or even to live. The one course was to push backward by the way we came. And if it had not been for the last two days' journey we should probably have chosen that way without hesitation. And even now if we could be sure of not meeting the blacks again, I think we might have tried it. It was true that we might wait here long enough to make sure that the blacks would have gone west-ward, but all the while we should wait, the tracks and the other waymarks would be gradually becoming obliterated. Besides, it was certain that we could not live by snaring birds and spearing fish for food as the blacks could, and our powder and shot would soon be done. Our better hope seemed to lie in the chance of finding white men somewhere near, and the strange proceedings of Bomero seemed surely to indicate the near presence of white men. He must have met some pioneers from the west coast. Such men were often known to treat the blacks as if they were mere wild beasts, and it seemed not unlikely that some act of reckless cruelty on the part of the white men might have been witnessed by him, or, at least, that he might have heard of such from some other blacks.

Jack had a little pocket telescope, and he examined the hill to westward with it. After a careful scrutiny he declared that he saw a man in one of the gaps on the top of the hill and that he was a white man. "Yes, I see him," said I, for I thought I observed something moving, "but I cannot say whether he is black or white." Jack handed me the glass, but I could not now distinguish even with the glass any sign of life or movement.

He took back the glass in a hurry and looked again, and then he declared that he could no longer see any man. "And yet," said he, "there was a man there, and he had on a long coat, and there was something odd and foreign in the look of him."

"Nonsense," I said, "you could never tell that at such a distance and with such a glass."

"Well, one would think not," he said, "and yet it was as I say."

I then went over my calculations with a view to determine whereabouts we were, but I could not by any means make our position far enough west to render it likely that we were near any settlement. We had no instrument by which we could make observations with any approach to accuracy. Our latitude was not much changed since we had left the wire; that much we could see from the stars. But our course had been so very zigzag that it was quite impossible to estimate our longtitude within a hundred or more miles. And even if our course had been due west all through I still could hardly hink that we were near the head waters of the western slope. After all, however, it seemed the wisest course to reconnoitre, first, this mountain or hill. If there was no one there it would be still Possible for us to return to where we were now, and to make a start eastward. Indeed, if the hill were not inhabited, that would be the only course that would be in the least degree hopeful. For certainly to strike westward without any guide er any knowledge of the way would be for us, and in such a country as Australia, to face certain death.

We made up our minds, therefore, to explore the hill at once. We put together somehow the remains of our breakfast, enough for two very spare meals each. We took a good drink of water and filled with water a small flask which would suffice to moisten our lips and throats in case we should find none at the hill. We reckoned that the hill was not quite ten miles away, and if that were all, we should get here in time to reconnoitre while it was still daylight, and if no prospect of help appeared we would return early in the morning. Then we took our farewell of poor Gioro's grave and set our faces to the hill. The way was quite easy; there was but little timber and the grass, although thick, was short. There were still evidences about us that the past season had been wet, but we did not find the ground boggy, and the atmosphere was fresh, clear, and bright. As we marched forward the shape of the hill became better and better defined, and more striking. It stood quite alone in the plain, from which it seemed to rise sheer upward with little or no slope.

It looked for all the world as if it had been dropped from the sky, so completely without connection was it with the surrounding landscape. As we drew nearer, it presented more the appearance of a huge irregular building which had become covered in the course of ages with vegetation. But, as we drear nearer still, these odd appearances gradually wore away, and began to look not very unlike other lonely and precipitous rocks which I have seen in Australia. Such a rock, for example, as the Hanging Rock, near Woodend, only very much larger, or such a rock as that other one a little north of the Billabong, and south of the Murrumbidgee, near the railway between Albury and Wagga.

As we drew near the foot of the precipice we made for the shadiest spot that we could find.

The various crags of which the hill was formed were covered almost everywhere with a foliage which differed but little from the prevailing Australian type.

There was abundance of the sweet smelling shrub which is common along the shores of Port Phillip. I pressed and rubbed a few of the leaves and the smell was just the same. There was less of the blue gum and more of the lightwood than I had elsewhere seen, and there were a good many pines. There were also a few remarkable shrubs that I have not seen elsewhere, and a few large and queer-looking flowers of a bright red colour.

We made for this particular spot not only because it was the shadiest but because it seemed to have a fresher and greener look than the rest of the hill; and our delight was great when upon reaching it, and after poking about a little while, we found a large basin or pond of water surrounded and shut off by rocks. It was nearly elliptical in shape but rather elongated: about thirty feet by ten. The water seemed at first as if it issued from the earth, but on closer inspection we had little doubt that it was due altogether to the rainfall percolating through the cliffs from the heights above.

Here we sat and refreshed ourselves for an hour or so before consulting as to our further progress.

It was later than we had reckoned on, for the journey to the hill had taken a longer time than we thought it would take; so we resolved to decide nothing further until the morning.

We chose not to light a fire although we knew by experience that the middle of the night would be very cold. We told ourselves that though we had seen no sign of any more natives there were probably some about, and therefore that it was better not to light a fire. Our prevailing reason, however, was an indefinite sense of dread which had come upon us and which we confessed to one another as we sat and ate.

We chose to attribute this dread to the strange and threatening shape of the hill as we approached it. Yet as we looked about us now we could not but acknowledge that we had seen many more awful cliffs and precipices without any of the unreasonable feeling which we could not but confess to now. A little while before sunset I noticed something which I tried to tell myself was most likely nothing, but which, nevertheless, increased this indefinite fear into a sense almost of horror.

The sky was perfectly cloudless, but for all that the shadow of a cloud fell on the ground quite near. The sun was very low and the shadows were nearly at their longest, and yet about this there was a shapeliness too definite for a cloud, a sort of shapeliness which might have reminded me at once of those other shadows of which I have told you, and yet it did not then remind me of them. It was the same sort of shadow, only elongated by the setting sun. It passed away very rapidly and I said nothing of it to my companion who was dozing.

Indeed, I felt the same unaccountable unwillingness to speak of it that I felt when I had seen the like of it before.

Next morning we awoke early, and found to our great delight a second well of water higher up the cliff. It was very much smaller—only a few feet across, but it was purer; and we determined if we remained long here to reserve it for drinking and to bathe in the larger one.

After we had bathed and had eaten the few scraps of food which remained to us, we began to reconnoitre, and we were both immediately struck by the appearance of the ground a few hundred yards to the south of where we had slept, but still at the foot of the cliff. The ground was worn away, it might be by water, it might be by some heavy mass being dragged along it.

It had a curious air of something like regularity, which suggested, and yet which need not suggest, art or design. We saw, however, at once, that it was the termination of a sort of hole in the cliff, apparently coming from above.

As this hole proved to be quite large enough for three or four men to stand up in it abreast, and as the ascent of it seemed not impracticable, we began to think of trying to ascend it.

Jack thought that it might lead us to the top more easily than the surface of the hill. Certainly no part of the cliff, as far as we had seen, seemed at all practicable, but I saw no reason to suspect that we should find a readier passage upward here. Still I agreed with Jack that we might as well try it. I insisted, however, that only one of us should go up, and that the other should await either his return or some signal from the top, if that were possible.

We agreed finally to cast lots to see who should stay behind, and the lot fell upon Jack. I immediately began the ascent, and found it very much easier than I had expected. The darkness increased only for a little while, and by and by it began to grow light, and I then discovered a sort of roadway with steps moulded out of the soil on either side.

After perhaps an hour of this work I came suddenly to a level. The passage opened into a spacious cave, which was dimly lit by a large opening in the rock, across which there seemed to be growing a thick scrub, not so thick, however, but that here and there the sunshine came freely enough through.

I had little doubt now that I was coming upon some hiding place of the blacks, and I proceeded with very great caution. I made slowly for the opening in the rock of which I had spoken, and when I had nearly reached it I saw that I could, without very much difficulty, force my way through the scrub. On a closer approach I observed with great astonishment that the scrub seemed to be arranged in two square pieces, which were certainly suggestive of a gateway.

There was a framework of dead branches, or rather two frames, and the scrub was roughly twisted in and out upon these. I thought it best now to make some preliminary observation from behind the screen of leaves and branches.

I soon found a small opening where I could see without any risk of being seen. I looked cautiously through. What I saw I will tell you in the next chapter.

Note.—I have never been able to come to any decisive conclusion as to the origin and use of this cave or underground passage by which I made the ascent to the gateway as above described. It was in no way necessary, as far as I could see, to the people of whom you will read in the following chapters. I should have thought it an old haunt of the blacks but for two reasons: If it had been so it must have been long disused by them, and yet it was evidently still, or quite recently, in use, but for what purpose I am unable even to guess. I tell you the facts as I find them.—R. E.

CHAPTER SEVEN
THE CARS

What I saw was this: a platform of rock extending before me a mile or nearly so, and about double the width of a very wide road. This platform ended in the cliff, which there bent suddenly into a line almost at right angles with the line of the platform. That was not straight but followed the slighter bends of the cliff. There were three flights of stone steps descending towards the valley, one of them at least, the broadest, reaching the whole way down. The valley itself seemed to be filled with houses and rows of trees, and certain enclosures that looked like gardens. The houses were odd-looking but unpretentious. One saw at a glance that their oddity was in the main owing to their lack of size, and to the absence of chimneys. One could not suppose them to be of much use for living in, and yet the whole appearance of the scene quite forbade one from accounting for their size by the poverty of the builders or from any other lack of resource.

But the scene closer at hand arrested my attention so forcibly that the more distant view left but a faint and general impression on my mind. On one side of the platform, the side next the valley, there were a number of men engaged at work of some sort, but their backs were just then turned to me: and I cannot tell you why, but the sight of men, probably civilised men, by no means gave me such hope or pleasure as our desolate condition would have justified.

On the other side of the platform, the side next the cliff, there were a number of objects which I must try to describe even at the risk of being tedious, as they proved to have a very decisive effect upon the progress and sequel of our adventures. They presented a most uncouth and bizarre appearance, and although they were all of one kind, almost identical in every detail, it was not until after several minutes' view of them that the fact of their likeness became apparent. Then I perceived that they were all some sort of conveyance consisting of an upper and lower framework. Here I saw a very odd-looking car resting on nothing at a distance of a few feet from the ground, and there I saw an elaborately constructed support which supported nothing. I saw, further, that the height of the supports was about as great as the distance of the cars from the ground, and I thought for a moment that by some unaccountable distortion of sight, the supports got the appearance of being separated from the things which were supported. But almost immediately I saw that this could not be the case, for in some instances it seemed as if the body of the car were cut into two parts, part only remaining and resting upon a complete frame; and then again, the body of the car was all there, and rested, for about half of its mass, on a supporting frame, half of which appeared to have been removed, while the other half of the body of the car appeared to be resting on nothing. A longer look at the scene offered an explanation, but it was an explanation which most urgently needed to be itself explained. At each of these objects a man stood, as it would seem, painting them, and he seemed to dip what I thought to be a brush in a bucket beside him. And at first I thought that he was painting the whole object, car and supporting framework, but presently I perceived that the brush which he was using and which showed a very irregular and jagged edge, never touched, or never at least was seen to touch anything at all, but that what it passed over disappeared. I watched the operation with breathless attention, and I saw the body of the car which had seemed to hang in the air gradually disappear as the brush passed over it, until nothing was left either above or below. I watched another which was complete in all parts until nearly the whole of the supporting framework disappeared beneath the brush. It looked for all the world as if some sort of invisible paint were being smeared over the conveyances. That they were conveyances of some sort I felt no doubt, but whether they were meant to travel on land or water I doubted. I saw no wheels, but these might be hidden by the framework, and there were things attached to each which might be said to have a remote resemblance to the screw of a steamboat. I may as well say at once that they proved to be carriages for travelling through the air.

Just then, some of the men who were working on the other side of the platform turned their faces towards me, and one of them, who seemed to be a sort of director or superintendent, came from behind them moving in the same direction. All kept moving towards where I stood until they were so near that I could clearly distinguish their features and their dress. The costume of all was exactly the same but unlike anything that I had ever seen. Each wore a low hat of a light colour and a broadish brim, a coat or smock reaching to the knee and fastened with a girdle, and some kind of shoe or sandal for the feet. That was all. As I noticed these points, the leader took a half-turn to the left and the men to the right, so that they and he stood facing one another with their side faces towards me. All the men were about as unlike one another as the same number of men picked up anywhere at random, excepting for one point. They had all an expression of malignity which was horrible to look upon, and which was worse, if possible, in the side face than in the full face. Not that there was anything deformed about their countenances; quite the contrary. Every feature considered by itself, whether from the front or side-view, was remarkably well formed. Eyes, mouth, nose, teeth, and hair, were of just the size, shape, and colour that you would say they ought to be. In fact, the symmetry of their faces was ideally perfect, and attracted more notice than anything else in their appearance except one thing, and that one thing was the malignity of their expression. That was utterly inhuman; it was diabolical. I declare that as I stood there behind the forest scrub and watched them, my very heart sank. I felt that I would rather see a dozen man-eating tigers or a herd of hungry wolves. I am not constitutionally timid and yet I repressed with difficulty a cry of despair.

As I looked in sheer horror and terror I thought I caught sight among the faces of a face that I knew. But surely I had never seen anything so frightful in my waking moments. Could I have dreamt of such a face, or could it be that amongst one's acquaintance an expression like that was to be found, only in an undeveloped stage? I can remember quite distinctly how that last thought flashed across my mind as I stood hesitating whether to run for bare life, or to wait for some further development of the situation. I think that nothing but the shame of manhood kept me from running away. Just then I suddenly perceived that the men were under some strange and very comprehensive system of drill. The man who seemed to be their leader held them, to all appearance, under very close control. And yet it seemed also as if their submission to his control were voluntary. It was like the way of a very perfect chorus with its conductor. Every glance of the leader's eye, every motion of his hand seemed to affect and direct them. But it did not seem as if there were anything absolutely compulsory about their obedience. They seemed not only to follow his eye and his hand but to look for the guidance of each. The very expression of their faces was moulded upon his, and I could well believe that the malignity which kindled it was kept alive by his.

As I looked more steadily I could see waves of expression, so to speak, going out from his face to them. What particulars these might be conveying I could not guess, but that there were particulars I could not doubt. Their variety, regularity, and distinctive character were as remarkable as if they were spoken words. His hands also moved in harmony with this change of expression, and the bodies of the men swayed with a slight rhythmic movement, which seemed to rise and fall as they watched his changing face. For several seconds I verily thought that I was dreaming, and I even had the feeling that a dreaming man has when he knows that he is about to waken.

Suddenly the leader turned away and the men fell to work as before. I saw then that in his passage along the platform he was encountering group after group of men, and that he was holding with each group, so far as I could guess at the distance, the same sort of silent interview which I have just now described. Then I suddenly remembered my promise to Jack, and I stole away from where I was and ran down the dark passage with breathless haste. Fortunately I received no hurt beyond several scratches in the face from some thorny bushes, which I had not encountered on my way up.

I found Jack very near where I had left him, sleeping under the shadow of a rock. I shook him, and he got up at once, quite broad awake. "Come," I said, "come; I have found men, if they are men." "White men?" he queried, briefly. "God knows," I said, my voice, I believe, quivering with agitation. Jack said no more for the moment, but he gave me a drink of water which I drank very greedily, and he was proceeding leisurely to light his pipe. The water had steadied me a bit, and I said, "No, never mind the pipe now, Jack; I'll tell you as we go along."

So we both went back together over my track, and when we got into the covered way I told him all that I have now told you. Then, when we had got nearly as far as the upper opening of the cave, we sat down and held a short and hurried consultation.

"Let them be what they will," Jack whispered, "we must go straight up and speak to them: if we don't get help soon we shall perish miserably."

"Agreed," I said; "but let us watch them for a little and wait for a favourable moment." And so we both crawled on to the opening of which I have already told you, and looked through.

Everything was just as before, except that the leader was now engaged with a group of men further away. After a brief survey of the surroundings, Jack pulled out his little telescope and looked steadily at the leader and the group of men he was engaged with, and then he handed the glass to me. I could see them with the glass about as plainly as I had seen the near group with the naked eye. Everything was the same, except that the malignant expression of the men and their leader was much less easily recognisable. I handed back the glass, and we both by one impulse drew back from the opening.

We drew further back still into a dark and retired corner, quite out of the rough pathway, and held a brief conference.

"It's a queer start," Jack said, "but we must go on with it; it is our only chance."

"It's queerer than you think," said I; "you haven't seen the fellows' faces as I saw them at first."

"No, no, I am taking account of that," said he. "I saw what you mean, although I might not have taken much notice of it if you had not mentioned it. I am afraid they are a very bad lot, or I should say rather he is a bad lot, for they are mere puppets in his hands."

"Not quite that," said I. "I don't suppose they would be much without him, but they are following him with a will."

"That may be," he replied; "but now tell me, how shall we work it? We have no time to lose, for he knows we are coming."

"I don't see how he could know it," said I, "unless he is the devil himself."

Jack gave a short but unpleasant chuckle; then he said,

"Well, perhaps he is; he is bad enough to be, or else I am much mistaken. Anyway, he knows we are coming; that is why the malignant look is partly hidden; he is getting ready for us."

I wished for the light that I might see Jack's face, for his voice began to have an odd ring about it. Then I said, "What can he want with us, Jack?"

"I don't know," he said, "but I made a study of his face just now. I'm not much on—what do you call it?—physiognomy? but that beggar's face told me a story."

"What was the story?"

"Well, that he knows we are coming, and that he wants us, and that he is going to make use of us. What are we going to do?"

"We will go straight up to him and ask him to help us."

"Very well," Jack said. "Rest, and a guide, and food, and fire. And what story shall we tell him of ourselves?"

"We will tell him the truth," said I.

"And shame the devil," said he, with another uncomfortable chuckle.

"What language shall I try him with?" said I.

"Bet you a pound he knows English," said Jack.

"Oh, that's the sort of devil you think he is; very well, I'll take your bet, though I dare say you are right enough." I declare, although I knew very well what ruffians outlawed Englishmen are apt to be, I felt quite light-hearted as I thought that perhaps after the men we were going to meet might be no worse than such. "Come on," I said, and we walked straight to the light. I pulled aside the rustic frame, which came with my hand quite easily; then I walked straight through, Jack following me closely.

The strange leader saw us at once, stood still, and looked at us. We walked forward and saluted him. I felt at the moment that Jack was right, that he knew that we were coming, although he wore an air of surprise, interested and self-possessed. I thought at the very first, "After all, he looks noble." But almost immediately I changed the word "noble" for "very strong."

He spoke to us in English. I looked at Jack, who smiled grimly and whispered, "Lost, old man." The strange leader said,

"Who are you, and whence do you come?" He spoke perfectly, quite perfectly, and in a commanding and confident tone. But there was a something, I know not what, about his accent, which told me that he was speaking a language foreign to him, and then and afterwards I noticed also that he did not use the conversational idiomatic English of any of those who speak English as their mother tongue.

"We are Englishmen," I said, "and we come from the eastward. We went among the blacks and they left us, and we do not know our way. Can you give us food and clothes, and guide us to the nearest English settlement?"

"I can give you both food and clothes," he said; "about guidance we shall speak further when you have made up your mind whither your purpose is to go."

I was about to thank him when I suddenly noticed the aspect of his men. They were looking at us eagerly, and it seemed as if they were waiting for some expected word of command. I could not help thinking that they were about to spring upon us, and I put my hand instinctively to the pocket where I kept my pistol.

The leader said shortly, "never mind that." Then he turned to his men. I could not see his face, but I saw that he lifted his hand. Presently the men were working away at their previous work, and were taking no more note at all of us.

"Come with me," said the leader, and he walked down the broad stone stairway. It was a very broad stairway, with stone balustrades on each side, light in appearance, but immensely strong. Every step, as well as the whole of the balustrade, was diversified with a variety of pictures and devices wrought upon stone by some method which rendered them proof against the weather. On this occasion I noticed little but the colours, but I observed them very closely afterwards. They appeared not only here, but everywhere in the valley, whether under cover or in the open air, where-ever there was any space to receive them, on walls, floors, ceilings, pillars, and doors.

All these pictures and devices presented one pervading idea; and as one passed backward and forward over steps and through doors, past pillars and balustrades, and walls, this idea gradually wrought its way into one's mind, until it seemed to dominate, or at least to claim to dominate everywhere. The idea so presented was that of an unequal but very determined conflict. Sometimes there was a simple device, a heavy drawn sword, for one, falling sheer, a cloud hiding the arm that sped it, and a gauntleted hand raised in resistance. This hand was but small and slight as compared with the sword, but there was expression in every sinew of it and in its very poise.

Again, you would see a hand coming out of a cloud and wielding a flash of lightning, and underneath two smaller hands lifted up as if trying to catch the extremities of the zigzag line of light. But the eeriest of all the devices was that of the two eyes: the larger eye was above and the lesser beneath, and how such expression could be given to an eye by itself I do not understand, but certainly there it was. Either eye was looking steadfastly into the other, and in the upper eye you saw conscious power, harsh, stern, and unrelenting; and in the lower and lesser one you saw, quite as plainly, the spirit of hopeless but unquelled resistance. The same idea was repeated in many pictures. In one of them you saw a great host bearing down upon a few antagonists of determined if despairing aspect. And in the background a dark mass of cloud, forest, and rock hid all but the forefront of the mightier combatants and gave you the notion of unseen and inscrutable power. Still, the simpler devices, I think, suggested with more awful certainty the actual presence of desperate and deadly struggle.

As I have said, however, I was conscious of but little of all this as I walked down the broad stone stair. I was weary, and hungry, and thirsty, and utterly taken by surprise, and I was quite ready to attribute to these feelings the sense of eeriness and fear which was creeping over me.

Our host conducted us down the stair with stately courtesy, and he gave us briefly to understand that he was about to ask us to refresh ourselves with food and rest and change of raiment. At the foot of the stair a very broad roadway led straight on toward the other end of the valley, but our host beckoned us to the right by a shorter and narrower way. We entered one of the low buildings which I had seen from above. These were not very large, but they proved to be considerably larger than I had supposed. We passed through a little porch into a fair-sized room, the floor of which was covered with a stuff of curious texture. It looked like some sort of metal; it felt beneath the feet like the softest pile. The walls on one side of the room exhibited a number of drawers with handles. Both drawers and handles were of strange and irregular shapes, exhibiting, nevertheless, a sort of regular recurrence in their very irregularities. In the centre of each of the remaining walls was a picture wrought upon the surface of the wall and occupying about a third of the whole wall, and over the rest of the wall there was inscribed a variety of devices. Both picture and devices were of the sort which I have already indicated.

There was an elliptical table in the middle of the room, and here and there on the floor were several chairs and a few couches, all of a very bizarre pattern, and all—tables, couches, chairs, drawers, and floorcloth—were covered with devices, some similar in form and all similar in spirit to those upon the wall. In the wall opposite the drawers there was a door, and our host, opening this, showed us into a room of lesser size where there were all sorts of appliances for bathing and for dressing. Clothes also, like those worn by himself and his men, hung round on racks. The walls and furniture, here as well as elsewhere, presented repetitions under various forms of the same pictured idea.

Before taking us into the bath-room, our host pulled out three drawers, calling our attention to the numbers marked upon them. Out of each he took a number of little round cakes or lozenges, each of a little less than the circumference of a two-shilling piece, but rather thicker. These he placed on several dishes, a different sort on each dish, and two spoons, or like spoons, on each dish also. He told us to take each, after the bath, a few of these, and he told us in what order we were to take them. Then, with a salutation, he left us to ourselves.

We bathed quickly, and after our bath we availed ourselves gladly of the change of raiment which our host had placed at our disposal. We exchanged a very few words, and those few did not attempt to deal with the mystery which was thickening about us. Jack's face expressed a mixture of surprise and mistrust, each in an extreme degree. My own face, as Jack told me later on, expressed sheer bewilderment. Certainly that was my feeling until far into the middle of the next day. I did not really believe that I was awake and in my senses, and I kept going back and back in my thoughts trying to find out when and where I fell asleep or was stunned.

After our bath we returned into the larger room. We were then very hungry, and we lay down each upon a couch, expecting to be soon summoned to the evening meal, for by this time the afternoon was well advanced. The weather was pleasantly warm, and we would have dropped asleep if we had not been kept awake by hunger. We both remembered at the same moment the plates of confections which our host had offered us. We took first one and then another of each kind in the order which he had indicated, letting them slowly melt in our mouths. The taste of them, although pleasant, was rather strange, but yet not altogether unfamiliar. The taste of the first sort faintly resembled the taste of roast beef; of the second, of pine-apple; of the third, of sweet wine, specially of muscatel. The effect of them was extraordinary; we felt that we had partaken of an agreeable and substantial meal; our hunger and thirst were gone, and we were quite refreshed. And then, as will happen when one dines well after a laborious and exciting day, we both fell sound asleep. We slept all through the night and on until a little after sunrise, and, not to go into details, we rose immediately and breakfasted as we had dined. We had scarce finished our meal when we became aware of the tramp of many men at no great distance from us, and we hurried to the door. We saw then, what neither of us had noticed the evening before, that the broad road, out of which we had turned in order to reach our present resting-place, opened out at the distance of about two hundred yards from the flight of steps into a large square, formed as the road itself was formed, and planted around the borders with trees, under the shade of which were several benches.

In the square were some two or three hundred men, undergoing some sort of review by the leader, with whom we had already become acquainted. Whatever degree of mistrust either of us felt we thought it as well not to show it, so we came forward leisurely until we were within a few score paces of the men, and then we stood and looked. We were not at once perceived, as neither the leader nor his men were looking straight in our direction, and we were partly shaded by a tree. The men were evidently of a much higher stamp intellectually than those whom we had seen the day before, excepting the leader. The men, yesterday, seemed to differ from automatic machines in one single point, namely, that they seemed to have a will of their own, although they had surrendered it to their leader. They seemed, you would say, quite incapable of action except as prompted by him, although they gave themselves up to his prompting, no doubt, because of sympathy and unity of purpose with him. The men to-day seemed, on the contrary, to be men of considerable intelligence. You would suppose them to be quite capable of being leaders themselves, and able to carry out in full detail instructions which they might receive in the merest outline. It was evident that they were now receiving instructions. These were being given, partly by expressions and signs, and partly by some spoken language. The language, which I heard several times in the next two days, bore no resemblance at all to any language that I knew. It seemed to be very artificial and elliptical. The former quality was suggested by the regular recurrence and gradation of certain sounds, and the latter quality was suggested by its great brevity. A word or two seemed to suffice where we should require one or more sentences.

When the leader had given his instructions, one and another, and then another, of the men stood out from the ranks and spoke to him, and in each case he replied. The men who spoke I judged to be in some subordinate command. All the men stood in files now, one man behind another, facing the leader, and in each case the man who spoke stood in front of his file. These files formed themselves quite suddenly and with great precision after the leader had given his first orders and before the other men spoke. It seemed as if the subordinate leaders were making suggestions or inquiries respecting the details of the work about which they had just received instructions in outline.

Then followed what seemed like a numbering of the men, and it soon became apparent that one file had two men missing, that is to say, supposing all the files to have been at first equal in number. As the deficiency became apparent a flash of baffled but furious malignity passed across the leader's face. Then I knew that when I had seen the like expression yesterday I was not dreaming. Jack and I exchanged a momentary glance. Some words, as I judged of inquiry and satisfactory reply, passed between the leader and one of his subordinates, and then, in the progress of the drill, the men made a partial turn by which they brought us into full view. In a moment they saw us, and in a moment the same eager and threatening look came over their faces which we had seen in the other men's faces yesterday. Jack and I both believed for that moment that our last hour was come.

But the leader withheld them with a word and sign. What he said or signified of course I did not really know, but I felt sure, nevertheless, that it was to this effect, that we should supply the places of their comrades who had disappeared. The same thought occurred to Jack. His word was received with a sound like a laugh, but it was a very horrible and ghastly laugh. One sometimes hears of the horror of a maniac's laugh; but the maniac's laugh is horrible by reason of its vacancy. This laugh was by no means vacant, it was full of expression, but it was the expression of relentless malignity.

Then the leader dismissed the men and they moved away towards the further end of the valley. Then he turned and moved slowly towards us and we moved slowly to meet him. He met us with the same stately courtesy as before and we exchanged salutations. He led us to the square where the men had been and he invited us to sit down. Then he inquired briefly concerning our personal comfort and we both expressed briefly our thanks and satisfaction. Then I went on to say,

"My name, sir, is Easterley, and my friend is Mr. Wilbraham, and we have only now to ask you by what name we are to know our host, and to ask that he will add to the obligation under which he has placed us, by giving us a guide to the nearest station or settlement of English colonists."

"I have more names than one," he replied, "among your people, but when I was last in Italy, which is a country that I know better than most, I was known as Niccolo Davelli. I was an analytical chemist and something of an engineer, and I did, well, a little political work among the country folk." He said all this with a very easy manner but with a very unpleasant smile. "Signor Davelli," I replied, speaking in Italian, "I am proud to thank you by name on behalf of myself and my friend, and I trust you will find no difficulty in giving the guidance we ask." "Surely not," he answered in the same language, "but you will stay here for a little, will you not? I have some curious things to show you, and you may perhaps meet some old friends among my people, and my work is so interesting and important that I have some hope that you will see your way to cast in your lot with us altogether. But," said he, "you need not use Italian, for I am not any more skilful in that than in your own equally famous tongue." Here again was the unpleasant smile, and I noticed that although he spoke Italian, as far as I could judge quite perfectly, he used this language as well as English with the deliberate and measured enunciation of a foreigner.

"As you will," I replied, returning to English, "we shall be glad to see what you have to show us."

Signor Davelli rose up at the word and invited us to follow him. He went up the stair by which we had come down the day before, and led us to the platform on which we had first seen him. He told us briefly that his sojourn here was in fulfilment of a purpose to which he and certain others of his fellowship were pledged. That they were all acting in concert and that certain of them were leaders, and that each leader had command of a station such as this, of which there were several in different parts of the world. That it was essential to the work that it should be carried on from regions far removed from the haunts of men, at least of civilised men, for they could repel the interference of savage races without endangering the fulfilment of their purpose. He went on to tell us that in this station of his he had two classes of work to do, one class consisting of intellectual work of a high order, and affecting more directly the fulfilment of the common purpose, the other class consisting of merely mechanical work, affecting the routine of life and its conditions here. "The men," he went on to say, "who carry out the former are of high and independent mental faculties and rank accordingly; these men you have seen to-day. The men who carry out the latter are of a very acute capacity to receive and execute instructions, but have no originating power of conception or design. These are they whom you saw yesterday. Their work is mainly the making of our food and clothes, and the construction of our means of locomotion, and of the machinery by which the work is done. That machinery is designed and executed in model at the other end of the valley by the other men in the intervals of their more important work. That work, however, you cannot understand until you become better acquainted with us."

We had now reached the platform, and we saw the men at work just as we had seen them the day before. Signor Davelli uttered a single word which I did not understand, and on hearing it the men turned, and then followed for a very few minutes the same sort of pantomimic action which I had already seen and have described. Then they resumed work.

Signor Davelli then took us to the works and invited us to observe the construction of the various machines in use.

I must not, however, run the risk of tiring you by any minute account of them here. Let it suffice to say that there was a much higher degree of mechanical skill exhibited in their construction than I have ever seen anywhere before or since, and that besides there was much that suggested the application of chemical and electrical science in a manner greatly in advance of anything that is commonly known; and further that there were certain complicated arrangements of prisms and mirrors which indicated as I thought some use of the agency of light which was quite new to me and which I did not understand. One set of machines proved to be used for the manufacture of the compressed food which we had already found so effective. Another set of much simpler construction carried it away and stored it when made. Yet another set was used for the manufacture of that invisible paint, the use of which had so astonished me. These last were the machines which attracted my curiosity most of all, and which implied not only a use which I did not comprehend of agencies which I recognised, but the existence of other agencies of which I knew nothing at all. I observed, however, as carefully as possible and I made, later on, very full notes of what I did observe, and I shall be happy to communicate these to our men of science in whose hands they can hardly fail to become of much practical value. I need hardly say that I asked a good many questions about this last set of machines, but somehow I got very little information. Whether Signor Davelli was unwilling to explain, or whether there was something in the process which I was incapable of understanding, I am not quite sure. All I could get from him was that there are some rays at either end of the spectrum which are not visible, and that it is possible to treat some substances so as to cause them to reflect these rays only, just as other substances reflect only the yellow or only the red. But from a word or two which he spoke, I suspect inadvertently, I gathered that the rays he spoke of, which are invisible to us, were visible to him, and differed as much from yellow, red, or blue, as these from one another.

We now crossed the platform to the place where the cars were being painted. I perceived as soon as I came upon the spot that the cars were built at one level, and then raised by machinery to another level at which they were painted, and that when painted they were raised to a third level. Along each of these levels they were moved by rollers of quite simple construction. Yesterday I had only seen those on the second level; those on the first were too low to come within the field of my view, and those on the third were invisible.

On this third level, however, one was to-day visible. As I afterwards learned, Signor Davelli had caused it to be left unpainted. It was otherwise finished. He caused it now to be rolled along to the extremity of the platform, which ended to the southward in a sheer precipice of some hundreds of feet. There was a ledge to keep it from rolling over. Signor Davelli led us to this car and invited us to enter it.

There was plenty of accommodation for two or three people. There were easy benches and couches, and there were three boxes with distinctive marks like numbers on the lids. At the end of the car which was furthest from the ledge, the inside end, there was a great deal of machinery, but not of such a size as I should have expected considering the size of the car. This machinery consisted of two batteries resembling galvanic batteries in many ways, but the stuff used up in work was not fluid but solid; it consisted of large squares of matter, which I think was wholly or mainly metallic. The batteries were connected with a strong round bar, made, as I thought, of some sort of metal[4] running through the car and supporting a pair of huge paddles, or wings, one on each side of the car. At each end of the bar were certain little wheels and cranks, devised not so as to cause the paddles to revolve, but so as to give them a wing-like motion. At the forward part of the car were several vessels of a form which suggested a chemical apparatus for generating gas. And on each side of the car, constructed and placed with an evident view to balance or trim it, were two balloons, which seemed absurdly small in view of the size of the car. These were connected with the chemical apparatus just mentioned, and were filled by it, when occasion required, with a gas vastly lighter than hydrogen.

Signor Davelli, Jack, and I entered the car, and the Signor took a bottle of liquid out of one of the numbered boxes and poured it into one of the vessels. Then in all the vessels there seemed to be a sound like boiling, and presently the balloons became inflated and raised the car very gently and quite evenly. When we had been thus lifted to a height of about a hundred feet from the platform, he put on a dark-looking pair of gloves and laid hold of a strong thick wire, which I had not seen before, which was fastened to the bar which I had supposed to be of metal on the side further from where I sat. This wire he connected with the batteries of either end, and immediately took off the gloves. Presently the paddles began to move with a wing-like action, driving the car straight forward through the air. All this time we were still rising slowly, but when we had attained a high degree of speed Signor Davelli turned the key of a valve which communicated with both balloons and they presently collapsed, the action of the paddles being now sufficient both to sustain us and to urge us forward. The motion was easier than that of any conveyance that I had ever yet travelled in. The seat on which Signor Davelli sat was placed so that with one hand he could turn the key of the valve, and with the other grasp either of two handles, by one of which he managed the batteries, and by the other of which he changed at need the direction of the paddles. I perceived, upon looking more closely, that the key of the valve was fixed at the intersection of two tubes shaped like a T, one at right angles to the other, the horizontal tube joining the balloons and the perpendicular tube connected with the vessels from which the sound of boiling still proceeded.

After we had gone, as I thought, a few miles, Signor Davelli changed the direction of the paddles and swept round in a longish curve, until the forward part of the car was turned to our starting point. When we had travelled about half way back he turned the valve again and refilled the balloons, and then he stopped the paddles and we lay floating in the air, rising very slowly and gently. Then he bade me look to the west and say if I saw anything. I could see nothing at all, the day was

---

[4] I discovered afterwards that it was not metallic.

quite cloudless. Then he bade me look downward, but still to the west. Then I saw a shadow, as I thought, of a great bird, but I could see no bird to cast the shadow. The sun was now declining a little, and he bade me turn and look downward again, but now to the east. Then I saw the shadow of our own car, and although the point of view was not the same, there was no room to doubt but that the other shadow was cast by a car like ours. The moment I saw the likeness my old Welsh experience came with a flash to my mind. These were just the same queer sort of shadows that I had seen long ago at Penruddock the day James Redpath had disappeared; yes, and surely the evening before the day we reached the valley, the evening of the day that we lost poor Gioro I had seen just the same sort of shadow. And— Could it be? Yes, it surely was—the dreadful face that I recognised yesterday was no other than James Redpath's own! How it was that I did not identify him before I do not know, but now I knew very surely that I had seen himself indeed. Such was the tumult of mixed feelings that now took possession of me that although we moved rapidly forward again until we had passed quite over the valley and then wheeled round once more, I took no notice of our movements until I found that we were descending to the spot where we had started, the front of the car facing southward as before. I looked at Signor Davelli, and I read in his face an expression of gratified pride and a strong sense of power. There was nothing repulsive in his aspect now, at least nothing repulsive to me. I felt also that I was being somehow dominated by his will, and that I was not altogether unwilling that it should be so. I felt certainly some remnant of the horror with which I had looked yesterday on his face and the faces of his men, but I was conscious that my horror was rapidly merging into simple wonder. I felt something of the sort of awe which the suspected presence of the supernatural produces in most minds; but the feeling which dominated for the present all other feelings in me was a devouring curiosity. Just then the sacred allegory of the Fall passed before my mind rather as if presented than recalled. In my mind's eye I saw the very Tree itself which was to be desired to make one wise, and the legend written under it—

"Eritis sicut Deus scientes bonum et malum;"

but neither device nor motto seemed to have any other effect upon me than to stimulate my curiosity.

Just then we touched ground, and I started, as if coming to my senses, and looked over at Jack. His face was partly turned away, and I could see little more than his side face. He wore an abstracted air, such as I had never seen him wear before. There was also a sweetness and earnestness of expression about him which were certainly not foreign to his face, but which I had never before seen there in such intense degree. Strange to say, there came upon me for the moment a sort of contempt for his understanding which seemed strongly to repel me from him. This,

I have now no doubt, was produced by some evil influence acting I know not how, for assuredly there was nothing in my knowledge of him that it could build upon, and all that happened after justified it, if possible, even less. Just then he turned and looked upon me, and there was in his eyes so much care and kindness, kindness to me and care on my account, that my heart was touched and awakened at once. I cannot analyze or account for the effect which this look produced on me; I can only say that as I stepped from the car the tumult of mixed feelings, which so disturbed me, seemed to pass away like a bad dream that might or might not return.

After a few words of courteous inquiry as to our necessities and comforts, Signor Davelli made an appointment to meet us next day on the square where we had met this morning; and then we parted from him for the night, and Jack and I slowly returned to our place.

"Jack," said I, as we were going down, "what do you think of it all?"

"We won't talk of it now," he replied, "we are too tired, and perhaps excited; we had better sleep over it. To-morrow we must rise early, look out a quiet place, and talk the matter all round."

Nothing more but some words of course passed between us until the morning.

CHAPTER EIGHT
SIGNOR DAVELLI

Early the next morning Jack and I were ready for a scramble over the cliff. We wished to have a quiet talk together, and we wished further, although we had not yet named the wish one to another, to ascertain as far as possible whether or not we were in effect prisoners. There was one fact which told heavily against any such notion. That was the large quantity of portable provisions which had been deliberately put in our way. For we could each carry, without inconvenience, enough to last us for a long time, quite long enough to enable us to push westward as far as the coast, or to go back eastward as far as the wire. Nevertheless, I was firmly of opinion that we would not be permitted to escape, and that if we attempted to our lives would not be worth much. As I learned afterwards, Jack was of the same opinion. The events of this morning removed doubt on the subject.

We found quite a practicable ascent of the cliff on the side of the stair which was further from the platform. And, after climbing this, we found a fairly even space of several hundred yards, and then an easy descent upon the other side. We did not, however, attempt the descent, but sat down and talked. Jack began—

"Bob," he said, "we must keep cool, for we are playing for very high stakes."

"For life and death, you think."

"More than that, perhaps. I wonder what selling your soul meant in the old times?"

"I suppose," I said, "whatever else it meant, it meant acting dishonourably or treacherously for the sake of some personal gain."

"But some fellows have sold their souls who could never be persuaded to act either treacherously or dishonourably for the sake of any personal gain."

"I daresay," said I, not seeing nor caring what he was driving at.

"Now, Bob, if I were the devil, and if I wanted to get you to sell me your soul, I know what I should do."

I was getting a little vexed, but I replied simply—"Well, what would you do?"

"I would endeavour to pique your curiosity, and then I would show you that you could gratify it by putting yourself in my power, and then I would have your body even if you still insisted on keeping your soul."

"And which do you think it would be?"

"Well, I should have to be satisfied with your body, except in one event."

"And, pray, what would that be?"

"I might by the exhibition of some special or unaccounted-for power gain such influence over you as to get you to put your conscience at my disposal. Then you would be mine soul and body."

I was beginning to get vexed partly because I suppose I saw more truth in what he said than I liked, so I said shortly—

"What do you mean just now by all this?"

"I think our friend, the signor, is the devil himself. I don't mean any fee-faw-fum. I daresay there are a good many other men as much devils as he is, but he has all the power which great and special practical knowledge gives a man, and he is as full of malice as an egg is full of meat, and he is up to some very big villainy and, what is more to the purpose, he has a design upon you."

"He has done us no harm that I can see."

"He has done us a great deal of harm; he is persuading you to trust yourself to him, and he is worthy of no trust whatever, d—n him."

Now this from Jack was rather startling; for he was not in the least prone to use bad language. I never heard "the Englishman's prayer" from his lips before or since. But his earnestness irritated me more than his profanity surprised me.

"Don't you see," I said rather sullenly, "that if your hypothesis is correct your prayer is rather superfluous?"

"Well, yes, it is superfluous," he said with a harsh laugh quite unlike him; "he is damned already sure enough."

"I don't see much sign of damnation about him," I said, "not if misery be an essential park of damnation."

"Well, yes, the misery that comes of malice, and if ever malice and misery were written in a man's face, they were written in his yesterday when they missed those men. And mark me," Jack added, raising his voice, "his damnation has got something to do with the loss of those men."

I was now getting very angry, so I rose to my feet and said hastily—"If we have nothing to talk about, don't you think that we may as well go back?"

Jack rose and said, "No, Bob, we'll not go back yet awhile. Don't be vexed with me, old fellow. You are in more danger than I am, but your danger is mine." As he said this I saw the same expression on his face which I had seen yesterday, an expression of kindness and anxiety, and it had much the same effect on me now.

"Jack," I said, "forgive me, I declare I believe you are partly right; I believe there is some devilish influence at work trying to set me against you. I caught myself yesterday despising you for not being clever, and there were two devils in that, for you are twice as clever as I am, and even if you were not you are ten times as good."

"Ah Bob, my boy, there is plenty of reason to suspect me of stupidity without supposing that the devil is in the dance.

'Nec deus (or diabolus) intersit nisi dignus vindice nodus.'

You see I have a stock verse or two to quote at a pinch. But although I don't see as far, perhaps, into the game as you, it may be that just for that reason I see the near points a little more clearly. Now sit down again and tell me what you think of it all."

We didn't sit but kept walking up and down. "I don't know what to think," I said; "I was nearly sure yesterday that I was either mad or dreaming, but I have given over thinking that. I suppose there is a desperate and widely spread conspiracy against civilised society, and that these men are in it. You talk about fee-faw-fum, but I remembered some things yesterday while we were in that car that made me feel as if the whole world were nothing but what you call fee-faw-fum."

"What were they, Bob?"

I told him all that I have written in the first two chapters of this book. He listened most attentively, and made me repeat two or three times over parts of the conversation between the two doctors. But when I wound up my story by telling him that I had recognised James Redpath among the men on the platform, he stopped suddenly, turned right round and looked at me. "Good heavens!" he said. And then after a pause, "Do you think that you saw him carried away that morning from your Welsh village?"

"I didn't see him, but I have little doubt that I saw the shadow of the car in which he was carried away."

"Do you think that we have stumbled on your friend Dr. Leopold's non-human intelligence? and that there is a manufactory of black death or plague somewhere in the neighbourhood?"

"I have hardly a doubt of these men's malignity, but there is one thing I am surer of. Now that I am here I want to know all about the matter—and I mean to. Mr. Leopold may have stumbled upon half a truth."

"Well, my position is just the reverse of yours. I am curious enough about the matter, but I am so sure of these men's desperate malignity that my first wish is that we should make our escape from this place. And mind," he went on to say, "if you want to burst them up that is the way to do it. If you and I get back to civilisation others will soon be on our track. And once there is a settlement of English colonists near here these men will be played out, and they know it. Don't you remember what the fellow himself said? He said that they could keep the blacks at a distance, but that it does not suit them to carry on their work—whatever it is—in the presence of civilised men!"

"I remember," said I; "but if you are right, depend upon it they have made up their minds that you and I will never leave this place alive."

"Not quite that," said he, "or they would have murdered us before now."

"Well, they were going to do so twice."

"Yes, but Signor Niccolo restrained them. You see Signor Niccolo has a design upon you; he wants to make you one of his men. He doesn't care much about me, but he is willing to throw me into the bargain. Now if you and I refuse to join him our lives will be the forfeit."

"And if we don't refuse?"

"Why then," said he, "more than our lives."

"Well then," said I, "what in the name of common sense do you think they are?"

"Well," he replied, "I don't altogether agree with Dr. Leopold. I can't quite believe in the 'non-human' business; these men are flesh and blood safe enough; though I confess I am startled to see so much applied science, so much in advance of ours, in the possession of men of such malignity as these are." He paused for a moment and then proceeded. "What you said just now is most likely right. They belong most likely to some brotherhood of conspirators, some advanced guard of Nihilists, or the like, who propose to make war upon civilised society."

"What do you advise?"

"For all reasons the sooner we get away the better. My proposition is that we fill our pockets with these cakes of theirs and make a bolt of it the very first opportunity."

"Do you think we shall find an opportunity?"

"Well, the event will show. We may have to start in the dark and for a while to travel by night. But you see these cakes of theirs are meat and drink, and we can make a bee-line for the wire."

"Don't you think they will track us?"

"I doubt if they will be able. Their intelligence is very high, and their modes of procedure are very artificial; and the best trackers are men of mere instinct. Still I wish we could get hold of one of their cars; if we could, a few hours' start would save us."

"Look to the right," I said, "we are watched and followed now."

By this time the sun had risen a little way, the sky was clear, and here and there, slowly moving along the face of the cliff below us, were several shadows of the sort I have already more than once described. These plainly indicated the presence of several of the cars at no great distance from the ground, and at a lower level than the cliff on which we stood. Whether there were any or how many at a higher level no one could say just yet, and on the left everything lay still in shadow. We walked in the same direction, quickening our steps a little, the cliff all the while sloping downward slowly. Presently the sun was at a higher level than the ground we walked on, and the number of the shadows greatly increased, and there were very many now on all sides of us. Just then it seemed as if a cloud were passing over us quite near. We looked upward quickly, but there was no cloud, only a great shadow cast, as it would seem, by nothing. In a few seconds it was gone, and presently after we heard the swish—sh—sh right over us of the wing-like paddles, and we could even detect the small regular rattle of the machinery. It was evident that we were being closely guarded, and perhaps we were overheard.

Silently but with one impulse we turned and walked slowly back to the rooms that had been assigned to us.

We refreshed ourselves with food and we had an hour's rest before it was time to keep our appointment with our host. We agreed meanwhile to observe everything very closely and to compare notes at night.

"But," said I, "is it safe for us to separate?"

"Nothing, of course," Jack answered, "is altogether safe, but for a little while I think that we are not in any more danger apart than together."

"But you know, Jack, you said that you thought he had some special design on me and that he didn't want you. So he may have you quietly put out of the way if you go alone."

"He is bad enough for anything," was the answer, "but he knows that to put me out of the way would so disturb you as to baffle his designs upon you. Your attention would be entirely diverted from the matters in which you are now taking so deep an interest, and by means of which he hopes to secure you. He would have to put you out of the way too, and he doesn't want to do that. So he is going, as I have said, to throw me into the bargain."

"What course do you suggest then, when we are next left to ourselves?"

"You try to get an interview with—what's his name?—your old Welsh friend?"

"James Redpath."

"Just so, and I will try to pick up some information about the navigation of the cars."

At the appointed hour, which was rather early in the afternoon, we went together to the square, and we had hardly reached it when Signor Davelli arrived there too. His appearance was decidedly changed: his robe was ampler and longer, and this as well as his hat and sandals were apparently made of richer and lighter stuff than those which he had worn before, also there were various mottoes and devices wrought upon them. The devices were all of the sort I have before told you of, and the mottoes, or what I deemed such, were in a variety of characters, most of them altogether unknown to me. A few of them, however, were in languages that I knew. There was only one in English, and strange to say, I cannot remember what it was. On the front of the hat was an inscription in Hebrew characters, but so oddly formed that I did not at first recognise them. I am not much skilled in Hebrew but I have no doubt that the inscription was written, however, in a character ⁵כאלהים closely resembling that of the Palmyra inscriptions. As I came slowly to recognise the meaning of this inscription, it came to me much more forcibly (and with another sort of force), than if I had at once recognised it for what it was. And I would have at once recognised it if it had been in the ordinary square characters as I have written it here.

Signor Davelli's manner was, as I thought, very stately and even majestic, and yet at the same time quite easy and affable. Once or twice only I observed an air of effort, and even that seemed as of an effort graciously undertaken even if painful. Once or twice also a sort of spasm crossed his face as of self-repression of some sort. And once it seemed as if he were about to spring forward but checked himself, and his face then reminded me of the faces of his men yesterday in this very square when they first recognised our presence.

He bade us be seated, and he took a seat himself and began to talk to us. Our seats faced his and there was a pathway like a garden walk between us. I remember noticing as he began to speak that the same strange flowers and shrubs which I had seen outside grew in great abundance along this pathway.

Signor Davelli led the conversation quickly, but not at all with violence, to themes of an abstract character, and he presently settled down to the discussion of no less a subject than free will.

You would not thank me if I were to give you (supposing I could do so) a full account of all that he said. I will, therefore, not make any such attempt. I will only say that his remarks were bold and interesting, although he presented no aspect of the question which was absolutely new to me, and that he spoke apparently with strong feeling and fervour, and even sometimes with a bitter air of desperation. Then he looked at me with an air of inquiry.

After a long pause I said,

"I see, Signor Davelli, that you are not a materialist."

---

⁵ "As gods," Gen. iii. 5.

"Materialist?" he said, with a very unpleasant mixture of smile and sneer. "No; materialism is very well for a beginning; but one must face the facts at last if one is to deal with them at all successfully."

"But," said I, "some teach that matter is the very ultimate of all fact."

"It is perhaps well," he said, with a renewal of the same sneer and smile, "that they should teach so, but you and I know better; matter is evidence of the fact, but not the fact itself."

"And free will in your view is real?"

"Yes, it is real, doubtless, although so given as to make it for all but the very boldest practically unreal."

"So given, you say; it is a gift then?"

"Yes, it is a gift, if you call that 'given' which you use at your peril."

"And who gives it?" said I.

"Never mind that," he said, with a bitter scowl, which recalled for the moment, his malignant expression of the day but one before. "Call Him the Giver: a cursed way of giving is His. You know that you can use His gift if you dare, and you know that if you dare use it as you please He will scald you with what His bond-slaves call 'the vials of His wrath'; that I think is the phrase."

"Perhaps," I said, "the scalding is one's own doing: power to use the gift is power to use it rightly or wrongly: if one choose to use it wrongly one takes the consequences."

"Right and wrong," he said, "what are they?" and he spoke now with great coolness and without a sign of sneer; "trace back the ideas to their origin. Right is what I will, and wrong is what I will not. So it is with the Giver, and why should it not be so with you and me?" I observed that as he said this some of the mottoes on his dress grew bright and even flashed. Among them was that in Hebrew letters which I told you of just now. "But I know there are slaves," he went on to say, "slaves (you surely are not one of them) who are afraid of liberty, and who are jealous of those who are not afraid of it. And these," he said, and here the scowl returned, "these make use of such words as right and wrong to perpetuate the tyrannous rule of Him who gives with a curse, and who takes again with a fresh curse."

"Is He," I said, "the tyrant on whom you are making war?"

"Oh, yes," he said, "for all tyrants hold from Him; they are His hired bullies whom he pampers and lashes as you might lash and pamper your dog."

"You say that He gives and takes, will He take the gift of the freedom of will from you?"

If I had foreseen the effect which this question would have produced, I should certainly have been afraid to have asked it. His face became at once full of deadly fury and frenzy; "Yes," he said, "curse Him! He will at last if He can!" And then he sprang up and caught at the air with both his hands, just like the hands, in the device of which I have told you, grasping at the forked lightning.

In a moment, however, he resumed the quiet, stately and affable air, which he had worn before, and he sat down, and began to talk again quite calmly.

"Yes," he said, "free will is no doubt real to the bold and desperate spirit. To all others it is in effect unreal. To make it in effect real to all, every free being ought to be able to do as he will, not only without let or hindrance, but also without what you I suppose would call penal consequences."

"It seems to me," I said, "that our little world is too limited for such freedom as you desire. We should speedily come into collision with each other if there were no limit of any sort to our freedom."

"Yes, if your world were the only world."

I did not notice at the time his use of the pronoun "your" for "our." I only replied, "If our world were multiplied a hundred thousand fold, and I can well believe that there may be a hundred thousand such worlds, still the limits of habitable space must ultimately be a limit to freedom so that it cannot be unconditional."

"There are no limits," he said, "to habitable space."

I began to think that he was a very clever madman, and I said nothing.

"For such as you," he continued, "the limit exists, but not for me, nor for such as I."

Now I was sure he was mad, and I still kept silence.

"Nor yet for you," he added, "either, if you have courage enough to overleap the limit."

Now I began to be afraid that the form of mania which affected him was homicidal, and that he would presently require me, as he said, "to overleap the limit." But he rose to his feet with such a collected air, and looked so full of proud intellect and power that I began to change my mind and to think that I was going mad myself.

He spoke again, stretching out his hand, "Space is unlimited, and wherever space is there is a dwelling-place for me. This form in which I live here is but my dress, which I assume when I come to live among you. I can put it off and live in space, I can put it on again and come back to you. See here!"

Both his hands were now stretched upward, and his eyes were fixed on me with a domineering gaze, and mine on him with a mixture of wonder and of dread. Then he looked away straight out into the southern sky.

Suppose now a great mass of metal to be so quickly molten and vaporized that it has no time to fall to the earth as fluid before it rises into the air as gas. That was how it seemed to happen to the body of this extraordinary man. As I looked at him I saw no longer his body, but a great mass of apparently fluid substance, moved with a continuous ripple all through. Then it increased in volume vastly and spread upward like the smoke from an immense furnace. And as it spread it became thinner and finer, and still thinner and finer, until presently there was not the slightest trace of it any longer to be distinguished. How long a time it took to complete this transformation I could not at all guess from my experience of it. As far as my recollection of that goes, it might have occupied hours, but I know from external facts such as the shadows of the trees and the clouds that it could have been little more than five minutes at most, and on comparing notes afterwards with Jack I became inclined to believe that although I had certainly observed a succession of changes the whole transformation and disappearance was practically instantaneous.

Jack and I said not a word, we were both quite stupefied for the moment. Partly recovering ourselves we both walked up to the spot where Signor Davelli had stood, and we saw what seemed to be the remains of the sandals, hat, and coat, which he had worn. Jack took them up one after another, looked at them, and handed them to me. The texture of none of them was in any way destroyed. But they were now wholly colourless, and not the least trace of any letter or device was anywhere to be seen on them.

After the lapse of about ten minutes a slight explosion was heard a little way over our heads, and then a slight vapour appeared in the air very widely spread. Then I saw the same changes as before but in reverse order. The vapour thickened into smoke, the smoke became condensed into a fluid rapidly rippling throughout. This presently settled down over the spot where the discarded dress was lying, and became solidified; and as I looked I saw Signor Davelli with the same pose and attitude as before his disappearance, and with the same dress bearing the very same inscriptions and devices.

As before, I am inclined to believe that the reappearance and transformation, although presented to me as a succession of changes, were practically instantaneous.

I stood looking at him, transfixed with wonder and horror. He signed to me to sit down; then he sat down himself, and began to speak again quite gently and persuasively. Jack stood for a minute or two as if in hesitation about something; then he, too, sat down and listened.

Signor Davelli. Do not be alarmed, there is no occasion for alarm nor even for surprise. Nothing has been done but what is quite as fully susceptible of explanation as any simple chemical experiment.

Easterley. That can hardly be so. Much even of what we saw yesterday far exceeded any results of experimental science known to me, but I could readily believe it all to be explicable upon principles which I have studied, and which I partly understand. But the experiment which I have just witnessed (if I may call it an experiment) surely implies principles which far transcend any with which I am in the slightest degree acquainted.

Davelli. "Transcend" them, yes, but are nevertheless closely related to them, and are never at variance with them. But I can put you through an experience quite similar to that which I have myself just undergone. You shall judge for yourself then."

He came quite near me, and went on to speak in a tone at once masterful and persuasive.

"You shall experience my power," he said, "and you shall criticise it. I will send you hence and back in quite a little time. You will remember what you see, and you shall compare it with what you know of your own world, and you shall say then whether it is not worth your while to come and join us. If you join us you will know nothing of what you call death, for death cannot touch the dwellers in space."

As he said these last words I felt a shudder pass through me; it reminded me of something, I knew not what, but afterwards I remembered.

"Cannot death touch you?" I said. "Not even when you are dwelling here with us?"

"No," he replied; "anything that would kill you would simply drive us back into space."

I have a very trustworthy instinct as to the truth or falsehood of those who speak to me, and I felt now that Signor Davelli was speaking the truth in this particular, but that he was deceiving me somehow.

"Do you propose," I said, "to send me among the dwellers in space and to fetch me back now?"

I detected just the faintest turn of his eye towards Jack, and as he answered I knew that he was lying, and that if need were he would lie more.

"You cannot acquire at once," he said, "the powers of a dweller in space. But I shall send you out of this world and I will fetch you back, and your journey will help you to acquire the power to become a dweller in space by-and-by."

I distrusted him profoundly and I was not without fear of him. It was fear, however, that I could not easily define. Certainly it was not fear of death, for I feel quite sure that he was not going to kill me. I felt a consuming desire to know all about him, and I was willing to risk much in order to satisfy my desire. I felt also the influence of his masterful will. My distrust of him weighed one way, and the strength of his will the other way, and my lust of knowledge turned the scale.

So I said, "Send me where you will then."

The words were scarce out of my mouth when he raised his hand, and in a moment I lost all power of active motion, and could neither see nor hear, although my consciousness not only remained but became abnormally distinct.

Of course I had never experienced exactly such a state, but I remember once, in my college days, I had mastered a very abstract philosophical discussion, and I lay down on the hearthrug and thought it over until my power of thought seemed to merge into something clearer and fuller, and once later in life I stood on the deck of a ship gazing on the ocean—

"Until the sea and sky
Seemed one, and I seemed one with them and all
Seemed one, and there was only one, and time
And space and thought were one eternity."[6]

On both of these occasions I experienced something not unlike the intensely vivid consciousness which I experienced now.

It was mainly a consciousness of expectancy. The events of the last few days seemed to hang before my mind like a semi-transparent veil which was trembling under the action of the hand that was about to withdraw it in order to discover something wonderful behind.

Then I seemed to be borne onward, I knew not whither, with an inconceivably rapid motion. Then again I lay at rest. Then my power of sight returned, and I think my power of hearing, but there was at first nothing to hear. I seemed to be lying on a hard bank within the mouth of a cave not far below the surface of what seemed to be the earth. A light streamed into the cave, and I could see right opposite me a tract of mountain, wild and rugged beyond all description. The light was not diffused except within the cave. The space outside the cave's mouth seemed quite dark, and then the rugged mountain side beyond shone out quite brilliantly. Looking round I saw nothing but barren rock, and I could hear no sound either around or above, but as I moved my head from side to side I heard a sound from beneath as of a dull "thud, thud," and then a sound strangely like whispering voices.

I had been in a sitting position and I had lain back, and so now I looked up into the sky, and, notwithstanding the apparent daylight, I saw the stars quite plainly, and a monstrous moon, a little past the new phase, nearly overhead, with very distinct markings upon it. I watched steadily the markings near the edge, and I saw that they were moving very slowly, like the minute hand of a huge clock. Looking steadily still, I recognised the markings. I was looking at the earth. I could even distinguish some of the coasts and seas and islands, as it seemed to me, quite plainly recognisable. Now I knew where I was and I started to my feet. I had intended to stand up, but the force which I had exerted with that purpose in view made me bound several feet from the ground, so that my head reached beyond the edge of the cave. I felt as if my breath were suddenly stopped, and I fell back gasping to the ground again.

Then I gave myself up for lost, but in a moment sight and hearing again left me, and the strangely vivid consciousness came back. Then I felt a sense of rapid motion, and presently I found myself sitting on the bench with Signor Davelli bending over me and Jack standing by. Immediately I glanced at the shadows round

---

[6] "Nay, then God be wi' you, an you talk in blank verse."—J.W.

me, and I saw in a moment that my journey, whatever was its nature, had lasted much longer than Signor Davelli's. I knew at once that he had deceived me, that my lust of knowledge was baulked, and that I had been no nearer to his world than I was now.

I cried out, "You have shown me the moon, perhaps in trance, perhaps you have transferred me there. But what of that? You've shown me nothing of the dwellers in space."

"Be quiet," he said, lifting his hand, and again using the same tone, masterful and yet persuasive, "you have done very well for once;" and then he added in a lower and quite different tone, "and so have I."

I never could make you understand the mixture of contending feelings which began to harass me now. No one, I think, could understand it without undergoing it. I was astonished at what had happened to myself, and yet I was grievously disappointed.

Even if I had been sure that I had been actually transferred to the surface of the moon, that would have seemed as nothing to me now. For what I had looked for was a far greater thing. I had long learned to regard the ether which pervades the interplanatory spaces as the hidden storehouse of material out of which the visible worlds are made, and yet the ether is utterly impalpable to any of the senses, and we know of its existence only by roundabout processes of reasoning, and I had been fool enough to believe that I was going to be put in possession of powers of sense which would enable me to examine the ether just as one might examine any of the ordinary material with which we are familiar. I thought I was going to have a near view of the secret forces which lie behind all mechanical, chemical, and electrical action. And what, in view of such a prospect, did I care about seeing the surface of the moon, even if I did really see it? I knew that on the surface of the moon I should only see, under different conditions, the same sort of material as that with which I was already familiar. And I felt sure, or nearly sure, besides, that I had not seen anything but some picture which this wonderful and mysterious being contrived to impress upon my mind.

Besides, I felt sure now that he was deliberately deceiving me, and the sense of horror and repulsion with which he had more or less affected me from the first were now very greatly increased.

Besides, I felt that his power over me was great and was growing greater, and I began to doubt if I could ever shake it off.

But, above all—and now for the first time a bitter sense of remorse filled me on account of my own action in respect of him—I saw that I had been paltering with my conscience, and playing with right and wrong, for the sake of mere intellectual attainment. I knew that I had been doing this ever since this man or devil had first spoken to me. And I felt that my own words deliberately spoken but a little while ago had brought my wrong-doing to a crisis. I felt now that when the words, "Send me where you will, then," had passed my lips I had put myself, to what extent I knew not, within the power of one whom I deeply suspected of some horrible plot against humanity.

I must not say that I was overwhelmed by these feelings, for stronger than any of them was the resolve I now made, with the whole force of my being, that I would never again surrender my will to him on any pretext whatever. And yet I felt very nearly in despair, for I could not but seriously doubt if I had now the power to keep this resolve. I feared that I might be like the drunkard who has taken the first glass.

I suppose there is hardly a man anywhere who has never really prayed. And so I think every reader will understand me when I say, that I lifted up my heart to God silently, and on the moment, with far deeper energy and fervour and self-distrust than ever I thought possible before.

Just then I became aware that Signor Davelli's eyes were off me and that he was talking to Jack: his manner to him was quite courteous and gracious. He was, as it seemed, apologising to him.

"You must pardon me," said he; "I am afraid that my interest in your friend's conversation has diverted my attention unduly from my other guest." Then, after a slight pause, he added, "Now I propose to take your friend to-morrow on an aerial journey, to see the other extremity of the valley, and some of the operations there. I can only take one at a time: you will probably like to come again. But, for to-morrow, how shall we provide for your amusement? we shall be back early in the afternoon."

Jack replied civilly, but with an air of indifference which I thought was feigned, "*I* should be glad of an opportunity of examining some of the curious engines that we have seen yonder." He pointed as he spoke in the direction of the platform.

"Very well," was the reply; "I will see that you have a guide." As he spoke he took an odd-looking little instrument from a pocket at his girdle, and whistled upon it. The resulting sound consisted of a few recurring notes, with a wild, odd strain of music in them.

In a few moments a man appeared. He came from some place towards the further end of the valley, and he was no doubt one of those whom we had seen on this very square the day before. Signor Davelli spoke to the man. "You will meet this gentleman," he said, "here, to-morrow; his name is Mr. Wilbraham. Meet him at whatever hour he pleases, and show him whatever he wishes to see." Then he spoke a few words in the same strange language as before, and accompanied his words with the same sort of action.

Then he turned to me and said, "Will you meet me here at nine o'clock to-morrow, and I will take you to see what we are doing at the further end of the valley?"

I hesitated for a moment, and then I said, "Yes, I will meet you."

Whether my hesitation, or anything in my tone, indicated that I meant not to commit myself to more than to meet him, I cannot say, but as I spoke a scowl passed over his face. It came and went in a moment, and then he said, "Very well," rather curtly, to me. And then, addressing us both in the same gracious manner as before, "And now you are tired," he said, "and it is getting late; I hope you find your quarters convenient and your commissariat sufficient."

We assured him on both points briefly, made our parting salutation, and retired. I may here mention that the salutations which passed between us and him were never anything more than a formal inclination of the head.

Two more facts must be put on record before I close the account of this eventful day.

We met near the foot of the great stairway the man whom I supposed to be James Redpath. He appeared to be engaged in setting right some detail of the machinery made use of by the workers on the platform. I could not but think as I looked upon him that he had all the appearance of being a machine himself, worked by an intellect not his own. Yet he was evidently working with a will.

I stepped forward and stood before him, having first made a sign to Jack.

"James Redpath," I said; "surely it must be James Redpath?"

He started, and looked at me with a surly scowl, but said nothing. The name (of course I used his real name) seemed to remind him of something, but there was no recognition in his eyes. "Don't you remember Bob Easterley?" I said. He looked at me and then his eyes wandered. There was a muddled, wicked look about him, such as you will sometimes see in the eyes of a very bad-tempered man when he is drunk. "Don't you remember Penruddock?" I said, again of course using the real name. He started again, and I thought he brightened, but it was a queer sort of brightening.

"Penruddock?" he said. "Penruddock and Bob Easterly: curse him and curse the little beggar!" And then he gave a nasty laugh. His voice was thick, like the voice of a man half stupefied with drink or suffering from active brain disease. I thought at first that the name Penruddock had awakened no recollection in his mind, but that he mistook it for the name of a man. Since then, however, I have thought that perhaps "the little beggar" was the boy that he was cruel to, and that the name of Penruddock had reminded him of the matter. Anyhow he turned and looked steadily at me and said slowly, "Oh, so the governor has got you; I wish you joy of the governor." And then he laughed a coarse, harsh kind of laugh. It was not loud, and there was not much expression in it, but what there was was cruel. Then he made as if to pass us, and we let him pass: there was nothing to be got out of him. I am not absolutely sure to this day whether he was James Redpath or not.

That night Jack and I talked long and earnestly. I told him as I have told you my latest thoughts about the matter, and then we talked of our engagements for the coming day.

Wilbraham. There's a crisis near, Bob. It is as likely to come to-morrow as not.

Easterly. How do you think it will come?

Wilbraham. Well, this way. Davelli, I think, overrates the power that he has contrived to get over you. The disappointment you speak of, and your distrust of him and resolve against him have somehow checked the effect of his action on your will, and he does not know that. Not knowing it, he will reveal some villainy to you to-morrow. You will revolt and he will try to kill you. If you are on your guard you may escape yet. The minute you defy him shoot him through the body.

Easterly. What harm will that do him?

Wilbraham. Not much, but some. Did you notice what he said yesterday?

Easterly. Yes, and he was telling the truth. The shot would probably send him to his own place, but he will be back again presently.

Wilbraham. Yes, but meanwhile you will have got a start, and if you are in one of the cars and can manage it you may escape.

Easterly. Not very likely; but supposing I did, what is to become of you?

Wilbraham. I shall be working for myself all the time. Look here: this fellow who is to guide me will either try to kill me or to put me in the way of killing myself. I believe that he has instructions to that effect. I'll watch him, and if I see any treachery I'll send him to his own place and make off if only I can manage the car. For I intend that he shall take me into one of the cars. Then I will try to join you and we shall have perhaps a start of an hour or so before they get back and make ready to follow us.

I didn't see much chance of success in his plan. You couldn't look at it anywhere, I thought, without finding a flaw in it, and I told him as much.

"Never mind," said he, "it is the unlikely thing that happens: let us be on the watch."

Easterly. On the watch, certainly; but look here, Jack: you and I are in imminent danger of death, but I am in danger of worse than death.

Wilbraham. Yesterday, perhaps; but not now, Bob.

Easterly. In one sense, more now than yesterday. I have given him power over me to-day; not so much perhaps as he thinks—you may be right there—but more than I may now be able to withstand. Besides, mark me, he is not going to bring things to a crisis yet.

Wilbraham. Well, if he is not, we shall bring things to a crisis ourselves, and we shall defy him. Then let him kill us if he can. I shouldn't wonder if he couldn't after all. Anyhow, I shall learn something to-morrow, and don't you put yourself in his power any more.

Easterly. I have told you that I am not sure if I can escape him now, but, God helping me, I will do my best.

There our talk ceased for the night, and I may as well say at once that the crisis did not come next day, and that it was not left either to Signor Davelli or to ourselves to bring it about. If it had been so left I do not think this book would ever have been written.

We were now sitting in the inner chamber, from one of the windows of which you could see the door of the outer chamber. The inner chamber opened into the outer, and the outer chamber, without any porch or passage, opened upon the path which led either to the square or the great stairway. As I sat near the window I saw a bright light shining upon the outer door, so that no one could go in or out without being plainly seen. I started up at once and looked for a shadow, for it occurred to me immediately that this light was thrown from one of the invisible cars. But there was no moonlight, for the moon was just then hidden by clouds, and so there was no shadow except such as the light itself might cause. But presently, by walking backward from the window and again towards it, and then this way and that way before it, I discovered a star which appeared and disappeared as I walked. On further inspection it became evident that when the star disappeared it was hidden by some object which, though dark itself, was nevertheless that from which the light before the door proceeded. There could be no doubt that the light in question was thrown from one of the cars, and that the car from which it was thrown was not a hundred feet from the ground.

"Look," I said, "look! we are closely watched even here." But Jack was already fast asleep. I threw myself upon my bed and lay for hours broad awake.

CHAPTER NINE
THE SEED BEDS

As I lay awake the events of the last few days passed and repassed before my mind, and the more I thought over them the less I felt myself able to give any satisfactory account of them or to see any way of escape. I could make up my mind to no plan of action, to nothing except passive but obstinate resistance.

But although I did not see any way of escape I did not feel as if we were going to die. I suppose that youth and a sanguine temper enabled me to keep hoping. Anyhow I found myself again and again reckoning upon a return to civilisation.

But what kept my thoughts busiest was the fact that Jack and I were to be separated next day, and I asked myself over and over again, what could be the purpose of such separation. And here, after a while, I thought I saw my way a little. Such and such at least I felt I could say is not the purpose. Foul play is no doubt what our host is quite capable of; but what is to be gained by foul play? Why not kill either or both of us openly if he wishes? And when I had gotten as far as that I began to see, clearly enough, part at least of his purpose in separating us. And the revelation was greatly more flattering to Jack than to myself. Then I fell asleep and slept quite soundly for some hours, and I got up quite refreshed.

After we had dressed and refreshed ourselves there still remained an hour before it would be time to keep our appointments. For Jack had arranged with the man who had been told off to keep him company to meet him at nine o'clock, the same hour at which I was to meet Signor Davelli. And here I may as well mention that these men or whatever they were, understood our way of reckoning time. But they did not, as far as I could see, make use of it themselves. They had a method of reckoning time but I was not able to discover exactly what it was. I have sometimes thought since then that they were able to measure the earth's diurnal motion directly. But they used no clockwork nor (as far as I could see) any observation of the altitude of sun or stars.

In some of the cars which were fitted for long voyages there was fixed an instrument about a foot long, and this consisted of a hand moving along a graduated scale. I made sure (so far as my very brief opportunity of observation permitted) that this hand did not move by clockwork, but I was quite unable to discover by what power it did move.

I told Jack very briefly about the light I had seen last night, and then we held a brief conference before we parted.

"Jack," said I, "you thought yesterday that Signor Niccolo had given his man instructions either to kill you or to put you in the way of killing yourself?"

"Yes," he said, "under certain circumstances. If I attempt to make my escape the fellow is undoubtedly under orders to compass my death. But not otherwise; certainly not at present. And I need not say that I am not going to attempt my escape without you. If you and I agree to force a crisis, good and well; then we shall both run the risk of our lives. But you seem to think, and I am disposed to agree with you, that we had better for the present keep on the watch and let things take their course. Very well, then, I shall not be in any special danger to-morrow."

"Why do you think so?"

"Because, as I have said before, this man, or call him what you will, has got some design upon you. What that design is will probably appear shortly. And he will not hinder the success of it by allowing anything to happen to me."

"And if it succeeds?"

"Then it will depend on circumstances not now evident what will become of me."

"And if it fails?"

"Then I think that you and I are certain to be put to death unless we can manage to make our escape from this place."

"Which appears hardly to be expected."

"Yes, hardly to be expected, but the unexpected happens."

"And now, Jack," said I, "I agree with you in all that you have said; but do you know why he is sending you away?"

"Well, no, I don't."

"I'll tell you why: he fears your influence over me. I came to that conclusion as I lay awake last night. And he means to try on some new game to-day or to begin to try. But as I thought over all that I couldn't but go on to ask, why does he want me and not you, and why is he shy of you? What do you think?"

"I can't say, Bob, unless it be that I am not clever enough."

"Clever! you're a modest man, Jack, I know, but if I did not know you to be genuine I should say now that some of the modesty was put on. Not clever enough? You've seen through this fellow sooner and farther than I. You might better say too clever, but that is not it either."

"Well, what is it, then?"

"You are too good for him. You have too quick and clear a perception of what is right, and you are not ready enough to let the lust of knowledge blind your conscience. But, please God, this fellow will find that I am not after all quite the sort of man he takes me to be."

"My dear Bob, I am just as likely as you are to have dust thrown in the eyes of my conscience, only a different sort of dust. Your turn has come first, that is all. You'll baffle him and then my turn perhaps won't come at all. Let us both keep our eyes open to-day. If I can learn how to manage those cars of theirs, and if they give us half a chance, we will make a run for it."

"Do you forget the light last night?"

"I forget nothing, but we will give them the slip somehow."

"Well, perhaps we may, for one thing is clear me, Jack: those fellows once they come among us have to work under the same conditions as we."

"Did not Dr. Leopold say something of that sort?"

"Yes, and he was right; all that we have seen proves it: everything that they do is done by some chemical or mechanical or other contrivance, they have to get round their work just as we have; they know more of nature than we do, and so they can do more. But if we knew as much we could do as much as they."

"Well, all that is so much in our favour."

We were now at the foot of the stairway, and it was within a few minutes of nine. So we shook hands and parted. Jack went up the stairway, and I made my way to the square.

I saw in the centre of the square a car somewhat smaller than that in which we had travelled previously, but, like it, visible throughout. It was just alighting as I came up. Signor Davelli was standing in the square, and the man in the car was the same whom he had assigned yesterday to Jack, and as he alighted he addressed him with a few words and signs as before, and the man went away towards the stairway.

Signor Niccolo turned to me, and, after the usual salutation, he said shortly but civilly, "I have had a car prepared like the other. As we use them ourselves, you might find them awkward and even dangerous. I have left the larger car for your friend."

"Thank you," I replied. "I daresay we shall both do very well."

I was glad to know that Jack would have the opportunity that he wished for, and I felt sure that he would make the most of it. I felt confident now that we were on the verge of a desperate effort for freedom. It was likely enough, indeed most likely, that the issue of such an effort would be immediately fatal to us, but, if not immediately fatal, then I thought that we might escape. Meanwhile I was determined to observe as closely as possible every person and thing that should come under my notice to-day.

There was no difference between this car and the other except in respect of size. This one was a shade smaller. Also this one was furnished with some instruments which I had not observed in the other. There were two good field-glasses and a very powerful microscope. There were also some instruments whose use I did not recognise, but they seemed to suggest spectrum analysis. In addition to these there were some glass instruments that looked like test tubes, and other chemical apparatus of apparently simple construction, but quite unfamiliar to me.

We got under way just as formerly, and we moved rapidly towards the western end of the valley. I reckon that it was two miles, or perhaps a little more, from the eastern to the western extremity. The valley was bounded all round by hills. But I seemed to see to-day more than ever before an air of artificial construction about these. From some points of view this disappeared altogether, while from other points the evidence of it was all but conclusive. I made sure sometimes that I could detect the junction of a great embankment with the hills on either side, but in each case after I had got another view I was not quite so sure. Just the same impression, as I have told you, was produced on me by the view of the hills when I first approached them from the east; but the appearance or impression of artificial construction was very much stronger now.

I had on this day a very full view of the arrangement of the valley from end to end. You remember the large square in which on the second day we had seen the men drilled, and in which on the day after we had witnessed our host's wonderful disappearance and reappearance. You remember also the broad walk which led from the eastern stairway to the square. Very well; at the further end of the square that walk was continued. It was the same breadth all the way through, and it was planted with trees and with flowering shrubs, mostly of a kind which I had never seen elsewhere. On each side of it narrower ways branched off, leading to houses of the same style as those in which Jack and I were lodged. There was an air of trimness and regularity about the whole but no beauty. I can imagine one looking at the scene and pronouncing it stiff and formal and nothing more. But as

I looked I felt that if there was no beauty there was at least an eerie suggestiveness that took the place of beauty. Seen from above, as we saw, even trimness and regularity have an odd look. But after all the trimness and regularity of the scene were its least remarkable characteristics. The frowning hills with rampart-like ridges between them that might be walls or that might be natural embankments; the silence broken only by the whirr of our motion through the air, for there was no bird in the valley from end to end, and indeed no living creature of any sort except its human (if they were human) inhabitants, and I think a few snakes; the uncouth aspect of the chimneyless and smokeless houses; the absence of every object that might remind one of the cares and pleasures of life: no garden, or orchard, or playground, no child or woman;—all this formed altogether a picture as unearthly and inhuman as the barren surface of the moon. The odd-looking trees and shrubs which, as I have told you, were planted along the roadway, made this worse and not better. Their approach to naturalness made the unnaturalness of all the rest only the more apparent. Besides, their very presence made you feel that it was not nature, as on the surface of the moon, which caused the silence and desolation, but some foul and maleficent influence which was external to nature. The broad walk and the rows of houses both ended abruptly, abutting upon a belt of timber artificially planted. The trees were like the blue gum, they were so close together that no passage between them was possible, and as far as I could judge the intervals from tree to tree were quite equal and regular. This plantation extended a good way up the cliff on both sides, and it was a hundred yards across, or more. Beyond it was a space of about twenty feet, and then another row of trees of quite a different kind, and like nothing that I had ever seen. But as far as I could guess from such a height the leaves were as thick as the gum leaves, but in other ways much larger. This row of trees was nearly of the same depth as the other, and extended like it high up on either side of the cliff. I have little doubt that all these trees were intended as a defence against the vapours which were generated by certain works which were carried on beyond, and of which I must now try to tell you what I saw.

From what I have said it will be clear to you that there was only one way from the eastern part of the valley to the western, and that was through the air. No one could pass through either belt of timber. And as we floated over them I noticed that Signor Niccolo at once raised the car several hundred feet, and kept well away to the south. Then he stopped; then he lowered the car a little and asked me what I saw.

I saw several very unequal belts of what seemed to be cultivated ground. But it was a very queer-looking sort of cultivation. There was almost no green from end to end of it, and what green there was looked like the scum that you sometimes see floating upon the surface of a stagnant pool. And even this was only to be seen at the southern extremity of the cultivated ground. As you looked north the growth was more and more foul and offensive, and thick, filthy looking vapours floated over it here and there. I thought of Shelley's ruined garden, where—

"Agaric and fungi with mildew and mould
Started like mist from the wet ground cold."

Only that here certainly it was not lack of care that produced all the foulness, for there was plenty of evidence of care everywhere. The beds were divided according to a well-marked plan: they were six in all. The bed on the southern extremity must have been over two hundred and fifty feet wide, and it had several narrow pathways through it, well formed from end to end. Then there was a wide pathway, say about eight feet in width, separating it from the next bed. The next bed was only half the width, with about half as many narrow pathways through it, and then a walk twice as wide as that which separated it from the first bed. Then the third bed was only half the width of the second, with a separating walk of about thirty-two feet across. And so on, the width of the beds decreasing and the width of the walks increasing in geometrical progression, so that the last bed was only about eight feet wide, while the walk beyond it was about two hundred and fifty feet wide.

All the beds and walks were the same length. As I was making these approximate measurements mentally, with the aid of a powerful field-glass, I observed another fact that seems worthy of notice. The foul growths and vapours which, as I have told you, increased from the southern extremity of the ground northward, came absolutely to an end with the last bed but one. But the last bed, which was the narrowest, with the walks on either side of it which were the widest, occupied more than a third of the whole extent of the cultivated ground. The true extent of the foul growths and vapours was about this: they covered rather more than a third of the ground, and the space which they covered was rather nearer the southern end than the northern end. I had reason to believe before the close of the day that these vapours were deadly; but I had reason also to believe that there was something in the bed to the north beyond them which was deadlier still.

There were many men employed at all the beds, much the greater number at the first bed, but the work at the sixth bed seemed to be far the more important; certainly it proceeded, as far as I was able to judge, with far more care and deliberation. Not, however, that there was anything slovenly about any of the work or of the workers.

I first turned my attention to the first bed, and there I saw a number of men at about equal distances on each of the walks, each provided with an instrument like an elaborate sort of hoe, and having a box slung round his shoulders, and hanging directly under his face. Looking along these rows of men to the far edge of the beds, I saw that the valley ended at the west end with a platform, and on this platform several men were standing who were evidently working in concert with the workers at the beds. This platform was not so high as that at the east end, but, unlike that, it extended the whole width of the valley. It consisted of two terraces connected by steps, and on the lower terrace were the men whom I have mentioned who were working in concert with the workers at the beds. One man stood at the end of each walk, and handed to the nearest man on the walk a parcel, and then another and another. He took these parcels out of a little box on wheels that stood beside him. These parcels were marked and numbered. At least so I concluded from the manner in which the man on the walk received each parcel, glanced at it, and passed it on. This distribution of the marked parcels had commenced before I began to observe.

Looking to the boxes on wheels, I saw that they were standing on rafts, and were constructed so as to run on the same principle as the little waggons at the eastern end. Following with my glass the course of the rails on which they ran, I saw on the upper platform whither the rails led several machines in general appearance not unlike some of those at the other end. The glass which I was using was very powerful, much more powerful than any field-glass I had ever seen. Still, I could not observe with any such exactness as if I were standing by the machines. The car that I sat in, although there was not a breath of wind, was not absolutely still. I should not perhaps have noticed this if I had sat still and talked, or even read, but the moment I began to observe closely some object not on the car, I became conscious of a motion such as would be felt at sea on a calm day if there were a long but very gentle swell.

I saw with enough exactness, however, to conclude that the processes which were being carried on here were not mechanical, but most likely chemical. I could see many jars and retorts and instruments of similar aspect, and I thought I could make sure that electricity was being largely applied, and that some strange use was being made of light. It seemed as if there were some substances in certain small vessels on which now and then light greatly magnified was being thrown. These vessels were arranged in order within the machines in such way that they could be subjected at the will of the worker to the various light, magnifying, and chemical and electric processes which it seemed to be the function of the machine to keep in action.

I did not feel sure at first whether the substances in the vessels were being simply examined, or whether they were being treated with a view to effect some change in them. But I soon saw that the latter was the more likely purpose. For I perceived on further observation that they were subjected to a very severe and exact scrutiny before they were placed in the vessels. At one end of the row of machines was a very long table along which, near the middle, a trough ran from end to end. A man stood at the table who seemed to be examining something in the trough with a microscope, or at least with some sort of magnifying apparatus. Then he laid aside the magnifying apparatus, and poured from a little bottle either some fluid or powder, I could not tell which, on the objects which he was examining; then he would apply the magnifier again, and so on. Last of all, from this trough he would take up something or other with a little shovel or trowel, and place it in certain tiny waggons or boxes on wheels which communicated, apparently by automatic means such as I have before described, with the different machines, emptying their contents into the small vessels of which I have told you. All the machines appeared to be of the same sort, and engaged in the same work. I concluded that the man at the table with the trough in it was examining certain substances, and that these were being treated by the men at the machines with a view to some modification of their nature. And I had no doubt that this work, whatever it was, stood in some direct relation to the work at the seed beds.

If I had had any such doubt it would have been removed by what I observed at the other end of the row of machines. There I saw a table just like an enormous billiard table, only there were no pockets, and at this table stood four or five men busily at work. This table was connected with the seed beds by the rails, along which ran the boxes on wheels. Indeed, it was to it that my look had first been directed when I followed, with my glass, the course of these boxes. But the more curious aspect of the machines had attracted my attention, and I had observed the whole row of them to the other end and the table with the trough in it which stood there, before observing this end more particularly. I now saw that the substances which had been examined in the trough and treated in the machines were carried, still by automatic machinery, to this enormous table and emptied upon it. There they were very rapidly sorted and distributed into parcels by the five or six men at work there. These men must have had great accuracy of eye and touch, and their way of working reminded me of the man in the Mint who rings the coin. The parcels which were so made up were distributed among the workers in the seed beds in the way already described.

It was clear to me now that some substances, probably germs of one kind or another, were being examined and treated by scientific methods, and were being subjected afterwards to some sort of discriminating culture. I began to guess at the purpose of all this, and quite suddenly a suspicion broke upon me which almost made me drop my glass with horror. And I may as well say here at once that knowledge which I obtained later on confirmed this horrible suspicion.

Recovering myself, I turned my attention to workers at the seed beds. The men engaged at the first bed went slowly along the walks taking every now and then something out of the boxes which were slung one over the shoulder of each, and planting it in the ground and covering it over. I saw that they examined also something already planted, and sometimes took it up and put it into the box. I could not tell, owing to the distance and the motion, whether or not what they took up exhibited any visible growth. The substances, whatever they were, which were thus taken up, were placed in a little waggon which ran at the eastern end of the bed at right angles to the walks, and conveyed its contents to the walks which separated the first bed from the second, and were dealt with by the workers there. If you ask me how I knew that it was the substances exhumed and not the substances in the parcels that were thus passed, I can only say that such was my conclusion from the whole aspect of the movement, for I could not accurately distinguish small objects at the distance.

The way of working at the next four beds was not so different from what I have described, as to make it worth while attempting a detailed account. It will suffice to say that the mode of procedure was to sow something in each bed, and to take up something which had been down in order to transfer it to the next bed, and this latter process evidently involved much careful examination and discrimination. I should also mention that at the third bed and onward the workers wore masks, apparently wire masks of some elaborate construction. They wore them, not continuously, but whenever they stooped to the ground or examined very closely the substances with which they were dealing. At other times the masks hung at the girdles. At the fourth bed the workers wore the masks more frequently, and at the fifth they only removed them occasionally. The way of working at the sixth bed was different and will need a fuller description.

But before attempting to describe it I should say that just as I was beginning to observe the sixth bed, a slight change came in the weather which made two considerable changes, each in a different direction, in my opportunities of observation. It had been quite calm and at the same time cloudy. Now a light breeze began to blow and the sun shone out. The effect of the breeze was, at first, so to increase the motion of the car as to make very close observation impossible. But Signor Davelli presently applied a sort of ballasting machinery, which had the effect of greatly steadying the car. I was so much interested in what was going on below that I did not very accurately observe how this was done. But I think that it was somehow in this way. He moved, by mechanical contrivance, certain weights in the car, so as to change the centre of gravity in such manner as to render the part of it which we occupied subject to less motion than the rest. I have not much skill in such matters and I hardly know if this is possible, but so it seemed to me. But even after this was done the car was not by any means as steady as before.

At the same time, however, the sunshine which now appeared disclosed some features of the scene which I should otherwise have missed. For now, at the northern end of the beds, on a platform at right angles with the western platform, I saw several shadows which indicated to my now skilled eyesight the presence of several of the invisible cars. They were standing all still when I first saw them, but presently one moved, rose quickly from the earth, and passed gradually out of sight to the northward. I followed its course with my glass for several minutes, till it was nearly out of sight. I then turned again to the seed-beds. The men at the sixth bed were very few, only five in all, and each was working apparently on his own account. But they were all doing exactly the same kind of work. They were, as I thought, making a final selection of the germs which had undergone so careful a process of cultivation. Each of them had three boxes, instead of one, slung in front of him, and a long instrument in his hand with which he extracted certain substances from the ground. This instrument was constructed so as to hold in a little receptacle what was lifted from the ground. Each of the workers, also, had slung over his shoulder what looked like a small frame. I selected one of the five at random, and watched his proceedings more particularly. Now and then he would unsling the frame and place it on the ground. Then he would give it a little twist, whereupon it would assume a form very like that of a lady's work-table. I saw him do this many times, and each time he took something out of the closed receptacle which I have just mentioned, and placed it on the table, and observed it carefully with some kind of instrument that might have been a kind of microscope. After a more or less minute observation each time, he placed the substance observed in one of the boxes at his girdle, which he opened each time and carefully closed again. By-and-by he seemed to discover some substance which challenged his attention specially, for after a longer observation than usual, he took another instrument from his girdle and observed it more carefully and for a longer time. Then I could see that he called his neighbour, for he looked, and I almost thought that I could see his lips moving, and immediately the other looked up and came towards him. Then the first man handed his observing instrument to the second, who examined very carefully the substance on the little table. Some discussion seemed to follow, an animated conversation as I thought, with certainly a rapid pantomime accompaniment.

Then a very strange thing happened. As the first man stooped towards the table his mask fell off. My glass was so good that I saw it quite plainly come loose at one side, and I saw the man's hand lifted up to catch it. But before he could reach it, it fell off as I have said. Then in a moment the man's body became a mass of rapidly seething fluid, and the fluid became a dark cloud of smoke, which spread into the air and disappeared. Just so I had seen Signor Davelli's body transformed and disappear the day before. The second man at once caught up the mask and stood apparently waiting. Presently a diffused vapour appeared. This became denser and denser, until it assumed the appearance of a seething fluid, as before. This quickly became consolidated and assumed the form of a body, the body of the man who had just disappeared. Then the other man, who was standing ready with the mask in his hand, fitted it again upon the first man, and both men proceeded to examine the substance before them, and to converse, as if nothing had happened to interrupt them. All this time (which, however, was a very short time, although the change was by no means instantaneous, as the like change seemed to be yesterday) the other men worked away without, as far as I could see, taking any notice whatever of what was going on.

I exclaimed slightly and started, and this attracted Signor Davelli's attention. He had been, I think, examining and preparing some instruments. "What do you see?" he said. I answered without taking my eyes from the glass. "A man over there disappeared and appeared again just as you did yesterday."

"Careless wretches!" he said, looking towards the place that I was observing.

"I suppose," I said, "that these substances which they are examining must be very deadly, for his mask fell off just before he disappeared, and I remember you said yesterday that what would kill us only drove you back into space."

"And you infer, I suppose, that if you had been in his place you would have dropped down dead."

"That is what I think," said I.

"Then you see if you become one of us you escape death." He said this with a strongly persuasive manner, and as he spoke a slight shudder seemed to pass over me, and I expected him to say more. But he said no more, and he returned to the task in which he had been engaged.

I then turned my attention again to my examination of the workers at the sixth bed.

You will understand that a very broad walk lay between the bed and the northern platform. This walk was to all appearance formed of some hard stuff like flags or asphalt, and I now perceived by the aid of the sunlight that some of the cars had alighted upon this pathway and were standing there.

I could see that there were five of them, and presently the five workers went over to the cars, one to each car. There was a man in each or beside each, I could not say which. For as you will remember I could only see the shadows of the cars, and the sun was now very high, and very near the zenith, and the shadows were proportionately small. The five workers took the boxes, each one from his girdle, one after another, and handed them, one after another, each worker to one of the men in or beside each car. Then the workers went back to the bed, and the cars rose from the ground. I could see that they rose almost perpendicularly at first for the shadows hardly moved, but became smaller and smaller; then they lengthened and passed away to the north-east, and rapidly disappeared. I looked up in the direction which seemed indicated by the lengthening shadows, and I could see distinctly for a few minutes something like a queer little cloud, and another and another until I counted the five. Then I lost sight of them.

If the north platform was the port of departure for the cars it seemed as if the south platform was the port of arrival. For now on looking straight below I saw that many cars were standing there, and some arrived as I looked. The bright sunshine enabled me to count them as they stood and to see them coming; and my position in respect of them enabled me to estimate the size of these cars by their shadows much more exactly than that of those which I had been just observing at the other end. A little further observation showed me that the cargo they were laden with consisted of the same sort of substances as those which were so carefully treated on the platform, and in the seed beds, and, finally, in a modified condition exported for use elsewhere. I had evidence already of the care which was given to the preparation and final distribution of these, and I now had evidence that the same kind of care was given to their first selection. Signor Davelli lowered the car to the platform, alighted, and called a man to his side. I alighted at the same time. The man came at once, and it was clear that he knew what he was called for; for he brought with him something that looked like a little glass case or tray, in which were a multitude of little matters which proved to be germs of some sort, part of them of animal and part of vegetable growth, and these, as I gathered, had been selected from a great number of similar matters which had just come in, and they were now submitted to Signor Davelli for his examination and approval. He examined them carefully in some ways that I understood, and in some ways also that I did not understand at all. As an instance of the latter I may mention the following. He extracted one of the germs from the case and placed it on an elliptical piece of opaque ware which was very slightly depressed in the middle. The germ was so small that he had to work with a magnifying-glass of enormous power, and with instruments of extreme delicacy. He showed me the germ through the glass. It was egg-shaped and colourless, with a tiny dark spot under a partly transparent substance. Without the glass it was to me absolutely invisible. Then he got a little glass tube into which he put something out of a very small bottle, which he took from a number of others which lay side by side in a little case which he took out of a pocket in the side of the car. Whether what he took out of the bottle was powder or fluid I could not tell, though I was now so near what I was observing. But I noticed that when poured into the tube it seemed to change colour. Then Signor Davelli handed the tube to the man who had come in answer to his call, and this man, who appeared to know exactly what was expected of him, took the tube and blew through it upon the germ. I could not see that anything came through the tube, but in a few seconds a kind of cream-coloured spray began to rise from the germ, and Signor Davelli observed this, not the germ but the spray, very carefully through the magnifier. He seemed highly pleased; he selected a few more germs which he said were of the same sort as this; he spoke of them as particularly "promising," and he indicated, as I thought (for just here he began to speak in a tongue unknown to me), the treatment which in his judgment they ought to receive.

  When I could no longer understand him I looked again to the workers at the beds. There were now a great many more workers at the first bed, and the work all through was proceeding in a very rapid and orderly manner. I followed quickly the whole process from first to last: the gathering in of the germs, their preliminary examination, the treatment which they underwent on the platform, the tests to which they were subjected before and after that treatment, their gradual passage through the several stages of cultivation, and finally their dispersion, in their cultivated condition, whither I could not certainly say, but presumably to the ends of the earth.

One thing especially puzzled me: I could not estimate at all the amount of time which the process of cultivation consumed in the case of each germ. There were germs constantly going into cultivation and frequently coming out; but how long it was from the time that each one went in until the same one came out again, whether they took different periods of time or uniform, or nearly uniform periods, I could not at all guess. The rapidly decreasing size of the beds implied certainly that the process of cultivation was a process of elimination. It seemed that not one in a hundred of those which passed through the first stage could ever have reached the final stage. And I think also that it might be inferred with much probability from the same fact that the process of cultivation lasted in most cases for a long time. For otherwise they might surely have made up for losses during culture by an increase of the numbers put under cultivation. For what I saw left me no room to doubt that such an increase in quantity was at their disposal. Making a rough estimate, I should say that hundreds of germs cultivated up to the highest pitch were sent away every day, and that hundreds of thousands went under cultivation.

While I was making these calculations, I became aware of a disturbance at the first bed. Turning my glass hastily to the spot I saw that one of the men had fallen down, and it struck me at first that there was going to be a repetition of the sort of disappearance and reappearance which I had already witnessed, and which I now understood. But I very soon saw that this was quite a different matter. There was a panic, and the men ran in all directions away from the man who had fallen. I followed for a moment with my glass the course of some of the fugitives. Turning the glass back towards the spot where the man had fallen, I could perceive nothing at all. Every trace of his body was lost. Then I heard a long and loud whistle, and in almost as little time as it takes me to tell it the panic had ceased and the men were working away just as before. Just then I heard what seemed like a deep and desperate curse from Signor Davelli, and looking towards him I saw him standing with his arm half way up, holding the glass. He seemed to have just taken it away from his eyes, and a scowl was passing over his face, made up as it seemed to me of malignity, ferocity, and fear. It reminded me at once of the expression which had passed over his countenance on the second day when the men were gathered in the square and when one or two of them proved to be missing, and I remembered also Jack's words, "Depend upon it his damnation has got something or other to do with the loss of these men."

To conceal my horror I turned my glass again to the workers, but I really observed nothing more, and presently at a signal from Signor Davelli I resumed my place in the car. He raised the car just as before, made a curve to the south, and then turned the prow of the car towards the east end of the valley. We alighted at the same point whence we had started, and then he spoke—

"Mr. Easterley, you know something of my power now."

I looked at him, I suppose, interrogatively, for he went on to say—

"Among your kings who is the most powerful? Is it not he who possesses the deadliest weapons and can use them with the most facility and precision?"

I said nothing for a moment, for I knew he was misleading me, or perhaps I should not say I knew, but I felt so, not indeed because of any opinion that I had formed about the purpose of the cultivated germs, but because of the profound distrust with which he had inspired me. Then, as he seemed to be waiting for my reply I said briefly, "I have no doubt at all of your power."

"Very well," he said; "we shall see to-morrow if you are worthy to share it."

I said nothing. The words that formed themselves in my mind were, "I hope that I am not sufficiently unworthy," but for obvious reasons I kept silence.

Then he said, "We meet here to-morrow two hours before noon, and now you can return to your friend; I can see him coming towards us on the stair."

I could not see, for I had left the glass in the car; but I exchanged a parting salute with my companion, walked slowly to the stair and began to ascend it. Before beginning the ascent I had seen Jack standing half way up the stair, looking towards me.

After a hearty grip of the hand we turned back and walked slowly towards the pathway that we had taken on the second morning of our stay here. We spoke almost in whispers. I gave Jack a brief account of what I had seen. He said that it indicated something of which we could hardly guess the whole import, but he agreed with me that such import was probably as bad as it could be.

"We must try to escape," he said, "as soon as possible. I know now exactly how to work and steer the cars, and I know, too, how to lay my hands on a second battery."

"What do we want with a second battery?" said I.

"Well," said he, "I don't know what these batteries are made of; they are of solid stuff, not fluid, and yet they all waste very quickly. I doubt if any one of them will carry us as far as we may want to go; indeed, I am not sure that any two of them will be enough."

"But how are we to get away," said I; "we are so closely watched?"

"I'll tell you what I propose," he said. "We shall not retire to-night until an hour after dark, nor the next night, then we may hope that they will take it as a matter of course that we shall not retire on the third night until the same hour. But on the third night, immediately after dark, we shall make a bolt of it, and so we may hope for an hour's start."

"In the car?"

"Well, so I propose. I am aware that there is much to be said in favour of an attempt to escape on foot. These lozenges of theirs are meat and drink. We have had nothing else for several days, and we want nothing else, and we know now how many of them we should require, and it is certain that we could easily carry enough to last us three weeks or more. And if we make a bee-line for the wire we ought to reach it within three weeks or less. Besides, if we escape on foot they will not know where to look for us. We shall have cover among the trees, whereas in the air we shall have no cover."

"Not even if we escape in an invisible car?"

"There is none of the cars invisible to them."

"Ah! so I was beginning to think."

"I am quite sure of it."

"Well, go on."

"Still, three weeks may not be enough. We may not be able to make a bee-line. Probably we shall meet with some impassable scrub, or other obstacle, and so our food may run out, and we may die miserably after all. But if we escape in one of the cars the whole risk will be over, and our fate will be decided one way or another within twenty-four hours."

"Very well," said I, "we shall try it the night after next."

Then I told him of my appointment next day with Signor Davelli.

He looked very grave. "That's the biggest risk of all," he said. "If you give in to him we're both done for."

"I won't give in to him."

"Good; but if he knows for certain that you are resisting him, he may take immediate action, and then also we shall be done for."

"He will give me more than one trial."

"I think he will, but, any way, we are not likely to have as much time as we thought. I would say, let us try to-night, but we are watched so closely, that it is not possible. We had better say to-morrow night."

"So be it," said I.

Then we went to our quarters and had some food and a little rest. Then we walked backward and forward on the same path again. About an hour after dark we retired for the night, and when we had passed into the inner room we could see the bright light already shining before the doors. The watch upon us was close and constant.

CHAPTER TEN
LEÄFAR

That night we lay both of us in the outer chamber, partly for company, and partly because neither of us wished to be within sight of the light which lay all night before the door, and which could be seen from the window of the inner chamber. There was nothing, indeed, strange or ugly about the light itself; it was very bright, and, under other circumstances, might have been pleasant. But to us, guessing whence it was and what was its purpose, it had come to have a weird look of doom about it.

We lay still, scarcely speaking. Only from time to time a word or two passed between us, either suggestive of preparation, or of some topic of encouragement. By and by we lapsed into silence, and thence into an imperfect sleep. There was no artificial light in our chamber, we had no occasion for any, although day and night were nearly of equal length. Sometime in the evening before dusk we used to take a second bath (if one may use the consuetudinal for so short a period), and then to throw off our hats and sandals and to exchange the long robe, which was our only other garment, for another of the same sort, was the whole of our preparation for the night.

I do not know how long I had been sleeping, but it could not have been very long, when I woke up with a start. Surely there was a light in the room? Yes, there was, and it was growing slowly brighter. I looked over to the couch where Jack lay; it was very near my own, but not near enough to permit me to touch him without rising.

I sat up and put on my sandals. The light had now become so much brighter that I could see Jack plainly. He was awake and watching as I was. The light was now increasing much more quickly, and in a few minutes the room was quite brilliantly illuminated, and there was a sort of core of brightness beginning to appear in the centre of the light. This presently assumed a wavering aspect, and by-and-by became a bubbling fluid. I was prepared to expect the appearance of a form of human similitude, for I had witnessed as you will remember, the same thing twice already. The same, and yet not the same, for the dark vapour which I had seen in the former cases was replaced in this case by a bright rose-coloured light. I suppose it was partly because of this obvious difference that I felt now no fear, but hope. I began to think that help was coming, and that we were not going to be left to fight out a desperate battle alone.

As I looked, the bubbling fluid became consolidated and assumed, as I had expected, a human form. A man of, it might be middle age, stood before us. I should have said much under middle age only that his expression indicated, as I thought, a ripeness of experience and a calm wisdom seldom seen in very young men. There was a stately beauty and benignity in his features and demeanour, a mingled tone of love and command and entreaty; all the direct reverse of what we had seen in Signor Davelli and his men. He wore a flowing robe of much the same pattern as ours, but it was of a very bright, indeed of a luminous material, and it had somehow a strange air of being part of his body. His head was uncovered; his hair was brown, short, and slightly curled, and his eyes were blue.

We both started to our feet, and made, almost involuntarily, a profound salutation.

"Friends," he said, "you are in urgent danger, and I come to inform and counsel and help you." He spoke the English language with a very sweet and firm intonation, and yet his accent was in some way suggestive of an outland or foreign origin. "I am a friend," he said, "and in some sort a guide of men. It was my mission long ages ago to warn your first father of the designs of an enemy of the same order as this one of yours, but far mightier than he. Later on in the plains of Assyria, under the name and form of a man, I baffled the designs of another of the same evil race. And many times in more modern days I have rendered help of which no record remains to man and to the friends of man. Speak to me freely; you may call me Leäfar."

I was meditating whether or not I should begin with a confession of my own faults, when Jack stepped forward, prevented me, and spoke.

"Sir Leäfar," he said, "tell us first of all who these men are into whose power we seem to have fallen, and from whom we desire to escape."

"Yes," answered he who called himself Leäfar, "it is best that you should have information first; counsel and help will follow.

"These men and I have one thing in common. We are inhabitants not of earth, but of ether; as they have themselves told you, we are dwellers in space. But they are not, as they would have you think, a fair sample of the race which inhabits the ether, for although very many as compared with the inhabitants of earth, they are very few in comparison of those who hold with me."

"How is it possible," said I, "that you and they, although dwellers in space, or inhabitants of the ether, can assume as you do the form of men, and at least in some measure their nature?"

"I cannot," he replied, "unfold the matter to you in full detail, for you have not the faculties needful to enable you so to apprehend it; but if you will attend I will try to show you by analogies how it is possible for us to pass from our world to yours. But sit down," he said; "you will be weary, for I have much to say, and there is no time to lose."

Hereupon he sat down, having first indicated to us with a gracious air where we were to sit. We both sat in front of him, but each one a little to one side. Then he began. "The material," he said, "of your world and of such worlds as yours is limited. The material of our world envelops and pervades it all, and extends to immeasurable distances, as I believe to infinity, but the knowledge of infinity is reserved to the Infinite One Himself.

"The material of our world is the basis of the material of yours. The latter is made out of the former by a simple process of agglomeration. All the material of worlds like yours is resolvable ultimately into extremely minute particles, each of which is just a little twist of the ether. You may compare these particles to knots that you make upon a cord. Just as the parts of the cord in the knot act upon one another in a way in which they could not act if they remained in one continuous line, so the knotted or twisted ether becomes capable of a great variety of interactions which are not possible to it in its original state, and as the knots increase in complexity these possible interactions are multiplied. The motion by which the first agglomeration of ether is formed generates the various processes which are known to you as heat, magnetism, electricity, and the different chemical affinities, and so the matter of your world is built up. The bodies of the dwellers in ether are composed of ether in the simple state, and by a process which is simple enough although not fully explicable to you, we can transform them into the material of which your bodies are made and retransform them again.

"Two analogies, one mechanical and one chemical, may help you, if not to understand the process at least to see how it is possible. Suppose a string of immense length so thin as to be quite invisible; and suppose it to be knitted and woven and re-woven until it be formed into a piece of cloth, compact but very small. Suppose the process of knitting or weaving to be performed very quickly, and then suppose the web so formed to be as rapidly unravelled again. In that case the piece of cloth would appear and disappear just as you have seen our bodies do.

"Or suppose two vast masses of oxygen and hydrogen in the proportions in which they exist together as water. Suppose them to be brought together and subjected to the chemical process which is needed in order to make them combine: what happens? A small quantity of water suddenly appears. Reverse the process and it disappears.

"By means roughly analogous to these we are able to assume terrestrial bodies and to pass into the ether again. But while our bodies are in terrestrial form they are subject to the same laws as yours; we need food and sleep, and we are subject to the various accidents and conditions of humanity."

Here he paused for a moment and Jack spoke.

"But you are not subject to death as we are. Any cause that would kill us only resolves your material bodies into their ethereal form."

"That is the case," he said; "but the difference is not such as you suppose. All the material of your bodies is ultimately resolved into ethereal matter, but not all of it is essential to your being, and that which is essential is resolved by a much speedier process.

"But to speak of ourselves: while we remain in our own world we have instruments of sensation fitted to our condition and analogous to yours, just as hearing is analogous to seeing. But I cannot explain to you any more exactly our means of sensation, just as you could not explain sight to a man born blind.

"But our sensations are throughout strictly analogous to yours and pass into yours when we assume terrestrial bodies."

Here he paused again, and I asked, "Can you see our worlds from yours?"

"No," he replied. "The ether as far as we know pervades the universe and passes freely through worlds like yours, and we, while dwelling in the ether, have no more cognisance of your world than you of ours.

"But there are certain links," he added, "which bind both worlds together, and two of these are known to you as *light* and *gravity*. Our world is for ever in motion; motion is of the essence of its being, and it communicates its motion to all that is formed out of it and continued by it as your worlds are. Such motion is communicated in exact proportion to the vastly varied complexities of the matter of your worlds, and out of this proportionate communication arise the movements and the laws of movement of all the stars and planets, all of which movements and laws of movement are amenable to calculation. Much of this is already known to you, and the day will probably come when your men of science will be able to calculate the proper motion of the remotest star that your instruments can discover with as much precision as they now calculate the motions of your moon.

"Light is another link between your worlds and ours. And light is the one means which we have of detecting from our world the presence of yours. Not that we see light as you see it. The sort of perception that you have by means of light we have in our world by analogous but higher means. The presence of light is known to us when in our own world only by a slight shuddering motion of the ether. Just as you perceive a difference in the mode of motion when you travel on land and on the water or in the air; just so we perceive an analogous difference when we pass to the regions of light from the regions where light is not. A shuddering motion of the material of our world warns that we are where your worlds are. And just as for you sometimes the motion of the air or water passes into a hurricane or a whirlpool, so to us a vastly increased movement of the ether (not the regular movement which is the cause of gravity, but a quivering movement) indicates the presence of one of the secular outbursts of conflagration which form part of the process by which your worlds become fitted for your occupation."

"But how," inquired I, "can you come into our world without having any direct sensation of its whereabouts?"

"Once we have been here," he said, "it is a matter of easy calculation to us to fix the locality; and we can communicate the elements of the calculation to others who have not been here."

Here he paused, and rose to his feet, and as we were about to rise he signed to us to keep sitting.

"Now," he said, "hearken carefully while I tell you of those into whose power you are fallen." And as he spoke it seemed to me that his attention was directed more especially to myself.

He went on—"The Infinite One, ages before your worlds were formed, called the ethereal host into being. And at first they were like your brute creatures, only with vastly greater powers and intelligence; yet, like them, for their vast powers were not under the control of any will of their own, for there was no such thing then as will, except the will of the Infinite One.

"But it pleased the Infinite One at last to give His creatures will. That which is His own prerogative He communicated to them in order that He might give manifold scope to the eternal love which is His essence. That will of theirs it was His will that they should exercise in conformity with that eternal love. But being free it might oppose that eternal love, not indeed to eternity, but for incalculable cycles of time.

"A few, a very few, as compared to the whole number, opposed themselves to Him, and as the ages passed these grew ever more evil, and ever more full of hatred of Him and of all who hold with Him. A very few they were as compared with those who held with Him, but a great many when compared with all the men who inhabit this little world of yours, or who ever have inhabited it."

Here he paused again, and there was dead silence for a space, and then Jack spoke, and his voice was like that of a man hurried and somewhat overawed.

"But how did the will to resist the will of the Infinite One ever come into being at all?"

"It was a possibility from the moment when the first free being was created, and it became actual by the gradual and undue admixture of things in themselves good. The desire to do great things is good, and the joy to be able to do great things is good. But if these two good things are suffered to govern the whole being, they become the possible germs, inert as yet, of self-assertion and pride. And then when the call for self-sacrifice comes, as it must, to the finite in the presence of the Infinite, the will, the spark of divine life which the Creator has committed to the creature, rises up against the sacrifice, and by its action fertilises the germs of self-assertion and pride.

"So began the deadly war of the finite with the Infinite. That had its origin in 'worlds before the man,' and it speedily passed over into man's world, and would long ago have destroyed it had not the Infinite One Himself become human in order to teach men by His own example and in His own Person the divine lesson of self-sacrifice."

Here Leäfar paused again and sat down, and seemed to wait for some question from us. I was quite powerless to speak. I felt quite awe-stricken and shamed, but presently I heard Jack's voice ringing out clearly and confidently like the voice of a fearless and innocent child.

"Sir Leäfar," he said, "do the men who inhabit this valley belong to the evil race you speak of?"

"Yes," he replied, "they are some of the least powerful, though not the least evil among them."

"And what is their purpose here?"

"Their purpose in general is to set the inhabitants of your world against the will and purpose of the Infinite One, to teach them to call evil good and good evil. And they work out this purpose by a great variety of methods.

"They assume human forms, and they have dwellings in the most inaccessible parts of your worlds, near the summits of the loftiest mountain ranges, and in the polar regions, and in remote islands, and in deserts as here. When civilised men move into their neighbourhood they move away; and they destroy most of the marks of their occupation. Sometimes nothing remains; sometimes, it may be, a few huge rocks standing on end, or piled one upon another. Such remains, when you discover them, you account for by attributing their formation to races of men who have passed away.

"From these remote settlements of theirs they make excursions into the inhabited world; they mingle sometimes among men, stirring them to murder and rapine, sowing discontent among the people, and prompting rulers to tyrannous deeds of cruelty and violence. This Niccolo Davelli, as he calls himself, was very active in the most corrupt and violent years of the tenth century, when he was the active adviser of an Italian bandit baron.

"But they have seldom taken prominent action in their own persons in more modern times, although here and there they appear in subordinate characters, stirring up strife and all kinds of evil, and then they pass elsewhither.

"But this Davelli has lately taken up a line of action against God and man which some of the more powerful of his kind took up ages ago with far wider success; he has established here, and in the inaccessible parts of the Himalayas, and in one or two other places, artificial seed-beds of pestilence. His emissaries gather, from all quarters, germs of natural and healthful growth, and submit them to a special cultivation under which they become obnoxious and hurtful to human nature. And then they sow them here and there in the most likely places, and thus produce disease, death, and disaster among men. The black death, and the plague, and smallpox, and cholera, and typhus and typhoid fevers have all had their origin in this way, and some of these are kept alive since by the carelessness of men. But of later years men are beginning to understand health and disease better, and so the power of these evil beings is becoming greatly restricted in this direction."

Here he paused again, and I took heart and said—

"Is it simply to gratify their love of inflicting pain that they cultivate and propagate these plagues?"

"Partly that, no doubt," he said, "but, above all, their purpose is to set men against the Infinite One by making them believe Him to be the Creator of painful and abominable diseases."

"But why should they not blame Him," said I, "if He has called into existence those evil beings who invent such diseases?"

"Suppose," replied Leäfar, "that a human enemy were to poison your water supply. Would you blame God or man?"

"Man, I suppose," replied I.

"Yes," he said, "for you would recognise the fact that man, being man, is free, and that once his freedom absolutely ceases he is no longer man. The Infinite One may, if He so please, take away his freedom, but by so doing He annihilates the man."

"You raise a hard question," said I; "is the Infinite One, then, committed to the eternal prevalence of evil? Is He pledged never to annihilate the power to do evil?"

Leäfar answered very slowly and solemnly, and yet there was a smile upon his countenance as he spoke.

"There is one thing impossible to the Eternal Love, and that is to annihilate Himself: and it would be to annihilate Himself if He were to permit the existence of Eternal hatred."

"Then," said I, "if I understand you rightly, these beings are doomed to annihilation?"

He smiled again and said, "Surely the freedom which opposes and continues to oppose God must perish: it is self-doomed; that is as certain as that the Love of God is infinite. The creature who so misuses his freedom must lose it at last, and then he is as if he had never possessed it. And so his moral being is, as you say, annihilated. All his other powers remain, but his will is dead. He becomes, like the brute, or like the earliest of the ethereal creation; nothing but an instrument in the hand of God. Such is the eternal doom of those who choose evil and abide by their choice. No pain remains, no hatred remains, no sin remains, because no opposition to God remains. But no real soul remains. The moral being is dead and done with, only an intellectual being remains."

"And what becomes of them?"

"They become the beasts of burden of the universe: they become instruments for carrying on the various mechanisms of the visible creation. They become subject to us just as your horse is to you. Many such are under my own direction and control."

Here Jack started and almost interrupted him, then hesitated and said, "I beg your pardon."

"Say on," replied Leäfar, quite softly and kindly.

"What I was going to say," said Jack, "was this: It seems to me that the final doom of which you tell us must have come to some of them before this."

"Some of them are meeting it every day," said he. "The mightiest of them can hold out for periods of secular vastness without losing their power of will in any appreciable degree; others, again, lose it all after a period comparable with the life of a man."

"And do they all know that they must lose it?"

"As well as you know that you must die."

"Ah!" said Jack, "I thought so, and now, sir, tell me one thing more: if this doom comes upon them while they are in human form, what happens then?"

"They pass back at once into their own world and are dealt with as I have told you there."

"Yes, I see it now. Two of the men here appeared to be missing the other morning, and when Davelli missed them I saw his face change with terror and malignity. I said to my friend here, 'Depend upon it the loss of these men has got something to do with his damnation.' Did I not say so, Bob?"

I nodded assent.

"It is true," said Leäfar.

"Then surely," said I, "they must be dying out rapidly."

"Dying out, certainly, but not as rapidly as you might suppose."

"Have they," said I, "the power to reproduce their kind?"

"No," said he; "the dwellers in the ether 'neither marry nor are given in marriage.' But they recruit their failing ranks from amongst men and from races analogous to man in other worlds like yours; they win them over to their side here and then claim them when they pass over there. Sometimes they steal them away from this world. Their purpose is to steal you away, one of you or both."

"Steal us! Surely that would not be permitted?"

"It is not possible unless you yourselves give yourselves away."

"How should we give ourselves away?"

"If you submit your will to theirs they get power over you, power which is hard to shake off, and which is very easily increased."

Here he paused, and the smile which usually attended his pauses did not appear. A sad expression, severe yet very gentle, took its place. There was a silence of several seconds. Then I stood up and spoke, standing.

"Hear me, sir. I remember and repent my faults. I knew that this man was a bad man. Nay, I had begun to suspect that he was something other and worse than a bad man. But I saw that he knew things which I longed to know, and so I suffered myself to forget his badness and I did for the moment submit myself to his will. He exercised his power upon me and he deceived me in its exercise. He transferred me to the surface of the moon, or showed it me in a trance, I know not which. I am conscious ever since of being somehow in bondage to him; although I am now determined to resist him to the death. Is there any hope?"

"Yes, there is hope, surely, although you may have, as you say, to resist him to the death. But if you die resisting him he will have no power over you after death. I am come to rescue both you and your friend. He runs no such risk as you do, although you are both in great danger of your lives."

"And but for my compliance, I suppose neither of us would have run any risk at all."

"Not so. You were both of you in great danger of your lives, and your friend is still so. But any further compliance on your part will make you the slave of this man, living or dead."

I shuddered and said, "What is to be done?"

"Your penitence and your present purpose are accepted, and you will have one more opportunity of asserting your own will against this Davelli. Tell me what has passed between you since your first compliance."

I told him in brief all that I have told you in the last chapter.

"It is clear," said Leäfar, "that he is going to make one more attempt upon you. He will make it, no doubt, when you meet him to-morrow. If you surrender your will to him again I see no hope. If you resist, then he will have no power but over your body."

"And what will he do then?"

"I cannot certainly say. He may kill you in his unrestrained fury. It is not altogether unlikely that he will. But that is all that he can do. You will have escaped him, and I will be able most probably to extricate your friend. But I think it more probable that he will resolve to make one other effort to enslave you, and, in that case, before the effort is made, I shall probably be able to extricate you both. I have little or no doubt that I shall be able, although the strife will be hard."

It occurred to me to ask him why he would not rescue us at once, without waiting for any further conference between Davelli and me. But I knew what the answer would be, and I felt its force. I knew that I should be fit for nothing in earth or heaven until I had asserted my will against this evil being, so I answered simply, "How shall I resist him?"

"He will probably endeavour to throw you into a trance again, and if you give your will to him for a moment, he will succeed. But if you hold your soul firmly, then he will fail. Call inwardly upon God and give yourself to God with your whole purpose. Think all the time of the holiest event in the history of mankind when the power of evil flung its whole force against One that was human, and was baffled, and the victory was won through suffering. So you will keep your will unsurrendered, and your adversary will be beaten back."

"And then?"

"Then, as I have said, he may kill your body in his disappointment and humiliation and rage, but you will be safe from him all the same."

"Let me escape him, and I am willing to die."

"That is the true temper; keep to that, and you need have no fear. And now listen to my further counsel."

But here again Jack interrupted him. "Surely, sir," he said, "it is better, is it not, to act at once? Why expose my friend here to a fearful risk? Lead us now, and we will follow you any whither. Let the risk, then, be what it may be, it cannot be more than the risk of death."

"Sir," said Leäfar, "I deeply honour your spirit and feeling, but you do not know the nature of the case. It is true that I might be able to rescue both of you from the place without any further contact between your friend and him whom you call Niccolo Davelli. I might be able and yet I might not, for although I am stronger than these men they have great odds against me here. But that is not the question, for suppose that I were quite certain that I could take you both alive out of this place, your friend remaining as he now is, I should not try to do so, for his own sake I would not. Wherever he would be, the power which this evil being has gained over him would remain and might be exercised at the most inopportune time for him. Davelli would select his own time, and that would be, no doubt, when your friend would be not so likely as now to resist him successfully. I see that you are willing to risk your life on his account, and your willingness will, no doubt, help him greatly. But not even all the wealth of sacrifice can save a man against his will. You may win his will but you cannot dispense with its exercise as long as he is man, or no less than man. Believe me that the very best thing that can be done for your friend is to let him take at once the opportunity which presents itself of asserting his will against the will of this evil one. He never can be more favourably disposed to do so than he is now."

It seemed as if Jack was going to answer, and I tried to catch his eye to dissuade him, for I felt very certain that what Leäfar said was true. But I could not catch his eye, and he tried to speak, but hesitated before a word came. Leäfar waited courteously. Jack made a further attempt. "But, sir," he began, and then again hesitated. At last he said, "No doubt, sir, you know best; let me not interrupt you further."

Then Leäfar continued, addressing himself to me. "I will suppose, now, that you have been successful in your endeavour to resist your enemy, and that he has resolved to make one other attempt to subdue your will. For certain reasons, of which I am well aware, but which I have now no time to explain, I know that in that case another night will have to pass before the next attempt is made. And during that night you must make your endeavour to escape. Come back at once when Davelli leaves you and meet your friend at or near the entrance to these rooms. Go and take some rest and refreshment, for you will need them, and provide yourselves with as much food as you can carry with ease. Then wander whither you will, only not far, and keep well within the bounds of the valley. Make no attempt whatsoever at concealment while the daylight lasts. As the darkness comes on return hitherward and rest awhile within sight of these chambers.

"Wait there until you see two men about your own size enter the room and until you see the light settle down as usual before the door. Then go both of you to the car"—(here he addressed himself especially to Jack)—"the car, I mean, in which you rode yesterday; start at once; lose no time, there is none to lose, for if you are pursued at all, you will be pursued before daylight. I will see that the car is well stored with food and provided with a spare battery and with glasses and light."

Here he added some further instructions, which I lost. Then I heard him say further,

"If you are followed I will follow, and I will help you as far as I may. There is everything to hope, and by that time there will be but little to fear. Barring unforeseen accidents you will escape with your lives. A brave man does all he can to save his life, but he is not afraid to lose it.

"Be sure, at any rate, that one good result will come of your adventure. These men will desert this place. No whiteman before you ever set his foot here, and these beings always conceal their earthly dwelling-places from civilised men. The next pioneers will find nothing here but, perhaps, a few odd-looking rocks.

"You may not need my assistance any more, but if your enemies follow you look up for a white flag and you will see that you are not alone."

Here he ceased and stood up, and we also stood up and bent our heads. He lifted his hand simply, and said "God keep you."

Then he disappeared in the same way in which he had appeared, but much more quickly.

It was still quite dark in our quarters although the day may have been beginning to break, and after exchanging a few hopeful words we tried to sleep. Strange to say I slept soundly, and I did not awake until it was full daylight.

When the appointed hour came I wrung Jack's hand in silence, and went to meet Signor Davelli. I reached the place of meeting only a few minutes too soon, and presently I saw him coming.

I knew that this was the hour of destiny for me, and I remember thinking that a man does not always know the hour of destiny when it comes, and that it would be better for him if he did. Then, of a sudden, it struck me that such reflection indicated a coolness that was hardly native to me, and, was it a good sign or a bad? I thought it was good, and yet that it was overdone. And I remembered to have read, "Let him that thinketh he standeth take heed lest he fall."

Just then Davelli came up, and I silently committed myself to God and awaited his onset. It came without any delay, but without any demonstration. He wasted no time, and he was evidently very confident. I was standing when he arrived, and after the usual exchange of salutations he invited me to sit down. I did so, and he sat down too, not beside me but opposite me. Then, almost immediately, he rose up again and looked straight into my face; rather, I should say, straight into my eyes. Should I look away from him? No; straight back into his eyes, and let him do his best. Then, as our eyes met, there began for me a series of desperate encounters of which there was absolutely no outward sign.

First, it seemed as if I were enduring the most imperious cravings of appetite—appetite as relentless and cruel as that which drove the Samaritan mother to devour her son; such appetite as has ever been ready to trample upon honour and hope and shame and love, for the sake of its own immediate gratification. Such keen, hungry sense of desire goaded me now, and along with its urgency came the consciousness, full, clear, and strong, that it would be gratified at once, if I would simply change the look of resistance with which I was meeting my enemy's eye for a look of acquiescence.

I do not know how long this lasted, it could hardly have been an hour, but it seemed like days and years to me. But at last there was a change, and of a sudden I became conscious of pain—physical pain multiplied and intensified indefinitely beyond all my experience or imagination—

> "All fiery pangs on battle-fields
> On fever beds where sick men toss."

All these seemed to wring me, and rack me, and strive to wrench the soul out of me, and ever as the pain grew, there grew also the consciousness that if I would but meet my enemy's eye with one moment's glance of acquiescence all the pain would be exchanged for ease; and oh! how delicious the very thought of ease appeared to be, more delicious than all the delights of all the senses.

Meantime, I was conscious of nothing external except the eyes of my adversary, the expression of which was an extraordinary mixture of persuasiveness and deadly determination, now and then crossed, however, by a furious flash of malignity, and again by a flash of hideous and awful terror.

But all the time also I was doing with all my might what Leäfar had bade me do, and it seemed to me as if my will were growing one with God's will, and it seemed to me as if I stood under the cross, and felt in my own flesh and sinews the very nails and thorns which pierced the Divine Sufferer.

Again there was a change; all at once there began to crowd into my mind in rapid succession all the questionings of life and of thought, of knowing and of being, that ever have tantalized the mind of man. And it seemed to me that only a thin veil was lying between me and the answers to them all. It seemed to me that the key of all knowledge was lying within my reach; as if the solution of all the moral and intellectual riddles that ever have plagued humanity were there now ready to my hand; as if all mysteries might be unsealed for me in one way, and only one way, and as if that way once again were to change my attitude of resistance, if only for a moment, for an attitude of acquiescence.

And now the burning lust of knowledge seemed to grow into a force, far exceeding all the other forces that had been brought to bear upon me. Rather it seemed to draw them all up into itself, and then to let them loose upon me. And for one dreadful moment I felt as if I must surrender. But with a sheer and last effort I offered myself to God.

And then a whisper seemed to speak within, and say that the solution of all mysteries was only to be found in the Divine Self-Sacrifice. And then it seemed as if the cross and the figure upon the cross filled all my sight, and the evil glare of the eyes that had been fixed upon me slowly passed away.

I don't know if I fainted, I suppose I did, but if I did I was roused by a loud and furious curse, and starting into consciousness I saw Signor Niccolo looking at me with a look of baffled malignity, hatred, and fear.

"Wretch!" he said, "you have resisted me and you must die. And yet not now, nor easily. Go back to prison. To-morrow you shall suffer again all and more than all that you have suffered to-day. You are in my power beyond hope of escape; you must yield to me or die."

Then he put a little phial to his mouth, and his body seemed first to melt and then to boil, and then to pass into a dark vapour, and then to disappear almost as quickly as I have written the words.

After a few minutes I rose to my feet, saying, Thank God! I found that I was quite exhausted and scarce able for any exertion. I walked very slowly away.

I soon saw Jack standing near the foot of the eastern stairway. I made a signal to him and he hurried towards me. We met in a few minutes more; and in answer to Jack's look of anxious inquiry, I whispered, "I have beaten him," and Jack said, "Thank God!" and strange as it may seem, not another word on that part of the subject passed between us for months after.

We returned to our quarters and rested and refreshed ourselves, and then we compared notes briefly. We knew exactly what we had to do, and the time was at hand. About an hour before sunset we left our quarters for the last time, and wandered about without any attempt at concealment, and exchanging only a brief word or two now and then.

The night came on cloudy and dark, and still we stayed without. It was about an hour after dark when we saw such a light as that which rested every night before our door moving about hither and thither. It seemed as if the bearers of the light were in search of us, and we were beginning to wonder how best we should baffle their scrutiny. Just then we saw the figures of two men walk up to the door of our quarters and enter. Then the door was closed, and the light settled down before the door and all was quiet.

CHAPTER ELEVEN
ESCAPE

When we saw the light settle down before the door it was about eight o'clock, a little more than two hours after sunset. It was very cloudy but not absolutely dark. We turned our steps at once toward the stair. We had no expectation of any difficulty just yet. The watch which was kept upon us during the night was effectually neutralised; for the watchers, no doubt, supposed that we were safely housed, and that we could not stir without betraying our movements to them. Nevertheless, we walked very softly and spoke almost nothing until we reached the summit of the stair. Then we stopped and held a very brief conference. There were various points of detail as to which it was needful that we should understand one another more perfectly. But after glancing at them it seemed better that we should make a start first, and then we could converse without losing time.

So we hurried along the platform to the car. It was on the very spot where we saw it first, on the evening when we made our first voyage in it. Everything was ready. One battery was in position, and another lay by it ready to take its place. There was a pocket on one side of the car filled with the lozenge-like articles of diet on which we had lived since we came here. There were two glasses like that with which I had observed the seed-beds, and Jack, after examination, pronounced that there was an abundant store of the matters required for the production of the gas which was needed for the inflation of the balloons. The light by which we saw all this stood in the fore part of the car just over a little binnacle where a compass was fixed. Leäfar had more than fulfilled his promise.

I had noticed before in the cars a framework like this in which the compass was housed, but it never struck me what it was for. The compass card was very like ours. It had sixteen points only instead of thirty-two, and these were distinguished by colours and combinations of colours. The light was no doubt electric, for it was to all appearance produced by a battery acting on a system of wires. The wire did not seem to consume very rapidly, and it was supplied by automatic machinery from a large coil fixed under the binnacle. I have said "no doubt electric." I ought to add that the machinery which produced the light had no perceptible effect on the car's compasses nor yet on mine.

As soon as we got into the car Jack proceeded to raise it, as Niccolo Davelli had done, by inflating the balloons. This cannot be quickly done by any but a practised hand. If one who has had no practice tries it, the balloons are apt to get unequally inflated, and so the operator in bringing them every now and then to a state of equal inflation works the car from side to side with a rolling motion. Signor Davelli raised it quickly, without any rolling motion at all. This was only the second day of practice for Jack, but he managed by raising the car slowly to produce very little of the rolling motion.

As soon as he had attained what he judged a sufficient height he connected the batteries with the paddles, and as the wind was, as the sailors say, "dead aft," we soon began to make very great speed.

I noticed now a point in the machinery which I had not observed before. There was a valve to each balloon, and both valves were worked by a sort of movable tap, one tap for both. The effect of these valves appeared to be the maintenance of the cars at a uniform height, or higher or lower as the driver wished. The tap was worked by the same machinery that drove the paddles. And if the driver for any reason wished to make the balloon act independently of the paddles he could disconnect the tap which worked the valves from the machinery which worked the paddles. The connection and disconnection was made by a handle within easy reach of the driver.

After we had got well under way Jack began to speak.

"Now, Bob," he said, "do you think that you can steer while I speak? I have something to say. Here is the handle that you steer by: you see it is fixed so that you pull the way you want to go. That bright blue mark on the compass is East. Never mind the balloons, I will attend to them if there is need. You will have nothing to do but just keep the head of the car due east."

I found but little difficulty in managing the car as he directed, and after about twenty minutes' practice I was able to steer and listen at the same time.

Then Jack began, in a business-like manner, "You have seen the battery that we are driving by now; very well, here is the spare battery which, according to Leäfar's promise, I find." He pointed to the spare battery, which was placed on a sort of bracket within my sight. He took it off, or rather out of, the bracket with his two hands and put it back again.

"I see," said I, "that it is larger; it seems heavier than the other, and in some details different: what of that?"

"Thereby hangs a tale," he said. "I have not been able to learn anything about the way of making these batteries. Indeed, I did not try; there was no time to spare from the more urgent matters. What I have learned is that they have two kinds of battery, one much more easily made and which wastes very much more quickly, but which drives the cars faster while it lasts. That is the sort that we are using now. The other sort is more difficult of production and wastes very much more slowly, and drives the cars more slowly. On long voyages, as I understand, they use the latter sort mainly, reserving the former sort for short voyages and for spurts. Now the spare battery is of the sort that wastes more slowly and drives the car more slowly; whereas it is a battery of the other sort that has been put into operation, what does that mean? I don't know how Leäfar got the batteries, and I don't know what he knows about their use. I think it would not be safe to assume that he is beyond the risk of making mistakes. They have to learn things just as we have."

"He got the battery for us," I replied, "and it seems the safer thing to conclude that he knows more about it than we do. But what does it matter any way?"

"I'll tell you as near as I can. Don't mind a bit of rigmarole or what seems to be such. Trust me for coming to the point all the time."

"Go ahead," said I.

"Very well," he said, "I want to know, or to make as near a guess as possible, at two or three things.

"(1.) How fast are we going now, and how far are we from the wire? or how far were we when we started? That means, how soon shall we reach the wire?

"(2.) What are we to do if we overshoot the wire? We have no way of telling the longitude; my watch indeed is a capital chronometer, but I have altered it by the sun two or three times as near as I could. Besides, we cannot get the sun's place near enough. Now, if we overshoot the wire, we shall either have to cross the continent or else to make southward and look out for the Darling or for the Murray; or, failing either, for the sea.

"I do not think that we can have made much more than three hundred miles of westing from the Daly Waters, and suppose that we are now travelling at the rate of thirty miles an hour, which is not unlikely, we ought, if we keep up the rate, to make the wire at seven or eight o'clock in the morning. If I have overrated the distance or underrated our speed only a little, we may cross the wire before sunrise.

"So far, then, it seems clear to me that we ought to be travelling at the slow rate instead of the quick rate. I thought of this before, but I saw no means of securing one of the larger batteries, and I knew that I could slow the speed of the smaller one.

"Why don't I slow it now? you will say. Well, because I found the smaller and quicker battery put on, although the other was there: why was it put on unless to use all possible speed? I cannot but think that Leäfar considers the prospect of pursuit so great that speed is in his view the first necessity. I may be wrong, but, somehow, this view of the case makes me unwilling to slow the machinery."

"I think you are right," I said; "still it is quite possible that there may be nothing in it. The workers whom Leäfar employs may have been simply bidden to secure the batteries, and to put one of them on; the difference between the batteries may have been altogether overlooked."

"It may be so," he said, "and one must not overlook the possibility, but I don't think it likely."

"Then you see something in the presence of the larger battery?"

"That's it," he said. "If only the voyage to the wire were in view a second one of the smaller batteries would have given us an ample margin for contingencies. I think that the chance of our overshooting the wire has been reckoned upon, and for that reason the other battery has been provided. The smaller battery wastes in less than twenty-four hours, the other lasts, I believe, about four weeks. But the speed of the larger is not much more than half the speed of the smaller. Now, if we do overshoot the wire, a spare battery of the smaller kind would fail us in the midst of the bush, while the larger one would enable us to reach some settlement.

"Just one word more. We are now at full speed, and I found the machinery fixed for full speed when we came on board. Besides, the wind has not in any way changed since the middle of the day, and it is full in our favour now. Our speed is at the very highest, and whosoever put in the battery must have known that it would be so; even if the wind were to fall the difference would not be very great. Now, what do you say?"

Easterly. I think we must go as we are going until dawn of day anyway. If we are not pursued before then, we shall not be pursued at all.

Wilbraham. Why do you think that?

Easterly. It seems to be the way of these fellows to keep as clear of civilised men as is consistent with the pursuit of their malevolent purposes.

Wilbraham. What do you suppose to be their motive?

Easterly. Well, it doesn't seem very far to seek. Among civilised men there is very little belief in the existence of such beings; what little there is is usually not active, and so far as it is active it attributes to them, just as the belief of savage men does, powers greatly in excess of those which they really possess. Either state of mind is highly favourable to their ends, and anything substituted for either; a state of mind like neither would of course be avoided by them. They might almost live among savages without in any way detracting from a highly exaggerated view of their powers; but any decisive appearance of them among civilised men; any experience such as we have had, if established and accepted, would cause their powers to be examined and understood.

Wilbraham. I see; we should take their measure and know how to manage them.

Easterly. That's it; as Mr. Morley says of the clergy, we should explain them.

Wilbraham. And that would be worse for them than a sheer denial of their existence?

Easterly. Very much worse. Their motives and purposes would be known and canvassed like other matters of fact, and much that holds up its head in the world now would be discredited in consequence.

Wilbraham. In short, we may put our confidence in Leäfar's opinion, and we may conclude that they will not pursue us into the civilised settlements.

Easterly. I think so, and therefore my opinion is that when daylight comes if we find no trace of pursuit we may slack speed, and lower the car and look for the wire.

Wilbraham. Agreed. And now what do you think? Shall we be followed?

Easterly. On the whole I think we shall, but it depends on circumstances that we can only guess at.

Wilbraham. Why do you think we shall be followed?

Easterly. Well, it seems to me likely that patrols of some kind are kept, and in that case the absence of the car will be discovered, perhaps is now discovered.

Wilbraham. And what then?

Easterly. Then our quarters will be searched, and our escape will immediately become known.

Wilbraham. How can they tell in which direction to follow us?

Easterly. They cannot tell, but they may very well conclude that we shall make either for the west coast or for the wire, and they may send after us both ways. I wonder if Leäfar knows which course we have taken?

Wilbraham. Yes, he knows. I thought you were not attending when I said it, but I spoke plainly enough. I said, "If we escape shall we go eastward or westward? My purpose is to make for the wire." And he said in reply "Yes, that is the better course." It was near the end of his talk.

"Well, now," said I, "suppose we get through safely, what shall we do with the car?"

"I have thought that over, Bob," he said, "and I have come to rather an odd conclusion."

Easterly. Do you mind telling a fellow what it is?

Wilbraham. Not at all. Suppose now that we should steer this car to Melbourne or to Sydney and exhibit it. We should make a great noise, no doubt, and perhaps a pot of money, but we should ruin ourselves for all that. Even if we go to work like gentlemen, even if we make no attempt to make money out of it, but simply hand over the car to some public body with any statement we like to make, we shall be ruined all the same.

Easterly. I dare say you are right.

Wilbraham. Yes, I am right. For in the first place suppose we make a true statement, and neither of us would consent to do else, what will follow? Either we shall be set down as impostors without any more ado, or else an expedition will be organized to examine the country we have been in. But if Leäfar is right, as no doubt he is, nothing will be found to justify our story. Suppose we warn them beforehand that they will find nothing, that will be accepted as only one proof more that we are lying.

Suppose, now, for the sake of argument, that we do lie, and say that we ourselves invented and constructed the car, then we shall be expected and invited to make another. But we know next to nothing about the manner of producing the gas which inflates the balloons or about the constitution of the batteries. If we should attempt to substitute larger balloons filled with hydrogen, and batteries of such construction as we understand, the almost certain result would be that our car would be added to the long list of discredited flying machines, and ourselves to the much longer list of exposed impostors. How do you like the prospect?

Easterly. Not at all; and I believe you are right. But what do you propose to do?

Wilbraham. If we discover the wire I propose to go back two or three miles and abandon the car. I should like to break it up but we have no tools. I can dismantle it, however, so that nobody will be able to make anything of it if it is found.

Easterly. But if we escape we must give some account of our escape; we are not going to tell lies.

Wilbraham. Not lies; we shall tell the whole truth about the blacks, and for the rest we shall confine ourselves to generalities which will be true as far as they go. They may think us a little bit off our heads, "a shingle short," as Tim Blundel would say, but that won't matter, it will be set down to our wanderings in the bush. For the present at least we had better keep the whole matter as quiet as we can. If we ever see a chance of doing any good by speaking out we shall speak out. But now to more immediate business. Can we try to estimate the rate at which we are travelling?

By this time it was much brighter, the clouds were quite cleared away, and the moon, which was only two or three days past the full, was fairly well up in the sky.

So I said to Jack, "Lower the car a little, then take the steering gear in hand and let me try to estimate our speed. He let the car descend slowly until he could distinguish the trees and other prominent features of the landscape. Then he took the steering gear into his own hand and I looked over the side of the car. The forest was thick in parts, but there were wide spaces of treeless plain; and we were just passing over a range of hills which I think I am right in identifying with a range that we had observed at a distance of several miles when we were among the blacks.

I took particular notice of the larger trees, trying to guess their distance each from the other and referring to my watch every few seconds.

"What do you make of it?" said Jack at last, when he had raised the car to its former height.

"It is hard to fix it," said I, "but I cannot think that we are travelling less than twenty-five miles an hour and I should say much more probably thirty."

Wilbraham. Ah! and how far do you suppose that we have to travel from the start?

Easterly. Say fifteen days passed from our parting with Mr. Fetherston until we reached the valley, and I am pretty sure we made an average of thirty miles a day. But of course that was nearly all westing. I don't think that our furthest point could be quite as much as three hundred miles from the wire. I don't think that your own estimate can be much out of the way, but we are perhaps a little under the mark.

Wilbraham. Ah! if the figures are right the sum is easy; we ought to cross the wire about six o'clock.

Easterly. Yes, but look here; thirty miles an hour is possibly an overestimate of our speed; and three hundred miles is possibly an underestimate of our distance. Besides, we shall not be able to keep up our present speed. The wind is already falling, and may be against us in an hour or two. That would knock, say, ten miles an hour off the rate of speed at which we are now travelling.

Wilbraham. It might, but that is another over-estimate; we may fairly reckon on travelling all night at within five miles of our present rate of speed.

Easterly. I suppose so. Nevertheless, the chances are that if we stop the car about sunrise we shall still be west of the wire. Then we can lower the car, move north, and watch for the wire, then go slowly, still eastward, keeping a sharp look-out as we go.

We were now both very tired, and as there were still some hours to pass before we could expect to get sight of the wire, we agreed to divide the time till dawn into half-hour watches. Each of us wished the other to take the first rest, and so we had to settle the dispute by lot. I told Jack to hide some lozenges, and to let me guess odd or even. Jack won, but our mode of settling the question was not without important effects. For Jack said, when he was putting back the lozenges into his pocket, "By-the-way, I may as well put these with the others in the car pocket," and he did so.

When my turn came I lay down on the floor of the car, as Jack had done, with my hat for a pillow. The lozenges in my pocket were a little in my way; not much, but just enough to remind me of what Jack had done. Still, I didn't rise, only turned over. Then some of the lozenges rolled out of my pocket. Then I jumped up, and said, "I may as well put mine with yours." I did so, and lay down again and slept.

So now we had all our eggs in one basket, and it never occurred to us that we were incurring any risk at all.

It was eleven o'clock when Jack lay down for his first sleep, and we took regular half-hour turns until five o'clock, when my sixth half-hour was up. It was now dawn, and the light was increasing rapidly. We had had enough rest, and it was getting near sunrise. It was time to think of lowering the car and reconnoitring. The morning was very fine, but there was rather a heavy bank of clouds in the east where the sun was rising. We lowered the car a little, and slackened our speed. Presently we disconnected the battery, and so stopped the car. Then we rested at about four to five hundred feet from the ground. I swept the whole field of sight with the car's glasses in search of the wire, but could find no trace of it. Then I looked westward long and anxiously, but could see nothing specially worthy of notice. At last I fell to admiring the beauty of the clouds; they were beginning to reflect the glory of the sun which was now risen, but still hidden by them. There was in the air that sort of shimmering which portends a dry, hot day. I picked out a small bank of clouds to the west, on the near side of which the shimmering which I have mentioned appeared to be greater than elsewhere. I was quietly speculating on the cause of this when the sun extricated himself from the clouds to the eastward, and his rays fell straight and full upon the clouds to westward. Then I saw strike upon the cloud upon which I had been gazing two shadows which I recognised with horror. I cried out to Jack to look, and I lifted the glasses which were in my hand and turned them to the shadows on the cloud, and I saw that he did the same with his glasses. You will remember that we were now at rest, excepting for the motion caused by the breeze which had almost ceased to blow.

The sun was now shining brightly, and we could make out two dark masses moving towards us. I suppose we ought to have got in motion again as quickly as possible, although I doubt if it would have made any difference at all. At any rate, we did not make the slightest attempt to move, but watched in dead silence the shadows of the contending cars. For that they were somehow contending there could be no doubt at all. The one was trying to block the way of the other, and the other was trying to dodge it. The former was pursuing, and the latter was pursued. The two shadows passed right over us, and as they did, the cars, considering the position of the sun, must have been a little way to the eastward of us; and now it seemed as if the pursuing car was underneath the other, and so nearer to us, and as if the pursued car was being forced upward. Just then, however, the pursued car made a very quick turn westward. The movement was followed by the other car, but it seemed, as it followed, to lose just a little ground. Mind, we could see nothing but shadows, but the shadows were wonderfully distinct. Then the shadows passed over us again, and they were now much nearer, and they quite darkened our car. And now it seemed as if the pursued car had given the other the slip, for it was now the nearer of the two; and then both were straight over our heads. It seemed as if something clashed against us, and we perceived immediately that a missile of some sort had been driven right through the side and floor of our car. It had passed between us, and if it were intended to kill either of us, it had certainly missed its aim. We saw that our car remained steady, and we were too much absorbed in the strife going on above us to notice anything else. Then the same manœuvre seemed to be repeated, for the shadows passed over us again, but this time they were much higher, and the pursuing car was again underneath.

A fourth time the shadows fell across us, but they were still higher this time, and the pursuing car still held its place nearer to us. And now the pursued car seemed to give up the contest, for it held its way westward until we lost all trace of it, and the pursuing car stopped and turned, and came towards us until the shadow was all but over us, and then out of the shadow, as it seemed, there fell a long white streamer. It waved one moment backward and forward, and then disappeared. We swung off our hats together, and gave a lusty cheer.

Then the shadow of the car passed away westward and was lost to sight.

So we had been pursued, and the pursuit was over and our lives were saved. So it seemed, and our joy was great; but it was very soon changed for something very like despair. The car in which we rode had canted over to one side, so that it was becoming difficult either to sit or stand straight in it. We soon saw why.

One of the balloons was slowly collapsing, and on examination we found that it had been slightly grazed by the missile which had passed through the car. It was clear that we must lower the car to the ground as quickly as possible, and it was very doubtful if we could raise it again. A closer examination revealed a far worse loss. The missile in question had been driven straight through the wall-bag which held our provisions, and nearly all of them had fallen through the hole which had been pierced through the floor of the car. It was surely no chance which had given the missile its precise direction. It was almost incredible skill and altogether diabolical malignity. We thought that our enemy had aimed at our bodies and had missed his aim: he knew better: the purpose of his missile was to cause our miserable death in the wilderness.

Jack put in action the machinery by which the balloons were filled, and endeavoured to trim them so as to act together. But it proved quite impossible to do so. The rent in the injured balloon was increasing slowly under the pressure of the gas, and it was evident that it would very soon be quite useless. Jack sang out to me to connect the batteries and to set the paddles in motion. I did so at once and I soon perceived why I was told to do so. The injured balloon was now collapsing so rapidly that we were in great danger of being upset by the one-sided buoyancy of the car. It was necessary to empty the other balloon as quickly as possible in order to keep the car in such a position that we could keep our seats. And the rapid emptying of the balloons would have dashed us to the ground but for the motion of the paddles. As it was we were half turned over before we reached the ground, and we fell with rather a severe crash but without any serious injury. I managed to gather up a few of the lozenges which were left on the floor of the car, as they were rolling off the car when we were fifty or sixty feet from the ground.

Here we were now in a condition almost as bad as when the blacks left us; quite as bad, indeed, or worse, for although we were now probably much nearer to help than then, we did not know where to look for it, and we had no time to spend in finding it. When we were left alone before, we had plenty of water and the means of procuring food for at least some weeks. Now the doubt was if we could survive the second day unless help should reach us before its close.

Besides we were not now as ready to stand hardships as then. We were then in splendid condition. But the nervous excitement consequent upon the startling experiences of the few days which had intervened since then had heavily told on both of us; and anxiety and broken rest had also had their effect. I was myself much worn, but I saw now, or thought I saw, that Jack was on the very verge of collapsing. He was brave enough and ready enough, and very much more hopeful than I was, but there was a look about his eyes and mouth which alarmed me.

"What do you think now, Jack?" I said.

"Well, it's rather a bad business about the lozenges," he replied, "but as for the car, he has only done what I should have liked to do myself; we are well rid of it."

Easterley. But where's the wire?

Wilbraham. Well, old man, the wire is not five miles off, you may be sure of that: most likely not half so far.

Easterley. Why do you think so?

Wilbraham. Leäfar would never have left unless he knew that we were near enough. Besides, all our calculations look the same way.

Easterley. I wish I could see the situation in the same light. Our calculations are based on guesses, and may easily be fifty or a hundred miles astray. And Leäfar most likely did not know that our car was badly damaged and our food lost. Besides, the other one seemed to be quite satisfied with what he had done; for he sailed straight away. But he has not done much after all if he has only dropped us without hurt within a few miles of the wire.

Wilbraham. Well, not much as it has happened, but he was very near smashing us to pieces, and the spilling of the food was a clever extra touch. He had got to do something, and he had about a minute to do it in, and he did his best, or his worst: and as for sailing away, I take it he was beaten away.

Easterley. I hope you may be right. We must never say die, anyway. But you don't look well, Jack, though you speak so cheerfully.

Wilbraham. I am a bit seedy, I am sure I don't know why, but I daresay it will pass off soon.

Easterley. I suppose we had better push on, we have most of the day before us yet, and we had better take some of the food that is left. But look! what's that?

Wilbraham. A horse, by George! didn't I tell you?

And a horse it was, but its presence proved after all not to be such a very good sign as we supposed. We thought at first that it must belong to some of the telegraph people, but as we drew nearer we saw that it was Jack's own horse which had been abandoned in the bush on account of lameness. Still it was a good sign. Its presence made it much more likely that we were still west of the wire, and we might possibly make use of it for travelling, but above all it seemed as if there must be water near, and that if we stuck to the horse we should find it.

It was quite an easy matter to catch the horse; he had been well broken in, and his ten or twelve days in the bush had not made him at all forget his training. He seemed to recognise us, and we thought at first that his lameness was quite gone.

Then we reckoned up our store of food. We had saved just nine of the lozenges. We resolved now to take three each, reserving three for the evening.

If Jack was right we should hardly have need of them. And yet we might, for the telegraph stations were far apart, and it might be quite beyond our power to walk to the nearest, and we would not know in which direction to travel in order to reach the nearest. But then, as Jack said, if all came to all we should cut the wire, and that would soon bring us help.

The food quite restored me, but I did not think that it had the same good effect on Jack. He was quite cheerful, brave, and hopeful, but still there was undoubtedly something amiss. So I proposed that Jack should have the horse and that I should walk beside him. "I don't mind," he said, "if I have the first ride." And so it was arranged.

But riding even a very tame horse without either saddle or bridle is neither a pleasant nor a quick way of travelling, and besides the horse's lameness came on again as soon as he had weight to carry, and it became clear before long that we could get no good of him that way. I had improvised a sort of halter out of slips cut from our coats, and so when Jack dismounted, we tried to lead the horse; he showed a decided tendency, both when ridden and led, to go north. "Let him have his way," Jack said, "provided he doesn't make any westing. I will not go away from the wire." The end of it was that we led the horse, or let him lead us, for several hours. We travelled very slowly, indeed, but still we must have got over twelve or thirteen miles, going mainly northward, and making perhaps a mile of easting all the time.

The country that we travelled over consisted of a series of plains which were separated by thin belts of timber. There was little or no scrub. At last we came, as it seemed, to a small dried-up watercourse; but it proved to be not quite dried up, for the horse trotted over to one of the sand-beds where the ponds had been, and found a little hole of water which he drank very greedily. The hole was so small that we did not care to drink after him if it could be helped; but by digging with our hands in the sand a little higher up we got a sufficient supply of water that was fairly good.

We had now got all out of the horse that we were likely to get. This water meant life for a day or two longer. It seemed now to be the best course for us to start from this point due east. If the wire were even within twenty miles of us we might escape. If not, our death seemed certain.

But Jack's increasing debility, which was beginning to make me very anxious, made it out of the question to go farther to-night. Indeed, it was already getting on for sundown. So we took each, one of our three remaining lozenges, and made our camp as best we could. The trees near the watercourse were shadier than elsewhere, and the weather was mild. We had no tobacco. By some mischance we had left it behind us in our escape from the valley. Indeed, such was our excitement and anxiety that we had never smoked once all the time we were there. But now we missed our pipes very much.

Before going to sleep, however, I made a discovery that cheered us up a little. I found two more lozenges in the corner of my pocket. These would give us a shadow of breakfast.

I slept rather well, but Jack was troubled with restlessness and with dreams. And in the morning he was no better.

Things were looking very black indeed. After making our shadow of breakfast we had but one lozenge left, and then nothing but a little water to live upon. Jack was beginning to show signs of collapse. "I know, old fellow," he said, "that I could not persuade you to abandon me, but I'll die very soon, and after I am dead you will still have time to look for the wire."

"Jack," said I, "look here, shall I go and look for the wire now? I'll come back in two hours whether I find it or not, and then we shall stay together while we live. I daresay we have both of us pretty well done with this world, but while there's life there's hope. What do you say?"

"Well," he said, "I think I can live for more than two hours with the help of this water; yes, old fellow, go and look for it; that's the best chance."

I made him as comfortable as I could near the water under the shade, and then I started with but little hope. I was already getting weak with hunger, although otherwise I was well enough. I crossed the plain eastward to one of the belts of timber I told you of. The distance was about a quarter or a third of a mile. Then I marked a tree, and on passing through the belt of timber, which was only a few yards across, I marked another. I was now in a second plain just like the first. I crossed it slowly to the eastward, came to another belt of timber, and marked another tree.

Then I began to think it was of no use to make any further exertion. Half an hour was already gone; I must in any case turn back in half an hour more. "Oh Leäfar, Leäfar," I said, and I wrung my hand, "how could you leave us in such misery?" And then I remembered how little Leäfar seemed to think of death in comparison with the doom I had escaped, and I was ashamed of myself, and I said—

"The will of God be done."

I had crossed the second belt of timber, and I was marking another tree on the east side of it. I was acting quite mechanically and without conscious purpose, for I had made up my mind to return at once, and so I should not need another marked tree. All in a moment I became conscious of this, and I thought that perhaps my mind was going. Then I turned round to look at the plain which I had just entered, and was just about to leave, and, good heavens! there was the wire! This plain was of about the same dimensions as the other two, and right across it ran the telegraph poles.

I just said, "Thank God," and I ran back as fast as my legs could carry me.

Jack was taking a drink of water, and I thought looking a little brighter. I was quite out of breath, and before I could speak he had time to say—

"Why, Bob, you've hardly been away an hour."

"I have found it!" I cried, "I have found it!"

"Take it easy, man," he said; "take a drink of water. Didn't I tell you we were near it?"

We took near two hours to reach it, for we were both weak for want of food, and Jack was ill. Then we sat down under one of the posts and consulted.

"Jack," said I, "we may die of starvation yet, unless you can cut that wire. I couldn't climb the pole, poor devil that I am, not to save your life and my own."

(You will remember, no doubt, that I have already told you that Jack was a very clever athlete.)

He replied after a silence of a minute or so, letting his words drop slowly: "I should have thought but little of it yesterday morning. I am sure I don't know if I can do it now. I'll try."

"I have one lozenge left," I said; "take it before you try;" and I handed him the lozenge.

"I'll take my share of it," he answered, "but not yours too."

"Now be reasonable, Jack," said I; "my life as well as yours depends on your cutting that wire. If the lozenge helps you to cut it, don't you see that it is best for us both that you should have it."

"Very well," he replied; "I believe you are right; give it me," and he ate it without more ado. And then after feeling for his knife he began to climb.

Presently it became clear that he could not get up the pole without some protection to his knees. I cut off the sleeves of my coat and we slipped them up over his legs; they fitted him so tightly that no fastening was needed.

Then he began to climb again with more success, but such was his weakness that it seemed several times as if he would have to give over the attempt. At last he reached the top, and after hanging for a while to rest he began to cut at the wire.

I watched the process with great anxiety. He gave over several times, and once I thought he was going to faint, and I ran up to the post to try and break his fall. But he began hacking at the wire again, and in a few seconds more it fell apart, and one end of it lay on the ground.

Then he began to slide down the post, and before he was down his arms relaxed their hold, and he almost fell into my arms as I stood underneath.

We both fell to the ground, but without any severe shock, and we were quite unhurt. I staggered to my feet and dragged him to some thick shrubs near at hand, where I propped him up as well as I could manage. He did not quite lose his senses, and I whispered, "We are all right now, Jack; we shall have help soon." Then I lay down beside him.

I do not think that I was more than half an hour lying there when I heard the noise of horses, and in about fifteen minutes more a party of horsemen rode up.

We might have lain there for several hours, however, if it had not been for a combination of favourable circumstances. We were only three miles from a telegraph station to the north, and a sharp look-out had been kept for us. It had been kept indeed since the third or fourth day after our departure, and it had been quickened a few days ago by a lying rumour which proved to be unintentionally true. Some blacks had come into the camp who knew both Gioro and Bomero, and they told Mr. Fetherston that Gioro had been killed some days before. Now, as far as I could make out, Gioro had been killed a day or two after they told the story. So they were certainly lying. But it seemed as if every one who knew anything about the matter expected that Gioro would be killed if Bomero's protection were withdrawn. And so it happened as you have heard, and thus their lie came true.

So there was a bright look-out kept for about fifty miles on each side of the Daly Waters, and a party had gone westward into the bush in search of us a few days before, and the moment the communication by wire was broken a party of horsemen started for the point where the break was made. We were now nearly thirty miles north of the Daly Waters.

We were speedily taken to the nearest station and treated with all the attention that we needed. I needed only food and clothes, but Jack proved to be sickening for colonial fever, and was in rather a critical state for some time. He did not seem to me to be dangerously ill. Much languor and a little wandering and extreme prostration were his principal symptoms. I was not very anxious about him, but Mr. Fetherston thought more of the illness than he chose to say. I did not know the nature of the complaint; I have learnt better since then.

Mr. Fetherston asked me several questions, and I told him all about the blacks, dwelling especially on Bomero's panic and Gioro's death. Then I said that after that we had got among some people that had given us food and clothes. He looked very carefully at the coats and hats, and he said, "Why, these must have come from Java, or perhaps from the Philippines. I had no idea that there was any communication."

I said that I was inclined to believe that the people I had met were not of the same race as the blacks, their colour was much lighter, I said, and they had some curious knowledge.

Mr. Fetherstone looked at me with some anxiety and suspicion, and the same evening I heard him say to Tim Blundell that people who wandered among the blacks often got off their heads for a while.

After that I held my peace.

In about six weeks Jack was able to travel, and Mr. Fetherston gave us an escort to Port Darwin.

After about ten days there, we were so fortunate as to get a passage to King George's Sound in a Government steamer. We reached Adelaide about the first week in September.

CONCLUSION

My story is told now, and there is no occasion to detain you much longer. Our life ever since we came back to Adelaide, until the visit to Gippsland which led to the writing of this book, was all of a piece. It was all spent in Australia and Tasmania. We did some squatting, and we just glanced at agricultural and mining life. In every year we spent some weeks in town, and we made some acquaintance everywhere. But we settled down to nothing. We became very little richer, but no poorer. We seldom talked about our adventures to each other, and never to anyone else. But I think they were always more or less in our minds and kept us unsettled.

Sometimes when we seemed to be forgetting them, or when their effect upon us appeared to be passing away, something or other would happen to revive their memory and unsettle us again.

Once, for instance, I was in Sydney with Jack making arrangements for the purchase of a share in a small station. I was dining out one evening on the North Shore and as it chanced Jack was not with me. There was a physician of the company who was a clever talker, and after the ladies had gone away we got him to tell us some of his Australian experiences, which were curious and varied. He told us among other things that he was employed by Government to make a report on some cases in Tarban Creek Lunatic Asylum. After he had examined these cases the superintendent of the asylum said,

"By the bye, doctor, I have a queer fellow here that I sometimes think ought not to be here at all. He is an interesting fellow, too, and I should be much obliged if you would have a look at him."

"I did have a look at him," said the physician, "and I found him just a steady old bush hand, with an uncommon degree of intelligence and good sense, and a lot of information about the country and the aborigines. I was just wondering what on earth they could have sent him here for when he told me with the gravest face the following story:—He had been more than a year among the blacks and he did not know how he was to get back to his own people. It was away in the north-west somewhere, the far north-west. Well, one day, he said, there was a sort of panic among the blacks, he didn't know the cause of it, and he wandered away a mile or two from the camp. He said that when these panics take them they are jealous of the presence of strangers. He had a loaded revolver with him.

"There was no sun and he began to think he might lose his way, and so he made up his mind to return to the blacks' camp. Just then he heard a sort of rustle in the air above him, and presently a man, so he said, jumped out of the clouds and caught him by the collar of his coat. He said that this man never touched the ground himself, but tried to lift him off the ground. He drew his revolver and fired.

"Then he said—'Look here, doctor, I'm blest if the fellow didn't turn into bilin' water and then into steam and then into nothin' at all, and while I was wonderin' what in the mischief was the matter with me back he comes again, fust steam, and then bilin' water, and then an ugly tawny-looking beggar, neither nigger nor white man, and makes another grab at me. So I said, Man or devil, have at you again, and I gave him the contents of another barrel, and I'm blest if he didn't go of in a bile again and I took to my heels and ran as I never ran before until I got back to the darkles' camp.' That was his story," said the physician, "and it appears that he was picked up some months later on the headwaters of the Oakover River by some explorers, and so he got round to Adelaide, and thence to Sydney, and so found his way to the asylum."

In answer to further questions the physician said, "I told the superintendent of the asylum that the man was quite sane, or at least sane enough for the purposes of life; that he was no doubt under some strange delusion, but that I had observed that people who had been much among the blacks were liable to such delusions, and that in my opinion he was quite harmless and that it was cruel to keep him shut up in an asylum, and I made a memorandum in the visitors' book to that effect."

I told this story to Jack that night and we went off the very next day to Turban Creek to look for the man. He had been discharged and was now working as a clerk on a station on the Murrumbidgee. So the superintendent of the asylum told us.

We hurried off to the Murrumbidgee and found the station where he had been employed. It was somewhere near Balranald. But he had gone away to America about six months before, and we could find no means of tracing him. This affair unsettled us again and was indirectly the cause of our letting the negotiation in which we were engaged drift away from us.

But it is now quite a year since we have made a clean breast of it and committed our story to paper, although we have not at the moment of writing made up our minds about its publication. And the effect upon us both has been decidedly good. Jack says we have done better than the Ancient Mariner, for he had to tell his tale over and over again whenever he met a man whose doom it was to hear him; but we have just told our tale once for all and let the doomed ones read it. And now we have actually settled down to business and have become part owners of a station in Queensland and have our homes within ten miles of each other; that is to say we are quite next door neighbours, and I may as well finish by giving you the details of a conversation which passed between myself and Jack only a few months ago.

We were both staying with some friends at a pleasant little place very near a station on the Southern Railway, about thirty miles from Sydney. I say a little place, for it looked so; but when you came to know it well it turned out to be a very big place. There were as many bedrooms as its hospitable owner could fill with guests; and not to speak of dining and drawing-rooms, which were large and airy and very pretty, there were bath-rooms, billiard-rooms, and smoking-rooms without stint.

It was a quiet, unpretending place to look at, but it was really a most luxurious place. There were pictures and books and musical instruments everywhere; and most delightful contrivances, part couch, part hammock, part swing; and hothouse fruits and flowers; and horses of easiest pace if you wanted them, but somehow you seldom did want them. And whenever there were guests there, and that was three parts of the year, there was the best company in all Australia, and as good as there is anywhere in the world.

Just now the broad verandah, which ran along the main front, was covered with banksia roses, jessamine, and woodbine, and between this and the neat wicket-gate, which was the main entrance to this little paradise, were all sorts of spring and early summer flowers.

At the gate Jack and I were standing; he had come up from Sydney about an hour before. And this was what we said:—

Wilbraham. Well, Bob, can you tell me when you are going to be married?

Easterley. I cannot quite say, but it will be soon. Bessie and I have talked it over and she has listened to reason. She promised me that her friend, Violet Fanshawe, shall fix the day, and Violet is coming here to-morrow.

Wilbraham. And you can trust Violet?

Easterley. I think I can.

Wilbraham. Do you know, Bob, I saw Miss Fanshawe yesterday, and we were talking about you. But she didn't seem to know that she was to decide so momentous a question.

Easterley. Perhaps she didn't know.

Wilbraham. Perhaps not; but, Bob, I think I should like, if it could be so arranged, to be married on the same day as you and Bessie.

Easterley. Jack, I am very glad indeed, but I never guessed it, though I did wonder what was taking you to Sydney so often.

Wilbraham. It was not that; it was, in the first place, to leave you and Bessie together; but sure enough it led to that.

Easterley. But who is she? Oh, Jack, I hope we shall not be worse friends after we are married.

Wilbraham (with a knowing smile). Somehow, Bob, I don't think we will.

Easterley. Surely it is not Violet?

Wilbraham. Yes, it's Violet; so she and Bessie may as well settle both days in one.

Easterley. Well, I am very glad; but how is it that Bessie never told me, for surely Violet must have told her.

Wilbraham. No, she didn't. It was only settled yesterday. But there is Bessie on the verandah, and she has just got a letter.

We both went up to her; indeed we had parted from her scarce half an hour ago. I saw that the letter was Violet's writing. "I'll tell you," I said, "what's in that letter, Bessie. Violet is going to marry Jack."

It was very sudden, and she turned pale and red and then opened the letter. Then, after a few seconds, she cried, "Oh, Bob, I'm so glad!" and she kissed me, and I think she was very near kissing Jack.

So Violet came the next day and the conclave was held and the day was fixed, and just four weeks later Jack and Violet, Bessie and I, were married at All Saints, St. Kilda, for Bessie and Violet were Victorian girls and lived near Melbourne.

And now, as I have already told you, we are living in Queensland, in homes only ten miles apart.

I thought you might like just a little bit of human interest after so much of the other thing.

So now—Farewell!

THE END

SHORT STORIES OF RUDYARD KIPLING

WITH THE NIGHT MAIL: A STORY OF 2000 A.D.
(UNITED KINGDOM, 1909)

At nine o'clock of a gusty winter night I stood on the lower stages of one of the G. P. O. outward mail towers. My purpose was a run to Quebec in "Postal Packet 162 or such other as may be appointed"; and the Postmaster-General himself countersigned the order. This talisman opened all doors, even those in the despatching-caisson at the foot of the tower, where they were delivering the sorted Continental mail. The bags lay packed close as herrings in the long gray underbodies which our G. P. O. still calls "coaches." Five such coaches were filled as I watched, and were shot up the guides to be locked on to their waiting packets three hundred feet nearer the stars.

From the despatching-caisson I was conducted by a courteous and wonderfully learned official—Mr. L. L. Geary, Second Despatcher of the Western Route—to the Captains' Room (this wakes an echo of old romance), where the mail captains come on for their turn of duty. He introduces me to the Captain of "162"— Captain Purnall, and his relief, Captain Hodgson. The one is small and dark; the other large and red; but each has the brooding sheathed glance characteristic of eagles and aëronauts. You can see it in the pictures of our racing professionals, from L. V. Rautsch to little Ada Warrleigh—that fathomless abstraction of eyes habitually turned through naked space.

On the notice-board in the Captains' Room, the pulsing arrows of some twenty indicators register, degree by geographical degree, the progress of as many homeward-bound packets. The word "Cape" rises across the face of a dial; a gong strikes: the South African mid-weekly mail is in at the Highgate Receiving Towers. That is all. It reminds one comically of the traitorous little bell which in pigeon-fanciers' lofts notifies the return of a homer.

"Time for us to be on the move," says Captain Purnall, and we are shot up by the passenger-lift to the top of the despatch-towers. "Our coach will lock on when it is filled and the clerks are aboard."...

"No. 162" waits for us in Slip E of the topmost stage. The great curve of her back shines frostily under the lights, and some minute alteration of trim makes her rock a little in her holding-down slips.

Captain Purnall frowns and dives inside. Hissing softly, "162" comes to rest as level as a rule. From her North Atlantic Winter nose-cap (worn bright as diamond with boring through uncounted leagues of hail, snow, and ice) to the inset of her three built-out propeller-shafts is some two hundred and forty feet. Her extreme diameter, carried well forward, is thirty-seven. Contrast this with the nine hundred by ninety-five of any crack liner and you will realize the power that must drive a hull through all weathers at more than the emergency-speed of the "Cyclonic"!

The eye detects no joint in her skin plating save the sweeping hair-crack of the bow-rudder—Magniac's rudder that assured us the dominion of the unstable air and left its inventor penniless and half-blind. It is calculated to Castelli's "gull-wing" curve. Raise a few feet of that all but invisible plate three-eighths of an inch and she will yaw five miles to port or starboard ere she is under control again. Give her full helm and she returns on her track like a whip-lash. Cant the whole forward—a touch on the wheel will suffice—and she sweeps at your good direction up or down. Open the complete circle and she presents to the air a mushroom-head that will bring her up all standing within a half mile.

"Yes," says Captain Hodgson, answering my thought, "Castelli thought he'd discovered the secret of controlling aëroplanes when he'd only found out how to steer dirigible balloons. Magniac invented his rudder to help war-boats ram each other; and war went out of fashion and Magniac he went out of his mind because he said he couldn't serve his country any more. I wonder if any of us ever know what we're really doing."

"If you want to see the coach locked you'd better go aboard. It's due now," says Mr. Geary. I enter through the door amidships. There is nothing here for display. The inner skin of the gas-tanks comes down to within a foot or two of my head and turns over just short of the turn of the bilges. Liners and yachts disguise their tanks with decoration, but the G. P. O. serves them raw under a lick of gray official paint. The inner skin shuts off fifty feet of the bow and as much of the stern, but the bow-bulkhead is recessed for the lift-shunting apparatus as the stern is pierced for the shaft-tunnels. The engine-room lies almost amidships. Forward of it, extending to the turn of the bow tanks, is an aperture—a bottomless hatch at present—into which our coach will be locked. One looks down over the coamings three hundred feet to the despatching-caisson whence voices boom upward. The light below is obscured to a sound of thunder, as our coach rises on its guides. It enlarges rapidly from a postage-stamp to a playing-card; to a punt and last a pontoon. The two clerks, its crew, do not even look up as it comes into place. The Quebec letters fly under their fingers and leap into the docketed racks, while both captains and Mr. Geary satisfy themselves that the coach is locked home. A clerk passes the waybill over the hatch-coaming. Captain Purnall thumb-marks and passes it to Mr. Geary. Receipt has been given and taken. "Pleasant run," says Mr. Geary, and disappears through the door which a foot-high pneumatic compressor locks after him.

"A-ah!" sighs the compressor released. Our holding-down clips part with a tang. We are clear.

Captain Hodgson opens the great colloid underbody-porthole through which I watch million-lighted London slide eastward as the gale gets hold of us. The first of the low winter clouds cuts off the well-known view and darkens Middlesex. On the south edge of it I can see a postal packet's light ploughing through the white fleece. For an instant she gleams like a star ere she drops toward the Highgate Receiving Towers. "The Bombay Mail," says Captain Hodgson, and looks at his watch. "She's forty minutes late."

"What's our level?" I ask.

"Four thousand. Aren't you coming up on the bridge?"

The bridge (let us ever bless the G. P. O. as a repository of ancientest tradition!) is represented by a view of Captain Hodgson's legs where he stands on the control platform that runs thwartships overhead. The bow colloid is unshuttered and Captain Purnall, one hand on the wheel, is feeling for a fair slant. The dial shows 4,300 feet.

"It's steep to-night," he mutters, as tier on tier of cloud drops under. "We generally pick up an easterly draught below three thousand at this time o' the year. I hate slathering through fluff."

"So does Van Cutsem. Look at him huntin' for a slant!" says Captain Hodgson. A fog-light breaks cloud a hundred fathoms below. The Antwerp Night Mail makes her signal and rises between two racing clouds far to port, her flanks blood-red in the glare of Sheerness Double Light. The gale will have us over the North Sea in half an hour, but Captain Purnall lets her go composedly—nosing to every point of the compass as she rises.

"Five thousand—six, six thousand eight hundred"—the dip-dial reads ere we find the easterly drift, heralded by a flurry of snow at the thousand-fathom level. Captain Purnall rings up the engines and keys down the governor on the switch before him. There is no sense in urging machinery when Æolus himself gives you good knots for nothing. We are away in earnest now—our nose notched home on our chosen star. At this level the lower clouds are laid out all neatly combed by the dry fingers of the East. Below that again is the strong westerly blow through which we rose. Overhead, a film of southerly drifting mist draws a theatrical gauze across the firmament. The moonlight turns the lower strata to silver without a stain except where our shadow underruns us. Bristol and Cardiff Double Lights (those statelily inclined beams over Severnmouth) are dead ahead of us; for we keep the Southern Winter Route. Coventry Central, the pivot of the English system, stabs upward once in ten seconds its spear of diamond light to the north; and a point or two off our starboard bow The Leek, the great cloud-breaker of Saint David's Head, swings its unmistakable green beam twenty-five degrees each way. There must be half a mile of fluff over it in this weather, but it does not affect The Leek.

"Our planet's overlighted if anything," says Captain Purnall at the wheel, as Cardiff-Bristol slides under. "I remember the old days of common white verticals that 'ud show two or three thousand feet up in a mist, if you knew where to look for 'em. In really fluffy weather they might as well have been under your hat. One could get lost coming home then, an' have some fun. Now, it's like driving down Piccadilly."

He points to the pillars of light where the cloud-breakers bore through the cloud-floor. We see nothing of England's outlines: only a white pavement pierced in all directions by these manholes of variously coloured fire—Holy Island's white and red—St. Bee's interrupted white, and so on as far as the eye can reach. Blessed be Sargent, Ahrens, and the Dubois brothers, who invented the cloud-breakers of the world whereby we travel in security!

"Are you going to lift for The Shamrock?" asks Captain Hodgson. Cork Light (green, fixed) enlarges as we rush to it. Captain Purnall nods. There is heavy traffic hereabouts—the cloud-bank beneath us is streaked with running fissures of flame where the Atlantic boats are hurrying Londonward just clear of the fluff. Mail-packets are supposed, under the Conference rules, to have the five-thousand-foot lanes to themselves, but the foreigner in a hurry is apt to take liberties with English air. "No. 162" lifts to a long-drawn wail of the breeze in the fore-flange of the rudder and we make Valencia (white, green, white) at a safe 7,000 feet, dipping our beam to an incoming Washington packet.

There is no cloud on the Atlantic, and faint streaks of cream round Dingle Bay show where the driven seas hammer the coast. A big S. A. T. A. liner (Société Anonyme des Transports Aëriens) is diving and lifting half a mile below us in search of some break in the solid west wind. Lower still lies a disabled Dane: she is telling the liner all about it in International. Our General Communication dial has caught her talk and begins to eavesdrop. Captain Hodgson makes a motion to shut it off but checks himself. "Perhaps you'd like to listen," he says.

"'Argol' of St. Thomas," the Dane whimpers. "Report owners three starboard shaft collar-bearings fused. Can make Flores as we are, but impossible further. Shall we buy spares at Fayal?"

The liner acknowledges and recommends inverting the bearings. The "Argol" answers that she has already done so without effect, and begins to relieve her mind about cheap German enamels for collar-bearings. The Frenchman assents cordially, cries "Courage, mon ami," and switches off.

Their lights sink under the curve of the ocean.

"That's one of Lundt & Bleamers's boats," says Captain Hodgson. "Serves 'em right for putting German compos in their thrust-blocks. She won't be in Fayal to-night! By the way, wouldn't you like to look round the engine-room?"

I have been waiting eagerly for this invitation and I follow Captain Hodgson from the control-platform, stooping low to avoid the bulge of the tanks. We know that Fleury's gas can lift anything, as the world-famous trials of '89 showed, but its almost indefinite powers of expansion necessitate vast tank room. Even in this thin air the lift-shunts are busy taking out one-third of its normal lift, and still "162" must be checked by an occasional downdraw of the rudder or our flight would become a climb to the stars. Captain Purnall prefers an overlifted to an underlifted ship; but no two captains trim ship alike. "When I take the bridge," says Captain Hodgson, "you'll see me shunt forty per cent. of the lift out of the gas and run her on the upper rudder. With a swoop upwards instead of a swoop downwards, as you say. Either way will do. It's only habit. Watch our dip-dial! Tim fetches her down once every thirty knots as regularly as breathing."

So is it shown on the dip-dial. For five or six minutes the arrow creeps from 6,700 to 7,300. There is the faint "szgee" of the rudder, and back slides the arrow to 6,500 on a falling slant of ten or fifteen knots.

"In heavy weather you jockey her with the screws as well," says Captain Hodgson, and, unclipping the jointed bar which divides the engine-room from the bare deck, he leads me on to the floor.

Here we find Fleury's Paradox of the Bulkheaded Vacuum—which we accept now without thought—literally in full blast. The three engines are H. T. & T. assisted-vacuo Fleury turbines running from 3,000 to the Limit—that is to say, up to the point when the blades make the air "bell"—cut out a vacuum for themselves precisely as over-driven marine propellers used to do. "162's" Limit is low on account of the small size of her nine screws, which, though handier than the old colloid Thelussons, "bell" sooner. The midships engine, generally used as a reinforce, is not running; so the port and starboard turbine vacuum-chambers draw direct into the return-mains.

The turbines whistle reflectively. From the low-arched expansion-tanks on either side the valves descend pillarwise to the turbine-chests, and thence the obedient gas whirls through the spirals of blades with a force that would whip the teeth out of a power-saw. Behind, is its own pressure held in leash or spurred on by the lift-shunts; before it, the vacuum where Fleury's Ray dances in violet-green bands and whirled turbillions of flame. The jointed U-tubes of the vacuum-chamber are pressure-tempered colloid (no glass would endure the strain for an instant) and a junior engineer with tinted spectacles watches the Ray intently. It is the very heart of the machine—a mystery to this day. Even Fleury who begat it and, unlike Magniac, died a multi-millionaire, could not explain how the restless little imp shuddering in the U-tube can, in the fractional fraction of a second, strike the furious blast of gas into a chill grayish-green liquid that drains (you can hear it trickle) from the far end of the vacuum through the eduction-pipes and the mains back to the bilges. Here it returns to its gaseous, one had almost written sagacious, state and climbs to work afresh. Bilge-tank, upper tank, dorsal-tank, expansion-chamber, vacuum, main-return (as a liquid), and bilge-tank once more is the ordained cycle. Fleury's Ray sees to that; and the engineer with the tinted spectacles sees to Fleury's Ray. If a speck of oil, if even the natural grease of the human finger touch the hooded terminals Fleury's Ray will wink and disappear and must be laboriously built up again. This means half a day's work for all hands and an expense of one hundred and seventy-odd pounds to the G. P. O. for radium-salts and such trifles.

"Now look at our thrust-collars. You won't find much German compo there. Full-jewelled, you see," says Captain Hodgson as the engineer shunts open the top of a cap. Our shaft-bearings are C. M. C. (Commercial Minerals Company) stones, ground with as much care as the lens of a telescope. They cost £37 apiece. So far we have not arrived at their term of life. These bearings came from "No. 97," which took them over from the old "Dominion of Light," which had them out of the wreck of the "Perseus" aëroplane in the years when men still flew linen kites over thorium engines!

They are a shining reproof to all low-grade German "ruby" enamels, so-called "boort" facings, and the dangerous and unsatisfactory alumina compounds which please dividend-hunting owners and turn skippers crazy.

The rudder-gear and the gas lift-shunt, seated side by side under the engine-room dials, are the only machines in visible motion. The former sighs from time to time as the oil plunger rises and falls half an inch. The latter, cased and guarded like the U-tube aft, exhibits another Fleury Ray, but inverted and more green than violet. Its function is to shunt the lift out of the gas, and this it will do without watching. That is all! A tiny pump-rod wheezing and whining to itself beside a sputtering green lamp. A hundred and fifty feet aft down the flat-topped tunnel of the tanks a violet light, restless and irresolute. Between the two, three white-painted turbine-trunks, like eel-baskets laid on their side, accentuate the empty perspectives. You can hear the trickle of the liquefied gas flowing from the vacuum into the bilge-tanks and the soft gluck-glock of gas-locks closing as Captain Purnall brings "162" down by the head. The hum of the turbines and the boom of the air on our skin is no more than a cotton-wool wrapping to the universal stillness. And we are running an eighteen-second mile.

I peer from the fore end of the engine-room over the hatch-coamings into the coach. The mail-clerks are sorting the Winnipeg, Calgary, and Medicine Hat bags: but there is a pack of cards ready on the table.

Suddenly a bell thrills; the engineers run to the turbine-valves and stand by; but the spectacled slave of the Ray in the U-tube never lifts his head. He must watch where he is. We are hard-braked and going astern; there is language from the control-platform.

"Tim's sparking badly about something," says the unruffled Captain Hodgson. "Let's look."

Captain Purnall is not the suave man we left half an hour since, but the embodied authority of the G. P. O. Ahead of us floats an ancient, aluminum-patched, twin-screw tramp of the dingiest, with no more right to the 5,000 foot lane than has a horse-cart to a modern town. She carries an obsolete "barbette" conning-tower—a six-foot affair with railed platform forward—and our warning beam plays on the top of it as a policeman's lantern flashes on the area sneak. Like a sneak-thief, too, emerges a shock-headed navigator in his shirt-sleeves. Captain Purnall wrenches open the colloid to talk with him man to man. There are times when Science does not satisfy.

"What under the stars are you doing here, you sky-scraping chimney-sweep?" he shouts as we two drift side by side. "Do you know this is a Mail-lane? You call yourself a sailor, sir? You ain't fit to peddle toy balloons to an Esquimaux. Your name and number! Report and get down, and be——!"

"I've been blown up once," the shock-headed man cries, hoarsely, as a dog barking. "I don't care two flips of a contact for anything you can do, Postey."

"Don't you, sir? But I'll make you care. I'll have you towed stern first to Disko and broke up. You can't recover insurance if you're broke for obstruction. Do you understand that?"

Then the stranger bellows: "Look at my propellers! There's been a wulli-wa down under that has knocked us into umbrella-frames! We've been blown up about forty thousand feet! We're all one conjuror's watch inside! My mate's arm's broke; my engineer's head's cut open; my Ray went out when the engines smashed; and ... and ... for pity's sake give me my height, Captain! We doubt we're dropping."

"Six thousand eight hundred. Can you hold it?" Captain Purnall overlooks all insults, and leans half out of the colloid, staring and snuffing. The stranger leaks pungently.

"We ought to blow into St. John's with luck. We're trying to plug the fore-tank now, but she's simply whistling it away," her captain wails.

"She's sinking like a log," says Captain Purnall in an undertone. "Call up the Banks Mark Boat, George." Our dip-dial shows that we, keeping abreast the tramp, have dropped five hundred feet the last few minutes.

Captain Purnall presses a switch and our signal beam begins to swing through the night, twizzling spokes of light across infinity.

"That'll fetch something," he says, while Captain Hodgson watches the General Communicator. He has called up the North Banks Mark Boat, a few hundred miles west, and is reporting the case.

"I'll stand by you," Captain Purnall roars to the lone figure on the conning-tower.

"Is it as bad as that?" comes the answer. "She isn't insured, she's mine."

"Might have guessed as much," mutters Hodgson. "Owner's risk is the worst risk of all!"

"Can't I fetch St. John's—not even with this breeze?" the voice quavers.

"Stand by to abandon ship. Haven't you any lift in you, fore or aft?"

"Nothing but the midship tanks and they're none too tight. You see, my Ray gave out and—" he coughs in the reek of the escaping gas.

"You poor devil!" This does not reach our friend. "What does the Mark Boat say, George?"

"Wants to know if there's any danger to traffic. Says she's in a bit of weather herself and can't quit station. I've turned in a General Call, so even if they don't see our beam some one's bound to help—or else we must. Shall I clear our slings. Hold on! Here we are! A Planet liner, too! She'll be up in a tick!"

"Tell her to have her slings ready," cries his brother captain. "There won't be much time to spare.... Tie up your mate," he roars to the tramp.

"My mate's all right. It's my engineer. He's gone crazy."

"Shunt the lift out of him with a spanner. Hurry!"

"But I can make St. John's if you'll stand by."

"You'll make the deep, wet Atlantic in twenty minutes. You're less than fifty-eight hundred now. Get your papers."

A Planet liner, east bound, heaves up in a superb spiral and takes the air of us humming. Her underbody colloid is open and her transporter-slings hang down like tentacles. We shut off our beam as she adjusts herself—steering to a hair—over the tramp's conning-tower. The mate comes up, his arm strapped to his side, and stumbles into the cradle. A man with a ghastly scarlet head follows, shouting that he must go back and build up his Ray. The mate assures him that he will find a nice new Ray all ready in the liner's engine-room. The bandaged head goes up wagging excitedly. A youth and a woman follow. The liner cheers hollowly above us, and we see the passengers' faces at the saloon colloid.

"That's a good girl. What's the fool waiting for now?" says Captain Purnall.

The skipper comes up, still appealing to us to stand by and see him fetch St. John's. He dives below and returns—at which we little human beings in the void cheer louder than ever—with the ship's kitten. Up fly the liner's hissing slings; her underbody crashes home and she hurtles away again. The dial shows less than 3,000 feet.

The Mark Boat signals we must attend to the derelict, now whistling her death song, as she falls beneath us in long sick zigzags.

"Keep our beam on her and send out a General Warning," says Captain Purnall, following her down.

There is no need. Not a liner in air but knows the meaning of that vertical beam and gives us and our quarry a wide berth.

"But she'll drown in the water, won't she?" I ask.

"Not always," is his answer. "I've known a derelict up-end and sift her engines out of herself and flicker round the Lower Lanes for three weeks on her forward tanks only. We'll run no risks. Pith her, George, and look sharp. There's weather ahead."

Captain Hodgson opens the underbody colloid, swings the heavy pithing-iron out of its rack which in liners is generally cased as a settee, and at two hundred feet releases the catch. We hear the whir of the crescent-shaped arms opening as they descend. The derelict's forehead is punched in, starred across, and rent diagonally. She falls stern first, our beam upon her; slides like a lost soul down that pitiless ladder of light, and the Atlantic takes her.

"A filthy business," says Hodgson. "I wonder what it must have been like in the old days."

The thought had crossed my mind too. What if that wavering carcass had been filled with International-speaking men of all the Internationalities, each one of them taught (that is the horror of it!) that after death he would very possibly go forever to unspeakable torment?

And not half a century since, we (one knows now that we are only our fathers re-enlarged upon the earth), we, I say, ripped and rammed and pithed to admiration.

Here Tim, from the control-platform, shouts that we are to get into our inflators and to bring him his at once.

We hurry into the heavy rubber suits—and the engineers are already dressed—and inflate at the air-pump taps. G. P. O. inflators are thrice as thick as a racing man's "flickers," and chafe abominably under the armpits. George takes the wheel until Tim has blown himself up to the extreme of rotundity. If you kicked him off the c. p. to the deck he would bounce back. But it is "162" that will do the kicking.

"The Mark Boat's mad—stark ravin' crazy," he snorts, returning to command. "She says there's a bad blow-out ahead and wants me to pull over to Greenland. I'll see her pithed first! We wasted an hour and a quarter over that dead duck down under, and now I'm expected to go rubbin' my back all round the Pole. What does she think a postal packet's made of? Gummed silk? Tell her we're coming on straight, George."

George buckles him into the Frame and switches on the Direct Control. Now under Tim's left toe lies the port-engine Accelerator; under his left heel the Reverse, and so with the other foot. The lift-shunt stops stand out on the rim of the steering-wheel where the fingers of his left hand can play on them. At his right hand is the midships engine lever ready to be thrown into gear at a moment's notice. He leans forward in his belt, eyes glued to the colloid, and one ear cocked toward the General Communicator. Henceforth he is the strength and direction of "162," through whatever may befall.

The Banks Mark Boat is reeling out pages of A. B. C. Directions to the traffic at large. We are to secure all "loose objects"; hood up our Fleury Rays; and "on no account to attempt to clear snow from our conning-towers till the weather abates." Under-powered craft, we are told, can ascend to the limit of their lift, mail-packets to look out for them accordingly; the lower lanes westward are pitting very badly, "with frequent blow-outs, vortices, laterals, etc."

Still the clear dark holds up unblemished. The only warning is the electric skin-tension (I feel as though I were a lace-maker's pillow) and an irritability which the gibbering of the General Communicator increases almost to hysteria.

We have made eight thousand feet since we pithed the tramp and our turbines are giving us an honest two hundred and ten knots.

Very far to the west an elongated blur of red, low down, shows us the North Banks Mark Boat. There are specks of fire round her rising and falling—bewildered planets about an unstable sun—helpless shipping hanging on to her light for company's sake. No wonder she could not quit station.

She warns us to look out for the backwash of the bad vortex in which (her beam shows it) she is even now reeling.

The pits of gloom about us begin to fill with very faintly luminous films—wreathing and uneasy shapes. One forms itself into a globe of pale flame that waits shivering with eagerness till we sweep by. It leaps monstrously across the blackness, alights on the precise tip of our nose, pirouettes there an instant, and swings off. Our roaring bow sinks as though that light were lead—sinks and recovers to lurch and stumble again beneath the next blow-out. Tim's fingers on the lift-shunt strike chords of numbers—1:4:7:—2:4:6:—7:5:3, and so on; for he is running by his tanks only, lifting or lowering her against the uneasy air. All three engines are at work, for the sooner we have skated over this thin ice the better. Higher we dare not go. The whole upper vault is charged with pale krypton vapours, which our skin friction may excite to unholy manifestations. Between the upper and the lower levels—5,000, and 7,000, hints the Mark Boat—we may perhaps bolt through if.... Our bow clothes itself in blue flame and falls like a sword. No human skill can keep pace with the changing tensions. A vortex has us by the beak and we dive down a two-thousand-foot slant at an angle (the dip-dial and my bouncing body record it) of thirty-five. Our turbines scream shrilly; the propellers cannot bite on the thin air; Tim shunts the lift out of five tanks at once and by sheer weight drives her bulletwise through the maelstrom till she cushions with a jar on an up-gust, three thousand feet below.

"Now we've done it," says George in my ear. "Our skin-friction that last slide, has played Old Harry with the tensions! Look out for laterals, Tim, she'll want some holding."

"I've got her," is the answer. "Come up, old woman."

She comes up nobly, but the laterals buffet her left and right like the pinions of angry angels. She is jolted off her course in four ways at once, and cuffed into place again, only to be swung aside and dropped into a new chaos. We are never without a corposant grinning on our bows or rolling head over heels from nose to midships, and to the crackle of electricity around and within us is added once or twice the rattle of hail—hail that will never fall on any sea. Slow we must or we may break our back, pitch-poling.

"Air's a perfectly elastic fluid," roars George above the tumult. "About as elastic as a head sea off the Fastnet, aint it?"

He is less than just to the good element. If one intrudes on the Heavens when they are balancing their volt-accounts; if one disturbs the High Gods' market-rates by hurling steel hulls at ninety knots across tremblingly adjusted electric tensions, one must not complain of any rudeness in the reception. Tim met it with an unmoved countenance, one corner of his under lip caught up on a tooth, his eyes fleeting into the blackness twenty miles ahead, and the fierce sparks flying from his knuckles at every turn of the hand. Now and again he shook his head to clear the sweat trickling from his eyebrows, and it was then that George, watching his chance, would slide down the life-rail and swab his face quickly with a big red handkerchief. I never imagined that a human being could so continuously labour and so collectedly think as did Tim through that Hell's half hour when the flurry was at its worst. We were dragged hither and yon by warm or frozen suctions, belched up on the tops of wulli-was, spun down by vortices and clubbed aside by laterals under a dizzying rush of stars in the company of a drunken moon. I heard the rushing click of the midship-engine-lever sliding in and out, the low growl of the lift-shunts, and, louder than the yelling winds without, the scream of the bow-rudder gouging into any lull that promised hold for an instant. At last we began to claw up on a cant, bow-rudder and port-propeller together; only the nicest balancing of tanks saved us from spinning like the rifle-bullet of the old days.

"We've got to hitch to windward of that Mark Boat somehow," George cried.

"There's no windward," I protested feebly, where I swung shackled to a stanchion. "How can there be?"

He laughed—as we pitched into a thousand foot blow-out—that red man laughed beneath his inflated hood!

"Look!" he said. "We must clear those refugees with a high lift."

The Mark Boat was below and a little to the sou'west of us, fluctuating in the centre of her distraught galaxy. The air was thick with moving lights at every level. I take it most of them were trying to lie head to wind but, not being hydras, they failed. An under-tanked Moghrabi boat had risen to the limit of her lift and, finding no improvement, had dropped a couple of thousand. There she met a superb wulli-wa and was blown up spinning like a dead leaf. Instead of shutting off she went astern and, naturally, rebounded as from a wall almost into the Mark Boat, whose language (our G. C. took it in) was humanly simple.

"If they'd only ride it out quietly it 'ud be better," said George in a calm, as we climbed like a bat above them all. "But some skippers will navigate without enough lift. What does that Tad-boat think she is doing, Tim?"

"Playin' kiss in the ring," was Tim's unmoved reply. A Trans-Asiatic Direct liner had found a smooth and butted into it full power. But there was a vortex at the tail of that smooth, so the T. A. D. was flipped out like a pea from off a fingernail, braking madly as she fled down and all but over-ending.

"Now I hope she's satisfied," said Tim. "I'm glad I'm not a Mark Boat.... Do I want help?" The C. G. dial had caught his ear. "George, you may tell that gentleman with my love—love, remember, George—that I do not want help. Who is the officious sardine-tin?"

"A Rimouski drogher on the lookout for a tow."

"Very kind of the Rimouski drogher. This postal packet isn't being towed at present."

"Those droghers will go anywhere on a chance of salvage," George explained. "We call 'em kittiwakes."

A long-beaked, bright steel ninety-footer floated at ease for one instant within hail of us, her slings coiled ready for rescues, and a single hand in her open tower. He was smoking. Surrendered to the insurrection of the airs through which we tore our way, he lay in absolute peace. I saw the smoke of his pipe ascend untroubled ere his boat dropped, it seemed, like a stone in a well.

We had just cleared the Mark Boat and her disorderly neighbours when the storm ended as suddenly as it had begun. A shooting-star to northward filled the sky with the green blink of a meteorite dissipating itself in our atmosphere.

Said George: "That may iron out all the tensions." Even as he spoke, the conflicting winds came to rest; the levels filled; the laterals died out in long easy swells; the airways were smoothed before us. In less than three minutes the covey round the Mark Boat had shipped their power-lights and whirred away upon their businesses.

"What's happened?" I gasped. The nerve-storm within and the volt-tingle without had passed: my inflators weighed like lead.

"God, He knows!" said Captain George, soberly. "That old shooting-star's skin-friction has discharged the different levels. I've seen it happen before. Phew! What a relief!"

We dropped from ten to six thousand and got rid of our clammy suits. Tim shut off and stepped out of the Frame. The Mark Boat was coming up behind us. He opened the colloid in that heavenly stillness and mopped his face.

"Hello, Williams!" he cried. "A degree or two out o' station, ain't you?"

"May be," was the answer from the Mark Boat. "I've had some company this evening."

"So I noticed. Wasn't that quite a little draught?"

"I warned you. Why didn't you pull out round by Disko? The east-bound packets have."

"Me? Not till I'm running a Polar consumptives' Sanatorium boat. I was squinting through a colloid before you were out of your cradle, my son."

"I'd be the last man to deny it," the captain of the Mark Boat replies softly. "The way you handled her just now—I'm a pretty fair judge of traffic in a volt-flurry—it was a thousand revolutions beyond anything even I've ever seen."

Tim's back supples visibly to this oiling. Captain George on the c. p. winks and points to the portrait of a singularly attractive maiden pinned up on Tim's telescope-bracket above the steering-wheel.

I see. Wholly and entirely do I see!

There is some talk overhead of "coming round to tea on Friday," a brief report of the derelict's fate, and Tim volunteers as he descends: "For an A. B. C. man young Williams is less of a high-tension fool than some.... Were you thinking of taking her on, George? Then I'll just have a look round that port-thrust—seems to me it's a trifle warm—and we'll jog along."

The Mark Boat hums off joyously and hangs herself up in her appointed eyrie. Here she will stay, a shutterless observatory; a life-boat station; a salvage tug; a court of ultimate appeal-cum-meteorological bureau for three hundred miles in all directions, till Wednesday next when her relief slides across the stars to take her buffeted place. Her black hull, double conning-tower, and ever-ready slings represent all that remains to the planet of that odd old word authority. She is responsible only to the Aërial Board of Control—the A. B. C. of which Tim speaks so flippantly. But that semi-elected, semi-nominated body of a few score persons of both sexes, controls this planet. "Transportation is Civilization," our motto runs. Theoretically, we do what we please so long as we do not interfere with the traffic and all it implies. Practically, the A. B. C. confirms or annuls all international arrangements and, to judge from its last report, finds our tolerant, humorous, lazy little planet only too ready to shift the whole burden of private administration on its shoulders.

I discuss this with Tim, sipping maté on the c. p. while George fans her along over the white blur of the Banks in beautiful upward curves of fifty miles each. The dip-dial translates them on the tape in flowing freehand.

Tim gathers up a skein of it and surveys the last few feet, which record "162's" path through the volt-flurry.

"I haven't had a fever-chart like this to show up in five years," he says ruefully.

A postal packet's dip-dial records every yard of every run. The tapes then go to the A. B. C., which collates and makes composite photographs of them for the instruction of captains. Tim studies his irrevocable past, shaking his head.

"Hello! Here's a fifteen-hundred-foot drop at eighty-five degrees! We must have been standing on our heads then, George."

"You don't say so," George answers. "I fancied I noticed it at the time."

George may not have Captain Purnall's catlike swiftness, but he is all an artist to the tips of the broad fingers that play on the shunt-stops. The delicious flight-curves come away on the tape with never a waver. The Mark Boat's vertical spindle of light lies down to eastward, setting in the face of the following stars. Westward, where no planet should rise, the triple verticals of Trinity Bay (we keep still to the Southern route) make a low-lifting haze. We seem the only thing at rest under all the heavens; floating at ease till the earth's revolution shall turn up our landing-towers.

And minute by minute our silent clock gives us a sixteen-second mile.

"Some fine night," says Tim. "We'll be even with that clock's Master."

"He's coming now," says George, over his shoulder. "I'm chasing the night west."

The stars ahead dim no more than if a film of mist had been drawn under unobserved, but the deep air-boom on our skin changes to a joyful shout.

"The dawn-gust," says Tim. "It'll go on to meet the Sun. Look! Look! There's the dark being crammed back over our bow! Come to the after-colloid. I'll show you something."

The engine-room is hot and stuffy; the clerks in the coach are asleep, and the Slave of the Ray is near to follow them. Tim slides open the aft colloid and reveals the curve of the world—the ocean's deepest purple—edged with fuming and intolerable gold. Then the Sun rises and through the colloid strikes out our lamps. Tim scowls in his face.

"Squirrels in a cage," he mutters. "That's all we are. Squirrels in a cage! He's going twice as fast as us. Just you wait a few years, my shining friend and we'll take steps that will amaze you. We'll Joshua you!"

Yes, that is our dream: to turn all earth into the Vale of Ajalon at our pleasure. So far, we can drag out the dawn to twice its normal length in these latitudes. But some day—even on the Equator—we shall hold the Sun level in his full stride.

Now we look down on a sea thronged with heavy traffic. A big submersible breaks water suddenly. Another and another follow with a swash and a suck and a savage bubbling of relieved pressures. The deep-sea freighters are rising to lung up after the long night, and the leisurely ocean is all patterned with peacock's eyes of foam.

"We'll lung up, too," says Tim, and when we return to the c. p. George shuts off, the colloids are opened, and the fresh air sweeps her out. There is no hurry. The old contracts (they will be revised at the end of the year) allow twelve hours for a run which any packet can put behind her in ten. So we breakfast in the arms of an easterly slant which pushes us along at a languid twenty.

To enjoy life, and tobacco, begin both on a sunny morning half a mile or so above the dappled Atlantic cloud-belts and after a volt-flurry which has cleared and tempered your nerves. While we discussed the thickening traffic with the superiority that comes of having a high level reserved to ourselves, we heard (and I for the first time) the morning hymn on a Hospital boat.

She was cloaked by a skein of ravelled fluff beneath us and we caught the chant before she rose into the sunlight. "Oh, ye Winds of God," sang the unseen voices: "bless ye the Lord! Praise Him and magnify Him forever!"

We slid off our caps and joined in. When our shadow fell across her great open platforms they looked up and stretched out their hands neighbourly while they sang. We could see the doctors and the nurses and the white-button-like faces of the cot-patients. She passed slowly beneath us, heading northward, her hull, wet with the dews of the night, all ablaze in the sunshine. So took she the shadow of a cloud and vanished, her song continuing. Oh, ye holy and humble men of heart, bless ye the Lord! Praise Him and magnify Him forever.

"She's a public lunger or she wouldn't have been singing the Benedicite; and she's a Greenlander or she wouldn't have snow-blinds over her colloids," said George at last. "She'll be bound for Frederikshavn or one of the Glacier sanatoriums for a month. If she was an accident ward she'd be hung up at the eight-thousand-foot level. Yes—consumptives."

"Funny how the new things are the old things. I've read in books," Tim answered, "that savages used to haul their sick and wounded up to the tops of hills because microbes were fewer there. We hoist 'em into sterilized air for a while. Same idea. How much do the doctors say we've added to the average life of a man?"

"Thirty years," says George with a twinkle in his eye. "Are we going to spend 'em all up here, Tim?"

"Flap along, then. Flap along. Who's hindering?" the senior captain laughed, as we went in.

We held a good lift to clear the coastwise and Continental shipping; and we had need of it. Though our route is in no sense a populated one, there is a steady trickle of traffic this way along. We met Hudson Bay furriers out of the Great Preserve, hurrying to make their departure from Bonavista with sable and black fox for the insatiable markets. We over-crossed Keewatin liners, small and cramped; but their captains, who see no land between Trepassy and Blanco, know what gold they bring back from West Africa. Trans-Asiatic Directs, we met, soberly ringing the world round the Fiftieth Meridian at an honest seventy knots; and white-painted Ackroyd & Hunt fruiters out of the south fled beneath us, their ventilated hulls whistling like Chinese kites. Their market is in the North among the northern sanatoria where you can smell their grapefruit and bananas across the cold snows. Argentine beef boats we sighted too, of enormous capacity and unlovely outline. They, too, feed the northern health stations in ice-bound ports where submersibles dare not rise.

Yellow-bellied ore-flats and Ungava petrol-tanks punted down leisurely out of the north like strings of unfrightened wild duck. It does not pay to "fly" minerals and oil a mile farther than is necessary; but the risks of transhipping to submersibles in the ice-pack off Nain or Hebron are so great that these heavy freighters fly down to Halifax direct, and scent the air as they go. They are the biggest tramps aloft except the Athabasca grain-tubs. But these last, now that the wheat is moved, are busy, over the world's shoulder, timber-lifting in Siberia.

We held to the St. Lawrence (it is astonishing how the old water-ways still pull us children of the air), and followed his broad line of black between its drifting ice blocks, all down the Park that the wisdom of our fathers—but every one knows the Quebec run.

We dropped to the Heights Receiving Towers twenty minutes ahead of time and there hung at ease till the Yokohama Intermediate Packet could pull out and give us our proper slip. It was curious to watch the action of the holding-down clips all along the frosty river front as the boats cleared or came to rest. A big Hamburger was leaving Pont Levis and her crew, unshipping the platform railings, began to sing "Elsinore"—the oldest of our chanteys. You know it of course:

> Mother Rugen's tea-house on the Baltic—
> Forty couple waltzing on the floor!
> And you can watch my Ray,
> For I must go away
> And dance with Ella Sweyn at Elsinore!

Then, while they sweated home the covering-plates:

> Nor-Nor-Nor-Nor-
> West from Sourabaya to the Baltic—
> Ninety knot an hour to the Skaw!
> Mother Rugen's tea-house on the Baltic
> And a dance with Ella Sweyn at Elsinore!

The clips parted with a gesture of indignant dismissal, as though Quebec, glittering under her snows, were casting out these light and unworthy lovers. Our signal came from the Heights. Tim turned and floated up, but surely then it was with passionate appeal that the great tower arms flung open—or did I think so because on the upper staging a little hooded figure also opened her arms wide towards her father?

In ten seconds the coach with its clerks clashed down to the receiving-caisson; the hostlers displaced the engineers at the idle turbines, and Tim, prouder of this than all, introduced me to the maiden of the photograph on the shelf. "And by the way," said he to her, stepping forth in sunshine under the hat of civil life, "I saw young Williams in the Mark Boat. I've asked him to tea on Friday."

EASY AS ABC: A TALE OF 2150 A.D.
(UNITED KINGDOM, 1912)

Isn't it almost time that our Planet took some interest in the proceedings of the Aerial Board of Control? One knows that easy communications nowadays, and lack of privacy in the past, have killed all curiosity among mankind, but as the Board's Official Reporter I am bound to tell my tale.

At 9.30 A.M. on August 26, the Board, sitting in London, was informed by De Forest (U.S.) that the District of Northern Illinois had riotously cut itself out of all systems and would remain disconnected till the Board should take over and administer it direct.

Every Northern Illinois freight and passenger tower was, he reported, out of action; all District main, local, and guiding lights had been extinguished; all

General Communications were dumb, and through traffic had been diverted. No reason had been given, but he gathered unofficially from the Mayor of Chicago that the District complained of "crowd-making and invasion of privacy."

As a matter of fact, it is of no importance whether Northern Illinois stay in or out of planetary circuit; as a matter of policy, any complaint of invasion of privacy needs immediate investigation, lest worse follow.

By 9.45 A.M. De Forest, Dragomiroff (Russia), Takahira (Japan), and Pirolo (Italy) were empowered to visit Illinois and "to take such steps as might be necessary for the resumption of traffic and all that that implies." By 10 A.M. the Hall was empty, and the four Members and I were aboard what Pirolo insisted on calling "my leetle godchild" - that is to say, the new Victor Pirolo. Our Planet prefers to know Victor Pirolo as a gentle, grey-haired enthusiast who spends his time near Foggia, inventing or creating new breeds of Spanish-Italian olive-trees; but there is another side to his nature - the manufacture of quaint inventions, of which the Victor Pirolo is perhaps, not the least surprising. She and a few score sister-craft of the same type embody his latest ideas. But she is not comfortable. An A.B.C. boat does not take the air with the level-keeled lift of a liner, but shoots up rocket-fashion like the "aeroplane" of our ancestors, and makes her height at top-speed from the first. That is why I found myself sitting suddenly on the large lap of Eustace Arnott, who commands the A.B.C. Fleet. One knows vaguely that there is such a thing as a Fleet somewhere on the Planet, and that, theoretically, it exists for the purposes of what used to be known as "war." Only a week before, while visiting a glacier sanatorium behind Gothaven, I had seen some squadrons making false auroras far to the north while they manoeuvred round the Pole; but, naturally, it had never occurred to me that the things could be used in earnest.

Said Arnott to De Forest as I staggered to a seat on the chart-room divan: "We're tremendously grateful to 'em in Illinois. We've never had a chance of exercising all the Fleet together. I've turned in a General Call, and I expect we'll have at least two hundred keels aloft this evening."

"Well aloft?" De Forest asked.

"Of course, sir. Out of sight till they're called for."

Arnott laughed as he lolled over the transparent chart-table where the map of the summer-blue Atlantic slid along, degree by degree, in exact answer to our progress. Our dial already showed 320 m.p.h. and we were two thousand feet above the uppermost traffic lines.

"Now, where is this Illinois District of yours?" said Dragomiroff. "One travels so much, one sees so little. Oh, I remember! It is in North America."

De Forest, whose business it is to know the out districts, told us that it lay at the foot of Lake Michigan, on a road to nowhere in particular, was about half an hour's run from end to end, and, except in one corner, as flat as the sea. Like most flat countries nowadays, it was heavily guarded against invasion of privacy by forced timber - fifty-foot spruce and tamarack, grown in five years. The population was close on two millions, largely migratory between Florida and California, with a backbone of small farms (they call a thousand acres a farm in Illinois) whose owners come into Chicago for amusements and society during the winter. They were, he said noticeably kind, quiet folk, but a little exacting, as all flat countries must be, in their notions of privacy. There had, for instance, been no printed news-sheet in Illinois for twenty-seven years. Chicago argued that engines for printed news sooner or later developed into engines for invasion of privacy, which in turn might bring the old terror of Crowds and blackmail back to the Planet. So news-sheets were not.

"And that's Illinois," De Forest concluded. "You see, in the Old Days, she was in the fore-front of what they used to call 'progress,' and Chicago—"

'Chicago?" said Takahira. "That's the little place where there is Salati's Statue of the Nigger in Flames. A fine bit of old work."

"When did you see it?" asked De Forest quickly. "They only unveil it once a year."

"I know. At Thanksgiving. It was then," said Takahira, with a shudder. "And they sang MacDonough's Song, too."

"Whew!" De Forest whistled. "I did not know that! I wish you'd told me before. MacDonough's Song may have had its uses when it was composed, but it was an infernal legacy for any man to leave behind."

"It's protective instinct, my dear fellows,' said Pirolo, rolling a cigarette. "The Planet, she has had her dose of popular government. She suffers from inherited agoraphobia. She has no - ah - use for crowds."

Dragomiroff leaned forward to give him a light. "Certainly," said the white-bearded Russian, "the Planet has taken all precautions against crowds for the past hundred years. What is our total population today? Six hundred million, we hope; five hundred, we think; but - but if next year's census shows more than four hundred and fifty, I myself will eat all the extra little babies. We have cut the birth-rate out - right out! For a long time we have said to Almighty God, 'Thank You, Sir, but we do not much like Your game of life, so we will not play.'"

"Anyhow," said Arnott defiantly, "men live a century apiece on the average now."

"Oh, that is quite well! I am rich - you are rich - we are all rich and happy because we are so few and we live so long. Only I think Almighty God He will remember what the Planet was like in the time of Crowds and the Plague. Perhaps He will send us nerves. Eh, Pirolo?"

The Italian blinked into space. "Perhaps," he said, "He has sent them already. Anyhow, you cannot argue with the Planet. She does not forget the Old

Days, and - what can you do?"

"For sure we can't remake the world." De Forest glanced at the map flowing smoothly across the table from west to east. "We ought to be over our ground by nine to-night. There won't be much sleep afterwards."

On which hint we dispersed, and I slept till Takahira waked me for dinner. Our ancestors thought nine hours' sleep ample for their little lives. We, living thirty years longer, feel ourselves defrauded with less than eleven out of the twenty-four.

By ten o'clock we were over Lake Michigan. The west shore was lightless, except for a dull ground-glare at Chicago, and a single traffic-directing light - its leading beam pointing north - at Waukegan on our starboard bow. None of the Lake villages gave any sign of life; and inland, westward, so far as we could see, blackness lay unbroken on the level earth. We swooped down and skimmed low across the dark, throwing calls county by county. Now and again we picked up the faint glimmer of a house-light, or heard the rasp and rend of a cultivator being played across the fields, but Northern Illinois as a whole was one inky, apparently uninhabited, waste of high, forced woods. Only our illuminated map, with its little pointer switching from county to county, as we wheeled and twisted, gave us any idea of our position. Our calls, urgent, pleading, coaxing or commanding, through the General Communicator brought no answer. Illinois strictly maintained her own privacy in the timber which she grew for that purpose.

"Oh, this is absurd!" said De Forest. "We're like an owl trying to work a wheat-field. Is this Bureau Creek? Let's land, Arnott, and get hold of someone."

We brushed over a belt of forced woodland - fifteen-year-old maple sixty feet high - grounded on a private meadow-dock, none too big, where we moored to our own grapnels, and hurried out through the warm dark night towards a light in a verandah. As we neared the garden gate I could have sworn we had stepped knee-deep in quicksand, for we could scarcely drag our feet against the prickling currents that clogged them. After five paces we stopped, wiping our foreheads, as hopelessly stuck on dry smooth turf as so many cows in a bog.

"Pest!" cried Pirolo angrily. "We are ground-circuited. And it is my own system of ground-circuits too! I know the pull."

"Good evening," said a girl's voice from the verandah. "Oh, I'm sorry! We've locked up. Wait a minute."

We heard the click of a switch, and almost fell forward as the currents round our knees were withdrawn.

The girl laughed, and laid aside her knitting. An old-fashioned Controller stood at her elbow, which she reversed from time to time, and we could hear the snort and clank of the obedient cultivator half a mile away, behind the guardian woods.

"Come in and sit down," she said. "I'm only playing a plough. Dad's gone to Chicago to - Ah! Then it was your call I heard just now!"

She had caught sight of Arnott's Board uniform, leaped to the switch, and turned it full on.

We were checked, gasping, waist-deep in current this time, three yards from the verandah.

"We only want to know what's the matter with Illinois," said De Forest placidly.

"Then hadn't you better go to Chicago and find out?" she answered. "There's nothing wrong here. We own ourselves."

"How can we go anywhere if you won't loose us?" De Forest went on, while Arnott scowled. Admirals of Fleets are still quite human when their dignity is touched.

"Stop a minute - you don't know how funny you look!" She put her hands on her hips and laughed mercilessly.

"Don't worry about that," said Arnott, and whistled. A voice answered from the Victor Pirolo in the meadow.

"Only a single-fuse ground-circuit!" Arnott called. "Sort it out gently, please."

We heard the ping of a breaking lamp; a fuse blew out somewhere in the verandah roof, frightening a nest full of birds. The groud-circuit was open. We stooped and rubbed our tingling ankles.

"How rude - how very rude of you!" the maiden cried.

"Sorry, but we haven't time to look funny," said Arnott. "We've got to go to Chicago; and if I were you, young lady, I'd go into the cellars for the next two hours, and take mother with me."

Off he strode, with us at his heels, muttering indignantly, till the humour of the thing struck and doubled him up with laughter at the foot of the gangway-ladder.

"The Board hasn't shown what you might call a fat spark on this occasion," said De Forest, wiping his eyes. "I hope I didn't look as big a fool as you did, Arnott! Hullo! What on earth is that? Dad coming home from Chicago?"

There was a rattle and a rush, and a five-plough cultivator, blades in air like so many teeth, trundled itself at us round the edge of the timber, fuming and sparking furiously.

"Jump!" said Arnott, as we hurled ourselves through the none-too-wide door. "Never mind about shutting it. Up!"

The Victor Pirolo lifted like a bubble, and the vicious machine shot just underneath us, clawing high as it passed.

"There's a nice little spit-kitten for you!" said Arnott, dusting his knees. "We ask her a civil question. First she circuits us and then she plays a cultivator at us!"

"And then we fly," said Dragomirof. "If I were forty years more young, I would go back and kiss her. Ho! Ho!"

"I," said Pirolo, "would smack her! My pet ship has been chased by a dirty plough; a - how do you say? - agricultural implement."

"Oh, that is Illinois all over," said De Forest. "They don't content themselves with talking about privacy. They arrange to have it. And now, where's your alleged fleet, Arnott? We must assert ourselves against this wench."

Arnott pointed to the black heavens. "Waiting on - up there," said he. "Shall I give them the whole installation, sir?"

"Oh, I don't think the young lady is quite worth that," said De Forest. "Get over Chicago, and perhaps we'll see something."

In a few minutes we were hanging at two thousand feet over an oblong block of incandescence in the centre of the little town.

"That looks like the old City Hall. Yes, there's Salati's Statue in front of it," said Takahira. "But what on earth are they doing to the place? I thought they used it for a market nowadays! Drop a little, please."

We could hear the sputter and crackle of road-surfacing machines - the cheap Western type which fuse stone and rubbish into lava-like ribbed glass for their rough country roads. Three or four surfacers worked on each side of a square of ruins. The brick and stone wreckage crumbled, slid forward, and presently spread out into white-hot pools of sticky slag, which the levelling-rods smoothed more or less flat. Already a third of the big block had been so treated, and was cooling to dull red before our astonished eyes.

"It is the Old Market," said De Forest. "Well, there's nothing to prevent Illinois from making a road through a market. It doesn't interfere with traffic, that I can see."

"Hsh!" said Arnott, gripping me by the shoulder. "Listen! They're singing. Why on the earth are they singing?"

We dropped again till we could see the black fringe of people at the edge of that glowing square.

At first they only roared against the roar of the surfacers and levellers. Then the words came up clearly - the words of the Forbidden Song that all men knew, and none let pass their lips - poor Pat MacDonough's Song, made in the days of the Crowds and the Plague - every silly word of it loaded to sparking-point with the Planet's inherited memories of horror, panic, fear and cruelty. And Chicago - innocent, contented little Chicago - was singing it aloud to the infernal tune that carried riot, pestilence and lunacy round our Planet a few generations ago!

"Once there was The People - Terror gave it birth;

Once there was The People, and it made a hell of earth!"

(Then the stamp and pause):

"Earth arose and crushed it. Listen, oh, ye slain!
Once there was The People - it shall never be again!"

The levellers thrust in savagely against the ruins as the song renewed itself again, again and again, louder than the crash of the melting walls.

De Forest frowned.

I don't like that," he said. "They've broken back to the Old Days! They'll be killing somebody soon. I think we'd better divert 'em, Arnott."

"Ay, ay, sir." Arnott's hand went to his cap, and we heard the hull of the Victor Pirolo ring to the command: "Lamps! Both watches stand by! Lamps! Lamps! Lamps!"

"Keep still!" Takahira whispered to me. "Blinkers, please, quartermaster."

"It's all right - all right!" said Pirolo from behind, and to my horror slipped over my head some sort of rubber helmet that locked with a snap. I could feel thick colloid bosses before my eyes, but I stood in absolute darkness.

"To save the sight," he explained, and pushed me on to the chart-room divan. "You will see in a minute."

As he spoke I became aware of a thin thread of almost intolerable light, let down from heaven at an immense distance - one vertical hairs breadth of frozen lightning.

"Those are our flanking ships," said Arnott at my elbow. "That one is over Galena. Look south - that other one's over Keithburg. Vincennes is behind us, and north yonder is Winthrop Woods. The Fleet's in position, sir" - this to De Forest. "As soon as you give the word."

"Ah no! No!" cried Dragomiroff at my side. I could feel the old man tremble. "I do not know all that you can do, but be kind! I ask you to be a little kind to them below! This is horrible horrible!"

"When a Woman kills a Chicken,
Dynasties and Empires sicken,"

Takahira quoted. "It is too late to be gentle now."

"Then take off my helmet! Take off my helmet!" Dragomiroff began hysterically.

Pirolo must have put his arm round him.

"Hush," he said, "I am here. It is all right, Ivan, my dear fellow."

"I'll just send our little girl in Bureau County a warning," said Arnott. "She don't deserve it, but we'll allow her a minute or two to take mamma to the cellar."

In the utter hush that followed the growling spark after Arnott had linked up his Service Communicator with the invisible Fleet, we heard MacDonough's Song from the city beneath us grow fainter as we rose to position. Then I clapped my hand before my mask lenses, for it was as though the floor of Heaven had been riddled and all the inconceivable blaze of suns in the making was poured through the manholes.

"You needn't count," said Arnott. I had had no thought of such a thing. "There are two hundred and fifty keels up there, five miles apart. Full power, please, for another twelve seconds."

The firmament, as far as eye could reach, stood on pillars of white fire. One fell on the glowing square at Chicago, and turned it black.

"Oh! Oh! Oh! Can men be allowed to do such things?" Dragomiroff cried, and fell across our knees.

"Glass of water, please," said Takahira to a helmeted shape that leaped forward. "He is a little faint."

The lights switched off, and the darkness stunned like an avalanche. We could hear Dragomiroff's teeth on the glass edge.

Pirolo was comforting him.

"All right, all ra-ight," he repeated. "Come and lie down. Come below and take off your mask. I give you my word, old friend, it is all right. They are my siege-lights. Little Victor Pirolo's leetle lights. You know me! I do not hurt people."

"Pardon!" Dragomiroff moaned. "I have never seen Death. I have never seen the Board take action. Shall we go down and burn them alive, or is that already done?"

"Oh, hush," said Pirolo, and I think he rocked him in his arms.

"Do we repeat, sir?" Arnott asked De Forest.

"Give 'em a minute's break," De Forest replied." They may need it."

We waited a minute, and then MacDonough's Song, broken but defiant, rose from undefeated Chicago.

"They seem fond of that tune," said De Forest. "I should let 'em have it, Arnott."

"Very good, sir," said Arnott, and felt his way to the Communicator keys.

No lights broke forth, but the hollow of the skies made herself the mouth for one note that touched the raw fibre of the brain. Men hear such sounds in delirium, advancing like tides from horizons beyond the ruled foreshores of space.

"That's our pitch-pipe," said Arnott. "We may be a bit ragged. I've never conducted two hundred and fifty performers before." He pulled out the couplers, and struck a full chord on the Service Communicators.

The beams of light leaped down again, and danced, solemnly and awfully, a stilt-dance, sweeping thirty or forty miles left and right at each stiff-legged kick, while the darkness delivered itself - there is no scale to measure against that utterance - of the tune to which they kept time. Certain notes - one learnt to expect them with terror - cut through one's marrow, but, after three minutes, thought and emotion passed in indescribable agony.

We saw, we heard, but I think we were in some sort swooning. The two hundred and fifty beams shifted, re-formed, straddled and split, narrowed, widened, rippled in ribbons, broke into a thousand white-hot parallel lines, melted and revolved in interwoven rings like old-fashioned engine-turning, flung up to the zenith, made as if to descend and renew the torment, halted at the last instant, twizzled insanely round the horizon, and vanished, to bring back for the hundredth time darkness more shattering than their instantly renewed light over all Illinois. Then the tune and lights ceased together, and we heard one single devastating wail that shook all the horizon as a rubbed wet finger shakes the rim of a bowl.

"Ah, that is my new siren," said Pirolo. "You can break an iceberg in half, if you find the proper pitch. They will whistle by squadrons now. It is the wind through pierced shutters in the bows."

I had collapsed beside Dragomiroff, broken and snivelling feebly, because I had been delivered before my time to all the terrors of Judgment Day, and the Archangels of the Resurrection were hailing me naked across the Universe to the sound of the music of the spheres.

Then I saw De Forest smacking Arnott's helmet with his open hand. The wailing died down in a long shriek as a black shadow swooped past us, and returned to her place above the lower clouds.

"I hate to interrupt a specialist when he's enjoying himself," said De Forest. "But, as a matter of fact, all Illinois has been asking us to stop for these last fifteen seconds."

"What a pity." Arnott slipped off his mask. "I wanted you to hear us really hum. Our lower C can lift street-paving."

"It is Hell - Hell!" cried Dragomiroff, and sobbed aloud.

Arnott looked away as he answered: "It's a few thousand volts ahead of the old shoot-'em-and-sink-'em game, but I should scarcely call it that. What shall I tell the Fleet, sir?"

Tell 'em we're very pleased and impressed. I don't think they need wait on any longer. There isn't a spark left down there." De Forest pointed. "They'll be deaf and blind."

"Oh, I think not, sir. The demonstration lasted less than ten minutes."

"Marvellous!" Takahira sighed. "I should have said it was half a night. Now, shall we go down and pick up the pieces?"

"But first a small drink," said Pirolo. "The Board must not arrive weeping at its own works."

"I am an old fool - an old fool!" Dragomiroff began piteously. "I did not know what would happen. It is all new to me. We reason with them in Little Russia."

Chicago North landing-tower was unlighted, and Arnott worked his ship into the clips by her own lights. As soon as these broke out we heard groanings of horror and appeal from many people below.

"All right," shouted Arnott into the darkness. "We aren't beginning again!" We descended by the stairs, to find ourselves knee deep in a grovelling crowd, some crying that they were blind, others beseeching us not to make any more noises, but the greater part writhing face downward, their hands or their caps before their eyes.

It was Pirolo who came to our rescue. He climbed the side of a surfacing-machine, and there, gesticulating as though they could see, made oration to those afflicted people of Illinois.

"You stchewpids!" he began. "There is nothing to fuss for. Of course, your eyes will smart and be red to-morrow. You will look as if you and your wives had drunk too much, but in a little while you will see again as well as before. I tell you this, and I - I am Pirolo. Victor Pirolo!"

The crowd with one accord shuddered, for many legends attach to Victor Pirolo of Foggia, deep in the secrets of God.

"Pirolo?" An unsteady voice lifted itself. "Then tell us was there anything except light in those lights of yours just now?"

The question was repeated from every corner of the darkness.

Pirolo laughed.

"No!" he thundered. (Why have small men such large voices?) "I give you my word and the Board's word that there was nothing except light - just light! You stchewpids! Your birth-rate is too low already as it is. Some day I must invent something to send it up, but send it down - never!"

"Is that true? - We thought - somebody said -'

One could feel the tension relax all round.

"You too big fools," Pirolo cried. "You could have sent us a call and we would have told you."

"Send you a call!" a deep voice shouted. "I wish you had been at our end of the wire."

"I'm glad I wasn't," said De Forest. "It was bad enough from behind the lamps. Never mind! It's over now. Is there any one here I can talk business with? I'm De Forest - for the Board."

"You might begin with me, for one - I'm Mayor," the bass voice replied.

A BIG man rose unsteadily from the street, and staggered towards us where we sat on the broad turf-edging, in front of the garden fences.

"I ought to be the first on my feet. Am I?" said he.

"Yes," said De Forest, and steadied him as he dropped down beside us.

"Hello, Andy. Is that you?" a voice called.

"Excuse me," said the Mayor; "that sounds like my Chief of Police, Bluthner!"

"Bluthner it is; and here's Mulligan and Keefe – on their feet."

"Bring 'em up please, Blut. We're supposed to be the Four in charge of this hamlet. What we says, goes. And, De Forest, what do you say?"

"Nothing – yet," De Forest answered, as we made room for the panting, reeling men. "You've cut out of system. Well?"

"Tell the steward to send down drinks, please," Arnott whispered to an orderly at his side.

"Good!" said the Mayor, smacking his dry lips. "Now I suppose we can take it, De Forest, that henceforward the Board will administer us direct?"

"Not if the Board can avoid it," De Forest laughed. "The A.B.C. is responsible for the planetary traffic only."

"And all that that implies." The big Four who ran Chicago chanted their Magna Charta like children at school.

"Well, get on," said De Forest wearily. "What is your silly trouble anyway?"

"Too much dam' Democracy," said the Mayor, laying his hand on De Forest's knee.

"So? I thought Illinois had had her dose of that."

"She has. That's why. Blut, what did you do with our prisoners last night?"

"Locked 'em in the water-tower to prevent the women killing 'em," the Chief of Police replied. "I'm too blind to move just yet, but –"

"Arnott, send some of your people, please, and fetch 'em along," said De Forest.

"They're triple-circuited," the Mayor called. "You'll have to blow out three fuses." He turned to De Forest, his large outline just visible in the paling darkness. "I hate to throw any more work on the Board. I'm an administrator myself, but we've had a little fuss with our Serviles. What? In a big city there's bound to be a few men and women who can't live without listening to themselves, and who prefer drinking out of pipes they don't own both ends of. They inhabit flats and hotels all the year round. They say it saves 'em trouble. Anyway, it gives 'em more time to make trouble for their neighbours. We call 'em Serviles locally. And they are apt to be tuberculous."

"Just so!" said the man called Mulligan. "Transportation is Civilisation. Democracy is Disease. I've proved it by the blood-test, every time."

"Mulligan's our Health Officer, and a one-idea man," said the Mayor, laughing. "But it's true that most Serviles haven't much control. They will talk; and when people take to talking as a business, anything may arrive - mayn't it, De Forest?"

"Anything - except the facts of the case," said De Forest, laughing.

"I'll give you those in a minute," said the Mayor. "Our Serviles got to talking - first in their houses and then on the streets, telling men and women how to manage their own affairs. (You can't teach a Servile not to finger his neighbour's soul.) That's invasion of privacy, of course, but in Chicago we'll suffer anything sooner than make crowds. Nobody took much notice, and so I let 'em alone. My fault! I was warned there would be trouble, but there hasn't been a crowd or murder in Illinois for nineteen years."

"Twenty-two," said his Chief of Police.

"Likely. Anyway, we'd forgot such things. So, from talking in the houses and on the streets, our Serviles go to calling a meeting at the Old Market yonder." He nodded across the square where the wrecked buildings heaved up grey in the dawn-glimmer behind the square-cased statue of The Negro in Flames. "There's nothing to prevent anyone calling meetings except that it's against human nature to stand in a crowd, besides being bad for the health. I ought to have known by the way our men and women attended that first meeting that trouble was brewing. There were as many as a thousand in the market-place, touching each other. Touching! Then the Serviles turned in all tongue-switches and talked, and we -"

"What did they talk about?" said Takahira.

"First, how badly things were managed in the city. That pleased us Four - we were on the platform - because we hoped to catch one or two good men for City work. You know how rare executive capacity is. Even if we didn't it's - it's refreshing to find any one interested enough in our job to damn our eyes. You don't know what it means to work, year in, year out, without a spark of difference with a living soul."

"Oh, don't we!" said De Forest. "There are times on the Board when we'd give our positions if any one would kick us out and take hold of things themselves."

"But they won't," said the Mayor ruefully. "I assure you, sir, we Four have done things in Chicago, in the hope of rousing people, that would have discredited Nero. But what do they say? "Very good, Andy. Have it your own way. Anything's better than a crowd. I'll go back to my land." You can't do anything with folk who can go where they please, and don't want anything on God's earth except their own way. There isn't a kick or a kicker left on the Planet."

"Then I suppose that little shed yonder fell down by itself?" said De Forest. We could see the bare and still smoking ruins, and hear the slag-pools crackle as they hardened and set.

"Oh, that's only amusement. "Tell you later. As I was saying, our Serviles held the meeting, and pretty soon we had to ground-circuit the platform to save 'em from being killed. And that didn't make our people any more pacific."

How d'you mean?" I ventured to ask.

"If you've ever been ground-circuited," said the Mayor, "you'll know it don't improve any man's temper to be held up straining against nothing. No, sir! Eight or nine hundred folk kept pawing and buzzing like flies in treacle for two hours, while a pack of perfectly safe Serviles invades their mental and spiritual privacy, may be amusing to watch, but they are not pleasant to handle afterwards."

Pirolo chuckled.

"Our folk own themselves. They were of opinion things were going too far and too fiery. I warned the Serviles; but they're born house-dwellers. Unless a fact hits 'em on the head, they cannot see it. Would you believe me, they went on to talk of what they called 'popular government'? They did! They wanted us to go back to the old Voodoo-business of voting with papers and wooden boxes, and word-drunk people and printed formulas, and news-sheets! They said they practised it among themselves about what they'd have to eat in their flats and hotels."

"Yes, sir! They stood up behind Bluthner's doubled ground-circuits, and they said that, in this present year of grace, to self-owning men and women, on that very spot! Then they finished" - he lowered his voice cautiously - "by talking about 'The People.' And then Bluthner he had to sit up all night in charge of the circuits because he couldn't trust his men to keep 'em shut."

"It was trying 'em too high," the Chief of Police broke in. "But we couldn't hold the crowd ground-circuited for ever. I gathered in all the Serviles on charge of crowd-making, and put 'em in the water-tower, and then I let things cut loose. I had to! The District lit like a sparked gas-tank!"

"The news was out over seven degrees of country," the Mayor continued; "and when once it's a question of invasion of privacy, good-bye to right and reason in Illinois! They began turning out traffic-lights and locking up landing-towers on Thursday night. Friday, they stopped all traffic and asked for the Board to take over. Then they wanted to clean Chicago off the side of the Lake and rebuild elsewhere - just for a souvenir of 'The People' that the Serviles talked about. I suggested that they should slag the Old Market where the meeting was held, while I turned in a call to you all on the Board. That kept 'em quiet till you came along. And - and now you can take hold of the situation."

"Any chance of their quieting down?" De Forest asked.

"You can try," said the Mayor.

De Forest raised his voice in the face of the reviving crowd that had edged in towards us. Day was come.

"Don't you think this business can be arranged?" he began. But there was a roar of angry voices:

"We've finished with Crowds! We aren't going back to the Old Days! Take us over! Take the Serviles away! Administer direct or we'll kill 'em! Down with The People!"

An attempt was made to begin MacDonough's Song. It got no further than the first line, for the Victor Pirolo sent down a warning drone on one stopped horn. A wrecked side-wall of the Old Market tottered and fell inwards on the slag-pools. None spoke or moved till the last of the dust had settled down again, turning the steel case of Salati's Statue ashy grey.

"You see you'll just have to take us over," the Mayor whispered.

De Forest shrugged his shoulders.

"You talk as if executive capacity could be snatched out of the air like so much horse-power. Can't you manage yourselves on any terms?" he said.

"We can, if you say so. It will only cost those few lives to begin with."

The Mayor pointed across the square, where Arnott's men guided a stumbling group of ten or twelve men and women to the lake front and halted them under the Statue.

"Now I think," said Takahira under his breath, "there will be trouble."

The mass in front of us growled like beasts.

At that moment the sun rose clear, and revealed the blinking assembly to itself. As soon as it realised that it was a crowd we saw the shiver of horror and mutual repulsion shoot across it precisely as the steely flaws shot across the lake outside. Nothing was said, and, being half blind, of course it moved slowly. Yet in less than fifteen minutes most of that vast multitude - three thousand at the lowest count - melted away like frost on south eaves. The remnant stretched themselves on the grass, where a crowd feels and looks less like a crowd.

"These mean business," the Mayor whispered to Takahira. "There are a goodish few women there who've borne children. I don't like it."

The morning draught off the lake stirred the trees round us with promise of a hot day; the sun reflected itself dazzlingly on the canister-shaped covering of Salati's Statue; cocks crew in the gardens, and we could hear gate-latches clicking in the distance as people stumblingly resought their homes.

"I'm afraid there won't be any morning deliveries," said De Forest. "We rather upset things in the country last night."

"That makes no odds," the Mayor returned. "We're all provisioned for six months. We take no chances."

Nor, when you come to think of it, does anyone else. It must be three-quarters of a generation since any house or city faced a food shortage. Yet is there house or city on the Planet today that has not half a year's provisions laid in? We are like the shipwrecked seamen in the old books, who, having once nearly starved to death, ever afterwards hide away bits of food and biscuit. Truly we trust no Crowds, nor system based on Crowds!

De Forest waited till the last footstep had died away. Meantime the prisoners at the base of the Statue shuffled, posed and fidgeted, with the shamelessness of quite little children. None of them were more than six feet high, and many of them were as grey-haired as the ravaged, harassed heads of old pictures. They huddled together in actual touch, while the crowd, spaced at large intervals, looked at them with congested eyes.

Suddenly a man among them began to talk. The Mayor had not in the least exaggerated. It appeared that our Planet lay sunk in slavery beneath the heel of the Aerial Board of Control. The orator urged us to arise in our might, burst our prison doors and break our fetters (all his metaphors, by the way, were of the most medieval). Next he demanded that every matter of daily life, including most of the physical functions, should be submitted for decision at any time of the week, month, or year to, I gathered, anybody who happened to be passing by or residing within a certain radius, and that everybody should forthwith abandon his concerns to settle the matter, first by crowd-making, next by talking to the crowds made, and lastly by describing crosses on pieces of paper, which rubbish should later be counted with certain mystic ceremonies and oaths. Out of this amazing play, he assured us, would automatically arise a higher, nobler, and kinder world, based – he demonstrated this with the awful lucidity of the insane – based on the sanctity of the Crowd and the villainy of the single person. In conclusion, he called loudly upon God to testify to his personal merits and integrity. When the flow ceased, I turned bewildered to Takahira, who was nodding solemnly.

"Quite correct," said he. "It is all in the old books. He has left nothing out, not even the war-talk."

"But I don't see how this stuff can upset a child, much less a district," I replied.

"Ah, you are too young," said Dragomiroff. "For another thing, you are not a mamma. Please look at the mammas."

Ten or fifteen women who remained had separated themselves from the silent men, and were drawing in towards the prisoners. It reminded one of the stealthy encircling, before the rush in at the quarry, of wolves round musk oxen in the North. The prisoners saw, and drew together more closely. The Mayor covered his face with his hands for an instant. De Forest, bareheaded, stepped forward between the prisoners and the slowly, stiffly moving line.

"That's all very interesting," he said to the dry-lipped orator. "But the point seems that you've been making crowds and invading privacy."

A woman stepped forward, and would have spoken, but there was a quick assenting murmur from the men, who realised that De Forest was trying to pull the situation down to ground-line.

"Yes! Yes!" they cried. "We cut out because they made crowds and invaded privacy! Stick to that! Keep on that switch! Lift the Serviles out of this! The Board's in charge! Hsh!"

"Yes, the Board's in charge," said De Forest.

"I'll take formal evidence of crowd-making if you like, but the Members of the Board can testify to it. Will that do?"

The women had closed in another pace, with hands that clenched and unclenched at their sides.

"Good! Good enough!" the men cried. "We're content. Only take them away quickly."

"Come along up!" said De Forest to the captives. "Breakfast is quite ready."

It appeared, however, that they did not wish to go. They intended to remain in Chicago and make crowds. They pointed out that De Forest's proposal was gross invasion of privacy.

"My dear fellow," said Pirolo to the most voluble of the leaders, "you hurry, or your crowd that can't be wrong will kill you!"

"But that would be murder," answered the believer in crowds; and there was a roar of laughter from all sides that seemed to show the crisis had broken.

A woman stepped forward from the line of women, laughing, I protest, as merrily as any of the company. One hand, of course, shaded her eyes, the other was at her throat.

"Oh, they needn't be afraid of being killed!" she called.

"Not in the least," said De Forest. But don't you think that, now the Board's in charge, you might go home while we get these people away?"

"I shall be home long before that. It - it has been rather a trying day."

She stood up to her full height, dwarfing even De Forest's six-foot-eight, and smiled, with eyes closed against the fierce light.

"Yes, rather," said De Forest. I'm afraid you feel the glare a little. We'll have the ship down."

He motioned to the Pirolo to drop between us and the sun, and at the same time to loop-circuit the prisoners, who were a trifle unsteady. We saw them stiffen to the current where they stood. The woman's voice went on, sweet and deep and unshaken:

"I don't suppose you men realise how much this - this sort of thing means to a woman. I've borne three. We women don't want our children given to Crowds. It must be an inherited instinct. Crowds make trouble. They bring back the Old Days. Hate, fear, blackmail, publicity, 'The People' - That! That! That!" She pointed to the Statue, and the crowd growled once more.

"Yes, if they are allowed to go on," said De Forest. "But this little affair–"

"It means so much to us women that this – this little affair should never happen again. Of course, never's a big word, but one feels so strongly that it is important to stop crowds at the very beginning. Those creatures' – she pointed with her left hand at the prisoners swaying like seaweed in a tide way as the circuit pulled them – "those people have friends and wives and children in the city and elsewhere. One doesn't want anything done to them, you know. It's terrible to force a human being out of fifty or sixty years of good life. I'm only forty myself. I know. But, at the same time, one feels that an example should be made, because no price is too heavy to pay if – if these people and all that they imply can be put an end to. Do you quite understand or would you be kind enough to tell your men to take the casing off the Statue? It's worth looking at."

"I understand perfectly. But I don't think anybody here wants to see the Statue on an empty stomach. Excuse me one moment." De Forest called up to the ship, "A flying loop ready on the port side, if you please." Then to the woman he said with some crispness, "You might leave us a little discretion in the matter."

"Oh, of course. Thank you for being so patient. I know my arguments are silly, but–" She half turned away and went on in a changed voice, "Perhaps this will help you to decide."

She threw out her right arm with a knife in it. Before the blade could be returned to her throat or her bosom it was twitched from her grip, sparked as it flew out of the shadow of the ship above, and fell flashing in the sunshine at the foot of the Statue fifty yards away. The outflung arm was arrested, rigid as a bar for an instant, till the releasing circuit permitted her to bring it slowly to her side. The other women shrank back silent among the men.

Pirolo rubbed his hands, and Takahira nodded.

"That was clever of you, De Forest," said he.

"What a glorious pose!" Dragomiroff murmured, for the frightened woman was on the edge of tears.

"Why did you stop me? I would have done it!" she cried.

"I have no doubt you would," said De Forest. "But we can't waste a life like yours on these people. I hope the arrest didn't sprain your wrist; it's so hard to regulate a flying loop. But I think you are quite right about those persons' women and children. We'll take them all away with us if you promise not to do anything stupid to yourself."

"I promise – I promise." She controlled herself with an effort. "But it is so important to us women. We know what it means; and I thought if you saw I was in earnest–"

"I saw you were, and you've gained your point. I shall take all your Serviles away with me at once. The Mayor will make lists of their friends and families in the city and the district, and he'll ship them after us this afternoon."

"Sure," said the Mayor, rising to his feet. "Keefe, if you can see, hadn't you better finish levelling off the Old Market? It don't look sightly the way it is now, and we shan't use it for crowds any more."

"I think you had better wipe out that Statue as well, Mr. Mayor," said De Forest. "I don't question its merits as a work of art, but I believe it's a shade morbid."

"Certainly, sir. Oh, Keefe! Slag the Nigger before you go on to fuse the Market. I'll get to the Communicators and tell the District that the Board is in charge. Are you making any special appointments, sir?"

"None. We haven't men to waste on these backwoods. Carry on as before, but under the Board. Arnott, run your Serviles aboard, please. Ground ship and pass them through the bilge-doors. We'll wait till we've finished with this work of art."

The prisoners trailed past him, talking fluently, but unable to gesticulate in the drag of the current. Then the surfacers rolled up, two on each side of the Statue. With one accord the spectators looked elsewhere, but there was no need. Keefe turned on full power, and the thing simply melted within its case. All I saw was a surge of white-hot metal pouring over the plinth, a glimpse of Salati's inscription, "To the Eternal Memory of the Justice of the People," ere the stone base itself cracked and powdered into finest lime. The crowd cheered.

"Thank you," said De Forest; "but we want our breakfasts, and I expect you do too. Good-bye, Mr. Mayor! Delighted to see you at any time, but I hope I shan't have to, officially, for the next thirty years. Good-bye, madam. Yes. We're all given to nerves nowadays. I suffer from them myself. Good-bye, gentlemen all! You're under the tyrannous heel of the Board from this moment, but if ever you feel like breaking your fetters you've only to let us know. This is no treat to us. Good luck!"

We embarked amid shouts, and did not check our lift till they had dwindled into whispers. Then De Forest flung himself on the chart room divan and mopped his forehead.

"I don't mind men," he panted, "but women are the devil!"

"Still the devil," said Pirolo cheerfully. "That one would have suicided."

"I know it. That was why I signalled for the flying loop to be clapped on her. I owe you an apology for that, Arnott. I hadn't time to catch your eye, and you were busy with our caitiffs. By the way, who actually answered my signal? It was a smart piece of work."

"Ilroy," said Arnott; "but he overloaded the wave. It may be pretty gallery-work to knock a knife out of a lady's hand, but didn't you notice how she rubbed 'em? He scorched her fingers. Slovenly, I call it."

"Far be it from me to interfere with Fleet discipline, but don't be too hard on the boy. If that woman had killed herself they would have killed every Servile and everything related to a Servile throughout the district by nightfall."

"That was what she was playing for," Takahira said. "And with our Fleet gone we could have done nothing to hold them."

"I may be ass enough to walk into a ground-circuit," said Arnott, "but I don't dismiss my Fleet till I'm reasonably sure that trouble is over. They're in position still, and I intend to keep 'em there till the Serviles are shipped out of the district. That last little crowd meant murder, my friends."

"Nerves! All nerves!" said Pirolo. "You cannot argue with agoraphobia."

"And it is not as if they had seen much dead - or is it?" said Takahira.

"In all my ninety years I have never seen death." Dragomiroff spoke as one who would excuse himself. "Perhaps that was why - last night -"

Then it came out as we sat over breakfast, that, with the exception of Arnott and Pirolo, none of us had ever seen a corpse, or knew in what manner the spirit passes.

"We're a nice lot to flap about governing the Planet," De Forest laughed. "I confess, now it's all over, that my main fear was I mightn't be able to pull it off without losing a life."

"I thought of that too," said Arnott; "but there's no death reported, and I've inquired everywhere. What are we supposed to do with our passengers? I've fed 'em."

"We're between two switches," De Forest drawled. "If we drop them in any place that isn't under the Board, the natives will make their presence an excuse for cutting out, same as Illinois did, and forcing the Board to take over. If we drop them in any place under the Board's control they'll be killed as soon as our backs are turned."

"If you say so," said Pirolo thoughtfully, "I can guarantee that they will become extinct in process of time, quite happily. What is their birth-rate now?"

"Go down and ask 'em," said De Forest.

"I think they might become nervous and tear me to bits," the philosopher of Foggia replied.

"Not really? Well?"

"Open the bilge-doors," said Takahira with a downward jerk of the thumb.

"Scarcely - after all the trouble we've taken to save 'em," said De Forest.

"Try London," Arnott suggested. "You could turn Satan himself loose there, and they'd only ask him to dinner."

"Good man! You've given me an idea. Vincent! Oh, Vincent!" He threw the General Communicator open so that we could all hear, and in a few minutes the chartroom filled with the rich, fruity voice of Leopold Vincent, who has purveyed all London her choicest amusements for the last thirty years. We answered with expectant grins, as though we were actually in the stalls of, say, the Combination on a first night.

"We've picked up something in your line," De Forest began.

"That's good, dear man. If it's old enough. There's nothing to beat the old things for business purposes. Have you seen London, Chatham, and Dover at Earl's Court? No? I thought I missed you there. Im-mense! I've had the real steam locomotive engines built from the old designs and the iron rails cast specially by hand. Cloth cushions in the carriages, too! Im-mense! And paper railway tickets. And Polly Milton."

"Polly Milton back again!" said Arnott rapturously. "Book me two stalls for to-morrow night. What's she singing now, bless her?"

"The old songs. Nothing comes up to the old touch. Listen to this, dear men." Vincent carolled with flourishes:

Oh, cruel lamps of London,
If tears your light could drown,
Your victims' eyes would weep them,
Oh, lights of London Town!

"Then they weep."

"You see?" Pirolo waved his hands at us. "The old world always weeped when it saw crowds together. It did not know why, but it weeped. We know why, but we do not weep, except when we pay to be made to by fat, wicked old Vincent."

"Old, yourself!" Vincent laughed. "I'm a public benefactor, I keep the world soft and united."

"And I'm De Forest of the Board," said De Forest acidly, "trying to get a little business done. As I was saying, I've picked up a few people in Chicago."

"I cut out. Chicago is –'

"Do listen! They're perfectly unique."

"Do they build houses of baked mud blocks while you wait – eh? That's an old contact."

"They're an untouched primitive community, with all the old ideas."

"Sewing-machines and maypole-dances? Cooking on coal-gas stoves, lighting pipes with matches, and driving horses? Gerolstein tried that last year. An absolute blow-out!"

De Forest plugged him wrathfully, and poured out the story of our doings for the last twenty-four hours on the top-note.

"And they do it all in public," he concluded. "You can't stop 'em. The more public, the better they are pleased. They'll talk for hours - like you! Now you can come in again!"

"Do you really mean they know how to vote?" said Vincent. "Can they act it?"

"Act? It's their life to 'em! And you never saw such faces! Scarred like volcanoes. Envy, hatred, and malice in plain sight. Wonderfully flexible voices. They weep, too."

"Aloud? In public?"

"I guarantee. Not a spark of shame or reticence in the entire installation. It's the chance of your career."

"D'you say you've brought their voting props along - those papers and ballot-box things?"

"No, confound you! I'm not a luggage-lifter. Apply direct to the Mayor of Chicago. He'll forward you everything. Well?"

"Wait a minute. Did Chicago want to kill 'em? That 'ud look well on the Communicators."

"Yes! They were only rescued with difficulty from a howling mob - if you know what that is."

"But I don't," answered the Great Vincent simply.

"Well then, they'll tell you themselves. They can make speeches hours long."

"How many are there?"

"By the time we ship 'em all over they'll be perhaps a hundred, counting children. An old world in miniature. Can't you see it?"

"M-yes; but I've got to pay for it if it's a blow-out, dear man."

"They can sing the old war songs in the streets. They can get word-drunk, and make crowds, and invade privacy in the genuine old-fashioned way; and they'll do the voting trick as often as you ask 'em a question."

"Too good!" said Vincent.

"You unbelieving Jew! I've got a dozen head aboard here. I'll put you through direct. Sample 'em yourself."

He lifted the switch and we listened. Our passengers on the lower deck at once, but not less than five at a time, explained themselves to Vincent. They had been taken from the bosom of their families, stripped of their possessions, given food without finger-bowls, and cast into captivity in a noisome dungeon.

"But look here," said Arnott aghast; "they're saying what isn't true. My lower deck isn't noisome, and I saw to the finger-bowls myself."

My people talk like that sometimes in Little Russia," said Dragomiroff. "We reason with them. We never kill. No!"

"But it's not true," Arnott insisted. "What can you do with people who don't tell facts? They're mad!"

"Hsh!" said Pirolo, his hand to his ear. "It is such a little time since all the Planet told lies."

We heard Vincent silkily sympathetic. Would they, he asked, repeat their assertions in public - before a vast public? Only let Vincent give them a chance, and the Planet, they vowed, should ring with their wrongs. Their aim in life - two women and a man explained it together - was to reform the world. Oddly enough, this also had been Vincent's life-dream. He offered them an arena in which to explain, and by their living example to raise the Planet to loftier levels. He was eloquent on the moral uplift of a simple, old-world life presented in its entirety to a deboshed civilisation.

Could they - would they - for three months certain, devote themselves under his auspices, as missionaries, to the elevation of mankind at a place called Earl's Court, which he said, with some truth, was one of the intellectual centres of the Planet? They thanked him, and demanded (we could hear his chuckle of delight) time to discuss and to vote on the matter. The vote, solemnly managed by counting heads - one head, one vote - was favourable. His offer, therefore, was accepted, and they moved a vote of thanks to him in two speeches - one by what they called the "proposer" and the other by the "seconder."

Vincent threw over to us, his voice shaking with gratitude:

"I've got 'em! Did you hear those speeches? That's Nature, dear men. Art can't teach that. And they voted as easily as lying. I've never had a troupe of natural liars before. Bless you, dear men! Remember, you're on my free lists for ever, anywhere - all of you. Oh, Gerolstein will be sick - sick!"

"Then you think they'll do?" said De Forest.

"Do? The Little Village'll go crazy! I'll knock up a series of old-world plays for 'em. Their voices will make you laugh and cry. My God, dear men, where do you suppose they picked up all their misery from, on this sweet earth? I'll have a pageant of the world's beginnings, and Mosenthal shall do the music. I'll -"

"Go and knock up a village for 'em by to-night. We'll meet you at No. 15 West Landing Tower," said De Forest. "Remember the rest will be coming along to-morrow."

"Let 'em all come!" said Vincent. "You don't know how hard it is nowadays even for me, to find something that really gets under the public's damned iridium-plated hide. But I've got it at last. Good-bye!"

"Well," said De Forest when we had finished laughing, "if any one understood corruption in London I might have played off Vincent against Gerolstein, and sold my captives at enormous prices. As it is, I shall have to be their legal adviser to-night when the contracts are signed. And they won't exactly press any commission on me, either."

"Meantime," said Takahira, "we cannot, of course, confine members of Leopold Vincent's last-engaged company. Chairs for the ladies, please, Arnott."

"Then I go to bed," said De Forest. "I can't face any more women!" And he vanished.

When our passengers were released and given another meal (finger-bowls came first this time) they told us what they thought of us and the Board; and, like Vincent, we all marvelled how they had contrived to extract and secrete so much bitter poison and unrest out of the good life God gives us. They raged, they stormed, they palpitated, flushed and exhausted their poor, torn nerves, panted themselves into silence, and renewed the senseless, shameless attacks.

"But can't you understand," said Pirolo pathetically to a shrieking woman, "that if we'd left you in Chicago you'd have been killed?"

"No, we shouldn't. You were bound to save us from being murdered."

"Then we should have had to kill a lot of other people."

"That doesn't matter. We were preaching the Truth. You can't stop us. We shall go on preaching in London; and then you'll see!"

"You can see now," said Pirolo, and opened a lower shutter.

We were closing on the Little Village, with her three million people spread out at ease inside her ring of girdling Main-Traffic lights - those eight fixed beams at Chatham, Tonbridge, Redhill, Dorking, Woking, St. Albans, Chipping Ongar, and Southend.

Leopold Vincent's new company looked, with small pale faces, at the silence, the size, and the separated houses.

Then some began to weep aloud, shamelessly - always without shame.

THE END

ANNO DOMINI 2000, OR WOMAN'S DESTINY BY SIR JULIUS VOGEL (NEW ZEALAND, 1889)

PROLOGUE
A.D. 1920

George Claude Sonsius in his early youth appeared to have before him a fair, prosperous future. His father and mother were of good family, but neither of them inherited wealth. When young Sonsius finished his university career, the small fortune which his father possessed was swept away by the failure of a large banking company. All that remained from the wreck was a trifling annuity payable during the lives of his father and mother, and this they did not live long to enjoy. They died within a year of each other, but they had been able to obtain for their son a fairly good position in a large mercantile house as foreign correspondent. At twenty-five the young man married; and three years afterwards he unfortunately met with a serious accident, that made him for two years a helpless invalid and at the end of the time left him with his right hand incapable of use. Meanwhile his appointment had lapsed, his wife's small fortune had disappeared, and during several years his existence had been one continual struggle with ever-increasing want and penury. The end was approaching. The father and mother and their one crippled son, twelve years old, dwelt in the miserable attic of a most dilapidated house in one of the poorest neighbourhoods of London. The roof over their heads did not even protect them from the weather. The room was denuded of every article of furniture with the exception of two worthless wooden cases and a horsehair mattress on which the unhappy boy stretched his pain-wrung limbs.

Early in life this child suffered only from weakness of the spine, but his parents could afford no prolonged remedial measures. Not that they were unkind to him. On the contrary, they devoted to him every minute they could spare, and lavished on him all the attention that affection comparatively powerless from want of means could dictate. But the food they were able to give him was scant instead of, as his condition demanded, varied and nutritious. At length chronic disease of the spine set in, and his life became one long misery.

Parochial aid was refused unless they would go into the poor-house, but the one thing Mrs. Sonsius could not bring herself to endure was the separation from her son which was demanded of her as a condition of relief.

For thirty hours they had been without food, when the father, maddened by the moanings of his wife and child, rushed into the street, and passing a baker's shop which appeared to be empty, stole from it a loaf of bread. The proprietor, however, saw the action from an inner room. He caught Sonsius just as he was leaving the shop. He did not care to give the thief in charge, necessitating as it would several attendances at the police court. He took the administration of justice into his own hands, and dealt the unhappy man two severe blows in the face. To a healthy person the punishment would have done comparatively little harm, but Sonsius was weakened by disease and starvation, and the shock of the blows was too much for him. He fell prone on the pavement, and all attempts to restore him to consciousness proved unavailing.

Then his history became public property. Scores of people remembered the pleasant-mannered, well-looking young man who had distinguished himself at college, and for whom life seemed to promise a pleasant journey. The horrible condition of his wife and child, the desperation that drove him to the one lapse from an otherwise stainless life, the frightful contrast between the hidden poverty and the gorgeous wealth of the great metropolis, became themes upon which every newspaper dilated after its own fashion. Some papers even went so far as to ask, "Was it a crime for a man to steal a loaf of bread to save his wife and child from starvation?"

In grim contrast with the terrible conclusion of his wretched career, the publicity cast upon it elicited the fact that a few weeks earlier he had inherited by the death of a distant relative an enormous fortune, all efforts to trace him through the changes of residence that increasing poverty had necessitated having proved unavailing. Now that the wretched father and husband was dead, the wife for whom the bread was stolen had become a great lady, the boy was at length to receive the aid that wealth could give him. Poor George Claude Sonsius has nothing to do with our story, but his fate led to the alleviation of a great deal of misery that otherwise might have been in store for millions of human beings.

Loud and clear rang out the cry, "What was the use of denouncing slavery when want like this was allowed to pass unheeded by the side of superfluous wealth?" The slave-owner has sufficient interest in his slaves, it was alleged, as a rule, to care for their well-being. Even criminals were clothed and fed.

Had not, it was asked, every human being the right to demand from a world which through the resources of experience and science became constantly more productive a sufficiency of sustenance?

The inquest room was crowded. The coroner and jury were strongly affected as they viewed the body laid out in a luxuriously appointed coffin. Wealth denied to the living was lavished on the dead. No longer in rags and tatters, the lifeless body seemed to revert to the past. Shrunken as was the frame, and emaciated the features, there remained evidence sufficient to show that the now inanimate form was once a fine and handsome man.

The evidence was short, and the summing up of the coroner decisive. He insisted that the baker had not wilfully committed wrong and should not be made responsible for the consequences that followed his rough recovery of his property. A butcher and a general provision dealer on the jury took strongly the same view. How were poor tradesmen to protect themselves? They must take the law in their own hands, they argued, otherwise it would be better to submit to being robbed rather than waste their time in police courts. They wanted a verdict of justifiable homicide. Another juryman (a small builder) urged a verdict of misadventure; at first he called it peradventure. But the rest of the jury felt otherwise. Some desired a verdict of manslaughter, and it was long before the compromise of "Death by accident" was agreed to.

Deep groans filled the room as the result was announced. That same night a large crowd of men and women assembled outside the baker's shop with hostile demonstrations. The windows were destroyed, and an attempt made to break in the door. A serious riot would probably have ensued but for the arrival of a large body of police.

Again the fate of George Sonsius became the familiar topic of the press. But the impression was not an ephemeral one.

The fierce spirit of discontent which for years had been smouldering burst into flames. A secret society called the "Live and Let Live" was formed, with ramifications throughout the world. The force of numbers, the force of brute strength, was appealed to.

A bold and outspoken declaration was made that every human being had an inherent right to sufficient food and clothing and comfortable lodging. Truly poor George Sonsius died for the good of many millions of his fellow-creatures. Our history will show the point at length achieved.

Shortly after poor Sonsius' death a remarkable meeting was held in the city of London. The representatives of six of the largest financial houses throughout the globe assembled by agreement to discuss the present material condition of the world and its future prospects. There was Lord de Cardrosse, head of the English house of that name and chief, moreover, of the family, whose branches presided over princely houses of finance in six of the chief cities of the continent of Europe. Second only in power in Great Britain, the house of Bisdat and Co. was represented by Charles James Bisdat, a man of scarcely forty, but held to be the greatest living authority on abstruse financial questions. The Dutch house of Von Serge Brothers was represented by its head, Cornelius Julius Von Serge. The greatest finance house in America, Rorgon, Bryce and Co., appeared by its chief, Henry Tudor Rorgon; and the scarcely less powerful house of Lockay, Stanfield and Co., of San Francisco, Melbourne, Sydney, and Wellington, was represented by its chief, Alfred Demetrius. The German and African house of Werther, Scribe and Co. was present in the person of its head, Baron Scribe; and the French and Continental houses of the De Cardrosse family were represented by the future head of the family, the Baroness de Cardrosse. The deliberations were carried on in French.

Two or more of these houses had no doubt from time to time worked together in one transaction; but their uniform position was one of independence towards each other, verging more towards antagonism than to union. In fact, the junction for ordinary purposes of such vast powers as these kings of finance wielded would be fatal to liberty and freedom.

A single instance will suffice to show the power referred to, which even one group of financiers could wield.

Five years previously all Europe was in a ferment. War was expected from every quarter. It depended not on one, but on many questions. The alliances were doubtful. Nothing seemed certain but that neutrality would be impossible, and that the Continent would be divided into two or more great camps. The final decision appeared to rest with Great Britain. There an ominous disposition for war was displaying itself. The inclination of the Sovereign and the Cabinet was supposed to be in that direction. But the family of De Cardrosses throughout Europe was for peace. The chief of the family was the head of the English house, and it was decided he should interview the Prime Minister of England and acquaint him with the views of this great financial group. His reception was not flattering; but if he felt mortified, he did not show it. He expressed himself deeply sensible of the honour done to him by his being allowed to state his opinions; and with a reverential inclination he bowed himself from the presence of the greatest statesman of his day, the Right Honourable Randolph Stanley. That afternoon it was bruited about that, in view of coming possibilities, the De Cardrosse family had determined to realise securities all over Europe and send gold to America. The next morning a disposition to sell was reported from every direction, and five millions sterling of gold were collected for despatch to New York. In twenty-four hours there was a panic throughout Great

Britain and Europe. The Bank of England asked for permission to suspend specie payments, but could indicate no limit to which such a permission should be set. It seemed as if Europe would be drained of gold.

The great rivals of the De Cardrosses looked on and either could not or would not interfere. A hurried Cabinet meeting was convened, and as a result a conference by telephone was arranged between the Prime Minister of Great Britain and the Ministers of the Great Powers of Europe. Commencing by twos and threes, the conference developed into an assemblage for conversational purposes of at least twenty of the chief statesmen and diplomatists of the Old World. Rumour said that even monarchs in two or three cases were present and inspired the telephonic utterances of their Ministers. How the result was arrived at was known best to those who took part in the conference, but peace and disarmament were agreed on if certain contingencies involving the exercise of vast power and the expenditure of enormous capital could be provided for. No other conclusion could be arrived at, and one way or the other the outcome had to be settled within twenty-four hours. The conference had lasted from ten o'clock to four. At five o'clock by invitation Lord de Cardrosse waited on the Prime Minister, who received him much more cordially than before.

"You have caused me," he said, "to learn a great deal during the last forty-eight hours."

"I could not presume to teach you anything. Events have spoken," was the reply.

"And who controlled them if not the houses of De Cardrosse?"

"You do us too much honour. It is you who govern; we are of those who are governed."

"The alliance between power and modesty," said the Prime Minister, with pardonable irony, "is irresistible. Tell me, my Lord, is it too late for your views to prevail?"

A slight, almost imperceptible start was the only movement the De Cardrosse made. The enormous self-repression he was exercising cannot be exaggerated. The future strength of the family depended on the issue. There was, however, no tremor in his voice when he answered, "If you adopt them, I do not think it is too late."

"But do you realise the sacrifices in all directions that have to be made?" said the Minister in faltering tones.

"I think I do."

"And you think to secure peace those sacrifices should be made?"

"I do."

"Will you tell me what those sacrifices are?" he asked.

Lord de Cardrosse smiled. "You desire me," he said, "to tell you what you already know." Then he proceeded to describe to the amazed Prime Minister in brief but pregnant terms one after the other the conditions that had been agreed on. Once only he paused and indicated that the condition he was describing he accepted reluctantly.

"I do not conceal," said the astounded Prime Minister, "my surprise at the extent of your knowledge; and clearly you approve the only compromise possible. It is needless to tell you that the acceptance of this compromise requires the use of means not at the disposal of the Governments. In one word, will it suit you to supply them?"

"I might," responded Lord de Cardrosse, "ask you until two o'clock to-morrow to give an answer; but I do not wish to add to your anxiety. If you will undertake to entirely and absolutely confine within your own breast the knowledge of what my answer will be, I will undertake that that answer at two o'clock to-morrow shall be 'Yes.'"

Silently they shook hands. Probably these two men had never before so thoroughly appreciated the strength and speciality of their several powers.

The panic continued until two o'clock the following day, when an enormous reaction took place. The part the De Cardrosse family played in securing peace was suspected by a few only. Its full extent the Prime Minister alone knew. He it was who enjoyed the credit for saving the world from a desolating war.

And now, after an interval of five years, the sovereigns of finance met in conclave. In obedience to the generally expressed wish, Lord de Cardrosse took the chair. "I need scarcely say," he began, "that I am deeply sensible of the compliment you pay me in asking me to preside over such a meeting. We in this room represent a living power throughout the globe, before which the reigning sovereigns of the world are comparatively helpless. But, because of our great strength, it is undesirable that we should work unitedly except for very great and humane objects. For the mere purpose of money-making, I feel assured you all agree with me in desiring no combination, no monopoly, that would pit us against the rest of the world."

He paused for a moment, evidently desiring to disguise the strength of the emotion with which he spoke.

He resumed in slower and apparently more mastered words. "I wish I could put it to you sufficiently strongly that our houses would not have considered any good that could result to them and to you a sufficient excuse for inviting such a combination. We hold that the only cause that could justify it is the conviction that for the good of mankind a vast power requires to be wielded which is not to be found in the ordinary machinery of government."

A murmur of applause went round the table; and Mr. Demetrius, with much feeling, said, "You make me very happy by the assurance you have given. I will not conceal from you that our house anticipated as much, or it would not have been represented. We are too largely concerned with States in which free institutions are permanent not to avoid anything which might savour of a disposition to combine financial forces for the benefit of financial houses."

Lord de Cardrosse then proceeded to explain that his family, in serious and prolonged conclave, could come to no other conclusion than that certain influences were at work which would cause great suffering to mankind and sap and destroy the best institutions which civilisation and science had combined to create. The time had come to answer the question, Should human knowledge, human wants, and human skill continue to advance to an extent to which no limit could be put, or should the survival of the fittest and strongest be fought out in a period of anarchy?

"It amounts," he said in a tone of profound conviction, "to this: the ills under which the masses suffer accumulate. There is no use in comparing what they have to-day with what they had fifty years ago. A person who grows from infancy to manhood in a prison may feel contented until he knows what the liberty is that others enjoy. The born blind are happier than those who become blind by accident. To our masses the knowledge of liberty is open, and they feel they are needlessly deprived of it. Wider and wider to their increasing knowledge opens out the horizon of possible delights; more and more do they feel that they are deprived of what of right belongs to them."

He paused, as if inviting some remarks from his hearers.

Mr. Bisdat, who spoke in an interrogative rather than an affirmative tone, took up the thread.

"I am right, I think, in concluding that your remarks do not point against or in favour of any school of politics or doctrines of party. You direct our notice to causes below the surface to which the Government of the day—I had almost said the hour,—do not penetrate, causes which you believe, if left to unchecked operation, will undermine the whole social fabric."

"It is so," emphatically replied Lord de Cardrosse. "The evils are not only apparent; but equally apparent is it that no remedy is being applied, and that we are riding headlong to anarchy."

Again he paused, and Mr. Rorgon took up the discussion. "If we," he said, "the princes of finance, do not find a remedy, how long will the enlarged intelligence of the people submit to conditions which are at war with the theory of the equality and liberty of mankind?"

"Yes," said the Baroness de Cardrosse, speaking for the first time, "it is clear that there is a limit to the inequality of fortune to which men and women will submit. Equality of possessions there cannot be; but, if I may indulge in metaphor, we cannot expect that the bulk of humankind will be content with being entirely shut out from the sunlight of existence."

The gentlemen present bowed low in approval; and Mr. Demetrius said, "The simile of the Baroness is singularly appropriate. There are myriads of human beings to whom the sunshine of life is denied. A too universal evil invites resistance by means which in lesser cases might be scouted. In short, if the remedy is left to anarchy, anarchy there will be. Even in our young lands the shadow of the coming evil is beginning to show itself. Indeed," he added, with an air of musing abstraction, "it is not unfair to deduce from what has been said, that, even if the evils are less in the new lands of the West and the South, superior general intelligence may more than proportionally increase the wants of the multitude and the sense of wrong under which they labour."

The conference extended over three days. Every one agreed that interference with the ordinary conditions of finance was inexpedient except in extreme cases, but they were unanimous in thinking that an extreme case had to be dealt with. They finally decided by the use of an extended paper currency, with its necessary guarantees, to increase the circulating medium and to raise the prices both of products and labour. Some other decisions were adopted having especial reference to the employment of labour and insurance against want in cases of disablement through illness, accident, or old age.

So ended the most remarkable conference of any age or time.

CHAPTER ONE
THE YEAR 2000—UNITED BRITAIN

Time has passed. There have been many alterations, few of an extreme character. The changes are mostly the results of gradual developments worked out by the natural progress of natural laws. But as constant dropping wears away a stone, constant progression, comparatively imperceptible in its course, attains to immense distances after the lapse of time. This applies though the momentum continually increases the rate of the progress. Thus the well-being of the human kind has undoubtedly increased much more largely during the period between 1900 and 2000 than during the previous century, but equally in either century would it be difficult to select any five years as an example of the turning-point of advancement. Progression, progression, always progression, has been the history of the centuries since the birth of Christ. Doubtless the century we have now entered on will be yet more fruitful of human advancement than any of its predecessors. The strongest point of the century which

"Has gone, with its thorns and its roses,

With the dust of dead ages to mix,"

has been the astonishing improvement of the condition of mankind and the no less striking advancement of the intellectual power of woman.

The barriers which man in his own interest set to the occupation of woman having once been broken down, the progress of woman in all pursuits requiring judgment and intellect has been continuous; and the sum of that progress is enormous. It has, in fact, come to be accepted that the bodily power is greater in man, and the mental power larger in woman. So to speak, woman has become the guiding, man the executive, force of the world. Progress has necessarily become greater because it is found that women bring to the aid of more subtle intellectual capabilities faculties of imagination that are the necessary adjuncts of improvement. The arts and caprices which in old days were called feminine proved to be the silken chains fastened by men on women to lull them into inaction. Without abating any of their charms, women have long ceased to submit to be the playthings of men. They lead men, as of yore, but not so much through the fancy or the senses as through the legitimate consciousness of the man that in following woman's guidance he is tending to higher purposes. We are generalising of course to a certain extent. The variable extent of women's influence is now, as it has been throughout the ages past, the point on which most of the dramas of the human race depend.

The increased enjoyment of mankind is a no less striking feature of the last hundred years. Long since a general recognition was given to the theory that, whilst equality of possession was an impossible and indeed undesirable ideal, there should be a minimum of enjoyment of which no human being should be deprived unless on account of crime. Crime as an occupation has become unknown, and hereditary crime rendered impossible. On the other hand, the law has constituted such provisions for reserves of wealth that anything more than temporary destitution is precluded. Such temporary destitution can only be the result of sheer improvidence, the expenditure, for instance, within a day of what should be expended in a week. The moment it becomes evident, its recurrence is rendered impossible, because the assistance, instead of being given weekly, is rendered daily. Private charity has been minimised; indeed, it is considered to be injurious: and all laws for the recovery of debts have been abolished. The decision as to whether there is debt and its amount is still to be obtained, but the satisfaction of all debt depends solely on the sense of honour or expediency of the debtor. The posting the name of a debtor who refuses to satisfy his liabilities has been found to be far more efficacious than any process of law.

The enjoyment of what in the past would have been considered luxuries has become general. The poorest household has with respect to comforts and provisions a profusion which a hundred years since was wanting in households of the advanced classes.

Long since there dawned upon the world the conviction—

First. That labour or work of some kind was the only condition of general happiness.

Second. That every human being was entitled to a certain proportion of the world's good things.

Third. That, as the capacity of machinery and the population of the world increased production, the theory of the need of labour could not be realised unless with a corresponding increase of the wants of mankind; and that, instead of encouraging a degraded style of living, it was in the interests of the happiness of mankind to encourage a style of living in which the refinements of life received marked consideration.

Great Britain, as it used to be called, has long ceased to be a bundle of sticks. The British dominions have been consolidated into the empire of United Britain; and not only is it the most powerful empire on the globe, but at present no sign is shown of any tendency to weakness or decay. Yet there was a time—about the year 1920—when the utter disintegration of the Empire seemed not only possible, but probable.

The Irish question was still undecided. For many years it had continued to be the sport of Ministers. Cabinet succeeded Cabinet; each had its Irish nostrum; each seemed to think that the Irish question was a good means of delaying questions nearer home. The power of the nation sensibly waned. What nation could be strong with pronounced disaffection festering in its midst? At length, when rumours of a great war were rife upon the result of which the very existence of Great Britain as a nation might depend, the Colonies interposed. By this time the Canadian, Australasian, and Cape colonies had become rich, populous, and powerful. United, they far exceeded in importance the original mother-country.

At the instigation of the Premier of Canada, a confidential intercolonial conference was held. In consequence of the deliberations that ensued, a united representation was made to the Prime Minister of England to the effect that the Colonies could no longer regard without concern the prolonged disquiet prevailing in Ireland. They would suffer should any disaster overtake the Empire, and disaster was courted by permitting the continuation of Irish disaffection. Besides, the Colonies, enjoying as they did local government, could see no reason why Ireland should be treated differently. The message was a mandate, and was meant to be so. The Prime Minister of England, however, puffed up with the pride of old traditions, did not or would not so understand it, and returned an insolent answer. Within twenty-four hours the Colonial Ministers sent a joint respectful address to the King of England representing that they were equally his Majesty's advisers with his Ministers residing in England, and refusing to make any further communications to or through his present advisers.

The Ministry had to retire; a new one was formed. Ireland received the boon it had long claimed of local government, and the whole Empire was federated on the condition that the federation was irrevocable and that every part of it should fight to the last to preserve the union. The King of England and Emperor of India was crowned amidst great pomp Emperor of Britain. All parts of the Empire joined their strength and resources. A federal fleet was formed on the basis that it was to equal in power in every respect the united fleets of all the rest of the world. Conferences with the Great Powers took place in consequence of which Egypt, Belgium, and the whole of the ports bordering the English Channel and Straits of Dover, and the whole of South Africa became incorporated into the empire of Britain. Some concessions, however, were made in other directions. These results were achieved within fifteen years of the interference by the Colonies in federal affairs, and the foundation was laid for the powerful empire which Britain has become. Two other empires and one republic alone approach it in power, and a cordial understanding exists between them to repress war to the utmost extent possible. They constitute the police of the world. Each portion of the Emperor of Britain's possessions enjoys local government, but the federal government is irresistibly strong. It is difficult to say which is the seat of government, as the Federal Parliament is held in different parts of the world, and the Emperor resides in many places. With the utmost comfort he can go from end to end of his dominions in twelve days.

If a headquarter does remain, it may probably be conceded that Alexandria fulfils that position.

The House of Lords has ceased to exist as a separate chamber. The peers began to feel ashamed of holding positions not in virtue of their abilities, but because of the accident of birth. It was they who first sought and ultimately obtained the right to hold seats in the elective branch of the Legislature; and finally it was decided that the peerage should elect a certain number of its own members to represent it in the Federal Parliament: in other words, the accidents of birth were controlled by the selection of the fittest.

Our scene opens in Melbourne, in the year 2000—a few years prior to the date at which we are writing. The Federal Parliament was sitting there that year. The Emperor occupied his magnificent palace on the banks of the Yarra, above Melbourne, which city and its suburbs possessed a population of nearly two millions.

In a large and handsome room in the Federal buildings, a young woman of about twenty-three years of age was seated. She was born in New Zealand. She entered the local parliament before she was twenty. At twenty-two she was elected to the Federal Parliament, and she had now become Under-Secretary of State for

Home Affairs. From her earliest youth she had never failed in any intellectual exercise. Her intelligence was considered phenomenal. Her name was Hilda Richmond Fitzherbert. She was descended from families which for upwards of a century produced distinguished statesmen—a word, it should be mentioned, which includes both sexes. She was fair to look at in both face and figure. Dark violet eyes, brown hair flecked with a golden tinge, clearly cut features, and a glorious complexion made up a face artistically perfect; but these charms were what the observer least noticed. The expression of the face was by far its chief attraction, and words fail to do justice to it. There was about it a luminous intelligence, a purity, and a pathos that seemed to belong to another world. No trace of passion yet stamped it. If the love given to all humanity ever became a love devoted to one person, the expression of the features might descend from the spiritual to the passionate. Even then to human gaze it might become more fascinating. But that test had not come. As she rose from her chair you saw that she was well formed, though slight in figure and of full height. She went to an instrument at a side-table, and spoke to it, the materials for some half-dozen letters referring to groups of papers that lay on the table. When she concluded, she summoned a secretary, who removed the papers and the phonogram on which her voice had been impressed. These letters were reproduced, and brought to her for signature. Copies attached to the several papers were initialled. Meanwhile she paced up and down the room in evident deep distraction. At length she summoned a messenger, and asked him to tell the Countess of Middlesex that she wished to see her. In a few minutes Lady Middlesex entered the room. She was about thirty years of age, of middle height, and pleasing appearance, though a close observer might imagine he saw something sinister in the expression of her countenance. After a somewhat ceremonious greeting, Miss Fitzherbert commenced: "I have carefully considered what passed at our last interview. It is difficult to separate our official and unofficial relations. I am still at a loss to determine whether you have spoken to me as the Assistant Under-Secretary to the Under-Secretary or as woman to woman."

Lady Middlesex quickly rejoined, "Will you let me speak to you as woman to woman, and forget for a moment our official relations?"

"Can you doubt it?" replied Miss Fitzherbert. "But remember that our wishes are not always under our control, and that, though I may not desire to remember to your prejudice what you say, I may not be able to free myself from recollection."

"And yet," said Lady Middlesex, with scarcely veiled irony, "the world says Miss Fitzherbert does not know what prejudice means!"

The slightest possible movement of impatience was all the rejoinder vouchsafed to this speech.

Lady Middlesex continued, "I spoke to you as strongly as I dared, as strongly as my position permitted, about my brother Reginald—Lord Reginald Paramatta. He suffers under a sense of injury. He is miserable. He feels that it is to you that he owes his removal to a distant station. He loves you, and does not know if he may venture to tell you so."

"No woman," replied Miss Fitzherbert, "is warranted in regarding with anger the love of a good man; but you know, or ought to know, that my life is consecrated to objects that are inconsistent with my entertaining the love you speak of."

"But," said Lady Middlesex, "can you be sure that it always will be so?"

"We can be sure of nothing."

"Nay," replied Lady Middlesex, "do not generalise. Let me at least enjoy the liberty you have accorded me. If you did not feel that there were possibilities for Reginald in conflict with your indifference, why should you trouble yourself with his removal?"

"I have not admitted that I am concerned in his removal."

"You know you are; you cannot deny it."

Miss Fitzherbert was dismayed at the position into which she had allowed herself to be forced. She must either state what truth forbade or admit that to some extent Lord Reginald had obtained a hold on her thoughts.

"Other men," pursued Lady Middlesex, with remorseless directness, "have aspired as Reginald does; and you have known how to dispose of their aspirations without such a course as that of which my brother has been the object."

"I have understood," said Miss Fitzherbert, "that Lord Reginald is promoted to an important position, one that ought to be intensely gratifying to so comparatively young a man."

"My brother has only one wish, and you are its centre. He desires only one position."

"I did not infer, Lady Middlesex," said Miss Fitzherbert, with some haughtiness, "that you designed to use the permission you asked of me to become a suitor on your brother's behalf."

"Why else should I have asked such permission?" replied Lady Middlesex, with equal haughtiness. Then, with a sudden change of mood and manner, "Miss Fitzherbert, forgive me. My brother is all in all to me. My husband and my only child are dead. My brother is all that is left to me to remind me of a once happy home. Do not, I pray, I entreat you, embitter his life. Ask yourself— forgive me for saying so—if ambition rather than consecration to a special career may not influence you; and if your conscience replies affirmatively, remember the time will come to you, as it has come to other women, when success, the applause of the crowd, and a knowledge of great deeds effected will prove a poor consolation for the want of one single human being on whom to lavish a woman's love. Most faculties become smaller by disuse, but it is not so with the affections; they revenge themselves on those who have dared to disbelieve in their force."

"You assume," said Miss Fitzherbert, "that I love your brother."

"Is it not so?"

"No! a thousand times no!"

"You feel that you might love him. That is the dawn of love."

"Listen, Lady Middlesex. That dawn has not opened to me. I will not deny, I have felt a prepossession in favour of your brother; but I have the strongest conviction that my life will be better and happier because of my refusing to give way to it. For me there is no love of the kind. In lonely maidenhood I will live and die. If my choice is unwise, I will be the sufferer; and I have surely the right to make it. My lady, our interview is at an end."

Lady Middlesex rose and bowed her adieu, but another thought seemed to occur to her. "You will," she said, "at least see my brother before he goes. Indeed, otherwise I doubt his leaving. He told me this morning that he would resign."

Miss Fitzherbert after a moment's thought replied, "I will see your brother. Bid him call on me in two hours' time. Good-bye."

As she was left alone a look of agony came over her face. "Am I wise?" she said. "That subtle woman knew how to wound me. She is right. I could love; I could adore the man I loved. Will all the triumphs of the world and the sense of the good I do to others console me during the years to come for the sunshine of love to which every woman has a claim? Yes, I do not deny the claim, high as my conception is of a woman's destiny." After a few moments' pause, she started up indignantly. "Am I then," she ejaculated half aloud, "that detestable thing a woman with a mission, and does the sense of that mission restrain me from yielding to my inclination?" Again she paused, and then resumed, "No, it is not so. I have too easily accepted Lady Middlesex's insinuation. I am neither ambitious nor philanthropic to excess. It is a powerful instinct that speaks to me about Lord Reginald. To a certain extent I am drawn to him, but I doubt him, and it is that which restrains me. I am more disposed to be frightened of than to love him. Why do I doubt him? Some strong impulse teaches me to do so. What do I doubt? I doubt his loving me with a love that will endure, I doubt our proving congenial companions, and—why may I not say it to myself?—I doubt his character. I question his sincerity. The happiness of a few months might be followed by a life of misery. I must be no weak fool to allow myself to be persuaded."

Hilda Fitzherbert was a thoroughly good, true-hearted, and lovable girl. Clever, well informed, and cultivated to the utmost, she had no disposition to prudery or priggishness. She was rather inclined to under- than over-value herself. Lady Middlesex's clever insinuations had caused her for the moment to doubt her own conduct; but reflection returned in time, and once more she became conscious that she felt for Lord Reginald no more attachment than any woman might entertain for a handsome, accomplished man who persistently displayed his admiration. She was well aware that under ordinary circumstances such feelings as she had, might develop into strong love if there were no reverse to the picture; but in this case conviction—call it, if you will, an instinct—persuaded her there was an opposite side. She felt that Lord Reginald was playing a part; that, if his true character stood revealed to her, an unfathomable abyss would yawn between them.

Her reflections were disturbed by the entrance of a lady of very distinguished mien. She might indeed look distinguished, for the Right Honourable Mrs. Hardinge was not only Prime Minister of the empire of Britain, but the most powerful and foremost statesman in the world. In her youth she had been a lovely girl; and even now, though not less than forty years of age, she was a beautiful—it might be more correct to say, a grand—woman. A tall, dignified, and stately figure was set off by a face of which every feature was artistically correct and capable of much variety of expression; and over that expression she held entire command. She had, if she wished it, an arch and winning manner, such as no one but a cultivated Irishwoman possesses; the purest Irish blood ran through her veins. She could say "No" in a manner that more delighted the person whose request she was refusing than would "Yes" from other lips. An adept in all the arts of conversation, she could elicit information from the most inscrutable statesmen, who under her influence would fancy she was more confidential to them than they to her. By indomitable strength she had fought down an early inclination to impulsiveness. The appearance still remained, but no statesman was more slow to form opinions and less prone to change them. She could, if necessary, in case of emergency, act with lightning rapidity; but she had schooled herself to so act only in cases of extreme need. She had a warm heart, and in the private relations of life no one was better liked.

Hilda Fitzherbert worshipped her; and Mrs. Hardinge, childless and with few relations, loved and admired the girl with a strength and tenacity that made their official relations singularly pleasant.

"My dear Hilda," she said, "why do you look so disturbed, and how is it you are idle? It is rare to find you unoccupied."

Hilda, almost in tears, responded, "Dear Mrs. Hardinge, tell me, do tell me, what do you really think of Lord Reginald Paramatta?"

If Mrs. Hardinge felt any surprise at the extraordinary abruptness of the question, she did not permit it to be visible.

"My dear, the less you think of him the better. I will tell you how I read his character. He is unstable and insincere, capable of any exertion to attain the object on which he has set his mind; the moment he has gained it the victory becomes distasteful to him. I have offered him the command of our London forces to please you, but I tell you frankly I did so with reluctance. Nor would I have promoted him to the post but that it has long ceased to possess more than traditional importance. Those chartered sybarites the Londoners can receive little harm from Lord Reginald, and the time has long passed for him to receive any good. Such as it is, his character is moulded; and professionally he is no doubt an accomplished officer and brave soldier. Besides that, he possesses more than the ordinary abilities of a man."

Hilda looked her thanks, but said no more than "Your opinion does not surprise me, and it tallies with my own judgment."

"Dear girl, do not try to dispute that judgment. And now to affairs of much importance. I have come from the Emperor, and I see great difficulties in store for us."

Probably Hilda had never felt so grateful to Mrs. Hardinge as she did now for the few words in which she had expressed so much, with such fine tact. An appearance of sympathy or surprise would have deeply wounded the girl.

"Dear mamma," she said—as sometimes in private in moments of affection she was used to do—"does his Highness still show a disinclination to the settlement to which he has almost agreed?"

"He shows the most marked disinclination, for he told me with strong emotion that he felt he would be sacrificing the convictions of his race."

The position of the Emperor was indeed a difficult one. A young, high-spirited, generous, and brave man, he was asked by his Cabinet to take a step which in his heart he abhorred. A short explanation is necessary to make the case clear. When the Imperial Constitution of Britain was promulgated, women were beginning to acquire more power; but no one thought of suggesting that the preferential succession to the direct heirs male should be withdrawn.

Meanwhile women advanced, and in all other classes of life they gained perfect equality with regard to the laws of succession and other matters, but the custom still remained by which the eldest daughter of the Emperor would be excluded in favour of the eldest son. Some negotiations had proceeded concerning the marriage of the Emperor to the daughter of the lady who enjoyed the position of President of the United States, an intense advocate of woman's equality. She was disposed, if not determined, to make it a condition of the marriage that the eldest child, whether son or daughter, should succeed. The Emperor's Cabinet had the same view, and it was one widely held throughout the Empire. But there were strong opinions on the other side. The increasing number of women elected by popular suffrage to all representative positions and the power which women invariably possessed in the Cabinet aroused the jealous anger of men. True, the feeling was not in the ascendant, and other disabilities of women were removed; but in this particular case, the last, it may be said, of women's disabilities, a separate feeling had to be taken into account. The ultra-Conservatives throughout the Empire, including both men and women, were superstitiously tenacious of upholding the Constitution in its integrity and averse to its being changed in the smallest particular. They felt that everything important to the Empire depended upon the irrevocable nature of the Constitution, and that the smallest change might be succeeded by the most organic alterations. The merits of the question mattered nothing in their opinion in comparison with the principle which they held it was a matter of life and death not to disturb.

It was now proposed to introduce a Bill to enable the Emperor to declare that the succession should be to the eldest child. The Cabinet were strongly in favour of it, and to a great extent their existence as a Government depended on it. The Emperor was well disposed to his present advisers, but, it was no secret, was strongly averse to this one proposal. The contemplated match was an affair of State policy rather than of inclination. He had seldom met his intended bride, and was not prepossessed with her. She was good-looking and a fine girl; but she had unmistakably red hair, an adornment not to his taste. Besides, she was excessively firm in her opinions as to the superiority of women over men; and he strongly suspected she would be for ever striving to rule not only the household, but the Empire. It is difficult to fathom the motives of the human mind, difficult not only to others, but to the persons themselves concerned. The Emperor thought that his opposition to placing the succession on an equality between male and female was purely one of loyalty to his ancestors and to the traditions of the Empire. But who could say that he did not see in a refusal to pass the necessary Act a means of escaping the distasteful nuptials? Mrs. Hardinge had come from a long interview with him, and it was evident that she greatly doubted his continued support. She resumed, "His Highness seems very seriously to oppose the measure, and indeed quite ready to give up his intended marriage. I wonder," she said, looking keenly at Hilda, "whether he has seen any girl he prefers."

The utter unconsciousness with which Hilda heard this veiled surmise appeared to satisfy Mrs. Hardinge; and she continued, "Tell me, dear, what do you think?"

"I am hardly in a position to judge. Does the Emperor give no reasons for his opposition?"

"Yes, he has plenty of reasons; but his strongest appears to be that whoever is ruler of the Empire should be able to lead its armies."

"I thought," said Miss Fitzherbert, "that he had some good reason."

"Do you consider this a good reason?" inquired Mrs. Hardinge sharply.

"From his point of view, yes; from ours, no," said Hilda gently, but promptly.

"Then you do not think that we should retreat from our position even if retreat were possible?"

"No," replied Hilda. "Far better to leave office than to make a concession of which we do not approve in order to retain it."

"You are a strange girl," said Mrs. Hardinge. "If I understand you rightly, you think both sides are correct."

"I think that there is a great deal to be said on both sides, and this is constantly the case with important controversies. Between the metal and the flint the spark of truth is struck. I should think it no disgrace to be defeated on a subject about which we could show good cause. I might even come to think that better cause had been shown against us after the discussion was over; but to flee the discussion, to sacrifice conviction to expediency—that would be disgraceful."

"Then," said Mrs. Hardinge, with some interest, "if the Emperor were to ask your opinion, you would try to persuade him to our side?"

"Yes and no. I would urge strongly my sense of the question and my opinion that it is better to settle at once a controversy about which there is so much difference of opinion. But I should respect his views; and if they were conscientious, I should not dare to advise him to sacrifice them."

An interruption unexpected by Miss Fitzherbert, but apparently not surprising to Mrs. Hardinge, occurred. An aide-de-camp of the Emperor entered. After bowing low to the ladies, he briefly said, "His Imperial Majesty desires the presence of Miss Fitzherbert."

A summons so unusual raised a flush to the girl's cheek. She looked at Mrs. Hardinge.

"I had intended to tell you," said that lady, "that the Emperor mentioned he would like to speak to you on the subject we have been considering." Then, turning to the aide-de-camp, she said, "Miss Fitzherbert will immediately wait on his Majesty."

The officer left the room.

Hilda archly turned to Mrs. Hardinge. "So, dear mamma, you were preparing me for this interview?"

"Dear child," said the elder lady, "you want no preparation. Whatever the consequences to me, I will not ask you to put any restraint on the expression of your opinions."

CHAPTER TWO
THE EMPEROR AND HILDA FITZHERBERT

The Emperor received Miss Fitzherbert with a cordial grace, infinitely pleasing and flattering to that young lady. She of course had often seen his Majesty at Court functions, but never before had he summoned her to a separate audience.

And indeed, high though her official position and reputation were, she did not hold Cabinet rank; and a special audience was a rare compliment, such as perhaps no one in her position had ever previously enjoyed.

The Emperor was a tall man of spare and muscular frame, with the dignity and bearing of a practised soldier. It was impossible not to recognise that he was possessed of immense strength and power of endurance. He had just celebrated his twenty-seventh birthday, and looked no more than his age. His face was of the fair Saxon type. His eyes were blue, varying with his moods from almost dark violet to a cold steel tint. Few persons were able to disguise from him their thoughts when he fixed on them his eyes, with the piercing enquiry of which they were capable. His eyes were indeed singularly capable of a great variety of expression. He could at will make them denote the thoughts and feelings which he wished to make apparent to those with whom he conversed. Apart from his position, no one could look at him without feeling that he was a distinguished man. He was of a kindly disposition, but capable of great severity, especially towards any one guilty of a mean or cowardly action. He was of a highly honourable disposition, and possessed an exalted sense of duty. He rarely allowed personal inclination to interfere with public engagements; indeed, he was tenaciously sensitive on the point, and sometimes fancied that he permitted his judgment to be obscured by his prepossessions when he had really good grounds for his conclusions. On the very subject of his marriage he was constantly filled with doubt as to whether his objection to the proposed alteration in the law of succession was well founded on public grounds or whether he was unconsciously influenced by his personal disinclination to the contemplated union. He realised the truth of the saying of a very old author—

"Uneasy lies the head that wears a crown."

After indicating to Miss Fitzherbert his wish that she should be seated, he said to her, "I have been induced to ask your attendance by a long conversation I have had with Mrs. Hardinge. I have heard the opinions she has formed, and they seem to me the result of matured experience. It occurred to me that I would like to hear the opinions of one who, possessed of no less ability, has been less subject to official and diplomatic exigencies. I may gather from you how much of personal feeling should be allowed to influence State affairs."

"Your Majesty is very gracious," faltered Hilda, "but Mrs. Hardinge has already told you the opinion of the Cabinet. Even if I differed from it, which I do not, I could not venture to obtrude my view on your Majesty."

"Yes, you could," said the Emperor, "if I asked you, or let me say commanded you."

"Sir, your wishes are commands. I do not pretend to have deeply studied the matter. I think the time has come to finally settle a long-mooted question and to withdraw from woman the last disability under which she labours."

"My objection," interposed the Emperor, "or hesitation is in no manner caused by any doubt as to woman's deserving to be on a par with man in every intellectual position."

"Then, Sir, may I ask, why do you hesitate? The greatest Sovereign that ever reigned over Great Britain, as it was formerly called, was a woman."

"I cordially agree with you. No Sovereign ever deserved better of the subjects of the realm than my venerated ancestress Queen Victoria. But again I say, I do not question woman's ability to occupy the throne to the greatest advantage."

"Why, may I ask, then does your Majesty hesitate?"

"I can scarcely reply to my own satisfaction. I give great heed to the objections commonly stated against altering the Constitution, but I do not feel certain that these alone guide me. There is another, and to me very important, reason. It appeals to me not as Sovereign only, but as soldier. My father and my grandfather led the troops of the Empire when they went forth to battle. Happily in our day war is a remote contingency, but it is not impossible. We preserve peace by being prepared for war. It seems to me a terrible responsibility to submit to a change which might result in the event of war in the army not being led by its emperor."

"Your Majesty," said Miss Fitzherbert, "what am I to say? To deny the cogency of your reasons is like seeking to retain power, for you know the fate of the Cabinet depends upon this measure, to which it has pledged itself."

"Miss Fitzherbert," said the Emperor gravely, "no one will suspect you of seeking to retain office for selfish purposes, and least of all would I suppose it, or I would not ask your counsel. Tell me now," he said, with a winning look, "as woman to man, not as subject to Sovereign, what does your heart dictate?"

"Sir," said Miss Fitzherbert with great dignity, rising from her seat, "I am deeply sensible of the honour you do me; and I cannot excuse myself from responding to it. In the affairs of life, and more especially State affairs, I have noticed that both sides to a controversy have frequently good grounds for their advocacy; and, moreover, it often happens that previous association fastens on each side the views it holds. I am strong in the belief, we are right in wishing this measure to pass; but since you insist on my opinion, I cannot avoid declaring as far as I, a non-militant woman, can judge, that, were I in your place, I would hold the sentiment you express and refuse my sanction."

Hilda spoke with great fervour, as one inspired. The Emperor scarcely concealed his admiration; but he merely bowed courteously, and ended the interview with the words, "I am greatly indebted to you for your frankness and candour."

CHAPTER THREE
LORD REGINALD PARAMATTA

As Miss Fitzherbert returned to her room, she did not know whether to feel angry or pleased with herself. She was conscious she had not served the interest of her party or of herself, but she realised that she was placed in a situation in which candour was demanded of her, and it seemed to her that the Emperor was the embodiment of all that was gracious and noble in man.

Her secretary informed her that Lord Reginald Paramatta was waiting to see her by appointment.

Lord Reginald was a man of noticeable presence. Above the ordinary height, he seemed yet taller because of the extreme thinness of his frame. Yet he by no means wore an appearance of delicacy. On the contrary, he was exceedingly muscular; and his bearing was erect and soldierlike. He was well known as a brilliant officer, who had deeply studied his profession. But he was not only known as a soldier: he held a high political position. He had for many years continued to represent an Australian constituency in the Federal Parliament. His naturally dark complexion was further bronzed by exposure to the sun. His features were good and strikingly like those of his sister, the Countess of Middlesex. He had also the same sinister expression. The Paramattas were a very old New South Wales family. They were originally sheep-farmers, or squatters as they used to be called. They owned large estates in New South Wales and nearly half of a thriving city. The first lord was called to the peerage in 1930, in recognition of the immense sums that he had devoted to philanthropic and educational purposes. Lord Reginald was the second son of the third and brother of the fourth peer. He inherited from his mother a large estate in the interior of New South Wales.

Miss Fitzherbert greeted Lord Reginald with marked coolness. "Your sister," she said, "told me you were kind enough to desire to wish me farewell before you left to take the London command, upon which allow me to congratulate you."

"Thanks!" briefly replied his Lordship. "An appointment that places me so far from you is not to my mind a subject of congratulation."

Miss Fitzherbert drew herself up, and with warmth remarked, "I am surprised that you should say this to me."

"You ought not to be surprised," replied Lord Reginald. "My sister told you of my feelings towards you, if indeed I have not already sufficiently betrayed them."

"Your sister must have also told you what I said in reply. Pray, my lord, do not inflict on both of us unnecessary pain."

"Do not mistake my passion for a transitory one. Miss Fitzherbert, Hilda, my life is bound up in yours. It depends on you to send me forth the most happy or the most miserable of men."

"Your happiness would not last. I am convinced we are utterly unsuited to each other. My answer is 'No' in both our interests."

"Do not say so finally. Take time. Tell me I may ask you again after the lapse of some few months."

"To tell you so would be to deceive. My answer can never change."

"You love some one else, then?"

"The question, my lord, is not fair nor seemly, nor have you the right to put it. Nevertheless I will say there is no foundation for your surmise."

"Then why finally reject me? Give me time to prove to you how thoroughly I am in earnest."

"I have not said I doubted it. But no lapse of years can alter the determination I have come to. I hope, Lord Reginald, that you will be happy, and that amidst the distractions of London you will soon forget me."

"That would be impossible, but it will not be put to the test. I shall not go to London. I believe it is your wish that we should be separated."

"I have no wish on the subject. There is nothing more to be said," replied Hilda, with extreme coldness.

"Yes, there is. Do not think that I abandon my hope. I will remain near you. I will not let you forget me. I leave you in the conviction that some day you will give me a different answer. When the world is less kind to you than hitherto, you may learn to value the love of one devoted being. There is no good-bye between us."

Hilda suppressed the intense annoyance that both his words and manner occasioned. She merely remarked, with supreme hauteur, "You will at least be good enough to rid me of your presence here."

Her coldness seemed to excite the fury of Lord Reginald beyond the point of control. "As I live, you shall repent this in the future," he muttered in audible accents.

Shortly afterwards a letter from Lord Reginald was laid before the Premier. He was gratified, he wrote, for the consideration the official appointment displayed; but he could not accept it: his parliamentary duties forbade his doing so. If, he continued, it was considered that his duty as an officer demanded his accepting the offer, he would send in his papers and retire from the service, though of course he would retain his position in the Volunteer force unless the Emperor wished otherwise.

It should be explained that the Volunteer force was of at least equal importance to the regular service. Officers had precedence interchangeably according to seniority. Long since the absurdity had been recognised of placing the Volunteer force on a lower footing than the paid forces. Regular officers eagerly sought to be elected to commands in Volunteer regiments, and the colonel of a Volunteer regiment enjoyed fully as much consideration in every respect as the colonel of any of the paid regiments. The duty of defending all parts of the Empire from invasion was specially assigned to volunteers. The Volunteer force throughout the Empire numbered at least two million, besides which there was a Volunteer reserve force of three quarters of a million, which comprised the best men selected from the volunteers. The vacancies were filled up each year by fresh selections to make up the full number. The Volunteer reserve force could be mobilised at short notice, and was available for service anywhere. Its members enjoyed many prized social distinctions. The regular force of the Empire was comparatively small. In order to understand the availability of the Volunteer reserve force, regard must be had to the immense improvement in education. No child attained man or woman's estate without a large theoretical and practical knowledge of scientific laws and their ordinary application. For example, few adults were so ignorant as not to understand the modes by which motive power of various descriptions was obtained and the principles on which the working depended—each person was more or less an engineer. A hundred years since, education was deemed to be the mastering of a little knowledge about a great variety of subjects. Thoroughness was scarcely regarded, and the superficial apology for preferring quantity to quality was "Education does not so much mean imparting knowledge as training the faculties to acquire it." This plausible plea afforded the excuse for wasting the first twenty years of life of both sexes in desultory efforts to acquire a mastery over the dead languages. "It is a good training to the mind and a useful means of learning the living languages" was in brief the defence for the shocking waste of time.

Early in the last century it fell to the lot of the then Prince of Wales, great-grandfather to the present Emperor, to prick this educational bladder. He stoutly declared that his sons should learn neither Latin nor Greek. "Why," he said, "should we learn ancient Italian any more than the Italians should learn the dialects of the ancient Britons?"

"There is a Greek and Latin literature," was the reply, "but no literature of ancient Britain."

"Yes," replied the Prince, "there is a literature; but does our means of learning the dead languages enable two persons in ten thousand after years of study to take up promiscuously a Latin or Greek book and read it with ease and comfort? They spend much more time in learning Latin and Greek than their own language, but who ever buys a Latin or Greek book to read when he is travelling?"

"But a knowledge of Latin is so useful in acquiring living languages."

"Fudge!" said this unceremonious prince, who, by the way, was more than an average classical scholar. "If I want to go to Liverpool, I do not proceed there by way of New York. I will back a boy to learn how to speak and read with interest three European languages before he shall be able, even with the aid of a dictionary, to laboriously master the meaning of a Latin book he has not before studied." He continued, "Do you think one person out of fifty thousand who have learnt Greek is so truly imbued with the spirit of the Iliad as are those whose only acquaintance with it is through the translations of Derby, Gladstone, or even Pope? It is partly snobbishness," he proceeded, with increased warmth. "The fact is, it is expensive and wasteful to learn Greek and Latin; and so the rich use the acquirement as another means of walling up class against class. At any rate, I will destroy the fashion; and so that there shall be no loss of learning, I will have every Greek and Latin work not yet translated that can be read with advantage by decent and modest people rendered into the English language, if it cost me a hundred thousand pounds: and then there will be no longer an excuse for the waste of millions on dead languages, to say nothing of the loss occasioned by the want of education in other subjects that is consequent on the prominence given to the so-called classical attainments."

The Prince was equal to his word. Science and art, mathematical and technical acquirements, took the place of the classics; and people became really well informed. Living languages, it was found, could be easily learnt in a few months by personal intercourse with a fluent speaker.

This digression has been necessary to explain how it was that the volunteers were capable of acquiring all the scientific knowledge necessary to the ranks of a force trained to the highest military duties. As to the officers, the position was sufficiently coveted to induce competitors for command in Volunteer regiments to study the most advanced branches of the profession.

It will be understood Lord Reginald, while offering to retire from the regular service, but intending to retain his Volunteer command, really made no military sacrifice, whilst he took up a high ground embarrassing to the authorities. He forced them either to accept his refusal of the London command, and be a party to the breach of discipline involved in a soldier declining to render service wherever it was demanded, or to require his retirement from the regular service, with the certainty of all kinds of questions being asked and surmises made.

It was no doubt unusual to offer him such a splendid command without ascertaining that he was ready to accept it, and there was a great risk of Miss Fitzherbert's name being brought up in an unpleasant manner. Women lived in the full light of day, and several journals were in the habit of declaring that the likes and dislikes of women were allowed far too much influence. What an opportunity would be afforded to them if they could hang ever so slightly Lord Reginald's retirement on some affair of the heart connected with that much-envied young statesman Miss Fitzherbert!

Mrs. Hardinge rapidly realised all the features of the case. "He means mischief, this man," she said; "but he shall not hurt Hilda if I can help it." Then she minuted "Write Lord Reginald that I regret he is unable to accept an appointment which I thought would give him pleasure, and which he is so qualified to adorn." She laughed over this sentence. "He will understand its irony," she thought, "and smart under it." She continued, "Add that I see no reason for his retirement from the regular service. It was through accident he was not consulted before the offer was officially made. I should be sorry to deprive the Empire of his brilliant services. Mark 'Confidential.'" Then she thought to herself, "This is the best way out of it. He has gained to a certain extent a triumph, but he cannot make capital out of it."

CHAPTER FOUR
PARTIAL VICTORY

Parliament was about to meet, and the Emperor was to open it with a speech delivered by himself. Much difference of opinion existed as to whether reference should be made to the question of altering the nature of the succession. The Emperor desired that all reference to it should be omitted. He told Mrs. Hardinge frankly he had decided not to agree to an alteration, but he said his greatest pain in refusing was the consciousness that it might deprive him of his present advisers. If the recommendation were formally made, he should be compelled to say that he would not concur until he had recourse to other advisers. He wished her not to impose on him such a necessity.

"But," said Mrs. Hardinge, "your Majesty is asking us to hold office at the expense of our opinions."

"Not so," replied his Majesty. "All pressing need of dealing with the question is over. I have resolved to break off the negotiations with the President of the United States for her daughter's hand. I do not think the union would be happy for either, and I take exception to the strong terms in which the President has urged a change in the succession of our imperial line. You see that the question is no longer an urgent one."

"I hardly know to which direction our duty points," Mrs. Hardinge said. "We think the question urgent whether or not your Majesty marries at once."

"Pray do not take that view. There is another reason. I have determined, as I have said, not to accept such advice without summoning other advisers. In adopting this step, I am strictly within my constitutional rights; and I do not say, if a new Cabinet also recommends an alteration in the law of succession I will refuse to accept the advice. I will never voluntarily decline to recognise the constitutional rights which I have sworn to uphold. So it might be that a change of Cabinet would not alter the result, and then it would be held that I had strained my constitutional power in making the change. I do not wish to appear in this or any other question to hold individual opinions. Frankly I will tell you that I doubt if you have the strength to carry your proposed change even if I permitted you to submit it. If I am correct in my conjecture, the question will be forced on you from the other side; and you will be defeated on it. In that case I shall not have interfered; and, as I have said, I prefer not to do so. So you see, Mrs. Hardinge, that I am selfish in wishing you to hold back the question. It is in my own interest that I do so, and you may dismiss all feeling of compunction."

"Your Majesty has graciously satisfied me that I may do as you suggest without feeling that I am actuated by undue desire to continue in office. I agree with your Majesty the parliamentary result is doubtful. It greatly depends on the line taken by Lord Reginald Paramatta and the forty or fifty members who habitually follow him."

The Emperor's speech was received with profound respect. But as soon as he left the council-chamber a murmur of astonishment ran round. It was generally anticipated that the announcement of the royal marriage would be made.

The Federal Chamber was of magnificent dimensions. It accommodated with comfort the seven hundred and fifty members and one thousand persons besides. The Chamber was of circular shape. A line across the centre divided the portion devoted to the members from that occupied by the audience. The latter were seated tier on tier, but not crowded. The members had each a comfortable chair and a little desk in front, on which he could either write or by the hand telegraph communicate telegrams to his friends outside for retransmission if he desired it. He could receive messages also, and in neither case was the least noise made by the instrument.

The council-chamber possessed astonishing acoustic powers. Vast as were its dimensions, a comparatively feeble voice could be clearly heard at the remotest distance. As soon as some routine business was concluded the leader of the Opposition, a lady of great reputation for statesmanship, rose, and, partly by way of interrogation, expressed surprise that no intimation had been made respecting the future happiness of the reigning family. This was about as near a reference to the person of the Sovereign as the rules of the House permitted. Mrs. Hardinge curtly replied that she had no intimation to make, a reply which was received with a general murmur of amazement. The House seemed to be on the point of proceeding to the ordinary business, when Lord Reginald Paramatta rose and said "he ventured to ask, as no reference was made to the subject in the speech, what were the intentions of the Government on the question of altering the law of succession of the imperial family."

This interruption was received with much surprise. Lord Reginald had long been a member possessed of great influence. He had a considerable following, numbering perhaps not less than fifty. His rule of conduct hitherto had been to deprecate party warfare. He tried to hold the balance, and neither side had yet been able to number him and his following as partisans. That he should lead the way to an attack of an extreme party character seemed most astonishing. The few words that he had uttered were rapidly translated into meaning that he intended to throw in his lot with the Opposition. Mrs. Hardinge, however, appeared to feel no concern as she quietly replied that she was not aware that the question pressed for treatment. "I am afraid," said Lord Reginald, "that I am unable to agree with this opinion; and it is my duty to test the feelings of the House on the subject." Then he read to the intently listening members a resolution of which he gave notice that it was desirable, in order that no uncertainty should exist on the subject, to record the opinion of the House that the law of succession should not be altered. Loud cheers followed the announcement; and the leader of the Opposition, who was equally taken by surprise, congratulated Lord Reginald, with some little irony, on the decided position he had at last assumed. Mrs. Hardinge, without any trace of emotion or anxiety, rose amidst the cheers of her side of the House. The noble and gallant member, she said, had given notice of a resolution which the Government would consider challenged its position. It would be better to take it before proceeding to other business, and if, as she expected, the reply to the Imperial speech would not occasion discussion, to-morrow could be devoted to it. Lord Reginald replied to-morrow would suit him, and the sitting soon came to an end.

 Mrs. Hardinge could not but feel surprise at the accuracy of the Emperor's anticipation. She was sure he was not aware of Lord Reginald's intention, and she knew that the latter was acting in revenge for the slight he had received at the hands of Hilda Fitzherbert. She felt that the prospect of the motion being carried was largely increased through Lord Reginald having so cleverly appropriated it to himself. But it was equally evident from the cordiality with which the proposal was received that, if Lord Reginald had not brought it on, some one else would. She saw also that the Countess of Cairo (the leader of the Opposition) had rapidly decided to support Lord Reginald, though she might have reasonably objected to his appropriating the subject. "He is clever," Mrs. Hardinge reflected. "He accurately gauged Lady Cairo's action. What a pity neither Hilda nor I can trust him! He is as bad in disposition as he is able in mind."

 The next day, after the routine business was disposed of, Lord Reginald's resolution was called on. That it excited immense interest the crowded state of the hall in every part attested. Two of the Emperor's aides-de-camp were there, each with a noiseless telegraph apparatus in front of him to wire alternately the progress of the debate. Reporters were similarly communicating with the Argus, Age, and Telegraph in Melbourne, and with the principal papers in Sydney, Brisbane, Adelaide, and New Zealand.

Lord Reginald rose amidst loud cheers from the Opposition side of the House. He made a temperate but exceedingly able speech. He would explain before he concluded why he had taken the lead in bringing the question on. Hitherto he had not sought to take a prominent place in politics. He was a soldier by profession, and he would infinitely prefer distinguishing himself as a soldier than as a politician; and, as he would show, it was as a soldier that he came forward. He disclaimed any hostility to the equality of the sexes or any objection to the increasing power in public affairs to which women were attaining. He fully recognised that the immense progress of the world during the last hundred years was largely due to the intellectual advancement of women. He equally rejected the idea that women were unfitted to rule over a constitutionally governed empire.

Then he dwelt at great length on the inexpediency of permitting the Constitution to be altered in any one particular, and this part of his speech was warmly cheered by a considerable section on each side of the Chamber. The effect of these remarks was, however, marred as far as the Government party were concerned by a sneering reference to their disposition to changes of all kinds; and he attempted a feeble joke by insinuating that the most desirable change of all might be a change of government.

Then he came to his main argument and explained that it was this consideration which had impelled him to take up the question. He was, as he had said, a soldier; but he was not one who overlooked the misery caused by war. He did not long for war, nor did he think that war was a probable contingency; but he felt that the British Empire should always be ready for war as the best means of avoiding it, and as a soldier he believed no greater prestige could be given to the forces of their vast dominions than the knowledge that the Emperor was ready to lead them in person. "I would not," he said, "exclude the female line; but I would not give it larger probabilities of succession than it enjoys at present. Again, as a soldier I declare that the interests of the Empire forbid our doing anything to limit the presence at the head of his forces of the ruler of the Empire."

Lord Reginald sat down amidst cheers. He had been listened to with profound attention, and parts of his speech were warmly applauded. Still, on the whole, the speech was not a success. Every one felt that there was something wanting. The speaker seemed to be deficient in sincerity. The impression left was that he had some object in view. The malign air with which the little joke was uttered about a change of government was most repelling. It came with singularly bad grace from one who tried to make out that he was unwillingly forced into opposition to a Government with which he had been friendly.

Mrs. Hardinge rose amidst loud and continuous cheers. She combated each argument of the last speaker. She admitted her great disinclination to change the Constitution, but, she asked, was reverence for the Constitution promoted by upholding it on the ground not of its merits, but of the inexpediency of varying it? She freely admitted that her feelings were in favour of changing the laws of succession, but she had not brought forward any proposal to that effect, nor, as an advocate of a change, did she see any immediate or early need of bringing down proposals. Was it a good precedent to make great Ministerial changes depend on resolutions affecting not questions before the House, not proposals made by the Government, but sentiments or opinions they were supposed to entertain? This was a great change in parliamentary procedure, a larger one than those changes which the noble lord had sneeringly credited her with advocating. Then she gave Lord Reginald a very unpleasant quarter of an hour. She pictured him as head of the Government in consequence of carrying his resolution; she selected certain unpopular sentiments which he was known to entertain, and, amidst great laughter, travestied Lord Reginald's defence of his fads in response to resolutions of the same kind as they were now discussing. She grew eloquent even to inspiration in describing the abilities of the female Sovereigns of the past. And as to the soldier's point of view she asked did not history tell them that the arms of the country had been as successful under female as under male rulers? The noble lord, she said, amidst roars of laughter, had intended to come forward as a soldier; but, for her part, she thought he had posed as a courtier, and sarcastically she hinted that he was as able in one capacity as the other. "He is sad, sir," she continued, "over the possibility that any one but the Emperor should lead the forces; but if all that is said as to the noble lord's ambition be correct, he would prefer leading the troops himself to following the lead of the most exalted commander." She concluded with an eloquent appeal to her own party. She did not deny the opinions of her colleagues and herself, but asked was it wise to allow a great party to be broken up by a theoretical discussion upon a subject not yet before the country, and which for a long while might not come before it? Mrs. Hardinge's speech was received most enthusiastically, and at its conclusion it was clear that she had saved her party from breaking up. Not a vote would be lost to it. The result merely depended on what addition Lord Reginald's own following could bring to the usual strength of the Opposition. After some more debating a division ensued, and the resolution was lost by two votes only. Both sides cheered, but there was breathless silence when Mrs. Hardinge rose. She made no reference to the debate beyond the very significant one of asking that the House should adjourn for a week.

CHAPTER FIVE
CABINET NEGOTIATIONS

Mrs. Hardinge tendered the resignation of the Government to the

Emperor, who at once sent for Lady Cairo, the leader of the Opposition. He asked her to form an administration.

"Your Majesty," she said, "knows that, though I am in opposition to the present Premier, I greatly admire both her ability and honesty of purpose. I am not at all satisfied that she is called on to resign, or that the small majority she had on the late resolution indicates that she has not a large following on other questions."

"I hold," said the Emperor, "the balance evenly between the great parties of the State; and I respect the functions of the Opposition no less than those of the Government. It is the opinion of my present advisers that a strong administration is necessary, and that, after such a division as that of the other night, the Opposition should have the opportunity offered to them of forming a Government."

"I respect," replied Lady Cairo, "Mrs. Hardinge's action, and under like circumstances would have pursued a like course. But though Mrs. Hardinge is right in offering us the opportunity, it does not follow that we should be wise in accepting it."

"You are of that," replied the Emperor, "of course the best judge. But I should not like so grave a step as the one which Mrs. Hardinge has felt it her duty to take to be construed into a formality for effacing the effect of a vote of the House. I am averse," said the wise ruler, "to anything which might even remotely make me appear as the medium of, or interferer with, parliamentary action. I esteem Mrs. Hardinge, and I esteem you, Lady Cairo; but if the resignation now tendered to me went no further than at present, it might justly be surmised that I had permitted myself to be the means of strengthening what Mrs. Hardinge considered an insufficient parliamentary confidence. I therefore ask you not to give me a hasty answer, but to consult your friends and endeavour to form a strong Government."

No more could be said. Lady Cairo, with becoming reverence, signified her submission to the Emperor's wishes. She summoned her chief friends and colleagues, and had many earnest conferences with them separately and collectively. It was readily admitted that, if they formed a Government, there was a considerable number of members who, though not their supporters, would protect them in a fair trial. It was indeed certain that Mrs. Hardinge would be too generous to indulge in factious opposition, and that, if they avoided any notoriously controversial measure, she would herself help them to get through the session. But Lady Cairo was a large-minded statesman. She loved power, but, because she loved it, was averse to exercising it on sufferance. She could not but be sensible such would be her position, and that she would have to trust less to the strength of her own party than to the forbearance of her opponents. Besides, there was a point about which a great difference of opinion existed. She could not attempt to form a Government unless in combination with Lord Reginald, who moved the resolution. The animosity he had displayed to the Government made it probable, almost certain, that he would do what he could to aid her; it might even be expected that he would induce all or nearly all of his followers to come over to her; but again and again she asked herself the question would such an alliance be agreeable to her? Joint action during an animated debate was widely different from the continued intimacy of official comradeship. She liked Lord Reginald no better than other persons liked him. She had very clear perceptions, and was of a high and honourable nature. Lord Reginald inspired her with distrust. It was his misfortune to awaken that feeling in the minds of those persons with whom he came into contact. Her most trusted colleagues were generally of the same opinion, though several prominent members of the party thought it a mistake not to accept the opportunity and test its chances.

Her intimate friends expressed their opinion with diffidence. They would not accept the responsibility of dissuading her from taking office. They knew that it was a high position and one to which individually she would do justice, and they knew also that many contingencies might convert a Government weak at the outset into a strong one. But she could read between the lines, the more especially that she shared the distrust at which they hinted. Two of the colleagues she most valued went so far as to leave her to understand that they would not join her Government, though of course they would support it. They excused themselves on private grounds; but she was shrewd enough to see these were the ostensible, not the real, reasons. Lady Cairo was not one of those persons who habitually try to persuade themselves to what their inclinations lead. What she had said to the Emperor satisfied the most fastidious loyalty. She was perfectly free to take office. No one could question either her action or her motive. She need not fear the world's opinion if she consulted her own inclination, and nineteen out of twenty persons would have been satisfied. She was not; she still saw before her the necessity of acting with one colleague at least, Lord Reginald, who would be distasteful to her: and as a strong party statesman, she was not well disposed generally to the bulk of his followers, whose inclination led them to endeavour to hold the balance of power between contending parties. She determined on consulting her aged mother, now a confirmed invalid, but once a brilliant and powerful statesman, noted for her high sense of honour.

"My dear," said this helpless lady when she had heard all her daughter had to tell her, "no one but yourself can measure the strength or the justice of the distaste you feel for the alliance you must make if you accept the splendid responsibilities offered to you. But the distaste exists, and it is not likely to become less. I doubt if you are justified in disregarding it. Your time will come, my dear; and it will be a pleasure to you to think that you have not sought it at the expense of a personal sacrifice of doubts, that would not exist if all grounds for them were wanting. You must decide. I will go no further than to say this. I cannot persuade you to allow your inclination for office to overrule your disinclination to a powerful section of those who must share your responsibilities. It is sadly often the case that the instinct to sacrifice inclination is more reliable than the disposition to follow it."

Three days after their last interview the Emperor again received Lady Cairo.

"Your Majesty, I have to decline, with great respect and much gratitude for the confidence you reposed in me, the task of forming a Government with which you graciously charged me."

"Is this your deliberate decision? I am told that you would have no difficulty in carrying on the business of the session if Lord Reginald and his party supported you."

"That is a contingency, Sir, on which I could not count."

"How! He has not promised to support you?"

"I have not asked him. Our chance presence in the same division lobby did not appear to me a sufficient basis of agreement."

"Then," said the Emperor, "the mover of the resolution that has occasioned so much trouble has not been consulted?"

"It is so, your Majesty, as far as I am concerned. I did not understand that you made coalition with him a condition of my attempt to form a Government. I hope, Sir, you acquit me of having disregarded your wishes."

"I do, Lady Cairo. I made no conditions, nor was I entitled to do so. I left you quite free. Only it seemed to me you must act with the support of Lord Reginald and his following, and that therefore you would necessarily consult him."

"I would not say anything in disparagement of Lord Reginald; but may it not be that my party do not think there has been such habitual agreement with him as to warrant our assuming that a coalition would be for the public interest, to say nothing of our own comfort?"

"I see," muttered the Emperor in barely audible voice, "always the same distrust of this man, able and brave though he be." Then aloud, "Lady Cairo, what am I to do? Should I send for Lord Reginald and ask him to attempt to form a Government?"

"I implore your Majesty not to ask me for advice. Mrs. Hardinge is still in power. May I," she said in a tone of pathetic entreaty, "utter half a dozen words not officially, but confidentially?"

"Certainly you have my permission."

"Then, Sir, you will understand me when I say that personal opinions, confidence, trust, and liking may have so much to do with the matter that it will be graciously kind of your Majesty to allow me to state only this much in my place in the House: that, after considering the charge you entrusted to me, I felt compelled to refuse it, not believing that I could form a Government which would enjoy the confidence of a majority of the House."

"Let it be so," said the Emperor good-humouredly. "That may be your version. I must not put my troubles upon you."

"Your Majesty is most good, most kind. I can never be sufficiently grateful."

The Emperor had gained one more devoted admirer. Few who came into personal contact with him failed to be fascinated by his wonderful sympathy and grace. All human character appeared an open book to his discernment.

He sent for Mrs. Hardinge. "I fear," he said, "you will not be pleased at what I am about to say. Lady Cairo has declined to form a Government. I may have to refuse to accept your resignation, or rather to ask you to withdraw it. First, however, I wish your advice; but before I formally seek it tell me would it be distasteful to you to give it."

He paused to afford an opportunity to Mrs. Hardinge to speak, of which she did not avail herself.

"Lady Cairo," he continued, "did not communicate at all with the mover of the resolution, Lord Reginald. Will you be averse to my asking you to advise me on the subject?"

It will be observed that he did not ask for the advice. He well knew, if he did so, Mrs. Hardinge would be bound to declare that he had asked for advice, and whether she gave it or not, would still be unable to conceal that it was sought from her. The Emperor now only put his question on the footing of whether she was willing that he should seek her opinion. Mrs. Hardinge appreciated his consideration. It all came back to the point that the objection to Lord Reginald was of a personal nature, and as such it was in the last degree distasteful to every one to be mixed up with its consideration.

"Your Majesty," said Mrs. Hardinge, "has a claim to seek my advice on the subject; but there are reasons which make me very averse to giving it. If I can avoid doing so, you will make me very grateful."

The Emperor mused. "Whatever the special reasons may be, why should I force on so valuable a public servant the necessity of making a lifelong enemy of this unscrupulous man? To me his enmity matters little. I will myself decide the point. Lord Reginald did not carry his resolution, and Mrs. Hardinge need not have tendered her resignation. She did offer it; and, guided by constitutional rule, I sent for the leader of the Opposition. I did not take advice from Mrs. Hardinge as to whether I should send for Lord Reginald or Lady Cairo. I acted on my own responsibility, as in such cases I prefer doing. I am opposed to the principle of a retiring Minister selecting his or her successor. I had the right to suppose that Lady Cairo would consult Lord Reginald, though not to complain of her failing to do so. If I send for Lord Reginald, it must be of my own initiative There is no reason why I should consult Mrs. Hardinge now, seeing that I did not consult her at first. So much then is settled. Now I must myself decide if I will send for Lord Reginald. It will be distasteful to me to do so. I have no confidence in the man, and it would be a meaningless compliment, for he cannot form a Government. Why should I make a request I know cannot be complied with? Constitutional usage does not demand it; in fact, the precedent will be injurious. Because of a sudden accidental combination, the representative of a small party has no right to be elevated into the most important leader. Such a practice would encourage combinations injurious to party government. If I had intended to send for Lord Reginald, I ought to have summoned him before I sought Lady Cairo. I am quite satisfied that the course I pursued was constitutional and wise, and I should throw doubt upon it by sending for Lord Reginald now." These reflections were made in less time than it takes to write them down.

"Mrs. Hardinge," said the Emperor, "we now begin our official interview. Be kind enough to efface from your mind what has hitherto passed. I have to ask you to withdraw your resignation. Lady Cairo, the leader of the Opposition, has declined to act, on the ground that she cannot form a Government which will sufficiently possess the confidence of a majority of the House."

"It shall be as your Majesty wishes," said Mrs. Hardinge.

When the House met, Mrs. Hardinge, by agreement with Lady Cairo, merely stated that, after the division of last week, she had felt it her duty to tender the resignation of her Government to the Emperor.

Lady Cairo in very few words explained that the Emperor had sent for her and entrusted her with the formation of a Government, and that, after sufficient consideration, she resolved it was not desirable she should undertake the task, as she could not rely on a majority in the House and could not submit to lead it on sufferance.

Mrs. Hardinge again rose, and explained that, at the request of the Emperor, she had withdrawn her resignation. Loud cheers from all sides of the House followed the intimation.

Public feeling during the week had abundantly shown itself to be against a change of government upon what really amounted to a theoretical question, as the matter was not before the House upon which the resolution was nearly carried. It was argued that even if carried it would have been a most unsatisfactory reason for a change of government.

There was one member in the Chamber to whom all that had passed was gall and wormwood. Lord Reginald left the House last week a marked and distinguished man. For the first twenty-four hours he received from those persons throughout the Empire who made it their business to stand well with "the powers that be" congratulations of a most flattering description. To-day there was "none so poor to do him reverence."

The change was intolerable to a man of his proud and haughty disposition. The worst feature of it was that he could not single out any one specially for complaint. There was no disguising from himself what every one in the House knew, and what every one throughout the Empire soon would know: that the Emperor himself and the leaders of both the great parties did not think him worthy of consideration. As we have seen, there was no actual slight; that is to say, constitutional usages had been followed. But to his mind he had been slighted in a most marked and offensive fashion. Why was he not sent for at first? Why did not Lady Cairo consult him? Why was Mrs. Hardinge asked to withdraw her resignation without his assistance being sought—he, the mover of the resolution; he, the man who brought on the crisis about which miles of newspaper columns had since been written? He forgot that no one had asked him to take the action he did, that he had sought no advice on the subject, and that politicians who elect to act on their own account have no right to complain of the isolation they court. Scarcely any one spoke to him. A member near him, noticing his extreme pallor, asked him if he was unwell; but no one seemed to care about him or to remember that he had had anything to do with the crisis which, to the rejoicing of all sides, was over. "The newspapers," he thought, "will not forget." They had blamed him during the last week; now they would ridicule and laugh at him. He writhed at the reflection; and when he reached the quiet of his own home, he paced his large study as one demented. "I will be revenged," he muttered over and over again. "I will show them I am not so powerless a being; they shall all repent the insult they have put on me: and as for that girl, that image of snow—she has set Mrs. Hardinge against me. She shall grovel at my feet; she shall implore me to marry her."

CHAPTER SIX
BAFFLED REVENGE

Hilda's most confidential secretary was her sister, Maud Fitzherbert. She was some two or three years younger, a lovely, graceful girl, and possessed of scarcely less intellectual power than Hilda. She had perhaps less inclination for public life; but both the girls were learned in physical laws, in mathematics, in living languages, in everything, in short, to which they devoted their extraordinary mental powers. They adored each other, and Maud looked up to Hilda as to a divinity.

The latter was writing in her room. Maud came to her. "Lord Montreal is most anxious to see you for a few minutes."

Lord Montreal was a fine-looking, handsome young man of twenty-five years of age. He was a brave soldier, a genial companion, and a general favourite. He was the second son of the Duke of Ontario. He had known the Fitzherberts since they were children, and the families were intimate. Hilda greeted him cordially.

"I will not detain you," he said; "but I have had important information confided to me in strict secrecy. I cannot tell you who was my informant, and you must not use my name. Will you accept the conditions?"

"I must, I suppose, if you insist on them."

"I must insist on them. My information much concerns my commanding officer, Lord Reginald Paramatta, with whom I am only on formal terms; and therefore my name must not appear. As to my informant, his condition was absolute secrecy as to his name. The gist of what he told me was that Lord Reginald is organising a secret society, with objects certainly not loyal to the Emperor, if indeed they are not treasonable. I gathered that there is something more contemplated than theoretical utterances, and that action of a most disastrous character may follow if steps to arrest it be not at once taken. The information was imparted to me in order that I might bring it to you. I feel that I have been placed in a false position by being made the recipient without proof of statements so damaging to my superior officer; and though I fear that I may be placing a trouble upon you, I have on reflection not thought myself warranted in withholding the statement, as it was made to me with the object of its reaching you. Never again will I give assurances about statements the nature of which I do not know."

Miss Fitzherbert seemed to be destined to annoyance through Lord Reginald. She was now called to set the detective power in force against a man who a few days since so eagerly sought her hand.

"I certainly wish," she said, "that you will not give promises which will land you into bringing me information of this kind."

"You surely," said Montreal, "do not care for Lord Reginald?"

"I may not and do not care for him, but it is not agreeable to be asked to search out criminal designs on the part of a person with whom one is acquainted."

"Forgive me, Hilda," said Montreal. "It was thoughtless of me not to think that I might give you pain. But, you see, I regard you as indifferent to everything but public affairs. Now Maud is different;" and he looked at the fair girl who still remained in the room, with eyes in which warm affection was plainly visible.

"Maud has a heart, of course; but I have not," said Hilda, with more irritation than she was accustomed to display.

The poor girl had suffered much annoyance during the last few days, and the climax was attained that afternoon when she read in a paper purposely sent to her a strangely inverted account of her relations with Lord Reginald. According to this journal, Mrs. Hardinge had treated Lord Reginald cruelly because she could not induce him to respond to the affection which her protegée Hilda Fitzherbert felt for the great soldier. In spite of, or perhaps on account of, her vast mental power, Hilda was possessed of a singularly sensitive character. She gave herself up to public affairs in the full conviction that women could do so without sacrificing in the smallest degree their self-respect. She had a high conception of the purity and holiness of woman's individual existence, and it seemed to her a sacrilege to make the public life of a woman the excuse for dragging before the eyes of the world anything that affected her private feelings. She was intensely annoyed at this paragraph. In the end, we may say in anticipation, Lord Reginald did not come out of it with advantage. The next issue of the paper contained the following passage: "In reference to what appeared in our columns last week about Miss Fitzherbert, we must apologise to that lady. We are informed by Mrs. Hardinge that the facts were absolutely inverted. It is not Lord Reginald who is unwilling. It is Lord Reginald who has received a decidedly negative reply."

Hilda was not one to readily inflict her own annoyances on others. She recovered herself in a moment as she saw the pained look on Maud's face. "Forgive me, Montreal; forgive me, Maud," she said. "I have much to disturb me. I did not mean to be unkind. Of course, Montreal, I should have liked your aid in this matter; but as you cannot give it, I must see what I can do without it. Good-bye, Montreal. Maud dear, send at once to Colonel Laurient, and ask him if he will do me the kindness to come to see me at once."

Colonel Laurient was a very remarkable man. He was on his mother's side of an ancient Jewish family, possessing innumerable branches all over the world. At various times members of the family had distinguished themselves both in public life and in scientific, commercial, and financial pursuits. Colonel Laurient was the second son of one of the principal partners in the De Childrosse group, the largest and most wealthy financial house in the world. When his education was completed, he decided not to enter into the business, as his father gave him the option of doing. He had inherited an enormous fortune from his aunt, the most celebrated scientific chemist and inventor of her day. She had left him all the law permitted her to leave to one relation. He entered the army, and also obtained a seat in Parliament. As a soldier he gained a reputation for extreme skill and discretion in the guerilla warfare that sometimes was forced on the authorities in the British Asiatic possessions. On one occasion by diplomatic action he changed a powerful foe on the frontier of the Indian possessions to a devoted friend, his knowledge of languages and Asiatic lore standing him in good stead. This action brought him to the notice of the Emperor, who soon attached him to his personal service, and, it was said, put more faith in his opinions than in those of any person living. He was rather the personal friend than the servant of the Emperor.

Some twenty years before the date of our story it was found necessary to give to the then Sovereign a private service of able and devoted men. It was the habit of the Emperor of United Britain to travel about the whole of his vast dominions. The means of travelling were greatly enlarged, and what would at one time have been considered a long and fatiguing expedition ceased to possess any difficulty or inconvenience. A journey from London to Melbourne was looked upon with as much indifference as one from London to the Continent used to be. It became apparent that either the freedom of the Emperor to roam about at pleasure must be much curtailed, or that he must be able to travel without encroaching on the ordinary public duty of his constitutional advisers. Thus a species of personal bodyguard grew up, with the members of which, according as his temperament dictated, the Sovereign became on more or less intimate personal terms. The officers holding this coveted position had no official status. If there was any payment, the Emperor made it. There was no absolute knowledge of the existence of the force, if such it could be called, or of who composed it. That the Sovereign had intimate followers was of course known, and it was occasionally surmised that they held recognised and defined positions. But it was merely surmise, after all; and not half a dozen people outside of Cabinet rank could have positively named the friends of the Emperor who were members of the bodyguard.

Colonel Laurient retired from Parliament, where he had rather distinguished himself in the treatment of questions requiring large geographical and historical knowledge; and it was commonly supposed, he wished to give more attention to his military duties. In reality he became chief of the Emperor's bodyguard, and, it might be said, was the eyes and ears of the Sovereign. With consummate ability he organised a secret intelligence department, and from one end of the dominions to the other he became aware of everything that was passing. Not infrequently the Emperor amazed Cabinet Ministers with the extent of his knowledge of immediate events. Colonel Laurient never admitted that he held any official position, and literally he did not hold any such position. He received no pay, and his duties were not defined. He loved the Emperor personally for himself, and the Emperor returned the feeling. Really the most correct designation to give to his position was to term him the Emperor's most devoted friend and to consider that in virtue thereof the members of the bodyguard regarded him as their head, because he stood to them in the place of the Emperor himself.

Hilda Fitzherbert knew something, and conjectured more, as to his position. She was frequently brought into communication with him, and after she heard Lord Montreal's story she instantly determined to consult him. He came quickly on her invitation. He was always pleased to meet her.

Colonel Laurient was a tall, slender man, apparently of about thirty-five years of age. His complexion was very dark; and his silky, curly hair was almost of raven blackness. His features were small and regular, and of that sad but intellectual type common to some of the pure-bred Asiatic races. You would deem him a man who knew how to "suffer and be strong;" you would equally deem him one whom no difficulty could frighten, no obstacle baffle. You would expect to see his face light up to enjoyment not because of the prospect of ordinary pleasure, but because of affairs of exceeding gravity which called for treatment by a strong hand and subtle brain. His manner was pleasing and deferential; and he had a voice of rare harmony, over which he possessed complete control. Cordial greetings passed between him and Miss Fitzherbert. There was no affectation of apology being necessary for sending for him or of pleasure on his part at the summons. Briefly she told him of Lord Montreal's communication. He listened attentively, then carelessly remarked, "Lord Reginald's conduct has been very peculiar lately."

Do what she would, the girl could not help giving a slight start at this remark, made as it was with intention. Colonel Laurient at once perceived that there was more to be told than he already was aware of. He knew a great deal that had passed with Lord Reginald, and guessed more; and gradually, with an apparently careless manner, he managed to elicit so much from Hilda that she thought it wiser to tell him precisely all that had occurred, especially the account of her last interview with Lord Reginald and his subsequent letter resigning his appointment.

"Confidences with me," he said, "are entirely safe. Now I understand his motives, you and I start on fair terms, which we could not do whilst you knew more than I did."

Then they discussed what had better be done. "It may be," Colonel Laurient said, "that there is nothing in it. There is a possibility that it is a pure invention, and it is even possible that Lord Reginald may have himself caused the invention to reach you for the purpose of giving you annoyance. Montreal's informant may have been instigated by Lord Reginald. Then there is the possibility—we may say probability—that the purposes of the society do not comprise a larger amount of disaffection or dissatisfaction than the law permits. And, lastly, there is let us say the barest possibility that Lord Reginald, enraged to madness, may have determined on some really treasonable action. You know in old days it was said, 'Hell has no fury like a woman scorned;' but in our time we would not give the precedence for wounded vanity to woman; man is not wanting in the same susceptibility, and Lord Reginald has passed through a whole series of humiliating experiences. I knew some of them before I saw you this afternoon. You have filled up the list with a bitter from which he doubtless suffers more than from all the rest."

Miss Fitzherbert appeared to care little for this strain of conjecture. "What is the use of it?" she said. "However infinitesimal the risk of treasonable designs, the Emperor must not be allowed to run it."

"You are right," said Colonel Laurient. "I do not, as you know, appear in these matters; but I have means of obtaining information of secret things. Within twenty-four hours I will see you again and let you know what it all means. We can then decide the course to take."

Some explanation is necessary to enable Colonel Laurient's remarks about the limits of disaffection to be understood. Freedom of thought and expression was amongst the cardinal liberties of the subject most prized. In order to recognise its value, it was long since determined that a line should be drawn beyond which the liberty should not extend. It was argued that nothing could be more cruel than to play with disaffection of a dangerous nature. Not only was it the means of increasing the disaffection, but of gradually drawing eminent people into compromising positions. The line then was drawn at this point:—upon any subject that did not affect the fundamental principles of the Constitution change might be permissible, but any advocacy or even suggestion of destroying those fundamental principles was regarded as treasonable. The Constitution was so framed as to indicate within itself the principles which were susceptible of modification or change, such, for example, as the conditions of the franchise and the modes of conducting elections. But there were three fundamental points concerning which no change was allowable, and these were—first, that the Empire should continue an empire; secondly, that the sovereignty should remain in the present reigning family; and thirdly, that the union of the different parts of the dominion was irrevocable and indissoluble. It will be remembered that a great aversion had been expressed by the upholders of the Constitution to the proposal to change the law of succession within the imperial family. It could not be said to touch on the second fundamental principle, as it did not involve a change of dynasty; yet many thought it too nearly approached one of the sacred, unchangeable principles.

As regards the fundamental principles, no discussion was permissible. To question even the wisdom of continuing the Empire, of preserving the succession in the imperial family, or of permitting a separation of any of the dominions was held to be rank treason; and no mercy was shown to an offender. Outside of these points changes could be made, and organisations to promote changes were legitimate, however freely they indulged in plain speech. The conduct of the Emperor himself was legitimately a subject of comment, especially on any point in which he appeared to fail in respect to the Constitution he had sworn to uphold. It need scarcely be said that the Constitution was no longer an ill-defined and unwritten one. Such a Constitution worked well enough as long as the different parts of the Empire were united only during pleasure. When the union became irrevocable, it was a natural necessity that the conditions of union should be defined.

It may be convenient here to state some of the broad features of the governing and social system. It has already been said that, without approaching to communism, it had long since been decided that every human being was entitled to a share in the good things of the world, and that destitution was abhorrent. It was also recognised that the happiest condition of humanity was a reasonable amount of work and labour. For that very reason, it was decided not to make the labour distasteful by imposing it as a necessity. The love of work, not its necessity, was the feeling it was desirable to implant. Manual work carried with it no degradation, and there was little work to be done which did not require intelligence. Mere brute force was superseded by the remarkable contrivances for affording power and saving labour which were brought even to the humblest homes. The waves, tides, and winds stored up power which was convertible into electricity or compressed air; and either of these aids to labour-saving could be carried from house to house as easily as water. If men and women wished to be idle and State pensioners, it was open to them to follow their inclination; but they had to wear uniforms, and they were regarded as inferior by the healthy body politic. The aged, infirm, and helpless might enjoy State aid without being subjected to such a humiliation or to any disability. The starting-point was that, if a person was not sufficiently criminal to be the inmate of a prison, he should not be relegated to a brutal existence. It was at first argued that such a system would encourage inaction and idleness; the State would be deluged with pensioners. But subtler counsels prevailed. Far-seeing men and women argued that the condition of the world was becoming one of contracted human labour; and if the viciously inclined refused to work, there would be more left to those who had the ambition to be industrious. "But," was the rejoinder, "you are stifling ambition by making the lowest round of the ladder so comfortable and luxurious." To this was replied, "Your argument is superficial. Survey mankind; and you will see that, however lowly its lowest position, there is a ceaseless, persistent effort to rise on the part of nearly every well-disposed person, from the lowliest to the most exalted." Ambition, it was urged, was natural to man, but it was least active amongst the poverty-crushed classes. Mankind as a whole might be described as myriads of units striving to ascend a mountain. The number of those contented to rest on the plateaus to which they had climbed was infinitesimal compared with the whole. It would be as difficult to select them as it would be to pick out a lazy bee from a whole hive. Whether you started at the lowest class, with individuals always on the point of starvation, with families herded together with less decency than beasts of the fields, and with thousands of human beings who from cradle to grave knew not what happiness meant, or made the start from a higher elevation, upon which destitution was impossible, there would still continue the climbing of myriads to greater heights and the resting on plateaus of infinitesimally few; indeed, as poverty tended to crush ambition, there would be a larger range of aspiration accompanying an improvement in the condition of the lowliest class. And so it proved.

    The system of government and taxation followed the theory of the range above destitution. Taxes were exacted in proportion to the ability to pay them. The payments for the many services the Post Office rendered were not regarded as taxation. The customs duties were looked upon as payments made in proportion to the desires of the people to use dutiable goods. If high customs duties meant high prices, they also meant high wages.

The Empire, following the practice of other countries, was utterly averse to giving employment to the peoples of foreign nations. Every separate local dominion within the Empire was at liberty to impose by its legislature what duties it pleased as between itself and other parts of the Empire, but it was imperatively required to collect three times the same duties on commodities from foreign countries. This was of course meant to be prohibitive of foreign importations, and was practicable because the countries within the Empire could supply every commodity in the world. It was argued that to encourage foreign importations merely meant to pit cheap labour against the price for labour within the Empire. Besides the customs duties, the revenue was almost entirely made up of income tax and succession duties. Stamp duties, as obstacles to business, were considered an evidence of the ignorance of the past. The first five hundred pounds a year of income was free; but beyond that amount the State appropriated one clear fourth of all incomes. Similarly one quarter of the value of all successions, real or personal, in excess of ten thousand pounds, was payable to the State; and disposition by gifts before death came within the succession values. A man or woman was compelled to leave half his or her property, after payment of succession duty, in defined proportion to the children and wife or husband, as the case might be, or failing these to near relations; the other half he or she might dispose of at pleasure. It was argued that to a certain extent the amasser of wealth had only a life interest in it, and that it was not for the happiness of the successors of deceased people to come into such wealth that the ambition to work and labour would be wanting. The system did not discourage the amassment of wealth; on the contrary, larger fortunes were made than in former times. Higher prices gave to fortunes of course a comparatively less purchasing power; but taking the higher prices into consideration, the accumulation of wealth became a more honourable ambition and a pleasanter task when it ceased to be purchased at the expense of the comfort of the working classes.

The customs duties belonged to the separate Governments that collected them, and the quarter-income tax and succession duties were equally divided between the Imperial and the Dominion Governments. Thus the friction between them was minimised. The Imperial Government and the Dominion Governments both enjoyed during most years far more revenue than they required, and so large a reserve fund was accumulated that no inconvenience was felt in years of depression. Part of the surplus revenues arising from the reserve fund was employed in large educational and benevolent works and undertakings. The result of the system was that pecuniary suffering in all directions was at an end; but the ambition to acquire wealth, with its concomitant powers, was in no degree abated.

Of course there was not universal content—such a condition would be impossible—but the controversies were, as a rule, less bitter than the former ones which prevailed between different classes. The man-and-woman struggle was one of the large points of constant difference, and again there was much difference of opinion as to whether the quarter-income and succession duties might be reduced to a fifth. It was argued, on the one hand, that the reserve funds were becoming too large, and that the present generation was working too much for its successors. On the other hand, it was urged that the present generation in working for its successors was merely perpetuating the gift which it had inherited, and that by preserving the reserve funds great strength was given to contend against any reverses that the future might have in store. Another point of controversy was the strength of the naval and military forces. A comparatively small school of public men argued that the cost and strength might be materially reduced without risk or danger, but the general feeling was not with them.

This has been a long digression, but it was necessary to the comprehension of our story. It will easily be understood from what has been said that, supposing the alleged action of Lord Reginald was dictated by revenge, it was difficult to see, unless he resorted to treasonable efforts, what satisfaction he could derive from any agitation.

Colonel Laurient the next afternoon fulfilled his promise of waiting on Hilda. She had suffered great anxiety during the interval—the anxiety natural to ill-defined fears and doubts. He looked careworn, and his manner was more serious than on the previous day. "I have found out all about it," he said; "and I am sorry there is more cause for anxiety than we thought yesterday. It is undoubtedly true that Lord Reginald is organising some combination; and although the proof is wanting, there is much reason to fear that his objects are not of a legitimate nature. It is impossible to believe, he would take the trouble which he is assuming, to deal only with questions to which he has never shown an inclination. I am persuaded that behind the cloak of his ostensible objects lies ambition or revenge, or perhaps both, pointing to extreme and highly dangerous action."

"You are probably right," said Miss Fitzherbert, who knew from the manner of the Emperor's favourite that he was much disturbed by what he had heard. "But even so, what obstacle lies in the way of putting an end to the projected action, whatever its nature?"

"There is a great obstacle," promptly replied the Colonel; "and that is the doubt as to what the nature of the project is. Lord Reginald is a clever man; and notwithstanding his late failure, he has plenty of friends and admirers, especially among his own sex, and amongst soldiers, both volunteers and regulars. I have ascertained enough to show me that the leaders intend to keep within ostensibly legitimate limits until the time comes to unfold their full design to their followers, and that then they will trust to the comradeship of the latter and to their fears of being already compromised."

Hilda was quick of apprehension. "I see they will organise to complain perhaps of the nature of the taxation, and only expose their treasonable objects at a later time."

Colonel Laurient gazed on her with admiration. "How readily you comprehend!" he said. "I believe you alone can grapple with the situation."

The girl flushed, and then grew pale. She did not know what physical fear meant. Probably, if her feelings were analysed, it would have been found that the ruling sensation she experienced was an almost delirious pleasure at the idea that she could do a signal service to the Emperor.

She replied, however, with singular self-repression. "I am not quick enough," she said, with a slight smile, "to understand how I can be of any use."

"The organisation has been proceeding some time, although I fancy Lord Reginald has only lately joined and accepted the leadership. It numbers thousands who believe themselves banded together only to take strong measures to reduce taxation, on the ground that the reserve funds have become amply large enough to permit such reduction. But the leaders have other views; and I have ascertained that they propose to hold a meeting three days hence, at which it is possible—nay, I think, probable—there will be an unreserved disclosure."

"Why not," said Miss Fitzherbert, "arrest them in the midst of their machinations?"

"There lies the difficulty," responded the Colonel. "It entirely depends on the nature of the disclosures whether the Government authorities are entitled to take any action. If the disclosures fall short of being treasonable, it would be held that there was interference of a most unpardonable character with freedom of speech and thought; and the last of it would never be heard. Dear Miss Fitzherbert," he said caressingly, "we want some one at the meeting with a judgment so evenly balanced and accurate that she will be able on the instant to decide if the treasonable intentions are sufficiently expressed or if it would be safer not to interfere. I know no one so quick and at the same time so logical in her judgment as you. In vain have I thought of any one else whom it would be nearly so safe to employ."

"But how could it be managed?" inquired Hilda. "Every one knows my appearance. My presence would be immediately detected."

"Pray listen to me," said the Colonel, delighted at having met with no strenuous opposition. He had feared, he would have great difficulty in persuading Miss Fitzherbert to take the part he intended for her; and, to his surprise, she seemed inclined to meet him half-way. Then he explained that the meeting was to be held in the Parliamentary Hall, a celebrated place of meeting. It had been constructed with the express purpose of making it impossible that any one not inside the Hall could hear what was taking place. The edifice was an enormous one of stone. Inside this building, about fifteen feet from the walls all round, and twenty feet from the roof, was a second erection, composed entirely of glass. So that as long as the external building was better lighted than the interior one the presence of a human being could be detected outside the walls or on the roof of the hall of meeting. The chamber was artificially cooled, as indeed were most of the houses in the cities of Australia, excepting during the winter months.

"This is the place of all others," said Miss Fitzherbert, "where it would be difficult for an unauthorised person to be present."

"Not so," replied Colonel Laurient. "The inside hall is to be in darkness, and the exterior dimly lighted. Only the vague outlines of each person's form will be revealed; and every one is to come cloaked, and with a large overshadowing hat. From what I can gather, the revelation is to be gradual and only to be completed if it should seem to be approved during its progress. I expect Lord Reginald will be the last to give in his adhesion, so that it might be said he was deceived as to the purpose of the meeting if he should see fit to withdraw from the declaration of its real object. Mind, you are to be sole judge as to whether the meeting transgresses the line which divides the legitimate from the treasonable."

"Why not act yourself?" said Hilda.

"If you think for a moment," he replied, "you will understand my influence is maintained only so long as it is hidden. If I appeared to act, it would cease altogether. Unfortunately I must often let others do what I would gladly do myself. Believe me, it is painful to me to put tasks on you of any kind, much less a task of so grave a nature. By heavens!" he exclaimed, carried away for a moment, "there is a reason known to me only why I might well dread for myself the great service you will do the Emperor."

He was recalled to himself by the amazed look of the girl. "Forgive me," he ejaculated. "I did not mean anything. But there is no danger to you; of that be assured."

"Colonel Laurient," said Hilda gravely, "you ought to know me well enough not to suppose I am guided by fear."

"I do know it," he answered, "otherwise I should not have asked you to undertake the great task I have set before you. No woman whose mind was disturbed by alarm could do justice to it."

He told her that in some way, he did not mention how, he had control over the manager of the building, who had let it under a false impression, and asked her if she was aware of the comparatively late discovery of how to produce artificial magnetism.

"I ought to be," she replied, with a smile, "for I am credited with having been the first to discover the principle of the remote branch of muscular magnetising electricity on which it depends."

"I had forgotten," he said, with an answering smile. "One may be forgiven for forgetting for a moment the wide nature of your investigations and discoveries."

Then he explained to her that the principle could be put into practice with perfect certainty and safety, and that he would take care everything was properly arranged. He would see her again and tell her the pass-words, the part of the Hall she was to occupy, and the mode she was to adopt to summon assistance.

The evening of the meeting came, and for half an hour there were numerous arrivals at the many doors of the huge building. Each person had separately to interchange the pass-words at both the outer and inner doors. At length about twelve hundred people were assembled. The lights outside the glass hall were comparatively feeble. The powerful electric lamps were not turned on. The inner hall was unlighted, and received only a dull reflection from the outer lights. Some surprise was expressed by the usual frequenters of the Hall at the appearance inside the glass wall of a wooden dais, sufficiently large to hold three or four people, and with shallow steps on one side leading up to it. Inquiry was made as to its object. The doorkeeper, suitably instructed, replied carelessly it was thought, they might require a stage from which the speakers could address the audience. The present meeting certainly did not want it. The speakers had no desire to individually bring themselves into notice. Hilda, muffled up as were the rest, quietly took a seat close to the steps of the dais. No president was appointed; no one appeared to have any control; yet as the meeting proceeded it was evident that its tactics had been carefully thought out, and that most, if not all, of the speakers were fulfilling the parts allotted to them.

First a tall, elderly man rose, and with considerable force and fluency enlarged upon the evils of the present large taxation. He went into figures, and his speech ought to have been effective, only no one seemed to take any interest in it. Then there loomed on the meeting the person apparently of a middle-aged woman. The cloaks and hats carefully mystified the identities of the sexes and individual peculiarities. This speaker went a little further. She explained that maintaining the Empire as a whole entailed the sacrifice of regulating the taxation so as to suit the least wealthy portions. She carefully guarded herself from being more than explanatory. The comparative poverty of England and the exactions of the self-indulgent Londoners, she said, necessitated a scale of taxation that hardy and rich Australia, New Zealand, and Canada did not require. Then a historically disposed young woman rose and dwelt upon the time when England thought a great deal more of herself than of the Colonies and to curry favour with foreign countries placed them on the same footing as her own dominions. Little by little various speakers progressed, testing at every step the feelings of the audience, until at last one went so far as to ask the question whether the time would ever come when

Australia would be found to be quite large and powerful enough to constitute an empire of itself. "Mind," said he, "I do not say the time will come." Then an apparently excited Australian arose. She would not, she said, say a word in favour of such an empire; but she, an Australian bred and born, and with a long line of Australian ancestors, was not going to listen to any doubts being thrown on Australia or Australians. The country and the people, she declared, amidst murmuring signs of assent, were fit for any destiny to which they might be called. Then a logical speaker rose and asked why were they forbidden to discuss the question as to whether it was desirable to retain the present limits of the Empire or to divide it. He would not state what his opinion was, but he would say this: that he could not properly estimate the arguments in favour of preserving the integrity of the Empire unless he was at liberty to hear the arguments and answer them of those who held an opposite opinion. When this speaker sat down, there was a momentary pause. It seemed as if there was a short consultation between those who were guiding the progress of the meeting. Whether or not this was the case, some determination appeared to be arrived at; and a short, portly man arose and said he did not care for anybody or anything. He would answer the question to which they had at length attained by saying that in his opinion the present empire was too large, that Australia ought to be formed into a separate empire, and that she would be quite strong enough to take care of herself.

The low murmur of fear with which this bold announcement was heard soon developed into loud cheers, especially from that part of the Hall where the controlling influence seemed to be held. Then all restraint was cast aside; and speaker after speaker affirmed, in all varieties of eloquence, that Australia must be an empire. Some discussed whether New Zealand should be included, but the general opinion appeared to be that she should be left to her own decision in the matter. Then the climax was approached. A speaker rose and said there appeared to be no doubt in the mind of the meeting as to the Empire of Australia; he hoped there was no doubt that Lord Reginald Paramatta should be the first Emperor. The meeting seemed to be getting beyond the control of its leaders. It did not appear to have been part of their programme to put forward Lord Reginald's name at this stage. It was an awkward fix, for no person by name was supposed to be present, so that he could neither disclaim the honour nor express his thanks for it. One of the controllers, a grave, tall woman, long past middle age, dealt with this difficulty. They must not, she said, go too far at first; it was for them now to say whether Australia should be an empire. She loved to hear the enthusiasm with which Lord Reginald Paramatta's name was received. Australia boasted no greater or more distinguished family than the Paramattas; and as for Lord Reginald, every one knew that a braver and better soldier did not live. Still they must decide on the Empire before the Emperor, and each person present must answer the question was he or she favourable to Australia being constructed into a separate empire? They could not in this light distinguish hands held up. Each person must rise and throw off his or her cloak and hat and utter the words, "I declare that I am favourable to Australia being constituted an empire." Then, evidently with the intention of making the controllers and Lord Reginald speak last, she asked the occupant of the seat to the extreme left of the part of the Hall most distant from her to be the first to declare. Probably he and a few others had been placed there for that purpose. At any rate, he rose without hesitation, threw off his cloak, removed his hat, and said, "I declare myself in favour of Australia being constituted an empire." Person after person from left to right and from right to left of each line of chairs followed the same action and uttered the same words, and throughout the Hall there was a general removal of cloaks and hats. At length it came to Hilda Fitzherbert's turn. Without a moment's hesitation, the brave girl rose, dropped her cloak and hat, and in a voice distinctly heard from end to end of the Hall said, "I declare I am not in favour of Australia being constituted an empire."

For a second there was a pause of consternation. Then arose a Babel of sounds: "Spy!" "Traitor!" "It is Hilda Fitzherbert;" "She must not leave the Hall alive;" "We have been betrayed." Shrieks and sobs were amongst the cries to be distinguished. Then there arose a mighty roar of "She must die," and a movement towards her. It was stilled for a moment. Lord Reginald rose, and, with a voice heard above all the rest, he thundered forth, "She shall not die. She shall live on one condition. Leave her to me;" and he strode towards her.

In one second the girl, like a fawn, sprang up the steps of the dais, and touched a button concealed in the wall, and then a second button. Words are insufficient to describe the effect.

The first button was connected with wires that ran through the flooring and communicated to every being in the Hall excepting to Hilda, on the insulated dais, a shock of magnetic electricity, the effect of which was to throw them into instantaneous motionless rigidity. No limb or muscle could be moved; as the shock found them they remained. And the pressure of the second button left no doubt of the fact, for it turned on the electric current to all the lamps inside and outside of the Hall, until the chamber became a blaze of dazzling light. There was no longer disguise of face or person, and every visage was at its worst. Fear, terror, cruelty, or revenge was the mastering expression on nearly every countenance. Some faces showed that the owners had been entrapped and betrayed into a situation they had not sought. But these were few, and could be easily read. On the majority of the countenances there was branded a mixture of greed, thwarted ambition, personal malignity, and cruelty horrible to observe. The pose of the persons lent a ludicrous aspect to the scene. Lord Reginald, for instance, had one foot in front of the other in the progress he was making towards Hilda. His body was bent forward. His face wore an expression of triumphant revenge and brutal love terrible to look at. Evidently he had thought there "was joy at last for my love and my revenge." Hilda shuddered as she glanced down upon the sardonic faces beneath her, and touched a third button. An answering clarionet at once struck out the signal to advance, and the measured tread of troops in all directions was heard. The poor wretches in the Hall preserved consciousness of what was passing around, though they could not exercise their muscular powers and felt no bodily pain. An officer at the door close to the dais saluted Miss Fitzherbert. "Be careful," she said, "to put your foot at once on the dais and come up to me." He approached her. "Have you your orders?" she asked.

"My orders," he said, "are to come from you. We have photographers at hand."

"Have a photograph," she instructed him, "taken of the whole scene, then of separate groups, and lastly of each individual. Have it done quickly," she added, "for the poor wretches suffer mental, if not physical, pain. Then every one may go free excepting the occupants of the three top rows. The police should see that these do not leave Melbourne."

She bowed to the officer, and sprang down the steps and out of the Hall. At the outer door a tall form met her. She did not require to look—she was blinded by the light within—to be convinced that it was Colonel Laurient who received her and placed her in a carriage. She was overcome. The terrible scene she had passed through had been too much for her. She did not faint; she appeared to be in a state of numbed inertness, as if she had lost all mental and physical power. Colonel Laurient almost carried her into the house, and, with a face of deathly pallor, consigned her to the care of her sister. Maud had been partly prepared to expect that Hilda would be strongly agitated by some painful scene, and she was less struck by her momentary helplessness than by the agonised agitation of that usually self-commanding being Colonel Laurient. Probably no one had ever seen him like this before. It may be that he felt concern not only for Hilda herself, but for the part he had played in placing her in so agitating a position.

CHAPTER SEVEN
HEROINE WORSHIP

It was nearly twelve o'clock before Hilda roused herself from a long and dreamless slumber, consequent upon the fatigue and excitement of the previous evening. She still felt somewhat exhausted, but no physician could have administered a remedy so efficacious as the one she found ready to hand. On the table beside her was a small packet sealed with the imperial arms. She removed the covering; and opening the case beneath, a beautifully painted portrait of the Emperor on an ivory medallion met her enraptured gaze. The portrait was set round with magnificent diamonds. But she scarcely noticed them; it was the painting itself that charmed her. The Emperor looked just as he appeared when he said to her, "Tell me now as woman to man, not as subject to emperor." There was the same winning smile, the same caressing yet commanding look. She involuntarily raised the medallion to her lips, and then blushed rosy red over face and shoulders. She turned the medallion, and on the back she found these words engraved: "Albert Edward to Hilda, in testimony of his admiration and gratitude." He must have had these words engraved during the night.

The maid entered. "Miss Fitzherbert," she said, "during the last two hours there have been hundreds of cards left for you. There is quite a continuous line of carriages coming to the door, and there have been bundles of telegrams. Miss Maud is opening them."

Hilda realised the meaning of the line—

"Do good by stealth, and blush to find it fame."

Then the maid told her Mrs. Hardinge was most anxious to see her and was waiting. She would not allow her to be awakened. Hilda said she would have her bath and see Mrs. Hardinge in the little boudoir adjoining her dressing-room in a few minutes.

Quite recovered from her last night's agitation, Hilda looked her best in a charmingly fashioned dressing-gown as she entered the room where Mrs. Hardinge was waiting to receive her.

"My dear, dear girl," said that lady as she embraced her, "I am delighted. You are well again? I need not ask. Your looks proclaim it. You are the heroine of the hour. The Emperor learnt everything last night, and the papers all over the world are full of it to-day. Maud says the telegrams are from every part of the globe, not only within our own empire, but from Europe, and the United States, and South America. You are a brave girl."

"Pray do not say so, Mrs. Hardinge. I only did my duty—what any one in my place would have done. Tell me all that has happened."

Mrs. Hardinge, nothing reluctant, replied with animated looks and gestures. "Laurient has told me everything. You instructed the officer, it seems, to keep a watch over only the occupants of the three further rows. Lord Reginald had left those, and was approaching you. The officer, following your words literally, allowed him to leave unwatched. Some sixty only of the people were placed under espionage. Nearly every one of the rest who were present is supposed to have left Melbourne, including Lord Reginald. We sent to his house to arrest him, but he had departed in one of his fastest long-distance air-cruisers. It is supposed that he has gone to Europe, or to America, or to one of his remote estates in the interior of this continent. I am not sure that the Emperor was displeased at his departure. When the intelligence reached him, he said to me, 'That will save Miss Fitzherbert from appearing in public to give evidence. As for the rest, it does not matter. They have been fooled to serve that man's ends.' So now they are free. But their names are known; indeed, their ridiculous appearance is immortalised. A likeness was taken of every one, but the tout ensemble is superbly grotesque. It is well so few people know the secret of artificial magnetism."

Hilda showed Mrs. Hardinge the Emperor's magnificent present, and asked what was she to do. Should she write a letter of thanks?

"Do so," said the shrewd woman of the world. "Who knows that he will not value the acknowledgment as you value the gift?"

Again Hilda's face was suffused in red. "I must go away," she said to herself, "until I can better command myself." Then she begged Mrs. Hardinge not to mention about the Emperor's gift. "I shall only tell Maud of it. I felt it was right to tell you."

"Of course it was," said Mrs. Hardinge; "but it may be well not to mention it further. There are thousands of persons who honour and admire you; but there are thousands also who already envy you, and who will not envy you the less because of this great deed."

Then she told Hilda that the Emperor wished to do her public honour by making her a countess in her own right. Hilda shrank from the distinction. "It will lose me my seat in Parliament," she said.

"No. You will only have to stand for re-election, and no one will oppose you."

"But," said the girl, "I am not rich enough."

"If report is correct, you soon will be. The river-works in New Zealand are nearly finished; they will make you, it is said, a millionaire."

"I had forgotten them for the moment, but it is not safe to count on their success until the test is actually made. This reminds me that they will be finished next week; and my friends in New Zealand think that my sister and I ought to be present, if only in honour of our dear grandfather, who left us the interest we hold in the river. Can you spare me for ten days?"

"Of course I can, Hilda dear. The change will do you good. Laurient is going. He is said to have an interest in the works. And Montreal is going also. He too had an interest, but I think he parted with it."

They discussed whether Hilda should go to the fête that was to be held on Monday to celebrate the centenary of the completion of the irrigation of the Malee Scrub Plains.

These plains were once about as desolate and unromantic a locality as could be found; but a Canadian firm, Messrs. Chaffey Brothers, had undertaken to turn the wilderness into a garden by irrigation, and they had entirely succeeded. An enormous population now inhabited the redeemed lands, and a fête was to be held in commemoration of the century that had elapsed since the great work was completed. The Emperor himself had agreed to be there. Hilda begged to be excused. Her nerves were shaken. She would dread the many congratulations she would receive and the requests to repeat over and over again the particulars of the scene which inspired her now with only horror and repulsion.

"You must not show yourself to-day," Mrs. Hardinge said; "and I will cry you off to-morrow on the ground of illness. Next day go to New Zealand, and by the time you return you will be yourself again."

"You may say too I am abundantly occupied," said Hilda archly as Maud entered the room with an enormous package of open telegrams in her hands. "Dear Hilda, you do look well to-day. I am so pleased," said the delighted girl as she flung down the telegrams and embraced her sister. There was something singularly pathetic in the love of these two girls. Mrs. Hardinge left them together. Hilda showed the medallion in strict confidence. Maud was literally enraptured with it. "How noble, how handsome, he is! I know only one other man so beautiful." Then she paused in confusion; and Hilda rather doubted the exception, though she knew it was their old playfellow Montreal who was intended.

"Who is the traitor," she said, "you dare to compare with your Sovereign?"

Maud, almost in tears, declared she did not mean what she said. The Emperor was very handsome.

"Do not be ashamed, my dear, to be true to your feelings," said Hilda sententiously. "A woman's heart is an empire of itself, and he who rules over it may be well content with a single loyal subject."

"Nonsense, Hilda! Do not tease me. An emperor, too, may rule over a woman's heart."

This was rather carrying the war into the opposite camp. Miss Fitzherbert thought it time to change the subject. They discussed the telegrams. Then Maud told Hilda how frightfully agitated Laurient was the previous evening. Finally they decided they would go to New Zealand the day after the next. They debated if they should proceed in their own air-cruiser or in the public one that left early every morning. It was about a sixteen hours' journey in the public conveyance, but in their own it would take less time. Besides, they wished to go straight to Dunedin, where the girls had a beautiful residence, and where their friends were chiefly located. Hilda represented Dunedin in the New Zealand Parliament, and local government honours had been freely open to her; but, under the tutelage of Mrs. Hardinge, she had preferred entering into federal politics, though she continued in the New Zealand Parliament. Most of the leading federal statesmen interested themselves with one or other Dominion government. There was such an absence of friction between the federal and the separate dominion governments that no inconvenience resulted from the dual attention, while it led to a more intimate knowledge of local duties. Maud bashfully remembered that Lady Taieri had asked them to go to Dunedin on her beautiful cruiser. "She was making up a party," said Maud; "and she mentioned that Colonel Laurient and Lord Montreal were amongst the number."

Hilda saw the wistful look in Maud's eyes. "Let us go with Lady Taieri," she said; and so it was arranged.

CHAPTER EIGHT
AIR-CRUISERS

We trust our readers will not be wearied because it is necessary to give them at some length an explanation concerning the aerial machines to which reference has so often been made as air-cruisers. It need scarcely be said that from time immemorial a great deal of attention has been directed to the question whether aerial travelling could be made subservient to the purposes of man. Balloons, as they were called, made of strong fabrics filled with a gas lighter than air, were to some extent used, but rarely for practical purposes. They were in considerable request for military objects, and it is recorded that Gambetta managed to get out of Paris in a balloon when that city was beleaguered by the German army in 1871. The principle of the balloon was the use of a vessel which, weighing, with all its contents, less than a similar volume of the atmosphere, would consequently rise in the air. But evidently no great progress could be made with such an apparatus. The low specific gravity of the atmosphere forbade the hope of its being possible to carry a heavy weight in great quantity on a machine that depended for its buoyancy on a less specific gravity. Besides, there was danger in using a fabric because of its liability to irreparable destruction by the smallest puncture.

The question then was mooted, Could not an aerial machine be devised to work although of higher specific gravity than the air? Birds, it was argued, kept themselves afloat by the motion of their wings, although their weight was considerably greater than a similar volume of the air through which they travelled. This idea was pursued. The cheap production of aluminium, a strong but light metal, gave an impulse to the experiment; and it was at length proved quite satisfactorily that aerial travelling was practicable in vessels considerably heavier than the air, by the use of quickly revolving fans working in the directions that were found to be suitable to the progress of the vessel. But great power was required to make the fans revolve, and the machinery to yield great power was proportionately heavy. It was especially heavy if applied separately to a portion of the fans, whilst it was dangerous to rely on one set of machinery, since any accident to it would mean cessation of the movement of the whole of the fans and consequently instant destruction. It was considered that, for safety's sake, there should be at least three sets of fans, worked by separate machinery, and that any one set should be able to preserve sufficient buoyancy although the other two were disabled. But whilst it was easy to define the conditions of safety, it was not easy to give them effect. All applications of known engines, whether of steam, water gas, electricity, compressed air, or petroleum, were found to be too bulky; and although three sets of machines were considered necessary, one set only was generally used, and many accidents occurred in consequence. The aerial mode of travelling was much employed by the adventurous, but hundreds of people lost their lives annually.

At length that grand association the Inventors' Institution came to the rescue. The founders of the Inventors' Institution, though working really with the object of benefiting humanity, were much too wise to place the undertaking on a purely philanthropic basis. On the contrary, they constructed it on a commercial basis. The object was to encourage the progress of valuable inventions, and they were willing to lend sums from trifling amounts to very large ones to aid the development of any invention of which they approved. They might lend only a trifle to obtain a patent or a large sum to make exhaustive experiments. The borrower had to enter into a bond to repay the amount tenfold or to any less extent demanded by the Institution at its own discretion. It was clearly laid down that, when the invention proved a failure through no fault of the inventor, he would not be asked for any repayment. In case of moderate success, he would only be asked for moderate repayment, and so on. The fairness of the Institution's exercise of discretion was rarely, if ever, called into question. Once they lent nearly thirty thousand pounds to finally develop an invention. Within four years they called upon the inventor to repay nearly three hundred thousand, but he was nothing loath. The invention was a great commercial success and yielding him at the rate of nearly a million per annum. This association offered a large reward for the best suggestion as to the nature of an invention to render aerial travelling safe, quick, and economical. A remarkable paper gained the prize.

The writer was an eminent chemist. He expressed the opinion that the one possible means of success was the use of a power which, as in the case of explosives, could be easily produced from substances of comparative light weight. He urged, it was only of late years that any real knowledge of the nature of explosives was obtained. It was nearly four hundred years after the discovery of gunpowder before any possible substitutes were invented. It was again a long time before it was discovered that explosives partook of two distinctly separate characters. One was the quick or shattering compound producing instantaneous effect; the other was the slow or rending compound of more protracted action. He dwelt on the fact that in all cases the force yielded by explosives was through the change of a solid into a gaseous body, and that the volume of the gaseous body was greatly increased by the expansion consequent on the heat evolved during decomposition. The total amount of heat evolved during decomposition did not differ, but evidently the concentration of heat at any one time depended on the rapidity of the decomposition. The volume of gas, independent of expansion by heat, varied also with different substances. Blasting oil, for instance, gave nearly thirteen hundred times its own volume of gas, and this was increased more than eight times by the concentration of heat; gunpowder only yielded in gas expanded by heat eight hundred times its own volume: or, in other words, the one yielded through decomposition thirteen times the volume of the other. He went on to argue that what was required was the leisurely chemical decomposition of a solid into a gas without sensible explosion, and of such a slow character as to avoid the production of great heat. He referred, as an example of the change resulting from the contact of two bodies, to the effect of safety matches. The match would only ignite by contact with a specially prepared surface. This match was as great an improvement on the old primitive match, as would be a decomposing material the force of which could be controlled, an improvement on the present means of obtaining power. He expressed a positive opinion that substances could be found whose rapidity of decomposition, and consequent heat and strength, could be nicely regulated, so that a force could be employed which would not be too sudden nor too strong to be used in substitution of steam or compressed air. He was, moreover, of opinion that, instead of the substances being mixed ready for use, with the concurrent danger, a mode could be devised of bringing the different component parts into contact in a not dissimilar manner to the application of the safety match, thereby assuring absolute immunity from danger in the carriage of the materials. This discovery could be made, he went on to say; and upon it depended improvement in aerial travelling. Each fan could be impelled by a separate machine of a light weight, worked with perfect safety by a cheap material; for the probabilities were, the substance would be cheaply producible. Each aerial vessel should carry three or four times the number of separate fans and machinery necessary to obtain buoyancy. The same substances probably could be used to procure buoyancy in the improbable event of all the machines breaking down. Supposing, as he suspected would be the case, that the resultant gas of the decomposition was lighter than air, a hollow case of a strong elastic fabric could be fastened to the whole of the outside exposed surface of the machine; and this could be rapidly inflated by the use of the same material. The movement of a button should be sufficient to produce decomposition, and as a consequence to charge the whole of this casing with gas lighter than the air. As the heat attending the decomposition subsided the elastic fabric would sufficiently collapse. The danger then would not be so much of descending too rapidly through the atmosphere as of remaining in it; a difficulty, however, which a system of valves would easily overcome.

The Institution offered twenty-five thousand pounds for a discovery on the lines indicated; and the Government offered seventy-five thousand pounds more on the condition that they should have the right to purchase the invention and preserve it as a secret, they supplying the material for civil purposes, but retaining absolute control over it for military purposes. This proviso was inserted because of the opinion of the writer that the effects he looked for might not so much depend on the chemical composition of the substances as on their molecular conditions, and that these might defy the efforts of analysts. If he was wrong, and the nature of the compound could be ascertained by analysis, the Government need not buy the invention; they could leave the discoverer to enjoy its advantages by patenting it, and share with other nations the uses that could be made of it for purposes of warfare.

It was some time before the investigations were completely successful. There was no lack of attention to the subject, the inducements being so splendid. Many fatal accidents occurred through the widely spread attention given to the properties of explosives and to the possibility of modifying their effects. On one occasion it was thought that success was attained. Laboratory experiments were entirely satisfactory, and at length it was determined to have a grand trial of the substance. A large quantity was prepared, and it was applied to the production of power in various descriptions of machinery. Many distinguished people were present, including a Cabinet Minister, a Lord of the Admiralty, the Under-Secretary for Defence, the President of the Inventors' Institution, several members of Parliament, a dozen or more distinguished men and women of science, and the inventor himself. The assemblage was a brilliant one; but, alas! not one of those present lived to record an opinion of the invention. The substance discovered was evidently not wanting in power. How far it was successful no one ever learnt. It may have been faultily made or injudiciously employed. But the very nature of the composition was lost, for the inventor went with the rest. An explosion occurred; and all the men and women within the building were scattered miles around, with fragments of the edifice itself. The largest recognisable human remains discovered were the well-defined joint of a little finger. A great commotion followed. The eminent chemist who wrote the paper suggesting the discovery was covered with obloquy. Suggestions were made that the law should restrain such investigations. Some people went so far as to describe them as diabolical. All things, however, come to those who wait; and at length a discovery was made faithfully resembling the one prognosticated by the great chemist.

Strange to say, the inventor or discoverer was a young Jewish woman not yet thirty years of age. From childhood she had taken an intense interest in the question, and the terrible accident above recorded seemed to spur her on to further exertion. She had a wonderful knowledge of ancient languages, and she searched for information concerning chemical secrets which she believed lost to the present day. She had a notion that the atomic structure of substances was better known to students in the early ages. It was said that the hint she acted on was conveyed to her by some passage in a Chaldean inscription of great antiquity. She neither admitted nor denied it. Perhaps the susceptibilities of an intensely Eastern nature led her to welcome the halo of romance cast over her discovery. Be that as it may, it is certain she discovered a substance, or rather substances which, brought into contact with each other, faithfully fulfilled all that the chemist had ventured to suggest. Together with unwavering efficiency there was perfect safety; and so much of the action depended on the structure, not the composition, that the efforts of thousands of savants failed to discover the secret of the invention. What the substances were in composition, and what they became after decomposition was easily determined, but how to make them in a form that fulfilled the purpose required defied every investigation.

The inventor did not patent her invention. After making an enormous fortune from it, she sold it to the Government, who took over the manufactory and its secrets; and whilst they sold it in quantity for ordinary use, they jealously guarded against its accumulation in foreign countries for possible warlike purposes. This invention, as much almost as its vast naval and military forces, gave to the empire of Britain the great power it possessed. The United States alone affected to underrate that power. It was the habit of Americans to declare that they did not believe in standing armies or fleets. If they wanted to fight, they could afford to spend any amount of treasure; and they could do more in the way of organising than any nation in the world. They were not going to spend money on keeping themselves in readiness for what might never happen. But we have not now to consider the aerial ships from their warlike point of view.

It should be mentioned that the inventor of this new form of power was the aunt of Colonel Laurient. She died nearly twenty years before this history, and left to him, her favourite nephew, so much of her gigantic fortune as the law permitted her to devise to one inheritor.

CHAPTER NINE
TOO STRANGE NOT TO BE TRUE

A little after sunrise on a prematurely early spring morning at the end of August Lady Taieri's air-cruiser left Melbourne. There was sufficient heat to make the southerly course not too severe, and it was decided to call at Stewart's Island to examine its vast fishery establishments. A gay and happy party was on board. Lord and Lady Taieri were genial, lively people, and liked by a large circle of friends. They loved nothing better than to assemble around them pleasant companions, and to entertain them with profuse hospitality. No provision was wanting to amuse the party, which consisted, besides the two Miss Fitzherberts, Lord Montreal, and Colonel Laurient, of nearly twenty happy young people of both sexes. General and Lady Buller also were there. The General was the descendant of an old New Zealand family which had acquired immense wealth by turning to profitable use large areas of pumice-stone land previously supposed to be useless.

The Bullers were always scientifically disposed; and one lady of the family, a professor of agricultural science, was convinced that the pumice-stone land could be made productive. It was not wanting in fertilising properties; but the difficulty was that on account of its porous nature, it could not retain moisture. Professor Buller first had numerous artesian wells bored, and obtained at regular distances an ample supply of water over a quarter of a million of acres of pumice land, which she purchased for two shillings an acre. After a great many experiments, she devised a mixture of soil, clay, and fertilising agents capable of being held in water by suspension. She drenched the land with the water thus mixed. The pumice acted as a filter, retaining the particles and filtering the water. As the land dried it became less porous. Grass seed was surface-sown. Another irrigation of the charged water and a third, after some delay, of clear water, completed the work. When once vegetation commenced, there was no difficulty. The land was found particularly suitable for subtropical fruits and for grapes. Vast fruit-canning works were established; and a special effervescent wine known as Bullerite was produced, and was held in higher estimation than the best champagne. Whilst more exhilarating, it was less intoxicating. It fetched a very high price, for it could be produced nowhere but on redeemed pumice land. Not a little proud was General Buller of his ancestor's achievement. He was in the habit of declaring that he did not care for the wealth he inherited in consequence; it was the genius that devised and carried out the reclamation, he said, which was to him its greatest glory. Nevertheless in practice he did not seem to disregard the substantial results he enjoyed. General Buller was a soldier of great scientific attainments. His only child, Phœbe, a beautiful girl of seventeen, was with them. She was the object of admiration of most of the young men on board, Lord Montreal alone excepted. Beyond some conventional civilities, he seemed unconscious of the presence of any one but Maud Fitzherbert; and she was nothing reluctant to receive his attentions.

The cruiser was beautifully constructed of pure aluminium. Everything conducive to the comfort of the passengers was provided. The machinery was very powerful, and the cruiser rose and fell with the grace and ease of a bird. After clearing the land, it kept at about a height of fifty feet above the sea, and, without any strain on the machinery, made easily a hundred miles an hour.

About four o'clock in the afternoon a descent was made on Stewart's Island. The fishing establishments here were of immense extent and value. They comprised not only huge factories for tinning the fresh fish caught on the banks to the south-east, but large establishments for dressing the seal-skins brought from the far south, as also for sorting and preparing for the market the stores of ivory brought from near the Antarctic Pole, the remnants of prehistoric animals which in the regions of eternal cold had been preserved intact for countless ages.

To New Zealand mainly belonged the credit of Antarctic research. Commenced in the interests of science, it soon became endowed with permanent activity on account of its commercial results. A large island, easily accessible, which received the name of Antarctica, was discovered within ten degrees of the Pole, stretching towards it, so that its southern point was not more than ten miles from the southern apex of the world. From causes satisfactorily explained by scientists, the temperature within a hundred-mile circle of the Pole was comparatively mild. There was no wind; and although the cold was severe, it was bearable, and in comparison with the near northern latitudes it was pleasant. On this island an extraordinary discovery was made. There were many thousands of a race of human beings whose existence was hitherto unsuspected. The instincts of man for navigating the ocean are well known. A famous scientific authority, Sir Charles Lyell, once declared that, if all the world excepting one remote little island were left unpeopled, the people of that island would spread themselves in time over every portion of the earth's surface. The Antarctic Esquimaux were evidently of the same origin as the Kanaka race. They spoke a language curiously little different from the Maori dialect, although long centuries must have elapsed since the migrating Malays, carried to the south probably against their own will, found a resting-place in Antarctica. Nature had generously assimilated them to the wants of the climate. Their faces and bodies were covered with a thick growth of short curly hair, which, though it detracted from their beauty, greatly added to their comfort. They were a docile, peaceful, intelligent people. They loved to come up to Stewart's Island during the winter and to return before the summer made it too hot for them to exist, laden with the presents which were always showered upon them. They were too useful to the traders of Stewart's Island not to receive consideration at their hands. The seal-skins and the ivory obtained from Antarctica were the finest in the world, and the latter was procured in immense quantities from the ice-buried remains of animals long since extinct as a living race.

Lady Taieri's friends spent a most pleasant two hours on the island. Some recent arrivals from Antarctica were objects of great interest. A young chief especially entertained them by his description of the wonders of Antarctica and his unsophisticated admiration of the novelties around him. He appeared to be particularly impressed with Phœbe Buller. The poor girl blushed very much; and her companions were highly amused when the interpreter told them that the young chief said she would be very good-looking if her face was covered with hair, and that he would be willing to take her back with him to Antarctica. Lady Taieri proposed that they should all visit the island and be present at the wedding. This sally was too much. Phœbe Buller retired to her cabin on the cruiser, and was not seen again until the well-lighted farms and residences on the beautiful Taieri plains, beneath the flying vessel, reminded its occupants that they were close to their destination.

During the next six days Lady Taieri gave a series of magnificent entertainments. There were dances, dinner-parties, picnics, a visit to the glacier region of Mount Cook, and finally a ball in Dunedin of unsurpassed splendour. This was on the eve of the opening of the river-works; and all the authorities of Wellington, including the Governor and his Ministers, honoured the ball with their presence.

An account of the river-works will not be unacceptable. So long since as 1863 it was discovered that the river Molyneux, or Clutha as it was sometimes called, contained over a great length rich gold deposits. More or less considerable quantities of the precious metal were obtained from time to time when the river was unusually low. But at no time was much of the banks and parts adjacent thereto uncovered. Dredging was resorted to, and a great deal of gold obtained; but it was pointed out that the search in that manner was something like the proverbial exploration for a needle in a haystack. A great scientist, Sir Julius Von Haast, declared that during the glacial period the mountains adjacent to the valley of the Molyneux were ground down by the action of glaciers from an average height of several thousand feet. Every ounce of the pulverised matter must have passed through the valley drained by the river; and he made a calculation which showed that, if the stuff averaged a grain to the ton, there must be in the interstices of the river bed many thousands of tons of gold.

Nearly fifty years before the period of this history the grandfather of Hilda and Maud Fitzherbert set himself seriously to unravel the problem. His design was to deepen the bed of the Mataura river, running through Southland, and to make an outlet to it from Lake Whakatip. Simultaneously he proposed to close the outlet from the lake into the Molyneux and, by the aid of other channels, cut at different parts of the river to divert the tributary streams, to lay bare and clear from water fully fifty miles of the river bed between Lake Whakatip and the Dunstan. It was an enormous work. The cost alone of obtaining the various riparian and residential rights absorbed over two millions sterling. Twice, too, were the works on the point of completion, and twice were they destroyed by floods and storms.

Mr. Fitzherbert had to take several partners, and his own enormous fortune was nearly dissipated. He had lost his son and his son's wife when his grandchildren, Hilda and Maud, were of tender age. After his death the two girls found a letter from him in which he told them he had settled on each of them three thousand pounds a year and left to them jointly his house and garden near Dunedin, with the furniture, just as they had always lived in it. Beyond this comparatively inconsiderable bequest, he wrote, he had devoted everything to the completion of the great work of his life. It was certain now that the river would be uncovered; and if he was right in his expectations, they would become enormously wealthy. If it should prove he was wrong, "which," he continued, "I consider impossible, you will not think unkindly of the old grandfather whose dearest hope it was to make you the richest girls in the world." The time had come when these works, upon which so much energy had been expended, and which had been fruitful of so many disappointments, were to be finished; and a great deal of curiosity as to the result was felt in every part of the Empire. Hilda and Maud Fitzherbert had two and a half tenths each of the undertaking, and Montreal and his younger brother had each one tenth, which they had inherited, but it was understood that Montreal had parted with his own share to Colonel Laurient; two tenths were reserved for division amongst those people whose riparian and other rights Mr. Fitzherbert had originally purchased; and of the remaining tenth one half was the property of Sir Central Vincent Stout, Baronet, a young though very able lawyer, the other half belonged to Lord Larnach, one of the wealthiest private bankers in the Empire. There was by no means unanimity of opinion concerning the result of the works. Some people held, they would prove a total failure, and that the money spent on them had been wasted by visionary enthusiasts; others thought, a moderate amount of gold might be obtained; while very few shared the sanguine expectations which had led old Fitzherbert to complacently spend the huge sums he had devoted to his life's ideal. And now the result of fifty years of toil and anxiety was to be decided. It was an exceptionally fine day, and thousands of people from all parts of New Zealand thronged to the ceremony. Some preferred watching the river Molyneux subside as the waters gradually ran out; others considered the grander sight to be the filling of the new channel of the Mataura river.

It had been arranged that two small levers pressed by a child would respectively have the effect of opening the gates that barred the new channel to the Mataura and of closing the gates that admitted the lake waters to the Molyneux. As the levers were pressed a signal was to run down the two rivers, in response to which guns stationed at frequent intervals were to thunder out a salute.

Precisely at twelve the loud roar of artillery announced the transfer of the waters. Undoubtedly the grander sight was on the Mataura river. The progress of the liberated water as it rushed onward in a great seething, foaming, swirling mass, gleaming under the bright rays of the sun, formed a picture not easily to be forgotten. But the other river attracted more attention, for there not only nature played a part, but the last scene was to be enacted in a drama of great human interest. And this scene was more slowly progressing. The subsidence of the water was not very quick. The Molyneux was a quaint, many-featured river, partly fed by melted snow, partly by large surface drainage, both finding their way to the river through the lake, and by independent tributaries. At times the Molyneux was of great volume and swiftness. On the present occasion it was on moderate terms— neither at its slowest nor fastest. But as the river flowed on without its usual accession from the lake and the diverted tributaries, an idealist might have fancied that it was fading away through grief at the desertion of its allies. Lady Taieri's party were located on a dais erected on the banks of the river about twenty miles from the lake. After an hour or so the subsidence of the water became well marked; and occasionally heaps of crushed quartz, called tailings, from gold workings on the banks, became visible. Some natural impediments had prevented these from flowing down the river and built them up several feet in height. Here and there crevices, deep and narrow or shallow and wide, became apparent.

The time was approaching when it would be known if there was utter failure or entire success or something midway between. It had been arranged that, if any conspicuous deposit of gold became apparent, a signal should be given, in response to which all the guns along the river banks should be fired.

At a quarter past one o'clock the guns pealed forth; and loud as was the noise they made, it seemed trifling compared with the cheers which ran up and down the river from both banks from the throats of the countless thousands of spectators. The announcement of success occasioned almost delirious joy. It seemed as if every person in the vast crowd had an individual interest in the undertaking. The telephone soon announced that at a turn in the river about seven miles from the lake what appeared to be a large pool of fine gold was uncovered. Even as the news became circulated there appeared in the middle of the river right opposite Lady Taieri's stand a faint yellow glow beneath the water. Gradually it grew brighter and brighter, until at length to the eyes of the fascinated beholders there appeared a long, irregular fissure of about twenty-five feet in length by about six or seven in width which appeared to be filled with gold. Some of the company now rushed forward, and, amidst the deafening cheers of the onlookers, dug out into boxes which had been prepared for the purpose shovelsful of gold. Fresh boxes were sent for, but the gold appeared to be inexhaustible. Each box held five thousand ounces; and supposing the gold to be nearly pure, fifty boxes would represent the value of a million sterling.

Five hundred boxes were filled, and still the pool opposite Hilda was not emptied, and it was reported two equally rich receptacles were being drained in other parts. Guards of the Volunteer forces were told off to protect the gold until it could be placed in safety.

Hilda and Maud were high-minded, generous girls, with nothing of a sordid nature in their composition; but they were human, and what human being could be brought into contact with the evidence of the acquisition of such vast wealth without feelings of quickened, vivid emotion? It is only justice to them to say that their feelings were not in the nature of a sense of personal gratification so much as one of ecstatic pleasure at the visions of the enormous power for good which this wealth would place in their hands. Every one crowded round with congratulations. As Colonel Laurient joined the throng Hilda said to him, "Why should I not equally congratulate you? You share the gold with us."

"Do I?" he said, with his inscrutable smile. "I had forgotten."

Lord Montreal, with a face in which every vestige of colour was wanting, gravely congratulated Hilda, then, turning to her sister, said in a voice the agitation of which he could not conceal, "No one, Miss Maud, more warmly congratulates you or more fervently wishes you happiness."

Before the astonished girl could reply he had left the scene. It may safely be said that Maud now bitterly regretted the success of the works. She understood that Montreal, a poor man, was too proud to owe to any woman enormous wealth. "What can I do with it? How can I get rid of it?" she wailed to Hilda, who in a moment took in the situation.

"Maud dearest," she said, "control yourself. All will be well." And she led her sister off the dais into the cruiser, in which they returned to Lady Taieri's house. They met Montreal in the gallery leading to their apartments. He bowed gravely.

Maud could not restrain herself. "You will kill me, Montreal," she said. "What do I care for wealth?"

"Maud, you would not have me sacrifice my self-respect," he said, and passed on.

He seemed almost unconscious where he was going. He was roused from his bitter reverie.

"Colonel Laurient will be greatly obliged if you will go to him at once," said a servant.

"Show me to his room," replied Montreal briefly.

"Laurient," said Montreal, "believe me, I am not jealous of your good fortune."

"My good fortune!" said Laurient. "I do not know of anything very good. I always felt sure that you would pay me what you owe me."

"Pay you what I owe you!" said Montreal, in a voice of amazement.

"Yes," replied Laurient. "You know that I come of a race of money-lenders, and I have sent for you to ask you for my money and interest."

But Montreal was too sad to understand a joke; and Laurient had noticed what passed with Maud, and formed a shrewd conjecture that the gold had not made either of them happy.

"Listen to me," he continued. "It is three years since you came to me and asked me to buy your share in the Molyneux works, as you had need of the money. I replied by asking what you wanted for your interest. You named a sum much below what I thought its value—a belief which to-day's results have proved to be correct. I am not in the habit of acquiring anything from a friend in distress at less than its proper value, and I was about to say so when I thought, 'I will lend this money on the security offered. I will not worry Montreal by letting him think that he is in debt and has to find the interest every half-year. There is quite sufficient margin for interest and principal too; and when the gold is struck, he will repay me.' I made this arrangement apparent in my will and by the execution of a deed of trust. The share is still yours, and out of the first money you receive you can repay me. Nay," he said, stopping Montreal's enthusiastic thanks. "I said I was a money-lender. Here is a memorandum of the interest, and you will see each year I have charged interest on the previous arrears—perfect usury. Go, my dear boy. I hate thanks, and I do not want money."

Montreal could not control himself to speak. Two minutes afterwards he was in Hilda and Maud's sitting-room. "Forgive me, Maud darling! I have the share. I thought I had lost it," he said incoherently; but he made his meaning clear by the unmistakable caress of a lover.

Hilda left the room—an example the historian must follow.

CHAPTER TEN
LORD REGINALD AGAIN

The following telegram reached Hilda next morning: "I heartily congratulate you, dear Hilda, on the success of your grandfather's great undertaking. The Emperor summoned me and desired me to send you his congratulations. I am also to say that he wishes as a remarkable event of his reign to show his approval of the patience, skill, and enterprise combined in the enormous works successfully concluded yesterday. The honour is to come to you as your grandfather's representative. Besides that, on account of your noble deed last week he wished to raise you to the peerage. He will now raise you to the rank of duchess, and suggests the title of Duchess of New Zealand; but that of course is as you wish. You must, my dear, accept it. A duchess cannot be an under-secretary, and I am not willing to lose you. Mr. Hazelmere has repeated his wish to resign; and I now beg you to enter the Cabinet as Lord President of the Board of Education, a position for which your acquirements peculiarly fit you. Your re-election to Parliament will be a mere ceremony. Make a speech to your constituents in Dunedin. Then take the waters at Rotomahana and Waiwera. In two months you can join us in London, where the next session of Parliament will be held. You will be quite recovered from all your fatigue by then."

In less than two weeks Hilda, Duchess of New Zealand, was re-elected to Parliament by her Dunedin constituents. Next day she left for Rotomahana with a numerous party of friends who were to be her guests. She had engaged the entire accommodation of one of the hotels.

Maud and Hilda before they left Dunedin placed at the disposal of the Mayor half a million sterling to be handed to a properly constituted trust for the purpose of encouraging mining pursuits, and developing mining undertakings.

New Zealand was celebrated for the wonderfully curative power of its waters. At Rotomahana, Te Aroha, and Waiwera in the North Island, and at Hammer Plains and several other localities in the Middle Island innumerable springs, hot and cold, existed, possessing a great variety of medicinal properties. There was scarcely a disease for which the waters of New Zealand did not possess either cure or alleviation. At one part of the colony or another these springs were in use the whole year round. People flocked to them from all quarters of the world. It was estimated that the year previous to the commencement of this history, more than a million people visited the various springs. Rotomahana, Te Aroha, and Waiwera were particularly pleasant during the months of October, November, and December. Hilda proposed passing nearly three weeks at each. Rotomahana was a city of hotels of all sizes and descriptions. Some were constructed to hold only a comparatively few guests and to entertain them on a scale of great magnificence. Every season these houses were occupied by distinguished visitors. Not infrequently crowned heads resorted to them for relief from the maladies from which even royalty is not exempt. Others of the hotels were of great size, capable indeed of accommodating several thousands of visitors. The Grandissimo Hotel comfortably entertained five thousand people. Most of the houses were built of ground volcanic scoria, pressed into bricks. Some of them were constructed of Oamaru stone, dressed with a peculiar compound that at the same time hardened and gave it the appearance of marble. The house that Hilda took appeared like a solid block of Carrara marble, relieved with huge glass windows and with balconies constructed of gilt aluminium. Balconies of plain or gilt aluminium adorned most of the hotels, and gave them a very pretty appearance. Te Aroha was a yet larger city than Rotomahana, as, besides its use as a health resort, it was the central town of an extensive and rich mining district. Waiwera was on a smaller scale, but in point of appearance the most attractive. Who indeed could do justice to thy charms, sweet Waiwera? A splendid beach of sand, upon which at short intervals two picturesque rivers debouched to the sea, surrounded with wooded heights of all degrees of altitude, and with many variations in the colour of the foliage, it is not to be wondered at that persons managed in this charming scene to forget the world and to reveal whatever of poetry lay dormant in their composition. Few who visited Waiwera did not sometimes realise the sentiment—

"I love not man the less, but nature more."

Hilda had duly passed through the Rotomahana and Te Aroha cures, and she had been a week at Waiwera, when one morning two hours after sunrise, as she returned from her bath, she was delighted at the receipt of the following letter, signed by Mrs. Hardinge: "I have prepared a surprise for you, dearest Hilda. Mr. Decimus has lent me his yacht, and I am ready to receive you on board. Come off at once by yourself. We can talk over many things better here than on shore."

A beautifully appointed yacht lay in the offing six hundred yards from the shore, and a well-manned boat was waiting to take Hilda on board. She flew to her room, completed her toilet, and in ten minutes was on the boat and rowing off to the yacht. She ascended the companion ladder, and was received on deck by a young officer. "I am to ask your Grace to wait a few minutes," he said. Hilda gazed round the entrancing view on sea, land, and river, beaming beneath a bright and gorgeous sun, forgetting everything but the sense of the loveliness around her. She could never tell how long she was so absorbed. She aroused herself with a start to feel the vessel moving and to see before her the dreaded figure of Lord Reginald Paramatta.

Meanwhile the spectators on the shore were amazed to see Hilda go off to the yacht alone, and the vessel weigh anchor and steam away swiftly. Maud and Lady Taieri, returning from their baths along the beautiful avenue of trees, were speedily told of the occurrence, and a council rapidly held with Laurient and Montreal. Mrs. Hardinge's letter was found in Hilda's room.

"Probably," said Lady Taieri, "the morning is so fine that Mrs. Hardinge is taking the Duchess for a cruise while they talk together."

"I do not think so," said the Colonel. "Look at the speed the vessel is making. They would not proceed at such a rate if a pleasant sail were the only object. She is going at the rate of thirty miles an hour."

Maud started with surprise, and again glanced at the letter. "You are right, Colonel Laurient," she said, with fearful agitation; "this writing is like that of Mrs. Hardinge, but it is not hers. I know her writing too well not to be sure it is an imitation. Oh, help Hilda; do help her! Montreal, you must aid. She is the victim of a plot."

Meanwhile the vessel raced on; but with a powerful glass they could make out that there was only one female figure on board, and that a male figure stood beside her.

"Hilda," said Lord Reginald, bowing low, "forgive me. All is fair in love and war. My life without you is a misery."

"Do you think, my lord," said the girl, very pale but still courageous, "that this course you have adopted is one that will commend you to my liking?"

"I will teach you to love me. You cannot remain unresponsive to the intense affection I bear you."

"True love, Lord Reginald, is not steeped in selfishness; it has regard for the happiness of its object. Do you think you can make me happy by tearing me from my friends by an artifice like this?"

"I will make it up to you. I implore your forgiveness. Try to excuse me."

Hilda during this rapid dialogue did not lose her self-possession. She knew the fears of her friends on shore would soon be aroused. She wondered at her own want of suspicion. Time, she felt, was everything. When once doubt was aroused, pursuit in the powerful aerial cruiser they had on shore would be rapid.

"I entreat you, Lord Reginald," she said, "to turn back. Have pity on me. See how defenceless I am against such a conspiracy as this."

Lord Reginald was by nature brave, and the wretched cheat he was playing affected him more because of its cowardly nature than by reason of its outrageous turpitude. He was a slave to his passions and desires. He would have led a decently good life if all his wishes were capable of gratification, but there was no limit to the wickedness of which he might be guilty in the pursuit of desires he could not satisfy. He either was, or fancied himself to be, desperately in love with Hilda; and he believed, though without reason, that she had to some extent coquetted with him. Even in despite of reason and evidence to the contrary, he imagined she felt a prepossession in his favour, that an act of bravery like this might stir into love. He did not sufficiently understand woman. To his mind courage was the highest human quality, and he thought an exhibition of signal bravery even at the expense of the woman entrapped by it would find favour in her eyes. Hilda's words touched him keenly, though in some measure he thought they savoured of submission. "She is imploring now," he thought, "instead of commanding."

"Ask me," he said, in a tone of exceeding gentleness, "anything but to turn back. O Hilda, you can do with me what you like if you will only consent to command!"

"Leave me then," she replied, "for a time. Let me think over my dreadful position."

"I will leave you for a quarter of an hour, but do not say the position is dreadful."

He walked away, and the girl was left the solitary occupant of the deck. The beautiful landscape was still in sight. It seemed a mockery that all should appear the same as yesterday, and she in such dreadful misery. Smaller and smaller loomed the features on the shore as the wretched girl mused on. Suddenly a small object appeared to mount in the air.

"It is the cruiser," she exclaimed aloud, with delight. "They are in pursuit."

"No, Hilda," said Lord Reginald, who suddenly appeared at her side, "I do not think it is the cruiser; and if it be, it can render you no aid. Look round this vessel; you will observe guns at every degree of elevation. No cruiser can approach us without instant destruction."

"But you would not be guilty of such frightful wickedness. Lord Reginald, let me think better of you. Relent. Admit that you did not sufficiently reflect on what you were doing, and that you are ready to make the only reparation in your power."

"No," said Lord Reginald, much moved, "I cannot give you up. Ask me for anything but that. See! you are right; the cruiser is following us. It is going four miles to our one. Save the tragedy that must ensue. I have a clergyman in the cabin yonder. Marry me at once, and your friends shall come on board and congratulate you as Lady Paramatta."

"That I will never be. I would prefer to face death."

"Is it so bitter a lot?" said Lord Reginald, stung into irritation. "If persuasion is useless, I must insist. Come to the cabin with me at once."

"Dare you affect to command me?" said Hilda, drawing herself up with a dignity that was at once grave and pathetic.

"I will dare everything for you. It is useless," he said as she waved her handkerchief to the fast-approaching cruiser. "If it come too close, its doom is sealed. Be ready to fire," he roared out to the captain; and brief, stern words were passed from end to end of the vessel. "Now, Hilda, come. The scene is not one fit for you. Come you shall," he said, approaching her and placing his arm round her waist.

"Never! I would rather render my soul to God," exclaimed the brave, excited girl.

With one spring she stood on the rail of the bulwarks, and with another leapt far out into the ocean. Lord Reginald gazed on her in speechless horror, and was about to follow overboard.

"It is useless," the captain said, restraining him. "The boat will save her."

In two minutes it was lowered, but such was the way on the yacht that the girl floating on the water was already nearly a mile distant. The cruiser and the boat raced to meet her. The yacht's head also was turned; and she rapidly approached the scene, firing at the cruiser as she did so. The latter reached Hilda first. Colonel Laurient jumped into the water, and caught hold of the girl. The beat was near enough for one of its occupants with a boathook to strike him a terrible blow on the arm. The disabled limb fell to his side, but he held her with iron strength with his other arm. The occupants of the cruiser dragged them both on board; and Colonel Laurient before he fainted away had just time to cry out, "Mount into the air, and fly as fast as you can." The scene that followed was tragical. Two of the occupants of the boat had grasped the sides of the cruiser, and were carried aloft with it. Before they could be dragged on board a shot from the yacht struck them both, and crushed in part of the side of the vessel, besides injuring many sets of fans. Another shot did damage on the opposite side. But still she rose, and to aid her buoyancy the casing was inflated. Soon she was out of reach of the yacht; and, with less speed than she left it, she returned to Waiwera. The yacht turned round, and steamed out to sea at full speed.

Hilda's immersion did her no harm, but her nerves were much shaken, and for many days she feared to be left alone. Colonel Laurient's arm was dreadfully shattered. The doctor at first proposed amputation, but the Colonel sternly rejected the suggestion. With considerable skill it was set, and in a few days the doctors announced that the limb was saved. Colonel Laurient, however, was very ill. For a time, indeed, even his life was in danger. He suffered from more than the wounded arm. Perhaps the anxiety during the dreadful pursuit as to what might be happening on board the yacht had something to do with it.

Hilda was untiring in her attention to Laurient; no sister could have nursed him more tenderly, and indeed it was as a sister she felt for him.

One afternoon, as he lay pale and weak, but convalescent, on a sofa by the window, gazing out at the sea, Hilda entered the room with a cup of soup and a glass of bullerite. "You must take this," she said.

"I will do anything you tell me," he replied, "if only in acknowledgment of your infinite kindness."

"Why should you talk of kindness?" said the girl, with tears in her eyes. "Can I ever repay you for what you have done?"

"Yes, Hilda, you could repay me; but indeed there is nothing to repay, for I suffered more than you did during that terrible time of uncertainty."

The girl looked very sad. The Colonel marked her countenance, and over his own there came a look of weariness and despair. But he was brave still, as he always was. "Hilda, dearest Hilda," he said, "I will not put a question to you that I know you cannot answer as I would wish; it would only pain you and stand in the way perhaps of the sisterly affection you bear for me. I am not one to say all or nothing. The sense of your presence is a consolation to me. No, I will not ask you. You know my heart, and I know yours. Your destiny will be a higher and happier one than that of the wife of a simple soldier."

"Hush!" she said. "Ambition has no place in my heart. Be always a brother to me. You can be to me no more." And she flew from the room.

CHAPTER ELEVEN
GRATEFUL IRELAND

At the end of October Maud was married from the house of the two sisters in Dunedin. No attribute of wealth and pomp was wanting to make the wedding a grand one. Both Maud and Montreal were general favourites, and the number and value of the presents they received were unprecedented. Hilda gave her sister a suite of diamonds and one of pearls, each of priceless value. One of the most gratifying gifts was from the Emperor; it was a small miniature on ivory of Hilda, beautifully set in a diamond bracelet. It was painted by a celebrated artist. The Emperor had specially requested the Duchess to sit for it immediately Maud's engagement became known. It was surmised that the artist had a commission to paint a copy as well as the original.

Immediately after the wedding Lord and Lady Montreal left in an air-cruiser to pass their honeymoon in Canada, and the Duchess of New Zealand at once proceeded to London, where she was rapturously received by Mrs. Hardinge. She reached London in time to be present at its greatest yearly fête, the Lord Mayor's Show, on the 9th November. According to old chronicles, there was a time when these annual shows were barbarous exhibitions of execrable taste, suitably accompanied with scenes of coarse vulgarity. All this had long since changed. The annual Lord Mayor's Show had become a real work of elaborated art. Either it was made to represent some particular event, some connected thread of history, or some classical author's works. For example, there had been a close and accurate representation of Queen Victoria's Jubilee procession, again a series of tableaux depicting the life of the virtuous though unhappy Mary Queen of Scots, a portrayal of Shakespeare's heroes and heroines, and a copy of the procession that celebrated the establishment of local government in Ireland. The present year was devoted to a representation of all the kings and queens of England up to the proclamation of the Empire. It began with the "British warrior queen," Boadicea, and ended with the grandfather of the present Emperor. Each monarch was represented with his or her retinue in the exact costumes of the respective periods. No expense was spared on these shows. They were generally monumental works of research and activity, and were in course of preparation for several years.

In many respects London still continued to be the greatest city of the Empire. Its population was certainly the largest, and no other place could compare with it in the possession of wealthy inhabitants. But wealth was unequally distributed. Although there were more people than elsewhere enjoying great riches, the aggregate possessions were not as large in proportion to the population as in other cities, such as Melbourne, Sydney, and Dublin. The Londoners were luxurious to the verge of effeminacy. A door left open, a draught at a theatre, were considered to seriously reflect on the moral character of the persons responsible for the same. A servant summarily dismissed for neglecting to close a door could not recover any arrears of wages due to him or her. Said a great lady once to an Australian gentleman, "Are not these easterly winds dreadful? I hope you have nothing of the kind in your charming country."

"We have colder winds than those you have from the east," he replied. "We have blasts direct from the South Pole, and we enjoy them. My lady, we would not be what we are," drawing himself up, "if the extremes of heat and cold were distasteful to us."

She looked at him with something of curiosity mixed with envy.

"You are right," she said. "It is a manly philosophy to endeavour to enjoy that which cannot be remedied."

The use of coal and gas having long since been abandoned in favour of heat and light from electricity, the buildings in London had lost their begrimed appearance, and the old dense fogs had disappeared. A city of magnificent buildings, almost a city of palaces, London might be termed. Where there used to be rookeries for the poor there were now splendid edifices of many stories, with constant self-acting elevators. It was the same with regard to residence as with food and clothing. The comforts of life were not denied to people of humble means.

Parliament was opened with much pomp and magnificence, and a mysterious allusion, in the speech from the throne, to large fiscal changes proposed, excited much attention. The Budget was delivered at an early date amidst intense excitement, which turned into unrestrained delight when its secrets were revealed. The Chancellor of the Exchequer, the Right Honourable Gladstone Churchill, examined critically the state of the finances, the enormous accumulations of the reserve funds all over the dominions, and the continued increase of income from the main sources of revenue. "The Government," he said, "are convinced the time has come to make material reductions in the taxation. They propose that the untaxable minimum of income shall be increased from five to six hundred pounds, and the untaxable minimum of succession value from ten to twelve thousand pounds, and that, instead of a fourth of the residue in each case reverting to the State, a fifth shall be substituted." Then he showed by figures and calculations that not only was the relief justifiable, but that further relief might be expected in the course of a few years. He only made one exception to the proposed reductions. Incomes derived from foreign loans and the capital value of such loans were still to be subject to the present taxation. Foreign loans, he said, were mischievous in more than one respect. They armed foreign nations, necessitating greater expense to the British Empire in consequence. They also created hybrid subjects of the Empire, with sympathies divided between their own country and foreign countries. There was room for the expenditure of incalculable millions on important works within the Empire, and those who preferred to place their means abroad must contribute in greater proportion to the cost of government at home. They had not, he declared, any prejudice against foreign countries. It was better for them and for Britain that each country should attend to its own interests and its own people. Probably no Budget had been received with so much acclamation since that in which the Chancellor of the Exchequer declared the policy of the Empire to be one of severe protection to the industries of its vast dominions.

Singularly, it was Lord Gladstone Churchill, great-grandfather of the present Chancellor of the Exchequer, who made the announcement, seventy years previously, that the time had arrived for abandoning the free trade which however he admitted had been of benefit to the parent country prior to federation.

The proposed fiscal reforms were rapidly confirmed; and Parliament rose towards the middle of December, in time to allow members to be present at the great annual fête in Dublin. We have already described how it was that the federation of the Empire, including local government in Ireland, was brought about by the intervention of the Colonies. The Irish people, warm-hearted and grateful, felt they could never be sufficiently thankful. They would not allow the declaration of the Empire to be so great an occasion of celebration, as the anniversary of the day on which the premiers of the six Australasian colonies, of the Dominion of Canada, and of the South African Dominion met and despatched the famous cablegram which, after destroying one administration, resulted in the federation of the empire of Britain. A magnificent group representing these prime ministers, moulded in life-size, was erected, and has always remained the most prominent object, in Dublin. The progress of Ireland after the establishment of the Empire was phenomenal, and it has since generally been regarded as the most prosperous country in the world. Under the vivifying influence of Protection, the manufactures of Ireland advanced with great strides. Provisions were made by which the evils of absenteeism were abated. Formerly enormous fortunes were drawn from Ireland by persons who never visited it. An Act was passed by which persons owning large estates but constantly absent from the country were compelled to dispose of their property at a full, or rather, it might be said, an excessive, value. The Government of Ireland declared that the cost of doing away with the evils of absenteeism was a secondary consideration. The population of Ireland became very large. Hundreds of thousands of persons descended from those who had gone to America from Ireland came to the country, bringing with them that practical genius for progress of all sorts which so distinguishes the American people. The improvement of Ireland was always in evidence to show the advantages of the federation of the Empire and of the policy of making the prosperity of its own people the first object of a nation.

The Irish fête-day that year was regarded with even more than the usual fervour, and that is saying a great deal. It was to be marked by a historical address which Mrs. Hardinge had consented to deliver. Mrs. Hardinge was the idol of the Irish. With the best blood of celebrated Celtic patriots in her veins, she never allowed cosmopolitan or national politics to make her forget that she was thoroughly Irish. She gloried in her country, and was credited with being better acquainted with its history and traditions than any other living being. She spoke in a large hall in Dublin to thousands of persons, who had no difficulty in hearing every note of the flexible, penetrating, musical voice they loved so well. She spoke of the long series of difficulties that had occurred before Ireland and England had hit upon a mode of living beneficial and happy to both, because the susceptibilities of the people of either country were no longer in conflict. "Undoubtedly," she said, "Ireland has benefited materially from the uses she has made of local government; but the historian would commit a great mistake who allowed it to be supposed that aspirations of a material and sordid kind have been at the root of the long struggle the Irish have made for self-government. I put it to you," she continued, amidst the intense enthusiasm of her hearers, "supposing we suffered from the utmost depression, instead of enjoying as we do so much prosperity, and we were to be offered as the price of relinquishing self-government every benefit that follows in the train of vast wealth, would we consent to the change?" The vehement "No" which she uttered in reply to her own question was re-echoed from thousands of throats. She directed particular attention to what she called the Parnell period. "Looked at from this distance," she said, "it was ludicrous in the extreme. Government succeeded Government; and each adopted whilst in office the same system of partial coercion, partial coaxing, which it condemned its successor for pursuing. The Irish contingent went from party to party as they thought each oscillated towards them. Many Irish members divided their time between Parliament and prison. The Governments of the day adopted the medium course: they would not repress the incipient revolution, and they would not yield to it. Agrarian outrages were committed by blind partisans and weak tools who thought that an exhibition of unscrupulous ferocity might aid the cause. The leaders of the Irish party were consequently placed on the horns of a dilemma. They had either to discredit their supporters, or to admit themselves favourable to criminal action. They were members of Parliament. They had to take the oath of allegiance. They did not dare to proclaim themselves incipient rebels." Then Mrs. Hardinge quoted, amidst demonstrative enthusiasm, Moore's celebrated lines—

"Rebellion, foul, dishonouring word,
Whose wrongful blight so oft has stained
The holiest cause that tongue or sword

Of mortal ever lost or gained—
How many a spirit born to bless
Has shrunk beneath that withering name
Whom but a day an hour's success,
Had wafted to eternal fame."

"But, my dear friends," pursued Mrs. Hardinge, "do not think that I excuse crime. The end does not justify the means. Even the harm from which good results is to be execrated. The saddest actors in history are those who by their own infamy benefited or hoped to benefit others.

"For one sad losel soils a name for aye,
However mighty in the olden time;
Not all that heralds rake from coffined clay,
Nor florid prose, nor honeyed words of rhyme
Can blazon evil deeds or consecrate a crime."

When the applause these lines elicited subsided, Mrs. Hardinge dilated on the proposed Home Rule that Mr. Gladstone offered. Naturally the Irish party accepted it, but a close consideration convinced her that it was fortunate it was not carried into effect. The local powers Mr. Gladstone offered were very moderate, far less than the Colonies then possessed, whilst, as the price of them, Ireland was asked to virtually relinquish all share in the government of the country. Gladstone saw insuperable difficulties in the way of establishing a federal parliament; and without it his proposals, if carried into operation, would have made Ireland still more governed from England than it was without the so-called Home Rule. In fact, the fruition of Mr. Gladstone's proposals would have driven Ireland to fight for independence. "We Irish are not disposed," declared Mrs. Hardinge, "to submit to be excluded from a share in the government of the nation to which we belong. Mr. Gladstone would virtually have so excluded us; and if we had taken as a boon the small instalment of self-government he offered, we could only have taken it with the determination to use the power we acquired for the purpose of seeking more or of gaining independence. Yes, my fellow-countrymen," she continued amidst loud cheers, "it was good for us, seeing how happily we now live with England, that we did not take Mr. Gladstone's half-measure. Yet there was great suffering and great delay. Weariness and concession stilled the question for a time; but the Irish continued in a state of more or less suppressed irritation, both from the sense of the indignity of not being permitted local government, and from the actual evils resulting from absenteeism. Relief came at length. It came from the great Colonies the energy of all of us—Irish, English, and Scotch—had built up." Long, continuous cheering interrupted the speaker. "You may well cheer," she continued. "The memory of the great colonial heroes whose action we this day commemorate, and whom, as usual, we will crown with wreaths of laurel, will always remain as green in our memory as the Isle of Erin itself." She proceeded to describe individually the prime ministers of the Colonies who had brought the pressure to bear upon the Central Government. "The Colonies," she said, "became every day, as they advanced in wealth and progress, more interested in the nation to which they belonged. They saw that nation weakened and discredited at home and abroad by the ever-present contingency of Irish disaffection. They felt, besides, that the Colonies, which had grown not only materially, but socially, happy under the influence of free institutions, could not regard with indifference the denial of the same freedom to an important territory of the nation. Their action did equal honour to their intellect and virtue."

Mrs. Hardinge concluded by describing with inimitable grace the various benefits which had arisen from satisfying Ireland's wants. "The boon she received," the speaker declared, "Ireland has returned tenfold. It was owing to her that the Empire was federated; at one moment it stood in the balance whether this great cluster of States should be consolidated into the present happy and united Empire or become a number of disintegrated communities, threatened with all the woes to which weak States are subject."

After this address Mrs. Hardinge, in the presence of an immense multitude, placed a crown of laurel on the head of each of the statues of the colonial statesmen, commencing with the Prime Minister of Canada. Those statues later in the day were almost hidden from sight, for they were covered with a mass of many thousand garlands.

CHAPTER TWELVE
THE EMPEROR PLANS A CAMPAIGN

One day early in May Colonel Laurient was alone with the Emperor, who was walking up and down the room in a state of great excitement. His eyes glittered with an expression of almost ferocity. The veins in his forehead stood out clear and defined, like cords. No one had seen him like this before. "To think they should dare to enter my territory! They shall never cease to regret it," he declared as he paced the room. Two hours before, the Emperor had been informed that the troops of the United States had crossed into Canada, the excuse, some dispute about the fisheries, the real cause, chagrin of the President at the Emperor's rejection of her daughter's hand.

"This shall be a bitter lesson to the Yankees," continued the Emperor.

"They do not know with whom they have to deal. I grant they were right to seek independence, because the Government of my ancestor goaded them to it. But they shall learn there is a limit to their power, and that they are weak as water compared with the parent country they abandoned. Listen, Laurient," he went on more calmly as he took a seat by a table on which was spread a large map of the United States and Canada. "I have made up my mind what to do, and you are to help me. You are now my first military aide-de-camp. In that capacity and as head of the bodyguard you may appear in evidence."

"I shall only be too glad to render any assistance in my power. I suppose that the troops will at once proceed to Canada?"

"Would you have me," said the Emperor, "do such a wrong to my Canadian subjects? You know, by the constitution of the Empire, each State is bound to protect itself from invasion. Do you think that my Canadian volunteers are not able to perform this duty?"

"I know, your Majesty, that no finer body of troops is to be found in the Empire than the Canadian volunteers and Volunteer reserve. But I thought you seemed disinclined to refrain from action."

"There you are right, nor do I mean to remain idle. No; I intend a gigantic revenge. I will invade the States myself."

Colonel Laurient's eyes glittered. He recognised the splendid audacity of the idea, and he was not one to feel fear. "Carry the war into the enemy's camp!" he said. "I ought to have thought of it. It is an undertaking worthy of you, Sir."

"I have arranged everything with my advisers, who have given me, as commander of the forces, full executive discretion. You have a great deal to do. You will give, in strict confidence, to some person information which he is to cause to be published in the various papers. That information will be that all the ships and a large force are ordered immediately to the waters of the St. Lawrence. To give reality to the intelligence, the newspapers are to be severely blamed and threatened for publishing it. But you are to select trustworthy members of the bodyguard who are verbally to communicate to the admirals and captains what is really to be done. Nothing is to be put in writing beyond the evidence of your authority to give instructions, which I now hand to you. Those instructions are to be by word of mouth. All the large, powerful vessels on the West Indian, Mediterranean, and Channel stations are to meet at Sandy Hook, off New York, on the seventeenth evening from this, with the exception of twenty which are to proceed to Boston. They are to carry with them one hundred thousand of the Volunteer reserve force, fifty thousand of the regular troops, and fifty thousand ordinary volunteers who may choose to offer their services. In every case the ostensible destination is Quebec. My faithful volunteers will not object to the deceit. Part of the force may be carried in air-cruisers, of which there must be in attendance at least three hundred of the best in the service. The air-cruisers as soon as it is dark on the evening appointed are to range all round New York for miles and cut and destroy the telegraph wires in every direction. Twenty of the most powerful, carrying a strong force of men, are to proceed to Washington during the night and bring the President of the United States a prisoner to the flagship, the British Empire. They are to leave Washington without destroying property. About ten o'clock the men are to disembark at New York from the air-cruisers, and take possession of every public building and railway station. They are also during the night to disembark from the vessels. There will be little fighting. The Yankees boast of keeping no standing army. They have had a difficulty to get together the hundred and fifty thousand men they have marched into Canada. Similar action to that at New York is to be adopted at Boston. As soon as sufficient troops are disembarked I will march them into Canada at the rear of the invaders, and my Canadian forces are to attack them in front. I will either destroy the United States forces or take them prisoners. All means of transport by rail or river are to be seized, and also the newspaper offices. The morning publication of the newspapers in New York and Boston is to be suppressed; and if all be well managed, only a few New York and Boston people will know until late the day after our arrival that their cities are in my hands. My largest yacht, the Victoria, is to go to New York. I will join it there in an air-cruiser. Confidential information of all these plans is to be verbally communicated to the Governor of Canada by an aide-de-camp, who will proceed to Ottawa to-morrow morning in a swift air-cruiser. During this night you must arrange for all the information being distributed by trusty men. I wish the intended invasion to be kept a profound secret, excepting from those specially informed. Every one is to suppose that Canada is the destination. I want the United States to strengthen its army in Canada to the utmost. As to its fleet, as soon as my vessels have disembarked the troops they can proceed to destroy or capture such of the United States vessels of war as have dared to intrude on our Canadian waters."

The Emperor paused. Colonel Laurient had taken in every instruction. His eyes sparkled with animation and rejoicing, but he did not venture to express his admiration. The Emperor disliked praise. "Laurient," he continued as he grasped his favourite's hand, "go. I will detain you no longer. I trust you as myself." The Colonel bowed low and hastened away.

It may seem that the proposed mobilization was incredible. But all the forces of the Empire were constantly trained to unexpected calls to arms. Formerly intended emergency measures were designed for weeks in advance; and though they purported to be secret, every intended particular was published in the newspapers. This was playing at soldiering. The Minister presiding over all the land and sea forces has long since become more practical. He orders for mobilization without notice or warning, and practice has secured extraordinarily rapid results.

CHAPTER THIRTEEN
LOVE AND WAR

We seldom give to Hilda her title of Duchess of New Zealand, for she is endeared to us, not on account of her worldly successes, but because of her bright, lovable, unsullied womanly nature. She was dear to all who had the privilege of knowing her. The fascination she exercised was as powerful as it was unstudied. Her success in no degree changed her kindly, sympathetic nature. She always was, and always would be, unselfish and unexacting. She was staying with Mrs. Hardinge whilst the house she had purchased in London was being prepared for her. When Maud was married, she had taken Phœbe Buller for her principal private secretary. Miss Buller was devoted to Hilda, and showed herself to be a very able and industrious secretary. She had gained Hilda's confidence, and was entrusted with many offices requiring for their discharge both tact and judgment. She was much liked in London society, and was not averse to general admiration. She was slightly inclined to flirtation, but she excused this disposition to herself by the reflection that it was her duty to her chief to learn as much as she could from, and about every one. She had a devoted admirer in Cecil Fielding, a very able barrister. As a rule, the most successful counsel were females. Men seldom had much chance with juries. But Cecil Fielding was an exception. Besides great logical powers, he possessed a voice of much variety of expression and of persuasive sympathy. But however successful he was with juries, he was less fortunate with Phœbe. That young lady did not respond to his affection. She inclined more to the military profession generally and to Captain Douglas Garstairs in particular. He was one of the bodyguard, and now that war was declared was next to Colonel Laurient the chief aide-de-camp. By the Colonel's directions, the morning after the interview with the Emperor, he waited on the Duchess of New Zealand to confer with her as to the selection of a woman to take charge of the ambulance corps to accompany the forces on the ostensible expedition to Canada. Hilda summoned Phœbe and told her to take Captain Garstairs to see Mary Maudesley, and ascertain if that able young woman would accept the position on so short a notice.

Hilda had always taken great interest in the organisation of all institutions dedicated to dealing with disease. Lately she had contributed large sums to several of these establishments in want of means, and she had specially endowed an ambulance institution to train persons to treat cases of emergency consequent on illness or accident. She had thus been brought into contact with Mary Maudesley, and had noticed her astonishing power of organisation and her tenderness for suffering. Mary Maudesley was the daughter of parents in humble life. She was about twenty-seven years of age. Her father was subforeman in a large metal factory. He had risen to the position by his assiduity, ability, and trustworthiness. He received good wages; but having a large family, he continued to live in the same humble condition as when he was one of the ordinary hands at the factory. He occupied a flat on the eighth story of a large residential building in Portman Square, which had once been an eminently fashionable neighbourhood. Besides the necessary sleeping accommodation, he had a sitting-room and kitchen. His residence might be considered the type of the accommodation to which the humblest labourers were accustomed. No one in the British Empire was satisfied with less than sufficient house accommodation, substantial though plain food, and convenient, decent attire.

Mary when little more than fourteen years old had been present at an accident by which a little child of six years old was knocked down and had one leg and both arms broken. The father of the child had recently lost his wife. He lived in the same building as the Maudesleys, and Mary day and night attended to the poor little sufferer until it regained health and strength. Probably this gave direction to the devotion which she subsequently showed to attendance on the sick. She joined an institution where nurses were trained to attend cases of illness in the homes of the humble. She was perfectly fearless, notwithstanding she had been twice stricken down with dangerous illness, the result of infection from patients she had nursed.

Miss Buller thought it desirable to see Miss Maudesley at her own house, both because it might be necessary to consult her further, and because she wished to observe what were her domestic surroundings. They were pleased with what they saw. The flat was simply but usefully furnished. There was no striving after display. Everything was substantial and good of its kind without being needlessly expensive. Grace and beauty were not wanting. Some excellent drawings and water-coloured paintings by Mr. Maudesley and one or two of his children decorated the walls. There were two or three small models of inventions of Mr. Maudesley's and one item of luxury in great beauty in the shape of flowers, with which the sitting-room was amply decorated. We are perhaps wrong in terming flowers luxuries, for after all, luxuries are things with which people can dispense; and there were few families who did not regard flowers as a necessary ornament of a home, however humble it and its surroundings might be.

Miss Buller explained to Miss Maudesley that the usual head of the war ambulance corps required a substitute, as she was unable to join the expedition. It was her wish as well as that of the Duchess of New Zealand that Miss Maudesley should take her place. Fortunately Miss Maudesley's engagements were sufficiently disposable to enable her to accept the notable distinction thus offered to her. Miss Buller was greatly pleased with the unaffected manner in which she expressed her thanks and her willingness to act.

Captain Garstairs returned with Phœbe Buller to her official room. "Good-bye, Miss Buller," he said. "I hope you will allow me to call on you when I return, if indeed the exigencies of war allow me to return."

"Of course you will return. And why do you call me Miss Buller?" said the girl, with downcast eyes and pale face. For the time all traces of coquetry were wanting.

"May I call you Phœbe? And do you wish me to return?"

"Why not? Good-bye."

The cold words were belied by the moistened eyes. The bold soldier saw his opportunity. Before he left the room they were engaged to be married.

It is curious how war brings incidents of this kind to a crisis. At the risk of wearying our readers with a monotony of events, another scene in the same mansion must be described.

The Emperor did Mrs. Hardinge the honour of visiting her at her own house. So little did she seem surprised, that it almost appeared she expected him. She, however, pleaded an urgent engagement, and asked permission to leave Hilda as her substitute. The readiness with which the permission was granted seemed also to be prearranged, and the astonished girl found herself alone with the Emperor before she had fully realised that he had come to see Mrs. Hardinge. He turned to her a bright and happy face, but his manner was signally deferential.

"You cannot realise, Duchess, how I have longed to see you alone once more."

Hilda, confused beyond expression, turned to him a face from which every trace of colour had departed.

"Do you remember," he proceeded, "the last time we were alone? You allowed me then to ask you a question as from man to woman. May I again do so?"

He took her silence for consent, and went on in a tone from which he vainly endeavoured to banish the agitation that overmastered him. "Hilda, from that time there has been but one woman in the world for me. My first, my only, love, will you be my wife?"

"Your Majesty," said the girl, who as his agitation increased appeared to recover some presence of mind, "what would the world say? The Emperor may not wed with a subject."

"Why not? Am I to be told that, with all the power that has come to me, I am to be less free to secure my own happiness than the humblest of my subjects? Hilda, I prefer you to the throne if the choice had to be made. But it has not. I will remain the Emperor in order to make you the Empress. But say you can love the man, not the monarch."

"I do not love the Emperor," said the girl, almost in a whisper.

These unflattering words seemed highly satisfactory to Albert Edward as he sought from her sweet lips a ratification of her love not for the Emperor, but the man.

They both thought Mrs. Hardinge's absence a very short one when she returned, and yet she had been away an hour.

"Dear Mrs. Hardinge," said the Emperor, with radiant face, "Hilda has consented to make me the happiest man in all my wide dominions."

Mrs. Hardinge caught Hilda in her arms, and embraced her with the affection of a mother. "Your Majesty," she said at length, "does Hilda great honour. Yet I am sure you will never regret it."

"Indeed I shall not," he replied, with signal promptitude. "And it is she who does me honour. When I return from America and announce my engagement, I will take care that I let the world think so."

On the evening which had been fixed, the war and transport vessels and air-cruisers met off New York; and in a few hours the city was in the hands of the Emperor's forces. There was a little desultory fighting as well as some casualties, but there were few compared with the magnitude of the operation. The railway and telegraph stations, public buildings, and newspaper offices were in the hands of the invaders. Colonel Laurient himself led the force to Washington. At about four o'clock in the morning between twenty and thirty air-cruisers, crowded with armed soldiers, reached that city. With a little fighting, the Treasury and Arsenal were taken possession of, and the newspaper offices occupied. About one thousand men invaded the White House, some entering by means of the air-cruisers through the roof and others forcing their way through the lower part of the palace. There was but little resistance; and within an hour the President of the United States, in response to Colonel Laurient's urgent demand, received him in one of the principal rooms. She was a fine, handsome woman of apparently about thirty-five years of age. Her daughter, a young lady of seventeen, was in attendance on her. They did not show much sign of the alarm to which they had been subjected or of the haste with which they had prepared themselves to meet the British envoy. They received Colonel Laurient with all the high-bred dignity they might have exhibited on a happier occasion. Throughout the interview his manner, though firm, was most deferential.

"Madam," he said, bowing low to the President, "my imperial master the Emperor of Britain, in response to what he considers your wanton invasion of British territory in his Canadian dominions, has taken possession of New York, and requires me to lead you a prisoner to the British flagship stationed off that city. I need scarcely say that personally the task so far as it is painful to you is not agreeable to me. I have ten thousand men with me and a large number of air-cruisers. I regret to have to ask you to leave immediately."

The President, deeply affected, asked if she might be allowed to take her daughter and personal attendants with her.

"Most certainly, Madam," replied Laurient. "I am only too happy to do anything to conduce to your personal comfort. You may be sure, you will suffer from no want of respect and attention."

Within an hour the President, her daughter, and attendants left Washington in Colonel Laurient's own air-cruiser. An hour afterwards a second cruiser followed with the ladies' luggage. Meanwhile the telegraph lines round Washington were destroyed, and the officers of the forces stationed at Washington were made prisoners of war and taken on board the cruisers. At six o'clock in the morning the whole of the remaining cruisers left, and rapidly made their way to New York. The President, Mrs. Washington-Lawrence, and her daughter were received on board the flagship with the utmost respect. The officers vied with each other in showing them attention, but they were not permitted to make any communication with the shore. About noon the squadron, after disembarking the land forces, left for the St. Lawrence waters, and succeeded in capturing twenty-five of the finest vessels belonging to the United States, besides innumerable smaller ones. The Emperor left fifty thousand men, well supplied with guns, arms, and ammunition, in charge of New York, and at the head of an army of one hundred thousand men, the flower of the British force in the Northern Hemisphere, proceeded rapidly to the Canadian frontier. About a hundred miles on the other side of the frontier they came upon traces of the near presence of the American forces.

Here it was that the most conspicuous act of personal courage was displayed, and the hero was Lord Reginald Paramatta. He happened to be in London when war was announced, and he volunteered to accompany one of the battalions. It should be mentioned that no proceedings had been initiated against Lord Reginald either for his presence at the treasonable meeting, or for his attempted abduction of Hilda. Her friends were entirely averse to any action being taken, as the publicity would have been most repugnant to her. It became necessary early in the night to ascertain the exact position of the American forces, and to communicate with the Canadian forces on the other side, with the view to joint action. The locality was too unknown and the night too dark to make the air-cruisers serviceable. The reconnoitring party were to make their way as best they could through the American lines, communicate with the Canadian commander, and return as soon as possible in an air-cruiser. Each man carried with him an electric battery of intense force, by means of which he could either produce a strong light, or under certain conditions a very powerful offensive and defensive weapon.

Only fifty men were to compose the force, and Lord Reginald's offer to lead them was heartily accepted. His bravery, judgment, and coolness in action were undeniable. At midnight he started, and, with the assistance of a guide, soon penetrated to an eminence from which the lights of the large United States camp below could be plainly discerned. The forces were camped on the plain skirted by the range of hills from one of which Lord Reginald made his observations. The plain was of peculiar shape, resembling nearly the figure that two long isosceles triangles joined at the base would represent. The force was in its greatest strength at the middle, and tapered down towards each end. Far away on the other edge of the plain, evidence of the Canadian camp could be dimly perceived. The ceaseless movements in the American camp betokened preparations for early action. After a long and critical survey both of the plain and of the range of hills, Lord Reginald determined to cross at the extreme left. The scouts of the Americans were stationed far up upon the chain of hills, and Lord Reginald saw that it would be impossible to traverse unnoticed the range from where he stood to the point at which he had determined to descend to the plain. He had to retire to the other side of the range and make his progress to the west (the camp faced the north) on the outer side of the range that skirted the camp. The hill from which he had decided to descend was nearly two miles distant from the point at which he made his observation. But the way was rough and tortuous, and it took nearly two hours to reach a comparatively low hill skirting the plain at the narrowest point. The force below was also narrowed out. Less than half a mile in depth seemed to be occupied by the American camp at this point. The Canadian camp was less extended. Its extreme west appeared to be attainable by a diagonal line of about two miles in length, with an inclination from the straight of about seventy degrees. Lord Reginald had thus to force his way through nearly half a mile of the camp, and then to cross nearly two miles between both forces.

  The commander halted his followers, and in a low tone proceeded to give his instructions. The men were to march in file two deep, about six feet were to separate each rank, and the files were to be twenty feet apart. Each two men of the same file were to carry extended between them the flexible platinum aluminium electric wire, capable of bearing an enormous strain, that upon a touch of the button of the battery, carried by each man, would destroy any living thing which came in contact with it. Lord Reginald and the officer next to him in rank, who was none other than Captain Douglas Garstairs, were to lead the way. In a few moments the wires between each two men were adjusted. They were to proceed very slowly down the hill until they were observed, then with a rush, to skirt the outside of the camp. Once past the camp, the wires were to be disconnected, and the men, as much separated as possible, were to make to the opposite camp with the utmost expedition. Slowly and noiselessly amidst the intense shadow of the hill Lord Reginald and his companion led the way towards the extreme end of the camp. They had nearly reached the level ground when at three feet distance a sentry stood before them and shouted, "Who goes there?" Poor wretch, they were his last words. Lord Reginald and his companion with a rapid movement rushed on either side of him, and the moment the wire touched him he sank to the ground a lifeless mass. Then ensued a commotion almost impossible to describe. Lord Reginald and Captain Garstairs were noted runners. They proceeded at a strong pace outside of the tents. As the men rushed out to stop them, the fatal wire performed its ghastly execution. Three times three men sank lifeless in their path, before they cleared the outside of the tents. The Americans could only fire at intervals, for fear of hitting their own men. Of the twenty-five couples of Lord Reginald's force, fifteen passed the tents; twenty of the brave men were stricken down, whilst the way was strewn with the bodies of the Americans who had succumbed to the mysterious electric force. And now the time had come for each one to save himself. The wires were disconnected, the batteries thrown down, and for dear life every one rushed towards the Canadian camp. But the noise had been heard along the line, and a wonderful consequence ensued. From end to end of the American camp the electric lights were turned on to the strength of many millions of candle-power. The lights left the camp in darkness; the rays were turned outwards to the spare ground that separated the camps. The Canadians responded by turning on their lights, and the plain between the two camps was irradiated with a dazzling brightness which even the sunlight could not emulate. The forlorn hope dashed on. Thousands of pieces were fired at the straggling men. It was fortunate they were so much apart, as it led to the same man being shot at many times. Of the thirty who passed the tents ten men at intervals fell before the murderous fire. Lord Reginald had been grazed by a shot the effects of which he scarcely felt. He and his companions were within a hundred yards of safety. But that safety was not to be. Captain Garstairs was struck. "Good-bye, Reginald. Tell Phœbe Buller——" He could say no more. Lord Reginald arrested his progress, and as coolly as if he were in a drawing-room lifted the wounded man tenderly and carefully in his arms, and without haste or fear covered the intervening distance to the Canadian camp. He was not struck. Who indeed shall say that he was aimed at? His great deed was equally seen by each army in the bright blaze of light; and when he reached the haven of safety, a cheer went up from each side, for there were brave men in both armies, ready to admire deeds of valour. Only ten men reached the Canadian camp; but, under the sanction of a flag of truce, five more were brought in alive, and they subsequently recovered from their wounds. Captain Garstairs was shot in the leg both above and below the knee. He remained in the Canadian camp that day. At first it was feared he would lose the limb. But, to anticipate events, when the Emperor's forces joined the Canadian, Mary Maudesley took charge of him; and Captain Garstairs had ample cause to congratulate himself on the visit he had paid to secure the services of that lady. He was in the habit of declaring afterwards that it was the most successful expedition of his life, for it was the means of securing him a wife and of saving him a limb.

Lord Reginald rapidly explained the situation to the Canadian commander-in-chief. The Emperor's army could come up in three hours. It was evident from the movements under the hills opposite, as shown by the electric light, that the Americans did not mean to waste time. It was probable that at the first dawn of day they would set their army in motion; and it was arranged that the Canadians, without hastening the action, should, on the Americans advancing, proceed to meet them, so that they would be nearer the Emperor's forces as these advanced in rear of the enemy. Scarcely half an hour after he reached the Canadian lines Lord Reginald ascended in a swift air-cruiser, and passing high above the American camp, reached the Emperor's forces before day dawned.

Lord Reginald briefly communicated the result of his expedition. He took no credit to himself, did not dwell on the dangerous passage nor his heroic rescue of Captain Garstairs. Nevertheless the incident soon became known, and enhanced Lord Reginald's popularity.

The army was rapidly in motion; and after the Canadian and American forces became engaged, the British army, led by the Emperor in person, appeared on the crest of the hills and descended towards the plains. The American commander-in-chief knew nothing of the British army in his rear. Tidings had not reached him of the occupation of New York and Boston. The incident of the rush of Lord Reginald and his party across the plain from camp to camp and the return of an air-cruiser towards the United States frontier had occasioned him surprise; but his mind did not dwell on it in the midst of the immediate responsible duties he had to perform. On the other hand, he was expecting reinforcements from the States; and when the new force appeared on the summit of the hills, he congratulated himself mentally; for the battle with the Canadian army threatened to go hard with him. Before he was undeceived the British troops came thundering down the hills, and he was a prisoner to an officer of the Emperor's own staff. The British troops went onwards, and the destruction of the American forces was imminent. But the Emperor could not bear the idea of the carnage inflicted on persons speaking the same language, and whose forefathers were the subjects of his own ancestors. "Spare them," he appealed to the commander-in-chief. "They are hopelessly at our mercy. Let them surrender."

The battle was stayed as speedily as possible; and the British and Canadian forces found themselves in possession of over one hundred and thirty thousand prisoners, besides all the arms, ammunition, artillery, and camp equipage. It was a tremendous victory.

CHAPTER FOURTEEN
THE FOURTH OF JULY RETRIEVED

The prisoners were left at Quebec suitably guarded; but the British and Canadian forces, as fast as the railways could carry them, returned to New York. The United States Constitution had not made provision for the imprisonment or abduction of the President of the Republic, and there was some doubt as to how the place of the chief of the executive should be supplied. It was decided that, as in the President's absence on ordinary occasions the deputy President represented him, so the same precedent should be followed in the case of the present extraordinary absence.

The President, however, was not anxious to resume her position. It was to her headstrong action that the invasion of Canada was owing. The President of the United States possesses more individual power in the way of moving armies and declaring war than any other monarch. This has always been the case. A warlike spirit is easily fostered in any nation. Still the wise and prudent were aghast at the President's hasty action on what seemed the slight provocation of the renewal of the immemorial fisheries dispute. Of course public opinion could not gauge the sense of wrong that the rejection by the Emperor of her daughter's hand had occasioned in the mind of the President. Now that the episode was over, and the empire of Britain had won a triumph which amply redeemed the humiliation of centuries back, when the English colonies of America won their independence by force of arms, public opinion was very bitter against the President. The glorious 4th of July was virtually abolished. How could they celebrate the independence and forget to commemorate the retrieval by their old mother-country of all her power and prestige? No wonder then that Mrs. Washington-Lawrence did not care to return to the States!

"My dear," she said to her daughter in one of the luxurious cabins assigned to them on the flagship, "do you think that I ought to send in my resignation?"

"I cannot judge," replied the young lady. "You appear quite out of it. Negotiations are said to be proceeding, but you are not consulted or even informed of what is going on."

"If it were not for you," said the elder lady, "I would never again set foot on the United States soil. Captain Hamilton" (alluding to the captain of the vessel they were on, the British Empire) "says I ought not to do so."

"I do not see that his advice matters," promptly answered the young lady. "If Admiral Benedict had said so, I might have considered it more important."

"I think more of the captain's opinion," said Mrs. Washington-Lawrence.

"Perhaps he thinks more of yours," retorted the unceremonious daughter. "But what do you mean about returning for my sake?"

"My dear, you are very young, and cannot remain by yourself. Besides, you will want to settle in the United States when you marry, to look after the large property your father left you, and that will come to you when you are twenty-one."

"I think, mother, you have interfered quite sufficiently about my marrying. We should not be here now but for your anxiety to dispose of me."

Mrs. Washington-Lawrence thought this very ungrateful, for her efforts were not at the time at all repugnant to the ambitious young lady. However, a quarrel was averted; and milder counsels prevailed. At length the elder lady confessed, with many blushes, Captain Hamilton had proposed to her, and that she would have accepted him but for the thought of her daughter's probable dissatisfaction.

This aroused an answering confession from Miss Washington-Lawrence. The admiral, it appeared, had twice proposed to her; and she had consented to his obtaining the Emperor's permission, a condition considered necessary under the peculiar circumstances.

The Emperor readily gave his consent. It was an answer to those of his own subjects who had wished him to marry the New England girl with the red hair, and opened the way to his announcing his marriage with Hilda.

The two weddings of mother and daughter took place amidst much rejoicing throughout the whole squadron. The Emperor gave to each bride a magnificent set of diamonds. Negotiations meanwhile with the United States proceeded as to the terms on which the Emperor would consent to peace, a month's truce having been declared in the meanwhile. Mrs. Hardinge and Hilda met the chief ministers of the two powerful empires in Europe, and satisfied them that the British Government would not ask anything prejudicial to their interests.

The terms were finally arranged. The United States were to pay the empire of Britain six hundred millions sterling and to salute the British flag. The Childrosse family and Rorgon, Mose and Co. undertook to find the money for the United States Government. The Emperor consented to retire from New York in six months unless within that time a plebiscite of that State and the New English States declared by a majority of two to one the desire of the people to again become the subjects of the British Empire, in which case New York would be constituted the capital of the Dominion of Canada. To anticipate events, it may at once be said that the majority in favour of reannexation was over four to one, and that the union was celebrated with enormous rejoicing. Most of the United States vessels were returned to her, and the British Government, on behalf of the Empire, voluntarily relinquished the money payment, in favour of its being handed to the States seceding from the Republic to join the Canadian Dominion. This provision was a wise one, for otherwise the new States of the Canadian Dominion would have been less wealthy than those they joined.

CHAPTER FIFTEEN
CONCLUSION

The Emperor went to Quebec for a week, and thence returned to London, in the month of July. There he announced his intended marriage, and that it would very soon take place. The ovations showered on the Emperor in consequence of his successful operations in the United States defy description. He was recognised as the first military genius of the day. Many declared that he excelled all military heroes of the past, and that a better-devised and more ably carried-into-effect military movement was not to be found in the pages of history, ancient or modern.

At such a time, had the marriage been really unpopular, much would have been conceded to the desire to do honour to his military successes. But the marriage was not unpopular in a personal sense. There was great difference of opinion as to the wisdom of an emperor marrying a subject instead of seeking a foreign alliance. On the one hand, difficulties of court etiquette were alleged; on the other, it was contended that Britain had nothing to gain from foreign marriage alliances, that she was strong enough without them, and that they frequently were sources of weakness rather than strength.

The Duchess of New Zealand sat alone in her study in the new mansion in London of which she had just taken possession. It was magnificently furnished and decorated, but she would soon cease to have a use for it. She was to be married in a week, and the Empress of Britain would have royal residences in all parts of her wide dominions. She intended to make a present of her new house, with its contents, to Phœbe Buller on her marriage with Colonel Garstairs. He won his promotion in the United States war. She was writing a letter to her sister, Lady Montreal. A slight noise attracted her attention. She looked up, and with dismay beheld the face of Lord Reginald Paramatta. "How dare you thus intrude?" she said, in an accent of strong indignation, though she could scarcely restrain a feeling of pity, so ill and careworn did he look.

"Do not grudge me," he said, in deprecatory tones, "a few moments of your presence. I am dying for the want of you."

"My lord," replied Hilda, "you should be sensible that nothing could be more distasteful to me than such a visit after your past conduct."

"I do not deny your cause of complaint; but, Hilda—let me call you so this once—remember it was all for love of you."

"I cannot remember anything of the kind. True love seeks the happiness of the object it cherishes, not its misery."

"You once looked kindly on me."

"Lord Reginald, I never loved you, nor did I ever lead you to believe so. A deep and true instinct told me from the first that I could not be happy with you."

"You crush me with your cruel words," said Lord Reginald. "When I am away from you, I persuade myself that I have not sufficiently pleaded my cause; and then with irresistible force I long to see you."

"All your wishes," said the girl, "are irresistible because you have never learned to govern them. If you truly loved me, you would have the strength to sacrifice your love to the conviction that it would wreck my happiness." The girl paused. Then, with a look of impassioned sincerity, she went on, "Lord Reginald, let me appeal to your better nature. You are brave. No one more rejoiced than I did over your great deed in Canada. I forgot your late conduct, and thought only of our earlier friendship. Be brave now morally as well as physically. Renounce the feelings I cannot reciprocate; and when next I meet you, let me acknowledge in you the hero who has conquered himself."

"In vain. In vain. I cannot do it. There is no alternative for me but you or death. Hilda, I will not trifle with time. I am here to carry you away. You must be mine."

"Dare you threaten me," said she, "and in my own house?" Her hand was on the button on the table to summon assistance, but he arrested the movement and put his arm round her waist. With a loud and piercing scream, Hilda flew towards the door. Before she reached it, it opened; and there entered a tall man, with features almost indistinguishable from the profuse beard, whiskers, and moustache with which they were covered. Hilda screamed out, "Help me. Protect me."

"I am Laurient," he whispered to the agitated girl. "Go to the back room, and this whistle will bring immediate aid. The lower part of the house and staircase are crowded with that man's followers." Hilda rushed from the room before Lord Reginald could reach her. Colonel Laurient closed the door, and pulled from his face its hirsute adornments. "I am Colonel Laurient, at your service. You have to reckon with me for your cruel persecution of that poor girl."

"How came you here?" asked Lord Reginald, who was almost stunned with astonishment.

"My lord," replied Laurient, "since your attempt at Waiwera to carry the Duchess away you have been unceasingly shadowed. Your personal attendants were in the pay of those who watched over that fair girl's safety. Your departure from Canada was noted, the object of your stay in London suspected. Your intended visit to-day was guessed at, and I was one of the followers who accompanied you. But there is no time for explanation. You shall account to me as a friend of the Emperor for your conduct to the noble woman he is about to marry. She shall be persecuted no longer; one or both of us shall not leave this room alive."

He pulled out two small firing-pieces, each with three barrels. "Select one," he said briefly. "Both weapons are loaded. We shall stand at opposite ends of this large room."

At no time would Lord Reginald have been likely to refuse a challenge of this kind, and least of all now. His one desire was revenge on some one to satisfy the terrible cravings of his baffled passions. "I am under the impression," he said, with studied calmness, "that I already owe something to your interference. I am not reluctant to acquit myself of the debt."

In a few minutes the help Hilda summoned arrived. Laurient had taken care to provide assistance near at hand. When the officers in charge of the aid entered the room, a sad sight presented itself. Both Lord Reginald and Colonel Laurient were prostrate on the ground, the former evidently fatally stricken, the latter scarcely less seriously wounded.

They did not venture to move Lord Reginald. At his earnest entreaty, Hilda came to him. It was a terrible ordeal for her. It was likely both men would die, and their death would be the consequence of their vain love for her. But how different the nature of the love, the one unselfish and sacrificing, seeking only her happiness, the other brutally indifferent to all but its own uncontrollable impulses. It seemed absurd to call by the same name sentiments so widely opposite, the one so ennobling, the other so debasing.

She stood beside the couch on which they had lifted him. "Hilda," he whispered in a tone so low, she could scarcely distinguish what he said, "the death I spoke of has come; and I do not regret it. It was you or death, as I told you; and death has conquered." He paused for a few moments, then resumed, "My time is short. Say you forgive me all the unhappiness I have caused you."

Hilda was much affected. "Reginald," she faltered, "I fully, freely forgive you for all your wrongs to me; but can I forget that Colonel Laurient may also meet his death?"

"A happy death, for it will have been gained in your service."

"Reginald, dear Reginald, if your sad anticipation is to be realised, should you not cease to think of earthly things?"

"Pray for me," he eagerly replied. "You were right in saying my passions were ungovernable, but I have never forgotten the faith of my childhood. I am past forgiveness, for I sinned and knew that I was sinning."

"God is all-merciful," said the tearful girl. She sank upon her knees before the couch, and in low tones prayed the prayers familiar to her, and something besides extemporised from her own heart. She thought of Reginald as she first knew him, of the great deeds of which he had been capable, of the melancholy consequence of his uncontrolled love for herself. She prayed with an intense earnestness that he might be forgiven; and as she prayed a faint smile irradiated the face of the dying man, and with an effort to say, "Amen," he drew his last breath.

Three days later Hilda stood beside another deathbed. All that care and science could effect was useless; Colonel Laurient was dying. The fiat had gone forth; life was impossible. The black horses would once more come to the door of the new mansion. He who loved Hilda so truly, so unselfishly, was to share the fate of that other unworthy lover. Hilda's grief was of extreme poignancy, and scarcely less grieved was the Emperor himself. He had passed most of his time since he had learnt Laurient's danger beside his couch, and now the end was approaching. On one side of the bed was the Emperor, on the other Hilda, Duchess of New Zealand. How puerile the title seemed in the presence of the dread executioner who recognises no distinction between peasant and monarch. The mightiest man on earth was utterly powerless to save his friend, and the day would come when he and the lovely girl who was to be his bride would be equally powerless to prolong their own lives. In such a presence the distinctions of earth seemed narrowed and distorted.

"Sir," said the dying man, "my last prayer is that you and Hilda may be happy. She is the noblest woman I have ever met. You once told me," he said, turning to her, "that you felt for me a sister's love. Will you before I die give me a sister's kiss and blessing?" Hilda, utterly unable to control her sobs, bent down and pressed a kiss upon his lips. It seemed as if life passed away at that very moment. He never moved or spoke again. He was buried in the grounds of one of the royal residences, and the Emperor and Hilda erected a splendid monument to his memory. No year ever passed without their visiting the grave of the man who had served them so well.

Their marriage was deferred for a month in consequence of Colonel Laurient's death, but the ceremony was a grand one. Nothing was wanting in the way of pomp and display to invest it with the utmost importance. Throughout the whole Empire there were great rejoicings. It really appeared as if the Emperor could not have made a more popular marriage, and that unalloyed happiness was in store for him and his bride.

EPILOGUE

Twenty years have passed. The Emperor is nearly fifty, and the Empress is no longer young. They have preserved their good looks; but on the countenance of each is a settled melancholy expression, wanting in the days which preceded their marriage. Their union seemed to promise a happy life, no cloud showed itself on the horizon of their new existence, and yet sadness proved to be its prominent feature. A year after their marriage a son was born, amidst extravagant rejoicings throughout the Empire. Another year witnessed the birth of a daughter, and a third child was shortly expected, when a terrible event occurred. A small dog, a great favourite of the child, slightly bit the young prince. The animal proved to be mad, a fact unsuspected until too late to apply adequate remedial measures to the boy, and the heir to the Empire died amidst horrible suffering. The grief of the parents may be better imagined than described. The third child, a boy, was prematurely born, and grew up weak and sickly. Two more children were subsequently born, but both died in early childhood. The princess, the elder-born of the two survivors, grew into a beautiful woman. She was over eighteen years old when this history reopens. Her brother was a year younger. The contrast between the two was remarkable. Princess Victoria was a fine, healthy girl, with a lovely complexion. She inherited her mother's beauty and her father's dignity and grace of manner. She was the idol of every one with whom she came in contact. The charm and fascination of her demeanour were enhanced by the dignity of presence which never forsook her. Her brother, poor boy, was thin and delicate-looking, and a constant invalid, though not afflicted with any organic disease. They both were clever, but their tastes were widely apart. The Princess was an accomplished linguist; and few excelled her in knowledge of history, past and contemporaneous. She took great interest in public affairs. No statesman was better acquainted with the innumerable conditions which cumbered the outward seeming of affairs of state. Prince Albert Edward, on the contrary, took no heed of public affairs. He rarely read a newspaper; but he was a profound mathematician, a constant student of physical laws: and, above all, he had a love for the study of human character. When only sixteen, he gained a gold medal for a paper sent in anonymously to the Imperial Institute, dealing with the influence of circumstances and events upon mental and moral development. The essay was very deep, and embodied some new and rather startling theories, closely reasoned, as to the effects of training and education.

  The Princess was her father's idol; and though he was too just to wish to prejudice his son's rights, he could not without bitter regret remember that but for his action long ago his daughter would have been heiress to the throne. Fate, with strange irony, had made the Empress also alter her views. The weak and sickly son had been the special object of long years of care. The poor mother, bereaved of three children out of five, clung to this weak offspring as the shipwrecked sailor to the plank which is his sole chance of life. The very notion of the loved son losing the succession was a cruel shock to her. The theoretical views which she shared with Mrs. Hardinge years since, were a weak barrier to the promptings of maternal love.

  So it happened that the Emperor ardently regretted that he had prevented the proposed change in the order of succession, and the Empress as much rejoiced that the views of her party had not prevailed. But the Emperor was essentially a just man. He recognised that before children had been born to him the question was open to treatment, but that it was different now when his son enjoyed personal rights. Ardently as he desired his daughter should reign, he would not on any consideration agree that his son should be set aside without his own free and full consent. What annoyed him most was the fallacy of his own arguments long ago. It will be remembered, he had laid chief stress on the probability that the female succession would reduce the chance of the armies being led by the Emperor in person in case of war. But it was certain that, if his son succeeded, he would not head the army in battle. The young Prince had passed through the military training prescribed for every male subject of the Empire, but he had no taste for military knowledge. Not that he wanted courage; on the contrary, he had displayed conspicuous bravery on several occasions. Once he had jumped off a yacht in rough weather to save one of his staff who had fallen overboard; and on another occasion, when a fire took place at sea, he was cooler and less terror-stricken than any of the persons who surrounded him. But for objects and studies of a militant character he had an aversion, almost a contempt; and it was certain he never would become a great general. The fallacy of his principal objection to the change in the order of succession was thus brought home to the Emperor with bitter emphasis.

Perhaps the worst effect of all was the wall of estrangement that was being built up between him and the Empress. When two people constantly in communication feel themselves prevented from discussing the subject nearest to the heart and most constant to the mind of each, estrangement must grow up, no matter how great may be their mutual love. The Emperor and Empress loved each other as much as ever, but to both the discussion of the question of succession was fraught with bitter pain.

The time had, however, come when they must discuss it. The Princess had already reached her legal majority, and the Prince would shortly arrive at the age which was prescribed as the majority of the heir to the throne. His own unfitness for the sovereignty and the exceeding suitability of his sister were widely known, and the newspapers had just commenced a warm discussion on the subject. The Cabinet, too, were inclined to take action. Many years since, Mrs. Hardinge died quite suddenly of heart disease; and Lady Cairo had for a long period filled the post of Prime Minister. Lady Garstairs, née Phœbe Buller, was leader of the Opposition. She was still a close friend of the Empress, and she shared the opinion of her imperial mistress that the subject had better not be dealt with. But Lady Cairo, who had always thought it ought to have been settled before the Emperor's marriage, was very much embarrassed now by the strong and general demand that the question should be immediately reopened. She had several interviews with the

Emperor on the subject. His Majesty did not conceal his personal desire that his daughter should succeed, or his opinion that she was signally fitted for the position; but nothing, he declared, would induce him to allow his son's rights to be assailed without the Prince's full and free consent. Meanwhile the Prince showed no sign. It seemed as if he alone of all the subjects of the Empire knew and cared nothing about the matter. He rarely spoke of public affairs, and scarcely ever read the newspapers, especially those portions of them devoted to politics.

The Emperor felt a discussion with the Empress could no longer be avoided; and we meet them once more at a long and painful interview, in which they unburdened the thoughts which each had concealed from the other for years past.

"Dear Hilda," said the Emperor, "do not misunderstand me. I would rather renounce the crown than allow our son's rights to be prejudiced without his approval."

"Yes, yes, I understand that," said the Empress; "and I recognise your sense of justice. I do not think that you love Albert as much as you do Victoria, and you certainly have not that pride in him which you have in her; whilst I—I love my boy, and cannot bear that he should suffer."

"My dear," said the Emperor, "that is where we differ. I love Albert, and I admire his high character; but I do not think it would be for his happiness that he should reign, nor that he should now relinquish all the studies in which he delights, in order to take his proper position as heir to the throne. In a few weeks he will be of age; and if he is to succeed me, duties of a most onerous and constant character will devolve on him. He is, I will do him the justice to say, too conscientious to neglect his duty; and I believe he will endeavour to attend to public affairs and cast away all those studies that most delight him: but the change will make him miserable."

"You are a wise judge of the hearts and ways of men and women, and it would ill become me to disregard your opinion; but, Albert, does it not occur to you that our Albert might live to regret any renunciation he made in earlier life?"

"I admit the possibility," said the Emperor; "but he is stable and mature beyond his years. His dream is to benefit mankind by the studies he pursues. He has already met with great success in those studies, and I think they will bring their own reward; but should anything occur to make him renounce them, he may, I admit, lament too late the might-have-been."

"Supposing," said the Empress, "he married an ambitious wife and had sons like you were, dear Albert, in your young manhood?"

"One cannot judge one's self; yet I think I should have accepted whatever was my position, and not have allowed vain repinings to prevent my endeavouring to perform the duties that devolved on me."

"Forgive me, Albert, for doubting it. You would, I am sure, have been true to yourself."

"You confirm my own impression. Recollect, Hilda, true ambition prompts to legitimate effort, not to vain grief for the unattainable. It may be that Victoria's own children will succeed; but Albert's children, if they are ambitious, will not be denied a brilliant career."

"I cannot argue the matter, for it is useless to deny that I refuse to see our son as he is. I love him to devotion, yet the grief is always with me that the son is not like the father."

"Hilda dear, he is not like the father in some respects; but the very difference perhaps partakes of the higher life. When the last day comes to him and to me, who shall say that he will not look back to his conduct through life with more satisfaction than I shall be able to do?"

"I will not allow you to underrate yourself. You are faultless in my eyes. No human being has ever had cause to complain of you."

"Tut! tut! You are too partial a judge." But he kissed her tenderly, and his eyes gleamed with a pleasure for a very long while unknown to them, as she brought to him the conviction that the love and admiration of her youth had survived all the sorrows of their after-lives.

At this juncture the Prince entered the room. "Pardon me," he said. "I thought my mother was alone;" and he was about to retire. The Emperor looked at the Empress, and he gathered from her answering glance that she shared with him the desire that all reserve and concealment should be at an end. In a moment his resolution was formed. His son should know everything and decide for himself.

"Stay, Albert," he said. "I am glad to have an opportunity of talking with you in the presence of your mother."

"I am equally glad, Sir. Indeed, I should have asked you later in the day to have given me an audience."

"Why do you wish to see me?" said the Emperor, who in a moment suspected what proved to be the case: that his son anticipated his own wish for an exchange of confidence.

"During the last few days it has become known to me, Sir, that a controversy is going on respecting the order of succession to the throne. I have," producing a small package, "cuttings from some of the principal newspapers from which I gather there is a strong opinion in favour of a change in the order of succession. I glean from them that by far the larger number are agreed on the point that it would be better my sister should succeed to you." He paused a moment, and then in a clear and distinct tone said, "I am of the same opinion."

The Empress interposed. "Are you sure of your own mind? Do you recognise what it is you would renounce—the position of foremost ruler on the wide globe?"

"I think I realise it. I am not much given to the study of contemporaneous history, but I am well acquainted with all the circumstances of my father's great career." The parents looked at each other in surprise. "Yes; there is no one," he resumed, "who is more proud of the Emperor than his only son."

With much emotion the father clasped the son's hand. "What is it you wish, Albert?" he said.

"I would like Victoria to be present if you would not mind," replied the Prince, looking at his mother. "May I fetch her?"

The Empress nodded. "You will find her in the next room."

The Princess Victoria was a lovely and splendid girl. It was impossible to look at her without feeling that she would adorn the highest position. The Emperor's face lighted up as he glanced at her; and the Empress, much impressed with what her husband had said, kissed the Princess with unusual tenderness. She probably wished her daughter to feel that she was not averse to any issue which might result from the momentous interview about to take place.

"Sir," said the young Prince, addressing his father, "I know how important your time is, so I will not prolong what I wish to say. Until I saw these papers," holding up the extracts, "I confess I was unaware of the great interest which is now being taken in the question of the succession. But I cannot assert that the subject is new to me; on the contrary, I have thought it over deeply, and it was my intention to speak to you about it when in a few weeks I should attain my majority."

"My dear boy, pray believe that it was through consideration to you I have refrained from speaking to you on the subject."

"I know it, Sir, and thank you," said the boy with feeling; "but the time has come when there must be no longer any reserve between us. You know, I do not take much interest in public affairs, and I fear it has grieved you that my inclinations have been so alien to what my position as heir to the throne required. But I am not unacquainted with the principles of the constitution of the Empire. I will not pretend that I have studied them from a statesman's point of view. They have absorbed my attention in the course of my favourite study of human character. I have closely (if it did not seem conceited, I might say philosophically) investigated the Constitution with the object of determining to what extent it operates as an educational medium affecting the character of the nation. The question of the succession is settled by the Constitution Act, and no alteration is possible in justice, that does not fully reserve the rights of all living beings. I am first in the order of succession, and no law of man can take it from me excepting with my full consent."

"Albert," interrupted the Emperor, "you say rightly; and I assure you that I am fully prepared to adopt this view. No consideration will induce me to consent to any alteration which will prejudice you excepting with your own desire; and indeed I am doubtful if even with your desire I should be justified in allowing you at so early a period of your life to make a renunciation."

"I am grateful, Sir, for this assurance. Its memory will live in my mind. And now let me say that, having for a long while considered the subject with the utmost attention I could give to it, I am of opinion that the present law by which the female succession is partly barred is not a just one. I will not, however, say that it ought to be altered against a living representative; but I decidedly think that it should be amended as regards those unborn. The decision I have come to then does not depend upon the amendment in the Constitution which I believe to be desirable. It arises from personal causes. I believe that my sister Victoria is as specially fitted for the dignity and functions of empress, as I am the reverse."

The Princess Victoria started up in great agitation. She was not without ambition, and it could not be questioned that the position of empress had fascinating attraction for her active mind and courageous spirit. But she dearly loved her brother, and her predominant feeling at the moment was regard for his interests. "Albert," she said with great energy, "I will not have you make any sacrifice for me. You will be a good and clever man, and will adorn whatever position you are called to."

"I thank you, Victoria," said the boy gravely. "I am delighted that you think so well of me. But you must not consider I am making a sacrifice. My inclinations are entirely against public life. The position of next heir, and in time of emperor, would give me no pleasure. My ambition—and I am not without it—points to triumphs of a different kind. No success in the council or in the field would give me the gratification that the reception of my paper by the Imperial Institute occasioned me, and the gold medal which I gained without my name as author being known. Why I have dwelt on your fitness for the position, Victoria, is because I do not believe that I should be justified in renouncing the succession unless I could honestly feel that a better person would take my place."

"Albert," interposed the Empress, "let your mother say a word before you proceed further. I will not interfere with any decision that may be arrived at. I leave that to your father, in whose wisdom I have implicit faith. But I must ask you, Have you thought over all contingencies, not only of what has happened in the past or of what is now occurring, but of what the future may have in store?"

"I have, my mother, thought over the future as well as the past."

"You may marry, Albert. Your wife may grieve for the position you have renounced; you may have children: they may inherit your father's grand qualities. Will you yourself not grieve to see them subordinate to their cousins, your sister's children?"

"Mother, I probably shall not marry; and if I do, my renunciation of the succession will justify me in marrying as my heart dictates, and not to satisfy State exigencies. I shall be well assured that whomever I marry will be content to take me for myself, and not for what I might have been. As to the children, they will be educated to the station to which they will belong, surely a sufficiently exalted one."

The Emperor now interposed. "You are young," he said, "to speak of wife and children; but you have spoken with the sense and discretion of mature years. I understand, that if you renounce the succession, you will do so in the full belief that you will be consulting your own happiness and not injuring those who might be your subjects, because you leave to them a good substitute in your sister."

"You have rightly described my sentiments," said the boy.

"Then, Albert," said the Emperor, "I will give my consent to the introduction of a measure that, preserving your rights, will as regards the future give to females an equal right with males to the succession. As regards yourself, I think the Act should give you after your majority a right, entirely depending on your own discretion, of renunciation in favour of your sister, and provide that such renunciation shall be finally operative."

Our history for the present ends with the passage of the Act described by the Emperor; an Act considered to be especially memorable, since it removed the last disability under which the female sex laboured.

It is perhaps desirable to explain that three leading features have been kept in view in the production of the foregoing anticipation of the future.

First, it has been designed to show that a recognised dominance of either sex is unnecessary, and that men and women may take part in the affairs of the world on terms of equality, each member of either sex enjoying the position to which he or she is entitled by reason of his or her qualifications.

The second object is to suggest that the materials are to hand for forming the dominions of Great Britain into a powerful and beneficent empire.

The third purpose is to attract consideration to the question as to whether it is not possible to relieve the misery under which a large portion of mankind languishes on account of extreme poverty and destitution. The writer has a strong conviction that every human being is entitled to a sufficiency of food and clothing and to decent lodging whether or not he or she is willing to or capable of work. He hates the idea of anything approaching to Communism, as it would be fatal to energy and ambition, two of the most ennobling qualities with which human beings are endowed. But there is no reason to fear that ambition would be deadened because the lowest scale of life commenced with sufficiency of sustenance. Experience, on the contrary, shows that the higher the social status the more keen ambition becomes. Aspiration is most numbed in those whose existence is walled round with constant privation. Figures would of course indicate that the cost of the additional provision would be enormous, but the increase is more seeming than real. Every commodity that man uses is obtained by an expenditure of more or less human labour. The extra cost would mean extra employment and profit to vast numbers of people, and the earth itself is capable of an indefinite increase of the products which are necessary to man's use. The additional employment available would in time make work a privilege, not a burden; and the objects of the truest sympathy would be those who would not or who could not work. The theory of forcing a person to labour would be no more recognised than one of forcing a person to listen to music or to view works of art. Of course it will be urged that natives of countries where the earth is prolific are not, as a rule, industrious. But this fact must be viewed in connection with that other fact that to these countries the higher aims which grow in the path of civilisation have not penetrated. An incalculable increase of wealth, position, and authority would accompany an ameliorated condition of the proletariat, so that the scope of ambition would be proportionately enlarged. There would still be much variety of human woe and joy; and though the lowest rung of the ladder would not descend to the present abysmal depth of destitution and degradation, the intensely comprehensive line of the poet would continue as monumental as ever,—

"The meanest hind in misery's sad train still looks beneath him."

THE END

SULTANA'S DREAM
BY BEGUM ROKEYA SAKHAWAT HUSSAIN
(BANGLADESH, 1905)

One evening I was lounging in an easy chair in my bedroom and thinking lazily of the condition of Indian womanhood. I am not sure whether I dozed off or not. But, as far as I remember, I was wide awake. I saw the moonlit sky sparkling with thousands of diamond-like stars, very distinctly.

All on a sudden a lady stood before me; how she came in, I do not know. I took her for my friend, Sister Sara.

"Good morning," said Sister Sara. I smiled inwardly as I knew it was not morning, but starry night. However, I replied to her, saying, "How do you do?"

"I am all right, thank you. Will you please come out and have a look at our garden?"

I looked again at the moon through the open window, and thought there was no harm in going out at that time. The men-servants outside were fast asleep just then, and I could have a pleasant walk with Sister Sara.

I used to have my walks with Sister Sara, when we were at Darjeeling. Many a time did we walk hand in hand and talk light-heartedly in the botanical gardens there. I fancied, Sister Sara had probably come to take me to some such garden and I readily accepted her offer and went out with her.

When walking I found to my surprise that it was a fine morning. The town was fully awake and the streets alive with bustling crowds. I was feeling very shy, thinking I was walking in the street in broad daylight, but there was not a single man visible.

Some of the passers-by made jokes at me. Though I could not understand their language, yet I felt sure they were joking. I asked my friend, "What do they say?"

"The women say that you look very mannish."

"Mannish?" said I, "What do they mean by that?"

"They mean that you are shy and timid like men."

"Shy and timid like men?" It was really a joke. I became very nervous, when I found that my companion was not Sister Sara, but a stranger. Oh, what a fool had I been to mistake this lady for my dear old friend, Sister Sara.

She felt my fingers tremble in her hand, as we were walking hand in hand.

"What is the matter, dear?" she said affectionately. "I feel somewhat awkward," I said in a rather apologizing tone, "as being a purdahnishin woman I am not accustomed to walking about unveiled."

"You need not be afraid of coming across a man here. This is Ladyland, free from sin and harm. Virtue herself reigns here."

By and by I was enjoying the scenery. Really it was very grand. I mistook a patch of green grass for a velvet cushion. Feeling as if I were walking on a soft carpet, I looked down and found the path covered with moss and flowers.

"How nice it is," said I.

"Do you like it?" asked Sister Sara. (I continued calling her "Sister Sara," and she kept calling me by my name).

"Yes, very much; but I do not like to tread on the tender and sweet flowers."

"Never mind, dear Sultana; your treading will not harm them; they are street flowers."

"The whole place looks like a garden," said I admiringly. "You have arranged every plant so skillfully."

"Your Calcutta could become a nicer garden than this if only your countrymen wanted to make it so."

"They would think it useless to give so much attention to horticulture, while they have so many other things to do."

"They could not find a better excuse," said she with smile.

I became very curious to know where the men were. I met more than a hundred women while walking there, but not a single man.

"Where are the men?" I asked her.

"In their proper places, where they ought to be."

"Pray let me know what you mean by 'their proper places'."

"O, I see my mistake, you cannot know our customs, as you were never here before. We shut our men indoors."

"Just as we are kept in the zenana?"

"Exactly so."

"How funny," I burst into a laugh. Sister Sara laughed too.

"But dear Sultana, how unfair it is to shut in the harmless women and let loose the men."

"Why? It is not safe for us to come out of the zenana, as we are naturally weak."

"Yes, it is not safe so long as there are men about the streets, nor is it so when a wild animal enters a marketplace."

"Of course not."

"Suppose, some lunatics escape from the asylum and begin to do all sorts of mischief to men, horses and other creatures; in that case what will your countrymen do?"

"They will try to capture them and put them back into their asylum."

"Thank you! And you do not think it wise to keep sane people inside an asylum and let loose the insane?"

"Of course not!" said I laughing lightly.

"As a matter of fact, in your country this very thing is done! Men, who do or at least are capable of doing no end of mischief, are let loose and the innocent women, shut up in the zenana! How can you trust those untrained men out of doors?"

"We have no hand or voice in the management of our social affairs. In India man is lord and master, he has taken to himself all powers and privileges and shut up the women in the zenana."

"Why do you allow yourselves to be shut up?"

"Because it cannot be helped as they are stronger than women."

"A lion is stronger than a man, but it does not enable him to dominate the human race. You have neglected the duty you owe to yourselves and you have lost your natural rights by shutting your eyes to your own interests."

"But my dear Sister Sara, if we do everything by ourselves, what will the men do then?"

"They should not do anything, excuse me; they are fit for nothing. Only catch them and put them into the zenana."

"But would it be very easy to catch and put them inside the four walls?" said I. "And even if this were done, would all their business – political and commercial – also go with them into the zenana?"

Sister Sara made no reply. She only smiled sweetly. Perhaps she thought it useless to argue with one who was no better than a frog in a well.

By this time we reached Sister Sara's house. It was situated in a beautiful heart-shaped garden. It was a bungalow with a corrugated iron roof. It was cooler and nicer than any of our rich buildings. I cannot describe how neat and how nicely furnished and how tastefully decorated it was.

We sat side by side. She brought out of the parlour a piece of embroidery work and began putting on a fresh design.

"Do you know knitting and needle work?"

"Yes; we have nothing else to do in our zenana."

"But we do not trust our zenana members with embroidery!" she said laughing, "as a man has not patience enough to pass thread through a needlehole even!"

"Have you done all this work yourself?" I asked her pointing to the various pieces of embroidered teapoy cloths.

"Yes."

"How can you find time to do all these? You have to do the office work as well? Have you not?"

"Yes. I do not stick to the laboratory all day long. I finish my work in two hours."

"In two hours! How do you manage? In our land the officers, - magistrates, for instance - work seven hours daily."

"I have seen some of them doing their work. Do you think they work all the seven hours?"

"Certainly they do!"

"No, dear Sultana, they do not. They dawdle away their time in smoking. Some smoke two or three choroots during the office time. They talk much about their work, but do little. Suppose one choroot takes half an hour to burn off, and a man smokes twelve choroots daily; then you see, he wastes six hours every day in sheer smoking."

We talked on various subjects, and I learned that they were not subject to any kind of epidemic disease, nor did they suffer from mosquito bites as we do. I was very much astonished to hear that in Ladyland no one died in youth except by rare accident.

"Will you care to see our kitchen?" she asked me.

"With pleasure," said I, and we went to see it. Of course the men had been asked to clear off when I was going there. The kitchen was situated in a beautiful vegetable garden. Every creeper, every tomato plant was itself an ornament. I found no smoke, nor any chimney either in the kitchen -- it was clean and bright; the windows were decorated with flower gardens. There was no sign of coal or fire.

"How do you cook?" I asked.

"With solar heat," she said, at the same time showing me the pipe, through which passed the concentrated sunlight and heat. And she cooked something then and there to show me the process.

"How did you manage to gather and store up the sun-heat?" I asked her in amazement.

"Let me tell you a little of our past history then. Thirty years ago, when our present Queen was thirteen years old, she inherited the throne. She was Queen in name only, the Prime Minister really ruling the country.

"Our good Queen liked science very much. She circulated an order that all the women in her country should be educated. Accordingly a number of girls" schools were founded and supported by the government. Education was spread far and wide among women. And early marriage also was stopped. No woman was to be allowed to marry before she was twenty-one. I must tell you that, before this change we had been kept in strict purdah."

"How the tables are turned," I interposed with a laugh.

"But the seclusion is the same," she said. "In a few years we had separate universities, where no men were admitted."

"In the capital, where our Queen lives, there are two universities. One of these invented a wonderful balloon, to which they attached a number of pipes. By means of this captive balloon which they managed to keep afloat above the cloud-land, they could draw as much water from the atmosphere as they pleased. As the water was incessantly being drawn by the university people no cloud gathered and the ingenious Lady Principal stopped rain and storms thereby."

"Really! Now I understand why there is no mud here!" said I. But I could not understand how it was possible to accumulate water in the pipes. She explained to me how it was done, but I was unable to understand her, as my scientific knowledge was very limited. However, she went on, "When the other university came to know of this, they became exceedingly jealous and tried to do something more extraordinary still. They invented an instrument by which they could collect as much sun-heat as they wanted. And they kept the heat stored up to be distributed among others as required.

"While the women were engaged in scientific research, the men of this country were busy increasing their military power. When they came to know that the female universities were able to draw water from the atmosphere and collect heat from the sun, they only laughed at the members of the universities and called the whole thing 'a sentimental nightmare'!"

"Your achievements are very wonderful indeed! But tell me, how you managed to put the men of your country into the zenana. Did you entrap them first?"

"No."

"It is not likely that they would surrender their free and open air life of their own accord and confine themselves within the four walls of the zenana! They must have been overpowered."

"Yes, they have been!"

"By whom? By some lady-warriors, I suppose?"

"No, not by arms."

"Yes, it cannot be so. Men's arms are stronger than women's. Then?"

"By brain."

"Even their brains are bigger and heavier than women's. Are they not?"

"Yes, but what of that? An elephant also has got a bigger and heavier brain than a man has. Yet man can enchain elephants and employ them, according to their own wishes."

"Well said, but tell me please, how it all actually happened. I am dying to know it!"

"Women's brains are somewhat quicker than men's. Ten years ago, when the military officers called our scientific discoveries "a sentimental nightmare," some of the young ladies wanted to say something in reply to those remarks. But both the Lady Principals restrained them and said, they should reply not by word, but by deed, if ever they got the opportunity. And they had not long to wait for that opportunity."

"How marvelous!" I heartily clapped my hands. "And now the proud gentlemen are dreaming sentimental dreams themselves."

"Soon afterwards certain persons came from a neighbouring country and took shelter in ours. They were in trouble having committed some political offense. The king who cared more for power than for good government asked our kind-hearted Queen to hand them over to his officers. She refused, as it was against her principle to turn out refugees. For this refusal the king declared war against our country.

"Our military officers sprang to their feet at once and marched out to meet the enemy. The enemy however, was too strong for them. Our soldiers fought bravely, no doubt. But in spite of all their bravery the foreign army advanced step by step to invade our country.

"Nearly all the men had gone out to fight; even a boy of sixteen was not left home. Most of our warriors were killed, the rest driven back and the enemy came within twenty-five miles of the capital.

"A meeting of a number of wise ladies was held at the Queen's palace to advise as to what should be done to save the land. Some proposed to fight like soldiers; others objected and said that women were not trained to fight with swords and guns, nor were they accustomed to fighting with any weapons. A third party regretfully remarked that they were hopelessly weak of body.

"'If you cannot save your country for lack of physical strength,' said the Queen, 'try to do so by brain power.'

"There was a dead silence for a few minutes. Her Royal Highness said again, 'I must commit suicide if the land and my honour are lost.'

"Then the Lady Principal of the second university (who had collected sun-heat), who had been silently thinking during the consultation, remarked that they were all but lost, and there was little hope left for them. There was, however, one plan which she would like to try, and this would be her first and last efforts; if she failed in this, there would be nothing left but to commit suicide. All present solemnly vowed that they would never allow themselves to be enslaved, no matter what happened.

"The Queen thanked them heartily, and asked the Lady Principal to try her plan. The Lady Principal rose again and said, 'before we go out the men must enter the zenanas. I make this prayer for the sake of purdah.' 'Yes, of course,' replied Her Royal Highness.

"On the following day the Queen called upon all men to retire into zenanas for the sake of honour and liberty. Wounded and tired as they were, they took that order rather for a boon! They bowed low and entered the zenanas without uttering a single word of protest. They were sure that there was no hope for this country at all.

"Then the Lady Principal with her two thousand students marched to the battle field, and arriving there directed all the rays of the concentrated sunlight and heat towards the enemy.

"The heat and light were too much for them to bear. They all ran away panic-stricken, not knowing in their bewilderment how to counteract that scorching heat. When they fled away leaving their guns and other ammunitions of war, they were burnt down by means of the same sun-heat. Since then no one has tried to invade our country any more."

"And since then your countrymen never tried to come out of the zenana?"

"Yes, they wanted to be free. Some of the police commissioners and district magistrates sent word to the Queen to the effect that the military officers certainly deserved to be imprisoned for their failure; but they never neglected their duty and therefore they should not be punished and they prayed to be restored to their respective offices.

"Her Royal Highness sent them a circular letter intimating to them that if their services should ever be needed they would be sent for, and that in the meanwhile they should remain where they were. Now that they are accustomed to the purdah system and have ceased to grumble at their seclusion, we call the system 'Mardana' instead of 'zenana'."

"But how do you manage," I asked Sister Sara, "to do without the police or magistrates in case of theft or murder?"

"Since the 'Mardana' system has been established, there has been no more crime or sin; therefore we do not require a policeman to find out a culprit, nor do we want a magistrate to try a criminal case."

"That is very good, indeed. I suppose if there was any dishonest person, you could very easily chastise her. As you gained a decisive victory without shedding a single drop of blood, you could drive off crime and criminals too without much difficulty!"

"Now, dear Sultana, will you sit here or come to my parlour?" she asked me.

"Your kitchen is not inferior to a queen's boudoir!" I replied with a pleasant smile, "but we must leave it now; for the gentlemen may be cursing me for keeping them away from their duties in the kitchen so long." We both laughed heartily.

"How my friends at home will be amused and amazed, when I go back and tell them that in the far-off Ladyland, ladies rule over the country and control all social matters, while gentlemen are kept in the Mardanas to mind babies, to cook and to do all sorts of domestic work; and that cooking is so easy a thing that it is simply a pleasure to cook!"

"Yes, tell them about all that you see here."

"Please let me know, how you carry on land cultivation and how you plough the land and do other hard manual work."

"Our fields are tilled by means of electricity, which supplies motive power for other hard work as well, and we employ it for our aerial conveyances too. We have no rail road nor any paved streets here."

"Therefore neither street nor railway accidents occur here," said I. "Do not you ever suffer from want of rainwater?" I asked.

"Never since the 'water balloon' has been set up. You see the big balloon and pipes attached thereto. By their aid we can draw as much rainwater as we require. Nor do we ever suffer from flood or thunderstorms. We are all very busy making nature yield as much as she can. We do not find time to quarrel with one another as we never sit idle. Our noble Queen is exceedingly fond of botany; it is her ambition to convert the whole country into one grand garden."

"The idea is excellent. What is your chief food?"

"Fruits."

"How do you keep your country cool in hot weather? We regard the rainfall in summer as a blessing from heaven."

"When the heat becomes unbearable, we sprinkle the ground with plentiful showers drawn from the artificial fountains. And in cold weather we keep our room warm with sun-heat."

She showed me her bathroom, the roof of which was removable. She could enjoy a shower bath whenever she liked, by simply removing the roof (which was like the lid of a box) and turning on the tap of the shower pipe.

"You are a lucky people!" ejaculated I. "You know no want. What is your religion, may I ask?"

"Our religion is based on Love and Truth. It is our religious duty to love one another and to be absolutely truthful. If any person lies, she or he is...."

"Punished with death?"

"No, not with death. We do not take pleasure in killing a creature of God, especially a human being. The liar is asked to leave this land for good and never to come to it again."

"Is an offender never forgiven?"

"Yes, if that person repents sincerely."

"Are you not allowed to see any man, except your own relations?"

"No one except sacred relations."

"Our circle of sacred relations is very limited; even first cousins are not sacred."

"But ours is very large; a distant cousin is as sacred as a brother."

"That is very good. I see purity itself reigns over your land. I should like to see the good Queen, who is so sagacious and far-sighted and who has made all these rules."

"All right," said Sister Sara.

Then she screwed a couple of seats onto a square piece of plank. To this plank she attached two smooth and well-polished balls. When I asked her what the balls were for, she said they were hydrogen balls and they were used to overcome the force of gravity. The balls were of different capacities to be used according to the different weights desired to be overcome. She then fastened to the air-car two wing-like blades, which, she said, were worked by electricity. After we were comfortably seated she touched a knob and the blades began to whirl, moving faster and faster every moment. At first we were raised to the height of about six or seven feet and then off we flew. And before I could realize that we had commenced moving, we reached the garden of the Queen.

My friend lowered the air-car by reversing the action of the machine, and when the car touched the ground the machine was stopped and we got out.

I had seen from the air-car the Queen walking on a garden path with her little daughter (who was four years old) and her maids of honour.

"Halloo! You here!" cried the Queen addressing Sister Sara. I was introduced to Her Royal Highness and was received by her cordially without any ceremony.

I was very much delighted to make her acquaintance. In the course of the conversation I had with her, the Queen told me that she had no objection to permitting her subjects to trade with other countries. "But," she continued, "no trade was possible with countries where the women were kept in the zenanas and so unable to come and trade with us. Men, we find, are rather of lower morals and so we do not like dealing with them. We do not covet other people's land, we do not fight for a piece of diamond though it may be a thousand-fold brighter than the Koh-i-Noor, nor do we grudge a ruler his Peacock Throne. We dive deep into the ocean of knowledge and try to find out the precious gems, which nature has kept in store for us. We enjoy nature's gifts as much as we can."

After taking leave of the Queen, I visited the famous universities, and was shown some of their manufactories, laboratories and observatories.

After visiting the above places of interest we got again into the air-car, but as soon as it began moving, I somehow slipped down and the fall startled me out of my dream. And on opening my eyes, I found myself in my own bedroom still lounging in the easy-chair!

THE END

THE REPUBLIC OF ORISSÁ: ANNALS FROM THE PAGES OF THE TWENTIETH CENTURY BY SHOSHEE CHUNDER DUTT (INDIA, 1905)

The republic of Orissá was comprised, till a recent period, within the dominions of the British Crown, and extended from the confines of Bengal on the north, to those of the Circárs on the south. Berár formed its western boundary, and the Bay of Bengal washed it on the east. But the boundaries of the new republic have been, by an Act of its Congress, passed in the year of Christ 1925, extended in a western and southern direction over a considerable portion of Berár, and to the whole of the Circárs. On the east, also, it has increased its empire over the alluvial land left by the retreating waters of the sea.

This delightful country, some seventy years ago, was inhabited by a weak and niggard race of aborigines, some scores of white settlers, a few Asiatic foreigners, and a horde of wild animals. But, year after year, since the earthquake of 1899, which is supposed by the superstitious nations of Europe to have effected a complete change in the constitution of the world, the enormous herds of the wilderness have been swept away with resistless rapidity, making room for wilder and more fearful denizens — untamed men. Amongst the various tribes that roam over the interior of Orissá, the name of the Kingáries, or hill-tribes, has long been the most terrible to the neighbouring powers. The preeminence of these tribes is not only secured by their superiority in numbers, but by a combination of great physical strength with an intrepidity and courage unknown to any other people of the world. They stray in large predatory bands, pillaging without distinction all whose unguarded attitude tempts their cupidity. Their chief arms are battle-axes and spears; but the deadly use of a Nágpore rifle is not unknown to them. However the name of these tribes may be connected with cruelty, robbery, and blood-shed, still it is one which is emblazoned on the triumphant flag of freedom; for Orissá owes her liberty to the daring adventures of her Kingáries.

On the 25th June, of the year 1916, was passed, in the Council Chamber at Pillibheet (the capital of British India), an Act, permitting a system of oppression revolting to the refined ideas of the Indian public. The purport of it was, that, it being found cheaper to support Indian labourers as slaves than to employ them at fixed wages, slavery was from that time forward to be re-established in British India, against all provisions to the contrary. And the Act stated—

1. That the title to a slave was established by its being proved that he or she was the issue of parents known and acknowledged to be Hindus by birth, and had voluntarily sold his or her freedom, or had his or her freedom sold by such parents.

2. That parents had a right to sell their children, and all children thus sold were to be considered as slaves.

3. That slaves were to be reckoned as the personal property of their owners, and liable to perform any service required of them, and disposable in any way their proprietors might choose.

4. That a master beating, or otherwise grossly ill-using his slave, without great and notorious cause of offence, was to be amenable to punishment; but when such cause had been given, a slave was liable to be tortured even with red-hot iron.

5. That a slave dying intestate, his owner was to become his heir-at-law, and inherit all his lands and effects.

An enactment so harsh and oppressive necessarily irritated the feelings of the native community. The odious distinction it made between the conquerors and the conquered struck them to the quick. The despotism of the British Government had for some time been regarded with the greatest hatred and dissatisfaction. But nothing — not the dishonest and inefficient administration of justice, not the gross corruption that prevailed in the highest functionaries of the Government, not oven the total exclusion of the whole native population from every legitimate object of ambition, and every honourable species of employment — had spread such dissatisfaction, is this injudicious and disgraceful enactment. At first, from all quarters poured in entreaties, and appeals to good feeling. The *Morning Star*, *the Bengal Hurkaru*, and the *Agra Gazette* took up the cause of "poor, oppressed India." But entreaties, appeals to good feeling, and editorial declamations were of no avail. Then came the *Indian Patriot*, denouncing the British Government, predicting its coming overthrow, philosophizing on the future, and calling on the slumbering genii of India to extirpate the foreigners. But the liberty of the Press was violated by the tyrannic Government, and the editor, proprietor, and printer were ordered to be imprisoned. This changed the state of affairs. The spirit of the populace was kindled. On the north and on the south, on the east and on the west

— everywhere, except in Pillibheet, the seat of empire — was raised the cry of revolt. All the provinces were in motion — thousands daily joined the standard of rebellion, and first and foremost ranked the insurgents of Orissá.

But the road was yet open for peace; though ripe for a revolt, the Indian army was, on proper terms, prepared to close the breach. But, elated with some heroic achievements on the frontiers of Cooch Behár, the Government refused to make the slightest concession; and this denial was made more poignant to the patriots by a very declamatory article in the *Government Advocate*, which denounced and ridiculed their exertions. The following is the article alluded to:—

"We think the glaring impolicy of taking up arms against the Government, adopted as it has been by the patriots of India, will be admitted by those who have their eyes open and their senses awake. Does it not strike the mind of every sensible man, that India, for centuries to come, will not be able to wrest the supremacy from the grasp of her conquerors? When we view the disparity in numbers between the black and white population, the result of this rebellion may be feared; but we shudder not for our brethren when we consider the comparative physical and moral courage of the parties pitted against each other. As well might you overpower the rushing leopard with a flock of sheep, as make Bheekoo Bárik, with a hundred *souwárs* at his back, confront the fiery visage of an English drunkard. Even if that were possible, would it not be the wiser plan for the patriots moderately to pursue that course which in time may place them on an equal footing with their conquerors, as regards the cultivation of intellect and the rules of civilized life, than to begin at the wrong end, and seek for freedom without having acquired the simplest lessons of government to secure that liberty? Do they presumes like the genii of Aláddin's lamp, to erect in one night a fair palace fit for the habitation of their deity? Are the Juggomohuns and Gocooldáses, the Opertis and Bindábun Sirdárs fit persons to be intrusted with the management of a vast empire? Though the liberty of India be a consummation devoutly to be wished for, yet must it be admitted that length of time is needful to erect that fabric. Says the common adage, 'Rome was not built in a day.' That under the British Government the Hindus at prospering, and will prosper in spite of their ingratitude, cannot be denied. Go a century or two backwards, take notes of other days, and compare India as it *was* with India as it *is*, and mark the result. But not yet are the Indians fit to be a free people. Perhaps, as time rolls on, the day may come when it will be unjust to refuse to, and perhaps impossible to withhold from the Indians the rights of liberty, and then England may possibly think it just and proper to relinquish her sovereignty over them — but not till then. The Hindus are like children. They want what they cannot understand, fret because with paternal care we refuse to indulge them, and cry because we are deaf to their entreaties. After all, what is there in the last enactment, which is held up as the immediate cause of sedition, to irritate their feelings? The harsher and more outrageous features of slavery have now no existence. Slavery, as now constituted, hardly approaches the 'durance vile' of a common every-day labourer. To all intents and purposes the slave is as good as the *free* (?) labourer. But 'why does the enactment exclude Europeans from slavery?' they ask. *Why*, dear patriots? Because ye are the conquered, we the conquerors. Are you answered?

"Ere taking leave of the subject, we will give a piece of advice to the insurgent chiefs, which we hope and wish for their own sakes they may not wholly despise. They should immediately disband their followers, come to the capital, and on their knees sue for pardon from the Government. We believe the Governor-General in Council may think it proper to excuse them and the people, on an adequate sum being raised for the erection of a palace, now in contemplation for the accommodation of his lordship's family. This measure, if they think proper to adopt should be taken before it is too late. We understand his lordship intends very soon to direct Sir George Proudfoot and the forces under his command to proceed, from the frontiers of Cooch Behár, where they are at present stationed, against the insurgent army now assembled at Beerbhoom.— 29th Dec. 1917."

This article highly incensed the patriot chiefs; and Bheekoo Bárik, the chief of the Kingáries of Orissá, was heard to say, "My *sowárs* can confront the devil when he is mad, leave aside drunkards, English, Scotch, or Irish!" A convention of delegates from the insurgent forces of Bengal, Behár, and Orissá was held at Mulhárpore, on the 8th September, 1918; and it was there resolved that the British Government, having infringed the rules of good government, by introducing slavery into India, and by making various other innovations in the administration of the laws, which innovations were found upon experience to be highly injurious and despotic, it was necessary to adopt bold measures to prevent misrule, and the warriors all vowed to shed the last drops of their blood in the cause of freedom, if bloodshed should be necessary. It was also resolved that the insurgent army should be divided into two bodies — those of Bengal and Behár comprising one, and those of Orissá the other. Gokool Dás Treebaidy was chosen leader of the former, and Operti Sirdár of the latter.

It is not our purpose to give minute details of the wars that followed. An army of ten thousand Irish soldiers, under the command of Sir G. Proudfoot, was directed to proceed first against the forces of Bengal and Behár, and soon subjugating that body, marched in the winter of 1919 for Orissá. The invasion of Orissá was also attended with success at the outset; and success was attended with the most revolting cruelties. The fortress of Rádánuggur was taken at the point of the bayonet, no quarter was given, and the whole garrison was put to the sword; the sacred shrine of Sreekhettur was sacrilegiously pillaged; and Operti Sirdár was well-nigh overpowered the plains of Parbutná, when the mounted troopers of Bheekoo Bárik rushed boldly to the teeth of the enemy, and scattered the whole army in complete rout.

This decisive victory of the Ooryáhs led to promises of concession on the part of the British Government; and, pleased with the prospects of peace, the patriot insurgents fell off. The British Council, in the meantime, perceiving that the immediate danger had passed away, forgot its promises, or deceitfully deferred fulfilling them. Matters were thus circumstanced, when a private wrong brought this uncertain state of affairs to a conclusion.

Lukhun Dás Khundáti, a hero of the good old times, who held a conspicuous station amongst his countrymen, and whose valour was known far beyond the confines of his nation, had a daughter named Nuleeny, a paragon of loveliness. This beauty was early betrothed to one Jugoo Dás Mytheepo, a young man of a very promising character, and, what is more consonant to the taste of women, cast in the best proportions of strength and manly beauty. Bred in the camp, and under the particular care and example of Lukhun Khundáti, he had imbibed all the manners that conspicuously marked the character of that hardy veteran. In every deed of desperation he had a heart to resolve, a head to contrive, and a hand to perform. This youth, while signalizing himself in a sally party by the most desperate feats of gallantry, had fallen prisoner into the hands of one Subadár Báhádoor Gopee Dás, an Ooryáh by birth, and a rejected admirer of Nuleeny, who had enlisted in the service of the enemies of his country on account of domestic differences. From him Jugoo Dás expected no fair treatment, and received none. His highest powers of endurance were put to the test; and his captor, making the public cause subservient his private feelings, refused all proffers of a ransom and exchange of prisoners, and kept him chained and strictly guarded, no intercourse being allowed to be held with him.

It must not be imagined that, during this period, Lukhun Dás and his friends were unmindful of the valiant as Jugoo. They tried every means for effecting his release; but Gopee Dás was deaf to their proffers and entreaties. Young hearts, however, are not easily put down; and the beautiful daughter of the Khundáti veteran was still planning and plotting for the escape of her lover, though hopelessness was depicted on the countenance of her father and the other elders of her country. With a spirit of chivalry which, in this age, is common amongst the women of no other country but Orissá, she left her father's house alone, disguised in the mean habiliments of a wandering *fakir*, to seek her beloved Jugoo among the hated Ferángees. What miseries and privations she suffered on the way, and how, when she did reach the place of her destination, she managed to ingratiate herself with her lover's captor, our deponent saith not; but that she succeeded in all this is placed beyond doubt by the fact that, in the course of a short time, having laid aside the dress of a *fakir*, and assumed that of a soldier, she was enlisted amongst his keepers. Not to make a romance of a simple matter of history we will at once inform our readers that, in this capacity, she managed to secure his liberty — not however so effectually as to prevent pursuit. Furious and foaming Gopee Dás gave chase, with half a dozen *sowárs* at his back; but Jugoo and his fair deliverer, being mounted on the fleetest horse ever transported from the happy shores of Arabia, were far out of harm's way.

It was not till they had reached the hills of Ghotá Nágpore that their pursuers got sight of them. The *sowărs* pressed hard; and their cheers and the clatter of their horses' hoofs, sounded fearfully near in the ears of the fugitives. Every moment lessened the distance between them, till the space was reduced to an arm's length. The horse on which Jugoo and his betrothed were mounted, had cleared a greater space than any horse ever did, and could proceed no more. Now was the desperate moment. The young Mytheepo dismounted, and, like a lion at bay, turned back upon his pursuers, and single-handed opposed them all, resolved to sell his life as dearly as he could. Two of his assailants were levelled with the ground, and he was on the point of despatching a third, when a robust hávildár caught him by the neck and brought him down on his knees, and would have killed him, but that the beautiful Nuleeny, joining in the *mêlée*, plunged a dagger into the hávildár's heart. In the meantime, warding off the blows which were dealt at him from all sides, Jugoo kept rapidly retreating, until, gaining the brow of a steep declivity, he flung himself over to the opposite side, and was instantly lost to view. A desperate escape! And did he escape alone, leaving his liberator, his own Nuleeny, in the hands of his bitterest enemy? Even so. Not that he valued his life more than hers, but because he felt persuaded that she could meet no wrong from one who had long professed to be her lover. Gopee Dás was an Ooryáh, and Jugoo knew that his countrymen, of all nations in the world, were the most chivalrously devoted the fair sex. How could Gopee, then, he reasoned internally, harm a woman? Unfortunately, he did not consider that an Ooryáh who had so far demeaned himself as to enter into the service of the Ferángees — *m'lechhas*, whose very touch is pollution — and to take up arms against his native country, could not possibly retain the noble nature of his race. Alas! sad was the fate of Nuleeny! But that fate was quickly avenged.

Lukhun Dás Khundáti was no sooner informed of his daughter's death, than he repaired to the Kingáries, or hill- tribes. He raked up the fire that was slumbering beneath the ashes, urged home the despotism of the British Government, and at the head of eighty thousand men, began his terrible march towards the English seat of empire, sweeping all petty detachments like dust before his path. The whole kingdom was once again in arms, and all with one accord shouted for battle. On the 15th of October, 1921, took place the memorable engagement of the Jumná, so named because fought on the banks of that sacred river. The English generals were totally defeated — their army cut down to a man. Jugoo Dás and Gopee Dás were found dead on the field of battle, locked fiercely in each other's arms! On the 13th January of the following year Orissá proclaimed her independence, and though the Government of Pillibheet refused to recognise it, their armies completely evacuated that province, after a few vain efforts to disturb its independence.

      Years have passed over those events. The British Empire is sinking fast into that state of weakness and internal division which is the sure forerunner of the fall of kingdoms. Its former glory is now no more. But, with the usual inconsistency of human pride its tone was never more haughty, nor the exterior of its court ever more ostentatious.

<blockquote>"The shadow lengthens as the sun declines."</blockquote>

      We regret for its fallen grandeur; we regret to see an imperial bird, shorn of, its wings and plumage of pride, coming down precipitately from its aëry height. The Council is still sitting, and is a scene of wrangling and confusion — a shadow of what it was, and a lively example of the insufficiency of regulation in a declining State. In the meantime, from this picture of fallen glory, and of the vicissitudes of human greatness, the eye is attracted by the morning splendour of a brilliant luminary. A splendid spectacle is presented to the eyes of wondering millions, of a nation emerging from the chaos of ignorance and slavery, and hastening to occupy its orbit on the grand system of civilization. The Republic of Orissá has become the predominant star in Hindustán.

THE END

THE MAN IN ASBESTOS:
AN ALLEGORY OF THE FUTURE
BY STEPHEN LEACOCK
(CANADA, 1911)

To begin with let me admit that I did it on purpose. Perhaps it was partly from jealousy.

It seemed unfair that other writers should be able at will to drop into a sleep of four or five hundred years, and to plunge head-first into a distant future and be a witness of its marvels.

I wanted to do that too.

I always had been, I still am, a passionate student of social problems. The world of to-day with its roaring machinery, the unceasing toil of its working classes, its strife, its poverty, its war, its cruelty, appals me as I look at it. I love to think of the time that must come some day when man will have conquered nature, and the toil-worn human race enter upon an era of peace.

I loved to think of it, and I longed to see it.

So I set about the thing deliberately.

What I wanted to do was to fall asleep after the customary fashion, for two or three hundred years at least, and wake and find myself in the marvel world of the future.

I made my preparations for the sleep.

I bought all the comic papers that I could find, even the illustrated ones. I carried them up to my room in my hotel: with them I brought up a pork pie and dozens and dozens of doughnuts. I ate the pie and the doughnuts, then sat back in the bed and read the comic papers one after the other. Finally, as I felt the awful lethargy stealing upon me, I reached out my hand for the *London Weekly Times*, and held up the editorial page before my eye.

It was, in a way, clear, straight suicide, but I did it.

I could feel my senses leaving me. In the room across the hall there was a man singing. His voice, that had been loud, came fainter and fainter through the transom. I fell into a sleep, the deep immeasurable sleep in which the very existence of the outer world was hushed. Dimly I could feel the days go past, then the years, and then the long passage of the centuries.

Then, not as it were gradually, but quite suddenly, I woke up, sat up, and looked about me.

Where was I?

Well might I ask myself.

I found myself lying, or rather sitting up, on a broad couch. I was in a great room, dim, gloomy, and dilapidated in its general appearance, and apparently, from its glass cases and the stuffed figures that they contained, some kind of museum.

Beside me sat a man. His face was hairless, but neither old nor young. He wore clothes that looked like the grey ashes of paper that had burned and kept its shape. He was looking at me quietly, but with no particular surprise or interest.

"Quick," I said, eager to begin; "where am I? Who are you? What year is this; is it the year 3000, or what is it?"

He drew in his breath with a look of annoyance on his face.

"What a queer, excited way you have of speaking," he said.

"Tell me," I said again, "is this the year 3000?"

"I think I know what you mean," he said; "but really I haven't the faintest idea. I should think it must be at least that, within a hundred years or so; but nobody has kept track of them for so long, it's hard to say."

"Don't you keep track of them any more?" I gasped.

"We used to," said the man. "I myself can remember that a century or two ago there were still a number of people who used to try to keep track of the year, but it died out along with so many other faddish things of that kind. Why," he continued, showing for the first time a sort of animation in his talk, "what was the use of it? You see, after we eliminated death——"

"Eliminated death!" I cried, sitting upright. "Good God!"

"What was that expression you used?" queried the man.

"Good God!" I repeated.

"Ah," he said, "never heard it before. But I was saying that after we had eliminated Death, and Food, and Change, we had practically got rid of Events, and——"

"Stop!" I said, my brain reeling. "Tell me one thing at a time."

"Humph!" he ejaculated. "I see, you must have been asleep a long time. Go on then and ask questions. Only, if you don't mind, just as few as possible, and please don't get interested or excited."

Oddly enough the first question that sprang to my lips was—

"What are those clothes made of?"

"Asbestos," answered the man. "They last hundreds of years. We have one suit each, and there are billions of them piled up, if anybody wants a new one."

"Thank you," I answered. "Now tell me where I am?"

"You are in a museum. The figures in the cases are specimens like yourself. But here," he said, "if you want really to find out about what is evidently a new epoch to you, get off your platform and come out on Broadway and sit on a bench."

I got down.

As we passed through the dim and dust-covered buildings I looked curiously at the figures in the cases.

"By Jove!" I said looking at one figure in blue clothes with a belt and baton, "that's a policeman!"

"Really," said my new acquaintance, "is *that* what a *policeman* was? I've often wondered. What used they to be used for?"

"Used for?" I repeated in perplexity. "Why, they stood at the corner of the street."

"Ah, yes, I see," he said, "so as to shoot at the people. You must excuse my ignorance," he continued, "as to some of your social customs in the past. When I took my education I was operated upon for social history, but the stuff they used was very inferior."

I didn't in the least understand what the man meant, but had no time to question him, for at that moment we came out upon the street, and I stood riveted in astonishment.

Broadway! Was it possible? The change was absolutely appalling! In place of the roaring thoroughfare that I had known, this silent, moss-grown desolation. Great buildings fallen into ruin through the sheer stress of centuries of wind and weather, the sides of them coated over with a growth of fungus and moss! The place was soundless. Not a vehicle moved. There were no wires overhead—no sound of life or movement except, here and there, there passed slowly to and fro human figures dressed in the same asbestos clothes as my acquaintance, with the same hairless faces, and the same look of infinite age upon them.

Good heavens! And was this the era of the Conquest that I had hoped to see! I had always taken for granted, I do not know why, that humanity was destined to move forward. This picture of what seemed desolation on the ruins of our civilisation rendered me almost speechless.

There were little benches placed here and there on the street. We sat down.

"Improved, isn't it," said man in asbestos, "since the days when you remember it?"

He seemed to speak quite proudly.

I gasped out a question.

"Where are the street cars and the motors?"

"Oh, done away with long ago," he said; "how awful they must have been. The noise of them!" and his asbestos clothes rustled with a shudder.

"But how do you get about?"

"We don't," he answered. "Why should we? It's just the same being here as being anywhere else." He looked at me with an infinity of dreariness in his face.

A thousand questions surged into my mind at once. I asked one of the simplest.

"But how do you get back and forwards to your work?"

"Work!" he said. "There isn't any work. It's finished. The last of it was all done centuries ago."

I looked at him a moment open-mouthed. Then I turned and looked again at the grey desolation of the street with the asbestos figures moving here and there.

I tried to pull my senses together. I realised that if I was to unravel this new and undreamed-of future, I must go at it systematically and step by step.

"I see," I said after a pause, "that momentous things have happened since my time. I wish you would let me ask you about it all systematically, and would explain it to me bit by bit. First, what do you mean by saying that there is no work?"

"Why," answered my strange acquaintance, "it died out of itself. Machinery killed it. If I remember rightly, you had a certain amount of machinery even in your time. You had done very well with steam, made a good beginning with electricity, though I think radial energy had hardly as yet been put to use."

I nodded assent.

"But you found it did you no good. The better your machines, the harder you worked. The more things you had the more you wanted. The pace of life grew swifter and swifter. You cried out, but it would not stop. You were all caught in the cogs of your own machine. None of you could see the end."

"That is quite true," I said. "How do you know it all?"

"Oh," answered the Man in Asbestos, "that part of my education was very well operated—I see you do not know what I mean. Never mind, I can tell you that later. Well, then, there came, probably almost two hundred years after your time, the Era of the Great Conquest of Nature, the final victory of Man and Machinery."

"They did conquer it?" I asked quickly, with a thrill of the old hope in my veins again.

"Conquered it," he said, "beat it out! Fought it to a standstill! Things came one by one, then faster and faster, in a hundred years it was all done. In fact, just as soon as mankind turned its energy to decreasing its needs instead of increasing its desires, the whole thing was easy. Chemical Food came first. Heavens! the simplicity of it. And in your time thousands of millions of people tilled and grubbed at the soil from morning till night. I've seen specimens of them—farmers, they called them. There's one in the museum. After the invention of Chemical Food we piled up enough in the emporiums in a year to last for centuries. Agriculture went overboard. Eating and all that goes with it, domestic labour, housework—all ended. Nowadays one takes a concentrated pill every year or so, that's all. The whole digestive apparatus, as you knew it, was a clumsy thing that had been bloated up like a set of bagpipes through the evolution of its use!"

I could not forbear to interrupt. "Have you and these people," I said, "no stomachs—no apparatus?"

"Of course we have," he answered, "but we use it to some purpose. Mine is largely filled with my education—but there! I am anticipating again. Better let me go on as I was. Chemical Food came first: that cut off almost one-third of the work, and then came Asbestos Clothes. That was wonderful! In one year humanity made enough suits to last for ever and ever. That, of course, could never have been if it hadn't been connected with the revolt of women and the fall of Fashion."

"Have the Fashions gone," I asked, "that insane, extravagant idea of——" I was about to launch into one of my old-time harangues about the sheer vanity of decorative dress, when my eye rested on the moving figures in asbestos, and I stopped.

"All gone," said the Man in Asbestos. "Then next to that we killed, or practically killed, the changes of climate. I don't think that in your day you properly understood how much of your work was due to the shifts of what you called the weather. It meant the need of all kinds of special clothes and houses and shelters, a wilderness of work. How dreadful it must have been in your day—wind and storms, great wet masses—what did you call them?—clouds—flying through the air, the ocean full of salt, was it not?—tossed and torn by the wind, snow thrown all over everything, hail, rain—how awful!"

"Sometimes," I said, "it was very beautiful. But how did you alter it?"

"Killed the weather!" answered the Man in Asbestos. "Simple as anything—turned its forces loose one against the other, altered the composition of the sea so that the top became all more or less gelatinous. I really can't explain it, as it is an operation that I never took at school, but it made the sky grey, as you see it, and the sea gum-coloured, the weather all the same. It cut out fuel and houses and an infinity of work with them!"

He paused a moment. I began to realise something of the course of evolution that had happened.

"So," I said, "the conquest of nature meant that presently there was no more work to do?"

"Exactly," he said, "nothing left."

"Food enough for all?"

"Too much," he answered.

"Houses and clothes?"

"All you like," said the Man in Asbestos, waving his hand. "There they are. Go out and take them. Of course, they're falling down— slowly, very slowly. But they'll last for centuries yet, nobody need bother."

Then I realised, I think for the first time, just what work had meant in the old life, and how much of the texture of life itself had been bound up in the keen effort of it.

Presently my eyes looked upward: dangling at the top of a moss-grown building I saw what seemed to be the remains of telephone wires.

"What became of all that," I said, "the telegraph and the telephone and all the system of communication?"

"Ah," said the Man in Asbestos, "that was what a telephone meant, was it? I knew that it had been suppressed centuries ago. Just what was it for?"

"Why," I said with enthusiasm, "by means of the telephone we could talk to anybody, call up anybody, and talk at any distance."

"And anybody could call you up at any time and talk?" said the Man in Asbestos, with something like horror. "How awful! What a dreadful age yours was, to be sure. No, the telephone and all the rest of it, all the transportation and intercommunication was cut out and forbidden. There was no sense in it. You see," he added, "what you don't realise is that people after your day became gradually more and more reasonable. Take the railroad, what good was that? It brought into every town a lot of people from every other town. Who wanted them? Nobody. When work stopped and commerce ended, and food was needless, and the weather killed, it was foolish to move about. So it was all terminated. Anyway," he said, with a quick look of apprehension and a change in his voice, "it was dangerous!"

"So!" I said. "Dangerous! You still have danger?"

"Why, yes," he said, "there's always the danger of getting broken."

"What do you mean," I asked.

"Why," said the Man in Asbestos, "I suppose it's what you would call being dead. Of course, in one sense there's been no death for centuries past; we cut that out. Disease and death were simply a matter of germs. We found them one by one. I think that even in your day you had found one or two of the easier, the bigger ones?"

I nodded.

"Yes, you had found diphtheria and typhoid and, if I am right, there were some outstanding, like scarlet fever and smallpox, that you called ultra-microscopic, and which you were still hunting for, and others that you didn't even suspect. Well, we hunted them down one by one and destroyed them. Strange that it never occurred to any of you that Old Age was only a germ! It turned out to be quite a simple one, but it was so distributed in its action that you never even thought of it."

"And you mean to say," I ejaculated in amazement, looking at the Man in

Asbestos, "that nowadays you live for ever?"

"I wish," he said, "that you hadn't that peculiar, excitable way of talking; you speak as if everything *mattered* so tremendously. Yes," he continued, "we live for ever, unless, of course, we get broken. That happens sometimes. I mean that we may fall over a high place or bump on something, and snap ourselves. You see, we're just a little brittle still—some remnant, I suppose, of the Old Age germ—and we have to be careful. In fact," he continued, "I don't mind saying that accidents of this sort were the most distressing feature of our civilisation till we took steps to cut out all accidents. We forbid all street cars, street traffic, aeroplanes, and so on. The risks of your time," he said, with a shiver of his asbestos clothes, "must have been awful."

"They were," I answered, with a new kind of pride in my generation that I had never felt before, "but we thought it part of the duty of brave people to——"

"Yes, yes," said the Man in Asbestos impatiently, "please don't get excited. I know what you mean. It was quite irrational."

We sat silent for a long time. I looked about me at the crumbling buildings, the monotone, unchanging sky, and the dreary, empty street. Here, then, was the fruit of the Conquest, here was the elimination of work, the end of hunger and of cold, the cessation of the hard struggle, the downfall of change and death—nay, the very millennium of happiness. And yet, somehow, there seemed something wrong with it all. I pondered, then I put two or three rapid questions, hardly waiting to reflect upon the answers.

"Is there any war now?"

"Done with centuries ago. They took to settling international disputes with a slot machine. After that all foreign dealings were given up. Why have them? Everybody thinks foreigners awful."

"Are there any newspapers now?"

"Newspapers! What on earth would we want them for? If we should need them at any time there are thousands of old ones piled up. But what is in them, anyway; only things that *happen*, wars and accidents and work and death. When these went newspapers went too. Listen," continued the Man in Asbestos, "you seem to have been something of a social reformer, and yet you don't understand the new life at all. You don't understand how completely all our burdens have disappeared. Look at it this way. How used your people to spend all the early part of their lives?"

"Why," I said, "our first fifteen years or so were spent in getting education."

"Exactly," he answered; "now notice how we improved on all that. Education in our day is done by surgery. Strange that in your time nobody realised that education was simply a surgical operation. You hadn't the sense to see that what you really did was to slowly remodel, curve and convolute the inside of the brain by a long and painful mental operation. Everything learned was reproduced in a physical difference to the brain. You knew that, but you didn't see the full consequences. Then came the invention of surgical education—the simple system of opening the side of the skull and engrafting into it a piece of prepared brain. At first, of course, they had to use, I suppose, the brains of dead people, and that was ghastly"—here the Man in Asbestos shuddered like a leaf—"but very soon they found how to make moulds that did just as well. After that it was a mere nothing; an operation of a few minutes would suffice to let in poetry or foreign languages or history or anything else that one cared to have. Here, for instance," he added, pushing back the hair at the side of his head and showing a scar beneath it, "is the mark where I had my spherical trigonometry let in. That was, I admit, rather painful, but other things, such as English poetry or history, can be inserted absolutely without the least suffering. When I think of your painful, barbarous methods of education through the ear, I shudder at it. Oddly enough, we have found lately that for a great many things there is no need to use the head. We lodge them—things like philosophy and metaphysics, and so on—in what used to be the digestive apparatus. They fill it admirably."

He paused a moment. Then went on:

"Well, then, to continue, what used to occupy your time and effort after your education?"

"Why," I said, "one had, of course, to work, and then, to tell the truth, a great part of one's time and feeling was devoted toward the other sex, towards falling in love and finding some woman to share one's life."

"Ah," said the Man in Asbestos, with real interest. "I've heard about your arrangements with the women, but never quite understood them. Tell me; you say you selected some woman?"

"Yes."

"And she became what you called your wife?"

"Yes, of course."

"And you worked for her?" asked the Man in Asbestos in astonishment.

"Yes."

"And she did not work?"

"No," I answered, "of course not."

"And half of what you had was hers?"

"Yes."

"And she had the right to live in your house and use your things?"

"Of course," I answered.

"How dreadful!" said the Man in Asbestos. "I hadn't realised the horrors of your age till now."

He sat shivering slightly, with the same timid look in his face as before.

Then it suddenly struck me that of the figures on the street, all had looked alike.

"Tell me," I said, "are there no women now? Are they gone too?"

"Oh, no," answered the Man in Asbestos, "they're here just the same. Some of those are women. Only, you see, everything has been changed now. It all came as part of their great revolt, their desire to be like the men. Had that begun in your time?"

"Only a little." I answered; "they were beginning to ask for votes and equality."

"That's it," said my acquaintance, "I couldn't think of the word. Your women, I believe, were something awful, were they not? Covered with feathers and skins and dazzling colours made of dead things all over them? And they laughed, did they not, and had foolish teeth, and at any moment they could inveigle you into one of those contracts! Ugh!"

He shuddered.

"Asbestos," I said (I knew no other name to call him), as I turned on him in wrath, "Asbestos, do you think that those jelly-bag Equalities out on the street there, with their ash-barrel suits, can be compared for one moment with our unredeemed, unreformed, heaven-created, hobble-skirted women of the twentieth century?"

Then, suddenly, another thought flashed into my mind—

"The children," I said, "where are the children? Are there any?"

"Children," he said, "no! I have never heard of there being any such things for at least a century. Horrible little hobgoblins they must have been! Great big faces, and cried constantly! And *grew*, did they not? Like funguses! I believe they were longer each year than they had been the last, and—"

I rose.

"Asbestos!" I said, "this, then, is your coming Civilisation, your millennium. This dull, dead thing, with the work and the burden gone out of life, and with them all the joy and sweetness of it. For the old struggle—mere stagnation, and in place of danger and death, the dull monotony of security and the horror of an unending decay! Give me back," I cried, and I flung wide my arms to the dull air, "the old life of danger and stress, with its hard toil and its bitter chances, and its heartbreaks. I see its value! I know its worth! Give me no rest," I cried aloud—

"Yes, but give a rest to the rest of the corridor!" cried an angered voice that broke in upon my exultation.

Suddenly my sleep had gone.

I was back again in the room of my hotel, with the hum of the wicked, busy old world all about me, and loud in my ears the voice of the indignant man across the corridor.

"Quit your blatting, you infernal blatherskite," he was calling. "Come down to earth."

I came.

THE END

THE LOG OF THE FLYING FISH: A STORY OF AERIAL AND SUBMARINE PERIL AND ADVENTURE BY HARRY COLLINGWOOD (UNITED KINGDOM, 1886))

CHAPTER ONE
PROFESSOR VON SCHALCKENBERG MAKES A STARTLING SUGGESTION

The "Migrants'" Club stands on the most delightful site in all London; and it is, as the few who are intimately acquainted with it know full well, one of the most cosy and comfortable clubs in the great metropolis.

It is by no means a *famous* club; the building itself has a very simple, unpretentious elevation, with nothing whatever about it to attract the attention of the passer-by; but its interior is fitted up in such a style of combined elegance and comfort, and its domestic arrangements are so perfect, as to leave nothing to be desired.

Its numerous members are essentially wanderers upon the face of the earth—that is the one distinguishing characteristic wherein they most widely differ from their fellow-men—they are ceaseless travellers; mighty hunters in far-off lands; adventurous yachtsmen; eager explorers; with a small sprinkling of army and navy men. Their visits to their club are infrequent in the extreme; but, during the brief and widely separated intervals when they have the opportunity to put in an appearance there, they like to be made thoroughly comfortable; and no pains are spared to secure their complete gratification in this respect.

The smoke-room of the "Migrants'" presented an appearance of especial comfort and attractiveness on a certain cold and stormy February evening a few years ago. A large fire blazed in the polished steel grate and roared cheerfully up the chimney, in rivalry of the wind, which howled and scuffled and rumbled in the flue higher up. An agreeable temperature pervaded the room, making the lashing of the fierce rain on the window-panes sound almost pleasant as one basked in the light and warmth of the apartment and contrasted it with the state of cold and wet and misery which reigned supreme outside. A dozen opal-shaded gas-burners brilliantly lighted the room, and revealed the fact that it was handsomely and liberally furnished with luxurious divans, capacious easy-chairs, a piano, a table loaded with the papers and periodicals of the day, an enormous mirror over the black marble mantel-piece, a clock with a set of silvery chimes for the quarters, and a deep, mellow-toned gong for the hours, and so many pictures that the whole available surface of the walls was completely covered with them. These pictures—executed in both oil and water-colour—represented out-of-the-way scenes visited, or incidents participated in by the members who had executed them, and all possessed a considerable amount of artistic merit; it being a rule of the club that every picture should be submitted to a hanging committee of distinctly artistic members before it could be allowed a place upon the smoke-room walls.

The occupants of the room on the evening in question were four in number. One, a German, known as the Professor Heinrich von Schalckenberg, was half buried in the recesses of a huge arm-chair, from the depths of which he perused the pages of the *Science Monthly*, smoking meanwhile a pipe with a huge elaborately carved meerschaum bowl and a long cherry-wood stem. From the ferocious manner in which he glared through his spectacles at the pages of the magazine, from the impatience with which he from time to time dashed his disengaged hand through the masses of his iron-grey hair, and from the frequent ejaculations of "Pish!" "Psha!" "Ach!" and so on which escaped his lips, accompanied by vast volumes of smoke, it seemed evident that he was not altogether at one with the author whose article he was perusing. He was an explorer and a scientist.

Near the Herr Professor there reclined upon a divan the form of Sir Reginald Elphinstone, sometimes called by his friends "the handsome baronet," said to be *the* richest commoner in England. At the age of thirty-five, having freely exposed himself to all known sources of peril, except those involved in a trip to the Polar regions, in his eager pursuit of sport and adventure, Sir Reginald seemed, for the moment, to have no object left him in life but to shoot as many rings as possible of cigar-smoke through each other, as he lay there on the divan in an attitude more easy than elegant.

Square in front of the fire, dreamily puffing at his cigar and apparently studying the merits of a painting hanging behind him, and on the reflected image of which in the mirror before him his eyes lazily rested, sat Cyril Lethbridge, ex-colonel of the Royal Engineers, a successful gold-seeker, and almost everything else to which a spice of adventure could possibly attach itself.

And next him again, on the side of the fire-place opposite to the Herr Professor, lounged Lieutenant Edward Mildmay, R.N.

The lieutenant was skimming through the daily papers. Presently he looked up and remarked to the colonel:

"I see that some Frenchmen have been making experiments in the navigation of balloons."

"Ah, indeed!" responded the colonel, with his head thrown critically on one side, and his eyes still fixed on the reflection of the picture. "And with what result?"

"Oh, failure, of course."

"And failure it always will be. The thing is simply an impossibility," remarked the colonel.

"No, bardon me, colonel, id is not an imbossibilidy by any means."

This from the professor.

"Indeed? Then how do you account for it, professor, that all attempts to navigate a balloon have hitherto failed?" asked the colonel.

"Begause, my dear zir, the aeronauts have never yed realised all the requiremends of zuccess," replied the professor, laying down his magazine as though quite prepared to go thoroughly into the question.

The colonel accepted the challenge, and, rousing himself from his semi-recumbent posture, said:

"That is quite possible; but what *are* the requirements of success?"

The professor knocked the ashes out of his meerschaum, refilled it with the utmost deliberation, carefully lighted it, gave a few vigorous puffs, and replied:

"The requiremends of zuccess in balloon navigation are very zimilar to those which enable a man to draverse the ocean. If a man wants to make a voyage agross the ocean he embargs in a ship, not on a life-buoy. Now a balloon is nothing more than a life-buoy; id zusdains a man, but that is all. Id drifts aboud with the currends of air jusd as a life-buoy drifts aboud with the currends of ocean, and the only advandage which the aeronaud has over the man with the life-buoy is thad the former can ascend or descend in search of a favourable air currend, whereas the ladder is obliged do dake the ocean currends as they come."

"Very true," remarked the colonel; "and what do you deduce from that, professor?"

"I deduse from thad thad the man who wands to navigade the air musd do as his brother the sailor does, he musd have a *ship*."

"Well, is not a balloon a sort of air ship?"

"You may gall it zo iv you like, colonel, I do nod; I call it merely a buoy," returned the professor. "A *ship* is a zomething gabable of *moving* in the elemend which zustains it; a balloon is ingabable of any indebendend movement in the air;

it drifts aboud at the mercy of every idle wind that blows. Id is like a ship on a breathless sea; withoud any means of brobulsion the ship lies motionless, or drifts at the mercy of the currends. Bud give the ship a means of brobulsion, and navigation ad once begomes bossible. And zo will it be with balloons."

"Well, that has already been tried," remarked the colonel; "but the buoyancy of a balloon is too slight to permit of its being fitted with engines and a boiler."

"My vriendt," said the professor impressively, "whad would you think of the man who tried to pud the engines and boilers of an Atlantic liner in a leedle boad?"

"I should think him an unmitigated ass," retorted the colonel.

"Jusd so. Yed thad is whad the aeronauds have been doing; they have been drying to make the leedle boad-balloon garry the brobelling bower of the aerial ship. In other words, they have not made their balloons large enough."

"Then you think they have not yet reached the practical limit to the size of a balloon?" asked the colonel.

"They have—very nearly—if balloons are do be made only of silk," was the reply. "Bud if *navigable* balloons are to be gonsdrugded, aeronauds musd durn do other maderials and adobd another form. As I said before, they musd build a *shib*, and she musd be of sufficiend size to float in the air and to garry all her eguipments."

"But such an aerial ship would be a veritable *monster*" protested the colonel.

"Zo are the Adlandic liners of the presend day," quietly answered the professor.

"Phew!" whistled the colonel. The baronet rose from the divan, flung away the stump of his cigar, and settled himself to listen, and perhaps take part in the singular conversation.

"And of what would you build your aerial ship, professor?" asked the colonel when he had in some measure recovered from his astonishment.

"Of the lighdesd and, ad the zame dime, sdrongesd maderial I gould find," answered the professor. "Once get the aeronaud to realise thad greadly ingreased bulk and a differend form are necessary, and id will nod be long before he will find a suitable building maderial. Iv I were an aeronaud I should dry medal."

"Metal!" exclaimed the colonel. "Oh, come, professor; now you are romancing, you know. A ship of metal would never float in the atmosphere."

"A zimilar remarg was made nod zo very many years ago when id was suggesded that ocean shibs could be buildt of medal," retorted the professor. "Yed there are thousands of medal shibs in exisdenze do-day; and there can be no doubt as do the facd thad they fload. And zo will an aerial shib. The gread—in facd the *only* diffiguldy in the madder is thad air is eight hundred dimes lighder than wader; and an air shib of given dimensions musd therefore be ad leasd eight hundred dimes lighder than her ocean sisder do enable her do fload in the atmosphere. The broblem, then, is this: How are you to gonsdrugt a medal ship, of given dimensions, sdrong enough do hold dogether and withsdand the shock of goming do earth, yed of less weighd than her own bulk of air? With the medals hitherdoo ad our disbosal, I admid thad the dask is a diffiguld one; bud I maindain thad id is by no means an imbossibilidy. An ocean ship musd be buildt sdrong enough nod only do susdain the weighd of her gargo—often amounding do upwards of a thousand dons—bud also do withsdand the dremendous and incessandly varying sdrain do which she is exbosed when garrying thad gargo through a moundainous sea. This enormous sdrength necessidades the use of a gorresbonding thickness—and therefore weighd—of the medal used in her gonsdruction. Such brovision would of gourse be unnecessary in the gase of an aerial ship; begause no one would dream of garrying an ounze of unnecessary weighd through the air; and there are no moundain seas in the admosphere to sdrain a ship. A vasd saving in weighd would resuld from these zirgumsdances alone; and a further saving—zufficiend, I believe, to aggomblish the desired object—gan, no doubd, be effecded by skilful engineers, one of whose greadesd driumphs id is do design sdrugdures in which the maximum of sdrength is zecured with the minimum of weighd. Id musd nod be forgodden, either, thad an air ship musd, in one imbordand bardigular, be dreated exactly like her ocean sisder. An ocean ship gonsdrugded, say, of sdeel, will sink if filled with wader, begause sdeel is heavier than wader, bulk for bulk; bud bump oud all the wader from her inderior, and if she be broberly gonsdrugded, she will fload on the elemend she is indended do navigade. And the same with an air ship: bump out all or nearly all the air which she gondains, and if she be gonsdrugded in aggordanze with the brincibles I have indigaded, she will fload in the lighder elemend."

"Upon my word, professor, you have argued your case extremely well," exclaimed the colonel. "I can see only one difficulty in the way; and that is in the matter of *weight*."

"Which diffiguldy I have gombledely gonquered," triumphantly exclaimed the professor, rising excitedly from his seat with flushed cheeks and flashing eyes. "Do me, Heinrich von Schalckenberg, belongs the honour and glory of having made dwo mosd imbordand disgoveries, disgoveries of ingalgulable value do the worldt, disgoveries which will enable me do soar ad will indo the highesd regions of the embyrean, do skim the surface of the ocean, or do blunge do ids lowesd debths."

"Bravo, professor; that was positively dramatic!" exclaimed the baronet. "You have mistaken your business, my dear sir; you were undoubtedly born to be an actor. But what are these two most important discoveries of which you so exultantly speak?"

"They are a new medal and a new power," exclaimed the professor. Then, fumbling in his breast-pocket, he drew forth a wallet from which he extracted a small rectangular plate of—apparently—polished silver. It measured about five inches long by four inches broad, and was about a quarter of an inch thick.

"There, Sir Reginald," he exclaimed, offering the plate to the baronet, "dell me whad you think of thad."

"Very pretty indeed," commented Sir Reginald, as he held out his hand to take it. "What is it? Silver? Phew! No; it can't be that," as his fingers closed upon it; "it is far too light for silver. Why, it seems to be absolutely devoid of weight altogether. What is it, professor?"

"Thad, my good sir, is my new medal, which I gall '*aethereum*' begause of ids wonderful lighdness. See here."

There was a very handsome cut glass water-jug, full, standing on the table in a capacious salver of hammered brass. The professor took up the jug and emptied it into the salver, almost filling the latter. Then he laid the glittering slab of metal down on the surface of the water, where it floated as buoyantly as though it had been an empty box constructed of the lightest cardboard. The professor raised the salver from the table and agitated the water, to show that the metal actually floated.

"Why, it floats as lightly as a cork!" exclaimed the colonel in the utmost astonishment.

"Korg!" exclaimed the professor disdainfully, "korg is *heavy* gombared with this. This is the lighdesd solid known. Loog ad this."

The professor lifted the plate of metal out of the water, and, wiping it dry very carefully with his silk pocket-handkerchief, held it suspended, flat side downwards, between his finger and thumb. Then, when he had poised it as nearly horizontal as he could guess at, he let it go. It wavered about in the air as a thin sheet of paper would have done, and finally sailed aslant and very gently to the ground, amid the astonished exclamations of the beholders, by whom it was immediately examined with the utmost curiosity.

"You have seen for yourselves and gan therefore judge how marvellously lighd this medal is," continued the professor when the plate had been handed back to him; "bud ids *sdrength* you musd dake my word for, as I have no means ad hand do illusdrade id. Ids sdrength is as wonderful as ids lighdness, being—zo var as I have had obbordunidy do desd id—exactly one hundred dimes thad of the besd sdeel."

"If that be the case, professor, then I should say you have solved the problem of aerial navigation," remarked the colonel. "But you spoke of having also discovered a new power. What is it?"

The professor once more instituted a search in his pockets, and at length produced a small paper packet, which, on being opened, was found to contain about a table-spoonful of green metallic-looking crystals.

"There id is," he said, handing the packet to the colonel for inspection.

"Um!" ejaculated the colonel, turning the crystals over slowly with his finger. "Quite new to me; I don't recognise them at all. And what is the nature of the power derivable from these crystals?"

"Dreated in one way they give off elegdricidy; dreated in another way they yield an exbansive gas, which may be subsdiduded for either gunbowder or sdeam," answered the professor.

"Are they explosive, then?" asked the colonel.

"Nod in their bresend form. You mighd doss all those crysdals indo the fire with imbunidy; but bowder them and mix indo a baste with a zerdain acid, and whad you now hold in your hand would develop exblosive bower enough to demolish this building," was the quiet reply.

The professor's little audience looked at him incredulously; a look to which he responded by saying:

"Id is quide drue, I assure you," in such convincing tones as left no room for further doubt. They knew the professor well; knew him to be quite incapable of the slightest attempt at deception or exaggeration.

"Then, if I have understood you aright, you will construct your aerial ship of your new metal, and apply your new power to give motion to her machinery?" said the colonel.

"Yes. Thad is do say, I *would* if I bossessed the means do build such a ship as I have described. Bud I am a scientist, and therefore boor. Never mind; I have no doubt thad, when I make my discoveries known, I shall find some wealthy man who, for the sake of science, will find der money," said the professor hopefully.

"How much would it cost to build an aerial ship such as you have been speaking of?" asked the baronet.

"Oh! I cannod say. Nod zo very much. Berhabs a hundred thousandt bounds," was the reply.

"Phew! That's rather 'steep,' as the Yankees say. But—'a fool and his money are soon parted'—if you are convinced that your scheme is really practicable, professor, I will find the needful," remarked the baronet.

"Bragdigable! My dear sir, id is as bragdigable as id is to build a shib which will navigade the ocean. I have thoughd the madder oudt, and there is nod a single weak boindt anywhere in my scheme. Led me have der money and I will brovide you with the means of zoaring above the grest of Mount Everest, or of exbloring the deepest ocean valleys," exclaimed the professor enthusiastically.

"Good!" remarked the baronet quietly. "That is a bargain. Meet me here at noon to-morrow, and we will go together to my bankers, where I will transfer one hundred thousand pounds to your account. And—what say you, gentlemen?—when this wonderful ship is completed will you join the professor and me in an experimental trip round the world?"

"I shall be delighted," exclaimed the colonel.

"Nothing would please me better," remarked the lieutenant.

And so it was agreed.

"Well," remarked the baronet reflectively, and as though he already began to feel doubtful as to the wisdom of his agreement with the professor, "if it has no other good result it will at least afford employment to a few of the unfortunate fellows who are now hanging about idle day after day."

The professor looked up sharply.

"What!" he exclaimed. "Of whom are you sbeaging, my dear Sir Reginald?"

"I am speaking of the unfortunate individual known as 'the British Workman,'" was the baronet's quiet reply.

"Am I do understandt thad you make the embloymend of English workmen a gondition of the underdaking?" asked the professor somewhat sharply.

"By no means, my dear sir," answered Sir Reginald; "I shall not attempt to impose conditions of any kind upon you. But I should naturally expect that, if English workmen are as capable of executing the work as foreigners, the former would be given the preference in a matter involving the expenditure of say a hundred thousand pounds of an Englishman's money."

"Quide zo," concurred the professor; "and you would be perfectly justified in such an expegdation *if* the Bridish workman was the steady, indusdrious, reliable fellow he once was. Bud, unfordunadely, he is *nod* the same, zo var ad leasd as *reliabilidy* is concerned. You gannod any longer debend ubon him. Id is no longer bossible to underdake a work of any imbordance withoudt the gonsdand haunting fear that your brogress will be inderrubted—berhaps ad a most cridical juncture—by a 'sdrike,' The greadt quesdion which, above all others, do-day agidades the British mind is: 'Do whadt cause is the bresendt debression of drade addribudable?' And, in my obinion, gendlemen, the answer to that quesdion is thad id is very largely due do the consdandly recurring sdrikes which have become almosdt *a habid* with the Bridish workman. The 'sdrike' is the most formidable engine which has ever been broughd indo oberation do seddle the differences bedween embloyer and embloyed; and, whilst I am willing to admid thad in certain cases id has resulded in the repression and redress of long-sdanding oppression and injusdice, id has been used with such a lack of discrimination as do have almost ruined the drade of the goundry. With the invention of the 'sdrike' the workman thoughd he had ad lasd discovered the means of enriching himself ad the expense of his embloyer, or of securing his fair and righdful share of the brofids of his labour, as *he* described id; and, udderly ignorand of the laws of bolidigal egonomy, recognising in the 'sdrike' merely an insdrumend for forcing a higher rade of wages from his embloyer, he has gone on recklessly using id undil the unfordunade gabidalist, finding himself unable do produce his wares ad a cost which will enable him do successfully gompede with the manufagdurers of other goundries, has been gombelled to glose his works and remove his gabidal and his energies to a spodt where he gan find workmen less unreasonable in their demands. There is no more capable or valuable workman in existence than the English artisan, if he gould only be induced to do his honest *best* for his embloyer; there is hardly any branch of industry in which he is nod ad leasd the equal, if not very greadly the superior of the foreigner; and id is even yet in his power to recover the command of the world's market by the suberior excellence of his broductions, if he could only be brevailed upon do abandon sdrikes and do be satisfied with a wage which will allow the cabidalist a fair and moderate redurn for the use of his money and brains and for the risks he has do run. If the British workman would gollecdively make up his mind to do this, and would acquaindt the gabidalist with his decision, we should speedily see a revival of drade and embloymend for every really capable workman. Bud in the meantime there unfordunadely seems do be very little chance of this; and in so delicate a madder as the gonsdrugdion of this ship of ours, it would be nod only unwise, but also unfair to you to run the risk of a failure through the embloymendt of untractable or unreliable workmen; and if, therefore, you had insisted on my embloying Englishmen, I should have been relugdandly gombelled do wash my hands of the whole affair. Ad the same dime I feel id due do myself do say thad, even had you nod mendioned the madder, I should have done my best to secure Englishmen for the work, as of course I shall now; bud I do nod feel very sanguine as do the resuldt."

"My dear professor!" exclaimed the baronet, smiling at the intense earnestness of the German, "are you not laying on the colour rather thickly? I admit with sorrow that your portrait is only *too* truthful—as a portrait—still I cannot help thinking it rather highly coloured. They are surely not *all* as despicable as you have painted them?"

"No," answered the professor with enthusiasm, "no they are nod. Id was only a few weeks ago thad I read of the workmen of a cerdain firm bresending their employers with a full week's work *free*, in order to helb the firm out of their beguniary diffiguldies. Now, *they*, I admit, were fine, noble, sensible fellows; they had indelligence enough to regognize the diffiguldies of the siduation, and do grabble with them in a sensible way. I warrand you *they* always worked honesdly and efficiendly whether their embloyer's eye was on them or nod. And they will find their reward in due time; their embloyers will never rest until they have recouped the men for their generous sacrifice. But where will you find another body of men like them? They are only the one noble, grand exception which goes do brove my rule."

"Well, professor, though what you have said is, in the main, only *too* true, I cannot agree with you altogether; I believe there are a few good, intelligent, reliable men to be found here and there, in addition to those splendid fellows of whom you have just told us," said the baronet. "But," he continued, "I will not attempt to constrain you in any way. If you cannot find exactly what you want here, import men from abroad, by all means. I have a great deal of sympathy for want and suffering when they are the result of misfortune; but when they are brought on by a man's own laziness or perversity he must go elsewhere for sympathy and help; I have none to spare for people of that sort."

CHAPTER TWO
THE REALISATION OF A SCIENTIST'S DREAM

Punctual to the moment, Professor von Schalckenberg opened the door of the smoke-room at the "Migrants'," and entered the apartment as the deep-toned notes of Big Ben were heard sounding the hour of noon on the day following that upon which occurred the conversation recorded in the preceding chapter. Sir Reginald Elphinstone was already there; and after a few words of greeting the two men left the club together, and, entering the baronet's cab, which was in waiting, drove away to the banker's, where the business of the money transfer was soon concluded.

The pair then separated; and for the next fortnight the professor was busy all day, and during a great part of the night, with his drawings and calculations. At the end of that time, having completed his work on paper to his satisfaction, he took advantage of a fine day to make a little excursion. Proceeding to London Bridge, he embarked in a river steamer, about ten o'clock in the morning, and indulged himself in a run down the river. He kept his eyes sharply about him as the boat sped down the stream; and just before reaching Blackwall he saw what he thought would suit him. It was a ship-building yard, "for sale, or to let, with immediate possession", as an immense notice-board informed him. Landing at the pier, he made his way back to the yard, and, having with some difficulty found the man in charge of the keys, proceeded to inspect the premises. They turned out to be as nearly what he wanted as he could reasonably hope to find, being very spacious, with a full supply of "plant," in perfect working order, and with enough spare room to allow of the laying down of the special "plant" necessary for the manufacture of his new metal. Having satisfied himself upon this point, he next obtained the address of the parties who had the letting of the yard and works, and proceeded back to town by rail. The parties of whom he was now in search proved to be a firm of solicitors having offices in Lincoln's Inn; and by them, when he had stated the object of his call, he was received with—figuratively—open arms. The premises had been lying idle and profitless for some time; and they were only too glad to let them to him upon a two years' lease upon terms highly advantageous to him and his client the baronet.

This important business settled, the next thing was to lay down the special plant already referred to; and so energetic was the professor in his management of this and the other necessary preliminaries that six months sufficed to place the yard in a fit state for the commencement of actual operations.

And now the professor's troubles began in real earnest. Impressed with the idea that he was perhaps wrong after all, and the baronet right, in his judgment of the British workman, Herr von Schalckenberg determined to run the risk of giving the Englishmen another trial. He had no difficulty whatever in engaging an efficient office staff; but when it came to securing the services of foremen, mechanics, and labourers, the unhappy German was driven almost to despair. He advertised his wants widely, of course, and, in response to his advertisements, the applications for employment poured in almost literally without number. The great entrance-gates of the works were fairly besieged, and the roadway outside blocked by the great army of applicants, who were admitted into the presence of the professor in gangs of twenty at a time. The professor had set out with the resolve that he would deal as liberally with his employés as he possibly could, consistently with justice to his client, the baronet; and with this object he had spared no pains to ascertain the rate of wages then ruling for such men as he wanted. With the data thus obtained he had drawn up a scale of pay which he was prepared to offer, and beyond which he had resolved not to go. Armed with this, he interviewed the countless applicants as they presented themselves before him; and the result was enough to drive to distraction even a more patient man than Herr von Schalckenberg. The applicants proved to be, almost without exception, trades-unionists, out on strike because their employers had declined or had been unable to accede to the exorbitant demands of the workmen. These workmen had in many cases been idle for months; yet they now unhesitatingly refused employment, and refused it insolently too, because the wages offered by the professor, though fully equal to those paid by other employers, were less than they chose to consider themselves entitled to. Their wives and children were, by their own admission, naked and starving, and here was an opportunity to clothe and feed them, yet they rejected it scornfully. And naked, starving though the families of these wretches might be and actually were, almost every man of them, bearing out the professor's criticism of them, had a short dirty pipe in his mouth and smelt strongly of drink. There were a few exceptions to this rule—about one in every fifty applicants, perhaps—and they were almost all non-union men, who eagerly and thankfully accepted employment, careless of the sneers, gibes, and threats of the others; and these proved to be, with scarcely a single exception, steady, reliable, honest, and capable men, who soon worked themselves into leading positions. The professor wanted about two hundred men, and he succeeded in securing twenty; after which his overtasked patience gave out, and in despair he obtained the remainder from Germany.

All this took time; and it was not until nearly eight months after the conversation in the "Migrants'" smoke-room that the professor was actually able to commence work in the building yard. Then, however, the operations proceeded apace. Day after day long mineral trains jolted and clanked noisily along the siding and into the yard, where they disgorged their loads and made way for still other trains; day after day clumsy steam colliers hauled in alongside the yard wharf and under the fussy steam-cranes to discharge their cargoes; and very soon the lofty furnace chimneys began to belch forth a never-ending cloud of inky smoke. Very soon, too, the belated wayfarer might possibly, had he been so disposed, have obtained a chance glimpse, through accidental chinks in the close palisading, of a long range of brilliantly lighted buildings, wherein, if the doors happened to be inadvertently left open, he would have witnessed huge outpourings of dazzling molten metal, which, after being subjected to the action of certain chemicals, and passing through divers strange processes, was passed as it solidified through a series of powerful rolling mills, which relentlessly squeezed and flattened it out, until it finally emerged, still glowing red with fervent heat, in the shape of long flat symmetrically shaped sheets, or angle-bars and girders of various sections. And, a little later on, an inquisitive individual, could he have obtained a peep into the jealously boarded-in building shed, might have seen a far-reaching series of light circular ribs of glittering silver-like metal, of gradually decreasing diameter as they spread each way from the central rib, rearing themselves far aloft toward the ground-glass skylight which surmounted the roof of the building. But perhaps the strangest sight of all, could one but have gained admission into the forge to see it, was the huge main shaft of the ship, which, after having been mercilessly pounded and battered into shape by the giant Nasmith hammers, was coolly seized by only a couple of men, and by them easily carried into the machine-shop, there to receive its finishing touches in the lathe.

  And so the work went on, steadily yet rapidly, until at length it so nearly approached completion that the professor was every week enabled to dispense with the services of and pay off an increasingly large number of men. Finally, the day arrived when the score or so of painters and decorators, who then constituted the sole remnant of the professor's late army of workmen, completed their task of beautifying the interior of the aerial ship, and, receiving their pay, were dismissed to seek a new field of labour. The official staff now alone remained, and to these, after making them a pleasant little complimentary speech expressing his appreciation of the zeal and ability with which they had discharged their duties, Herr von Schalckenberg announced the pleasant intelligence that, although he had now no further need of their services, Sir Reginald Elphinstone had, upon his—the professor's—earnest recommendation, successfully used his influence to secure them other and immediate employment. The professor then handed each man a cheque for his salary, including three months' extra pay in lieu of the usual notice of dismissal to which he was entitled, together with a letter of introduction to his new employer, and, shaking hands with the staff all round, bade them good-bye, wishing them individually success in their new posts. Then, watching them file out of the office for the last time, he waited until all had left the premises, when he turned the key in the door, and making his way into the interior of the building shed, found himself at length alone with his completed work.

How the professor spent the next few hours no man but himself can say; but it is reasonable to suppose that, man of science though he was, he was still sufficiently human to regard with critical yet innocent pride and exultation the wonderful fabric which owed its existence to the inventive ingenuity of his fertile brain. It is probable, too, that when he had at length gratified himself with an exhaustive contemplation of its many points of interest, he went on board the ship, and with his own eyes and hands made a final inspection and trial of all her machinery, to satisfy himself that everything was complete and ready. At all events, however the professor may have passed those few hours of precious solitude, when he finally handed over the keys to the yard watchman and bade him "good-night" late on that summer evening, his whole bearing and appearance was that of a thoroughly happy and satisfied man.

CHAPTER THREE
THE "FLYING FISH"

During the whole of the following week stores of various kinds necessary to the comfort and sustenance of the voyagers were being constantly delivered at the building yard, where they were received by the valet and cook of Sir Reginald Elphinstone—the only servants or assistants of any kind who were to accompany the expedition—and promptly stowed away by them, under the direction of the professor, who was exceedingly anxious to accurately preserve the proper "trim" of the vessel—a much more important and difficult matter than it would have been had she been designed to navigate the ocean only. By mid-day on Saturday the last article had been received, including the personal belongings of the travellers, the stowage was completed, and everything was ready for an immediate start.

At three o'clock on the following Monday afternoon the voyagers met in the smoke-room of the "Migrants'" as a convenient and appropriate rendezvous, and, without having dropped the slightest hint to anyone respecting the novel nature of their intended journey, quietly said "Good-bye" to the two or three men who happened to be there, and, chartering a couple of hansoms, made the best of their way to Fenchurch Street railway station, from whence they took the train to Blackwall. On emerging from the latter station they placed themselves under the guidance of the professor, and were by him conducted in a few minutes to the building yard. The professor was the only one of the quartette who had as yet set eyes on the vessel in which they were about to embark; and the remaining three naturally felt a little flutter of curiosity as they passed through the gateway and saw before them the enormous closely-boarded shed which jealously hid from all unprivileged eyes the latest marvel of science. But they were Englishmen, and as such it was a part of their creed to preserve an absolutely unruffled equanimity under every conceivable combination of circumstances, so between the whiffs of their cigars they chatted carelessly about anything and everything but the object upon which their thoughts were just then centred.

But the baronet's equanimity was for a moment upset when the professor, after a perhaps unnecessarily prolonged fumbling with the key, threw open the wicket which gave admission to the interior of the shed, and, stepping back to allow his companions to precede him, exclaimed in tones of exultant pride, in that broken English of his which it is unnecessary to further reproduce:

"Behold, gentlemen, the embodiment of a scientist's dream—the *Flying Fish!*"

The baronet advanced a pace or two, then stopped short, aghast.

"Good heavens!" he ejaculated. "What, in the name of madness, have you done, professor? That huge object will *never* float in the air; and I should say it will be a pretty expensive business to get her into the *water*, if indeed it is worth while to put her there."

The other two, the representatives of the army and of the navy, though probably as much astonished as the baronet, said nothing. They knew considerably more than the latter about the capabilities of science; and though they might possibly entertain grave doubts as to the success of the professor's experiment, they did not feel called upon to express an off-hand opinion that it would prove a failure.

The baronet might well be excused his hasty expression of incredulity. Towering above and in front of him, filling up the entire space of the enormous shed from end to end and from ground to roof-timbers, he saw an immense cylinder, pointed at both ends, and constructed entirely of the polished silver-like metal which the professor had called aethereum. The sides of the ship from stem to stern formed a series of faultless curves; the conical bow or fore body of the ship being somewhat longer, and therefore sharper, than the after body, which partook more of the form of an ellipse than of a cone; the curvilinear hull was supported steadily in position by two deep broad bilge-keels, one on either side and about one-third the extreme length of the ship; and, attached to the stern of the vessel by an ingeniously devised ball-and-socket joint in such a manner as to render a rudder unnecessary, was to be seen a huge propeller having four tremendously broad sickle-shaped blades, the palms of which were hollowed in such a manner as to gather in and concentrate the air, or water, about the boss and powerfully project it thence in a direct line with the longitudinal axis of the ship. Crowning the whole there was a low superstructure immediately over and of the same length as the bilge-keels, very much resembling the upper works of a double-bowed vessel such as are some of the small Thames river steamers. This was decked over, and afforded a promenade about two hundred feet long by thirty feet wide. And, lastly, rising from the centre of this deck there was a spacious pilot-house with a dome-like roof, from the interior of which the movements of the vessel could be completely controlled. The entire hull of the vessel, excepting the double-bowed superstructure, was left unpainted, and it shone like a polished mirror. The superstructure, however, was painted a delicate grey tint, with the relief of a massive richly gilded cable moulding all round the shear-strake and the further adornment of a broad ribbon of a rich crimson hue rippling through graceful wreaths of gilded scroll-work at bow and stern, the name *Flying Fish* being inscribed on the ribbon in gold letters. Altogether, notwithstanding her unusual form, the aerial ship was an exceedingly graceful and elegant object, and, but for her enormous proportions, looked admirably adapted for her work.

Under other circumstances the professor would probably have been seriously offended at the baronet's incredulous exclamation; but as it was he was so confident of his success—so gratified and triumphant altogether—that he could afford to be not only forgiving but actually tolerant. He therefore replied to Sir Reginald only with a mute smile of amused compassion for the baronet's lamentable ignorance and unbelief.

The professor's smile somewhat reassured Sir Reginald, though he still continued to eye his novel possession very dubiously.

"You once spoke of Atlantic liners," he at last remarked to the professor; "but surely this craft is larger than the largest Atlantic liner afloat. What are her dimensions?"

"She is six hundred feet long, by sixty feet diameter at the point of her greatest girth," quietly replied the professor.

"And do you mean to tell me that such a monster will ever float in the air?" ejaculated the baronet, his incredulity returning and taking possession of him with tenfold tenacity.

"I do," answered the professor firmly, his self-love at length becoming slightly ruffled. "In that ship you shall to-night soar higher into the empyrean than mortal has ever soared before; and after that you shall, if you choose, sleep calmly until morning at the bottom of the English Channel. By and by at the dinner-table I will endeavour to demonstrate to you, my dear friend, that it is her immense proportions alone which will enable her to float in so thin a fluid as air."

"Very well," said the baronet in the tones of a man still utterly unconvinced; "if you say so, I suppose I must doubt no more. Now, please, introduce to us the novel details of this wonderful craft of yours."

"With pleasure," answered the professor, his brow clearing and a gratified smile suffusing his countenance. "A few minutes will suffice to show you all that can be seen from the outside. Those small circular pieces of glass which you perceive let into the hull here and there are, as you have no doubt already surmised, windows to enable us to observe what is passing outside. The larger windows at the bow and stern protect powerful electric lamps, and are exclusively for the purpose of lighting up our surroundings when we are at the bottom of the sea. This,"—pointing to what looked like a circular trap-door in the bottom of the ship, some fifteen feet from the centre on the port side—"is the anchor recess; and this,"—pointing to a corresponding arrangement on the starboard side—"is the door through which we shall obtain egress from and access to the ship when she is at the bottom of the sea."

"Do you mean by that, that we are going to leave the ship and walk about on the bed of the ocean?" asked the baronet.

"Certainly," answered the professor with a look of surprise. "Our exploration of the ocean's bed will probably be one of the most interesting incidents of the expedition."

The baronet shrugged his shoulders and the professor continued:

"These bilge-keels serve a threefold purpose; they enable the ship to rest steadily and firmly on the ground, as you see, which, from her peculiar form, she could not otherwise do; they also form the sheaths, so to speak, of four anchors to fasten her securely to the ground either above or beneath the water—a most necessary precaution, believe me; and they also add considerably to the cubical contents of the water-chambers, with which they communicate, which will help to sink the ship to the bottom. Lastly, there is the propeller, the only peculiarities of which are its great diameter—fifty feet—its enormous surface area, and the fact that it is attached to the hull in such a way as to admit of its being turned freely in any direction, thus dispensing with all necessity for a rudder."

"Why have you left the hull unpainted, professor? I suppose you had some good reason for so doing?" remarked the colonel, chiming into the conversation.

"I had no less than *three* good reasons for leaving the hull of the ship unpainted," answered the professor. "In the first place, aethereum is quite insensible to the attacks of air and water—it never oxidises, and paint was therefore unnecessary for its preservation. In the next place, the quantity of paint necessary to cover that enormous surface would weigh something considerable; and, as I have throughout the work taken the utmost pains to keep down all the weight to the lowest ounce consistent with absolute safety, I rejected it on that account. And lastly, I take it that we are anxious to avoid all unnecessary observation; and I believe this cannot be better accomplished than by preserving the brilliant metallic lustre of the hull, which, especially when we are floating in mid-air, will reflect the tints of the surrounding atmosphere, and so make it almost impossible to distinguish us."

"Except when the sun's rays fall directly upon us, eh, professor?" remarked Mildmay.

"In that case," returned the professor, "observers will see a dazzling flash of light in which all shape will be indistinguishable."

"And we shall thus be mistaken for a meteorite," exclaimed the baronet somewhat sarcastically. "Excellent! admirable! I really must congratulate you, professor, upon the wonderful foresight with which you seem to have provided for every possible and impossible emergency. Now, what is the next marvel?"

"There is nothing more down here. We will now proceed on board, if you please, gentlemen," said the professor; and he forthwith led the way up a ladder which leaned against the vessel's lofty side. This conducted them as far as the upper curve of her cylindrical bilge, at which point they encountered a flight of light ornamental openwork steps permanently attached to the ship's side, up which they passed to the gangway in the stout metal railing which served instead of bulwark, and so reached the spacious promenade deck. Looking down into the yard from this coign of vantage, they seemed to be an enormous height from the ground; and the baronet shrugged his shoulders more expressively than ever as he glanced first below and then around him, realising more fully than ever, as he did so, the immense proportions of his new possession. He said nothing, however, but turned inquiringly to the professor.

"This way, gentlemen, if you please," said the German, in answer to the look; and he led them aft to what may be styled the quarter-deck.

"You spoke about the weight of a coat of paint on the hull just now, but I see you have planked the deck. The weight of all this planking must be something considerable," remarked Mildmay.

"A mere trifle; it is only a thin veneering just to give a secure and comfortable foothold," remarked the professor. He paused at what looked like a trap-door in the deck and said:

"We shall not be always soaring in the air nor groping about at the bottom of the sea; we shall sometimes be riding on the surface; and I have therefore thought it advisable to provide a couple of boats. Here is one of them."

He stooped down, seized hold of and turned a ring in the flap, and raised the trap-door, disclosing a dark pit-like recess of considerable dimensions. Letting the flap fold back flat on the deck, the professor then stooped down and grasped the handle of a horizontal lever which lay just below the level of the deck, and drew it up into a perpendicular position, and, as he did so, a pair of davits, the upper portions of which had been plainly visible, rose through the aperture close to the protecting railing, bringing with them a handsomely modelled boat hanging from the tackles. The professor deftly turned the davits outward, and there hung the boat at the quarter in the exact position she would have occupied in an ordinary ship.

"Bravo, professor; very clever indeed!" exclaimed Mildmay. "But what is the object of those four curved tubes projecting through the boat's bottom?"

"Those tubes," answered the professor, "are the boat's means of propulsion. You see," he explained, "being built of aethereum, the boat is extremely light, and draws so little water that a screw propeller would be quite useless to her. So I have substituted those tubes instead. One pair, you will observe, points toward the stern, and one pair toward the bow. The boat's engine is a powerful three-cylinder pump, and it sucks the water strongly in through the tubes which point forward, discharging it as powerfully out through those which point astern; thus drawing and driving the boat along at a speed of about twelve knots per hour, which is as fast, I fancy, as we shall ever want her to go. If you want to go astern the movement of a single lever reverses the whole process. There is a similar boat on the other side."

The boat having been returned to her hiding-place, the professor next led his friends to the structure which occupied the centre of the deck. It was a perfectly plain erection, with curved sides meeting in a kind of stem and stern-post at its forward and after ends, with a curved dome-like roof, several small circular windows all round its sides, and no apparent means of entry.

"Why, how is this, professor? You have actually built your pilot-house—for such I suppose it is—without a door," exclaimed the baronet with returning good-humour as he perceived that, even in the event of the *Flying Fish* failing to fly, he would still have a very wonderful ship for his money.

"As you have rightly supposed, this *is* the pilot-house," answered the professor, with one hand pressing lightly against the gleaming wall of the structure. "But as to its being without a door, you are mistaken, for there it is."

And as he spoke a door, hitherto unnoticed in the side of the building, flew open.

"Why, you are a veritable magician, professor! How on earth did you manage that?" exclaimed the colonel.

"Easily enough," answered the professor. "Just look here, all of you. This is a secret door which it is necessary you should all know how to open. Now, there are four of us, are there not? Very well; find the fourth rivet from the bottom in the fourth row from the after end of the building—here it is—push it to your left—*not* press it; pressing is no good—and open flies the door. Push the rivet to the *right* when the door is open, and you shut it—so," suiting the action to the word. "Now, Sir Reginald, let me see if you can open that door."

The baronet opened and closed the door without difficulty; and then the other two essayed the attempt with similarly successful results.

"That is all right," commented the professor. "Now step inside, please; and close the door—so: when you want to open it from the inside you simply turn this handle—so, and open it comes."

The quartette now found themselves inside the pilothouse, which proved to be two stories in height. On their right hand they beheld the companion-way leading to the interior of the ship, with a wide flight of stairs of delightfully easy descent, handsomely carpeted, and a magnificent massive handrail and balusters of gleaming aethereum. The square opening to the companion-way was also protected by a similar handrail and balusters, producing an exceedingly rich effect and seeming to promise a corresponding sumptuousness of fitting in the saloons below.

Just clear of the head of the companion staircase and leading up one side of the pilot-house was another light staircase of open grid-work leading to the floor above, which, at a height of seven feet, spanned the building from side to side. This floor was also of light open gridwork, affording easy verbal communication between persons occupying the different stories in the pilot-house. Through this open grid-floor could be seen various apparatus, the objects of which the new-comers were naturally anxious to learn; and to this floor the professor accordingly led his companions up the staircase.

The first object to which he directed attention was a long straight bar of aethereum handsomely moulded into the form of a thick cable, and finished off at the outer end with the semblance of a "Matthew Walker" knot. This bar issued at its inner end from a handsomely panelled and moulded casing which extended down through both floors of the pilot-house, presumably covering in and protecting the mechanism with which the bar was obviously connected.

"This," said the professor, laying his hand on the bar, "is the steering apparatus—the tiller as you call it—of the ship. It moves, as you see, in all directions, and communicates a corresponding movement to the propeller—as you may see, if you will take the trouble to look out through one of those windows."

The trio immediately did so, and saw, as the professor had stated, that with every movement of the tiller, right or left, up or down, the propeller inclined itself at a corresponding angle. A handsome binnacle compass stood immediately in front of the tiller, but the professor did not call attention to it, rightly assuming that his companions were fully acquainted with its use and purpose.

On the professor's right, as he stood at the tiller, was an upright lever working in a quadrant, and communicating, like the tiller—and indeed all the other apparatus—with the interior of the ship.

"This," said the professor, directing attention to the lever, "is the lever which controls the valves of the main engines. I have fashioned and arranged it exactly like the corresponding lever in a locomotive. Placed vertically, thus, the engines remain motionless. Thrown forward, thus, the engines will turn ahead. And thrown backward, thus, they will turn astern. That is simple enough. And so is this," directing attention to a dial on his left hand which stood facing him. The dial had a single hand which was obviously intended to travel over a carefully graduated arc of ninety degrees painted on the dial-face, and which, in addition to the graduations, was marked in the proper positions with the words "Stop;" "Quarter speed;" "Half speed;" "Full speed;" and also with two arrows pointing in opposite directions marked "On" and "Off" respectively. Just beneath the dial was a small wheel with a crank-handle projecting from one of its spokes, and on this crank-handle the professor now laid his hand.

"This," he said, "regulates the valve which admits vapour into the engine; and the dial-hand shows the extent to which the valve is opened. Turn the wheel in the direction of the arrow marked 'On'—thus, and you admit vapour into the engine. You will observe that, as I turn the wheel, the hand on the dial travels over the arc and indicates the extent to which the valve is open. There; now it is fully open, and the cylinders are full of vapour." Then he quickly reversed the wheel and sent the index hand back to "Stop," keeping a wary eye on his companions as he did so.

"These are dangerous things to meddle with," he remarked apologetically. "The engines are of one hundred thousand horse-power; and, full as the ship now is of air at the atmospheric pressure, they would drive her irresistibly along the ground and through all obstacles. I must beg that none of you will meddle with the machinery until you are fully acquainted with its tremendous power."

"What is this pendulum-looking affair, professor?" asked the colonel, pointing to a pendulum the point of which hung in a shallow basin-like depression thickly studded with needle-points which the pendulum just cleared by a hair's-breadth.

"That," explained the professor, "is a device for automatically regulating the balance, or 'trim' as you call it, of the ship when she is floating in the air. You will readily understand that when freed of air, and thus deprived of weight, as it were, the most trifling matter will suffice to derange her equilibrium; one of us, walking from side to side, or from one end of the deck to the other, would very seriously incline her from the horizontal, and thus alter the direction of her flight, possibly with disastrous results; so I have devised this little apparatus to prevent all that. This pendulum, as you see, is so delicately poised that it will instantly respond to the slightest deviation from a horizontal position, and, swaying over one of these needle-points, will send an electric current to the air-pump, causing it to promptly inject a sufficient quantity of air into the proper chamber to restore the equilibrium. But, as we may desire occasionally to direct the flight of the ship in an upward or a downward direction, I have so arranged matters that the apparatus shall be thrown out of gear when the tiller is sloped in either direction out of the horizontal; and as we shall not require it when the ship is on or below the surface of the ocean, I have here provided a small knob by pressing which inwards the apparatus can also be thrown out of gear until it is again wanted."

"Excellent!" exclaimed the baronet. "I must again congratulate you, professor, on your truly wonderful forethought. And what is this, pray?"

"That," said the German, "is the controlling lever of the air-pump. When we want to sink into the depths of the ocean, I thrust this lever over—so; and the pump at once begins to pump air into the air-chambers."

"*Out* of them, I suppose you mean," interrupted the baronet.

"*Into* them, I mean," insisted the professor. "You must understand," he continued, noting the baronet's look of astonishment, "that air, like everything else, has *weight*. Feathers are light; but you may pack them so tightly into a receptacle as to make them very weighty; and so is it with air: the more air you force into a receptacle of given size the heavier you make that receptacle; and, provided that both your forcing apparatus and your receptacle are strong enough to endure the tremendous pressure, you may at last force enough air into the receptacle to sink it. And that is precisely what we shall do; we shall force air into our air-chambers until the ship is on the point of sinking, and we shall then close the valves, stop the air-pump, and, opening the sea-cocks of the water-chambers, admit water enough into the ship to send her to the bottom like a stone."

"Well! you astonish me, I freely admit," gasped the baronet. "This is the first time I ever heard of a ship being sunk by filling her with air. And then the cool way in which you talk of our 'sinking to the bottom like a stone!' I undertook this enterprise because I wanted to experience a new sensation; and it appears to me that there are a good many of them in store for me. However, it is all right; go on with your explanations, my dear sir."

"These," said the professor, indicating several levers marked with distinguishing labels ranged all along one side of the pilot-house, "are the levers opening and closing the valves of the air and water chambers, and need no further description. This," he continued, pointing to a small box with a little knob projecting out of the top of it, "is the apparatus for firing our torpedo shells."

The baronet glanced mutely round at his companions, and shrugged his shoulders expressively, as who should say, "What next?"

The colonel and the lieutenant nodded approvingly, however, and the latter said:

"That is capital, professor; we ought to have the means of fighting the ship, if necessary; but I was beginning to fear you had overlooked that matter, having seen no provision for anything of the kind. But where is your torpedo port? you omitted to point that out to us when we were under the ship's bottom."

"There was nothing to show," replied the professor; "and I can explain the matter just as well up here as I could have done when we were down below. The conical point which forms the extreme forward end of the ship is solid and movable. Under ordinary circumstances it remains firmly fixed in position; but when it becomes necessary to fire a torpedo-shell the solid point is made to slide in along a grooved tube for a certain distance; the shell is then placed in the tube and fired, when the solid point follows it out and becomes again securely fixed in its former position. In addition to this arrangement, I have two large guns which can be worked through ports in the dining-saloon, and six wonderful magazine rifles invented by a Mr. Maxim, a friend of mine. They are perhaps the most wonderful pieces of mechanism in the ship, for when the first shot has been fired they will go on firing themselves at the marvellous rate of six hundred shots per minute so long as you keep them supplied with cartridges. Then I have also provided an ample supply of ordinary guns and rifles, swords, pikes, pistols, and in fact everything we are likely to require for the purposes of sport or defence. These small knobs afford the means of lighting the electric lamp in the lantern on the top of the pilot-house and those in the bow and stern of the ship. And that is all to which I think I need direct your attention here at present. Now, if you please, we will go down and look at the machinery."

The party accordingly left the pilot-house and directed their steps below by way of the grand staircase. At the bottom of this they found themselves upon a spacious landing magnificently carpeted, and lighted at each end by a circular window in the side of the ship. In front of them as they descended the staircase, and at a distance of about twelve feet from its base, a partition stretched from side to side of the ship, evidently forming one of the saloon bulkheads. Along the face of this a series of Corinthian pilasters, supporting a noble cornice at the junction of wall and ceiling, divided up the partition into a corresponding number of panels, which were enriched with elegant mouldings of fanciful scroll-work and painted in creamy white and gold. In two instances, however, at points which divided the partition into three equal parts, the panels were replaced by handsome massively moulded doors of unpainted aethereum, imparting a very rich and handsome effect. These doors were, however, closed, and the curiosity of the new-comers as to what was to be seen on the other side of them had to remain for a short time ungratified.

Passing round to the back of the grand staircase (in which direction lay the sleeping apartments, bath-rooms, and domestic offices) they found themselves at the head of another staircase much narrower than the former. The one now before them was only about four feet wide, winding cork-screw fashion round the tube which encased the communications between the pilot-house and the engine-room, etcetera, and it was in its turn encased in a cylindrical bulk-head, in which, on their way below, they passed several doors giving access, as the professor explained, to the different decks.

Winding their way downward for a considerable distance they at length reached the foot of the staircase and passed at once through a doorway marked "Engine Room." The first sensation of those who now visited this apartment for the first time was disappointment. The room, though full of machinery, was small, absurdly so, it seemed to them. So also with the machinery itself. The main engines, consisting of a pair of three-cylinder compound engines, though made throughout of aethereum, and consequently presenting an exceedingly handsome appearance, suggested more the idea of an exquisite model in silver than anything else, the pair occupying very little more space than those of one of the larger Thames river steamers. The impression of diminutiveness and inadequacy of power passed away, however, when the professor informed his companions that the vapour would enter the high-pressure cylinder at the astounding pressure of five thousand pounds to the square inch, and that, though the engines themselves would only make fifty revolutions per minute, the propeller, would be made, by means of speed-multiplying gear, to revolve at the rate of one thousand times per minute in air of ordinary atmospheric pressure.

"But how on earth do you manage to get your vapour up to that tremendous pressure?" asked the colonel.

"Oh!" answered the professor, "that is a mere matter of mixing. According to the proportions in which the crystals and the acid are mingled together, so is the pressure of the vapour."

"And how do you mingle them together?" asked the lieutenant.

"This," said the professor, leading them up to a small boiler-like vessel, "is the generator. The crystals are placed in a hopper at one end, and the acid in that small tank at the other, from whence they are respectively conducted along tubes into a small well in the bottom of the generator, where, their proportions being regulated by the size of the tubes through which they pass, they mingle and generate a vapour having a pressure of five thousand pounds on the square inch. See, there is the gauge, and it is now registering a pressure of five thousand pounds."

"Good Heavens, man!" exclaimed the baronet, starting back; "you don't mean to say that your generator is *now*, at this moment, subjected to that enormous pressure of more than two tons per square inch? Supposing it exploded, what would become of us?"

"We should be consumed in an instant by the fierce heat of the liberated vapour," replied the professor calmly. "But," he continued, "you need have no apprehension of an explosion. When that generator was being made I had a second one constructed at the same time, precisely similar in every respect, and this second one I tested to destruction, with the satisfactory result that it endured without distress a pressure of thirty-five tons per square inch, showed the first signs of weakness when it became subjected to a pressure of thirty-eight tons, and burst at a joint when under a pressure of forty-three tons per square inch. You may therefore feel quite satisfied that the generator is fully equal to a continuous pressure of at least fifteen tons, instead of the trifle over two which it will have to sustain."

The remainder of the machinery possessing no very startling or novel features, it was passed by with merely an admiring glance at its exquisite finish; and the quartette, leaving the engine-room, passed round on the other side of the spiral staircase to a room marked "Diving Room."

Entering this they found themselves in an apartment about twenty feet square, one side of which was wholly occupied by four cupboards labelled respectively "Sir Reginald Elphinstone," "Colonel Lethbridge," "Lieutenant Mildmay," and "Von Schalckenberg."

"This," explained the professor, "is the room wherein we shall equip ourselves for our submarine rambles; and here," opening one of the cupboards, "are the costumes which we shall wear upon such occasions."

The opened cupboard contained an ordinary indiarubber diving-dress, a sort of double knapsack, a number of heterogeneous articles, and, lastly, a suit of armour.

"Why, professor, what, in the name of all that is comical, is the meaning of this? Are we to walk forth among the fishes equipped like the knights of old?" asked the baronet, pointing to the armour.

"I will explain," said the professor. "In an ordinary diving-dress a man can only descend to a depth of something like fifteen fathoms. Instances have certainly occurred where this depth has been exceeded, a Liverpool diver named Hooper having descended as far as thirty-four fathoms, if my information is correct; but this was quite an exceptional circumstance; and, as I have said, fifteen fathoms may be taken as the average depth at which a man can move about and work in comfort. The reason for this limit is that beyond it the pressure of the water on the exposed hands is so great as to drive the blood to the head and bring on a fainting fit, if nothing worse; besides which, the volume of air inside the dress necessary to counteract the outside pressure of the water would be so great as to speedily result in suffocation. Now, if our explorations were limited to a depth of fifteen fathoms only they would hardly be worth the undertaking; so I have devised these suits of armour, in which we may safely explore the profoundest depths of the ocean to which the *Flying Fish* can penetrate. The armour is, as you see, composed of a number of small scales or plates of aethereum, and is so constructed that, whilst it is perfectly flexible, permitting the utmost freedom of movement to the wearer, it is also absolutely water-tight and incompressible, no matter how great the exterior pressure to which it is subjected. The wearer of it will consequently be perfectly protected at all points from the enormous water pressure; and he will be able to breathe in comfort, his air being supplied to him at the normal atmospheric pressure. In equipping himself the diver will first don the india-rubber diving-dress in the usual way. Then he will assume this double-haversack, the larger chamber of which, worn on the back, will contain a supply of air, whilst the smaller of the two, worn on the chest, is charged with a supply of chemicals for the purification of the air after it has been breathed. The two are connected together by a pair of flexible tubes, as you may perceive, and the mere expansion and contraction of the chest, in the act of breathing, sets in motion the simple apparatus which produces the necessary circulation of air between the two chambers. Having secured this haversack in position the diver next dons his body armour, and straps about his waist this belt, with its electric lamp and its dagger. The dagger, as you see, is double-bladed; it has a haft of insulating material, and the blades have connected to them this insulated wire at the point where the blades and the handle unite. You thus have a weapon which, on being plunged into the body of a foe, not only inflicts a severe wound, but also administers an electric shock of such terrible intensity as must result in instant death. The last portion of the armour to be assumed is the helmet, on the top of which is securely fixed an electric lamp, which, with the aid of the one at the belt, will give us, I imagine, as much light as we are likely to need.

"Having donned our armour we pass out of this chamber into the next, which I call the chamber of egress, carefully closing the door behind us."

The professor, suiting the action to the word, ushered his companions into the next chamber, closing the door behind him, and they found themselves in a small room some ten feet square by seven feet in height. This room, in common with the diving-room, was brilliantly lighted by an electric lamp inclosed in a lantern of abnormally thick glass.

"Arrived here," continued the professor, "we are all ready to sally forth upon our submarine explorations; all we have to do therefore is, first to fill the chamber with water by means of this valve, then open the trap-door and step forth upon the bottom of the sea."

As the professor said this he released the fastenings of the door, and it fell down, forming a sort of inclined plane, over which they passed, to find themselves once more on the solid earth, under the ship's bottom, with the starboard bilge-keel rising like a wall of silver before them. They passed along the lane formed by this keel and the cylindrical bottom of the ship, and then stepped back with one accord to take another glance aloft at the huge bulk of the ship as she towered high above them. They now became conscious of the sounds of vigorous hammering and of men's voices in the direction of the river gable of the building shed, and on looking in that direction they saw that the contractor, whom the professor had engaged for the purpose, was already at work with his men removing the boarding which had hitherto concealed the *Flying Fish* from passers-by on the river, thus making a way for the exit of the ship a little later on.

The little party had re-entered the hull by way of the trap-door, and the professor had just made the fastenings once more secure, when, far away aloft from somewhere within the recesses of the ship, they heard the loud, sonorous, sustained note of a gong.

"Ah, that is good!" exclaimed Herr von Schalckenberg, rubbing his hands; "that is the dinner gong; and I am hungry. Come, my friends, to the dining saloon, and let us partake of the first of, I hope, many pleasant meals on board the *Flying Fish.*"

CHAPTER FOUR
THE NOVEL BEGINNING OF A SINGULAR VOYAGE

On reaching the head of the spiral staircase the professor paused for a moment to direct the attention of his companions to a long passage which extended apparently along the middle of the ship to the fore-end of the superstructure. The passage was about five feet wide, and the ceiling was of ground glass, through which a flood of light streamed brilliantly down.

"In that direction," said the professor, "are to be found, first, the kitchen, pantry, larder, and store-room; then next to them come my laboratory and workshop, with the armoury and magazine on the opposite side; then the quarters of the cook and the valet; next these again are the bath-rooms and lavatories; and finally, at the extreme end of the passage, there are the state-rooms or sleeping apartments, eight in number—four for ourselves and four spare ones."

George, the valet—whose duties, however, on board the *Flying Fish* were to be rather those of steward and general handy man—stood during the progress of this brief explanation with his hand on the handle of the saloon door; and now, as the professor turned and nodded, he flung the door wide open and stood aside for the baronet and his friends to enter.

They now found themselves in the dining-saloon, an apartment thirty feet square and about ten feet high to the lower edge of the cornice. The walls, of unpainted aethereum, were broken up into panels by fluted pilasters with richly-moulded capitals, each panel having a frosted border covered with delicate tracery, whilst the central portion of the panel was left plain and polished, serving the purpose of a mirror, in which the room and its multiplied reflections on the opposite wall was again reflected in a long perspective. The floor was covered with a rich Turkey carpet, into which one sank ankle deep; the chairs, sofas, the massive sideboard, the wide table, in fact all the furniture in the room, was constructed of aethereum and modelled after the choicest designs, the upholstery being in rich embossed velvet of a delicate light-blue shade. The table glittered with a brilliant array of plate and glass; and the entire apartment was suffused with rich, soft, rainbow-tinted light, streaming down through the magnificent coved skylight of stained glass, which served instead of ceiling to the saloon.

"Superb!"

"Magnificent!"

"Exquisite!"

Such were the exclamations which burst from the professor's companions as they paused to look about them and take in all the details of the splendidly furnished and decorated apartment. A dozen eager questions rushed from their lips; but Herr von Schalckenberg was hungry, and the dinner was served, he therefore contented himself with bowing profoundly and pointing to the dinner-table.

"Come, gentlemen," exclaimed the baronet laughingly, "take your seats, I beg. It is evident that we have quite exhausted both the professor's patience and his strength, and that we shall get no more information out of him until both have been restored by a good dinner."

With which remark Sir Reginald set the example by taking his place at the head of the table, as he was entitled to do in virtue of his ownership of the *Flying Fish*.

The dinner was an admirable one, in all respects quite worthy the exceptional nature of the occasion; and under its genial influence, and that of the choice wines which accompanied it, the conversation soon grew extremely animated. The topic was, of course, the aerial ship and the novel and interesting character of her various equipments. The professor speedily redeemed his afternoon's promise to the baronet, and at length succeeded in completely convincing that hitherto sceptical individual that, so far from the enormous proportions of the *Flying Fish* being detrimental to her, they constituted the principal basis upon which he was justified in his anticipations of her success as an *aerial* ship.

Having at length made this perfectly plain, he was next called upon by Lieutenant Mildmay to explain a certain peculiarity in the binnacle compass, which had attracted that gentleman's notice and excited his curiosity.

"I observed," he said, "that the compass-card bore round its outer rim, at every quarter point, a small upright needle. As everything on board here, however apparently insignificant, seems to have its own especial purpose, I should like to know the purpose which those small needles are designed to serve."

"Ha, ha, my friend! so you noticed them, did you? I quite expected that, as a seaman, you very soon would," said the professor. "Well, I will tell you what they are. They form part of a little device of mine to render the ship self-steering, or, more correctly, to make the compass itself steer her in any given direction. Having noticed those needles, you doubtless also noticed that across the 'lubber's mark' there was a small slit some six inches long in the side of the compass-box?"

The lieutenant nodded.

"Good!" ejaculated the professor. "Had you looked outside the box you would also have observed two long slender arms pivoted close together, their outer and longer extremities being united, and carrying a small needle which travels, point downwards, along the arc of a circle. Now the action of the instrument is this. Supposing that you wish the ship to travel along, say, a southerly course, you manipulate the helm in the usual manner until the south point of the compass-card swings round to the lubber's mark. The moment that these two accurately coincide you pull toward you a small lever within easy reach of your hand, and the two arms glide in through the slit in the side of the compass-box, passing one on each side of the needle on the edge of the card, and your apparatus is then connected up ready for action. Now, so long as the ship's bows remain pointed accurately to the south, the south point on the compass-card continues coincident with the lubber's mark, and nothing happens. But should the ship deviate ever so slightly from her proper course the heavy, yet sensitive, compass needle at once swings round in sympathy; the small needle on the edge of the card moves the two slender arms which embrace it; the downward-pointing needle at the further extremity of these arms travels along the arc; and electric communication is at once established with the steering machinery, which promptly acts in such a way as to bring back the ship to her original course."

"Capital! Admirable!" ejaculated Sir Reginald and the lieutenant together, the former continuing:

"Upon my word, professor, you are a veritable wizard—a magician with powers exceeding those of the most potent of your brethren referred to in the 'Arabian Nights.'"

The professor made a laughing disclaimer. "No, no, my dear sir," said he, "I am no magician, but only a poor scientist. Nevertheless, the wonders of science far exceed those of the 'Arabian Nights,' and will well repay the man who cares to patiently study them."

Enlivened by conversation of a character so interesting to all present, the sitting was prolonged to quite an inordinate length, and though no one, except perhaps the professor, noted the fact, it was past midnight when the adventurous quartette rose from the table, and taking their wine and cigars with them, moved into the music-room, at the same time dismissing the patient George for the night.

The music-room was a much larger apartment than the dining saloon, being, like the latter, the full width of the superstructure, and measuring forty feet between the fore and the after bulkheads. It was the next room abaft the dining saloon, and was even more elaborately furnished and decorated than the latter. The walls, divided up in the same manner as those of the other apartment, were adorned with choice pictures, and exquisite statues of frosted aethereum were grouped on pedestals at frequent intervals all round the room. A coved and panelled ceiling of decorated aethereum sprang from the upper edge of the richly moulded cornice; and a skylight of magnificent stained glass, somewhat similar to that of the dining saloon, surmounted the whole. A grand piano and a noble chamber organ, both in superbly modelled aethereum cases, occupied opposite sides of the apartment; a very handsome clock, with a set of silvery chimes for the quarters and a deep rich-toned gong for the hours, occupied a conspicuous position on a wall bracket; chairs, couches, and divans of seductive shape and ample capacity were dotted here and there about the rich carpet; and a handsome table occupied the centre of the room, supporting and reflecting in the silvery depths of its undraped top a noble épergne of choice hot-house flowers.

"Why, how is this?" exclaimed the colonel as he sank into the luxurious depths of a most inviting arm-chair; "my watch must be all wrong, and your clock there is also wrong, professor; they both assert that it is half-past twelve o'clock, yet the sun has not yet set," pointing aloft to the skylight, through which a brilliant flood of sunshine was streaming down into the magnificent apartment.

"The sun has not yet set? Then we will soon make it do so," laughingly remarked the professor, rising from his seat and approaching one of the walls of the apartment, whilst the baronet and the lieutenant stared in dismay at their own watch-faces. The German began to manipulate a couple of tiny knobs which occupied unobtrusive positions in the base of one of the pilasters, and the sunlight gradually deepened into a rich orange hue, then changed to a soft pearly grey, which gradually deepened into a dim delicious twilight in which little was visible save the pictured glass in the skylight above; then it gradually brightened again, and presently a flood of glorious silvery moonlight streamed down through the skylight and suffused the room. Finally, with an instantaneous change, the brilliant sunlight was again restored. "Another wonder!" exclaimed Sir Reginald. "How do you manage it, professor?"

"Oh! that is a very simple matter," was the reply; "it is merely a cunning arrangement of variously tinted glass shades interposed between the electric light above the centre of the skylight and the mirrors which reflect the light down through the stained glass into the room. As you probably noticed when on the deck, there are no actual skylights in the usual acceptation of the term; ours are only make-believes; but they struck me as affording an agreeable means of lighting the saloons, so I introduced them."

In further conversation, diversified by music, the time slipped rapidly away; and at length the clock on the bracket proclaimed that it was two hours after midnight.

As the sonorous strokes of the gong announced the fact, the professor rose to his feet, and in a voice tremulous with sudden nervous excitement, said:

"Gentlemen, the hour for our departure, the hour which is to witness the success or failure of our grand experiment, has arrived. The river and the streets of the great city are by this time nearly or quite deserted; and we may therefore hope that our movements will attract little or no notice. Are you ready?"

"Ready!" ejaculated the baronet; "of course we are, my dear sir. Is not this the moment to which we have all been anxiously looking forward for more than two years? Proceed, professor, we will follow you; and whatever orders you may give us shall be obeyed to the letter."

"Come, then," said the professor; and he led the way through the dining saloon and up the grand staircase to the lower compartment of the pilot-house, and thence out on deck.

To their eyes, fresh from the brilliantly lighted saloons, the night appeared intensely dark; but in a minute or two, becoming accustomed to the gloom, they were able to perceive that the ladder had been taken away from the ship's side, and also that the contractor had completed his task of removing the planking at the river end of the shed, thus clearing a way for the exit of the great ship. They walked to the after extremity of the deck, and from that point were not only able, in the breathless stillness then prevailing, to distinctly hear the gurgle and rush of the river, but also to dimly make out the shining, swirling surface of the water as the flood-tide swept past them.

"The air is absolutely motionless," said the professor. "No more favourable moment could possibly have been chosen for the difficult task of moving the *Flying Fish* out of her present cramped quarters, and we will at once avail ourselves of it. Lieutenant, I will ask you to return here presently on the 'look-out,' as you sailors term it. Your duty will be to see that when we move out of the shed we do not come into collision with anything. Perhaps you, colonel, will kindly go to the other end the deck, also on the 'look-out;' and, as for you, Sir Reginald, I must ask you to stand on the deck just outside the pilothouse, to see that the electric lamp on the top of it does not come into collision with the roof-timbers, and so drag the roof off the shed. But as it is necessary that you should all become acquainted with the working of the ship, you had better be with me in the pilot-house until we are actually ready to move."

"Now," continued the professor when the quartette had made their way to the upper floor of the pilot-house, which was moderately illuminated by an electric lamp of small power, "the first thing to be done is to place the tiller of the ship in a horizontal position, and thus bring into action the automatic balancing gear. So! It is done. The next thing is to expel the air from the entire hull of the ship, excepting, of course, the comparatively insignificant portion reserved for habitation, and this I do by injecting vapour into the several compartments. The vapour drives out the air, and then, condensing like steam, creates, if required, a perfect vacuum. This large wheel controls the valve which we now want to open. I turn it this way, so—and now we shall see what will happen."

Two large dials were attached to the side of the pilothouse, close together; and upon these the professor now intently fixed his gaze. The index-hands of both were seen to be moving. A period of perhaps half a minute elapsed, and then the professor, suddenly shutting off the vapour, went over and closely inspected both dials.

"Good!" he exclaimed, after a single keen glance at each of them. "Gentlemen, let us congratulate each other. Our experiment is a *Signal Success*!"

"How do you know that, professor? How can you tell?" eagerly asked his companions.

"Look at these two dials; they will tell you," replied the professor. "This dial," tapping one with his finger, "indicates the weight of the ship, or the pressure with which she bears upon the ground. This one," indicating the other, "shows the pressure of air inside the hull of the ship. The first, as you see, shows that the ship is now pressing upon the ground with a force of less than a single ton—in other words, she now weighs less than one ton. The air-gauge shows that there is still an air pressure of six pounds per square inch inside the hull, and we therefore have, as I expected we should, a large margin of buoyancy. Now, lieutenant, do me the favour to turn on the vapour once more, very cautiously. Steady! *Stop*! There, Sir Reginald, the index has reached zero, and your ship is now as nearly as possible without weight; and if a man were now underneath her, he might, notwithstanding her gigantic proportions, easily raise her upon his shoulders. Now comes the delicate part of our operation. To your stations on the deck quickly, gentlemen, if you please."

The professor's companions, just a trifle excited, perhaps, hurried away to their posts, and the scientist was left alone. The circular windows in the sides of the pilothouse were all left open, and in through them presently floated the voice of the lieutenant shouting:

"All ready abaft, professor."

"All ready at this end," replied the colonel.

The professor reversed the engines, turned on the vapour *very* cautiously indeed, and simultaneously, with the engines below only just barely moving, the huge propeller began to whirl round at a speed of some sixty revolutions a minute.

A breathless pause of perhaps two seconds followed, and then the professor, his forehead damp with nervous perspiration, heard:

"Hurrah! She's away!" from the lieutenant.

"She moves; she moves!" from the colonel.

And, "By Jove, she is actually moving!" from the baronet.

Slowly but surely the *Flying Fish* backed out of the building-shed, until nearly half her immense length projected beyond the walls. Then the voice of the baronet was heard exclaiming:

"Ho! stop her! The electric lamp will not clear the roof, I am afraid. Can you give us a little light on the subject, professor?"

By way of reply the professor pressed a knob, and the lamp itself flashed its dazzling light upon the scene, when it became apparent that the ship had gradually risen from the ground, bringing the top of her lamp just above the level of the last tie-rod of the roof.

"Can you drop her a little? Six inches will do it," said the baronet.

The professor opened the air-valve and the ship at once began to settle down.

"So! That will do; all clear. You may go astern again now as fast as you please," said the baronet.

Once more the great propeller began to revolve, and presently the baronet, from his position under the foremost end of the pilot-house, remarked:

"Now she is all clear, professor; the whole of the pilothouse is outside the shed. A bold dash astern now and we shall be clear fore and aft in another moment."

The professor extinguished the electric lamp; gave the wheel connected with the vapour-valve another turn; the engines increased their speed; and the great ship at once shot rapidly out over the stream and clear of everything. Then the professor stopped the engines, turned a thin stream of vapour into the air chambers, and the huge fabric began to slowly rise perpendicularly in the air. Herr von Schalckenberg waited until he saw that they were fairly above the level of the roofs on both sides of the river; then he left the pilot-house and, joining the baronet on the deck outside, said, in a voice of undisguised exultation:

"Well, Sir Reginald, what think you *now* of the *Flying Fish?*"

"I think her, professor, a wonderful creation of a still more wonderful man. I see that we are steadily rising in the air, as you assured us would be the case, but I cannot yet fully realise the fact; I feel like a man in a dream; you must give me time to become familiar with this new marvel—this new triumph of science. But there can no longer be any doubt as to the success of your labours; and I accordingly offer you my most hearty thanks and congratulations."

The colonel and the lieutenant also hastened to offer theirs, and then the whole party sauntered to the side, and, leaning upon the guard-rail which took the place of bulwarks, stood gazing upon the scene below. Not that there was very much to see; the sky was obscured by a thin almost motionless canopy of cloud, and the moon, in her last quarter, had not yet risen; the darkness was therefore profound. At the same time it was novel and interesting to watch how, as the huge ship rose steadily higher in the air, the long lines of lighted gas-lamps in street after street became visible, until gradually the whole of the great city lay spread out below them like a map, with the thoroughfares indicated by faint twinkling lines of fire. And, as they continued to rise, the various disjointed sounds which, even at that early hour, pervaded the city, began to reach their ears: the rumbling of a wagon or the rattle of a cab over the stone-paved streets, the barking of a dog, the crow of some unnaturally wakeful rooster, the clank of shunting trucks at one or another of the many goods stations dotted here and there all over the metropolis, the distant whistle and rattle of a train speeding along in the open country beyond; all floated up to them with almost startling distinctness at first, then fainter and fainter, until at length they died completely away as the *Flying Fish* gradually attained a higher altitude. Then they entered the bank of cloud which overspread the city, and the air, which had hitherto been warm, became suddenly chill and damp.

"Now, my friends," said the professor, "there will be little or nothing more to see until we again descend; I therefore propose that we return to the pilot-house, shut ourselves in, and at once test the soaring powers of the ship by rising to the highest attainable altitude."

"Agreed!" said the baronet. "But why shut ourselves in?"

"Because," answered the professor, "it will not only grow rapidly colder as we rise, but, if we remain outside, we shall also find it increasingly difficult to breathe as we reach the more rarefied air; whereas, by remaining inside, we shall be sheltered from the cold and shall be able to breathe the denser air which we shall take up with us."

They accordingly entered the pilot-house, shutting the door after them, and closing all the windows; then the professor turned a full jet of vapour into the air-chambers for a moment, producing a perfect vacuum therein, and the ship at once began to mount into the ether with greatly accelerated speed, as they could easily see by watching the barometer, the bulb of which, completely protected, was situate outside the walls of the pilot-house.

It was no very easy matter for cold to penetrate through the thin yet obdurate walls of the pilot-house; but by the time that the barometer had fallen to fifteen inches the voyagers experienced a distinct sensation of chilliness, whilst the windows of the pilot-house were thickly coated with a delicate frost tracery. Still the barometer continued to fall steadily, though not so rapidly as at first, indicating that the ship was still soaring upward; and with every inch fall of the mercury the professor became an increasingly interesting study of mingled delight and anxiety. At length the mercury, still falling, registered a height of eleven inches only, and the professor gave vent to a great sigh of relief. And when it further dropped to ten inches he could no longer contain himself.

"Gentlemen," he exclaimed, "rejoice with me. The conquest of the mountains is ours. We are now as nearly as possible on a level with the topmost peak of Everest, the most lofty projection on the earth's surface; and in due time I hope we shall have the unique felicity of planting our feet on that as yet untrodden spot, and of leaving a record to that effect behind us."

At length the mercury fell to a little below eight inches, and there it stopped; the limit of the *Flying Fish's* buoyancy was reached.

The professor stood intently regarding the barometer tube for some time; then he turned and said to his companions:

"Gentlemen, behold the indisputably lowest reading of the barometer which man has ever witnessed, and which indicates that we are at this moment farther from our mother earth than mortal has ever journeyed before. Humboldt and Bonpland ascended Chimborazo to a height of eighteen thousand five hundred and seventy-six feet. Gay-Lussac rose in his balloon to the much higher elevation of twenty-three thousand feet, only to be eclipsed by your own countryman, Green, who soared to the astounding height of twenty-seven thousand six hundred feet. But it was left for *us*, my friends, to achieve the crowning feat of aeronautical science, by attaining to the extraordinary altitude of thirty-four thousand six hundred feet, or more than six and a half miles of perpendicular elevation above the sea-level. *Now*, Sir Reginald, what think you of your latest acquisition, the *Flying Fish*?"

"I think her by far the most wonderful creation of which I have ever heard or read, and," (with a bow to the professor) "every way worthy of the truly remarkable man to whom she owes her existence. If her power to penetrate the hitherto unexplored depths of the ocean is at all commensurate with her ability to reach the higher regions of the air, I foresee that our voyage is likely to be fruitful in startling incident and in the discovery of many hitherto unsuspected secrets of nature. Now, what do you propose that we shall next do, professor?"

"I propose," said von Schalckenberg, "that, having tested the *Flying Fish's* capabilities of merely rising into the air, we should now ascertain what she can do in the way of *navigating* the atmosphere; after which we will try her powers as a submarine ship. The lowest depression in the English Channel is to be found in a submarine valley called the 'Hurd Deep;' it is situate about six miles north of the 'Casquets,' and lies ninety-four fathoms (or five hundred and sixty-four feet) below the surface of the water. I propose (subject to your approval) to make for this spot and there sink to the bottom, taking advantage of our presence there to make a first trial of our diving armour. Does this meet with your approval?"

The baronet and his companions thought it a very capital idea, and the professor took immediate steps for carrying it out. Opening a case he produced therefrom a chart of the English Channel, and, directing his companions' attention to the spot which he proposed to visit, requested Lieutenant Mildmay to lay off the course and measure the distance in a straight line. The latter was found to be about one hundred and fifty miles.

"Which distance," remarked the professor, "I expect we shall accomplish, in the present calm state of the atmosphere, in about an hour and a quarter. This high rate of speed will necessitate our remaining in the pilothouse; but it will, perhaps, be worth while to put up with that temporary inconvenience on the present occasion, since we have so exceptionally favourable an opportunity of testing the actual speed of the ship through the air. If, however, you prefer to be on deck in the open air, we can of course moderate our speed sufficiently to render such a mode of travelling pleasant."

It was unanimously decided, however, to remain inside and give the speed of the ship a fair trial. The professor accordingly turned the vapour into the engines, slowly at first, but in gradually increasing volume, until they were revolving at full speed, and the ship's head was pointed in the proper direction, the automatic steering gear being at the same time thrown into action to test its capabilities. This done the professor opened the main air-valve, gradually admitting a certain quantity of air into the ship's interior, and she at once began to drop once more earthward.

"We will descend to within about a thousand feet of the sea level," said the professor. "This will restore us to a more genial temperature, will give the propeller a denser atmosphere in which to work, and will also enable us to see somewhat of the country over which we are flying; whilst our elevation will be ample to take us clear of everything. Leith Hill, nine hundred and sixty-seven feet in height, is the greatest elevation at all near our path; but we shall pass some three miles or so to the westward of it, if the air remains calm; and Saint Catherine's Point, over which we shall pass, is only seven hundred and seventy-five feet high. So that we have nothing to fear."

In a few minutes the *Flying Fish* had dropped to within the proposed distance of the earth; and, on clearing the windows of the accumulated frost, it was discovered that the moon (then in her third quarter) had risen and was suffusing the earth with her feeble ghostly light, which, slight as it was, enabled the voyagers to perceive that they were skimming through the air at a tremendous speed. The engines, though working at their full power, were perfectly noiseless; and the propeller, though revolving at a rate of fully one thousand revolutions per minute, caused not the slightest perceptible vibration in the hull of the ship. A loud humming sound, however, proceeded from it, audible even above the rush of the air against the sides of the pilot-house.

Leith Hill was soon passed, the waters of the Channel—distinguished in the faint light only by a thin tremulous line of glimmering silver under the crescent moon—were sighted, and, almost before they had time to realise the fact, they had skimmed over the anchorage at Spithead, across the Isle of Wight, and were floating above the waters of the Channel. By this time the eastern sky had begun to pale perceptibly before the coming dawn; the lights of Saint Catherine behind them and the Casquets ahead gleamed with steadily diminishing power in the gathering daylight; the half-dozen or so of ships and steamers in sight, one after the other extinguished their signal lamps; and, just as they reached their destination and settled lightly as a snow-flake upon the glassy surface of the water, up rose the glorious sun, flashing his brilliant beams over land and sea, and awakening all nature into light and life once more.

As the *Flying Fish* alighted on the surface of the water, the professor pulled out his watch and remarked, with evident satisfaction:

"One hundred and fifty miles in just one hour and a quarter! That is good travelling, and proves the speed of our ship to be exactly what I estimated it would be. We will now set the force-pump to work; and I hope, that by the time we are ready to descend, that brilliant sun will have enshrouded our movements in a concealing mist. We are surrounded by fishing-boats, as you see, and I have no doubt that we have also been observed by the light-keepers on the Casquets. It will never do to disappear before so many curious eyes; they would be filled with horror at the supposed catastrophe. In the meantime we may as well go out on deck to enjoy the fresh morning air. As for me, I propose to indulge in the luxury of a swim."

The main engines had, in the meantime, been stopped, and the force-pump put slowly in motion, so that the submersion of the hull might be sufficiently gradual to escape notice.

Five minutes later the professor and his three companions were gambolling round the ship like so many porpoises—or dolphins, if they would prefer the latter metaphor—enjoying to the full the invigorating luxury of their bath in the cool, pure sea-water.

By the time that they were on board again and dressed, the intelligent George had arranged for them on deck a nice little light breakfast of chocolate, biscuits, and fruit, for which their swim had given them an unbounded relish. The meal was partaken of at leisure, and followed by a cigar, over which they dawdled so long that the *Flying Fish* was submerged to the deck before the last stump had been reluctantly thrown away. The mist which the professor had prognosticated having, meanwhile, gathered sufficiently to cloak their movements, a cast of the lead was taken and the ship was found to be in ninety fathoms of water. The professor, for reasons of his own, deemed this sufficiently near the deepest point to justify an immediate descent. They accordingly entered the pilot-house forthwith, closing the door securely after them—the air-pump was stopped, the sea-cock communicating with the water-chambers was opened, and the *Flying Fish*, with an easy imperceptible motion, sank gently beneath the placid waters, to rest, a minute or two later, on a bed of gravel at the bottom of the Channel.

"Now," said the professor, looking at his watch when the ship had fairly settled into her strange berth, and had been securely anchored there, "it is just eight o'clock. We are all somewhat fatigued, and our bath and breakfast have prepared us nicely to enjoy a few hours' repose. I therefore propose, gentlemen, that we retire to our sleeping apartments until two o'clock p.m. George shall call us at that hour and have a bit of luncheon ready for us, after which we shall have ample time to test our diving apparatus before dinner."

This proposal met with a very cordial reception, and was duly carried out, with the result that, half an hour later, the four adventurous voyagers were sleeping as calmly in their novel resting-place as though they had been accustomed from their earliest infancy to take their repose at the bottom of the sea.

CHAPTER FIVE
A SUBMARINE EXCURSION

At the appointed hour the imperturbable George, who never could be betrayed into the slightest exhibition of astonishment at finding himself in any extraordinary situation which he might happen to be sharing with his somewhat eccentric master, duly aroused the four sleepers, and when they were ready, laid luncheon before them with the same indomitable *sangfroid* which he would have exhibited had the transaction been conducted on *terra firma*.

The meal over, the professor led the way below to the diving chamber, where the adventurous four carefully donned their diving dresses, inclusive of the armour which Sir Reginald felt so strongly disposed to ridicule. As this was the first occasion of inducting themselves into their novel costume, they were rather a long time about it; but when once they were fairly encased, they were fain to admit that, strange as might be their appearance, they felt exceedingly comfortable. The professor was the last to assume the dress, having busied himself in the first instance in assisting the others; but at length all was ready, and they filed into the exit chamber, carefully closing the door behind them. This chamber was illuminated by an electric lamp, the light of which clearly revealed the whereabouts of the sea-cock, and of the fastenings to the trap-door, all of which the professor pointed out to his companions, at the same time explaining the method of working them. The sea-cock was then opened, and the chamber began to slowly fill with water.

"Now," explained the professor, "please listen to me. If now, or at any future time, either of you should experience the slightest sensation of discomfort as the water rises round you, all you have to do is simply to open this air-cock, which communicates with the air-chambers, and the condensed air will at once rush in and expel the water again; then close the sea and air cocks; open this relief valve, which will allow the condensed air to disperse itself in the habitable portions of the hull, and you can at once open the door of communication to the diving chamber, and disencumber yourself of your dress, remembering always to close the door behind you. Now, do either of you feel at all uncomfortable?"

The exit chamber was by this time full of water, and its occupants were, therefore, completely submerged, and subject to the same pressure of water as they would be outside, but the armour proved fully equal to its work in every respect, and its wearers were able to move with just as much freedom and ease as if they had been on dry land. They accordingly replied to the professor's inquiry with a brisk negative.

"And can you hear distinctly what I say?" continued the professor.

They replied that they could hear every word perfectly, only realising when the question was asked that they were completely sheathed in metal from head to foot, and that, consequently, the fact of their being able to hear at all was somewhat singular.

"That is all right," exclaimed the professor. "I thought it would be convenient if we could communicate freely with each other under water, so I introduced a couple of small microphones into each helmet, hoping they would answer the purpose. Mine are simply perfect, but I was anxious to know if yours were also. Now, if you are quite ready I will open the door."

The next moment the trap-door fell open, and a great black aperture yawned before them.

"Light both your lamps," exclaimed the professor, "and pick your footsteps. Remember, you are about to tread on strange ground."

The professor led the way, his armour-clad figure looming up black and gigantic against the two overlapping discs of illuminated water before him, and the other three followed closely in his footsteps. On emerging from the trap-door they turned sharp to the left, and made their way toward the bow along the tunnel-like passage between the ship's bottom and the starboard bilge keel. This was soon traversed, and they then found themselves on a tolerably firm, level, gravelly bottom. Emerging from underneath the ship's bottom, they now extinguished their lamps for a moment by way of experiment, and found that so clear was the water that even at the great depth of ninety fathoms it was not absolutely dark, a sombre greenish blue twilight prevailing in which the hull of the ship towered above them vast and shadowy, yet with tolerable distinctness. This twilight, however, was strongly illuminated at both ends of the ship by the powerful electric lamps at the bow and stern, all of which the professor had taken the precaution to light before descending to the diving chamber.

"Those are our beacons," said the professor, pointing to these lamps, "and we must be exceedingly careful not to stray beyond the reach of their rays, otherwise we might experience great difficulty in finding our way back to the ship. Are you all pretty comfortable in this great depth of water? We are now five hundred and forty feet beneath the surface of the sea, or three hundred and thirty-six feet deeper than man has ever reached before. Why, if we were to accomplish nothing more than this, we have already achieved a great triumph! Now, let us make our way toward the deepest spot in this submarine valley; I have an idea that we shall see something curious when we reach it. This way, gentlemen; our course is about due west, and we cannot well lose our way if we descend the slope which seems to commence yonder."

The little party pressed forward, experiencing no inconvenience or difficulty whatever, save that of making their way through water of such a density as that which enveloped them, and soon reached the edge of a rather steep declivity, evidently leading down to the lowest part of the depression. Before venturing down this declivity they paused to glance backward, and saw that, though the ship herself had become invisible in the sombre twilight, all the electric lights were distinctly visible, the very powerful one on the top of the pilot-house especially gleaming like the illuminated lantern of a lighthouse. So far, therefore, all was well; they were still within range of the lights, and they at once turned and plunged fearlessly into the depression. They had not far to go, the sides of the depression being steep, and in about two minutes they found themselves at the bottom, and standing before an immense confused heap of wreckage of almost every imaginable description. Shattered stumps of spars, waterlogged and weighed down with a thick incrustation of barnacles, the accumulated growth of years of immersion; part of the hull of a ship, so overgrown with "sea grass" as to be distinguishable as such only from the fact that the channels and channel irons with their dead-eyes, and even the frayed ends of the shroud lanyards still remained attached; a twisted and tangled-up mass of iron rods which looked as though it might at some distant period have been the paddle-wheel of a steamer, and near it the evident remains of a boiler and some machinery; the beam of a trawl-net, and bales, boxes, packing-cases, barrels, and, in short, every conceivable description of covering in which ships' cargoes are usually stowed were mixed up in inextricable confusion with heaps of coal, large stones, and other anomalous substances.

"Just as I anticipated," exclaimed the professor, pointing to the heap and addressing his companions. "And this, I expect, is the sort of thing which we shall see in every depression of the ocean's bed which we may visit. All these matters have been swept hither and thither over the ground by the action of the tidal and other currents, until they have happened to drift over this spot, and here they have finally settled owing to the inability of the currents to move them up the steep sides of the depression. Let us walk round the heap; we may see something of interest before we have completed the circuit."

And so they did, though the interest was hardly the kind of which the professor had been thinking when he spoke. For, whilst standing on the opposite side of the heap, contemplating the remains of an ancient and grass-grown wreck, they were startled by the appearance of a sharp snake-like head with a pair of fierce gleaming eyes which was suddenly protruded from a gap in the ship's side, and in another moment the creature—a conger-eel of truly gigantic proportions—emerged from its hiding-place, and, possibly attracted by the brilliancy of the electric lights which the party carried, swam boldly toward them.

"What a horrible monster!" ejaculated the colonel, at the same moment that Lieutenant Mildmay, struck with the savage look of the creature, exclaimed:

"Why, I believe the brute means to attack us!"

"And, by Jove, here come some more of them!" exclaimed the baronet, pointing to the hole from which the creature had emerged.

"Draw your daggers, gentlemen!" shouted the professor. "And be not dismayed; they and our armour are quite sufficient for our protection."

It was perhaps just as well that the professor had sufficient presence of mind at that moment to say what he did; for his companions, though their courage had been proved a thousand times before, were now in a new and strange element to which they had scarcely had time to accustom themselves; and, moreover, the aspect of the fierce fish as they rushed forward with open jaws, disclosing their formidable teeth, was sufficiently weird and uncanny to at least momentarily dismay the stoutest heart.

Lieutenant Mildmay's anticipation as to the intentions of the fish proved quite correct. On they came, some thirty or forty in number; and before the attacked could quite recover from their confusion they found themselves fairly in the clutches of the snake-like creatures. The attack was made with the utmost determination and ferocity, the eels twining themselves so powerfully about the bodies of their foes that it was almost impossible for the latter to move hand or foot; whilst the sharp teeth rasped strongly but ineffectually against the scales of the aethereum armour. The fight, however, though fiercely waged on the part of the assailants, was soon over, a single stroke of the keen double-edged dagger—as soon as the assailed could get their hands free—proving sufficient to instantly destroy the individual fish upon which it happened to fall. But so fierce were the eels that the conflict ended only with the slaughter of the last of them. The fish were of truly enormous size, two or three specimens measuring, as nearly as could be estimated, fully eighteen feet in length, whilst none were less than ten feet long. The tour of exploration was then completed without further adventure; the powerful electric lights of the ship enabled them to find her without difficulty the moment that they climbed up out of the depression; and they made good their return with no worse result than that of excessive fatigue due to their unwonted efforts in forcing their way through so dense a medium as water of ninety fathoms depth.

So novel an experience as theirs had that day been naturally furnished the chief topic of conversation at the dinner-table; the professor especially entertaining his companions with many interesting anecdotes of strange adventures which had happened to, and curious sights witnessed by divers at various times and places. At length, during a lull in the conversation, he said:

"There still remain two trials to which the *Flying Fish* must be subjected before we can say that we are fully acquainted with her powers, namely, a trial of her speed through the water when fully submerged; and a trial of her behaviour as an ordinary ocean-going ship. And these trials, I think, should—if you approve, Sir Reginald—be carried out before we do anything else."

The baronet gave his willing assent to the professor's proposal; and it was finally arranged that the trials, or, at all events, one of them, should take place on the morrow.

It having been arranged that early rising should be the order of the day throughout the voyage, they were aroused at seven o'clock on the following morning, and sat down to breakfast at eight prompt. By nine o'clock the meal was over, and the party, pipe or cigar in mouth, mustered in the pilot-house. Here the first thing the professor did was to produce a chart, to which, on spreading it open on the table, he called Lieutenant Mildmay's attention, saying:

"Being a seaman by profession, you are undoubtedly the most skilful navigator of the party; and I therefore propose—with Sir Reginald's full approval, which I have already obtained—to confide the navigation of the *Flying Fish* to you. Now this,"—making a pencil mark on the chart—"is our present position; and this,"—

pointing to another pencil mark off Cape Finisterre, which presented the appearance of having been very carefully laid down—"is the point to which I wish you to navigate us in the first instance."

"Very good," said Mildmay. "I undertake the charge with pleasure. Only I must stipulate, that when making long passages you will rise to the surface occasionally, in order that I may be enabled to take the observations necessary to verify our position."

"Of course, of course," answered the professor. "Now, are we all ready to start?"

An answer in the affirmative was given; and von Schalckenberg thereupon moved the lever which actuated the simple machinery controlling the four anchors in the bilge keels. The ship being thus released from the ground, he next opened the cocks connecting the air and water chambers; a stream of compressed air at once rushed into the latter, forcing out a certain quantity of water, and the ship began to rise.

"We will so adjust our position that the top of the lantern surmounting the pilot-house shall be submerged to a depth of six fathoms; at which depth we shall not only be enabled to pass clear of all ships, but shall also, if the water be clear, be enabled to see pretty well what is before and above us," said the professor, fixing his eyes upon a gauge before him. "There," he continued, closing the air-cocks as the index pointed to six fathoms, "now we shall do very well. Are you ready to set the course, Mildmay?"

"A run of six hundred and fifty miles, upon a west-south-west course, will take us to about the spot you have indicated," answered Mildmay.

"Which is a trifle less than five and a half hours' run, if our speed under water is equal to what it was through the air. But I anticipate that we shall do better than that; the resistance of water is considerably greater than that of air to the vessel's passage through it, I admit; but I anticipate that this will be more than counterbalanced by the greater power of the propeller in the denser fluid. We shall soon see."

So saying, the professor set the engines in motion, and the *Flying Fish* began to glide smoothly yet soon with marvellous rapidity through the water.

"My surmise was correct, you see," said the professor some ten minutes afterwards, as he pointed to another gauge on the wall of the pilot-house. "We are now running steadily at a speed of one hundred and fifty miles per hour; and we have already travelled twelve miles from our starting-point. The gauge is, as you see, self-registering, and shows on that piece of paper the exact distance run through or along the surface of the water (but not through the *air*) between any two given points. When the ship's course is altered, or you desire for any other reason to commence the register afresh, all you have to do is, press that ivory knob, and the instrument will draw a line across the paper and, at the same moment, spring back to zero."

The water, at the depth at which they were travelling, proved to be almost as transparent as crystal, of a dark olive-green tint beneath them, merging by imperceptible gradations to a faint greenish-blue above; the surface being discernible by the shifting lace work of gold incessantly playing over it where the sun's beams caught the ridges of the faint rippling wavelets raised by the languid summer breeze. Even small objects, such as medusae, and fragments of weed floating in mid-sea, were distinguishable at a considerable distance; and fishing-boats could be clearly made out at the distance of a mile. A very novel and curious effect was witnessed when objects floating on the surface (such as ships, fishing-boats, or aquatic birds) came into view, the submerged portions of them being as clearly defined as though they were floating in air, whilst the parts *above* the surface were wavering and indistinct. A flock of diving gulls, for instance, which they passed at no great distance, presented the curious spectacle of little more than dark dots furnished with pairs of quickly-moving webbed feet whilst they floated on the placid surface; but directly a bird dived its whole body became distinctly visible, with a long stream of air-bubbles trailing behind it.

At length it became apparent that they were approaching a large fleet of ships making their way up channel.

A smile passed over the professor's features as he gazed out at them, and turning to his companions he remarked:

"I feel mischievously inclined this morning. I think we will give the crews of those ships a little surprise, and furnish them with a new topic for conversation."

"Ah, indeed!" said the baronet. "How do you propose to do it?"

"By rising to the surface in the midst of the fleet. Our engine power is quite sufficient, I believe, to send us to the surface or to plunge us several fathoms deeper than we now are without our interfering with the water chambers or altering in any way the weight of the ship. There is a nice clear space just ahead, with ample room in which to show ourselves and to make a downward plunge again beneath that large ship, the barnacle-covered bottom of which seems to tell of a long voyage through tropic seas. Now take up your stations of observation, gentlemen, and note the consternation which our unexpected appearance will produce."

The professor's companions placed themselves at the windows of the pilot-house, and Herr von Schalckenberg at the same moment suddenly pressed the end of the tiller vertically downward. Obedient to the helm, the *Flying Fish's* sharp snout immediately swerved upward, and with a tremendous swirl and commotion of the water the great ship rushed to the surface, throwing half her length out of the sea, only to disappear again the next moment with a graceful plunging motion and a still greater disturbance of the water by her immense rapidly revolving propeller.

A single swift glance around them was all that the travellers were able to obtain of the state of affairs above water; but that sufficed to show them that their appearance, sudden though it was, had attracted a considerable amount of notice. They saw that the *Flying Fish* had broken water in the very centre of a large fleet of ships, most of which were making their way up channel under every stitch of canvas they could spread before a very light westerly air. Many of these ships were evidently, from their weather-beaten appearance, traders from far-distant foreign ports; and their crews, taking advantage of the beautifully fine weather and smooth water, were either occupied on stages slung over the sides in giving the hulls a touch of fresh paint to brighten up their appearance previous to going into port, or aloft, scraping, painting, and varnishing the spars, or tarring down the rigging, with a similar object. All eyes seemed to be directed toward the apparition which had made its sudden appearance in their midst; and the shouts of astonishment and dismay evoked by that sudden appearance were distinctly audible to the occupants of the *Flying Fish's* pilot-house. The hurried way in which the crew of the large ship immediately ahead of them sprang to their feet and scrambled in over the bulwarks from the stages on which they were working, or slid down the freshly-tarred backstays to the deck as they saw the immense object rushing directly toward them, was particularly amusing, and drew a hearty laugh from the beholders on board the *Flying Fish*. Another moment, and the cause of all this commotion was plunging fathoms deep beneath the keel of the last-mentioned ship, to reappear on the surface a minute later, beyond the farthest outskirts of the fleet. A judicious manipulation of the helm kept the *Flying Fish* this time on the surface for perhaps a quarter of a minute, just long enough, in fact, to satisfy the wondering beholders that their eyes had not deceived them, when she once more disappeared, this time finally, from the view of the fleet.

"That escapade of ours will produce a tremendously sensational paragraph for the newspapers, and we must keep a look-out for it," said the colonel. "I wonder what they will make of it!"

Sure enough, the paragraph appeared in due course, to the following effect, as copied from a cutting which is still preserved in the professor's scrap-book:—

Appearance Of A Gigantic Sea Monster In The English Channel.
Extraordinary Story.

"On Wednesday morning last, the 27th instant, a fleet of some hundred and fifty sail of vessels was off the Start and about in mid-channel, making its way to the eastward before a light westerly air, the weather at the time being fine, the water smooth, and the atmosphere perfectly clear. A portion of the crews belonging to several of the craft in question were at work in the rigging when their attention was attracted by a curious commotion which suddenly appeared on the surface of the water at a considerable distance to the eastward. The disturbance was in the form of a long wedge-like ripple, the appearance being very pronounced and distinct at its forward or pointed extremity, but less so at its rear end, where it spread widely out and became gradually merged and lost in the gentle ripple caused by the wind. It was travelling directly towards the fleet at a speed far exceeding that of the fastest express train, and it bore all the appearance of being the 'wake' of some enormous body moving at no great distance beneath the surface. While the seamen were still watching it in wonder and perplexity, mingled with no little alarm, it had reached the fleet, the rippling swell spreading out on each side and curling over into a breaker which dashed against the sides of the several vessels, causing the smaller craft to rock and toss perceptibly. It clove its irresistible way to the very centre of the fleet, where there happened to be a large open space of water, and here there suddenly shot into view above the surface a gigantic fish, the length of which is variously estimated by those who saw it as from four hundred to eight hundred feet, with a girth of between one and two hundred feet. The creature, apparently startled at finding itself in the midst of so many vessels, immediately dived below the surface again, passing directly beneath the keel of the barque *Olivia*, of London, from Bangkok, William Rogers master. The crew of this ship had a most distinct view of the monster, as it broke water at not more than half a cable's length (or some three hundred feet) from them, and immediately afterwards shaved the keel of the ship so closely as almost to touch it. Captain Rogers, who was on deck at the time, describes the creature, and his description tallies perfectly with that of the other witnesses, as being somewhat like a saw-fish, without the saw, in general shape, but with a proportionately longer and more sharply pointed head, in which *four* eyes, two in the upper and two in the lower part of the head, were distinctly seen. The body was a beautiful silvery white, glistening in the sun like polished metal. On the back of the immense fish was a curious flat protuberance, above which rose another in the form of a dome-shaped hump, with, if we may venture to repeat so incredible a story, eyes all round it, and surmounted by an object having a very marked resemblance to a silver crown. This extraordinary creature had no fins so far as could be seen, but propelled itself solely by its tail, which it moved with such wonderful rapidity as rendered it utterly impossible to detect the shape of it. The creature was evidently an air-breather, for it had no sooner completely cleared the fleet, which it did in about one minute, the distance travelled in that time being fully three miles, than it rose once more to the surface, remaining there for perhaps half a minute, evidently for the purpose of getting a fresh supply of air, when it again dived and was seen no more."

CHAPTER SIX
IN SEARCH OF A SUBMERGED WRECK

To return to the *Flying Fish*. It was exactly two o'clock p.m. when

Lieutenant Mildmay announced that, according to his "dead reckoning," they were now on or very near the spot indicated on the chart by the professor, and that, if there was no objection, he should like to rise to the surface in order to obtain the astronomical observations necessary to verify the ship's position. The engines were accordingly stopped, and the water being ejected from the water chambers, the travellers once more found themselves above water, advantage being taken of the opportunity to throw open the door of the pilot-house and step out on deck.

The first discovery made by them was that a moderate breeze was blowing from the westward, with a corresponding amount of sea and a very long heavy swell, which, however, to their great gratification, affected the *Flying Fish* only to a very trifling extent. When end-on to the sea she pitched a little, it is true, but when broadside-on she simply rose and fell with the run of the sea, being as completely free from rolling motion as though she had still been on the stocks.

Their next discovery was that a large steamer was in sight, some seven miles distant; and, whilst they stood watching the way in which the craft plunged along over the heavy swell, pitching "bows under" occasionally, she suddenly altered her course and steered direct toward them, her crew having apparently only that moment sighted the *Flying Fish*, and being evidently in great perplexity as to what she could possibly be.

"Be as quick as you can with your observations, Mildmay, and let us get under water again," said the baronet. "We shall perhaps be expected to explain who and what we are if that steamer gets within hail of us, and I am not particularly anxious to do that."

The sights were taken, and, whilst the steamer was yet some five miles distant, the *Flying Fish* quietly sank once more beneath the waves; doubtless to the intense astonishment of those who were making such haste to get alongside her.

Rapidly, yet steadily, and with a perfectly level deck, the craft sank lower and lower, the light diminishing momentarily, until it at length vanished altogether, and the darkness became so intense that it was impossible for the occupants of the pilot-house to discern each other; whilst the silence which prevailed around them was first oppressive and then awe-inspiring in its intensity.

Suddenly a light shuffling sound arose within the pilot-house, and in another moment the inky depths through which they were descending became brilliantly illuminated with a clear white penetrating light, in which every detail of the ship's hull fore and aft stood out distinctly visible, whilst here and there, above, below, and on either side of them, a momentary gleam revealed the presence of some startled and hastily retreating denizen of the deep. The professor had lighted up the electric lanterns, the especial purpose of which was to illuminate the sea around the ship, leaving the interior of the pilot-house still in darkness, in order that its occupants might enjoy, to the fullest extent, the novelty of the scene thus suddenly revealed to them, and also that, on reaching the bottom, they might the better be able to distinguish external objects.

Lower and lower sank the *Flying Fish*, and at length, after what seemed to the travellers an almost interminable descent, she reached the bottom.

"Now, gentlemen," exclaimed the professor, with some slight evidences of excitement in the tones of his voice, "look around you, and see if you can discover anything unusual in our neighbourhood."

The persons addressed did as they were requested, the professor himself also peering eagerly out of each of the pilot-house windows in turn, but without result; the electric lamps, though they brilliantly illuminated the scene on all sides for fully fifty yards, and rendered objects distinguishable for at least three times that distance, revealed nothing but a plain completely covered with rocks and boulders, some of which were of enormous size, and all thickly overgrown with sea-weed.

"What is it you expected to find down here, professor?" asked the colonel, when it had become perfectly evident that nothing but rocks lay within their range of vision.

"The hull of a ship," answered the professor. "She foundered on or near the spot indicated by me, and cannot be far off; unless, indeed, we are out in our reckoning. Have you worked out your calculations, Mildmay?"

"Not yet," answered the lieutenant, "but I soon will do so if you will oblige us with a little light inside here."

"Ah, true! I had forgotten," murmured the professor apologetically, and he lighted the lamp which hung suspended above the table in the pilot-house.

The lieutenant sat down and rapidly worked out his observations, with the resulting discovery that they were exactly two miles north-east of the spot they were seeking, having doubtless been swept that much out of their proper position by the tide. The *Flying Fish* was accordingly raised some fifty feet from the bottom, her engines were once more set in motion, slowly this time, however, and the ship's head laid in the proper direction, the occupants of the pilot-house stationing themselves at the windows and peering out eagerly ahead on the look-out for the object of their search.

The engines being set to work dead slow and stopped at intervals when the speed became too high, the speed of the *Flying Fish* was kept down to about twelve knots per hour, at which rate she would occupy ten minutes in traversing the required distance. She had been under weigh exactly nine minutes when Mildmay exclaimed:

"Sail ho! That is to say, there is a large object of some kind dead ahead. Port *hard*, professor, or we shall be into it."

The professor, who was not absolutely ignorant of nautical phraseology, promptly ported his helm and at the same moment stopped the engines, by which manoeuvre the *Flying Fish* glided close past the object so slowly that it was easily distinguishable as a huge pinnacle of rock.

They were now on the exact spot indicated by the professor on the chart, but nothing in the slightest degree resembling the hull of a ship was in sight. Rocks in the form of pinnacles, huge fantastic boulders, and boldly-jutting reefs appeared all round, as far as the powerful lamps of the ship could project their rays, but no ship was to be seen. They rose some fifty feet higher, in order to see over the more lofty rocks, some of which intercepted their view, but with no more successful result.

"There is no ship here, professor," at last remarked the baronet, after all hands had carefully inspected the whole of the ground within their ken. "Are you quite sure of the accuracy of your information?"

"My information has reference only to an *approximate* position; the ship is hereabout—within a few miles of this spot—and I considered that our best chance of discovering her lay in coming here first, and, if necessary, prosecuting our search with this position as a starting-point."

"Very good. Then, as the object of our quest is manifestly not here, I propose that we proceed with our search at once."

By way of reply the professor put the helm hard over, and once more set the engines slowly in motion, thus causing the ship to travel in a circle about the spot; all hands going, as before, to the windows of the pilot-house on the look-out.

The circle described by the *Flying Fish* was a very small one—not more than two hundred feet in diameter—and the inmates of the pilot-house were therefore able to carefully examine every inch of ground within its circumference. One complete circuit having been accomplished without result, the helm was very slightly altered, and the ship then went on in a continually widening spiral which must necessarily at length take her to the object of her search, if indeed it actually existed.

That it did so was ultimately demonstrated, the professor himself being the first to make its discovery.

The wreck, when first sighted, was distant about one hundred yards on their starboard hand, and only just within range of the circle of electric light. The ship's head was at once turned in that direction, the engines being at the same time stopped, to permit of a very gradual approach.

All eyes were of course intently fixed upon the strange object; and they had neared it to within about one hundred feet, when Lieutenant Mildmay exclaimed in a low, awe-struck voice:

"Just as I suspected! It is the *Daedalus!*"

"Yes," replied the professor very quietly; "it is that most unfortunate ship. And now, gentlemen, with your permission I will anchor the *Flying Fish*, and pay a visit—unaccompanied—to the wreck."

It was evident, from the extreme gravity of the professor's demeanour, that his proposed visit was prompted by some other motive than that of mere idle curiosity; his companions therefore simply bowed in token of acquiescence, and permitted von Schalckenberg to follow undisturbed the bent of his own inclinations.

The *Flying Fish*, meanwhile, had been caused to descend to the bottom, to which she was at once secured by her four grip-anchors; immediately after which the professor, with a somewhat hurried and incoherent apology, left his companions and descended to the diving-room.

Left to themselves, the trio occupying the pilot-house had ample leisure to note the position and surroundings of the ill-fated steamer.

She had settled down upon a flat ledge of level rock, and rested, keel downwards, in a perfectly upright position, having apparently recovered herself whilst settling down. She was greatly damaged, both in hull and rigging; the spar-deck and forecastle being swept away, and her main deck blown up in midships, very possibly through the explosion of her boilers. Her bowsprit and mizzen-mast were gone, as was also her fore topmast; and the mainmast, with topmast and all attached, was leaning aft, and so far over the side that the observers would not have been surprised to see it fall at any moment. Loose ropes were trailing in all directions; and the tattered remains of sails still hung from some of the yards and stays, swaying occasionally in a slow, weird, ghostly manner, with the mysterious intermittent under-currents of the sea.

The trio were still discussing the particulars of the sad disaster, which, on a stormy September night, had resulted in the drowning of nearly five hundred people, and the plunging of the ship herself to the depths wherein they had so strangely found her, when the figure of the professor, clad in his suit of diving armour and dwindled in apparent dimensions by his great distance below them, was seen to emerge from the black shadow of the *Flying Fish's* hull and make his way slowly and laboriously over the rocky bottom toward the wreck. A couple of minutes sufficed him to perform the short journey; and; scrambling up the side by the aid of some of the dangling gear, he entered the poop cabin and disappeared.

The party in the pilot-house finished their chat; and then sauntered down into the music saloon, of which they had seen nothing since the night of their departure from London—actually only two nights before, but they had since then been so satiated with novel sights and experiences that it really seemed as though at least a month had elapsed since they last passed the threshold. Here they beguiled the time so effectually with music, vocal and instrumental, that it was not until George appeared announcing dinner that it occurred to either of them that the professor had been out of the ship nearly three hours.

"Where can the man be? Surely some accident must have befallen him!" exclaimed the baronet, starting up in alarm.

"Not necessarily," replied the colonel. "The professor is pretty well able to take care of himself. It is much more probable that he has discovered some object of exceptional interest on board the wreck, or has fallen into a scientific reverie as to the actual cause of the disaster—the cause, I mean, from a *scientist's* point of view. Sound the gong, George; water is a good conductor, and he may possibly hear it and be awakened to a consciousness that time flies."

The gong was accordingly struck, and the three companions hastened to the pilot-house to watch for results. The call proved effectual, for in less than five minutes afterwards the professor made his appearance on the deck of the wreck, soon afterwards rejoining his friends on board the *Flying Fish* in the vestibule outside the saloons. He carried in his hand a small compact package, which he deposited carefully on the sideboard, and then, with a much more cheerful mien than he had worn when setting out upon his solitary journey, took his accustomed place at the table, apparently quite prepared to do full justice to the meal which was about to be served.

The soup and fish were discussed in silence; a glass of wine was then imbibed with much apparent enjoyment, and this unlocked the professor's lips.

"I feel it to be due to you, gentlemen—and more especially to *you*, Sir Reginald—to offer some explanation of the motive which influenced me in my proposal that we should come hither," he remarked, setting his wine-glass down on the table. "I had a threefold object in view. In the first place, I felt curious to know whether it would be possible to find, *at the bottom of the sea*, an object the position of which is only approximately known. In the second place, I was anxious to secure a relic. And in the third place, I was almost equally anxious to recover a most valuable document which I was convinced had gone down in the unfortunate *Daedalus*. With regard to the first-named object, you have already witnessed our complete success. I have also been successful in the remaining two."

The speaker paused here; but it was so evident from his manner that he had not yet said all he had to say upon the subject that his companions contented themselves with mere simple monosyllabic murmurs of polite congratulation, and then awaited in silence a further communication.

The professor continued silent and evidently plunged deep in a somewhat sombre reverie for several minutes; then he lifted his head and said somewhat hesitatingly:

"You will perhaps be surprised to learn that my life has not been left wholly ungilded by the halo of romance. Five-and-twenty years ago, when Science had perhaps not obtained so tight a grip upon me as she now has, it was my fate to meet the loveliest woman I have ever beheld. She was an only daughter, of English parentage; and chance threw us somewhat more intimately together than is usual with people who become acquainted casually and informally. I fell blindly, madly in love with this peerless creature; and, gentlemen, I have since—and alas, too late!— had reason to believe that, strange as such a circumstance may appear to you, she did not altogether escape a reciprocal passion. But my studious habits had brought with them one serious disadvantage—I was indescribably diffident and shy; so much so that when the time arrived that I must either unbosom myself or let her pass away out of my life, perhaps for ever, I found myself without the courage to make the necessary declaration. We parted without a word of love having passed between us. She remained single for five years—to give me an opportunity of declaring myself, as I now know—and then married a man far more worthy of her than I could ever have proved. Gentlemen, her only child, a lad of fifteen, went down with the ill-fated *Daedalus*; and the mother is to-day breaking her heart because, by some perverse chance, she does not possess a single memento of her lost boy. My visit to the wreck, however, will remove that source of grief; for I shall have the melancholy satisfaction of transmitting to the dear lady, by the first safe conveyance which offers itself, the watch and chain and the signet-ring which he wore when he bade her a final farewell. In the moment that I conquered the last difficulty connected with the construction of this ship, and felt assured that she would prove a success, I vowed to myself that, by the courtesy of our amiable host, I would avail myself of the means she would offer for securing some memento of that poor lad; and I have to-day at once performed my vow and passed through scenes of such surpassing horror as probably no mortal has ever witnessed before, and which language has no words to describe.

"The third object of my visit to the wreck is before you in the shape of yonder package. It is a manuscript book filled with jottings and memoranda, the result of some thirty years of profound research in the many bypaths of science. It was the property of an officer of the ship with whom I had corresponded for many years; and, knowing how greatly I coveted the book, he left it me in his will, probably little thinking, poor fellow! that it was fated to go with him to the bottom of the sea. On being made acquainted with the circumstances of his death, and also with his bequest, I surmised at once that the precious volume must have been in his immediate possession when the ship foundered. And having visited him on board, as well as had occasion to notice the place in which the book was ordinarily kept, I had very little difficulty in placing my hand upon it."

"I suppose matters are in a very terrible state on board the wreck?" asked the baronet.

"So bad," was the reply, "that, knowing what I now know, I cannot think of any motive powerful enough to induce me to repeat my visit. I had two very strong motives for going on board the ship; and, as each successive horror presented itself, I thought, surely there can be nothing worse than this; and I pressed onward, only to encounter greater and still greater horrors at every step. But I would not go there again even to achieve what I have achieved to-day."

"Ah!" said the baronet, "I have a great curiosity to see what the ship herself looks like after such a tremendous catastrophe; but, if the sights to be witnessed on board her be one-tenth part so bad as your words would lead one to suppose, I would not go near her for the world."

"Nor I," said the colonel.

"Nor I," added Mildmay.

"You are wise, gentlemen," remarked the professor. "I can quite understand your curiosity; but, were you to gratify it, your pleasure would be effectually destroyed for the remainder of the voyage."

"That reminds me to ask the question, Where are we going next?" said Sir Reginald.

The professor shrugged his shoulders and spread out his hands, palms upwards.

"The world is all before you where to choose," he replied. "You have only to name a place, and it will be strange indeed if we cannot get there."

"Well, for my own part, I am of opinion that it will be wise for us to devote this trip as far as possible to the visiting of such spots as it is difficult or impossible to reach by any other means. What say you, gentlemen?"

This from the baronet.

The others expressed their full coincidence in this opinion.

"Very well, then," continued Sir Reginald; "my proposal is that, as the days are now at their longest, and this is therefore the most favourable time for such an expedition—and as, moreover, the *Flying Fish's* stores have as yet been barely broached—we make the best of our way forthwith *to the North Pole*, there to enjoy a little of the choice sport which we may reasonably hope to find among animals that have never yet seen the face of man."

"A most admirable proposal, and one which we are especially well adapted to successfully carry out," exclaimed the professor enthusiastically. The colonel and Mildmay also gave their cordial assent to the plan.

"Very well, then; that is settled," remarked von Schalckenberg. "Now, to revert for a moment to the subject of the wreck. You have not been on board her, as I have; but, even with the comparatively distant view you have had of her, I think you must have seen that she is injured beyond all possibility of repair; to say nothing of the fact that she is lying in a spot from which it would be difficult—quite impossible, indeed, without our assistance—to recover her. Now, it has occurred to me that, all things taken into consideration, it would be a good deed to destroy her. What say you, gentlemen? It would afford us an excellent opportunity for making trial of one of our shells."

"Destroy her, by all means," said the baronet.

"I can see no possible objection," observed the colonel.

"Nor I," remarked Mildmay. "As to assisting in her recovery, I would not stir so much as my little finger to do it; she has already drowned some five hundred human beings, which is quite enough mischief for one ship."

"Quite so," coincided the professor. "Then we will do the deed after dinner."

Accordingly, half an hour later, the party rose from the table and made their way to the pilot-house, where the professor delivered a little lecture on the mode of firing the shells. Then, accompanied by the colonel, who had proffered his assistance, von Schalckenberg proceeded to the fore end of the ship to make the requisite arrangements. It being a first experiment, the preparation occupied fully ten minutes—or ten times as long as he should allow himself in future, the professor remarked. Then, all being ready, a return was made to the pilothouse; the anchors were withdrawn from the ground, and the *Flying Fish* was got under weigh. The monster circled once or twice round the doomed wreck, seeking the most suitable point of attack, which having been decided upon, the sharp nose of the submarine ship was pointed straight at the *Daedalus*, and the professor touched a knob. At the same instant—so it appeared, so rapid was the discharge—there was a blinding flash of light on board the wreck, a terrific concussion, but no sound, and the wreck *vanished*; that is the only word which adequately describes the suddenness and completeness of her destruction. The concussion was so violent that it jarred the *Flying Fish* throughout the whole of her vast frame; indeed, but for her tremendous strength she would in all probability have herself been destroyed. As it was, no damage or harm whatever was done on board beyond throwing the four occupants of the pilothouse somewhat violently to the floor, and terrifying the cook and the hitherto sedate George almost out of their senses.

But perhaps even they were less frightened than were the captain and crew of a small Levant trader which happened at the moment to be almost directly above the scene of the explosion. All hands felt the jar; the watch below frantically sprang on deck under the impression that they had collided with another vessel; and the skipper, who happened to be standing near the taffrail, was horrified beyond expression to see an immense cone of water some thirty feet high rise out of the sea just astern of his vessel, to fall next moment with a deafening splash and an accompanying surge which tossed the little vessel as helplessly about for a moment or two as though she had been the merest cockle-shell. It took that skipper nearly half an hour to fully recover his faculties; and when he did so, his first act was to go below and solemnly make an entry in his official log to the effect that, on such and such a date at such an hour, in latitude and longitude so and so, the weather at the time being fine, with a moderate breeze from S.W., the schooner *Pomona* had experienced a terrific shock of earthquake with an accompanying disturbance of water which nearly swamped the ship. This entry he signed in the presence of the mate, secured that officer's signature to it also, and then, reviving his courage with a glass of grog stiff enough to float a marlinespike, he retired to his bunk.

CHAPTER SEVEN
EN ROUTE FOR THE NORTH POLE

The destruction of the wreck having been effected, the *Flying Fish* moved a few miles northward until she reached a small level sandy patch affording a good berth for the night, and there she was once more placed upon the ground and anchored.

Nothing whatever occurred to disturb the repose of the travellers; and, after passing a tranquil night, they assembled at the breakfast table punctually at eight o'clock on the following morning. An hour later, having finished their meal, the quartette rose, and made their way to the pilot-house, where preparations were at once commenced for an ascent to the surface. On this occasion the professor being anxious that the other members of the party should become conversant with the method of handling the ship, the baronet placed himself at the tiller—from which post the entire apparatus controlling the movements of the vessel could be reached—and, with von Schalckenberg at his elbow to correct him in the event of a possible mistake, the ascent was begun. This, from prudential motives, was slowly accomplished, and at a distance of five fathoms from the surface a pause was made for the purpose of taking a good look round and thus avoiding all possibility of inflicting damage on passing ships in the act of breaking water. It was well that this precaution was observed; for their first glance revealed to them the bottom of a large steamer close at hand and coming rapidly straight toward them; and had the *Flying Fish* continued to rise she would have broken water directly under the stranger's bows. As it was, by backing astern a few yards they gave the steamer good room to pass; and it was both interesting and novel to see the great mass go plunging heavily past with the long sea-grass waving and trailing from her bottom, and the great propeller spinning rapidly round, now completely immersed, and anon lifted almost entirely out of the water. Once clear of her, the *Flying Fish* sank to a depth of ten fathoms, and after a ten-mile run at full speed, once more paused to reconnoitre. This time the sea was clear for at least a mile in every direction—which was as far as they could see in the then condition of the water—and they at once rose to the surface.

The horizon proved to be clear in every direction save to the southward, in which quarter the upper spars of the steamer they had so lately encountered were still visible. The wind was blowing a moderate breeze from S.S.E.—almost a dead fair wind for the *Flying Fish*—the weather also was delightfully fine and clear; it was therefore promptly resolved to take to the air once more and thus wing their way northward.

The valves of the air-chambers were accordingly thrown open to their full extent, when, with a screaming roar, the highly compressed air at once rushed forth, and in less than half a minute the huge bulk of the ship was lying poised as lightly as an air-bubble on the surface of the heaving water. The main vapour-valve was then cautiously opened, and a partial vacuum produced, when, as easily as a seabird, the *Flying Fish* rose at once into the air. The engines were next turned ahead, the helm adjusted, and the northward journey was fairly begun.

The wind was blowing at the rate of about fifteen miles an hour, and nearly dead fair; the engines were therefore set so as just to turn round and no more; this gave the ship a speed of about twelve knots through the air, which, added to the rate of the wind, gave a total speed of twenty-seven knots over the ground—or rather over, the water—and at this pace they calculated that, after making the necessary allowance in their course for the set of the wind, they would reach the Irish coast, in the vicinity of Cape Clear, at about five o'clock the next morning. Their reason for not travelling faster was that, as the baronet said, they were on a pleasure cruise, and having been pent up inside the hull for fully thirty-six hours, they felt that a few hours in the open air would be an acceptable change.

They pursued their flight throughout the day at an altitude of only a thousand feet above the sea, except when they encountered a ship—which happened only once during the hours of daylight—and when this occurred they rose, on the instant of sighting her, to the highest attainable distance, in pursuance of their resolve to attract as little attention as possible, descending again to their former level as soon as they had passed beyond her range of vision. At this latter elevation they were able to enjoy to the full the health-giving properties of the pure sea-breeze, and to revel in a prospect—though it was only that of the restless sea—of nearly forty nautical miles on every side; the horizon, that is to say, forming a circle of little less than eighty miles diameter round about them. And though it may be hastily thought that, with a sea bare of craft there was little or nothing to interest the travellers, this was by no means the case; for at their height the water was clear and transparent for a long distance below the surface, and the gambols of the fish, of which there were great numbers visible, including several schools of porpoises and a solitary whale, could be seen distinctly, affording a most interesting sight; and when they grew tired of this they promenaded the spacious deck, or lounged about in chairs, smoking their cigars or pipes, and discussing with much animation their future prospects. And now, for the first time, a fact in connection with the automatic balancing apparatus brought itself under their notice. It was this. They found that, let them walk about the ship where and as much as they chose, the balance of the ship always remained perfect; but the little jets of air which, at their every movement, were admitted into the hull to maintain its equilibrium, soon had a perceptible influence on the vessel's buoyancy, causing her to slowly but steadily descend toward the surface of the sea, thus necessitating periodic visits to the pilot-house to renew the vacuum. This set the professor's brain to work, and by nightfall he succeeded—with the aid of a second barometer having a small piece of highly magnetised steel floating on the top of the mercurial column, and a couple of magnetised steel bars—

in constructing a somewhat rude but thoroughly efficient apparatus for automatically maintaining the ship at any desired height, unaffected by the movements, be they few or many, of those on board.

By the time that this apparatus had been fixed, and subjected to the test of an hour's conscientious walking fore and aft the deck by the entire party, the dinner-hour had arrived, and they retired below with such appetites as only a day's exposure to the tonic effects of a sea-breeze—minus all uncomfortable motion—could produce. The fullest justice was consequently done to the meal, after which they made their way once more to the deck, and there, under a brilliant star-lit sky, gave themselves up to the soothing influence of *the weed* and the renewed enjoyment of their novel position. Midnight found them quite ready for their state-rooms, and at that hour they accordingly retired; the professor first of all, as a matter of precaution, increasing the ship's altitude to four thousand feet above the sea-level, and then paying a visit of inspection to the engine-room. Matters were found to be all right there; the engines were working smoothly and noiselessly, the bearings were quite cool, and the automatic feed was doing its work to perfection. The ship, then, being at such a height as to be clear of all danger, and steering herself in the required direction, with all the machinery in perfect working order, the weather also being fine and wearing a settled aspect, von Schalckenberg told himself that there was not the slightest necessity for the maintenance of a look-out, and he therefore also retired. A quarter of an hour later the whole of the crew were sunk in profound repose, and the *Flying Fish*, left to herself, was leisurely wending her way northward at a height of nearly a mile above the earth's surface.

The first of the quartette to put in an appearance on deck next morning was the professor, who was awakened just as day was breaking by the faint sound of a steam whistle. Springing hastily from his very comfortable couch, he rushed up the companion way and into the open air, without even pausing to don his nether garments. Springing to the guard rail he looked around and below him, and the half-formed fear that something had gone amiss, and that the ship was in danger, was at once dissipated. He saw that the *Flying Fish* was moving rapidly along with the land beneath her, the breeze having freshened during the night, whilst still blowing from the same quarter, causing them to reach the Irish coast sooner than had been anticipated. The mercury stood at the same height in the tube as it had done when they retired to rest on the preceding night; the ship had consequently maintained her approximate height above the sea-level, the only variation being that due to the greater or lesser density of the atmosphere; which was eminently satisfactory, as it showed that the professor's hastily constructed apparatus for maintaining an uniform level had been faithfully performing its duty.

These facts ascertained, von Schalckenberg cast his glance over the scene spread out beneath him, in order to ascertain, if possible, his position. The morning was beautifully clear, the atmosphere being entirely destitute of clouds, and the only obstacle to uninterrupted vision was a thick mist which overspread the earth outstretched below him like an immense map. This, to a certain extent, rendered prompt identification of the locality difficult; but a lake of very irregular triangular shape was immediately underneath the ship, and from S. round to about W.S.W., at a distance of about eight miles, extended a range of hills which, from their height, the professor easily identified as Macgillicuddy's Reeks, the lake below being Killarney. Other hills towered up out of the mist all round the ship, and, at a distance of some twenty miles straight ahead, appeared the Stack Mountains. Towns, villages, farm buildings, and solitary cabins were dotted about all over the country, and beyond all, from S.S.E. round by S. and W. to N., could be seen the blue sea, dotted here and there with the brown sails of the fishing craft or the scarcely whiter canvas of the coasters.

Satisfied that all was right, the professor returned to the pilot-house, and, closing the doors to exclude the intense cold of the higher atmospheric region, perfected the vacuum in the air chambers, causing the ship to immediately soar aloft to the enormous height of thirty-five thousand feet; having done which he made his way below again and plunged into his bath.

On meeting his companions at the breakfast-table, von Schalckenberg informed them of the position and elevation of the ship, and they at once expressed an ardent desire to go out on deck immediately after breakfast to view the magnificent prospect spread out around and beneath them.

"You will have to put on your diving suits then, gentlemen," remarked the scientist, "for you would find it quite impossible to breathe in the extremely rarefied atmosphere which now supports us; moreover, it is so intensely cold that, unless exceedingly well protected, you would soon freeze to death. But I quite agree with you that the prospect, embracing as it does a circle of—let me see," and he made a hasty calculation on the back of an envelope—"yes, a circle of very nearly four hundred and sixty miles in diameter, must be well worth looking at."

Accordingly, on the completion of the meal, the quartette descended to the diving-room, and there donned their armour, taking the additional precaution of adding a flannel overall to their ordinary inner diving dress. Thus equipped, they made their way to the pilot-house, carefully closing all doors behind them on the way, and sallied out on deck.

The spectacle which then met their gaze was novel beyond all power of description, and can only be feebly suggested. The sky overhead was of an intense ultramarine hue, approaching in depth to indigo, gradually changing, as the eye travelled downward from the zenith toward the horizon, to a pallid colourless hue. The stars—excepting those near the horizon—were almost as distinctly visible as at midnight; whilst the sun, shorn of his rays, hung in the sky like a great ball of molten copper; the moon also, reduced to a thin silver thread-like crescent, had followed the sun into the sky, and hung a few degrees only above the eastern horizon.

So lost in wonder were the travellers at this most extraordinary sight that it was several minutes before they could withdraw their gaze from the heavens and allow it to travel earthward. When at length they did so a scarcely less enchanting spectacle greeted them. They were hovering just over the inner extremity of an arm of the sea, which the colonel—who was well acquainted with the south-west of Ireland—at once identified as Dingle Bay. Westward of them stretched the broad Atlantic, its foam-flecked waters tinted a lovely sea-green immediately below them, which gradually changed to a delicate sapphire blue as it stretched away toward the invisible horizon (the atmosphere not proving sufficiently clear to allow of their seeing to the utmost possible limits of distance), the colour growing gradually fainter and more faint until it became lost in a soft silvery grey mist. Northward lay the Dingle peninsula, and beyond it again could be seen Tralee Bay, the mouth of the Shannon, and Loop Head; then Galway Bay and the Isles of Arran, and, further on, just discernible in the misty distance, the indented shore and hills of Connemara. From thence, all round to the eastern point of the compass, could be seen, with more or less distinctness, the whole of county Clare, with part of county Galway, the Doon Mountains, and a considerable portion of Tipperary; the Galtee and Knockmeledown Mountains, and, in the extreme distance, a faint misty blue, which the colonel declared was the sea just about Dungarvan harbour. And from thence, round to the southward, the sea and the southern coast-line became more and more distinctly visible as the eye travelled round the compass, Cork Harbour being just discernible, whilst Cape Clear Island, Bantry Bay, and the Kenmare river seemed little more than a stone's-throw distant. Altogether it was perhaps the most magnificent prospect upon which the human eye had ever rested; it certainly exceeded anything which the travellers had ever witnessed before, and their expressions of admiration and delight were unbounded.

When at last they had become somewhat accustomed to even this unique experience, and had found leisure to take note of themselves, as it were, the baronet remarked to the professor:

"But how is this, professor? The engines are working, yet we do not appear to be making any headway. So far as I can judge we seem to be simply drifting bodily to the westward and more toward the open sea."

"It is so," answered the professor. "We have risen above the range of the variable winds, and are now feeling the influence of an adverse air current, which, in this latitude, invariably blows *from* the northward; and if we were to maintain our present altitude, for which, however, there is not the slightest necessity, we should have to struggle against it for the next eight or nine hundred miles, in fact until we reach the neighbourhood of the Arctic circle. There, or thereabout, we should again have a fair wind, of which we may possibly yet be glad to avail ourselves. In the meantime, however, we will increase our speed, if you please—at all events, until we are clear of the land, when we can once more descend into a favourable current.

And as, until then, our rate of travelling will be such as to make it difficult, if not impossible, to maintain our footing on the deck, I would suggest the advisability of a retreat to the pilot-house."

This suggestion having been promptly carried out, the speed of the ship was increased to its utmost limit, whereby the rate of progression over the ground was raised from nothing to about one hundred and eight miles per hour. This rate of travelling—the adverse wind fortunately remaining moderate—enabled them to reach Erris Head, the north-western corner of county Mayo, in an hour and a half, or about eleven o'clock A.M., at which hour they found themselves just running clear of the land, with the bay and county of Donegal on their right hand, and the broad expanse of the North Atlantic ahead.

At this point the professor turned to his companions and said:

"It now becomes necessary that we should come to a definite decision as to the course to be steered. All routes are of course equally open to us; but there are two which especially commend themselves to our preference. One is the direct northerly route to the Pole, which will take us to the eastward of Iceland, straight to the island of Jan Mayen, and thence, between Greenland and Spitzbergen, into an icy sea which has been but little explored. And the other is the usual route taken by nearly all the great Arctic explorers, namely, up Davis Strait, through Baffin's Bay, and thence, by way of Smith Sound and Kennedy Channel, into the open Polar Sea, if such should actually exist. By the one route we shall have an opportunity of surveying the eastern coast of Greenland, and thus accurately determining much that is at present mere matter of conjecture; and by the other we shall have an opportunity of beholding with our own eyes many spots of interest associated with the researches of former explorers. Now, which is it to be?"

The colonel and Mildmay naturally glanced at Sir Reginald, as an intimation that he, in his character of founder of the expedition, was entitled to the first expression of opinion; and, thus appealed to, the baronet, after a short pause for reflection, replied:

"Well, so far as I am concerned, if I have a preference at all, I think I am inclined to favour the Baffin's Bay route. I confess I should like to go over the ground traversed so painfully by former explorers, and see for myself the nature of the obstacles with which they have had to grapple. And I should also like to look with my bodily eyes upon the spots where they sought refuge during the rigours of the Arctic winter, and those other spots where, the forces of nature finally proving too great for them, they were reluctantly compelled to abandon further effort, and, confessing themselves beaten, turn their faces once more southward. But if either of you happens to have a preference for another route, I beg that you will say so, uninfluenced by my remarks."

The colonel and Mildmay now looked at each other interrogatively; and at length the latter said:

"My predilections are naturally in favour of the route proposed by Sir Reginald, that being the one followed by so many of my distinguished predecessors in the service. But what says the professor? Which route does he, as a scientist, think would be the most interesting?"

"Exactly; that, it seems to me, is the point of view from which we ought to regard the question," exclaimed the baronet and the colonel in a breath.

"From a purely scientific point of view they would probably prove equally interesting," answered the professor. "But, taking the other circumstances into consideration, I am inclined to record my vote in favour of Sir Reginalds suggestion."

"Then let that decide it," remarked the colonel; "I am sure we shall have no cause to regret the choice."

The Baffin's Bay route was accordingly agreed upon; and the ship's head was forthwith laid in a west-north-westerly direction for Cape Farewell.

For the next hour the ship's altitude above the sea-level was maintained unaltered; but at noon, the ocean proving clear of ships as far as the eye could reach, a descent was made to within one thousand feet of the sea, at which height a favourable breeze and a clear atmosphere was again met with. On returning to the pilothouse after luncheon, or about half-past three o'clock in the afternoon, three icebergs were discovered, two ahead and one astern; but they were very small, and it was therefore deemed hardly worth while to pause and examine them. At the same time a large steamer was observed, steering east, on the extreme verge of the southern horizon; and by the aid of their very powerful telescopes the travellers were able to identify her as one of the Atlantic liners. Half an hour later a sail was discovered on the starboard bow; and, from the fact that she was heading to the northward under easy canvas, they rightly concluded that she was a whaler. They passed this vessel within a distance of a dozen miles, and at this point were able to so minutely examine her with their telescopes that they could distinctly make out the figure of a man perched aloft in the "crow's nest" on the look-out, as well as the figures of her crew moving about the deck; but, although within such comparatively close proximity to her, they were quite unable to detect any sign of their being observed, which the professor attributed to the almost total absence of colour about the hull; indeed, he gave it as his opinion that, unless the rays of the sun happened to be reflected from the polished surface of the aethereum directly toward an observer, the *Flying Fish* might easily pass within half a dozen miles unnoticed.

Before this whaler had been left out of sight astern other icebergs had risen into view above the western horizon, and within half an hour they found themselves flying above a sea thickly dotted with ice in every direction, showing that they were rapidly nearing the entrance to Davis Straits. At six o'clock the sound of the gong summoned them below to dinner; and just as they were on the point of leaving the pilot-house, Mildmay, who, with the instinct of the seaman, had paused to take a last look round, sighted a faint blue cloud-like appearance on the horizon, about a point on the starboard bow, and raised a joyful shout of:

"Land, ho!"

The professor glanced at the clock, and, muttering to himself, "Yes, it is about the right time," took his telescope and carefully examined the distant cloud-like appearance.

"You are right, Mildmay," he exclaimed, as he closed the instrument, "that is the land; it is Cape Farewell, the most southerly point of that great *terra incognita*, Greenland. With your permission, Sir Reginald, I will reduce the speed of the ship to about twenty miles per hour, and slightly alter her course; and, from the look of the weather, I think I may promise that, when we go on deck to smoke our cigars after dinner, you will see a sight well worth looking at."

CHAPTER EIGHT
A SUPERB SPECTACLE

Upon one pretext or another the professor purposely delayed the rising of the party from the table until nine o'clock; and when they at length reached the deck they found the somewhat rash promise made by von Schalckenberg abundantly fulfilled. A scene of surpassing loveliness met their delighted gaze, and, to enjoy it more fully and completely, it was promptly decided to descend to the ocean's surface. The sea on all sides was thickly covered with detached masses of floating ice, from the diminutive fragment of drift-ice, measuring not more than two or three square yards in area, to gigantic bergs, measuring, in one or two instances, from a half to three quarters of a mile long, and towering from two to three hundred feet above the surface of the water. The sun was nearing the horizon, and, with his golden beams falling full upon them, these huge masses of ice glittered against the rosy grey of the horizon like burnished metal or solid flame. Two of these bergs in particular were the objects of the travellers' especial wonder and admiration. One, at a distance of some six miles to the eastward, resembled an island of crystal capped with an assemblage of marble ruins. Its perpendicular sides were rent here and there with deep fissures, and in the centre there yawned an immense cavern, the interior of which displayed every conceivable shade of the most lovely green, from the transparent tint of the emerald to the opaque colour of the malachite, a projecting bluff near at hand casting a strangely-contrasting shadow of the deepest, purest ultramarine. The ruined pinnacles on the summit of the berg gleamed with every tint of the rainbow, from palest yellow, through orange and crimson, to a blue varying from the most delicate cobalt to a deep violet, almost undistinguishable from black. And, to complete the fairy-like beauty of the picture, the body of the berg, a pure marble-like white in the centre, gradually assumed a translucent appearance toward the edges, in which the rays of the sun gleamed and sparkled so brilliantly that the mass resembled nothing so much as a gigantic opal.

The other large berg, which in the first instance was only remarkable for its enormous size, lay on the western horizon at a distance of some eleven miles, and, when the travellers first directed their gaze upon it, presented the appearance of a vast mass of a uniform very pale tint of opaque blue rising above the rosy waters. But as they looked upon it the setting sun drew round toward its rear, and then the pale blue opaque tint gradually quickened into translucency and quivered here and there with sudden golden and roseate gleams of indescribable beauty. As the sun neared the berg these gleams and flashes deepened in tint and became mingled in the most bewildering and delightful manner with rays of rich sea-green, warm violet, and delicate purple. Finally the sun, just skimming the edge of the horizon, passed behind the berg, when it at once flamed out into a dazzling blinding blaze, as though the berg had taken fire. For a space of perhaps half a minute this dazzling spectacle continued with scarcely diminished brilliancy; then the blaze deepened from gold to crimson, momentarily subsiding in intensity and increasing in depth of colour until it stood out against the horizon an immense mass of blood-red hue. The red deepened into purple, the purple into violet, and at last, probably when the sun had entirely sunk beneath the horizon, the violet faded gradually to a pale cold lifeless grey.

"Superb!"

"Magnificent!"

"Delightful!"

"Beautiful as a dream!"

Such were the exclamations which burst from the lips of the travellers as they turned away with a sigh at the transitory nature of the beauties they had just been witnessing, when lo! the scene to the eastward had donned new glories. The sun had vanished below the horizon, and the lower portions of the bergs were therefore in cold blue shadow; but as the glance travelled upwards the blue became merged by imperceptible degrees into a delicate amethystine tint, which, growing gradually warmer and more ruddy, passed by a thousand gradations through the richest rose and orange tints to the purest golden-yellow, out of which the projecting points and pinnacles of ice flashed and sparkled like living flame. This fairy-like spectacle lasted for a short time only, however; the golden flashes vanished one by one; the yellow became orange, the orange deepened into crimson, and the crimson in its turn slowly merged into a cold cobalt blue as the light died out of the western sky; and finally the stars came out one by one until the entire firmament was thickly studded with them. It was "nightfall on the sea."

Enthralled by the surpassing witchery of the scene, some time elapsed before either of the travellers cared to break the silence. At length, however, the baronet turned to the professor and said:

"I owe you a debt of never-dying gratitude, professor, for having been the means of introducing me to a scene of such indescribable beauty as that which we have just witnessed; I have looked upon many a fair scene during the course of my wanderings, but never upon anything to equal this. We must have been exceptionally fortunate to-night, have we not? for surely the Polar world can have no spectacle more enchanting than the one which we have just witnessed?"

"We *have* been fortunate; there is no doubt about that," was the reply. "But you have not yet seen the midnight sun nor the aurora borealis, both of which sights far exceed in beauty what we have looked upon to-night. But it grows chilly and an insidious fog is gathering round us; we must take measures for passing the night in safety, for, were we by chance to be caught between two icebergs of even ordinary size, not even the enormous strength of the *Flying Fish* would save her from destruction."

"And what do you propose to do, then, professor, in order to ensure our safety?"

"There are two courses open to us. One is to sink to the bottom of the sea, which is here deep enough to secure us from all danger of being struck by floating bergs. And the other is to ascend into the calm belt, where the night can be passed in a state of absolute safety."

"Very well, then; let us ascend into the 'calm belt,' by all means," said the baronet. "And, by the way, I should feel extremely obliged if you would kindly explain to us what the 'calm belt' is; I for one never heard of it before."

"I will do so with pleasure," replied the professor. "You must know, then, in the first place, that there are certain atmospheric currents as regular and precise in their action as those of the ocean, both being created by the same cause—namely, the tendency of a warm fluid to rise and of a colder one to flow into the vacated space. Thus the air on the equator, being heated by the vertical rays of the sun, rises, creating a partial vacuum which the cold air from the poles rushes equatorward to fill, the warm air moving toward the poles to restore the balance. Thus at a few degrees north of the equator the upper stratum of air will always be found to be travelling northward. And it continues so to do until it reaches the vicinity of the thirtieth parallel of latitude, when, having lost most of its heat by constant exposure to open space, it becomes cold enough to descend, taking the place of the polar current, which meanwhile has been warmed by passing over the temperate zone. The equatorial current, though it has descended to the surface of the earth, still makes its gradual way northward, as well as local circumstances will permit, in order to replace the southward-flying polar current; and by the time that it reaches the Arctic circle, it has again, by contact with the earth, become the warmer of the two currents, when it once more rises into the upper regions of the atmosphere, to descend no more until it reaches the vicinity of the pole, when it sinks, and at the same time turns southward as the polar current. And the same thing happens in the southern hemisphere. Thus in each hemisphere we have two great atmospheric currents—one flowing from the pole to the equator, and the other flowing from the equator to the pole. The lower current, or that which sweeps along the surface of the earth, meets with so many disturbing local influences that it is frequently deflected greatly from its proper course, sometimes so much so that its course becomes completely reversed for a time; but in the upper regions of the atmosphere these disturbing influences are very little if at all felt. Now, if I have succeeded in making this plain to you, you will readily understand that where the top of the lower current and the bottom of the upper current touch each other there will be so much friction that a neutral or 'calm belt' will occur in which the air will be motionless. And it is in this calm belt—which occurs between the altitudes of three thousand and twelve thousand feet above the earth's surface—that I propose we should take refuge to-night."

The professor's small audience duly expressed their thanks for the extremely interesting lecture to which they had just been treated, and then the party retreated to the pilot-house; the door was closed to exclude the cold air of the upper regions which they were about to visit; and an ascent was made to an altitude of eight thousand feet, where the night was passed in an atmosphere so completely motionless that, on their descent next morning, Lieutenant Mildmay's observations showed them to be in the exact spot which they had occupied on the previous evening.

It was decided over the breakfast-table that morning, that the journey northward should be prosecuted, as far as possible, upon the surface of the sea; and the *Flying Fish* was accordingly put in motion on the required course immediately upon her descent. Their rate of progress was particularly slow, not exceeding, on the average, a speed of six miles per hour, as drift ice was remarkably abundant, mostly in small detached blocks, though they occasionally encountered a floe of several acres in extent; and, far away to the northward, quite a large assemblage of bergs were seen. This slow rate of progress would have been wearisome to a veteran Arctic navigator in possession of such means for the accomplishment of a quick passage as those enjoyed by the inmates of the *Flying Fish's* pilot-house; but to them everything was novel and interesting, and, almost before they knew it, they found themselves in the immediate vicinity of the bergs. These varied greatly in size, some of them being no larger than a dwelling-house of moderate dimensions, whilst others fully equalled, if, indeed, they did not exceed, the proportions of the monsters seen on the previous evening. They were grouped so closely together that a passage between them seemed to be not wholly unattended with danger; and the party were in the act of discussing the question which channel it would be most prudent to take, their eyes being meanwhile fixed on the huge towering cliffs of ice before them, when a gigantic overhanging mass was seen to detach itself from its parent berg and plunge, a distance of some two hundred and fifty feet, with a terrific splash into the water and disappear. The deep thunderous roar of its plunge smote the ears of the watchers next moment, and they looked on with breathless interest to see what would follow. The mass, from its enormous size, would weigh, they considered, fully five thousand tons; and they were not surprised to see that the loss of so much weight had seriously disturbed the balance of the berg, which at once began to rock ponderously to and fro, creating a terrific commotion in the water when conjoined with that caused by the plunge into the sea and the reappearance a second or two later of the detached mass. The sea was seen to heap itself up in a long well-defined ridge, similar—though, of course, on a tremendously magnified scale—to that caused by the plunge of a stone into the water. This ridge spread out in a circular form all round the spot where the mass had fallen, and at once began to travel outward in the form of an immense breaker some six or seven feet in height. Onward it rolled, its smooth glassy front capped with a foaming crest presenting a singular and somewhat alarming spectacle. The fears of the beholders, however, if they had any, were groundless, for, though the threatening wave swept forward with a velocity of some twelve knots per hour, it swept harmlessly enough over and along the cylindrical sides of the *Flying Fish*, hissing and roaring most ominously, but failing to throw so much as a single drop of spray on her deck. This wave was quickly followed by several others, each of which, however, was less formidable than the preceding one. Meanwhile, the drama, it appeared, had only begun. The oscillation of the parent berg, though it was probably quite unaffected by the portion of the circular wave which dashed furiously against its sides, became momentarily more and more violent, accompanied by a rapidly increasing agitation of the sea in its neighbourhood, an agitation so great that the surface of the ocean soon assumed the appearance of a boiling cauldron, the foaming surges leaping wildly hither and thither with a continuous roar like that of the surf beating on a rocky shore, and soon assuming such dimensions that they even broke over the deck of the *Flying Fish*, and dashed themselves into a cloud of spray against the strong walls of the pilot-house. Other fragments now began to detach themselves with dull heavy roaring crashes from the rocking berg; and, as though the action were contagious—or more probably, in consequence of the jarring vibration of the air from such a strong volume of sound—one after the other, the remaining bergs began to go to pieces. Then, indeed, the sight and the accompanying sounds became truly awe-inspiring. The air resounded with the continuous roar of the dismembering bergs; the eye grew dizzy and bewildered as it watched their swaying forms; and the surface of the ocean was momentarily stirred into a wilder frenzy as the surges swept madly hither and thither, and, meeting in mid-career, shattered each other into a wild tempest of leaping foam, in the midst of which huge masses of ice were seen every now and then to be tossed high into the air as though they had been fragments of cork. So mad was the commotion, and so furiously were even the larger masses of ice dashed to and fro, that it was deemed prudent to remove the *Flying Fish* out of harm's way; and she was accordingly raised a few fathoms above the surface of the raging commotion which leaped and roared around her. Scarcely had this been accomplished—the whole of the drama occupying not one-tenth part of the time which it takes to describe it—when the largest of the bergs was seen to roll completely over, raising in the act so awful a surge that it visibly affected even the immense masses of the other bergs, which, in their turn, rolled slowly over one after the other, to the accompaniment of one long loud echoing roar of rending ice as their dismemberment thus became accelerated. The resulting ocean disturbance was, as may easily be imagined, appallingly grand and utterly indescribable; and it no doubt contributed in no inconsiderable degree to the total destruction of the bergs, which, once started, continued to roll over and over, every lurch causing a further dismemberment until the fragments became so small as to be incapable of further division. Then ensued comparative silence, the only sounds being those of the hoarse roar of the angry surges and the grinding crash of ice-blocks dashed violently together. Gradually these too subsided; and, in half an hour from the commencement of the spectacle, the ice-strewn waters were again rippling crisply under the influence of a moderate breeze, and no sign remained to tell a new arrival upon the scene—had there been one—what an awful tempest of destruction had raged there so short a time before.

Pushing northward, the travellers sighted the coast of Greenland about noon; the land made being a lofty snow-covered mountain, the conical summit of which gleamed like silver in the brilliant sunshine. As they neared the coast the water became more open; and at length they emerged into a broad channel completely free of ice, up which the *Flying Fish* was urged at a trifle less than half-speed, or at the rate of about sixty miles per hour. At eight o'clock that night they crossed, according to their "dead reckoning," the Arctic circle; and midnight found them abreast of Disko Island, gazing with delighted eyes upon the glorious spectacle of the midnight sun, the lower edge of his ruddy disc just skimming the northern horizon.

At this point the channel between the Greenland coast and the pack-ice narrowed very considerably; and their rate of progress northward next day was reduced to a speed of between two and three miles per hour; the engines needing to be just started, and then stopped again for a few minutes in order to keep the speed down to this very low limit. But they were all as yet so new to Arctic scenery—everything was so entirely novel to them—that even this snail's pace failed to prove wearisome, especially as the weather continued gloriously fine.

Strange to say, up to this time they had not set eyes on a single Arctic animal; but now, as they were busily threading their way through a narrow channel in the ice, a white bear was seen about half a mile ahead rapidly making his way across the pack toward them, whilst, a quarter of a mile nearer, an animal which they at once took for a seal was seen basking in the sun on the ice close to the water.

It speedily became evident that the bear was after the seal, which, seemingly all unconscious of the proximity of its enemy, raised its head now and then as though in keen enjoyment of the warm glow. The colonel hurried below for rifles, as eager as a schoolboy, to obtain a shot at one or both of the animals; and when he returned to the pilot-house with the weapons both the seal and the bear were within range. He raised one of the rifles to his shoulder, and was covering the seal with it, when Sir Reginald, who was watching the animals through a telescope, said:

"Do not fire, Lethbridge; there is something very curious about this; *that seal is armed with a bow.*"

The colonel stared incredulously at his companion, and then, dropping the rifle, took and applied to his eye the telescope which Sir Reginald handed to him.

"By George, you are right!" he exclaimed. "What a very extraordinary thing. Why," he continued, "it is not a seal at all, it is a man, an Esquimaux. Now, look out and you will see some sport; the fellow is fitting an arrow to his string, and how cautiously he is doing it, too. It is my belief that he has got himself up as a seal and has been simulating the actions of the animal in order to entice that deluded bear within range. There! he has shot his arrow and hit the mark, but the bear does not seem to be very much the worse. Aha! now you have to run for it, my good fellow. By Jove, the matter grows exciting!"

The Esquimaux had indeed been compelled to "run for it," the only apparent effect of the arrow being to irritate the bear. The man ran fairly well, although hampered with an immense amount of clothing, but the bear proved the faster of the two. He rapidly gained upon the man, and seemed about to spring upon him when the party in the pilot-house poured in a general fusillade from their rifles. There was just a perceptible click from the locks of the weapons, but neither fire nor smoke appeared, neither was there any report. At that moment the bear rose upon his hind-legs and, reaching forward with his fore-paws, aimed a terrific blow at the flying hunter. The man, who had been intently watching his enemy all the while, nimbly leaped aside, and, quick as thought, plunged a light lance fairly under the creature's armpit and deep into his body. The bear uttered a single roar of pain and baffled rage, staggered a moment, and fell upon the ice, dead.

"Bravo! very cleverly done, indeed," exclaimed the colonel, apostrophising the distant Esquimaux; "that was a lucky stroke for you, my man. But, I say, professor, what in the world is the matter with these wretched rifles? Every one of them missed fire, and, so far as we are concerned, that unfortunate Esquimaux might have been killed."

"He might—yes, that is quite true," answered the professor with provoking composure; "but if he had been it would have been our fault, not that of the rifles; it was we who missed, not they. Every one of them duly discharged its bullet, and we simply missed our mark. But had we—or rather had *I*—preserved my presence of mind, I could still have saved the man, for each of these weapons is a magazine rifle, firing twenty shots—a fact which I had forgotten for the moment, and which it now seems I have never yet explained to you. Fortunately, the poor man has proved quite able to take care of himself; but the shameful way in which we all missed the bear, and our failure to fire again, is a lesson on the folly of using untried weapons in an emergency. We must practise, gentlemen; we must practise."

And, without troubling themselves further as to what became of the Esquimaux and his game, the deeply mortified party set themselves forthwith first to listen to the professor's explanation of the peculiarities of the weapons, and next, to practise diligently with them for a full hour; at the expiration of which, as the rifles were really a splendid arm and simple enough to handle when their action had been clearly explained, the quartette had fully regained their confidence in themselves and each other, having done some most excellent shooting.

Meanwhile the channel hourly grew more narrow and intricate; and, to add still further to the difficulties of the passage, the wind shifted round and began to blow freshly from the northward, bringing with it a dense and bitterly cold fog. The travellers struggled gallantly against these adverse circumstances as long as any progress northward was at all possible, being desirous of realising, as fully as might be, for themselves the difficulties experienced by explorers in these high latitudes; but at length they found themselves so completely hemmed in by vast floes and drifting masses of pack-ice that to prolong the struggle would only be endangering the ship, and they were reluctantly compelled to own themselves beaten and to rise into the air.

They rose to a height of five hundred feet above the sea-level, and, at this elevation, found themselves entirely free of the fog. So far this was well, but the dense masses of heavy grey snow-laden cloud which obscured the heavens above them, and the threatening aspect of the sky to windward, told them that their holiday weather was, at all events for the present, gone, and that they were about to experience the terrors of a polar gale. The temperature fell with astounding rapidity; and they were compelled to beat a rapid retreat to their state-rooms, there to don additional garments. This done, they sallied out on deck, to find that during the short period of their retirement a heavy snow-storm had set in, the air being so full of the great white blinding flakes that, standing abreast the pilot-house, it was impossible to see either end of the ship. Floating in the air as they were it was, of course, impossible for them to estimate the strength of the gale, the only apparent movement of the atmosphere being that due to their own passage through it. Though heading to the northward, with the engines making a sufficient number of revolutions per minute to propel them through still air at the rate of thirty miles per hour, it was quite on the cards that the adverse wind might be travelling at a higher speed than this, in which event they would actually be driving more or less rapidly astern, notwithstanding their apparent forward motion. It thus became necessary to post a look-out at each end of the ship, in order to avoid all possibility of collision with some towering iceberg, unless they chose to rise high enough in the air to be clear of all danger; and this they were reluctant to do, as they wished to experience, for at least once in their lives, all the terrors of a polar gale. The baronet accordingly volunteered to look out forward and the colonel to do the same aft, and they hastened at once to their respective stations, Mildmay and the professor superintending meanwhile the engine levers and other appliances controlling the motion of the ship. It was well for them that these precautions were so promptly taken, for the colonel had scarcely reached his post when, through the thick whirling snow which scurried past him, he descried a huge white ghostly mass looming vaguely up in the semi-darkness directly astern, and before he well had time to make up his mind that he actually saw something, the top of a gigantic berg revealed itself close at hand, and his prompt warning cry was only raised in barely sufficient time to prevent the *Flying Fish* driving stern foremost into it, when the loss of her propeller must inevitably have resulted. Mildmay, however, whose quick ear first caught the sound, promptly sent the engines at full speed ahead, and the danger was averted.

Meanwhile, though the snow whirled so thickly around them and the fog was so dense beneath that they were unable to see anything, they were not allowed to remain entirely in ignorance of what was happening in their near proximity. The howling of the bitter blast over the frozen waste beneath resounded in their ears like the diapason of some huge organ played by giant fingers, and mingled with these deeper tones there rose up to them a constant grinding crunching sound with occasional rifle-like reports, telling of the tremendous destruction going on among the ice-floes beneath.

Suddenly the snow ceased, the fog was swept away upon the wings of the gale, and the entire scene in all its terrific grandeur burst at once upon their gaze. They were hovering immediately over the spot where two immense floes had come into collision, and for miles to the right and left of them the contiguous margins were being ground to pieces by the enormous pressure, and the splintered fragments heaped up one above another in the wildest confusion, to a height of from fifty to eighty feet above the surface of the floe. The ice, which was about fifteen feet thick, crumbled away like fragile glass, and it was only by observing the manner in which masses weighing hundreds of tons were wildly tossed hither and thither like corks that even an approximate idea of the tremendous power at work could be obtained.

A mile ahead another grand sight presented itself. The northern and larger of the two floes, acted strongly upon by the gale, and opposed by the smaller floe, was slowly but irresistibly swinging round, and in its sweep it had come into contact with a very large berg, which, influenced apparently by some undercurrent, was with equally irresistible force actually making its way to windward in the teeth of the gale.

The result was a scene of wild chaos and confusion and destruction compared with which that upon which they had just looked was as nothing. The berg simply tore its way through the floe as a plough does through a furrow, splitting up the thick ice before it, and tossing the huge fragments hither and thither until its path through the field was marked by a black band of open water churned into fleecy froth by the breath of the tempest, and bordered on either side by an immense wall of ice-blocks, each of which constituted a small berg in itself.

The cold had by this time so increased in intensity that the colonel and the baronet were only too glad to abandon their posts, now that there was no further necessity for maintaining them, and retreat to the friendly shelter of the pilot-house, where they lost no time in closing themselves in.

CHAPTER NINE
AN EXCITING ADVENTURE AND A RESCUE

It was at this moment that Mildmay caught a momentary glimpse of an object far away on the northern horizon, which his practised eye at once told him was a sail of some sort. He instantly seized one of the telescopes suspended in the pilot-house, and brought the instrument to bear in her direction. For nearly a minute he was unsuccessful in his endeavour to find her; but at length she reappeared from behind an intervening berg; and it appeared to him that she was in a situation of considerable peril. She was a barque, under close-reefed topsails, reefed courses, fore topmast staysail, and mizzen; and she appeared to be embayed in the bight of a huge floe, with a whole fleet of bergs in dangerous proximity and apparently bearing down upon her. Perhaps the strangest peculiarity about her was that, notwithstanding her perilous position, she was dressed with flags, from her mast-heads downward, as though it were a gala day on board.

Mildmay's anxious attitude and expression of face, together with his earnest devotion to his telescope, soon attracted the notice of the rest of the party; and the baronet asked him what object it was that so riveted his attention.

He withdrew his eyes for a moment from the instrument, and, pointing out the small and scarcely distinguishable dark spot on the horizon, said:

"Do you see that object, gentlemen? Well, that is a barque embayed in the ice, and evidently making a supreme effort to free herself—an effort which to me, and at this distance, appears quite hopeless. It is my opinion that, unless the wind changes, or something equally unforeseen occurs, she will within the next half hour be smashed into matchwood—unless, indeed, *we* can help her."

"Help her? Of course we can," said the professor; and without waiting for further discussion, he laid his hand on the engine lever and sent the machinery ahead at nearly half-speed.

The *Flying Fish* darted forward like a swallow in full flight; and the professor, leaving the baronet in charge of the engines and the steering-gear, summoned Mildmay and the colonel to follow him. The trio hastened to the after part of the deck, and, raising a trap-door which the professor indicated, withdrew therefrom a thin pliant wire hawser—made, like almost everything else in the ship, of aethereum—which, having secured one end of it to a ring-bolt in the after extremity of the deck, they coiled down in readiness for use as a tow-line.

"There!" ejaculated the professor in a gratified tone of voice, "we will give her the end of that rope; and it shall go hard with us, but we will tow her into some place of at least temporary safety."

"That is all right," responded Mildmay; "but how are we going to get it on board her? Its weight is a mere nothing, it is true, but it is rather too bulky to heave on board. Have you nothing smaller that we can bend on to the eye of the hawser and use as a heaving-line?"

"Certainly I have," replied the professor. "I had not thought of that. 'Every man to his trade.'" And, diving down the hatchway, he rummaged about for a few minutes and finally reappeared with a small coil of very thin light pliant wire line, which Mildmay, pronouncing it to be exactly the thing, proceeded at once to attach to the eye of the hawser.

Meanwhile, the baronet had been anxiously watching the barque through the telescope, and had seen so much to increase his anxiety for her safety that, forgetful of the exposed situation of his companions, he had gradually increased the pace of the *Flying Fish* until he had brought it up to full speed. This, of course, created so tremendous a draught that not only was it quite impossible for the party aft to make headway against it and thus regain the pilot-house, but they actually had to fling themselves flat on the deck to avoid being blown overboard; and even thus it was only with the utmost difficulty that they were able to save themselves.

And this, unfortunately, was not the worst of it. The light hawser, acted upon by so powerful a draught, was for an instant slightly lifted off the deck, and that slight lift did the mischief. The next moment the coils went streaming away astern one after the other, and, almost before those who witnessed the accident could tell what had happened, the propeller had been fouled and the hawser snapped like a thread.

The powerful jerk thus occasioned caused the baronet to turn his head; and he then saw in a moment what mischief he had done. He, luckily, had presence of mind enough to stop the engines at once; the *Flying Fish's* course was stayed, and she immediately began to drive swiftly astern in apparently a dead calm, but actually swept along upon the wings of the gale.

The professor at once scrambled to his feet, and, followed by his companions, hurried to the pilot-house, where, without wasting time in useless words, he at once set himself to look out for a suitable spot upon which to alight, it being absolutely necessary to clear the propeller before again moving the engines, lest in doing so a complete break-down should result.

A favourable spot was at length found—but not until they had drifted completely out of sight of the apparently doomed barque—and the *Flying Fish* was carefully lowered to the surface of a large floe, her anchor being first let go in order to "bring her up" and prevent her being driven along by the wind over the smooth surface. It was a task more difficult of accomplishment than they had anticipated, the anchor for some time refusing to bite, but it caught at last in a crevice, and immediately on the vessel touching, the grip-anchors were extended and the ship secured.

No sooner was the *Flying Fish* fairly settled on the ice than Mildmay, who knew exactly what ought to be done, descended to the lower recesses of the ship, and, opening the trap-door in her bottom, made his way out on the ice, dragging with him a ladder which was always kept in the diving-room. He soon reached the stern of the vessel, and, rearing the ladder in a suitable position against the propeller, nimbly ran aloft and began to throw off the convolutions of the entangled hawser. Twenty minutes sufficed, not only to complete the work, but also to assure him that no damage had been done to the hull of the vessel; and, his three companions having followed him and removed the hawser to the interior of the vessel, he re-entered the hull, secured the trap-door after him, and ascended to the deck. He here found Sir Reginald and the colonel busily engaged in adjusting a new hawser ready for use, and, with his assistance, this task was completed in another five minutes, and the ship was once more ready for service.

As the *Flying Fish* was in the act of rising from off the ice, Sir Reginald asked:

"Should we not make better speed by taking at once to the water, professor?"

"Undoubtedly we should," was the answer. "Such a course would also have the additional advantage of enabling us to immerse the hull to the proper depth as we go along, thus giving us that hold upon the water necessary to cope successfully with the weight of a large ship like the one of which we are going in search. We *might*, whilst floating in the air, be able to tow her out of danger, but I am a little doubtful on the point; and, as this is a case in which it will not do to incur any risk by trying experiments, we will take to the water as soon as we can discover a suitable channel. It appears to me that there is something of the kind about six miles ahead and a little to our right."

There certainly was a channel through the ice at the point indicated by the professor, but whether it was a true channel, or merely a *cul de sac*, they were for the moment unable to decide. On nearing it to within a mile, however, they found it to be the latter; but about a couple of miles beyond it another streak of water was seen extending, unbroken, as far as the eye could reach. For this they steered, and in a very few minutes afterwards the *Flying Fish* was once more afloat, with her water-chambers full and her air-compressor working to the full extent of its power.

The hawser being this time temporarily secured in such a manner as to render a repetition of their late accident impossible, and the entire party being, moreover, safely ensconced in the pilot-house, there was no hesitation about again pressing the ship forward at full speed, the channel, luckily, being straight enough to allow of this; and very soon the group of icebergs in which the unfortunate barque was entangled once more appeared in view. Mildmay was at the helm, with the professor standing by the engines; but Sir Reginald and the colonel no sooner saw the bergs than they seized their telescopes and began at once to look out for the barque.

At first they could see nothing of her, but presently she glided into view from behind an intervening berg, and a single glance was sufficient to assure them that another five minutes would decide her fate. She had gradually set down into the triangular extremity of the bight in which she was embayed, so that every tack she made became shorter than the one preceding it, and very soon the water space would become so circumscribed as to leave no room for her to manoeuvre. But this was not the worst feature of the case. As desperate diseases are sometimes combated with desperate remedies, so in her desperate condition the hazardous and almost hopeless expedient of berthing her alongside one of the edges of the floe might have been attempted. But this last resource was denied to the despairing seamen, from the fact that two enormous bergs, the vanguard of the fleet, had already reached the edge of the floe, on opposite sides of the bay, to windward of the entrapped barque, and were rapidly rasping their way down toward the apex of the triangle where the whaler was already shooting into stays for what must evidently be her last tack. This would be so short that she could scarcely fail to miss stays on her next attempt, when she would drift helplessly down into the corner of the bight, and be ground out of existence by the berg which first happened to reach that point.

It was at this critical moment that a cry of dismay arose simultaneously from the lips of the party in the *Flying Fish's* pilot-house. A slight turn in the channel had revealed to them the appalling fact that it, also, terminated in a *cul de sac*, a neck of solid ice, some fifty yards in width, dividing it from the open water in which the barque was still battling for her life.

What was to be done? There was no time to discuss the question; but a happy inspiration flashed through the baronet's brain.

"We must *leap* the barrier!" he exclaimed.

"Right! I understand," was the professor's brief reply; and, turning the compressed air into the water-chambers, he forced out the water and succeeded in raising the sharp nose of the *Flying Fish* just above the level of the floe a single instant before she reached it.

It was a tremendous risk to run—one which would never have been thought of in cold blood, as the ship was rushing forward at full speed, and there was no knowing what might happen; but the sympathies of the party were now so fully aroused by the awful peril of the barque—which, in the midst of all her danger, was still gaily dressed in flags—that they never paused to think of the possible consequences, but sent the ship at the barrier as a huntsman sends his horse to a desperate leap. For an infinitesimal fraction of time the four adventurous travellers were thrilled with a feeling of wild exultation as they held their breath and braced themselves for the expected shock. Then the smooth polished hull of the *Flying Fish* met the ice, and, rising like a hunter to the leap, slid smoothly, and without the slightest jar, up on to the surface of the floe, across the narrow barrier, and into the water beyond.

"Stop her!" shouted Mildmay, checking the exultant cheer which rose to the lips of his companions. "Sheer as close alongside the barque as you can go, Sir Reginald, and give me a chance to get our heaving line on board. Then, as soon as I wave my hand, go ahead gently until you have brought a strain upon the hawser, when you may increase the speed to about twelve knots—not more, or you will tear the windlass out of the barque. Steer straight out between those two bergs, and remember that *moments* are now precious."

With these words the lieutenant hurried out on deck and made his way aft, where he at once began to clear away the heaving line and make ready for a cast.

The engines meanwhile had been stopped in obedience to Mildmay's command, his companions intuitively recognising that he was the man to cope with the present emergency, and the *Flying Fish* answering the helm, which the baronet, an experienced yachtsman, was deftly manipulating, shot cleverly up along the weather side of the barque.

"Look out for our line, lads!" hailed Mildmay to the crew of the vessel, who were gaping in open-mouthed astonishment at the extraordinary apparition which had thus abruptly put in an appearance alongside them.

"Ay, ay, sir; heave!" answered one smart fellow, who, notwithstanding his surprise, still seemed to have his wits about him. Mildmay hove the line with all a seaman's skill, and a couple of bights settled down round the neck and shoulders of the expectant tar.

"Haul in, and throw the eye of the hawser over your windlass bitts," ordered Mildmay; "we will soon have you clear of your present pickle."

"Thank you, sir," hailed the skipper; "haul in smart there, for'ard, and take a turn *anywhere*; those bergs are driving down upon us mighty fast."

With a joyous "hurrah" at the timely arrival of such unexpected assistance, the men roused the hawser on board, threw the eye over the bitts, passed two or three turns of the slack round the barrel of the windlass, and adjusted the rope in a "fair-lead" with lightning rapidity. Mildmay, who was intently watching their movements, waved his hand as a signal to the baronet the instant he saw that the hawser was properly fast on board the barque, and the *Flying Fish* immediately began to glide ahead. The baronet was evidently bent on retrieving his character and making up for his past carelessness, for he handled his strangely-shaped vessel with most consummate skill, bringing the strain upon the hawser very gradually, and, when he had done so, coaxing the barque's head round until her nose and that of the *Flying Fish* pointed straight toward the rapidly narrowing passage between the bergs. Then, indeed, the thin but tough hawser straightened out taut as a bowstring between the two vessels as the baronet sent his engines powerfully ahead; the barque's windlass bitts creaked and groaned with the tremendous strain to which they were suddenly subjected; a foaming surge gathered and hissed under her bows, and as her harassed crew, active as wild-cats, skipped about the decks busily letting go and clewing up, away went the two craft toward the closing gap.

It was like steering into the jaws of death. The two bergs were by this time within a bare cable's-length of the *Flying Fish's* conical stem; and as they swept irresistibly onward, their pinnacled summits towering five hundred feet into the air, their rugged sides rasping horribly along the edges of the floe with an awful crushing, grinding sound, and their contiguous sides approaching each other more and more nearly every moment, there was not a man on either of those two vessels who did not hold his breath and stand fascinated in awestricken suspense, gazing upon those menacing walls of ice and waiting for the shock which should be the herald of their destruction.

Rapidly—yet slower than a snail's pace, as it seemed to those anxious men— the space narrowed between the bergs and the ships; the grinding crash and crackle of the ice grew momentarily more loud and distracting; the freezing wind from the bergs cut their faces like an invisible razor as it swept down upon them in sudden powerful gusts, apparently intent upon retarding their progress until the last hope of escape should be cut off; the gigantic icy cliffs lowered more and more threateningly down upon them; and at last, when the feeling of doubt and suspense was at its highest, the *Flying Fish* entered the gap. The channel had by this time become so narrow that for the *Flying Fish* to pass through it seemed utterly impossible; indeed, it looked as though there remained scarcely room for the barque with her much narrower beam; and as the towering crystal walls closed in upon them every man present felt that the final moment had now come. Everything depended upon Sir Reginald; if at this critical instant his nerve failed him there was nothing but quick destruction and a horrible death for every man there. But the baronet's nerve did *not* fail him. With a face pale and teeth clenched with excitement, but with a steady pulse and an unquailing eye, he stood with one hand on the tiller and the other on the engine lever, guiding his ship exactly midway through the narrow gorge; and precisely at the right moment, when the *Flying Fish's* sides were actually grazing the ice on either side, he increased the pressure of his hand upon the lever, the engines revolved a shade more rapidly, and the flying ship slid through the narrowest part of the pass uninjured, but escaping by the merest hair's breadth.

But would the barque also get through? She was fully two hundred feet astern of the *Flying Fish*, and the bergs were revolving on their own centres in such a manner that ere many seconds were past they must inevitably come together with a force which would literally annihilate whatever might happen to be between them. And as for the barque—the way in which her bows were burying themselves in the hissing wave that foamed and surged about her cutwater, and the terrified looks of her crew as they glanced, now aloft at the formidable bergs, and now at the straining hawser—from which they stood warily aloof lest it should part, and in so doing inflict upon some of them a deadly injury—told the baronet that he must not increase by a single ounce the strain upon the rope, lest something should give way on board the whaler and leave her there helpless in the very grip of those awful floating mountains of ice.

It was a race between the bergs and the barque; and Mildmay, standing there by the after rail, told himself, as he breathlessly watched the progress of events, that the bergs would win. The contiguous sides of these monsters were slightly concave in shape; and whilst the whaler, still some dozen yards or so within the passage had a foot or two of clear water on either side of her, the projecting extremities of the bergs had neared each other to within a distance of twenty feet, or some five feet less than the breadth of the imprisoned ship.

Suddenly a tremendous crash was heard, and the party on board the *Flying Fish* looked to see the unfortunate barque collapse and crumple into a shapeless mass of splintered wood before their eyes. But, to their inexpressible astonishment, nothing of the sort occurred. There was a reverberating sound as of muffled thunder, which echoed and re-echoed in the confined space between the two bergs; a series of tremendous splashes just astern of the whaler; the bergs recoiled violently from each other; the baronet, more by instinct than anything else, threw the engine lever still further forward, and before anyone had time even to draw a breath of relief, the apparently doomed vessel was dragged, with a foaming surge heaped up round her bows as high as the figurehead, out from the reopened portal and clear of all danger a single instant before the two gigantic masses of ice again closed in upon each other with a horrible grinding *crunch* which must have been audible for miles.

It was not until the barque had been dragged, almost bows under, some fifty or sixty fathoms away from the still grinding and rasping bergs, that her crew were able to realise the astounding fact of their safety, but when they did so they sent up a wild cheer which was as distinct an expression of gratitude to God for their deliverance as ever issued from human lips. Their escape, though it could easily be accounted for, might indeed well be called miraculous, for at the moment when their last hope was extinguished—apparently their last chance gone—two huge overhanging projections on the summits of the bergs had come into contact with such violence that both the projecting masses of ice had become detached and had gone thundering down into the water, fortunately at some few yards' distance astern of the whaler, and the shock of collision had been so great as to compel the momentary recoil of the bergs, with the fortunate result already described.

Directly it was seen that the barque had indeed escaped, the *Flying Fish's* engines were slowed down to their lowest speed, and the whaler, relieved of the enormous tugging strain upon her, once more floated on her normal water-lines. The two craft were now in comparatively open water, the channel being between two and three miles wide, and still widening ahead of them, with a few small bergs in their vicinity, it is true, but with no ice at hand likely to cause them immediate peril. The barque was towed to windward of all these, and then the baronet stopped the *Flying Fish* altogether, and hailed the skipper of the whaler to know whither he was bound. Upon this the worthy man lowered one of his boats and pulled alongside his strange consort to return thanks in person for his recent rescue.

He was a very fine specimen of a seaman, not very tall, but bluff and hearty-looking in his manifold wraps surmounted by a dreadnought pilot jacket, sealskin cap, and water boots reaching to his thighs; and it was amusing to see his look of surprise as he came up the *Flying Fish's* side-ladder and stepped in upon her roomy deck unencumbered by anything but the pilot-house. The four companions of course stepped out on deck in a body to meet him, and after they had all heartily shaken hands with him and deprecatingly received his thanks for the important service rendered in the rescue of his ship from the ice, he was invited to accompany them below to cement the newly-made acquaintance over a glass of grog. And if the worthy seaman was surprised at the exterior of the strange craft he was now visiting, how much greater was his astonishment when he entered her magnificent saloons, revelled in their grateful warmth, and looked round bewildered upon the rich carpets, the handsome furniture, the superb pictures and statuary, and the choice *bric à brac*, all glowing under the brilliant but cunningly modified electric light. And if he was surprised at all these unwonted sights, his astonishment may be imagined when he was informed that the four refined and cultured men who welcomed him so hospitably, constituted, with the exception of the cook and the steward, the entire crew of the immense craft, and that the owner of all the magnificence he beheld had dared the terrors of the polar regions solely by way of pastime.

"Well, gentlemen," he remarked, "it's an old saying that tastes differ, and what you've just told me proves it. I've been a whaler for nigh on to twenty-five years, but it has been a case of necessity, not choice, with me; and after the first two or three years of the life—when the novelty had worn off a bit, as you may say—I've looked forward to only one thing, and that is the scraping together of enough money to retire and get quit of it all for ever. I took to it first as a hand before the mast, and have regularly passed through all the grades—boat-steerer, third, second, and chief mate, master, and at last owner of my own ship, always with the same object ahead. And when, little more than a year ago, I put the savings of a lifetime into the purchase of the old *Walrus* there, I thought that the dream of my life was soon to be realised, and that one trip more to the nor'ard would bring me in a sufficiency to last me the remainder of my days, and enable me to enjoy 'em in the company of my wife and my little daughter. God bless the child! if she's still alive she's five years old to-day."

"Ah!" interrupted Mildmay, "then that, I suppose, accounts for the flags flying on board you, and the meaning of which we were so utterly unable to guess?"

"That's it, sir," was the reply. "I 'dressed ship' at eight o'clock this morning in honour of my little Florrie's birthday, and I hadn't the heart to haul down the flags even when we found ourselves in such a precious pickle amongst the ice yonder. I thought that if so be it was God's will that we was to go, we might as well go with the buntin' still flying in Florrie's honour as not."

"And what success have you met with, captain?" asked Sir Reginald.

"Precious little, sir. We've been out now more'n a twelvemonth, and we've only killed three fish in all that time. Got jammed up here in the ice all last winter. I stayed in hopes of doin' something in the sealing line, and only got some three hundred skins after all. It's been a bad speculation for me. An old friend of mine came this way the year before last, and, the season being an open one and not much ice about, he reached as far north as Baffin's Bay and through Jones' Sound, fillin' his ship with oil and bone in a single season. He was lucky enough to hit upon a spot where the sea was fairly alive with whales, and he filled the ship right up in that very spot. The fish seemed tame, as though they hadn't been interfered with for years; and bein' an old friend, as I said before, he gave me the latitude and longitude of the place as a great secret, and I've been trying to reach the spot ever since we came north, but have been kept back by the ice and the contrary winds. If I could get there, even now, it would make the trip profitable enough to serve my purpose; but I see no chance of it, and the men are getting disheartened."

"Never mind, captain, cheer up; all may yet be well," exclaimed the baronet. "We can't drag your ship *over* the ice, but if there is only a passage for her we can drag her *through* it, and for little Florrie's sake we will. If it is in our power to get you to the spot you wish to reach, you shall go there. Now, as the present open water affords an opportunity too good to be lost, return to your ship, secure our hawser in such a way that we may put a big strain upon it without damaging the vessel, and send a trustworthy hand aloft into the crow's-nest to look out for the best channels. We will tow you to the northward as long as a channel can be found through the ice, and at seven o'clock I hope you will give us the pleasure of your company on board here to dinner, when we will drink 'many happy returns of the day' to Florrie in the best champagne the *Flying Fish's* cellar affords."

The captain of the whaler returned to his own ship in a state of such mingled astonishment and elation that his people were at first inclined to think he had suddenly gone demented. However, the order which he gave them to secure the towing hawser in such a manner as would enable the ship to withstand a heavy strain was intelligible enough; it told them that, with the assistance of their strange rescuers, a supreme effort was now to be made to reach those prolific fishing-grounds which had from the first been the goal of their voyage; and that, best of all, that effort was to be unaccompanied by any of the usual harassing labour of working the ship to windward through the ice, and they set to with a will. A sufficient length of the hawser was hauled on board to enable them to take a couple of turns round the barrel of the windlass and two more round the heel of the foremast, the eye of the hawser being further secured by tackles to every ring-bolt in the ship capable of bearing a good substantial strain; and then, the skipper himself going aloft to the crow's-nest, the signal was given for the *Flying Fish* to go ahead.

CHAPTER TEN
THE "HUMBOLDT" GLACIER

The two ships were at this time floating in a tolerably broad expanse of open water; but at a distance of some seven miles ahead the pack-ice stretched, apparently unbroken, across their track for miles. The skipper of the whaler, however, shouted down to them from his elevated perch the intelligence that a somewhat intricate but continuous channel extended through this ice in a northerly direction as far as the eye could reach. Toward this channel, then, away they went at a speed of something like sixteen knots per hour, the barque with her string of colours still fluttering bravely in defiance of the adverse gale, and the *Flying Fish* with the white ensign of the Royal Yacht Squadron, of which Sir Reginald was a member, streaming from her ensign staff in honour of little Florrie. It was a strange sight, even in that region of fantastic phantasmagoria, to see the two ships, one of which, moreover, wore such an unaccustomed shape, dashing rapidly along through the black foam-flecked water, with ice in every conceivable form heaped and piled around them, and their bright-hued flags fluttering against the dark and dismal background of a stormy sky; and the skipper of the whaler possesses to this day a spirited water-colour sketch of the scene, executed on the spot by the colonel, which he exhibits with becoming pride whenever he relates the story of his wonderful escape from the threatening icebergs.

Half an hour later they entered the channel through the ice. Narrow and tortuous at first, it gradually widened out, and, after a journey of some fourteen or fifteen miles, turned sharply off in a direction almost due west. About the same time the gale broke, the sun made his appearance through the rifted clouds, and by seven o'clock that evening, at which hour Florrie's father duly put in an appearance on board the *Flying Fish*, the engines having been temporarily stopped to receive him, they found themselves in open water, or rather in a straight channel some twelve miles in width and entirely free from ice, with a clear sky overhead, a light easterly wind blowing, and the evening sun lighting up the snow-clad peaks of the extensive island called North Devon. An hour later, dinner having been postponed on account of their near proximity to the land, the two vessels entered a commodious natural harbour called Hyde Bay, and anchored there for the night, in order to give the whaler's exhausted crew an opportunity to snatch a few hours of much-needed rest.

The master of the *Walrus*, who answered, by the way, to the name of Hudson, though only a bluff hearty seaman, and somewhat shy for the first half-hour or so in such unaccustomed company as that of his four well-bred easy-mannered entertainers, gradually thawed out under the genial influence of the baronet's champagne, and proved himself a tolerably well informed and by no means disagreeable companion. He possessed a fund of interesting anecdote and information with respect to the peculiarities of the region his hosts were now visiting for the first time, and imparted to them many valuable hints as to the best means of protecting themselves from the ice; but, as they did not see fit to inform him of the aerial capabilities of the *Flying Fish*, he laughed to scorn their project of reaching the North Pole, which he assured them most solemnly was an utter impossibility. They duly drank the unconscious Florrie's health, treated her father to some excellent music, gave him a file of the latest newspapers they had brought with them, and sent him back to his own ship at midnight a thoroughly happy man.

On the following morning about half-past eight, whilst the party on board the *Flying Fish* were sitting down to breakfast, the sound of oars was heard close alongside; and a minute later Captain Hudson, ushered by George, made his appearance in the saloon. He was in a great hurry and almost breathlessly explained that he had come on board to repeat his thanks and those of his crew for their rescue of the previous day, and to say "Good-bye," as he was about to weigh and proceed to sea in chase of a large school of whales which had just been seen spouting at a distance of some twelve miles in the offing. The baronet was good-natured enough to offer to tow him to the scene of action; but this service he gratefully declined, saying that there was a fine fair wind blowing and that his anchor was already a-trip. The party therefore shook hands heartily with him, wishing him "Good luck," and he departed, leaving Sir Reginald and his friends to finish their meal at their leisure.

An hour later the *Flying Fish* also weighed and stood out to sea after the *Walrus*, now nearly hull down, to witness the sport.

The engines had scarcely begun to move when the whaler was seen to heave to; and when the *Flying Fish* ranged up alongside her, some ten minutes afterwards, three whale-boats were in the water and pulling lustily toward a school of some forty whales which were lazily sporting, apparently quite unconscious of danger, about two miles away.

"Those whales do not appear in the least alarmed at the presence of the boats," remarked Mildmay; "evidently they have not been chased for a considerable period. If we only had the means of killing a few, now, what a splendid opportunity there would be to do that poor fellow Hudson a good turn."

"Well thought of!" exclaimed the professor. "Follow me, gentlemen; we can do our friend a good turn, and, at the same time, test the powers of our large-bore rifles with explosive shells for big game."

The party hurried below to the armoury, and each selected one of the weapons indicated by the professor, providing himself at the same time with a supply of cartridges from a large chest near at hand.

The rifles were truly formidable, being repeating weapons each capable of firing ten shots without reloading. The barrels were not very long, measuring only three feet from breech to muzzle, but they were of one-and-a-half-inch bore and fired a conical shell four and a half inches in length. Notwithstanding their somewhat ponderous appearance they were very light, being constructed of aethereum throughout.

When the party returned to the deck they had the satisfaction of seeing that, though each of the whale-boats had succeeded in fastening to a fish, the remainder of the school manifested very little alarm, the stricken whales having started to "run" in different directions and quite away from their companions.

The *Flying Fish* was moved as gently as possible into the very centre of the herd, the huge monsters taking no apparent notice of her, and perhaps mistaking her for one of themselves. They were swimming lazily about, rolling over on their sides until their pectoral fins appeared above the surface, and occasionally throwing themselves entirely out of the water.

The engines being stopped the four sportsmen took up their positions, two on each side of the deck, and, having loaded their weapons, waited for a favourable opportunity to use them.

The baronet was the first to fire. He had selected for his victim a huge bull, fully eighty feet in length, and this creature he patiently watched, hoping for an opportunity to inflict a fatal wound. It soon came. The animal rolled lazily over on its right side, exposing the whole of its left fin, and before it could recover itself Sir Reginald had levelled and discharged his piece. There was a very faint puff of thin fleecy vapour, but no report or sound of any kind save the by no means loud click of the hammer, above which could be distinctly heard the dull thud of the shell. The whale shuddered visibly at the blow, and made as though about to "sound" or dive; but before it had power to do so the shell must have exploded, for the immense creature made a sudden violent writhing motion, half leapt out of the water, and rolled over on its side, dead. The professor scored the next success, closely followed by the colonel, Lieutenant Mildmay signalising his first essay with the new arm by making a palpable miss, much to his disgust. His failure, however, taught him a valuable lesson, and he succeeded in killing two whales before either of the others had been able to secure another shot. In ten minutes eight whales had been killed, and the professor, who was very rigid in his objection to the wanton sacrifice of life, then suggested that probably as many had been killed as the whaler could successfully deal with at one time, especially as the boats now had signals flying which showed that each had killed her fish. The *Flying Fish* was accordingly ranged up close alongside the *Walrus*, and the baronet hailed:

"*Walrus* ahoy! how many fish can you 'cut in' at one operation?"

"I wish I had the chance of trying my hand upon half a dozen," was the reply, given, the baronet thought, in rather a sulky tone.

"Well," returned Sir Reginald, "there are eight which we have killed and three taken by your boats, making eleven altogether. Can you handle any more? because, if so, we will kill them for you; but, if not, we think it best not to disturb them further."

"Do you mean to say that you've killed those fish on my account, then?" asked Hudson with great animation.

"To be sure we did. You surely did not suppose that we wanted them for ourselves, did you?"

The whaling skipper muttered a few unintelligible words to himself, and then shouted back in unmistakably hearty tones:

"Thank'ee, gentlemen, thank'ee with all my heart. That's another favour I'm in your debt. That being the case, I think, if it's all the same to you, I'd rather that the rest of the school be left to go their ways in peace. I don't want them to be frightened; and eleven fish is as much as we can well handle at one time."

"In that case, then," returned Sir Reginald, "we will wish you 'Good-bye,' and a prosperous voyage."

"Thank'ee, gentlemen; the same to you, and best thanks for all favours," replied Hudson.

And with mutual hand-wavings and dipping of colours the two craft separated, the *Walrus* bearing up to intercept her boats, and the *Flying Fish* heading northward at a speed of about twenty knots.

For about a couple of hours the adventurous voyagers were able to maintain that speed; but toward noon they found themselves once more surrounded by ice; and they had no choice but either to materially reduce their speed and slowly thread their way through narrow and tortuous channels, or once more take flight into the air. They chose the latter alternative; and for the next two hours the flying ship sped northward through Smith's Sound, for the most part over an unbroken field of pack-ice which, to any ordinary vessel, would have opposed an utterly impassable barrier. At two o'clock in the afternoon, however, the Greenland shore suddenly trended to the north-eastward; and after following it for a short time the ice once more began to be intersected with water channels, short and narrow at first, but wider as they proceeded, until at length they found themselves once more able to descend in a water lane some four miles in width.

"And now," said the professor, as they were nearing a bold rocky headland on their starboard bow, "we are about to be introduced to one of *the* sights *par excellence* of the Arctic regions."

"What is it?" was the question which burst simultaneously from the lips of his three companions.

"Wait and see," answered the professor, nodding mysteriously.

Sure enough, the moment that the *Flying Fish* rounded the point a magnificent spectacle burst upon the travellers' enraptured gaze. It was neither more nor less than an immense cliff of the clearest crystal ice, towering some three hundred feet above the water's edge, and extending so far northward along the coast that its northern extremity lay far below the horizon. It was the magnificent Humboldt Glacier. The afternoon sun was shining full upon its rugged face, causing the enormous mass to flash and gleam like a gigantic diamond. As they coasted slowly along, at a distance of about half a mile from its face, the dazzling flashes of light were reproduced one after the other, changing rapidly from one colour to another through every conceivable tint of the rainbow, until the beholders' eyes fairly ached with the contemplation of so much splendour, all of which was reflected with the most charming variation in the mirror-like surface of the deep still water below. The wind had died away to a dead calm, as if to give the bold explorers an opportunity of witnessing this unrivalled sight to the best advantage; and every now and then the still air resounded with the sharp rifle-like *crack* which told that, though apparently so motionless and solid, hidden forces were at work within the heart of the glacier, slowly but surely tending to its ultimate dismemberment.

Suddenly a crashing report, so loud that it resembled the simultaneous discharge of a whole army of rifles, smote upon their ears; and then, as they stood in a trance of breathless expectation, wondering what was about to happen, an immense section of the icy cliff was seen to be in motion. Slowly at first, but with ever-increasing rapidity, it slid downward into the water, with a continuous roaring reverberating crash, to which even the awful pealing of thunder was as nothing, until in a wild turmoil of madly leaping and foaming surges it disappeared entirely below the water. The sea rushed irresistibly after it from all sides, pouring like a foaming cataract into the hollow watery basin it had left, and dragging the *Flying Fish* helplessly toward the yawning vortex. Then the inward rush suddenly ceased; a gleaming white crest of ice reappeared above the foam, and with a mighty upward rush and a resounding roar the gigantic submerged mass once more upreared itself above the again maddened waters, swaying heavily to and fro, whilst a thousand gleaming torrents poured down its sparkling sides. And, as a fitting *finale* to the thrilling spectacle, a huge wall of water suddenly heaped itself up about the rocking mass and began to rush rapidly outward in an ever-widening circle, its towering crest surmounted by a roaring curling fringe of snow-white foam. Increasing in height and in speed as it advanced, it rapidly attained an altitude of fully sixty feet, bearing down upon the *Flying Fish* so menacingly that, for a few seconds, the party in the pilot-house stood paralysed with consternation, expecting nothing less than that they would be helplessly overwhelmed. The first to recover his presence of mind was Mildmay, who, springing to the rods which controlled the air-valves, pressed them powerfully down, throwing them all wide open and at once ejecting from the hull both the water and the compressed air, and causing the ship to rise until she floated lightly as an air-bubble on the water. He then injected a dense body of vapour into the air and water chambers, completing the vacuum; and the ship rose into the air just in time to avoid the gigantic surge, which went hissing and roaring close beneath them with a power and fury which fully revealed to them the extent of the disturbance from which they had so narrowly escaped. Other surges followed in quick rotation; but each was less formidable than its predecessor, and in another ten minutes the surface had once more subsided into a state of comparative calm.

As the *Flying Fish* once more settled down upon the water and the air-pump was set going, the professor turned to his companions and remarked:

"We have especial reason to congratulate ourselves and each other, gentlemen, for we have to-day not only looked upon the magnificent Humboldt Glacier under most highly favourable conditions, but we have been also permitted to witness that even rarer sight, *the birth of an iceberg*!"

They had indeed witnessed the birth of an iceberg, and that too of quite unusual size; for, as soon as they dared, they approached the newly fallen mass of ice closely enough to make a tolerably accurate measurement of it; and they found that it was of nearly square shape, measuring fully three-quarters of a mile along each of its four sides, and towering to an average height of about three hundred and fifteen feet above the surface of the water. The visible portion of the berg constituted, however, only a small portion of its entire bulk, since fresh-water ice floating in salt water shows above the surface only one-eighth of its entire depth. This enormous berg, therefore, must have measured in its entirety about four thousand feet square by about two thousand five hundred feet deep! And its weight must have approximated closely upon two thousand millions of tons! Bergs of equal, or even greater dimensions, have occasionally been encountered in the Arctic seas; but how few of earth's inhabitants have ever been privileged to witness the disruption of so enormous a mass from its parent glacier!

After witnessing so thrilling a spectacle as this—probably the grandest and most impressive which the Arctic regions can exhibit—it is perhaps not to be wondered at that even the beauties of the glacier itself appeared somewhat tame and uninteresting to the voyagers. But their interest was once more awakened when, having at length coasted along the face of the glacier for a distance of not less than *sixty miles*, they reached its northern extremity and found the succeeding Greenland coast to be magnificently picturesque, the greenstone and sandstone cliffs in some cases towering abruptly from the water's edge to a height of a thousand feet or more, not in a smooth unbroken face, or even with the usual everyday rugged aspect of a rocky precipice, but presenting to the enraptured eye an ever-varying perspective of ruined buttresses, pinnacles, arches, and even more fantastic architectural semblances. In one spot which caused them to pause in sheer admiration, the crumbling *débris* at the foot of the cliff had shaped itself into the likeness of a huge causeway such as might have been constructed by one of the giants of fabulous times, leading into a deep wild rocky gorge rich in soft purple shadows, at the further edge of which rose a gigantic rock hewn by the storms of ten thousand winters into the exact similitude of a castle flanked by three lofty detached towers all bathed in the dreamy roseate haze of the evening sunshine. And, somewhat further on, they came to a single greenstone cliff the skyline of which was boldly chiselled into the likeness of the ruined ramparts of an extensive city, whilst at its northern extremity, at the edge of a deep ravine, a solitary column nearly five hundred feet high, and standing upon a base or pedestal nearly three hundred feet high, shot straight and smooth up into the deep blue of the northern sky.

Tearing themselves unwillingly away from this region of weird enchantment, the voyagers pushed onward along Kennedy and Robeson Channels, sometimes winding their way through intricate water lanes in the ice, and sometimes skimming lightly a few yards above the surface of the solid pack, until they reached the latitude of 82 degrees 30 minutes North, when the land abruptly trended away to their right and left, and they found themselves hovering over an immense field of pack-ice which extended in an unbroken mass as far northward as the eye could reach.

Up to the present, from the time of their passing Disko Island, the voyagers had seen plenty of seals and walruses, with an occasional white bear, a few Arctic foxes, a herd or two of reindeer, and even a few specimens of the elk and musk-ox, to say nothing of birds, such as snow-geese, eider and long-tailed ducks, sea-eagles, divers, auks, and gulls. Moreover, they had been favoured with, on the whole, exceptionally fine weather—due as much as anything, perhaps, to the fact that they had been fortunate enough to enter the Arctic circle during the prevalence of a "spell" of fine weather, and that they had accomplished in a very few days a distance which it would occupy an ordinary craft months of weary toil to cover. But, on passing the edge of this gigantic ice barrier, they left all life behind them; even the very gulls—which had followed them in clouds whenever the speed of the *Flying Fish* was low enough to permit of such a proceeding—after wheeling agitatedly about the ship for a few minutes with discordant screams, as of warning to the travellers not to venture into so vast and gloomy a solitude, forsook them and retraced their way to the southward. The weather, too, changed, the sky becoming overcast with a pall of dull grey snow—laden cloud accompanied by a dismal murky atmosphere and a temperature of ten degrees below zero. The wind sighed and moaned over the icy waste; but, excepting for this dreary and depressing sound, there was absolute silence, the silence of a dead world.

The ice bore at first the same appearance as all the other ice which they had hitherto encountered, but by the time that they had advanced a distance of thirty miles into the frozen desert they became conscious of a change. The hummocks were not so lofty as heretofore, the hollows between them having the appearance of being to a considerable extent filled up with hard frozen snow; the ice itself, too, instead of being a pure white, was tinged with yellow of the hue of very old ivory; the sharp angles, also, were all worn away as if by long-continued abrasion; the ice, in fact, bore unmistakable evidence of extreme age.

At the professor's suggestion a pause was made and a descent effected, in order that he might carefully investigate the nature of the ice; and, warmly clad in furs, the entire party left the ship for this purpose.

"It is as I feared," said von Schalckenberg, after they had toiled painfully over the surface for some time; "we have reached the region of paleocrystic or ancient ice; and my cherished theory of an open sea about the North Pole vanishes into thin air. Look at this ice here, where a portion of the original hummock still remains bare—it is yellow and rotten, not with the rottenness which precedes a thaw, but with extreme age. See, it crumbles at a kick or a blow, but the fragments do not melt; it is years—possibly *ages*—since this ice was water. And look at the edges of the blocks; they are rounded and worn away by the constant abrading action of the wind, the snow, the hail, and possibly the rain, which has beaten upon them through unnumbered years. It is no wonder that this is a lifeless solitude; there is nothing here capable of sustaining the life of even the meanest insect. Let us return to the ship, my friends, and hasten over this part of our journey; we shall meet with nothing worthy of interest until we reach the Pole, which itself will probably prove to be merely an undistinguishable spot in just such a waste as this."

The professor was, however mistaken; a most interesting discovery awaited them at no very great distance ahead. They returned to the ship oppressed with a vague feeling of melancholy foreboding for which they could not account, but which was doubtless attributable to the gloomy cheerless aspect of their surroundings, and, releasing the ship from the hold of her grip-anchors, resumed their way northward at the *Flying Fish's* utmost speed.

Half an hour later, however, they suddenly checked their flight and diverged a mile to the eastward of their former course to examine an object which Mildmay's quick eye had detected. The object—or objects rather, for there were two of them—proved to be short poles or spars about twenty-five feet apart, projecting about twelve feet out of the ice, and surmounted by the skeleton framework of what seemed to have been at one time small bulwarked platforms. Wondering what they could possibly be, and by whom placed in so out-of-the-way a region, but thinking they might possibly mark cairns or places of deposit inclosing the records of some long-lost expedition, they resolved to stop and institute a thorough examination.

They were fortunate enough to find a smooth and level spot suitable for grounding the *Flying Fish* upon, at a distance of barely a quarter of a mile from the objects of their interest; and it being by that time six o'clock in the evening, and too late to do any good before dinner, they secured the ship there for the night—taking the precaution of fully weighting her down with compressed air in addition to mooring her firmly to the ice by her four grip-anchors. It was a most happy inspiration which impelled them to take this precaution; for when they arose next morning a terrific gale from the northward was blowing, accompanied by a heavy ceaseless fall of snow; and, well secured as the ship was both by her weight and by her anchors, she fairly trembled at times with the violence of the blast. Had she been dependent only upon her anchors and her own unassisted weight—which the reader will remember was very trifling notwithstanding her immense dimensions—she would infallibly have been whirled away like a bubble upon the wings of the gale. The highly-compressed air, however, held her securely down upon her icy bed, and, beyond imparting an occasional tremor, as already mentioned, the tempest, fierce as it was, had no power to move her.

In such terrible weather it was of course useless to think of pursuing their investigations; it would, indeed, have been the sheerest madness to have attempted to face the furious gale, with its deadly cold and the blinding whirling snow. The travellers were therefore compelled to spend an inactive day. For this, however, they were by no means sorry; they had been keeping rather late hours since entering the Arctic circle, and this interval of inaction afforded them an opportunity of securing their arrears of rest. Besides this there were sketches to complete, and a thousand little odd matters to attend to—to such an extent, indeed, that when they once began work they wondered at their own thoughtlessness in not having attended to them before. Thus employed, with occasional interludes of meditative gazing out upon the ceaseless whirling rush of the snow, the day passed rapidly and pleasantly away, wound up by an hour or two of vocal and instrumental music after dinner. They retired early to their warm comfortable state-rooms that night, and were lulled to sweet dreamless slumber by the howling of the gale outside.

The four following days were spent in the same manner—the gale lasting all that time with unabated fury, accompanied by an almost ceaseless fall of snow. But on the fifth day the weather moderated; the snow ceased, or at all events fell only intermittently; the wind backed round and blew from the south-west; and the exterior temperature, which during the gale had fallen to thirty-three degrees below zero, rose twenty degrees. The sky was still overcast and lowering, it is true, and the cold was still intense. But notwithstanding this the weather, compared with that of the preceding five days, seemed positively fine; and, wrapping themselves up in their warmest clothing, and arming themselves with pick and shovel, they set out to discover if possible what lay concealed beneath the two queer-looking poles.

CHAPTER ELEVEN
AN INTERESTING RELIC

They issued from the ship through the trap-door in her bottom; and no sooner did they find themselves in the open air than an almost uncontrollable impulse seized them to go back again. The contrast between the warm comfortable temperature of the ship's interior and the bitter piercing cold without was so great that at first the latter felt quite unendurable. They, however, persevered; and, after perhaps ten minutes of intense suffering, the severe exercise of scrambling over the rotten slippery hummocks somewhat restored their impeded circulation, and they began to feel that, perhaps, after all, they might be able to do something toward the execution of their self-imposed task. The mere act of breathing, however, continued to be exceedingly painful; and when they at length reached the spot of which they were in search, they were able to fully realise, for the first time in their lives, the incredible difficulties attendant upon the exploration of the regions within the polar circles.

On a nearer inspection of the two poles they proved to be stout spars about the thickness of a man's leg; and, from the appearance in each of a sort of sheave-hole, Lieutenant Mildmay declared his conviction that they were the masts of a small ship. They were very rotten, however, and, if Mildmay's surmise was indeed correct, the craft must have been under the ice for a very long time. The mere suggestion was enough to fully arouse their curiosity; and, forgetful for the moment of the intense cold, to which they were already in a measure growing accustomed, they set to work with a will plying pick-axe and shovel upon the ice with such small dexterity as they possessed.

The task to which they had devoted themselves was, after all, not a very difficult one, the ice, especially that of ancient formation, yielding readily before the vigorous strokes of their picks; and it soon became evident that they could work to greater advantage by dividing themselves into two gangs of two each; one gang breaking up the ice with the pick, and the other shovelling away the débris. The low temperature, however, made the work very exhausting; and by lunch time they had only succeeded in excavating a hole some twenty-five feet long—or the distance between the two masts—by six feet wide and four feet deep. They had widened this excavation by a couple of feet and sunk it some four feet deeper by six o'clock that evening; and then they knocked off work for the day, returning to the *Flying Fish* stiff, and exhausted with their unwonted exertions, but with more voracious appetites than they ever remembered experiencing before.

In this way they laboured day after day for ten days; being greatly hindered in their operations by frequent showers of snow, which filled up their excavation almost as rapidly as they made it, until, beginning to lose patience at their slow progress, they resolved to run a little risk, and the professor was induced to employ a minute portion of his explosive compound in blowing away the sides of the pit to a sufficient extent to allow of the snow drifting out with the wind instead of lodging in the bottom. This engineering feat was successfully accomplished without apparent damage to the object they sought to bring to light; and, thus encouraged, they further cautiously employed the compound in breaking up the ice, with the triumphant result that, on the evening of the thirteenth day before giving up work, they succeeded in uncovering the deck of a craft measuring eighty feet long over all by sixteen feet beam. They were now intensely excited and elated, as they had every reason to believe that—judging from certain peculiarities of build which had already revealed themselves—they had discovered a most interesting relic.

The next morning was most fortunately as fine as they could reasonably expect it to be in that stormy and desolate region; and, commencing work at an early hour—having, moreover, by this time acquired quite a respectable dexterity in the use of their tools—they succeeded by lunch time in laying completely bare the entire hull of what proved most unmistakably to be a veritable ancient Viking ship.

This intensely interesting relic was, as already stated, eighty feet long by sixteen feet beam; with a depth of hold in midships, as they now found, of eight feet; she must therefore have been at the time of her launch quite a noble specimen of naval architecture. She was of course built of wood, and was beautifully moulded fore and aft; her stem and stern-posts were carried to a height of five feet above her rail; and the former was finished off with a rather roughly hewn but vigorously modelled horse's head, whilst the latter terminated in an elaborately carved piece of scroll-work. She was fully decked, with a sort of monkey-poop aft, about two and a half feet high and twenty feet long, beneath which was her principal cabin. Her bulwarks and rail were very solidly constructed; the former being pierced with rowlock holes for sixteen oars or sweeps of a side, in addition to holes abaft, one on each side of, and near the stern-post, for the short broad-bladed steering paddles. Both of these paddles, together with twenty-three oars and two square sails, shaped somewhat like lugs and still attached to their yards, were found stowed fore and aft amidships on the vessel's deck. They were all in an excellent state of preservation, as were also the lower portions of the masts; indeed it was only that portion of these spars which had been long exposed to the air which showed signs of rot, the upper extremities being most rotten, whilst the parts close to the deck were perfectly sound.

Having fully satisfied their curiosity with regard to the exterior of this interesting craft, they next essayed to penetrate below by forcing open the after hatch. On removing the cover a small and almost perpendicular ladder was revealed, down which Mildmay rapidly made his way. On reaching the bottom he found himself in a small vestibule or ante-room, the floor, sides, and ceiling of which were thickly cased with smooth glassy ice, long icicles of varying thicknesses also depending from the beams and deck planking overhead. He could trace the existence of a door in the middle of the bulkhead facing him; but it was hermetically sealed with the thick coating of ice before mentioned, and the removal of this occupied over half an hour. Whilst he was thus engaged the rest of the party at his suggestion returned to the *Flying Fish* for the small electric lamps used in their diving operations; and when they returned he was just about ready to force open the door of the after cabin. This was accomplished without much difficulty, and a faint sickly odour at once became apparent, issuing from the interior of the cabin.

Consumed by curiosity, the party pressed eagerly forward through the doorway, and a most extraordinary sight at once revealed itself. The cabin was a tolerably roomy apartment for the size of the vessel, having for furniture a solid handsomely carved oaken table in the centre, shaped to suit the narrowing dimensions of the vessel abaft, and side benches or lockers all round the sides. The walls or inner planking of the ship were thickly covered with seal, walrus, and white bear skins, evidently hung there to prevent, as far as possible, the penetration of the extreme cold through the ship's sides; and upon large nails, driven through these and into the planks, were hung various trophies of weapons, such as long two-handed swords, small shields or targets, maces with heavy iron-spiked heads, short-handled battle-axes, spears, unstrung bows, and quivers of arrows. But it was not these objects, interesting as they were, which first riveted the attention of the intruders; it was upon *the occupants of the cabin* that their startled glances fixed themselves. Yes, strange as it may seem, the four nineteenth-century travellers found themselves face to face with some at least of the hardy crew who had stood on the deck waving their last good-bye to wives, children, or sweethearts—who shall say how many years ago?—when that stout galley swept out of harbour with pennons flying, oars flashing, and arms glancing, maybe, in the brilliant sunshine, as she started on the enterprise of wild adventure from which she was never to return. The inmates were four in number. Three of them were reclining on the lockers, their heads pillowed upon, and their bodies thickly covered with skins, whilst the fourth, doubtless the master spirit of the expedition, sat as in life at the narrow or after end of the table, his body supported in a massive quaintly carved oaken chair.

The bodies, the floor, the table, and every article in the cabin were thickly coated with frost-rime, which glittered with a diamond-like lustre in the cold keen light of the electric lamps, and the first act of the visitors was to carefully remove and clear away this frost coating. To their intense satisfaction this task was accomplished by gentle brushing without the slightest difficulty, and they were then able to minutely inspect the bodies of these ancient sea kings. They were in a state of surprisingly perfect preservation, and indeed had the appearance of having only recently fallen asleep, the intense cold having seized upon them with such fierce rapidity that their bodies had completely congealed before even the primary stages of decay had had time to manifest themselves. Indeed, judging from appearances, they had succumbed, in the first instance, to starvation, and, overcome by weakness, had been frozen to death. They were all of lofty stature and muscular build, with fair hair and tawny beards and moustaches, the latter worn extremely long. They were fully clad, all in garments of the same general character, excepting that those of the seated figure appeared to be of somewhat finer material than those of his companions. These garments, the outer ones, that is to say, consisted of a thick leathern tunic confined at the waist by a broad belt, and leather drawers reaching from the waist to the ankles, thick leather socks or stockings, and sandals laced to the feet and legs by leather thongs. The tunic of the chief was elaborately embroidered on the breast in silk, a winged black horse being the central and most conspicuous design. The trophy hanging at the back of the sitter's chair consisted of a small circular shield, with a formidable axe, double-handed sword, and mace crossing each other, behind it, the whole being surmounted by a handsome bronze headpiece, or helmet without a visor, having a large pair of finely modelled wings starting from the sides and near the crown. The helmets of the other three occupants were of similar shape, but without ornament of any kind. Two drinking horns were upon the table, one being plainly mounted in bronze, and the other elaborately mounted in silver and supported upon three legs modelled after those of the horse, the fourth leg being lifted in the attitude of pawing the ground.

But perhaps the most interesting object of all was a sheet of parchment which lay stretched upon the table before the sitter, and which he had evidently been studying when the drowsiness of death seized him, and, sinking back in his chair, he had closed his eyes for ever. This parchment was, of course, stiff with the frost of centuries; but by exercising the utmost care the finders succeeded in conveying it intact to the *Flying Fish*, and in thawing it out, when it was found to be covered with a rude but vigorously drawn sketch or chart, representing with surprising accuracy of outline—but without much attention to scale—the whole of the channel between the west coast of Greenland and the east coast of America, and showing, at the top or northern margin, an irregular line *evidently intended to represent land*. And in the top left-hand corner of the chart was a square space marked off as a separate and distinct chart, the centre of which was occupied by an island, the southern coast-line of which corresponded in shape with the line drawn next the northern margin of the main or principal chart. Rudely drawn figures of the whale, narwhal, walrus, seal, and polar bear were sketched here and there upon the chart, as though to indicate spots where these animals had been seen by the author of the document; and on the island shown in the small subsidiary chart, great numbers of animals were drawn, among those represented being hares, foxes, deer, seals, and *elephants*, besides others which the travellers failed to identify. There was also a sketch of a ship—very similar in appearance to the craft from which the chart had been taken—represented as *sailing away from the island*. This particular sketch was the source of much speculation on the part of the quartette; Sir Reginald and the colonel being disposed to regard it as an insertion for the purpose merely of giving a more effective appearance to the chart, whilst the professor and Mildmay were of opinion that it was intended to convey an intimation that the mysterious island had actually been visited.

The above particulars, it need scarcely be said, were ascertained and the surmises discussed after dinner that day; the party not leaving the galley until they had effected a thorough and exhaustive examination of her from stem to stern. They found little else of interest on board her, however, except ten more bodies in the large fore-cabin or forecastle of the craft. The store-rooms occupied the central portion of the vessel, being accessible only from the after end, and the fact that they were clean swept of everything which could by any possibility have served for food, tended to confirm the impression that the expedition had perished of starvation. One or two documents and a massive vellum-bound book were discovered, and these, together with some of the armour and weapons found on board, were taken possession of, but the documents and book proved to be written in a tongue wholly unknown to either of the discoverers, and they were therefore destined to remain for some time longer in ignorance of the history of the long-lost expedition. One fact only was it possible to discover in connection with it, which was that the hardy and resolute crew had undoubtedly cut their way for a very considerable distance into the heart of that vast field of everlasting ice. This was most conclusively ascertained by Sir Reginald and his friends, who, on board the *Flying Fish*, were able to follow quite unmistakable traces of the channel cut by the unknown explorers for a distance of fully forty miles to the southward of the galley itself.

The examination of this strange and interesting craft being at length completed, the cabin doors were closed, the hatches replaced, and the ship, with all that she contained, left to the mercy of the weather, there being no doubt that the excavation so laboriously accomplished would soon be again filled up by the almost ceaseless snow-fall, and the ship again concealed in all probability for ever.

The first thing after breakfast on the following morning, the northward journey was resumed in the face of a perfect hurricane from the northward, accompanied by so tremendous and incessant a fall of snow that it was utterly impossible to see anything at a distance of more than twenty feet in any direction. It was, of course, quite out of the question for anyone to venture outside the door of the pilot-house in such terrible weather; and the cold even inside on the steering platform was so intense that the breath of the travellers was condensed on their moustaches, and, instantly congealing, rapidly formed into a mass of ice which effectually prevented the opening of their mouths. An attempt was made to elude the storm by rising into the higher regions of the atmosphere; but the cold there proved to be so unbearable, notwithstanding the protection afforded by the stubbornly non-conducting material of which the *Flying Fish* was built, that they were compelled to descend once more, and their journey was continued at about a height of one thousand feet above the ice, and at a speed of ninety miles per hour, at which rate of travel they considered that they were stemming the gale, and perhaps actually progressing to windward some ten miles or so every hour.

The dreary day lagged slowly on, with the occurrence of no event of importance, until about four o'clock in the afternoon, at which time the travellers became conscious of a decided rise of temperature. By five o'clock the cold had so greatly diminished that they were compelled to throw off their thick fur outer clothing; and half an hour later, the thick dreadnought jackets, which constituted their ordinary outer covering in bad weather, were also discarded; the snow meanwhile giving place to sleet, and the sleet in its turn yielding to a deluge of driving rain. And, whilst they were still wondering what this singular phenomenon might portend, a hoarse low muffled roar, accompanied by an occasional grinding crash, smote upon their ears through the heavy *swish* of the rain; the dull white monotonous expanse of the ice-field was abruptly broken into by a jagged irregular-shaped black blot ahead; and, almost before they had time to realise the extraordinary change, the *Flying Fish* had swept beyond the northern boundary of the immense expanse of paleocrystic ice, and was careering northward, at an elevation of about a thousand feet, above the surface of a liquid sea which raged and chafed and tossed its foamy arms to heaven under the influence of the fast-diminishing gale.

"Hurrah!" ejaculated the professor; "hurrah! Scoresby and Kane spoke the truth; and my pet theory turns out to be correct, after all. Gentlemen, look round and feast your eyes upon the glorious spectacle of *an open Polar Sea*!"

Whether it actually *was* an open sea, or only an unusually wide channel between two ice-fields, was now the question to be settled. It certainly looked like the former; it was completely free of floating ice, large or small, except the cakes which were broken away by the waves from the edge of the enormous floe just left behind, and they were kept by the wind close to their parent mass; the sea ran so high and was so regular as to convey the idea of a very considerable extent of "fetch;" and, lastly, there was neither ice nor ice-blink to be seen anywhere along the whole stretch of the northern horizon.

Impatient to solve this momentous and interesting question, the *Flying Fish* was pushed to her utmost speed, causing her to make headway over the ground, and against the fresh breeze still blowing, at a pace of about ninety miles per hour. A quarter of an hour later the rain ceased, and the flying ship plunged into the midst of a dense fog, so thick that it was impossible to see even so far as the guard-rail on either side of the deck. The temperature had by this time, however, risen to *thirty-three degrees above zero (Fahrenheit)*, and the travellers therefore at once resolved to again brave the rigours of the upper atmosphere. An immediate ascent was accordingly made, with the satisfactory result, that at an elevation of three thousand feet above the sea-level they found themselves once more clear of the fog, with no perceptible fall of the thermometer, and with a clear view ahead. Twenty minutes more of travelling, and the northern skirts of the fog-bank were past, the clouds broke away, and the westering sun cast his ruddy beams upon the surface of the heaving waters. The sea was still without a vestige of ice, and the horizon was perfectly clear ahead.

Consumed with enthusiasm and impatience, the travellers now effected a descent to the surface of the sea, that having been proved to be the situation in which the *Flying Fish* made her greatest speed, and the journey was promptly proceeded with. A further run of twenty miles found them beneath a cloudless sky, with the wind, soft and balmy, fallen to the gentlest of zephyrs, and the temperature risen to the extraordinary height of forty-five degrees above zero. Their delight, especially that of the professor, was excessive at this wonderful change in their surroundings within so short a time; indeed von Schalckenberg became positively extravagant in his demonstrations, dancing about the deck like a schoolboy, laughing, cheering, clapping his hands, and uttering the most extraordinary prophecies as to what awaited them at the now not far distant pole. The moment was favourable for an astronomical observation; and the ship, notwithstanding their eagerness to press forward, was accordingly stopped for a few minutes to take the necessary sights, after which "Northward ho!" again became their watchword. A few minutes sufficed Mildmay to complete his calculations, and then, amidst vociferous cheering on the part of his companions, he announced to them the gratifying intelligence that they had approached to within a distance of *only one hundred and sixty miles of the North Pole.*

At the moment when this announcement was made it was exactly ten minutes after six o'clock p.m. The speed gauge showed that the *Flying Fish* was then making her way through the water at the rate of one hundred and fifty miles per hour; in a trifle over one hour more, therefore, if nothing prevented, they would reach the goal of their northward journey. Their enthusiasm became almost painful in its intensity; and as the *Flying Fish* rushed at headlong speed through the rippling waters, tossing the wavelets aside in a great outward-curling fringe of sparkling foam, and as the minutes lagged slowly away, the eyes of the quartette in the pilot-house were strained with ever-increasing intensity in their vain efforts to pierce the mysteries of the horizon ahead.

At exactly twenty minutes to seven o'clock, Mildmay electrified his companions, and put the finishing touch to their excitement, by raising an exultant shout of:

"Land ho!"

"Where?" "Show it me!" "I can't see it. You must be mistaken!" exclaimed his companions in chorus, after a breathless moment of vain peering into the pearly northern horizon.

"There it is, directly ahead, looking just like the edge of a flat grey cloud showing above the water's edge," was the reply.

Sure enough it *was* land; for when once their eyes had been directed to the proper point there was little difficulty in discerning it. Moreover, as the ship sped on, it rose rapidly above the horizon, the grey tint growing every moment darker and more distinct, and a few minutes later other land, more sharply defined in outline and more distinctive in colour, rose above the horizon immediately below it, showing that the table-land first made out lay at some distance from the southern shore.

And at this auspicious moment the sea began to exhibit signs of the life which teemed within its depths. An accidental glance astern showed an enormous school of whales spouting on the southern horizon; porpoises undulated sportively to windward; a troop of dolphins suddenly appeared for a moment alongside the ship, evidently straining every nerve to keep pace with her; and an occasional sea-otter rose now and then to the surface of the placid sea, to dive out of sight again the next instant in quite a ridiculous state of consternation at so unwonted a sight as the rushing form of the *Flying Fish*. Flocks of sea-birds of various, and indeed some of hitherto unknown, kinds next made their appearance, industriously pursuing their avocation of fishermen, and—unlike the sea-otters—paying little or no attention to their strange visitors. And finally, as they drew nearer in with the land, seals of various kinds were passed, sportively chasing each other, and pausing for a moment to raise their heads inquisitively and turn their mild glances upon the flying ship.

When within some ten miles of the land, it was deemed advisable to rise out of the water and to complete the journey at a few feet above its surface, thus taking the most effectual of precautions against accidental collision with a sunken rock. As the ship drew in still closer with the land, her speed was reduced; and, at a quarter after seven o'clock on that calm July evening, she once more settled down, like a wearied sea-fowl, upon the surface of the water, and let go her anchor in a depth of twelve fathoms, at a distance of half a mile from the shore, in a fine roomy well-sheltered bay of crescent form, the two horns or outer extremities of which rose sheer out of the water in the form of a pair of bold rocky spurs, backed up on the landward side by a sweep of low grassy hills, crowned, at a short distance from the shore, with a forest of majestic pines.

"Well!" ejaculated the professor, as he finally turned away and went below to dinner, after feasting his eyes on the splendid landscape, gloriously lighted up by the rays of the evening sun, "I was prepared to see many unexpected sights in the event of our reaching the North Pole, but grass and trees!—well, I was *not* prepared to find *them*."

CHAPTER TWELVE
ANOTHER STARTLING DISCOVERY

Notwithstanding the state of excitement which the travellers had been thrown into by the successful accomplishment of this, the first, and, perhaps, the most difficult part of their novel enterprise, they managed to secure a tolerably sound night's rest—if one may venture to term night any part of the twenty-four hours at that season and in that region, where the sun had never once sunk beneath the horizon since the twenty-first of the preceding March, and where the day had still two months more to run before it should wane into the long six-months' night of winter. But, as might be expected, they were up bright and early on the following morning, eager to explore this strange new polar land, and scarcely patient enough to sit down and consume with becoming leisure the appetising breakfast which the still imperturbable George had provided for them.

The meal, however, like most other matters, had an end at last; and the travellers felt themselves free to follow the bent of their impatient inclinations. But the expedition upon which they were about to enter was one not to be undertaken without due foresight and preparation. It was only to be a preliminary exploration, it is true, only a journey of some three or four miles into the interior; but the country and the climate having already proved so extraordinarily at variance with all their preconceived ideas, who could say what new and strange forms of animal life might not possibly be lurking within those vast forest depths? It therefore behoved them to adopt at least a reasonable amount of precaution, and so to equip themselves that, in the event of their encountering new and hitherto unsuspected dangers, they might not find themselves in a wholly defenceless condition.

The question of the kind of clothing to be worn was soon settled. The temperature stood at the extraordinary height (for that latitude) of fifty-seven degrees Fahrenheit; and the air, actually cool and bracing, felt almost oppressively warm to them after the rigours of the paleocrystic ice-field; they therefore donned a suit of rough serviceable cloth of moderate thickness, and stout waterproof leather walking boots. Then, for arms, as they were merely going on a reconnoitring and not a hunting expedition, they decided to take their large-bore repeating rifles, which, with the explosive shells constituting their ammunition, would enable the explorers to face anything. And lastly, as accident or design might cause them to extend their ramble beyond its originally intended limits, they adopted the precaution of providing themselves each with a small light knapsack of provisions. Thus equipped they proceeded on deck, raised the two boats with their davits out of the snug below-deck compartments in which they had hitherto been concealed, and, lowering the smaller boat of the two, stepped into her, and were quickly conveyed to the shore.

It was with a curiously mingled feeling of awe and exultation that they sprang from the boat to the strand, and planted their feet for the first time upon this hitherto unknown and unvisited ground.

"Behold!" exclaimed the baronet, pointing to their footprints in the sand; "behold the first human footprints ever impressed upon this soil." And stepping rapidly forward until he had passed beyond the high-water mark, he unfurled a small union-jack which he carried in his hand, and, forcing the butt-end of the staff into the yielding sand, exclaimed:

"In the name of her most gracious majesty Victoria, Queen of Great Britain and Ireland, I annex this land as a dependency of the British crown!"

Then they all took off their hats and gave three cheers for the queen; after which Colonel Lethbridge proposed that the newly-discovered country be called "Elphinstone Land," a proposition which was carried with acclamation by a majority of three to one, the dissenting voice being that of the baronet, who modestly disclaimed the honour of having the country named after himself.

But *were* theirs, after all, the first human footprints which had ever been impressed upon that soil? A decided answer in the negative awaited them; for they had not advanced very many yards from the shore when they came upon an object which, upon examination, proved to be an ancient and much-rusted spear-head broken short off but with some six inches of the haft still attached to it. The travellers felt, greatly disconcerted at this discovery; it robbed them at once irretrievably of the honour of being the first discoverers of the North Pole, and showed them that, at some unknown period in the remote past, there must have existed a man, or more probably a body of men, who, not only without the exceptional facilities offered by the possession of such a ship as the *Flying Fish*, but with, in all probability, ships infinitely inferior to the worst of those used by modern explorers, had actually achieved the hitherto deemed impossible feat of piercing the great ice-barrier and actually reaching the northern pole of the earth.

Who were they? Of what country could they possibly have been natives? And why was the fact of their important discovery suffered to sink into oblivion? Such were the questions which at once rose to the minds of the baronet and his companions, and to which their lips spontaneously gave utterance.

"I think there can be little doubt as to who and what they were," remarked the professor. "They were *Vikings*; and their leader it must unquestionably have been who drew the chart found by us in the Viking ship buried in the ice of the paleocrystic sea. It is his ship which we see delineated upon the chart; this is the land from which she is represented as sailing triumphantly away; and it was doubtless this land which the Viking ship, discovered by us, was making so desperate an effort to reach when death claimed her crew as its prey. The other question, as to why the discovery of this land was suffered to remain an unknown fact, is not by any means so easy to answer. Perhaps the man before whose dead body the chart lay spread open upon the table may have been its author and the original discoverer of this land; perhaps the ship represented on the chart and the ship discovered by us may have been one and the same; she may have been on her homeward voyage; and, finding the channels to the southward completely blocked with ice, may have been attempting to force her way back into the open Polar Sea when her fate overtook her."

"But, admitting for the moment that such may possibly have been the case," remarked the baronet, "how do you account for the fact that, whilst she must necessarily have forced her way twice through the ancient ice, she should have failed in her third attempt?"

"Her third attempt may have been made late in the season," answered the professor. "But it is just possible that her final attempt may have been to force not a *third* but a *second* passage through the ice. She may have been attempting to return *southward* instead of northward, as I just now suggested. My impression, with respect to the vast field of paleocrystic ice, is that at certain seasons—as when, for instance, two or three very mild winters have occurred in succession in the Arctic circle, followed possibly by exceptionally hot summers—it undergoes partial disruption, splitting up, in fact, into several lesser fields which drift for longer or shorter distances out into the open Polar Sea. The fact that Scoresby, Penny, and Kane all beheld, at different periods, an open Polar sea, tends to confirm this impression; and the circumstance that the bows of the galley discovered by us were pointing to the northward may be due, not to the fact that she was actually making her way north when finally frozen in, but to the accident of that portion of the field by which she was surrounded being subsequently turned completely round whilst adrift. But what object do I see yonder? Surely it is not a human habitation?"

It was, however, or at least had been, at some more or less distant period. It was the roofless ruin of a once most substantially built log-hut, measuring some twenty-five feet long by sixteen feet broad. The roof had fallen in; the log sides were decayed and moss-grown; and the interior was overgrown with long grass and brambles, with a stately pine springing to a height of some ninety feet from the very centre of the structure—all of which incontestably proved its antiquity; but that it was the work of man—most probably those who had left behind them the rusty spear-head—there could be no possible doubt.

The party minutely inspected this interesting ruin, but without making any further discovery, and then pressed forward through the heart of a belt of pine forest which they had by this time reached.

The walking was not difficult and they made tolerably rapid progress. That the country was not absolutely tenantless they soon had abundant proof, for they had not advanced more than half a mile before an Arctic fox was discovered gliding rapidly away before them. A little further on they came unexpectedly upon a herd of moose-deer. The behaviour of these animals—naturally extremely shy—conclusively proved that they had never before met such an enemy as man, for, instead of bounding rapidly away, as is their wont, they merely ceased feeding for a moment to stand and gaze curiously upon the new-comers, and then went on browsing again with the utmost composure. Their fearlessness offered a strong temptation to such inveterate sportsmen as Sir Reginald and the colonel; but not being in actual need of their flesh, and being, moreover, anxious not to disturb them just then, the party passed quietly on without firing a shot. A huge brown bear was the next animal encountered, and this time the baronet's love of sport overcame his humanity, bruin falling an easy victim to the noiseless but deadly percussion shell of Sir Reginald's large-bore rifle. A solitary prowling wolf next fell before the equally deadly weapon of the colonel; and then the explorers emerged on the other side of the forest-belt, and found themselves on the borders of an extensive tract of tolerably level country intersected here and there by low hills, with occasional patches of marshy land, the high flat table-land, which had been the first object sighted by them when approaching these shores from the southward, looming up, still misty and grey, at a long distance in the extreme background of the landscape.

Heading directly for this mountain, as a conspicuous landmark, the party again pressed forward, and were speedily delighted to observe several flocks of ptarmigan busily feeding on the crests of the low hills which here and there crossed the route. These birds proved rather shy, though not so much so as to have prevented the sportsmen making a very decent bag had they been provided with fowling-pieces. As it was, however, the birds were, of course, permitted to go free and undisturbed. A mile further on a small drove of musk-oxen were seen grazing in the distance, and, whilst some of the party were watching the animals and discussing the possibility of stalking them, Mildmay, who had been intently gazing through his binocular in another direction, startled his companions by exclaiming, in an almost horrified tone of voice:

"What on earth are those immense creatures moving slowly about in the valley away yonder? Surely they *can't* be elephants?"

"Elephants! my dear fellow, don't be absurd," remonstrated the baronet. "Where are they? Oh, ah! now I have them," as he brought his glass to bear in the right direction. "By George, they *are* elephants, though, and monsters into the bargain. And, I declare, it seems to me that they are covered with a thick coat of shaggy hair. Why, I never saw such a thing in my life."

"*Elephants? Covered with hair?*" exclaimed the professor in a voice so eager that it almost amounted to a scream. "Lend me a binocular, somebody; with my usual luck I have left mine at home—on board, I mean. A thousand thanks, Mildmay, my dear fellow. Now, where are these elephants of yours? Quick, show me where to look for them. Good heavens! if it should really be so. Ah! now I see them. Yes—yes—they are—they *must* be—Gentlemen, as I am a man of science, I solemnly declare to you the stupendous fact that those extraordinary animals are neither more nor less than living Mammoths. I congratulate you, gentlemen—I congratulate myself. Ach, himmel! to think that it should ever be my good fortune to actually behold, not only one, but a whole herd of living mammoths! I cannot believe it—yet—yes, there they are; it is no freak of a disordered imagination, but an actual, positive, undeniable reality."

The worthy professor was so excited that he could scarcely hold the binocular firmly enough to look through it, and it was really laughable—to his companions—to hear his "Ach's" and "Pish's" of impatience as he vainly strove to steady his trembling hands and get another good look at the herd of hitherto believed extinct monsters, which were quietly feeding at a distance of about two miles away. At length he, with a comical gesture of despair, restored the borrowed binocular to Mildmay, and, turning to his companions, exclaimed in a voice of feverish earnestness:

"Come, my dear friends, why do we stand idly gaping here and wasting valuable time, when we really have not a moment to lose? We may never have such a priceless opportunity again. Let us press forward, then, and at all risks secure a specimen of so unique an animal as the mammoth. If we were to achieve this and nothing more our success would be ample repayment for all the anxious thought devoted to the designing of our vessel, and all the money spent in her construction."

His excitement was contagious, and the baronet, after briefly arranging with the colonel a plan of operations, invited von Schalckenberg to follow him; Lethbridge and Mildmay going off in another direction, with the object of getting on the other side of the animals, and, in co-operation with the other party, driving them, if possible, within easy distance of the harbour in which the *Flying Fish* lay at anchor.

To do this a wide détour was necessary, and it was nearly an hour and a half later when the four men found themselves in a proper position to commence the operation of "driving." They had arranged themselves in the form of a semicircle round the herd, at a distance of about a quarter of a mile away, and, at a signal from the baronet, all hands advanced toward the huge creatures, shouting and gesticulating to the utmost extent of their several powers.

The mammoths, utterly unsuspicious of danger, had been quietly feeding among the long grass during the approach of their enemies; but on the baronet's first signal shout they paused, and, facing rapidly round in the direction of the noise, raised their trunks in the air and waved them slowly from side to side as though scenting the air. The hunters now redoubled their exertions, fully expecting that, on seeing them, the animals would wheel about and shamble off in the required direction. But, to their dismay, the creatures, instead of doing this, no sooner caught sight of the party than, with upraised trunks and harsh trumpet-like screams of rage and defiance, they charged furiously straight down upon them. The herd numbered ten individuals, four of which appeared to instantly constitute themselves the defenders of the party; and each of these promptly selected his own particular enemy, occupying his attention so fully that the remaining members of the herd were afforded every facility for escape.

It was a nervous moment for the hunters, who, never having faced such a creature before, had not the most remote idea of its fighting tactics; moreover, the aspect of the monsters, with their towering stature of fully fifteen feet, their thick shaggy coats of rusty brown hair, their enormous spirally curving tusks, and their small eyes blazing with fury as they rushed forward to the attack, all combined to produce such a hideous *tout ensemble* as might well strike terror to the boldest heart. But neither Sir Reginald nor the colonel were the men to shrink from an encounter when game was before them; Mildmay possessed all the cool daring and recklessness of the British seaman; and as for the professor, he would willingly have faced a thousand deaths to secure so new and rare a specimen of natural history as the creature before him.

The four sportsmen pulled trigger almost simultaneously. The baronet and the colonel had each selected the same spot, the eye, as the object of their aim, and both had been equally successful, the shell in each case passing upward through the eyeball into the brain, exploding there and causing instant death. The professor's fascinated gaze being riveted upon the wide-open mouth of his own particular adversary, he seemed to think that the yawning cavern thus revealed would be as good a place as any to empty his rifle into; and he did so—just in bare time to bring down his game and save himself from being trampled to a jelly. Mildmay, however, was not so fortunate. He seemed to think that it mattered very little where he directed his aim, so long as he made sure of hitting the brute *somewhere*, and he therefore fired point-blank at the chest of the mammoth which was menacing him. The shell sped true, but, encountering the thick shaggy coat and the enormously tough hide of the creature, failed to penetrate the body, and, exploding outside, only inflicted such wounds as further excited the already angry monster to a perfect frenzy of rage. Even at this critical moment there was time for another shot; but Mildmay most unfortunately forgot that he had nine loaded chambers still available, and instead of firing again he flung away his piece and ran for his life. The race was a disastrously short one, however; he had not run more than twenty yards when the huge creature was upon him. The great uplifted trunk gave one whirl in the air and descended with force enough to slay an ox. It struck poor Mildmay on his right side, and, but for the fortunate accident of his having at that moment tripped and fallen forward, the lieutenant would there and then have lost the number of his mess. As it was, he was sent whirling through the air like a cricket-ball, to fall senseless, and bleeding from the nose and mouth, fully forty feet away. The vindictive brute instantly turned short off with the evident intention of trampling his victim to death; but before he could reach the prostrate body a shell from the colonel's rifle sent him crashing lifeless to the ground. The remainder of the herd, evidently dismayed at the slaughter of their companions, now abandoned a half-formed intention which they had at first manifested to stay and fight it out, and went off in full retreat with horrible trumpetings of anger and alarm.

The colonel was the first to reach the side of his unfortunate friend, the professor and the baronet joining him as speedily as their legs could convey them to the spot. Very fortunately von Schalckenberg, among his other multitudinous acquirements, possessed a very fair knowledge of medicine and surgery; and his skilful fingers were soon at work removing the lieutenant's clothing so far as was necessary to investigate the nature and extent of his injuries. Singularly enough these were found to be comparatively trifling, a fractured rib and several very severe bruises being the sum of them. A little brandy forced between the lips of the sufferer soon restored him to consciousness, and he was able to sit up.

On attempting to rise to his feet, however, he experienced such severe pain that it was then and there resolved to let him remain where he was, two of his companions also remaining to mount guard over him and see that he came to no harm; whilst the third was to hurry back with all speed to the ship and bring her out on to the plain close by the spot where the accident occurred, when it would be a comparatively easy matter to convey the lieutenant from the spot where he then lay to his own bed on board the *Flying Fish*.

The professor, having first made Mildmay as easy and comfortable as circumstances permitted, volunteered for the service of moving the ship, explaining to his companions that, in the event of an attack of any kind, they, as seasoned sportsmen, would be able to far more effectually defend the wounded man than he could possibly hope to do; and then, Sir Reginald and the colonel quite concurring in this view, he set off for the bay, shouting back an assurance as he went that he would not be absent one moment longer than should prove absolutely necessary.

The worthy scientist was as good as his word; for in less than an hour from the moment of his departure the immense bulk of the *Flying Fish* was seen to rise into the air beyond the tops of the distant pine-trees, and, with her polished hull gleaming and flashing in the rays of the sun, to sweep gracefully round until she was heading straight in the direction of the anxious watchers. Under the professor's able pilotage she was soon brought to the ground and secured within a dozen yards of the spot occupied by them, when it was the work of a few minutes only to convey the injured man to his own stateroom, where his hurts were at once properly attended to and himself made thoroughly comfortable.

As soon as luncheon was over Sir Reginald and the colonel set out for the spot were they had shot the bear in the morning, one of them being armed with a large-bore rifle and the other carrying a fowling-piece; and on their return somewhat late in the afternoon they bore not only the skin, skull, and claws of the defunct bruin, but also a goodly bag of ptarmigan. During their absence the professor had also been very busy, dividing his attention pretty evenly between Mildmay and the finest specimen of the slain mammoths, the latter of which he had succeeded in nearly half-denuding of its skin. With the assistance of his two able-bodied friends this task was completed by dinner-time; and by the corresponding hour next evening not only was the enormous hide undergoing the first stage of preparation for the taxidermist, but the indefatigable labourers had also succeeded in hewing out the tusks of the other slaughtered mammoths. For health's sake the ship was then moved about a mile further inland, and the carcasses were left to the wolves, which had already gathered in large numbers in the vicinity.

Under the skilful treatment of the professor Mildmay made steady and rapid progress toward recovery from the very first; the baronet and the colonel had therefore no hesitation about carrying out a project which had been under discussion between them for the last two or three days, and which was neither more nor less than a pedestrian excursion to the far distant table-land which they had first sighted from the sea. They estimated that this goal of their journey, upon which they expected to find the actual site of the Northern Pole of the earth, must be about sixty miles distant from the ship; and they considered that the trip there and back would occupy them about six days. It would of course have been very much easier, and more convenient in every way, to have made the journey on board the *Flying Fish*, but the professor was busy with the preparation of his mammoth, the skin of which he had carefully stretched and pegged out on the ground alongside the ship, and was so averse to the losing sight of it, even for a few hours, that it was soon decided the *Flying Fish* must not be moved for the present. After all, the journey would probably not involve any very great amount of hardship; it simply meant camping out for five or six nights, or at least those hours of the twenty-four which did duty for night. And this the two seasoned hunters looked forward to as rather a pleasant change than otherwise.

The necessary preparations were all made on the previous evening, and after breakfast on the appointed day the two adventurers set out, taking leave of Mildmay—who was already out of bed again—and of the professor, who, to tell the truth, was heartily glad to be left to the uninterrupted prosecution of his task.

They were in light marching order, having resolved to carry nothing which they could possibly do without; their previous experience of the country had taught them that game was pretty plentiful, and that they might safely depend upon their guns for the supply of their larder; and their stock of provisions consisted solely, therefore, of a few biscuits and a substantial flask of brandy each. The temperature was decidedly mild, and had been so ever since their arrival at "Elphinstone Land," with settled fine weather, and they therefore carried nothing in the shape of extra clothing save a light macintosh each, which they bore securely strapped on the top of their knapsacks. The remainder of their *impedimenta* consisted of a double-barrelled gun for each man—one barrel being rifled and the other a smooth bore—two cartridge belts, one for the waist and the other for the shoulder, fully stocked; a formidable double-edged hunting knife each; a capacious waterproof bag containing a reserve supply of cartridges, and a small stock of matches and tobacco.

Their road for the first five or six miles led up a gentle acclivity, just sufficient to make itself felt, but not steep enough to render walking difficult or fatiguing. Then came a stretch of flat country, bounded on each side by the projecting spurs of a range of rugged hills of fantastic outline which stretched immediately across their path at a distance of some three or four miles or so. The pedestrians had not progressed very far across this plain before their attention became arrested by a curious phenomenon. The atmosphere immediately behind the range of hills last mentioned was thick with fleecy vapour, now so thin that the distant table-land could be dimly seen through it as through a veil, and anon so dense that it assumed a decided cloud-like shape upon which the unsetting sun shone with dazzling brilliancy. This thickening of the vapour seemed to occur at tolerably regular intervals of about twenty minutes each, and was immediately preceded by a sudden silvery gleam succeeded by a most brilliant and perfectly formed rainbow. The periodical recurrence of this singular phenomenon under a perfectly cloudless sky of course greatly excited the curiosity of the pedestrians, and they pushed rapidly forward, eager to ascertain the cause.

As they advanced, the encircling hills thrust their projecting spurs further and further into the narrowing plain, their slopes became steeper and more rugged, and rocks began to crop out here and there with increasing frequency through the lessening soil. A corresponding change of course occurred in the character of the landscape; it grew increasingly picturesque and wild at every step, and at length the travellers found themselves at the mouth of a narrow rocky boulder-strewn gorge bounded on either side by titanic masses of volcanic rock, rugged and moss-grown, with little patches of herbage here and there, or an occasional stunted pine growing out of an almost imperceptible fissure. The only signs of life in this wild spot consisted of a diminutive musk-ox here and there cropping the scanty herbage half-way up the apparently inaccessible height in spots from which it appeared equally impossible for the creature to advance or to retreat.

Plunging into this defile, the travellers advanced with steadily increasing difficulty, the boulders with which their path was strewed growing ever larger and more numerous until at length the narrowing road became completely choked with them, and the only mode of progression was that of a slow, toilsome, dangerous scramble. Still the pair pushed resolutely on, every minute hoping that the difficulties of the journey would come to an end, and every minute less willing to turn back and again encounter the obstacles already surmounted. At length the path became so narrow that one enormous boulder sufficed to completely block the way, whilst the perpendicular rocky walls of the chasm towered so far aloft that only the merest thread of sky was visible; the air grew chill and damp, and so deep a twilight gloom pervaded the place that it was difficult to distinguish any object more than half a dozen yards distant.

The weary travellers looked at each other in dismay. Was this to be the ineffectual ending of that long and toilsome scramble through the ravine? There was just one single narrow crevice between the huge boulder which blocked their way, and one of the precipitous walls which pressed so closely in upon them—a crevice left by the irregular shape of the block, and affording barely space enough for a man of robust proportions to squeeze himself through—and they determined that, before retracing their steps, they would at least satisfy their curiosity so far as to creep through this crevice and see what lay on the farther side. The baronet with some little difficulty squeezed through first, and his exclamation of astonishment quickly took the colonel to his side.

The pair found themselves in a narrow rent between the two vertical faces of rock—the projections of the one accurately corresponding with the indentations of the other, and clearly demonstrating that, at some distant period of the earth's history, that mighty chasm had been suddenly torn open by a great natural convulsion awful in its intensity beyond all power of imagination. The rent was roofed in as it were by boulders which thickly hung suspended and jammed in at varying heights between the almost touching walls of the rift; and the adventurous explorers could not repress a shudder as they glanced aloft at these huge masses and thought of the consequences to themselves which would ensue should a projecting corner just then yield and suffer its parent rock to come crashing down to the bottom. Their first impulse was to beat a precipitate retreat; their second, to go forward; for at only a few yards' distance before them the rift closed altogether, except at the very bottom, where a low cavern-like fissure dimly appeared. A hasty consultation passed between them, resulting in a determination to go forward and explore the fissure.

Fortunately for their purpose they had, at an early stage of their difficulties, provided themselves with a couple of stoutish pine branches—wrenched from their parent stems and hurled into the ravine perchance by some winter storm—to aid them in surmounting the difficulties of the way, and these they now determined to utilise if possible as torches.

With some little difficulty the smaller ends of these brands were induced to kindle; but, once fairly ignited, they blazed up bravely, and thus provided with the necessary lights the adventurers boldly pushed forward and plunged into the recesses of the fissure.

CHAPTER THIRTEEN
AT THE NORTH POLE

The opening was so low and so narrow, that for the first fifty or sixty feet the explorers were I obliged to creep forward on their hands and knees; then it widened and became gradually higher, so that by the time they had penetrated a couple of hundred feet they were able to resume a perpendicular attitude. The cavern, if such it could be called, still however remained so narrow that it was only here and there possible for them to walk side by side. It was also very tortuous; and the heights varied momentarily, at one time compelling them to stoop almost double in order to pass beneath some immense projection, and anon increasing so greatly that the light of their torches failed to reach and reveal the roof. They observed several rifts or crevices to the right and left of them as they pressed forward, but, with one or two exceptions, these were quite impassable, and those which were not so were still so cramped that they offered no inducement to deviate from the main passage.

Groping thus in semi-darkness over painfully rough and broken ground, a full hour was spent, and the colonel was just expressing his conviction that they must have traversed a distance of fully two miles when a faint glimmer of daylight revealed itself on one of the rocky walls of the passage; and, turning sharply round an angle, the pair suddenly found themselves once more within a few yards of the open air.

Emerging into broad daylight a most wonderful spectacle greeted the two adventurous explorers. They found themselves standing on a narrow strip of coarse sandy beach at the bottom of an immense basin, measuring fully a mile in diameter, the sides of which were formed of lofty precipitous cliffs of volcanic rock, so smooth and so nearly vertical that nowhere, at least in their immediate neighbourhood, could they discover a spot capable of being scaled. Before them, and occupying the whole bottom of this enormous basin, stretched a placid lake, the water of which was as clear as crystal. A thin filmy veil of vapour rose everywhere from the surface of the water, softening the hard outlines of the more distant landscape, and imparting an aspect of dreamlike witchery and unreality which it would certainly have otherwise lacked.

"Why, the water is tepid!" exclaimed Sir Reginald, plunging his hand into the lake and raising a small quantity of its water in his palm, to ascertain by taste whether it was fresh or salt.

The colonel thereupon thrust *his* hand down, and satisfied himself by experiment of the truth of his companion's statement. It was even more than tepid, it was positively *warm*.

The two were still discussing the probable reason for this phenomenon when their attention was suddenly arrested by a curious movement of the water in the centre of the lake. First a few tremulous ripples appeared, spreading outward from the centre; then the disturbance became more pronounced, until, within a minute, an area of some thirty or forty yards in diameter had assumed an appearance of violent ebullition. Suddenly a jet of steam and spray shot up out of the centre of this disturbed spot; and then, before either of the two bewildered spectators could find time to remark upon so curious a phenomenon, an immense column of purest crystal water shot into the air to a height of at least two hundred feet, and, gleaming and flashing in the sunbeams as it soared away above the level of the encircling cliffs, spread out into a dome-like sheet, and, leaving behind it aloft a dense cloud of vapour of dazzling whiteness, fell again into the lake in the form of a shower of boiling water.

"A geyser!" exclaimed the baronet. "A geyser! and of such grandeur that the Great Geyser of Iceland, which I have seen, sinks into the utmost insignificance compared with it."

"You are right," acquiesced Lethbridge. "I too have seen the so-called Great Geyser, and admired it immensely; but after this—"

He finished with a shrug of the shoulders so expressive that there was not the slightest need for words to explain his meaning.

"We must bring the professor to see this," he continued after a slight pause. "And—look here, Elphinstone—if you wish to intensely gratify the worthy man, call this geyser after him—'The Von Schalckenberg Geyser'—eh? It doesn't sound half bad, does it?"

The baronet laughingly consented to his friend's proposal, the more readily as he knew that what Lethbridge had said as to the professor's gratification was perfectly true; and then the wanderers resumed their journey, passing along the narrow strip of sand which divided the edge of the water from the base of the cliffs.

"There is no doubt, I think, that this geyser produces the cloud of vapour and the sudden flashing gleam, at tolerably regular intervals, which so aroused our curiosity this morning," remarked the baronet as they plodded somewhat wearily along side by side over the sand.

His companion assented, and then they both paused, and finally flung themselves down upon the sand to witness a repetition of the eruption, the premonitory signs of which at that moment made their appearance. Then, when it was over, finding themselves very comfortable—and very hungry—they concluded to take luncheon before again moving; and, this being followed by a pipe, it was after four o'clock in the afternoon when they once more made a move.

A saunter for three-quarters of an hour along the margin of the lake enabled them to reach a spot almost directly opposite that where they had emerged into daylight from the interior of the cavern; and here they found the point of overflow from the lake. The chain of hills, which from their first point of sight had appeared to completely surround the sheet of water, was here pierced by a narrow valley, through which a small shallow stream, emanating from the geyser lake, made its devious way. As the course of this valley appeared to trend generally in a northerly direction, or toward the high table-land of which the travellers were in quest, and as, moreover, the valley appeared to offer the only exit from the lake basin in a northerly direction, the travellers decided to follow its course, which they did by keeping close to the margin of the stream. This mode of procedure, whilst it afforded them tolerably easy walking, also enabled them to estimate more accurately than they had hitherto done, the enormous quantity of water projected into the air by the geyser; for whilst the stream normally consisted of a body of water some ten feet wide by three or four inches deep, it was swollen—at regular intervals of twenty minutes each, corresponding with the periodical discharge of the geyser—into a rushing and foaming torrent of about ten feet wide and four feet deep, lasting thus for about a minute, when the stream again rapidly subsided to its previous depth.

For a distance of about two miles the stream wound its way over a bed of exposed rock, beyond which occurred a considerable stretch of coarse gravelly soil, thickly overgrown with long grass. The constant flow of water for untold ages through this bed of gravel had scoured out a channel nearly forty feet wide by half that depth; the banks being perfectly vertical, except in a few places where the gravel had crumbled away to a rather steep slope.

It was whilst the wanderers were passing one of these places that—the sun being by this time in the western quarter of the heavens, and his level rays falling directly upon the right bank of the stream—the baronet's attention was arrested by the appearance of several bright sparkling gleams emanating from among the *débris* of the crumbling bank. He directed the colonel's attention to these, whereupon the latter, seized with sudden excitement, scrambled down the bank, waded across the shallow stream, and in another instant flung himself down upon his knees on the gravel. Before the astonished baronet could follow him he leaped to his feet again, and, whilst he waved some glittering object above his head, shouted:

"Hurrah! hurrah! Elphinstone, my dear fellow, we are in luck to-day. Here is a fabulous fortune for every one of us, to be had merely for the trouble of picking up. *This is a bed of diamondiferous gravel.*"

Sir Reginald hastened across the stream, and, scrambling half-way up the bank, joined his companion on the spot where the latter had halted.

"Look here!" exclaimed Lethbridge, holding out for inspection a crystal as large as a pigeon's egg; "what think you of that for a first find? And it is of the first water, too."

The baronet took it in his hand and examined it critically. Then he handed it back with the remark:

"Well, my dear fellow, I am no judge of diamonds, at least in their natural uncut state; but if your supposition—that you have discovered a 'bed' or 'pocket,' or whatever you call it, of diamonds—be correct, I most heartily congratulate you."

"You—congratulate—*me*?" gasped the colonel. "Why, my dear Elphinstone, what on earth do you mean? I am much obliged for your congratulations, certainly; but whether the diamonds here be many or few, we shall of course all share alike, so you may also congratulate yourself and our absent friends at the same time. And as to my supposition being correct, I have had too much experience at the South African diamond-fields to make a mistake in such a matter. Why," he continued, looking round and picking up two or three more stones, "they are positively sown broadcast just here—an hour's diligent work in this spot will make us all rich beyond the power of computation."

"If that be the case," returned the baronet, "then here goes to help you. But, mind, I am a rich man already; and not a single stone will I accept until all three of you are perfectly satisfied that you have abundantly sufficient for all your requirements."

"Very well," said the colonel. "Go ahead with that understanding if you like. I feel pretty confident that, even upon such terms, you will be able to take back to England, if all goes well, sufficient gems to make the future Lady Elphinstone—should there ever be such a personage—a diamond suite which shall cause her to be the envied of all beholders."

Sir Reginald laughed gleefully. "I have never yet met a woman charming enough to induce me to yield up my freedom of action and movement for her sake, and I do not think it likely I ever shall," he said.

Lethbridge shook his head a little doubtfully, but he was just then so busy digging down into the gravel with his hunting-knife that he had no breath to waste in the words of a disclaimer.

The baronet moved away to a distance of some twenty feet, and began poking about the gravel in a very careless, half-hearted sort of way, occasionally picking up and slipping into one of his capacious pockets such crystals as he thought likely to be of value.

Half an hour of this work sufficed him; and, rising to his feet, he cried: "Spell, ho! as our friend Mildmay would probably observe. Now, Lethbridge," as he sauntered up to his companion, "let us compare the results of our labour."

With this he flung himself down upon the gravel, and, plunging his hand into his pocket three or four times, produced a goodly little heap of gems of all sizes, ranging from that of a pea up to stones of fully one ounce in weight. Meanwhile the colonel brought his collection to light, and a very fine one it was, the stones being nearly twice as many as those gathered by the baronet, though many of them were much smaller.

"Is that all?" asked Sir Reginald.

"*All?*" echoed Lethbridge; "why, my dear sir, what would you have? If, after we have quite exhausted the ground here, my share amounts to such a handsome collection as this, I can assure you I shall be exceedingly well satisfied. You have made a most excellent haul too, but I think mine is the more valuable of the two."

"Perhaps," said the baronet, "*this* will go some way toward equalising our finds." And as he spoke he quietly slipped his hand into his pocket and smilingly produced a stone fully as large as a hen's egg.

The colonel took it into his hands and critically examined it for several minutes. It was most unmistakably a diamond, and that, too, of the very finest water, without the faintest trace of a flaw of any kind. He remained silent so long that Sir Reginald grew impatient and finally blurted out:

"Well, man, what is it? Is it a diamond, or is it merely a worthless piece of crystal? Why don't you speak?"

"Simply," said the colonel as he took a final look at it against the light and then handed it back, "because I am at a loss for words to express my admiration. It *is* a diamond, and, so far as I know, the finest that has ever yet been brought to light. Its value must be simply fabulous, and I heartily congratulate you on its discovery. Where did you find it? Was it deep in the gravel?"

"Come with me and I'll show you," was the reply; and, leading the colonel back to the spot, Sir Reginald quietly pointed to a hole about eighteen inches deep which he had excavated, and wherein lay, side by side, seven other gems equally as fine as the one he had produced.

"Help yourself, my dear fellow," he said with a laugh, "and then let us be moving; we have our dinner to find yet, you know."

Lethbridge fairly gasped for breath as his eyes first fell upon the magnificent jewels; but he lost no time in transferring them to his pocket, and then he turned to the baronet and asked what would be the best thing for them to do next.

"Let us simply continue our journey," answered the baronet. "Of course if these stones which we have found are really diamonds, which I do not doubt, since you assure me that they are, I am as fully alive as yourself to the fact that a mine of incalculable wealth lies here at our feet. But it will not run away within the next few days. Let us finish our exploration and return to the *Flying Fish*. We will then move her to this spot, and all hands of us can then go to work at diamond-hunting in good earnest. Meanwhile, if these large stones are of such inestimable value, it seems to me that they are likely to prove, after all, practically valueless, for the simple reason that nobody will be found willing to spend the enormous sum which would enable him to become a purchaser."

"That is very true," answered the colonel with a laugh. "The stones of moderate size are what we must hope to realise upon; nevertheless, I shall not pass over such large ones as may happen to thrust themselves under my notice, for if we should fail to dispose of them, they will still come in handy as ornaments for our future wives, in which, notwithstanding a remark you made a little while ago, I somehow have a profound belief. Now, if you are ready to march, so am I."

The pair accordingly shouldered their guns, and, turning their backs for the time being upon the diamond mine, continued their course down the valley.

Half an hour later a herd of reindeer was discovered browsing upon the lichens and mosses which grew plentifully on the rocky spurs of the range of hills from which the travellers were now emerging, and one of these was soon afterwards killed with little or no difficulty by means of a bullet from one of the rifles. To such experienced hunters as Sir Reginald and the colonel the task of "breaking up" the deer was an easy one, and, that done, they went into camp on the spot, and feasted royally that night upon reindeer tongue and marrow-bones.

The two following days passed uneventfully, that is to say the travellers met with no adventure specially worth recording. They passed through extensive tracts of pine forest, and saw plenty of game, to say nothing of such valuable fur-bearing animals as the sable and ermine, both of which animals seemed to be extraordinarily abundant, and late on the evening of the third day they found themselves at the base of the table-land, after a somewhat fatiguing but most enjoyable tramp.

The next day was devoted to a thorough examination of the somewhat remarkable object which they had set out to visit. It proved to be an enormous mass of rock, nearly circular in shape, about three miles in circumference, and towering aloft from the surface of the surrounding plain to a height of between three and four thousand feet, as nearly as could be measured without the aid of instruments. Their idea had of course been not only to reach this enormous rock, but also to ascend to its summit, but this they found to be quite impracticable, a journey round it demonstrating the fact that on all sides its cliffs rose perpendicularly and without a single break from the base to the flat summit. For that time at least they were defeated; but when they finally turned their backs upon "Mount Mildmay," as they determined to name it, it was with a fixed resolve that, before many days were over, they would reach the summit with the aid of the *Flying Fish*.

Their journey back to the ship was marked by no more noteworthy incident than the sighting in the distance of a herd of mammoths, apparently the identical animals with which they had already had an encounter. They followed a somewhat different route from their outward one, making a détour round the group of hills which inclosed the "Schalckenberg Geyser," and arrived at the ship late on the evening of the sixth day from their departure, weary and somewhat foot-sore it is true, but in all other respects in the very best of health, and with thoroughly pleasant memories of their journey.

They were of course welcomed with open arms by the two friends they had left behind them. Mildmay, under the professor's skilful treatment, was rapidly advancing toward complete recovery; and as for the scientist himself, he was jubilant in the highest degree over the fact that he had been thoroughly successful in his preparation of that gigantic "specimen," the mammoth. A great deal of desultory conversation of course took place within the first hour of the wanderers' return; but at last the party settled down, and then followed a recital by Sir Reginald of the particulars of the journey. Both the professor and Mildmay were of course intensely interested in the story, but in different ways. Mildmay's interest was merely that of the ordinary travelled man of culture, but von Schalckenberg was disposed to regard everything from the scientist's view-point, and incessantly broke the continuity of the narrative by a whole string of questions which neither Sir Reginald nor the colonel could possibly answer. He was extravagantly delighted with both the description of the geyser and the sight of the diamonds, and it was difficult to say which pleased him most; perhaps the most gratifying circumstance to him was the information that the geyser had been named after him, at all events he begged most pathetically that the projected visit to this most interesting object might be allowed to take precedence of that to the diamond mine.

Such being the case, it will readily be understood that no pen of mere ordinary graphic power could hope to adequately portray the ecstasy of enthusiasm with which the worthy man, two days later, actually viewed the geyser itself from so advantageous a stand-point as the deck of the *Flying Fish*; such a task is utterly beyond the powers of the present narrator and must be left to the vivid imagination of the indulgent reader. For over two hours did that amiable and learned scientist sit immovably in his deck chair with a meerschaum of abnormal dimensions in his mouth, and with his eyes beaming in a rapt admiration, which was almost adoration, upon the magnificent spectacle; and it was not until he had been solemnly assured by the others that he would be excused from all participation in the task of diamond-hunting and have full liberty to return to the geyser and spend there the whole of the time during which the rest of the party might be so engaged, that he consented to leave the spot at all.

Three days were spent at the diamond mine; and, with the aid of proper tools obtained from the ship, this time proved sufficient for the accumulation of such a hoard of priceless gems as would, if disposed of at even half their market value, realise a magnificent fortune for each of the lucky finders.

The next move was to the summit of the flat tableland, which was of course easily reached by the *Flying Fish*. It proved to be, as had already been surmised, merely an enormous mass of bare rock, without a scrap of soil or vegetation of any kind about its surface, and useful only as a citadel, into which, had it been planted in some more accessible spot on the earth's surface, it would undoubtedly have been converted, in which case it would have eclipsed even Gibraltar itself in the matter of impregnability. Useless as it was, however, where it stood, its summit afforded an admirable look-out; and from that point of vantage the travellers made the discovery that "Elphinstone Land" was an island, the horizon at that elevation being bounded by the sea on every side. The rock was roughly circular in shape, with a circumference of about three miles, and the travellers made the circuit of the summit in about an hour and a half, pausing at frequent intervals to admire and enjoy the magnificent panorama of woods and hills and streams which lay spread out beneath them. Herds of elk, reindeer, and musk-oxen were seen dotted about here and there on the plains below, as well as a skulking wolf or two, a few Arctic foxes, and other wild animals. The herd of mammoths—apparently the only herd in the island—was also seen; and, with the aid of their telescopes, the travellers were also able to make out, far away at sea, certain dark moving spots which, from their alternate appearance above and disappearance beneath the surface, they judged to be whales.

The chief business of the travellers, however, on the summit of "Mount Mildmay" was to ascertain whether or no the North Pole of the earth was or was not situated within its circumference. This was rightly regarded as a matter of such great importance that several days were unhesitatingly devoted to its settlement; and Mildmay, the professor, and Colonel Lethbridge were busy from breakfast time in the morning until dinner-time at night, making the most careful observations and working out the necessary calculations. These were at length satisfactorily completed—not one moment too soon, for the sun was daily dropping nearer and nearer to the horizon—and the trio were enabled, not only to say that the North Pole *was* contained within the limits of the summit, but to plant their feet upon it and to say unhesitatingly and authoritatively:

"This is the North Pole!"

The position having thus been accurately determined, the next thing was to mark the spot.

With this object a large triangle was first described about it, and a point was carefully marked off on each of its sides in such a position that a line tightly strained from such point to the opposite angle of the triangle would pass directly through the pole. This done, an excavation six feet deep in the solid rock was made, and in its bottom was deposited a tightly-sealed bottle containing a small parchment scroll, on which was inscribed a brief statement of the circumstances connected with the discovery of the spot, with the date, and the signatures of the joint discoverers. This bottle was carefully packed in and buried up with small fragments of rock, and made finally secure by a covering of excellent concrete, the materials for compounding which had been carefully and with infinite labour prepared by the professor. Then, when the concrete had become properly hardened, a substantial flagstaff of aethereum was stepped into the hole in a position accurately corresponding with the North Pole of the earth, and also made secure by being built in or "set" in concrete, which completely filled the hole. The professor next, with the aid of a diamond, engraved on the staff, in bold conspicuous characters, at a height of five feet from the ground, the words:

"*This staff marks the exact position of the North Pole of the earth.*" And finally, amid cheers from the rest of the party, Sir Reginald Elphinstone ran the Union Jack up to the staff head and knotted the halliards so that it would remain there, thus formally claiming for the British nation the honour of actual discovery.

CHAPTER FOURTEEN
SOUTHWARD HO!

So important a matter as the localisation of the Pole having thus been satisfactorily disposed of, it was next resolved to effect a thorough exploration of the entire island, including its circumnavigation. This, with the aid of the *Flying Fish*, was pretty effectually accomplished in a fortnight, after which the ship returned to her original anchorage in the harbour, on the south side of the island, now named Lethbridge Cove.

Both the forests and the adjacent waters of this favoured hyperborean land were found to be literally swarming with game and other animals, some of which afforded in their flesh a welcome change from the preserved meats with which the ship's larder was stocked, whilst the chief value of others lay in their "pelts" or skins; and, the hydrographic features of the island having been carefully ascertained and recorded, the party, with the exception of von Schalckenberg, now gave themselves up unreservedly to the pleasures of the chase. The professor's tastes lay more in the direction of geology, mineralogy, and botany, though he was also an enthusiastic naturalist, and thus, whilst he sallied forth every morning armed with gun, hammer, specimen box for his botanical treasures, and bag for his minerals, the three others went their several ways, either armed with traps and guns in search of game, or in one of the boats, duly provided with dredger, net, and line, in quest of ocean spoils.

Thus employed, the short remainder of the Arctic summer swiftly passed away; the sun daily sank nearer and nearer the horizon; the temperature fell; frost made its appearance, hardening the soil beneath the tread and coating the pools and puddles and morasses with an ever-thickening sheet of ice and the vegetation with a delicate tracery of silver; and at length the day came when the anchor was lifted and the *Flying Fish* moved some few miles out to sea to enable her occupants to witness the final disappearance of the sun beneath the southern horizon. Some anxiety had been experienced by the travellers for the last few days, as clouds had been gathering in the sky, with every indication of a speedy change of weather, and it was feared that the sight, which they had long been promising themselves, would, after all, be denied them; but at the last moment, or rather at the last hour, fortune proved favourable to them; the cloud-bank broke up along the south-western horizon, the vapours grouped themselves into a series of imposingly picturesque masses, all aflame with the most gorgeous tints of sunset, and from a little after eleven o'clock until shortly after noon the thin golden upper edge of the luminary's disc was visible sweeping imperceptibly along the purple horizon, until finally, as it reached the point of disappearance, it glimmered feebly for a moment, and, whilst the travellers stood watching it bare-headed, sank out of sight. The Arctic day was over, and the six months of night and winter had set in. Not, it must be understood, that darkness set in immediately—far from it; for several succeeding days there ensued a weird, delicious, magic, and ever-deepening twilight; but by the eighth day after the sun's final disappearance this also had vanished, and night reigned with undisputed sway.

And now, too, winter laid its icy hand with unrelenting grasp upon this beauteous polar island; not, however, to desolate it with storm and howling tempest and the deadly cold with which he visits less favoured climes, but only to add newer and more unaccustomed beauties to the scene. It is true that for the first fortnight after the disappearance of the sun the weather wore a more or less unsettled aspect. The sky became overcast with a canopy of cloud which, light and fleecy at first, steadily increased in density; and at length, on the travellers emerging from the pilot-house one morning after breakfast, they found the motionless air thick with falling snow, which, settling noiselessly down, had already covered the deck to a depth of some three inches. The darkness was of course intense, so much so, indeed, that it was impossible to see for a distance of half the length of the ship, and for all that they could see of the land it might as well have been a hundred miles distant.

This state of things lasted without intermission for the ensuing four days and kept the travellers close prisoners on board their ship. This, however, they in nowise regretted; indeed this short breathing space was positively welcome to them, for they had plenty of work to do; and, shut up warm and snug on board the *Flying Fish*, with all her saloons, cabins, and corridors brilliantly illuminated by the electric light, they busied themselves in carefully preparing and curing the many unique specimens of natural history and the various choice skins and furs they had already accumulated.

But on the morning of the fifth day they found that another change of weather had taken place, and, on going out on deck, a glorious spectacle greeted their delighted eyes. The snowfall had ceased, the sky was once more cloudless, and the deep sapphire blue was studded with countless myriads of scintillating stars that gleamed with the cold sharp lustre which is seen only in periods of very severe frost. But it was not the brilliant starlight, beautiful though that was, which drew ejaculations of wonder and delight from the lips of the entranced beholders; it was another and a rarer sight which excited their admiration. As they looked, the sky immediately overhead, and for a distance of some twenty degrees all round from the zenith, became tinged with the softest and most delicate rose-colour, bordering which there suddenly appeared a broad circle of flashing rays of light, blood-red at the inner rim of the circle, and merging from thence through the richest purple into brilliant blue, and from thence, through green of every conceivable tint, into a clear dazzling yellow at the points of the rays. These superbly-tinted rays were animated by a constant motion; now withdrawing themselves into the main body of the circle as into a sheath, and anon darting out again until they almost reached the horizon; and so delicately transparent were they that, notwithstanding their brilliant colour, the stars were distinctly perceptible through them. This magnificent spectacle continued for a full hour with ever-increasing brilliancy, suffusing sea and land with a quivering glow of prismatic light, and imparting an aspect of magic, unearthly, indescribable beauty to the scene. Then the colours gradually faded, the flashes became more feeble, and the darting rays ever shorter and shorter, until they finally faded completely away, to be succeeded shortly afterwards by the keen silvery radiance of the young crescent moon which slowly rolled upwards from the horizon, and, shedding her subdued light upon the snow-clad landscape, invested it with an air of bewitching mystery and unreality which was distinctly heightened by the profound impressive silence of the long Arctic night.

With nature thus presenting herself to the travellers in so novel and attractive a guise a month swiftly passed away, during which they tended their traps or prosecuted their hunting expeditions under the glorious light of the aurora, the cold steel-like radiance of the silver moon, or the dim mysterious starlight; alternating these open-air employments with assiduous devotion to their easels, in sufficiently clever but altogether unsuccessful efforts to adequately transfer to canvas the entrancing beauties of the Arctic scenery and phenomena which constantly charmed their delighted eyes.

Toward the end of October, however, the temperature had fallen so low that ice had begun to form all along the coast-line of Elphinstone Land, and the weather had taken a decided change for the worse. Moreover, the party had accumulated so much extra weight in the shape of valuable skins, natural history specimens, and other curiosities, as to seriously affect the buoyancy of the *Flying Fish* as an aerial ship; and they therefore at last—more than half-reluctantly—came to the determination to desert the enchanted region of the Pole and wend their way southward.

Accordingly, on the morning of the first day of November the anchor was hove up; the vapour was turned into the air and water chambers, producing an almost perfect vacuum; and, rising into the air to an altitude of about ten thousand feet, the *Flying Fish* turned her nose southward, and, illumined by the dazzling effulgence of the most glorious aurora the voyagers had ever seen, was sent ahead at the utmost limit of her speed.

It was determined to return to England forthwith, and without pause or stoppage of any kind, unless some unforeseen necessity should arise, the object being to dispose of their various acquisitions previous to a renewal of their wanderings. The elevation at starting was therefore maintained, and the ship pursued her headlong flight to the southward with only one man—Mildmay—in the pilot-house to take charge and enact the part of look-out; the remainder busying themselves in packing up their various treasures for transference to safe-keeping on shore. The pilot-house, like every other habitable portion of the ship, was maintained at a comfortable temperature by means of pipes communicating with the vapour-generating chamber in the engine-room below; and, reclining at his ease in a most luxurious lounging chair, the lieutenant had nothing to do but maintain a vigilant lookout through the circular windows, and solace himself with his pipe meanwhile. The ship's speed through the air was about one hundred and twenty miles per hour; and by their calculations they expected to overtake the sun in about latitude 79 degrees 49 minutes north; if, therefore, the *Flying Fish* maintained her speed, the sun ought to appear once more above the horizon in four hours thirty-five and a half minutes from the time of starting—Lethbridge Cove being situated in exactly 89 degrees 0 minutes North latitude. It was exactly nine o'clock in the morning when they started; consequently, if their calculations were right, the sun ought to make his appearance at thirty-five and a half minutes past one; and it was this phenomenon for which Mildmay was chiefly watching, his companions being anxious to have the unique experience of seeing the luminary rise an hour and a half past mid-day. And it was for this reason, and in order that they might not on the one hand be taken by surprise by being hurried southward on the wings of a favouring gale, or on the other hand be delayed by a possible adverse one, that the elevation of ten thousand feet had been selected, this being well within the limits of the *neutral belt*, or zone of motionless air.

Not to be caught napping, Mildmay extinguished the electric light in the pilot-house as the musical gong of the clock suspended therein struck the hour of one; after which he rose to his feet and took a good look round on all sides. There was, however, nothing to be seen save a vast sea of cloud beneath his feet and on all sides, as far as the eye could reach, softly illumined by the light of the star-studded heavens above. But even as he looked a just perceptible paleness in the deep velvety blue of the sky to the southward attracted his attention. He looked more intently. Yes, there could be no mistake about it; that pallor of the southern sky was undoubtedly the first faint indication of the approaching dawn; and he at once struck two strokes—the appointed signal—upon the great mellow-toned bell which hung in the pilot-house.

The call was promptly answered by the appearance of his three fellow-voyagers, who, abandoning whatever they had in hand, rushed helter-skelter up the saloon staircase and into the pilot-house, anxious to lose no scrap of that, to them, now novel sight, sunrise.

Rapidly yet imperceptibly the pale dawn stole upward into the sky; the lustrous stars waxed dim before it, and one by one twinkled out of sight; a faint roseate flush tinged the sky along the horizon, brightened first into a rich orange, then into purest amber, the colours being faintly reflected on the most distant edges of the vast cloud-bank floating below; and at length, just as the hands of the clock marked thirty-five minutes after one, an arrowy shaft of pure white light shot upward into the sky, swiftly followed by another and another; and then, with a dazzling flash of golden light, the upper edge of the sun's disc rose slowly into view, soaring higher and higher until the whole of the glorious luminary was revealed, whilst the rolling sea of cloud above which the *Flying Fish* skimmed glowed softly beneath his beams with varying tints of the most exquisite opal.

This return to the realms of day had a curious effect upon the travellers. They had not been conscious of the least depression of spirits consequent upon their sojourn of more than a month in the region of uninterrupted night, but it must have affected them, however unconsciously, to no inconsiderable extent, for now, at the first glimpse of sunshine, their spirits rose to an extravagant height; they felt as though they had just effected their escape from some terrible doom, and they were irresistibly impelled to shake hands with each other, to exchange congratulations, and to talk all together, laughing uproariously at even the feeblest attempt at jocularity.

The thoughts of the quartette were, however, speedily diverted by the ever-imperturbable George, who now sounded the gong for luncheon, and the whole party at once trundled below, leaving the ship to take care of herself, as they very safely might, seeing that she was now travelling down the "first" meridian, or that of Greenwich, with no land ahead nearer than the Shetland Islands, more than a thousand miles distant.

After luncheon, however, the whole party returned to the pilot-house, where they spent the time smoking and chatting, talking over their past adventures, and maturing their further plans, until sunset, when, their short day having come to an end, they once more retired below to complete their preparations for a flying visit to London previous to a resumption of their wanderings.

The question of the disposal of the *Flying Fish* during the short period of their absence from her had greatly exercised their minds for a time. They were anxious still to avoid for the present, if possible, anything approaching to notoriety or the attraction of public notice to their proceedings, and they felt that this could scarcely be done if they ventured to take so singularly modelled a ship into any British port, however insignificant; moreover, there are very few harbours or havens on the British coast capable of receiving a ship with such an excessive draught of water—namely, forty feet—as that of the *Flying Fish*. So they finally decided to sink her off the Isle of Wight (first of all, of course, taking the precaution to accurately ascertain the bearings of her berth), and to proceed to Portsmouth in the two boats, taking with them the spoils of their polar expedition, and trusting to their own ingenuity to evade such suspicions and speculations as might be engendered by the somewhat singular circumstances connected with their arrival, especially as the hour—about half-past four o'clock on the following morning—at which they would reach the Wight would be favourable to the execution of their plan.

The night was intensely dark, with a fresh north-easterly gale blowing, accompanied by frequent rain-squalls, as the voyagers found on descending to within about a thousand feet of the level of the sea at midnight, in order to discover, if possible, their whereabouts. But they could see nothing save the lights of a few ships and fishing craft dotted about here and there; the appearance of the latter indicating that they had already approached to within a short distance of the land; nor did they sight anything by which to fix their position until first the light on Flamborough Head and then that on Spurn Point flashed into view out of the murky darkness. Then indeed, having satisfactorily identified those lights, they knew exactly where they were; the course was altered and shaped anew directly for the spot of their intended descent, and the ship once more soared to her former elevation.

At twenty minutes after four o'clock a.m. a second descent was made, when it was found that they were passing over hilly country which they surmised to be that situated about the borders of the three counties of Surrey, Hants, and Sussex; and almost immediately afterwards the lights on the forts in progress of construction at Spithead came into view, together with the anchor-lights of two or three men-o'-war in the roadstead, and they knew that the first part of their journey was almost accomplished.

Precisely at half-past four o'clock the *Flying Fish* took the water about two miles to the eastward of the "Noman" fort, and her occupants at once began the search for a suitable berth for her—a berth, that is to say, in a position where she would not be likely to be discovered by the fishermen, and where the depth of water would be sufficient to permit of the largest man-o'-war passing over her submerged hull without striking upon it. To discover such a spot proved by no means an easy task; but it was accomplished at last, though at a distance considerably farther out to sea than they had bargained for, and at half-past five o'clock her anchor was let go in the selected berth. Cross bearings were then most carefully taken and entered in each of the travellers' pocket-books, after which the next task was to get their varied spoils into the boats and the boats themselves into the water. This was soon done, and then all hands, including George and the *chef*, but excluding the professor, entered the boats and shoved off a few fathoms from the ship's side, where they anchored.

The first faint signs of dawn were just appearing in the eastern sky when it became apparent to those in the boats that the huge bulk of the *Flying Fish* was disappearing. Steadily but imperceptibly she settled lower and lower in the water until her deck was awash and nothing but her pilot-house remained visible in the dim ghostly light of the early morning. A minute more and this too had disappeared, and, as the waves washed over its top, the baronet carefully lowered over the side of his boat a rope-ladder, well weighted at the bottom and with an unlit electric lamp attached to it in such a position as to hang suspended at a height of about six feet above the bed of the sea. This lamp was of course attached to a battery in the boat, and as soon as Sir Reginald felt the weights at the foot of the ladder touch bottom he sent the current through the insulated wire, a patch of vivid white light, like a patch of moonlight, immediately shining out beneath the waves and showing that the lantern was properly performing its duty. Then they waited.

Not for very long, however. An interval of perhaps five minutes elapsed, and then a quivering jerky motion became communicated to the rope-ladder, followed a minute later by the appearance of von Schalckenberg in his suit of diving armour. He stepped quietly into the boat, and whilst he busied himself in doffing his glittering panoply, the lamp was extinguished, the ladder hauled inboard, the anchors tripped, and the two boats made their way slowly to the westward, heading in for Nettlestone Point and the Solent.

They arrived at Portsmouth about half-past seven o'clock, and Sir Reginald at once made his way to the Custom House to get the boats' cargoes cleared. He was fortunate enough to find in the collector a man with whom he had had several previous transactions, and who was consequently pretty well acquainted with him. This facilitated matters greatly, and by half-past eight the duty (a very considerable sum) had been paid and the goods passed, so that nothing further remained but to land everything and have it conveyed to the railway-station for transmission to town. This done the two boats were taken into "The Camber" and put under the care of a trustworthy man, after which the party breakfasted at the "George," proceeding to town directly afterwards by the twelve-o'clock express.

CHAPTER FIFTEEN
A TROOP OF UNICORNS

A week later, the four friends once more found themselves beneath the roof of "The Migrants'", where it had been arranged that they were to meet and take luncheon together prior to their journey down to Portsmouth to rejoin the *Flying Fish*. On comparing notes it was found that each had, according to his own views, made the best possible use of his time, the professor having not only placed the mammoth's skin in the hands of an eminent taxidermist, but also prepared and read before the Royal Society a paper on "The Open Polar Sea," which had created a profound impression on the collective mind of that august body; Lethbridge and Mildmay had seized the opportunity for paying a too-long-deferred visit to their respective mothers; and Sir Reginald had, acting upon the best obtainable advice, conveyed the four parcels of diamonds belonging to the party over to Amsterdam, where they had been left in the care of a thoroughly trustworthy diamond merchant, with instructions that certain of the jewels were to be cut and set in the handsomest possible manner, whilst the rest were to be disposed of as opportunity might offer. The furs were also satisfactorily got rid of; some of them having been sold, and the remainder (consisting of all the choicest skins) placed in the hands of the furriers to be cured and taken care of until their owners should return to claim them.

The luncheon was a very lively meal; the conversation naturally turning to the last occasion upon which the travellers had met there; and upon its conclusion the four friends chartered a couple of hansoms, which conveyed them to Waterloo station in good time for the Portsmouth express.

On their arrival at the Harbour station they found George and his French friend, the cook (both of whom had been granted a week's leave), dutifully awaiting them on the platform. The boats, under the care of the man who had been placed in charge of them, were lying alongside the adjacent slipway, in accordance with a telegraphed arrangement which had preceded the travellers; and, entering these, the party at once proceeded down the harbour, past Southsea and its castle, and out toward Nettlestone Point. It was by this time quite dark, save for the light of the young moon, which was already near her setting, and the boats were consequently at once urged to their full speed in the direction where the *Flying Fish* had been left.

Having originally taken their cross bearings wholly from the shore lights, the voyagers had now no difficulty whatever in placing the boats in their proper position. Arrived on the spot, a sounding-line was dropped over the side, and the first cast showed that they were floating exactly over the submerged ship. The boats were therefore allowed to drift with the tide until they were clear of the *Flying Fish*, when Sir Reginald dropped his anchor and ladder, and the professor, who had already routed out from the stern locker and donned his diving armour, stepped over the side, adjusted his weights, and quietly disappeared beneath the surface of the water. A lapse of perhaps a minute occurred, when the ladder was found to be hanging limp and loose; a bright white light flashed upward through the water for a moment, as a signal from the professor that he had reached the bottom all right; and then the luminous beam was seen moving slowly forward over the bottom in the direction of the submerged ship. Suddenly the light vanished.

"He has reached the ship," the baronet reported to those in the other boat, who were alternately drifting with the tide and moving up against it to maintain an easy speaking distance from their consort. A quarter of an hour passed, and then a brilliant, dazzling flood of light streamed out for about ten seconds at apparently no great distance below the surface, then vanished again.

"All right," remarked Sir Reginald as soon as he saw this; "he has reached the pilot-house. Now, George, up with the anchor, my good fellow, and we will back off a few yards out of harm's way."

The boats accordingly did so, von Schalckenberg allowing them ten minutes for the operation; then, with a sudden rush and swirl of water, the huge bulk of the *Flying Fish* appeared above the surface, looming black, vast, and mysterious against the faintly luminous horizon. A moment more, and the windows of the pilot-house shone out a series of luminous discs against the darkness, showing that the professor had lighted up the interior, and that individual himself appeared on deck hailing the invisible boats with:

"It is all right; everything is just as we left it, and you may come on board as soon as you like."

Ten minutes later the boats had been hoisted in and stowed away, and the *Flying Fish*, at an elevation of some three hundred feet above the sea-level, was moving to the southward and eastward across the placid waters of the Channel, at the moderate rate of some five-and-twenty miles per hour. At midnight, however, after a little music and conversation, the pace was quickened to about one hundred miles per hour; the altitude was at the same time increased to ten thousand feet; the course was set to south, by compass, and the travellers, with a feeling of perfect security, retired to rest, confident that the professor's clever automatic devices would not only maintain the ship at her then elevation, but would also steer her straight in the required direction.

On the following morning at daybreak the travellers found themselves hovering over the blue Mediterranean, with the African coast at no great distance, and a town of considerable size directly ahead. This town was soon identified as Tunis (near which is the site of ancient Carthage), and they shortly afterwards passed over it, not unnoticed by the inhabitants, who, with the aid of the telescope, could be seen pointing upward at the ship in evident consternation. Then on over the chain of hills beyond the town, and they once more found themselves with the sea beneath them, the ship's course causing her to just skirt the Gulf of Hammamet, whilst they obtained a splendid view of Lake Kairwan and the three streams which it absorbs. Then past Capes Dimas and Kadijah, across the Gulf of Cabes, and so on to Tripoli, which was reached and passed soon after the party had risen from breakfast. At this point the Mediterranean was finally left behind, and the ship's speed was shortly afterwards reduced to a rate of about fifteen knots through the air; her altitude being also decreased to about one thousand feet above the ground level.

The course was now altered to about south by west (true), and the travellers passed slowly over the Fezzan country, the borders of the Libyan Desert, the Soudan, and Dar Zaleh; the prospect beneath and around them varying with every hour of their progress, from the most fertile and highly cultivated district, dotted here and there with straggling villages, to the most sterile and sandy wastes. They saw but little game during this portion of their journey, and only descended to the ground at night, when the vessel was secured by her four grip-anchors during the hours which her crew devoted to rest.

This uneventful state of affairs continued until they arrived in ten degrees of north latitude and twenty degrees of east longitude, when they found themselves fairly beyond the limits of even the most rudimentary civilisation, and in a country of alternating wooded hill and grassy, well-watered plain, which had all the appearance of a very promising hunting district. The country was very thinly populated, the native villages being in some cases as much as fifty or sixty miles apart, whilst in no instance were two villages found within a shorter distance than twenty miles. The inhabitants were, as far as could be seen, fine stalwart specimens of the negro race, evidently skilled in the chase and, presumably, also in all the arts of savage warfare; but it was not very easy to form a reliable opinion upon their habits and mode of life, as whenever the *Flying Fish* appeared upon the scene they invariably took to their heels with yells of terror and sought shelter in the thickest covert they could find.

As the travellers penetrated further in toward the heart of this district, their anticipations in the matter of game became ever more abundantly realised; vast herds of antelope of various descriptions, and including more than one new species, being constantly visible from the ship's deck whenever she was raised a few hundred feet in the air. And, in addition to antelope, a few elephants, an occasional herd of buffalo, a troop or two of wild horses, a rhinoceros, a family of lions, a skulking leopard, or a gorilla, was a by no means unusual sight; to say nothing of the countless troops of monkeys and other unimportant game with which the country seemed to be literally swarming.

Such a district seemed to be the very realisation of a sportsman's or a naturalist's dream of paradise; and it was quickly decided that a halt should be called, and at least a few days devoted to the pursuit of game and the collection of natural history specimens. A suitable spot in which to bring the *Flying Fish* to earth was accordingly sought for, and found in a small open space of about thirty acres, almost entirely surrounded by bush, and in close proximity to a tiny streamlet which emptied itself into a small shallow lake about half a mile distant from the selected site.

Here they hunted with moderate success for a week, not killing any very large amount of game—for they soon discovered that they could do very little without horses—but managing, by patient stalking and the secreting of themselves in artfully devised ambushes, to secure a few choice and rare skins and horns, besides the tusks of eight elephants and the plumage of over a dozen ostriches.

On the day of their departure from this temporary halting-place, however, a piece of surprising and wholly unexpected good fortune befell them. It was one of those especially glorious mornings which are never encountered anywhere but in the tropics. A very heavy dew had fallen during the night, revivifying the vegetation parched by the fervid heat of the previous day, and causing the foliage and flowers to glow for a brief period in their brightest and freshest tints, whilst they exhaled their choicest odours; and a light cool northerly breeze imparted a temporary freshness to the early morning air, as yet uninfluenced by the scarcely risen sun.

They had "broken camp," and had risen to a height of about one thousand feet above the ground level, preparatory to the resumption of their southward journey. An awning was spread over the deck, fore and aft, under the protecting shade of which they proposed to take breakfast; and whilst waiting for the meal to be served, the travellers, each seated in a deck chair, were amusing themselves by inspecting the magnificent prospect which lay spread out around and beneath them, the more distant parts of which were being diligently investigated with the aid of their telescopes.

They were thus engaged when George announced that breakfast was served; and the professor was just on the point of laying down his instrument, preparatory to seating himself at the table, when a small group of animals, which were grazing upon the crest of a distant eminence, swept for a moment across his field of view. A certain something of peculiarity and strangeness in the appearance of the creatures caused the motion of the telescope to be arrested in mid-sweep, and in another instant von Schalckenberg, deaf to the calls of his companions and the respectful reminder of the faithful steward, had his instrument focused full upon the group of animals. They were, however, a long way off, and the mist was now rising so thickly from the surface of the ground that it was impossible to clearly distinguish them; so the professor contented himself by going to the pilot-house and directing the ship's head straight toward the point occupied by the animals. After which he carefully noted the time, made a little mental calculation, and seated himself at the breakfast table, with his watch carefully propped up before his plate.

His friends were, by this time, so accustomed to the professor's little peculiarities that no one thought of asking any questions, feeling sure that an explanation would come all in good time. Neither did they make any remark or evince any surprise, beyond a shrug of the shoulders and an amused elevation of the eyebrows, when the *savant*, glancing at his watch, hastily rose from the table, and, in his absent-mindedness carrying with him a fork with a morsel of venison-steak impaled upon its prongs, hurried away to the pilot-house. A moment or two later a gentle jar was felt as the ship came to the ground; but the mist was by this time so thick that it was difficult to see objects more than a couple of hundred feet distant, and all that could be clearly made out was that they had stopped close to a clump of bush of considerable extent.

By the time that breakfast was over, the morning mist, true to its proverbially evanescent character, had completely passed away, and the travellers found that they had come to earth on the crest of a slight eminence, from which an uninterrupted view, of several miles extent over the surrounding plains, could be obtained in every direction save one, namely, that between which and the ship stretched the belt of bush.

And now came the professor's explanation:

"You have, doubtless, wondered, gentlemen," said he, "why I have thus early, and without warning, interrupted our journey. I will now tell you. I have lately been glancing through the book which, you will remember, I succeeded in recovering from the wreck of the *Daedalus*, and therein I met with a passage of a most surpassingly interesting character. This passage related to the rumoured penetration into this region of a certain unnamed traveller who is stated to have positively asserted that he here saw, on more than one occasion, an animal absolutely identical with the fabled unicorn. This remarkable statement at once reminded me that I had, many years ago, seen a paragraph in a Berlin paper to a similar effect. The statement was accompanied by an expression of strong doubt, if not of absolute incredulity, as to its veracity; an expression which impressed me at the time as being most cruel and unfair to the claimant for the honours of a new discovery in natural history; since the discovery was alleged to have been made in a region which had never before—nor, indeed, has since, until now—been penetrated by civilised man; or from which, at all events, no civilised traveller has ever again emerged, if indeed he had been successful in penetrating it. Such being the case, as the course we were pursuing would take us through the very heart of this unknown and unvisited region, I resolved to maintain a most careful watch for these creatures. I have done so, and I am sanguine that I have this morning actually seen a troop of them. Unfortunately, the mist and the distance together prevented a clear and distinct view of the animals to which I refer; but, whatever they may be, I have an idea that they are at this moment feeding at no great distance on the other side of this belt of bush. Should such be the case, we have the wind of the animals and ought to have no great difficulty in stalking them; a proceeding which, if patiently and cautiously executed, ought to enable us not only to secure a specimen or two, but also to obtain a slight insight into the habits of the creature."

The trio addressed felt, one and all, slightly incredulous as to the realisation of von Schalckenberg's sanguine surmises; but, remembering the mammoths, they prudently kept their own counsel, and hastened away to secure their rifles and to make their preparations for a possibly long and tedious stalk. They exchanged their suits of dazzling white nankeen for others of a thin, tough serge of a light greenish-grey tint, which admirably matched the colour of the long grass through which the stalk would have to be performed; and, in about a quarter of an hour from the commencement of their preparations, found themselves standing outside the huge hull of the ship, and in its shadow, making their final dispositions for the chase. These arrangements were soon made. Sir Reginald and the professor were to constitute one contingent, Lethbridge and Mildmay the other;

these last being impressively instructed by von Schalckenberg to take up the most advantageous position possible for intercepting the flight of the game, but on no account to shoot until the others had first opened fire.

The two parties then went their several ways, reaching, at about the same moment, the opposite extremities of the bush belt. The utmost caution now became necessary in order to avoid startling the game, if indeed the professor was right in his conjectures, and the hunters sank down upon their knees and began a slow and tedious progress through the long grass. The professor was fairly quivering with excitement, and all his companion's efforts were ineffectual to prevent his rising cautiously to his feet as soon as they had cleared the bush sufficiently to allow of his obtaining a view beyond. For a moment or two he glared anxiously around him, then dropped to his knees again as if shot.

"They are there," he gasped almost inarticulately, "sixteen of them; not more than half a mile away."

"And what do '*they*' actually prove to be?" murmured the baronet. "Not unicorns, of course?"

"Yes, *unicorns*! Animals with only one horn—the males, that is to say. Some have no horns, and those I take to be females."

This was too much for Sir Reginald's curiosity. He, in his turn, rose to his feet, ignoring the professor's agonised entreaties for caution, and, sure enough, within half a mile of where he stood was a herd of animals so closely resembling the unicorn which figures as one of the supporters of the royal arms of England that he could hardly credit his eyes. He counted the creatures, and found that, as the professor had stated, there were sixteen of them, all apparently full-grown. They very closely approached the zebra in general shape, but were considerably larger animals, standing about fourteen hands high. They were of a beautiful deep cream colour, their legs black below the knee, and they had short black manes, black switched tails very similar to that of the gemsbok, and, in the case of four of the animals then in view, were provided with a single straight black pointed horn projecting from the very centre of the forehead, just above the level of the eyes.

At length, yielding to the professor's entreaties and remonstrances, the baronet again sank to his knees and the stalk was resumed.

Soon, however, it became apparent that, from some cause or other, the animals were growing restless and uneasy. They frequently ceased feeding suddenly and gazed about them with an anxious, inquiring look, as though suspicious of but unable to detect the approach of danger, and instead of steadily cropping at the grass in one particular spot they would snatch a few hasty mouthfuls and then move on some ten or a dozen yards. And, as it unfortunately happened, their progress was directly away from the hunters, so that the latter soon found they were booked for a very long, tedious, and wearisome task. The stalkers were at first disposed to regard the uneasiness of the game as due to their own presence, yet, upon further reflection, this seemed scarcely possible, for, in the first place, they were all, even to Mildmay and the professor, tolerably experienced hunters, and were conducting the stalk in the most approved and sportsmanlike manner, and, in the next place, they were dead to leeward of the animals, and it was consequently impossible that the creatures could have scented them. Both Sir Reginald and the colonel were thoroughly puzzled; and at length they—almost simultaneously, as it afterwards appeared—arrived at the same conclusion, namely, that the unicorns were being stalked by somebody or something besides themselves, or else that a storm was brewing.

In support of the first idea there was no evidence beyond the mere fact of the animals' restlessness; but the aspect of the heavens soon became such as to strongly favour the second. Whilst the hunters had been sedulously pursuing their task the sky had gradually lost its pristine purity of blue and had become a pale colourless grey, in which the sun seemed to hang like a ghastly white radiant ball, shorn of his beams. The distant landscape first became unnaturally clear and distinct in all its details and then became veiled in a sort of murky haze. Presently a sharply defined ridge of cloud made its appearance above the south-western horizon, spreading rapidly toward the zenith, and the hunters began to realise that they were in for a thorough wetting, if for nothing worse. Mildmay, indeed, who was perhaps better acquainted than anyone else in the party with the character of the tropics, strongly urged upon his companion, Lethbridge, the desirability of abandoning the chase and returning with all speed to the ship; and the latter, impressed by the lieutenant's earnestness, once rose cautiously to his feet with the intention of signalling a return to the other contingent, but the baronet and the scientist were at that moment invisible, so the colonel sank once more on all-fours and the chase went on.

Suddenly a sound like a low growling roar, closely followed by a shrill scream, came floating down to the hunters upon the wings of the almost stagnant breeze, and, springing hastily to their feet, they saw that a magnificent leopard had sprung upon the back of one of the hornless unicorns, and was tearing savagely at its neck and throat with its teeth and claws, the rest of the herd, with one exception, being in full flight. The exception was a fine male unicorn, which, with bristling mane and half-averted body, stood motionless save for a quick angry stamping of his fore-feet upon the ground, watching the unavailing struggles of his hapless companion. These were of very short duration, a staggering gallop of a few yards sufficing to exhaust the victim's strength, when she reeled and fell headlong to the ground with her savage rider still clinging tenaciously to her back. This, apparently, was the moment which the male unicorn had been waiting for. Bounding forward at lightning speed and with lowered head he charged full upon the prostrate pair, and, as the leopard faced round toward him with an angry snarl, the long straight pointed horn was levelled and in another instant the great cat was hurled ruthlessly from the quivering body of his victim, transfixed through eye and brain by the formidable weapon of his vengeful antagonist. The unicorn stood for a moment tossing his head, apparently half stunned with the tremendous shock; but he quickly recovered, and was evidently preparing to renew his terrible onslaught when his quick eye detected the presence of the hunters, who, completely carried away by the exciting spectacle they had just witnessed, were standing at their full height in the long grass, fully exposed from their waists upward, and with the light glancing brightly from the polished silver-like barrels of their rifles. A moment's pause was sufficient for the unicorn; some subtle instinct doubtless taught him that in the strange beings who had thus unexpectedly revealed themselves he beheld enemies more dangerous than the most deadly of his four-footed foes; and, wheeling quickly about, he uttered a curious barking kind of neigh and dashed off at a headlong gallop in the direction already taken by the rest of his companions.

"Good Heavens, we have lost them!" groaned the professor in a perfect agony of despair.

"Yes," assented the baronet, who next turned to his more distant companions and hailed them with:

"We have had our trouble for nothing, after all. The best thing we can now do is to make our way back to the ship with all speed, when we can renew the pursuit, unless, as seems only too probable, we are about to have our hands full with the coming storm. We have not a moment to lose, I should say; so I would suggest that each of us put his best foot foremost."

"Ay, ay," replied Mildmay, "crowd sail we must; for, unless I am greatly mistaken, we are about to have a regular tornado."

"A tornado!" gasped the professor. "Run—run for your lives; I verily believe *I forgot to moor the ship*!"

Forgot to moor the ship! Could such fatal carelessness be possible? If so, they must indeed run for their lives; for should the storm burst before they reached the ship she would be whirled away over the plain like an empty bladder before the blast, to what distance and with what results it was difficult just then to foreshadow; but among the possibilities which instantly presented themselves to the mind was that of death to the two inmates of the ship, irreparable damage to the craft herself, and four persons left to shift for themselves in the very centre of Africa, with nothing but the clothes they wore, the rifles they carried, and about a dozen rounds of ammunition apiece. The prospect was appalling enough to send a momentary spasm of horror thrilling through the stoutest heart there, but it also at the same time endowed them with a temporary access of almost supernatural energy; and the four men at once started for the ship at a speed which, even at the moment and to themselves, seemed incredible.

The distance they had to traverse was but short, a mere half-mile or so perhaps; but to the runners it seemed, notwithstanding their speed, as though they would *never* reach their goal. The grass was long and tangled, and rapid progress through it was possible only by a series of leaps or bounds; any other mode of progression would simply have resulted in their being tripped up at every other step. This, to men unaccustomed to such exercise, was in itself a sufficiently fatiguing process; but in addition to this they had to contend with the stifling heat of the stagnant atmosphere, which had been oppressive enough even whilst they had been in a condition of comparative inactivity; now it seemed to completely sap their strength and cause their limbs to hang heavy as lead about them. Then, too, the air had become so rarefied that it seemed impossible to breathe, whilst the blood rushed to their heads, and their hearts thumped against their ribs until it seemed as though nature could bear the tremendous exertion no more, and that the runners must drop dead upon the plain. Still, however, the men sped on, the portentous aspect of the heavens serving as an effectual spur to their flagging energies. The dark slate-coloured cloud had already reached the zenith, deepening in tint meanwhile until it had grown almost literally as black as ink. Presently a few great drops of hot rain splashed down upon the panting runners; and, as they rounded the end of the bush clump and came within view of the *Flying Fish*, a blinding flash of lightning blazed out from the sable canopy overhead, accompanied by a deafening peal of thunder which rattled and crashed and boomed and rumbled and rolled until its echoes gradually died away in the distance. A perfect deluge of rain almost immediately followed, wetting the runners to the skin in an instant as effectually as though they had been plunged into the sea. This lasted for perhaps ten seconds, during which every object, even to the racing figures of their companions, was hidden from view by the dense volume of falling water. Then the rain ceased as abruptly as it had begun, the travellers finding themselves at the same instant close to the towering hull of the *Flying Fish*.

"Last man in, close the trap!" gasped the baronet as he dashed up first to the opening in the ship's bottom. The others were only a few yards behind him and heard his command; so he wasted no more time in conversation, but bounded up the long spiral staircase leading to the pilot-house, having reached which he laid his hands upon the engine lever and tiller, and gaspingly awaited the signal shout which should tell him he might move the ship, gazing anxiously out through the windows meanwhile on the watch for some sign of the bursting of the hurricane.

He had not long to wait. Almost before he had found time to remove his hat and wipe the perspiration from his brow a shout came echoing up the staircase shaft from the bottom of the ship, announcing the fact that the trap-door was securely closed; and Sir Reginald instantly raised the ship from the ground, sending the engines gently ahead at the same moment, and putting the helm hard over so as to bring the *Flying Fish* stem-on to the direction from which he expected the hurricane.

CHAPTER SIXTEEN
A BATTLE ON LAKE TANGANYIKA

The ship had risen about one hundred feet from the ground, and her engines had just completed a single revolution, when the black pall of murky cloud suddenly burst apart on the south-western horizon, revealing a broad patch of livid coppery-looking sky behind it; and at the same moment a low moaning sound became audible in the breathless air. A dull smoky grey veil of vapour seemed at the same time to overspread the more distant features of the landscape in that quarter, and through it the baronet and his three companions, who had now rejoined him, saw the trees and foliage of the most remote clumps of bush bowing themselves almost to the ground before some mighty invisible force. The moaning sound rapidly increased in power and volume, the cloud of vapour rushed down toward them with appalling speed; the long billowy grass was flattened down to the earth, as if under the pressure of a heavy roller; the successive clumps of bush were seen to yield one after the other to the resistless power of the hurricane, and the air in that direction grew dark with the leaves and branches which were torn from the trees.

"Raise the ship higher. Lift her above the power of the hurricane altogether if you have still time to do so," shouted the professor in Sir Reginald's ear, as the roar of the approaching tornado thundered in their ears with almost deafening intensity.

"No," shouted back the baronet; "I am going to try the experiment of seeing how she will bear the stroke of the gale. Hold on tight all of you!"

And as he spoke he sent the engines ahead at full speed, and drove the ship forward right in the teeth of the hurricane.

The next instant, with an appalling burst of sound, the gale was upon them. Contrary to their expectations, there was scarcely any perceptible shock, but the ship's speed was rapidly checked much as is the speed of an express train when the brakes are suddenly and powerfully applied, and in some six seconds, though the engines were still going ahead at their utmost speed, the progress of the *Flying Fish* over the ground was as effectually checked as though she had been lying at anchor.

Meanwhile the air was one vast volume of awful sound, and thick with the clouds of dust, and tufts of grass, and leaves, and hurtling branches which were being whirled furiously along upon the wings of the tornado, so that the inmates of the pilot-house could neither hear each other speak nor see any object beyond a quarter of a mile away on either side. This lasted for perhaps three minutes, when the wind suddenly lulled, and the ship at once began to forge rapidly ahead. The lull lasted perhaps half a minute, and then ensued a repetition of all that had gone before, excepting that perhaps the wind was not *quite* so strong as at the first outburst. But it was of longer duration, the second instalment of the gale lasting fully half an hour, after which the wind gradually dropped to a gentle breeze, the sky cleared, the sun reappeared in all his wonted splendour, and the air resumed its usual transparency.

But what a sight was now presented to the view of the travellers; what a scene of devastation was that which lay outspread around them! The long grass was pressed so flat to the ground that it would scarcely have afforded cover to the smallest animal; stately trees were lying prostrate, either uprooted altogether, or their massive trunks snapped short off, whilst others still retained their upright position indeed, but stood denuded of every branch. Other trees again, whilst less mutilated as to their branches, retained only a few straggling leaves here and there, and the same thing applied to those dense patches of creeper-like tangled growth known as "bush," the upper portions of which presented merely a bristling array of leafless twigs. And in some spots could be seen huge clumps of "bush" which had been torn bodily out of the ground and swept remorselessly along for perhaps miles of distance.

But the strangest sight of all was presented by the animals. From a height of one thousand feet, to which the *Flying Fish* had by this time risen, a very wide extent of the plateau below could be surveyed, and on this in every direction could be seen the wild creatures of the forest, the jungle, and the plain, many of them suffering from injuries more or less severe, received during the progress of the tornado, and all of them exhibiting unmistakable and in some instances surprising evidences of demoralisation and terror. Deer and antelopes of various species lay crouched upon the ground palpably quivering with fear, or limped painfully about on three legs, the fourth being doubtless injured through the creature having been hurled violently to the ground, or struck by some falling branch. The lion and his mate could be seen here and there wandering harmlessly and aimlessly to and fro in the midst of hundreds of creatures which on ordinary occasions would afford them a welcome prey, but which were now too completely overcome with terror to notice their presence. In one place a fine elephant lay prostrate, his massive spine apparently broken by the fall of an enormous tree, the trunk of which had pinned him to the ground; and in another, an immense assemblage of animals of the most mixed and antagonistic species were seen huddled promiscuously together under the lee of an immense belt of bush, where they seemed to have found a shelter from which they were evidently still afraid to venture.

At length, having seen enough to afford them a tolerably clear idea of the destruction wrought by the storm, the professor suggested the retracing of their steps with the object of again finding, if possible, the troop of unicorns. The ship was accordingly put about, and in a short time the spot was reached on which still lay the carcasses of the leopard and the female unicorn. Here she was again brought temporarily to the ground in order that the party might secure the two skins, which was done; but the hide of the unicorn was so dreadfully lacerated by the claws of the leopard that the professor was plunged into the lowest depths of chagrin and despondency. The pursuit of the lost animals was now once more taken up; the ship rising to a height of five thousand feet into the air and then going ahead dead slow in the direction taken by the unicorns, the four gentlemen, armed with their most powerful telescopes, posting themselves in advantageous positions on deck and minutely examining every yard of the ground over which they passed. This method of proceeding was continued until nightfall without result; and it then became evident that the animals of which they were in pursuit had somehow eluded them.

"Well," said the professor, endeavouring to put a good face upon his disappointment, as, the ship having been carefully brought to earth and securely moored for the night, the party left the pilot-house and went below to take their evening bath previous to dinner, "it is disappointing, but it cannot be helped. Perhaps we shall be fortunate enough to encounter them or others to-morrow as we wend our way southward. And, *à propos* of our next destination, I have a suggestion which I should like to make, and which I will lay before you when we meet at the dinner-table."

Accordingly, when they had fairly settled down to the meal that evening, Sir Reginald called upon the scientist for his suggestion or proposal.

"I must preface it," said von Schalckenberg, "by informing you that I have again been diving into my lamented friend's note-book, which I may say *en passant* is the most remarkable volume I have ever come across. And in it I find, under the heading of 'Africa,' a most clever and scholarly disquisition on 'the site of ancient Ophir,' the place from which it is recorded that David obtained gold for the building of Solomon's temple. I need not inflict upon you the various arguments and authorities which are cited in the endeavour to identity the position of this most interesting spot; suffice it to say, that I am morally convinced I can lay my finger upon it on the map. The principal, indeed I may say the *only* reasons why the region has never yet been explored are, first, its extreme difficulty of access except by sea; and secondly, the fact that all recorded attempts to penetrate it have been thwarted by the inhabitants, who are a most jealous, warlike, and savage race of people. *We*, however, are fortunately possessed of exceptional, or I should rather say unique, means of approach to this unknown country; and my suggestion is that we should—"

"Do it," interrupted the baronet. "Most certainly we *will*, my dear sir, and I am exceedingly obliged to you for the proposal. The adventure will doubtless possess a piquant flavouring of danger about it, but I presume that will scarcely be regarded by any of us as a drawback?" glancing across the table to the colonel and Mildmay.

"Scarcely," echoed Lethbridge lazily, as he held his glass of wine up critically to the light.

"Did you say 'danger?'" laughed Mildmay. "This craft of yours is so confoundedly safe, Sir Reginald, that upon my word I have almost forgotten what danger is; so if you really think you can find a place where we may once more come within hail of it, pray take us there without loss of time. For my part, I am becoming positively effeminate, and unless I can speedily have a chance of getting my head broken I shall be utterly ruined for 'the service' when I go back to it."

"So be it," said the baronet. "Ancient Ophir is our next destination; and we will start to-morrow morning. You, professor, I know will not shrink from danger when the solving of so interesting a question is concerned."

"Ah, ah! try me," laughed the professor joyously—"try me, my friend, and you shall see."

Accordingly, on the following morning after breakfast a general adjournment was made to the pilot-house, where, with map and chart spread out before them, and the professor's treasured volume beside them for reference, the probable site of ancient Ophir was at length definitely located; when the course and distance were ascertained, and a start made.

Being anxious to see as much as possible of the country during their passage over it, a low rate of speed—averaging about twenty miles per hour—was maintained; the day's journey beginning at six o'clock in the morning, and terminating at the same hour in the evening, when a halt was called and the ship brought to earth for the night.

On the fourth day of this part of their journey, shortly after effecting their morning's start, they came within sight of an immense lake; and a slight deviation from their prescribed course was made in order that a thorough examination of it might be effected. A long range of hills, which had been sighted on the previous day, lay on their left hand; and, on clearing the southern spurs of these, they found that another large body of water lay beyond or to the eastward of them; a river connecting the two lakes, afterwards identified by them as lakes Albert Nyanza and Tanganyika. Rising in the air to a height of about ten thousand feet, they slowly traversed the latter from its northern extremity, reaching its widest part—which they estimated to be about sixty miles across—at mid-day.

And here a most exciting scene presented itself. An hour previously a dark mass had been sighted near the western shore of the lake, which mass had at first been taken for an island; but, on a nearer approach, the supposed island had resolved itself into an immense fleet of canoes, in number about three hundred, manned by from four to twenty men in each, rapidly making its way toward the western shore. So large a concourse of craft, coupled with the fact that the crews were elaborately "got up" with paint, feathers, and skins, and were well provided with bows and arrows, spears, shields, and clubs—to say nothing of a few very antiquated-looking muskets which the travellers' glasses revealed here and there—

seemed to point to the conclusion that a hostile expedition was afoot, or, rather, afloat; and the explorers resolved upon a temporary pause in order to watch the course of events.

The natives were so intent upon their paddling that—facing forward as they all were, with the *Flying Fish* somewhat in their rear and nearly a mile above them—not one of them seemed to have detected the near vicinity of the aerial ship; and the fleet diligently pursued its course landward, the short broad-bladed paddles moving to the time of a deep, sonorous, but somewhat monotonous song, which, issuing as it did from the throats of probably quite two thousand warriors, was distinctly audible on board the *Flying Fish*, and really had quite an impressive effect.

The flotilla had reached within about four miles of the shore, and of a tolerably extensive native settlement built thereon on both sides of a river which at that point emptied itself into the lake, when a sudden confused beating of drums and blowing of horns seemed to indicate that the menaced tribe had at last become awakened to the unpleasant fact that an invasion of their territory was imminent. The summons was responded to with very commendable celerity, the men swarming out of the settlement like ants out of an ant-heap; and in less than ten minutes nearly a hundred canoes were launched and manned, and advancing boldly to meet the enemy, whilst the laggards pushed off by twos and threes as soon afterwards as they could get down to the beach, all making the most strenuous efforts to join the main body.

To the observers on board the *Flying Fish* it seemed that the attacked party had made a grave mistake in thus taking to their canoes and advancing in them to meet the enemy; the colonel's impression being that they would have done better if they had awaited their foes on the beach and harassed them during their attempt to effect a landing. But it soon became evident that the threatened tribe knew perfectly well what they were about, their canoes being larger and steadier than those of their opponents, and their method of handling them greatly superior.

The opposing forces encountered each other at a distance of about two miles from the western shore of the lake, when a simultaneous discharge of arrows was poured in by both sides, after which the two fleets closed, and a most determined and sanguinary battle commenced. The invaders outnumbered their opponents nearly in the proportion of two to one; yet the latter not only gallantly held their own, but actually appeared now and then to gain some slight temporary advantage. Spears were thrown and arrows were shot by hundreds; the heavily-knobbed war-clubs were wielded with untiring activity and terrible effect; and, occasionally, a flash and a faint puff of smoke followed by a report told that one of the ancient muskets had been brought into play. The shouting of commands, the cries of anguish or defiance, the shrieks of the wounded, and the yells of triumph united in the creation of a most deafening din; and that it was not noise only, but work as well, was speedily manifested by the numerous bodies, splashing and struggling in the agonies of death, or floating quiescent on the surface of the lake.

"How stubbornly the rascals fight!" remarked Lethbridge at last, when the battle had been hotly raging for fully three-quarters of an hour without yielding to either side any decided advantage. "I wonder what the quarrel is all about?"

"It is difficult to say," answered the professor, who seemed to consider the question as addressed to himself; "it may be a simple case of tribal animosity; it may be an attack of retaliation; or it may be a slave-hunting expedition. It is pretty sure to be one or the other of those three, but it is impossible to say which."

"Well," remarked Mildmay, "whatever the cause of the fight, my sympathies are all with the weaker side. Cannot we help the poor wretches a little? A shot or two from our rifles—"

"Would ensure to either party a victory," interrupted the baronet. "Yes; that is quite true. But how can we tell which party—if either—is fighting in the cause of right and justice? We cannot take the part of either the aggressors or the defenders without a certain lurking doubt that in so doing we may perhaps be unwittingly giving aid and encouragement to the evil-doer. My sympathies are, like yours, on the side of the defenders; but I am afraid we must let them fight it out unaided."

And fight it out they did in the most gallant manner, the invaded baffling all attempts on the part of the invaders to get even a small portion of their force between them and the shore; and finally, by what looked like a last supreme and desperate effort, putting the foe to flight, and pursuing him triumphantly and persistently in his retreat, harassing his rear, cutting off and capturing stragglers, and in every possible way worrying and annoying him so thoroughly that, to those on board the *Flying Fish*, it looked unlikely in the extreme that the attack, whether provoked or not, would ever be repeated.

The combatants had evidently been far too busy to notice the extraordinary apparition floating in the sky above them; but just as the battle was about to commence a crowd of women and children, with a few decrepit old men, had assembled on the beach, seemingly to watch the conflict; and on bringing the telescopes to bear on these it soon became apparent, by their gestures and cries of amazement, that they had seen the ship.

"Yes," said the professor, peering through his telescope, "they see us undoubtedly, but they can detect neither form nor details. The sun is immediately behind them, you will observe; consequently, as it is shining full upon our burnished hull, those people, in the position they now occupy, will be able to see nothing but a shapeless blaze of dazzling effulgence, which they will doubtless take as an outward manifestation of their particular deity's favour, and an indication that he is present to crown their cause with victory."

And indeed there was plenty of evidence to support this singular opinion, for the people, though evidently astonished beyond measure, manifested delight rather than fear at what they saw, stretching out their hands, palms upward, by way of greeting and salute, whilst many were seen to hurry away to the village and back, bringing with them offerings of fruit, goats, and fowls, which they ranged in a line ("in order to make the most of them," as Mildmay suggested) along the margin of the lake. The proffered offering was, however, unaccepted, and, the battle being over, the *Flying Fish* resumed her course along the centre line of the lake, reaching its southern extremity in time to select a halting-place before sunset.

The fourth day following found them within easy distance of their destination; and the disappointment of the travellers, arising from the fact that no more unicorns had been seen, was to a very great extent swallowed up in curiosity as to what lay before them. Shortly after effecting their morning's start the fertile region over which they had hitherto been travelling came abruptly to an end, and they found themselves passing over an arid sandy desert, utterly destitute of even the feeblest suggestion of vegetation, without a trace of water or even of moisture, and of course with no sign of a living creature anywhere upon it. So uninteresting a region offered no temptation for loitering or dalliance, and the speed of the ship was accordingly increased to about sixty miles an hour over the ground, the pace being maintained until two o'clock in the afternoon, when a low range of rocky precipitous hills was reached, beyond which fertility and life once more resumed their sway. The travellers computed the stretch of desert over which they had passed as being fully three hundred miles in extent, and they could therefore fully understand the difficulty—not to say impossibility—of approaching Ophir, at all events from a north-westerly direction. Speed was now once more reduced, the ship gently gliding through the hot afternoon air at the rate of about eighteen knots, over a somewhat rugged, well-wooded country, watered by numerous streams, with native villages dotted here and there along the banks, in the midst of well-cultivated maize and tobacco fields, with an occasional patch of sugar-cane. Large herds of cattle were also frequently passed, and it soon became evident that to the natives in charge of these, and indeed to the inhabitants generally, the apparition of the aerial ship was productive of a vast amount of curiosity, excitement, and wonder. These natives appeared to possess the same power or gift attributed to the Montenegrins, namely, that of projecting the voice for incredible distances through the air; and it was speedily apparent that the arrival of the monster aerial visitor to the country was being orally telegraphed forward in the direction of her course. Mounted men were seen dashing madly along until they reached some eminence favourably situated for the exercise of their powers, when, dismounting, the messenger would raise his hands to his lips, and, in a peculiar high-pitched tone of voice which seemed to have the power of penetrating the air for an immense distance, send his message echoing forward over hill and dale, to be instantly caught up and repeated by another. So smartly was this novel system of telegraphy performed, that the message actually outsped the ship, and the travellers found the inhabitants of every village along their route awaiting *en masse* their appearance, which was instantly greeted with loud shouts of astonishment. At one village or settlement, which, from its size, appeared to be of more than ordinary importance, they found, in addition to the general inhabitants, a squadron of about fifty mounted warriors awaiting them, fully armed with bow, spear, and shield, and upon the appearance of the *Flying Fish* these troops most pluckily ranged themselves directly across her course and prepared to treat her to a shower of arrows.

"Now is our time to create a wholesome impression of our invincibility upon these fellows," remarked the baronet, and hurrying to the pilot-house he caused the ship to sink well within range of the projected salute.

In an instant every bow was drawn to its utmost tension, a second or two sufficed the warriors to steady their aim, and then, with a simultaneous *twang* of bowstrings, the fifty arrows sped through the air, and, rattling harmlessly against the ship's gleaming hull, glanced off and fell to the earth again. The baronet smartly raised the fore end of the tiller, and, obedient to her helm, the *Flying Fish* made a sudden swoop earthward in the direction of the audacious cavalry, who, already disconcerted at the utter failure of their attack, at once wheeled short about, and, with piercing yells of terror, took headlong flight, jostling and overthrowing each other without the least compunction in their frantic eagerness to escape.

"There," remarked the baronet, as, steadying the helm, the ship once more soared to her former elevation, "I hope that will suffice to convince them that we are not to be attacked with impunity. If not, we shall be compelled to read them a sharper lesson."

After that no further attempt at molestation was ventured upon, the inhabitants simply congregating in close proximity to the doors of their huts to see the ship go past, watching her stately progress in silent, awestruck wonder, and obviously holding themselves ready for an instant dive beneath the fancied shelter of their thatched roofs in the event of any hostile demonstration on the part of the Mysterious Visitant.

At about half-past five in the evening the hilly character of the country gave place to that of a wide-stretching level plain, thickly overgrown with long rank grass, with occasional isolated clumps of bush, and here and there a tall feathery palm, or a grove of wild plantains or bamboo. The faint grey glimmer of the sea appeared on the utmost verge of the distant horizon, and certain huge shapeless irregularities in the extreme distance gradually revealed themselves as the colossal remains of what must at one time have been a city of extraordinary extent and magnificence. The ship was brought to earth and secured exactly at six o'clock, at a distance of some eight or nine miles from the sea, and the travellers then found themselves surrounded on all sides by gigantic ruined walls, arches, columns, erect and overturned, huge fragments of pediments, shattered entablatures, ruined capitals, splintered pedestals, and crumbling mutilated statues of men and animals, all of colossal proportions, the buildings being of a massive but ornate and imposing style of architecture, quite unknown to civilisation. The ship had found a resting-place as nearly as possible in the centre of the ruins, which extended all round her for a distance of nearly three miles, the eastern half being all aglow with the golden radiance of the sunset, whilst the western half loomed up black, imposing, and solemnly mysterious against the clear orange of the evening sky.

"Well," said the professor, as the party slowly paced the deck, watching in almost silent rapture the swiftly changing glories of the dying day, the rapid but exquisite gradations of tint on the mouldering ruins which accompanied the fading light, and the almost instantaneous appearance of the stars in the darkening heavens—"well, I am equally surprised and delighted at the result of our resolve to come hither. Here we find ourselves in the very heart of savagedom surrounded by the vast remains of a remote but civilised and evidently highly cultivated race; and though at present we have nothing more than the merest surmise to help us to their identification, I have little doubt that the result of our explorations and investigations will be to satisfy us that we have in very deed found in these ponderous ruins the remains of Ancient Ophir."

CHAPTER SEVENTEEN
A NATIVE CHIEFTAN'S VISIT TO CLOUDLAND

The travellers, safely shut up in that impregnable fortress, the hull of the *Flying Fish*, passed the night in peaceful slumber, undisturbed, in the confidence begotten of a sense of perfect security, by the weird cries of the night birds, the incessant howling of the jackals, the maniacal laugh of the prowling hyena, the occasional roar of the lion, the loud *whirr* of myriads of insects, the croaking of bull-frogs, and the other multitudinous nocturnal sounds which floated in through the open windows of their state-rooms. They were early astir in the morning, eager to commence their investigations as are school-boys to plunge into the enjoyments of a long-anticipated holiday. Moved by a common impulse, they all went out on deck to witness the ruins under the effect of sunrise previous to their plunge into the matutinal bath; and it was whilst they were admiring the exquisite beauty of the scene that the keen-eyed colonel became conscious of the fact that they were beleaguered by a host of lurking savages.

"Umph!" he commented, "I expected as much."

"You expected as much as what? What is it, Lethbridge?" asked Sir Reginald.

"Look there," was the reply; "and there, and there, and there. Do you notice anything peculiar in the appearance of the undergrowth about us, especially where it is thickest?"

"N-o, I can't say that I do—unless you refer to those occasional quick gleams which come and go here and there. What are they? At first I thought it was the flash of the sun on the dew-laden grass and leaves as they wave in the wind, but it can hardly be that, or we should see more of it."

"No," said the colonel, "it is not that; it is the occasional glint of the sun on a native spear-head. I have been through the Kaffir war, and have seen the same thing before, though not so distinctly as now, our present towering height above the ground giving us an advantage in that respect which we sadly lacked before. We are beset by the natives. You cannot see *one*, I know, but they are all about us, all the same. Ah! look there, just behind that magnolia bush. Do you see a small dark object rising slowly into view? That is the head of a savage, and he is—ah! now he has ducked again, having caught sight of us."

"And what do you suppose the fellows want?" asked the baronet. "They cannot attack us, you know."

"No; but *they* don't know it. Their object is to steal up as close as possible to us in order, in the first place, to satisfy their curiosity, and, in the second place, to make a sudden swoop if they see any fancied chance of being successful."

"Well," said Sir Reginald. "I should like to see the savage who can reach us so long as we stick to the *Flying Fish*. But we don't want to stick to her, so we will leave them undisturbed to satisfy their curiosity to its fullest extent until after breakfast, when we must adopt measures either to conciliate them or to terrorise them into leaving us alone. Come, gentlemen, we shall be late for breakfast. What a superb mass of ruins it is!—beats the Acropolis; don't you think so?"

If the thousand or more savages, who had spent nearly half the night in accomplishing the engirdlement of the *Flying Fish*, could have heard and understood the airy way in which the fact of their close proximity was dismissed by the baronet as a matter of the most trivial importance, they would have been intensely disgusted. Happily for their dignity they were blissfully unconscious of it; and whilst Sir Reginald and his companions were luxuriating in the bath, and afterwards dallying with a light but dainty breakfast, the sable warriors continued to close cautiously in upon the huge white gleaming object which had come into their midst in so unexpected and extraordinary a manner. Slowly, cautiously, with untiring patience, and practising every known art of savage warfare, the band drew closer and closer, until they found themselves within about a hundred feet of the hull, and almost overshadowed by her enormous bulk, when considerations of personal safety prevailed over the ardour of the warrior burning to distinguish himself, and further advance was, as by unanimous consent, checked. The huge monster, with its gleaming silvery skin and its curiously-shaped tail, lay so ominously still and silent, with its enormous circular black eyes so wide open and fixed, that, having heard of its threatening demonstration against the cavalry who attacked it on the previous day, they felt certain it meant mischief, and was only waiting for some foolhardy wight to venture within its reach, to seize and devour him. They had been despatched by a despotic king to capture or kill the creature; but, whilst every man there would have emulated his neighbour in rushing to certain death against the ranks of an enemy, there seemed to be so little glory in furnishing a breakfast to this monster that every individual there inwardly resolved that some other man than himself should be the first to offer himself as a sacrifice. And, equally afraid to advance or to retire, there they remained motionless, and in a state of breathless suspense, waiting for events to develop themselves. And there they were distinctly visible from the lofty stand-point of the *Flying Fish's* deck when the quartette, cigar in mouth, emerged from the pilot-house after breakfast.

The situation was decidedly comical, and the travellers indulged in a hearty laugh at the expense of the discomfited savages. But it was obvious that matters could not be allowed to remain in that condition; the natives must be impressed with the conviction that hostilities were neither necessary nor desirable, and that it would be to their advantage to be on terms of amity with the newcomers. How could this be achieved? A parley offered the most ready solution of the difficulty; and the professor—who was a perfect polyglot dictionary in human form—offered to essay the task of conducting it. This was by no means his first introduction to savages; he had encountered them in various parts of the world before, and had never experienced any very serious difficulty in communicating with them, so that he felt tolerably sanguine of success on the present occasion.

"The matter is very simple, I think," remarked the German, as he led the way to the larboard gangway. "We want these people to understand that we are friendly disposed toward them; that they have nothing whatever to fear from us; that we have not come here to rob them of one tittle of their possessions; that we merely wish to explore and examine these ancient ruins; and that, if they will receive us among them as friends, they will be distinct and decided gainers by the transaction. Is not that so?"

"Certainly," remarked the baronet. "Tell them—if you can—that all we ask is permission to investigate and explore unmolested; and that if they will accord us this privilege they shall be substantially rewarded."

"Very good; I will do my best. And that reminds me that you had better order George to bring on deck and open a small case of those beads and nick-nacks that we provided for such occasions as the present," remarked the professor.

The baronet returned to the pilot-house to give the order; and von Schalckenberg drew out his white pocket-handkerchief, waved it two or three times in the air, and then demanded, in the language he thought most likely to be intelligible:

"What chief commands the warriors who have assembled to pay homage to the four Spirits of the Winds?"

Most luckily for the professor's prestige and reputation as an all-wise

Spirit, the dialect he had adopted, though not the language actually spoken by the tribe he addressed, was so far similar that his question was understood; and whilst the astounded blacks started to their feet in dismay at finding themselves at last actually face to face with and addressed by an avowed Spirit, one of them hesitatingly and timorously advanced a few paces, threw himself prostrate on the ground, and, maintaining his posture of humility, stammered out:

"I, Lualamba, am the leader of these warriors, O most potent Spirit."

"Approach, brave Lualamba, and ascend to us by the ladder which we will let down to you. We have that to say which must be heard by your ear alone," commanded the professor, waving his hand majestically.

A rope-ladder was attached to the lower extremity of the side-ladder and let down to the ground; and the chief, in a state of mind about equally divided between the extremity of bodily fear on the one hand and pride at being selected as the recipient of a special communication from the Spirit Land on the other, hesitatingly and falteringly, and with many doubtful pauses, advanced until he reached the foot of the ladder, when his courage failed him, and he came to a dead halt.

"Ascend, and fear not," called out the professor encouragingly; "we are the friends of your nation, and have forgiven the attack which some of your people (not knowing us) made upon us yesterday. We have come hither to shower gifts and benefits upon you—if you are obedient; but if you reject our friendship, beware!"

Upon this the savage, no doubt feeling that, by placing himself at the head of this most unlucky expedition, he had already gone too far to permit of withdrawal, summoned up all his courage, and, with the air of a man who knew himself to be treading on mined ground, scrambled up the swaying ladder, and finally stepped in through the gangway on to the spacious deck of the *Flying Fish*, upon which he prostrated himself on his face, laying his shield and weapons—his most valued possessions—as an offering at the feet of the professor.

The latter, touching him lightly on the shoulder, at once bade him rise; and, as the chief gathered himself up and regained his feet, von Schalckenberg threw round the quaking but gratified savage's neck a string of large opaque, turquoise-blue glass beads, and over his naked shoulders a length of gaudily-flowered chintz. A loud shout of admiration from the crowd of natives below proclaimed the fact that they had witnessed the bestowal of these gifts, whilst Lualamba, notwithstanding the august presence in which he found himself, could not restrain the broad grin of delight which spontaneously overspread his features.

A few judicious questions, artfully put, soon elicited from the savage the information that the travellers were now in the country belonging to M'Bongwele, a fierce, cruel, and jealous despot, so suspicious of foreigners that the most stringent orders were in force to allow none such to cross his borders upon any pretence whatever. This king had been duly apprised, through the medium of the curious voice-telegraphic mode of communication already described, of the mysterious arrival in his dominions on the day previous; and had been so greatly disconcerted and enraged at the news that he had forthwith issued the most peremptory orders for the capture or slaughter of the monstrous visitant; and he was now, according to Lualamba, impatiently awaiting in his palace, a few miles distant, the intelligence that his order had been executed. The chief, during the conversation which elicited these facts, had so far recovered his self-possession and equanimity as to be able to make the best possible use of his eyes; and, being a very shrewd fellow, he was not long in arriving at the conclusion that the gigantic monster on whose back he stood was, after all, nothing more nor less than an inanimate, though unquestionably wonderful, *vehicle* of some sort; and that the fair-skinned beings to whom he was talking, though they claimed to be the four Spirits of the Winds, were very similar in many respects to certain white men whom he had seen only a few moons ago. The wily savage accordingly made up his mind that, if he could only induce these beings to accompany him into the king's presence, he would, after all, have most satisfactorily accomplished his mission; and he forthwith proceeded, with all the craft and subtlety of which he was master, to urge upon them the desirability of an immediate visit to king M'Bongwele, who, averse as he was to the prying visits of strange *men*, would, he assured them, be highly gratified at the honour of having as his guests the four Spirits of the Winds.

This proposition, however, by no means accorded with the views of the travellers; and von Schalckenberg somewhat sternly intimated that, whilst an interview with M'Bongwele was undoubtedly desirable, it was *he* who must visit and pay homage to *them*, and not they to him. They had entered the country with the most friendly disposition toward M'Bongwele and his people, and that friendly disposition would be manifested to the distinct advantage of the entire nation if the king showed himself properly appreciative of the honour done him by this visit. But if not, king and people would be very severely punished for the insult offered to their potent visitors, "and," continued the professor, "in order that Lualamba might see for himself that, in making this threat, they were indulging in no mere empty boast, he would give the chief and his followers a single specimen of their power."

Mildmay having, during the progress of this conversation, received a hint from the professor how to act, had quietly, and as if not particularly interested in what was going forward, sauntered off to the pilot-house, where, stationing himself at the engine and other levers controlling the movements of the ship, he awaited further instructions.

The professor, having promised to give the savages a specimen of their visitors' power, now waved his right hand very slowly and impressively skyward, as a signal to the watchful Mildmay, loudly exclaiming as he did so:

"Lualamba will now accompany the four Spirits of the Winds to yonder cloud," pointing, as he spoke, to a single small white fleecy cloud which was floating at the moment across the sun's disc.

Dexterously manipulating the various valves, Mildmay caused the *Flying Fish* to rise with a gentle and almost imperceptible motion from the earth. So gentle was the movement that Lualamba was utterly unconscious of it, and it was not until some seconds had elapsed that he fully realised what was happening. The savages below, however, no sooner heard von Schalckenberg's exclamation than, to their inexpressible horror, they beheld the huge structure, round which they were standing, lift itself off the earth without the slightest visible effort and begin to rise into the air. Many of them were so overpowered by astonishment that they could only stand, open-mouthed and as motionless as statues, staring at the extraordinary sight; others, however, remembering the stringent orders of the king, and feeling that the prize which they had believed to be so secure was not only escaping them but also carrying off one of their number, rushed forward, and, whilst some fruitlessly attempted to grasp and hold the smooth and polished hull, others seized and clung tenaciously to the rope-ladder. The weight of some seven or eight natives clinging to the dangling ladder had, of course, no visible effect upon the movement of the great ship; and, finding themselves being helplessly dragged skyward, they let go their hold with a yell of dismay when they were some four or five yards from the earth, upon which they dropped back heavily.

The ship once fairly off the ground, Mildmay increased the rarefaction of the air in the air-chambers to an almost perfect vacuum, and the immense structure soared skyward with great rapidity. Lualamba, hearing the shouts of his people from below, stepped to the gangway to ascertain the cause; and it was then that, to his inexpressible dismay, he saw the earth apparently falling from under him, and the upturned faces of his followers rapidly dwindling until they became unrecognisable. In the first extremity of his terror he would have flung himself headlong from the deck had he not been prevented; failing in this he prostrated himself, and for some time lay motionless, with his face hidden in his hands. At length, however, somewhat reassured by the encouraging adjurations of the professor and the apparent absence of movement in the ship, he ventured first of all to uncover his eyes and then to rise slowly to his feet. He glanced wildly about him, but could see nothing, save a thick white mist which completely enveloped the ship (for she had just plunged into the centre of the cloud), with the sun dimly visible through it; and a fresh paroxysm of terror seized him, for the horrible thought at once suggested itself that he had looked his last upon mother Earth. The professor, however, speedily reassured him upon this point, and, leading him to the guard-rail which ran round the deck, bade him look downward. Terrified into the most servile obedience, the wretched chief did as he was bidden, and in a few minutes, the mist growing thinner and thinner, he once more caught sight of the earth at an immense distance below, the gigantic ruins above which they were hovering dwarfed to a mere sprinkling of boulders over the plain; the trees, the clumps of bush, and the meandering streams stretching away to the horizon in almost illimitable perspective, and to the eastward the sea, with just one solitary sail upon it, barely visible above its gleaming rim.

Ignorant savage though he was, Lualamba was quite intelligent enough to appreciate the novel beauty of the scene upon which his eyes now rested; and, forgetting for the moment all his terrors, he leaned upon the rail, lost in wonder and admiration. And when, after a minute or two, he became conscious that the ship was again nearing the earth, his delight knew no bounds, for he felt that, as the hero of so unique an experience as he was now passing through, he must henceforth be a person of much greater consequence among his countrymen than he had ever been before.

Meanwhile the travellers had availed themselves of their recent ascent to sharply scrutinise the face of the country immediately adjacent to the ruins, and had at length discovered, on the summit of a distant hill, an extensive village or settlement, strongly defended by a circular stockade, which they shrewdly suspected to be the headquarters of king M'Bongwele. The single street, which ran through the centre of the village from end to end, was crowded with people all gazing skyward at the unwonted apparition of the aerial ship; and, with the aid of their telescopes, the travellers could see in the central square a small group of persons (who they conjectured to be the king and his suite) similarly engaged, surrounded and protected from the rabble by a phalanx of armed men.

The ship swept rapidly onward until she hovered immediately over the last-named party (just to impress upon the king a wholesome conviction of the utter uselessness of his stockade as a protection against such a foe as the *Flying Fish*), and then, making a majestic sweep, came gently to earth immediately opposite the principal gate in the stockade.

"Now, go," said the professor, addressing Lualamba, "and inform king M'Bongwele that we await him on the spot among the ruins where you found us this morning."

The bewildered chief, scarcely able to realise the fact that he had actually been brought safely back to *terra firma*, lost no time in availing himself of the permission given him to depart, and, scrambling down the ship's side and the rope-ladder, he reached the ground and bounded off like a startled deer toward the gate, which was hastily thrown open to admit him, and as hastily closed and barred again the moment he had passed through. The *Flying Fish* then rose once more into the air and leisurely made her way back to the ruins, passing, *en route*, the force which had been sent out to capture her, and which was now making the best of its way back to the village to report the result of the expedition.

Meanwhile Lualamba made his way rapidly up through the village to the king's palace (which was, after all, merely the largest hut in the inclosure), having gained which he besought an immediate audience with M'Bongwele on a matter of the utmost importance. The king, who had already been made acquainted with the circumstance of the chief's involuntary journey into the upper regions, was, of course, all curiosity to learn the fullest details of the adventure, and the desired audience was accordingly at once granted. Conscious of the fact that, for the first time in his life, he had failed to execute the mission intrusted to him, and extremely doubtful as to the reception which would be accorded to the message of which he was the unwilling bearer, Lualamba deemed it best on this occasion to tell a plain unvarnished tale, and, commencing his narrative at the point where he and his warriors had first come within sight of the huge object of which they were in quest, he described in full detail all his subsequent adventures, with the thoughts, feelings, and impressions resulting therefrom, and wound up falteringly with the message.

His story was received by the king and his suite with ejaculations of wonder and incredulity, interspersed with many sharp commands from the monarch to repeat or to explain more fully certain passages; and when the message was delivered a profound silence reigned for fully an hour. King M'Bongwele was a despot, accustomed to issue his commands in the most heedless manner and to have them executed at all costs; but to *receive* a command was an entirely novel and decidedly disagreeable experience, and he was thoroughly puzzled how to act. His first feeling was one of speechless indignation at the insolence of these audacious strangers; his second, a wholesome fear of the consequences of disobedience. For if these mysterious visitants had the power of soaring into the air by a mere wave of the hand, what might it not be possible for them to do in the event of their being seriously provoked. Besides, he had already received a practical assurance of his impotency so far as they were concerned; moreover, he was consumed by curiosity to see for himself the marvels so graphically described by his lieutenant, to receive a moiety of those magnificent gifts which the strangers seemed prepared to lavish broadcast upon all with whom they chanced to come into contact, and, above all, to satisfy himself with respect to certain conjectures which had flitted through his brain whilst listening to the astonishing narrative of Lualamba. M'Bongwele was an ignorant savage, it is true, but he was possessed of a dauntless courage, a persistency of purpose, and an unscrupulous craftiness and ambitiousness of character which would have won him distinction of a certain unenviable kind in any community. Already his brain was teeming with vague unformed plots of the wildest and most audaciously extravagant description, the possibility of which he was determined to ascertain for himself, and the maturing of which he was quite prepared to leave to time. He therefore ultimately resolved to obey the summons sent him by the strangers; but, remembering his kingly dignity, he postponed obedience as long as he dared, and it was not until four o'clock in the afternoon that he set out for the ruins, attired in all his native finery, consisting of a lion-skin mantle and magnificent gold coronet adorned with flamingo's feathers—the emblems of his regal power—

gold bangles on his arms and ankles, a necklace of lion's teeth and claws round his neck, and a short petticoat of leopard's skin about his loins. He was armed with a sheaf of light javelins or assegais, he carried in his left hand a long narrow shield of rhinoceros hide decorated with ostrich plumes, and he was mounted on a superb black horse (which he rode bare-backed and managed with the skill of a finished equestrian). His followers, numbering about five hundred, were also fully armed and excellently mounted, they being, indeed, with the exception of a few court officials, his regiment of household cavalry, the pick of his native warriors and the very flower of his army. He was anxious to make the profoundest possible impression of his power and greatness upon the mysterious beings he was about to visit; and, indeed, the cavalcade, as it swept at a hand-gallop out through the wide gateway which formed the principal opening in the stockade, constituted, with its tossing plumes, its fluttering mantles, its glancing weapons, and its prancing horses, a sight to make a soldier's heart bound with appreciative delight.

CHAPTER EIGHTEEN
KING M'BONGWELE IS TEMPORARILY REDUCED TO SUBMISSION

In the return of the *Flying Fish* to her former berth the subject of the reception to be accorded to king M'Bongwele, in the event of his obeying their summons, was somewhat anxiously discussed by the travellers. They had already seen and heard enough to convince them that the individual in question was a sovereign of considerable power, as African kings go, and former experience among savages had taught them that he would, as likely as not, prove to be a crafty, unscrupulous, and slippery customer to deal with. To satisfactorily carry out the object of their visit to this man's country—namely, the examination and exploration of the mysterious and very interesting ruins which surrounded them—it would be absolutely necessary that they should be able to pass to and fro, freely and unmolested, between the ship and the various points selected for examination; and, in order to secure this perfect freedom, it would be necessary not only to conciliate this powerful ruler and his people, but also to so thoroughly impress him and them with the mysterious and wonderful attributes of their unbidden guests that they should, one and all, be absolutely *afraid* to interfere with them. The question was, how could this be most effectually achieved? The first part of the programme, namely the conciliation of sovereign and subjects, appeared simple enough; the obvious pride and delight with which Lualamba had received his flashy presents of beads and Manchester finery furnished a key to the satisfactory solution of this difficulty; but how was the second and equally important part of the programme to be carried out? Lualamba, it was true, had been effectually cowed by the simple expedient of carrying him a few thousand feet up into the air; but something more than the mere repetition of this experiment would be necessary to produce the required impression upon M'Bongwele and the crowd of warriors he would be certain to bring with him. The matter was placed in the hands of the professor for settlement, and he promptly avowed himself to be fully equal to the task.

"Science, my friends," he remarked, "is constantly revealing wonders which surprise and astound even the most cultured minds of the civilised world; how much more capable is it then of overawing the uncultured savage, however shrewd and clever he may be in those simple matters which affect his everyday life! Leave it to me; we have ample scientific means at our command to quell this man and his followers, and to reduce them to a state of the most abject and servile subjection."

Von Schalckenberg then retired to make his preparations, which were soon complete. When next he appeared he carried upon one arm a glittering mass of what at first sight appeared to be drapery, but which, on his unfolding it, proved to be three suits of chain armour (minus helmet and gauntlets), constructed of very small fine links of aethereum, light and flexible as silk.

"I think," said he, "it will be unadvisable to make any change in our outward appearance in preparing to receive this royal savage; any such change would be certainly noticed, and as certainly regarded as an indication of the importance we attach to his visit. Now, our policy is to treat the whole affair as a matter of no moment whatever, and we will therefore (if you agree with my views) continue to wear the white flannel suits in which we received Lualamba this morning. But I would recommend that each of you don a suit of this mail under your clothing (I have already assumed mine), and we shall then be pretty well prepared for emergencies. These savages are often exceedingly treacherous fellows, and it is quite among the possibilities that certain of this king's followers may have received instructions to test our supposed invulnerability by a sly stab in the back or something of that kind; it will be well, therefore, that we should be properly prepared for anything of the kind. I had in view some such occasion as the present when I arranged for the construction of these suits. There is a helmet and gauntlets for each; but we shall scarcely need them today, I think, and it would hardly be politic to wear any *visible* defensive armour."

The luncheon hour arrived and passed without sign or token of the presence of a single savage in the neighbourhood, and as the afternoon waned with still no indication of human vicinity, the travellers—but for the absolute impregnability of the *Flying Fish*—would have begun to feel uneasy. About half-past four o'clock, however, as the quartette were languidly puffing at their cigars, lolling meanwhile in the most luxurious of deck-chairs, a huge cloud of yellow dust rising into the air beyond the ruins announced the approach of the cavalcade, and a minute or two later king M'Bongwele at the head of his cavalry swept like a whirlwind into the open space occupied by the great ship, and, charging in a solid square close up to her, suddenly wheeled right and left into line, and came to an abrupt halt. The evolution was very brilliantly executed, and as Lethbridge lazily scanned the performers through the thin filmy smoke of his cigar, he could not restrain a low murmur of admiration, followed by the remark:

"By George! what splendid soldiers those fellows would make with a couple of months' training!"

"Y-e-s," agreed the baronet, "that was very well done; but I suppose that particular evolution is the one in which they most excel, and of course it was done purely for effect. Ah! the individual now dismounting is, I suppose, our royal visitor."

The baronet was quite right in his conjecture. As the party halted, some ten or a dozen individuals, including Lualamba, flung themselves from their horses, and, advancing reverentially, grouped themselves about the royal charger. Two of them then stepped to the creature's head and grasped the bridle, whilst two more assisted the king to dismount. The horse was then handed over to the care of a warrior, and the king, closely followed by the members of his suite, advanced to the foot of the rope-ladder, which had been lowered for their accommodation; the professor at the same time stepping to the gangway and inviting the party to ascend.

M'Bongwele looked somewhat doubtfully at the swaying ladder for a moment or two, and then essayed the ascent; but the oscillation set up by his movements proved too much for his nerves—or his dignity—and, much chagrined, he was obliged to desist. The professor then in compassion suggested the steadying of the ladder at its foot, when the king, promptly giving the necessary order to his suite, ascended to the deck, leaving those who followed him to manage as best they could.

The first glance of the travellers satisfied them that in king M'Bongwele they had a man of more than ordinary intelligence to deal with. The colour of his skin and complexion was a rich deep brown, he stood nearly six feet high on his naked feet, and, but for his somewhat excessive corpulence, he would have been a man of magnificent proportions. His lips were rather thick, and his nose somewhat flattened, but not nearly as much so as in the case of the genuine negro. His forehead was broad and lofty, though receding, his eyes keen, restless, and piercing, and there was a crafty, cruel, resolute look about the lower part of his face which taught his hosts that they would have to be exceedingly cautious in their dealings with him. He was accommodated with a chair between Sir Reginald and the professor, the former being flanked by Lethbridge (Mildmay, in accordance with previous arrangements, had ensconced himself in the pilothouse); Lualamba and the rest of the suite were quietly allowed to squat in a semicircle before them on the deck.

The king opened the conversation by somewhat abruptly demanding the reason for the strangers' visit to his dominions; to which the professor replied by pointing to the ruins, explaining that they were believed to be the remains of a great city built many ages ago by a very interesting race of people of whom but little was known, and he and his companions were anxious to minutely examine and explore what was left, in the hope of discovering some sculptured or other record bearing upon the origin, habits, and history of the builders.

A few minutes of profound meditation on the part of the king followed this announcement, and then he suddenly demanded where the travellers had come from. The professor replied by a comprehensive sweep of the hand skyward.

"But," objected M'Bongwele, "if you are spirits you should know all that you want to know about these ruins without coming here to investigate. The spirits know everything."

A low murmur of applause from the king's adherents followed this enunciation, showing that they evidently considered their monarch to be getting the better of the strangers, and a smile of gratification flickered for an instant over M'Bongwele's features.

"Not everything," corrected the professor. "We know a great many things, but not everything. And what we know we have been obliged to find out by investigation. We spend the greater part of our existence in passing from place to place investigating and finding out things."

"Then I have been misinformed, and the spirits are neither so wise nor so powerful as I thought them to be," retorted the king.

"Perhaps so," quietly remarked the professor. "Nevertheless we are very powerful—sufficiently so to destroy you and your whole army in a moment, should we choose to do so. Would you like to witness a specimen or two of our power?"

M'Bongwele glanced somewhat nervously about him for a second or two, and then with an obvious effort answered:

"Yes."

"I see that some of your followers here are armed with bows," continued the professor. "Are they good marksmen?"

"The best in the world," answered the king proudly.

The professor in his turn hesitated an instant; he was about to make a dangerous experiment. Then he drew from his pocket a small crimson silk rosette, and, placing it in M'Bongwele's hand, said:

"I will attach this to any part of my dress you choose to point out; then order one of your archers to shoot an arrow at it, and observe the result."

The king took the rosette in his hand, examined it carefully, and passed it round among his suite for inspection. On receiving it back he suddenly wheeled round in his chair, and, reaching over, laid his finger on Lethbridge's breast exactly over the heart.

"Fasten it *there*," he said with a scornful smile, "and I will shoot at it myself."

The professor was disconcerted. The danger of the experiment consisted in the possibility that the archer, instead of aiming at the rosette, would select an eye or some part of the head for a mark, in which case the result would be fatal. He was quite willing to incur the risk himself, trusting that the archer's vanity would impel him to aim at the right spot; but he had never contemplated the turn which affairs had now taken.

Lethbridge, however, with a languid smile and a shrug of the shoulders, rose to his feet, and, nonchalantly flicking the ash off the end of his cigar, waited for the professor to affix the rosette.

A happy inspiration just then occurred to von Schalckenberg. "It is a very small mark," he murmured confidentially to M'Bongwele; "I do not believe you can hit it. Shall I get something larger?"

The king would not listen to any such proposal; he was evidently anxious to exhibit his skill; and the professor, reassured, attached the rosette to Lethbridge's coat in the exact spot indicated, M'Bongwele and his companions watching the operation with the keenest interest.

The colonel, glancing round for a good background against which to place himself, noticed a large clump of trees with olive-green foliage growing at a short distance directly astern of the ship. Against these his white-clad figure would stand out in strong relief. He accordingly stepped leisurely out to a suitable position on the deck, and, with one hand in his pocket and his smouldering cigar in the other, patiently awaited the decisive moment. M'Bongwele in the meantime snatched a bow from one of his followers, and, selecting a long straight arrow from the sheaf, retired to the other end of the deck, a distance of about one hundred and fifty feet from his living target. He strung the bow carefully, adjusted the arrow to the string with the utmost nicety, drew it to the head, and then paused for a full minute, apparently waiting for some indication of flinching on Lethbridge's part. In this, however, he was disappointed, not the faintest suggestion of uneasiness could be detected in the colonel's face—indeed, he seemed to be absorbed in a critical contemplation of the smoke which lazily wreathed upward from the end of the cigar. Suddenly the bow twanged loudly, the arrow whizzed through the air, and, striking fair upon the rosette, fell in splinters to the deck. Lethbridge somewhat contemptuously kicked the fragments aside, unpinned the rosette from the breast of his coat, and sauntered back to his former seat. The group of chiefs gathered on the deck glanced at each other and uttered suppressed ejaculations of dismay. As for M'Bongwele, he was thoroughly discomfited; he had been shrewd enough to suspect in the professor's proposal some preconcerted arrangement, which he flattered himself he had skilfully baffled; instead of which his *ruse* had simply redounded to his own more complete confusion.

The professor rose and picked up the pierced rosette, which he handed to the king.

"You are very skilful," he remarked, pointing to the puncture; "I compliment you." Then, changing his tone, he continued: "We have allowed you to do this in order that you may be thoroughly convinced of the impossibility of injuring us. Now you shall have a further example of our power. Order your warriors to dismount and try their best to lift this ship from off the ground."

The king turned to Lualamba and gave him the necessary order; whereupon the chief, descending the ladder to the ground, advanced to the troops, and, dismounting them, assembled them all round the hull; then, at a given signal, the entire body exerted themselves to the utmost to lift the immense fabric from the ground—of course without effect, as her chambers were full of air.

"Now," said the professor when the savages had pretty well exhausted themselves, "let all but one man retire."

This was done, Mildmay meanwhile exhausting the chambers until the gauge showed that the ship weighed only a few pounds. The professor glanced carelessly at the pilot-house, caught the signal that all was in readiness, and said to the king:

"Now order that man to lift the ship on to his shoulders."

M'Bongwele duly repeated the order, without the slightest expectation that it would be fulfilled; and the man—who would have plunged into a blazing bonfire if he had been so ordered—advanced, and, to the unutterable astonishment of himself, the king, and in fact the whole concourse of natives, raised the gigantic structure to his shoulders and held it there with scarcely an effort.

"Now, tell him to toss us into the air," commanded von Schalckenberg, shouting down from the gangway to Lualamba.

And in another second the terrified king and his suite felt a slight movement, and saw the earth sinking far away beneath them. This was altogether too much for the suite, who grovelled on the deck in mortal fear; and even king M'Bongwele felt his courage rapidly oozing away as he sat uneasily in his deck-chair convulsively gripping its arms and glancing anxiously about him.

The ascent was continued to a height of about fifteen thousand feet, at which altitude the wretched savages were shivering even more with cold than they had hitherto done with fear. The ship was then headed straight for the sea, which she soon reached, and, speeding onward at the rate of thirty miles an hour, her course was continued, accompanied by a gradual descent until the land was lost sight of; when a wide sweep was made, and, at a height of only one hundred feet above the waves, the return journey was commenced. This experience proved sufficient, and more than sufficient, for M'Bongwele; he was completely cowed; and when he found himself hovering over the illimitable sea, without a sign of land in any direction, he flung himself upon his knees before the professor and piteously entreated to be restored to his home and people, abjectly promising that he and they would be the willing slaves of the White Spirits for ever; and as for the ruins, the Spirits might do whatever they chose with them, freely and without let or hindrance. This was all very well, but von Schalckenberg had not yet fully carried out his programme; he had still one more item in the entertainment which he was determined to produce, and which he fully believed would render M'Bongwele's subjugation not only complete but permanent.

Accordingly, on returning to their starting-place (by which time it was nearly dark), the demoralised warriors, who had all but given up their king as lost, were set to work by von Schalckenberg's orders to collect wood for a gigantic bonfire. This was soon done, and the fire was kindled; but, much of the wood being green, an immense cloud of smoke was raised, with very little flame, which exactly suited the professor's purpose. When the fire was fairly alight, the troops were re-formed in line as close to the ship as possible, and M'Bongwele and his suite were arranged in position on the deck immediately beneath the pilot-house walls. By this time it was perfectly dark, save for the starlight and the flickering gleam of the bonfire; and the air was stark calm.

Gradually and imperceptibly the dense cloud of smoke which hung motionless over the smouldering pile became faintly luminous. The radiance grew stronger and stronger, and presently an immense circular disc of light appeared reflected on the slowly-rising cloud of vapour, in which a host of forms were indistinctly traceable. Another moment and a loud ejaculation of astonishment burst from the savage spectators, for, with another sudden brightening of the luminous disc there appeared the phantom presentment of M'Bongwele's troops drawn up as they had appeared a couple of hours before, when the king had first boarded the *Flying Fish* So clear and vivid was the representation that it met with instant recognition, amid loud murmurs of amazement from the beholders; the king being quite as strongly moved as any of his subjects.

"Do you recognise the vision?" demanded the professor sternly of M'Bongwele.

"I do, I do. Those are the spirits of my bravest soldiers," murmured the king. "Truly the Spirits of the Winds have wondrous powers."

"You say well," answered von Schalckenberg. "Now, look again and you shall see a few of *our* warriors."

As he spoke the picture became blurred and indistinct, prismatic colours began to come and go upon the curtain of vapour, and suddenly out flashed the image of a wide-stretching sun-lit plain, upon which were drawn up on parade, in illimitable perspective, a countless host of British troops, infantry, cavalry, and artillery, with bayonets, swords, and lance-points gleaming in the sun, with colours uncased, guns limbered up, and all apparently ready and waiting for the order to march. So realistic was the picture that even the baronet and Lethbridge could scarcely repress an exclamation of astonishment, and as for M'Bongwele and his people, they were perfectly breathless with surprise. The picture was allowed to remain clear, brilliant, and distinct for some ten minutes, then the radiant disc rapidly faded until it vanished altogether, and nothing remained but the red glimmer of the smouldering fire.

A heavy sigh issued from M'Bongwele's breast, and he rose to his feet.

"It is enough," he said. "Let me go home."

He advanced gropingly to the gangway (for it was now very dark), when, in an instant, every one of the electric lights in the ship flashed out at their fullest brightness, brilliantly illuminating the deck, and turning night into day for fully a mile round, and, under the clear steely radiance thus unexpectedly furnished him, the king slowly made his way to the ground, mounted his horse in silence, and galloped away at the head of his followers. The illumination of the ship was maintained until the cavalcade was well clear of the ruins, when the side-ladder was drawn up, the lights extinguished, and M'Bongwele was left to make the remainder of his way as best he could in the darkness.

"Well," said the professor as the quartette wended their way below to dinner, "how have I managed?"

"Admirably," answered Sir Reginald and the colonel together. "Never, surely," continued the latter, "was African king so completely overawed in so short a time as this fellow has been to-day."

"We all, and I especially, owe you thanks, colonel, for the sublime *sang froid* with which you stood up and allowed yourself to be made a target of to-day," said von Schalckenberg. "Believe me, I would never have made the proposal I did had I suspected that the part of target would have been so cleverly transferred to someone else. But the crafty fellow evidently suspected what you English call 'a plant'—a prearranged plan—and he thought that by adopting the course he did he would have us at advantage."

"Oh," laughed the colonel scornfully, "that was a mere trifle, less than nothing. I saw that the fellow was confident of his skill as a marksman and anxious to show off, so I felt perfectly easy in my mind. Had it been one of our own men, now—" An expressive shrug of the shoulders finished the sentence.

"Yes," remarked the baronet reflectively, "what a pity it is that they are not trained to individually select and aim at a particular object. If they were, no troops in the world could stand up for ten minutes before them. But, speaking of troops, professor, what a master-stroke that was of yours to give the darkies an opportunity of comparing their own soldiers with ours. How on earth did you manage it?"

"Oh, easily enough," laughed the professor. "A magic lantern and a couple of slides did the whole business. The throwing of the pictures upon the smoke-wreath certainly enhanced its effectiveness a good deal, but it is quite an old trick, which I have often done before with excellent results. Everyone who is going much among savages ought to include a lantern and an assortment of good startling slides in his outfit if possible."

"But how did you get the first of your two slides? That was surely a representation of M'Bongwele's own people."

"Certainly. And our friend Mildmay very cleverly secured it with a camera which I set up and prepared for him in the pilot-house. He only had to release a spring at the right moment, and the thing was done. He developed the picture whilst we were making our little excursion out to sea and back. Well, the whole thing was a farce; but I believe it has effectually secured us from interruption during our researches among the ruins; and if so, it was worth playing."

CHAPTER NINETEEN
KING M'BONGWELE TURNS THE TABLES UPON HIS VISITORS

In reaching his palace that night king M'Bongwele dismissed his followers with but scant ceremony, and at once retired to rest. He passed a very disturbed night of alternate sleeplessness and harassing fitful dreams, and arose next morning in a particularly bad temper. He was anxious, annoyed, and uneasy in the extreme at the unexpected and unwelcome presence of these extraordinary visitors to his dominions—these spirits, or men, whichever they happened to be, who had taken such pains to show him that they despised his power, and were quite prepared to ride rough-shod over him unless he slavishly conformed to all their wishes; who had frightened and humiliated him in the presence of his immediate followers and most powerful chiefs, and entailed upon him a loss of prestige which it would be difficult if not impossible to recover. He was childishly jealous of the slightest interference with his supreme authority, and he fretted and chafed himself into a state of fury almost bordering upon madness as he reflected upon the veiled menaces to himself which had been only too distinctly recognisable in every manifestation of these strangers' extraordinary power on the preceding day. He recognised that their deliberate intention had been to show him that during their sojourn in his country he must in all respects conform to their wishes, and model his conduct strictly in accordance with their ideas of what was right and proper, or take the consequences. And what were those consequences likely to be? Judging from what he had already seen, his dethronement and utter humiliation seemed to be among the least severe of future possibilities. Instead of remaining the irresponsible autocrat he had hitherto been, he would, during the sojourn of these strangers in his vicinity, be obliged to carefully weigh and consider his every word and action, in order that he might neither say nor do anything which could by any possibility prove distasteful to them. And if this state of servile, abject, slavish submission was to be his condition during the period of their stay—which might last the Great Fetisch himself only knew how long—his life would not be worth having, it would simply be a grinding, insupportable burden to him.

As these unwelcome reflections thronged through his mind he grew so madly ferocious that he issued orders for the instant execution of certain white prisoners which had fallen into his hands a few months before, countermanding the order almost immediately afterwards—and, happily, in good time—partly because they were women, and he still hoped, notwithstanding present difficulties and frequent former failures, to add them to his harem; and partly because he was under the apprehension that, among their other attributes, his mysterious visitors might possess that of omniscience, and, getting knowledge of the execution, object to and call him to account for it. It was a similar consideration alone which deterred him from solacing himself by the impalement of half a dozen or so of his principal ministers, the entire suite having an exceedingly lively time of it that morning, and being infinitely thankful when they were at last dismissed with whole skins.

The question which harassed and perplexed M'Bongwele for the remainder of that day was: could the visit of these extraordinary beings be by any means shortened or terminated? And, if so, how? Or if the visit could not be cut short, was there any possibility of subjugating the visitors? This particular African monarch possessed at least one virtue, that of perseverance under difficulties. He was not at all the sort of man to sit down and tamely submit to evils if he thought there was even the most remote and slender possibility of overcoming them. He had, on a previous occasion, encountered certain fair-skinned men so similar in appearance, and in every other respect, except dress, to these present troublesome visitors of his that they might well have been taken for beings of the same race; yet *they* had proved so thoroughly mortal that he had had no difficulty whatever in disposing of them. True, he had shot an arrow at one of these visitants yesterday, striking him fair upon the breast, and the arrow, instead of piercing him through and through, had fallen splintered to pieces at his feet. Yet this very extraordinary incident was not, to M'Bongwele, wholly conclusive evidence as to their invulnerability. Lualamba had on the previous day made certain suggestive remarks tending to strengthen his monarch's belief that if these persons could by any means be separated from the huge structure which seemed to be their home they might possibly prove to be very ordinary mortals after all. He was inclined to believe that a great deal, if not the whole, of their power was centred in the gigantic fabric which they called a ship. And, if that should indeed prove to be the case, all that they had done on the previous day could be done by anyone into whose hands the ship might happen to fall. It could be done by *him*. As this reflection flashed across his brain he pictured to himself the immense accession of power and prestige which would come to him with the possession of that wonderful structure; of the conquests it would enable him to make, and of the boundless extension of his dominions which it would enable him to secure; and his eyes flashed and his bosom heaved with unsuppressed excitement as he inwardly vowed that he would achieve its possession or die in the attempt. All the conditions of his life, he angrily told himself, had been violently and permanently disarranged by the incidents of the previous day; he had been publicly threatened; publicly terrified into a cowardly and disgraceful state of submission; and it was quite impossible that he could permanently continue as he then was. He must fully recover all his lost prestige and add immeasurably to it, or must be content to see some ambitious chief rise up and wrest the kingdom from him. These presumptuous strangers had forced him into enmity against them, and they must take the consequences.

Lualamba was one of M'Bongwele's most trusted chiefs, and shortly before sunset he and the head witch-doctor were summoned to a special conference with the king.

Meanwhile the travellers, having enjoyed a most excellent night's rest, rose betimes in the morning and prepared for a thorough systematic investigation of the ruins. They bathed and breakfasted in due course, and then, armed to the teeth, set out upon a tour of general inspection, the professor carrying his camera, and Sir Reginald his sketch-block and colour-box, whilst Mildmay and the colonel, provided with a box-sextant and a light measuring chain, set themselves the task of making a rough survey of the ruins and a portion of the surrounding country. The tour of the ruins, the taking of an occasional sketch or photograph, and the making of the survey, kept the party fully occupied for the whole of the first day; and they returned to the ship just before sunset, tired and hungry, but thoroughly satisfied with their day's work, and fully convinced that their success in penetrating to this interesting spot would alone more than repay them for all the trouble and expense connected with the outfit of the expedition. One important fact at least had been clearly ascertained by them in the course of the day, which was, that the ruins were extremely ancient, their antiquity being demonstrated by the circumstance that during successive ages the soil had gradually accumulated about the ruins until they were nearly half buried. The most interesting discovery made by them during the day was that of an enormous block of ruins, which, from its extent and the imposing character of its architecture, they felt convinced must have been a temple or other public building, and it was resolved that their investigations should commence with it. It was situated about a mile distant from the spot occupied by the *Flying Fish*, and their first intention had been to move the ship somewhat nearer; but an inspection of the intervening ground had shown it to be so encumbered with ruins that it was soon apparent that she must be left where she was.

A very large amount of excavation—much more than they could possibly manage alone—would be necessary before the lower portion of the walls and the pavement of the building could be laid bare, and they decided to go over to M'Bongwele's village on the following morning and arrange with him if possible for the hire of some fifty or a hundred men. This, however, proved to be unnecessary, for whilst they were at breakfast next day the sound of a horn was heard without, and, going on deck, they discovered Lualamba below in charge of a party of some twenty women bearing a present of milk (in closely woven grass baskets), eggs, fowls, and fruit, and a message from the king asking whether his visitors required assistance of any kind in the pursuit of their investigations.

"Capital!" exclaimed the baronet when von Schalckenberg had translated the message. "This is as it should be. Lower the ladder, professor, and ask Lualamba to come on deck. We must send back a present to the king in return for that which he has sent us; and we can at the same time forward a message explaining our wants."

Lualamba quickly made his appearance on deck, where, after receiving a further small present for himself and a cast-off soldier's coat, battered cocked-hat, an old pair of uniform trousers, the seams of which were trimmed with tarnished gold braid, and half a dozen strings of beads, as a present for the king, the wants of the travellers were explained to him. The chief shook his head; he feared it would be difficult, if not impossible, to meet the wishes of the illustrious strangers in the particular manner spoken of. The male inhabitants of the village were all warriors, to whom work of any description would be an unspeakable degradation. But he would see what could be done. If women, now, would serve the strangers' purpose as well as men, the thing could easily be arranged.

Had the travellers been less experienced than they were this suggestion as to the employment of women would have come upon them as a surprise; but they were well aware that among many savage races labour is looked upon as degrading, and therefore imposed solely upon the women; so they merely thanked Lualamba for his promise, and intimated that women would serve them equally as well as men. Upon which Lualamba withdrew, promising that a gang of at least fifty should be at the ruined temple—or whatever it was—"before the sun reached the top of the sky;" in other words, before noon. This promise was faithfully fulfilled, for at eleven o'clock the explorers saw the gang of labourers come filing in among the ruins, armed with rude wooden mattocks and spades, and provided with large baskets in which to convey away the soil as it was dug out. They were as unprepossessing a lot of specimens of female humanity as could well be imagined. Naked, save for a filthy ragged skin petticoat round their waists and reaching to the knee, their faces wore, without exception, an expression of sullen stupidity, and they looked as though they had never experienced a joyous moment in their lives; but they were active and muscular, and soon showed that they thoroughly understood how to use their clumsy tools to the best advantage. They were led by and worked under the directorship of a lean, shrunken, withered old grey-haired hag of superlative ugliness, who did no work herself, but went constantly back and forth along the line of workers, bearing in her hand a long thin pliant rattan, which she did not hesitate to smartly apply to the shoulders of those who seemed to her to be doing less than their fair share of the work in hand. This bit of petty cruelty was, however, as a matter of course, promptly stopped by the professor, who thereby won for himself a look of withering scorn from the hag aforesaid, and glances of stupid wonder—in which in some cases could be also detected faint traces of an expression of gratitude—from the unfortunate sisterhood who laboured under her.

The amount of work performed was, as might naturally be expected, nothing approaching to that which would have been accomplished in the same time by the same number of white labourers; indeed, a gang of half a dozen good honest hard-working English navvies would have accomplished fully as much per diem as the fifty women who laboured among the ruins. But the explorers were quite satisfied; they were in no particular hurry; the climate was delightful; M'Bongwele was wonderfully civil, sending large supplies of provisions, fruit, and milk to the ship daily, accompanied by the most solicitous inquiries through Lualamba as to whether all things were going well with his visitors. There was no attempt whatever, so far as they could discover, to pry into their doings, not a single warrior, save Lualamba, having been seen by them since the day of the king's visit, and everything seemed to be favourable to a thorough and leisurely execution of their purpose.

On the fourth day from the commencement of the excavation the explorers were gratified by the uncovering of a yard or two of what appeared to be a magnificent tesselated pavement of white and variegated marble; and by the end of a fortnight fully half of its supposed area was exposed, showing it to be of an entirely novel and exquisitely graceful design, the intricate outline of the pattern being emphasised by the insertion of plates of gold about a quarter of an inch wide between the tesserae. The pavement was smooth, level, and in perfect preservation, and the explorers were in the very highest of spirits at their exceptional good luck.

At the outset of the work the four friends had been in the habit of returning every day to the ship for luncheon, but as time passed on they felt that to do this in the very hottest part of the day was a wholly unnecessary waste of energy, and they accordingly transferred from the ship to the scene of their operations a spacious umbrella-tent (that is to say, a tent with a top but no sides), together with a small table and four chairs. And under the shadow of this tent they were wont to partake of the mid-day meal (usually a cold collation), which they generally finished off with a cup of chocolate or coffee and a cigar, the potables being prepared by a particular one of the women labourers, who speedily developed quite a special aptitude for the task, and who at length fell into the habit of regularly bringing with her, every day, the milk needed for the purpose. The tent being pitched on a spot which commanded a full view of the operations in progress, the quartette gradually acquired the habit of lingering somewhat over their luncheon, and especially over the final coffee and cigar, the inevitable result of which was that, for the next hour or two, they experienced a feeling of delicious languor and drowsiness, and an almost unconquerable disinclination to exchange the grateful shade of the tent for the scorching heat of the afternoon sun. At first they struggled resolutely and manfully against this overpowering temptation to idleness; but finding, or fancying, that they could supervise the work as efficiently from the tent as they could at a yard or two from its shelter, they gradually gave up the struggle, yielding day after day more completely to the seductive feeling of lassitude which seemed to have laid hold upon them.

Finally, one hot afternoon, overcome by the drowsy influence of the warm perfumed air which played about their languid bodies, they all fell asleep.

Unknown to and wholly unsuspected by them, the old crone who was in charge of the gang of female labourers had, for some days past, been keeping a sharply watchful eye upon the investigators, and upon the day in question she had been, if possible, more sharply watchful than ever. So interested in them did she at last become that, turning her back upon the women and leaving them to work or not as they saw fit, she advanced until she entered the shadow of the tent, where she paused, eagerly scanning the features of the slumberers. For some ten minutes or so she stood motionless as a statue, her sunken glittering eyes turning from one placid face to the other; then she stepped to the baronet's side and, seizing him by the shoulder, shook him sharply. The sleeper might have been dead for all the consciousness which he exhibited at her rude touch. Another and more violent shake proved equally unproductive of results. Then she passed on to the colonel, to Mildmay, and to the professor, experimenting in like manner with each. If she wished to arouse them, her efforts were useless; they were, one and all, locked fast in the embrace of sleep—profound, unnatural, death-like sleep. A scornful laugh grated harshly from her lips, and, wheeling sharply upon her heel, she rejoined the gang of excavators, exclaiming:

"Cease this useless labour; there is no further need of it. The witch-potion has done its work, and you may all return to the village. I go to summon the warriors."

The women, without further ado, gathered up their tools and baskets, and, breaking into a low monotonous song, to which their feet kept time, took the trail leading to the village, and soon disappeared among the scattered ruins and the bush which clustered thickly about them.

Ten minutes later a band of dusky warriors, fully armed and numbering about a hundred, made their appearance, and, led by Lualamba, advanced to the tent, which they surrounded. Four grass hammocks, each of which was stretched between two long bamboo poles, were then brought forward, and, by the directions of the chief, the unconscious white men were carefully lifted from their seats and deposited at full length in them. The tent was then struck, and, with its simple furniture, taken in charge by certain members of the band told off for the purpose, when each of the hammocks, with its sleeping burden, was carefully raised from the ground and shouldered by four savages, and, the remainder of the warriors forming round them as an escort, the band took the trail to the village, and marched rapidly away.

On reaching their destination the prisoners (for such they evidently were) were carried to a new hut, which had all the appearance of having been specially constructed for them, and, once inside, the poles of the hammocks were carefully laid in the forked ends of upright posts, firmly fixed in the ground, the whole forming a sufficiently comfortable bed. Four young women then entered the building, and, taking their places, one at the head of each sleeper, proceeded, with the aid of large feather fans, to protect their helpless charges from the attacks of the mosquitoes and other insect torments with which the village swarmed; when the hammock-bearers filed out, and the white men were left to sleep off, undisturbed, the effects of the potent drug which had been artfully mingled with the milk with which their coffee had that day been prepared.

The hut in which our four friends were thus left had been erected in a spacious palisaded quadrangle which surrounded the king's palace, so that M'Bongwele might, as it were, always have them under his own eye; and the fact that, having got them into his power, the king was determined, if possible, to keep them there, was made manifest by the presence of a strong cordon of guards, who, on the passage of the prisoners within the portal, immediately ranged themselves round the hut outside. The hut was only some twelve feet square, and entirely open at one end, the open end being, however, protected from the sun by a continuation of the roof in the form of a broad verandah supported at the eaves upon two stout verandah-posts; and round this diminutive structure were ranged twenty picked men, facing inward, fully armed with bow, spear, and shield; it was pretty evident, therefore, that, unless the prisoners had the power to render themselves invisible, or of paralysing their guards, there was little probability of their effecting their escape.

The posting of the guard having been effected to Lualamba's satisfaction, he entered the palace to make his report to the king, who was anxiously expecting him. M'Bongwele listened attentively to all the details of the capture, and, upon its completion, rose and, accompanied by the chief, made his way to the hut, which he cautiously entered, placing himself at the foot of each hammock in succession, and long and anxiously regarding the countenances of the sleepers. He had been successful in his bold enterprise beyond his most sanguine hopes; but it was evident that even in the very moment of his triumph he was anxious and disturbed in his mind. He trembled at the audacity which had led him to pit himself against these extraordinary beings, and the very ease with which he had accomplished his purpose frightened him. Had these men—if men they were—been encountered and overcome awake, and in the full possession of their senses, he would have been happy, for he would then have felt that his own power was superior to theirs. But they had been surprised whilst under the influence of a subtle and potent drug prepared by the chief witch-doctor; and when they awoke and discovered what had been done to them, what might not the consequence be? But what was done was done; he had now gone too far to retreat; besides which, his ambition overmastered his fears, and he determined to go on and risk the consequences.

Having obtained possession of the persons of these formidable beings, obviously the next thing would be to secure that wonderful thing which they called a "ship;" and this M'Bongwele determined to do at once: who knew but that its possession might give him a much-needed and decisive power over its former owners? He accordingly retired from the prison hut, and gave orders for the immediate assembling of all his available cavalry; at the head of which he soon dashed off in the direction of the ruins, leaving Lualamba in charge of the guard and of the prisoners, a position of responsibility which that chief by no means coveted, and which he accepted with much inward perturbation.

Proceeding at a gallop, the impatient M'Bongwele and his troopers soon reached the *Flying Fish*, which they immediately surrounded. The king then dismounting, and summoning some fifty of his most famous braves to follow him, cautiously approached the ship, with the purpose of boarding her. But the rope-ladder, by means of which he had on a former occasion accomplished this feat, was no longer there; and, as he glanced upward at the gleaming cylindrical sides of the towering structure, it began to dawn upon him that the task he had undertaken was, after all, not without its difficulties. Presently, however, a brilliant idea occurred to him, and, selecting a dozen men, he gave them certain orders which sent them scurrying off at a gallop. Half an hour later they returned, dragging behind them two long stout bamboos and a considerable quantity of tough pliant "monkey-rope" or creeper. With these materials the men, under M'Bongwele's instructions, proceeded to construct a ladder, which, when completed, they reared against the side of the ship; and by this means the king and his fifty chosen warriors ascended and triumphantly reached the deck.

M'Bongwele now regarded himself as completely successful; he had gained possession of the wonderful structure; and all that remained was to make use of it in a similar manner to that of its former owners. He accordingly advanced pompously to the gangway, and ordered his troopers to first remove the ladder from the ship's side, and then return to the village with all speed, adding exultantly that he and those with him on the "flying horse's back" would be there long before them.

Resolved to give the cavalcade a good start, he watched it disappear in a cloud of dust among the ruins, and then, assuming his most commanding attitude and manner, raised his right hand aloft and exclaimed:

"We will now return through the air to the village—keeping as close to the ground as possible," he added with some trepidation as he nervously grasped the guard rail in anticipation of the expected movement.

The ship, however, remained motionless. Something was evidently wrong, but what it might be he could not imagine; surely he had not forgotten or misunderstood the formula as stated to him by Lualamba? He now most heartily wished that he had brought that trusty chief with him, and so provided against all possibility of error; however, the omission could not be helped, and he would try again, adopting a somewhat different form of words. This time he stamped rather impatiently on the deck, exclaiming:

"Take us back to the village, good flying horse, but gently, and not very far above the ground."

Still no movement. The king began to look puzzled, and to feel as vexed as he dared, with the consciousness weighing heavily upon him that he was playing with frightfully keen edged tools. He did not know what to make of this persistent immobility; it was uncanny, sinister, portentous, almost appalling. He would try again. He *did* try again, not once but nearly a dozen times, varying the form of words, more or less, every time; and, of course, with the same ill success. At length, in chagrin and disgust, he gave up the attempt to move the ship, and turned his attention to an examination of her interior. He advanced to the pilot-house, complacently reflecting that here, at least, he could not possibly be beaten; he had only to walk up to the door and enter. But here, again, surprise and confusion awaited him; for, after *twice* making the circuit of the building, he was unable to find a door; there was no perceptible entrance anywhere excepting the circular windows, which, however, were all open. Summoning his followers to his assistance, he made them give him a "back;" and, scrambling up on their shoulders, he at length contrived to raise himself to the level of these openings and to look in. He saw a great many levers, and knobs, and buttons, and short lengths of insulated wire; in fact, he got a glimpse of pretty nearly all the apparatus contained in the pilothouse; but that did not help him in the least, for he had not the most remote idea of what all these things were for; and when he essayed an entrance by one of the windows he was again foiled; it was much too small. At length, after a great deal of ineffectual wriggling and struggling—which occasioned serious inconvenience and anxiety to the human supports who were with the utmost difficulty maintaining a state of very unstable equilibrium beneath his feet—his patience completely failed him, and, in a fit of childish anger and spite, he sent a series of truly blood-curdling yells echoing into the interior of the pilot-house. These cries were of course distinctly heard by George and the *chef,* but (acting upon a concise code of instructions furnished to them when they were first engaged for the voyage, and which provided for almost every conceivable emergency), neither of these individuals condescended to take any notice of them. Having thus given vent to a portion of his spleen, king M'Bongwele, paying but scanty attention to the comfort or dignity of his supporters, scrambled down from his elevated position to the deck, and sat down to reflect upon the next steps to be taken. He would gladly now have left the ship and made the best of his way back to the village, even though the journey would have had to be performed on foot; but the ladder had, by his own command, been removed, and his retreat was thus effectually cut off, a drop of about forty feet from the bottom of the metal accommodation ladder to the ground being a something not to be thought of.

CHAPTER TWENTY
THE HISTORY OF CERTAIN DISTRESSED DAMSELS

Meanwhile Seketulo, the chief in command of king M'Bongwele's household cavalry, returned to the village in due course, and lost no time in dismissing his men, chuckling to himself as he reflected that, after all, he had beaten his monarch in the race homeward.

Time passed on; the sun set; the evanescent twilight faded out of the sky; the stars twinkled forth in all the mellow radiance characteristic of the tropics; and still the adventurous M'Bongwele and his wondrous prize came not. Hour after hour lagged slowly away; and at length the expectant villagers, who had poured into the open air to witness the triumphant arrival of the king, returned to their huts—their transient enthusiasm overcome by their habitual apathy and indolence—and surrendered themselves willingly enough to the blandishments of sleep. All, with the exception, that is to say, of the guard detailed to watch over the prisoners, the anxious Lualamba, and Seketulo. These were all wakeful enough, the latter perhaps even more so than any of the others. For, as the night waxed and the great full moon rolled slowly upward into the sky, the powerful chief, who had won for himself the envied position of commander of the king's cavalry (a position equivalent to that of commander-in-chief of the whole army), felt the hope growing within him that the foolhardy king and those with him had been carried off to the nether regions for a permanency by the wondrous Thing of which they had so audaciously sought to secure the possession. And in that case (M'Bongwele being without sons, and having, in order to avoid possible future complications, carefully slaughtered all his brothers and other relations on his accession to the throne) there would be a vacancy in that particular country for a king, which vacancy Seketulo believed himself powerful enough to secure and fill.

Giving free rein to these ambitious ideas and aspirations, the chief paced thoughtfully to and fro in a retired corner of the village until about ten o'clock that night, when his impatience could no longer be curbed, and he felt that he *must* sally forth to ascertain, if possible, the fate of M'Bongwele and his party. Accordingly, mounting his horse, he took his way out of the village, passing through the principal gateway, and heading for the ruins at a gallop. He was greatly disconcerted, on reaching his destination, to discover that the *Flying Fish* still peacefully reposed in her usual berth; and his disgust was supreme when he further noticed, crouched on her lofty deck, a disconsolate-looking group, which his fears only too truly assured him must be the king and his companions. His first impulse was to retire and leave them to their merited fate; but the unwelcome reflection suggesting itself to him that they might possibly be discovered and rescued in the morning, he altered his purpose, and, making a virtue of what was almost a necessity, advanced with the intention of proffering a respectful inquiry as to whether any unfortunate accident had delayed the royal return. He was, however, forestalled by the king and his party, who, the instant they saw him, hailed his appearance with joyous shouts and an almost piteous entreaty to him to replace the ladder. This he, still making a virtue of necessity, at once attempted to do; but the clumsy construction proved too much for his strength. A happy idea, however, now flashed through the mind of one of the party; and, unstringing their bows, they joined the strings together into one continuous line, which, luckily for them, reached the ground; and Seketulo bending the lower end on to the ladder, the latter was soon, by the exertions of all hands, reared into position. The party, thoroughly crestfallen, now lost no time in making their way to the ground, when M'Bongwele at once requisitioned Seketulo's horse, and galloped off homeward at top speed, the chief and the rest of the party being left to plod back to the village at their leisure and as best they could.

Notwithstanding this most dismal failure, M'Bongwele still entertained hopes of being able to possess himself of the coveted ship; and early next morning every available man and woman was marched to the scene of the preceding day's discomfiture to attempt the task of *carrying the Flying Fish to the village*! This attempt, it is scarcely necessary to say, also resulted in complete failure, and with this failure king M'Bongwele was at last compelled to recognise himself as beaten. It became clear to him that the mysterious beings whose persons he had so rashly seized possessed certain peculiar and wonderful powers; and the only course now open to him seemed to be to make the best terms he could with them for their co-operation in the furtherance of his schemes. And he felt heartily glad—pluming himself at the same time upon his prudence—that he had not taken advantage of their seemingly helpless condition, when brought to the village, to attempt the putting of a period to their existence.

Meanwhile, Seketulo, though greatly chagrined at the turn of affairs, by no means abandoned hope. He felt that though disappointment had for once overtaken him, it by no means followed that such would always be the case; and if his ambitious dreams could not be realised in one way, they still might be in another. The king, unfortunately, had not been carried off to perdition; but, figuratively speaking, that seemed to be his ultimate and speedy destination. For, had he not pitted his own power against that of the mysterious strangers, and lost the game? He had inflicted a most grievous outrage upon them, and had ineffectually attempted to seize their wonderful ship; yet not a particle of gain or advantage of any description had been secured, and the wrath of these strangers had yet to be faced; the penalty of his audacious deeds had yet to be paid. Did not all this point to M'Bongwele's speedy downfall? And if such a state of things should happily be in the near future, would it not be worth his (Seketulo's) while to approach the strangers in a friendly spirit and (after cautiously feeling his way) with offers of assistance? He decided that it undoubtedly would, and that he would forthwith adopt that line of policy, cautiously, yet without losing a single favourable opportunity.

So far as M'Bongwele was concerned, he found himself in a greater strait than ever. He had not only failed completely in his ambitious schemes, but he had also lost prestige with his own people and had made enemies of the strangers. His situation was distinctly worse than if he had done nothing at all; and how to make his way out of the imbroglio he knew not, nor could any of his ministers advise anything. He now fervently wished he had adopted other and more friendly measures with his visitors; but it was too late; he fully recognised that, with the odium of failure fresh upon him, any attempt at conciliation would be utterly hopeless; the only course still open to him appearing to be that of "masterly inactivity." This would, at all events, leave time for events to shape themselves, and afford him an opportunity of regulating his conduct in accordance therewith; and this course he accordingly determined to pursue; at the same time issuing the most imperative orders that the prisoners were to be treated with the utmost courtesy and consideration consistent with their safe-keeping.

In accordance with these orders, the prisoners found that, after the second day of their seizure, they had very little of which to complain beyond the actual loss of their liberty. They were abundantly supplied with provisions of all kinds within the resources of the village; the four young women originally detailed to watch over them during their drugged slumber were permanently appointed to attend upon them, do their cooking, keep their hut clean, and so on; and they were allowed to take unrestricted exercise within the bounds of the compound. Their attendants and guards were allowed to answer any questions except such as related to the king's recent attempt to possess himself of their property; and hints were freely offered to the effect that M'Bongwele was most anxious to secure their friendship, and would gladly afford them an audience whenever they might desire it. But they had no intention whatever of seeking an audience with the king; they had a very shrewd suspicion of what had actually taken place; and having by this time formed a tolerably accurate estimate of the royal character, they felt convinced that their only chance of advantageously dealing with M'Bongwele lay in forcing upon *him* the character of a suitor to *them*.

Thus matters stood for nearly a fortnight from the date of their seizure—Seketulo doing his best to effectually ingratiate himself in the strangers' favour before venturing to tender his proposed offer of assistance; and M'Bongwele waiting with daily growing impatience for overtures from his prisoners—when an event occurred which, simple though it seemed at the moment, was destined to have an important bearing on the fortunes of certain other white prisoners then in the king's power.

It happened thus. The quartette were sitting under the verandah of their hut one morning, whining away the very last remains of their carefully hoarded stock of tobacco, when a soft thud, followed by a low startled cry of pain and terror from one of their female attendants caused them to glance hastily round. The sight which then met their eyes was startling enough to make them spring instantly to their feet. A snake fully seven feet long, and of the most deadly venomous kind (which had evidently just dropped out of the thatch of the hut), had flung its coils round the bare leg of one of the women, and, before help could be rendered, had struck its fangs deep into the flesh. The cruel heart-shaped head, with its wicked eyes glowing like a couple of carbuncles, was already drawn back to repeat the stroke when Lethbridge sprang forward, and, seizing a small pliant rattan which happened to be handy at the moment, dealt the reptile a swift downward cut across the body, dividing the creature almost in two; following up the blow by a rapid dart of his hand, grasping the reptile by the neck and tearing the quivering coils away from the wounded limb. Another second, and the head was being fiercely ground into the dust under the thick solid leather of his boot-heel, the wounded body twisting and writhing in the most horrible contortions meanwhile.

Two out of Lethbridge's three companions stood helplessly aghast whilst this tragedy was in progress; but the professor, ever alert in the interests of science, promptly compelled the wounded girl to lie down, and instantly applied his lips to the wound made by the poisonous fangs of the snake, sucking vigorously until he had induced as copious a flow of blood as could reasonably be expected from the two tiny punctures. Then, fumbling in his waistcoat pocket, he drew forth a small stick of lunar caustic (with which he had some time previously provided himself in anticipation of possible snake-bites) and effectually cauterised the wound. The result of which prompt treatment was that the girl, after enduring some three hours' slight suffering and inconvenience from the pain and subsequent swelling of the wound, recovered, and in a day or two was as well again as ever.

This incident was, as might be expected, much talked about in the village, and it very soon reached M'Bongwele's ears. That monarch happened, just then, to be plunged into a state of serious domestic affliction; and, inspired by the above occurrence with a brilliant idea, he, after much painful cogitation, resolved to seek the aid of his prisoners. Briefly stated, the difficulty was this. His youngest and favourite wife had just added another to his already too numerous family of daughters, thus disgusting and seriously disappointing the king, who had confidently looked forward to being this time blessed with a son. This was by no means the first disappointment of the kind that the monarch had been called upon to endure; and it had been his wont, on such occasions, to banish the offending wife from his presence, replacing her with a new one. He proposed to follow the same rule upon the present occasion; and the only difficulty which lay in his way consisted in suitably filling up the vacancy. There were, of course, hundreds of sable damsels within the limits of his dominions who would gladly have accepted the responsibilities of the position, but that would no longer suit king M'Bongwele; the women of his own race had, one and all, so far as he had tried them, failed disgracefully in their duty of providing him with an heir, and he was now determined to try elsewhere. He happened to have in his possession, as prisoners, four white women, one of whom was somewhat elderly, whilst the remaining three were young, and, though by no means sufficiently *embonpoint* to be strictly handsome, from an African savage's point of view, still attractive enough to justify his choice of either of them as a wife. The difficulty with these women was that they were unfortunately all insane—a circumstance which (in accordance with one of the many superstitious beliefs of the natives, and quite apart from the equally important objection of consequent unsuitability) effectually precluded any resort to threats or compulsion for enabling the king to carry out his plans. And it was for the purpose of securing these unfortunate creatures' restoration to reason that M'Bongwele now resolved to invoke the potent aid of his new prisoners. When making up his mind to this course he was at first greatly puzzled as to how he should approach the individuals he had so basely betrayed, and how explain and excuse his conduct; but at last the happy idea suggested itself of ignoring his ill-behaviour altogether; and acting upon this, and without giving himself time for further consideration, he hurried off to the hut and presented himself before his prisoners.

Seating himself jauntily upon one of the bedsteads, he opened the negotiations by explaining that he had come to express his admiration of, and his thanks for, the wonderful manner in which the woman had been saved from the deadly effects of the snake-bite; and then, without affording an opportunity for interruption, he went on to state, in full detail, his further business.

The indignation excited in the breasts of his listeners by the cool impudence of the king soon subsided under the influence of the interesting news that four white women were captives in the village; and when M'Bongwele closed his explanation and proffered his request, the professor, instead of loading his captor with reproaches, followed the latter's example of ignoring all cause for unpleasantness, and simply stated that no promise of any kind could be made until the four friends had been afforded an interview with the afflicted women. To this proposition the king eagerly assented, overjoyed at so unexpected a measure of success, indeed he volunteered to personally conduct the quartette into the presence of his female prisoners; but this was promptly negatived, the professor declaring that if he and his friends went to see the women at all they must go entirely unattended, and at such time as might be most convenient to themselves. It would have suited M'Bongwele very much better to have been present at this interview, for he was suspicious to a really absurd degree; but, finding the white men firm upon this point, and, apparently, wholly indifferent in the matter, and being also unable to discover any cause for suspicion in their conduct, he at length yielded his assent and retired, giving the necessary instructions to the guard as he passed out of the hut.

The next morning, about eleven o'clock, having previously talked this curious matter carefully over together, they paid their promised visit; the women's prison (to which they were carefully escorted by their entire guard) being situated close to the principal opening in the palisading which surrounded the village; the same guard being apparently made to serve for both the prison and the gateway. The building was an almost exact facsimile of their own place of confinement, both in shape and dimensions; but at the very threshold the visitors encountered evidences of female delicacy and refinement in the shape of finely woven grass curtains or *portières* across the otherwise unclosed entrance, and these trifling elegances were multiplied a hundred-fold in the interior, converting the little building into a veritable miniature palace in comparison with their own unadorned domicile.

But these little interior adornments did not attract the visitors' notice until later on; their whole attention was at once claimed, upon their entrance, by the occupants of the building, or at least by the fairer portion of them. There were eight altogether—four white and four black, the ebony damsels evidently filling the position of attendants. Of the white women three were young—that is to say, they apparently ranged between nineteen and twenty-five years of age—whilst the fourth seemed to be somewhere between forty and fifty. This lady was of medium height, with a figure slightly inclined toward stoutness, brown hair with just a single streak of silver discernible here and there amongst it, a complexion still in fairly good preservation, a pair of keen but kindly grey eyes, an excellent set of teeth, shapely hands and feet, and a pleasant smile which at once prepossessed the beholder in its possessor's favour. Of the three younger women, two, aged respectively twenty-one and nineteen, were sisters; whilst the third, aged twenty-five, was their cousin, the elderly lady being aunt to all three.

On entering the hut, in response to the cry of "Come in" which followed their knock on the framework of the portal, the visitors at once found themselves face to face with the four ladies, who had risen to their feet to meet them; the sable attendants crouching at the rear end of the apartment with a grin of sympathetic curiosity overspreading their shining visages.

"You are most welcome, gentlemen," said the elderly lady, advancing and offering her hand to each of her visitors in succession. "We have been expecting you. Allow me to perform the ceremony of introduction. I am Mrs. Scott, widow of Brigadier-general Scott of her majesty's forces in India. This lady is Miss Sabine, my niece and the only daughter of Major-general Sabine; and these are respectively Miss Rose and Miss Lucilla Lumsden, the daughters of an Indian judge."

The gentlemen bowed low as each name was mentioned, and, upon Mrs.

Scott making a somewhat significant pause, the baronet took up his parable, remarking:

"We are greatly honoured and delighted, ladies, at thus unexpectedly making your acquaintance in this out-of-the-way spot, and we sincerely hope that the acquaintanceship will redound to our mutual advantage. I am Sir Reginald Elphinstone. This gentleman is Colonel Lethbridge; this is Lieutenant Mildmay, of her majesty's navy; and, last but by no means least, this gentleman is Professor von Schalckenberg, an eminent German scientist, a most delightful companion, and a man clever enough, I firmly believe, to help us all out of our present difficulties."

A general shaking of hands ensued; and then Mrs. Scott laughingly invited the gentlemen to seat themselves on the four bamboo pallets which occupied opposite sides of the apartment, apologising at the same time for the lack of suitable sitting accommodation.

"And now," said Mrs. Scott laughingly, "to which of you gentlemen are we to look for the cure of our madness?"

"It is expected, I believe," said Sir Reginald, "that we shall each aid, to the best of our ability, in the good work. But," he continued in a lower and more cautious tone of voice, "is it not rather imprudent of you to behave in so very sane a manner before these women?"

"Oh," said Mrs. Scott, "they are all right. They are perfectly trustworthy—indeed, they are actively aiding and abetting us in the exceedingly disagreeable but necessary deception we are practising upon king M'Bongwele. The wretch!" she continued, starting indignantly to her feet. "Would you believe it? He actually has the audacity and impudence to—to—to—"

"To aspire to a matrimonial alliance with one, if not all, of you. Yes, I am aware of his ambition," said the baronet with a smile; "and whilst we are here to-day, at his request, to remove the obstacle which your most deplorable insanity interposes, I hope that the ultimate result will be your speedy deliverance, with our own, from his power. We are, like yourselves, prisoners, but we are by no means hopeless of escape, and I pledge you my word that we will not leave until we can take you all with us."

Mrs. Scott shook her head somewhat doubtfully. "We are all infinitely obliged to you for your generous promise," she said with a sigh; "but I greatly fear you are somewhat overrating your powers. The difficulties of escape—in the first place, from this village, and, in the next place, from the country itself—are so formidable that we have almost given up all hope. May I ask what strange accident brought you hither?"

"Assuredly," answered the baronet. "And when I have informed you of the facts, you will see that the difficulties of escape are, after all, not so very enormous, and I trust that you will all take heart once more."

Sir Reginald then proceeded to give a detailed description of the *Flying*

Fish; and of his own and his companions' adventures in her; winding up with an account of their capture—so far as they were aware of its details—and a recital of the grounds upon which they founded their hopes of escape.

The ladies listened to Sir Reginald's singular story with an astonishment which they vainly strove to conceal, and had it been uncorroborated, they would probably have suspected in him a touch of the same malady with which they were supposed to be afflicted; but, as matters were, they had no choice but to credit the tale, and very much gratified they were to learn that there existed a means of conveyance affording, if they could but once gain access to it, a safe, easy, and speedy escape from the realms of king M'Bongwele.

Sir Reginald, having brought his story to an end, requested that he and his companions might be favoured with an account of the manner in which the ladies had fallen into the hands of the savages, which request Mrs. Scott complied with, somewhat in the following terms:

"It is, to a great extent, my fault that these poor girls find themselves in the unfortunate position which they occupy to-day. I have been a widow for nearly seven years; but, having been early left an orphan, with no friends in England and many in India, I did not, as many newly-made widows do, turn my face homeward immediately on my husband's death; on the contrary, I determined rather to remain in the country of my adoption, and, being left in tolerably comfortable circumstances, made arrangements to reside alternately in Delhi and Simla. These arrangements I duly carried into effect, and nothing occurred to disturb them until about a year ago, when my brother, Sir James Lumsden, died, leaving his motherless daughters—Rose and Lucilla here—in my care, with an earnest entreaty that I would convey them, at my earliest convenience, home to their grandfather, who owns a very fine place in Hampshire, and who would, doubtless, be glad to receive them. I, of course, very willingly undertook the duty—not the less so, perhaps, from the fact that I was myself somewhat ailing, and had been strongly urged by my medical adviser to try the effect of change and a long sea voyage. Our preparations were soon completed, and we journeyed down to Bombay, at which place I happened to meet my brother-in-law, General Sabine. He, poor man, was in a great difficulty just then, being under orders to proceed at once to Afghanistan, and not knowing what to do with his daughter, who, I ought to explain, has been motherless from her infancy. The best way I could see out of the difficulty was for her to take the trip home to Europe with us, and, upon my making the proposal, it was joyfully adopted. So far all was well; but at this point our difficulties were to begin. We, unfortunately, took passage for London in a sailing ship for my health's sake. We, or the ship rather, had to call at the Cape, and, three weeks after we sailed, the captain died. The chief mate then assumed the command of the vessel, and in a few days afterwards we found that he was giving way to drink. That was, doubtless, the cause of the disaster which followed, for on a dark and stormy night, whilst the chief mate—or captain, rather, I suppose I ought to call him—was lying in his berth in a state of almost helpless intoxication, and the ship was flying before the rising gale under all the sail the sailors could spread, *we struck*! the masts snapped short off at the deck, and in a moment all was confusion and panic. The mate, or captain, staggered up on deck to see what was the matter, and he had scarcely reached the poop when a breaker swept down upon the wreck and washed the unhappy wretch overboard, never to be seen again. The next officer—a brave energetic young fellow - then took command, and by his coolness and courage soon restored order among the crew. He commanded the lead-line to be dropped overboard, and by its means ascertained that the ship was being rapidly driven shoreward by the force of the waves. Meanwhile the shocks of the ship striking against the ground gradually grew less and less severe, until they ceased altogether, and the vessel became motionless save for an occasional sickening lurch when an exceptionally heavy wave struck her. By this time it was ascertained that the hold was nearly full of water, a circumstance from which the young officer in charge came to the conclusion that the hull was irretrievably damaged, and he then gave orders to lower the boats. This task the sailors with great difficulty accomplished, and then, there being at the moment no immediate prospect of the wreck going to pieces, the boats were secured under the shelter of the ship, and it was determined to defer until daylight our attempt at landing, when the dangers of the enterprise could be distinctly seen and more easily avoided. About two hours elapsed between the first striking of the vessel and the launching of the boats, during which time I and my nieces were on deck in our night-dresses, supplemented by such wraps as we had been able to hastily snatch on the moment of the first alarm. But when the boats had been safely lowered into the sea and secured, Mr. Snelgrove (the young officer who had last assumed the command) came to us, and, in the kindest manner possible, begged us to retire to our cabins, assuring us that we might do so with perfect safety, and that we might depend on him to summon us in good time to attempt a landing with the rest of the crew. We accordingly took his advice, glad to get back to the shelter of the saloon, where we at once discarded our wet garments and proceeded to make ourselves as comfortable as the circumstances permitted. Day broke at length, and then Mr. Snelgrove made his appearance in the saloon, informing us that the weather had moderated, the sea gone down a good deal, and the tide had ebbed, rendering it a favourable moment to attempt a landing, which he believed might be effected without much danger; he further added that the seamen were then passing provisions and water into the boats, and that he would allow us ten minutes wherein to select and pack a small bundle of such clothing and effects as might be deemed by us most necessary. At length the eventful moment arrived for us to pass down into the boats, and though we were assured by the sailors that there was no danger, I never was so thoroughly frightened in my life, for the sea was still very rough, leaping, curling, and foaming all round us. However, we all managed to embark without accident, and then our boat (which was the second to make the attempt) pushed off and made for the shore. The breakers were appalling, and the boat was turned round with her bow pointing seaward, and 'backed'—I think they called it—toward the shore. The sea broke over us several times, half filling the boat; but two men were kept constantly baling with buckets, and at length—thanks to Mr. Snelgrove's admirable management—we safely reached the beach, but wet to the skin as a matter of course. Meanwhile, the first boat, in charge of the boatswain, had discharged her cargo on the beach, and was now sent back with four men to the wreck to bring on shore the remainder of the crew and whatever of value they could lay their hands upon. This going to and fro between the beach and the ship lasted nearly all day, and by nightfall we had quite a large quantity of provisions, water, canvas, spars, and other matters, and last, but not least, all my nieces' and my own boxes. The sailors constructed two tents in a sheltered spot high up on the beach—one for themselves and one for us—and we at length retired to spend our first night in the character of castaways.

"About an hour before daybreak we were rudely awakened—to find ourselves in the power of the savages. I am of opinion that we must have been watched during the whole of the previous day, for the surprise of the camp was complete; we had been noiselessly surrounded, and, whilst we unfortunate women were spared, the equally unfortunate men were, for the most part, slain in their sleep; not one had escaped—at least we never afterwards saw any of them alive. The camp was of course ransacked, and when every man had possessed himself of whatever happened to take his fancy, we were placed in the centre of the band and conveyed to this place, where we have been detained close prisoners ever since. The scattered contents of the camp must afterwards, I fancy, have been collected and brought to this village, for a few days later our boxes—broken open and the contents in a dreadfully soiled and disordered condition—were brought to us, and upon our replying in the affirmative to the questions put to us by signs as to whether they were our property, were left in our possession. I have only to add that the wreck, and the horrors which succeeded it, proved too much for poor Lucilla in her then somewhat weak state of health, and she fell into a low fever with delirium, which prostrated her for nearly three months, and from the effects of which she has even now not wholly recovered. It was during this dreadfully anxious period that those four poor black creatures were appointed to attend upon us. They have been most zealous and faithful in their efforts to help us; they have instructed us to some extent in their simple language; and they have informed us, not only that they are cast-off wives of the king, but that he was, and still is, anxious to secure one (if not more) of my nieces for a wife, and that the only hope of escape from such a fate lay in our simulating insanity, which, most reluctantly, we have been compelled to do whenever M'Bongwele or any of his emissaries have visited us. But, beyond our close confinement and this horrible ever-impending danger, we have no very great cause for complaint, all our expressed wants being instantly satisfied so far as the resources of the king will permit."

Mrs. Scott having thus brought her story to an end, the gentlemen expressed their sympathy and condolences, and the conversation gradually grew more general. At length, much as they would have liked to prolong the interview, they felt that they had already lengthened it out almost beyond the bounds of prudence, so they rose to take leave, uttering a few encouraging remarks, which Sir Reginald rounded off with an exhortation to them to be ever on the watch, and to hold themselves in readiness for flight at a moment's notice, adding that one or other of the gentlemen would visit them as often as possible and keep them well informed upon the progress of events.

CHAPTER TWENTY ONE
RETRIBUTION OVERTAKES KING M'BONGWELE

King M'Bongwele had evidently been keenly on the watch for the return of the four prisoners, for they had scarcely had time to enter their hut when the monarch presented himself before them, and, with some little impatience of manner, began his interrogations with the single word:

"Well?"

"We can cure them," briefly answered the professor.

"Good!" ejaculated the king, his impatience yielding to almost childish delight. "When is the cure to be performed?"

"Within one span of the sun's journey through the sky after we have administered a certain medicine, which we must procure from the ship. Provide us each with a horse to go and fetch this medicine, and I promise you, that before you see the stars to-night those women shall be in as full possession of their reason as you are."

"No," said the king, eyeing the professor keenly, "I will arrange better than that. You shall tell Lualamba where to find this wonderful medicine, and he shall fetch it for you."

"That will not do at all," answered the professor. "Lualamba could never find the medicine; he could not even gain access to the ship. We must fetch it ourselves."

M'Bongwele rested his chin in his hand for some minutes, pondering deeply. Then he rose to his feet and stalked out of the hut again without vouchsafing a word, either "yea" or "nay."

"He is not quite such a fool as he looks," was the baronet's sole comment upon this strange behaviour, and then they sat down to luncheon.

The king, upon re-entering his palace, at once sent for Lualamba, and, upon that chief making his appearance, issued strict orders that every available man, woman, and child, not only in the village but in the entire district, should be mustered by noon next day, to make one grand and final attempt to move the ship to the village, pending which the king decided to hold no further communications with his prisoners. The attempt was made in due course, and, like the others, it proved, as might be expected, a miserable failure. Poor M'Bongwele was now completely at a loss; he knew not what to do. He was most anxious to have the white women cured; but he had a powerful presentiment that if those singular beings, whom he certainly to some extent had in his power, once again set foot upon that curious thing they called a "ship," his power over them would be gone for ever. And in such a case he felt that his fate was certain; he had laid unholy hands upon them, and dire would be his punishment. No; he was convinced that at all costs they must be debarred from access to that terrible "ship," unless he could first of all gain their forgiveness, amity, and good-will, and interest them in his fortunes to the extent of securing their active co-operation in his schemes of conquest and aggrandisement. How to do this was, however, the question which puzzled king M'Bongwele; and it puzzled him so long that—but stay, we must not forestall the story.

Thus engaged in a futile endeavour to discover a way out of his dilemma, the king kept himself strictly secluded in his palace day after day, allowing no one access to him unless upon business of the utmost urgency and importance. Meanwhile, Seketulo, deeming the period a favourable one for the furtherance of his own schemes, first exhibited an increased amount of precaution in the proper posting of the guard over the prisoners, and then a gradually growing disposition to converse with the prisoners themselves. From this he proceeded to develop an interest, which, after a suitable lapse of time, was allowed to merge into anxiety for their welfare and greater comfort, and, finding these cautious advances well received, he then set to work in real earnest upon the delicate task of unfolding his proposals. He was so very cautious, however, and took so long a time about this, that he missed his opportunity altogether, and that, too, through a very simple accident.

It happened one night that, after an unusually long, disjointed, and desultory conversation with this same chief, Mildmay failed to get to sleep with his usual promptitude, and he lay tossing restlessly upon his pallet until he became impatient and finally exasperated at his want of success. The hut felt hot and stuffy to the verge of suffocation, and the lieutenant at length came to the conclusion that there was no hope of his getting to sleep until he had taken a turn or two up and down the compound, in the comparatively cool night air.

He accordingly scrambled to his feet, and, groping his way in the intense darkness, made for the verandah. Here he paused for a moment, glancing upward to the sky, which he found to be obscured by a dense canopy of heavy black cloud, portending rain, which sufficiently accounted for the pitchy darkness. His eyes at length becoming accustomed to the obscurity, he looked round for the guard; and he eventually discovered the various members faithfully occupying their posts, but, one and all, squatted upon the ground evidently fast asleep. He stalked out toward the centre of the compound and took two or three turns up and down its length, his footsteps falling noiselessly upon the light sandy soil, and not one of the savages manifested the slightest consciousness of his presence. Then he gradually extended his walk until he reached the gate in the palisade, and here too the guard was fast asleep. An idea presented itself to him; and he was about to make an attempt to noiselessly remove the bars and open the gate, when prudence suggested another and a better plan. He tiptoed lightly back to the hut, and, gently awakening each of his companions in turn, whispered in their ears:

"Up at once! There is an opportunity for us to effect our escape!"

The aroused sleepers instinctively comprehended the situation and sprang to their feet. Another minute, and four shadowy shapes stole noiselessly across the compound, to vanish almost instantly in the deeper shadows of the palisading. The closed gate was reached and passed, and presently the fugitives found themselves in the angle of the compound most distant from the slumbering guard. Here Mildmay offered a "back" to the baronet, whispering:

"You go first."

Without a word Sir Reginald complied, clambering first upon his companion's back and thence noiselessly to the top of the palisading. In another second a faint thud on the outside told that the first adventurer had successfully scaled the barrier. "You go next," whispered Mildmay to the colonel, "and remain on the top of the palisade to give the professor a hand."

Up went the colonel, and up after him went the professor. The latter, with the baronet's assistance from below on the outside, accomplished his descent in safety; and then the colonel, reaching as far down as he could, assisted Mildmay to the top. The rest was easy; and a minute later they were cautiously making their way up the road to the top end of the village, or that which was most thinly inhabited. At this moment down came the rain, a regular tropical deluge, which was undoubtedly a most fortunate circumstance for the fugitives, as they could otherwise have scarcely hoped to escape the vigilance of the numerous prowling curs belonging to the village, who, as it was, were driven by the rain to take refuge in their masters' huts.

Five minutes sufficed the travellers to reach the stout lofty palisade which inclosed the village; and this, the framework all being on the inner side, they were easily enabled to surmount. Once outside this obstacle, Mildmay assumed the leadership, confidently declaring his ability to find the ship, though he had only once before, consciously, passed over the ground between the village and the ruins.

The party made their way in the first place along the outer side of the palisading until they reached the main entrance gate to the village; and from this point Mildmay "took his departure." A well-defined pathway led for some distance down into the plain, and this they traversed until the lieutenant believed he had reached the point at which to turn off. Here he paused for a full minute, looking about him and peering into the darkness. The rain was still pelting down, though not so heavily as at first; and away to the eastward the clouds were already beginning to break, allowing a star to peep through here and there. At length Mildmay thought he had got his bearings right; and, selecting a star to steer by, away he plunged into the long thick wet grass, his companions following closely behind. A few minutes later the rain ceased, the clouds vanished from the sky, and the stars shone calmly out in all their beauty, affording an ample sufficiency of light to distinctly reveal to the wayfarers the nearer clumps of bush, trees, and other large objects. Mildmay now paused again, and, shading his eyes with his hand, once more keenly surveyed the horizon.

"All right," he murmured. "We are going just right, I believe. I can indistinctly make out something away there on the horizon, just ahead, which I feel certain must be the ruins. Come along, my hearties; heave ahead!"

Again they pushed forward, dripping wet, drenched to the skin with the recent shower, and stumbling every now and then as their feet became entangled in the long matted grass; now swerving to the right to avoid a clump of bush, then to the left for the same purpose; but ever keeping one particular star, low down on the horizon, as nearly straight ahead as possible. Though the rest of the party felt themselves utterly lost, without the faintest notion of where they were going, and though neither of them could distinguish anything even remotely resembling the ruins, Mildmay still persisted that he was right; and he continued to press rapidly forward, the rest following him, since they could do no better. At length they struck a narrow path through the grass, and Mildmay at once announced his intention of following it.

"It is a little off our course," he said, "but the walking is so much easier here that we shall gain more than we shall lose by following it; and I should not be surprised to find that it leads to the ruins."

Half an hour later a brilliant star suddenly appeared in the dense darkness ahead. It shone steadily for nearly a minute, disappeared, and almost instantly appeared again.

"Hurrah!" ejaculated the lieutenant joyously, "there is the ship's light. Now we *know* that we are right. Another hour's tramp will, if all be well, take us alongside. How I wish I had a pipe of tobacco!"

"Don't mention it!" fervently ejaculated the professor, who was an ardent lover of the weed. "However, in another hour, as you say—ah!"

The professor's "ah!" was so very expressive of anticipated pleasure that his companions with one accord burst into a hearty laugh, which, however, was abruptly cut short by a low savage growl and a sudden rustling in the grass close by.

"What was that?" was the simultaneous inquiry as the party came abruptly to a dead halt.

"Push on, push on!" urged the professor. "It is some nocturnal animal prowling in search of prey. At this moment he is more frightened than we are; but if we wait here until he has regained his courage he will perhaps spring on one of us."

The march was accordingly resumed, with perhaps some little precipitation; and at length Mildmay's companions began to be conscious of the presence of certain shapeless blotches of blackness rising up against the sky ahead of them and occasionally obscuring for a few seconds the now brilliant light which gleamed from the top of the *Flying Fish's* pilot-house. These shapeless blotches of blackness increased in size with almost startling rapidity; and in a few minutes the travellers, still following the footpath, found themselves in the midst of them, winding in and out between great blocks of masonry which suddenly rose up in front of them in the darkness, and stumbling over loose boulders and fragments of stone. At length they found themselves in the clear open space occupied by the *Flying Fish*; and in another quarter of an hour the party passed into the black tunnel formed by the bilge-keel and the side of the ship, and began to feel with their feet for the open trap-door. This was soon reached; the party entered the opening, closed the flap, and, with a murmured "Thank God, we are safe at last!" began to feel for the button which was to open the door giving access to the interior proper of the ship. Another second and this door swung open, and the party found themselves at the foot of the cylindrical staircase, in the full blaze of the electric lamps.

"Now," said the baronet, "ten minutes in which to strip, rub down, and don dry garments, and then we will be off to the rescue of those poor women, after which I think we must give our friend M'Bongwele a salutary lesson on the evil and impolicy of treachery."

The allotted ten minutes had not quite expired when the professor, the last of the party, made his appearance in the pilot-house, by which time the *Flying Fish* was some five hundred feet in the air, with her nose pointing in the direction of M'Bongwele's village, and her propeller driving her ahead at full speed. The electric lights of the ship were all called into requisition for the illumination of the landscape, producing a weird and ghostlike effect as the trees and clumps of bush first caught the light and then brightened into full radiance as they flashed past, to instantly fade again into obscurity. A startled howl or two smote upon the ears of the travellers, and the forms of hastily retreating animals were momentarily caught sight of; but all eyes were intently directed ahead in anxious expectancy of catching sight of the village, and presently it came into view. The speed was at once reduced and the vessel's flight directed earthward, and in another moment she dashed through the palisade, shivering the principal entrance gate to splinters, and (as was intended) frightening the guard clean out of their senses. With one shrill, piercing scream of terror, as they caught sight of the dazzling bow lights of the ship, the sable warriors took to their heels and vanished in the darkness, whilst the *Flying Fish* was dexterously brought to earth close alongside the hut tenanted by Mrs. Scott and her nieces. That appalling yell effectually awakened the entire occupants of the hut; and whilst they were sitting up on their pallets, rubbing their eyes and wondering what the terrible sound might portend, the portière was pushed aside and the professor, bearing a hand-lamp, unceremoniously made his appearance before them with an earnest request that they would dress with all speed and join him on the outside of the hut, where he would await them, the hour of their deliverance having arrived.

A quarter of an hour later the bewildered ladies were conducted by von Schalckenberg in through the trapdoor in the bottom of the *Flying Fish* and up the cylindrical staircase to the saloon, where they were warmly welcomed by the other three gentlemen, who, after a few congratulatory remarks on their fortunate escape, retired to secure and convey on board the boxes containing the remainder of their guests' wardrobes. This done, Mrs. Scott and her nieces were conducted to the cabins assigned for their use, and the gentlemen then retreated to the pilot-house, where, over a keenly enjoyed pipe, a hasty council was held as to what should be done with M'Bongwele.

This question was settled just as the first faint streaks of approaching dawn began to brighten the eastern horizon, when the ship was moved up into the great square before the king's house, where the whole of the king's body-guard were drawn up under arms, and, beyond them, the remaining inhabitants of the village, a dense, surging, excited, squabbling crowd.

On the approach of the *Flying Fish* the latter flung themselves face downwards, in abject terror, to the ground, and the armed and mounted warriors betrayed a disposition to stampede which was only with the utmost difficulty checked and restrained by Seketulo. Even this chief found himself unable to wholly conceal the feeling of nervousness which agitated him; but he in this trying moment enjoyed a consciousness, unshared by any other man there present, of having done his best to make the erstwhile prisoners comfortable.

As the huge ship settled quietly down in the centre of the great square a profound and deathlike silence suddenly succeeded the confused babbling sound which had hitherto prevailed, and when the four travellers stepped out from the pilot-house to the deck and appeared at the gangway a visible shudder ran through the entire concourse of people there assembled. They dreaded they knew not what, and their fears were only in a very trifling degree allayed by the promise of intercession on their behalf which Seketulo had made to them.

The professor was of course to be spokesman for the occasion; it was he, therefore, who broke the terrible silence by exclaiming, in a loud, commanding tone of voice:

"Seketulo, we are your friends. Advance, therefore, and listen to the commands which we are about to lay upon you!"

The reassured and now happy chief struck with his spurred heels the sides of his charger, and the animal, bounding and caracoling, advanced to within a few yards of the ship's side, where his rider dismounted and, with bowed head and bended knee, waited for such communication as might be vouchsafed him.

"Listen, O Seketulo!" continued the professor. "We entered this country animated by feelings of the most amicable nature to its king and to every one of its inhabitants. We showed this by distributing presents of beads, cloth, and other matters when Lualamba and his warriors first visited us. And we asked for nothing in return save permission to examine and explore the ruins on yonder plain; offering to pay promptly and liberally for whatever assistance we might need. Is not this the truth?"

"It is, O most mighty wizard," answered Seketulo humbly; some of the braver warriors also venturing to murmur:

"It is! It is!"

"And how have we been treated?" asked the professor. "Your king, not satisfied with our friendship and the presents we gave him, wickedly and treacherously devised a scheme to get us into his power—a scheme which, in order to try him, we permitted to succeed. And, having done that, he further attempted to gain possession of this ship,"—this fact having leaked out in Seketulo's previous conversations—"profanely and audaciously thinking he could subdue her to his will and control her as we do. Now, therefore, be it understood by all present that, for his base treachery, *M'Bongwele is dethroned*, and Seketulo will, from this moment, reign in his stead. Let a detachment of the guard enter the palace and bring M'Bongwele forth to hear his sentence!"

In an instant Lualamba—anxious above all things to please the powers that be, and having, moreover, in revengeful remembrance many little gratuitous slights and insults which he had suffered at the king's hands—dismounted a squadron of the guard, and, surrounding the palace, himself entered the building at the head of half a dozen men. Two or three minutes later the party reappeared with the dethroned monarch in their midst. They advanced until almost level with the spot occupied by Seketulo, when, at a sign from the professor, they halted; the guards disposing themselves round M'Bongwele in such a manner that, whilst to escape was an utter impossibility, he could still see and hear the individual who, perched far aloft in the gangway of the ship, was about to address him.

M'Bongwele never, perhaps, looked more kingly than whilst he thus stood to receive his sentence of dethronement. He was fully conscious of his treacherous behaviour to his guests, but he felt no shame threat, for he had been schooled in the belief that treachery, falsehood, ay, even deliberate, cold-blooded murder, was perfectly justifiable in the pursuit of power. His only feeling was that he had played a bold game for a high stake and had lost it. The moment of reckoning had now arrived, the penalty of failure had to be paid, and though he knew not what that penalty might be—though his brain was teeming with all sorts of possible and impossible horrors—he never for a moment forgot that he was a monarch, that the eyes of his people were on him, noting his every look and gesture, and he summoned all his fortitude to his aid, in order that, since fall he must, he should fall as becomes a king.

So there he stood in the bright sunlight of the early morning—an unarmed man, surrounded by those who, whilst they would yesterday have poured out their heart's blood at his command, were now prepared to hew him in pieces at the bidding of a white-skinned stranger—with arms folded across the muscular naked chest which throbbed visibly with the intensity of his hardly repressed emotions, his head thrown back, his brows knitted, his lips firmly closed over his rigidly set teeth, and his eyes unquailingly fixed upon the group of white men whom he recognised and tacitly acknowledged as his conquerors and judges. And when the sentence of dethronement, separation from his family, and instant banishment for life from his country, was pronounced upon him, he offered no plea for pardon or mitigation of his punishment; he urged nothing in extenuation or justification of his conduct, but simply bowed his head in token of his submission to the inevitable, and begged a respite of a few minutes in which to bid farewell to his family before setting out upon his journey to the frontier, whither he was to be escorted by a small well-armed party, in whom Seketulo knew he could place implicit trust.

This somewhat painful scene over, the troops and people there present were required to swear allegiance and fidelity to their new king, which they readily did with all the formalities customary among them on such occasions; after which the crown of gold and feathers worn by M'Bongwele was brought forward and placed upon Seketulo's head; and the new king was then invited on board the ship to confer with—and in reality to receive instructions respecting his future policy and conduct from—the men who had raised him to the supreme dignity. The advice—given with sufficient firmness and emphasis to constitute a command—comprised many valuable hints for the wise and humane government of the nation, and was concluded with a powerful exhortation to treat with fairness, justice, humanity, and hospitality all strangers who might be brought by accident or otherwise into the country; to succour, nourish, and carefully protect them from molestation or spoliation of any and every kind whilst within its borders; and to afford them every help and facility to leave whensoever they might desire. And, finally, a satisfactory arrangement was made whereby the baronet and his companions were enabled to continue and complete their exploration and examination of the ruins.

The *Flying Fish* and her inmates remained in the country for rather more than three months from that date; quite long enough to satisfy the party that they had really acted wisely, and for the benefit of the nation, in deposing M'Bongwele;

and long enough to enable them to make several most surprising and interesting discoveries among the ruins—discoveries which it is not necessary to describe or particularise here, since the professor has prepared, and is now revising for the press, an elaborate and exhaustive treatise upon the subject.

CHAPTER TWENTY TWO
AN ADVENTURE ON THE TOP OF MOUNT EVEREST

Leaving the country at last—to the very great regret of the inhabitants, who found that every little service rendered to the white strangers was munificently rewarded by a present of beads, buttons, party-coloured cloth, or perhaps a small hand mirror—the travellers made the best of their way to Bombay, at which place Mrs. Scott and her nieces were anxious to be landed, and there they bade their fair guests a reluctant adieu. Thence, starting under cover of night and rising to a height of about ten thousand feet above the ground surface, the travellers made their way across the Indian peninsula in a north-easterly direction, travelling at a speed of about one hundred miles per hour, and arriving about eight o'clock the next morning at the foot of Mount Everest, the summit of which—towering into the sky to the enormous altitude of twenty-nine thousand feet above the sea-level, and believed to be the most lofty spot of earth on the surface of our globe—they intended attempting to reach.

Here, on a magnificent grassy plateau surrounded by trees, and with not a single sign of human life at hand, the *Flying Fish* was brought to earth and temporarily secured whilst the party took breakfast.

"Now," said the professor as they rose from the breakfast-table, "in seeking to plant our feet upon the topmost peak of Mount Everest we are about to enter upon a task of no ordinary difficulty and danger, and it is desirable that no avoidable risks should be run. The danger arises from two causes—the excessive cold, and the highly rarefied state of the atmosphere at so enormous an elevation. The first can be guarded against by suitable clothing; the second can only be overcome by the assumption of our diving dresses. The latter, no doubt, seems to you a strange precaution; but it is a fact, that on the top of Mount Everest the air is too thin to support life, at all events in comfort, and for any but the briefest possible time; so we must take up our air with us. Let us therefore go and make these necessary changes of costume before we attempt moving the ship from her present position."

Half an hour later, the party, accoutred in their diving armour—between which and their ordinary clothing they had interposed stout warm flannel overalls—and armed with small ice-hatchets, mustered in the pilot-house; the ship was released from the ground, a vacuum created in her air-chambers, and upward she at once shot into the clear blue cloudless sky. A few minutes only sufficed her to soar to the height of ten thousand feet, after which her progress upward, as indicated by the steadily falling column of mercury in the tube of the barometer, gradually decreased in velocity. At the height of twenty-nine thousand feet the mercury ceased to fall, or the ship ceased to rise, which amounted to the same thing, and Mount Everest lay before them, its snowy peak glistening in the sun ten miles away, and its topmost pinnacle still towering somewhere about five hundred feet above the line of their horizon.

"Well," said the professor, remarking upon their failure to attain a greater altitude, "I anticipated this; I was quite prepared to find that here, where the sun is so much more nearly vertical than it is with us in England, we should meet with a more rarefied atmosphere. However, we cannot help it. We must do what we can; and if we fail to reach the summit we shall simply be obliged to descend again, rid ourselves temporarily of a few of our more weighty matters, and then renew the attempt. Perhaps we may be enabled to *force* her up that remaining five hundred feet by the power of her engines. Let us try."

The engines were sent ahead at full speed, and the *Flying Fish* rushed toward the glittering peak, the professor so adjusting the helm as to give the ship's bows a slight upward inclination. The experiment resulted in partial success, an additional elevation of some two hundred feet being attained, but beyond that it was found impossible to go; even then it was necessary to keep the ship moving at full speed, and to maintain the upward inclination of her bows, in order to preserve the slight additional height gained, her tendency being to sink immediately upon any relaxation of speed. It was resolved to be satisfied with this, to effect a landing somewhere, and to attempt surmounting the remaining three hundred feet by climbing. A landing-place was next sought for, and this was at length found on the northern side of the mountain, on a sidelong slanting snow-bank, which seemed to have accumulated between two projecting crags. It was by no means a desirable spot on which to effect a landing, the area of the bank being very small, and the surface sloping most awkwardly; however, it was the best place the travellers could find, and they were therefore obliged to rest content with it; so the ship was headed toward it, and in another second or two a harsh grating sound, accompanied by an upward surge, showed that she had taken the ground, or rather the snow-bank. The engines were then stopped, and the grip-anchors brought into requisition to secure her in her somewhat precarious berth.

"Well, here we are," exclaimed the baronet; "and the next thing, I suppose, is to land and commence our climb without loss of time. What a wild-looking spot it is, to be sure; if I were to stand looking at it long I believe I should lose my nerve and shirk the task."

"Better not look at it any longer, then, until we can contemplate the prospect from the peak away up aloft there," remarked the practical Mildmay. "But," he continued, "I don't half like the idea of going out upon that sloping slippery surface of frozen snow that the ship has grounded upon; a single slip or false step and away one would go over the edge, to bring up, perhaps, on a rock a thousand feet below. I shall hook on the rope-ladder, and endeavour to make a start from yonder naked spur of rock."

The others also seemed to think this the wisest plan, and in a few minutes they were making their way cautiously down the rope-ladder one after the other, the baronet, an experienced mountaineer, leading, and Mildmay bringing up the rear.

The adventurers soon found that their task was likely to be a great deal more difficult and hazardous than they had at all contemplated. The snow-bank upon which the *Flying Fish* rested proved to be the only even approximately level spot at that elevation; the rocks rising almost sheer above them everywhere, with only an occasional crevice here and there by way of foothold, and in many places the precipice was coated with treacherous frozen snow, sometimes tenacious enough to afford a momentary support, but more often crumbling away beneath the weight of the body. Slowly and steadily, however, they worked their way upward—now occupying perhaps five minutes to advance as many feet, and anon hitting upon a favourable spot where twenty or thirty feet might be gained in a single minute. At length, after a toilsome and hazardous climb of more than an hour's duration, the baronet found himself clinging to a slender pinnacle of rock about seven feet high and four feet in diameter, upon the top of which he next moment triumphantly seated himself. The colonel, the professor, and Mildmay speedily followed, and there they sat, undoubtedly the first human beings who had ever reached the topmost pinnacle of Mount Everest.

Having accomplished the ascent, they now settled themselves down as comfortably as they could upon their narrow perch to enjoy at leisure the magnificent view spread out around them, a view such as no human eye had ever before looked upon, and which even *they* would probably never have another opportunity of beholding. The atmosphere, most fortunately, was exceptionally clear and transparent, not a vestige of cloud or vapour being anywhere visible; the view was therefore unobstructed to the very verge of the horizon, which extended round them in a gigantic circle measuring *four hundred and eighteen miles in diameter.*

Northward of them stretched the vast plains of Thibet, the only object worthy of notice being the river Sampoo, which, although sixty miles distant, was distinctly seen as it issued from the purplish-grey haze of the extreme distance on their left, meandering along the plain beneath for a visible distance of nearly two hundred miles before its course became again lost in the haze on their right hand. Eight and left of them stretched the vast mountain chain of the Himalayas, their wooded slopes and countless peaks and cones presenting a bewildering yet charming picture of variegated colour, sunlight and shadow, as they dwindled away on either hand until all suggestion of local colouring was swallowed up and lost in an enchanting succession of increasingly pure and delicate soft pearly greys, which merged and melted at last into the vague shapeless all-pervading purple-grey of the horizon. Glancing immediately around and beneath them their blood curdled and their brains whirled with the vertigo which seized them as they peered appalled and shrinkingly down upon the sharp crags, the sheer precipices, the steeply-sloping snow-fields with their lower edges generally overhanging some fathomless abyss, the great glaciers, the awful crevasses spanned here and there by crumbling snow bridges—the effect of the scene being heightened and intensified in its impressive grandeur by the deathlike silence which prevailed, broken only by the occasional thunderous roar of an avalanche far below. The scene was absolutely fascinating in its appalling sublimity; but it was a relief to turn the eye further afield until it rested to the eastward upon the grandly towering mass of Everest's rival, snow-capped Kunchinjinga, which reared its giant crest aloft to a height of twenty-eight thousand five hundred feet above the sea-level, and which, though it was eighty-five miles away, appeared to be almost within rifle-shot. And still more was it a relief to turn the eye in an opposite direction, and to allow it to rest upon the glittering summit of Dhawalagiri, which, at a distance of no less than *two hundred and forty miles*, gleamed faint and softly opalescent out of the western haze. And, lastly, to the southward of them they beheld the fertile province of Nepaul, watered by countless tributaries to the mighty Ganges; and, beyond it again, the still more fertile province of Oudh. The professor, totally forgetful of his exceedingly perilous position, was enthusiastically expatiating, after his usual manner, upon the marvellous extent and beauty of the prospect, and interrupting the flow of his eloquence at short intervals to assure his companions that a—to them—invisible object on the far horizon *must* be the town of Patna, when a terrific crackling crash just below them drew the eyes of the party in that direction, just in time for them to see the supposed projecting crag—in reality an enormous mass of ice—which supported the snow-bank on which the *Flying Fish* rested, break off and go thundering down into the unfathomable depths below. The spectators clung to each other in helpless nerveless terror at so appalling a spectacle as the falling of this mass, weighing probably millions of tons; but the full significance and import of the catastrophe did not present itself to their dazed and bewildered senses until they beheld the *Flying Fish*, after following the falling mass for a couple of hundred feet, recover herself and float jauntily in the air, *adrift*, at a distance of fully two thousand feet from the mountain side. Then, indeed, the full horror of their position began to slowly dawn upon them, and they looked at each other with eyes in which could be read a despair too deep and too complete to need or find expression in words. Their long search for a landing-place that morning had unconsciously impressed upon them a fact which now—and not till now—took intelligible shape within their brains, and it was this: they could descend the mountain as far as the spot at which they had left the *Flying Fish, but no further*; beyond that point further descent, with the means at their disposal, was impossible. Which meant, in plain language and few words, that, sooner or later, they would try to get down, and either be dashed to pieces in the attempt or perish miserably of starvation upon the edge of some ghastly impassable precipice.

It took but a moment for these ideas to shape themselves intelligibly, and then a general movement was made to commence the descent and thus cut short a state of suspense which would soon become unbearable.

But at this moment the colonel interposed with a word of caution.

"One moment," said he. "Before we start let each one of us clearly understand that perfect coolness and presence of mind is imperatively necessary if we would emerge from this strait alive. We *may* perhaps find a way down after all, but in order to do so we must have our wits completely about us; let no man move, therefore, until he has fully recovered the control of his nerves; when all have done so we will make a start, and I will go last."

"And I first," exclaimed the baronet, "because, next to you, I believe I am the most experienced mountaineer of the party."

The colonel's little speech produced a most beneficial effect upon the nerves of the whole party, his own included; and now, without further ado, a general start was made, the baronet going first and directing and helping the professor, who followed him; Mildmay going third, also helping von Schalckenberg, and being helped in his turn by Lethbridge, and the latter bringing up the rear.

The descent, owing to the perpendicular precipices over which they had to pass, and the extremely dangerous character, generally, of the road, proved to be even more tedious and difficult than the ascent; and within the first quarter of an hour (during which they had accomplished only about one hundred feet of perpendicular descent) every one of the party had experienced at least one narrow escape from certain death.

Steadily, however, they toiled on; foot by foot they crept down the face of the icy precipice, and at length they reached a ledge nearly a foot in width, upon which the entire party were enabled to pause for a minute or two to rest and relieve their tired and quivering muscles.

When their feet were safely planted upon this ledge Mildmay spoke.

"I may now venture," he said, "to call your attention to a fact which I feared to mention before, lest it should upset the balance of your nerves and produce a catastrophe. It is this. The *Flying Fish*, floating undisturbed in this motionless air, is, in obedience to the law of gravitation, slowly but steadily being drawn in toward the side of the mountain; and if—which God grant—it remains perfectly calm up here for another quarter of an hour, she will be once more alongside, and we may yet regain access to her. To do this, however, we must edge away more toward the eastern side of the mountain, where I fear we shall encounter even greater difficulties than we have yet met with. We can but try, however, and I think the sooner we push on the better."

"Forward, then, at once," cried the baronet; "and take heed to your steps, my friends, for this ice is terribly smooth and slippery."

Once more was the journey resumed, the baronet availing himself of the ledge, as far as it extended, to work his way round the shoulder of the hill in the required direction; and by the time they reached a point where actual descent had again become necessary, they had once more come within sight of the ship, and had the satisfaction of seeing that she had drawn sensibly nearer to the cliff.

"All right," exclaimed Sir Reginald cheerfully, "I see the spot we must aim for—that pinnacle of bare rock yonder, and there is a tolerably easy road down to it, moreover."

Away they now went, their spirits at the very highest pitch of exhilaration, and their nerves by so much the steadier, and such rapid progress did they make that ten minutes later saw them clustered together clinging to the rocky pinnacle before mentioned. And a gruesome-enough looking spot it was—a sharp projecting point of rock overhanging a sheer precipice some two hundred feet deep, with a narrow snow-bank immediately beneath, and then another frightful abyss of unknown depth beyond. And, to the right and left of it, an almost vertical face of bare rock coated with smooth, slippery, transparent ice, any attempt to traverse which would be courting death in its most horrible form.

The *Flying Fish* seemed to be drifting steadily in toward this pinnacle of rock, though at a depth of some twenty feet below it, and it was resolved to pause there and allow events to develop somewhat before exerting themselves further.

Slowly, very slowly, the *Flying Fish* drifted nearer and nearer in; the little party clustered upon the rock watching her with bated breath, and every moment dreading that a faint air of wind might after all waft her beyond their reach. But nothing of the sort occurred; in she steadily came, until at last her starboard gangway was immediately underneath the party.

"Now or never!" exclaimed Sir Reginald. "I am going to make a jump for her. We shall scarcely have a better chance; and breeze may at any moment sweep round the face of the rock and carry her away from us. Lethbridge and Mildmay, let me steady myself by your shoulders whilst I stand on the extreme point of the rock. Stand firm, now; I am about to jump. Are you ready? Then—one—*two*—*three*!"

The body of the baronet darted outward from the face of the rock, Mildmay and the colonel retaining their footing with the utmost difficulty under the recoil from the outward impulse; and then the three men left behind on the rock craned their necks over the precipice to watch the result.

The sight which met their eyes caused their hair to bristle and their blood to curdle with horror. Sir Reginald had either miscalculated his distance, or his foot had slipped in the act of springing, for instead of alighting upon the ship's deck, as he had intended, he had fallen on the circular bilge of the vessel, from whence, after an unavailing struggle to secure a footing, he slid off, and, with a piercing scream, went whirling downward until he alighted on the narrow snow-bank some two hundred feet below. His horror-stricken companions fully expected to see him rebound and go plunging over the edge of the next precipice, but luckily the snow upon which he had fallen was so deep that his body sank into it, and there he lay, motionless.

"Merciful Heaven, he is killed!" ejaculated the colonel with stammering lips.

"Perhaps not," returned Mildmay; "at all events we will hope for the best. Let me see if I can do better. *Quick*—out of the way—ah! The wind after all! We are too late!"

And even as he spoke the bows of the *Flying Fish* swung slowly round, and her hull was swept gently away from the face of the cliff by a capricious zephyr which just then came creeping along the mountain side.

CHAPTER TWENTY THREE
HOW THE ADVENTURE TERMINATED

The silence of despair again settled upon the three remaining travellers; they had lost one of their party, and were a second time left stranded upon that terrible mountain top, from which it now began to appear that there was no possibility of escape. One thing at least was certain, which was, that on their side of the mountain there was no means of further descent; the pinnacle of rock upon which they then stood was the lowest accessible point; there was no possible way even of reaching poor Sir Reginald's body, and the way downward, if indeed such existed, must be sought elsewhere.

They crouched where they were, in helpless bewilderment, watching the ship until she slowly drifted out of sight round a projecting bluff; and then, in a dazed, halfhearted way, and with nerves all unstrung by disappointment and the dreadful accident which had befallen the baronet, they began to slowly retrace their steps, in the faint hope of stumbling upon some means of escape.

Led this time by the colonel, Mildmay bringing up the rear, the little party at last made their way back to the narrow ledge where they had previously paused to rest, and here they again made a momentary halt, afterwards following the ledge in the other direction until it terminated abruptly in an almost perpendicular wall of smooth rock. Another ledge was here discovered, about eighteen feet further down, but it was certainly not more than a foot wide, with apparently a vertical fall of several hundred feet beyond. This ledge extended right and left beyond their range of vision, and had evidently been traversed by them in their original ascent, for their footprints were plainly visible in the snow with which it was covered; if, therefore, they could reach it, it would at least be possible to return to their original starting-point, which would certainly be something gained. But how to get down to it was the question. They had grown bewildered in their gropings round about the summit, and knew not in which direction to go to regain the lost path. They might, of course, go on climbing until they were once more at the very top of the mountain, and commence their descent afresh, but this was a task so full of difficulty and peril as not to be thought of, save as a last resort. Besides, the day was already on the wane, and it was of the utmost importance that they should reach some place of comparative safety before nightfall. At length Mildmay hit upon a bold though terribly dangerous mode of mastering the difficulty.

"Look here," he said, "it is no use hesitating here; we shall never do any good at this rate. Let me offer a suggestion. I will lower myself down over the ledge until I hang from it by my hands alone; then you, Lethbridge, must climb down over me, using my body as a ladder (or a rope, rather), and when you are hanging at arm's-length from my feet there will only remain a very trifling drop to the lower ledge, which you can surely accomplish in safety. That done you must stand by to steady me and prevent me, if possible, from going backward over the precipice; and, with us two safely on the ledge, we are surely men enough to catch the professor when he makes the drop. What say you to the plan?"

"It is frightfully dangerous, but it is perhaps worth trying—if you think you have the strength for it. What say you, professor? Have you nerve enough to make the drop, trusting to us to catch you?"

"Anything is better than this," answered the professor. "Your own and Mildmay's are the most difficult portions of the task. If you are equal to your parts I will perform mine; but my strength is not sufficient to justify my offering to change places with either of you."

"Then let us try it," exclaimed the colonel decisively. "Will you go first, Mildmay, or shall I?"

"You go first," answered Mildmay. "I am pretty strong in the arms, and think the method I have proposed the safest, on the whole."

"All right, then. I am ready whenever you are."

"Stand firm, then, and let me steady myself down over the ledge by your leg—we shall be down, one way or another, all the sooner. Now, look out, I am going!"

The colonel braced himself as firmly as possible against the strain, and Mildmay lowered himself cautiously down until he hung from the ledge by both hands. Then, without wasting a moment, Lethbridge carefully placed himself in position, got down on his knees, lowered one foot until it rested on Mildmay's shoulder, then the other; firmly grasped the ledge with both hands, outside Mildmay's; got his knees down on Mildmay's shoulders, and then, warning the lieutenant to hold firm, grasped him by both wrists and proceeded as rapidly and carefully as possible to slide down his body until he hung to him by a firm handgrasp round the ankles. The muscles of poor Mildmay's hands and arms quivered and fairly cracked with the terrible strain thrown upon them during the latter part of this manoeuvre; but he set his teeth hard, remembering that the lives of the whole party depended upon him just then, and hung on. It was not for long. The colonel paused only for a moment to give one downward glance at the spot upon which he was about to drop, and then let go. He pitched fairly on the ledge, slipped, staggered for a moment, *almost* went over, but recovered himself and stood firm. Then moving a little to one side he prepared to receive Mildmay, and gave him the word to drop. It came none too soon, for the lieutenant's quivering muscles were already failing him, his nerveless fingers were already relaxing their grasp, and he felt that he must let go, whether or not, in another moment. At the cry from Lethbridge he released his hold, and next moment, with the colonel's arm thrown firmly round his waist, stood safely on the ledge.

It was next the professor's turn; but now that the critical moment had arrived for him too to drop from one ledge to another, the unwelcome discovery was made that his nerves were unequal to the task, and for some time persuasion, cajolery, entreaties, and threats proved equally unavailing to tempt him to the enterprise. At length, however, in a fit of desperation he essayed the task, hurried over it, missed his hold, and went whirling outward from the face of the cliff. In another instant he would have been over the precipice, and plunging headlong downward to the death which awaited him thousands of feet below, but most fortunately both Mildmay and the colonel saw the mishap, and made a simultaneous snatch at him; the former succeeded in grasping him by the arm, and, before either of the trio had time to fully realise what had actually happened, poor von Schalckenberg was dragged—pale, breathless, and completely unnerved—in upon the ledge.

A few minutes were allowed the unhappy professor in which to recover his presence of mind, and then the little party cautiously worked their way downward along the ledge, finally arriving half an hour later on the narrow platform of ice which was now all that remained of the plateau whereon the *Flying Fish* had been grounded.

It had been the intention of the unfortunate adventurers to make a temporary halt here, for the purpose of recruiting their exhausted energies so far as it might be done by taking a few minutes' rest, but the ice was so shivered by the shock of its recent rupture as to present a very insecure appearance, and they were therefore constrained to keep moving notwithstanding their fatigue. Very fortunately the breaking away of the snow-bank had, in one place, laid bare the surface of the rock, which here was very jagged and uneven (which would probably account for the original accumulation of the snow in that spot), and these irregularities were promptly utilised as a means of further descent. By their aid an additional two hundred feet of downward movement was slowly and painfully accomplished, and then Mildmay (who was now leading the way) found himself within a foot or two of the lower edge of an almost perpendicular slope overhanging an awful abyss of unfathomable depth, his further progress downward being barred by the fact that beneath him the rock sloped *inwards*! A single downward glance sufficed not only to reveal to him his appalling situation, but also to wring from his lips such a piercing cry of horror as effectually warned his friends from following him any further. Then he pressed his body close to the face of the rock, and clung there convulsively with feet and hands to the trifling irregularities of surface which alone afforded him a hold, his blood curdling and his brain reeling at the thought of the horrible deadly danger which menaced him. A single slip of hand or foot, a momentary failure of a muscle, the slightest seizure of cramp or vertigo, and he would go whirling headlong downward at least five hundred feet sheer through the air before reaching the ground below. He was so unnerved that he was actually incapable of replying to the colonel's anxious hail as to what was the matter.

It was whilst he stood thus vainly striving to recover his self-control—a growing conviction of the impossibility of escape meanwhile forcing itself with momentarily increasing intensity upon him—that a huge moving mass suddenly swung into view round a projection on his left, and a simultaneous cry of surprise from his two waiting and wondering companions told that they too had caught sight of it. It was the *Flying Fish* slowly drifting round the mountain, stern on, and that too so closely that her propeller actually touched the rocky projection, some thirty feet off, as she passed it. The force of the contact, though very gentle, was sufficient to give her a slight outward impulse; and though she continued to drift round toward the rock to which the adventurers were clinging, it appeared as though she would pass it at such a distance as would *just* preclude the possibility of their reaching her.

"We must shout," exclaimed Mildmay, finding his voice all at once; "we must shout to George. Perhaps our cries may reach him and bring him on deck, in which event we shall be able to tell him what to do."

And shout they did, simultaneously, and at the full power of their lungs; but it was of no avail—George and the cook were both at that moment in the innermost recesses of the ship busily engaged on their respective avocations, and in all likelihood profoundly ignorant of the state of affairs. At all events there was no response, and the ship went drifting slowly past. She was floating almost level with the little party clinging there desperately to the face of the naked rock, the boss of her propeller being at just about the same height as the colonel's head. As she drove almost imperceptibly along it seemed to Mildmay that she was also being drawn inward toward the face of the rock; and he began to ask himself whether an active man might not, after all, be able to overleap the intervening space and grasp one of the propeller-blades. The craft was so tantalisingly close that it seemed to him almost a cowardly thing to let this chance pass; yet, when he glanced downward at the darkening abyss over which he hung, he shudderingly confessed to himself that the leap was an impossibility, and that they must retreat upward with all speed to gain some comparatively secure spot upon which to pass the night now gathering about them. He was about to put this thought into words, and to propose an immediate upward movement, when he turned to take (as he believed) a last parting glance at the *Flying Fish*, now immediately behind him. In doing so his fingers slipped and lost their grip upon the rock, and before he could recover his hold he found himself going over backwards. He felt that he was lost; but, with the instinct of self-preservation, turned quickly on his feet, and as they too were slipping off the minute projections on which he had been supporting himself, he made a vigorous desperate spring outward from the face of the rock, reaching forward into space toward the curved end of the propeller-blade which he saw in front of him. Despair must have leant him extra strength when making that last awful leap, for, though the distance was fully twenty feet, he actually reached and succeeded in grasping the end of the blade. To swing himself up astride upon it was the work of a moment; and then he paused to rest and recover from this last shock to his nervous system. Not for long, however; he knew that his companions must be nearly exhausted, and that their lives now probably depended solely on his activity and the celerity with which he might be able to go to their rescue; so he pulled himself together, shouted to them the encouraging news of his success, and then devoted himself in earnest to the difficult and perilous task of reaching the deck of the ship. He had hardly begun this task before he realised that it was one which would tax his strength, energy, and ingenuity to their utmost extent. The propeller-blade upon which he was perched happened to be at the very lowest point of its revolution; and his first task must be to reach the boss, which was about seventeen feet above his head. The peculiar shape of the blades rendered it impossible for him to achieve this by climbing up the edge of any one of them; his only chance consisted in working his way from one to the other. The blade to his right seemed to him the most easily accessible, and he forthwith set about the work of reaching it. To do this he had to climb about ten feet up the fore *edge* of the blade upon which he was perched, and to anyone but a sailor this would have been an impossibility. Even to Mildmay it proved a most difficult as well as hazardous feat; but after a couple of failures success crowned his efforts, and he found himself high enough to reach the point of the next blade. This was so far away, however, that he could only touch it with his finger-tips, and in order to grasp it—even with *one* hand—he found that he would be obliged to overbalance himself so much that, if he missed, a fall must inevitably result. The risk had to be taken, however; and he took it, fortunately with success. This left him swinging by *one* hand from the point of the propeller-blade; but in another second he had grasped it with his other hand, and, after a struggle or two, managed to get fairly astride the edge. His next task was to work himself in along the edge until he was abreast the after edge of the blade he had just left, when he had to reach over to the utmost stretch of his arms, grasp the blade, and in that awkward position scramble to his feet. This he also managed, when a further comparatively easy climb enabled him to reach the boss. He now found himself standing on the boss and leaning against the smooth elliptical stern of the vessel. His next task was to climb up over this smooth rounded surface and so make his way along the upper surface of the hull to the superstructure, when he would soon find means to reach the deck. This also, though a task of immense difficulty, he actually accomplished; finally reaching the deck in so prostrate a condition that he fell insensible before he could gain the pilot-house.

His fit of insensibility, however, did not last long—the latent consciousness of responsibility effectually prevented that; and he was soon able to rise and stagger to the pilot-house. Once there, he forthwith made his way below and availed himself of the stimulus afforded by a glass of neat brandy, after which he felt equal to the task which yet lay before him. Having swallowed the brandy, he at once returned to the deck and shifted the rope-ladder over to the larboard gangway. He then looked about him to ascertain the whereabouts of the ship, which he found to be about half a mile distant from the spot where he had left his friends, and gradually drifting further away under the influence of a gentle night-breeze which had just sprung up—thus proving indubitably that, had he not reached the craft when he did, she would probably have been lost to them all for ever. Having attached the ladder securely, Mildmay next entered the pilot-house, and—night having by this time completely fallen—turned on the electric lights; after which he set the engines in motion and returned to the side of the mountain in search of the two companions he had left clinging in so dangerous a situation. These were found just as he had left them, and were speedily taken on board—they too being completely overcome by the revulsion of feeling following upon their rescue.

A glass of brandy each quickly revived them, however, and then they devoted their united energies to a search for the baronet. With some little difficulty the scene of the accident was discovered; and a minute or two later Sir Reginald was observed, not dead, as they had feared to find him, but sitting up on the snow-bank upon which he had fallen, a prisoner to the spot, from the fact that there was no possible way of retreat from it either upward or downward; but in other respects very little the worse for his terrible fall, the snow, happily, proving so deep that it served as a cushion or buffer, allowing the baronet to escape with only a few somewhat severe bruises. The adventure being thus happily terminated, the ship was quickly navigated to the berth she had occupied on the preceding night; and the party then sat down to dinner, over which meal they came to the conclusion that they had had enough mountain-climbing that day to suffice them for the remainder of their lives.

CHAPTER TWENTY FOUR
THE FOUNDERING OF THE "MERCURY"

The nerves of the adventurers were so shaken by the vicissitudes of their day's adventure that they found it impossible to obtain sound and refreshing sleep that night, notwithstanding their terrible fatigue; their slumbers were broken by horrible dreams, and further disturbed by the cries of wild beasts of various descriptions which kept the forest in a perfect uproar the whole night long. So great, indeed, was the disturbance from the latter cause, that, on comparing notes over the breakfast table next morning, the party came to the conclusion that they must be in a district literally swarming with big game, and that it might be worth their while to spend a few days there hunting. This they did; with such success that their stay was prolonged for nearly a month, by which time they had collected such a quantity of skins, horns, tusks, skulls, and other trophies of the chase that even they, inveterate sportsmen as they were, acknowledged themselves satisfied. The professor, meanwhile, had devoted himself enthusiastically to the forming of a collection of rare birds, beetles, and butterflies, in which pursuit he had been fully as successful as his companions in theirs; so that when the time came for them to leave this delightful spot they did so in the highest possible state of health and spirits; the remembrance of their ugly adventure on Everest disturbing them no more than would the memory of a troublesome dream.

Their next destination was the island of Borneo; and they arranged their departure so as to pass over Calcutta and enter the Bay of Bengal during the hours of darkness, their intention being to make the latter part of the trip by water rather than by air.

They descended to the surface of the sea at daylight, the land being at that time invisible from the elevation of ten thousand feet at which they had been travelling during the night. Not a sail of any description was in sight; the sparkling sea was only moderately ruffled by the north-east monsoon; and appearances seemed to warrant a belief that the passage would be a thoroughly pleasant one. The travellers were in no hurry whatever, and they were, moreover, longing for a sniff of the good wholesome sea-breeze; the *Flying Fish* therefore proceeded very leisurely on her course, her engines revolving dead slow, which gave her a speed of about sixteen knots through the water.

They proceeded thus during the whole of that day and the succeeding night, finding themselves at daybreak next morning within sight of one of the lesser islands of the Andaman group. And at this point of their journey a gradual fall of the mercury in their barometers warned them that they were about to experience a change of weather. The atmospheric indications remained unchanged, however, until about two o'clock in the afternoon, when the wind lulled, the mercury experienced a sudden further fall, and a great mass of murky cloud began to bank up in the south-western quarter. This rapidly overspread the sky, until the whole of the visible heavens became obscured by a thick curtain of flying scud. The sea, inky black, suddenly became agitated, and formed itself into a confusion of irregular waves without any "run," but which reared themselves tremblingly aloft, and then subsided again, only to be instantly succeeded by others. The wind fell away to a dead calm, which continued for about a quarter of an hour, during which an alarmingly rapid fall of the mercury, combined with a low weird moaning in the atmosphere, seemed to forebode the approach of some dire disaster. This was followed by a sudden blast of wind from the eastward—which came and was gone again in an instant—and which preceded a brief but terrific downpour of rain. This lasted for perhaps three minutes, when it ceased as suddenly as it had commenced.

"Now, look out for the wind," exclaimed Mildmay. "Ah! here it comes—a regular hurricane! Thank Heaven, there is no sail to shorten on board the *Flying Fish*!"

He might well say so; for sore indeed would be the plight of the unwary seaman who should find himself under similar circumstances, unprepared. A long line of white foam suddenly appeared on their starboard bow, racing down toward them and spreading out right and left with frightful rapidity, until the whole horizon, from some four points on the larboard bow right round to broad on their starboard beam, was marked by a continuous line of flying foam and spindrift. They watched with eager curiosity this remarkable phenomenon, noticed the astounding rapidity with which it travelled, and saw that the sea on their starboard hand, ay, and even well on their starboard quarter, was lashed into a perfect frenzy by the hurricane before it reached the ship. Then, with a wild rush and a deafening roar, the gale struck them, and the *Flying Fish*—stout ship as she was—fairly shuddered under the force of the blow. In an instant the air became so thick with the driving scud-water that every window in the pilot-house had to be closed to prevent the inmates being drenched to the skin. In less than five minutes the deck was wet fore and aft with the flying spray; and before a quarter of an hour had elapsed the *Flying Fish* was pitching her fore-deck clean under water.

At its commencement the gale blew from about south-east, or dead in their teeth; and the revolutions of the engines were increased to a rate which, under ordinary circumstances, would have given the ship a speed of some twenty-five knots, but which now drove her ahead at the rate of only some fifteen knots against the gale. As the afternoon wore on, the wind gradually "backed," until, at four p.m., it was blowing from due south. This confirmed Mildmay in his suspicion that they had fallen in with one of those most terrible of storms—*a cyclone*!

At half-past four o'clock—at which time the gale was raging with hurricane force—a sail was made out, bearing about one point on the *Flying Fish's* port bow, and about four miles distant. As well as could be made out, she appeared to be barque-rigged; and, on approaching her more closely, this proved to be the case. She was a vessel of some four hundred tons register, pretty deep in the water; and—though she was hove-to under close-reefed fore and main topsails—was making frightfully bad weather of it, the seas sweeping clear and clean over her, fore and aft, every time she met them.

The moment that the stranger was first sighted, Mildmay opened one of the windows—at the risk of getting drenched to the skin—and brought a telescope to bear upon her. He had scarcely brought her within the field of vision when he exclaimed agitatedly:

"Good Heavens! what is the man about? He has hove-to his ship *on the port tack*; does he not know he is in a cyclone?"

"What does it matter which tack the vessel is hove-to upon?" asked Sir Reginald with a smile at Mildmay's excitement.

"All the difference in the world, my dear sir," was the reply. "We are in the Northern Hemisphere; in which—as you have already had an opportunity of observing—cyclones *invariably* revolve *against* the apparent course of the sun. A knowledge of this fact teaches the wary seaman to heave-to on the *starboard* tack; by doing which his ship dodges *away from* the fatal centre or 'eye' of the storm. This fellow, however, by heaving-to on the port tack, is steadily nearing the centre, which must eventually pass over him, when his ship will be suddenly becalmed, only to be struck aback a few moments later, when she will—almost to a dead certainty—founder with all hands. For Heaven's sake let us bear down upon him and warn him ere it be too late. And we have no time to lose about it either; for, if I may judge from the fury of the gale, the centre of the storm is not far off."

The speed of the *Flying Fish* was promptly increased, her course being at the same time so far altered as to admit of her intercepting the barque, and a few minutes later she passed under the stranger's stern and hauled close up on her weather quarter, the travellers thus having an opportunity of ascertaining the name of the vessel, which proved to be the *Mercury* of Bristol. They were now also able to realise more fully than they had yet the tremendous strength of the gale and power of the sea; the unfortunate barque careening gunwale-to under the pressure of the wind upon her scanty canvas, whilst the sea deluged her decks fore and aft; the whole of her lee and a considerable portion of her weather bulwarks having already been carried away, together with her spare spars; whilst every sea which broke on board her swept something or other off the deck and into the sea to leeward. The long-boat and pinnace, stowed over the main hatchway, were stove and rendered unserviceable; and, even as the *Flying Fish* ranged up alongside, their destruction was completed and their shattered planks and timbers torn out of the "gripes." The crew of the ship had, for safety's sake, assembled aft on the full poop; and among them could be seen a female figure crouching down under the meagre shelter of the cabin skylight evidently in a state of extreme terror.

"You go out and hail them, Mildmay; you know what to say," remarked Sir Reginald, as he steered the *Flying Fish* into a favourable position for communicating.

The lieutenant needed no second bidding; he felt that the crisis was imminent; and, stepping out on deck, where he had to cling tightly to the lee guard-rail to escape being washed overboard, he hailed:

"Barque ahoy! do you know that you are in a cyclone, and hove-to on the wrong tack? I would very strongly advise you to wear round at once and get the ship on the starboard tack. If the eye of the storm catches you you will surely founder."

To his intense astonishment an answer came back—from a great black-bearded savage-looking fellow—couched in the words, as nearly as he could make them out for the howling of the wind and the rush of the sea:

"You mind your own business! Nobody on board this ship wants your advice."

"But I am giving it you for your own safety's sake, and that of the ship," persisted Mildmay.

The answer was unintelligible, but, as it was accompanied by an impatient wave of the hand and a turning of the speaker's back upon him, Mildmay rightly concluded that the individual was one of those obstinate, pig-headed people, who, having once made a mistake, will persist in it at all hazards rather than take advice, and so admit the possibility of their having done wrong; he accordingly turned away somewhat disgusted, and made his way back to the shelter of the pilot-house.

The lieutenant was in the act of describing to his companions the unsatisfactory nature of the foregoing brief colloquy, when suddenly—*instantaneously*—there occurred an awful pause in the fury of the hurricane; the wind lulled at once to a dead calm; the air cleared; the sea, no longer thrashed down by the gale, reared itself aloft as though it would scale the very heavens; and the canvas of the barque flapped with a single loud thunderous report as she rolled heavily to windward.

"Now, look out!" gasped Mildmay. And, even as the words escaped his lips, down came the hurricane again in a sudden mad burst of relentless fury; but *now* the wind blew from the *northward*, the point of the compass exactly opposite that from which it had been blowing a minute before.

The *Flying Fish*, having neither sails nor spars exposed to the blast, received this second stroke of the gale with impunity; but with the devoted barque it was, alas, very different. She was struck flat aback and borne irresistibly over on her beam-ends, gathering stern-way at the same time. The crew, at last fully alive to the extreme peril of their situation, scrambled along the deck and made their way to the braces in a futile attempt to haul round the yards, the helmsman at the same time jamming the wheel hard down that the ship might have a chance to pay off. The yards, however, were jammed fast against the weather rigging, and could not be moved; neither would the ship's head pay off; meanwhile, her stern-way was rapidly increasing, the sea already foaming up level with her taffrail; and presently it curled in over her lee quarter, sweeping in a steadily increasing volume along her deck. The catastrophe which followed took place with startling rapidity. The stern of the barque, now buried beneath the surge, seemed at once to lose all its buoyancy, and, powerfully depressed by the leverage of the topsails on the masts, plunged at once deeply below the surface of the hungrily leaping sea, the rest of the hull following so quickly that, before the horrified spectators in the *Flying Fish's* pilot-house fully realised what was happening, the entire hull had disappeared, the masts, yards, and top-hamper generally only remaining in sight a moment longer, as though to impress upon them unmistakably the fact that a ship was foundering before their eyes.

"Come back and close the door!" thundered Sir Reginald to Mildmay, laying his hand upon certain valve-handles as the lieutenant sprang out on deck, urged by some indefinite purpose of rendering help where help was obviously no longer possible.

Mildmay stood for a moment, as one in a dream, watching the submergence of the ill-fated *Mercury's* jib-boom end and fore-topgallant mast-head (the last of her spars to disappear) beneath the swirl where her hull had just vanished, and then, dazedly, he obeyed the baronet's sharply reiterated command.

No sooner did the door clang to than Sir Reginald rapidly threw open all the valves of the water chambers, and the *Flying Fish* at once began to follow the barque to the bottom. In less than five seconds the travellers found themselves clear of all the wild commotion raging on the surface, and descending silently, rapidly, yet steadily deeper and deeper into the recesses of the cool twilight which prevailed around them, deepest blue below and an ever-darkening green above. They quickly overtook the *Mercury* and continued the descent almost side by side with her, watching, with awe-struck curiosity yet overwhelming pity and horror, the death-struggles of those who were being helplessly dragged down with her. They observed, with a feeling of intense relief, that the struggle for life ceased, in almost every case, in less than a minute, the expression of horror on the dying men's faces passing away still earlier and giving place to one of profound peace and contentment; thus confirming, to a great extent the current belief that death by drowning is a painless mode of dissolution.

The crew had, without exception, at the moment of the barque's foundering, grasped some rope or other portion of the vessel's equipment, the death-clutch upon which was in no single instance relaxed; hence they were, one and all, dragged hopelessly to the bottom with the wreck. With the female, however, it was different. She had been crouching in a kneeling attitude upon the deck, under the imperfect shelter of the cabin skylight, and when the poop deck became submerged she was swept forward, still in the same attitude, with her hands clasped as in prayer, until her body was washed clear of the poop rail, when the suction of the sinking ship dragged her below the surface. As the hull of the barque settled down it gradually recovered its balance and assumed an almost level position, due, to some extent, no doubt, to the pressure of the water upon the sails; and, with every fathom of descent, the downward motion grew increasingly slower. The wreck had sunk to a depth of perhaps twenty or five-and-twenty fathoms, when the absorbed spectators in the *Flying Fish's* pilot-house were startled by observing a sudden convulsive motion in the body of the female. Her hands were unclasped, her arms were flung wildly out above her head, and her body was slowly straightened out. At the same moment the space between her and the sinking wreck widened; the vessel was sinking more rapidly than the body. The descent of the *Flying Fish* was instantly checked, and in another moment it became apparent that the body *was rising to the surface*.

In eager, breathless anxiety the watchers noted the steady downward progress of the *Mercury's* spars and cordage past the now struggling form of the woman, victims of alternate dismay and hope as they saw the body now fouled by some portion of the complicated net-work of standing and running gear between the main and mizzen masts, and anon drifting clear of it again. A few seconds, which to the quartette in the pilot-house seemed spun out to the duration of ages, and the last of these perils was evaded, upon which the body, still feebly struggling, resumed its upward journey.

With a great sigh of intense relief, echoed by each of his companions, Sir Reginald swiftly backed the *Flying Fish* astern, causing her at the same time, by a movement of the tiller, to swerve with her bow directly toward the body, now some five or six feet above the level of the deck. Then, quick as thought, the ship was sent ahead until her deck was immediately beneath the body, when, the valves of the air and water chambers being simultaneously thrown open, she rushed upward to the surface, overtaking the drowning woman and carrying her upward also.

In another instant, a vacuum having been created in the air-chambers, the *Flying Fish* broke water with a tremendous rush and swirl, and, without a moment's pause, rose into the air, the senseless body on deck being prevented from washing off again only by the guard-rail which stood in place of bulwarks.

"Take charge, please, and do not rise too high," hurriedly exclaimed the baronet to Mildmay, springing, as he spoke, for the door of the pilot-house, which he flung open, rushing out on deck and seizing the body as though fearful that it might yet be snatched away from him.

Gently raising it in his arms he turned and bore the slender form to the shelter of the pilot-house, at the door of which he was met by the professor, who felt that his medical skill might yet perhaps serve the unfortunate girl in good stead. Together they conveyed her below to one of the state-rooms, and, without a moment's loss of time, the most approved methods of resuscitation were vigorously resorted to. For fully half an hour their utmost efforts proved all unavailing; but von Schalckenberg so positively asserted life was not extinct that they persevered, and at length a slight return of warmth to the body and colour to the lips, followed by a fluttering sigh, assured them that success was about to reward their endeavours. Another minute, and a pair of glorious brown eyes were disclosed by their opening lids, a faint moan escaped the quivering lips, the head moved uneasily upon the pillow, and the sufferer murmured a few inarticulate words.

"Thank God, we have saved her, I believe," ejaculated Sir Reginald, in a whisper, to the professor. "Now, doctor, I will retire and leave you to complete her restoration, so that the poor girl may be spared embarrassment as far as possible on the full recovery of consciousness. But I shall establish myself outside the door of the state-room, within easy reach of your voice should you need anything; and do not forget that the whole resources of the ship are at your absolute disposal."

"All right," answered the professor. "Now go, for the patient is coming to herself rapidly."

Half an hour later von Schalckenberg crept out on tiptoe, his kindly face beaming and his eyes sparkling with exultation.

"It is all right," he whispered in his broadest German-English. "I have fully restored the circulation, and the young patient is now in a sound sleep, from which she must not be disturbed on any account. I shall keep watch by her side, and when she awakes you shall all be duly informed of the circumstance. You may now go about your business, my good friend, your services are no longer required here."

The worthy professor kept sedulous watch over his patient until satisfied that she was completely out of danger, presenting her to his companions only when they assembled in the saloon for dinner some four-and-twenty hours after the catastrophe which had thrown her into their society.

The colonel and Mildmay were stricken absolutely, though only temporarily, dumb with astonishment and admiration at the vision of remarkable beauty which met their gaze as the saloon door opened, and von Schalckenberg, stepping hastily forward with a most courtly bow, met the fair stranger at the threshold, taking her hand and leading her forward into the apartment preliminary to the ceremony of introduction. Even Sir Reginald, though he had not failed to notice the beauty of the pale and apparently lifeless girl he had raised from the wet deck and borne so carefully below on the preceding evening, was startled at her radiant loveliness as she, somewhat shrinkingly and with a momentary vivid blush, responded to the introductions and congratulatory greetings which immediately followed. All night long, and throughout the day, she had been haunted by the dreamy recollection of another face than that of the kindly professor who had so assiduously nursed her back to life—a bronzed handsome face, with tender pitiful blue eyes, close-cut auburn hair clustering wavily about the small shapely head, and luxuriant auburn moustache and beard, bending anxiously over her as she lay weak, helpless, suffering, and with the feebly-returning consciousness of having recently experienced some terrible calamity; of having passed through some awful and harrowing ordeal; and now, as she gave her hand to Sir Reginald, and shyly glanced up into his handsome face and read the tender sympathy for her expressed by the kindly blue eyes, she recognised the embodiment of the vision which had haunted her so persistently, and knew that she had not been merely dreaming. The circumstances in which she thus found herself placed were certainly somewhat embarrassing; but, with the tact of a true gentleman, Sir Reginald at once led the conversation into a channel which soon made the poor girl forget her embarrassment, and almost immediately afterwards the party sat down to dinner.

During the progress of this meal—which, however, their guest scarcely tasted—the gentlemen were made aware of the circumstances which led to this lovely girl being thrown, helpless and friendless, into their society and upon their hospitality.

Her name, she informed them, was Olivia D'Arcy. She was an orphan. Her brother, formerly a lieutenant in the royal navy, had been compelled by straitened circumstances to quit the service and enter the mercantile marine, in which he had without much difficulty succeeded in securing a command. By practising the most rigid economy he had contrived to maintain his only sister, Olivia, and educate her at a first-class school, and on her education being completed he had decided, as the simplest way out of many difficulties, financial and otherwise, to take her to sea with him. This had been her first voyage with him, as it had been his first in command of the *Mercury*. The ship had been to Manilla, and at the time of her loss was homeward-bound, with instructions to call at Madras *en route*. The voyage had been an unfortunate one in many respects, even from its commencement, and Olivia thought the climax had been reached when, a week before her wreck, the *Mercury* had been attacked by pirates in the Straits of Malacca, and her brother slain by the pirates' last shot, as they retired defeated. The cruel shot, she declared in a burst of uncontrollable grief, had robbed her, in her brother, of her sole relative; and whilst she was deeply grateful to those she addressed for preserving her life, she felt that it would perhaps have been better for her had she been allowed to perish.

Such a story was calculated to excite the deepest sympathy and commiseration in the breasts of those who listened to it; and it did; in Sir Reginald's case, indeed, the feeling was even warmer than either of those mentioned, especially when he learned, upon further inquiry, that Olivia's brother had been none other than the George D'Arcy who, in the days of their mutual boyhood, had fought many a battle on his behalf at Eton when certain first-form bullies had shown a disposition to tyrannise over the then delicate curly-headed "Miss Reggie" (as Elphinstone was dubbed when he first entered the school), and the sorrowing girl was assured that, so far from being friendless, she would find in her then companions four men upon whom she might always rely for the warmest sympathy, the most kindly counsel, and the most substantial help so long as their lives might last.

The accession of such a guest as Olivia D'Arcy to the little party on board the *Flying Fish* occasioned, it will readily be understood, a complete and immediate change in all their plans. In the first moment that they gave to the consideration of the matter they saw that it would never do for a young, beautiful, and unprotected girl to accompany them hither and thither in their wanderings, even were she willing to do so, which they felt well assured she would not be. Two alternatives then presented themselves to the choice of the party: the one being to land her at the nearest port, and, furnishing her with the necessary means, leave her to make her way to England alone and unprotected as best she could; the other alternative involving the temporary abandonment of their further projects and the immediate return of the *Flying Fish* to England. The first project was named only to be abruptly and unanimously rejected by the entire party, the second being gladly adopted by Sir Reginald upon his receiving from his three friends the assurance of their hearty approval and acquiescence.

This decision was arrived at shortly before midnight on the evening following Olivia's formal introduction by the professor to the remaining members of the party, and thereupon—the *Flying Fish* being at the time afloat and making her way leisurely southward toward the Straits of Malacca—an ascent to the upper regions of the atmosphere was at once made, and the ship's head pointed homeward. The distance to be traversed was considerable, but it was calculated that by travelling at the ship's utmost speed along the arc of a great circle (the shortest possible route between any two places on the earth's surface), the journey might be accomplished in about forty-five hours, which, allowing for the difference of longitude in time between their then position and the English Channel, would enable them to reach the latter place at about two o'clock in the afternoon of the day but one following. This was rather an awkward time, if they still intended to maintain their secrecy of movement and avoid observation, but under the circumstances they resolved to risk it. Soaring, therefore, to a height of ten thousand feet—the elevation which experience had taught them to be most suitable for the performance of long-distance journeys—the *Flying Fish* was put to her utmost speed, and, with the gentlemen keeping watch by turns in the pilot-house, the journey was commenced.

Swiftly the wonderful fabric sped forward upon her homeward way, and, without incident of any kind worthy of mention, and almost at the very minute calculated upon, the waters of the English Channel were sighted; an unobserved descent being effected some twenty miles seaward of the little town of Saint Valery on the French coast. A course was now shaped for the Isle of Wight, and, a few hours later, one of the boats belonging to the *Flying Fish* quietly glided into Portsmouth harbour in charge of Lieutenant Mildmay. Three passengers—Olivia

D'Arcy, the professor, and Colonel Lethbridge—landed from her without attracting any attention, and found themselves just in good time to take the London express, which they did, Mildmay making his solitary way out of the harbour again immediately.

In accordance with arrangements previously made by Sir Reginald, Miss D'Arcy was escorted by her two cavaliers straight to the town residence of a certain aunt of the baronet's, and handed over to the care and protection of the old lady, with whom (to make short of a long story) for the ensuing twelve months she found a most comfortable and happy home; Sir Reginald and Mildmay turning up in town two days later laden with their African spoils, the equitable division of which, and their ultimate disposal, occupied the party for several months.

Thus ended the cruise of the *Flying Fish*. What remains to be told may be said in a very few words. Will the sagacious reader be very much surprised to learn that Sir Reginald Elphinstone suddenly discovered, in the aunt who had kindly taken Olivia D'Arcy under her protection, an old lady whose good graces were worth the most assiduous cultivation? Such, at all events, was the fact, and, this much having been stated, the aforesaid sagacious reader will perhaps be not altogether unprepared to learn that, about a year after the return of the *Flying Fish* to England, a wedding took place from that old lady's house; in which ceremony Olivia enacted most charmingly the part of bride, with Sir Reginald as bridegroom, supported by the three staunch friends who had shared with him so many perils.

And what about the *Flying Fish*, does somebody ask? When last heard of she was—where she probably still is—lying safe and unsuspected at the bottom of the "Hurd Deep," in the identical spot where she made her first descent into the waters of the English Channel.

Whether she will ever again be put into commission—and, if so, under what circumstances—time alone will show.

THE END

THE BALL AND THE CROSS
BY G.K. CHESTERTON
(UNITED KINGDOM, 1909)

CHAPTER ONE
A DISCUSSION SOMEWHAT IN THE AIR

The flying ship of Professor Lucifer sang through the skies like a silver arrow; the bleak white steel of it, gleaming in the bleak blue emptiness of the evening. That it was far above the earth was no expression for it; to the two men in it, it seemed to be far above the stars. The professor had himself invented the flying machine, and had also invented nearly everything in it. Every sort of tool or apparatus had, in consequence, to the full, that fantastic and distorted look which belongs to the miracles of science. For the world of science and evolution is far more nameless and elusive and like a dream than the world of poetry and religion; since in the latter images and ideas remain themselves eternally, while it is the whole idea of evolution that identities melt into each other as they do in a nightmare.

All the tools of Professor Lucifer were the ancient human tools gone mad, grown into unrecognizable shapes, forgetful of their origin, forgetful of their names. That thing which looked like an enormous key with three wheels was really a patent and very deadly revolver. That object which seemed to be created by the entanglement of two corkscrews was really the key. The thing which might have been mistaken for a tricycle turned upside-down was the inexpressibly important instrument to which the corkscrew was the key. All these things, as I say, the professor had invented; he had invented everything in the flying ship, with the exception, perhaps, of himself. This he had been born too late actually to inaugurate, but he believed at least, that he had considerably improved it.

There was, however, another man on board, so to speak, at the time. Him, also, by a curious coincidence, the professor had not invented, and him he had not even very greatly improved, though he had fished him up with a lasso out of his own back garden, in Western Bulgaria, with the pure object of improving him. He was an exceedingly holy man, almost entirely covered with white hair. You could see nothing but his eyes, and he seemed to talk with them. A monk of immense learning and acute intellect he had made himself happy in a little stone hut and a little stony garden in the Balkans, chiefly by writing the most crushing refutations of exposures of certain heresies, the last professors of which had been burnt (generally by each other) precisely 1,119 years previously. They were really very plausible and thoughtful heresies, and it was really a creditable or even glorious circumstance, that the old monk had been intellectual enough to detect their fallacy; the only misfortune was that nobody in the modern world was intellectual enough even to understand their argument. The old monk, one of whose names was Michael, and the other a name quite impossible to remember or repeat in our Western civilization, had, however, as I have said, made himself quite happy while he was in a mountain hermitage in the society of wild animals. And now that his luck had lifted him above all the mountains in the society of a wild physicist, he made himself happy still.

"I have no intention, my good Michael," said Professor Lucifer, "of endeavouring to convert you by argument. The imbecility of your traditions can be quite finally exhibited to anybody with mere ordinary knowledge of the world, the same kind of knowledge which teaches us not to sit in draughts or not to encourage friendliness in impecunious people. It is folly to talk of this or that demonstrating the rationalist philosophy. Everything demonstrates it. Rubbing shoulders with men of all kinds——"

"You will forgive me," said the monk, meekly from under loads of white beard, "but I fear I do not understand; was it in order that I might rub my shoulder against men of all kinds that you put me inside this thing?"

"An entertaining retort, in the narrow and deductive manner of the Middle Ages," replied the Professor, calmly, "but even upon your own basis I will illustrate my point. We are up in the sky. In your religion and all the religions, as far as I know (and I know everything), the sky is made the symbol of everything that is sacred and merciful. Well, now you are in the sky, you know better. Phrase it how you like, twist it how you like, you know that you know better. You know what are a man's real feelings about the heavens, when he finds himself alone in the heavens, surrounded by the heavens. You know the truth, and the truth is this. The heavens are evil, the sky is evil, the stars are evil. This mere space, this mere quantity, terrifies a man more than tigers or the terrible plague. You know that since our science has spoken, the bottom has fallen out of the Universe. Now, heaven is the hopeless thing, more hopeless than any hell. Now, if there be any comfort for all your miserable progeny of morbid apes, it must be in the earth, underneath you, under the roots of the grass, in the place where hell was of old. The fiery crypts, the lurid cellars of the underworld, to which you once condemned the wicked, are hideous enough, but at least they are more homely than the heaven in which we ride. And the time will come when you will all hide in them, to escape the horror of the stars."

"I hope you will excuse my interrupting you," said Michael, with a slight cough, "but I have always noticed——"

"Go on, pray go on," said Professor Lucifer, radiantly, "I really like to draw out your simple ideas."

"Well, the fact is," said the other, "that much as I admire your rhetoric and the rhetoric of your school, from a purely verbal point of view, such little study of you and your school in human history as I have been enabled to make has led me to—er—rather singular conclusion, which I find great difficulty in expressing, especially in a foreign language."

"Come, come," said the Professor, encouragingly, "I'll help you out. How did my view strike you?"

"Well, the truth is, I know I don't express it properly, but somehow it seemed to me that you always convey ideas of that kind with most eloquence, when—er—when——"

"Oh! get on," cried Lucifer, boisterously.

"Well, in point of fact when your flying ship is just going to run into something. I thought you wouldn't mind my mentioning it, but it's running into something now."

Lucifer exploded with an oath and leapt erect, leaning hard upon the handle that acted as a helm to the vessel. For the last ten minutes they had been shooting downwards into great cracks and caverns of cloud. Now, through a sort of purple haze, could be seen comparatively near to them what seemed to be the upper part of a huge, dark orb or sphere, islanded in a sea of cloud. The Professor's eyes were blazing like a maniac's.

"It is a new world," he cried, with a dreadful mirth. "It is a new planet and it shall bear my name. This star and not that other vulgar one shall be 'Lucifer, sun of the morning.' Here we will have no chartered lunacies, here we will have no gods. Here man shall be as innocent as the daisies, as innocent and as cruel—here the intellect——"

"There seems," said Michael, timidly, "to be something sticking up in the middle of it."

"So there is," said the Professor, leaning over the side of the ship, his spectacles shining with intellectual excitement. "What can it be? It might of course be merely a——"

Then a shriek indescribable broke out of him of a sudden, and he flung up his arms like a lost spirit. The monk took the helm in a tired way; he did not seem much astonished for he came from an ignorant part of the world in which it is not uncommon for lost spirits to shriek when they see the curious shape which the Professor had just seen on the top of the mysterious ball, but he took the helm only just in time, and by driving it hard to the left he prevented the flying ship from smashing into St. Paul's Cathedral.

A plain of sad-coloured cloud lay along the level of the top of the Cathedral dome, so that the ball and the cross looked like a buoy riding on a leaden sea. As the flying ship swept towards it, this plain of cloud looked as dry and definite and rocky as any grey desert. Hence it gave to the mind and body a sharp and unearthly sensation when the ship cut and sank into the cloud as into any common mist, a thing without resistance. There was, as it were, a deadly shock in the fact that there was no shock. It was as if they had cloven into ancient cliffs like so much butter. But sensations awaited them which were much stranger than those of sinking through the solid earth. For a moment their eyes and nostrils were stopped with darkness and opaque cloud; then the darkness warmed into a kind of brown fog. And far, far below them the brown fog fell until it warmed into fire. Through the dense London atmosphere they could see below them the flaming London lights; lights which lay beneath them in squares and oblongs of fire. The fog and fire were mixed in a passionate vapour; you might say that the fog was drowning the flames; or you might say that the flames had set the fog on fire. Beside the ship and beneath it (for it swung just under the ball), the immeasurable dome itself shot out and down into the dark like a combination of voiceless cataracts. Or it was like some cyclopean sea-beast sitting above London and letting down its tentacles bewilderingly on every side, a monstrosity in that starless heaven. For the clouds that belonged to London had closed over the heads of the voyagers sealing up the entrance of the upper air. They had broken through a roof and come into a temple of twilight.

They were so near to the ball that Lucifer leaned his hand against it, holding the vessel away, as men push a boat off from a bank. Above it the cross already draped in the dark mists of the borderland was shadowy and more awful in shape and size.

Professor Lucifer slapped his hand twice upon the surface of the great orb as if he were caressing some enormous animal. "This is the fellow," he said, "this is the one for my money."

"May I with all respect inquire," asked the old monk, "what on earth you are talking about?"

"Why this," cried Lucifer, smiting the ball again, "here is the only symbol, my boy. So fat. So satisfied. Not like that scraggy individual, stretching his arms in stark weariness." And he pointed up to the cross, his face dark with a grin. "I was telling you just now, Michael, that I can prove the best part of the rationalist case and the Christian humbug from any symbol you liked to give me, from any instance I came across. Here is an instance with a vengeance. What could possibly express your philosophy and my philosophy better than the shape of that cross and the shape of this ball? This globe is reasonable; that cross is unreasonable. It is a four-legged animal, with one leg longer than the others. The globe is inevitable. The cross is arbitrary. Above all the globe is at unity with itself; the cross is primarily and above all things at enmity with itself. The cross is the conflict of two hostile lines, of irreconcilable direction. That silent thing up there is essentially a collision, a crash, a struggle in stone. Pah! that sacred symbol of yours has actually given its name to a description of desperation and muddle. When we speak of men at once ignorant of each other and frustrated by each other, we say they are at cross-purposes. Away with the thing! The very shape of it is a contradiction in terms."

"What you say is perfectly true," said Michael, with serenity. "But we like contradictions in terms. Man is a contradiction in terms; he is a beast whose superiority to other beasts consists in having fallen. That cross is, as you say, an eternal collision; so am I. That is a struggle in stone. Every form of life is a struggle in flesh. The shape of the cross is irrational, just as the shape of the human animal is irrational. You say the cross is a quadruped with one limb longer than the rest. I say man is a quadruped who only uses two of his legs."

The Professor frowned thoughtfully for an instant, and said: "Of course everything is relative, and I would not deny that the element of struggle and self-contradiction, represented by that cross, has a necessary place at a certain evolutionary stage. But surely the cross is the lower development and the sphere the higher. After all it is easy enough to see what is really wrong with Wren's architectural arrangement."

"And what is that, pray?" inquired Michael, meekly.

"The cross is on top of the ball," said Professor Lucifer, simply. "That is surely wrong. The ball should be on top of the cross. The cross is a mere barbaric prop; the ball is perfection. The cross at its best is but the bitter tree of man's history; the ball is the rounded, the ripe and final fruit. And the fruit should be at the top of the tree, not at the bottom of it."

"Oh!" said the monk, a wrinkle coming into his forehead, "so you think that in a rationalistic scheme of symbolism the ball should be on top of the cross?"

"It sums up my whole allegory," said the professor.

"Well, that is really very interesting," resumed Michael slowly, "because I think in that case you would see a most singular effect, an effect that has generally been achieved by all those able and powerful systems which rationalism, or the religion of the ball, has produced to lead or teach mankind. You would see, I think, that thing happen which is always the ultimate embodiment and logical outcome of your logical scheme."

"What are you talking about?" asked Lucifer. "What would happen?"

"I mean it would fall down," said the monk, looking wistfully into the void.

Lucifer made an angry movement and opened his mouth to speak, but

Michael, with all his air of deliberation, was proceeding before he could bring out a word.

"I once knew a man like you, Lucifer," he said, with a maddening monotony and slowness of articulation. "He took this——"

"There is no man like me," cried Lucifer, with a violence that shook the ship.

"As I was observing," continued Michael, "this man also took the view that the symbol of Christianity was a symbol of savagery and all unreason. His history is rather amusing. It is also a perfect allegory of what happens to rationalists like yourself. He began, of course, by refusing to allow a crucifix in his house, or round his wife's neck, or even in a picture. He said, as you say, that it was an arbitrary and fantastic shape, that it was a monstrosity, loved because it was paradoxical. Then he began to grow fiercer and more eccentric; he would batter the crosses by the roadside; for he lived in a Roman Catholic country. Finally in a height of frenzy he climbed the steeple of the Parish Church and tore down the cross, waving it in the air, and uttering wild soliloquies up there under the stars. Then one still summer evening as he was wending his way homewards, along a lane, the devil of his madness came upon him with a violence and transfiguration which changes the world. He was standing smoking, for a moment, in the front of an interminable line of palings, when his eyes were opened. Not a light shifted, not a leaf stirred, but he saw as if by a sudden change in the eyesight that this paling was an army of innumerable crosses linked together over hill and dale. And he whirled up his heavy stick and went at it as if at an army. Mile after mile along his homeward path he broke it down and tore it up. For he hated the cross and every paling is a wall of crosses. When he returned to his house he was a literal madman. He sat upon a chair and then started up from it for the cross-bars of the carpentry repeated the intolerable image. He flung himself upon a bed only to remember that this, too, like all workmanlike things, was constructed on the accursed plan. He broke his furniture because it was made of crosses. He burnt his house because it was made of crosses. He was found in the river."

Lucifer was looking at him with a bitten lip.

"Is that story really true?" he asked.

"Oh, no," said Michael, airily. "It is a parable. It is a parable of you and all your rationalists. You begin by breaking up the Cross; but you end by breaking up the habitable world. We leave you saying that nobody ought to join the Church against his will. When we meet you again you are saying that no one has any will to join it with. We leave you saying that there is no such place as Eden. We find you saying that there is no such place as Ireland. You start by hating the irrational and you come to hate everything, for everything is irrational and so——"

Lucifer leapt upon him with a cry like a wild beast's. "Ah," he screamed, "to every man his madness. You are mad on the cross. Let it save you."

And with a herculean energy he forced the monk backwards out of the reeling car on to the upper part of the stone ball. Michael, with as abrupt an agility, caught one of the beams of the cross and saved himself from falling. At the same instant Lucifer drove down a lever and the ship shot up with him in it alone.

"Ha! ha!" he yelled, "what sort of a support do you find it, old fellow?"

"For practical purposes of support," replied Michael grimly, "it is at any rate a great deal better than the ball. May I ask if you are going to leave me here?"

"Yes, yes. I mount! I mount!" cried the professor in ungovernable excitement. "*Altiora peto.* My path is upward."

"How often have you told me, Professor, that there is really no up or down in space?" said the monk. "I shall mount up as much as you will."

"Indeed," said Lucifer, leering over the side of the flying ship. "May I ask what you are going to do?"

The monk pointed downward at Ludgate Hill. "I am going," he said, "to climb up into a star."

Those who look at the matter most superficially regard paradox as something which belongs to jesting and light journalism. Paradox of this kind is to be found in the saying of the dandy, in the decadent comedy, "Life is much too important to be taken seriously." Those who look at the matter a little more deeply or delicately see that paradox is a thing which especially belongs to all religions. Paradox of this kind is to be found in such a saying as "The meek shall inherit the earth." But those who see and feel the fundamental fact of the matter know that paradox is a thing which belongs not to religion only, but to all vivid and violent practical crises of human living. This kind of paradox may be clearly perceived by anybody who happens to be hanging in mid-space, clinging to one arm of the Cross of St. Paul's.

Father Michael in spite of his years, and in spite of his asceticism (or because of it, for all I know), was a very healthy and happy old gentleman. And as he swung on a bar above the sickening emptiness of air, he realized, with that sort of dead detachment which belongs to the brains of those in peril, the deathless and hopeless contradiction which is involved in the mere idea of courage. He was a happy and healthy old gentleman and therefore he was quite careless about it. And he felt as every man feels in the taut moment of such terror that his chief danger was terror itself; his only possible strength would be a coolness amounting to carelessness, a carelessness amounting almost to a suicidal swagger. His one wild chance of coming out safely would be in not too desperately desiring to be safe. There might be footholds down that awful facade, if only he could not care whether they were footholds or no. If he were foolhardy he might escape; if he were wise he would stop where he was till he dropped from the cross like a stone. And this antinomy kept on repeating itself in his mind, a contradiction as large and staring as the immense contradiction of the Cross; he remembered having often heard the words, "Whosoever shall lose his life the same shall save it." He remembered with a sort of strange pity that this had always been made to mean that whoever lost his physical life should save his spiritual life. Now he knew the truth that is known to all fighters, and hunters, and climbers of cliffs. He knew that even his animal life could only be saved by a considerable readiness to lose it.

Some will think it improbable that a human soul swinging desperately in mid-air should think about philosophical inconsistencies. But such extreme states are dangerous things to dogmatize about. Frequently they produce a certain useless and joyless activity of the mere intellect, thought not only divorced from hope but even from desire. And if it is impossible to dogmatize about such states, it is still more impossible to describe them. To this spasm of sanity and clarity in Michael's mind succeeded a spasm of the elemental terror; the terror of the animal in us which regards the whole universe as its enemy; which, when it is victorious, has no pity, and so, when it is defeated has no imaginable hope. Of that ten minutes of terror it is not possible to speak in human words. But then again in that damnable darkness there began to grow a strange dawn as of grey and pale silver. And of this ultimate resignation or certainty it is even less possible to write; it is something stranger than hell itself; it is perhaps the last of the secrets of God. At the highest crisis of some incurable anguish there will suddenly fall upon the man the stillness of an insane contentment. It is not hope, for hope is broken and romantic and concerned with the future; this is complete and of the present. It is not faith, for faith by its very nature is fierce, and as it were at once doubtful and defiant; but this is simply a satisfaction. It is not knowledge, for the intellect seems to have no particular part in it. Nor is it (as the modern idiots would certainly say it is) a mere numbness or negative paralysis of the powers of grief. It is not negative in the least; it is as positive as good news. In some sense, indeed, it is good news. It seems almost as if there were some equality among things, some balance in all possible contingencies which we are not permitted to know lest we should learn indifference to good and evil, but which is sometimes shown to us for an instant as a last aid in our last agony.

Michael certainly could not have given any sort of rational account of this vast unmeaning satisfaction which soaked through him and filled him to the brim. He felt with a sort of half-witted lucidity that the cross was there, and the ball was there, and the dome was there, that he was going to climb down from them, and that he did not mind in the least whether he was killed or not. This mysterious mood lasted long enough to start him on his dreadful descent and to force him to continue it. But six times before he reached the highest of the outer galleries terror had returned on him like a flying storm of darkness and thunder. By the time he had reached that place of safety he almost felt (as in some impossible fit of drunkenness) that he had two heads; one was calm, careless, and efficient; the other saw the danger like a deadly map, was wise, careful, and useless. He had fancied that he would have to let himself vertically down the face of the whole building. When he dropped into the upper gallery he still felt as far from the terrestrial globe as if he had only dropped from the sun to the moon. He paused a little, panting in the gallery under the ball, and idly kicked his heels, moving a few yards along it. And as he did so a thunderbolt struck his soul. A man, a heavy, ordinary man, with a composed indifferent face, and a prosaic sort of uniform, with a row of buttons, blocked his way. Michael had no mind to wonder whether this solid astonished man, with the brown moustache and the nickel buttons, had also come on a flying ship. He merely let his mind float in an endless felicity about the man. He thought how nice it would be if he had to live up in that gallery with that one man for ever. He thought how he would luxuriate in the nameless shades of this man's soul and then hear with an endless excitement about the nameless shades of the souls of all his aunts and uncles. A moment before he had been dying alone. Now he was living in the same world with a man; an inexhaustible ecstasy. In the gallery below the ball Father Michael had found that man who is the noblest and most divine and most lovable of all men, better than all the saints, greater than all the heroes—man Friday.

In the confused colour and music of his new paradise, Michael heard only in a faint and distant fashion some remarks that this beautiful solid man seemed to be making to him; remarks about something or other being after hours and against orders. He also seemed to be asking how Michael "got up" there. This beautiful man evidently felt as Michael did that the earth was a star and was set in heaven.

At length Michael sated himself with the mere sensual music of the voice of the man in buttons. He began to listen to what he said, and even to make some attempt at answering a question which appeared to have been put several times and was now put with some excess of emphasis. Michael realized that the image of God in nickel buttons was asking him how he had come there. He said that he had come in Lucifer's ship. On his giving this answer the demeanour of the image of God underwent a remarkable change. From addressing Michael gruffly, as if he were a malefactor, he began suddenly to speak to him with a sort of eager and feverish amiability as if he were a child. He seemed particularly anxious to coax him away from the balustrade. He led him by the arm towards a door leading into the building itself, soothing him all the time. He gave what even Michael (slight as was his knowledge of the world) felt to be an improbable account of the sumptuous pleasures and varied advantages awaiting him downstairs. Michael followed him, however, if only out of politeness, down an apparently interminable spiral of staircase. At one point a door opened. Michael stepped through it, and the unaccountable man in buttons leapt after him and pinioned him where he stood. But he only wished to stand; to stand and stare. He had stepped as it were into another infinity, out under the dome of another heaven. But this was a dome of heaven made by man. The gold and green and crimson of its sunset were not in the shapeless clouds but in shapes of cherubim and seraphim, awful human shapes with a passionate plumage. Its stars were not above but far below, like fallen stars still in unbroken constellations; the dome itself was full of darkness. And far below, lower even than the lights, could be seen creeping or motionless, great black masses of men. The tongue of a terrible organ seemed to shake the very air in the whole void; and through it there came up to Michael the sound of a tongue more terrible; the dreadful everlasting voice of man, calling to his gods from the beginning to the end of the world. Michael felt almost as if he were a god, and all the voices were hurled at him.

"No, the pretty things aren't here," said the demi-god in buttons, caressingly. "The pretty things are downstairs. You come along with me. There's something that will surprise you downstairs; something you want very much to see."

Evidently the man in buttons did not feel like a god, so Michael made no attempt to explain his feelings to him, but followed him meekly enough down the trail of the serpentine staircase. He had no notion where or at what level he was. He was still full of the cold splendour of space, and of what a French writer has brilliantly named the "vertigo of the infinite," when another door opened, and with a shock indescribable he found himself on the familiar level, in a street full of faces, with the houses and even the lamp-posts above his head. He felt suddenly happy and suddenly indescribably small. He fancied he had been changed into a child again; his eyes sought the pavement seriously as children's do, as if it were a thing with which something satisfactory could be done. He felt the full warmth of that pleasure from which the proud shut themselves out; the pleasure which not only goes with humiliation, but which almost is humiliation. Men who have escaped death by a hair have it, and men whose love is returned by a woman unexpectedly, and men whose sins are forgiven them. Everything his eye fell on it feasted on, not aesthetically, but with a plain, jolly appetite as of a boy eating buns. He relished the squareness of the houses; he liked their clean angles as if he had just cut them with a knife. The lit squares of the shop windows excited him as the young are excited by the lit stage of some promising pantomime. He happened to see in one shop which projected with a bulging bravery on to the pavement some square tins of potted meat, and it seemed like a hint of a hundred hilarious high teas in a hundred streets of the world. He was, perhaps, the happiest of all the children of men. For in that unendurable instant when he hung, half slipping, to the ball of St. Paul's, the whole universe had been destroyed and re-created.

Suddenly through all the din of the dark streets came a crash of glass. With that mysterious suddenness of the Cockney mob, a rush was made in the right direction, a dingy office, next to the shop of the potted meat. The pane of glass was lying in splinters about the pavement. And the police already had their hands on a very tall young man, with dark, lank hair and dark, dazed eyes, with a grey plaid over his shoulder, who had just smashed the shop window with a single blow of his stick.

"I'd do it again," said the young man, with a furious white face. "Anybody would have done it. Did you see what it said? I swear I'd do it again." Then his eyes encountered the monkish habit of Michael, and he pulled off his grey tam-o'-shanter with the gesture of a Catholic.

"Father, did you see what they said?" he cried, trembling. "Did you see what they dared to say? I didn't understand it at first. I read it half through before I broke the window."

Michael felt he knew not how. The whole peace of the world was pent up painfully in his heart. The new and childlike world which he had seen so suddenly, men had not seen at all. Here they were still at their old bewildering, pardonable, useless quarrels, with so much to be said on both sides, and so little that need be said at all. A fierce inspiration fell on him suddenly; he would strike them where they stood with the love of God. They should not move till they saw their own sweet and startling existence. They should not go from that place till they went home embracing like brothers and shouting like men delivered. From the Cross from which he had fallen fell the shadow of its fantastic mercy; and the first three words he spoke in a voice like a silver trumpet, held men as still as stones. Perhaps if he had spoken there for an hour in his illumination he might have founded a religion on Ludgate Hill. But the heavy hand of his guide fell suddenly on his shoulder.

"This poor fellow is dotty," he said good-humouredly to the crowd. "I found him wandering in the Cathedral. Says he came in a flying ship. Is there a constable to spare to take care of him?"

There was a constable to spare. Two other constables attended to the tall young man in grey; a fourth concerned himself with the owner of the shop, who showed some tendency to be turbulent. They took the tall young man away to a magistrate, whither we shall follow him in an ensuing chapter. And they took the happiest man in the world away to an asylum.

CHAPTER TWO
THE RELIGION OF THE STIPENDIARY MAGISTRATE

The editorial office of *The Atheist* had for some years past become less and less prominently interesting as a feature of Ludgate Hill. The paper was unsuited to the atmosphere. It showed an interest in the Bible unknown in the district, and a knowledge of that volume to which nobody else on Ludgate Hill could make any conspicuous claim. It was in vain that the editor of *The Atheist* filled his front window with fierce and final demands as to what Noah in the Ark did with the neck of the giraffe. It was in vain that he asked violently, as for the last time, how the statement "God is Spirit" could be reconciled with the statement "The earth is His footstool." It was in vain that he cried with an accusing energy that the Bishop of London was paid L12,000 a year for pretending to believe that the whale swallowed Jonah. It was in vain that he hung in conspicuous places the most thrilling scientific calculations about the width of the throat of a whale. Was it nothing to them all they that passed by? Did his sudden and splendid and truly sincere indignation never stir any of the people pouring down Ludgate Hill? Never. The little man who edited *The Atheist* would rush from his shop on starlit evenings and shake his fist at St. Paul's in the passion of his holy war upon the holy place. He might have spared his emotion. The cross at the top of St. Paul's and *The Atheist* shop at the foot of it were alike remote from the world. The shop and the Cross were equally uplifted and alone in the empty heavens.

To the little man who edited *The Atheist*, a fiery little Scotchman, with fiery, red hair and beard, going by the name of Turnbull, all this decline in public importance seemed not so much sad or even mad, but merely bewildering and unaccountable. He had said the worst thing that could be said; and it seemed accepted and ignored like the ordinary second best of the politicians. Every day his blasphemies looked more glaring, and every day the dust lay thicker upon them. It made him feel as if he were moving in a world of idiots. He seemed among a race of men who smiled when told of their own death, or looked vacantly at the Day of Judgement. Year after year went by, and year after year the death of God in a shop in Ludgate became a less and less important occurrence. All the forward men of his age discouraged Turnbull. The socialists said he was cursing priests when he should be cursing capitalists. The artists said that the soul was most spiritual, not when freed from religion, but when freed from morality. Year after year went by, and at least a man came by who treated Mr. Turnbull's secularist shop with a real respect and seriousness. He was a young man in a grey plaid, and he smashed the window.

He was a young man, born in the Bay of Arisaig, opposite Rum and the Isle of Skye. His high, hawklike features and snaky black hair bore the mark of that unknown historic thing which is crudely called Celtic, but which is probably far older than the Celts, whoever they were. He was in name and stock a Highlander of the Macdonalds; but his family took, as was common in such cases, the name of a subordinate sept as a surname, and for all the purposes which could be answered in London, he called himself Evan MacIan. He had been brought up in some loneliness and seclusion as a strict Roman Catholic, in the midst of that little wedge of Roman Catholics which is driven into the Western Highlands. And he had found his way as far as Fleet Street, seeking some half-promised employment, without having properly realized that there were in the world any people who were not Roman Catholics. He had uncovered himself for a few moments before the statue of Queen Anne, in front of St. Paul's Cathedral, under the firm impression that it was a figure of the Virgin Mary. He was somewhat surprised at the lack of deference shown to the figure by the people bustling by. He did not understand that their one essential historical principle, the one law truly graven on their hearts, was the great and comforting statement that Queen Anne is dead. This faith was as fundamental as his faith, that Our Lady was alive. Any persons he had talked to since he had touched the fringe of our fashion or civilization had been by a coincidence, sympathetic or hypocritical. Or if they had spoken some established blasphemies, he had been unable to understand them merely owing to the preoccupied satisfaction of his mind.

On that fantastic fringe of the Gaelic land where he walked as a boy, the cliffs were as fantastic as the clouds. Heaven seemed to humble itself and come closer to the earth. The common paths of his little village began to climb quite suddenly and seemed resolved to go to heaven. The sky seemed to fall down towards the hills; the hills took hold upon the sky. In the sumptuous sunset of gold and purple and peacock green cloudlets and islets were the same. Evan lived like a man walking on a borderland, the borderland between this world and another. Like so many men and nations who grow up with nature and the common things, he understood the supernatural before he understood the natural. He had looked at dim angels standing knee-deep in the grass before he had looked at the grass. He knew that Our Lady's robes were blue before he knew the wild roses round her feet were red. The deeper his memory plunged into the dark house of childhood the nearer and nearer he came to the things that cannot be named. All through his life he thought of the daylight world as a sort of divine debris, the broken remainder of his first vision. The skies and mountains were the splendid off-scourings of another place. The stars were lost jewels of the Queen. Our Lady had gone and left the stars by accident.

His private tradition was equally wild and unworldly. His great-grandfather had been cut down at Culloden, certain in his last instant that God would restore the King. His grandfather, then a boy of ten, had taken the terrible claymore from the hand of the dead and hung it up in his house, burnishing it and sharpening it for sixty years, to be ready for the next rebellion. His father, the youngest son and the last left alive, had refused to attend on Queen Victoria in Scotland. And Evan himself had been of one piece with his progenitors; and was not dead with them, but alive in the twentieth century. He was not in the least the pathetic Jacobite of whom we read, left behind by a final advance of all things. He was, in his own fancy, a conspirator, fierce and up to date. In the long, dark afternoons of the Highland winter, he plotted and fumed in the dark. He drew plans of the capture of London on the desolate sand of Arisaig.

When he came up to capture London, it was not with an army of white cockades, but with a stick and a satchel. London overawed him a little, not because he thought it grand or even terrible, but because it bewildered him; it was not the Golden City or even hell; it was Limbo. He had one shock of sentiment, when he turned that wonderful corner of Fleet Street and saw St. Paul's sitting in the sky.

"Ah," he said, after a long pause, "that sort of thing was built under the Stuarts!" Then with a sour grin he asked himself what was the corresponding monument of the Brunswicks and the Protestant Constitution. After some warning, he selected a sky-sign of some pill.

Half an hour afterwards his emotions left him with an emptied mind on the same spot. And it was in a mood of mere idle investigation that he happened to come to a standstill opposite the office of *The Atheist*. He did not see the word "atheist", or if he did, it is quite possible that he did not know the meaning of the word. Even as it was, the document would not have shocked even the innocent Highlander, but for the troublesome and quite unforeseen fact that the innocent Highlander read it stolidly to the end; a thing unknown among the most enthusiastic subscribers to the paper, and calculated in any case to create a new situation.

With a smart journalistic instinct characteristic of all his school, the editor of *The Atheist* had put first in his paper and most prominently in his window an article called "The Mesopotamian Mythology and its Effects on Syriac Folk Lore." Mr. Evan MacIan began to read this quite idly, as he would have read a public statement beginning with a young girl dying in Brighton and ending with Bile Beans. He received the very considerable amount of information accumulated by the author with that tired clearness of the mind which children have on heavy summer afternoons—that tired clearness which leads them to go on asking questions long after they have lost interest in the subject and are as bored as their nurse. The streets were full of people and empty of adventures. He might as well know about the gods of Mesopotamia as not; so he flattened his long, lean face against the dim bleak pane of the window and read all there was to read about Mesopotamian gods. He read how the Mesopotamians had a god named Sho (sometimes pronounced Ji), and that he was described as being very powerful, a striking similarity to some expressions about Jahveh, who is also described as having power. Evan had never heard of Jahveh in his life, and imagining him to be some other Mesopotamian idol, read on with a dull curiosity. He learnt that the name Sho, under its third form of Psa, occurs in an early legend which describes how the deity, after the manner of Jupiter on so many occasions, seduced a Virgin and begat a hero. This hero, whose name is not essential to our existence, was, it was said, the chief hero and Saviour of the Mesopotamian ethical scheme. Then followed a paragraph giving other examples of such heroes and Saviours being born of some profligate intercourse between God and mortal. Then followed a paragraph—but Evan did not understand it. He read it again and then again. Then he did understand it. The glass fell in ringing fragments on to the pavement, and Evan sprang over the barrier into the shop, brandishing his stick.

"What is this?" cried little Mr. Turnbull, starting up with hair aflame. "How dare you break my window?"

"Because it was the quickest cut to you," cried Evan, stamping. "Stand up and fight, you crapulous coward. You dirty lunatic, stand up, will you? Have you any weapons here?"

"Are you mad?" asked Turnbull, glaring.

"Are you?" cried Evan. "Can you be anything else when you plaster your own house with that God-defying filth? Stand up and fight, I say."

A great light like dawn came into Mr. Turnbull's face. Behind his red hair and beard he turned deadly pale with pleasure. Here, after twenty lone years of useless toil, he had his reward. Someone was angry with the paper. He bounded to his feet like a boy; he saw a new youth opening before him. And as not unfrequently happens to middle-aged gentlemen when they see a new youth opening before them, he found himself in the presence of the police.

The policemen, after some ponderous questionings, collared both the two enthusiasts. They were more respectful, however, to the young man who had smashed the window, than to the miscreant who had had his window smashed. There was an air of refined mystery about Evan MacIan, which did not exist in the irate little shopkeeper, an air of refined mystery which appealed to the policemen, for policemen, like most other English types, are at once snobs and poets. MacIan might possibly be a gentleman, they felt; the editor manifestly was not. And the editor's fine rational republican appeals to his respect for law, and his ardour to be tried by his fellow citizens, seemed to the police quite as much gibberish as Evan's mysticism could have done. The police were not used to hearing principles, even the principles of their own existence.

The police magistrate, before whom they were hurried and tried, was a Mr. Cumberland Vane, a cheerful, middle-aged gentleman, honourably celebrated for the lightness of his sentences and the lightness of his conversation. He occasionally worked himself up into a sort of theoretic rage about certain particular offenders, such as the men who took pokers to their wives, talked in a loose, sentimental way about the desirability of flogging them, and was hopelessly bewildered by the fact that the wives seemed even more angry with him than with their husbands. He was a tall, spruce man, with a twist of black moustache and incomparable morning dress. He looked like a gentleman, and yet, somehow, like a stage gentleman.

He had often treated serious crimes against mere order or property with a humane flippancy. Hence, about the mere breaking of an editor's window, he was almost uproarious.

"Come, Mr. MacIan, come," he said, leaning back in his chair, "do you generally enter you friends' houses by walking through the glass?" (Laughter.)

"He is not my friend," said Evan, with the stolidity of a dull child.

"Not your friend, eh?" said the magistrate, sparkling. "Is he your brother-in-law?" (Loud and prolonged laughter.)

"He is my enemy," said Evan, simply; "he is the enemy of God."

Mr. Vane shifted sharply in his seat, dropping the eye-glass out of his eye in a momentary and not unmanly embarrassment.

"You mustn't talk like that here," he said, roughly, and in a kind of hurry, "that has nothing to do with us."

Evan opened his great, blue eyes; "God," he began.

"Be quiet," said the magistrate, angrily, "it is most undesirable that things of that sort should be spoken about—a—in public, and in an ordinary Court of Justice. Religion is—a—too personal a matter to be mentioned in such a place."

"Is it?" answered the Highlander, "then what did those policemen swear by just now?"

"That is no parallel," answered Vane, rather irritably; "of course there is a form of oath—to be taken reverently—reverently, and there's an end of it. But to talk in a public place about one's most sacred and private sentiments—well, I call it bad taste. (Slight applause.) I call it irreverent. I call it irreverent, and I'm not specially orthodox either."

"I see you are not," said Evan, "but I am."

"We are wondering from the point," said the police magistrate, pulling himself together.

"May I ask why you smashed this worthy citizen's window?"

Evan turned a little pale at the mere memory, but he answered with the same cold and deadly literalism that he showed throughout.

"Because he blasphemed Our Lady."

"I tell you once and for all," cried Mr. Cumberland Vane, rapping his knuckles angrily on the table, "I tell you, once and for all, my man, that I will not have you turning on any religious rant or cant here. Don't imagine that it will impress me. The most religious people are not those who talk about it. (Applause.) You answer the questions and do nothing else."

"I did nothing else," said Evan, with a slight smile.

"Eh," cried Vane, glaring through his eye-glass.

"You asked me why I broke his window," said MacIan, with a face of wood. "I answered, 'Because he blasphemed Our Lady.' I had no other reason. So I have no other answer." Vane continued to gaze at him with a sternness not habitual to him.

"You are not going the right way to work, Sir," he said, with severity. "You are not going the right way to work to—a—have your case treated with special consideration. If you had simply expressed regret for what you had done, I should have been strongly inclined to dismiss the matter as an outbreak of temper. Even now, if you say that you are sorry I shall only——"

"But I am not in the least sorry," said Evan, "I am very pleased."

"I really believe you are insane," said the stipendiary, indignantly, for he had really been doing his best as a good-natured man, to compose the dispute.

"What conceivable right have you to break other people's windows because their opinions do not agree with yours? This man only gave expression to his sincere belief."

"So did I," said the Highlander.

"And who are you?" exploded Vane. "Are your views necessarily the right ones? Are you necessarily in possession of the truth?"

"Yes," said MacIan.

The magistrate broke into a contemptuous laugh.

"Oh, you want a nurse to look after you," he said. "You must pay L10."

Evan MacIan plunged his hands into his loose grey garment and drew out a queer looking leather purse. It contained exactly twelve sovereigns. He paid down the ten, coin by coin, in silence, and equally silently returned the remaining two to the receptacle. Then he said, "May I say a word, your worship?"

Cumberland Vane seemed half hypnotized with the silence and automatic movements of the stranger; he made a movement with his head which might have been either "yes" or "no". "I only wished to say, your worship," said MacIan, putting back the purse in his trouser pocket, "that smashing that shop window was, I confess, a useless and rather irregular business. It may be excused, however, as a mere preliminary to further proceedings, a sort of preface. Wherever and whenever I meet that man," and he pointed to the editor of *The Atheist*, "whether it be outside this door in ten minutes from now, or twenty years hence in some distant country, wherever and whenever I meet that man, I will fight him. Do not be afraid. I will not rush at him like a bully, or bear him down with any brute superiority. I will fight him like a gentleman; I will fight him as our fathers fought. He shall choose how, sword or pistol, horse or foot. But if he refuses, I will write his cowardice on every wall in the world. If he had said of my mother what he said of the Mother of God, there is not a club of clean men in Europe that would deny my right to call him out. If he had said it of my wife, you English would yourselves have pardoned me for beating him like a dog in the market place. Your worship, I have no mother; I have no wife. I have only that which the poor have equally with the rich; which the lonely have equally with the man of many friends. To me this whole strange world is homely, because in the heart of it there is a home; to me this cruel world is kindly, because higher than the heavens there is something more human than humanity. If a man must not fight for this, may he fight for anything? I would fight for my friend, but if I lost my friend, I should still be there. I would fight for my country, but if I lost my country, I should still exist. But if what that devil dreams were true, I should not be—I should burst like a bubble and be gone. I could not live in that imbecile universe. Shall I not fight for my own existence?"

The magistrate recovered his voice and his presence of mind. The first part of the speech, the bombastic and brutally practical challenge, stunned him with surprise; but the rest of Evan's remarks, branching off as they did into theoretic phrases, gave his vague and very English mind (full of memories of the hedging and compromise in English public speaking) an indistinct sensation of relief, as if the man, though mad, were not so dangerous as he had thought. He went into a sort of weary laughter.

"For Heaven's sake, man," he said, "don't talk so much. Let other people have a chance (laughter). I trust all that you said about asking Mr. Turnbull to fight, may be regarded as rubbish. In case of accidents, however, I must bind you over to keep the peace."

"To keep the peace," repeated Evan, "with whom?"

"With Mr. Turnbull," said Vane.

"Certainly not," answered MacIan. "What has he to do with peace?"

"Do you mean to say," began the magistrate, "that you refuse to..." The voice of Turnbull himself clove in for the first time.

"Might I suggest," he said, "That I, your worship, can settle to some extent this absurd matter myself. This rather wild gentleman promises that he will not attack me with any ordinary assault—and if he does, you may be sure the police shall hear of it. But he says he will not. He says he will challenge me to a duel; and I cannot say anything stronger about his mental state than to say that I think that it is highly probable that he will. (Laughter.) But it takes two to make a duel, your worship (renewed laughter). I do not in the least mind being described on every wall in the world as the coward who would not fight a man in Fleet Street, about whether the Virgin Mary had a parallel in Mesopotamian mythology. No, your worship. You need not trouble to bind him over to keep the peace. I bind myself over to keep the peace, and you may rest quite satisfied that there will be no duel with me in it."

Mr. Cumberland Vane rolled about, laughing in a sort of relief.

"You're like a breath of April, sir," he cried. "You're ozone after that fellow. You're perfectly right. Perhaps I have taken the thing too seriously. I should love to see him sending you challenges and to see you smiling. Well, well."

Evan went out of the Court of Justice free, but strangely shaken, like a sick man. Any punishment of suppression he would have felt as natural; but the sudden juncture between the laughter of his judge and the laughter of the man he had wronged, made him feel suddenly small, or at least, defeated. It was really true that the whole modern world regarded his world as a bubble. No cruelty could have shown it, but their kindness showed it with a ghastly clearness. As he was brooding, he suddenly became conscious of a small, stern figure, fronting him in silence. Its eyes were grey and awful, and its beard red. It was Turnbull.

"Well, sir," said the editor of *The Atheist*, "where is the fight to be? Name the field, sir."

Evan stood thunderstruck. He stammered out something, he knew not what; he only guessed it by the answer of the other.

"Do I want to fight? Do I want to fight?" cried the furious Free-thinker. "Why, you moonstruck scarecrow of superstition, do you think your dirty saints are the only people who can die? Haven't you hung atheists, and burned them, and boiled them, and did they ever deny their faith? Do you think we don't want to fight? Night and day I have prayed—I have longed—for an atheist revolution—I have longed to see your blood and ours on the streets. Let it be yours or mine?"

"But you said..." began MacIan.

"I know," said Turnbull scornfully. "And what did you say? You damned fool, you said things that might have got us locked up for a year, and shadowed by the coppers for half a decade. If you wanted to fight, why did you tell that ass you wanted to? I got you out, to fight if you want to. Now, fight if you dare."

"I swear to you, then," said MacIan, after a pause. "I swear to you that nothing shall come between us. I swear to you that nothing shall be in my heart or in my head till our swords clash together. I swear it by the God you have denied, by the Blessed Lady you have blasphemed; I swear it by the seven swords in her heart. I swear it by the Holy Island where my fathers are, by the honour of my mother, by the secret of my people, and by the chalice of the Blood of God."

The atheist drew up his head. "And I," he said, "give my word."

CHAPTER THREE
SOME OLD CURIOSITIES

The evening sky, a dome of solid gold, unflaked even by a single sunset cloud, steeped the meanest sights of London in a strange and mellow light. It made a little greasy street of St. Martin's Lane look as if it were paved with gold. It made the pawnbroker's half-way down it shine as if it were really that Mountain of Piety that the French poetic instinct has named it; it made the mean pseudo-French bookshop, next but one to it, a shop packed with dreary indecency, show for a moment a kind of Parisian colour. And the shop that stood between the pawnshop and the shop of dreary indecency, showed with quite a blaze of old world beauty, for it was, by accident, a shop not unbeautiful in itself. The front window had a glimmer of bronze and blue steel, lit, as by a few stars, by the sparks of what were alleged to be jewels; for it was in brief, a shop of bric-a-brac and old curiosities. A row of half-burnished seventeenth-century swords ran like an ornate railing along the front of the window; behind was a darker glimmer of old oak and old armour; and higher up hung the most extraordinary looking South Sea tools or utensils, whether designed for killing enemies or merely for cooking them, no mere white man could possibly conjecture. But the romance of the eye, which really on this rich evening, clung about the shop, had its main source in the accident of two doors standing open, the front door that opened on the street and a back door that opened on an odd green square of garden, that the sun turned to a square of gold. There is nothing more beautiful than thus to look as it were through the archway of a house; as if the open sky were an interior chamber, and the sun a secret lamp of the place.

I have suggested that the sunset light made everything lovely. To say that it made the keeper of the curiosity shop lovely would be a tribute to it perhaps too extreme. It would easily have made him beautiful if he had been merely squalid; if he had been a Jew of the Fagin type. But he was a Jew of another and much less admirable type; a Jew with a very well-sounding name. For though there are no hard tests for separating the tares and the wheat of any people, one rude but efficient guide is that the nice Jew is called Moses Solomon, and the nasty Jew is called Thornton Percy. The keeper of the curiosity shop was of the Thornton Percy branch of the chosen people; he belonged to those Lost Ten Tribes whose industrious object is to lose themselves. He was a man still young, but already corpulent, with sleek dark hair, heavy handsome clothes, and a full, fat, permanent smile, which looked at the first glance kindly, and at the second cowardly. The name over his shop was Henry Gordon, but two Scotchmen who were in his shop that evening could come upon no trace of a Scotch accent.

These two Scotchmen in this shop were careful purchasers, but free-handed payers. One of them who seemed to be the principal and the authority (whom, indeed, Mr. Henry Gordon fancied he had seen somewhere before), was a small, sturdy fellow, with fine grey eyes, a square red tie and a square red beard, that he carried aggressively forward as if he defied anyone to pull it. The other kept so much in the background in comparison that he looked almost ghostly in his grey cloak or plaid, a tall, sallow, silent young man.

The two Scotchmen were interested in seventeenth-century swords. They were fastidious about them. They had a whole armoury of these weapons brought out and rolled clattering about the counter, until they found two of precisely the same length. Presumably they desired the exact symmetry for some decorative trophy. Even then they felt the points, poised the swords for balance and bent them in a circle to see that they sprang straight again; which, for decorative purposes, seems carrying realism rather far.

"These will do," said the strange person with the red beard. "And perhaps I had better pay for them at once. And as you are the challenger, Mr. MacIan, perhaps you had better explain the situation."

The tall Scotchman in grey took a step forward and spoke in a voice quite clear and bold, and yet somehow lifeless, like a man going through an ancient formality.

"The fact is, Mr. Gordon, we have to place our honour in your hands. Words have passed between Mr. Turnbull and myself on a grave and invaluable matter, which can only be atoned for by fighting. Unfortunately, as the police are in some sense pursuing us, we are hurried, and must fight now and without seconds.

But if you will be so kind as to take us into your little garden and see far play, we shall feel how—"

The shopman recovered himself from a stunning surprise and burst out:

"Gentlemen, are you drunk? A duel! A duel in my garden. Go home, gentlemen, go home. Why, what did you quarrel about?"

"We quarrelled," said Evan, in the same dead voice, "about religion." The fat shopkeeper rolled about in his chair with enjoyment.

"Well, this is a funny game," he said. "So you want to commit murder on behalf of religion. Well, well my religion is a little respect for humanity, and—"

"Excuse me," cut in Turnbull, suddenly and fiercely, pointing towards the pawnbroker's next door. "Don't you own that shop?"

"Why—er—yes," said Gordon.

"And don't you own that shop?" repeated the secularist, pointing backward to the pornographic bookseller.

"What if I do?"

"Why, then," cried Turnbull, with grating contempt. "I will leave the religion of humanity confidently in your hands; but I am sorry I troubled you about such a thing as honour. Look here, my man. I do believe in humanity. I do believe in liberty. My father died for it under the swords of the Yeomanry. I am going to die for it, if need be, under that sword on your counter. But if there is one sight that makes me doubt it it is your foul fat face. It is hard to believe you were not meant to be ruled like a dog or killed like a cockroach. Don't try your slave's philosophy on me. We are going to fight, and we are going to fight in your garden, with your swords. Be still! Raise your voice above a whisper, and I run you through the body."

Turnbull put the bright point of the sword against the gay waistcoat of the dealer, who stood choking with rage and fear, and an astonishment so crushing as to be greater than either.

"MacIan," said Turnbull, falling almost into the familiar tone of a business partner, "MacIan, tie up this fellow and put a gag in his mouth. Be still, I say, or I kill you where you stand."

The man was too frightened to scream, but he struggled wildly, while Evan MacIan, whose long, lean hands were unusually powerful, tightened some old curtain cords round him, strapped a rope gag in his mouth and rolled him on his back on the floor.

"There's nothing very strong here," said Evan, looking about him. "I'm afraid he'll work through that gag in half an hour or so."

"Yes," said Turnbull, "but one of us will be killed by that time."

"Well, let's hope so," said the Highlander, glancing doubtfully at the squirming thing on the floor.

"And now," said Turnbull, twirling his fiery moustache and fingering his sword, "let us go into the garden. What an exquisite summer evening!"

MacIan said nothing, but lifting his sword from the counter went out into the sun.

The brilliant light ran along the blades, filling the channels of them with white fire; the combatants stuck their swords in the turf and took off their hats, coats, waistcoats, and boots. Evan said a short Latin prayer to himself, during which Turnbull made something of a parade of lighting a cigarette which he flung away the instant after, when he saw MacIan apparently standing ready. Yet MacIan was not exactly ready. He stood staring like a man stricken with a trance.

"What are you staring at?" asked Turnbull. "Do you see the bobbies?"

"I see Jerusalem," said Evan, "all covered with the shields and standards of the Saracens."

"Jerusalem!" said Turnbull, laughing. "Well, we've taken the only inhabitant into captivity."

And he picked up his sword and made it whistle like a boy's wand.

"I beg your pardon," said MacIan, dryly. "Let us begin."

MacIan made a military salute with his weapon, which Turnbull copied or parodied with an impatient contempt; and in the stillness of the garden the swords came together with a clear sound like a bell. The instant the blades touched, each felt them tingle to their very points with a personal vitality, as if they were two naked nerves of steel. Evan had worn throughout an air of apathy, which might have been the stale apathy of one who wants nothing. But it was indeed the more dreadful apathy of one who wants something and will care for nothing else. And this was seen suddenly; for the instant Evan engaged he disengaged and lunged with an infernal violence. His opponent with a desperate promptitude parried and riposted; the parry only just succeeded, the riposte failed. Something big and unbearable seemed to have broken finally out of Evan in that first murderous lunge, leaving him lighter and cooler and quicker upon his feet. He fell to again, fiercely still, but now with a fierce caution. The next moment Turnbull lunged; MacIan seemed to catch the point and throw it away from him, and was thrusting back like a thunderbolt, when a sound paralysed him; another sound beside their ringing weapons. Turnbull, perhaps from an equal astonishment, perhaps from chivalry, stopped also and forebore to send his sword through his exposed enemy.

"What's that?" asked Evan, hoarsely.

A heavy scraping sound, as of a trunk being dragged along a littered floor, came from the dark shop behind them.

"The old Jew has broken one of his strings, and he's crawling about," said Turnbull. "Be quick! We must finish before he gets his gag out."

"Yes, yes, quick! On guard!" cried the Highlander. The blades crossed again with the same sound like song, and the men went to work again with the same white and watchful faces. Evan, in his impatience, went back a little to his wildness. He made windmills, as the French duellists say, and though he was probably a shade the better fencer of the two, he found the other's point pass his face twice so close as almost to graze his cheek. The second time he realized the actual possibility of defeat and pulled himself together under a shock of the sanity of anger. He narrowed, and, so to speak, tightened his operations: he fenced (as the swordsman's boast goes), in a wedding ring; he turned Turnbull's thrusts with a maddening and almost mechanical click, like that of a machine. Whenever Turnbull's sword sought to go over that other mere white streak it seemed to be caught in a complex network of steel. He turned one thrust, turned another, turned another. Then suddenly he went forward at the lunge with his whole living weight. Turnbull leaped back, but Evan lunged and lunged and lunged again like a devilish piston rod or battering ram. And high above all the sound of the struggle there broke into the silent evening a bellowing human voice, nasal, raucous, at the highest pitch of pain. "Help! Help! Police! Murder! Murder!" The gag was broken; and the tongue of terror was loose.

"Keep on!" gasped Turnbull. "One may be killed before they come."

The voice of the screaming shopkeeper was loud enough to drown not only the noise of the swords but all other noises around it, but even through its rending din there seemed to be some other stir or scurry. And Evan, in the very act of thrusting at Turnbull, saw something in his eyes that made him drop his sword. The atheist, with his grey eyes at their widest and wildest, was staring straight over his shoulder at the little archway of shop that opened on the street beyond. And he saw the archway blocked and blackened with strange figures.

"We must bolt, MacIan," he said abruptly. "And there isn't a damned second to lose either. Do as I do."

With a bound he was beside the little cluster of his clothes and boots that lay on the lawn; he snatched them up, without waiting to put any of them on; and tucking his sword under his other arm, went wildly at the wall at the bottom of the garden and swung himself over it. Three seconds after he had alighted in his socks on the other side, MacIan alighted beside him, also in his socks and also carrying clothes and sword in a desperate bundle.

They were in a by-street, very lean and lonely itself, but so close to a crowded thoroughfare that they could see the vague masses of vehicles going by, and could even see an individual hansom cab passing the corner at the instant. Turnbull put his fingers to his mouth like a gutter-snipe and whistled twice. Even as he did so he could hear the loud voices of the neighbours and the police coming down the garden.

The hansom swung sharply and came tearing down the little lane at his call. When the cabman saw his fares, however, two wild-haired men in their shirts and socks with naked swords under their arms, he not unnaturally brought his readiness to a rigid stop and stared suspiciously.

"You talk to him a minute," whispered Turnbull, and stepped back into the shadow of the wall.

"We want you," said MacIan to the cabman, with a superb Scotch drawl of indifference and assurance, "to drive us to St. Pancras Station—verra quick."

"Very sorry, sir," said the cabman, "but I'd like to know it was all right. Might I arst where you come from, sir?"

A second after he spoke MacIan heard a heavy voice on the other side of the wall, saying: "I suppose I'd better get over and look for them. Give me a back."

"Cabby," said MacIan, again assuming the most deliberate and lingering lowland Scotch intonation, "if ye're really verra anxious to ken whar a' come fra', I'll tell ye as a verra great secret. A' come from Scotland. And a'm gaein' to St. Pancras Station. Open the doors, cabby."

The cabman stared, but laughed. The heavy voice behind the wall said: "Now then, a better back this time, Mr. Price." And from the shadow of the wall Turnbull crept out. He had struggled wildly into his coat (leaving his waistcoat on the pavement), and he was with a fierce pale face climbing up the cab behind the cabman. MacIan had no glimmering notion of what he was up to, but an instinct of discipline, inherited from a hundred men of war, made him stick to his own part and trust the other man's.

"Open the doors, cabby," he repeated, with something of the obstinate solemnity of a drunkard, "open the doors. Did ye no hear me say St. Pancras Station?"

The top of a policeman's helmet appeared above the garden wall. The cabman did not see it, but he was still suspicious and began:

"Very sorry, sir, but..." and with that the catlike Turnbull tore him out of his seat and hurled him into the street below, where he lay suddenly stunned.

"Give me his hat," said Turnbull in a silver voice, that the other obeyed like a bugle. "And get inside with the swords."

And just as the red and raging face of a policeman appeared above the wall, Turnbull struck the horse with a terrible cut of the whip and the two went whirling away like a boomerang.

They had spun through seven streets and three or four squares before anything further happened. Then, in the neighbourhood of Maida Vale, the driver opened the trap and talked through it in a manner not wholly common in conversations through that aperture.

"Mr. MacIan," he said shortly and civilly.

"Mr. Turnbull," replied his motionless fare.

"Under circumstances such as those in which we were both recently placed there was no time for anything but very abrupt action. I trust therefore that you have no cause to complain of me if I have deferred until this moment a consultation with you on our present position or future action. Our present position, Mr. MacIan, I imagine that I am under no special necessity of describing. We have broken the law and we are fleeing from its officers. Our future action is a thing about which I myself entertain sufficiently strong views; but I have no right to assume or to anticipate yours, though I may have formed a decided conception of your character and a decided notion of what they will probably be. Still, by every principle of intellectual justice, I am bound to ask you now and seriously whether you wish to continue our interrupted relations."

MacIan leant his white and rather weary face back upon the cushions in order to speak up through the open door.

"Mr. Turnbull," he said, "I have nothing to add to what I have said before. It is strongly borne in upon me that you and I, the sole occupants of this runaway cab, are at this moment the two most important people in London, possibly in Europe. I have been looking at all the streets as we went past, I have been looking at all the shops as we went past, I have been looking at all the churches as we went past. At first, I felt a little dazed with the vastness of it all. I could not understand what it all meant. But now I know exactly what it all means. It means us. This whole civilization is only a dream. You and I are the realities."

"Religious symbolism," said Mr. Turnbull, through the trap, "does not, as you are probably aware, appeal ordinarily to thinkers of the school to which I belong. But in symbolism as you use it in this instance, I must, I think, concede a certain truth. We *must* fight this thing out somewhere; because, as you truly say, we have found each other's reality. We *must* kill each other—or convert each other. I used to think all Christians were hypocrites, and I felt quite mildly towards them really. But I know you are sincere—and my soul is mad against you. In the same way you used, I suppose, to think that all atheists thought atheism would leave them free for immorality—and yet in your heart you tolerated them entirely. Now you *know* that I am an honest man, and you are mad against me, as I am against you. Yes, that's it. You can't be angry with bad men. But a good man in the wrong— why one thirsts for his blood. Yes, you open for me a vista of thought."

"Don't run into anything," said Evan, immovably.

"There's something in that view of yours, too," said Turnbull, and shut down the trap.

They sped on through shining streets that shot by them like arrows. Mr. Turnbull had evidently a great deal of unused practical talent which was unrolling itself in this ridiculous adventure. They had got away with such stunning promptitude that the police chase had in all probability not even properly begun. But in case it had, the amateur cabman chose his dizzy course through London with a strange dexterity. He did not do what would have first occurred to any ordinary outsider desiring to destroy his tracks. He did not cut into by-ways or twist his way through mean streets. His amateur common sense told him that it was precisely the poor street, the side street, that would be likely to remember and report the passing of a hansom cab, like the passing of a royal procession. He kept chiefly to the great roads, so full of hansoms that a wilder pair than they might easily have passed in the press. In one of the quieter streets Evan put on his boots.

Towards the top of Albany Street the singular cabman again opened the trap.

"Mr. MacIan," he said, "I understand that we have now definitely settled that in the conventional language honour is not satisfied. Our action must at least go further than it has gone under recent interrupted conditions. That, I believe, is understood."

"Perfectly," replied the other with his bootlace in his teeth.

"Under those conditions," continued Turnbull, his voice coming through the hole with a slight note of trepidation very unusual with him, "I have a suggestion to make, if that can be called a suggestion, which has probably occurred to you as readily as to me. Until the actual event comes off we are practically in the position if not of comrades, at least of business partners. Until the event comes off, therefore I should suggest that quarrelling would be inconvenient and rather inartistic; while the ordinary exchange of politeness between man and man would be not only elegant but uncommonly practical."

"You are perfectly right," answered MacIan, with his melancholy voice, "in saying that all this has occurred to me. All duellists should behave like gentlemen to each other. But we, by the queerness of our position, are something much more than either duellists or gentlemen. We are, in the oddest and most exact sense of the term, brothers—in arms."

"Mr. MacIan," replied Turnbull, calmly, "no more need be said." And he closed the trap once more.

They had reached Finchley Road before he opened it again.

Then he said, "Mr. MacIan, may I offer you a cigar. It will be a touch of realism."

"Thank you," answered Evan. "You are very kind." And he began to smoke in the cab.

CHAPTER FOUR
A DISCUSSION AT DAWN

The duellists had from their own point of view escaped or conquered the chief powers of the modern world. They had satisfied the magistrate, they had tied the tradesman neck and heels, and they had left the police behind. As far as their own feelings went they had melted into a monstrous sea; they were but the fare and driver of one of the million hansoms that fill London streets. But they had forgotten something; they had forgotten journalism. They had forgotten that there exists in the modern world, perhaps for the first time in history, a class of people whose interest is not that things should happen well or happen badly, should happen successfully or happen unsuccessfully, should happen to the advantage of this party or the advantage of that part, but whose interest simply is that things should happen.

It is the one great weakness of journalism as a picture of our modern existence, that it must be a picture made up entirely of exceptions. We announce on flaring posters that a man has fallen off a scaffolding. We do not announce on flaring posters that a man has not fallen off a scaffolding. Yet this latter fact is fundamentally more exciting, as indicating that that moving tower of terror and mystery, a man, is still abroad upon the earth. That the man has not fallen off a scaffolding is really more sensational; and it is also some thousand times more common. But journalism cannot reasonably be expected thus to insist upon the permanent miracles. Busy editors cannot be expected to put on their posters, "Mr. Wilkinson Still Safe," or "Mr. Jones, of Worthing, Not Dead Yet." They cannot announce the happiness of mankind at all. They cannot describe all the forks that are not stolen, or all the marriages that are not judiciously dissolved. Hence the complete picture they give of life is of necessity fallacious; they can only represent what is unusual. However democratic they may be, they are only concerned with the minority.

The incident of the religious fanatic who broke a window on Ludgate Hill was alone enough to set them up in good copy for the night. But when the same man was brought before a magistrate and defied his enemy to mortal combat in the open court, then the columns would hardly hold the excruciating information, and the headlines were so large that there was hardly room for any of the text. The *Daily Telegraph* headed a column, "A Duel on Divinity," and there was a correspondence afterwards which lasted for months, about whether police magistrates ought to mention religion. The *Daily Mail* in its dull, sensible way, headed the events, "Wanted to fight for the Virgin." Mr. James Douglas, in *The Star*, presuming on his knowledge of philosophical and theological terms, described the Christian's outbreak under the title of "Dualist and Duellist." The *Daily News* inserted a colourless account of the matter, but was pursued and eaten up for some weeks, with letters from outlying ministers, headed "Murder and Mariolatry." But the journalistic temperature was steadily and consistently heated by all these influences; the journalists had tasted blood, prospectively, and were in the mood for more; everything in the matter prepared them for further outbursts of moral indignation. And when a gasping reporter rushed in in the last hours of the evening with the announcement that the two heroes of the Police Court had literally been found fighting in a London back garden, with a shopkeeper bound and gagged in the front of the house, the editors and sub-editors were stricken still as men are by great beatitudes.

The next morning, five or six of the great London dailies burst out simultaneously into great blossoms of eloquent leader-writing. Towards the end all the leaders tended to be the same, but they all began differently. The *Daily*

Telegraph, for instance began, "There will be little difference among our readers or among all truly English and law-abiding men touching the, etc. etc." The *Daily Mail* said, "People must learn, in the modern world, to keep their theological differences to themselves. The fracas, etc. etc." The *Daily News* started, "Nothing could be more inimical to the cause of true religion than, etc. etc." The *Times* began with something about Celtic disturbances of the equilibrium of Empire, and the *Daily Express* distinguished itself splendidly by omitting altogether so controversial a matter and substituting a leader about goloshes.

And the morning after that, the editors and the newspapers were in such a state, that, as the phrase is, there was no holding them. Whatever secret and elvish thing it is that broods over editors and suddenly turns their brains, that thing had seized on the story of the broken glass and the duel in the garden. It became monstrous and omnipresent, as do in our time the unimportant doings of the sect of the Agapemonites, or as did at an earlier time the dreary dishonesties of the Rhodesian financiers. Questions were asked about it, and even answered, in the House of Commons. The Government was solemnly denounced in the papers for not having done something, nobody knew what, to prevent the window being broken. An enormous subscription was started to reimburse Mr. Gordon, the man who had been gagged in the shop. Mr. MacIan, one of the combatants, became for some mysterious reason, singly and hugely popular as a comic figure in the comic papers and on the stage of the music hall. He was always represented (in defiance of fact), with red whiskers, and a very red nose, and in full Highland costume. And a song, consisting of an unimaginable number of verses, in which his name was rhymed with flat iron, the British Lion, sly 'un, dandelion, Spion (With Kop in the next line), was sung to crowded houses every night. The papers developed a devouring thirst for the capture of the fugitives; and when they had not been caught for forty-eight hours, they suddenly turned the whole matter into a detective mystery. Letters under the heading, "Where are They," poured in to every paper, with every conceivable kind of explanation, running them to earth in the Monument, the Twopenny Tube, Epping Forest, Westminster Abbey, rolled up in carpets at Shoolbreds, locked up in safes in Chancery Lane. Yes, the papers were very interesting, and Mr. Turnbull unrolled a whole bundle of them for the amusement of Mr. MacIan as they sat on a high common to the north of London, in the coming of the white dawn.

The darkness in the east had been broken with a bar of grey; the bar of grey was split with a sword of silver and morning lifted itself laboriously over London. From the spot where Turnbull and MacIan were sitting on one of the barren steeps behind Hampstead, they could see the whole of London shaping itself vaguely and largely in the grey and growing light, until the white sun stood over it and it lay at their feet, the splendid monstrosity that it is. Its bewildering squares and parallelograms were compact and perfect as a Chinese puzzle; an enormous hieroglyphic which man must decipher or die. There fell upon both of them, but upon Turnbull more than the other, because he know more what the scene signified, that quite indescribable sense as of a sublime and passionate and heart-moving futility, which is never evoked by deserts or dead men or men neglected and barbarous, which can only be invoked by the sight of the enormous genius of man applied to anything other than the best. Turnbull, the old idealistic democrat, had so often reviled the democracy and reviled them justly for their supineness, their snobbishness, their evil reverence for idle things. He was right enough; for our democracy has only one great fault; it is not democratic. And after denouncing so justly average modern men for so many years as sophists and as slaves, he looked down from an empty slope in Hampstead and saw what gods they are. Their achievement seemed all the more heroic and divine, because it seemed doubtful whether it was worth doing at all. There seemed to be something greater than mere accuracy in making such a mistake as London. And what was to be the end of it all? what was to be the ultimate transformation of this common and incredible London man, this workman on a tram in Battersea, his clerk on an omnibus in Cheapside? Turnbull, as he stared drearily, murmured to himself the words of the old atheistic and revolutionary Swinburne who had intoxicated his youth:

> *"And still we ask if God or man*
> *Can loosen thee Lazarus;*
> *Bid thee rise up republican,*
> *And save thyself and all of us.*
> *But no disciple's tongue can say*
> *If thou can'st take our sins away."*

Turnbull shivered slightly as if behind the earthly morning he felt the evening of the world, the sunset of so many hopes. Those words were from "Songs before Sunrise". But Turnbull's songs at their best were songs after sunrise, and sunrise had been no such great thing after all. Turnbull shivered again in the sharp morning air. MacIan was also gazing with his face towards the city, but there was that about his blind and mystical stare that told one, so to speak, that his eyes were turned inwards. When Turnbull said something to him about London, they seemed to move as at a summons and come out like two householders coming out into their doorways.

"Yes," he said, with a sort of stupidity. "It's a very big place."

There was a somewhat unmeaning silence, and then MacIan said again:

"It's a very big place. When I first came into it I was frightened of it. Frightened exactly as one would be frightened at the sight of a man forty feet high. I am used to big things where I come from, big mountains that seem to fill God's infinity, and the big sea that goes to the end of the world. But then these things are all shapeless and confused things, not made in any familiar form. But to see the plain, square, human things as large as that, houses so large and streets so large, and the town itself so large, was like having screwed some devil's magnifying glass into one's eye. It was like seeing a porridge bowl as big as a house, or a mouse-trap made to catch elephants."

"Like the land of the Brobdingnagians," said Turnbull, smiling.

"Oh! Where is that?" said MacIan.

Turnbull said bitterly, "In a book," and the silence fell suddenly between them again.

They were sitting in a sort of litter on the hillside; all the things they had hurriedly collected, in various places, for their flight, were strewn indiscriminately round them. The two swords with which they had lately sought each other's lives were flung down on the grass at random, like two idle walking-sticks. Some provisions they had bought last night, at a low public house, in case of undefined contingencies, were tossed about like the materials of an ordinary picnic, here a basket of chocolate, and there a bottle of wine. And to add to the disorder finally, there were strewn on top of everything, the most disorderly of modern things, newspapers, and more newspapers, and yet again newspapers, the ministers of the modern anarchy. Turnbull picked up one of them drearily, and took out a pipe.

"There's a lot about us," he said. "Do you mind if I light up?"

"Why should I mind?" asked MacIan.

Turnbull eyed with a certain studious interest, the man who did not understand any of the verbal courtesies; he lit his pipe and blew great clouds out of it.

"Yes," he resumed. "The matter on which you and I are engaged is at this moment really the best copy in England. I am a journalist, and I know. For the first time, perhaps, for many generations, the English are really more angry about a wrong thing done in England than they are about a wrong thing done in France."

"It is not a wrong thing," said MacIan.

Turnbull laughed. "You seem unable to understand the ordinary use of the human language. If I did not suspect that you were a genius, I should certainly know you were a blockhead. I fancy we had better be getting along and collecting our baggage."

And he jumped up and began shoving the luggage into his pockets, or strapping it on to his back. As he thrust a tin of canned meat, anyhow, into his bursting side pocket, he said casually:

"I only meant that you and I are the most prominent people in the English papers."

"Well, what did you expect?" asked MacIan, opening his great grave blue eyes.

"The papers are full of us," said Turnbull, stooping to pick up one of the swords.

MacIan stooped and picked up the other.

"Yes," he said, in his simple way. "I have read what they have to say. But they don't seem to understand the point."

"The point of what?" asked Turnbull.

"The point of the sword," said MacIan, violently, and planted the steel point in the soil like a man planting a tree.

"That is a point," said Turnbull, grimly, "that we will discuss later. Come along."

Turnbull tied the last tin of biscuits desperately to himself with string; and then spoke, like a diver girt for plunging, short and sharp.

"Now, Mr. MacIan, you must listen to me. You must listen to me, not merely because I know the country, which you might learn by looking at a map, but because I know the people of the country, whom you could not know by living here thirty years. That infernal city down there is awake; and it is awake against us. All those endless rows of windows and windows are all eyes staring at us. All those forests of chimneys are fingers pointing at us, as we stand here on the hillside. This thing has caught on. For the next six mortal months they will think of nothing but us, as for six mortal months they thought of nothing but the Dreyfus case. Oh, I know it's funny. They let starving children, who don't want to die, drop by the score without looking round. But because two gentlemen, from private feelings of delicacy, do want to die, they will mobilize the army and navy to prevent them. For half a year or more, you and I, Mr. MacIan, will be an obstacle to every reform in the British Empire. We shall prevent the Chinese being sent out of the Transvaal and the blocks being stopped in the Strand. We shall be the conversational substitute when anyone recommends Home Rule, or complains of sky signs. Therefore, do not imagine, in your innocence, that we have only to melt away among those English hills as a Highland cateran might into your god-forsaken Highland mountains. We must be eternally on our guard; we must live the hunted life of two distinguished criminals. We must expect to be recognized as much as if we were Napoleon escaping from Elba. We must be prepared for our descriptions being sent to every tiny village, and for our faces being recognized by every ambitious policeman. We must often sleep under the stars as if we were in Africa. Last and most important we must not dream of effecting our—our final settlement, which will be a thing as famous as the Phoenix Park murders, unless we have made real and precise arrangements for our isolation—I will not say our safety. We must not, in short, fight until we have thrown them off our scent, if only for a moment. For, take my word for it, Mr. MacIan, if the British Public once catches us up, the British Public will prevent the duel, if it is only by locking us both up in asylums for the rest of our days."

MacIan was looking at the horizon with a rather misty look.

"I am not at all surprised," he said, "at the world being against us. It makes me feel I was right to——"

"Yes?" said Turnbull.

"To smash your window," said MacIan. "I have woken up the world."

"Very well, then," said Turnbull, stolidly. "Let us look at a few final facts. Beyond that hill there is comparatively clear country. Fortunately, I know the part well, and if you will follow me exactly, and, when necessary, on your stomach, we may be able to get ten miles out of London, literally without meeting anyone at all, which will be the best possible beginning, at any rate. We have provisions for at least two days and two nights, three days if we do it carefully. We may be able to get fifty or sixty miles away without even walking into an inn door. I have the biscuits and the tinned meat, and the milk. You have the chocolate, I think? And the brandy?"

"Yes," said MacIan, like a soldier taking orders.

"Very well, then, come on. March. We turn under that third bush and so down into the valley." And he set off ahead at a swinging walk.

Then he stopped suddenly; for he realized that the other was not following. Evan MacIan was leaning on his sword with a lowering face, like a man suddenly smitten still with doubt.

"What on earth is the matter?" asked Turnbull, staring in some anger.

Evan made no reply.

"What the deuce is the matter with you?" demanded the leader, again, his face slowly growing as red as his beard; then he said, suddenly, and in a more human voice, "Are you in pain, MacIan?"

"Yes," replied the Highlander, without lifting his face.

"Take some brandy," cried Turnbull, walking forward hurriedly towards him. "You've got it."

"It's not in the body," said MacIan, in his dull, strange way. "The pain has come into my mind. A very dreadful thing has just come into my thoughts."

"What the devil are you talking about?" asked Turnbull.

MacIan broke out with a queer and living voice.

"We must fight now, Turnbull. We must fight now. A frightful thing has come upon me, and I know it must be now and here. I must kill you here," he cried, with a sort of tearful rage impossible to describe. "Here, here, upon this blessed grass."

"Why, you idiot," began Turnbull.

"The hour has come—the black hour God meant for it. Quick, it will soon be gone. Quick!"

And he flung the scabbard from him furiously, and stood with the sunlight sparkling along his sword.

"You confounded fool," repeated Turnbull. "Put that thing up again, you ass; people will come out of that house at the first clash of the steel."

"One of us will be dead before they come," said the other, hoarsely, "for this is the hour God meant."

"Well, I never thought much of God," said the editor of *The Atheist*, losing all patience. "And I think less now. Never mind what God meant. Kindly enlighten my pagan darkness as to what the devil *you* mean."

"The hour will soon be gone. In a moment it will be gone," said the madman. "It is now, now, now that I must nail your blaspheming body to the earth— now, now that I must avenge Our Lady on her vile slanderer. Now or never. For the dreadful thought is in my mind."

"And what thought," asked Turnbull, with frantic composure, "occupies what you call your mind?"

"I must kill you now," said the fanatic, "because——"

"Well, because," said Turnbull, patiently.

"Because I have begun to like you."

Turnbull's face had a sudden spasm in the sunlight, a change so instantaneous that it left no trace behind it; and his features seemed still carved into a cold stare. But when he spoke again he seemed like a man who was placidly pretending to misunderstand something that he understood perfectly well.

"Your affection expresses itself in an abrupt form," he began, but MacIan broke the brittle and frivolous speech to pieces with a violent voice. "Do not trouble to talk like that," he said. "You know what I mean as well as I know it. Come on and fight, I say. Perhaps you are feeling just as I do."

Turnbull's face flinched again in the fierce sunlight, but his attitude kept its contemptuous ease.

"Your Celtic mind really goes too fast for me," he said; "let me be permitted in my heavy Lowland way to understand this new development. My dear Mr. MacIan, what do you really mean?"

MacIan still kept the shining sword-point towards the other's breast.

"You know what I mean. You mean the same yourself. We must fight now or else——"

"Or else?" repeated Turnbull, staring at him with an almost blinding gravity.

"Or else we may not want to fight at all," answered Evan, and the end of his speech was like a despairing cry.

Turnbull took out his own sword suddenly as if to engage; then planting it point downwards for a moment, he said, "Before we begin, may I ask you a question?"

MacIan bowed patiently, but with burning eyes.

"You said, just now," continued Turnbull, presently, "that if we did not fight now, we might not want to fight at all. How would you feel about the matter if we came not to want to fight at all?"

"I should feel," answered the other, "just as I should feel if you had drawn your sword, and I had run away from it. I should feel that because I had been weak, justice had not been done."

"Justice," answered Turnbull, with a thoughtful smile, "but we are talking about your feelings. And what do you mean by justice, apart from your feelings?"

MacIan made a gesture of weary recognition! "Oh, Nominalism," he said, with a sort of sigh, "we had all that out in the twelfth century."

"I wish we could have it out now," replied the other, firmly. "Do you really mean that if you came to think me right, you would be certainly wrong?"

"If I had a blow on the back of my head, I might come to think you a green elephant," answered MacIan, "but have I not the right to say now, that if I thought that I should think wrong?"

"Then you are quite certain that it would be wrong to like me?" asked Turnbull, with a slight smile.

"No," said Evan, thoughtfully, "I do not say that. It may not be the devil, it may be some part of God I am not meant to know. But I had a work to do, and it is making the work difficult."

"And I suppose," said the atheist, quite gently, "that you and I know all about which part of God we ought to know."

MacIan burst out like a man driven back and explaining everything.

"The Church is not a thing like the Athenaeum Club," he cried. "If the Athenaeum Club lost all its members, the Athenaeum Club would dissolve and cease to exist. But when we belong to the Church we belong to something which is outside all of us; which is outside everything you talk about, outside the Cardinals and the Pope. They belong to it, but it does not belong to them. If we all fell dead suddenly, the Church would still somehow exist in God. Confound it all, don't you see that I am more sure of its existence than I am of my own existence? And yet you ask me to trust my temperament, my own temperament, which can be turned upside down by two bottles of claret or an attack of the jaundice. You ask me to trust that when it softens towards you and not to trust the thing which I believe to be outside myself and more real than the blood in my body."

"Stop a moment," said Turnbull, in the same easy tone, "Even in the very act of saying that you believe this or that, you imply that there is a part of yourself that you trust even if there are many parts which you mistrust. If it is only you that like me, surely, also, it is only you that believe in the Catholic Church."

Evan remained in an unmoved and grave attitude. "There is a part of me which is divine," he answered, "a part that can be trusted, but there are also affections which are entirely animal and idle."

"And you are quite certain, I suppose," continued Turnbull, "that if even you esteem me the esteem would be wholly animal and idle?" For the first time

MacIan started as if he had not expected the thing that was said to him. At last he said:

"Whatever in earth or heaven it is that has joined us two together, it seems to be something which makes it impossible to lie. No, I do not think that the movement in me towards you was...was that surface sort of thing. It may have been something deeper...something strange. I cannot understand the thing at all. But understand this and understand it thoroughly, if I loved you my love might be divine. No, it is not some trifle that we are fighting about. It is not some superstition or some symbol. When you wrote those words about Our Lady, you were in that act a wicked man doing a wicked thing. If I hate you it is because you have hated goodness. And if I like you...it is because you are good."

Turnbull's face wore an indecipherable expression.

"Well, shall we fight now?" he said.

"Yes," said MacIan, with a sudden contraction of his black brows, "yes, it must be now."

The bright swords crossed, and the first touch of them, travelling down blade and arm, told each combatant that the heart of the other was awakened. It was not in that way that the swords rang together when they had rushed on each other in the little garden behind the dealer's shop.

There was a pause, and then MacIan made a movement as if to thrust, and almost at the same moment Turnbull suddenly and calmly dropped his sword. Evan stared round in an unusual bewilderment, and then realized that a large man in pale clothes and a Panama hat was strolling serenely towards them.

CHAPTER FIVE
THE PEACEMAKER

When the combatants, with crossed swords, became suddenly conscious of a third party, they each made the same movement. It was as quick as the snap of a pistol, and they altered it instantaneously and recovered their original pose, but they had both made it, they had both seen it, and they both knew what it was. It was not a movement of anger at being interrupted. Say or think what they would, it was a movement of relief. A force within them, and yet quite beyond them, seemed slowly and pitilessly washing away the adamant of their oath. As mistaken lovers might watch the inevitable sunset of first love, these men watched the sunset of their first hatred.

Their hearts were growing weaker and weaker against each other. When their weapons rang and riposted in the little London garden, they could have been very certain that if a third party had interrupted them something at least would have happened. They would have killed each other or they would have killed him. But now nothing could undo or deny that flash of fact, that for a second they had been glad to be interrupted. Some new and strange thing was rising higher and higher in their hearts like a high sea at night. It was something that seemed all the more merciless, because it might turn out an enormous mercy. Was there, perhaps, some such fatalism in friendship as all lovers talk about in love? Did God make men love each other against their will?

"I'm sure you'll excuse my speaking to you," said the stranger, in a voice at once eager and deprecating.

The voice was too polite for good manners. It was incongruous with the eccentric spectacle of the duellists which ought to have startled a sane and free man. It was also incongruous with the full and healthy, though rather loose physique of the man who spoke. At the first glance he looked a fine animal, with curling gold beard and hair, and blue eyes, unusually bright. It was only at the second glance that the mind felt a sudden and perhaps unmeaning irritation at the way in which the gold beard retreated backwards into the waistcoat, and the way in which the finely shaped nose went forward as if smelling its way. And it was only, perhaps, at the hundredth glance that the bright blue eyes, which normally before and after the instant seemed brilliant with intelligence, seemed as it were to be brilliant with idiocy. He was a heavy, healthy-looking man, who looked all the larger because of the loose, light coloured clothes that he wore, and that had in their extreme lightness and looseness, almost a touch of the tropics. But a closer examination of his attire would have shown that even in the tropics it would have been unique; but it was all woven according to some hygienic texture which no human being had ever heard of before, and which was absolutely necessary even for a day's health. He wore a huge broad-brimmed hat, equally hygienic, very much at the back of his head, and his voice coming out of so heavy and hearty a type of man was, as I have said, startlingly shrill and deferential.

"I'm sure you'll excuse my speaking to you," he said. "Now, I wonder if you are in some little difficulty which, after all, we could settle very comfortably together? Now, you don't mind my saying this, do you?"

The face of both combatants remained somewhat solid under this appeal. But the stranger, probably taking their silence for a gathering shame, continued with a kind of gaiety:

"So you are the young men I have read about in the papers. Well, of course, when one is young, one is rather romantic. Do you know what I always say to young people?"

A blank silence followed this gay inquiry. Then Turnbull said in a colourless voice:

"As I was forty-seven last birthday, I probably came into the world too soon for the experience."

"Very good, very good," said the friendly person. "Dry Scotch humour.

Dry Scotch humour. Well now. I understand that you two people want to fight a duel. I suppose you aren't much up in the modern world. We've quite outgrown duelling, you know. In fact, Tolstoy tells us that we shall soon outgrow war, which he says is simply a duel between nations. A duel between nations. But there is no doubt about our having outgrown duelling."

Waiting for some effect upon his wooden auditors, the stranger stood beaming for a moment and then resumed:

"Now, they tell me in the newspapers that you are really wanting to fight about something connected with Roman Catholicism. Now, do you know what I always say to Roman Catholics?"

"No," said Turnbull, heavily. "Do *they*?" It seemed to be a characteristic of the hearty, hygienic gentleman that he always forgot the speech he had made the moment before. Without enlarging further on the fixed form of his appeal to the Church of Rome, he laughed cordially at Turnbull's answer; then his wandering blue eyes caught the sunlight on the swords, and he assumed a good-humoured gravity.

"But you know this is a serious matter," he said, eyeing Turnbull and MacIan, as if they had just been keeping the table in a roar with their frivolities. "I am sure that if I appealed to your higher natures...your higher natures. Every man has a higher nature and a lower nature. Now, let us put the matter very plainly, and without any romantic nonsense about honour or anything of that sort. Is not bloodshed a great sin?"

"No," said MacIan, speaking for the first time.

"Well, really, really!" said the peacemaker.

"Murder is a sin," said the immovable Highlander. "There is no sin of bloodshed."

"Well, we won't quarrel about a word," said the other, pleasantly.

"Why on earth not?" said MacIan, with a sudden asperity. "Why shouldn't we quarrel about a word? What is the good of words if they aren't important enough to quarrel over? Why do we choose one word more than another if there isn't any difference between them? If you called a woman a chimpanzee instead of an angel, wouldn't there be a quarrel about a word? If you're not going to argue about words, what are you going to argue about? Are you going to convey your meaning to me by moving your ears? The Church and the heresies always used to fight about words, because they are the only things worth fighting about. I say that murder is a sin, and bloodshed is not, and that there is as much difference between those words as there is between the word 'yes' and the word 'no'; or rather more difference, for 'yes' and 'no', at least, belong to the same category. Murder is a spiritual incident. Bloodshed is a physical incident. A surgeon commits bloodshed."

"Ah, you're a casuist!" said the large man, wagging his head. "Now, do you know what I always say to casuists...?"

MacIan made a violent gesture; and Turnbull broke into open laughter. The peacemaker did not seem to be in the least annoyed, but continued in unabated enjoyment.

"Well, well," he said, "let us get back to the point. Now Tolstoy has shown that force is no remedy; so you see the position in which I am placed. I am doing my best to stop what I'm sure you won't mind my calling this really useless violence, this really quite wrong violence of yours. But it's against my principles to call in the police against you, because the police are still on a lower moral plane, so to speak, because, in short, the police undoubtedly sometimes employ force. Tolstoy has shown that violence merely breeds violence in the person towards whom it is used, whereas Love, on the other hand, breeds Love. So you see how I am placed. I am reduced to use Love in order to stop you. I am obliged to use Love."

He gave to the word an indescribable sound of something hard and heavy, as if he were saying "boots". Turnbull suddenly gripped his sword and said, shortly, "I see how you are placed quite well, sir. You will not call the police. Mr. MacIan, shall we engage?" MacIan plucked his sword out of the grass.

"I must and will stop this shocking crime," cried the Tolstoian, crimson in the face. "It is against all modern ideas. It is against the principle of love. How you, sir, who pretend to be a Christian..."

MacIan turned upon him with a white face and bitter lip. "Sir," he said, "talk about the principle of love as much as you like. You seem to me colder than a lump of stone; but I am willing to believe that you may at some time have loved a cat, or a dog, or a child. When you were a baby, I suppose you loved your mother. Talk about love, then, till the world is sick of the word. But don't you talk about Christianity. Don't you dare to say one word, white or black, about it. Christianity is, as far as you are concerned, a horrible mystery. Keep clear of it, keep silent upon it, as you would upon an abomination. It is a thing that has made men slay and torture each other; and you will never know why. It is a thing that has made men do evil that good might come; and you will never understand the evil, let alone the good. Christianity is a thing that could only make you vomit, till you are other than you are. I would not justify it to you even if I could. Hate it, in God's name, as Turnbull does, who is a man. It is a monstrous thing, for which men die. And if you will stand here and talk about love for another ten minutes it is very probable that you will see a man die for it."

And he fell on guard. Turnbull was busy settling something loose in his elaborate hilt, and the pause was broken by the stranger.

"Suppose I call the police?" he said, with a heated face.

"And deny your most sacred dogma," said MacIan.

"Dogma!" cried the man, in a sort of dismay. "Oh, we have no *dogmas*, you know!"

There was another silence, and he said again, airily:

"You know, I think, there's something in what Shaw teaches about no moral principles being quite fixed. Have you ever read *The Quintessence of Ibsenism*? Of course he went very wrong over the war."

Turnbull, with a bent, flushed face, was tying up the loose piece of the pommel with string. With the string in his teeth, he said, "Oh, make up your damned mind and clear out!"

"It's a serious thing," said the philosopher, shaking his head. "I must be alone and consider which is the higher point of view. I rather feel that in a case so extreme as this..." and he went slowly away. As he disappeared among the trees, they heard him murmuring in a sing-song voice, "New occasions teach new duties," out of a poem by James Russell Lowell.

"Ah," said MacIan, drawing a deep breath. "Don't you believe in prayer now? I prayed for an angel."

"An hour ago," said the Highlander, in his heavy meditative voice, "I felt the devil weakening my heart and my oath against you, and I prayed that God would send an angel to my aid."

"Well?" inquired the other, finishing his mending and wrapping the rest of the string round his hand to get a firmer grip.

"Well?"

"Well, that man was an angel," said MacIan.

"I didn't know they were as bad as that," answered Turnbull.

"We know that devils sometimes quote Scripture and counterfeit good," replied the mystic. "Why should not angels sometimes come to show us the black abyss of evil on whose brink we stand. If that man had not tried to stop us...I might...I might have stopped."

"I know what you mean," said Turnbull, grimly.

"But then he came," broke out MacIan, "and my soul said to me: 'Give up fighting, and you will become like That. Give up vows and dogmas, and fixed things, and you may grow like That. You may learn, also, that fog of false philosophy. You may grow fond of that mire of crawling, cowardly morals, and you may come to think a blow bad, because it hurts, and not because it humiliates. You may come to think murder wrong, because it is violent, and not because it is unjust. Oh, you blasphemer of the good, an hour ago I almost loved you! But do not fear for me now. I have heard the word Love pronounced in *his* intonation; and I know exactly what it means. On guard!'"

The swords caught on each other with a dreadful clang and jar, full of the old energy and hate; and at once plunged and replunged. Once more each man's heart had become the magnet of a mad sword. Suddenly, furious as they were, they were frozen for a moment motionless.

"What noise is that?" asked the Highlander, hoarsely.

"I think I know," replied Turnbull.

"What?... What?" cried the other.

"The student of Shaw and Tolstoy has made up his remarkable mind," said Turnbull, quietly. "The police are coming up the hill."

CHAPTER SIX
THE OTHER PHILOSOPHER

Between high hedges in Hertfordshire, hedges so high as to create a kind of grove, two men were running. They did not run in a scampering or feverish manner, but in the steady swing of the pendulum. Across the great plains and uplands to the right and left of the lane, a long tide of sunset light rolled like a sea of ruby, lighting up the long terraces of the hills and picking out the few windows of the scattered hamlets in startling blood-red sparks. But the lane was cut deep in the hill and remained in an abrupt shadow. The two men running in it had an impression not uncommonly experienced between those wild green English walls; a sense of being led between the walls of a maze.

Though their pace was steady it was vigorous; their faces were heated and their eyes fixed and bright. There was, indeed, something a little mad in the contrast between the evening's stillness over the empty country-side, and these two figures fleeing wildly from nothing. They had the look of two lunatics, possibly they were.

"Are you all right?" said Turnbull, with civility. "Can you keep this up?"

"Quite easily, thank you," replied MacIan. "I run very well."

"Is that a qualification in a family of warriors?" asked Turnbull.

"Undoubtedly. Rapid movement is essential," answered MacIan, who never saw a joke in his life.

Turnbull broke out into a short laugh, and silence fell between them, the panting silence of runners.

Then MacIan said: "We run better than any of those policemen. They are too fat. Why do you make your policemen so fat?"

"I didn't do much towards making them fat myself," replied Turnbull, genially, "but I flatter myself that I am now doing something towards making them thin. You'll see they will be as lean as rakes by the time they catch us. They will look like your friend, Cardinal Manning."

"But they won't catch us," said MacIan, in his literal way.

"No, we beat them in the great military art of running away," returned the other. "They won't catch us unless——"

MacIan turned his long equine face inquiringly. "Unless what?" he said, for Turnbull had gone silent suddenly, and seemed to be listening intently as he ran as a horse does with his ears turned back.

"Unless what?" repeated the Highlander.

"Unless they do—what they have done. Listen." MacIan slackened his trot, and turned his head to the trail they had left behind them. Across two or three billows of the up and down lane came along the ground the unmistakable throbbing of horses' hoofs.

"They have put the mounted police on us," said Turnbull, shortly. "Good Lord, one would think we were a Revolution."

"So we are," said MacIan calmly. "What shall we do? Shall we turn on them with our points?"

"It may come to that," answered Turnbull, "though if it does, I reckon that will be the last act. We must put it off if we can." And he stared and peered about him between the bushes. "If we could hide somewhere the beasts might go by us," he said. "The police have their faults, but thank God they're inefficient. Why, here's the very thing. Be quick and quiet. Follow me."

He suddenly swung himself up the high bank on one side of the lane. It was almost as high and smooth as a wall, and on the top of it the black hedge stood out over them as an angle, almost like a thatched roof of the lane. And the burning evening sky looked down at them through the tangle with red eyes as of an army of goblins.

Turnbull hoisted himself up and broke the hedge with his body. As his head and shoulders rose above it they turned to flame in the full glow as if lit up by an immense firelight. His red hair and beard looked almost scarlet, and his pale face as bright as a boy's. Something violent, something that was at once love and hatred, surged in the strange heart of the Gael below him. He had an unutterable sense of epic importance, as if he were somehow lifting all humanity into a prouder and more passionate region of the air. As he swung himself up also into the evening light he felt as if he were rising on enormous wings.

Legends of the morning of the world which he had heard in childhood or read in youth came back upon him in a cloudy splendour, purple tales of wrath and friendship, like Roland and Oliver, or Balin and Balan, reminding him of emotional entanglements. Men who had loved each other and then fought each other; men who had fought each other and then loved each other, together made a mixed but monstrous sense of momentousness. The crimson seas of the sunset seemed to him like a bursting out of some sacred blood, as if the heart of the world had broken.

Turnbull was wholly unaffected by any written or spoken poetry; his was a powerful and prosaic mind. But even upon him there came for the moment something out of the earth and the passionate ends of the sky. The only evidence was in his voice, which was still practical but a shade more quiet.

"Do you see that summer-house-looking thing over there?" he asked shortly. "That will do for us very well."

Keeping himself free from the tangle of the hedge he strolled across a triangle of obscure kitchen garden, and approached a dismal shed or lodge a yard or two beyond it. It was a weather-stained hut of grey wood, which with all its desolation retained a tag or two of trivial ornament, which suggested that the thing had once been a sort of summer-house, and the place probably a sort of garden.

"That is quite invisible from the road," said Turnbull, as he entered it, "and it will cover us up for the night."

MacIan looked at him gravely for a few moments. "Sir," he said, "I ought to say something to you. I ought to say——"

"Hush," said Turnbull, suddenly lifting his hand; "be still, man."

In the sudden silence, the drumming of the distant horses grew louder and louder with inconceivable rapidity, and the cavalcade of police rushed by below them in the lane, almost with the roar and rattle of an express train.

"I ought to tell you," continued MacIan, still staring stolidly at the other, "that you are a great chief, and it is good to go to war behind you."

Turnbull said nothing, but turned and looked out of the foolish lattice of the little windows, then he said, "We must have food and sleep first."

When the last echo of their eluded pursuers had died in the distant uplands, Turnbull began to unpack the provisions with the easy air of a man at a picnic. He had just laid out the last items, put a bottle of wine on the floor, and a tin of salmon on the window-ledge, when the bottomless silence of that forgotten place was broken. And it was broken by three heavy blows of a stick delivered upon the door.

Turnbull looked up in the act of opening a tin and stared silently at his companion. MacIan's long, lean mouth had shut hard.

"Who the devil can that be?" said Turnbull.

"God knows," said the other. "It might be God."

Again the sound of the wooden stick reverberated on the wooden door. It was a curious sound and on consideration did not resemble the ordinary effects of knocking on a door for admittance. It was rather as if the point of a stick were plunged again and again at the panels in an absurd attempt to make a hole in them.

A wild look sprang into MacIan's eyes and he got up half stupidly, with a kind of stagger, put his hand out and caught one of the swords. "Let us fight at once," he cried, "it is the end of the world."

"You're overdone, MacIan," said Turnbull, putting him on one side. "It's only someone playing the goat. Let me open the door."

But he also picked up a sword as he stepped to open it.

He paused one moment with his hand on the handle and then flung the door open. Almost as he did so the ferrule of an ordinary bamboo cane came at his eyes, so that he had actually to parry it with the naked weapon in his hands. As the two touched, the point of the stick was dropped very abruptly, and the man with the stick stepped hurriedly back.

Against the heraldic background of sprawling crimson and gold offered him by the expiring sunset, the figure of the man with the stick showed at first merely black and fantastic. He was a small man with two wisps of long hair that curled up on each side, and seen in silhouette, looked like horns. He had a bow tie so big that the two ends showed on each side of his neck like unnatural stunted wings. He had his long black cane still tilted in his hand like a fencing foil and half presented at the open door. His large straw hat had fallen behind him as he leapt backwards.

"With reference to your suggestion, MacIan," said Turnbull, placidly, "I think it looks more like the Devil."

"Who on earth are you?" cried the stranger in a high shrill voice, brandishing his cane defensively.

"Let me see," said Turnbull, looking round to MacIan with the same blandness. "Who are we?"

"Come out," screamed the little man with the stick.

"Certainly," said Turnbull, and went outside with the sword, MacIan following.

Seen more fully, with the evening light on his face, the strange man looked a little less like a goblin. He wore a square pale-grey jacket suit, on which the grey butterfly tie was the only indisputable touch of affectation. Against the great sunset his figure had looked merely small: seen in a more equal light it looked tolerably compact and shapely. His reddish-brown hair, combed into two great curls, looked like the long, slow curling hair of the women in some pre-Raphaelite pictures. But within this feminine frame of hair his face was unexpectedly impudent, like a monkey's.

"What are you doing here?" he said, in a sharp small voice.

"Well," said MacIan, in his grave childish way, "what are *you* doing here?"

"I," said the man, indignantly, "I'm in my own garden."

"Oh," said MacIan, simply, "I apologize."

Turnbull was coolly curling his red moustache, and the stranger stared from one to the other, temporarily stunned by their innocent assurance.

"But, may I ask," he said at last, "what the devil you are doing in my summer-house?"

"Certainly," said MacIan. "We were just going to fight."

"To fight!" repeated the man.

"We had better tell this gentleman the whole business," broke in Turnbull. Then turning to the stranger he said firmly, "I am sorry, sir, but we have something to do that must be done. And I may as well tell you at the beginning and to avoid waste of time or language, that we cannot admit any interference."

"We were just going to take some slight refreshment when you interrupted us..."

The little man had a dawning expression of understanding and stooped and picked up the unused bottle of wine, eyeing it curiously.

Turnbull continued:

"But that refreshment was preparatory to something which I fear you will find less comprehensible, but on which our minds are entirely fixed, sir. We are forced to fight a duel. We are forced by honour and an internal intellectual need. Do not, for your own sake, attempt to stop us. I know all the excellent and ethical things that you will want to say to us. I know all about the essential requirements of civil order: I have written leading articles about them all my life. I know all about the sacredness of human life; I have bored all my friends with it. Try and understand our position. This man and I are alone in the modern world in that we think that God is essentially important. I think He does not exist; that is where the importance comes in for me. But this man thinks that He does exist, and thinking that very properly thinks Him more important than anything else. Now we wish to make a great demonstration and assertion—something that will set the world on fire like the first Christian persecutions. If you like, we are attempting a mutual martyrdom. The papers have posted up every town against us. Scotland Yard has fortified every police station with our enemies; we are driven therefore to the edge of a lonely lane, and indirectly to taking liberties with your summer-house in order to arrange our..."

"Stop!" roared the little man in the butterfly necktie. "Put me out of my intellectual misery. Are you really the two tomfools I have read of in all the papers? Are you the two people who wanted to spit each other in the Police Court? Are you? Are you?"

"Yes," said MacIan, "it began in a Police Court."

The little man slung the bottle of wine twenty yards away like a stone.

"Come up to my place," he said. "I've got better stuff than that. I've got the best Beaune within fifty miles of here. Come up. You're the very men I wanted to see."

Even Turnbull, with his typical invulnerability, was a little taken aback by this boisterous and almost brutal hospitality.

"Why...sir..." he began.

"Come up! Come in!" howled the little man, dancing with delight. "I'll give you a dinner. I'll give you a bed! I'll give you a green smooth lawn and your choice of swords and pistols. Why, you fools, I adore fighting! It's the only good thing in God's world! I've walked about these damned fields and longed to see somebody cut up and killed and the blood running. Ha! Ha!"

And he made sudden lunges with his stick at the trunk of a neighbouring tree so that the ferrule made fierce prints and punctures in the bark.

"Excuse me," said MacIan suddenly with the wide-eyed curiosity of a child, "excuse me, but..."

"Well?" said the small fighter, brandishing his wooden weapon.

"Excuse me," repeated MacIan, "but was that what you were doing at the door?"

The little man stared an instant and then said: "Yes," and Turnbull broke into a guffaw.

"Come on!" cried the little man, tucking his stick under his arm and taking quite suddenly to his heels. "Come on! Confound me, I'll see both of you eat and then I'll see one of you die. Lord bless me, the gods must exist after all—they have sent me one of my day-dreams! Lord! A duel!"

He had gone flying along a winding path between the borders of the kitchen garden, and in the increasing twilight he was as hard to follow as a flying hare. But at length the path after many twists betrayed its purpose and led abruptly up two or three steps to the door of a tiny but very clean cottage. There was nothing about the outside to distinguish it from other cottages, except indeed its ominous cleanliness and one thing that was out of all the custom and tradition of all cottages under the sun. In the middle of the little garden among the stocks and marigolds there surged up in shapeless stone a South Sea Island idol. There was something gross and even evil in that eyeless and alien god among the most innocent of the English flowers.

"Come in!" cried the creature again. "Come in! it's better inside!"

Whether or no it was better inside it was at least a surprise. The moment the two duellists had pushed open the door of that inoffensive, whitewashed cottage they found that its interior was lined with fiery gold. It was like stepping into a chamber in the Arabian Nights. The door that closed behind them shut out England and all the energies of the West. The ornaments that shone and shimmered on every side of them were subtly mixed from many periods and lands, but were all oriental. Cruel Assyrian bas-reliefs ran along the sides of the passage; cruel Turkish swords and daggers glinted above and below them; the two were separated by ages and fallen civilizations. Yet they seemed to sympathize since they were both harmonious and both merciless. The house seemed to consist of chamber within chamber and created that impression as of a dream which belongs also to the Arabian Nights themselves. The innermost room of all was like the inside of a jewel. The little man who owned it all threw himself on a heap of scarlet and golden cushions and struck his hands together. A negro in a white robe and turban appeared suddenly and silently behind them.

"Selim," said the host, "these two gentlemen are staying with me tonight. Send up the very best wine and dinner at once. And Selim, one of these gentlemen will probably die tomorrow. Make arrangements, please."

The negro bowed and withdrew.

Evan MacIan came out the next morning into the little garden to a fresh silver day, his long face looking more austere than ever in that cold light, his eyelids a little heavy. He carried one of the swords. Turnbull was in the little house behind him, demolishing the end of an early breakfast and humming a tune to himself, which could be heard through the open window. A moment or two later he leapt to his feet and came out into the sunlight, still munching toast, his own sword stuck under his arm like a walking-stick.

Their eccentric host had vanished from sight, with a polite gesture, some twenty minutes before. They imagined him to be occupied on some concerns in the interior of the house, and they waited for his emergence, stamping the garden in silence—the garden of tall, fresh country flowers, in the midst of which the monstrous South Sea idol lifted itself as abruptly as the prow of a ship riding on a sea of red and white and gold.

It was with a start, therefore, that they came upon the man himself already in the garden. They were all the more startled because of the still posture in which they found him. He was on his knees in front of the stone idol, rigid and motionless, like a saint in a trance or ecstasy. Yet when Turnbull's tread broke a twig, he was on his feet in a flash.

"Excuse me," he said with an irradiation of smiles, but yet with a kind of bewilderment. "So sorry...family prayers...old fashioned...mother's knee. Let us go on to the lawn behind."

And he ducked rapidly round the statue to an open space of grass on the other side of it.

"This will do us best, Mr. MacIan," said he. Then he made a gesture towards the heavy stone figure on the pedestal which had now its blank and shapeless back turned towards them. "Don't you be afraid," he added, "he can still see us."

MacIan turned his blue, blinking eyes, which seemed still misty with sleep (or sleeplessness) towards the idol, but his brows drew together.

The little man with the long hair also had his eyes on the back view of the god. His eyes were at once liquid and burning, and he rubbed his hands slowly against each other.

"Do you know," he said, "I think he can see us better this way. I often think that this blank thing is his real face, watching, though it cannot be watched. He! he! Yes, I think he looks nice from behind. He looks more cruel from behind, don't you think?"

"What the devil is the thing?" asked Turnbull gruffly.

"It is the only Thing there is," answered the other. "It is Force."

"Oh!" said Turnbull shortly.

"Yes, my friends," said the little man, with an animated countenance, fluttering his fingers in the air, "it was no chance that led you to this garden; surely it was the caprice of some old god, some happy, pitiless god. Perhaps it was his will, for he loves blood; and on that stone in front of him men have been butchered by hundreds in the fierce, feasting islands of the South. In this cursed, craven place I have not been permitted to kill men on his altar. Only rabbits and cats, sometimes."

In the stillness MacIan made a sudden movement, unmeaning apparently, and then remained rigid.

"But today, today," continued the small man in a shrill voice. "Today his hour is come. Today his will is done on earth as it is in heaven. Men, men, men will bleed before him today." And he bit his forefinger in a kind of fever.

Still, the two duellists stood with their swords as heavily as statues, and the silence seemed to cool the eccentric and call him back to more rational speech.

"Perhaps I express myself a little too lyrically," he said with an amicable abruptness. "My philosophy has its higher ecstasies, but perhaps you are hardly worked up to them yet. Let us confine ourselves to the unquestioned. You have found your way, gentlemen, by a beautiful accident, to the house of the only man in England (probably) who will favour and encourage your most reasonable project. From Cornwall to Cape Wrath this county is one horrible, solid block of humanitarianism. You will find men who will defend this or that war in a distant continent. They will defend it on the contemptible ground of commerce or the more contemptible ground of social good. But do not fancy that you will find one other person who will comprehend a strong man taking the sword in his hand and wiping out his enemy. My name is Wimpey, Morrice Wimpey. I had a Fellowship at Magdalen. But I assure you I had to drop it, owing to my having said something in a public lecture infringing the popular prejudice against those great gentlemen, the assassins of the Italian Renaissance. They let me say it at dinner and so on, and seemed to like it. But in a public lecture...so inconsistent. Well, as I say, here is your only refuge and temple of honour. Here you can fall back on that naked and awful arbitration which is the only thing that balances the stars—a still, continuous violence. *Vae Victis!* Down, down, down with the defeated! Victory is the only ultimate fact. Carthage *was* destroyed, the Red Indians are being exterminated: that is the single certainty. In an hour from now that sun will still be shining and that grass growing, and one of you will be conquered; one of you will be the conqueror. When it has been done, nothing will alter it. Heroes, I give you the hospitality fit for heroes. And I salute the survivor. Fall on!"

The two men took their swords. Then MacIan said steadily: "Mr. Turnbull, lend me your sword a moment."

Turnbull, with a questioning glance, handed him the weapon. MacIan took the second sword in his left hand and, with a violent gesture, hurled it at the feet of little Mr. Wimpey.

"Fight!" he said in a loud, harsh voice. "Fight me now!"

Wimpey took a step backward, and bewildered words bubbled on his lips.

"Pick up that sword and fight me," repeated MacIan, with brows as black as thunder.

The little man turned to Turnbull with a gesture, demanding judgement or protection.

"Really, sir," he began, "this gentleman confuses..."

"You stinking little coward," roared Turnbull, suddenly releasing his wrath. "Fight, if you're so fond of fighting! Fight, if you're so fond of all that filthy philosophy! If winning is everything, go in and win! If the weak must go to the wall, go to the wall! Fight, you rat! Fight, or if you won't fight—run!"

And he ran at Wimpey, with blazing eyes.

Wimpey staggered back a few paces like a man struggling with his own limbs. Then he felt the furious Scotchman coming at him like an express train, doubling his size every second, with eyes as big as windows and a sword as bright as the sun. Something broke inside him, and he found himself running away, tumbling over his own feet in terror, and crying out as he ran.

"Chase him!" shouted Turnbull as MacIan snatched up the sword and joined in the scamper. "Chase him over a county! Chase him into the sea! Shoo! Shoo! Shoo!"

The little man plunged like a rabbit among the tall flowers, the two duellists after him. Turnbull kept at his tail with savage ecstasy, still shooing him like a cat. But MacIan, as he ran past the South Sea idol, paused an instant to spring upon its pedestal. For five seconds he strained against the inert mass. Then it stirred; and he sent it over with a great crash among the flowers, that engulfed it altogether. Then he went bounding after the runaway.

In the energy of his alarm the ex-Fellow of Magdalen managed to leap the paling of his garden. The two pursuers went over it after him like flying birds. He fled frantically down a long lane with his two terrors on his trail till he came to a gap in the hedge and went across a steep meadow like the wind. The two Scotchmen, as they ran, kept up a cheery bellowing and waved their swords. Up three slanting meadows, down four slanting meadows on the other side, across another road, across a heath of snapping bracken, through a wood, across another road, and to the brink of a big pool, they pursued the flying philosopher. But when he came to the pool his pace was so precipitate that he could not stop it, and with a kind of lurching stagger, he fell splash into the greasy water. Getting dripping to his feet, with the water up to his knees, the worshipper of force and victory waded disconsolately to the other side and drew himself on to the bank. And Turnbull sat down on the grass and went off into reverberations of laughter. A second afterwards the most extraordinary grimaces were seen to distort the stiff face of MacIan, and unholy sounds came from within. He had never practised laughing, and it hurt him very much.

CHAPTER SEVEN
THE VILLAGE OF GRASSLEY-IN-THE-HOLE

At about half past one, under a strong blue sky, Turnbull got up out of the grass and fern in which he had been lying, and his still intermittent laughter ended in a kind of yawn.

"I'm hungry," he said shortly. "Are you?"

"I have not noticed," answered MacIan. "What are you going to do?"

"There's a village down the road, past the pool," answered Turnbull. "I can see it from here. I can see the whitewashed walls of some cottages and a kind of corner of the church. How jolly it all looks. It looks so—I don't know what the word is—so sensible. Don't fancy I'm under any illusions about Arcadian virtue and the innocent villagers. Men make beasts of themselves there with drink, but they don't deliberately make devils of themselves with mere talking. They kill wild animals in the wild woods, but they don't kill cats to the God of Victory. They don't——" He broke off and suddenly spat on the ground.

"Excuse me," he said; "it was ceremonial. One has to get the taste out of one's mouth."

"The taste of what?" asked MacIan.

"I don't know the exact name for it," replied Turnbull. "Perhaps it is the South Sea Islands, or it may be Magdalen College."

There was a long pause, and MacIan also lifted his large limbs off the ground—his eyes particularly dreamy.

"I know what you mean, Turnbull," he said, "but... I always thought you people agreed with all that."

"With all that about doing as one likes, and the individual, and Nature loving the strongest, and all the things which that cockroach talked about."

Turnbull's big blue-grey eyes stood open with a grave astonishment.

"Do you really mean to say, MacIan," he said, "that you fancied that we, the Free-thinkers, that Bradlaugh, or Holyoake, or Ingersoll, believe all that dirty, immoral mysticism about Nature? Damn Nature!"

"I supposed you did," said MacIan calmly. "It seems to me your most conclusive position."

"And you mean to tell me," rejoined the other, "that you broke my window, and challenged me to mortal combat, and tied a tradesman up with ropes, and chased an Oxford Fellow across five meadows—all under the impression that I am such an illiterate idiot as to believe in Nature!"

"I supposed you did," repeated MacIan with his usual mildness; "but I admit that I know little of the details of your belief—or disbelief."

Turnbull swung round quite suddenly, and set off towards the village.

"Come along," he cried. "Come down to the village. Come down to the nearest decent inhabitable pub. This is a case for beer."

"I do not quite follow you," said the Highlander.

"Yes, you do," answered Turnbull. "You follow me slap into the inn-parlour. I repeat, this is a case for beer. We must have the whole of this matter out thoroughly before we go a step farther. Do you know that an idea has just struck me of great simplicity and of some cogency. Do not by any means let us drop our intentions of settling our differences with two steel swords. But do you not think that with two pewter pots we might do what we really have never thought of doing yet—discover what our difference is?"

"It never occurred to me before," answered MacIan with tranquillity. "It is a good suggestion."

And they set out at an easy swing down the steep road to the village of Grassley-in-the-Hole.

Grassley-in-the-Hole was a rude parallelogram of buildings, with two thoroughfares which might have been called two high streets if it had been possible to call them streets. One of these ways was higher on the slope than the other, the whole parallelogram lying aslant, so to speak, on the side of the hill. The upper of these two roads was decorated with a big public house, a butcher's shop, a small public house, a sweetstuff shop, a very small public house, and an illegible signpost. The lower of the two roads boasted a horse-pond, a post office, a gentleman's garden with very high hedges, a microscopically small public house, and two cottages. Where all the people lived who supported all the public houses was in this, as in many other English villages, a silent and smiling mystery. The church lay a little above and beyond the village, with a square grey tower dominating it decisively.

But even the church was scarcely so central and solemn an institution as the large public house, the Valencourt Arms. It was named after some splendid family that had long gone bankrupt, and whose seat was occupied by a man who had invented a hygienic bootjack; but the unfathomable sentimentalism of the English people insisted in regarding the Inn, the seat and the sitter in it, as alike parts of a pure and marmoreal antiquity. And in the Valencourt Arms festivity itself had some solemnity and decorum; and beer was drunk with reverence, as it ought to be. Into the principal parlour of this place entered two strangers, who found themselves, as is always the case in such hostels, the object, not of fluttered curiosity or pert inquiry, but of steady, ceaseless, devouring ocular study. They had long coats down to their heels, and carried under each coat something that looked like a stick. One was tall and dark, the other short and red-haired. They ordered a pot of ale each.

"MacIan," said Turnbull, lifting his tankard, "the fool who wanted us to be friends made us want to go on fighting. It is only natural that the fool who wanted us to fight should make us friendly. MacIan, your health!"

Dusk was already dropping, the rustics in the tavern were already lurching and lumbering out of it by twos and threes, crying clamorous good nights to a solitary old toper that remained, before MacIan and Turnbull had reached the really important part of their discussion.

MacIan wore an expression of sad bewilderment not uncommon with him. "I am to understand, then," he said, "that you don't believe in nature."

"You may say so in a very special and emphatic sense," said Turnbull. "I do not believe in nature, just as I do not believe in Odin. She is a myth. It is not merely that I do not believe that nature can guide us. It is that I do not believe that nature exists."

"Exists?" said MacIan in his monotonous way, settling his pewter pot on the table.

"Yes, in a real sense nature does not exist. I mean that nobody can discover what the original nature of things would have been if things had not interfered with it. The first blade of grass began to tear up the earth and eat it; it was interfering with nature, if there is any nature. The first wild ox began to tear up the grass and eat it; he was interfering with nature, if there is any nature. In the same way," continued Turnbull, "the human when it asserts its dominance over nature is just as natural as the thing which it destroys."

"And in the same way," said MacIan almost dreamily, "the superhuman, the supernatural is just as natural as the nature which it destroys."

Turnbull took his head out of his pewter pot in some anger.

"The supernatural, of course," he said, "is quite another thing; the case of the supernatural is simple. The supernatural does not exist."

"Quite so," said MacIan in a rather dull voice; "you said the same about the natural. If the natural does not exist the supernatural obviously can't." And he yawned a little over his ale.

Turnbull turned for some reason a little red and remarked quickly, "That may be jolly clever, for all I know. But everyone does know that there is a division between the things that as a matter of fact do commonly happen and the things that don't. Things that break the evident laws of nature—"

"Which does not exist," put in MacIan sleepily. Turnbull struck the table with a sudden hand.

"Good Lord in heaven!" he cried—

"Who does not exist," murmured MacIan.

"Good Lord in heaven!" thundered Turnbull, without regarding the interruption. "Do you really mean to sit there and say that you, like anybody else, would not recognize the difference between a natural occurrence and a supernatural one—if there could be such a thing? If I flew up to the ceiling—"

"You would bump your head badly," cried MacIan, suddenly starting up. "One can't talk of this kind of thing under a ceiling at all. Come outside! Come outside and ascend into heaven!"

He burst the door open on a blue abyss of evening and they stepped out into it: it was suddenly and strangely cool.

"Turnbull," said MacIan, "you have said some things so true and some so false that I want to talk; and I will try to talk so that you understand. For at present you do not understand at all. We don't seem to mean the same things by the same words."

He stood silent for a second or two and then resumed.

"A minute or two ago I caught you out in a real contradiction. At that moment logically I was right. And at that moment I knew I was wrong. Yes, there is a real difference between the natural and the supernatural: if you flew up into that blue sky this instant, I should think that you were moved by God—or the devil. But if you want to know what I really think...I must explain."

He stopped again, abstractedly boring the point of his sword into the earth, and went on:

"I was born and bred and taught in a complete universe. The supernatural was not natural, but it was perfectly reasonable. Nay, the supernatural to me is more reasonable than the natural; for the supernatural is a direct message from God, who is reason. I was taught that some things are natural and some things divine. I mean that some things are mechanical and some things divine. But there is the great difficulty, Turnbull. The great difficulty is that, according to my teaching, you are divine."

"Me! Divine?" said Turnbull truculently. "What do you mean?"

"That is just the difficulty," continued MacIan thoughtfully. "I was told that there was a difference between the grass and a man's will; and the difference was that a man's will was special and divine. A man's free will, I heard, was supernatural."

"Rubbish!" said Turnbull.

"Oh," said MacIan patiently, "then if a man's free will isn't supernatural, why do your materialists deny that it exists?"

Turnbull was silent for a moment. Then he began to speak, but MacIan continued with the same steady voice and sad eyes:

"So what I feel is this: Here is the great divine creation I was taught to believe in. I can understand your disbelieving in it, but why disbelieve in a part of it? It was all one thing to me. God had authority because he was God. Man had authority because he was man. You cannot prove that God is better than a man; nor can you prove that a man is better than a horse. Why permit any ordinary thing? Why do you let a horse be saddled?"

"Some modern thinkers disapprove of it," said Turnbull a little doubtfully.

"I know," said MacIan grimly; "that man who talked about love, for instance."

Turnbull made a humorous grimace; then he said: "We seem to be talking in a kind of shorthand; but I won't pretend not to understand you. What you mean is this: that you learnt about all your saints and angels at the same time as you learnt about common morality, from the same people, in the same way. And you mean to say that if one may be disputed, so may the other. Well, let that pass for the moment. But let me ask you a question in turn. Did not this system of yours, which you swallowed whole, contain all sorts of things that were merely local, the respect for the chief of your clan, or such things; the village ghost, the family feud, or what not? Did you not take in those things, too, along with your theology?"

MacIan stared along the dim village road, down which the last straggler from the inn was trailing his way.

"What you say is not unreasonable," he said. "But it is not quite true. The distinction between the chief and us did exist; but it was never anything like the distinction between the human and the divine, or the human and the animal. It was more like the distinction between one animal and another. But—"

"Well?" said Turnbull.

MacIan was silent.

"Go on," repeated Turnbull; "what's the matter with you? What are you staring at?"

"I am staring," said MacIan at last, "at that which shall judge us both."

"Oh, yes," said Turnbull in a tired way, "I suppose you mean God."

"No, I don't," said MacIan, shaking his head. "I mean him."

And he pointed to the half-tipsy yokel who was ploughing down the road.

"What do you mean?" asked the atheist.

"I mean him," repeated MacIan with emphasis. "He goes out in the early dawn; he digs or he ploughs a field. Then he comes back and drinks ale, and then he sings a song. All your philosophies and political systems are young compared to him. All your hoary cathedrals, yes, even the Eternal Church on earth is new compared to him. The most mouldering gods in the British Museum are new facts beside him. It is he who in the end shall judge us all."

And MacIan rose to his feet with a vague excitement.

"What are you going to do?"

"I am going to ask him," cried MacIan, "which of us is right."

Turnbull broke into a kind of laugh. "Ask that intoxicated turnip-eater—" he began.

"Yes—which of us is right," cried MacIan violently. "Oh, you have long words and I have long words; and I talk of every man being the image of God; and you talk of every man being a citizen and enlightened enough to govern. But if every man typifies God, there is God. If every man is an enlightened citizen, there is your enlightened citizen. The first man one meets is always man. Let us catch him up."

And in gigantic strides the long, lean Highlander whirled away into the grey twilight, Turnbull following with a good-humoured oath.

The track of the rustic was easy to follow, even in the faltering dark; for he was enlivening his wavering walk with song. It was an interminable poem, beginning with some unspecified King William, who (it appeared) lived in London town and who after the second rise vanished rather abruptly from the train of thought. The rest was almost entirely about beer and was thick with local topography of a quite unrecognizable kind. The singer's step was neither very rapid, nor, indeed, exceptionally secure; so the song grew louder and louder and the two soon overtook him.

He was a man elderly or rather of any age, with lean grey hair and a lean red face, but with that remarkable rustic physiognomy in which it seems that all the features stand out independently from the face; the rugged red nose going out like a limb; the bleared blue eyes standing out like signals.

He gave them greeting with the elaborate urbanity of the slightly intoxicated. MacIan, who was vibrating with one of his silent, violent decisions, opened the question without delay. He explained the philosophic position in words as short and simple as possible. But the singular old man with the lank red face seemed to think uncommonly little of the short words. He fixed with a fierce affection upon one or two of the long ones.

"Atheists!" he repeated with luxurious scorn. "Atheists! I know their sort, master. Atheists! Don't talk to me about 'un. Atheists!"

The grounds of his disdain seemed a little dark and confused; but they were evidently sufficient. MacIan resumed in some encouragement:

"You think as I do, I hope; you think that a man should be connected with the Church; with the common Christian——"

The old man extended a quivering stick in the direction of a distant hill.

"There's the church," he said thickly. "Grassley old church that is. Pulled down it was, in the old squire's time, and——"

"I mean," explained MacIan elaborately, "that you think that there should be someone typifying religion, a priest——"

"Priests!" said the old man with sudden passion. "Priests! I know 'un. What they want in England? That's what I say. What they want in England?"

"They want you," said MacIan.

"Quite so," said Turnbull, "and me; but they won't get us. MacIan, your attempt on the primitive innocence does not seem very successful. Let me try. What you want, my friend, is your rights. You don't want any priests or churches. A vote, a right to speak is what you——"

"Who says I a'n't got a right to speak?" said the old man, facing round in an irrational frenzy. "I got a right to speak. I'm a man, I am. I don't want no votin' nor priests. I say a man's a man; that's what I say. If a man a'n't a man, what is he? That's what I say, if a man a'n't a man, what is he? When I sees a man, I sez 'e's a man."

"Quite so," said Turnbull, "a citizen."

"I say he's a man," said the rustic furiously, stopping and striking his stick on the ground. "Not a city or owt else. He's a man."

"You're perfectly right," said the sudden voice of MacIan, falling like a sword. "And you have kept close to something the whole world of today tries to forget."

"Good night."

And the old man went on wildly singing into the night.

"A jolly old creature," said Turnbull; "he didn't seem able to get much beyond that fact that a man is a man."

"Has anybody got beyond it?" asked MacIan.

Turnbull looked at him curiously. "Are you turning an agnostic?" he asked.

"Oh, you do not understand!" cried out MacIan. "We Catholics are all agnostics. We Catholics have only in that sense got as far as realizing that man is a man. But your Ibsens and your Zolas and your Shaws and your Tolstoys have not even got so far."

CHAPTER EIGHT
AN INTERLUDE OF ARGUMENT

Morning broke in bitter silver along the grey and level plain; and almost as it did so Turnbull and MacIan came out of a low, scrubby wood on to the empty and desolate flats. They had walked all night.

They had walked all night and talked all night also, and if the subject had been capable of being exhausted they would have exhausted it. Their long and changing argument had taken them through districts and landscapes equally changing. They had discussed Haeckel upon hills so high and steep that in spite of the coldness of the night it seemed as if the stars might burn them. They had explained and re-explained the Massacre of St. Bartholomew in little white lanes walled in with standing corn as with walls of gold. They had talked about Mr. Kensit in dim and twinkling pine woods, amid the bewildering monotony of the pines. And it was with the end of a long speech from MacIan, passionately defending the practical achievements and the solid prosperity of the Catholic tradition, that they came out upon the open land.

MacIan had learnt much and thought more since he came out of the cloudy hills of Arisaig. He had met many typical modern figures under circumstances which were sharply symbolic; and, moreover, he had absorbed the main modern atmosphere from the mere presence and chance phrases of

Turnbull, as such atmospheres can always be absorbed from the presence and the phrases of any man of great mental vitality. He had at last begun thoroughly to understand what are the grounds upon which the mass of the modern world solidly disapprove of her creed; and he threw himself into replying to them with a hot intellectual enjoyment.

"I begin to understand one or two of your dogmas, Mr. Turnbull," he had said emphatically as they ploughed heavily up a wooded hill. "And every one that I understand I deny. Take any one of them you like. You hold that your heretics and sceptics have helped the world forward and handed on a lamp of progress. I deny it. Nothing is plainer from real history than that each of your heretics invented a complete cosmos of his own which the next heretic smashed entirely to pieces. Who knows now exactly what Nestorius taught? Who cares? There are only two things that we know for certain about it. The first is that Nestorius, as a heretic, taught something quite opposite to the teaching of Arius, the heretic who came before him, and something quite useless to James Turnbull, the heretic who comes after. I defy you to go back to the Free-thinkers of the past and find any habitation for yourself at all. I defy you to read Godwin or Shelley or the deists of the eighteenth century of the nature-worshipping humanists of the Renaissance, without discovering that you differ from them twice as much as you differ from the Pope. You are a nineteenth-century sceptic, and you are always telling me that I ignore the cruelty of nature. If you had been an eighteenth-century sceptic you would have told me that I ignore the kindness and benevolence of nature. You are an atheist, and you praise the deists of the eighteenth century. Read them instead of praising them, and you will find that their whole universe stands or falls with the deity. You are a materialist, and you think Bruno a scientific hero. See what he said and you will think him an insane mystic. No, the great Free-thinker, with his genuine ability and honesty, does not in practice destroy Christianity. What he does destroy is the Free-thinker who went before. Free-thought may be suggestive, it may be inspiring, it may have as much as you please of the merits that come from vivacity and variety. But there is one thing Free-thought can never be by any possibility—Free-thought can never be progressive. It can never be progressive because it will accept nothing from the past; it begins every time again from the beginning; and it goes every time in a different direction. All the rational philosophers have gone along different roads, so it is impossible to say which has gone farthest. Who can discuss whether Emerson was a better optimist than Schopenhauer was pessimist? It is like asking if this corn is as yellow as that hill is steep. No; there are only two things that really progress; and they both accept accumulations of authority. They may be progressing uphill and down; they may be growing steadily better or steadily worse; but they have steadily increased in certain definable matters; they have steadily advanced in a certain definable direction; they are the only two things, it seems, that ever *can* progress. The first is strictly physical science. The second is the Catholic

Church."

"Physical science and the Catholic Church!" said Turnbull sarcastically; "and no doubt the first owes a great deal to the second."

"If you pressed that point I might reply that it was very probable," answered MacIan calmly. "I often fancy that your historical generalizations rest frequently on random instances; I should not be surprised if your vague notions of the Church as the persecutor of science was a generalization from Galileo. I should not be at all surprised if, when you counted the scientific investigations and discoveries since the fall of Rome, you found that a great mass of them had been made by monks. But the matter is irrelevant to my meaning. I say that if you want an example of anything which has progressed in the moral world by the same method as science in the material world, by continually adding to without unsettling what was there before, then I say that there *is* only one example of it. And that is Us."

"With this enormous difference," said Turnbull, "that however elaborate be the calculations of physical science, their net result can be tested. Granted that it took millions of books I never read and millions of men I never heard of to discover the electric light. Still I can see the electric light. But I cannot see the supreme virtue which is the result of all your theologies and sacraments."

"Catholic virtue is often invisible because it is the normal," answered MacIan. "Christianity is always out of fashion because it is always sane; and all fashions are mild insanities. When Italy is mad on art the Church seems too Puritanical; when England is mad on Puritanism the Church seems too artistic. When you quarrel with us now you class us with kingship and despotism; but when you quarrelled with us first it was because we would not accept the divine despotism of Henry VIII. The Church always seems to be behind the times, when it is really beyond the times; it is waiting till the last fad shall have seen its last summer. It keeps the key of a permanent virtue."

"Oh, I have heard all that!" said Turnbull with genial contempt. "I have heard that Christianity keeps the key of virtue, and that if you read Tom Paine you will cut your throat at Monte Carlo. It is such rubbish that I am not even angry at it. You say that Christianity is the prop of morals; but what more do you do? When a doctor attends you and could poison you with a pinch of salt, do you ask whether he is a Christian? You ask whether he is a gentleman, whether he is an M.D.— anything but that. When a soldier enlists to die for his country or disgrace it, do you ask whether he is a Christian? You are more likely to ask whether he is Oxford or Cambridge at the boat race. If you think your creed essential to morals why do you not make it a test for these things?"

"We once did make it a test for these things," said MacIan smiling, "and then you told us that we were imposing by force a faith unsupported by argument. It seems rather hard that having first been told that our creed must be false because we did use tests, we should now be told that it must be false because we don't. But I notice that most anti-Christian arguments are in the same inconsistent style."

"That is all very well as a debating-club answer," replied Turnbull good-humouredly, "but the question still remains: Why don't you confine yourself more to Christians if Christians are the only really good men?"

"Who talked of such folly?" asked MacIan disdainfully. "Do you suppose that the Catholic Church ever held that Christians were the only good men? Why, the Catholics of the Catholic Middle Ages talked about the virtues of all the virtuous Pagans until humanity was sick of the subject. No, if you really want to know what we mean when we say that Christianity has a special power of virtue, I will tell you. The Church is the only thing on earth that can perpetuate a type of virtue and make it something more than a fashion. The thing is so plain and historical that I hardly think you will ever deny it. You cannot deny that it is perfectly possible that tomorrow morning, in Ireland or in Italy, there might appear a man not only as good but good in exactly the same way as St. Francis of Assisi. Very well, now take the other types of human virtue; many of them splendid. The English gentleman of Elizabeth was chivalrous and idealistic. But can you stand still here in this meadow and *be* an English gentleman of Elizabeth? The austere republican of the eighteenth century, with his stern patriotism and his simple life, was a fine fellow. But have you ever seen him? have you ever seen an austere republican? Only a hundred years have passed and that volcano of revolutionary truth and valour is as cold as the mountains of the moon. And so it is and so it will be with the ethics which are buzzing down Fleet Street at this instant as I speak. What phrase would inspire the London clerk or workman just now? Perhaps that he is a son of the British Empire on which the sun never sets; perhaps that he is a prop of his Trades Union, or a class-conscious proletarian something or other; perhaps merely that he is a gentleman when he obviously is not. Those names and notions are all honourable; but how long will they last? Empires break; industrial conditions change; the suburbs will not last for ever. What will remain? I will tell you. The Catholic Saint will remain."

"And suppose I don't like him?" said Turnbull.

"On my theory the question is rather whether he will like you: or more probably whether he will ever have heard of you. But I grant the reasonableness of your query. You have a right, if you speak as the ordinary man, to ask if you will like the saint. But as the ordinary man you do like him. You revel in him. If you dislike him it is not because you are a nice ordinary man, but because you are (if you will excuse me) a sophisticated prig of a Fleet Street editor. That is just the funny part of it. The human race has always admired the Catholic virtues, however little it can practise them; and oddly enough it has admired most those of them that the modern world most sharply disputes. You complain of Catholicism for setting up an ideal of virginity; it did nothing of the kind. The whole human race set up an ideal of virginity; the Greeks in Athene, the Romans in the Vestal fire, set up an ideal of virginity. What then is your real quarrel with Catholicism? Your quarrel can only be, your quarrel really only is, that Catholicism has *achieved* an ideal of virginity; that it is no longer a mere piece of floating poetry. But if you, and a few feverish men, in top hats, running about in a street in London, choose to differ as to the ideal itself, not only from the Church, but from the Parthenon whose name means virginity, from the Roman Empire which went outwards from the virgin flame, from the whole legend and tradition of Europe, from the lion who will not touch virgins, from the unicorn who respects them, and who make up together the bearers of your own national shield, from the most living and lawless of your own poets, from Massinger, who wrote the *Virgin Martyr*, from Shakespeare, who wrote *Measure for Measure*—if you in Fleet Street differ from all this human experience, does it never strike you that it may be Fleet Street that is wrong?"

"No," answered Turnbull; "I trust that I am sufficiently fair-minded to canvass and consider the idea; but having considered it, I think Fleet Street is right, yes—even if the Parthenon is wrong. I think that as the world goes on new psychological atmospheres are generated, and in these atmospheres it is possible to find delicacies and combinations which in other times would have to be represented by some ruder symbol. Every man feels the need of some element of purity in sex; perhaps they can only typify purity as the absence of sex. You will laugh if I suggest that we may have made in Fleet Street an atmosphere in which a man can be so passionate as Sir Lancelot and as pure as Sir Galahad. But, after all, we have in the modern world erected many such atmospheres. We have, for instance, a new and imaginative appreciation of children."

"Quite so," replied MacIan with a singular smile. "It has been very well put by one of the brightest of your young authors, who said: 'Unless you become as little children ye shall in no wise enter the kingdom of heaven.' But you are quite right; there is a modern worship of children. And what, I ask you, is this modern worship of children? What, in the name of all the angels and devils, is it except a worship of virginity? Why should anyone worship a thing merely because it is small or immature? No; you have tried to escape from this thing, and the very thing you point to as the goal of your escape is only the thing again. Am I wrong in saying that these things seem to be eternal?"

And it was with these words that they came in sight of the great plains. They went a little way in silence, and then James Turnbull said suddenly, "But I *cannot* believe in the thing." MacIan answered nothing to the speech; perhaps it is unanswerable. And indeed they scarcely spoke another word to each other all that day.

CHAPTER NINE
THE STRANGE LADY

Moonrise with a great and growing moon opened over all those flats, making them seem flatter and larger than they were, turning them to a lake of blue light. The two companions trudged across the moonlit plain for half an hour in full silence. Then MacIan stopped suddenly and planted his sword-point in the ground like one who plants his tent-pole for the night. Leaving it standing there, he clutched his black-haired skull with his great claws of hands, as was his custom when forcing the pace of his brain. Then his hands dropped again and he spoke.

"I'm sure you're thinking the same as I am," he said; "how long are we to be on this damned seesaw?"

The other did not answer, but his silence seemed somehow solid as assent; and MacIan went on conversationally. Neither noticed that both had instinctively stood still before the sign of the fixed and standing sword.

"It is hard to guess what God means in this business. But he means something—or the other thing, or both. Whenever we have tried to fight each other something has stopped us. Whenever we have tried to be reconciled to each other, something has stopped us again. By the run of our luck we have never had time to be either friends or enemies. Something always jumped out of the bushes."

Turnbull nodded gravely and glanced round at the huge and hedgeless meadow which fell away towards the horizon into a glimmering high road.

"Nothing will jump out of bushes here anyhow," he said.

"That is what I meant," said MacIan, and stared steadily at the heavy hilt of his standing sword, which in the slight wind swayed on its tempered steel like some huge thistle on its stalk.

"That is what I meant; we are quite alone here. I have not heard a horse-hoof or a footstep or the hoot of a train for miles. So I think we might stop here and ask for a miracle."

"Oh! might we?" said the atheistic editor with a sort of gusto of disgust.

"I beg your pardon," said MacIan, meekly. "I forgot your prejudices." He eyed the wind-swung sword-hilt in sad meditation and resumed: "What I mean is, we might find out in this quiet place whether there really is any fate or any commandment against our enterprise. I will engage on my side, like Elijah, to accept a test from heaven. Turnbull, let us draw swords here in this moonlight and this monstrous solitude. And if here in this moonlight and solitude there happens anything to interrupt us—if it be lightning striking our sword-blades or a rabbit running under our legs—I will take it as a sign from God and we will shake hands for ever."

Turnbull's mouth twitched in angry humour under his red moustache. He said: "I will wait for signs from God until I have any signs of His existence; but

God—or Fate—forbid that a man of scientific culture should refuse any kind of experiment."

"Very well, then," said MacIan, shortly. "We are more quiet here than anywhere else; let us engage." And he plucked his sword-point out of the turf.

Turnbull regarded him for a second and a half with a baffling visage almost black against the moonrise; then his hand made a sharp movement to his hip and his sword shone in the moon.

As old chess-players open every game with established gambits, they opened with a thrust and parry, orthodox and even frankly ineffectual. But in MacIan's soul more formless storms were gathering, and he made a lunge or two so savage as first to surprise and then to enrage his opponent. Turnbull ground his teeth, kept his temper, and waiting for the third lunge, and the worst, had almost spitted the lunger when a shrill, small cry came from behind him, a cry such as is not made by any of the beasts that perish.

Turnbull must have been more superstitious than he knew, for he stopped in the act of going forward. MacIan was brazenly superstitious, and he dropped his sword. After all, he had challenged the universe to send an interruption; and this was an interruption, whatever else it was. An instant afterwards the sharp, weak cry was repeated. This time it was certain that it was human and that it was female.

MacIan stood rolling those great blue Gaelic eyes that contrasted with his dark hair. "It is the voice of God," he said again and again.

"God hasn't got much of a voice," said Turnbull, who snatched at every chance of cheap profanity. "As a matter of fact, MacIan, it isn't the voice of God, but it's something a jolly sight more important—it is the voice of man—or rather of woman. So I think we'd better scoot in its direction."

MacIan snatched up his fallen weapon without a word, and the two raced away towards that part of the distant road from which the cry was now constantly renewed.

They had to run over a curve of country that looked smooth but was very rough; a neglected field which they soon found to be full of the tallest grasses and the deepest rabbit-holes. Moreover, that great curve of the countryside which looked so slow and gentle when you glanced over it, proved to be highly precipitous when you scampered over it; and Turnbull was twice nearly flung on his face. MacIan, though much heavier, avoided such an overthrow only by having the quick and incalculable feet of the mountaineer; but both of them may be said to have leapt off a low cliff when they leapt into the road.

The moonlight lay on the white road with a more naked and electric glare than on the grey-green upland, and though the scene which it revealed was complicated, it was not difficult to get its first features at a glance.

A small but very neat black-and-yellow motor-car was standing stolidly, slightly to the left of the road. A somewhat larger light-green motor-car was tipped half-way into a ditch on the same side, and four flushed and staggering men in evening dress were tipped out of it. Three of them were standing about the road, giving their opinions to the moon with vague but echoing violence. The fourth, however, had already advanced on the chauffeur of the black-and-yellow car, and was threatening him with a stick. The chauffeur had risen to defend himself. By his side sat a young lady.

She was sitting bolt upright, a slender and rigid figure gripping the sides of her seat, and her first few cries had ceased. She was clad in close-fitting dark costume, a mass of warm brown hair went out in two wings or waves on each side of her forehead; and even at that distance it could be seen that her profile was of the aquiline and eager sort, like a young falcon hardly free of the nest.

Turnbull had concealed in him somewhere a fund of common sense and knowledge of the world of which he himself and his best friends were hardly aware. He was one of those who take in much of the shows of things absent-mindedly, and in an irrelevant reverie. As he stood at the door of his editorial shop on Ludgate Hill and meditated on the non-existence of God, he silently absorbed a good deal of varied knowledge about the existence of men. He had come to know types by instinct and dilemmas with a glance; he saw the crux of the situation in the road, and what he saw made him redouble his pace.

He knew that the men were rich; he knew that they were drunk; and he knew, what was worst of all, that they were fundamentally frightened. And he knew this also, that no common ruffian (such as attacks ladies in novels) is ever so savage and ruthless as a coarse kind of gentleman when he is really alarmed. The reason is not recondite; it is simply because the police-court is not such a menacing novelty to the poor ruffian as it is to the rich. When they came within hail and heard the voices, they confirmed all Turnbull's anticipations. The man in the middle of the road was shouting in a hoarse and groggy voice that the chauffeur had smashed their car on purpose; that they must get to the Cri that evening, and that he would jolly well have to take them there. The chauffeur had mildly objected that he was driving a lady. "Oh! we'll take care of the lady," said the red-faced young man, and went off into gurgling and almost senile laughter.

By the time the two champions came up, things had grown more serious. The intoxication of the man talking to the chauffeur had taken one of its perverse and catlike jumps into mere screaming spite and rage. He lifted his stick and struck at the chauffeur, who caught hold of it, and the drunkard fell backwards, dragging him out of his seat on the car. Another of the rowdies rushed forward booing in idiot excitement, fell over the chauffeur, and, either by accident or design, kicked him as he lay. The drunkard got to his feet again; but the chauffeur did not.

The man who had kicked kept a kind of half-witted conscience or cowardice, for he stood staring at the senseless body and murmuring words of inconsequent self-justification, making gestures with his hands as if he were arguing with somebody. But the other three, with a mere whoop and howl of victory, were boarding the car on three sides at once. It was exactly at this moment that Turnbull fell among them like one fallen from the sky. He tore one of the climbers backward by the collar, and with a hearty push sent him staggering over into the ditch upon his nose. One of the remaining two, who was too far gone to notice anything, continued to clamber ineffectually over the high back of the car, kicking and pouring forth a rivulet of soliloquy. But the other dropped at the interruption, turned upon Turnbull and began a battering bout of fisticuffs. At the same moment the man crawled out of the ditch in a masquerade of mud and rushed at his old enemy from behind. The whole had not taken a second; and an instant after MacIan was in the midst of them.

Turnbull had tossed away his sheathed sword, greatly preferring his hands, except in the avowed etiquette of the duel; for he had learnt to use his hands in the old street-battles of Bradlaugh. But to MacIan the sword even sheathed was a more natural weapon, and he laid about him on all sides with it as with a stick. The man who had the walking-stick found his blows parried with promptitude; and a second after, to his great astonishment, found his own stick fly up in the air as by a conjuring trick, with a turn of the swordsman's wrist. Another of the revellers picked the stick out of the ditch and ran in upon MacIan, calling to his companion to assist him.

"I haven't got a stick," grumbled the disarmed man, and looked vaguely about the ditch.

"Perhaps," said MacIan, politely, "you would like this one." With the word the drunkard found his hand that had grasped the stick suddenly twisted and empty; and the stick lay at the feet of his companion on the other side of the road. MacIan felt a faint stir behind him; the girl had risen to her feet and was leaning forward to stare at the fighters. Turnbull was still engaged in countering and pommelling with the third young man. The fourth young man was still engaged with himself, kicking his legs in helpless rotation on the back of the car and talking with melodious rationality.

At length Turnbull's opponent began to back before the battery of his heavy hands, still fighting, for he was the soberest and boldest of the four. If these are annals of military glory, it is due to him to say that he need not have abandoned the conflict; only that as he backed to the edge of the ditch his foot caught in a loop of grass and he went over in a flat and comfortable position from which it took him a considerable time to rise. By the time he had risen, Turnbull had come to the rescue of MacIan, who was at bay but belabouring his two enemies handsomely. The sight of the liberated reserve was to them like that of Blucher at Waterloo; the two set off at a sullen trot down the road, leaving even the walking-stick lying behind them in the moonlight. MacIan plucked the struggling and aspiring idiot off the back of the car like a stray cat, and left him swaying unsteadily in the moon. Then he approached the front part of the car in a somewhat embarrassed manner and pulled off his cap.

For some solid seconds the lady and he merely looked at each other, and MacIan had an irrational feeling of being in a picture hung on a wall. That is, he was motionless, even lifeless, and yet staringly significant, like a picture. The white moonlight on the road, when he was not looking at it, gave him a vision of the road being white with snow. The motor-car, when he was not looking at it, gave him a rude impression of a captured coach in the old days of highwaymen. And he whose whole soul was with the swords and stately manners of the eighteenth century, he who was a Jacobite risen from the dead, had an overwhelming sense of being once more in the picture, when he had so long been out of the picture.

In that short and strong silence he absorbed the lady from head to foot. He had never really looked at a human being before in his life. He saw her face and hair first, then that she had long suede gloves; then that there was a fur cap at the back of her brown hair. He might, perhaps, be excused for this hungry attention. He had prayed that some sign might come from heaven; and after an almost savage scrutiny he came to the conclusion that his one did. The lady's instantaneous arrest of speech might need more explaining; but she may well have been stunned with the squalid attack and the abrupt rescue. Yet it was she who remembered herself first and suddenly called out with self-accusing horror:

"Oh, that poor, poor man!"

They both swung round abruptly and saw that Turnbull, with his recovered sword under his arm-pit, was already lifting the fallen chauffeur into the car. He was only stunned and was slowly awakening, feebly waving his left arm.

The lady in long gloves and the fur cap leapt out and ran rapidly towards them, only to be reassured by Turnbull, who (unlike many of his school) really knew a little science when he invoked it to redeem the world. "He's all right," said he; "he's quite safe. But I'm afraid he won't be able to drive the car for half an hour or so."

"I can drive the car," said the young woman in the fur cap with stony practicability.

"Oh, in that case," began MacIan, uneasily; and that paralysing shyness which is a part of romance induced him to make a backward movement as if leaving her to herself. But Turnbull was more rational than he, being more indifferent.

"I don't think you ought to drive home alone, ma'am," he said, gruffly. "There seem to be a lot of rowdy parties along this road, and the man will be no use for an hour. If you will tell us where you are going, we will see you safely there and say good night."

The young lady exhibited all the abrupt disturbance of a person who is not commonly disturbed. She said almost sharply and yet with evident sincerity: "Of course I am awfully grateful to you for all you've done—and there's plenty of room if you'll come in."

Turnbull, with the complete innocence of an absolutely sound motive, immediately jumped into the car; but the girl cast an eye at MacIan, who stood in the road for an instant as if rooted like a tree. Then he also tumbled his long legs into the tonneau, having that sense of degradedly diving into heaven which so many have known in so many human houses when they consented to stop to tea or were allowed to stop to supper. The slowly reviving chauffeur was set in the back seat; Turnbull and MacIan had fallen into the middle one; the lady with a steely coolness had taken the driver's seat and all the handles of that headlong machine. A moment afterwards the engine started, with a throb and leap unfamiliar to Turnbull, who had only once been in a motor during a general election, and utterly unknown to MacIan, who in his present mood thought it was the end of the world. Almost at the same instant that the car plucked itself out of the mud and whipped away up the road, the man who had been flung into the ditch rose waveringly to his feet. When he saw the car escaping he ran after it and shouted something which, owing to the increasing distance, could not be heard. It is awful to reflect that, if his remark was valuable, it is quite lost to the world.

The car shot on up and down the shining moonlit lanes, and there was no sound in it except the occasional click or catch of its machinery; for through some cause or other no soul inside it could think of a word to say. The lady symbolized her feelings, whatever they were, by urging the machine faster and faster until scattered woodlands went by them in one black blotch and heavy hills and valleys seemed to ripple under the wheels like mere waves. A little while afterwards this mood seemed to slacken and she fell into a more ordinary pace; but still she did not speak. Turnbull, who kept a more common and sensible view of the case than anyone else, made some remark about the moonlight; but something indescribable made him also relapse into silence.

All this time MacIan had been in a sort of monstrous delirium, like some fabulous hero snatched up into the moon. The difference between this experience and common experiences was analogous to that between waking life and a dream. Yet he did not feel in the least as if he were dreaming; rather the other way; as waking was more actual than dreaming, so this seemed by another degree more actual than waking itself. But it was another life altogether, like a cosmos with a new dimension.

He felt he had been hurled into some new incarnation: into the midst of new relations, wrongs and rights, with towering responsibilities and almost tragic joys which he had as yet had no time to examine. Heaven had not merely sent him a message; Heaven itself had opened around him and given him an hour of its own ancient and star-shattering energy. He had never felt so much alive before; and yet he was like a man in a trance. And if you had asked him on what his throbbing happiness hung, he could only have told you that it hung on four or five visible facts, as a curtain hangs on four of five fixed nails. The fact that the lady had a little fur at her throat; the fact that the curve of her cheek was a low and lean curve and that the moonlight caught the height of her cheek-bone; the fact that her hands were small but heavily gloved as they gripped the steering-wheel; the fact that a white witch light was on the road; the fact that the brisk breeze of their passage stirred and fluttered a little not only the brown hair of her head but the black fur on her cap. All these facts were to him certain and incredible, like sacraments.

When they had driven half a mile farther, a big shadow was flung across the path, followed by its bulky owner, who eyed the car critically but let it pass. The silver moonlight picked out a piece or two of pewter ornament on his blue uniform; and as they went by they knew it was a sergeant of police. Three hundred yards farther on another policeman stepped out into the road as if to stop them, then seemed to doubt his own authority and stepped back again. The girl was a daughter of the rich; and this police suspicion (under which all the poor live day and night) stung her for the first time into speech.

"What can they mean?" she cried out in a kind of temper; "this car's going like a snail."

There was a short silence, and then Turnbull said: "It is certainly very odd, you are driving quietly enough."

"You are driving nobly," said MacIan, and his words (which had no meaning whatever) sounded hoarse and ungainly even in his own ears.

They passed the next mile and a half swiftly and smoothly; yet among the many things which they passed in the course of it was a clump of eager policemen standing at a cross-road. As they passed, one of the policemen shouted something to the others; but nothing else happened. Eight hundred yards farther on, Turnbull stood up suddenly in the swaying car.

"My God, MacIan!" he called out, showing his first emotion of that night. "I don't believe it's the pace; it couldn't be the pace. I believe it's us."

MacIan sat motionless for a few moments and then turned up at his companion a face that was as white as the moon above it.

"You may be right," he said at last; "if you are, I must tell her."

"I will tell the lady if you like," said Turnbull, with his unconquered good temper.

"You!" said MacIan, with a sort of sincere and instinctive astonishment. "Why should you—no, I must tell her, of course——"

And he leant forward and spoke to the lady in the fur cap.

"I am afraid, madam, that we may have got you into some trouble," he said, and even as he said it it sounded wrong, like everything he said to this particular person in the long gloves. "The fact is," he resumed, desperately, "the fact is, we are being chased by the police." Then the last flattening hammer fell upon poor Evan's embarrassment; for the fluffy brown head with the furry black cap did not turn by a section of the compass.

"We are chased by the police," repeated MacIan, vigorously; then he added, as if beginning an explanation, "You see, I am a Catholic."

The wind whipped back a curl of the brown hair so as to necessitate a new theory of aesthetics touching the line of the cheek-bone; but the head did not turn.

"You see," began MacIan, again blunderingly, "this gentleman wrote in his newspaper that Our Lady was a common woman, a bad woman, and so we agreed to fight; and we were fighting quite a little time ago—but that was before we saw you."

The young lady driving her car had half turned her face to listen; and it was not a reverent or a patient face that she showed him. Her Norman nose was tilted a trifle too high upon the slim stalk of her neck and body.

When MacIan saw that arrogant and uplifted profile pencilled plainly against the moonshine, he accepted an ultimate defeat. He had expected the angels to despise him if he were wrong, but not to despise him so much as this.

"You see," said the stumbling spokesman, "I was angry with him when he insulted the Mother of God, and I asked him to fight a duel with me; but the police are all trying to stop it."

Nothing seemed to waver or flicker in the fair young falcon profile; and it only opened its lips to say, after a silence: "I thought people in our time were supposed to respect each other's religion."

Under the shadow of that arrogant face MacIan could only fall back on the obvious answer: "But what about a man's irreligion?" The face only answered: "Well, you ought to be more broadminded."

If anyone else in the world had said the words, MacIan would have snorted with his equine neigh of scorn. But in this case he seemed knocked down by a superior simplicity, as if his eccentric attitude were rebuked by the innocence of a child. He could not dissociate anything that this woman said or did or wore from an idea of spiritual rarity and virtue. Like most others under the same elemental passion, his soul was at present soaked in ethics. He could have applied moral terms to the material objects of her environment. If someone had spoken of "her generous ribbon" or "her chivalrous gloves" or "her merciful shoe-buckle," it would not have seemed to him nonsense.

He was silent, and the girl went on in a lower key as if she were momentarily softened and a little saddened also. "It won't do, you know," she said; "you can't find out the truth in that way. There are such heaps of churches and people thinking different things nowadays, and they all think they are right. My uncle was a Swedenborgian."

MacIan sat with bowed head, listening hungrily to her voice but hardly to her words, and seeing his great world drama grow smaller and smaller before his eyes till it was no bigger than a child's toy theatre.

"The time's gone by for all that," she went on; "you can't find out the real thing like that—if there is really anything to find——" and she sighed rather drearily;

for, like many of the women of our wealthy class, she was old and broken in thought, though young and clean enough in her emotions.

"Our object," said Turnbull, shortly, "is to make an effective demonstration"; and after that word, MacIan looked at his vision again and found it smaller than ever.

"It would be in the newspapers, of course," said the girl. "People read the newspapers, but they don't believe them, or anything else, I think." And she sighed again.

She drove in silence a third of a mile before she added, as if completing the sentence: "Anyhow, the whole thing's quite absurd."

"I don't think," began Turnbull, "that you quite realize—Hullo! hullo—hullo—what's this?"

The amateur chauffeur had been forced to bring the car to a staggering stoppage, for a file of fat, blue policemen made a wall across the way. A sergeant came to the side and touched his peaked cap to the lady.

"Beg your pardon, miss," he said with some embarrassment, for he knew her for a daughter of a dominant house, "but we have reason to believe that the gentlemen in your car are—" and he hesitated for a polite phrase.

"I am Evan MacIan," said that gentleman, and stood up in a sort of gloomy pomp, not wholly without a touch of the sulks of a schoolboy.

"Yes, we will get out, sergeant," said Turnbull, more easily; "my name is James Turnbull. We must not incommode the lady."

"What are you taking them up for?" asked the young woman, looking straight in front of her along the road.

"It's under the new act," said the sergeant, almost apologetically. "Incurable disturbers of the peace."

"What will happen to them?" she asked, with the same frigid clearness.

"Westgate Adult Reformatory," he replied, briefly.

"Until when?"

"Until they are cured," said the official.

"Very well, sergeant," said the young lady, with a sort of tired common sense. "I am sure I don't want to protect criminals or go against the law; but I must tell you that these gentlemen have done me a considerable service; you won't mind drawing your men a little farther off while I say good night to them. Men like that always misunderstand."

The sergeant was profoundly disquieted from the beginning at the mere idea of arresting anyone in the company of a great lady; to refuse one of her minor requests was quite beyond his courage. The police fell back to a few yards behind the car. Turnbull took up the two swords that were their only luggage; the swords that, after so many half duels, they were now to surrender at last. MacIan, the blood thundering in his brain at the thought of that instant of farewell, bent over, fumbled at the handle and flung open the door to get out.

But he did not get out. He did not get out, because it is dangerous to jump out of a car when it is going at full speed. And the car was going at full speed, because the young lady, without turning her head or so much as saying a syllable, had driven down a handle that made the machine plunge forward like a buffalo and then fly over the landscape like a greyhound. The police made one rush to follow, and then dropped so grotesque and hopeless a chase. Away in the vanishing distance they could see the sergeant furiously making notes.

The open door, still left loose on its hinges, swung and banged quite crazily as they went whizzing up one road and down another. Nor did MacIan sit down; he stood up stunned and yet staring, as he would have stood up at the trumpet of the Last Day. A black dot in the distance sprang up a tall black forest, swallowed them and spat them out again at the other end. A railway bridge grew larger and larger till it leapt upon their backs bellowing, and was in its turn left behind. Avenues of poplars on both sides of the road chased each other like the figures in a zoetrope. Now and then with a shock and rattle they went through sleeping moonlit villages, which must have stirred an instant in their sleep as at the passing of a fugitive earthquake. Sometimes in an outlying house a light in one erratic, unexpected window would give them a nameless hint of the hundred human secrets which they left behind them with their dust. Sometimes even a slouching rustic would be afoot on the road and would look after them, as after a flying phantom. But still MacIan stood up staring at earth and heaven; and still the door he had flung open flapped loose like a flag. Turnbull, after a few minutes of dumb amazement, had yielded to the healthiest element in his nature and gone off into uncontrollable fits of laughter. The girl had not stirred an inch.

After another half mile that seemed a mere flash, Turnbull leant over and locked the door. Evan staggered at last into his seat and hid his throbbing head in his hands; and still the car flew on and its driver sat inflexible and silent. The moon had already gone down, and the whole darkness was faintly troubled with twilight and the first movement of beasts and fowls. It was that mysterious moment when light is coming as if it were something unknown whose nature one could not guess— a mere alteration in everything. They looked at the sky and it seemed as dark as ever; then they saw the black shape of a tower or tree against it and knew that it was already grey. Save that they were driving southward and had certainly passed the longitude of London, they knew nothing of their direction; but Turnbull, who had spent a year on the Hampshire coast in his youth, began to recognize the unmistakable but quite indescribable villages of the English south. Then a white witch fire began to burn between the black stems of the fir-trees; and, like so many things in nature, though not in books on evolution, the daybreak, when it did come, came much quicker than one would think. The gloomy heavens were ripped up and rolled away like a scroll, revealing splendours, as the car went roaring up the curve of a great hill; and above them and black against the broadening light, there stood one of those crouching and fantastic trees that are first signals of the sea.

CHAPTER TEN
THE SWORDS REJOINED

As they came over the hill and down on the other side of it, it is not too much to say that the whole universe of God opened over them and under them, like a thing unfolding to five times its size. Almost under their feet opened the enormous sea, at the bottom of a steep valley which fell down into a bay; and the sea under their feet blazed at them almost as lustrous and almost as empty as the sky. The sunrise opened above them like some cosmic explosion, shining and shattering and yet silent; as if the world were blown to pieces without a sound. Round the rays of the victorious sun swept a sort of rainbow of confused and conquered colours—brown and blue and green and flaming rose-colour; as though gold were driving before it all the colours of the world. The lines of the landscape down which they sped, were the simple, strict, yet swerving, lines of a rushing river; so that it was almost as if they were being sucked down in a huge still whirlpool. Turnbull had some such feeling, for he spoke for the first time for many hours.

"If we go down at this rate we shall be over the sea cliff," he said.

"How glorious!" said MacIan.

When, however, they had come into the wide hollow at the bottom of that landslide, the car took a calm and graceful curve along the side of the sea, melted into the fringe of a few trees, and quietly, yet astonishingly, stopped. A belated light was burning in the broad morning in the window of a sort of lodge- or gate-keepers' cottage; and the girl stood up in the car and turned her splendid face to the sun.

Evan seemed startled by the stillness, like one who had been born amid sound and speed. He wavered on his long legs as he stood up; he pulled himself together, and the only consequence was that he trembled from head to foot. Turnbull had already opened the door on his side and jumped out.

The moment he had done so the strange young woman had one more mad movement, and deliberately drove the car a few yards farther. Then she got out with an almost cruel coolness and began pulling off her long gloves and almost whistling.

"You can leave me here," she said, quite casually, as if they had met five minutes before. "That is the lodge of my father's place. Please come in, if you like—but I understood that you had some business."

Evan looked at that lifted face and found it merely lovely; he was far too much of a fool to see that it was working with a final fatigue and that its austerity was agony. He was even fool enough to ask it a question. "Why did you save us?" he said, quite humbly.

The girl tore off one of her gloves, as if she were tearing off her hand. "Oh, I don't know," she said, bitterly. "Now I come to think of it, I can't imagine."

Evan's thoughts, that had been piled up to the morning star, abruptly let him down with a crash into the very cellars of the emotional universe. He remained in a stunned silence for a long time; and that, if he had only known, was the wisest thing that he could possibly do at the moment.

Indeed, the silence and the sunrise had their healing effect, for when the extraordinary lady spoke again, her tone was more friendly and apologetic. "I'm not really ungrateful," she said; "it was very good of you to save me from those men."

"But why?" repeated the obstinate and dazed MacIan, "why did you save us from the other men? I mean the policemen?"

The girl's great brown eyes were lit up with a flash that was at once final desperation and the loosening of some private and passionate reserve.

"Oh, God knows!" she cried. "God knows that if there is a God He has turned His big back on everything. God knows I have had no pleasure in my life, though I am pretty and young and father has plenty of money. And then people come and tell me that I ought to do things and I do them and it's all drivel. They want you to do work among the poor; which means reading Ruskin and feeling self-righteous in the best room in a poor tenement. Or to help some cause or other, which always means bundling people out of crooked houses, in which they've always lived, into straight houses, in which they often die. And all the time you have inside only the horrid irony of your own empty head and empty heart. I am to give to the unfortunate, when my whole misfortune is that I have nothing to give. I am to teach, when I believe nothing at all that I was taught. I am to save the children from death, and I am not even certain that I should not be better dead. I suppose if I actually saw a child drowning I should save it. But that would be from the same motive from which I have saved you, or destroyed you, whichever it is that I have done."

"What was the motive?" asked Evan, in a low voice.

"My motive is too big for my mind," answered the girl.

Then, after a pause, as she stared with a rising colour at the glittering sea, she said: "It can't be described, and yet I am trying to describe it. It seems to me not only that I am unhappy, but that there is no way of being happy. Father is not happy, though he is a Member of Parliament—" She paused a moment and added with a ghost of a smile: "Nor Aunt Mabel, though a man from India has told her the secret of all creeds. But I may be wrong; there may be a way out. And for one stark, insane second, I felt that, after all, you had got the way out and that was why the world hated you. You see, if there were a way out, it would be sure to be something that looked very queer."

Evan put his hand to his forehead and began stumblingly: "Yes, I suppose we do seem—"

"Oh, yes, you look queer enough," she said, with ringing sincerity. "You'll be all the better for a wash and brush up."

"You forget our business, madam," said Evan, in a shaking voice; "we have no concern but to kill each other."

"Well, I shouldn't be killed looking like that if I were you," she replied, with inhuman honesty.

Evan stood and rolled his eyes in masculine bewilderment. Then came the final change in this Proteus, and she put out both her hands for an instant and said in a low tone on which he lived for days and nights:

"Don't you understand that I did not dare to stop you? What you are doing is so mad that it may be quite true. Somehow one can never really manage to be an atheist."

Turnbull stood staring at the sea; but his shoulders showed that he heard, and after one minute he turned his head. But the girl had only brushed Evan's hand with hers and had fled up the dark alley by the lodge gate.

Evan stood rooted upon the road, literally like some heavy statue hewn there in the age of the Druids. It seemed impossible that he should ever move. Turnbull grew restless with this rigidity, and at last, after calling his companion twice or thrice, went up and clapped him impatiently on one of his big shoulders. Evan winced and leapt away from him with a repulsion which was not the hate of an unclean thing nor the dread of a dangerous one, but was a spasm of awe and separation from something from which he was now sundered as by the sword of God. He did not hate the atheist; it is possible that he loved him. But Turnbull was now something more dreadful than an enemy: he was a thing sealed and devoted—a thing now hopelessly doomed to be either a corpse or an executioner.

"What is the matter with you?" asked Turnbull, with his hearty hand still in the air; and yet he knew more about it than his innocent action would allow.

"James," said Evan, speaking like one under strong bodily pain, "I asked for God's answer and I have got it—got it in my vitals. He knows how weak I am, and that I might forget the peril of the faith, forget the face of Our Lady—yes, even with your blow upon her cheek. But the honour of this earth has just this about it, that it can make a man's heart like iron. I am from the Lords of the Isles and I dare not be a mere deserter. Therefore, God has tied me by the chain of my worldly place and word, and there is nothing but fighting now."

"I think I understand you," said Turnbull, "but you say everything tail foremost."

"She wants us to do it," said Evan, in a voice crushed with passion. "She has hurt herself so that we might do it. She has left her good name and her good sleep and all her habits and dignity flung away on the other side of England in the hope that she may hear of us and that we have broken some hole into heaven."

"I thought I knew what you mean," said Turnbull, biting his beard; "it does seem as if we ought to do something after all she has done this night."

"I never liked you so much before," said MacIan, in bitter sorrow.

As he spoke, three solemn footmen came out of the lodge gate and assembled to assist the chauffeur to his room. The mere sight of them made the two wanderers flee as from a too frightful incongruity, and before they knew where they were, they were well upon the grassy ledge of England that overlooks the Channel. Evan said suddenly: "Will they let me see her in heaven once in a thousand ages?" and addressed the remark to the editor of *The Atheist*, as on which he would be likely or qualified to answer. But no answer came; a silence sank between the two.

Turnbull strode sturdily to the edge of the cliff and looked out, his companion following, somewhat more shaken by his recent agitation.

"If that's the view you take," said Turnbull, "and I don't say you are wrong, I think I know where we shall be best off for the business. As it happens, I know this part of the south coast pretty well. And unless I am mistaken there's a way down the cliff just here which will land us on a stretch of firm sand where no one is likely to follow us."

The Highlander made a gesture of assent and came also almost to the edge of the precipice. The sunrise, which was broadening over sea and shore, was one of those rare and splendid ones in which there seems to be no mist or doubt, and nothing but a universal clarification more and more complete. All the colours were transparent. It seemed like a triumphant prophecy of some perfect world where everything being innocent will be intelligible; a world where even our bodies, so to speak, may be as of burning glass. Such a world is faintly though fiercely figured in the coloured windows of Christian architecture. The sea that lay before them was like a pavement of emerald, bright and almost brittle; the sky against which its strict horizon hung was almost absolutely white, except that close to the sky line, like scarlet braids on the hem of a garment, lay strings of flaky cloud of so gleaming and gorgeous a red that they seemed cut out of some strange blood-red celestial metal, of which the mere gold of this earth is but a drab yellow imitation.

"The hand of Heaven is still pointing," muttered the man of superstition to himself. "And now it is a blood-red hand."

The cool voice of his companion cut in upon his monologue, calling to him from a little farther along the cliff, to tell him that he had found the ladder of descent. It began as a steep and somewhat greasy path, which then tumbled down twenty or thirty feet in the form of a fall of rough stone steps. After that, there was a rather awkward drop on to a ledge of stone and then the journey was undertaken easily and even elegantly by the remains of an ornamental staircase, such as might have belonged to some long-disused watering-place. All the time that the two travellers sank from stage to stage of this downward journey, there closed over their heads living bridges and caverns of the most varied foliage, all of which grew greener, redder, or more golden, in the growing sunlight of the morning. Life, too, of the more moving sort rose at the sun on every side of them. Birds whirred and fluttered in the undergrowth, as if imprisoned in green cages. Other birds were shaken up in great clouds from the tree-tops, as if they were blossoms detached and scattered up to heaven. Animals which Turnbull was too much of a Londoner and MacIan too much of a Northerner to know, slipped by among the tangle or ran pattering up the tree-trunks. Both the men, according to their several creeds, felt the full thunder of the psalm of life as they had never heard it before; MacIan felt God the Father, benignant in all His energies, and Turnbull that ultimate anonymous energy, that *Natura Naturans*, which is the whole theme of Lucretius. It was down this clamorous ladder of life that they went down to die.

They broke out upon a brown semicircle of sand, so free from human imprint as to justify Turnbull's profession. They strode out upon it, stuck their swords in the sand, and had a pause too important for speech. Turnbull eyed the coast curiously for a moment, like one awakening memories of childhood; then he said abruptly, like a man remembering somebody's name: "But, of course, we shall be better off still round the corner of Cragness Point; nobody ever comes there at all." And picking up his sword again, he began striding towards a big bluff of the rocks which stood out upon their left. MacIan followed him round the corner and found himself in what was certainly an even finer fencing court, of flat, firm sand, enclosed on three sides by white walls of rock, and on the fourth by the green wall of the advancing sea.

"We are quite safe here," said Turnbull, and, to the other's surprise, flung himself down, sitting on the brown beach.

"You see, I was brought up near here," he explained. "I was sent from Scotland to stop with my aunt. It is highly probable that I may die here. Do you mind if I light a pipe?"

"Of course, do whatever you like," said MacIan, with a choking voice, and he went and walked alone by himself along the wet, glistening sands.

Ten minutes afterwards he came back again, white with his own whirlwind of emotions; Turnbull was quite cheerful and was knocking out the end of his pipe.

"You see, we have to do it," said MacIan. "She tied us to it."

"Of course, my dear fellow," said the other, and leapt up as lightly as a monkey.

They took their places gravely in the very centre of the great square of sand, as if they had thousands of spectators. Before saluting, MacIan, who, being a mystic, was one inch nearer to Nature, cast his eye round the huge framework of their heroic folly. The three walls of rock all leant a little outward, though at various angles; but this impression was exaggerated in the direction of the incredible by the heavy load of living trees and thickets which each wall wore on its top like a huge shock of hair. On all that luxurious crest of life the risen and victorious sun was beating, burnishing it all like gold, and every bird that rose with that sunrise caught a light like a star upon it like the dove of the Holy Spirit. Imaginative life had never so much crowded upon MacIan. He felt that he could write whole books about the feelings of a single bird. He felt that for two centuries he would not tire of being a rabbit. He was in the Palace of Life, of which the very tapestries and curtains were alive. Then he recovered himself, and remembered his affairs. Both men saluted, and iron rang upon iron. It was exactly at the same moment that he realized that his enemy's left ankle was encircled with a ring of salt water that had crept up to his feet.

"What is the matter?" said Turnbull, stopping an instant, for he had grown used to every movement of his extraordinary fellow-traveller's face.

MacIan glanced again at that silver anklet of sea-water and then looked beyond at the next promontory round which a deep sea was boiling and leaping. Then he turned and looked back and saw heavy foam being shaken up to heaven about the base of Cragness Point.

"The sea has cut us off," he said, curtly.

"I have noticed it," said Turnbull with equal sobriety. "What view do you take of the development?"

Evan threw away his weapon, and, as his custom was, imprisoned his big head in his hands. Then he let them fall and said: "Yes, I know what it means; and I think it is the fairest thing. It is the finger of God—red as blood—still pointing. But now it points to two graves."

There was a space filled with the sound of the sea, and then MacIan spoke again in a voice pathetically reasonable: "You see, we both saved her—and she told us both to fight—and it would not be just that either should fail and fall alone, while the other——"

"You mean," said Turnbull, in a voice surprisingly soft and gentle, "that there is something fine about fighting in a place where even the conqueror must die?"

"Oh, you have got it right, you have got it right!" cried out Evan, in an extraordinary childish ecstasy. "Oh, I'm sure that you really believe in God!"

Turnbull answered not a word, but only took up his fallen sword.

For the third time Evan MacIan looked at those three sides of English cliff hung with their noisy load of life. He had been at a loss to understand the almost ironical magnificence of all those teeming creatures and tropical colours and smells that smoked happily to heaven. But now he knew that he was in the closed court of death and that all the gates were sealed.

He drank in the last green and the last red and the last gold, those unique and indescribable things of God, as a man drains good wine at the bottom of his glass. Then he turned and saluted his enemy once more, and the two stood up and fought till the foam flowed over their knees.

Then MacIan stepped backward suddenly with a splash and held up his hand. "Turnbull!" he cried; "I can't help it—fair fighting is more even than promises. And this is not fair fighting."

"What the deuce do you mean?" asked the other, staring.

"I've only just thought of it," cried Evan, brokenly. "We're very well matched—it may go on a good time—the tide is coming up fast—and I'm a foot and a half taller. You'll be washed away like seaweed before it's above my breeches. I'll not fight foul for all the girls and angels in the universe."

"Will you oblige me," said Turnbull, with staring grey eyes and a voice of distinct and violent politeness; "will you oblige me by jolly well minding your own business? Just you stand up and fight, and we'll see who will be washed away like seaweed. You wanted to finish this fight and you shall finish it, or I'll denounce you as a coward to the whole of that assembled company."

Evan looked very doubtful and offered a somewhat wavering weapon; but he was quickly brought back to his senses by his opponent's sword-point, which shot past him, shaving his shoulder by a hair. By this time the waves were well up Turnbull's thigh, and what was worse, they were beginning to roll and break heavily around them.

MacIan parried this first lunge perfectly, the next less perfectly; the third in all human probability he would not have parried at all; the Christian champion would have been pinned like a butterfly, and the atheistic champion left to drown like a rat, with such consolation as his view of the cosmos afforded him. But just as Turnbull launched his heaviest stroke, the sea, in which he stood up to his hips, launched a yet heavier one. A wave breaking beyond the others smote him heavily like a hammer of water. One leg gave way, he was swung round and sucked into the retreating sea, still gripping his sword.

MacIan put his sword between his teeth and plunged after his disappearing enemy. He had the sense of having the whole universe on top of him as crest after crest struck him down. It seemed to him quite a cosmic collapse, as if all the seven heavens were falling on him one after the other. But he got hold of the atheist's left leg and he did not let it go.

After some ten minutes of foam and frenzy, in which all the senses at once seemed blasted by the sea, Evan found himself laboriously swimming on a low, green swell, with the sword still in his teeth and the editor of *The Atheist* still under his arm. What he was going to do he had not even the most glimmering idea; so he merely kept his grip and swam somehow with one hand.

He ducked instinctively as there bulked above him a big, black wave, much higher than any that he had seen. Then he saw that it was hardly the shape of any possible wave. Then he saw that it was a fisherman's boat, and, leaping upward, caught hold of the bow. The boat pitched forward with its stern in the air for just as much time as was needed to see that there was nobody in it. After a moment or two of desperate clambering, however, there were two people in it, Mr. Evan MacIan, panting and sweating, and Mr. James Turnbull, uncommonly close to being drowned. After ten minutes' aimless tossing in the empty fishing-boat he recovered, however, stirred, stretched himself, and looked round on the rolling waters. Then, while taking no notice of the streams of salt water that were pouring from his hair, beard, coat, boots, and trousers, he carefully wiped the wet off his sword-blade to preserve it from the possibilities of rust.

MacIan found two oars in the bottom of the deserted boat and began somewhat drearily to row.

* * *

A rainy twilight was clearing to cold silver over the moaning sea, when the battered boat that had rolled and drifted almost aimlessly all night, came within sight of land, though of land which looked almost as lost and savage as the waves. All night there had been but little lifting in the leaden sea, only now and then the boat had been heaved up, as on a huge shoulder which slipped from under it; such occasional sea-quakes came probably from the swell of some steamer that had passed it in the dark; otherwise the waves were harmless though restless. But it was piercingly cold, and there was, from time to time, a splutter of rain like the splutter of the spray, which seemed almost to freeze as it fell. MacIan, more at home than his companion in this quite barbarous and elemental sort of adventure, had rowed toilsomely with the heavy oars whenever he saw anything that looked like land; but for the most part had trusted with grim transcendentalism to wind and tide. Among the implements of their first outfit the brandy alone had remained to him, and he gave it to his freezing companion in quantities which greatly alarmed that temperate Londoner; but MacIan came from the cold seas and mists where a man can drink a tumbler of raw whisky in a boat without it making him wink.

When the Highlander began to pull really hard upon the oars, Turnbull craned his dripping red head out of the boat to see the goal of his exertions. It was a sufficiently uninviting one; nothing so far as could be seen but a steep and shelving bank of shingle, made of loose little pebbles such as children like, but slanting up higher than a house. On the top of the mound, against the sky line, stood up the brown skeleton of some broken fence or breakwater. With the grey and watery dawn crawling up behind it, the fence really seemed to say to our philosophic adventurers that they had come at last to the other end of nowhere.

Bent by necessity to his labour, MacIan managed the heavy boat with real power and skill, and when at length he ran it up on a smoother part of the slope it caught and held so that they could clamber out, not sinking farther than their knees into the water and the shingle. A foot or two farther up their feet found the beach firmer, and a few moments afterwards they were leaning on the ragged breakwater and looking back at the sea they had escaped.

They had a dreary walk across wastes of grey shingle in the grey dawn before they began to come within hail of human fields or roads; nor had they any notion of what fields or roads they would be. Their boots were beginning to break up and the confusion of stones tried them severely, so that they were glad to lean on their swords, as if they were the staves of pilgrims. MacIan thought vaguely of a weird ballad of his own country which describes the soul in Purgatory as walking on a plain full of sharp stones, and only saved by its own charities upon earth.

> *If ever thou gavest hosen and shoon*
>   *Every night and all,*
> *Sit thee down and put them on,*
>   *And Christ receive thy soul.*

Turnbull had no such lyrical meditations, but he was in an even worse temper.

At length they came to a pale ribbon of road, edged by a shelf of rough and almost colourless turf; and a few feet up the slope there stood grey and weather-stained, one of those big wayside crucifixes which are seldom seen except in Catholic countries.

MacIan put his hand to his head and found that his bonnet was not there. Turnbull gave one glance at the crucifix—a glance at once sympathetic and bitter, in which was concentrated the whole of Swinburne's poem on the same occasion.

> *O hidden face of man, wherever*
>   *The years have woven a viewless veil,*
> *If thou wert verily man's lover*
>   *What did thy love or blood avail?*
> *Thy blood the priests mix poison of,*
>   *And in gold shekels coin thy love.*

Then, leaving MacIan in his attitude of prayer, Turnbull began to look right and left very sharply, like one looking for something. Suddenly, with a little cry, he saw it and ran forward. A few yards from them along the road a lean and starved sort of hedge came pitifully to an end. Caught upon its prickly angle, however, there was a very small and very dirty scrap of paper that might have hung there for months, since it escaped from someone tearing up a letter or making a spill out of a newspaper. Turnbull snatched at it and found it was the corner of a printed page, very coarsely printed, like a cheap novelette, and just large enough to contain the words: "*et c'est elle qui*—"

"Hurrah!" cried Turnbull, waving his fragment; "we are safe at last. We are free at last. We are somewhere better than England or Eden or Paradise. MacIan, we are in the Land of the Duel!"

"Where do you say?" said the other, looking at him heavily and with knitted brows, like one almost dazed with the grey doubts of desolate twilight and drifting sea.

"We are in France!" cried Turnbull, with a voice like a trumpet, "in the land where things really happen—*Tout arrive en France*. We arrive in France. Look at this little message," and he held out the scrap of paper. "There's an omen for you superstitious hill folk. *C'est elle qui—Mais oui, mais oui, c'est elle qui sauvera encore le monde.*"

"France!" repeated MacIan, and his eyes awoke again in his head like large lamps lighted.

"Yes, France!" said Turnbull, and all the rhetorical part of him came to the top, his face growing as red as his hair. "France, that has always been in rebellion for liberty and reason. France, that has always assailed superstition with the club of Rabelais or the rapier of Voltaire. France, at whose first council table sits the sublime figure of Julian the Apostate. France, where a man said only the other day those splendid unanswerable words"—with a superb gesture—"'we have extinguished in heaven those lights that men shall never light again.'"

"No," said MacIan, in a voice that shook with a controlled passion. "But France, which was taught by St. Bernard and led to war by Joan of Arc. France that made the crusades. France that saved the Church and scattered the heresies by the mouths of Bossuet and Massillon. France, which shows today the conquering march of Catholicism, as brain after brain surrenders to it, Brunetière, Coppée, Hauptmann, Barrès, Bourget, Lemaître."

"France!" asserted Turnbull with a sort of rollicking self-exaggeration, very unusual with him, "France, which is one torrent of splendid scepticism from Abelard to Anatole France."

"France," said MacIan, "which is one cataract of clear faith from St. Louis to Our Lady of Lourdes."

"France at least," cried Turnbull, throwing up his sword in schoolboy triumph, "in which these things are thought about and fought about. France, where reason and religion clash in one continual tournament. France, above all, where men understand the pride and passion which have plucked our blades from their scabbards. Here, at least, we shall not be chased and spied on by sickly parsons and greasy policemen, because we wish to put our lives on the game. Courage, my friend, we have come to the country of honour."

MacIan did not even notice the incongruous phrase "my friend", but nodding again and again, drew his sword and flung the scabbard far behind him in the road.

"Yes," he cried, in a voice of thunder, "we will fight here and *He* shall look on at it."

Turnbull glanced at the crucifix with a sort of scowling good-humour and then said: "He may look and see His cross defeated."

"The cross cannot be defeated," said MacIan, "for it is Defeat."

A second afterwards the two bright, blood-thirsty weapons made the sign of the cross in horrible parody upon each other.

They had not touched each other twice, however, when upon the hill, above the crucifix, there appeared another horrible parody of its shape; the figure of a man who appeared for an instant waving his outspread arms. He had vanished in an instant; but MacIan, whose fighting face was set that way, had seen the shape momentarily but quite photographically. And while it was like a comic repetition of the cross, it was also, in that place and hour, something more incredible. It had been only instantaneously on the retina of his eye; but unless his eye and mind were going mad together, the figure was that of an ordinary London policeman.

He tried to concentrate his senses on the sword-play; but one half of his brain was wrestling with the puzzle; the apocalyptic and almost seraphic apparition of a stout constable out of Clapham on top of a dreary and deserted hill in France. He did not, however, have to puzzle long. Before the duellists had exchanged half a dozen passes, the big, blue policeman appeared once more on the top of the hill, a palpable monstrosity in the eye of heaven. He was waving only one arm now and seemed to be shouting directions. At the same moment a mass of blue blocked the corner of the road behind the small, smart figure of Turnbull, and a small company of policemen in the English uniform came up at a kind of half-military double.

Turnbull saw the stare of consternation in his enemy's face and swung round to share its cause. When he saw it, cool as he was, he staggered back.

"What the devil are you doing here?" he called out in a high, shrill voice of authority, like one who finds a tramp in his own larder.

"Well, sir," said the sergeant in command, with that sort of heavy civility shown only to the evidently guilty, "seems to me we might ask what are you doing here?"

"We are having an affair of honour," said Turnbull, as if it were the most rational thing in the world. "If the French police like to interfere, let them interfere. But why the blue blazes should you interfere, you great blue blundering sausages?"

"I'm afraid, sir," said the sergeant with restraint, "I'm afraid I don't quite follow you."

"I mean, why don't the French police take this up if it's got to be taken up? I always heard that they were spry enough in their own way."

"Well, sir," said the sergeant reflectively, "you see, sir, the French police don't take this up—well, because you see, sir, this ain't France. This is His Majesty's dominions, same as 'Ampstead 'eath."

"Not France?" repeated Turnbull, with a sort of dull incredulity.

"No, sir," said the sergeant; "though most of the people talk French. This is the island called St. Loup, sir, an island in the Channel. We've been sent down specially from London, as you were such specially distinguished criminals, if you'll allow me to say so. Which reminds me to warn you that anything you say may be used against you at your trial."

"Quite so," said Turnbull, and lurched suddenly against the sergeant, so as to tip him over the edge of the road with a crash into the shingle below. Then leaving MacIan and the policemen equally and instantaneously nailed to the road, he ran a little way along it, leapt off on to a part of the beach, which he had found in his journey to be firmer, and went across it with a clatter of pebbles. His sudden calculation was successful; the police, unacquainted with the various levels of the loose beach, tried to overtake him by the shorter cut and found themselves, being heavy men, almost up to their knees in shoals of slippery shingle. Two who had been slower with their bodies were quicker with their minds, and seeing Turnbull's trick, ran along the edge of the road after him. Then MacIan finally awoke, and leaving half his sleeve in the grip of the only man who tried to hold him, took the two policemen in the small of their backs with the impetus of a cannon-ball and, sending them also flat among the stones, went tearing after his twin defier of the law.

As they were both good runners, the start they had gained was decisive. They dropped over a high breakwater farther on upon the beach, turned sharply, and scrambled up a line of ribbed rocks, crowned with a thicket, crawled through it, scratching their hands and faces, and dropped into another road; and there found that they could slacken their speed into a steady trot. In all this desperate dart and scramble, they still kept hold of their drawn swords, which now, indeed, in the vigorous phrase of Bunyan, seemed almost to grow out of their hands.

They had run another half mile or so when it became apparent that they were entering a sort of scattered village. One or two whitewashed cottages and even a shop had appeared along the side of the road. Then, for the first time, Turnbull twisted round his red bear to get a glimpse of his companion, who was a foot or two behind, and remarked abruptly: "Mr. MacIan, we've been going the wrong way to work all along. We're traced everywhere, because everybody knows about us. It's as if one went about with Kruger's beard on Mafeking Night."

"What do you mean?" said MacIan, innocently.

"I mean," said Turnbull, with steady conviction, "that what we want is a little diplomacy, and I am going to buy some in a shop."

CHAPTER ELEVEN
A SCANDAL IN THE VILLAGE

In the little hamlet of Haroc, in the Isle of St. Loup, there lived a man who—though living under the English flag—was absolutely untypical of the French tradition. He was quite unnoticeable, but that was exactly where he was quite himself. He was not even extraordinarily French; but then it is against the French tradition to be extraordinarily French. Ordinary Englishmen would only have thought him a little old-fashioned; imperialistic Englishmen would really have mistaken him for the old John Bull of the caricatures. He was stout; he was quite undistinguished; and he had side-whiskers, worn just a little longer than John Bull's. He was by name Pierre Durand; he was by trade a wine merchant; he was by politics a conservative republican; he had been brought up a Catholic, had always thought and acted as an agnostic, and was very mildly returning to the Church in his later years. He had a genius (if one can even use so wild a word in connexion with so tame a person) a genius for saying the conventional thing on every conceivable subject; or rather what we in England would call the conventional thing. For it was not convention with him, but solid and manly conviction. Convention implies cant or affectation, and he had not the faintest smell of either. He was simply an ordinary citizen with ordinary views; and if you had told him so he would have taken it as an ordinary compliment. If you had asked him about women, he would have said that one must preserve their domesticity and decorum; he would have used the stalest words, but he would have in reserve the strongest arguments. If you had asked him about government, he would have said that all citizens were free and equal, but he would have meant what he said. If you had asked him about education, he would have said that the young must be trained up in habits of industry and of respect for their parents. Still he would have set them the example of industry, and he would have been one of the parents whom they could respect. A state of mind so hopelessly central is depressing to the English instinct. But then in England a man announcing these platitudes is generally a fool and a frightened fool, announcing them out of mere social servility. But Durand was anything but a fool; he had read all the eighteenth century, and could have defended his platitudes round every angle of eighteenth-century argument. And certainly he was anything but a coward: swollen and sedentary as he was, he could have hit any man back who touched him with the instant violence of an automatic machine; and dying in a uniform would have seemed to him only the sort of thing that sometimes happens. I am afraid it is impossible to explain this monster amid the exaggerative sects and the eccentric clubs of my country. He was merely a man.

He lived in a little villa which was furnished well with comfortable chairs and tables and highly uncomfortable classical pictures and medallions. The art in his home contained nothing between the two extremes of hard, meagre designs of

Greek heads and Roman togas, and on the other side a few very vulgar Catholic images in the crudest colours; these were mostly in his daughter's room. He had recently lost his wife, whom he had loved heartily and rather heavily in complete silence, and upon whose grave he was constantly in the habit of placing hideous little wreaths, made out of a sort of black-and-white beads. To his only daughter he was equally devoted, though he restricted her a good deal under a sort of theoretic alarm about her innocence; an alarm which was peculiarly unnecessary, first, because she was an exceptionally reticent and religious girl, and secondly, because there was hardly anybody else in the place.

Madeleine Durand was physically a sleepy young woman, and might easily have been supposed to be morally a lazy one. It is, however, certain that the work of her house was done somehow, and it is even more rapidly ascertainable that nobody else did it. The logician is, therefore, driven back upon the assumption that she did it; and that lends a sort of mysterious interest to her personality at the beginning. She had very broad, low, and level brows, which seemed even lower because her warm yellow hair clustered down to her eyebrows; and she had a face just plump enough not to look as powerful as it was. Anything that was heavy in all this was abruptly lightened by two large, light china-blue eyes, lightened all of a sudden as if it had been lifted into the air by two big blue butterflies. The rest of her was less than middle-sized, and was of a casual and comfortable sort; and she had this difference from such girls as the girl in the motor-car, that one did not incline to take in her figure at all, but only her broad and leonine and innocent head.

Both the father and the daughter were of the sort that would normally have avoided all observation; that is, all observation in that extraordinary modern world which calls out everything except strength. Both of them had strength below the surface; they were like quiet peasants owning enormous and unquarried mines. The father with his square face and grey side whiskers, the daughter with her square face and golden fringe of hair, were both stronger than they know; stronger than anyone knew. The father believed in civilization, in the storied tower we have erected to affront nature; that is, the father believed in Man. The daughter believed in God; and was even stronger. They neither of them believed in themselves; for that is a decadent weakness.

The daughter was called a devotee. She left upon ordinary people the impression—the somewhat irritating impression—produced by such a person; it can only be described as the sense of strong water being perpetually poured into some abyss. She did her housework easily; she achieved her social relations sweetly; she was never neglectful and never unkind. This accounted for all that was soft in her, but not for all that was hard. She trod firmly as if going somewhere; she flung her face back as if defying something; she hardly spoke a cross word, yet there was often battle in her eyes. The modern man asked doubtfully where all this silent energy went to. He would have stared still more doubtfully if he had been told that it all went into her prayers.

The conventions of the Isle of St. Loup were necessarily a compromise or confusion between those of France and England; and it was vaguely possible for a respectable young lady to have half-attached lovers, in a way that would be impossible to the *bourgeoisie* of France. One man in particular had made himself an unmistakable figure in the track of this girl as she went to church. He was a short, prosperous-looking man, whose long, bushy black beard and clumsy black umbrella made him seem both shorter and older than he really was; but whose big, bold eyes, and step that spurned the ground, gave him an instant character of youth.

His name was Camille Bert, and he was a commercial traveller who had only been in the island an idle week before he began to hover in the tracks of Madeleine Durand. Since everyone knows everyone in so small a place, Madeleine certainly knew him to speak to; but it is not very evident that she ever spoke. He haunted her, however; especially at church, which was, indeed, one of the few certain places for finding her. In her home she had a habit of being invisible, sometimes through insatiable domesticity, sometimes through an equally insatiable solitude. M. Bert did not give the impression of a pious man, though he did give, especially with his eyes, the impression of an honest one. But he went to Mass with a simple exactitude that could not be mistaken for a pose, or even for a vulgar fascination. It was perhaps this religious regularity which eventually drew Madeleine into recognition of him. At least it is certain that she twice spoke to him with her square and open smile in the porch of the church; and there was human nature enough in the hamlet to turn even that into gossip.

But the real interest arose suddenly as a squall arises with the extraordinary affair that occurred about five days after. There was about a third of a mile beyond the village of Haroc a large but lonely hotel upon the London or Paris model, but commonly almost entirely empty. Among the accidental group of guests who had come to it at this season was a man whose nationality no one could fix and who bore the non-committal name of Count Gregory. He treated everybody with complete civility and almost in complete silence. On the few occasions when he spoke, he spoke either French, English, or once (to the priest) Latin; and the general opinion was that he spoke them all wrong. He was a large, lean man, with the stoop of an aged eagle, and even the eagle's nose to complete it; he had old-fashioned military whiskers and moustache dyed with a garish and highly incredible yellow. He had the dress of a showy gentleman and the manners of a decayed gentleman; he seemed (as with a sort of simplicity) to be trying to be a dandy when he was too old even to know that he was old. Ye he was decidedly a handsome figure with his curled yellow hair and lean fastidious face; and he wore a peculiar frock-coat of bright turquoise blue, with an unknown order pinned to it, and he carried a huge and heavy cane. Despite his silence and his dandified dress and whiskers, the island might never have heard of him but for the extraordinary event of which I have spoken, which fell about in the following way:

In such casual atmospheres only the enthusiastic go to Benediction; and as the warm blue twilight closed over the little candle-lit church and village, the line of worshippers who went home from the former to the latter thinned out until it broke. On one such evening at least no one was in church except the quiet, unconquerable Madeleine, four old women, one fisherman, and, of course, the irrepressible M. Camille Bert. The others seemed to melt away afterwards into the peacock colours of the dim green grass and the dark blue sky. Even Durand was invisible instead of being merely reverentially remote; and Madeleine set forth through the patch of black forest alone. She was not in the least afraid of loneliness, because she was not afraid of devils. I think they were afraid of her.

In a clearing of the wood, however, which was lit up with a last patch of the perishing sunlight, there advanced upon her suddenly one who was more startling than a devil. The incomprehensible Count Gregory, with his yellow hair like flame and his face like the white ashes of the flame, was advancing bareheaded towards her, flinging out his arms and his long fingers with a frantic gesture.

"We are alone here," he cried, "and you would be at my mercy, only that I am at yours."

Then his frantic hands fell by his sides and he looked up under his brows with an expression that went well with his hard breathing. Madeleine Durand had come to a halt at first in childish wonder, and now, with more than masculine self-control, "I fancy I know your face, sir," she said, as if to gain time.

"I know I shall not forget yours," said the other, and extended once more his ungainly arms in an unnatural gesture. Then of a sudden there came out of him a spout of wild and yet pompous phrases. "It is as well that you should know the worst and the best. I am a man who knows no limit; I am the most callous of criminals, the most unrepentant of sinners. There is no man in my dominions so vile as I. But my dominions stretch from the olives of Italy to the fir-woods of Denmark, and there is no nook of all of them in which I have not done a sin. But when I bear you away I shall be doing my first sacrilege, and also my first act of virtue." He seized her suddenly by the elbow; and she did not scream but only pulled and tugged. Yet though she had not screamed, someone astray in the woods seemed to have heard the struggle. A short but nimble figure came along the woodland path like a humming bullet and had caught Count Gregory a crack across the face before his own could be recognized. When it was recognized it was that of Camille, with the black elderly beard and the young ardent eyes.

Up to the moment when Camille had hit the Count, Madeleine had entertained no doubt that the Count was merely a madman. Now she was startled with a new sanity; for the tall man in the yellow whiskers and yellow moustache first returned the blow of Bert, as if it were a sort of duty, and then stepped back with a slight bow and an easy smile.

"This need go no further here, M. Bert," he said. "I need not remind you how far it should go elsewhere."

"Certainly, you need remind me of nothing," answered Camille, stolidly. "I am glad that you are just not too much of a scoundrel for a gentleman to fight."

"We are detaining the lady," said Count Gregory, with politeness; and, making a gesture suggesting that he would have taken off his hat if he had had one, he strode away up the avenue of trees and eventually disappeared. He was so complete an aristocrat that he could offer his back to them all the way up that avenue; and his back never once looked uncomfortable.

"You must allow me to see you home," said Bert to the girl, in a gruff and almost stifled voice; "I think we have only a little way to go."

"Only a little way," she said, and smiled once more that night, in spite of fatigue and fear and the world and the flesh and the devil. The glowing and transparent blue of twilight had long been covered by the opaque and slatelike blue of night, when he handed her into the lamp-lit interior of her home. He went out himself into the darkness, walking sturdily, but tearing at his black beard.

All the French or semi-French gentry of the district considered this a case in which a duel was natural and inevitable, and neither party had any difficulty in finding seconds, strangers as they were in the place. Two small landowners, who were careful, practising Catholics, willingly undertook to represent that strict church-goer Camille Burt; while the profligate but apparently powerful Count Gregory found friends in an energetic local doctor who was ready for social promotion and an accidental Californian tourist who was ready for anything. As no particular purpose could be served by delay, it was arranged that the affair should fall out three days afterwards. And when this was settled the whole community, as it were, turned over again in bed and thought no more about the matter. At least there was only one member of it who seemed to be restless, and that was she who was commonly most restful. On the next night Madeleine Durand went to church as usual; and as usual the stricken Camille was there also. What was not so usual was that when they were a bow-shot from the church Madeleine turned round and walked back to him. "Sir," she began, "it is not wrong of me to speak to you," and the very words gave him a jar of unexpected truth; for in all the novels he had ever read she would have begun: "It is wrong of me to speak to you." She went on with wide and serious eyes like an animal's: "It is not wrong of me to speak to you, because your soul, or anybody's soul, matters so much more than what the world says about anybody. I want to talk to you about what you are going to do."

Bert saw in front of him the inevitable heroine of the novels trying to prevent bloodshed; and his pale firm face became implacable.

"I would do anything but that for you," he said; "but no man can be called less than a man."

She looked at him for a moment with a face openly puzzled, and then broke into an odd and beautiful half-smile.

"Oh, I don't mean that," she said; "I don't talk about what I don't understand. No one has ever hit me; and if they had I should not feel as a man may. I am sure it is not the best thing to fight. It would be better to forgive—if one could really forgive. But when people dine with my father and say that fighting a duel is mere murder—of course I can see that is not just. It's all so different—having a reason—and letting the other man know—and using the same guns and things—and doing it in front of your friends. I'm awfully stupid, but I know that men like you aren't murderers. But it wasn't that that I meant."

"What did you mean?" asked the other, looking broodingly at the earth.

"Don't you know," she said, "there is only one more celebration? I thought that as you always go to church—I thought you would communicate this morning."

Bert stepped backward with a sort of action she had never seen in him before. It seemed to alter his whole body.

"You may be right or wrong to risk dying," said the girl, simply; "the poor women in our village risk it whenever they have a baby. You men are the other half of the world. I know nothing about when you ought to die. But surely if you are daring to try and find God beyond the grave and appeal to Him—you ought to let Him find you when He comes and stands there every morning in our little church."

And placid as she was, she made a little gesture of argument, of which the pathos wrung the heart.

M. Camille Bert was by no means placid. Before that incomplete gesture and frankly pleading face he retreated as if from the jaws of a dragon. His dark black hair and beard looked utterly unnatural against the startling pallor of his face. When at last he said something it was: "O God! I can't stand this!" He did not say it in French. Nor did he, strictly speaking, say it in English. The truth (interesting only to anthropologists) is that he said it in Scotch.

"There will be another mass in a matter of eight hours," said Madeleine, with a sort of business eagerness and energy, "and you can do it then before the fighting. You must forgive me, but I was so frightened that you would not do it at all."

Bert seemed to crush his teeth together until they broke, and managed to say between them: "And why should you suppose that I shouldn't do as you say—I mean not to do it at all?"

"You always go to Mass," answered the girl, opening her wide blue eyes, "and the Mass is very long and tiresome unless one loves God."

Then it was that Bert exploded with a brutality which might have come from Count Gregory, his criminal opponent. He advanced upon Madeleine with flaming eyes, and almost took her by the two shoulders. "I do not love God," he cried, speaking French with the broadest Scotch accent; "I do not want to find Him;

I do not think He is there to be found. I must burst up the show; I must and will say everything. You are the happiest and honestest thing I ever saw in this godless universe. And I am the dirtiest and most dishonest."

Madeleine looked at him doubtfully for an instant, and then said with a sudden simplicity and cheerfulness: "Oh, but if you are really sorry it is all right. If you are horribly sorry it is all the better. You have only to go and tell the priest so and he will give you God out of his own hands."

"I hate your priest and I deny your God!" cried the man, "and I tell you God is a lie and a fable and a mask. And for the first time in my life I do not feel superior to God."

"What can it all mean?" said Madeleine, in massive wonder.

"Because I am a fable also and a mask," said the man. He had been plucking fiercely at his black beard and hair all the time; now he suddenly plucked them off and flung them like moulted feathers in the mire. This extraordinary spoliation left in the sunlight the same face, but a much younger head—a head with close chestnut curls and a short chestnut beard.

"Now you know the truth," he answered, with hard eyes. "I am a cad who has played a crooked trick on a quiet village and a decent woman for a private reason of his own. I might have played it successfully on any other woman; I have hit the one woman on whom it cannot be played. It's just like my damned luck. The plain truth is," and here when he came to the plain truth he boggled and blundered as Evan had done in telling it to the girl in the motor-car.

"The plain truth is," he said at last, "that I am James Turnbull the atheist. The police are after me; not for atheism but for being ready to fight for it."

"I saw something about you in a newspaper," said the girl, with a simplicity which even surprise could never throw off its balance.

"Evan MacIan said there was a God," went on the other, stubbornly, "and I say there isn't. And I have come to fight for the fact that there is no God; it is for that that I have seen this cursed island and your blessed face."

"You want me really to believe," said Madeleine, with parted lips, "that you think——"

"I want you to hate me!" cried Turnbull, in agony. "I want you to be sick when you think of my name. I am sure there is no God."

"But there is," said Madeleine, quite quietly, and rather with the air of one telling children about an elephant. "Why, I touched His body only this morning."

"You touched a bit of bread," said Turnbull, biting his knuckles. "Oh, I will say anything that can madden you!"

"You think it is only a bit of bread," said the girl, and her lips tightened ever so little.

"I know it is only a bit of bread," said Turnbull, with violence.

She flung back her open face and smiled. "Then why did you refuse to eat it?" she said.

James Turnbull made a little step backward, and for the first time in his life there seemed to break out and blaze in his head thoughts that were not his own.

"Why, how silly of them," cried out Madeleine, with quite a schoolgirl gaiety, "why, how silly of them to call *you* a blasphemer! Why, you have wrecked your whole business because you would not commit blasphemy."

The man stood, a somewhat comic figure in his tragic bewilderment, with the honest red head of James Turnbull sticking out of the rich and fictitious garments of Camille Bert. But the startled pain of his face was strong enough to obliterate the oddity.

"You come down here," continued the lady, with that female emphasis which is so pulverizing in conversation and so feeble at a public meeting, "you and your MacIan come down here and put on false beards or noses in order to fight. You pretend to be a Catholic commercial traveller from France. Poor Mr. MacIan has to pretend to be a dissolute nobleman from nowhere. Your scheme succeeds; you pick a quite convincing quarrel; you arrange a quite respectable duel; the duel you have planned so long will come off tomorrow with absolute certainty and safety. And then you throw off your wig and throw up your scheme and throw over your colleague, because I ask you to go into a building and eat a bit of bread. And *then* you dare to tell me that you are sure there is nothing watching us. Then you say you know there is nothing on the very altar you run away from. You know——"

"I only know," said Turnbull, "that I must run away from you. This has got beyond any talking." And he plunged along into the village, leaving his black wig and beard lying behind him on the road.

As the market-place opened before him he saw Count Gregory, that distinguished foreigner, standing and smoking in elegant meditation at the corner of the local café. He immediately made his way rapidly towards him, considering that a consultation was urgent. But he had hardly crossed half of that stony quadrangle when a window burst open above him and a head was thrust out, shouting. The man was in his woollen undershirt, but Turnbull knew the energetic, apologetic head of the sergeant of police. He pointed furiously at Turnbull and shouted his name. A policeman ran excitedly from under an archway and tried to collar him. Two men selling vegetables dropped their baskets and joined in the chase. Turnbull dodged the constable, upset one of the men into his own basket, and bounding towards the distinguished foreign Count, called to him clamorously: "Come on, MacIan, the hunt is up again."

The prompt reply of Count Gregory was to pull off his large yellow whiskers and scatter them on the breeze with an air of considerable relief. Then he joined the flight of Turnbull, and even as he did so, with one wrench of his powerful hands rent and split the strange, thick stick that he carried. Inside it was a naked old-fashioned rapier. The two got a good start up the road before the whole town was awakened behind them; and half-way up it a similar transformation was seen to take place in Mr. Turnbull's singular umbrella.

The two had a long race for the harbour; but the English police were heavy and the French inhabitants were indifferent. In any case, they got used to the notion of the road being clear; and just as they had come to the cliffs MacIan banged into another gentleman with unmistakable surprise. How he knew he was another gentleman merely by banging into him, must remain a mystery. MacIan was a very poor and very sober Scotch gentleman. The other was a very drunk and very wealthy English gentleman. But there was something in the staggered and openly embarrassed apologies that made them understand each other as readily and as quickly and as much as two men talking French in the middle of China. The nearest expression of the type is that it either hits or apologizes; and in this case both apologized.

"You seem to be in a hurry," said the unknown Englishman, falling back a step or two in order to laugh with an unnatural heartiness. "What's it all about, eh?" Then before MacIan could get past his sprawling and staggering figure he ran forward again and said with a sort of shouting and ear-shattering whisper: "I say, my name is Wilkinson. *You* know—Wilkinson's Entire was my grandfather. Can't drink beer myself. Liver." And he shook his head with extraordinary sagacity.

"We really are in a hurry, as you say," said MacIan, summoning a sufficiently pleasant smile, "so if you will let us pass—"

"I'll tell you what, you fellows," said the sprawling gentleman, confidentially, while Evan's agonized ears heard behind him the first paces of the pursuit, "if you really are, as you say, in a hurry, I know what it is to be in a hurry—Lord, what a hurry I was in when we all came out of Cartwright's rooms—if you really are in a hurry"—and he seemed to steady his voice into a sort of solemnity—"if you are in a hurry, there's nothing like a good yacht for a man in a hurry."

"No doubt you're right," said MacIan, and dashed past him in despair. The head of the pursuing host was just showing over the top of the hill behind him. Turnbull had already ducked under the intoxicated gentleman's elbow and fled far in front.

"No, but look here," said Mr. Wilkinson, enthusiastically running after MacIan and catching him by the sleeve of his coat. "If you want to hurry you should take a yacht, and if"—he said, with a burst of rationality, like one leaping to a further point in logic—"if you want a yacht—you can have mine."

Evan pulled up abruptly and looked back at him. "We are really in the devil of a hurry," he said, "and if you really have a yacht, the truth is that we would give our ears for it."

"You'll find it in harbour," said Wilkinson, struggling with his speech. "Left side of harbour—called *Gibson Girl*—can't think why, old fellow, I never lent it you before."

With these words the benevolent Mr. Wilkinson fell flat on his face in the road, but continued to laugh softly, and turned towards his flying companion a face of peculiar peace and benignity. Evan's mind went through a crisis of instantaneous casuistry, in which it may be that he decided wrongly; but about how he decided his biographer can profess no doubt. Two minutes afterwards he had overtaken Turnbull and told the tale; ten minutes afterwards he and Turnbull had somehow tumbled into the yacht called the *Gibson Girl* and had somehow pushed off from the Isle of St. Loup.

CHAPTER TWELVE
THE DESERT ISLAND

Those who happen to hold the view (and Mr. Evan MacIan, now alive and comfortable, is among the number) that something supernatural, some eccentric kindness from god or fairy had guided our adventurers through all their absurd perils, might have found his strongest argument perhaps in their management or mismanagement of Mr. Wilkinson's yacht. Neither of them had the smallest qualification for managing such a vessel; but MacIan had a practical knowledge of the sea in much smaller and quite different boats, while Turnbull had an abstract knowledge of science and some of its applications to navigation, which was worse. The presence of the god or fairy can only be deduced from the fact that they never definitely ran into anything, either a boat, a rock, a quicksand, or a man-of-war. Apart from this negative description, their voyage would be difficult to describe. It took at least a fortnight, and MacIan, who was certainly the shrewder sailor of the two, realized that they were sailing west into the Atlantic and were probably by this time past the Scilly Isles. How much farther they stood out into the western sea it was impossible to conjecture. But they felt certain, at least, that they were far enough into that awful gulf between us and America to make it unlikely that they would soon see land again. It was therefore with legitimate excitement that one rainy morning after daybreak they saw that distinct shape of a solitary island standing up against the encircling strip of silver which ran round the skyline and separated the grey and green of the billows from the grey and mauve of the morning clouds.

"What can it be?" cried MacIan, in a dry-throated excitement. "I didn't know there were any Atlantic islands so far beyond the Scillies—Good Lord, it can't be Madeira, yet?"

"I thought you were fond of legends and lies and fables," said Turnbull, grimly. "Perhaps it's Atlantis."

"Of course, it might be," answered the other, quite innocently and gravely; "but I never thought the story about Atlantis was very solidly established."

"Whatever it is, we are running on to it," said Turnbull, equably, "and we shall be shipwrecked twice, at any rate."

The naked-looking nose of land projecting from the unknown island was, indeed, growing larger and larger, like the trunk of some terrible and advancing elephant. There seemed to be nothing in particular, at least on this side of the island, except shoals of shellfish lying so thick as almost to make it look like one of those toy grottos that the children make. In one place, however, the coast offered a soft, smooth bay of sand, and even the rudimentary ingenuity of the two amateur mariners managed to run up the little ship with her prow well on shore and her bowsprit pointing upward, as in a sort of idiotic triumph.

They tumbled on shore and began to unload the vessel, setting the stores out in rows upon the sand with something of the solemnity of boys playing at pirates. There were Mr. Wilkinson's cigar-boxes and Mr. Wilkinson's dozen of champagne and Mr. Wilkinson's tinned salmon and Mr. Wilkinson's tinned tongue and Mr. Wilkinson's tinned sardines, and every sort of preserved thing that could be seen at the Army and Navy stores. Then MacIan stopped with a jar of pickles in his hand and said abruptly:

"I don't know why we're doing all this; I suppose we ought really to fall to and get it over."

Then he added more thoughtfully: "Of course this island seems rather bare and the survivor—"

"The question is," said Turnbull, with cheerful speculation, "whether the survivor will be in a proper frame of mind for potted prawns."

MacIan looked down at the rows of tins and bottles, and the cloud of doubt still lowered upon his face.

"You will permit me two liberties, my dear sir," said Turnbull at last: "The first is to break open this box and light one of Mr. Wilkinson's excellent cigars, which will, I am sure, assist my meditations; the second is to offer a penny for your thoughts; or rather to convulse the already complex finances of this island by betting a penny that I know them."

"What on earth are you talking about?" asked MacIan, listlessly, in the manner of an inattentive child.

"I know what you are really thinking, MacIan," repeated Turnbull, laughing. "I know what I am thinking, anyhow. And I rather fancy it's the same."

"What are you thinking?" asked Evan.

"I am thinking and you are thinking," said Turnbull, "that it is damned silly to waste all that champagne."

Something like the spectre of a smile appeared on the unsmiling visage of the Gael; and he made at least no movement of dissent.

"We could drink all the wine and smoke all the cigars easily in a week," said Turnbull; "and that would be to die feasting like heroes."

"Yes, and there is something else," said MacIan, with slight hesitation. "You see, we are on an almost unknown rock, lost in the Atlantic. The police will never catch us; but then neither may the public ever hear of us; and that was one of the things we wanted." Then, after a pause, he said, drawing in the sand with his sword-point: "She may never hear of it at all."

"Well?" inquired the other, puffing at his cigar.

"Well," said MacIan, "we might occupy a day or two in drawing up a thorough and complete statement of what we did and why we did it, and all about both our points of view. Then we could leave one copy on the island whatever happens to us and put another in an empty bottle and send it out to sea, as they do in the books."

"A good idea," said Turnbull, "and now let us finish unpacking."

As MacIan, a tall, almost ghostly figure, paced along the edge of sand that ran round the islet, the purple but cloudy poetry which was his native element was piled up at its thickest upon his soul. The unique island and the endless sea emphasized the thing solely as an epic. There were no ladies or policemen here to give him a hint either of its farce or its tragedy.

"Perhaps when the morning stars were made," he said to himself, "God built this island up from the bottom of the world to be a tower and a theatre for the fight between yea and nay."

Then he wandered up to the highest level of the rock, where there was a roof or plateau of level stone. Half an hour afterwards, Turnbull found him clearing away the loose sand from this table-land and making it smooth and even.

"We will fight up here, Turnbull," said MacIan, "when the time comes. And till the time comes this place shall be sacred."

"I thought of having lunch up here," said Turnbull, who had a bottle of champagne in his hand.

"No, no—not up here," said MacIan, and came down from the height quite hastily. Before he descended, however, he fixed the two swords upright, one at each end of the platform, as if they were human sentinels to guard it under the stars.

Then they came down and lunched plentifully in a nest of loose rocks. In the same place that night they supped more plentifully still. The smoke of Mr. Wilkinson's cigars went up ceaseless and strong smelling, like a pagan sacrifice; the golden glories of Mr. Wilkinson's champagne rose to their heads and poured out of them in fancies and philosophies. And occasionally they would look up at the starlight and the rock and see the space guarded by the two cross-hilted swords, which looked like two black crosses at either end of a grave.

In this primitive and Homeric truce the week passed by; it consisted almost entirely of eating, drinking, smoking, talking, and occasionally singing. They wrote their records and cast loose their bottle. They never ascended to the ominous plateau; they had never stood there save for that single embarrassed minute when they had had no time to take stock of the seascape or the shape of the land. They did not even explore the island; for MacIan was partly concerned in prayer and Turnbull entirely concerned with tobacco; and both these forms of inspiration can be enjoyed by the secluded and even the sedentary. It was on a golden afternoon, the sun sinking over the sea, rayed like the very head of Apollo, when Turnbull tossed off the last half-pint from the emptied Wilkinsonian bottle, hurled the bottle into the sea with objectless energy, and went up to where his sword stood waiting for him on the hill. MacIan was already standing heavily by his with bent head and eyes reading the ground. He had not even troubled to throw a glance round the island or the horizon. But Turnbull being of a more active and birdlike type of mind did throw a glance round the scene. The consequence of which was that he nearly fell off the rock.

On three sides of this shelly and sandy islet the sea stretched blue and infinite without a speck of land or sail; the same as Turnbull had first seen it, except that the tide being out it showed a few yards more of slanting sand under the roots of the rocks. But on the fourth side the island exhibited a more extraordinary feature. In fact, it exhibited the extraordinary feature of not being an island at all. A long, curving neck of sand, as smooth and wet as the neck of the sea serpent, ran out into the sea and joined their rock to a line of low, billowing, and glistening sand-hills, which the sinking sea had just bared to the sun. Whether they were firm sand or quicksand it was difficult to guess; but there was at least no doubt that they lay on the edge of some larger land; for colourless hills appeared faintly behind them and no sea could be seen beyond.

"Sakes alive!" cried Turnbull, with rolling eyes; "this ain't an island in the Atlantic. We've butted the bally continent of America."

MacIan turned his head, and his face, already pale, grew a shade paler. He was by this time walking in a world of omens and hieroglyphics, and he could not read anything but what was baffling or menacing in this brown gigantic arm of the earth stretched out into the sea to seize him.

"MacIan," said Turnbull, in his temperate way, "whatever our eternal interrupted tete-a-tetes have taught us or not taught us, at least we need not fear the charge of fear. If it is essential to your emotions, I will cheerfully finish the fight here and now; but I must confess that if you kill me here I shall die with my curiosity highly excited and unsatisfied upon a minor point of geography."

"I do not want to stop now," said the other, in his elephantine simplicity, "but we must stop for a moment, because it is a sign—perhaps it is a miracle. We must see what is at the end of the road of sand; it may be a bridge built across the gulf by God."

"So long as you gratify my query," said Turnbull, laughing and letting back his blade into the sheath, "I do not care for what reason you choose to stop."

They clambered down the rocky peninsula and trudged along the sandy isthmus with the plodding resolution of men who seemed almost to have made up their minds to be wanderers on the face of the earth. Despite Turnbull's air of scientific eagerness, he was really the less impatient of the two; and the Highlander went on well ahead of him with passionate strides. By the time they had walked for about half an hour in the ups and downs of those dreary sands, the distance between the two had lengthened and MacIan was only a tall figure silhouetted for an instant upon the crest of some sand-dune and then disappearing behind it. This rather increased the Robinson Crusoe feeling in Mr. Turnbull, and he looked about almost disconsolately for some sign of life. What sort of life he expected it to be if it appeared, he did not very clearly know. He has since confessed that he thinks that in his subconsciousness he expected an alligator.

The first sign of life that he did see, however, was something more extraordinary than the largest alligator. It was nothing less than the notorious Mr. Evan MacIan coming bounding back across the sand-heaps breathless, without his cap and keeping the sword in his hand only by a habit now quite hardened.

"Take care, Turnbull," he cried out from a good distance as he ran, "I've seen a native."

"A native?" repeated his companion, whose scenery had of late been chiefly of shellfish, "what the deuce! Do you mean an oyster?"

"No," said MacIan, stopping and breathing hard, "I mean a savage. A black man."

"Why, where did you see him?" asked the staring editor.

"Over there—behind that hill," said the gasping MacIan. "He put up his black head and grinned at me."

Turnbull thrust his hands through his red hair like one who gives up the world as a bad riddle. "Lord love a duck," said he, "can it be Jamaica?"

Then glancing at his companion with a small frown, as of one slightly suspicious, he said: "I say, don't think me rude—but you're a visionary kind of fellow—and then we drank a great deal. Do you mind waiting here while I go and see for myself?"

"Shout if you get into trouble," said the Celt, with composure; "you will find it as I say."

Turnbull ran off ahead with a rapidity now far greater than his rival's, and soon vanished over the disputed sand-hill. Then five minutes passed, and then seven minutes; and MacIan bit his lip and swung his sword, and the other did not reappear. Finally, with a Gaelic oath, Evan started forward to the rescue, and almost at the same moment the small figure of the missing man appeared on the ridge against the sky.

Even at that distance, however, there was something odd about his attitude; so odd that MacIan continued to make his way in that direction. It looked as if he were wounded; or, still more, as if he were ill. He wavered as he came down the slope and seemed flinging himself into peculiar postures. But it was only when he came within three feet of MacIan's face, that that observer of mankind fully realized that Mr. James Turnbull was roaring with laughter.

"You are quit right," sobbed that wholly demoralized journalist. "He's black, oh, there's no doubt the black's all right—as far as it goes." And he went off again into convulsions of his humorous ailment.

"What ever is the matter with you?" asked MacIan, with stern impatience. "Did you see the nigger——"

"I saw the nigger," gasped Turnbull. "I saw the splendid barbarian Chief. I saw the Emperor of Ethiopia—oh, I saw him all right. The nigger's hands and face are a lovely colour—and the nigger——" And he was overtaken once more.

"Well, well, well," said Evan, stamping each monosyllable on the sand, "what about the nigger?"

"Well, the truth is," said Turnbull, suddenly and startlingly, becoming quite grave and precise, "the truth is, the nigger is a Margate nigger, and we are now on the edge of the Isle of Thanet, a few miles from Margate."

Then he had a momentary return of his hysteria and said: "I say, old boy, I should like to see a chart of our fortnight's cruise in Wilkinson's yacht."

MacIan had no smile in answer, but his eager lips opened as if parched for the truth. "You mean to say," he began——

"Yes, I mean to say," said Turnbull, "and I mean to say something funnier still. I have learnt everything I wanted to know from the partially black musician over there, who has taken a run in his war-paint to meet a friend in a quiet pub along the coast—the noble savage has told me all about it. The bottle containing our declaration, doctrines, and dying sentiments was washed up on Margate beach yesterday in the presence of one alderman, two bathing-machine men, three policemen, seven doctors, and a hundred and thirteen London clerks on a holiday, to all of whom, whether directly or indirectly, our composition gave enormous literary pleasure. Buck up, old man, this story of ours is a switchback. I have begun to understand the pulse and the time of it; now we are up in a cathedral and then we are down in a theatre, where they only play farces. Come, I am quite reconciled—let us enjoy the farce."

But MacIan said nothing, and an instant afterwards Turnbull himself called out in an entirely changed voice: "Oh, this is damnable! This is not to be borne!"

MacIan followed his eye along the sand-hills. He saw what looked like the momentary and waving figure of the nigger minstrel, and then he saw a heavy running policeman take the turn of the sand-hill with the smooth solemnity of a railway train.

CHAPTER THIRTEEN
THE GARDEN OF PEACE

Up to this instant Evan MacIan had really understood nothing; but when he saw the policeman he saw everything. He saw his enemies, all the powers and princes of the earth. He suddenly altered from a staring statue to a leaping man of the mountains.

"We must break away from him here," he cried, briefly, and went like a whirlwind over the sand ridge in a straight line and at a particular angle. When the policeman had finished his admirable railway curve, he found a wall of failing sand between him and the pursued. By the time he had scaled it thrice, slid down twice, and crested it in the third effort, the two flying figures were far in front. They found the sand harder farther on; it began to be crusted with scraps of turf and in a few moments they were flying easily over an open common of rank sea-grass. They had no easy business, however; for the bottle which they had so innocently sent into the chief gate of Thanet had called to life the police of half a county on their trail. From every side across the grey-green common figures could be seen running and closing in; and it was only when MacIan with his big body broke down the tangled barrier of a little wood, as men break down a door with the shoulder; it was only when they vanished crashing into the underworld of the black wood, that their hunters were even instantaneously thrown off the scent.

At the risk of struggling a little longer like flies in that black web of twigs and trunks, Evan (who had an instinct of the hunter or the hunted) took an incalculable course through the forest, which let them out at last by a forest opening—quite forgotten by the leaders of the chase. They ran a mile or two farther along the edge of the wood until they reached another and somewhat similar opening. Then MacIan stood utterly still and listened, as animals listen, for every sound in the universe. Then he said: "We are quit of them." And Turnbull said: "Where shall we go now?"

MacIan looked at the silver sunset that was closing in, barred by plumy lines of purple cloud; he looked at the high tree-tops that caught the last light and at the birds going heavily homeward, just as if all these things were bits of written advice that he could read.

Then he said: "The best place we can go to is to bed. If we can get some sleep in this wood, now everyone has cleared out of it, it will be worth a handicap of two hundred yards tomorrow."

Turnbull, who was exceptionally lively and laughing in his demeanour, kicked his legs about like a schoolboy and said he did not want to go to sleep. He walked incessantly and talked very brilliantly. And when at last he lay down on the hard earth, sleep struck him senseless like a hammer.

Indeed, he needed the strongest sleep he could get; for the earth was still full of darkness and a kind of morning fog when his fellow-fugitive shook him awake.

"No more sleep, I'm afraid," said Evan, in a heavy, almost submissive, voice of apology. "They've gone on past us right enough for a good thirty miles; but now they've found out their mistake, and they're coming back."

"Are you sure?" said Turnbull, sitting up and rubbing his red eyebrows with his hand.

The next moment, however, he had jumped up alive and leaping like a man struck with a shock of cold water, and he was plunging after MacIan along the woodland path. The shape of their old friend the constable had appeared against the pearl and pink of the sunrise. Somehow, it always looked a very funny shape when seen against the sunrise.

* * *

A wash of weary daylight was breaking over the country-side, and the fields and roads were full of white mist—the kind of white mist that clings in corners like cotton wool. The empty road, along which the chase had taken its turn, was overshadowed on one side by a very high discoloured wall, stained, and streaked green, as with seaweed—evidently the high-shouldered sentinel of some great gentleman's estate. A yard or two from the wall ran parallel to it a linked and tangled line of lime-trees, forming a kind of cloister along the side of the road. It was under this branching colonnade that the two fugitives fled, almost concealed from their pursuers by the twilight, the mist and the leaping zoetrope of shadows. Their feet, though beating the ground furiously, made but a faint noise; for they had kicked away their boots in the wood; their long, antiquated weapons made no jingle or clatter, for they had strapped them across their backs like guitars. They had all the advantages that invisibility and silence can add to speed.

A hundred and fifty yards behind them down the centre of the empty road the first of their pursuers came pounding and panting—a fat but powerful policeman who had distanced all the rest. He came on at a splendid pace for so portly a figure; but, like all heavy bodies in motion, he gave the impression that it would be easier for him to increase his pace than to slacken it suddenly. Nothing short of a brick wall could have abruptly brought him up. Turnbull turned his head slightly and found breath to say something to MacIan. MacIan nodded.

Pursuer and pursued were fixed in their distance as they fled, for some quarter of a mile, when they came to a place where two or three of the trees grew twistedly together, making a special obscurity. Past this place the pursuing policeman went thundering without thought or hesitation. But he was pursuing his shadow or the wind; for Turnbull had put one foot in a crack of the tree and gone up it as quickly and softly as a cat. Somewhat more laboriously but in equal silence the long legs of the Highlander had followed; and crouching in crucial silence in the cloud of leaves, they saw the whole posse of their pursuers go by and die into the dust and mists of the distance.

The white vapour lay, as it often does, in lean and palpable layers; and even the head of the tree was above it in the half-daylight, like a green ship swinging on a sea of foam. But higher yet behind them, and readier to catch the first coming of the sun, ran the rampart of the top of the wall, which in their excitement of escape looked at once indispensable and unattainable, like the wall of heaven. Here, however, it was MacIan's turn to have the advantage; for, though less light-limbed and feline, he was longer and stronger in the arms. In two seconds he had tugged up his chin over the wall like a horizontal bar; the next he sat astride of it, like a horse of stone. With his assistance Turnbull vaulted to the same perch, and the two began cautiously to shift along the wall in the direction by which they had come, doubling on their tracks to throw off the last pursuit. MacIan could not rid himself of the fancy of bestriding a steed; the long, grey coping of the wall shot out in front of him, like the long, grey neck of some nightmare Rosinante. He had the quaint thought that he and Turnbull were two knights on one steed on the old shield of the Templars.

The nightmare of the stone horse was increased by the white fog, which seemed thicker inside the wall than outside. They could make nothing of the enclosure upon which they were partial trespassers, except that the green and crooked branches of a big apple-tree came crawling at them out of the mist, like the tentacles of some green cuttlefish. Anything would serve, however, that was likely to confuse their trail, so they both decided without need of words to use this tree also as a ladder—a ladder of descent. When they dropped from the lowest branch to the ground their stockinged feet felt hard gravel beneath them.

They had alighted in the middle of a very broad garden path, and the clearing mist permitted them to see the edge of a well-clipped lawn. Though the white vapour was still a veil, it was like the gauzy veil of a transformation scene in a pantomime; for through it there glowed shapeless masses of colour, masses which might be clouds of sunrise or mosaics of gold and crimson, or ladies robed in ruby and emerald draperies. As it thinned yet farther they saw that it was only flowers; but flowers in such insolent mass and magnificence as can seldom be seen out of the tropics. Purple and crimson rhododendrons rose arrogantly, like rampant heraldic animals against their burning background of laburnum gold. The roses were red hot; the clematis was, so to speak, blue hot. And yet the mere whiteness of the syringa seemed the most violent colour of all. As the golden sunlight gradually conquered the mists, it had really something of the sensational sweetness of the slow opening of the gates of Eden. MacIan, whose mind was always haunted with such seraphic or titanic parallels, made some such remark to his companion. But Turnbull only cursed and said that it was the back garden of some damnable rich man.

When the last haze had faded from the ordered paths, the open lawns, and the flaming flower-beds, the two realized, not without an abrupt re-examination of their position, that they were not alone in the garden.

Down the centre of the central garden path, preceded by a blue cloud from a cigarette, was walking a gentleman who evidently understood all the relish of a garden in the very early morning. He was a slim yet satisfied figure, clad in a suit of pale-grey tweed, so subdued that the pattern was imperceptible—a costume that was casual but not by any means careless. His face, which was reflective and somewhat over-refined, was the face of a quite elderly man, though his stringy hair and moustache were still quite yellow. A double eye-glass, with a broad, black ribbon, drooped from his aquiline nose, and he smiled, as he communed with himself, with a self-content which was rare and almost irritating. The straw panama on his head was many shades shabbier than his clothes, as if he had caught it up by accident.

It needed the full shock of the huge shadow of MacIan, falling across his sunlit path, to rouse him from his smiling reverie. When this had fallen on him he lifted his head a little and blinked at the intruders with short-sighted benevolence, but with far less surprise than might have been expected. He was a gentleman; that is, he had social presence of mind, whether for kindness or for insolence.

"Can I do anything for you?" he said, at last.

MacIan bowed. "You can extend to us your pardon," he said, for he also came of a whole race of gentlemen—of gentlemen without shirts to their backs. "I am afraid we are trespassing. We have just come over the wall."

"Over the wall?" repeated the smiling old gentleman, still without letting his surprise come uppermost.

"I suppose I am not wrong, sir," continued MacIan, "in supposing that these grounds inside the wall belong to you?"

The man in the panama looked at the ground and smoked thoughtfully for a few moments, after which he said, with a sort of matured conviction:

"Yes, certainly; the grounds inside the wall really belong to me, and the grounds outside the wall, too."

"A large proprietor, I imagine," said Turnbull, with a truculent eye.

"Yes," answered the old gentleman, looking at him with a steady smile. "A large proprietor."

Turnbull's eye grew even more offensive, and he began biting his red beard; but MacIan seemed to recognize a type with which he could deal and continued quite easily:

"I am sure that a man like you will not need to be told that one sees and does a good many things that do not get into the newspapers. Things which, on the whole, had better not get into the newspapers."

The smile of the large proprietor broadened for a moment under his loose, light moustache, and the other continued with increased confidence:

"One sometimes wants to have it out with another man. The police won't allow it in the streets—and then there's the County Council—and in the fields even nothing's allowed but posters of pills. But in a gentleman's garden, now—"

The strange gentleman smiled again and said, easily enough: "Do you want to fight? What do you want to fight about?"

MacIan had understood his man pretty well up to that point; an instinct common to all men with the aristocratic tradition of Europe had guided him. He knew that the kind of man who in his own back garden wears good clothes and spoils them with a bad hat is not the kind of man who has an abstract horror of illegal actions of violence or the evasion of the police. But a man may understand ragging and yet be very far from understanding religious ragging. This seeming host of theirs might comprehend a quarrel of husband and lover or a difficulty at cards or even escape from a pursuing tailor; but it still remained doubtful whether he would feel the earth fail under him in that earthquake instant when the Virgin is compared to a goddess of Mesopotamia. Even MacIan, therefore (whose tact was far from being his strong point), felt the necessity for some compromise in the mode of approach. At last he said, and even then with hesitation:

"We are fighting about God; there can be nothing so important as that."

The tilted eye-glasses of the old gentleman fell abruptly from his nose, and he thrust his aristocratic chin so far forward that his lean neck seemed to shoot out longer like a telescope.

"About God?" he queried, in a key completely new.

"Look here!" cried Turnbull, taking his turn roughly, "I'll tell you what it's all about. I think that there's no God. I take it that it's nobody's business but mine—or God's, if there is one. This young gentleman from the Highlands happens to think that it's his business. In consequence, he first takes a walking-stick and smashes my shop; then he takes the same walking-stick and tries to smash me. To this I naturally object. I suggest that if it comes to that we should both have sticks. He improves on the suggestion and proposes that we should both have steel-pointed sticks. The police (with characteristic unreasonableness) will not accept either of our proposals; the result is that we run about dodging the police and have jumped over our garden wall into your magnificent garden to throw ourselves on your magnificent hospitality."

The face of the old gentleman had grown redder and redder during this address, but it was still smiling; and when he broke out it was with a kind of guffaw.

"So you really want to fight with drawn swords in my garden," he asked, "about whether there is really a God?"

"Why not?" said MacIan, with his simple monstrosity of speech; "all man's worship began when the Garden of Eden was founded."

"Yes, by——!" said Turnbull, with an oath, "and ended when the Zoological Gardens were founded."

"In this garden! In my presence!" cried the stranger, stamping up and down the gravel and choking with laughter, "whether there is a God!" And he went stamping up and down the garden, making it echo with his unintelligible laughter. Then he came back to them more composed and wiping his eyes.

"Why, how small the world is!" he cried at last. "I can settle the whole matter. Why, I am God!"

And he suddenly began to kick and wave his well-clad legs about the lawn.

"You are what?" repeated Turnbull, in a tone which is beyond description.

"Why, God, of course!" answered the other, thoroughly amused. "How funny it is to think that you have tumbled over a garden wall and fallen exactly on the right person! You might have gone floundering about in all sorts of churches and chapels and colleges and schools of philosophy looking for some evidence of the existence of God. Why, there is no evidence, except seeing him. And now you've seen him. You've seen him dance!"

And the obliging old gentleman instantly stood on one leg without relaxing at all the grave and cultured benignity of his expression.

"I understood that this garden——" began the bewildered MacIan.

"Quite so! Quite so!" said the man on one leg, nodding gravely. "I said this garden belonged to me and the land outside it. So they do. So does the country beyond that and the sea beyond that and all the rest of the earth. So does the moon. So do the sun and stars." And he added, with a smile of apology: "You see, I'm God."

Turnbull and MacIan looked at him for one moment with a sort of notion that perhaps he was not too old to be merely playing the fool. But after staring steadily for an instant Turnbull saw the hard and horrible earnestness in the man's eyes behind all his empty animation. Then Turnbull looked very gravely at the strict gravel walls and the gay flower-beds and the long rectangular red-brick building, which the mist had left evident beyond them. Then he looked at MacIan.

Almost at the same moment another man came walking quickly round the regal clump of rhododendrons. He had the look of a prosperous banker, wore a good tall silk hat, was almost stout enough to burst the buttons of a fine frock-coat; but he was talking to himself, and one of his elbows had a singular outward jerk as he went by.

CHAPTER FOURTEEN
A MUSEUM OF SOULS

The man with the good hat and the jumping elbow went by very quickly;

yet the man with the bad hat, who thought he was God, overtook him. He ran after him and jumped over a bed of geraniums to catch him.

"I beg your Majesty's pardon," he said, with mock humility, "but here is a quarrel which you ought really to judge."

Then as he led the heavy, silk-hatted man back towards the group, he caught MacIan's ear in order to whisper: "This poor gentleman is mad; he thinks he is Edward VII." At this the self-appointed Creator slightly winked. "Of course you won't trust him much; come to me for everything. But in my position one has to meet so many people. One has to be broadminded."

The big banker in the black frock-coat and hat was standing quite grave and dignified on the lawn, save for his slight twitch of one limb, and he did not seem by any means unworthy of the part which the other promptly forced upon him.

"My dear fellow," said the man in the straw hat, "these two gentlemen are going to fight a duel of the utmost importance. Your own royal position and my much humbler one surely indicate us as the proper seconds. Seconds—yes, seconds——" and here the speaker was once more shaken with his old malady of laughter.

"Yes, you and I are both seconds—and these two gentlemen can obviously fight in front of us. You, he-he, are the king. I am God; really, they could hardly have better supporters. They have come to the right place."

Then Turnbull, who had been staring with a frown at the fresh turf, burst out with a rather bitter laugh and cried, throwing his red head in the air:

"Yes, by God, MacIan, I think we have come to the right place!" And MacIan answered, with an adamantine stupidity:

"Any place is the right place where they will let us do it."

There was a long stillness, and their eyes involuntarily took in the landscape, as they had taken in all the landscapes of their everlasting combat; the bright, square garden behind the shop; the whole lift and leaning of the side of Hampstead Heath; the little garden of the decadent choked with flowers; the square of sand beside the sea at sunrise. They both felt at the same moment all the breadth and blossoming beauty of that paradise, the coloured trees, the natural and restful nooks and also the great wall of stone—more awful than the wall of China—from which no flesh could flee.

Turnbull was moodily balancing his sword in his hand as the other spoke; then he started, for a mouth whispered quite close to his ear. With a softness incredible in any cat, the huge, heavy man in the black hat and frock-coat had crept across the lawn from his own side and was saying in his ear: "Don't trust that second of yours. He's mad and not so mad, either; for he frightfully cunning and sharp. Don't believe the story he tells you about why I hate him. I know the story he'll tell; I overheard it when the housekeeper was talking to the postman. It's too long to talk about now, and I expect we're watched, but——"

Something in Turnbull made him want suddenly to be sick on the grass; the mere healthy and heathen horror of the unclean; the mere inhumane hatred of the inhuman state of madness. He seemed to hear all round him the hateful whispers of that place, innumerable as leaves whispering in the wind, and each of them telling eagerly some evil that had not happened or some terrific secret which was not true. All the rationalist and plain man revolted within him against bowing down for a moment in that forest of deception and egotistical darkness. He wanted to blow up that palace of delusions with dynamite; and in some wild way, which I will not defend, he tried to do it.

He looked across at MacIan and said: "Oh, I can't stand this!"

"Can't stand what?" asked his opponent, eyeing him doubtfully.

"Shall we say the atmosphere?" replied Turnbull; "one can't use uncivil expressions even to a—deity. The fact is, I don't like having God for my second."

"Sir!" said that being in a state of great offence, "in my position I am not used to having my favours refused. Do you know who I am?"

The editor of *The Atheist* turned upon him like one who has lost all patience, and exploded: "Yes, you are God, aren't you?" he said, abruptly, "why do we have two sets of teeth?"

"Teeth?" spluttered the genteel lunatic; "teeth?"

"Yes," cried Turnbull, advancing on him swiftly and with animated gestures, "why does teething hurt? Why do growing pains hurt? Why are measles catching? Why does a rose have thorns? Why do rhinoceroses have horns? Why is the horn on the top of the nose? Why haven't I a horn on the top of my nose, eh?" And he struck the bridge of his nose smartly with his forefinger to indicate the place of the omission and then wagged the finger menacingly at the Creator.

"I've often wanted to meet you," he resumed, sternly, after a pause, "to hold you accountable for all the idiocy and cruelty of this muddled and meaningless world of yours. You make a hundred seeds and only one bears fruit. You make a million worlds and only one seems inhabited. What do you mean by it, eh? What do you mean by it?"

The unhappy lunatic had fallen back before this quite novel form of attack, and lifted his burnt-out cigarette almost like one warding off a blow. Turnbull went on like a torrent.

"A man died yesterday in Ealing. You murdered him. A girl had the toothache in Croydon. You gave it her. Fifty sailors were drowned off Selsey Bill. You scuttled their ship. What have you got to say for yourself, eh?"

The representative of omnipotence looked as if he had left most of these things to his subordinates; he passed a hand over his wrinkling brow and said in a voice much saner than any he had yet used:

"Well, if you dislike my assistance, of course—perhaps the other gentleman——"

"The other gentleman," cried Turnbull, scornfully, "is a submissive and loyal and obedient gentleman. He likes the people who wear crowns, whether of diamonds or of stars. He believes in the divine right of kings, and it is appropriate enough that he should have the king for his second. But it is not appropriate to me that I should have God for my second. God is not good enough. I dislike and I deny the divine right of kings. But I dislike more and I deny more the divine right of divinity."

Then after a pause in which he swallowed his passion, he said to MacIan: "You have got the right second, anyhow."

The Highlander did not answer, but stood as if thunderstruck with one long and heavy thought. Then at last he turned abruptly to his second in the silk hat and said: "Who are you?"

The man in the silk hat blinked and bridled in affected surprise, like one who was in truth accustomed to be doubted.

"I am King Edward VII," he said, with shaky arrogance. "Do you doubt my word?"

"I do not doubt it in the least," answered MacIan.

"Then, why," said the large man in the silk hat, trembling from head to foot, "why do you wear your hat before the king?"

"Why should I take it off," retorted MacIan, with equal heat, "before a usurper?"

Turnbull swung round on his heel. "Well, really," he said, "I thought at least you were a loyal subject."

"I am the only loyal subject," answered the Gael. "For nearly thirty years I have walked these islands and have not found another."

"You are always hard to follow," remarked Turnbull, genially, "and sometimes so much so as to be hardly worth following."

"I alone am loyal," insisted MacIan; "for I alone am in rebellion. I am ready at any instant to restore the Stuarts. I am ready at any instant to defy the Hanoverian brood—and I defy it now even when face to face with the actual ruler of the enormous British Empire!"

And folding his arms and throwing back his lean, hawklike face, he haughtily confronted the man with the formal frock-coat and the eccentric elbow.

"What right had you stunted German squires," he cried, "to interfere in a quarrel between Scotch and English and Irish gentlemen? Who made you, whose fathers could not splutter English while they walked in Whitehall, who made you the judge between the republic of Sidney and the monarchy of Montrose? What had your sires to do with England that they should have the foul offering of the blood of Derwentwater and the heart of Jimmy Dawson? Where are the corpses of Culloden? Where is the blood of Lochiel?" MacIan advanced upon his opponent with a bony and pointed finger, as if indicating the exact pocket in which the blood of that Cameron was probably kept; and Edward VII fell back a few paces in considerable confusion.

"What good have you ever done to us?" he continued in harsher and harsher accents, forcing the other back towards the flower-beds. "What good have you ever done, you race of German sausages? Yards of barbarian etiquette, to throttle the freedom of aristocracy! Gas of northern metaphysics to blow up Broad Church bishops like balloons. Bad pictures and bad manners and pantheism and the Albert Memorial. Go back to Hanover, you humbug? Go to—"

Before the end of this tirade the arrogance of the monarch had entirely given way; he had fairly turned tail and was trundling away down the path. MacIan strode after him still preaching and flourishing his large, lean hands. The other two remained in the centre of the lawn—Turnbull in convulsions of laughter, the lunatic in convulsions of disgust. Almost at the same moment a third figure came stepping swiftly across the lawn.

The advancing figure walked with a stoop, and yet somehow flung his forked and narrow beard forward. That carefully cut and pointed yellow beard was, indeed, the most emphatic thing about him. When he clasped his hands behind him, under the tails of his coat, he would wag his beard at a man like a big forefinger. It performed almost all his gestures; it was more important than the glittering eye-glasses through which he looked or the beautiful bleating voice in which he spoke. His face and neck were of a lusty red, but lean and stringy; he always wore his expensive gold-rim eye-glasses slightly askew upon his aquiline nose; and he always showed two gleaming foreteeth under his moustache, in a smile so perpetual as to earn the reputation of a sneer. But for the crooked glasses his dress was always exquisite; and but for the smile he was perfectly and perennially depressed.

"Don't you think," said the new-comer, with a sort of supercilious entreaty, "that we had better all come into breakfast? It is such a mistake to wait for breakfast. It spoils one's temper so much."

"Quite so," replied Turnbull, seriously.

"There seems almost to have been a little quarrelling here," said the man with the goatish beard.

"It is rather a long story," said Turnbull, smiling. "Originally, it might be called a phase in the quarrel between science and religion."

The new-comer started slightly, and Turnbull replied to the question on his face.

"Oh, yes," he said, "I am science!"

"I congratulate you heartily," answered the other, "I am Doctor Quayle."

Turnbull's eyes did not move, but he realized that the man in the panama hat had lost all his ease of a landed proprietor and had withdrawn to a distance of thirty yards, where he stood glaring with all the contraction of fear and hatred that can stiffen a cat.

*   *   *

MacIan was sitting somewhat disconsolately on a stump of tree, his large black head half buried in his large brown hands, when Turnbull strode up to him chewing a cigarette. He did not look up, but his comrade and enemy addressed him like one who must free himself of his feelings.

"Well, I hope, at any rate," he said, "that you like your precious religion now. I hope you like the society of this poor devil whom your damned tracts and hymns and priests have driven out of his wits. Five men in this place, they tell me, five men in this place who might have been fathers of families, and every one of them thinks he is God the Father. Oh! you may talk about the ugliness of science, but there is no one here who thinks he is Protoplasm."

"They naturally prefer a bright part," said MacIan, wearily. "Protoplasm is not worth going mad about."

"At least," said Turnbull, savagely, "it was your Jesus Christ who started all this bosh about being God."

For one instant MacIan opened the eyes of battle; then his tightened lips took a crooked smile and he said, quite calmly:

"No, the idea is older; it was Satan who first said that he was God."

"Then, what," asked Turnbull, very slowly, as he softly picked a flower, "what is the difference between Christ and Satan?"

"It is quite simple," replied the Highlander. "Christ descended into hell; Satan fell into it."

"Does it make much odds?" asked the free-thinker.

"It makes all the odds," said the other. "One of them wanted to go up and went down; the other wanted to go down and went up. A god can be humble, a devil can only be humbled."

"Why are you always wanting to humble a man?" asked Turnbull, knitting his brows. "It affects me as ungenerous."

"Why were you wanting to humble a god when you found him in this garden?" asked MacIan.

"That was an extreme case of impudence," said Turnbull.

"Granting the man his almighty pretensions, I think he was very modest," said MacIan. "It is we who are arrogant, who know we are only men. The ordinary man in the street is more of a monster than that poor fellow; for the man in the street treats himself as God Almighty when he knows he isn't. He expects the universe to turn round him, though he knows he isn't the centre."

"Well," said Turnbull, sitting down on the grass, "this is a digression, anyhow. What I want to point out is, that your faith does end in asylums and my science doesn't."

"Doesn't it, by George!" cried MacIan, scornfully. "There are a few men here who are mad on God and a few who are mad on the Bible. But I bet there are many more who are simply mad on madness."

"Do you really believe it?" asked the other.

"Scores of them, I should say," answered MacIan. "Fellows who have read medical books or fellows whose fathers and uncles had something hereditary in their heads—the whole air they breathe is mad."

"All the same," said Turnbull, shrewdly, "I bet you haven't found a madman of that sort."

"I bet I have!" cried Evan, with unusual animation. "I've been walking about the garden talking to a poor chap all the morning. He's simply been broken down and driven raving by your damned science. Talk about believing one is God—why, it's quite an old, comfortable, fireside fancy compared with the sort of things this fellow believes. He believes that there is a God, but that he is better than God. He says God will be afraid to face him. He says one is always progressing beyond the best. He put his arm in mine and whispered in my ear, as if it were the apocalypse: 'Never trust a God that you can't improve on.'"

"What can he have meant?" said the atheist, with all his logic awake. "Obviously one should not trust any God that one can improve on."

"It is the way he talks," said MacIan, almost indifferently; "but he says rummier things than that. He says that a man's doctor ought to decide what woman he marries; and he says that children ought not to be brought up by their parents, because a physical partiality will then distort the judgement of the educator."

"Oh, dear!" said Turnbull, laughing, "you have certainly come across a pretty bad case, and incidentally proved your own. I suppose some men do lose their wits through science as through love and other good things."

"And he says," went on MacIan, monotonously, "that he cannot see why anyone should suppose that a triangle is a three-sided figure. He says that on some higher plane—"

Turnbull leapt to his feet as by an electric shock. "I never could have believed," he cried, "that you had humour enough to tell a lie. You've gone a bit too far, old man, with your little joke. Even in a lunatic asylum there can't be anybody who, having thought about the matter, thinks that a triangle has not got three sides. If he exists he must be a new era in human psychology. But he doesn't exist."

"I will go and fetch him," said MacIan, calmly; "I left the poor fellow wandering about by the nasturtium bed."

MacIan vanished, and in a few moments returned, trailing with him his own discovery among lunatics, who was a slender man with a fixed smile and an unfixed and rolling head. He had a goatlike beard just long enough to be shaken in a strong wind. Turnbull sprang to his feet and was like one who is speechless through choking a sudden shout of laughter.

"Why, you great donkey," he shouted, in an ear-shattering whisper, "that's not one of the patients at all. That's one of the doctors."

Evan looked back at the leering head with the long-pointed beard and repeated the word inquiringly: "One of the doctors?"

"Oh, you know what I mean," said Turnbull, impatiently. "The medical authorities of the place."

Evan was still staring back curiously at the beaming and bearded creature behind him.

"The mad doctors," said Turnbull, shortly.

"Quite so," said MacIan.

After a rather restless silence Turnbull plucked MacIan by the elbow and pulled him aside.

"For goodness sake," he said, "don't offend this fellow; he may be as mad as ten hatters, if you like, but he has us between his finger and thumb. This is the very time he appointed to talk with us about our—well, our exeat."

"But what can it matter?" asked the wondering MacIan. "He can't keep us in the asylum. We're not mad."

"Jackass!" said Turnbull, heartily, "of course we're not mad. Of course, if we are medically examined and the thing is thrashed out, they will find we are not mad. But don't you see that if the thing is thrashed out it will mean letters to this reference and telegrams to that; and at the first word of who we are, we shall be taken out of a madhouse, where we may smoke, to a jail, where we mayn't. No, if we manage this very quietly, he may merely let us out at the front door as stray revellers. If there's half an hour of inquiry, we are cooked."

MacIan looked at the grass frowningly for a few seconds, and then said in a new, small and childish voice: "I am awfully stupid, Mr. Turnbull; you must be patient with me."

Turnbull caught Evan's elbow again with quite another gesture. "Come," he cried, with the harsh voice of one who hides emotion, "come and let us be tactful in chorus."

The doctor with the pointed beard was already slanting it forward at a more than usually acute angle, with the smile that expressed expectancy.

"I hope I do not hurry you, gentlemen," he said, with the faintest suggestion of a sneer at their hurried consultation, "but I believe you wanted to see me at half past eleven."

"I am most awfully sorry, Doctor," said Turnbull, with ready amiability; "I never meant to keep you waiting; but the silly accident that has landed us in your garden may have some rather serious consequences to our friends elsewhere, and my friend here was just drawing my attention to some of them."

"Quite so! Quite so!" said the doctor, hurriedly. "If you really want to put anything before me, I can give you a few moments in my consulting-room."

He led them rapidly into a small but imposing apartment, which seemed to be built and furnished entirely in red-varnished wood. There was one desk occupied with carefully docketed papers; and there were several chairs of the red-varnished wood—though of different shape. All along the wall ran something that might have been a bookcase, only that it was not filled with books, but with flat, oblong slabs or cases of the same polished dark-red consistency. What those flat wooden cases were they could form no conception.

The doctor sat down with a polite impatience on his professional perch; MacIan remained standing, but Turnbull threw himself almost with luxury into a hard wooden arm-chair.

"This is a most absurd business, Doctor," he said, "and I am ashamed to take up the time of busy professional men with such pranks from outside. The plain fact is, that he and I and a pack of silly men and girls have organized a game across this part of the country—a sort of combination of hare and hounds and hide and seek—I dare say you've heard of it. We are the hares, and, seeing your high wall look so inviting, we tumbled over it, and naturally were a little startled with what we found on the other side."

"Quite so!" said the doctor, mildly. "I can understand that you were startled."

Turnbull had expected him to ask what place was the headquarters of the new exhilarating game, and who were the male and female enthusiasts who had brought it to such perfection; in fact, Turnbull was busy making up these personal and topographical particulars. As the doctor did not ask the question, he grew slightly uneasy, and risked the question: "I hope you will accept my assurance that the thing was an accident and that no intrusion was meant."

"Oh, yes, sir," replied the doctor, smiling, "I accept everything that you say."

"In that case," said Turnbull, rising genially, "we must not further interrupt your important duties. I suppose there will be someone to let us out?"

"No," said the doctor, still smiling steadily and pleasantly, "there will be no one to let you out."

"Can we let ourselves out, then?" asked Turnbull, in some surprise.

"Why, of course not," said the beaming scientist; "think how dangerous that would be in a place like this."

"Then, how the devil are we to get out?" cried Turnbull, losing his manners for the first time.

"It is a question of time, of receptivity, and treatment," said the doctor, arching his eyebrows indifferently. "I do not regard either of your cases as incurable."

And with that the man of the world was struck dumb, and, as in all intolerable moments, the word was with the unworldly.

MacIan took one stride to the table, leant across it, and said: "We can't stop here, we're not mad people!"

"We don't use the crude phrase," said the doctor, smiling at his patent-leather boots.

"But you *can't* think us mad," thundered MacIan. "You never saw us before. You know nothing about us. You haven't even examined us."

The doctor threw back his head and beard. "Oh, yes," he said, "very thoroughly."

"But you can't shut a man up on your mere impressions without documents or certificates or anything?"

The doctor got languidly to his feet. "Quite so," he said. "You certainly ought to see the documents."

He went across to the curious mock book-shelves and took down one of the flat mahogany cases. This he opened with a curious key at his watch-chain, and laying back a flap revealed a quire of foolscap covered with close but quite clear writing. The first three words were in such large copy-book hand that they caught the eye even at a distance. They were: "MacIan, Evan Stuart."

Evan bent his angry eagle face over it; yet something blurred it and he could never swear he saw it distinctly. He saw something that began: "Prenatal influences predisposing to mania. Grandfather believed in return of the Stuarts. Mother carried bone of St. Eulalia with which she touched children in sickness. Marked religious mania at early age—"

Evan fell back and fought for his speech. "Oh!" he burst out at last. "Oh! if all this world I have walked in had been as sane as my mother was."

Then he compressed his temples with his hands, as if to crush them. And then lifted suddenly a face that looked fresh and young, as if he had dipped and washed it in some holy well.

"Very well," he cried; "I will take the sour with the sweet. I will pay the penalty of having enjoyed God in this monstrous modern earth that cannot enjoy man or beast. I will die happy in your madhouse, only because I know what I know. Let it be granted, then—MacIan is a mystic; MacIan is a maniac. But this honest shopkeeper and editor whom I have dragged on my inhuman escapades, you cannot keep him. He will go free, thank God, he is not down in any damned document. His ancestor, I am certain, did not die at Culloden. His mother, I swear, had no relics. Let my friend out of your front door, and as for me—"

The doctor had already gone across to the laden shelves, and after a few minutes' short-sighted peering, had pulled down another parallelogram of dark-red wood.

This also he unlocked on the table, and with the same unerring egotistic eye on of the company saw the words, written in large letters: "Turnbull, James."

Hitherto Turnbull himself had somewhat scornfully surrendered his part in the whole business; but he was too honest and unaffected not to start at his own name. After the name, the inscription appeared to run: "Unique case of Eleutheromania. Parentage, as so often in such cases, prosaic and healthy. Eleutheromaniac signs occurred early, however, leading him to attach himself to the individualist Bradlaugh. Recent outbreak of pure anarchy—"

Turnbull slammed the case to, almost smashing it, and said with a burst of savage laughter: "Oh! come along, MacIan; I don't care so much, even about getting out of the madhouse, if only we get out of this room. You were right enough, MacIan, when you spoke about—about mad doctors."

Somehow they found themselves outside in the cool, green garden, and then, after a stunned silence, Turnbull said: "There is one thing that was puzzling me all the time, and I understand it now."

"What do you mean?" asked Evan.

"No man by will or wit," answered Turnbull, "can get out of this garden; and yet we got into it merely by jumping over a garden wall. The whole thing explains itself easily enough. That undefended wall was an open trap. It was a trap laid for two celebrated lunatics. They saw us get in right enough. And they will see that we do not get out."

Evan gazed at the garden wall, gravely for more than a minute, and then he nodded without a word.

CHAPTER FIFTEEN
THE DREAM OF MACIAN

The system of espionage in the asylum was so effective and complete that in practice the patients could often enjoy a sense of almost complete solitude. They could stray up so near to the wall in an apparently unwatched garden as to find it easy to jump over it. They would only have found the error of their calculations if they had tried to jump.

Under this insulting liberty, in this artificial loneliness, Evan MacIan was in the habit of creeping out into the garden after dark—especially upon moonlight nights. The moon, indeed, was for him always a positive magnet in a manner somewhat hard to explain to those of a robuster attitude. Evidently, Apollo is to the full as poetical as Diana; but it is not a question of poetry in the matured and intellectual sense of the word. It is a question of a certain solid and childish fancy. The sun is in the strict and literal sense invisible; that is to say, that by our bodily eyes it cannot properly be seen. But the moon is a much simpler thing; a naked and nursery sort of thing. It hangs in the sky quite solid and quite silver and quite useless; it is one huge celestial snowball. It was at least some such infantile facts and fancies which led Evan again and again during his dehumanized imprisonment to go out as if to shoot the moon.

He was out in the garden on one such luminous and ghostly night, when the steady moonshine toned down all the colours of the garden until almost the strongest tints to be seen were the strong soft blue of the sky and the large lemon moon. He was walking with his face turned up to it in that rather half-witted fashion which might have excused the error of his keepers; and as he gazed he became aware of something little and lustrous flying close to the lustrous orb, like a bright chip knocked off the moon. At first he thought it was a mere sparkle or refraction in his own eyesight; he blinked and cleared his eyes. Then he thought it was a falling star; only it did not fall. It jerked awkwardly up and down in a way unknown among meteors and strangely reminiscent of the works of man. The next moment the thing drove right across the moon, and from being silver upon blue, suddenly became black upon silver; then although it passed the field of light in a flash its outline was unmistakable though eccentric. It was a flying ship.

The vessel took one long and sweeping curve across the sky and came nearer and nearer to MacIan, like a steam-engine coming round a bend. It was of pure white steel, and in the moon it gleamed like the armour of Sir Galahad. The simile of such virginity is not inappropriate; for, as it grew larger and larger and lower and lower, Evan saw that the only figure in it was robed in white from head to foot and crowned with snow-white hair, on which the moonshine lay like a benediction. The figure stood so still that he could easily have supposed it to be a statue. Indeed, he thought it was until it spoke.

"Evan," said the voice, and it spoke with the simple authority of some forgotten father revisiting his children, "you have remained here long enough, and your sword is wanted elsewhere."

"Wanted for what?" asked the young man, accepting the monstrous event with a queer and clumsy naturalness; "what is my sword wanted for?"

"For all that you hold dear," said the man standing in the moonlight; "for the thrones of authority and for all ancient loyalty to law."

Evan looked up at the lunar orb again as if in irrational appeal—a moon calf bleating to his mother the moon. But the face of Luna seemed as witless as his own; there is no help in nature against the supernatural; and he looked again at the tall marble figure that might have been made out of solid moonlight.

Then he said in a loud voice: "Who are you?" and the next moment was seized by a sort of choking terror lest his question should be answered. But the unknown preserved an impenetrable silence for a long space and then only answered: "I must not say who I am until the end of the world; but I may say what I am. I am the law."

And he lifted his head so that the moon smote full upon his beautiful and ancient face.

The face was the face of a Greek god grown old, but not grown either weak or ugly; there was nothing to break its regularity except a rather long chin with a cleft in it, and this rather added distinction than lessened beauty. His strong, well-opened eyes were very brilliant but quite colourless like steel.

MacIan was one of those to whom a reverence and self-submission in ritual come quite easy, and are ordinary things. It was not artificial in him to bend slightly to this solemn apparition or to lower his voice when he said: "Do you bring me some message?"

"I do bring you a message," answered the man of moon and marble. "The king has returned."

Evan did not ask for or require any explanation. "I suppose you can take me to the war," he said, and the silent silver figure only bowed its head again. MacIan clambered into the silver boat, and it rose upward to the stars.

To say that it rose to the stars is no mere metaphor, for the sky had cleared to that occasional and astonishing transparency in which one can see plainly both stars and moon.

As the white-robed figure went upward in his white chariot, he said quite quietly to Evan: "There is an answer to all the folly talked about equality. Some stars are big and some small; some stand still and some circle around them as they stand. They can be orderly, but they cannot be equal."

"They are all very beautiful," said Evan, as if in doubt.

"They are all beautiful," answered the other, "because each is in his place and owns his superior. And now England will be beautiful after the same fashion. The earth will be as beautiful as the heavens, because our kings have come back to us."

"The Stuart——" began Evan, earnestly.

"Yes," answered the old man, "that which has returned is Stuart and yet older than Stuart. It is Capet and Plantagenet and Pendragon. It is all that good old time of which proverbs tell, that golden reign of Saturn against which gods and men were rebels. It is all that was ever lost by insolence and overwhelmed in rebellion. It is your own forefather, MacIan with the broken sword, bleeding without hope at Culloden. It is Charles refusing to answer the questions of the rebel court. It is Mary of the magic face confronting the gloomy and grasping peers and the boorish moralities of Knox. It is Richard, the last Plantagenet, giving his crown to Bolingbroke as to a common brigand. It is Arthur, overwhelmed in Lyonesse by heathen armies and dying in the mist, doubtful if ever he shall return."

"But now——" said Evan, in a low voice.

"But now!" said the old man; "he has returned."

"Is the war still raging?" asked MacIan.

"It rages like the pit itself beyond the sea whither I am taking you," answered the other. "But in England the king enjoys his own again. The people are once more taught and ruled as is best; they are happy knights, happy squires, happy servants, happy serfs, if you will; but free at last of that load of vexation and lonely vanity which was called being a citizen."

"Is England, indeed, so secure?" asked Evan.

"Look out and see," said the guide. "I fancy you have seen this place before."

They were driving through the air towards one region of the sky where the hollow of night seemed darkest and which was quite without stars. But against this black background there sprang up, picked out in glittering silver, a dome and a cross. It seemed that it was really newly covered with silver, which in the strong moonlight was like white flame. But, however, covered or painted, Evan had no difficult in knowing the place again. He saw the great thoroughfare that sloped upward to the base of its huge pedestal of steps. And he wondered whether the little shop was still by the side of it and whether its window had been mended.

As the flying ship swept round the dome he observed other alterations. The dome had been redecorated so as to give it a more solemn and somewhat more ecclesiastical note; the ball was draped or destroyed, and round the gallery, under the cross, ran what looked like a ring of silver statues, like the little leaden images that stood round the hat of Louis XI. Round the second gallery, at the base of the dome, ran a second rank of such images, and Evan thought there was another round the steps below. When they came closer he saw that they were figures in complete armour of steel or silver, each with a naked sword, point upward; and then he saw one of the swords move. These were not statues but an armed order of chivalry thrown in three circles round the cross. MacIan drew in his breath, as children do at anything they think utterly beautiful. For he could imagine nothing that so echoed his own visions of pontifical or chivalric art as this white dome sitting like a vast silver tiara over London, ringed with a triple crown of swords.

As they went sailing down Ludgate Hill, Evan saw that the state of the streets fully answered his companion's claim about the reintroduction of order. All the old blackcoated bustle with its cockney vivacity and vulgarity had disappeared. Groups of labourers, quietly but picturesquely clad, were passing up and down in sufficiently large numbers; but it required but a few mounted men to keep the streets in order. The mounted men were not common policemen, but knights with spurs and plume whose smooth and splendid armour glittered like diamond rather than steel. Only in one place—at the corner of Bouverie Street—did there appear to be a moment's confusion, and that was due to hurry rather than resistance. But one old grumbling man did not get out of the way quick enough, and the man on horseback struck him, not severely, across the shoulders with the flat of his sword.

"The soldier had no business to do that," said MacIan, sharply. "The old man was moving as quickly as he could."

"We attach great importance to discipline in the streets," said the man in white, with a slight smile.

"Discipline is not so important as justice," said MacIan.

The other did not answer.

Then after a swift silence that took them out across St. James's Park, he said: "The people must be taught to obey; they must learn their own ignorance. And I am not sure," he continued, turning his back on Evan and looking out of the prow of the ship into the darkness, "I am not sure that I agree with your little maxim about justice. Discipline for the whole society is surely more important than justice to an individual."

Evan, who was also leaning over the edge, swung round with startling suddenness and stared at the other's back.

"Discipline for society—" he repeated, very staccato, "more important—justice to individual?"

Then after a long silence he called out: "Who and what are you?"

"I am an angel," said the white-robed figure, without turning round.

"You are not a Catholic," said MacIan.

The other seemed to take no notice, but reverted to the main topic.

"In our armies up in heaven we learn to put a wholesome fear into subordinates."

MacIan sat craning his neck forward with an extraordinary and unaccountable eagerness.

"Go on!" he cried, twisting and untwisting his long, bony fingers, "go on!"

"Besides," continued he, in the prow, "you must allow for a certain high spirit and haughtiness in the superior type."

"Go on!" said Evan, with burning eyes.

"Just as the sight of sin offends God," said the unknown, "so does the sight of ugliness offend Apollo. The beautiful and princely must, of necessity, be impatient with the squalid and—"

"Why, you great fool!" cried MacIan, rising to the top of his tremendous stature, "did you think I would have doubted only for that rap with a sword? I know that noble orders have bad knights, that good knights have bad tempers, that the Church has rough priests and coarse cardinals; I have known it ever since I was born. You fool! you had only to say, 'Yes, it is rather a shame,' and I should have forgotten the affair. But I saw on your mouth the twitch of your infernal sophistry; I knew that something was wrong with you and your cathedrals. Something is wrong; everything is wrong. You are not an angel. That is not a church. It is not the rightful king who has come home."

"That is unfortunate," said the other, in a quiet but hard voice, "because you are going to see his Majesty."

"No," said MacIan, "I am going to jump over the side."

"Do you desire death?"

"No," said Evan, quite composedly, "I desire a miracle."

"From whom do you ask it? To whom do you appeal?" said his companion, sternly. "You have betrayed the king, renounced his cross on the cathedral, and insulted an archangel."

"I appeal to God," said Evan, and sprang up and stood upon the edge of the swaying ship.

The being in the prow turned slowly round; he looked at Evan with eyes which were like two suns, and put his hand to his mouth just too late to hide an awful smile.

"And how do you know," he said, "how do you know that I am not God?"

MacIan screamed. "Ah!" he cried. "Now I know who you really are. You are not God. You are not one of God's angels. But you were once."

The being's hand dropped from his mouth and Evan dropped out of the car.

CHAPTER SIXTEEN
THE DREAM OF TURNBULL

Turnbull was walking rather rampantly up and down the garden on a gusty evening chewing his cigar and in that mood when every man suppresses an instinct to spit. He was not, as a rule, a man much acquainted with moods; and the storms and sunbursts of MacIan's soul passed before him as an impressive but unmeaning panorama, like the anarchy of Highland scenery. Turnbull was one of those men in whom a continuous appetite and industry of the intellect leave the emotions very simple and steady. His heart was in the right place; but he was quite content to leave it there. It was his head that was his hobby. His mornings and evenings were marked not by impulses or thirsty desires, not by hope or by heart-break; they were filled with the fallacies he had detected, the problems he had made plain, the adverse theories he had wrestled with and thrown, the grand generalizations he had justified. But even the cheerful inner life of a logician may be upset by a lunatic asylum, to say nothing of whiffs of memory from a lady in Jersey, and the little red-bearded man on this windy evening was in a dangerous frame of mind.

Plain and positive as he was, the influence of earth and sky may have been greater on him than he imagined; and the weather that walked the world at that moment was as red and angry as Turnbull. Long strips and swirls of tattered and tawny cloud were dragged downward to the west exactly as torn red raiment would be dragged. And so strong and pitiless was the wind that it whipped away fragments of red-flowering bushes or of copper beech, and drove them also across the garden, a drift of red leaves, like the leaves of autumn, as in parody of the red and driven rags of cloud.

There was a sense in earth and heaven as of everything breaking up, and all the revolutionist in Turnbull rejoiced that it was breaking up. The trees were breaking up under the wind, even in the tall strength of their bloom: the clouds were breaking up and losing even their large heraldic shapes. Shards and shreds of copper cloud split off continually and floated by themselves, and for some reason the truculent eye of Turnbull was attracted to one of these careering cloudlets, which seemed to him to career in an exaggerated manner. Also it kept its shape, which is unusual with clouds shaken off; also its shape was of an odd sort.

Turnbull continued to stare at it, and in a little time occurred that crucial instant when a thing, however incredible, is accepted as a fact. The copper cloud was tumbling down towards the earth, like some gigantic leaf from the copper beeches. And as it came nearer it was evident, first, that it was not a cloud, and, second, that it was not itself of the colour of copper; only, being burnished like a mirror, it had reflected the red-brown colours of the burning clouds. As the thing whirled like a windswept leaf down towards the wall of the garden it was clear that it was some sort of air-ship made of metal, and slapping the air with big broad fins of steel. When it came about a hundred feet above the garden, a shaggy, lean figure leapt up in it, almost black against the bronze and scarlet of the west, and, flinging out a kind of hook or anchor, caught on to the green apple-tree just under the wall; and from that fixed holding ground the ship swung in the red tempest like a captive balloon.

While our friend stood frozen for an instant by his astonishment, the queer figure in the airy car tipped the vehicle almost upside down by leaping over the side of it, seemed to slide or drop down the rope like a monkey, and alighted (with impossible precision and placidity) seated on the edge of the wall, over which he kicked and dangled his legs as he grinned at Turnbull. The wind roared in the trees yet more ruinous and desolate, the red tails of the sunset were dragged downward like red dragons sucked down to death, and still on the top of the asylum wall sat the sinister figure with the grimace, swinging his feet in tune with the tempest; while above him, at the end of its tossing or tightened cord, the enormous iron air-ship floated as light and as little noticed as a baby's balloon upon its string.

Turnbull's first movement after sixty motionless seconds was to turn round and look at the large, luxuriant parallelogram of the garden and the long, low rectangular building beyond. There was not a soul or a stir of life within sight. And he had a quite meaningless sensation, as if there never really had been any one else there except he since the foundation of the world.

Stiffening in himself the masculine but mirthless courage of the atheist, he drew a little nearer to the wall and, catching the man at a slightly different angle of the evening light, could see his face and figure quite plain. Two facts about him stood out in the picked colours of some piratical schoolboy's story. The first was that his lean brown body was bare to the belt of his loose white trousers; the other that through hygiene, affectation, or whatever other cause, he had a scarlet handkerchief tied tightly but somewhat aslant across his brow. After these two facts had become emphatic, others appeared sufficiently important. One was that under the scarlet rag the hair was plentiful, but white as with the last snows of mortality. Another was that under the mop of white and senile hair the face was strong, handsome, and smiling, with a well-cut profile and a long cloven chin. The length of this lower part of the face and the strange cleft in it (which gave the man, in quite another sense from the common one, a double chin) faintly spoilt the claim of the face to absolute regularity, but it greatly assisted it in wearing the expression of half-smiling and half-sneering arrogance with which it was staring at all the stones, all the flowers, but especially at the solitary man.

"What do you want?" shouted Turnbull.

"I want you, Jimmy," said the eccentric man on the wall, and with the very word he had let himself down with a leap on to the centre of the lawn, where he bounded once literally like an India-rubber ball and then stood grinning with his legs astride. The only three facts that Turnbull could now add to his inventory were that the man had an ugly-looking knife swinging at his trousers belt, that his brown feet were as bare as his bronzed trunk and arms, and that his eyes had a singular bleak brilliancy which was of no particular colour.

"Excuse my not being in evening dress," said the newcomer with an urbane smile. "We scientific men, you know—I have to work my own engines—electrical engineer—very hot work."

"Look here," said Turnbull, sturdily clenching his fists in his trousers pockets, "I am bound to expect lunatics inside these four walls; but I do bar their coming from outside, bang out of the sunset clouds."

"And yet you came from the outside, too, Jim," said the stranger in a voice almost affectionate.

"What do you want?" asked Turnbull, with an explosion of temper as sudden as a pistol shot.

"I have already told you," said the man, lowering his voice and speaking with evident sincerity; "I want you."

"What do you want with me?"

"I want exactly what you want," said the new-comer with a new gravity. "I want the Revolution."

Turnbull looked at the fire-swept sky and the wind-stricken woodlands, and kept on repeating the word voicelessly to himself—the word that did indeed so thoroughly express his mood of rage as it had been among those red clouds and rocking tree-tops. "Revolution!" he said to himself. "The Revolution—yes, that is what I want right enough—anything, so long as it is a Revolution."

To some cause he could never explain he found himself completing the sentence on the top of the wall, having automatically followed the stranger so far.

But when the stranger silently indicated the rope that led to the machine, he found himself pausing and saying: "I can't leave MacIan behind in this den."

"We are going to destroy the Pope and all the kings," said the new-comer. "Would it be wiser to take him with us?"

Somehow the muttering Turnbull found himself in the flying ship also, and it swung up into the sunset.

"All the great rebels have been very little rebels," said the man with the red scarf. "They have been like fourth-form boys who sometimes venture to hit a fifth-form boy. That was all the worth of their French Revolution and regicide. The boys never really dared to defy the schoolmaster."

"Whom do you mean by the schoolmaster?" asked Turnbull.

"You know whom I mean," answered the strange man, as he lay back on cushions and looked up into the angry sky.

They seemed rising into stronger and stronger sunlight, as if it were sunrise rather than sunset. But when they looked down at the earth they saw it growing darker and darker. The lunatic asylum in its large rectangular grounds spread below them in a foreshortened and infantile plan, and looked for the first time the grotesque thing that it was. But the clear colours of the plan were growing darker every moment. The masses of rose or rhododendron deepened from crimson to violet. The maze of gravel pathways faded from gold to brown. By the time they had risen a few hundred feet higher nothing could be seen of that darkening landscape except the lines of lighted windows, each one of which, at least, was the light of one lost intelligence. But on them as they swept upward better and braver winds seemed to blow, and on them the ruby light of evening seemed struck, and splashed like red spurts from the grapes of Dionysus. Below them the fallen lights were literally the fallen stars of servitude. And above them all the red and raging clouds were like the leaping flags of liberty.

The man with the cloven chin seemed to have a singular power of understanding thoughts; for, as Turnbull felt the whole universe tilt and turn over his head, the stranger said exactly the right thing.

"Doesn't it seem as if everything were being upset?" said he; "and if once everything is upset, He will be upset on top of it."

Then, as Turnbull made no answer, his host continued:

"That is the really fine thing about space. It is topsy-turvy. You have only to climb far enough towards the morning star to feel that you are coming down to it. You have only to dive deep enough into the abyss to feel that you are rising. That is the only glory of this universe—it is a giddy universe."

Then, as Turnbull was still silent, he added:

"The heavens are full of revolution—of the real sort of revolution. All the high things are sinking low and all the big things looking small. All the people who think they are aspiring find they are falling head foremost. And all the people who think they are condescending find they are climbing up a precipice. That is the intoxication of space. That is the only joy of eternity—doubt. There is only one pleasure the angels can possibly have in flying, and that is, that they do not know whether they are on their head or their heels."

Then, finding his companion still mute, he fell himself into a smiling and motionless meditation, at the end of which he said suddenly:

"So MacIan converted you?"

Turnbull sprang up as if spurning the steel car from under his feet. "Converted me!" he cried. "What the devil do you mean? I have known him for a month, and I have not retracted a single——"

"This Catholicism is a curious thing," said the man of the cloven chin in uninterrupted reflectiveness, leaning his elegant elbows over the edge of the vessel; "it soaks and weakens men without their knowing it, just as I fear it has soaked and weakened you."

Turnbull stood in an attitude which might well have meant pitching the other man out of the flying ship.

"I am an atheist," he said, in a stifled voice. "I have always been an atheist. I am still an atheist." Then, addressing the other's indolent and indifferent back, he cried: "In God's name what do you mean?"

And the other answered without turning round:

"I mean nothing in God's name."

Turnbull spat over the edge of the car and fell back furiously into his seat.

The other continued still unruffled, and staring over the edge idly as an angler stares down at a stream.

"The truth is that we never thought that you could have been caught," he said; "we counted on you as the one red-hot revolutionary left in the world. But, of course, these men like MacIan are awfully clever, especially when they pretend to be stupid."

Turnbull leapt up again in a living fury and cried: "What have I got to do with MacIan? I believe all I ever believed, and disbelieve all I ever disbelieved. What does all this mean, and what do you want with me here?"

Then for the first time the other lifted himself from the edge of the car and faced him.

"I have brought you here," he answered, "to take part in the last war of the world."

"The last war!" repeated Turnbull, even in his dazed state a little touchy about such a dogma; "how do you know it will be the last?"

The man laid himself back in his reposeful attitude, and said:

"It is the last war, because if it does not cure the world for ever, it will destroy it."

"What do you mean?"

"I only mean what you mean," answered the unknown in a temperate voice. "What was it that you always meant on those million and one nights when you walked outside your Ludgate Hill shop and shook your hand in the air?"

"Still I do not see," said Turnbull, stubbornly.

"You will soon," said the other, and abruptly bent downward one iron handle of his huge machine. The engine stopped, stooped, and dived almost as deliberately as a man bathing; in their downward rush they swept within fifty yards of a big bulk of stone that Turnbull knew only too well. The last red anger of the sunset was ended; the dome of heaven was dark; the lanes of flaring light in the streets below hardly lit up the base of the building. But he saw that it was St. Paul's Cathedral, and he saw that on the top of it the ball was still standing erect, but the cross was stricken and had fallen sideways. Then only he cared to look down into the streets, and saw that they were inflamed with uproar and tossing passions.

"We arrive at a happy moment," said the man steering the ship. "The insurgents are bombarding the city, and a cannon-ball has just hit the cross. Many of the insurgents are simple people, and they naturally regard it as a happy omen."

"Quite so," said Turnbull, in a rather colourless voice.

"Yes," replied the other. "I thought you would be glad to see your prayer answered. Of course I apologize for the word prayer."

"Don't mention it," said Turnbull.

The flying ship had come down upon a sort of curve, and was now rising again. The higher and higher it rose the broader and broader became the scenes of flame and desolation underneath.

Ludgate Hill indeed had been an uncaptured and comparatively quiet height, altered only by the startling coincidence of the cross fallen awry. All the other thoroughfares on all sides of that hill were full of the pulsation and the pain of battle, full of shaking torches and shouting faces. When at length they had risen high enough to have a bird's-eye view of the whole campaign, Turnbull was already intoxicated. He had smelt gunpowder, which was the incense of his own revolutionary religion.

"Have the people really risen?" he asked, breathlessly. "What are they fighting about?"

"The programme is rather elaborate," said his entertainer with some indifference. "I think Dr. Hertz drew it up."

Turnbull wrinkled his forehead. "Are all the poor people with the Revolution?" he asked.

The other shrugged his shoulders. "All the instructed and class-conscious part of them without exception," he replied. "There were certainly a few districts; in fact, we are passing over them just now—"

Turnbull looked down and saw that the polished car was literally lit up from underneath by the far-flung fires from below. Underneath whole squares and solid districts were in flames, like prairies or forests on fire.

"Dr. Hertz has convinced everybody," said Turnbull's cicerone in a smooth voice, "that nothing can really be done with the real slums. His celebrated maxim has been quite adopted. I mean the three celebrated sentences: 'No man should be unemployed. Employ the employables. Destroy the unemployables.'"

There was a silence, and then Turnbull said in a rather strained voice: "And do I understand that this good work is going on under here?"

"Going on splendidly," replied his companion in the heartiest voice. "You see, these people were much too tired and weak even to join the social war. They were a definite hindrance to it."

"And so you are simply burning them out?"

"It *does* seem absurdly simple," said the man, with a beaming smile, "when one thinks of all the worry and talk about helping a hopeless slave population, when the future obviously was only crying to be rid of them. There are happy babes unborn ready to burst the doors when these drivellers are swept away."

"Will you permit me to say," said Turnbull, after reflection, "that I don't like all this?"

"And will you permit me to say," said the other, with a snap, "that I don't like Mr. Evan MacIan?"

Somewhat to the speaker's surprise this did not inflame the sensitive sceptic; he had the air of thinking thoroughly, and then he said: "No, I don't think it's my friend MacIan that taught me that. I think I should always have said that I don't like this. These people have rights."

"Rights!" repeated the unknown in a tone quite indescribable. Then he added with a more open sneer: "Perhaps they also have souls."

"They have lives!" said Turnbull, sternly; "that is quite enough for me. I understood you to say that you thought life sacred."

"Yes, indeed!" cried his mentor with a sort of idealistic animation. "Yes, indeed! Life is sacred—but lives are not sacred. We are improving Life by removing lives. Can you, as a free-thinker, find any fault in that?"

"Yes," said Turnbull with brevity.

"Yet you applaud tyrannicide," said the stranger with rationalistic gaiety. "How inconsistent! It really comes to this: You approve of taking away life from those to whom it is a triumph and a pleasure. But you will not take away life from those to whom it is a burden and a toil."

Turnbull rose to his feet in the car with considerable deliberation, but his face seemed oddly pale. The other went on with enthusiasm.

"Life, yes, Life is indeed sacred!" he cried; "but new lives for old! Good lives for bad! On that very place where now there sprawls one drunken wastrel of a pavement artist more or less wishing he were dead—on that very spot there shall in the future be living pictures; there shall be golden girls and boys leaping in the sun."

Turnbull, still standing up, opened his lips. "Will you put me down, please?" he said, quite calmly, like on stopping an omnibus.

"Put you down—what do you mean?" cried his leader. "I am taking you to the front of the revolutionary war, where you will be one of the first of the revolutionary leaders."

"Thank you," replied Turnbull with the same painful constraint. "I have heard about your revolutionary war, and I think on the whole that I would rather be anywhere else."

"Do you want to be taken to a monastery," snarled the other, "with MacIan and his winking Madonnas."

"I want to be taken to a madhouse," said Turnbull distinctly, giving the direction with a sort of precision. "I want to go back to exactly the same lunatic asylum from which I came."

"Why?" asked the unknown.

"Because I want a little sane and wholesome society," answered Turnbull.

There was a long and peculiar silence, and then the man driving the flying machine said quite coolly: "I won't take you back."

And then Turnbull said equally coolly: "Then I'll jump out of the car."

The unknown rose to his full height, and the expression in his eyes seemed to be made of ironies behind ironies, as two mirrors infinitely reflect each other. At last he said, very gravely: "Do you think I am the devil?"

"Yes," said Turnbull, violently. "For I think the devil is a dream, and so are you. I don't believe in you or your flying ship or your last fight of the world. It is all a nightmare. I say as a fact of dogma and faith that it is all a nightmare. And I will be a martyr for my faith as much as St. Catherine, for I will jump out of this ship and risk waking up safe in bed."

After swaying twice with the swaying vessel he dived over the side as one dives into the sea. For some incredible moments stars and space and planets seemed to shoot up past him as the sparks fly upward; and yet in that sickening descent he was full of some unnatural happiness. He could connect it with no idea except one that half escaped him—what Evan had said of the difference between Christ and Satan; that it was by Christ's own choice that He descended into hell.

When he again realized anything, he was lying on his elbow on the lawn of the lunatic asylum, and the last red of the sunset had not yet disappeared.

CHAPTER SEVENTEEN
THE IDIOT

Evan MacIan was standing a few yards off looking at him in absolute silence.

He had not the moral courage to ask MacIan if there had been anything astounding in the manner of his coming there, nor did MacIan seem to have any question to ask, or perhaps any need to ask it. The two men came slowly towards each other, and found the same expression on each other's faces. Then, for the first time in all their acquaintance, they shook hands.

Almost as if this were a kind of unconscious signal, it brought Dr. Quayle bounding out of a door and running across the lawn.

"Oh, there you are!" he exclaimed with a relieved giggle. "Will you come inside, please? I want to speak to you both."

They followed him into his shiny wooden office where their damning record was kept. Dr. Quayle sat down on a swivel chair and swung round to face them. His carved smile had suddenly disappeared.

"I will be plain with you gentlemen," he said, abruptly; "you know quite well we do our best for everybody here. Your cases have been under special consideration, and the Master himself has decided that you ought to be treated specially and—er—under somewhat simpler conditions."

"You mean treated worse, I suppose," said Turnbull, gruffly.

The doctor did not reply, and MacIan said: "I expected this." His eyes had begun to glow.

The doctor answered, looking at his desk and playing with a key: "Well, in certain cases that give anxiety—it is often better——"

"Give anxiety," said Turnbull, fiercely. "Confound your impudence! What do you mean? You imprison two perfectly sane men in a madhouse because you have made up a long word. They take it in good temper, walk and talk in your garden like monks who have found a vocation, are civil even to you, you damned druggists' hack! Behave not only more sanely than any of your patients, but more sanely than half the sane men outside, and you have the soul-stifling cheek to say that they give anxiety."

"The head of the asylum has settled it all," said Dr. Quayle, still looking down.

MacIan took one of his immense strides forward and stood over the doctor with flaming eyes.

"If the head has settled it let the head announce it," he said. "I won't take it from you. I believe you to be a low, gibbering degenerate. Let us see the head of the asylum."

"See the head of the asylum," repeated Dr. Quayle. "Certainly not."

The tall Highlander, bending over him, put one hand on his shoulder with fatherly interest.

"You don't seem to appreciate the peculiar advantages of my position as a lunatic," he said. "I could kill you with my left hand before such a rat as you could so much as squeak. And I wouldn't be hanged for it."

"I certainly agree with Mr. MacIan," said Turnbull with sobriety and perfect respectfulness, "that you had better let us see the head of the institution."

Dr. Quayle got to his feet in a mixture of sudden hysteria and clumsy presence of mind.

"Oh, certainly," he said with a weak laugh. "You can see the head of the asylum if you particularly want to." He almost ran out of the room, and the two followed swiftly on his flying coat tails. He knocked at an ordinary varnished door in the corridor. When a voice said, "Come in," MacIan's breath went hissing back through his teeth into his chest. Turnbull was more impetuous, and opened the door.

It was a neat and well-appointed room entirely lined with a medical library. At the other end of it was a ponderous and polished desk with an incandescent lamp on it, the light of which was just sufficient to show a slender, well-bred figure in an ordinary medical black frock-coat, whose head, quite silvered with age, was bent over neat piles of notes. This gentleman looked up for an instant as they entered, and the lamplight fell on his glittering spectacles and long, clean-shaven face—a face which would have been simply like an aristocrat's but that a certain lion poise of the head and long cleft in the chin made it look more like a very handsome actor's. It was only for a flash that his face was thus lifted. Then he bent his silver head over his notes once more, and said, without looking up again:

"I told you, Dr. Quayle, that these men were to go to cells B and C."

Turnbull and MacIan looked at each other, and said more than they could ever say with tongues or swords. Among other things they said that to that particular Head of the institution it was a waste of time to appeal, and they followed Dr. Quayle out of the room.

The instant they stepped out into the corridor four sturdy figures stepped from four sides, pinioned them, and ran them along the galleries. They might very likely have thrown their captors right and left had they been inclined to resist, but for some nameless reason they were more inclined to laugh. A mixture of mad irony with childish curiosity made them feel quite inclined to see what next twist would be taken by their imbecile luck. They were dragged down countless cold avenues lined with glazed tiles, different only in being of different lengths and set at different angles. They were so many and so monotonous that to escape back by them would have been far harder than fleeing from the Hampton Court maze. Only the fact that windows grew fewer, coming at longer intervals, and the fact that when the windows did come they seemed shadowed and let in less light, showed that they were winding into the core or belly of some enormous building. After a little time the glazed corridors began to be lit by electricity.

At last, when they had walked nearly a mile in those white and polished tunnels, they came with quite a shock to the futile finality of a cul-de-sac. All that white and weary journey ended suddenly in an oblong space and a blank white wall.

But in the white wall there were two iron doors painted white on which were written, respectively, in neat black capitals B and C.

"You go in here, sir," said the leader of the officials, quite respectfully, "and you in here."

But before the doors had clanged upon their dazed victims, MacIan had been able to say to Turnbull with a strange drawl of significance: "I wonder who A is."

Turnbull made an automatic struggle before he allowed himself to be thrown into the cell. Hence it happened that he was the last to enter, and was still full of the exhilaration of the adventures for at least five minutes after the echo of the clanging door had died away.

Then, when silence had sunk deep and nothing happened for two and a half hours, it suddenly occurred to him that this was the end of his life. He was hidden and sealed up in this little crack of stone until the flesh should fall off his bones. He was dead, and the world had won.

His cell was of an oblong shape, but very long in comparison with its width. It was just wide enough to permit the arms to be fully extended with the dumb-bells, which were hung up on the left wall, very dusty. It was, however, long enough for a man to walk one thirty-fifth part of a mile if he traversed it entirely. On the same principle a row of fixed holes, quite close together, let in to the cells by pipes what was alleged to be the freshest air. For these great scientific organizers insisted that a man should be healthy even if he was miserable. They provided a walk long enough to give him exercise and holes large enough to give him oxygen. There their interest in human nature suddenly ceased. It seemed never to have occurred to them that the benefit of exercise belongs partly to the benefit of liberty. They had not entertained the suggestion that the open air is only one of the advantages of the open sky. They administered air in secret, but in sufficient doses, as if it were a medicine. They suggested walking, as if no man had ever felt inclined to walk. Above all, the asylum authorities insisted on their own extraordinary cleanliness. Every morning, while Turnbull was still half asleep on his iron bedstead which was lifted half-way up the wall and clamped to it with iron, four sluices or metal mouths opened above him at the four corners of the chamber and washed it white of any defilement. Turnbull's solitary soul surged up against this sickening daily solemnity.

"I am buried alive!" he cried, bitterly; "they have hidden me under mountains. I shall be here till I rot. Why the blazes should it matter to them whether I am dirty or clean."

Every morning and evening an iron hatchway opened in his oblong cell, and a brown hairy hand or two thrust in a plate of perfectly cooked lentils and a big bowl of cocoa. He was not underfed any more than he was underexercised or asphyxiated. He had ample walking space, ample air, ample and even filling food. The only objection was that he had nothing to walk towards, nothing to feast about, and no reason whatever for drawing the breath of life.

Even the shape of his cell especially irritated him. It was a long, narrow parallelogram, which had a flat wall at one end and ought to have had a flat wall at the other; but that end was broken by a wedge or angle of space, like the prow of a ship. After three days of silence and cocoa, this angle at the end began to infuriate Turnbull. It maddened him to think that two lines came together and pointed at nothing. After the fifth day he was reckless, and poked his head into the corner. After twenty-five days he almost broke his head against it. Then he became quite cool and stupid again, and began to examine it like a sort of Robinson Crusoe.

Almost unconsciously it was his instinct to examine outlets, and he found himself paying particular attention to the row of holes which let in the air into his last house of life. He soon discovered that these air-holes were all the ends and mouths of long leaden tubes which doubtless carried air from some remote watering-place near Margate. One evening while he was engaged in the fifth investigation he noticed something like twilight in one of these dumb mouths, as compared with the darkness of the others. Thrusting his finger in as far as it would go, he found a hole and flapping edge in the tube. This he rent open and instantly saw a light behind; it was at least certain that he had struck some other cell.

It is a characteristic of all things now called "efficient", which means mechanical and calculated, that if they go wrong at all they go entirely wrong. There is no power of retrieving a defeat, as in simpler and more living organisms. A strong gun can conquer a strong elephant, but a wounded elephant can easily conquer a broken gun. Thus the Prussian monarchy in the eighteenth century, or now, can make a strong army merely by making the men afraid. But it does it with the permanent possibility that the men may some day be more afraid of their enemies than of their officers. Thus the drainage in our cities so long as it is quite solid means a general safety, but if there is one leak it means concentrated poison—an explosion of deathly germs like dynamite, a spirit of stink. Thus, indeed, all that excellent machinery which is the swiftest thing on earth in saving human labour is also the slowest thing on earth in resisting human interference. It may be easier to get chocolate for nothing out of a shopkeeper than out of an automatic machine. But if you did manage to steal the chocolate, the automatic machine would be much less likely to run after you.

Turnbull was not long in discovering this truth in connexion with the cold and colossal machinery of this great asylum. He had been shaken by many spiritual states since the instant when he was pitched head foremost into that private cell which was to be his private room till death. He had felt a high fit of pride and poetry, which had ebbed away and left him deadly cold. He had known a period of mere scientific curiosity, in the course of which he examined all the tiles of his cell, with the gratifying conclusion that they were all the same shape and size; but was greatly puzzled about the angle in the wall at the end, and also about an iron peg or spike that stood out from the wall, the object of which he does not know to this day. Then he had a period of mere madness not to be written of by decent men, but only by those few dirty novelists hallooed on by the infernal huntsman to hunt down and humiliate human nature. This also passed, but left behind it a feverish distaste for many of the mere objects around him. Long after he had returned to sanity and such hopeless cheerfulness as a man might have on a desert island, he disliked the regular squares of the pattern of wall and floor and the triangle that terminated his corridor. Above all, he had a hatred, deep as the hell he did not believe in, for the objectless iron peg in the wall.

But in all his moods, sane or insane, intolerant or stoical, he never really doubted this: that the machine held him as light and as hopelessly as he had from his birth been held by the hopeless cosmos of his own creed. He knew well the ruthless and inexhaustible resources of our scientific civilization. He no more expected rescue from a medical certificate than rescue from the solar system. In many of his Robinson Crusoe moods he thought kindly of MacIan as of some quarrelsome school-fellow who had long been dead. He thought of leaving in the cell when he died a rigid record of his opinions, and when he began to write them down on scraps of envelope in his pocket, he was startled to discover how much they had changed. Then he remembered the Beauchamp Tower, and tried to write his blazing scepticism on the wall, and discovered that it was all shiny tiles on which nothing could be either drawn or carved. Then for an instant there hung and broke above him like a high wave the whole horror of scientific imprisonment, which manages to deny a man not only liberty, but every accidental comfort of bondage. In the old filthy dungeons men could carve their prayers or protests in the rock. Here the white and slippery walls escaped even from bearing witness. The old prisoners could make a pet of a mouse or a beetle strayed out of a hole. Here the unpierceable walls were washed every morning by an automatic sluice. There was no natural corruption and no merciful decay by which a living thing could enter in. Then James Turnbull looked up and saw the high invincible hatefulness of the society in which he lived, and saw the hatefulness of something else also, which he told himself again and again was not the cosmos in which he believed. But all the time he had never once doubted that the five sides of his cell were for him the wall of the world henceforward, and it gave him a shock of surprise even to discover the faint light through the aperture in the ventilation tube. But he had forgotten how close efficiency has to pack everything together and how easily, therefore, a pipe here or there may leak.

Turnbull thrust his first finger down the aperture, and at last managed to make a slight further fissure in the piping. The light that came up from beyond was very faint, and apparently indirect; it seemed to fall from some hole or window higher up. As he was screwing his eye to peer at this grey and greasy twilight he was astonished to see another human finger very long and lean come down from above towards the broken pipe and hook it up to something higher. The lighted aperture was abruptly blackened and blocked, presumably by a face and mouth, for something human spoke down the tube, though the words were not clear.

"Who is that?" asked Turnbull, trembling with excitement, yet wary and quite resolved not to spoil any chance.

After a few indistinct sounds the voice came down with a strong Argyllshire accent:

"I say, Turnbull, we couldn't fight through this tube, could we?"

Sentiments beyond speech surged up in Turnbull and silenced him for a space just long enough to be painful. Then he said with his old gaiety: "I vote we talk a little first; I don't want to murder the first man I have met for ten million years."

"I know what you mean," answered the other. "It has been awful. For a mortal month I have been alone with God."

Turnbull started, and it was on the tip of his tongue to answer: "Alone with God! Then you do not know what loneliness is."

But he answered, after all, in his old defiant style: "Alone with God, were you? And I suppose you found his Majesty's society rather monotonous?"

"Oh, no," said MacIan, and his voice shuddered; "it was a great deal too exciting."

After a very long silence the voice of MacIan said: "What do you really hate most in your place?"

"You'd think I was really mad if I told you," answered Turnbull, bitterly.

"Then I expect it's the same as mine," said the other voice.

"I am sure it's not the same as anybody's," said Turnbull, "for it has no rhyme or reason. Perhaps my brain really has gone, but I detest that iron spike in the left wall more than the damned desolation or the damned cocoa. Have you got one in your cell?"

"Not now," replied MacIan with serenity. "I've pulled it out."

His fellow-prisoner could only repeat the words.

"I pulled it out the other day when I was off my head," continued the tranquil Highland voice. "It looked so unnecessary."

"You must be ghastly strong," said Turnbull.

"One is, when one is mad," was the careless reply, "and it had worn a little loose in the socket. Even now I've got it out I can't discover what it was for. But I've found out something a long sight funnier."

"What do you mean?" asked Turnbull.

"I have found out where A is," said the other.

Three weeks afterwards MacIan had managed to open up communications which made his meaning plain. By that time the two captives had fully discovered and demonstrated that weakness in the very nature of modern machinery to which we have already referred. The very fact that they were isolated from all companions meant that they were free from all spies, and as there were no gaolers to be bribed, so there were none to be baffled. Machinery brought them their cocoa and cleaned their cells; that machinery was as helpless as it was pitiless. A little patient violence, conducted day after day amid constant mutual suggestion, opened an irregular hole in the wall, large enough to let in a small man, in the exact place where there had been before the tiny ventilation holes. Turnbull tumbled somehow into MacIan's apartment, and his first glance found out that the iron spike was indeed plucked from its socket, and left, moreover, another ragged hole into some hollow place behind. But for this MacIan's cell was the duplicate of Turnbull's—a long oblong ending in a wedge and lined with cold and lustrous tiles. The small hole from which the peg had been displaced was in that short oblique wall at the end nearest to Turnbull's. That individual looked at it with a puzzled face.

"What is in there?" he asked.

MacIan answered briefly: "Another cell."

"But where can the door of it be?" said his companion, even more puzzled; "the doors of our cells are at the other end."

"It has no door," said Evan.

In the pause of perplexity that followed, an eerie and sinister feeling crept over Turnbull's stubborn soul in spite of himself. The notion of the doorless room chilled him with that sense of half-witted curiosity which one has when something horrible is half understood.

"James Turnbull," said MacIan, in a low and shaken voice, "these people hate us more than Nero hated Christians, and fear us more than any man feared Nero. They have filled England with frenzy and galloping in order to capture us and wipe us out—in order to kill us. And they have killed us, for you and I have only made a hole in our coffins. But though this hatred that they felt for us is bigger than they felt for Bonaparte, and more plain and practical than they would feel for Jack the Ripper, yet it is not we whom the people of this place hate most."

A cold and quivering impatience continued to crawl up Turnbull's spine; he had never felt so near to superstition and supernaturalism, and it was not a pretty sort of superstition either.

"There is another man more fearful and hateful," went on MacIan, in his low monotone voice, "and they have buried him even deeper. God knows how they did it, for he was let in by neither door nor window, nor lowered through any opening above. I expect these iron handles that we both hate have been part of some damned machinery for walling him up. He is there. I have looked through the hole at him; but I cannot stand looking at him long, because his face is turned away from me and he does not move."

Al Turnbull's unnatural and uncompleted feelings found their outlet in rushing to the aperture and looking into the unknown room.

It was a third oblong cell exactly like the other two except that it was doorless, and except that on one of the walls was painted a large black A like the B and C outside their own doors. The letter in this case was not painted outside, because this prison had no outside.

On the same kind of tiled floor, of which the monotonous squares had maddened Turnbull's eye and brain, was sitting a figure which was startlingly short even for a child, only that the enormous head was ringed with hair of a frosty grey. The figure was draped, both insecurely and insufficiently, in what looked like the remains of a brown flannel dressing-gown; an emptied cup of cocoa stood on the floor beside it, and the creature had his big grey head cocked at a particular angle of inquiry or attention which amid all that gathering gloom and mystery struck one as comic if not cocksure.

After six still seconds Turnbull could stand it no longer, but called out to the dwarfish thing—in what words heaven knows. The thing got up with the promptitude of an animal, and turning round offered the spectacle of two owlish eyes and a huge grey-and-white beard not unlike the plumage of an owl. This extraordinary beard covered him literally to his feet (not that that was very far), and perhaps it was as well that it did, for portions of his remaining clothing seemed to fall off whenever he moved. One talks trivially of a face like parchment, but this old man's face was so wrinkled that it was like a parchment loaded with hieroglyphics. The lines of his face were so deep and complex that one could see five or ten different faces besides the real one, as one can see them in an elaborate wall-paper. And yet while his face seemed like a scripture older than the gods, his eyes were quite bright, blue, and startled like those of a baby. They looked as if they had only an instant before been fitted into his head.

Everything depended so obviously upon whether this buried monster spoke that Turnbull did not know or care whether he himself had spoken. He said something or nothing. And then he waited for this dwarfish voice that had been hidden under the mountains of the world. At last it did speak, and spoke in English, with a foreign accent that was neither Latin nor Teutonic. He suddenly stretched out a long and very dirty forefinger, and cried in a voice of clear recognition, like a child's: "That's a hole."

He digested the discovery for some seconds, sucking his finger, and then he cried, with a crow of laughter: "And that's a head come through it."

The hilarious energy in this idiot attitude gave Turnbull another sick turn. He had grown to tolerate those dreary and mumbling madmen who trailed themselves about the beautiful asylum gardens. But there was something new and subversive of the universe in the combination of so much cheerful decision with a body without a brain.

"Why did they put you in such a place?" he asked at last with embarrassment.

"Good place. Yes," said the old man, nodding a great many times and beaming like a flattered landlord. "Good shape. Long and narrow, with a point. Like this," and he made lovingly with his hands a map of the room in the air.

"But that's not the best," he added, confidentially. "Squares very good; I have a nice long holiday, and can count them. But that's not the best."

"What is the best?" asked Turnbull in great distress.

"Spike is the best," said the old man, opening his blue eyes blazing; "it sticks out."

The words Turnbull spoke broke out of him in pure pity. "Can't we do anything for you?" he said.

"I am very happy," said the other, alphabetically. "You are a good man. Can I help you?"

"No, I don't think you can, sir," said Turnbull with rough pathos; "I am glad you are contented at least."

The weird old person opened his broad blue eyes and fixed Turnbull with a stare extraordinarily severe. "You are quite sure," he said, "I cannot help you?"

"Quite sure, thank you," said Turnbull with broken brevity. "Good day."

Then he turned to MacIan who was standing close behind him, and whose face, now familiar in all its moods, told him easily that Evan had heard the whole of the strange dialogue.

"Curse those cruel beasts!" cried Turnbull. "They've turned him to an imbecile just by burying him alive. His brain's like a pin-point now."

"You are sure he is a lunatic?" said Evan, slowly.

"Not a lunatic," said Turnbull, "an idiot. He just points to things and says that they stick out."

"He had a notion that he could help us," said MacIan moodily, and began to pace towards the other end of his cell.

"Yes, it was a bit pathetic," assented Turnbull; "such a Thing offering help, and besides— Hallo! Hallo! What's the matter?"

"God Almighty guide us all!" said MacIan.

He was standing heavy and still at the other end of the room and staring quietly at the door which for thirty days had sealed them up from the sun. Turnbull, following the other's eye, stared at the door likewise, and then he also uttered an exclamation. The iron door was standing about an inch and a half open.

"He said—" began Evan, in a trembling voice—"he offered—"

"Come along, you fool!" shouted Turnbull with a sudden and furious energy. "I see it all now, and it's the best stroke of luck in the world. You pulled out that iron handle that had screwed up his cell, and it somehow altered the machinery and opened all the doors."

Seizing MacIan by the elbow he bundled him bodily out into the open corridor and ran him on till they saw daylight through a half-darkened window.

"All the same," said Evan, like one answering in an ordinary conversation, "he did ask you whether he could help you."

All this wilderness of windowless passages was so built into the heart of that fortress of fear that it seemed more than an hour before the fugitives had any good glimpse of the outer world. They did not even know what hour of the day it was; and when, turning a corner, they saw the bare tunnel of the corridor end abruptly in a shining square of garden, the grass burning in that strong evening sunshine which makes it burnished gold rather than green, the abrupt opening on to the earth seemed like a hole knocked in the wall of heaven. Only once or twice in life is it permitted to a man thus to see the very universe from outside, and feel existence itself as an adorable adventure not yet begun. As they found this shining escape out of that hellish labyrinth they both had simultaneously the sensation of being babes unborn, of being asked by God if they would like to live upon the earth. They were looking in at one of the seven gates of Eden.

Turnbull was the first to leap into the garden, with an earth-spurning leap like that of one who could really spread his wings and fly. MacIan, who came an instant after, was less full of mere animal gusto and fuller of a more fearful and quivering pleasure in the clear and innocent flower colours and the high and holy trees. With one bound they were in that cool and cleared landscape, and they found just outside the door the black-clad gentleman with the cloven chin smilingly regarding them; and his chin seemed to grow longer and longer as he smiled.

CHAPTER EIGHTEEN
A RIDDLE OF FACES

Just behind him stood two other doctors: one, the familiar Dr. Quayle, of the blinking eyes and bleating voice; the other, a more commonplace but much more forcible figure, a stout young doctor with short, well-brushed hair and a round but resolute face. At the sight of the escape these two subordinates uttered a cry and sprang forward, but their superior remained motionless and smiling, and somehow the lack of his support seemed to arrest and freeze them in the very gesture of pursuit.

"Let them be," he cried in a voice that cut like a blade of ice; and not only of ice, but of some awful primordial ice that had never been water.

"I want no devoted champions," said the cutting voice; "even the folly of one's friends bores one at last. You don't suppose I should have let these lunatics out of their cells without good reason. I have the best and fullest reason. They can be let out of their cell today, because today the whole world has become their cell. I will have no more medieval mummery of chains and doors. Let them wander about the earth as they wandered about this garden, and I shall still be their easy master. Let them take the wings of the morning and abide in the uttermost parts of the sea—I am there. Whither shall they go from my presence and whither shall they flee from my spirit? Courage, Dr. Quayle, and do not be downhearted; the real days of tyranny are only beginning on this earth."

And with that the Master laughed and swung away from them, almost as if his laugh was a bad thing for people to see.

"Might I speak to you a moment?" said Turnbull, stepping forward with a respectful resolution. But the shoulders of the Master only seemed to take on a new and unexpected angle of mockery as he strode away.

Turnbull swung round with great abruptness to the other two doctors, and said, harshly: "What in snakes does he mean—and who are you?"

"My name is Hutton," said the short, stout man, "and I am—well, one of those whose business it is to uphold this establishment."

"My name is Turnbull," said the other; "I am one of those whose business it is to tear it to the ground."

The small doctor smiled, and Turnbull's anger seemed suddenly to steady him.

"But I don't want to talk about that," he said, calmly; "I only want to know what the Master of this asylum really means."

Dr. Hutton's smile broke into a laugh which, short as it was, had the suspicion of a shake in it. "I suppose you think that quite a simple question," he said.

"I think it a plain question," said Turnbull, "and one that deserves a plain answer. Why did the Master lock us up in a couple of cupboards like jars of pickles for a mortal month, and why does he now let us walk free in the garden again?"

"I understand," said Hutton, with arched eyebrows, "that your complaint is that you are now free to walk in the garden."

"My complaint is," said Turnbull, stubbornly, "that if I am fit to walk freely now, I have been as fit for the last month. No one has examined me, no one has come near me. Your chief says that I am only free because he has made other arrangements. What are those arrangements?"

The young man with the round face looked down for a little while and smoked reflectively. The other and elder doctor had gone pacing nervously by himself upon the lawn. At length the round face was lifted again, and showed two round blue eyes with a certain frankness in them.

"Well, I don't see that it can do any harm to tell you know," he said. "You were shut up just then because it was just during that month that the Master was bringing off his big scheme. He was getting his bill through Parliament, and organizing the new medical police. But of course you haven't heard of all that; in fact, you weren't meant to."

"Heard of all what?" asked the impatient inquirer.

"There's a new law now, and the asylum powers are greatly extended. Even if you did escape now, any policeman would take you up in the next town if you couldn't show a certificate of sanity from us."

"Well," continued Dr. Hutton, "the Master described before both Houses of Parliament the real scientific objection to all existing legislation about lunacy. As he very truly said, the mistake was in supposing insanity to be merely an exception or an extreme. Insanity, like forgetfulness, is simply a quality which enters more or less into all human beings; and for practical purposes it is more necessary to know whose mind is really trustworthy than whose has some accidental taint. We have therefore reversed the existing method, and people now have to prove that they are sane. In the first village you entered, the village constable would notice that you were not wearing on the left lapel of your coat the small pewter S which is now necessary to any one who walks about beyond asylum bounds or outside asylum hours."

"You mean to say," said Turnbull, "that this was what the Master of the asylum urged before the House of Commons?"

Dr. Hutton nodded with gravity.

"And you mean to say," cried Turnbull, with a vibrant snort, "that that proposal was passed in an assembly that calls itself democratic?"

The doctor showed his whole row of teeth in a smile. "Oh, the assembly calls itself Socialist now," he said, "But we explained to them that this was a question for men of science."

Turnbull gave one stamp upon the gravel, then pulled himself together, and resumed: "But why should your infernal head medicine-man lock us up in separate cells while he was turning England into a madhouse? I'm not the Prime Minister; we're not the House of Lords."

"He wasn't afraid of the Prime Minister," replied Dr. Hutton; "he isn't afraid of the House of Lords. But—"

"Well?" inquired Turnbull, stamping again.

"He is afraid of you," said Hutton, simply. "Why, didn't you know?"

MacIan, who had not spoken yet, made one stride forward and stood with shaking limbs and shining eyes.

"He was afraid!" began Evan, thickly. "You mean to say that we—"

"I mean to say the plain truth now that the danger is over," said Hutton, calmly; "most certainly you two were the only people he ever was afraid of." Then he added in a low but not inaudible voice: "Except one—whom he feared worse, and has buried deeper."

"Come away," cried MacIan, "this has to be thought about."

Turnbull followed him in silence as he strode away, but just before he vanished, turned and spoke again to the doctors.

"But what has got hold of people?" he asked, abruptly. "Why should all England have gone dotty on the mere subject of dottiness?"

Dr. Hutton smiled his open smile once more and bowed slightly. "As to that also," he replied, "I don't want to make you vain."

Turnbull swung round without a word, and he and his companion were lost in the lustrous leafage of the garden. They noticed nothing special about the scene, except that the garden seemed more exquisite than ever in the deepening sunset, and that there seemed to be many more people, whether patients or attendants, walking about in it.

From behind the two black-coated doctors as they stood on the lawn another figure somewhat similarly dressed strode hurriedly past them, having also grizzled hair and an open flapping frock-coat. Both his decisive step and dapper black array marked him out as another medical man, or at least a man in authority, and as he passed Turnbull the latter was aroused by a strong impression of having seen the man somewhere before. It was no one that he knew well, yet he was certain that it was someone at whom he had at sometime or other looked steadily. It was neither the face of a friend nor of an enemy; it aroused neither irritation nor tenderness, yet it was a face which had for some reason been of great importance in his life. Turning and returning, and making detours about the garden, he managed to study the man's face again and again—a moustached, somewhat military face with a monocle, the sort of face that is aristocratic without being distinguished. Turnbull could not remember any particular doctors in his decidedly healthy existence. Was the man a long-lost uncle, or was he only somebody who had sat opposite him regularly in a railway train? At that moment the man knocked down his own eye-glass with a gesture of annoyance; Turnbull remembered the gesture, and the truth sprang up solid in front of him. The man with the moustaches was Cumberland Vane, the London police magistrate before whom he and MacIan had once stood on their trial. The magistrate must have been transferred to some other official duties—to something connected with the inspection of asylums.

Turnbull's heart gave a leap of excitement which was half hope. As a magistrate Mr. Cumberland Vane had been somewhat careless and shallow, but certainly kindly, and not inaccessible to common sense so long as it was put to him in strictly conventional language. He was at least an authority of a more human and refreshing sort than the crank with the wagging beard or the fiend with the forked chin.

He went straight up to the magistrate, and said: "Good evening, Mr. Vane; I doubt if you remember me."

Cumberland Vane screwed the eye-glass into his scowling face for an instant, and then said curtly but not uncivilly: "Yes, I remember you, sir; assault or battery, wasn't it?—a fellow broke your window. A tall fellow—McSomething—case made rather a noise afterwards."

"MacIan is the name, sir," said Turnbull, respectfully; "I have him here with me."

"Eh!" said Vane very sharply. "Confound him! Has he got anything to do with this game?"

"Mr. Vane," said Turnbull, pacifically, "I will not pretend that either he or I acted quite decorously on that occasion. You were very lenient with us, and did not treat us as criminals when you very well might. So I am sure you will give us your testimony that, even if we were criminals, we are not lunatics in any legal or medical sense whatever. I am sure you will use your influence for us."

"My influence!" repeated the magistrate, with a slight start. "I don't quite understand you."

"I don't know in what capacity you are here," continued Turnbull, gravely, "but a legal authority of your distinction must certainly be here in an important one. Whether you are visiting and inspecting the place, or attached to it as some kind of permanent legal adviser, your opinion must still—"

Cumberland Vane exploded with a detonation of oaths; his face was transfigured with fury and contempt, and yet in some odd way he did not seem specially angry with Turnbull.

"But Lord bless us and save us!" he gasped, at length; "I'm not here as an official at all. I'm here as a patient. The cursed pack of rat-catching chemists all say that I've lost my wits."

"You!" cried Turnbull with terrible emphasis. "You! Lost your wits!"

In the rush of his real astonishment at this towering unreality Turnbull almost added: "Why, you haven't got any to lose." But he fortunately remembered the remains of his desperate diplomacy.

"This can't go on," he said, positively. "Men like MacIan and I may suffer unjustly all our lives, but a man like you must have influence."

"There is only one man who has any influence in England now," said Vane, and his high voice fell to a sudden and convincing quietude.

"Whom do you mean?" asked Turnbull.

"I mean that cursed fellow with the long split chin," said the other.

"Is it really true," asked Turnbull, "that he has been allowed to buy up and control such a lot? What put the country into such a state?"

Mr. Cumberland Vane laughed outright. "What put the country into such a state?" he asked. "Why, you did. When you were fool enough to agree to fight MacIan, after all, everybody was ready to believe that the Bank of England might paint itself pink with white spots."

"I don't understand," answered Turnbull. "Why should you be surprised at my fighting? I hope I have always fought."

"Well," said Cumberland Vane, airily, "you didn't believe in religion, you see—so we thought you were safe at any rate. You went further in your language than most of us wanted to go; no good in just hurting one's mother's feelings, I think. But of course we all knew you were right, and, really, we relied on you."

"Did you?" said the editor of *The Atheist* with a bursting heart. "I am sorry you did not tell me so at the time."

He walked away very rapidly and flung himself on a garden seat, and for some six minutes his own wrongs hid from him the huge and hilarious fact that Cumberland Vane had been locked up as a lunatic.

The garden of the madhouse was so perfectly planned, and answered so exquisitely to every hour of daylight, that one could almost fancy that the sunlight was caught there tangled in its tinted trees, as the wise men of Gotham tried to chain the spring to a bush. Or it seemed as if this ironic paradise still kept its unique dawn or its special sunset while the rest of the earthly globe rolled through its ordinary hours. There was one evening, or late afternoon, in particular, which Evan MacIan will remember in the last moments of death. It was what artists call a daffodil sky, but it is coarsened even by reference to a daffodil. It was of that innocent lonely yellow which has never heard of orange, though it might turn quite unconsciously into green. Against it the tops, one might say the turrets, of the clipt and ordered trees were outlined in that shade of veiled violet which tints the tops of lavender. A white early moon was hardly traceable upon that delicate yellow. MacIan, I say, will remember this tender and transparent evening, partly because of its virgin gold and silver, and partly because he passed beneath it through the most horrible instant of his life.

Turnbull was sitting on his seat on the lawn, and the golden evening impressed even his positive nature, as indeed it might have impressed the oxen in a field. He was shocked out of his idle mood of awe by seeing MacIan break from behind the bushes and run across the lawn with an action he had never seen in the man before, with all his experience of the eccentric humours of this Celt. MacIan fell on the bench, shaking it so that it rattled, and gripped it with his knees like one in dreadful pain of body. That particular run and tumble is typical only of a man who has been hit by some sudden and incurable evil, who is bitten by a viper or condemned to be hanged. Turnbull looked up in the white face of his friend and enemy, and almost turned cold at what he saw there. He had seen the blue but gloomy eyes of the western Highlander troubled by as many tempests as his own west Highland seas, but there had always been a fixed star of faith behind the storms. Now the star had gone out, and there was only misery.

Yet MacIan had the strength to answer the question where Turnbull, taken by surprise, had not the strength to ask it.

"They are right, they are right!" he cried. "O my God! they are right, Turnbull. I ought to be here!"

He went on with shapeless fluency as if he no longer had the heart to choose or check his speech. "I suppose I ought to have guessed long ago—all my big dreams and schemes—and everyone being against us—but I was stuck up, you know."

"Do tell me about it, really," cried the atheist, and, faced with the furnace of the other's pain, he did not notice that he spoke with the affection of a father.

"I am mad, Turnbull," said Evan, with a dead clearness of speech, and leant back against the garden seat.

"Nonsense," said the other, clutching at the obvious cue of benevolent brutality, "this is one of your silly moods."

MacIan shook his head. "I know enough about myself," he said, "to allow for any mood, though it opened heaven or hell. But to see things—to see them walking solid in the sun—things that can't be there—real mystics never do that, Turnbull."

"What things?" asked the other, incredulously.

MacIan lowered his voice. "I saw *her*," he said, "three minutes ago—walking here in this hell yard."

Between trying to look scornful and really looking startled, Turnbull's face was confused enough to emit no speech, and Evan went on in monotonous sincerity:

"I saw her walk behind those blessed trees against that holy sky of gold as plain as I can see her whenever I shut my eyes. I did shut them, and opened them again, and she was still there—that is, of course, she wasn't— She still had a little fur round her neck, but her dress was a shade brighter than when I really saw her."

"My dear fellow," cried Turnbull, rallying a hearty laugh, "the fancies have really got hold of you. You mistook some other poor girl here for her."

"Mistook some other—" said MacIan, and words failed him altogether.

They sat for some moments in the mellow silence of the evening garden, a silence that was stifling for the sceptic, but utterly empty and final for the man of faith. At last he broke out again with the words: "Well, anyhow, if I'm mad, I'm glad I'm mad on that."

Turnbull murmured some clumsy deprecation, and sat stolidly smoking to collect his thoughts; the next instant he had all his nerves engaged in the mere effort to sit still.

Across the clear space of cold silver and a pale lemon sky which was left by the gap in the ilex-trees there passed a slim, dark figure, a profile and the poise of a dark head like a bird's, which really pinned him to his seat with the point of coincidence. With an effort he got to his feet, and said with a voice of affected insouciance: "By George! MacIan, she is uncommonly like—"

"What!" cried MacIan, with a leap of eagerness that was heart-breaking, "do you see her, too?" And the blaze came back into the centre of his eyes.

Turnbull's tawny eyebrows were pulled together with a peculiar frown of curiosity, and all at once he walked quickly across the lawn. MacIan sat rigid, but peered after him with open and parched lips. He saw the sight which either proved him sane or proved the whole universe half-witted; he saw the man of flesh approach that beautiful phantom, saw their gestures of recognition, and saw them against the sunset joining hands.

He could stand it no longer, but ran across to the path, turned the corner and saw standing quite palpable in the evening sunlight, talking with a casual grace to Turnbull, the face and figure which had filled his midnights with frightfully vivid or desperately half-forgotten features. She advanced quite pleasantly and coolly, and put out her hand. The moment that he touched it he knew that he was sane even if the solar system was crazy.

She was entirely elegant and unembarrassed. That is the awful thing about women—they refuse to be emotional at emotional moments, upon some such ludicrous pretext as there being someone else there. But MacIan was in a condition of criticism much less than the average masculine one, being in fact merely overturned by the rushing riddle of the events.

Evan does not know to this day what particular question he asked, but he vividly remembers that she answered, and every line or fluctuation of her face as she said it.

"Oh, don't you know?" she said, smiling, and suddenly lifting her level brown eyebrows. "Haven't you heard the news? I'm a lunatic."

Then she added after a short pause, and with a sort of pride: "I've got a certificate."

Her manner, by the matchless social stoicism of her sex, was entirely suited to a drawing-room, but Evan's reply fell somewhat far short of such a standard, as he only said: "What the devil in hell does all this nonsense mean?"

"Really," said the young lady, and laughed.

"I beg your pardon," said the unhappy young man, rather wildly, "but what I mean is, why are you here in an asylum?"

The young woman broke again into one of the maddening and mysterious laughs of femininity. Then she composed her features, and replied with equal dignity: "Well, if it comes to that, why are you?"

The fact that Turnbull had strolled away and was investigating rhododendrons may have been due to Evan's successful prayers to the other world, or possibly to his own pretty successful experience of this one. But though they two were as isolated as a new Adam and Eve in a pretty ornamental Eden, the lady did not relax by an inch the rigour of her badinage.

"I am locked up in the madhouse," said Evan, with a sort of stiff pride, "because I tried to keep my promise to you."

"Quite so," answered the inexplicable lady, nodding with a perfectly blazing smile, "and I am locked up because it was to me you promised."

"It is outrageous!" cried Evan; "it is impossible!"

"Oh, you can see my certificate if you like," she replied with some hauteur.

MacIan stared at her and then at his boots, and then at the sky and then at her again. He was quite sure now that he himself was not mad, and the fact rather added to his perplexity.

Then he drew nearer to her, and said in a dry and dreadful voice: "Oh, don't condescend to play the fool with such a fool as me. Are you really locked up here as a patient—because you helped us to escape?"

"Yes," she said, still smiling, but her steady voice had a shake in it.

Evan flung his big elbow across his forehead and burst into tears.

The pure lemon of the sky faded into purer white as the great sunset silently collapsed. The birds settled back into the trees; the moon began to glow with its own light. Mr. James Turnbull continued his botanical researches into the structure of the rhododendron. But the lady did not move an inch until Evan had flung up his face again; and when he did he saw by the last gleam of sunlight that it was not only his face that was wet.

Mr. James Turnbull had all his life professed a profound interest in physical science, and the phenomena of a good garden were really a pleasure to him; but after three-quarters of an hour or so even the apostle of science began to find rhododendrus a bore, and was somewhat relieved when an unexpected development of events obliged him to transfer his researches to the equally interesting subject of hollyhocks, which grew some fifty feet farther along the path. The ostensible cause of his removal was the unexpected reappearance of his two other acquaintances walking and talking laboriously along the way, with the black head bent close to the brown one. Even hollyhocks detained Turnbull but a short time. Having rapidly absorbed all the important principles affecting the growth of those vegetables, he jumped over a flower-bed and walked back into the building. The other two came up along the slow course of the path talking and talking. No one but God knows what they said (for they certainly have forgotten), and if I remembered it I would not repeat it. When they parted at the head of the walk she put out her hand again in the same well-bred way, although it trembled; he seemed to restrain a gesture as he let it fall.

"If it is really always to be like this," he said, thickly, "it would not matter if we were here for ever."

"You tried to kill yourself four times for me," she said, unsteadily, "and I have been chained up as a madwoman for you. I really think that after that——"

"Yes, I know," said Evan in a low voice, looking down. "After that we belong to each other. We are sort of sold to each other—until the stars fall." Then he looked up suddenly, and said: "By the way, what is your name?"

"My name is Beatrice Drake," she replied with complete gravity. "You can see it on my certificate of lunacy."

CHAPTER NINETEEN
THE LAST PARLEY

Turnbull walked away, wildly trying to explain to himself the presence of two personal acquaintances so different as Vane and the girl. As he skirted a low hedge of laurel, an enormously tall young man leapt over it, stood in front of him, and almost fell on his neck as if seeking to embrace him.

"Don't you know me?" almost sobbed the young man, who was in the highest spirits. "Ain't I written on your heart, old boy? I say, what did you do with my yacht?"

"Take your arms off my neck," said Turnbull, irritably. "Are you mad?"

The young man sat down on the gravel path and went into ecstasies of laughter. "No, that's just the fun of it—I'm not mad," he replied. "They've shut me up in this place, and I'm not mad." And he went off again into mirth as innocent as wedding-bells.

Turnbull, whose powers of surprise were exhausted, rolled his round grey eyes and said, "Mr. Wilkinson, I think," because he could not think of anything else to say.

The tall man sitting on the gravel bowed with urbanity, and said: "Quite at your service. Not to be confused with the Wilkinsons of Cumberland; and as I say, old boy, what have you done with my yacht? You see, they've locked me up here—in this garden—and a yacht would be a sort of occupation for an unmarried man."

"I am really horribly sorry," began Turnbull, in the last stage of bated bewilderment and exasperation, "but really——"

"Oh, I can see you can't have it on you at the moment," said Mr. Wilkinson with much intellectual magnanimity.

"Well, the fact is——" began Turnbull again, and then the phrase was frozen on his mouth, for round the corner came the goatlike face and gleaming eye-glasses of Dr. Quayle.

"Ah, my dear Mr. Wilkinson," said the doctor, as if delighted at a coincidence; "and Mr. Turnbull, too. Why, I want to speak to Mr. Turnbull."

Mr. Turnbull made some movement rather of surrender than assent, and the doctor caught it up exquisitely, showing even more of his two front teeth. "I am sure Mr. Wilkinson will excuse us a moment." And with flying frock-coat he led Turnbull rapidly round the corner of a path.

"My dear sir," he said, in a quite affectionate manner, "I do not mind telling you—you are such a very hopeful case—you understand so well the scientific point of view; and I don't like to see you bothered by the really hopeless cases. They are monotonous and maddening. The man you have just been talking to, poor fellow, is one of the strongest cases of pure *idee fixe* that we have. It's very sad, and I'm afraid utterly incurable. He keeps on telling everybody"—and the doctor lowered his voice confidentially—"he tells everybody that two people have taken is yacht. His account of how he lost it is quite incoherent."

Turnbull stamped his foot on the gravel path, and called out: "Oh, I can't stand this. Really——"

"I know, I know," said the psychologist, mournfully; "it is a most melancholy case, and also fortunately a very rare one. It is so rare, in fact, that in one classification of these maladies it is entered under a heading by itself—Perdinavititis, mental inflammation creating the impression that one has lost a ship. Really," he added, with a kind of half-embarrassed guilt, "it's rather a feather in my cap. I discovered the only existing case of perdinavititis."

"But this won't do, doctor," said Turnbull, almost tearing his hair, "this really won't do. The man really did lose a ship. Indeed, not to put too fine a point on it, I took his ship."

Dr. Quayle swung round for an instant so that his silk-lined overcoat rustled, and stared singularly at Turnbull. Then he said with hurried amiability: "Why, of course you did. Quite so, quite so," and with courteous gestures went striding up the garden path. Under the first laburnum-tree he stopped, however, and pulling out his pencil and notebook wrote down feverishly: "Singular development in the Elenthero-maniac, Turnbull. Sudden manifestation of Rapinavititis—the delusion that one has stolen a ship. First case ever recorded."

Turnbull stood for an instant staggered into stillness. Then he ran raging round the garden to find MacIan, just as a husband, even a bad husband, will run raging to find his wife if he is full of a furious query. He found MacIan stalking moodily about the half-lit garden, after his extraordinary meeting with Beatrice. No one who saw his slouching stride and sunken head could have known that his soul was in the seventh heaven of ecstasy. He did not think; he did not even very definitely desire. He merely wallowed in memories, chiefly in material memories; words said with a certain cadence or trivial turns of the neck or wrist. Into the middle of his stationary and senseless enjoyment were thrust abruptly the projecting elbow and the projecting red beard of Turnbull. MacIan stepped back a little, and the soul in his eyes came very slowly to its windows. When James Turnbull had the glittering sword-point planted upon his breast he was in far less danger. For three pulsating seconds after the interruption MacIan was in a mood to have murdered his father.

And yet his whole emotional anger fell from him when he saw Turnbull's face, in which the eyes seemed to be bursting from the head like bullets. All the fire and fragrance even of young and honourable love faded for a moment before that stiff agony of interrogation.

"Are you hurt, Turnbull?" he asked, anxiously.

"I am dying," answered the other quite calmly. "I am in the quite literal sense of the words dying to know something. I want to know what all this can possibly mean."

MacIan did not answer, and he continued with asperity: "You are still thinking about that girl, but I tell you the whole thing is incredible. She's not the only person here. I've met the fellow Wilkinson, whose yacht we lost. I've met the very magistrate you were hauled up to when you broke my window. What can it mean—meeting all these old people again? One never meets such old friends again except in a dream."

Then after a silence he cried with a rending sincerity: "Are you really there, Evan? Have you ever been really there? Am I simply dreaming?"

MacIan had been listening with a living silence to every word, and now his face flamed with one of his rare revelations of life.

"No, you good atheist," he cried; "no, you clean, courteous, reverent, pious old blasphemer. No, you are not dreaming—you are waking up."

"What do you mean?"

"There are two states where one meets so many old friends," said MacIan; "one is a dream, the other is the end of the world."

"And you say——"

"I say this is not a dream," said Evan in a ringing voice.

"You really mean to suggest——" began Turnbull.

"Be silent! or I shall say it all wrong," said MacIan, breathing hard. "It's hard to explain, anyhow. An apocalypse is the opposite of a dream. A dream is falser than the outer life. But the end of the world is more actual than the world it ends. I don't say this is really the end of the world, but it's something like that—it's the end of something. All the people are crowding into one corner. Everything is coming to a point."

"What is the point?" asked Turnbull.

"I can't see it," said Evan; "it is too large and plain."

Then after a silence he said: "I can't see it—and yet I will try to describe it. Turnbull, three days ago I saw quite suddenly that our duel was not right after all."

"Three days ago!" repeated Turnbull. "When and why did this illumination occur?"

"I knew I was not quite right," answered Evan, "the moment I saw the round eyes of that old man in the cell."

"Old man in the cell!" repeated his wondering companion. "Do you mean the poor old idiot who likes spikes to stick out?"

"Yes," said MacIan, after a slight pause, "I mean the poor old idiot who likes spikes to stick out. When I saw his eyes and heard his old croaking accent, I knew that it would not really have been right to kill you. It would have been a venial sin."

"I am much obliged," said Turnbull, gruffly.

"You must give me time," said MacIan, quite patiently, "for I am trying to tell the whole truth. I am trying to tell more of it than I know."

"So you see I confess"—he went on with laborious distinctness—"I confess that all the people who called our duel mad were right in a way. I would confess it to old Cumberland Vane and his eye-glass. I would confess it even to that old ass in brown flannel who talked to us about Love. Yes, they are right in a way. I am a little mad."

He stopped and wiped his brow as if he were literally doing heavy labour. Then he went on:

"I am a little mad; but, after all, it is only a little madness. When hundreds of high-minded men had fought duels about a jostle with the elbow or the ace of spades, the whole world need not have gone wild over my one little wildness. Plenty of other people have killed themselves between then and now. But all England has gone into captivity in order to take us captive. All England has turned into a lunatic asylum in order to prove us lunatics. Compared with the general public, I might positively be called sane."

He stopped again, and went on with the same air of travailing with the truth:

"When I saw that, I saw everything; I saw the Church and the world. The Church in its earthly action has really touched morbid things—tortures and bleeding visions and blasts of extermination. The Church has had her madnesses, and I am one of them. I am the massacre of St. Bartholomew. I am the Inquisition of Spain. I do not say that we have never gone mad, but I say that we are fit to act as keepers to our enemies. Massacre is wicked even with a provocation, as in the Bartholomew. But your modern Nietzsche will tell you that massacre would be glorious without a provocation. Torture should be violently stopped, though the Church is doing it. But your modern Tolstoy will tell you that it ought not to be violently stopped whoever is doing it. In the long run, which is most mad—the Church or the world? Which is madder, the Spanish priest who permitted tyranny, or the Prussian sophist who admired it? Which is madder, the Russian priest who discourages righteous rebellion, or the Russian novelist who forbids it? That is the final and blasting test. The world left to itself grows wilder than any creed. A few days ago you and I were the maddest people in England. Now, by God! I believe we are the sanest. That is the only real question—whether the Church is really madder than the world. Let the rationalists run their own race, and let us see where *they* end. If the world has some healthy balance other than God, let the world find it. Does the world find it? Cut the world loose," he cried with a savage gesture. "Does the world stand on its own end? Does it stand, or does it stagger?"

Turnbull remained silent, and MacIan said to him, looking once more at the earth: "It staggers, Turnbull. It cannot stand by itself; you know it cannot. It has been the sorrow of your life. Turnbull, this garden is not a dream, but an apocalyptic fulfilment. This garden is the world gone mad."

Turnbull did not move his head, and he had been listening all the time; yet, somehow, the other knew that for the first time he was listening seriously.

"The world has gone mad," said MacIan, "and it has gone mad about Us. The world takes the trouble to make a big mistake about every little mistake made by the Church. That is why they have turned ten counties to a madhouse; that is why crowds of kindly people are poured into this filthy melting-pot. Now is the judgement of this world. The Prince of this World is judged, and he is judged exactly because he is judging. There is at last one simple solution to the quarrel between the ball and the cross—"

Turnbull for the first time started.

"The ball and—" he repeated.

"What is the matter with you?" asked MacIan.

"I had a dream," said Turnbull, thickly and obscurely, "in which I saw the cross struck crooked and the ball secure—"

"I had a dream," said MacIan, "in which I saw the cross erect and the ball invisible. They were both dreams from hell. There must be some round earth to plant the cross upon. But here is the awful difference—that the round world will not consent even to continue round. The astronomers are always telling us that it is shaped like an orange, or like an egg, or like a German sausage. They beat the old world about like a bladder and thump it into a thousand shapeless shapes. Turnbull, we cannot trust the ball to be always a ball; we cannot trust reason to be reasonable. In the end the great terrestrial globe will go quite lop-sided, and only the cross will stand upright."

There was a long silence, and then Turnbull said, hesitatingly: "Has it occurred to you that since—since those two dreams, or whatever they were—"

"Well?" murmured MacIan.

"Since then," went on Turnbull, in the same low voice, "since then we have never even looked for our swords."

"You are right," answered Evan almost inaudibly. "We have found something which we both hate more than we ever hated each other, and I think I know its name."

Turnbull seemed to frown and flinch for a moment. "It does not much matter what you call it," he said, "so long as you keep out of its way."

The bushes broke and snapped abruptly behind them, and a very tall figure towered above Turnbull with an arrogant stoop and a projecting chin, a chin of which the shape showed queerly even in its shadow upon the path.

"You see that is not so easy," said MacIan between his teeth.

They looked up into the eyes of the Master, but looked only for a moment. The eyes were full of a frozen and icy wrath, a kind of utterly heartless hatred. His voice was for the first time devoid of irony. There was no more sarcasm in it than there is in an iron club.

"You will be inside the building in three minutes," he said, with pulverizing precision, "or you will be fired on by the artillery at all the windows. There is too much talking in this garden; we intend to close it. You will be accommodated indoors."

"Ah!" said MacIan, with a long and satisfied sigh, "then I was right."

And he turned his back and walked obediently towards the building. Turnbull seemed to canvass for a few minutes the notion of knocking the Master down, and then fell under the same almost fairy fatalism as his companion. In some strange way it did seem that the more smoothly they yielded, the more swiftly would events sweep on to some great collision.

CHAPTER TWENTY
DIES IRAE

As they advanced towards the asylum they looked up at its rows on rows of windows, and understood the Master's material threat. By means of that complex but concealed machinery which ran like a network of nerves over the whole fabric, there had been shot out under every window-ledge rows and rows of polished-steel cylinders, the cold miracles of modern gunnery. They commanded the whole garden and the whole country-side, and could have blown to pieces an army corps.

This silent declaration of war had evidently had its complete effect. As MacIan and Turnbull walked steadily but slowly towards the entrance hall of the institution, they could see that most, or at least many, of the patients had already gathered there as well as the staff of doctors and the whole regiment of keepers and assistants. But when they entered the lamp-lit hall, and the high iron door was clashed to and locked behind them, yet a new amazement leapt into their eyes, and the stalwart Turnbull almost fell. For he saw a sight which was indeed, as MacIan had said—either the Day of Judgement or a dream.

Within a few feet of him at one corner of the square of standing people stood the girl he had known in Jersey, Madeleine Durand. She looked straight at him with a steady smile which lit up the scene of darkness and unreason like the light of some honest fireside. Her square face and throat were thrown back, as her habit was, and there was something almost sleepy in the geniality of her eyes. He saw her first, and for a few seconds saw her only; then the outer edge of his eyesight took in all the other staring faces, and he saw all the faces he had ever seen for weeks and months past. There was the Tolstoyan in Jaeger flannel, with the yellow beard that went backward and the foolish nose and eyes that went forward, with the curiosity of a crank. He was talking eagerly to Mr. Gordon, the corpulent Jew shopkeeper whom they had once gagged in his own shop. There was the tipsy old Hertfordshire rustic; he was talking energetically to himself. There was not only Mr.

Vane the magistrate, but the clerk of Mr. Vane, the magistrate. There was not only Miss Drake of the motor-car, but also Miss Drake's chauffeur. Nothing wild or unfamiliar could have produced upon Turnbull such a nightmare impression as that ring of familiar faces. Yet he had one intellectual shock which was greater than all the others. He stepped impulsively forward towards Madeleine, and then wavered with a kind of wild humility. As he did so he caught sight of another square face behind Madeleine's, a face with long grey whiskers and an austere stare. It was old Durand, the girls' father; and when Turnbull saw him he saw the last and worst marvel of that monstrous night. He remembered Durand; he remembered his monotonous, everlasting lucidity, his stupefyingly sensible views of everything, his colossal contentment with truisms merely because they were true. "Confound it all!" cried Turnbull to himself, "if *he* is in the asylum, there can't be anyone outside." He drew nearer to Madeleine, but still doubtfully and all the more so because she still smiled at him. MacIan had already gone across to Beatrice with an air of fright.

Then all these bewildered but partly amicable recognitions were cloven by a cruel voice which always made all human blood turn bitter. The Master was standing in the middle of the room surveying the scene like a great artist looking at a completed picture. Handsome as he looked, they had never seen so clearly what was really hateful in his face; and even then they could only express it by saying that the arched brows and the long emphatic chin gave it always a look of being lit from below, like the face of some infernal actor.

"This is indeed a cosy party," he said, with glittering eyes.

The Master evidently meant to say more, but before he could say anything M. Durand had stepped right up to him and was speaking.

He was speaking exactly as a French bourgeois speaks to the manager of a restaurant. That is, he spoke with rattling and breathless rapidity, but with no incoherence, and therefore with no emotion. It was a steady, monotonous vivacity, which came not seemingly from passion, but merely from the reason having been sent off at a gallop. He was saying something like this:

"You refuse me my half-bottle of Medoc, the drink the most wholesome and the most customary. You refuse me the company and obedience of my daughter, which Nature herself indicates. You refuse me the beef and mutton, without pretence that it is a fast of the Church. You now forbid me the promenade, a thing necessary to a person of my age. It is useless to tell me that you do all this by law. Law rests upon the social contract. If the citizen finds himself despoiled of such pleasures and powers as he would have had even in the savage state, the social contract is annulled."

"It's no good chattering away, Monsieur," said Hutton, for the Master was silent. "The place is covered with machine-guns. We've got to obey our orders, and so have you."

"The machinery is of the most perfect," assented Durand, somewhat irrelevantly; "worked by petroleum, I believe. I only ask you to admit that if such things fall below the comfort of barbarism, the social contract is annulled. It is a pretty little point of theory."

"Oh! I dare say," said Hutton.

Durand bowed quite civilly and withdrew.

"A cosy party," resumed the Master, scornfully, "and yet I believe some of you are in doubt about how we all came together. I will explain it, ladies and gentlemen; I will explain everything. To whom shall I specially address myself? To Mr. James Turnbull. He has a scientific mind."

Turnbull seemed to choke with sudden protest. The Master seemed only to cough out of pure politeness and proceeded: "Mr. Turnbull will agree with me," he said, "when I say that we long felt in scientific circles that great harm was done by such a legend as that of the Crucifixion."

Turnbull growled something which was presumably assent.

The Master went on smoothly: "It was in vain for us to urge that the incident was irrelevant; that there were many such fanatics, many such executions. We were forced to take the thing thoroughly in hand, to investigate it in the spirit of scientific history, and with the assistance of Mr. Turnbull and others we were happy in being able to announce that this alleged Crucifixion never occurred at all."

MacIan lifted his head and looked at the Master steadily, but Turnbull did not look up.

"This, we found, was the only way with all superstitions," continued the speaker; "it was necessary to deny them historically, and we have done it with great success in the case of miracles and such things. Now within our own time there arose an unfortunate fuss which threatened (as Mr. Turnbull would say) to galvanize the corpse of Christianity into a fictitious life—the alleged case of a Highland eccentric who wanted to fight for the Virgin."

MacIan, quite white, made a step forward, but the speaker did not alter his easy attitude or his flow of words. "Again we urged that this duel was not to be admired, that it was a mere brawl, but the people were ignorant and romantic. There were signs of treating this alleged Highlander and his alleged opponent as heroes. We tried all other means of arresting this reactionary hero worship. Working men who betted on the duel were imprisoned for gambling. Working men who drank the health of a duellist were imprisoned for drunkenness. But the popular excitement about the alleged duel continued, and we had to fall back on our old historical method. We investigated, on scientific principles, the story of MacIan's challenge, and we are happy to be able to inform you that the whole story of the attempted duel is a fable. There never was any challenge. There never was any man named MacIan. It is a melodramatic myth, like Calvary."

Not a soul moved save Turnbull, who lifted his head; yet there was the sense of a silent explosion.

"The whole story of the MacIan challenge," went on the Master, beaming at them all with a sinister benignity, "has been found to originate in the obsessions of a few pathological types, who are now all fortunately in our care. There is, for instance, a person here of the name of Gordon, formerly the keeper of a curiosity shop. He is a victim of the disease called Vinculomania—the impression that one has been bound or tied up. We have also a case of Fugacity (Mr. Whimpey), who imagines that he was chased by two men."

The indignant faces of the Jew shopkeeper and the Magdalen Don started out of the crowd in their indignation, but the speaker continued:

"One poor woman we have with us," he said, in a compassionate voice, "believes she was in a motor-car with two such men; this is the well-known illusion of speed on which I need not dwell. Another wretched woman has the simple egotistic mania that she has caused the duel. Madeleine Durand actually professes to have been the subject of the fight between MacIan and his enemy, a fight which, if it occurred at all, certainly began long before. But it never occurred at all. We have taken in hand every person who professed to have seen such a thing, and proved them all to be unbalanced. That is why they are here."

The Master looked round the room, just showing his perfect teeth with the perfection of artistic cruelty, exalted for a moment in the enormous simplicity of his success, and then walked across the hall and vanished through an inner door. His two lieutenants, Quayle and Hutton, were left standing at the head of the great army of servants and keepers.

"I hope we shall have no more trouble," said Dr. Quayle pleasantly enough, and addressing Turnbull, who was leaning heavily upon the back of a chair.

Still looking down, Turnbull lifted the chair an inch or two from the ground. Then he suddenly swung it above his head and sent it at the inquiring doctor with an awful crash which sent one of its wooden legs loose along the floor and crammed the doctor gasping into a corner. MacIan gave a great shout, snatched up the loose chair-leg, and, rushing on the other doctor, felled him with a blow. Twenty attendants rushed to capture the rebels; MacIan flung back three of them and Turnbull went over on top of one, when from behind them all came a shriek as of something quite fresh and frightful.

Two of the three passages leading out of the hall were choked with blue smoke. Another instant and the hall was full of the fog of it, and red sparks began to swarm like scarlet bees.

"The place is on fire!" cried Quayle with a scream of indecent terror. "Oh, who can have done it? How can it have happened?"

A light had come into Turnbull's eyes. "How did the French Revolution happen?" he asked.

"Oh, how should I know!" wailed the other.

"Then I will tell you," said Turnbull; "it happened because some people fancied that a French grocer was as respectable as he looked."

Even as he spoke, as if by confirmation, old Mr. Durand re-entered the smoky room quite placidly, wiping the petroleum from his hands with a handkerchief. He had set fire to the building in accordance with the strict principles of the social contract.

But MacIan had taken a stride forward and stood there shaken and terrible. "Now," he cried, panting, "now is the judgement of the world. The doctors will leave this place; the keepers will leave this place. They will leave us in charge of the machinery and the machine-guns at the windows. But we, the lunatics, will wait to be burned alive if only we may see them go."

"How do you know we shall go?" asked Hutton, fiercely.

"You believe nothing," said MacIan, simply, "and you are insupportably afraid of death."

"So this is suicide," sneered the doctor; "a somewhat doubtful sign of sanity."

"Not at all—this is vengeance," answered Turnbull, quite calmly; "a thing which is completely healthy."

"You think the doctors will go," said Hutton, savagely.

"The keepers have gone already," said Turnbull.

Even as they spoke the main doors were burst open in mere brutal panic, and all the officers and subordinates of the asylum rushed away across the garden pursued by the smoke. But among the ticketed maniacs not a man or woman moved.

"We hate dying," said Turnbull, with composure, "but we hate you even more. This is a successful revolution."

In the roof above their heads a panel shot back, showing a strip of star-lit sky and a huge thing made of white metal, with the shape and fins of a fish, swinging as if at anchor. At the same moment a steel ladder slid down from the opening and struck the floor, and the cleft chin of the mysterious Master was thrust into the opening. "Quayle, Hutton," he said, "you will escape with me." And they went up the ladder like automata of lead.

Long after they had clambered into the car, the creature with the cloven face continued to leer down upon the smoke-stung crowd below. Then at last he said in a silken voice and with a smile of final satisfaction:

"By the way, I fear I am very absent minded. There is one man specially whom, somehow, I always forget. I always leave him lying about. Once I mislaid him on the Cross of St. Paul's. So silly of me; and now I've forgotten him in one of those little cells where your fire is burning. Very unfortunate—especially for him." And nodding genially, he climbed into his flying ship.

MacIan stood motionless for two minutes, and then rushed down one of the suffocating corridors till he found the flames. Turnbull looked once at

Madeleine, and followed.

*   *   *

MacIan, with singed hair, smoking garments, and smarting hands and face, had already broken far enough through the first barriers of burning timber to come within cry of the cells he had once known. It was impossible, however, to see the spot where the old man lay dead or alive; not now through darkness, but through scorching and aching light. The site of the old half-wit's cell was now the heart of a standing forest of fire—the flames as thick and yellow as a cornfield. Their incessant shrieking and crackling was like a mob shouting against an orator. Yet through all that deafening density MacIan thought he heard a small and separate sound. When he heard it he rushed forward as if to plunge into that furnace, but Turnbull arrested him by an elbow.

"Let me go!" cried Evan, in agony; "it's the poor old beggar's voice—he's still alive, and shouting for help."

"Listen!" said Turnbull, and lifted one finger from his clenched hand.

"Or else he is shrieking with pain," protested MacIan. "I will not endure it."

"Listen!" repeated Turnbull, grimly. "Did you ever hear anyone shout for help or shriek with pain in that voice?"

The small shrill sounds which came through the crash of the conflagration were indeed of an odd sort, and MacIan turned a face of puzzled inquiry to his companion.

"He is singing," said Turnbull, simply.

A remaining rampart fell, crushing the fire, and through the diminished din of it the voice of the little old lunatic came clearer. In the heart of that white-hot hell he was singing like a bird. What he was singing it was not very easy to follow, but it seemed to be something about playing in the golden hay.

"Good Lord!" cried Turnbull, bitterly, "there seem to be some advantages in really being an idiot." Then advancing to the fringe of the fire he called out on chance to the invisible singer: "Can you come out? Are you cut off?"

"God help us all!" said MacIan, with a shudder; "he's laughing now."

At whatever stage of being burned alive the invisible now found himself, he was now shaking out peals of silvery and hilarious laughter. As he listened, MacIan's two eyes began to glow, as if a strange thought had come into his head.

"Fool, come out and save yourself!" shouted Turnbull.

"No, by Heaven! that is not the way," cried Evan, suddenly. "Father," he shouted, "come out and save us all!"

The fire, though it had dropped in one or two places, was, upon the whole, higher and more unconquerable than ever. Separate tall flames shot up and spread out above them like the fiery cloisters of some infernal cathedral, or like a grove of red tropical trees in the garden of the devil. Higher yet in the purple hollow of the night the topmost flames leapt again and again fruitlessly at the stars, like golden dragons chained but struggling. The towers and domes of the oppressive smoke seemed high and far enough to drown distant planets in a London fog. But if we exhausted all frantic similes for that frantic scene, the main impression about the fire would still be its ranked upstanding rigidity and a sort of roaring stillness. It was literally a wall of fire.

"Father," cried MacIan, once more, "come out of it and save us all!" Turnbull was staring at him as he cried.

The tall and steady forest of fire must have been already a portent visible to the whole circle of land and sea. The red flush of it lit up the long sides of white ships far out in the German Ocean, and picked out like piercing rubies the windows in the villages on the distant heights. If any villagers or sailors were looking towards it they must have seen a strange sight as MacIan cried out for the third time.

That forest of fire wavered, and was cloven in the centre; and then the whole of one half of it leaned one way as a cornfield leans all one way under the load of the wind. Indeed, it looked as if a great wind had sprung up and driven the great fire aslant. Its smoke was no longer sent up to choke the stars, but was trailed and dragged across county after county like one dreadful banner of defeat.

But it was not the wind; or, if it was the wind, it was two winds blowing in opposite directions. For while one half of the huge fire sloped one way towards the inland heights, the other half, at exactly the same angle, sloped out eastward towards the sea. So that earth and ocean could behold, where there had been a mere fiery mass, a thing divided like a V—a cloven tongue of flame. But if it were a prodigy for those distant, it was something beyond speech for those quite near. As the echoes of Evan's last appeal rang and died in the universal uproar, the fiery vault over his head opened down the middle, and, reeling back in two great golden billows, hung on each side as huge and harmless as two sloping hills lie on each side of a valley. Down the centre of this trough, or chasm, a little path ran, cleared of all but ashes, and down this little path was walking a little old man singing as if he were alone in a wood in spring.

When James Turnbull saw this he suddenly put out a hand and seemed to support himself on the strong shoulder of Madeleine Durand. Then after a moment's hesitation he put his other hand on the shoulder of MacIan. His blue eyes looked extraordinarily brilliant and beautiful. In many sceptical papers and magazines afterwards he was sadly or sternly rebuked for having abandoned the certainties of materialism. All his life up to that moment he had been most honestly certain that materialism was a fact. But he was unlike the writers in the magazines precisely in this—that he preferred a fact even to materialism.

As the little singing figure came nearer and nearer, Evan fell on his knees, and after an instant Beatrice followed; then Madeleine fell on her knees, and after a longer instant Turnbull followed. Then the little old man went past them singing down that corridor of flames. They had not looked at his face.

When he had passed they looked up. While the first light of the fire had shot east and west, painting the sides of ships with fire-light or striking red sparks out of windowed houses, it had not hitherto struck upward, for there was above it the ponderous and rococo cavern of its own monstrous coloured smoke. But now the fire was turned to left and right like a woman's hair parted in the middle, and now the shafts of its light could shoot up into empty heavens and strike anything, either bird or cloud. But it struck something that was neither cloud nor bird. Far, far away up in those huge hollows of space something was flying swiftly and shining brightly, something that shone too bright and flew too fast to be any of the fowls of the air, though the red light lit it from underneath like the breast of a bird. Everyone knew it was a flying ship, and everyone knew whose.

As they stared upward the little speck of light seemed slightly tilted, and two black dots dropped from the edge of it. All the eager, upturned faces watched the two dots as they grew bigger and bigger in their downward rush. Then someone screamed, and no one looked up any more. For the two bodies, larger every second flying, spread out and sprawling in the fire-light, were the dead bodies of the two doctors whom Professor Lucifer had carried with him—the weak and sneering Quayle, the cold and clumsy Hutton. They went with a crash into the thick of the fire.

"They are gone!" screamed Beatrice, hiding her head. "O God! The are lost!"

Evan put his arm about her, and remembered his own vision.

"No, they are not lost," he said. "They are saved. He has taken away no souls with him, after all."

He looked vaguely about at the fire that was already fading, and there among the ashes lay two shining things that had survived the fire, his sword and Turnbull's, fallen haphazard in the pattern of a cross.

THE END

About the Editor

Cory (C.W.) Gross is a Canadian heritage professional with over 20 years of experience in museum education. Cory is also the creator and writer of *Voyages Extraordinaires: Scientific Romances in a Bygone Age*, the preeminent weblog dedicated to Victorian-Edwardian science fiction, horror, fantasy, history, and retro-futurism.

Science Fiction of the British Empire: A Victorian-Edwardian Anthology

ALSO BY C.W. GROSS

Science Fiction of America's Gilded Age: An Anthology

Science Fiction of Antebellum America: An Anthology

Science Fiction of the British Empire: A Victorian-Edwardian Anthology

For more Victorian-Edwardian science fiction, horror, fantasy, history, and retro-futurism, visit

http://voyagesextraordinaires.blogspot.com/

Printed in Great Britain
by Amazon